GREAT NORTH ROAD

By Peter F. Hamilton

The Greg Mandel series

Mindstar Rising

A Quantum Murder

The Nano Flower

The Night's Dawn trilogy

The Reality Dysfunction

The Neutronium Alchemist

The Naked God

The Confederation Handbook
(a vital guide to the Night's Dawn trilogy)

Fallen Dragon

Misspent Youth

Great North Road

The Commonwealth Saga

Pandora's Star

Judas Unchained

The Void trilogy

The Dreaming Void

The Temporal Void

The Evolutionary Void

Short Story Collections

A Second Chance at Eden

Manhattan in Reverse

Peter F. Hamilton

GREAT NORTH ROAD

MACMILLAN

First published 2012 by Macmillan
an imprint of Pan Macmillan, a division of Macmillan Publishers Limited
Pan Macmillan, 20 New Wharf Road, London N1 9RR
Basingstoke and Oxford
Associated companies throughout the world
www.panmacmillan.com

ISBN 978-0-230-75005-0

9 8 7 6 5 4 3 2 1

A CIP catalogue record for this book is available from
the British Library.

Typeset by SetSystems Ltd, Saffron Walden, Essex
Printed and bound by CPI Group (UK) Ltd, Croydon, CR0 4YY

This one's for Lizzie, Tim, Judith, and Alan.

For all that quiet support down the years.

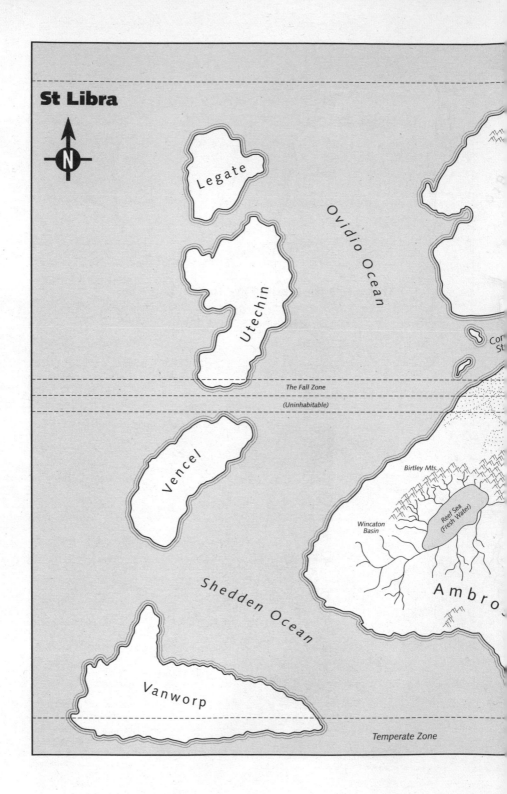

St Libra

N

Legate

Utechin

Ovidio Ocean

Cor
St

The Fall Zone

(Uninhabitable)

Vencel

Birtley Mts.

Reef Sea
(Fresh Water)

Wincaton
Basin

A m b r o

Shedden Ocean

Vanworp

Temperate Zone

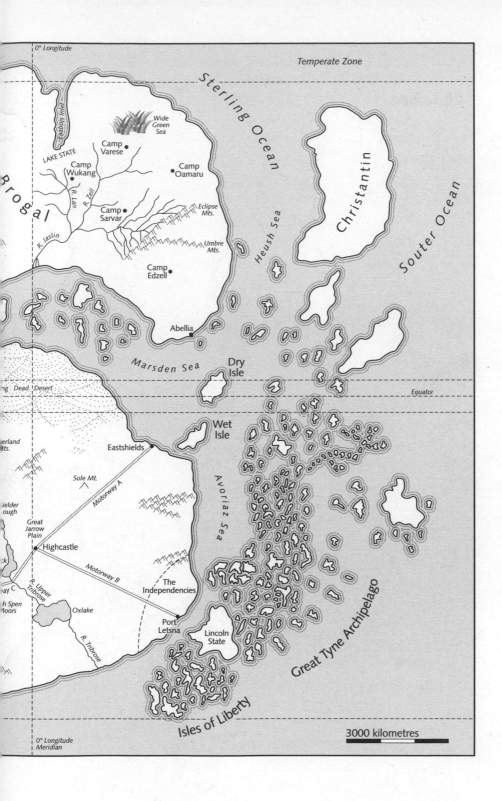

0° Longitude

Temperate Zone

Sterling Ocean

Christantin

Souter Ocean

Eaabois Inlet

LAKE STATE

Wide
Green
Sea

Camp
Varese

Camp
Wukang

Camp
Oamaru

R. Zell

R. Lan

Heush Sea

Camp
Sarvar

Eclipse
Mts.

Brogal

R. Jaslin

Umbre
Mts.

Camp
Edzell

Abellia

Marsden Sea

Dry
Isle

ng. Dead. Desert

Equator

Wet
Isle

erland
ts.

Eastshields

Avoriaz Sea

Sole Mt.

Motorway A

ielder
ough

Great
Jarrow
Plain

Highcastle

Motorway B

The
Independencies

ay C

R. Upper
Tribrose

h Spen
Moors

Oxlake

Port
Letsna

Lincoln
State

Great Tyne Archipelago

R. Tribrose

Isles of Liberty

0° Longitude
Meridian

3000 kilometres

Timeline

2003   Kane North injured by IED in Iraq.

2004   Kane receives honourable discharge from US Army. Moves to Edinburgh. Uses family trust money to recruit geneticists. Cloning programme begins.

2007   Brant North born, first clone of Kane North successfully carried to term. Large number of mental and physical defects; lives three years.

2009   Cicero North born. Severe learning difficulties, serious metabolic deficiency; lives to 2022.

2010   Forrest North born. High-spectrum autistic, lives to 2065.

2012   Augustine, Bartram, and Constantine North born.

2027   Wan Hi Chan presents his theory of trans-spacial connection.

2029   First 'connection' made at Princetown, 800m across campus. USA forms National Interstellar Agency (NIA).

2030   Europe forms European Trans-Space Bureau (ET-SB). China forms National Interstellar Transport Corporation (NITC). Russia, India, Israel, Brazil, Saudi Arabia, Pacific Alliance, North African

Coalition, and the Asian Federation all create agencies to begin interstellar exploration programs.

2031   NIA opens connection to Earth's moon.

2032–2038   Various national test programs produce 12 trans-spacial connections across solar system. Gateway technology perfected.

2034   Augustine, Bartram, and Constantine found Northumberland Interstellar Corp, using family corporate resources to fund gateway systems manufacture.

2039   NITC opens gateway to Proxima Centauri. Age of interstellar exploration begins.

2041   NIA opens New Washington for settlement.

2044   NIA opens gateway to Orleans.

2044   ET-SB opens New Brussels for settlement to EU citizens.

2045   India opens gateway to Kolhapur.

2045   NITC opens gateways to Taiyuan and Wuchow.

2047   Russia opens gateway to Nova Petersburg.

2047   Israel opens gateway to Ramla.

2047   US Senate expanded to take in ten new states from new worlds. Passes Federal Independent Landowner Act. Enforced off-Earth settlement of all long-term welfare recipients.

2048   Japan opens gateway to New Tokyo.

2048   France opens gateway to Rouen, for French citizens only.

2048   Earth economy stalling due to investment shift to new planets.

2049   Germany opens gateway to Odessa, for German citizens only.

2049	USA passes Illegals Dispersal Bill. All illegal immigrants in original states on Earth deported to the territories on new US planets.
2049	Saudi Arabia opens Riyadh for settlement, for Muslims only.
2050	ET-SB opens Minisa for 'all' Grande Europe citizens. Subsidized immigration begins for unemployed, later developing to 'opportunity immigration' policy, transporting millions of poor and jobless out of GE states on Earth.
2051	Northumberland Interstellar opens gateway to Sirius star system, discovers earth-giant planet, named St Libra. Cleared for human immigration.
2052	Brazil opens gateway to Sao Jeroni.
2052	North African gateway to Accra.
2053	First bioil algaepaddies established on St Libra. Start of bioil export to Earth. Massive investment into St Libra algaepaddies begins, establishment of Eight Great bioil companies in addition to NI.
2055	The Independencies founded on St Libra, constant mid-level immigration by GE dissidents, and other political refugees from across Earth.
2055–2070	Establishment of seven more human settled worlds. Earth's population in decline; its economy contracts. Enforced exodus of jobless instituted by most nations.
2063	Kane North dies, age 83.
2083	Rumour of True Jerusalem, a planet linked by a secret gateway from Ramla.
2087	Constantine North and Bartram North resign their directorships of Northumberland Interstellar. Company resources redistributed. The bulk remains with Augustine.

2088	Constantine North launches Jupiter habitat; 8,000 tonnes of cybernetic manufacturing equipment, and a 3,000-tonne mineral/chemical refinery all delivered to asteroid in Jupiter orbit via Newcastle gateway + 25,000-tonne life-support hostel. Several hundred supporters and all C Norths follow him there.
2089	Town of Abellia established on St Libra by Bartram. Bartram founds North Biogenetic Institute, begins serious research into human regeneration/ rejuvenation.
2092	Zanthswarm on Accra.
2093	Accra evacuated, gateway closed. Estimated human deaths: 8.2 million.
2093	Formation of Human Defence Alliance (HDA) to defend human race from the Zanth.
2094	Brinkelle North born.
2095	Large-scale trans-stellar financial instability as HDA budget approved. Bioil price increasing, reducing consumption. Markets falling.
2096–2111	Trans-stellar recession, affecting all worlds.
2111	Northumberland Interstellar-led cartel releases glut of low-price bioil, bankrupting many futures market speculators. Stability returns to bioil market. Trans-stellar share prices start to rise again.
2119	Zanthswarm on New Florida. Evacuation declared successful, deaths estimated at 108,000.
2119	Trans-stellar market downturn, lasts until 2123 – officially not a recession.
2121	Bartram North and his household slaughtered. Angela Tramelo convicted of mass murder, receives life sentence.

Principal Characters

The 2143 St Libra Northern Geogenetic Expedition

Charmonique Passam *Commissioner for the Grande Europe Bureau of alien evaluation*

Griffin Toyne *Major, HDA, head of expedition security*

CAMP WUKANG

Vance Elston *Colonel, Alien Intelligence Agency (AIA), Camp Commander*

Antrinell Viana *Captain, AIA, executive officer*

Administration

Jaysukhlal (Jay) Chomik

Norman Sliwinska

Forster Wardele

Bastian North *observer*

GE Legion squad

Pablo Botin *Lieutenant*

Raddon *Sergeant*

Paresh Evitts *Corporal*

Hiron *Corporal*

Privates

Mohammed Anwar

Atyeo

Ramon Beaken

DiRito

Leora Fawkes

Dave Guzman

Hanrahan

Gillian Kowalski

Omar Mihambo

Marty O'Riley

Peace-Davis

Audrie Sleath

Josh Justic

Xenobiology team

Angela Tramelo *civilian adviser*

Marvin Trambi

Roarke Kulwinder

Tamisha Smith

Miya

Smara Jacka

Iyel

Esther Coombes

Camm Montoto

Zhao

Helicopter pilots

Lorelei

Garrick

Juan-Fernando

Ravi Hendrik *ex-Thunderthorn SF-100 pilot*

AAV flight team

Ken Schmitt *chief*

Davinia Beirne *technician*

Chris Fiadeiro *technician*

Mackay *technician*

Medical

Dr Tamika Coniff

Mark Chitty *paramedic*

Juanitar Sakur *paramedic*

Engineering teams

Helicopters

Tork Ericson

Erius

Camp systems

Olrg Dorchev

Dean Creshaun

Lance

Ground vehicles

Leif Davdia

Darwin Sworowski

Microfacture

Karizma Wadhai

Ophelia Troy

General support personnel

Luther Katzen *supervisor*

Madeleine Hoque

Fuller Owusu

Lulu MacNamara

Winn Melia

Newcastle police

Sidney Hurst *Detective*

Royce O'Rouke *Chief Constable*

Ian Lanagin *Detective, surveillance specialist*

Eva Sealand *Visual interpretation constable*

Ralph Stevens *Special investigator, AIA*

Abner North *Detective, forensics specialist*

Ari North *Constable, data management specialist*

Aldred North *Northumberland Interstellar security director, legal liaison*

Hayfa Fullerton *Detective, Gang Task Force*

Kaneesha Saeed *Detective, retired, Chief of Gang Crime Office*

Tilly Lewis *Northern Forensics Corp, Grade-A team manager*

Chloe Healy *O'Rouke's media officer*

Saul Howard *Surfer and store-owner, St Libra*

Sunday 13th January 2143

As midnight approached, the wild neon colours of the borealis storm came shimmering through the soft snow falling gently across Newcastle upon Tyne. It was as if nature was partying along with the rest of the city, providing a jade and carmine lightshow far more elegant than any of the fireworks which had been bursting sporadically above the rooftops since Friday.

Detective, third grade, Sidney Hurst watched batches of late-night revellers staggering along the frozen pavement, calling out greetings or challenges depending on how toxed up they were. Ice, snow, and slush played havoc with the smart dust embedded in the tarmac, blacking out whole sections of the metamesh which governed the city's roads and therefore making driving with the vehicle's smartauto a dangerous gamble. Sid was steering the unmarked police car manually, but with the auto managing wheel torque on the slippery road. Their snow tyres provided reasonable traction, adding to stability and allowing him to make a decent thirty-five kilometres per hour along Collingwood Street past the cathedral. Radar kept throwing proximity symbols across the windscreen, designating a warning for the long filthy dunes of snow which the civic snowploughs had thrown off the centre of the road.

It had been snowing for two days now, and with the midday temperature spike sticking stubbornly below ten degrees there had been no thaw, allowing the elegant stone Georgian buildings of the city centre to become cloaked in Dickensian Yuletide splendour. Another proximity warning flashed scarlet, outlining a man running across the road directly in front of the car, laughing and jeering as Sid veered sharply round him. One last obscene gesture, and he was claimed by the swirling snow.

'He'll never last till dawn,' Ian Lanagin claimed from the front passenger seat.

Sid glanced over at his partner. 'Just another two-oh-one file,' he agreed. 'Welcome back, me.'

'Aye man, some Sunday night reunion this is.'

It was crazy so many people being out in this weather; though for once Newcastle's traditional nightclub dress code of T-shirt for the boys and short skirt with glitter heels for the girls had vanished under thick ankle-length coats. It was that cold. He'd even glimpsed a few sensible hats, which was almost a first in the fifteen years he'd been with the Newcastle police. Even now – married with two kids, a career that wasn't quite as dynamic as he'd originally envisaged – he was slightly surprised he was still in Newcastle. He'd followed a girl up here from London, where – like every twenty-something law graduate – he'd been arrowing down the smart and fast career path, alternating jobs between police and private security as if he were an electron bouncing between junction gates. To consummate the grand romantic gesture he applied for a transfer to the local city police, where the career track was equally valid for a couple of years, and the nights could still be spent in bed with Jacinta. Now, fifteen years' worth of Siberian winters and Saharan summers later, he was still here, married to Jacinta (which at least showed good judgement), with two kids and a career that had taken the kind of direction he'd always sneered at during those long-distant university years when he had passion and conviction and contempt for the way of a world screwed up by the current generation in power and the omnipresent lurking evil of the Zanth. Now, experience and its associate wisdom had flicked him onto the more rational track of time-serving and networking to make the final career switch which would see him through the last twenty years before retirement. Fifteen years of hard labour had taught him real life had a habit of doing that.

'They'll all sober up by tomorrow,' Sid said, switching his gaze back to the road.

'In this town?' Ian challenged.

'We've all got jobs now.'

Sid had been as surprised as anyone on Friday morning when Northumberland Interstellar had finally announced they were awarding contracts for five new fusion stations to be built at the Ellington energy complex north of the city. They should have been built years ago, but such was the way with all big projects that decade-long delays were built into corporate decisions as standard. And that was *before* regulators and politicians started to intervene to prove their worth. It meant the ageing tokamaks at Ellington that currently powered the Newcastle gateway to St Libra would have to be coaxed along way past their original design lifetime. Nobody cared about that, though, and euphoric Geordies had spent the weekend rejoicing at the announcement. It meant a new surge in the monumental tide of money which already coursed along the city streets, money which was channelled at every corner into St Libra, to be rewarded by the return flow of indispensable bioil back to the old motherworld. Bioil which kept cars and lorries moving across Grande Europe's still powerful trade arteries; valuable derivations allowing planes to fly and ships to voyage. This contract was nothing more than a ripple on that tide, to be sure, but even so it promised additional revenue for the ancient coal town's manufacturing and service industries, which would devour the digital cash with clever greed to fuel runaway expansion curves on the corporate market graphs. That meant there would be job opportunities at every level. Happy times were officially on their way.

None knew that better than Newcastle's extensive secondary economy of private lounges, pubs, clubs, pimps, and pushers, who were already salivating at the prospect. Like the rest of the city, they could look forward to a fresh decade of providing a good time to the army of middle-class salary-plus-bonus contractors who would descend upon them. To launch the new era, first drinks had been on the house all this weekend, with second drinks half price.

They had a lot of takers.

'There it is,' Ian Lanagin said, pointing through the symbols scrawling across the windscreen as they rolled into Mosley Street.

Up ahead, at the junction with Grey Street, the blue and green ambulance strobes were shimmering over the fractured ice, casting weird shadows across the walls as they competed with the light-haze seeping out of club doorways and shop windows to illuminate the scene. The big vehicle was parked at an angle, blocking half of the street. Sid nudged their car left, aiming to park behind the ambulance. Proximity radar sketched red caution brackets across the windscreen as the front bumper came to a halt a couple of centimetres from the mound of snow thrown up by the ploughs. He pulled his woollen hat down over his ears, zipped up the front of his quilted leather jacket, and stepped out into the bitter air.

The cold triggered a tear reflex which he blinked away rapidly, trying to focus on what he could see. Temperature didn't affect the ring of smartcells around his iris that shone minuscule laser pulses down his optic nerves, overlaying the street with sharp display graphics, correlating what he looked at with coordinate locations for the visual log he was running.

As per protocol, Sid's bodymesh – the interconnective network produced by all his smartcells – quested a link with Ian, making sure they remained in contact. Ian was represented by a small purple icon at the corner of his sight. The bodymesh also downloaded the visual log through the car's cell and into the police network.

It was a NorthernMetroServices agency constable who'd responded to the distress code. Sid didn't recognize him, though he knew the type well enough. His private Electronic-Identity (e-i) running inside his bodymesh performed a face-capture image, logging a man barely into his twenties – and walking about with

4

a swagger that was immediately depressing. Give him a uniform and a gram of authority and he thought he was running the city.

The agency constable's e-i identified him as Kraemer. It immediately quested Sid's e-i, which responded by confirming his own rank as well as activating the badge woven into his jacket, which now glowed a subtle amber. 'You caught this?' Sid asked.

'Aye, sir. On scene fifty seconds after the report was logged.'

Well inside the agency's contracted response period, Sid thought, which will help their stats at renewal time. Of course, it depended when the call was officially logged. NorthernMetroServices also ran the Newcastle emergency response centre. It wasn't unknown for the centre to alert an agency constable a minute or so before they entered the call into the log, so one of their people could always beat the response time.

'Aggravated thirteen-five. Culprits ran off before I arrived.'

'Fast runners,' Sid muttered. 'Seeing as you were here so quick.'

'Thump and grab, man,' Kraemer said.

'Victim name?'

'His e-i responded with Kenny Ansetal when I quested it. He was barely conscious; buggers gave him a good kicking. The paramedics have got him.'

'Okay.' Sid walked round to the back of the ambulance, where the paramedics had sat the mugging victim on its egress platform to perform triage. The man was in his early thirties, with facial features that Sid's best estimate placed as a mix of Asian and Southern Mediterranean origins – which was going to play hell when he came to filling out the ethnicity section of the case file. Of course that opinion's validity was slightly skewed by the amount of blood pouring out of the large gash on the victim's brow. There were deep lacerations on his cheeks, too, which Sid guessed had been caused by ringblades. That much blood tended to obscure the finer features of a person's skin.

'Hello, sir,' he called. 'We're city police. Can you tell me what happened?'

5

Kenny Ansetal glanced up at him and promptly vomited. Sid winced. The splatter just missed his shoes.

'I'll go gather some witness intel,' Ian said, already backing off.

'You're a shit,' Sid grunted.

Ian grinned, winked, and turned away. Despite the biting cold, the mugging had drawn a small crowd, who were still hanging round. What for, Sid never did understand. After all this time in the police it was about the one aspect of human instinctual psychology he could never get a handle on: people simply couldn't resist watching someone else's misfortune.

He waited for a minute while the paramedics managed to spray clotting foam onto Ansetal's forehead wound; then one was sorting out his cheeks while the other performed a quick body check, acting on the information coming out of Ansetal's body-mesh, fingers probing where smartcells were reporting damage. Judging by Ansetal's responses, he'd taken some blows to the ribs and a knee. Kicked when he was down, Sid decided. Common enough for a thirteen-five.

'Sir, can you tell me what happened?'

This time Kenny Ansetal managed to focus. 'Bastards,' he hissed.

'Try not to move your jaw too much,' the paramedic warned as he sealed up a cheek wound.

Sid recognized the anger and murmured commands to his e-i, which obediently paused the police log using an unauthorized non-department fix he just happened to have in a private cache. 'Did you recognize your attackers?'

Ansetal shook his head.

'How many of them?'

A hand was raised, two fingers extended.

'Male?'

Another nod. 'Fucking Chinese. Kids it were.'

Sid shook his head fractionally, pleased with himself for predicting Ansetal's answers. Of course, they were common enough. Ansetal didn't know it, but an expletive-linked ethnic identification was legally classified as a racist indicator. That would have opened up a whole world of misery for Ansetal in court if defence council got hold of a log with that on it.

'Did they take anything, sir?'

Ansetal juddered as some more sealant was applied to his cheek. 'My Apple – an i-3800.'

New model personal transnet cell, Sid recalled, and top-end. He was an idiot for carrying it round the city centre at this time of night. But idiocy wasn't a crime in itself. 'I'm just going to recover your visual records, sir.'

'Whatever.'

Sid held his hand close to Ansetal's forehead, and told his e-i to recover the visual memory. His palm had several smartcells configured for mesh reception, with fixes to handle most formats. The short-term memories from Ansetal's iris smartcells down-loaded into the police network. Sid watched what Ansetal had seen, closing his own eyes so he could study the images in the grid. The recording was a blur of motion. Two shadowy figures suddenly appearing, hoods drawn against the cold. Then every-thing degenerated into smears of motion as the beating began.

His e-i ran a capture, which showed him both assailants had the same face. Sid grunted at the familiar features: Lork Zai, the Chinese zone star who featured heavily on tabloid show hot lists these days.

'All right,' Sid said. 'Now, Kenny, I'm going to give you some unofficial advice. Best if you don't speak again.'

Ansetal gave him a puzzled look. Sid could almost see the middle-class thought processes clicking round behind his blood-painted skin. *I'm the victim here, why are the police giving me warnings?* The answer was simple enough, though they never got it: never say anything that a lawyer could gain traction on in court – so just don't say anything at all.

'Have you got full-comp crime insurance?' Judging by the relatively expensive clothes, that was a rhetorical question.

A cautious nod.

'Good. Use it. Call their emergency address. They'll dispatch a duty lawyer to your hospital. Now, the agency constable is going to accompany you there to take a full statement. Refuse to do so until your lawyer is present. You have that right. You also have the right to refuse blood composition analysis. Understand?'

'I suppose . . .'

Sid held a gloved finger to his lips.

A now worried Ansetal nodded. Sid heard a female giggle from somewhere behind the ambulance, and managed to suppress a frown. 'You'll do okay, Kenny. Just keep everything aboveboard and official. Wait for your lawyer. That's the way to go.'

Ansetal mouthed: 'Thank you.'

Sid murmured instructions to his e-i, clearing the paramedic crew to leave the crime scene, then went back to Kraemer. 'I've authorized Ansetal's release to the hospital. Go with him to take a statement.'

'Aye, I'll get to it.'

'Give him time to get some treatment and recover. That was a nasty pounding he got there.' He produced a friendly smile. 'It will keep you off the street for a while, too.'

'Appreciate that, man.'

'Then tomorrow I'll need you to pull all the local mesh sensor memories.' He gestured round at the buildings. The brickwork and concrete would be covered in smartdust, some of which might have escaped degradation from the snow. 'Forward them to my case file. He has insurance, so we can probably drag a budget from the company to run a track on the felons.'

'Right you are, man.'

Sid almost smiled – the young constable's Geordie accent was nearly as thick as Ian's. The paramedics closed the ambulance doors, firing up the siren as they pulled away. Ian was still talking to the remaining witnesses. Both of them young and female, Sid noticed without the slightest surprise. He'd been partnered with Ian for two years now – they knew each other better than brothers. As far as Ian was concerned the police force was simply the perfect vocation to legitimately meet girls. Dealing with actual criminals came in a very poor second. With not a little envy, Sid acknowledged Ian was very good at his chosen profession. A twenty-eight-year-old gym fanatic who spent his entire salary on good clothes and grooming, he knew every line in the file.

Both 'witnesses' were hanging on to his every word as Sid went over to them. Unlike the other onlookers who were now walking away, they had their coats open down the front, showing off their best nightclub dresses – what there was of them. Sid just knew he was getting old when all he could think was how cold the poor things must be. 'Anything useful in those statements, Detective?' he asked loudly.

Ian turned and gave him a derisory stare. 'Aye, sorry about this, ladies, my boss is being a pain again. But what can you do?'

They both giggled at how brave he was confronting his superior so directly, how confident and capable. Sid rolled his eyes. 'Just get in the car, man. We're done here.'

Ian's voice lowered an octave or two. 'I will be calling both of you for vital information. Like which is your favourite club, and when you're going there again.'

Sid closed his ears to further outbreaks of inane giggling.

It was wonderfully warm inside the car. The bioil fuel cell produced a lot of surplus heat, which the air-con chewed hungrily to redistribute evenly from the vents. Sid unzipped his jacket as he muttered instructions to his e-i, opening a new case file on the mugging. A sub-display on the bottom of his iris smartcell grid showed the file data building up.

'Oh yeah!' a delighted Ian said as he settled back into the passenger seat. 'I'm in there, man. Did you see those lassies? Up for it they were, both of them.'

'Our medical insurance doesn't provide unlimited penicillin, you know.'

Ian chuckled. 'You know what the world's greatest oxymoron is?'

'Happily married,' Sid said wearily.

'In one, pal. In one.'

'The case is a wash out. He was mugged by Lork Zai – two of him.'

'Crap on it! That man doesn't half get about. Got to be the most popular identity mask there is right now.'

Sid checked the time display. It was eleven thirty-eight. Their shift ended at midnight. 'We'll do one more circuit then park it.' Newcastle's central police station on Market Street was barely four hundred metres away, but it wouldn't look good to head straight home from an incident with another twenty minutes left on the clock. Some city accountant would fuss about that.

'What did they take?' Ian asked.

'An i-3800.'

'Nice bit of kit. That'll be a secondary down the Last Mile by lunchtime, mind.'

'Could be,' Sid admitted. Most of the city's petty crimes these days were committed by some desperate, impoverished refugee on their way to St Libra through the gateway. In the morning they'd be moving through the Last Mile, looking to barter whatever kit they'd acquired during the night along that huge sprawl of unregulated market leading up to the gateway, where everything you could ever possibly need to begin a new life on a fresh world was for sale. Such incidents were responsible for Newcastle's permanently dismal solved crimes rating: within hours of their crime spree the felons had run off to another world far beyond the reach of the city police.

Sid reversed the car away from the kerb. His iris smartcells flashed up green text in his grid, a message backed up by an identical read-out on the windscreen. His aural smartcells also started announcing the incident.

'A two-oh-five?' Ian said incredulously. 'Man, we've only got twenty minutes to go. They cannot do that.'

Sid closed his eyes for a moment – not that it banished the green text. He knew the night had been going too well, with just a few minor incidents in the whole six hours. Now this, a two-oh-five: a body discovered in suspicious circumstances. The only suspicious thing here was the timing – along with the location:

down on Quayside by the old Gateshead Millennium Bridge, a quarter of a mile away. According to the alert's text, the river police were only just confirming it was a body they were hauling from the water. Somebody somewhere was keen to get the incident logged fast. And he was the closest senior officer on patrol. 'Bastards,' he grunted.

'Welcome back, you,' Ian agreed.

Sid activated the strobes and siren, then told his e-i to authorize a clean route with the city's traffic management AI. Not that there was much traffic left now, mostly taxis hauling overtoxed revellers back home.

It might have been a short drive, but it was down Dean Street – a steep, sloping road underneath the ancient rail and road arches, canyoned by dark stone walls with blank windows – which took them down to the riverfront. As such, the car's auto struggled to keep them from slipping on the treacherous ice. Twice they started to fishtail before countertorque was applied and the snow tyres managed to grip. At the bottom, the tall buildings opened up to a broad road junction where the land-mark Tyne Bridge cut across the water high above. The big splash of spotlights illuminating its arched iron structure was almost lost in the swirl of snow, producing a weird crescent-shaped smear of luminosity hanging weightlessly in the air overhead. Sid steered carefully past the broad stone support pillar and headed down the deserted Quayside road.

'This is taking the piss a bit, isn't it?' Ian asked as they drove past the glass and pillar façade of the Court of Justice. 'This close and all?'

'Suspicious doesn't mean deliberate,' Sid reminded him. 'And this is a bad night.' He jabbed a finger at the dark river on the other side of the car. 'You fall in there tonight, you die. Fast.'

They took the right-hand fork after the government building. This stretch of pedestrianized road hadn't seen a snowplough since the middle of the afternoon. Radar showed the snow on the ground was now over ten centimetres thick, with a solid sheet of ice below that. Sid reduced their speed to a crawl. Up ahead, the twin arches of the Millennium Bridge curved across the river with the elegance of a swan's neck – the recently refurbished pearl-white surface of the upper arch glowing dimly under the shifting rainbow lights which illuminated it. Strobes on the roof of two patrol cars and a coroner's van flickered through the snow. Sid pulled in behind them.

It was the silence which surprised him when he stepped out of the car. Even with a waterside pub not forty metres further along Quayside, there was no sound apart from the murmurs of the three agency constables waiting by the promenade rails, looking down at the police boat below as it manoeuvred up to the quayside wall at the end of the bridge's glass-boxed wharf (which housed the axial pivot and its hydraulics that rotated the entire structure for bigger ships to pass underneath). Another constable was interviewing a young couple in a patrol car.

Sid waited until his bodymesh had quested into the ringlink – which the waiting constables had already established – and checked the log was working. A two-oh-five wasn't something you played loose with. His e-i identified and labelled them, along with the duty coroner's examiner who was just getting out of his van.

'So what have we got?' he asked.

The one who Sid's e-i tagged as Constable Saltz caught a pannier thrown up by the river boat crew. 'Clubbers walking across the bridge saw something snagged on the guides out there,' he said. 'Thought it looked like a body, so they called it in right away. They're just kids, nothing suspicious with them.'

Sid went over to the railings. He'd walked along Quayside's promenade a hundred times. It was a mix of old and new buildings which lined the waterfront, all soaked with money to produce the kind of grace and aura of wealth not seen in Northern England since the Victorian era two centuries before. The river here wasn't something the city council would allow to decay; it was the heart of the town, the showpiece that reflected the status of being Europe's fifth-wealthiest (per capita) city, with its iconic bridges and curved-glass, century-old cultural centre-piece, the Sage.

Tonight Sid couldn't even see the Gateshead bank opposite where the Sage building dominated the Tyne. All he could make out on the black water of the river was the police boat. On the other side of the boat, just visible in the middle of the water, were two sets of pillars, which supported the deep channel guides: like rails lying flat on the water, they made sure large boats passed directly under the centre of the Millennium Bridge's arches when they were cranked up to their highest position.

'Where was the body snagged?' Sid asked.

'This side,' Constable Mardine said. She gave the two detectives a grim smile. 'The tide's going out, so no telling how far it drifted downriver first.'

Saltz finished tying off the mooring rope. Sid clambered over the railings and started down the precarious metal ladder set into the vertical side of the quay, accompanied by the endless soundless fall of snow. Two specialist agency divers helped steady him as he reached the ice-coated deck. They were dressed in top-of-the-range heated water suits with flesh helmets, perfect for keeping them toasty warm while they splashed round in freezing, filthy saltwater, all the while trying to attach a harness to an awkward semi-submerged body. The helmets were peeled open to show off cheerful expressions decidedly out of context to the situation and weather, illustrating just how effective the suits were.

The captain at least was genuine city police: Detective Darian Foy. Sid knew him from way back.

'Permission to come aboard,' Sid said.

Darian gave him a knowing grin. 'Evening, Detective. Not a good find, I'm afraid.'

'Oh?' Something was very wrong with Darian's response. Too formal. It made Sid realize this was an important one – for the wrong reasons. He wished he had some kind of full-comp legal insurance like Kenny Ansetal, and that a smartarse solicitor would materialize at his side to make sure everything he said was court-formal perfect. Instead he just had to focus hard on procedure. Having the last three months off didn't help . . .

'Show me,' he said.

Ian was helped onto the boat behind him as Darian led him round to the rear of the small cabin. The body was laid out on a recovery stretcher that the midships winch had lowered onto the decking. A plastic sheet was on top. Two lights on the cabin roof were shining down on it, producing a white spectrum blaze at odds with the sombre night.

Darian gave him a last warning look, and pulled the plastic sheet aside.

Sid really hoped he didn't say the: 'Oh fuck,' out loud.

It certainly echoed round inside his skull for long enough. He suspected he had, though, because directly behind him Ian murmured: 'Aye, you can crap on that.'

The man's frozen-white body was naked. Which wasn't the bad thing. The nasty and unusual deep wound just above his heart wasn't the career-killer, either. No, the one thing that jumped out at Sid was the victim's identity.

He was a North.

That meant there would have to be a trial. One that ended with an utterly solid – beyond legal and media doubt – conviction. Fast.

Once upon a time – a hundred and thirty-one years ago to be precise – there were three brothers. They were triplets. Born to separate mothers. Perfect clones of their incredibly wealthy father, Kane North. He named them Augustine, Bartram, and Constantine.

Although they were excellent replicas of their brother/father – who in turn had possessed all their family's notorious drive, worship of money, and intellectual ability that all Norths inherited – they had a flaw. The genetic manipulation which produced them was a technology still in its infancy. Kane's DNA was fixed by rudimentary germline techniques inside the embryo. It meant that Kane's distinctive biological identity was locked in

14

and dominant in every cell throughout the new body, including the spermatozoon. Any woman having a child by one of the brothers produced yet another copy of the original. This was the flaw in the new dynastic order: as with all forms of replication, copies of copies inevitably saw some deterioration. Errors began to creep into the DNA as it reproduced itself. 2Norths, as the next generation were called, were almost as good as their fathers – but there were subtle deficiencies now. 3Norths were of an even lower quality. 4Norths had both physiological and psychological abnormalities. 5Norths tended not to survive very long. Rumour had it that after the first 5s appeared, 4s were quietly and diplomatically sterilized by the family.

Nonetheless, the triplets were outstanding men. It was they who embraced the new development of trans-spacial connection while it was in its formative years. They took the risk, and founded Northumberland Interstellar, which ultimately came to build the gateway to St Libra. In turn it was Northumberland Interstellar which pioneered the algaepaddies on the other side, where so much of Grande Europe's bioil was now produced. They were the board, directing the mighty company's direction for over fifty years until Bartram and Constantine parted to pursue their own, separate goals, leaving Augustine to lead the bioil colossus.

But it was the 2Norths who made up the higher echelons of the company management. 2Norths who devotedly ran things for their brother-fathers. 2Norths who had cast-iron links into the very heart of Grande Europe's political and commercial edifice. 2Norths who ruled their fiefdom of Newcastle with benign totality. 2Norths who would want to know who killed one of their brothers, and why. They'd want to know that with some considerable urgency.

Think! Sid ordered himself as he shut his eyes to eradicate the sight of his career-killer lying bright and still under the swirling snow. *Procedure. Procedure is king. Always.*

He took a breath, trying to summon up a smooth rational outlook: the unfazed take-charge man. An imaginary product of

15

a thousand boring management courses, like a stereotyped zone media cop.

He opened his eyes.

The dead North clone stared sightlessly up into the undulating colours of the borealis-plagued sky. His eyes were ruined. Fish? That was an unpleasant notion. Sid gave the odd chest wound a perplexed glance – as if the death wasn't enough, he couldn't work out what the hell had left such a puncture pattern. Still, at least something like that slicing into the heart would mean it was a quick death. The North wouldn't have suffered much. Karma was clearly choosing to spread that around everyone else.

Sid held his hand over the corpse's face, and ordered his e-i to quest a link with the dead man's bodymesh. The smartcells embedded in the icy dead flesh didn't care that it was dead. They should still be drawing power from the tweaked adenosine triphosphate (ATP) molecules that made up the core of their energy transfer system; an oxidative process that would continue to utilize surrounding fats and carbohydrates just like genuine cells, until the human meat finally started to decay.

There was no response. Every link icon in Sid's grid remained inert. The North didn't have an active bodymesh. 'He's been ripped,' Sid said. Reliving the last few moments of the North's life – watching the killer stab him through the heart – would probably have resolved the case immediately. Sid knew it would never be that easy, but procedure . . . He bent over, staring at the corpse's ruined eyes. It wasn't easy in the harsh glare thrown by the boat's spotlights, but he could just make out the tiny cuts in the eyeball's lens, as if an insect had been nibbling away. 'More than ripped, actually. Looks like they extracted the smartcells, too.'

'Aye, man. That'll be a pro hit, then,' Ian said.

'Yeah. Turn his hands over please,' he asked the divers with their rubber gloves. The skin on the tip of every white frozen finger was missing. Somebody was trying to make identification difficult, which might make sense for a normal crime victim, but a North . . . ?

'Okay,' Sid said abruptly. 'Get the examiner down here to clear and retrieve the body. I'm now officially reclassifying this case as a one-oh-one. All records to be backed up and forwarded to my case file.' He turned to the two divers. 'Was there anything else out there where you found the body?'

'No, sir.'

'Captain, once the body's been taken ashore I want this boat back out there, and the area where you found the body searched again.'

'Of course,' Darian said.

'Is it worth giving the area a sonar sweep?'

'It's not the best resolution, but we can certainly check for anything unusual.'

Both of them glanced back at the chest wound.

'Please do that.' Sid instructed his e-i to open a one-oh-one level case file. His iris smartcell grid showed the spherical green icon unfolding. Data from the log and the patrol boat began downloading.

'I want the couple who reported it taken down to the station for a full debrief,' he told Ian.

'You got it, boss,' Ian said sharply.

'Okay then.' Sid went over to the bottom of the ladder and waited until the duty examiner had come down. The man suddenly looked very nervous. 'I want every procedure carried out in perfect file compliance,' Sid told him.

As he climbed back up the ladder, he told his e-i to retrieve the Chief Constable's transnet access code. The icon appeared, a small red star glowing accusingly in front of him. Only when he got back up on the promenade and was holding the rail to make sure he didn't slip did he tell his e-i to make the call.

It took a minute for Royce O'Rouke to answer, which was reasonable enough, given the time. And when the icon did shift to blue it was an audio-only link, again reasonable. Sid could just picture him, half awake on the side of the bed, Mrs O'Rouke blinking in annoyance at the light switched on.

'What the fuck is it, Hurst?' Royce O'Rouke demanded.

17

'You've only been back for six hours. For Christ's sake, man, can you not even piss properly without someone holding your—'

'Sir!' Sid said quickly – he knew only too well the kind of language O'Rouke used at the best of times. 'I've just coded a case up to one-oh-one status.'

O'Rouke was silent as he adjusted to the implication; everything he said was part of the official case record. 'Go ahead, Detective.'

'A body has been found in the river. There's a nasty puncture wound on the chest. I suspect smartcell extraction, too.'

'I see.'

'Sir, our preliminary identification is a North.'

This time the silence really stretched out as grains of snow kissed Sid's nose and cheeks.

'Repeat please.'

'It's a North clone, sir. We're at the Millennium Bridge. The examiner's clearing the body to be brought ashore now. In addition, I have four agency constables with me on scene, two divers and Captain Foy on the boat. There are also two civilian witnesses having their statements taken.'

'I want a lockdown on the area right away. Everyone on scene is to be taken up to Market Street station immediately. No external communication, understood?'

'Yes, sir. I've ordered Captain Foy to sweep the discovery area again once the body is in the examiner's van.'

'That's good, right.'

'I'm fairly certain he didn't simply fall off the bridge. My preliminary theory is he was dumped upriver somewhere. Body looks like it's been immersed for a while, but I'll confirm when the examiner gets back to me. I was going to assign Detective Lanagin to accompany the coroner's van to the city morgue. He can ensure procedure is followed.'

'All right, that's a good start. Hurst, we do not want media attention drawn to this yet – we have to have a clear field to operate the investigation in. The chain of evidence must remain clean.'

'Yes, sir. Uh . . . Chief?'

'Yes?'

'How do you want to handle notifying next-of-kin?'

Pause again, shorter this time. 'I'll take care of that. You concentrate on securing the scene and starting the investigation properly.'

'Yes, sir. I'd like permission and authorization to coordinate with the coast guard. I want any ships sailing on the Tyne tonight identified and searched.'

'Good call. I'll have the authorization ready for you when you get to Market Street.'

'Thank you, sir.' Sid watched the icon flick back to purple, then vanish.

Ian stepped off the top of the ladder, back onto the powdery snow of the promenade.

'So?' Sid asked.

'Examiner doesn't want to commit himself. Naturally,' Ian said. 'But best he can do with the water temperature and exposure is confirm immersion for at least an hour.'

'He didn't fall off the bridge.'

'No. He didn't fall off the bridge. Too much tidal current.'

'Does our examiner want to go for time of death?'

Ian's mouth produced a thin smile. 'No. That's down to the autopsy.'

'All right. I've spoken to the Chief. You're going with the examiner back to the morgue. Make sure there are no glitches, procedure to be upheld at all times, no exceptions.'

'Aye.'

'I'm back to Market Street. The duty network staff can lock and download all the mesh surveillance memories from along the river for tonight. I need to chase ships, as well.'

Ian pulled a dubious expression. 'Nothing sailing tonight. Not in this.'

'We can't see more than a hundred metres, I can't even see the Baltic Exchange on the other side. There could be a super-tanker out there for all we know.'

19

'We'd know that, man.'

'Detective, we cover every possibility.'

Ian sobered, realizing how many people – and what rank – would review tonight's log. 'Aye, you're right.' He went over to the waiting agency constables. 'Okay, guys, we have to get the body up here. Hope you cleared your medical – it weighs something.'

Sid watched for a moment as the examiner and divers attached ropes to the stretcher so the body could be pulled up onto the promenade. He tried to work out if he'd missed anything. The basics had definitely been covered. He was sure of it. *Starting the investigation properly.* O'Rouke couldn't have been clearer. In the morning, senior detectives would be moved in to assume command of the case; no doubt aided by a dozen specialist advisers Aldred North would send along from Northumberland Interstellar's security division. By lunchtime, Sid wouldn't have to worry about a thing.

Monday 14th January 2143

The alarm clock's sharp buzz dragged Sid awake. He groaned and reached out for the snooze button.

'Oh no you don't.' Jacinta reached over him and caught his roaming hand.

He gave another groan, louder and frustrated. The alarm kept going. 'All right, Jesus, pet.' He swung his legs out of the bed. Only then did she agree to release his hand. He brought it down vindictively on the clock, and the wretched noise stopped. He yawned. His eyes were blurry and he felt like he'd had maybe ten minutes' sleep. The room was cold, even with the regen air-con whirring away behind the ceiling vents.

Jacinta was climbing out on her side of the bed. Sid picked up the clock and held it close to his face – the only way he could make out the glowing green figures.

6:57.

'Crap.' He couldn't stop yawning. His bodymesh had detected waking activity, and waited its preset one minute before activating displays and audio tones. The iris smartcells then unfolded a pantheon of ghosts across his sight, which was their basic icon grid.

'What time did you get in?' Jacinta asked. She was giving him a puzzled look. He managed to give her a weak grin in return, enjoying the sight of her. Jacinta was only three years younger than him, but she aged oh-so-much better. The dark hair was shorter now than when they had met back in London, but still as lush, and always wild this time in the morning. Her figure was similar to those days too, slimmer than anyone who'd had two children should reasonably expect. That was all down to determination in abundance. With fat expelled and muscles toned by solid, regular gymwork – gymwork that she was pointing out more and more would stop *his* recent upward weight-creep – she was enticingly fit. But it was her complexion which really belied her age, as she'd kept a clear skin that seemed to defy wrinkles. Fair enough, he thought, given that half her surgical nurse's salary was spent on creams, lotions, pharmaceutical gels, and many many other products from that section of the department store where real men fear to tread.

Sharp green eyes peered at him as the first of the hair clips went in. 'Well?'

'About three thirty,' he admitted.

'Aw, pet! Why? What happened?' Suddenly she was all sympathy again.

'I got a one-oh-one.'

'No! Your first night back? That's bad luck.'

'Worse,' he admitted. 'Not to be shouted about at work, okay, but it was a North.'

'Crap on that,' she breathed in astonishment.

'Yeah, well.' He shrugged. 'O'Rouke will take me off it about a minute into the morning shift.'

'You sure?'

'Oh yeah. This has to be a perfect investigation.'

'You can do that,' she said immediately, and with not a little indignation.

'Yes.' That was the shame of it: he knew he really could handle the investigation, and handle it well. In fact, he rather relished the challenge, half the night having been spent formulating a case strategy ready to begin as soon as the morning shift arrived at work. That was the thing with a career-killer – done right it could be a career-maker just as easily. 'But I'm only six hours back into the job.'

She gave him a significant look. 'Aye, pet, but let's not forget why, okay? The Norths will want someone they know is good.'

'Whatever . . .'

Loud thumps from the landing, followed by an outraged shout, announced the morning struggle between William and Zara for the bathroom. Will was abruptly banging on the door, yelling at his younger sister to let him in. 'I canna wait, you cow,' he yelled.

Her contemptuous response was muffled.

'You'll have to take them to school for me,' Sid announced quickly, hoping it would get overlooked in the general morning chaos.

'No bloody way!' Jacinta exclaimed. 'We agreed. I've got a full cardio replacement booked for this morning. Top-money vat-grown heart with DNA screening and everything. Her insurance pays full whack and bonus to theatre staff.'

'I've been dumped a one-oh-one with a North.'

'You just said you'll be taken straight off.'

'Oh away wi' ya, pet!'

She laughed contemptuously at his attempt to speak Geordie. 'My theatre has been in the diary since before Christmas.'

'But—'

Out on the landing there was another fast exchange of heated insults as Zara came out of the bathroom and Will rushed in.

'It's their first day back at school,' Jacinta said. 'You'd let them go alone? In this weather? What kind of father is that?'

'It's not like they're just starting there.' Sid knew it was coming, she knew it too. It was down to who broke first.

Him . . . of course.

'Can't you call Debra?'

She threw her hands up. 'She'll start bloody charging us, she's like a taxi service for our kids these days.'

'We do it for hers.'

'Aye, when there's a month with a Z in it.'

He gave her the *firm-bordering-on-exasperation* look. Because that made so much difference when you've been married for eleven years.

'I'll call,' Jacinta said with a sigh. 'Given as how you're so scared of her.'

'I am not—'

'But we'll need to have them round to dinner. To say thanks, an' all.'

'Oh, not John for a whole evening? If boring was a sport he'd be trans-space champion.'

'Are you taking them to school, or do you want me to make the call?'

Sid growled and shook his head furiously. 'Make the call.'

*

Even now, with Will eight years old and Zara six, Sid still couldn't quite get his head around seeing them in their school uniforms. They were babies, far too young to be wrenched out of the house each day. Yet there they were at breakfast, looking impossibly smart in dark-red sweaters and blue shirts, like miniaturized adults.

Sid busied himself making the porridge, checking the certification seals before opening the packets. There had been talk down at the station about companies slipping unregulated batches into their processing plants, importing them from some of the settled worlds where organic verification was nonexistent and cash was supreme. Nothing you'd ever find out about on the licensed news.

'Why is Debra taking us to school this morning?' Zara asked as Jacinta tried to brush her long hair into some kind of order.

'Both of us are busy, pet. Sorry,' Sid told her. The pan on the induction hob was boiling too strongly, so he turned it down to a simmer and set the timer for seven minutes.

'Are you working again, Dad?' Will asked, his face all earnest.

'Yeah, I'm working again.'

'Can we afford to move now, then?'

Sid exchanged a look with Jacinta. 'Yes, we're thinking about moving again.' They had lived in the three-bedroom house in Walkergate for five years now. A pleasant enough home, but its age meant it was never designed for the cold of today's winters, so it cost a fortune to heat. Only having one bathroom was a pain, and the zone room was also the dining room. Then there were the neighbours, who were wary about having a policeman on the street.

'What about school?' Zara protested. 'All my friends are there. I don't want to leave.'

'You'll stay at the same school,' Sid assured her. It was a private one, after all, which ate huge chunks out of his salary, and was the main reason he'd cultivated supplementary revenue streams income, despite the risks. But nobody sent their kids to public schools if they could afford an alternative.

'Actually I found one last night,' Jacinta said. 'I was reviewing estate agent files.'

'Really?' It was news to Sid. He sipped at a mug of coffee. The smartcells in his mouth detected the caffeine and flashed up a diet intake warning. It was his most sincere New Year resolution to eat better and do more exercise. But he'd barely had any sleep . . . You have to be realistic about such things. He told his e-i to cancel the warning, spooning an extra sugar into the mug in an act of petulant defiance.

'In Jesmond.'

'Jesmond's nice,' Will said admiringly. 'Sun Tu and Hinny live there.'

'Jesmond's expensive,' Sid said.

'You gets what you pays for,' Jacinta replied.

Sid took the porridge off the hob, and ladled it into the bowls. 'True.'

'So can I call the agent?' Jacinta asked.

'Sure, why not.' They could afford it – he'd stacked up a lot of money in his secondary account over the past few years. Now there was just the problem of how they used it to buy somewhere else without alerting the Tax Bureau. The reason they hadn't moved before Christmas was because of the attention it would have focused on him. Buying a house while he was on the reduced salary of a suspension would have triggered a host of Tax Bureau monitor programs.

'Mum,' Will pleaded. 'Does it have a proper zone room?'

'Yes, it has a proper zone room.'

'Cool!'

'What about en suites?' Zara asked urgently.

'Five bedrooms, two en suites, one family bathroom.'

Zara grinned contentedly to herself as she started to stir strawberry jam into her porridge. Just for a moment his family was happy and quiet; Sid felt he ought to put that in some kind of log. Dawn was bringing a harsh grey light to the misted-up kitchen window. It had stopped snowing. He began to have a good feeling about how the day was shaping up.

'If we're moving to a bigger house, does that mean we can have a puppy now?' Will asked.

*

Newcastle's central police station was a big glass and stone cube built in 2068, an impressive civic structure to reflect the new-found wealth that was benefiting the whole city as the bioil that flowed through the gateway increased on a near-daily basis. It had replaced the older station which had stood on the corner of Market Street and Pilgrim Street, providing all the facilities a modern police force could possibly want – if only it had the money to operate them.

The underground garage had four levels, capable of holding staff cars and a hundred and fifty official vehicles from mobile incident control rooms to patrol cars, prisoner vans to fast pursuit cars and smartdust dispenser trucks. A clear victory for design optimism over real-world practicality. Sid had never even seen anyone use the lowest level in all his fifteen years in Newcastle; the police simply didn't have that kind of fleet.

Every winter in the city, some councillor raised the idea of heating the roads Scandinavian-style to get rid of the snow and ice – at least in the centre of Newcastle – and each year it was deferred to an appraisal committee. Instead, long-term interests prevailed; low-wage crews and big snowploughs hit the roads and pavements on Monday morning, attempting to clear the weekend's snow for the armada of office workers heading in to the centre. They'd made a reasonable job leading up to the station's ramps; Sid drove his four-year-old Toyota Dayon down into the Market Street garage without worrying about sliding. He'd only seen two shunts on the way in, and it'd taken an acceptable fifteen minutes.

It was coming up on twenty past eight by the time he made it up to the third floor where the serious case offices were situated. The 2North murder had been assigned Office3, one of the larger ones, with two rows of zone console desks that could sit up to twelve specialist network operatives, a couple of zone cubicles, and five hi-rez, floor-to-ceiling wallscreens; one side was partitioned off into four private offices. Thermal exchange climate vents rattled as they produced a stream of air at a temperature three degrees below comfortable, the blue-grey carpet was worn and stained, the furniture was ten years old, but on the plus side, the network systems had all been upgraded last year. Sid knew that was what really counted; clearly O'Rouke knew it as well. Only five of the third-floor offices had been modernized in the last four years.

Detective Dobson was leading the night shift team, which consisted of three operatives establishing the procedures Sid had agreed with her at the shift handover last night. She acknowledged him with a quick nod and beckoned him into one of the glass-walled side offices.

'Basic datawork is laid out,' she told him. 'We've been downloading riverside surveillance mesh memories since five this morning. I've gone all the way upstream to the A1 bridge, and taken it two streets back on both sides.'

'Thanks. How far is it to the bridge?'

'Close on seven and a half kilometres, but I've included the corresponding road macromesh so you can observe the vehicle traffic. That's a lot of memory.' She hesitated before lowering her voice. 'There are some gaps.'

'Bound to be with this kind of snow.'

'Maybe. See what you think when you review it.'

'Hoookay. Do we have an identity, yet?'

She gave him a woeful glance. 'I think it could be a North.'

'Smartarse. Which one? Actually, do we even know how many there are?'

'It's a difficult figure to find. Northumberland Interstellar isn't exactly forthcoming about how many times Augustine has been a daddy.'

'Most of the 2s were born to surrogate mothers, weren't they? Those kids were popped out just to boost NI's management numbers.'

'Depends which non-licensed site loaded with disgraceful muck-raking gossip you access. But as best as I could find, there's just under a hundred of them. More 3s, mind; they're frisky boys, our Norths. But we're not riding an exponential curve here, thank God. The 2s aren't big breeders. Why would you, when you know your son's going to be a few neurones short of a headful? Shame the 3s don't have that much sense; and there are a lot of sharp little golddiggers out there ready to trap a 3 and collect their palimony, so we've no idea about how many 4s are wandering round loose.'

'Best guess?'

'Could be up to three hundred and fifty. I'm not guaranteeing that, mind.'

'And no one's called this one in missing?'

'He's been dead for eleven hours minimum now. Early days. Someone will start asking before lunch.'

Sid glanced back out into the office where Ian had just arrived and was chatting to the night shift. 'Has the media found out?'

'No. O'Rouke had two techs load monitor programs into the station network as we were setting up. He spoke to all of us direct about what he'd do if anyone leaked it. I think we're secure so far.'

'That's not going to last. But thanks for keeping it under wraps.'

'My pleasure. I'll handover now.'

'Sure.' Sid put his hand above the zone console's biometric pad, and told his e-i to log him in to the case. The station network acknowledged his request. The desk systems in the office switched to his personalized programs in their customized layout. 'Is there a pool?' he asked casually.

Dobson gave him a small grin. 'Certainly not, that would bring disgrace upon the force. Mind you, if you're still here in the room after lunch you'll owe me a hundred Eurofrancs.'

'Oh cheers, pet. Nice to know you have that much confidence.'

'You don't want it,' she said seriously. 'Not this one. Let one of O'Rouke's brown-nosers take it.'

'Aye, I might just.'

They went back out into the main office. Eva Sealand had just walked in, a senior constable specializing in visual interpretation, who'd reassigned from Leicester eighteen months ago. Sid had worked with her on a semi-permanent basis since she started at Newcastle, a cheerful redheaded Icelandic woman with three kids and a partner in some kind of company network management job which Sid never quite understood.

'Some work for you today,' he told her. 'And then some.'

She smiled as she pulled her hair back and twisted it through an elastic tie. 'I just heard,' she said quietly. 'For real? A North?'

'I was there when they pulled him out of the Tyne last night.'

'Who else have you got?'

'Lorelle should be here soon. I've requested some extra members, and I expect we'll just keep on expanding today.'

Eva leaned in close. 'Are you staying?'

'Dobson's running the sweep,' he muttered back. His main concern now was if he'd have anybody left to help with his other cases after O'Rouke shifted him back to normal duties. 'But I'm telling you, pet, there'll be some overtime to clock up on this, don't you—' He broke off, staring in astonishment at the two officers who'd just walked in. 'Aye, man,' he grunted.

Northumberland Interstellar didn't have a monopoly on employing 2Norths. Given the personality which Kane had been so desperate to duplicate, that trait he valued above all else – his determination – could switch them one of two ways: either they went straight to work in the family company, keen to push it further on so many fronts – financial, industrial, political, legal – one heading up every department with younger versions ready to assume top-dog position; or they struck out for themselves, equally resolute to show they didn't need family to get ahead. The second type were in a minority, and tended to set up businesses which ran in parallel with the interests of Northumberland Interstellar. An even smaller minority went into public service. In fact, Sid knew of only two: Abner 2North and Ari 2North, who were now standing in Office3's doorway, looking round expectantly.

Abner was the elder of the two, in his late forties, reaching detective second grade, specializing in forensic analysis. Sid had worked with him several times in the last decade, and always found him a very effective officer no matter what case they were assigned. The fact Abner hadn't reached a higher grade was always tied up with the biggest, longest-lasting gossip in the station: outside politics, what motivation any of them could possibly have for joining the force was anyone's guess. Sid didn't worry himself over that – it was results which counted in this game, and Abner had a respectable clean-up rate. Ari was maybe twelve years younger, still a senior constable in the data management track, and equally capable. There were few ways of telling them apart. The occasional difference in hair length helped; Norths had dark mouse-brown hair that curled beyond any cosmetic product's ability to tame, and didn't grey until they were well over fifty. But they all favoured keeping it cropped short, adding to the difficulty of separating them. Features didn't help either, as they were unnervingly identical: the flattish nose, rounded chin, grey-blue eyes, bushy eyebrows. They were also the same height, and Kane had clearly been one of those enviable people who didn't put on weight on an age-related basis. Voice was a uniform gravelly bass that always sounded slightly too loud. The most common way to guess their age (and therefore difference) was a quick scope of the neck, which thickened as they got older, a process Sid always compared to rings in a tree trunk. But it was a quick and easy tag, as some of the older Norths he'd seen had necks as wide as their head.

'Gentlemen,' Sid said quietly in greeting.

Abner gave him a tight smile. 'Morning, boss. Good to see you're taking the lead on this.'

'Thanks. So you understand who our victim is?'

'Aye,' Ari said.

'And you're okay with that?'

'Yes.'

Abner put a hand on Sid's shoulder. 'Don't worry. There'll be no bias. Procedure at all times, right?'

'Absolutely,' Ari confirmed.

It gave Sid an odd feeling talking to them – the same face he'd seen bloodless and frozen eight hours ago. Enough to make him question his own judgement. And as for whoever had the smart idea of assigning them to the case ... O'Rouke, of course. 'All right then, we still don't have his identity, and I need it. Once I have a name everything else should just fall into place. Find out for me. Any way you can.'

'There's no name yet?' Abner asked. He sounded surprised.

'Early days,' Sid said. It was a shabby thing to tell them, but he wasn't even sure if he should offer condolences for their loss. After all, the victim was family, right?

Lorelle Burdett, a generalist constable who was a regular on Sid's case teams, arrived a couple of footsteps ahead of Royce O'Rouke, and Sid stopped worrying about trivia like the etiquette of clone family ties. Newcastle's Chief Constable was dressed in his full uniform that morning, a dark tunic with an impressive number of coloured service award bands and plenty of gold braid. O'Rouke was a sixty-seven-year-old who had risen through the ranks by virtue of a respectable clean-up rate and an inordinately dirty political skill. You were either one of his players, showing total loyalty as a useful scapegoat, or you would spend your entire career stalled as you investigated one suspected illegal toxic waste tipping after another.

Two aides in smart dark suits slid in behind O'Rouke; Chloe Healy, the force's information officer, and Jenson San, the senior staff representative. Sid struggled not to give them the stone-face of contemptuous hatred. He really despised their type – enforcers and executioners of the regime – and as for their ability to misinterpret and misrepresent on behalf of their Dark Overlord, it was something that he could never master, let alone better.

Sid braced himself. This would be the moment when he was taken aside and given his new case assignment for the week. It was a shame – he could have done with the overtime.

O'Rouke shook his hand. 'How's it going, Detective?'

'Handover from the night shift almost complete, sir. The preliminary data I requested is downloaded. I'm about to outline the procedures I want followed, and designate assignments.' He was trying not to be obvious, glancing over O'Rouke's shoulder to see which senior crony was hovering in the corridor ready to be introduced. But Jenson San closed the office door, and the blue rim light came on to show the room was secure.

'That's good,' O'Rouke said; he turned to face the team. 'All right people, we all know the identity of the victim is going to create a storm of media interest. I want to emphasize that you do not make unauthorized statements. So we're perfectly clear: that is not one fucking word. Anything, any contact you have with reporter scum or unlicensed site reps, you refer to Chloe here.' He indicated the information officer. 'That directive is to be passed right down the chain of command to the police and agency staff you'll be multiplying your investigation with. I can assure you that whatever the budget requirement you have it will be met. For this I expect a positive result. Newcastle must send out a clear message that no one is above or beyond the law.

Nobody arrives here and commits this kind of crime against our most distinguished family and gets away with it. Understood?'

He was awarded a muttering of 'yes sir' from the team, and nodded gruffly at them. 'Good, I'm sure you will make me proud.' He inclined his head at Sid. 'Detective, a word.'

Here we go. Sid walked into the small office, watching as O'Rouke first went over to the two 2Norths and shook each of them by the hand, muttering: 'I'm so sorry for your loss.'

Bastard.

Surprisingly, the Chief didn't bring his aides with him as he joined Sid in the office. 'Good move calling me right away,' O'Rouke said.

'Frankly, I didn't know what else to do. A murder I can handle. But this . . . Fuck! A North!'

'Yeah. I'm not even going to tell you how much shit I've showered in already today. The Mayor is crapping bricks the size of a bungalow; and the city prosecution director has retained a London firm to handle the case when you take it to court – which you *will* be doing. You'll be getting a call from them in about half an hour to discuss strategy and the level of evidence they'll need.'

Sid leaned back slightly and looked at the imposing Chief Constable with slightly narrowed eyes. 'Me?'

'Yeah, you, Hurst.'

'Are you sure about that?'

'No other fucker on the second floor will step up and put his dick on the block. It's you.'

'Shit! Okay.'

'You screw up every now and then, who doesn't? But Chloe and Jenson went over your record after I woke them up at one o'clock this morning – they hate you for that by the way – but they say you're an okay detective, you know procedure, and you know the system. And face it, you can call down whatever covering fire you want with this one; Christ, you want to hire CERN for forensics, you got it. We have a tap directly into Northumberland Interstellar's primary credit account. Every agency we've ever dealt with is going to be calling in favours all over the station just for the privilege of meeting you so they can hand you and your boy season tickets to St James' Park for the next ten years.'

'Christ.' Despite the shock, Sid was actually enjoying the idea of being left in charge. Typical that everyone else was so shit-scared for their career they'd even risk defying O'Rouke. And that same second-floor 'everybody' thought he was on his way out – which he was, but just not in a way they imagined. Besides, unlimited budget for real, that was like watching the Gunners get a five nil result over Man U.

'So what have you got?' O'Rouke asked.

'Sweet FA so far. I don't even have a name yet, but I've put our pet Norths on finding out. I figured that was safest.'

'Okay, but they're not here just for show. Use the buggers, don't patronize them. They're going to provide Augustine the proof I need him to have about how effective and dedicated my force is to finding the bastard that did this.'

'Right . . .' Sid said cautiously.

'What?'

'Circumstances. He was naked, and that was a weird wound. This isn't some mugging that went wrong.'

'What are you saying?'

'I'm saying it could get unpleasant.'

'No shit, genius?'

'What if we find stuff the Norths don't want people knowing about them?'

'Then they're going to be seriously pissed off with *you*, aren't they?'

Sid took a long look at O'Rouke's face, ruddy from high blood pressure, the craggy skin arranged in a viciously belligerent ex-pression. Challenging him. Daring him. The same pissing contest as always.

'I'm due a promotion,' Sid said.

'You're just back off suspension.'

'Aye, but I'm covering your arse on this. You don't get that for free. I want grade-five or I walk.'

'Fucking walk then.'

Sid turned and went for the door. Calculated risk . . .

'You stop right there you little motherfucker,' O'Rouke snapped.

With his back to the Chief Constable, Sid grinned before turning round.

'If you don't solve this, and I mean get the bastard convicted, I will personally fry your balls for breakfast and feed them to the Norths,' O'Rouke said.

'Deal.'

O'Rouke jabbed a fat finger under Sid's nose. 'And be clear, there is no weird, no kinky, no tox involvement, nothing that drops a turd on the North family. He was a decent man murdered by scum.'

'That's what I believe. That's what we're working to prove.'

'Okay then, you and me get what this shit is about. Update me every two hours.' O'Rouke delivered one last warning glare before he pulled the door open. Chloe Healy and Jenson San fell in behind him as he left Office3 without a further word.

Everybody else turned to look at Sid with expressions ranging from curious to fascinated. He walked over to the door and shut it carefully, waiting until the blue rim light was on.

'All right then,' Sid told them. 'This is how it is. Last night a male we've preliminarily identified as a North was pulled from the river. There's a wound to the chest, and he was naked, which gives it a one-oh-one classification. What we're focusing on this morning is finding his identity and where he was dumped into the Tyne. Detective Dobson, what do we have by way of river traffic last night?'

'We identified three possibles,' she said. 'River police intercepted and inspected all of them.'

'Good work,' Sid said.

'Thanks. The first was the *Menthanine*: corporate charter boat, clean record, taking a group of four businessmen on a fishing trip. According to the captain, they'd been toxing up on board since late afternoon, and he was taking them out to the Scottish Isles overnight so they could start fishing when they were awake and sober.'

'Toxed argument that ended badly?' Ian queried.

'The trip had been booked for five weeks,' Dobson said. 'They were the only ones listed, and the crew confirms no one else was on board. But the *Menthanine* left from Dunston Marina, so I've acquired the mesh logs from its quay to review and see if our North came on board. I have to say: doubtful. The river police were satisfied their story was legitimate, too. However, they were ordered to make anchor off Tynemouth so we can run a forensic check this morning. Same goes for the *Bay Spirit*. That's a private yacht owned by a Tammie and Mark Haiah. It's just been refurbished, and starting on a round-the-world voyage; you can hire it for week-long periods between nice marinas and yacht clubs. First booking begins in Normandy in four days' time. This was the shakedown voyage; captain and the steward are a boyfriend-girlfriend crew. No one else on board.'

'And the third?' Sid asked.

'Another yacht. This seems to be the night for it. The *Dancer's Moon*, big floating gin palace, with a crew of seven owned by Corran Fiele. He's a director of several local service and engineering companies. He's taking his wife and three kids down to the Med for the rest of the winter. Again, doesn't look suspicious, but they're anchored with the others.'

'Okay, thanks, good work. I will sort getting forensics out there to clear them. So, we still need our two basics: name and crime location. Once we have them we can work our magic and plot his timeline. Now I'm expecting friend or family or workplace to call him in as missing soon enough, but I still want us to be checking. Abner and Ari, that's you to start with. The rest of you, I want all the riverside mesh memories confirmed then indexed on a map zone so we can see our field of coverage. It was high tide twenty-one forty-two hours last night, so begin with that as the dump time, as the body had to have been washed downstream. We'll narrow it down after the autopsy, but what I want to know is last night's blind spots in the mesh surveillance. This had purpose behind it – dumping the body was deliberate – and whoever did it isn't going to be waving at the smartdust.'

Sid was pleased to see the way they just got on with it. The team was competent. The night shift handed over codes and they began organizing data without any time spent on bullshit office who's-doing-what, I-want-this. They just each took a section of river, and began indexing the mesh memories.

After verifying the yachts were still in place and being watched by the river police, Sid called Osborne at Northern Forensics and arranged for each boat to be inspected. They were his preferred company; well equipped with decent personnel – and his second-ary got a cash deposit each time he threw work their way. The call was official, logged and recorded by the police network, so Osborne kept personal chat to a minimum, but he was quick to prioritize the case after Sid showed him the assigned financial rating. He was promised a team for the boats would be at Tynemouth within an hour.

'Three teams,' Sid said. 'One for each boat.'

Osborne took a moment to absorb that. 'It's Monday morning.'

'If you can't give me what I need, I'll take the contract to a company that can. I need this doing quickly and effectively.'

'Of course, I'll see to it personally. Three teams it is.'

'I'm sending an officer and three agency constables with each team in case they find any blood spill. They'll be at Tynemouth in thirty minutes; make sure your people are there in time.' He shouldn't have grinned at the blank screen after Osborne's pained expression faded to black, but if you couldn't act like a prima donna bitch on this one, then when could you?

With the first round of forensics sorted, Sid started helping with the surveillance logs. He sat at one of the spare zone consoles and the slim rectangular screen immediately curved towards him with an aquatic motion, forming a semicircle around his head.

Its projection interfaced with his iris smartcells, immersing him in a perfect holographic display, resembling a miniature zone. When he glanced down, his hands were hovering in the keyspace, a cube of air above the desk's keyboard. His personal operating topography materialized, icons with cog-like protrusions which he could spin and turn in three dimensions with an easy fingertip flip.

He took a section of the northern riverbank between the Tyne Bridge and the Redheugh Bridge. The city had sprayed a band of smartdust three metres up on all the ancient buildings set back on the other side of the road which ran above the river. That gave the pinhead-size particles a decent angle of view over the streets and the railings above the bank. Meshed together they should provide total coverage, showing him cars and pedestrians. Dobson had taken the memories from midday Sunday to two o'clock this morning. There were a few gaps, where individual smartdust motes had glitched or were smeared in pigeon crap or snow and ice had frozen over them, but the overall mesh memory had enough data to be formatted into a single 3D montage capable of being played inside a zone. That left the road macro-mesh, controlling and monitoring traffic, which had to be combined with the visual record to give an aggregate of the riverside.

Sid scanned through the midday Sunday visual image, as if he was gliding along the street, looking out across the river, establishing the baseline resolution quality. 'Aye, crap on it.' He stopped the replay when he was just east of the venerable swing bridge, leaving him looking out at a nightclub boat moored to the refurbished wooden pier that extended out from the bridge's southern support. 'Anyone know how many party boats are moored along the river these days?'

Ian looked up from his zone console, where he'd been reviewing meshed memories around the King Edward railway bridge. 'Five or six, I think,' he said.

'We're going to need all their surveillance.'

'Dobson already got them,' Eva said.

'Hell, she's good.'

By ten o'clock Abner and Ari still hadn't got a positive identification on the body. That was starting to bug Sid.

'We've got most 2Norths confirmed as alive,' Abner said by way of compensation.

Sid told them to stick with it. He was frontloading a lot of reliance on the autopsy now. Once they found method and estimated immersion time they'd have *something* to go on. Even so, a name would be a lot better.

Jenson San reappeared just before eleven. 'The North family have arranged for an observing coroner at the autopsy,' he told Sid. 'And we have the Chief Coroner himself performing the examination.'

'Thanks.'

'Do we have the victim's identity yet?'

Sid shook his head, irritated by the one crucial missing item. For a victim of this high profile it really didn't reflect well on himself and the team. And damn it, they were a good team.

'We need it,' Jenson muttered in a low voice.

'Yeah, I worked that one out for myself. Thanks, man.'

A quarter of an hour later Sid left for the city morgue, which was housed in a modern annex to the glass and steel towers of Arevalo Medical's Royal Victoria Infirmary.

As he drew into the car park next to the city morgue block Sid saw notices proclaiming that parking would be suspended in two months so footings could be sunk for the new oncology clinic. 'So where do we park?' he muttered to himself as he crunched his way over the snow and into the warm lobby.

For all its clean modern lines and well maintained interior, the morgue always depressed him. He'd lost track years ago of just how many grieving parents, partners, and family members he'd escorted in to identify a body. Thankfully there was no one in the lobby waiting for that grim task, though the little group standing beside the reception counter was almost as off-putting.

Chloe Healy turned from the two men she was talking to. 'Detective Hurst, this is Aldred North,' she said.

Aldred shook Sid's hand, showing a professional smile.

'Northumberland Interstellar security director.' He was in his late forties, wearing a suit and coat that must have been in the eight thousand Eurofranc range, a simple demonstration of exactly how far up the company hierarchy he was, which told everyone he was a 2North. 'Sorry, but officially I'm your insurance cover liaison for the case. Hope you don't mind. I'll try to be as unobtrusive as I can be.'

Sid gave him a neutral gaze, quite proud he could maintain such perfect composure. *Chloe must know. She's O'Rourke's creature, there's no way she can't.* 'That's fine, sir. I'm just sorry this had to happen at all.'

'Thank you. And this is Dr Fransun, our company's senior medical officer.'

'Doctor.' Sid shook hands, noticing how nervous the man was. But then as it was his boss's brother/son who'd been murdered last night, it was understandable enough.

'Do we know who it is yet?' Aldred asked.

From the corner of his eye, Sid caught Chloe wince. 'Not yet, no, which in itself is interesting.'

'How so?' Aldred asked.

'Whoever committed the murder knew what they were doing. The absence of data on this case indicates we're dealing with a professional, someone who knows how to cover up afterwards and make our job as difficult as possible.'

'You mean he was *hit*?'

'Until we know who he is and fill in some background, I can't speculate on why he was killed. Do you know of any member of your family being threatened?'

'Nothing outside the usual cranks, no.'

'Well if anything does come to light . . .'

'Absolutely.'

The city's Chief Coroner came out to greet them. 'I'm ready for you now,' he announced solemnly.

'Then I'm back to the office,' Chloe said. 'Keep me updated, please, Detective.'

Sid gave her his best insincere smile. 'Of course.'

'So how is O'Rouke?' Aldred asked as they walked along the corridors to the exam room.

'I believe he mentioned something about getting a result.'

Aldred snorted in sour amusement. 'My family wants a certainty here, Detective. We're prepared to wait for that. Don't cut corners on our account.'

'With the funding you've made available, I won't have to.'

The corpse was resting on a surgical-style table in the middle of the exam room. Directly above him, long segmented metal arms were attached to the ceiling around the bright lighting circle, each ending in a different kind of sensor. Around them were the holographic cameras to record the procedure. Screens made up one wall, while small sample desks lined the other, each with its own stock of instruments.

Sid and the others put on pale-blue smocks, with tight gloves to prevent any possible evidence contamination. Two assistants joined the coroner.

Under the harsh lighting the corpse somehow looked even worse than he had the night before on the boat. His skin had dried out and whitened to a classic pallor, leaving the big chest wound almost black by comparison.

The coroner activated the cameras and started his official commentary. His assistants wheeled instrument trolleys over to the examination table.

He began with a spectroscopic analysis, bringing down one of the sensor arms and sliding it smoothly across the body. 'Checking for contaminants,' he explained.

Sid thought that was taking procedure too far; the North had been in the Tyne for hours, he'd be saturated with pollution. He said nothing, though. Samples were taken from under the fingernails; hair was combed out. Swabs were applied to mouth, nose, and ears. Then they performed a thorough visual inspection.

'Note the minor abrasions on both heels,' the coroner said. 'They all run in one direction.'

'He was dragged,' Sid said.

'Correct. Post mortem.'

'He was dumped in the river after death,' Sid explained to Aldred.

'Early days, Detective,' the coroner said. He turned the left leg and indicated a three-centimetre graze. 'Again, post mortem, the wound is deeper at the top, indicating a snag of some kind punctured the skin and tore.' Another sensor was applied, along with a micro-camera which threw up a hugely magnified image on one of the screens. 'No residuals, I'm afraid. The river took care of that.'

The body was turned over, and the exam continued. Sid did his best not to flinch as one of the assistants took a swab sample from the body's anus. What that must be like for Aldred he couldn't imagine.

The coroner held up one of the hands, then the other, scanning the arms. 'There are small extraction marks everywhere. The smartcells were removed post mortem.'

'Roughly how long would that take?' Sid asked.

'I'll catalogue the exact number later, but if you're doing it properly, it takes about thirty seconds for each one. Most people have between ten and fifty depending on what level of transnet access you want, and how much of your health you like to monitor. They're actually quite easy to remove, since commercially available smartcells measure less than half a millimetre, except for the iris ones of course, they're a lot smaller. Obviously you have to locate them first, though. Judging by the mess they made of his eyeballs, I'd say they weren't too concerned about precision.'

'Each North family member has stealth smartcells,' Dr Fransun said. 'They won't activate and link without a code. They're embedded in case of abduction.'

Sid gave Aldred a sharp glance. 'And?'

'No response. I tried the general code as soon as we came in. Nothing.'

'So either he's not a true North, or they extracted the stealth smartcells as well.'

'Yes.'

'But if they're not active, how would they do that?'

'A sophisticated scan, or they tortured the codes out of him.'

'There's no sign of that,' the coroner said; he indicated the corpse's hands. 'There aren't even any defensive wounds. Whatever happened to him, it was quick.' He lifted the right hand to indicate the missing fingertip skin. 'Again, the skin was sliced off post mortem.'

'Are you sure you want to stay for this part?' Sid asked once the body was rolled onto its back again.

'Sure,' Aldred grunted.

The big C-shaped body sensor descended on two arms, and slowly moved the length of the corpse. They all watched the 3D image build up on a wallscreen. Sections were amplified on surrounding screens.

'No foreign matter visible,' the coroner said.

Dr Fransun walked over to the wall of screens, peering at one. 'That's unusual.'

The coroner joined him, the two of them peering at a blue and white image that seemed to show translucent sheets folded round each other in some complex origami. 'I see what you mean,' the coroner agreed.

'What's up?' Sid asked.

'There seems to be a lot of damage inside the chest cavity. That doesn't quite correspond to the surface wound.'

They returned to the corpse and swung a micro-camera across the wound. High-resolution images of the five puncture wounds were recorded, their dimensions measured exactly. Four of them were close together, in a slight curve, while the fifth, lower, puncture was a couple of centimetres from the rest.

'Each one is a slightly different size,' the coroner said. 'I thought it was one blade used repeatedly. Interesting, the weapon has five separate blades. That would be extremely difficult to use.'

'How so?' Aldred asked.

'To penetrate skin and bone – which is what's happened here – is hard enough for a single sharp blade. Human muscle can do it, obviously, but a considerable force has to be exerted. The body

43

provides significant resistance. Here, the assailant had to exert enough force for five blades to penetrate simultaneously. Most difficult.'

'Big man, then,' Sid said. He was staring at the wound pattern – something bothered him.

'Or frenzied,' the coroner said. 'But your first guess is probably the correct one. Let's check the angle of penetration.' He muttered to his e-i, and five green lines materialized on one of the screens. 'Oh, that's interesting. Judging by that angle I'd say victim and assailant were almost the same height.'

Sid walked round the examination table, then leaned forward and put his right hand on top of the wound, fingers extended. Each fingertip came to rest above a cut. His gave the coroner a quizzical glance.

'That is strange,' the coroner said slowly. 'A five-bladed knife designed to mimic the human hand.'

Sid backed away from the table. 'At least that should show up easily in the database,' he said, and began to instruct his e-i on the search.

'We'll open him up and sample the cellular structure,' the coroner said. 'Decay measurement will provide us with an accurate time of death.'

'Really,' Sid told Aldred. 'You should think about leaving now.'

'No. I need to see this through.'

The coroner started with a Y-shaped cut through the skin from both shoulders down to the base of the sternum, then carrying on down the abdomen to the root of the penis. Sid looked round as the flesh was peeled away; he'd seen this enough times. A camera recorded the punctures and cuts to the rib bones above the heart. Then a small powerblade was used to cut cleanly through the clavicles and ribs, allowing the coroner and his assistants to remove the breastbone, exposing the organs below.

Both the coroner and Dr Fransun were silent as they surveyed the damage. Sid peered over their shoulders.

'What the hell did that?' he asked in dismay. The North's

heart was in tatters, reduced to a purple-red mush surrounded by a jelly of clotted blood.

'The blades moved once they were inside,' the coroner said in shock. 'Praise be to Allah, blades like fingers stabbed into him then closed around the heart, completely shredding it.'

*

The transparent globe was made out of a carbon silicon compound whose particular superstrength molecular structure could be produced only in zero gee. It measured three metres across and had a small access airlock where it was attached to the mountain-sized space habitat's external axle spindle. Even with the material's impressive qualities, it was eight centimetres thick to ensure anyone inside would be well protected. Jupiter orbit was a notoriously hostile radiation environment.

But beautiful, Constantine North thought as he watched the black speck that was Ganymede's shadow traverse the gas giant's eternal storm bands. That was why he'd built the observation bubble, so he could float in a cross-legged yoga position like some kind of Buddha gyroscope and stare out at his bizarre yet wondrous chosen home. Some days he would gaze out at Jupiter's fantastic racing clouds and whirling moons for hours at a time.

As always, he watched the vast bands of variegated whites and pastel-browns and gentle blues gyrate against each other without any enhancements, content with everything his raw eyes could show him. From his vantage point, half a million kilometres above those frenetic clouds, the gas giant was a two-thirds crescent, big enough and bright enough to cast a spectral light across him. But cold. There was no heat in the pearl radiance that fell across his newly youthful face, no substance. Out here, beyond the Sun's habitable zone, light by itself wasn't strong enough to support planetary life.

Out there in the blackness, little flares of blue flame flickered briefly around a dazzling silver flower. The *Minantha* was returning from Earth, manoeuvring on its final approach to the habitat amalgamation. A slim cylinder a hundred and thirty metres long, it contained the fusion reactor for its high-density ion drive – along with the crew section and several hundred tons of cargo – all surrounded by the vast curving petals of the mirror-silver coolant radiators. Jupiter possessed three of the ferry craft, all of them flying twenty-seven-month loops between the gas giant and Earth.

Opening the Newcastle gateway to Jupiter orbit back in 2088 had been a one-time operation, allowing Constantine to deliver all the industrial machinery and initial wheel-hostel he needed to start his small empire in magnificent isolation. It had taken a day and a half to shunt everything through, a process which left the modules tumbling all around Jupiter space. Without an anchor mechanism turning it to a stable gateway, the open end of a trans-spacial connection would oscillate through spacetime around its exit coordinate like the tip of a tree in a hurricane. It had taken Constantine, his sons, and their followers a month to gather all the modules and factories and tanks and generators together into a stable constellation around their chosen carbonaceous chondritic asteroid so that they could begin mining and processing the minerals into raw. Only then could they begin construction of their new home.

Now, Constantine's only known contact with Earth was through the ferry ships, which brought cargo from Gibraltar; mainly seeds and genetic samples to expand the habitat's extensive genebank, but also specialist microfacture systems, and even sometimes a few people whom they'd recruited to add to their modest number of indigenous residents.

A bell rang in an old familiar tone, stirring Constantine from his reverie. Strange what his mind prioritized, but that particular hundred-and-ten-year-old memory of a telephone ringing in a marbled hallway had always drawn his attention. Every time it used to ring, Kane North would hurry to answer it and nothing else mattered, even if he was spending a rare moment with his three brother-sons.

Constantine closed his eyes against the icy splendour of the stormscape and the much closer glittering constellation of industrial systems which were his own creation. Still the ancient telephone bell rang, an impulse seeping into his brain at a much deeper level than any auditory nerve could reach. He let his consciousness rise through several levels of autonomous thoughts which now formed the strata of his resequenced brain until he reached the artificial layer, the one which stretched beyond his skull. His attention slipped across the multitude of connections until it reached the junction with the simplest nerve bundle that handled communications to the habitat AI. It opened like some third eye revealing a topology that could never exist in a Newtonian universe. The ethereal call of the telephone vanished.

'Yes?' he asked.

'Dad,' Coby replied. 'You have a message.'

'From whom?' There was no question of why he'd been disturbed. Coby, or indeed anyone at Jupiter, knew not to interrupt him when he was contemplating the universe. Whatever event occurred, it would have to be supremely important to warrant breaking his ruminations. The AI alone didn't have the authority unless they'd suffered a catastrophe, like a full-on asteroid impact. Therefore there were only a very limited number of people who could send a message that got bumped up the nominal chain of command to this exalted altitude. Two, in total, out of all humanity. He made a guess which it was.

'Augustine,' Coby said.

Right. Constantine breathed in, scenting the faintest tang of atmospheric filter purity, an air really too clean for humans. At the moment, time delay on a radio signal from Earth was forty minutes. This was not a conversation. And there were a limited number of things the brothers had left to say to one another. He made another guess as to the topic – and it wasn't good. After all, Augustine's medical and genetic technology wasn't as advanced as anything available at Jupiter. 'What does he want?'

'It's encrypted. A very heavy encryption. I'm assuming you have the key.'

'Let us hope so. Route it to me.'

The message began to play. Constantine's eyes snapped open.

His shocked consciousness viewed the autopsy images superimposed across supersonic cyclone spots the size of oceans charging along the storm bands to clash with counter-swirls in neighbouring bands amid explosion blooms of frozen ammonia and grubby ultraviolet-charged smog. An eerie backdrop indeed for the sharp functional graphics detailing cellular decay, blood chemistry composition, and hard-focus pictures of the sad butchered heart of a dead nephew-brother.

The message ended, leaving him trying to blink away the tears which would never otherwise flow free in zero gee. And how arrogantly wrong he'd been about the topic. Not that it was a bad thing, but the fright he was experiencing was akin to the sight of his own grave opening up. He was aware of his heart rate increasing, of adrenalin rushing through his blood, flushing the skin which radiated the new heat back out towards the lonely, majestic gas giant beyond the bubble. *No*, he told himself, *this is not fright. This is excitement that the challenge has finally come. It has been long enough.*

'Dad?' Coby asked. 'Is there a reply?'

'No. Just an acknowledgement that the message was received. I will prepare an appropriate message of sympathy later.'

'Right.'

'I'm coming down. Please have Clayton and Rebka meet me at home. And prep a lightwave ship for a trip to Earth.'

'Really?'

'Yes.'

*

Sid was watching the preliminary autopsy report slither across his iris smartcell grid. The neat tabulations on cellular decay and stomach contents were superimposed over the pasta he was twirling onto his fork. Around him, the bustle of the station canteen continued apace as people took their lunch break. He ignored it completely as he put the information together in a list he could use. The body had been immersed for barely two hours, which gave them some figures on how far it could have drifted down the Tyne. Which was almost irrelevant compared to the shock which was the estimated time of death: the morning of Friday the eleventh, three days ago. A North had been missing for three days and no one had called it in. That wasn't merely suspicious, realistically it was impossible – and that was down-right creepy.

He was beginning to think it was a domestic that had gone horribly wrong. Simple scenario. Some poor girl had found the North was cheating on her (everyone knew they could never keep it in their trousers) and picked up some weird brass ornament in fury, lashing out with typical *crime passionelle* strength. Explaining the body dumped in the river was a little more tricky. But not impossible, especially if you assumed her family had gang connections; brothers and cousins rushing round to her place and carting the corpse away – oh, and extracting the smartcells, which was a big stretch. She'd be out of town now, having a long weekend break with witness friends and with a little help from a bytehead running up place-and-time verifiable credit bills. So when she returned at the end of this week – why, surprise, her North boyfriend was nowhere to be found. Call the police and put on a worried voice to report it. *Yes Officer, I did think it was a little odd he didn't call while I was away, but he's been so busy lately . . .*

Sid munched down some garlic bread as he reviewed the premise. It simply wouldn't fly, no matter how much he wanted it to. Not even having gang family connections could explain away the missing stealth smartcells. And the murder weapon – the wound didn't allow for it to simply be a handy objet d'art you picked up in a moment of rage. Which in turn left him a huge problem. Fingerblades that could ram through a ribcage to shred the heart it protected? So far the database search had found nothing that matched. Not even close. No armament manufac-turer files, nothing from history. His e-i was constantly expanding the search.

'He needs you on the sixth floor.'

'Huh?' Sid looked up to see Jenson San standing beside the table. 'Aye, man, don't creep up on people like that.'

'I didn't. You were in a different universe.'

Sid pointed at his eyes. 'Autopsy results. It was a strange one, you know.'

'No I don't, actually. That information is case coded. And make sure you keep it that way.'

Sid wasn't sure if that was a bitch slap or not. 'I know *my* responsibilities, man.'

'Come on. He wants you.'

'This is my lunch break.'

'Not any more.'

'I have a call code you know.'

Jenson San's face remained impassive verging on contemptuous. 'If the Chief Constable had wanted to use that he would have. Instead he found out where you were and sent me to collect you. Do you understand, Detective?'

Punching the senior staff representative in the middle of a police canteen probably wasn't the best idea the day after you return from suspension. Satisfying, though.

Sid took a big bite of garlic and exhaled in Jenson San's direction. 'Lead on, then, man.'

O'Rouke had a corner office on the sixth floor. Of course. Sid hadn't been in it many times. He could've sworn it got bigger each time he did visit.

The Chief was sitting behind a broad desk which had a wall of screens that were rolling down as Sid walked in. 'Out,' he barked at Jenson San. The door closed and the blue secure seal lit up around it. Both window walls turned opaque.

'What?' Sid exclaimed as O'Rouke glared at him.

'Not you,' O'Rouke admitted. 'I've just had a message from the Brussels Security Commissioner himself. This case just became a whole lot more complicated. Access to all data is now restricted to those already working on the case. Nobody else is to be brought in, no external agency work is to be contracted until further notice. It's been reclassified: Global Restriction.'

'You could crap on that okay. Why?'

'They don't bother telling me that. All I know is that some specialist supervisor is coming up from London this afternoon to *take charge*. Fucking Brussels bastards. Take charge! This is my city. No government fuckface comes prancing up here and tells me what goes down on my streets.'

'Augustine must have stuck his oar in. Which is odd, since Aldred said they wouldn't.'

'This isn't the Norths. This is something else.'

And Sid could see that not knowing was hurting O'Rouke badly. 'Do they want me to close it down?'

'No. That's the weirdest piece of this crap. You're to keep going.'

'But if I can't call in experts when I need them, I can't get anywhere.'

'I know. Look, Hurst, you've built up a shitload of data this morning. Get it all processed ready for this supervisor dick. He's the one who's going to say where the investigation goes. Your priority now is to brief your team and make fucking sure nothing gets out. I'll send down some network nerds to beef up your systems security.'

'Okay. I'll get to it.'

'Are you anywhere near a suspect?'

'Chief, we don't even know who he was yet. And that can't be right, not for a North.'

'You've no idea? None?'

'No. But . . .'

'What? Give me something, man.'

'Autopsy said he was murdered on Friday.'

O'Rouke gave him a blank look. 'So?'

'Friday was when they announced the fusion stations contract.'

'Corporate crap,' O'Rouke hissed.

'I don't know. But that's a lot of money even for Northumberland Interstellar. And that much money becomes political. Now we've got Brussels interested. I'm joining dots, here.'

'Shit. All right, this prick will be here late afternoon, apparently. Keep the team at it until he arrives. And Hurst.'

'Yeah?'

'Be nice to have a name for the dead North when he gets here. Show the arsehole we don't need him for anything.'

'You got it.'

Sid went back down to the third floor, and found the team still busy at their zone consoles. 'A new brief for you,' he told them once the secure seal was on. 'This is bigger than we originally thought. So big that Brussels has decided to piss off O'Rouke and send an expert over here to take over from me.'

'What have they got that we haven't?' Eva asked indignantly. 'The Norths have given us an unlimited case budget. We can have this solved by tomorrow.'

'Uh huh,' Sid said. 'Ari, Abner, have you got a name for me?'

Abner shook his head diffidently. 'Sorry boss. Not yet.'

'According to the autopsy prelims, the victim was killed on Friday late morning,' Sid told them. 'In other words a North has been missing since then and nobody noticed. Come on, people! This was never a normal case to begin with. Now this. So . . . we carry on correlating our data, open up some fresh lines of enquiry ready to show our new super-detective when he arrives. Get to it, please.'

Sid went over to the consoles where Ari and Abner were working. 'Really?' he asked in a low voice. 'Nothing? Not even a brother who hasn't been seen for a while?'

Abner and Ari shared a troubled glance. It was eerie seeing the same features registering identical expressions. 'Not even a possibility,' Ari admitted.

'Okay. How far are you through the list? I assume you have a list; that you do know how many of you there are.'

'We know. There are three hundred and thirty two of us As.

We've already covered sixty per cent with personal calls to each of them to make completely sure.'

'As?' Sid asked warily.

'You know the original three brothers split up back in 2087?' Abner said. 'Well, all the 2s and 3s, even the 4s stuck by their tribal father – not that you heard me put it like that. All us As – Augustine's offspring – stayed here in Newcastle or Highcastle on St Libra, either to support Northumberland Interstellar or, like me and Ari, to build a life close by. The Bs and Cs went with their respective fathers to Abellia and Jupiter. One of them may have been visiting Newcastle on Friday; we don't know yet. It's not like they're forbidden ever to return, the split wasn't a divorce, and we do have plenty of contact with the family on Abellia. There's even the occasional visit from a Jupiter cousin when a ferry ship orbits.'

'Oh Jesus,' Sid muttered. 'How many total?'

'We're not sure,' Abner admitted. 'I've been putting in some calls all morning. Brinkelle's people have been helpful to a degree. But Jupiter . . . Augustine himself will have to ask that question for us.'

'Crap on it!' Sid had never considered that it could be anyone other than one of Augustine's descendants. No wonder the Security Commission was interested. 'The coroner took some samples to run a genetic scan with. It was Aldred's idea, he said they'd be able to tell if it was a 2 or 3 or 4.'

'According to the level of transcription breaks in the genome, yes,' Ari said. 'Good call. Especially if he was a 2. We tend to be more connected than our offspring.'

'Will the genetic read be able to tell if he was an A or B or C?' Sid asked.

'No. It only shows how far removed from Kane he is, not which branch of the family he was born to.'

'Okay. The Beijing Geonomics Institute is running it now, so the sequencing results should be in by mid-afternoon.'

'That'll really help us narrow the search,' Abner assured him. 'Once we know that for certain, it won't take much longer.'

'And if he was a C?' Sid asked.

'I'm not aware of any Cs on Earth right now.'

'As soon as you know . . .'

'Yes, boss.'

Sid sat at the spare zone console next to Ian. 'Any progress?' he enquired.

'Aye, man; I ran the party-boat memories myself. Facial feature recognition software picked three with a North going into them in the last week. It also counted them out again. He wasn't dumped over the side.'

'You reviewed a whole week? That's devotion to duty. Well done.'

'Aye, well, none of us can afford to bollox up this, now, can we?'

'Nice theory,' Sid agreed. 'Come on, let's find the possible dump points into the Tyne. Show that specialist tit how useless he is at doing our job.'

Two network technicians arrived, and began installing a dedicated memory core into Office3's network. 'Brand-new,' the lead tech announced as he plugged the football-sized device into the office cells. 'You guys must have a budget and a half for this case.'

All the data they'd accumulated so far was extracted from the station network and dumped inside the globe. Once the files were transferred, the techs set about eliminating any ghost copies left in the network's redundancy caches. Diode filter programs were loaded, preventing any data from leaving the core's dedicated zone consoles in Office3.

'Best we've got,' Sid was told. 'The only way anyone gets a look at those files now is if they come in here and physically tear the core out.'

An hour later Sid was standing in the office's largest zone booth, a translucent cylinder three metres in diameter, with ring projectors on the floor and ceiling. Eva was outside, running the synchronized image. The hologram which materialized around Sid was poor quality compared to the professional shows he was used to immersing in at home. It was to be expected. This was a composite from the multitude of smartdust meshes along the river, which were different brands, different ages, different resolution levels, and downloading into different memory formats. Despite the weird colour static, which skipped about him like iridescent rain, and the blurred outlines of anything which moved, he stood on the south shore below the curving glass façade of the Sage. Magnification was level one. 'Take the falling snow out, please,' he asked Eva.

Oddly, the image degraded slightly as the snow cleared away, leaving air that had somehow lost its full transparency. 'Best I can do,' Eva said.

'That's good, it's what I need,' he assured her. Now he could see directly across the Tyne to the Court of Justice. A single digital display hovering in mid-air told him it was fifteen hundred hours on Sunday. 'Take me up to twenty-one hundred hours and pause.'

Colour drained out of the zone as the digits accelerated, leaving the snow-cloaked buildings illuminated by weak, green-tinged streetlighting. Cars on the main roads were stationary, their headlight beams fixed.

Sid turned until he was facing straight along the southern road. Directly ahead of him streetlights produced pools of light that stretched away into the distance, each one separate from its neighbours. He brought both arms up and beckoned with closed fingers. The image began to slide past, taking him towards the Tyne Bridge. There was an empty slice just before he reached the support, as if a wedge of interplanetary space had fallen from the sky to lie across the road. He held his hands out, palms flat. The image halted. He circled an upraised finger, and everything rotated round him. 'Tag this: Gap one. It's about a metre and a half wide. Extends across the road and to the embankment wall.' He looked up at the concrete which was topped by a railed footpath before the ground continued to rise as a steep terracing of grass and overgrown ornamental trees.

'If anyone's trying to drag our North along that they're going to have to be very accurate,' Ian's voice announced.

'Something happened to the smartdust on the bridge support,' Eva said. 'Probably pigeon crap – they do like our bridges. There's been no mesh there since last winter – city hasn't got round to replacing the motes. This gap wasn't set up for the murder.'

'They'd have to get the body to the gap,' Ian said. 'If we're looking for a ten o'clock disposal, there were only eight cars went along that stretch of road between nine thirty and ten past ten. None of them stopped.'

'Show me,' Sid told them. Eva moved the simulation ahead half an hour. The cars swept along the road, flowing over and around him as he stood and watched. They were all moving slowly, the compacted snow was eight centimetres thick after all, but not slow enough to dump a body into the gap. 'Okay,' he told them. 'Take it back to twenty-one hundred hours. Let's find the next gap.'

*

Traffic Management assigned the car an Emergency Vehicle priority, and cars and lorries parted smoothly to allow Colonel Vance Elston of the HDA's Alien Intelligence Agency direct access to the autobahn's central reserved lane. This close to the gate-way, the commercial and private traffic was slowing up anyway, forming an orderly crawl-queue along the three lanes which led back to Earth. Now that he had a clear route, he floored the accelerator until he was doing a steady hundred and sixty kph. Beside the near-stationary cars, the sense of speed was exagger-ated; it was almost thrilling, the kind of rush a boy racer sought in a boosted car. Vance smiled at the idea. At forty-seven he was a long way beyond that kind of behaviour, though even with his service and doctrinal instilled discipline something about pure speed never failed to do it for the male psyche.

He flashed through the gateway leaving the German world of Odessa behind, emerging into a freezing Berlin winter afternoon; and immediately braked, taking the service off-ramp. An agency helicopter was waiting for him on the pad at the top of the embankment, its blades turning slowly. He abandoned the car and climbed aboard. It took him swiftly over the snow-clad capital to Schonefeld airport, where a ten-seater passenger jet was waiting. From there he flew directly to London Docklands airport. A black limousine drove right up to the airstairs to collect him. Major Vermekia was waiting in the back, wearing full dress uniform as everyone on the Human Defence Alliance general staff was required to do.

'You look impressive,' Vance told him as he settled back into the thick cushioning. Amid all the rows of decorations arrayed on the tunic like coloured bar codes was a single diamond and bronze pin with its tiny inlaid purple crucifix. It matched the one on Vance's suit collar. He'd long since stopped wearing a uniform on a day-to-day basis, instead favouring dark expensive suits in the tradition of spooks for centuries.

'Goes with the job,' Vermekia said simply. 'And you?'

'Busy, of course. Wish I wasn't, but that's human nature for you. You know five Zanth-worshipping cults have sprung up on Odessa in the last three years. All of them have leaders who claim to be attuned to the Zanth.'

'Morons.'

'Yes, but they need investigating. One was actually building a signalling device, claiming it could call the Zanth.'

Vermekia's eyebrows shot up. 'For real?'

'Sadly, yes. The techs at Frontline are examining the gadget. Something to do with setting up oscillations in a trans-spacial connection.'

'Oldest bunch of crap in the file. Everyone thinks it's the gateways that attract the Zanth.'

'Age gives credibility, which leads to belief. They had a lot of followers.'

Vermekia shook his head in bewilderment. 'Unbelievable.'

'Yeah. Unlike this.'

'Speak to me. I've never seen an alert like it. Some detective loaded a weapons identification request into the government network, and it's like a frigging fire alarm going off in the office.

I was expecting special forces guys to blow out the wall and snatch us to safety. Even the Supreme Commander himself is showing an interest.' He gave Vance a shrewd look over the top of his glasses. 'Lots of related files that even I couldn't get access to. But your name kept coming up.'

'It would.' Vance tried not to recall too many of those memories. Her screams and sobbing still flittered through his dreams, even now, twenty years later. *What's done is done. No regrets. The Lord knows the price of failure, of vigilance faltering, is too horrific to contemplate.* 'I was involved in the original case.'

'We'll have a beer one night, and you can tell me the gruesome details.'

'Right.'

The car was heading west through London, its auto steering them along the A13, taking them towards the Barbican and the start of the A1. As before, Vance had been given an Emergency Vehicle status by London's Traffic Management AI. They were travelling as fast as practical. Thin snow was drifting out of a leaden sky, but the roads had been kept clear by the city's winter weather crews.

When they reached Commercial Road another black sedan pulled in directly behind them.

'Who's on the visiting team?' Vance asked.

'Quite a little meet and greet committee, actually. There's you and me, two experts from the Brussels Interstellar Commission, three commanders from Human Defence Alliance GroundForce, an English cabinet office lawyer along with a rep from the Justice department. Now that is one department that is seriously worried – after all she's been locked up for twenty years.'

Vance shook his head in dismay. The levels of bureaucracy propping up the Human Defence Alliance dismayed him as much as it astonished.

How many twenty-second-century bureaucrats did it take to change a light panel?

We'll have a sub-committee meeting and get back to you with an estimate.

'Let me have their files,' he said as they finally turned onto Aldersgate Street, the bottom of the A1 – which was the modern designation of the original Great North Road, built by the Romans two thousand years ago to march its garrisons to the very edge of the empire three hundred miles to the north. Their duty was to reinforce Hadrian's Wall, keeping the outer darkness at bay and the empire safe. Today was likely to take him on that same journey, with a not too dissimilar duty.

Another two black government cars fell in behind them.

'They are good people,' Vermekia said. 'We've spent the last two hours sorting out the protocols. Everyone coming with us has the authority to make decisions.'

Vance began to skim their files as his e-i picked them up and fed them to his grid. They were only three hours into the alert, and already an organization was coming together. 'General Shaikh has made the decision already, hasn't he?'

'Yeah. His staff is establishing lines of command with Grande Europe's alien evaluation office and the Pentagon. Unless this murder turns out to be very mundane in the next twenty-four hours, I'd suggest packing some tropical travel clothes.'

Vance let himself sink back further into the car seat. 'Okay, so give me her file. What kind of prisoner has she been?'

'For a lifer, reasonably well behaved.'

Vance watched as his e-i flipped various prison records into his grid, where micro laserlight fired them directly into his brain. The life Angela Tramelo had lived for the last twenty years summarized in official evaluations and reports. Her fights with other inmates – inevitable, given the time spent incarcerated – punished by solitary confinement, which prison psychologists said never seemed to bother her as much as it was supposed to. No recorded tox usage – which was interesting, but then her determination was always fearsome. Education – she kept current on network systems and economics. Work record – competent. Health record – excellent. 'Hold,' he instructed his e-i, squeezing his eyelids shut. Angela's image steadied in front of him. He regarded it with mild exasperation. Fifty bureaucrats already getting with the programme and they still couldn't correlate files for shit. 'Can you get me a current image, please? This one is twenty years old.'

Vermekia's grin had a hint of malice. 'No it's not.'

'I met Angela twenty years ago. Trust me, this was taken back then.'

'That was taken six weeks ago. Check the prison date code, it's authentic.'

'This can't be right.' Vance closed his eyes again to regard the beautiful face with its harsh, aggressive stare. The hair was different now, shorter and unstyled. But those features: the cute little button nose, cheekbones sharp enough to cut diamond, a chin that was perfectly flat, wide flared lips, and green eyes with so much anger – even in the very heart of her anguish she held on to that anger – it was a decent resolution, the skin was as clear and lustrous as only the truly youthful possess. A face he would take to his grave given what he'd seen it endure. She'd been eighteen, and that was back in 2121. He'd only been twenty-five himself. Equally youthful, well built, a body he'd worked hard on to qualify for the college football team; a hundred and eighty-six centimetres tall, or six-one as they still called it back in Texas where he grew up, with black skin scarred from several game injuries and some best-forgotten adolescent rumbles. So diametrically opposite to her unblemished honey-gold, gym-toned flesh and white-blonde hair. The difference was fundamental: colour, wealth, class, upbringing, and culture – back then they'd taken one look at each other and knew the enmity which sparked immediately would last for ever, and that was before everything she'd undergone at Frontline. Now his flesh was showing wrinkles despite a good diet and all the usual middle-aged exercise tropes – gym, jogging, squash; the cheeks were rounding out, reflexes not quite the exultant lightning they had been on the football field, the hair obviously receding no matter how artfully he gelled it. But her, she looked barely twenty even now.

'It is,' Vermekia said cheerfully.

'But . . . that would mean she's a one-in-ten.'

'Yep. It would mean that.'

'We didn't know,' Vance said. One-in-ten germline treatment: where the DNA of a fertilized human egg was manipulated so that you aged one year biologically for every ten years which passed was rare even today, never mind back in . . . well, in 2103, according to her birth certificate – which they'd never thought to verify because that wasn't the line of enquiry and obviously she looked eighteen. He gave Vermekia an aghast stare. 'How could we not know that?'

'Does it matter?'

'Of course it matters. That was part of the calibration.'

'You mean for the interrogation?'

'Her file said she was eighteen, and she confirmed it. It was wrong. We asked her to confirm everything on her background file—'

'But you never bothered to check the file?'

'It came straight from the UK justice bureau. We assumed it was good.'

'Ah well. There's your first mistake right there. A government file. They reckon that up to twenty-five per cent of everything in an official database is crud. Personally I'd be one happy bunny if it ever gets that low.'

'Damnit! She could have lied about anything. No, actually, not in the final interview. That's still sound. Unless she was completely delusional.'

'Okay. I'll accept that last technique you went at her with produced valid data. But why was she lying about her age and everything else on her background file in the first place?'

'I have no idea. Damnit, the implications . . . Sweet Lord, what else did we overlook?'

Vermekia made an expressive gesture taking in the whole world. 'The fucking obvious by the looks of things.'

*

The five-car convoy turned into Parkhurst Road. Holloway Prison was on the right, a confined campus of functional concrete blocks with big metal grid gates already opening to allow the cars through into the parking yard. This latest version of the prison had been built in 2099; a kit that had been assembled on site by big cranes, methodical automata, and minimal human labour or skill. Rooms and corridors had all been pre-fitted with systems and wiring and plumbing in the cybernetic factory which mass-produced them to government standard; they were also painted and tiled to requirement. All anyone had to do to complete the integration and get a finished building was plug the wires together and join the pipes. That was the theory, which didn't quite explain why it was eight hundred million Eurofrancs over budget and seven years behind schedule when it finally did reopen for inmates in 2106.

Ever since the European Trans-Space Bureau (ET-SB) had opened a gateway to Minisa in 2050, which was backed first by subsidized settlement packages then latterly with the GE's Opportunity Immigration policy to transport the chronically un-employable along with low-level criminal offenders to the new lands, there had been a question about the need for prisons back on humanity's old homeworld. Simply locking offenders up had been going out of fashion for a long time, a social improvement trend accelerated by the opportunity to simply dump offenders lightyears from their offending environment where they were physically unable to repeat the offence – mainly because they found themselves in the middle of a wilderness with title to a hectare of land, a tent, a bag of seed corn, a toolbox, and a dis-appearing cloud of dust as the Resettlement Service bus trundled away to dump the next undesirable on a patch of impoverished soil half a mile away across the plains.

Some people however, despite the best efforts of psychiatrists, drugs, social workers, specialist education teachers, and good old-fashioned brutal guards, simply weren't fit to be released any-where no matter how many lightyears distant from frightened taxpayers. For the truly dangerous – the psychotic, the serial killers and paedophiles, the die-for-the-cause-fanatics and the just plain evil – prison remained the only option. In all such cases it was for life. And in 2143, life really did mean until you die.

Holloway Prison was for female inmates, one of only two in all of Grande Europe's United Kingdom region. Its bleak physical structure and smartdust tagging was all an acknowledgement that the only way those inmates would ever be coming out was as a pile of ash. To emphasize the point, it had its own crematorium tacked on to the back of the hospital block.

Life inside was regimented. All activities had a set period and routine ruled everything. It helped the warders keep life running as smoothly as possible when confining people who enjoyed the pain and suffering of others, and in many cases themselves.

Everyone knew the routine. Intimately. They obeyed it obsessively. They were attuned to it with a near-psychic intensity. It was the voltage running through the entire structure which powered them through each day. The slightest disturbance could be felt shivering subliminally along the pastel-green corridors and poster-covered cells and positively nineteenth-century workrooms.

At two o'clock, the governor was in her office for the scant privacy it afforded so she could receive a most unusual call. When she summoned three senior staff in to brief them, the result outside the administration block was the same as a wolfpack lifting their noses to the full moon and sniffing the blood of wounded prey.

Something was going down. Something new. Something different. The sensation howled through the interlinked blocks, sharp peaks and dips in the voltage flow. Aggression, always the twin of uncertainty in secure units, began to manifest. There were scuffles, arguments, abuse aimed at the staff. The handball game in the yard was stopped after the second broken nose.

At three o'clock the governor ordered everyone back to their cells to cool off. The routine was well and truly smashed and broken. Each cell wing resonated to the ragged chorus of obscene songs and screamed death threats. The governor herself led five warders down J-block, subjecting herself to a variety of innovative objects that could be hurled through the small window bars on each door. The obscenities she didn't even notice any more. It was almost ritual. What everyone really wanted to know was WTF was going down. After she passed their door, inmates would press up against the small barred windows and peer through eagerly.

The governor stopped outside cell 13, and put her hand on the palmkey pad. Two guards drew their taser batons in readiness. They needn't have bothered, the occupant was calm and silent.

Angela Tramelo stared out into the corridor with an unnervingly serene expression. Looking in at her, the prison staff all had the same disturbing thought: it was as though she'd been waiting twenty years for this moment, that she'd somehow always known it would arrive.

'Come with us, please, Angela,' the governor asked.

There was a moment's pause as the guards clutched their taser batons a fraction tighter, then Angela nodded. 'Of course.' She walked out of the cell into a cacophony of jeering and flaming, shit-smeared toilet rolls dropping from the upper cells, all of which she ignored.

The guards formed up to escort her as the governor led them back out of J-block. They didn't get too close, and held their batons ready at all times. Angela had never assaulted a prison employee in the twenty years of her incarceration, but they still didn't trust her. Not someone convicted for slaughtering fourteen people in one night.

The conference room she was taken to was in the administration block. It had a carpet, office chairs with leather cushioning, a table, wallscreens, and a big holographic pane. It was warm, the fans in the wall-mounted heaters rumbling away steadily. There was even a window, covered in a thick metal grid, that looked out onto the street. Angela glanced round the room almost in trepidation. This was a universe from memory so distant it was almost fiction, a world outside prison walls. The unfamiliarity of it, of what had once been her life, threatened to crack her resolution after all this time. *And how about that for irony?* she thought bitterly.

'Please sit,' the governor said.

Angela did as she was asked, taking the chair at the head of the table. The governor sat next to her. She seemed uncomfortable. Angela enjoyed that. The reversal finally beginning; somewhere in the background there must surely be the sound of giant cogwheels rumbling into motion, cogwheels big enough to turn the whole universe around.

'Angela,' the governor began. 'There's been an unusual development in relation to your case.'

'Bring them in.'

The governor gave her a frankly startled glance. 'Excuse me?'

'I'm not going to attack anybody. I'm not going to create a scene. Bring them in to tell me what kind of deal they're offering. That's what they're here for, isn't it?'

'I'm on your side, here, Angela. I'm trying to prepare you for what may be a shock.'

'Of course you are, that's very liberal, very *you*. Because after twenty years in here I'm a real fucking delicate flower. Now let's get on with it.'

The governor drew a breath. 'As you wish.'

Eight of them trooped in. Three women, five men; the civilians dressed in suits, the four Human Defence Alliance officers in smart uniforms. Officialdom at the top of their game, in positions which gave a solid kick up the arse of democratic accountability. And they were unaccustomed to being this nervous. It wasn't just being in the presence of a notoriously vicious murderess that had tensed up their muscles and produced unnatural body-language, it was what dark shadow might prove to be standing behind her which was their fear.

Angela ignored all of them except one. *He* was there, as she always knew he would be. Older of course, unlike her. That would anger him, she thought contentedly. He hadn't even been important back then, a junior brown-nose. But she'd known he would be somebody one day, he was that repellent, straight-arrow type, never going anywhere else but up.

She stared at him, keen to study his reactions, divining any emotional conflict their renewed proximity kindled behind his killer-cold brown eyes. Slowly and deliberately she parted her lips with a mirthless smile. It was raw mockery, and he'd know that. In response she perceived a tight flash of anger, quickly concealed. It made her smile broaden.

One of the civilians, some shitbag high-rank government lawyer, started telling her there was a possible change in her situation. His voice droned as irritatingly as a fly on a window. '... without prejudicing your legal position ...' She paid him no attention. '... full cooperation with an ongoing investigation would be regarded as ...' It was Vance Elston she was interested in. Vance Elston she wanted to twist and writhe in uncertainty and remorse. '... we can unfortunately offer no guarantee ...' Vance Elston's smug, self-righteous face weeping in terror as he finally confronted the hideous monster he'd tried so hard to deny ever existed.

Angela held her hand up, and the lawyer fell silent. They all regarded her with nervous expectancy. Still the only one she looked at was Elston. There was the sweetest-ever taste of victory in her voice as she asked him: 'It's come back, hasn't it?'

*

Ian and Sid took turns in the zone booth all afternoon. By six thirty that evening, they'd covered the Tyne all the way up to South Benwell on the north bank and the viaduct over the River Derwent where it spilled into the Tyne on the south bank. That was a lot higher upriver than the tidal flow current could carry a body in two hours, but Sid was being super-cautious. In total they found eleven possible gaps in the mesh surveillance, most of them a lot wider than the first by the Tyne Bridge support. After reviewing the entire Dunston Marina, Sid considered it the most likely place; there were just so many boats moored there that weren't fully covered by the local meshes.

'Eleven?' Eva said when Ian finished the final section. 'That's a lot of field work. And we've lost a day as well, so there's not going to be much evidence left.'

Sid yawned as he stretched his arms out. In front of him, one of the wallscreens was displaying a simple map with each of the eleven gaps. 'Not my problem.'

The zone booth door shut as Ian emerged. 'Are you at least allowed to cordon off the areas?'

'I don't know,' Sid admitted. 'I'll have to ask O'Rouke.' Which wasn't something he wanted to do. He swivelled the chair round. 'Abner?'

The two Norths looked at each other. 'No, sorry boss,' Abner replied.

'Seriously, man, no name at all?'

'The genetic sample confirmed he's a 2,' Ari said. 'We have spoken personally to all our brothers. They're all accounted for.'

'So he was a B or a C,' Sid said.

'Has to be,' Ari agreed. 'But Brinkelle's organization claims none of her 2s are missing.'

'And Jupiter?'

'Aldred talked to Augustine. A message was sent to Constantine. He claims no C 2s are on Earth.'

'This is bullshit,' Ian snapped at Abner and Ari. 'You're covering up for something.'

Abner stood up and walked over to Ian who wasn't giving ground. 'One of my brothers has been murdered, you cocksucking little twat.'

'Enough!' Sid said.

Ian and Abner glared at each other. Any second now a fist would fly. They didn't care about the internal sensors and official log. Sid knew he was going to have to get that log altered before the case file was folded and handed over to the prosecution office. There was a bytehead on the second floor he knew could help.

'Abner,' Sid said. 'Give me your best guess what's happened?'

With one final derisory sneer at Ian, Abner turned away. 'There's two possibles here: either there was a 2 we didn't know about. It's unlikely, but not impossible. Or Constantine and Brinkelle aren't being entirely truthful.'

'Why?' Ian asked.

Abner shrugged. 'I cannot think of a single reason.' He shot Ian a look. 'Certainly not corporate – not money.'

'Okay,' Sid said quickly.

'There's a third option,' Ari said.

Abner gave him a startled glance.

'Which is?' Sid asked.

'There have been attempts to imitate us in the past.'

'You said you'd talked to all the 2s,' Eva said.

'We did,' Ari said. 'But to be real, that was a thirty-second call to ask them if they're alive.'

'Pull them in,' Ian said. 'Interrogate them. Take DNA samples. It's the only way to find an imposter.'

'Good luck with that,' Abner said.

'We'd need Augustine's permission,' Sid mused. He didn't like to think of the fallout from that request to O'Rouke. Best to sound out Aldred first.

'His cooperation,' Ari corrected.

Sid was about to answer when they all heard the drone of a helicopter getting louder outside. Lorelle pushed off the console desk, letting her chair roll over to the nearest window, and peered up into the night sky. It had started snowing again. 'Kamov 130,' she said approvingly. 'Auxiliary tail prop. Those guys are fast. I don't know an agency that can afford one of those for police work.'

Everyone looked at Sid.

'Our new case chief?' Eva suggested.

'Well don't ask me,' Sid protested. 'I get told fuck all.'

'So what's next?' Ian asked.

Sid rubbed his hands across his face. All he wanted to do was go home, but that wasn't going to happen. 'No point in us all staying on. Wrap and seal your files, then get yourselves off home. I'll formulate the follow-ups that've come out of today's investigation ready to show the new bloke.'

*

He was still working on the official requests for forensic investigation of the river sites at seven thirty when O'Rouke finally summoned him up to the sixth floor. When he did get to the big corner office he wasn't entirely surprised to find a tall Afro-American in a dark suit waiting to greet him with a firm handshake and an appraising stare. Agent Vance Elston couldn't have been a more obvious covert government operative if he'd had SPOOK tattooed across his forehead. However, having Aldred waiting in the office as well was unexpected.

The final member of the meeting was secure i-conferencing from her own office in Brussels, showing on the wallscreen opposite the window. O'Rouke introduced her as Charmonique Passam, a commissioner for the Grande Europe Bureau of alien evaluation. Sid had never heard of her, nor her Bureau, but the type-recognition was instant. A politician: worst kind. She was in her early fifties, groomed and dressed in a painfully inadequate imitation of the genuinely wealthy. Suit from some Parisian couture house. Dark hair locked rigidly into place and streaked with brown highlights. Indian-heritage skin with pink and blue make-up shaded across cheeks and eyes. It all made her look even older, which Sid guessed might be the purpose. Her advisers must have told her age equated to gravitas. Quite how that much money and intellect could be exhausted to produce an image that was as comic as it was pitiful, Sid couldn't grasp. The one other thing he didn't understand was what she was doing i-conferencing here tonight. He didn't get to ask, either.

'Any progress?' O'Rouke began after he'd run the introductions.

Which was a great start, Sid thought. 'We've identified possible sites where the body was dumped in the river. However the most interesting aspect is the identity.'

'Who was it?' Vance Elston asked.

'We don't know.'

'And you think that's interesting?'

'Very. We've verified he was a 2North. Yet they're all accounted for. Our current belief is that an imposter is imitating a 2North, probably to advance some type of corporate scam. Once we've positively identified the site where the body was dumped into the river, we can begin a backtrack operation,' Sid replied levelly. 'I've prepared the procedures ready for authorization.'

'By whom?' Charmonique Passam enquired.

'I need to discuss that with the Chief Constable,' Sid replied cautiously. Her tone told him it was a loaded question, but then her tone was like someone from the Royal family spoke in a century-old recording. Patronizing. Sid realized just how bad his opinion of her was growing, and made an effort to stop being so cynical. He knew he'd resort to sarcasm if the meeting stretched on too long, and that wouldn't be good in any way.

'I'm not referring to which agency you contract. I'm interested in your team's composition.'

'I'm sorry?' Out of the corner of his eye Sid could see O'Rouke's face stiffen up as the skin slowly turned ruddy. That blood-pressure problem would kill him off one day not far away. Interestingly, there was no reaction from Elston, nothing at all, which was impressive. He was a parent waiting stoically for a toddler's tantrum to blow out.

'It seems very male-centric,' Charmonique Passam said. 'That's all I'm saying. But I am surprised to *have* to say it in this day and age, as I thought we were long past such issues after eighteen separate equality enforcement acts in the last hundred years. Very worthwhile acts, too, I might add.'

And what the fuck do you know about our duty rotas, let alone attracting anyone at all – least of all women – to do this job on the piss-poor pay and shit-mountain grief which government – YOU – give us. 'If you're dissatisfied with my team—' Sid started hotly.

70

'No. I did not express dissatisfaction, Detective, I simply made an observation.'

'I can talk with HR in the morning.'

'HR?'

'Human Resources.'

'In Brussels that kind of department is referred to as the Office for Personkind Enablement. Resources sounds like something you dig out of the ground. It's offensive to so many people given the historical rare earth mineral conflicts.'

'Right.' *Away man, you are a complete bollock-brain.*

'But I thank you for the courtesy of accommodating my concerns.'

'Okay, this is what's happening,' O'Rouke said. 'As of now the case is under HDA jurisdiction.'

'The Human Defence Alliance?' Sid asked in astonishment. He'd assumed some kind of Brussels-backed Interpol takeover.

'Yes, Detective,' Elston said. 'An agent called Ralph Stevens will be here tomorrow to act as our liaison to your team. As when the Norths were funding you, you will have unlimited budget and resources at your disposal, but we will be the paymasters now. We very much want you to find out exactly where this North was murdered.'

Sid stared back at him in bewilderment. 'You want me to carry on? Me?'

For the first time, Elston showed a small smile. 'Yes, Sid: you. We've all reviewed your file. You're highly competent; your actual detection rate is impressively high, especially in serious crime cases. Me, I don't have the first clue how to go about directing a major criminal investigation. Don't get me wrong, Ralph and I will be breathing fire down your neck the whole time. But we trust you to take point on this.'

'Thank you.' He didn't dare risk glancing at O'Rouke or Aldred. 'So what is really going on here? What's the HDA's interest?'

'The HDA is taking over for one simple reason,' Elston said.

'The murder method, or to be precise the instrument used to shred the victim's heart.'

'But ... we don't even know what the hell it is yet,' Sid protested.

'That's exactly what makes this so special. You see, the murder method has actually been employed once before.'

*

Town Moor was a huge area of parkland to the north-east of Newcastle's city centre, with a single road, the A189, running across the middle. To the western side of the intrusive tarmac strip was the golf course, where membership now cost nineteen thousand Eurofrancs a year, and the waiting list was a mere eight years, providing you had the right social contacts. To the east, the park was untended, a lush green wilderness amid the harsh urban bustle which surrounded it. In summer it was well used, providing people a pleasant refuge from their hectic lives: families had day-long picnics, runners chased over its rolling grass, lads played football, and kids flew their remote minibugs and planes and copters, buzzing innocent bystanders and dodging the wardens. In winter, visitors fell off dramatically. Now, after weeks of snow and constant sub-zero temperatures, even the most ardent dog walkers and fell runners were snubbing it until better weather returned.

The lightwave ship came down in the middle of Town Moor, barely a hundred metres from the A189. Anywhere else, at any other time, it would have been a complete impossibility to land an actual real live interplanetary spaceship smack in the centre of a human city without anyone noticing. But here it was, a featureless, thirty-metre-high stealth-black bubble cone, with five broad circular rings around its midsection – like curled-up wings – containing sections of the lightwave drive thrusters which lowered it down silently out of an invisible night sky amid thick flakes of snow.

It rested on three hemispherical bulges in the base, which compacted the snow underneath until the centre of the fuselage belly itself pressed against the fluffy white blanket. A rectangular airlock door dissolved, and a short aluminium airstair slid down. Clayton 2North emerged dressed in a quilted parka with a fur-lined hood pulled tight against his face. Rebka followed him, wearing an altogether more stylish fake-suede coat with big white buttons down the front, interrupted by a wide scarlet belt. Both wore sturdy boots. Rebka stood still and tipped her head back, opening her mouth as the snow settled on her skin. She licked avidly at the icy flakes, and started to laugh.

'This is fantastic,' she exclaimed. 'I never imagined anything like this.'

Clayton gave her a tolerant look and told his e-i to seal the spaceship. The airstair retracted and the airlock door shimmered back to existence. With a brief show of reluctance, Rebka double-looped her wide woollen scarf round her head, pulled on a bright-purple beret, and started walking through the swirling snow towards the road. They'd covered less than fifty metres before the spacecraft was lost behind them amid the darkness and snow. Rebka giggled.

'What?' Clayton asked.

'You all used to bitch about what a problem traffic and parking was in Newcastle.'

He had to grin at that. 'Well, let's hope the wardens don't swing by tonight. The fine for that baby would be out of this world.'

A minute later they found the road, though it was difficult. The snowploughs hadn't been through Town Moor for three hours. A couple of minutes later two city taxis crawled along the ice-coated tarmac. Clayton had ordered them from their permanent private Newcastle security team as soon as the ship's core had interfaced with the local net. He waved at the vehicles, laughing at himself for the no-brain redundancy – like there was anyone else waiting out here – as his e-i quested an identity. The return ping contained the confirmation code, and the vehicles stopped beside them.

The two drivers got out, staring at the visitors from another world with interest and respect.

'Take care,' Clayton told her.

She gave his arm an affectionate squeeze. 'You too. Be good.'

'As good as I can be.' His e-i sent out a connectivity quest, testing the secure connection between them. 'Don't break the link.'

'Not until I get there.'

There was an awkward moment. She gave him a quick platonic kiss, and climbed into the back of her taxi, smiling gratitude at the driver who was holding the door open for her.

Clayton went over to his taxi, and settled in the back seat, only to be overwhelmed by unexpected and unwelcome nostalgia. The cheap synthetic leather cushioning, smell of badly filtered air, gum pats on the floor. It was fifty-five years since he'd left Earth for good, and despite a few visits since, nothing had changed.

'I'm Ivan, sir,' the driver said. 'Where are we going?'

'Here,' Clayton's e-i sent the auto an address.

'Shouldn't be more than fifteen minutes, sir,' Ivan said.

'I expect the house will have an alarm system.'

'Nothing that will cause any trouble, sir. We can handle any kind of domestic protection system.'

'Good to hear.'

The taxi pulled out from the verge. Clayton saw the headlights of Rebka's taxi as it made a U-turn behind them, and within seconds its beams had vanished.

Tuesday 15th January 2143

Six fifty-six am. The alarm started its relentless electronic buzz. Sid groaned and reached for—

'No,' Jacinta warned him.

'Sod it.' He slowly swung his legs out of bed until he was sitting on the edge of the mattress and devoid of any duvet. The bedroom air was cold, maybe only a degree above freezing, and he could feel it chill-burning down his nasal passages and coughed brokenly. Only then did he smack the clock a good one, shutting it up. His yawn threatened to go on for ever.

'So what was it last night?' Jacinta asked as she rummaged round on her bedside cabinet for various clips and bands. Her wild mane of hair was slowly tamed, revealing a face that was both curious and concerned.

'The North case,' he sighed as his iris smartcells woke and displayed his grid. He hadn't got home until gone midnight; after the meeting with O'Rouke he'd spent hours with Elston, reading through the HDA briefing, then returning the favour by bringing Elston up to date on the team's case files and proposed avenues of enquiry.

'Well that's a big plus, isn't it, pet? You being left in charge?'

'Theoretically, yes. But there's a supervisor been brought in from—' He hesitated. 'Brussels.' He hated lying to her, but even O'Rouke had been worried last night. It would only take one unguarded word in the hospital canteen and his career really would be a blitzed ruin.

'Oh.' She contemplated that for a while. 'Did you make any progress yesterday?'

'Not much, which means it was a professional job.' Which, in turn, made what he'd been shown last night a mad paradox. 'But we do have an unlimited budget, which is going to help.'

'Good for you.' She gave him a quick kiss, then scurried out to get into the bathroom before the kids. Sid started searching round for a clean shirt and socks.

*

It was porridge again for breakfast. The snow had stopped some time during the night, but there was no sign of a thaw, although the clouds were thinning. Sid timed how long the thick mush simmered for, then poured it into bowls. Zara wanted honey with hers. Will, of course, wanted jam.

Sid finally found all the jars, plonked a carton of orange juice on the table, and fished some clean spoons out of the dishwasher. Jacinta sat down, bringing the cafetière with her.

'I need a new blazer for school,' Will announced.

'What's wrong with that one?' Sid asked.

Will held an arm out. The blazer cuff was short of his wrist by several centimetres.

'Fair enough,' Sid said. 'We'll get one at the weekend.' His bodymesh warned him his twenty-four-hour caffeine intake was now exceeding GE advisory limit. He told his e-i to shut it off.

Will rolled his eyes as he let out a wounded sigh. 'I can go tonight. By myself. Don't need you.'

'Sorry, but you see I actually want to be there to embarrass you. It's what fathers do best. We're all going together.'

Zara perked up. 'We can all go shopping together?'

'For things we *need*.' He knew that was never going to stick.

Zara dipped her head, not quite hiding a secret smile of satisfaction.

'Are we moving?' Will asked.

Sid had completely forgotten about the house in Jesmond. 'Oh yeah, how did that go?'

'I ran their catalogue virtual in our zone last night,' Jacinta said. 'It ticks a lot of boxes.'

'Great,' Sid said, on husband-auto.

'So now we have to go take a visit,' Jacinta pointed out.

Will frowned. 'Why? You've had a virtual.'

'Because a house is not just a lot of money,' Sid explained. 'It's all the money we have. So we don't just rely on a virtual catalogue, okay. The station has had cases where the house didn't actually exist, and the vendors didn't find out until they turned up on moving day with a vanload of furniture.'

'Away, man!' Will exclaimed.

'More common is an expanded scale, so you think it's bigger than it actually is. And the estate agent will add a room that isn't there. You have to go and see it. The transnet isn't perfect, you know; most of the data is unverified.'

'I get it,' Will said with a grump.

Sid grinned. If anyone ever found a way to download a person, Will's generation would dive headfirst down the fibre optic cable, never questioning.

'I'll set it up for the weekend,' Jacinta said.

'Okay.'

'You will be around, won't you?' she asked pointedly.

'I'll be here.' He smiled at the kids. 'And I'm taking you to school today.'

*

Vance Elston was waiting in the Office3 when Sid arrived at eight fifteen, well ahead of the team. He introduced Ralph Stevens who, apart from having Nordic-pale skin and thinning blond hair, seemed like a junior version of Elston himself. Sid started to wonder how many years he'd have to hang around either of them to see a single smile.

That sombre manner they both possessed was immediately picked up by the team as they arrived in the office. They turned up gripping their take-away cups of coffee or tea – in Eva's case, hot chocolate with cream and marshmallows – smiling and chattering, speculating on what was going to happen today, and how tough the new 'supervisor' would be. Then they caught sight of Elston and Stevens in the midst of their masters-of-misery act. Smiles blanked out and the chatter muted.

It wasn't a complete surprise to Sid when he saw Aldred turn up with Abner and Ari; after all, if anyone was going to take this seriously it would be the Norths. He waited until everyone was inside Office3 and the blue seal came on before starting the briefing. There were two additions to the team, which he'd arranged with Human Resources after last night's meeting: Constable Dedra Foyster and Constable Reannha Hall, both data-analysis specialists with high security clearance ratings. A clearance which had subsequently been checked and approved by HDA. Ralph had told him that. It was about the only thing he had said so far.

'Good morning,' Vance said formally. 'I'm sorry for the delay and confusion yesterday, and I thank you for your tolerance. This briefing will explain everything.' He walked over to a zone console and made a show of putting a chip in. The big central wallscreen flashed up file symbols that Sid hadn't seen before. They didn't open.

Sid saw Ian and Eva give each other a schoolkid grin.

'Can you . . .' Vance said to Abner.

Abner went over to the zone console. 'Sure thing.' The screen curved round him, and his hands hovered in the keyspace flicking at icons only he could see.

Nothing much happened. The chip's files remained stubbornly closed.

Sid waited with growing embarrassment. Abner even seemed to be having trouble with his own operating topography system, and as to resolving the format problem . . . It was going to reflect badly on Sid.

'What program is this?' Abner asked lamely.

Sid gave Reannha Hall an urgent gesture.

'It was recorded twenty years ago,' Vance said as Reannha sat down at the console next to Abner. Manicured fingers speed-flipped icons. 'Here you go,' she said as the file symbols on the wallscreen mutated to familiar modern symbols. 'They just needed a reformat, that's all.'

Abner's face was blank as he gave her a tight smile.

'Right then,' Vance said, reclaiming the briefing. 'The reason this case is now the most important event on the planet is because the murder method has been used precisely once before. You will not know this, because it was classified and not released into the public domain. How many of you are familiar with the name Angela Tramelo?'

Forewarned after last night, Sid was watching Abner and Ari. Both of them stiffened with shock. He wasn't surprised, since the name had triggered a whole bunch of neural connections which sent coldsparks trickling down his own spine.

Ian looked like he didn't give a shit, while Eva frowned thoughtfully. 'Wasn't she the, oh—' She broke off and gave the Norths a guilty look.

'Angela Tramelo was convicted of murdering Bartram North, and thirteen of his household,' Vance said. 'The atrocity was committed in one night, twenty-one years ago in Bartram's mansion on St Libra.'

One of the file icons migrated to a wallscreen and decompressed into a matrix of thumbnail pictures. Vance expanded the first. Sid tried not to grimace at the raw carnage it illustrated. The body was that of an older North, sprawled across the marble floor of some grandiose room, clothes saturated in blood, with yet more blood pooling around it. Another body was visible, lying crumpled across the sofa behind it. The image switched, showing a close-up of the kill wound: a fingerblade stab pattern above the heart. More wound pictures: long, deep slash marks across arms and backs, always running in parallel. Defensive wounds, Sid thought.

'As well as Bartram and six of his sons, three of Bartram's girlfriends were slaughtered along with four of his staff.' The screen began to slideshow the bodies. 'Bartram North kept a stable of between three and five girls living with him at the mansion at any one time. Thcy were recruited mainly from Earth. Angela Tramelo was one of them. She was caught at the Newcastle gateway two days later as she attempted to flee. Three months after that she was tried in London and found guilty: life sentence. No remission and no parole.'

'I don't understand,' Ian said. 'Has she escaped?'

Vance shook his head. 'I wish. No, she was secure in Holloway Prison at the time your victim was murdered. She's been there for twenty years; never been allowed to set foot outside the walls.'

'Then why all this? What's this to HDA?'

'Her defence,' Vance said. Another file expanded over the wallscreen into a paused AV image showing a courtroom with Angela Tramelo in the dock, flanked by two guards. 'This is her reaction to the guilty verdict; it explains quite a lot.'

The recording started to play. Angela was struggling against the hold the guards had her in, shouting furiously. The camera zoomed in on her beautiful face as it contorted with rage. 'No!' she shrieked. 'No no no, I didn't kill anybody. Why won't you *listen*, you stupid fucks. Listen to me! The alien did it. The monster. Do you understand? It ripped them apart. I swear it—' The image froze again, catching Angela's mouth open, spittle flying.

'She repeats that same claim for five minutes while she's dragged out,' Vance said. 'In fact, she never stopped claiming it.'

'An alien monster?' Ian asked quietly.

'That's what she said. That was her entire defence. But, of course, we all know there are no aliens on St Libra. No animals of any kind. The planet's evolution is botany only. And as we've never encountered anything remotely like she described in the century since the first trans-space connection was made to Proxima Centuri, it was clearly a ludicrous alibi concocted out of desperation. So we believed.'

'Then why did HDA classify information about the blade weapon?' Eva asked.

'Because it was never found,' Vance said. 'And it was . . . odd, as you all know from your own case. Theoretically, Angela's frenzy strength would be adequate to drive the five blades in. But that whole contraction thing, shredding the heart. A living claw-hand could theoretically cause that kind of damage. But what creature has one? We couldn't be sure she was lying, and the one thing humanity cannot afford is another hostile species out there. So we investigated as best we could at the time. Nothing came of it, so HDA also assumed she was guilty as well as delusional. A real basket case who had just enough smarts left to throw whatever nasty weapon she'd concocted over a cliff while she was running.'

Ian had sat on the edge of a desk, eyes narrowed as he gazed at Angela's manic features looming over all of them. 'What kind of monster was it? Did she say? Did she describe it?'

'Yes, which was the primary cause for disbelief at the time. She said it looked humanoid, which is ridiculous, because evolution simply doesn't work that way. And it certainly doesn't twice produce two legs, two arms, one head; same height as a man – again, her description. The only difference was its skin, which was, and I quote: leather turned to stone.'

'Man in a powered armour suit,' said Eva. 'That would even explain the human-style fingerblades.'

'Which fits everything,' Vance agreed. 'Except motive. Why would anyone do this?'

'But you accepted she did.' Ian waved an irritated hand at Angela's looming face.

'Angela Tramelo was judged a psychopath, and she was examined by several psychiatrists who all concurred. That is the only human motivation which fits for such a barbarity.'

'She's the psychopath, or the man in the power suit?'

'There was never a shred of evidence he existed. And how did she survive? The only one out of the entire household on the seventh floor that night. Nobody else survived an encounter.'

'She ran,' Eva said. 'That's what I would do. I mean, you caught her while she was running, didn't you?'

'Doesn't compute,' Vance said flatly. 'She said she fought the monster, then ran. Never changed that aspect of her story, stuck by it the whole time. An eighteen-year-old female going *mano a mano* with a hydraulically powered suit? One that has knives for fingers? And while we're on improbables: why did she run all the way back to Earth?'

'Very scared?' Ian said, but not convincingly.

'She didn't even call the local police,' Vance said.

'She fought the monster?' Sid asked; he hadn't been told that last night. 'Were there any injuries? As you say, she was a teenage girl back then.'

Vance gave him a sharp look, unhappy by being questioned by someone he thought was on side. 'There were no injuries, certainly nothing that would indicate a scrap like that – no cuts, no stab wounds. Check the arrest report. It was made here in Newcastle by this very force, I believe.'

Which was about the worst guarantee of quality you could get; but Sid held his opinion on that one.

'So you think there is a monster on the loose?' Ian asked with extreme scepticism. 'An alien one?'

'There are some disturbing unknowns,' Vance said. 'The identical murder of a North here in Newcastle last Friday does open up a highly embarrassing question over Angela Tramelo's conviction. If, and it is a colossal *if*, she did not perform the original slaughter, we are back to asking: who or what did? So, people, we have a choice of two. Either it was a psychopath with a grudge against the Norths, who has built himself a power armour suit with horror-drama fingers, and has now returned for the second round. Or . . .'

'Alien monster,' Sid said.

'Walking round Newcastle on a Friday morning,' Ian said scathingly. 'Aye man, do you think it stopped off for a burger first, maybe? Kind'a build up some energy, ready for the big slaughter rematch? Crap on this.'

'You will not *crap on this*,' Vance said in a coldly menacing tone. 'You will take it very seriously indeed. HDA needs to know just what the hell went down in this piss-poor excuse for a town last weekend. We have got to know if there is another sentient species out there intent on doing us harm. So, Detective *Second Grade* Lanagin, you *will* perform your duty to the best of your moronic ability, you *will* find out what went on here right under your inadequate nose last week, and you *will* find out if this is the start of the end of our entire species. Failure to comply, failure to give this task one hundred per cent of your utter devotion will result in me charging you with genocidal endangerment and collaboration with an enemy of humanity. For which, in case you don't know, the death penalty still applies; even here in your screwed-up *liberal* Grande Europe. Do we fully understand each other, now?'

Ian was glaring furiously at the HDA agent. Sid pointed a single warning finger at him, fearful he'd actually try to throw a punch.

'Where do you think it came from?' Lorelle Burdett asked.

Vance didn't take his eyes from Ian. 'Excuse me?'

'If this thing is an alien, then I'm sorry, but Ian is right. How did it get here? There's no way it can come through the gateway. The European Border Directorate has really strict reviews in place for people and cargo. Any refugee can walk across to St Libra without any questions, but it's a one-way street. Coming back is difficult. There's no way an alien, even a human-shaped one, could just sneak through to Earth.'

'We're going to be reviewing imported cargo as part of our expanded investigation,' Sid told her. He didn't like the amount of hostility and scepticism building in the office. The team had arrived expecting to be shat on by a grubby little political appointee, courtesy of the Norths; not be totally screwed by a paranoid spook who believed they were facing an alien Armageddon.

'You will be granted every gateway security record you want for review,' Aldred said. 'There are some pretty stringent precautions against people smuggling applied here. Grande Europe has quite the bug up its arse when it comes to St Libra. Europe, and every other Earth nation for that matter, has managed to offload a whole load of political undesirables on the St Libra independencies, and nobody wants them back. Northumberland International scans all crates and boxes coffin-sized or larger; and we also perform random physical searches as well. It's effective – we have electromagnetic scanners, X-ray, airborne chemical sampling, and good old-fashioned sniffer dogs. We have to be serious about it, because if anyone gets through we're hit with a huge fine, and I'm talking over ten million Eurofrancs for each incident. On the plus side, there's not too much for us to examine. The only real import from St Libra is bioil; because of its size the planet has no heavy metal ore in its crust, so it has bugger-all industry. Now this is all fine for snagging people, but if we are talking about an alien packaged up in some crate, our standard precautions clearly didn't catch it.'

'We can only go on Angela's description that it was man-sized, and though it pains me to admit it, she has no reason to lie,' Vance said. 'Therefore our conclusion is that if it is real it had to come through on the cargo route.'

'Okay,' Sid said, moving to stand in front of the screen so that Angela's face formed a snarling backdrop. 'For all the weird elements in play here, we're still left with a basic murder to solve. So first off, I'd really like a positive identity on our victim. Ari, Abner; you two carry on with that, please. Now Agent Elston has promised that he's going to lean on Brinkelle's people to thoroughly check out all their 2Norths, we might open up some new possibilities.'

'I have to say it's unlikely,' Aldred said. 'All Bartram's offspring, the 2s, are now quite old. None were born after Brinkelle herself, which makes the youngest of them fifty-one. That means there are no 2Norths on St Libra that match the victim's age of mid-forties.'

'That Bartram's family has yet admitted to,' Vance interjected. 'Commissioner Passam is flying to Abellia today to talk to Brinkelle directly. We may yet have some evidence on that front. After all, Bartram was still sugar-daddying those girls right up until his death.'

'Until anything extra turns up, we run a more thorough check on the 2Norths we do know about,' Sid said. 'Chase that imposter theory for me.'

'Yes, boss,' Ari said.

'Dedra and Reannha, I'm going to assign you to the cargo,' Sid told them. 'There's a lot of datawork correlation there, just your field. Start with a review of every piece in our size-bracket and above which came through the gateway in the two weeks prior to the murder, and prioritize those addressed locally. Once you have the item logged, call the company directly for verification that their delivery was intact. And when you do that, talk to a human – I don't want a smartnet response.'

'Yes boss.'

'That leaves the rest of us with the most important aspect: the riverside bodydump site. I'll be leading this part of the investigation personally. We identified eleven possible sites yesterday, which will be examined on an individual basis by one of us. Last night I had each site cordoned off by agency constables. They don't know why, and they never will. Remember that, please. Ian, Eva, Lorelle, and myself will each take out a forensics team this morning; we're going to sweep through each and every site to find some evidence of a body being dumped. I cannot emphasize enough how vital this part of the process is. We have got to find this place. Once we do, the rest is standard datawork.'

With the team starting their assignments, Sid went into his office with Vance and Ralph. Through the glass he could see Ian shaking his head in dismay as he grumbled to Eva. Aldred was settling in with Reannha and Dedra, routing them into the Northumberland Interstellar security network.

'I can get Abner taken off if you like,' Vance began. 'One call to O'Rouke.'

'Why would I want that?' Sid asked.

'The man can't even open a file. He's your chief forensics analyst? Come on!'

'Aye man, he's just had his brother murdered. Give him a moment.'

'I can't afford screw-ups, Sid. Nobody can, not on this one.'

'There won't be any. If he doesn't step up, I'll kick him out myself.'

'I will hold you to that.'

'We'll have the bodydump site by this afternoon,' Sid promised recklessly. 'After that it's going to get easier.'

'Explain.'

'The gap itself might not provide any information, but we can still watch who went in and out of it. They can be identified and better still, backtracked through the city's meshes. But I've got to tell you, Ian has a point. If there was an alien on the loose, then it would have been sighted. This is the age of total digitalization; everything is on line always.'

'Uh huh, and that's why our politicians are pure and clean, and the world works so well, is it? Because everybody knows everything and there's no hiding place.'

'I didn't—'

'There are things going on, Detective, which you have no idea about. Think yourself lucky about that. So now you just focus on your job, and find me some evidence; either that some nut-job has built himself a power suit in his basement and is targeting the Norths, or that we have ourselves one serious trans-stellar crisis.'

'Right.'

Vance studied him for a moment, making a judgement. 'I'm heading out to the local HDA base. You won't see me again, leastways not here. Ralph is your contact now. Clear?'

'Sure.'

'Make it good,' Vance said as he shook hands with Ralph.

Sid let out a long breath as Vance walked out through the office, not acknowledging any of the team as he passed them.

'Sorry about that,' Ralph said.

Sid was mildly surprised to see a sly smile on the man's face. 'Jesus, man.'

'He plays hardass because that's his way,' Ralph said. 'He thinks it shows his strength. He's right in a way. That's why he bitchslapped your guy out there. Just making everyone aware who the top dog is.'

'It isn't going to earn him any friends here.'

'He's not looking for friends. And, Sid, neither am I. This has been booted all the way up to General Shaikh himself. You have heard of General Shaikh, haven't you?'

'Aye. I know who he is.'

'Good. Then you truly understand how critical this situation is.'

'I think I'm getting there.'

*

The HDA maintained a large base close to every gateway on Earth in readiness for a Zanthswarm. Newcastle was no exception. The offices and barracks and primary staging area were situated in the Shipcote district, south of the river, exhibiting the kind of harsh brutalism which even Soviet architecture had eventually retreated from with an embarrassed shudder. Squatting atop the high ground, rigid concrete walls inset with narrow windows and topped by sophisticated sensors looked down on the unruly sprawl of Last Mile below like some stolid medieval castle dominating the hovels of the serfs.

Of course, as every Geordie knew from birth, it was just for show; if St Libra did ever have a Zanthswarm, the HDA and Grande Europe would simply slam the gateway shut. Nobody was going to dispatch wave after wave of humanity's finest to defend a world which housed nothing but corporate drones and bunches of malcontents.

Once he was installed in his new standard-military-issue office, Vance stared through the armoured glass window at the crawl of vehicles and even some pedestrians worming out of the end of Last Mile to the huge rectangular concrete burrow which housed the gateway machine. The end which faced Last Mile, the gateway itself, resembled a vertical pool of mist, writhing with silver phosphorescence. Only the upper third was actually visible to Vance, where a metal bridge-like ramp rose up from Last Mile to push its way into the trans-spacial connection, allowing free access to St Libra. Hidden below the elevated road was the narrow return lane, delivering all arrivals directly to the Border Directorate terminal. But underneath that, and taking up a good half of the gateway, were the twelve massive bioil pipelines that quickly sloped down into the underground tunnels, which led away to storage depots along the east coast and the Inter-Europe distribution grid. Billions of Eurofrancs' worth of harvested hydrocarbons were pumped through each day; helping to satisfy some of the voracious energy demand exerted by Grande Europe and its settled planets.

Only now, looking at the phenomenal enterprise, did Vance fully acknowledge the scale of responsibility that had settled on him. Protecting something of this magnitude and value from a vague yet persistent alien threat was something he could not, would not, shirk away from. He touched the small pin in his suit collar, rough skin rubbing the familiar outline. 'I have looked upon Zanth, and saw the face of the devil,' he whispered. It was the Lord who had brought him and Angela together twenty years ago. He knew that now. That simple encounter hadn't been fate, because today it had brought clarity to his life. *This* was why he had been born, this was the task his Lord had given him. 'I will be worthy, Jesus.'

The aural smartcells embedded in his ears bleeped, communication icons appearing in his grid. He told his e-i to quest the link. The conference screen opposite his desk showed the HDA top-secret logo, which promptly dissolved into General Khurram Shaikh. At sixty-two his hair was a short silver-fox cut atop a round face weighted by stress lines. He was dressed immaculately as always, appearing completely unruffled by the strange event in Newcastle. Vance did his best not to try and work out what time it was at Alice Springs. Part of the mystique surrounding Shaikh was his apparent permanent availability. Rumour had it he never slept, wilder rumour said there were three North-like clones of him working shifts.

'Good morning, Colonel,' General Shaikh said.

'Sir.'

'An eventful night in your part of the world, apparently.'

'Yes, sir.'

'We were beefing up the quantum field sensor coverage around Newcastle anyway, because of the gateway. This adds a sense of urgency to it.'

'Sir, this really doesn't look like a Zanth event.'

'No. But then we don't understand the Zanth. And if it isn't Zanth, then my strategists are assigning St Libra as the most likely origin of the creature. That's if it was a creature which did this.'

'It may be a human, a lone psychopath killing off Norths. At least this time we can launch a decent investigation.'

'Yes. There's a lot depending on the Newcastle police doing a good job. You need to keep the pressure on.'

'It's being done, sir.'

'Good. In the meantime, my strategists believe the most likely scenario is that the Norths have suppressed the fact that St Libra does have sentients. That way Northumberland Interstellar was free to develop their algaepaddies. Without them, the company would've been bankrupt from building the gateway.'

'I can agree with that. St Libra is a very big planet, and we are only really familiar with one continent, Ambrose; and nobody's even explored the western side of that. Who knows what could be skulking around the rest of the world.'

'Exactly. Has the Newcastle murder told us anything?'

'Not a thing. However, the detective in charge is convinced something is out of kilter. The fact that they cannot identify the victim is extremely unusual. Other than that, and the method, I'm not sure . . .'

'We weren't sure after the Bartram atrocity, either. And that's despite what AIA did to that poor girl. Another coincidence to consider, perhaps.'

'That there is never proof is proof? I suppose it makes as much sense as the rest of this. I'd hate to rely on that supposition alone.'

'I know. But there are a lot of factors pushing me to suspect that there is something on St Libra that has remained hidden until now. We have to know, Colonel, we cannot face two enemies across interstellar space. And this one is different, this one is smart and subtle. It eludes us. And I cannot allow that.'

'Yes, sir.'

'Unless the Newcastle police quickly provide some very strong evidence that this is a mundane, copy-cat human-on-human murder, the expedition will go ahead. I've always been uncomfortable about St Libra, there's too much we don't know about that world.'

'I'd like to go, sir.'

'Of course. The composition of the expedition is already being negotiated by the major government blocs, everyone is keen to have their presence felt. As it's St Libra, that wretched Charmonique Passam will be the official head to keep Grande Europe happy. You on the other hand will be the AIA's representative, and mine.'

'Thank you, sir.'

'I wouldn't thank me if I were you. The responsibility will be enormous. If you discover a threat you will have to determine right away if it can be tolerated. The Zanth we can do nothing about. Not yet. But this, this seems more physical, more animal. It is an intelligence we can perhaps comprehend. One that operates close to our level.'

'The noble savage.'

'This century's equivalent, perhaps. And we can't permit that. Precautions are in place against such a development. Detestable, yes; disgusting, morally bankrupt – all these things, but also essential.'

'I understand, sir. I won't let you down.'

*

Now, it is named Zanthworld 3. That wasn't always its name. Humans lived on it once. Eighteen million of them. Back then they called it New Florida. A world that was eerily Earth-like, hosting broad continents of lush vegetation and rugged coastlines.

Three small moons orbited, creating enchanting dapples of different coloured moonlight at night along with boisterous tides to pound the cliffs. Walking among its trees and skimming across the vast everglades the first settlers could so easily believe it was Earth itself in that peaceful time after the last ice age and before the rise of mechanized humankind. A time where unspoilt tranquillity reigned.

To a degree that admirable vista remained even after the gateway ushered through the eager people in their hundreds of thousands. The new settlers were proud of their world's majesty, and did their best not to repeat the hack-and-burn mistakes perpetrated against the old homeworld. Of course, there had to be development to bedrock an economy, something that would give them equal footing with the rest of the trans-stellar states of the United States of America, which even then incorporated three new planets in addition to the original continent back on Earth. But they kept it simple; it was always obvious that this planet's wealth lay in its land. Farming was its future.

Captain Antrinell Viana still occasionally caught sight of the odd farm building through the tough triple-layer windscreen of the excursion rover as it rumbled across Zanthworld 3's thoroughly alien landscape. The rover he drove was large at ten metres long, with a cabin that served both as living quarters and a lab fitted out with the most advanced analysis equipment available. Right at the back was the decontamination chamber where the HDA research team could suit up before venturing out across the Zanth. Power was delivered from five separate fuel cells, driving individual electric hub motors on each of the triple wheel sets. Puncture-proof tyres that stood as high as a man's shoulder in combination with long gas suspension pistons provided a reasonably smooth ride on the weird surfaces it was designed to traverse. And there was enough redundancy in the drive system to get the rover home if up to eighty per cent of the mechanics and electrics ever failed or went offline.

Knowing that, Antrinell could steer along the inclines and curving banks with a reasonable degree of confidence. He'd lost count now of how many missions he'd undertaken on various Zanthworlds in the twelve years since he'd qualified from the HDA academy. Well over a hundred, at any rate. A lot of staff on the deep research teams quit field work after twenty or thirty missions. Depression was the most common reason cited. Coming face to face with something so off-scale massive, a genuine irresistible force made real and completely in-your-face, eventually got to people. But Antrinell had his faith to comfort him; like everyone who answered the calling of the Gospel Warriors, he believed that Jesus would protect them, that God would ultimately show humans the way to salvation, and that the Zanth would eventually be broken. So he wasn't intimidated or disheartened by the Zanth, instead he saw it for what it was: hopeless evil arrogance, a cancer upon the glorious universe which God had created for life to flourish. By being here, by testing and experimenting, by discovering the Zanth's secrets, he was undertaking God's true work.

'Picking up the beacon signal,' Marvin Trambi said from the seat beside Antrinell. 'It hasn't shifted much.'

Antrinell got his e-i to lock the beacon signal onto the 3D radar image projected across the windscreen. It shone like a pink star, two and a half kilometres away, on a buttress shaft that was reasonably flat.

The Zanth might not intimidate Antrinell, but every time he ventured across Zanth he was disturbed by its sheer strangeness. Three hours ago they had emerged from the gateway onto a patch of land close to the coast, one of the last remaining clear spots on the planet which was still recognizably a terrestrial-match world, with grass and fern trees still alive despite the green-mist sky. Nervous surviving animals quivered behind bushes and skipped along gullies, triple-segment eyes staring out at the big vehicle which lumbered past. Blotting out the horizon was the Zanth, its boundary creeping forward inexorably towards the sea.

They drew closer to the perverted wonder that had become the ground, and eventually mounted the smooth aquamarine edge of the Zanth as if they were rising onto an ancient cooled lava spill. That impression only lasted a minute. This was no longer a geological landscape crafted by the stately thrust of ice age glaciers and underlying million-year tectonic currents. The Zanth had fallen upon the land, and subsumed its original quality, subverting it, twisting and reshaping both the solid profile and internal atomic structure, a conquest conducted at both the micro and macro levels. It was a process outside of nature, and which nature could never compete against.

The rover was now driving through a bizarre topology, as if the surface was transforming into a hive structure secreted by toxed-up mountain-sized bees. The Zanth consumed soil, rock, water, and vegetation alike, infusing the mass with its own purpose. Sink holes opened up, miles deep and tens of miles wide, the consumed material flowing up through vast columns of translucent matter resembling crystal, but never so static, so primitive. The interlocking lattice they wove through the sky was always an erratic asymmetrical labyrinth with strands arching tens of kilometres into the thinning air. Impossible had they been composed of ordinary matter. Pillars as broad as mountains and a hundred times taller: gravity would have brought them crashing down as soon as they curved away from the horizontal. But fundamental gravity didn't seem to bother Zanth in its formation phase, it possessed an interstice with quantum fields which defied scientific rationale.

Through this treacherous three-dimensional maze, Antrinell drove the rover, inching up curving slopes with inverse cambers; then back down into crater canyons where miles below them rivers of sludgy iridescent fog obscured the bottom, if indeed they had one. Across meandering bridges that multiplied at dangerously knobbly junctions, with few continuing strands keeping horizontal. Sometimes the surface below the tyres was as clear as glass before it slid away into a rainbow diffraction. Then there were times it seemed as insubstantial as the air which was mutating all around them.

A couple of kilometres from the beacon, Antrinell caught sight of a farmhouse. It was embedded in a purple-tinted column that was twelve hundred metres thick, with bent chrome-green buttress wings that themselves turned and intersected to form an arching bird's-nest roof a few hundred metres above, as if in tiny worshipful mimicry of the greater composition all around. The perfectly ordinary two-storey house was still resting on a scoop of raw soil, as if it had been ripped from the ground by a wild tornado. Now it hung a hundred and fifty metres above the excursion rover, tilted at a good fifty degrees from horizontal. Its symmetrical composite panel walls and strictly functional PV solar roof portrayed a complete contrast to the irrational chaos of the Zanth topology which had captured it. As Antrinell saw it now, the structure it was in the middle of was a disintegration drizzle, with each particle locked in a slo-mo spray away from the original outline. Recordings of similar embeddings always showed the inevitable absorption into the overall lattice of the Zanth as the structure's original molecules were methodically broken apart and distorted.

All that witnessing the sad, lost house did for him was reinforce the bitterly won knowledge that every human now laboured under: nothing evaded the Zanth. Nothing survived. Everything became Zanth in the end.

Antrinell began to steer the rover up a sharp incline. The equipment package which included the beacon was just above one of the intersections. Twelve strands curved together amid a cluster of fungal-profile protrusions and undulating hollows.

'I'm going to turn us round before we egress,' Antrinell said.

Marvin pointed at a pair of bulbous distensions thirty metres high, shimmering purple and grey in the weak light percolating through the fog. 'There's room between those two.'

'Okay.' Antrinell shifted the wheel slightly, and the rover tilted as it tracked along a sharp slope. Millimetre wave radar measured the gap between the bulbs. Marvin was right, it was big enough for the rover to pass through. If they got wedged stuck, it was a long walk back to the gateway. Everyone in the HDA's Frontline research division had seen the recordings of suited figures trapped inside Zanth material, long dead but with their edges dissolving. The fragments expanding. Vanishing.

There were some human sects, with mad perverted followers and manipulative leaders, who considered such transmutation to be the true path to immortality. That to be absorbed then merge with Zanth was the entrance to everlasting life, that your essence would be embraced by Zanth. That somewhere, somehow within its matrix of weird molecules and different quantum composition you would continue, that Zanth would cherish you for your gift of individuality, carry you down the galactic epochs and on through eternity. There was no afterlife, they preached, no truth in the primitive holy books. The Zanth brought a new life now and for ever.

Antrinell knew it did nothing of the sort. He'd seen enough Zanth to know it didn't care, didn't even notice humans, nor any biological life. He knew what a blight upon God's creation Zanth really was, and he never wavered from that truth.

The rover nosed through the gap and started down a thirty-degree incline. They were close to the rim of the junction now, front wheels barely five metres away, and the surface was a smooth curve of gold and scarlet diffraction patterns. Antrinell moved them on until they were a safer distance from the edge, and stopped.

Regulations were very clear that at least two people had to remain inside the vehicle at all times. Antrinell and Marvin suited up, leaving their three team-mates in the rover to monitor them constantly through a ringlink. Zanth environment suits weren't nearly as bulky and cumbersome as a spacesuit. They came in two sections, with a tight first skin like a neoprene wetsuit, which had a collar seal to attach the big bubble helmet to. A rebreather module and emergency oxygen bottle went on next, worn as a backpack. On top of it all went a one-piece, like a loose boiler suit with integrated boots. The outer layer was a white friction-less metalloceramic fabric, which had a small current constantly running through it. Electricity was about the only thing which could keep the Zanth at bay, though observation had shown it could take hours if not days for the absorption/transformation process to begin once ordinary matter came into contact with any Zanth. Someone in a suit would have to be lying down on the Zanth for a long time before they were in any danger. But still, people felt a lot safer with an electric barrier between them and doom; HDA certainly didn't begrudge them an extra layer of protection.

The airlock was a clinical-white cylindrical chamber with a ring of black titanium vents around the middle, and a circular door at each end. Antrinell and Marvin waited inside while their e-is ran a final batch of checks, then the vents hissed as the pressure was equalized. Rovers always maintained a positive pressure difference with the planetary atmosphere, which grew progressively easier as the Zanth consumed a planet. An atmosphere was clearly not a part of Zanth, the gases were absorbed and converted along with everything else it came into contact with. When the airlock's outer door swung open, Antrinell was first down the ladder. He tested the ground cautiously, making sure his boot soles had a reasonable traction. Sometimes the surface of the Zanth was as slippery as an ice rink. This time it was okay, and he gave Marvin the all clear.

Together they walked over to the equipment package. It seemed strangely old-fashioned in this age of smartdust and nanojunction processors. But as experience had shown, the smaller the gadget, the easier it was perverted and absorbed into the Zanth. HDA science teams had soon abandoned the meshed sensors which they took for granted on their own worlds in favour of solid retro blocks of electronics.

The last mission had set this one up on a tripod with two-metre-long telescoping legs that carried quite a high electrical charge. Antrinell was pleased to see the Zanth hadn't begun its absorption, all three legs remained an unblemished shiny stainless steel. Then he looked at the sensor equipment packages stacked together on top, covered in a plain thermal blanket – also conducting a charge. 'Hell.'

'What is it?' Marvin asked.

Antrinell leaned in for a better look, bringing his own helmet-mounted sensors in to focus. In total there were six square packages, twenty-five centimetres along a side, and maybe ten deep. The two in the middle had amber Zanth growing out of the tiny cracks between them. Slender fronds with mushroom tips spreading out from a single anchor point in starburst formation. Even fainter, were the threads that were staining the thermal blanket itself, radiating out from the base of the fronds. The similarity to terrestrial fungi was uncanny.

'Oh,' Marvin said uneasily. 'That's not good. Do you think it's growing resistant to electricity?'

'Who knows?' Antrinell waved a sensor wand over the packages. 'There's no defence charge running through the middle two units, but some of their internal circuitry is still functional.'

'Okay, I'll download the files. Maybe the guys back at Frontline can make something of it.'

Knowing what he would find, Antrinell walked over to the face of the spire which the equipment package was focused on. Two months ago they'd been here and applied a molecular virus to the surface of the Zanth. The stuff terrified most people, and Antrinell was no exception. No one outside of HDA even knew it existed. The precautions surrounding its handling were orders of magnitude stronger than those governing nukes. If it ever got loose on ordinary matter, it could conceivably devastate the entire world. There was one asteroid in a nameless star system where Frontline had opened a gateway that was now a seething mass of brittle fractal foam, its base-energy state lowered by the molecular metamorphosis. But the key was 'ordinary matter'.

Looking down on the virus, Antrinell could see it was dead. It had eaten its way into the Zanth, expanding progressively inwards until it was a dark-russet canker two metres across. At that point the Zanth somehow grew resistant, its own transformed molecules altering again, hardening themselves in some fashion so they could no longer be consumed by the virus. Unable to eat to grow, the molecular virus had simply died.

Antrinell unclipped the sample rod from his belt, and dipped it gingerly into the frail meringue-texture virus. It was like breaking the surface of very thin ice, a slight resistance that crumpled, then the solid-state probe slid down sluggishly. He watched the read-out in his optical grid, detailing the analysis. The virus was definitely dead, reduced to superfine dust with little cohesion. Strands were sucked into the sampler. 'Got it,' he said.

'And I have the sensor data,' Marvin said. He took a look at the deep puddle which the virus had become. 'Just great. That must have knocked out a good ten kilograms.' He looked round the massive opalescent structures enveloping them. 'Only another quizzillion tonnes to go.'

Antrinell grinned wide enough for Marvin to see his teeth through the darkened helmet. 'That's the optimism that'll see us all through this.'

'How many quit from despair?'

'You're not a quitter.' Antrinell pulled the sample probe out of the virus, and held it up like a victory cup. 'Besides, we made some progress today.'

'Progress? How exactly?'

'Elimination. That configuration doesn't work. We try another. Then another. Then another.'

'Yeah, right.'

They made their way back to the rover. Once they were inside the decontamination chamber the airlock door swung shut. White walls shone violet, and a thick oily mist sprayed out of the vents. They both stood still, holding their hands up like ballerinas caught in mid-pirouette. The oil formed a thin skin over the suit, and started dripping onto the floor. Then static arced through the chamber, producing a muffled roar as it strobed madly. Antrinell flinched, just like he did every time. There was enough voltage out there to knock him dead if the outer suit developed a break.

The vents reversed, pumping out the atmosphere. Antrinell could feel the inner suit stiffen as it kept him safe against the vacuum. The cycle was repeated three times, which should flush any Zanth substance molecules back out of the rover. No one had ever seen any evidence that Zanth could expand itself out of a microscopic fragment, it always seemed to achieve active status in chunks weighing in at over two hundred tonnes, but HDA wasn't going to take any chances.

As a final precaution, Antrinell and Marvin stripped off their outer suit layer and disposed of them through a chute. Another flush cycle began. Only then did they take off the inner suit. Those got dumped outside as well.

Dressed in fatigues again, Antrinell sat in the driver's seat, and fed power to the hub motors. It was always an anxious moment, finding out if the Zanth had begun to absorb the tyres. Fortunately, if that happened, they could shed the external layer of metallasized silicone tread like a snake skin.

The excursion rover moved away smoothly, and the team's tension drained away. They spent another hour driving carefully along the entangled strands to reach the end of the Zanth; arriving as dusk began to claim the already leaden sky, though they had another two hours of sunlight left. Zanthworld 3 used to have a day which lasted twenty-three hours and forty minutes; now with the Zanth somehow impinging on local gravity its rotation was slowing, already giving it thirty-seven-hour days, and the process still hadn't stopped. Dusk, like dawn, was a lingering affair.

Antrinell drove the rover down onto the natural land beyond, feeling an unexpected flush of relief. He knew the gouge they'd skirted was just one of hundreds of similar wounds that must have been sliced deep into the world. It wouldn't be much longer, a few years at most, before maintaining a gateway here would be too dangerous.

Five kilometres ahead, the gateway shimmered like a circle of entombed moonlight. Antrinell aimed the rover straight at it, eager to be home, to leave the Zanth's victory behind. A wave of rain lashed against the rover. Air temperature outside was only a couple of degrees above freezing. He could see now that the plants had given up. Their cyan leaves were growing flaccid as they shaded down to lime-green, with withered brittle edges flaking off. New shoots lacked vigour, more often pushing out malformed bracts. Native grass was patchy.

'Isn't that Okeechobee?' Marvin asked. He was leaning forward, craning to look up into the leaden sky.

Antrinell followed his gaze. The wispy clouds had parted, taking the rain with them and revealing a broad patch of clear sky. Almost directly above, blocking his view of the twilight stars, was a weird purple-green blob. The oddity was a rough sphere of loosely wound gossamer, with hundreds of spiky protrusions soaring outwards, like spume from clashing waves. Some were as long as the core's diameter.

'Yeah, that's Okeechobee,' he grunted. The smallest of the planet's original three moons. Zanth had completed its transformation of the dusty ball of regolith, now the structure was slowly growing as the strands of Zanth realigned themselves. Within a few decades, when Zanthworld 3 itself had stopped spinning and achieved tidal-lock with the star, Okeechobee and the other two moons would have shifted orbit until they all became stationary relative to each other. Once that configuration was achieved, they would slowly merge, then keep expanding until the whole local region of space was suffused by Zanth in the form of a diaphanous tangle of alien matter.

No one knew exactly what would happen after that. But then no one, theologians and cosmology theorists alike, could explain the origin or purpose of the Zanth. All they could do was shout questions into the sky like some pre-history priest asking his deity to explain the world he saw yet didn't understand.

Was the Zanth limited to this galaxy alone? Was it a runaway doomsday weapon? Or was it something more, an invasion from another universe, seeking to convert ours? A crusade which would take billions of years. Was there purpose? Or worse, was it accidental? And the biggest hope of all: was there another sentient species out there to join in battle against it?

The excursion rover passed through the gateway, emerging onto the wide concrete reception apron on Frontline, a reassuringly safe twenty-seven lightyears from Zanthworld 3. Frontline was a rock planet orbiting a red dwarf star, chosen because the strategists guessed, or prayed, that it would present an unattractive target to the Zanth. Antrinell believed they might just as well have sited it on a tropical paradise world, for all the difference that would make to Zanth motivation. If Zanth was attracted to gateways, Frontline was doomed anyway. Its personnel might at least benefit from a decent beach to relax on between shifts.

But nobody had asked him.

He drove the rover over to the first of the giant geodesic domes anchored to the rock. There were over twenty domes now; thick metal at the base, rising to a reinforced glass cap shielding circular patches of parkland which needed a lot of artificial lighting in order to grow properly. That white nurturing light glared out of each one, creating a thin haze in the minuscule atmosphere of freezing argon.

They passed through three separate sensor arches before they even reached the airlock's outer door. Inside, the robot systems of the decontamination area sluiced them down with a variety of chemicals. Smartdust dispensers fired jets of motes which settled on every surface and began scanning round. Molecular samplers ringing the drains analysed the effluent for the sign of any exotic molecules. The whole procedure took over an hour.

Eventually they were cleared to leave. A lab team came on board to retrieve the samples Antrinell had taken. Engineers began reviewing the rover's mechanics.

Antrinell and Marvin left it all behind, and took a tube train over to dome eight where there was a decent bar. It was ritual now after every mission. Tomorrow there would be a full debrief, but for now they were allowed some self-time.

The inside of the dome with its windowless metal-walled compartments and maze of corridors all lined with pipes and cables was how Antrinell imagined warships and submarines used to be like. Only when they got up to the upper park did the mild feeling of claustrophobia abate. Even then, the plants weren't exactly vigorous; they survived the strange environment rather than flourished. And it wasn't so much a park as a reasonable-sized garden.

But there was terrestrial greenery, and humidity, and flower scents, and even a few confused parrots flapping about between trees. The bar was a wide patio with tables that had tropical thatch parasols. It was all very laboured. Antrinell didn't mind, as it provided a pleasant counter to Zanth, and even Frontline itself. He just wanted to sit down with a beer and bitch about the mission, and command, and the lab which concocted the useless molecular virus.

Instead, when he came up the stairwell into the bar he saw who was waiting at the counter and his shoulders dropped. 'Oh hell,' he grunted.

Major Vermekia grinned broadly, and raised his fruit cocktail in greeting.

'So what's the mission?' Antrinell asked once he and Marvin had claimed their beers and allowed Vermekia to guide them over to a table on the edge of the patio.

'You're going to be looking for an alien,' Vermekia told them. 'A sentient. We believe it to be hostile.'

'Where?' asked Marvin. 'I haven't heard of anyone building a new gateway in five years.'

Vermekia's annoyingly superior grin broadened. 'St Libra.'

'You're kidding,' Antrinell said.

'Not at all. There's some uncomfortable evidence emerging that there might be some kind of sentient population hidden on Brogal – the northern continent.'

Antrinell sipped his beer as he listened to the major explain about the murder in Newcastle, and the connection to Bartram North's slaying. If it hadn't been for the major's immaculate uniform, reminding him this was coming directly from General Khurram Shaikh himself, he might have dismissed the whole notion. Although, he had to admit it was strange. And he was wearily familiar enough with HDA and high-level government bureaucracy to know that once a project acquired enough momentum at the top it became unstoppable. Shaikh was involved, as were the Presidents of the GE and USA along with the Chairman of the Unified Chinese Worlds; which alone guaranteed this wasn't going to be a ten-day digital exercise to be filed and forgotten. It was going to be big; short of an actual Zanthswarm, the biggest operation HDA would mount in a decade – in itself a telling point. Even in his short service time he'd noticed how brass-heavy the agency was becoming, how expensive civilian consultants were brought in to advise on everything, how essential equipment projects had fallen behind schedule and grown massive cost overruns. Depending on the outcome of the St Libra mission, some people were going to emerge from the other side with promotions and a massively enhanced career trajectory. Others were going to crash and burn. Quite a lot of others if the results weren't positive enough – about which he had his own suspicions. Clearly, Shaikh was going to prove that HDA had a vital non-Zanth role to play in human affairs, an expediency that would help keep all those grudging national treasuries in line.

'So what's our role?' Marvin asked.

'Genetic analysis,' Vermekia said. 'As the expedition makes its way north we need to know if evolution is starting to vary from the St Libra norm. You sample every odd-looking leaf to see just how odd it actually is, and if it's a progression.'

'We're looking for their equivalent of the Burgess Shale,' Antrinell decided.

Vermekia frowned. 'The what?'

'Burgess Shale. It's an area in Canada that preserved some unique species from the Cambrian Explosion. That was an evolutionary episode five hundred million years ago, basically the greatest biological diversity event which Earth has ever known, when unicellular organisms evolved into the kind of biologically complex animals and plants we are today. The fossils found in the Burgess Shale region gave palaeontologists a huge window into that period, allowing them to see the ancestors of nearly every species on Earth. But there were also others which have no modern descendants. The Shale had a boundary called the Cathedral Escarpment, so a lot of those unknown species never made it past that and out into the wider world. That's probably what Shaikh's advisers think has happened here – after all, Brogal covers an area greater than every one of Earth's continents put together. There's got to be a lot of isolated areas beyond Abellia.'

'I'm glad you're so receptive to the notion,' Vermekia said. 'And you're right; HDA is calling it enclave evolution.'

'But it's pretty weird that there's been no sign of any animal life anywhere on St Libra, not even an insect.'

'And that's a huge jump from nothing to a full sentient,' Marvin said.

'Well you might just be the ones who find the answer. They might even name them after you.'

'Wonderful, that's what I want to be known as for the rest of human history, a two-metre-high monster with knives for hands who goes around massacring people.'

'Ah,' Vermekia glanced round, checking the nearby tables were empty. 'That's the second part of your mission.'

*

Corporal Paresh Evitts of the Legion, the elite regiment of the GE Interstellar Defence Agency, was sorely puzzled by his charge. At twenty-five, Paresh had visited several planets for evacuation training exercises, including Wuchow in the Unified Chinese Worlds, which gave him a reasonable belief that he understood the way humanity's worlds worked, thus allowing him to be a decent judge of character.

Angela Tramelo sat on the other side of the aisle from him in the black fourteen-seat HDA minibus that was leading the convoy of ten identical vehicles up the A1, and he couldn't get a grip on her at all. Hot-looking, with her fuzzy blonde hair and elfin-delicate features; she wore standard-issue HDA fatigues: a dark-grey one-piece overall. It was too big for her, but not baggy enough to disguise a decent body when he glanced at her in the moments he thought she wasn't watching. A trim figure was to be expected, she was about twenty, maybe twenty-one max. Which was the first mystery. Her file, which was incredibly small – little more than an identity confirmation certificate to make sure they got the right person – said she was forty. No way.

Then the second enigma: why exactly was his entire squad assigned to pick her up from Holloway Prison at seven o'clock in the morning? She hadn't been designated a prisoner status. Strange, because Lieutenant Pablo Botin had ordered them to treat her like one; they were her official escort, and they had to get to Newcastle without 'incident'. But she wasn't dangerous; not dangerous enough to warrant issuing them with sidearms, apparently. So why then had Botin said: 'Watch the bitch close. She's fucking lethal when she wants to be.'

Sideways glances didn't give Paresh a clue where that warning came from. Fit she might be, but any one of his squad could snap her in two if she was dumb enough to try getting physical; even Private Audrie Sleath, who was a lot shorter than the not-prisoner. And thinking of physical . . . Paresh let his gaze linger a while. She was looking out of the window as the snow-coated outskirts of London slid past. Those legs would be quite some-thing wrapped round his neck. Oh yeah.

'What?' Angela asked. She was still looking at the window.

Too late Paresh realized his faint reflection on the glass was betraying him. 'Just trying to figure you out, is it,' Paresh explained. The rest of the squad roused themselves with a little flurry of grins and nudging elbows as they focused on the corporal and the babe. Question was: could he score? Cynics and supporters alike settled back to enjoy the show.

Angela turned, and gave him a smile which he couldn't quite believe was sincere. But it did bump her up still further on the beauty-scale. She really was a heart-buster – if they'd been in a bar he'd be pleading to buy her a drink. But the voice gave it away: steel hard. He'd seen that aspect of her this morning when they arrived at the prison to collect her. She hadn't been ready to leave.

Orders had them collecting her at seven sharp. Not a chance.

When he and the other two in the handover detail had arrived at the administration block she was arguing with the governor and two guards. Not arguing by shouting, but boy could she out-stubborn a cat. Insultingly slow words, and a body-pose that could be read as 'immovable object' by a blind dude.

'I have worked three days every week,' she said. 'I have spent at most ten per cent of that on your pitiful good behaviour store. Therefore this institution still owes me for ninety per cent of my hours. And I believe GE minimum wage legislation is fifty-eight Eurofrancs an hour.'

'You only get to spend that in here,' the disturbed governor protested.

'But I don't belong in here, do I? That's why we had yesterday's meeting. That's why you just extracted my smartcell tags.'

The governor tried to glance at her assistant, who managed to avoid all eye contact. 'I'll refer it to the Justice Department, first thing. You have my word.'

'Thank you.'

The governor gave a relieved smile, and gestured at Paresh. That was when Angela looked round at the detail, feigning interest. Then she addressed the governor direct: 'I'll wait.'

Paresh almost laughed at the stricken expression crawling across the governor's face.

'But they won't be in the office for another three hours,' the governor protested.

'Oh dear,' said Angela.

'Do you actually want to get out of here?' the governor snapped.

'I *am* getting out of here. We know that now, don't we? The question is: how? Do I go quietly now, as agreed? Or do I delete yesterday's agreement and wait until the expedition proves I'm innocent? After all, they're not going to keep the result quiet, now are they? Not with so much riding on this. Reputations a lot more important than yours are gambling on the outcome. Do you think the Justice Department will thank you for the publicity a month from now when I walk out of the front gate into a pack

106

of transnet reporters? Exactly how much compensation will that kind of miscarriage of justice net me do you think? And you could have bought me off with the money you owe me anyway. How's that going to scan?'

Paresh watched in admiration as the two women stared at each other. There was only ever going to be one result. The governor didn't even last a minute.

'All right! I'll authorize payment.'

'You can issue me with a European Social Bank account,' Angela said calmly. 'The standard for paroled criminals, I believe. Your office has the authority to do that. You see, allowing us access to education is a benefit.'

'Get it done,' the governor hissed at her assistant.

'But—'

'Do it!'

It had taken another thirty minutes for the process to be completed. Angela never moved from the spot the whole time. Paresh had to complain twice to the furious governor to try and speed things along.

'Not your concern,' Angela said without even turning to him. 'I either go back to my cell, or I leave with my money.'

Paresh didn't know how the hell to break the impasse – ordering his detail to physically lift her out was about the only option. He was nervous about that, his corporal stripe was only two months old. Screw the lieutenant for not making things clear.

Eventually, the assistant scuttled back into the room, and handed Angela a biometric card. She checked it registered her thumb, then they had to go over to a zone console and activate the account. Codes were assigned.

'Can we go now?' Paresh asked witheringly.

Angela grinned cheerfully at him. 'Of course we can. You didn't think I was going to stay in this shithole did you?'

Paresh was sure he could hear the governor's teeth grinding together. 'Your bag,' he said, gesturing helpfully at the small carryall Angela was walking away from.

'My butler always organizes delivery of my couture collection.'

Paresh and the detail had to hurry to catch up with Angela as buzzers sounded and big solid prison doors obediently opened for her.

*

'Nothing to figure out,' Angela said as they drove into the white wilderness of the Middlesex countryside. 'I was wrongly imprisoned, now I'm volunteering to help you guys out. I'm coming with you on the expedition.'

'What expedition?' DiRito asked from two seats down.

'Didn't they tell you? We're going alien hunting on St Libra.'

The squad exchanged a whole load of shocked glances. 'No shit?' Mohammed Anwar blurted.

'I'm sure you'll get your briefing when we arrive at Newcastle.'

'Hey,' Marty O'Riley said. 'What were you in there for?'

Angela turned round so she was facing all the curious faces, and hooked her arm over the top of the chair. 'They convicted me of slaughtering fourteen people in one go. Oh, that's more than all of you, isn't it?' Her lips parted at the startled silence which greeted that statement. 'Lucky for you, I didn't do it. Which is why your very embarrassed government has recruited me as a consultant on this trip.'

'What do you consult on?'

'I was the only one who survived. I saw the alien. I know what it looks like, I know what it sounds like, I know what it smells like. You don't forget that smell, not even after twenty years. When I smell it again, I'll know.'

Paresh couldn't resist. 'So what does a killer alien smell like?'

'Mint.'

Which was a complete load of bollocks, Paresh knew. She was just enjoying herself yanking their chains. But he knew who she was now. 'Bartram North,' he said quietly.

Those deadly green eyes stared at him. Then she grinned again. 'Smart boy.'

'Do my best.'

108

'Not good enough, though, is it?'

'How you reckon that?'

'You're on a trip to poke a stick into a monster's nest. It will kill you.' She raised her voice. 'It will kill all of you. You won't stand a chance.'

'You haven't seen what we can do,' Ramon Beaken asserted. 'No fucking alien gets on top of this squad, lady. We can handle ourselves.'

'Let's hope so. But if I do ever scent it, take me seriously. Your life depends on it.'

'You got out last time,' Paresh pointed out.

'That's because I'm tougher than you.'

No doubt about it, Paresh thought, she was a class-A bullshitter. That just made her more interesting. He wondered if he did stand a chance with her.

Angela didn't say much as the convoy rode along through the English midlands and into the north. The squad didn't know what the hell to make of her, so they by and large ignored her. Paresh didn't give up so easy. He saw the way she stared at the countryside, even though it was just drab frozen fields and denuded ice-gripped trees. She was entranced by it. The kind of delight anyone would have if they'd been denied that sight for twenty years. So if that part of the file was correct . . .

The convoy stopped at the Scotch Corner services so the vehicles could fill up with bioil. Everyone needed to take a pee, and after that they piled in to the Little Chef café franchise for a coffee and a donut, surprising the two waitresses who were suddenly rushed off their feet.

Angela climbed out of the HDA minibus and inhaled deeply. On the other side of the garage forecourt low sedans and twenty-four-wheel tankers carrying their cargo of raw were purring smoothly along the six lanes of the A1 in both directions, their thick winter tyres spraying the banks of snow which lined the road with a constant rain of filthy slush.

Paresh was entranced by the far-away expression on her face as she watched the continual stream of traffic. It made her appear vulnerable yet content at the same time, which he found quite bizarre. 'You're not going to try and run, are you?' he asked, not quite joking.

Her expression hardened, and that unnerving stare locked on to him again. 'No. I know exactly where I'm going, and that's back to Abellia.'

'Where?'

'The town where it happened on St Libra. I'm going to find that motherfucker, and when I do, it is going to *burn* – and I don't mean in hell. I'm not going to be that kind to it.'

'There really is a monster, isn't there?'

'Absolutely. So if you really are smart, Sergeant—'

'That's only corporal, and it's Paresh.'

'Paresh,' she acknowledged. 'If you're smart you'll be the one who runs.'

'Guess I'm stupid then.'

'We all are, in our own special ways.'

Which was the closest she'd come to making real conversation, even if it was kind of creepy. 'I know you've not been outside for a while,' he said. 'But it is bloody freezing standing here. Can I buy you a coffee?'

Angela glanced at the café franchise on the side of the station's large TravelMart store. The Legionnaires from the convoy were crowding every table, laughing as they joshed the harassed wait-resses. 'I bet you say that to all the girls.'

'Every one of them.'

'You know, this isn't quite the fantastic first meal I was planning on when I was free.'

'Best I can do.'

'Then I accept. Do you think they'd do hot chocolate with marshmallows?'

'Let's go find out.'

*

During the rest of the drive up to Newcastle, Angela did her best to behave as normally as she could. It wasn't easy, she had so few reference points left other than hazy memories, and those didn't exactly belong to a standard life. Acclimatizing herself to being out was proving more difficult than she had imagined. It was all so sudden – less than twenty-four hours ago she'd been brooding in the same cell she'd always been in, robotically performing the same tasks, eating the same food, not thinking about anything because that was how you survived each day. Now here she was, on the way back to St Libra, which was actually the last place in the galaxy she wanted to go.

The hot chocolate in the Little Chef had been surprisingly good. Good because it wasn't prison hot chocolate. The Danish pastry Paresh had bought her to go with it was also the best she'd tasted in twenty years. And then there was the laughter. For the last twenty years, laughter for her had been the twin of cruelty, the sound of vicious triumph which accompanied whimpering screams, not this carefree joy. That was something she knew would take a long time to get used to. All those young, confident Legionnaires crammed into the restaurant and misting up the windows with their boisterous joking, like a football team after the match. Watching their stupid schoolkid antics she couldn't feel anything but sorry for them. If the expedition was successful, they'd all be dead.

Once the minibuses filled their tanks with bioil the Legionnaires barged out of the Little Chef and hurried back to their vehicles. Angela nipped into the TravelMart and got the assistant manager to unlock the most expensive Spectrum basic smart-cell interface packet from the secure cabinet behind the counter. Not that there was a huge choice of brands. She hadn't had a direct meat-to-wi connection for over twenty years, not since she took out her cy-chips before Melyne Aslo recruited her. Smart-cells were a whole lot better than the old cy-chips, so the newer arrivals at Holloway told her.

She used the Social Bank card to buy the packet, and was moderately pleased when the transaction went through without any glitch, and even happier that the teen assistant manager girl didn't say anything when she waved the SBcard through the till's keyspace. It was like hearing the prison gates clanging shut behind her, but for real this time. She was out. She was free.

The HDA minibus's auto pulled out of the forecourt and slotted them into the northbound traffic. Angela watched the snowy landscape with a strangely neutral attitude. For years she'd been planning what to do on all the million possible variants of this day, but now it was here and she had to make some tough decisions. First one, the obvious one, she would go back to St Libra. It was where she could pick up the loose ends she'd abandoned twenty years ago. Besides, making a break for it now would be ridiculously tough. But in the meantime there were certain things to be done, preparations made as best she could.

Angela split the chic circular Spectrum packet open. Like the packet, the instruction booklet was simple, with monochrome diagrams just to make sure. She removed the little medical-style applicator tube, which had a short fat needle and a compressed gas cartridge, which she snapped together easily. Next out came a trim magazine of fourteen clearly marked pea-sized shells which clicked neatly into the back of the tube. The first shell contained an aural smartcell. She tucked the C-shaped plastic mould behind her left ear, which positioned the tube correctly, and pressed the trigger. 'Ow,' it was like getting stung by an infant bee. But the tube had inserted the smartcell close to her inner ear, where its vibrations would manifest as ordinary sounds. The sting turned cold as the tube released a drop of antiseptic gel. She ejected the empty shell, and shifted the mould to her right ear. The vocal smartcells followed, inside the back of the mouth, beside the lower rear molars. Hands: one in the palm, then each fingertip.

Finally she took out the contact lens case. Breaking the seal initiated them, so she dabbed the small thick transparent circles onto her eyes quickly, blinking against the sensation, and checking they were centred correctly with the little mirror provided in the case. Once she was satisfied, she triggered the pad which contained the unique bodymesh activation code. The contact lenses were the expensive part of the package, each containing a dozen iris smartcells, the smallest produced. Once they received the code, the lenses extended nanofilaments into her eyeball and injected the smartcells in a ring around the iris. They meshed together and orientated themselves, then fired off test pulses down her optic nerves.

The clarity was astonishing, she wasn't prepared for anything so sharp. For a second she was scared the smartcells would burn her retinas, they were so powerful. It was a bad déjà vu. But a basic grid of green lines appeared which reassured her. She closed her eyes like the booklet recommended, and her bodymesh began the full calibration sequence. Tones sounded in her ear. She muttered the words the grid display told her to so the interface could learn her speech patterns. It took a minute for the body-mesh software to build her personal configuration into a minimal e-i. With her voiceprint locked she worked with the e-i to define the colours and positioning of the grid, selecting icons. At the end she opened her eyes again to see the keyspace virtual the grid displayed, a red-edged cube above the empty seat beside her, with icons floating inside it. As her hands moved through it the bodymesh tracked their position so she could flick at the icons' cog-surface. Another couple of minutes' final calibration and familiarization, and she was done, a complete digital citizen again. The empty contact lenses peeled off, and she dropped them back into the packet along with the spent application tube and empty shells.

She told her e-i to quest a link to the minibus's net cell. And for the first time in twenty years Angela had an unmonitored, unrestricted channel into the transnet. The shoal of multi-coloured access route symbols which sprang up in her grid were familiar from her refresher lessons at Holloway, but now all of them were active. She used her SBcard account to buy her e-i an access code and a secure cache from a German service company, and launched herself into the virtual universe.

Her old Tramelo e-i was out there, of course, inactive in an eternity cache. But she'd given HDA those access codes long ago;

they would have run the entire store through AI analysis routines and planted monitors. There was nothing there for her now. Digitally there was very little she could do to reconnect with the one person she needed to, especially while using an HDA vehicle's cell as her transnet access point. She would have to wait until she had an independent, unmonitored connection. She'd already waited twenty years, a few more days were irrelevant.

Her e-i sent out half a dozen searches, harvesting exactly the kind of information the HDA would expect her to: tracers on the surviving girls from the mansion, summary of herself in news shows and sites, a list of decent Newcastle clothes shops and restaurants, a rundown on the city's HDA base, current news of St Libra with reference to any HDA activity, police reports on the murdered North, and, of course, the transnet address codes for the best GE civil liberties lawyers. But nothing about her mother from Nantes, no search to see if she was still alive, no access code listing. That particular farce didn't matter any more, Elston now knew the past on her file was a lie and he'd screwed up, missing his one chance to interrogate her about it. No matter what, she wouldn't be going back to Frontline again. Not alive.

'You know I can't quite place that accent of yours,' Paresh said, all boy-puppy smiles when she crumpled up the packet and tossed it into the waste bin below her seat.

'Really?' It was funny how this one game remained utterly constant down the decades, in jail or out. And nobody had ever had to teach her how to play to perfection. 'So what's your best guess?'

'Okay then. I'd say it's not quite pure UK region, so I'm going for: you lived in the States at some time.'

'Or I grew up in the States and then spent twenty years having UK English alone spoken to me in jail.'

'Oh, okay.' He didn't quite blush. 'So which part of the States, Earth or trans-stellar?'

'I didn't grow up in the States. My mother is French.'

He laughed. 'Damn, you're a tough nut.'

'Now you're just dreaming.'

'Your file says you're forty-two.'

'Never argue with a government file, they are wise.'

'If it's true that means you're a one-in-ten.'

'And that bothers you?'

'No. Not at all.'

'How very liberal of you.' Angela caught sight of the sign on the side of the A1; the turn-off for the A167 was just ahead. That meant they were only a few minutes out from the HDA base, and once she was in there she'd be confined inside its perimeter. Elston would make sure of that. She peered through the minibus's windscreen. 'Isn't that Last Mile up ahead?'

'Yeah, but we're going straight to the HDA base,' Paresh said.

'I'd like to make a quick detour, first. If you don't mind.'

'What?'

'Look, sometime soon after we get to the base, we're going to get shipped out to St Libra. You do know what the Last Mile is, don't you?'

'Sure. It sells you everything you need to live on St Libra. Why, you figure buying a farm there?'

'I'm not staying there – once we've found the alien I'm back to civilization.'

'So what do you want to visit Last Mile for?'

Angela raised her voice so everyone in the minibus could hear, insurrection targeting those precious hearts and minds. 'I've been to St Libra before.' She plucked at the coarse grey fatigues she was wearing. 'Trust me, you do not want to go there with just government-issue kit covering your ass.'

Paresh gaped incredulously. 'You want to go on a *shopping trip*?'

'Have you looked out of the window in the last fifteen minutes?'

'Do what?'

'Scope the traffic. Half of everything heading north with us right now is an HDA vehicle of some type. This is real, guys, the expedition is happening even if they haven't bothered to let you all in on it.'

She watched everyone suddenly start scanning the road.

'Okay,' Paresh admitted. 'We knew we were headed for St Libra. I'm not arguing that.'

'Good. Because visiting the Last Mile isn't some girlie mall blitz for pretty dresses. I want to survive the next month, thank you. And that means I want boots that aren't going to rot away in the humidity and swamp mud; more than one pair. Are you sure yours will last against everything St Libra's jungles can throw at them? And trust me, you need double-layer breathable socks no matter where you are on the planet. Are they HDA standard? Have you guys ever seen footrot fungus? I did while I was there before, plenty of times. Does HDA medic service provide enough nuflesh to cover the chunks they'll need to chop off you? And what about UV-resistant shirts and trousers; and factor 80 sunscreen? Without all of those in combination your skin's going to fry. Sirius is a white A-star, remember? Twenty-six times brighter than Earth's sun. You don't need a microwave to cook your frozen dinner, just hold the pack up to the sky for thirty seconds. Now name me the times when HDA gave you the right equipment for your exercise mission, then out of that big list, name one that's been rammed together faster than this expedition. So tell me the logistics corps in their air-conditioned offices back here on Earth are going to get it right for us poor front line sods eight and a half lightyears away. It's not just me that needs to take a visit to Last Mile. If you truly care for your squad, Paresh, you'll give them the chance to stock up with the most elementary kit they need for St Libra. And it's all lying there on the shelves at the cheapest prices anywhere across the trans-stellar worlds.'

Paresh held his hands up. 'Okay. Jesus, I get it.' He glanced along the aisle to see a bunch of expectant faces, silently demanding just one thing. 'All right, we don't have a scheduled arrival time, we just have to be there for a briefing at fifteen hundred hours, so we can sparc an hour maybe. No more.'

'I'll only need thirty minutes. And I'll be happy to advise you guys on what works and what's a rip-off.'

'All right, Atyeo, cancel the auto and take us to Last Mile.'

Up at the front of the minibus, Private Atyeo grinned in relief. 'Yes, Corporal.'

'Happy now?' Paresh was feigning exasperation.

'Thank you.'

They turned off at a junction just past the Angel of the North, that huge ancient ribbed steel statue which stood solitary guard over Tyneside. *Somebody back then had foresight,* Angela thought, *because if ever anywhere on this world needs divine protection, it's the city with a gateway to St Libra.* Although if Elston was correct about the latest North murder, it was too late already. The majestic, rusty old angel had been caught sleeping.

A couple of minutes later they turned into Last Mile. Here the elegance of Newcastle's Georgian centre and the utility logic of its residential estates had been abandoned in favour to the gods of commerce. The gentle valley had once been a sprawling industrial estate of light factories, wholesale markets, and warehouse stores. A lot of those original twenty-first-century frame and panel structures of the estate were still there. Their outlines invisible now, swamped under the twenty-third-century composites which automata had assembled around and over them like mechanical tumours.

Kingsway, the broad main road leading straight up to the gateway, was ruled by the major trans-stellar companies. Angela directed Atyeo into one of the avenues branching off the thoroughfare, where he parked in front of the Honda franchise. The glass wall of the showroom displayed a pageant of the latest models; but not for St Libra were the sleek sedans and roadsters that caught the eye, and were envied by school kids the trans-worlds over; this was the arena of utilities and farm trucks and land exploras, that could take anything nature at its most rugged could throw at them. The showroom took up less than a quarter of the building; the rest was occupied by tanks of raw feeding 3D printers and microfacture cells which produced customized components and interiors that assembly rigs could screw, bolt, click-lock, laser and epoxy onto a range of standard bodywork/ chassis combos shipped in from the more sophisticated principal factories.

Angela led them along the other side of the avenue, past the suppliers selling GM grain and seed which was guaranteed to sprout from St Libra's soil with its melange of vigorous alien bacteria. It ended in a wall of glass doors which led into the huge Birk-Unwin store.

'This was one of the first to sell stuff to people emigrating through the gateway,' Angela said as the squad filed in through the doors. 'Birk started out with a single stall back in the day.'

'How do you know all this crap?' Gillian Kowalski asked as she stared round at the cliff-like shelving rows.

'I've been here before,' Angela said, which wasn't quite true, and was stupid because it gave too much away. 'Their branch in Abellia, anyway,' she added.

Birk-Unwin was primarily a retail warehouse selling clothing and household items; the kind of products perfectly suited to its buy-it-cheap-and-pile-it-high philosophy. However, a small section at the side was given over exclusively to camping kit – and small was a relative term amid the store's cavernous interior. There were no assistants, they cost too much. Instead smartdust meshes watched and security guards patrolled to deter pilfering. Customers would pull an item from bins on the shelves and try it on; if it didn't fit they dropped it and reached for the next size. A small team of staff walked along the shelves, restocking and throwing stuff back that people had tried on.

In the camping section, Angela found herself a couple of pairs of excellent leather hiking boots from an established Austrian company (three seasons out of date) then had to scramble along a high shelf to track down the waterproof garters that fitted them. After that came eight pairs of proper (nonsynthetic) wool socks; long-sleeve T-shirts, three pairs of lightweight UV-proof trousers, and sunguard oil in litre bottles. She went for practical equipment next: a solar charger, a small hand-pumped torch, inertial guidance module, solid memory cache that could link to her bodymesh, and in a higher price bracket, two wraparound sun-glasses with smartlenses that provided night vision, infrared, and electronic magnification. Last of all she found a decent utility belt pre-loaded with a whole range of useful compact camping tools. It took a while to put it all together, as the squad members kept asking her opinion about stuff they found.

She was advising Leora Fawkes on a self-cooling bottle when she caught sight of Paresh stiffening. His mouth moved silently, a sure giveaway that he was on a call. Knowing what was coming, she dropped a couple of cotton sunhats into the collapsible weather-resistant bag on her trolley. The display on the handle registered their smartdust tags, and she tapped the Finish & Pay icon. Her e-i told her it had authorized payment to Birk-Unwin's account. Everything she'd chosen was in the bag; she zipped it up in a decisive motion.

'Everyone!' Paresh announced loudly. 'We're leaving. Now.'

Angela swung the bag round and pushed her arms through the shoulder straps. Paresh was suddenly standing beside her. He didn't look angry, exactly, more like troubled.

'Problem?' she asked.

'We have to go,' he said tightly.

'Sure.' Keeping it light. Not knowing what all the fuss was about. Couldn't envision that Elston had just gone into meltdown when he found out about their innocent little detour.

The minibus set off back along Kingsway and up to the HDA camp squatting on the slope above. It was crowded in the vehicle now, with the aisle full of store bags, and an air of apprehension building as they approached the high perimeter fence. Angela noted the innocuous matt-black spheres rolling along the run-track between the razor mesh, the lion and eagle emblem. A big sensor hoop curved over the entranceway in front of the red and white striped barrier. Guards in thick coats carrying automatic pistols in weather sheaths stood by the side, waiting for an alert from the AI which reviewed the deep scan of every vehicle that came in. She stared at the lion and eagle emblem, unable to look away. Her body's core temperature seemed to be dropping by the second, making it impossible to move as the memory came flooding back. The last time she'd passed through a fence with that same evil emblem glowing proudly on the posts had been twenty years ago . . .

*

That little shit Vance Elston had been sitting in the car with her. They'd told her it was the prisoner transfer vehicle – stupid stupid, since when did the UK region prison service agency use black limousines with opaque windows. It was the day after the court case had finished with its frightening, insane verdict, and she was still in a daze at being found guilty, so numb she never thought to question anything. Not that it would have done any good. She was meat now, no longer human with rights. Not that she had many in the first place.

She'd taken one look at Elston with his air of superiority and smart grey fatigues, and knew him for what he was – someone small, brown-nosing his way up the career pole with a whole flock of insecurities about his origins making him a rule-worshipping fascist. But the court had found her guilty and sentenced her, so she didn't care what kind of ass had been sent to escort her to Holloway. He walked her calmly and politely out of the court cells and she questioned nothing until she saw the limousine – which wasn't quite right.

'Where are we going?' she'd asked.

'A holding facility.'

Which should have started the alarm bells ringing loud and clear. But her mind just wasn't up to it – the horror of everything she'd seen at Bartram's mansion, the fear of being caught at the gateway, and the worry, so much worry that everything had gone wrong. But there had been no sign of him, no word, no mention by the dumb police who questioned her. So it must have been okay. The money transfer had worked. That thought alone held her steadfast through the farce of a trial.

Even then, driving through London on the way to the prison where the judge wanted her to spend the rest of her life, she

120

clung to that one precious chunk of knowledge. *They didn't know.* Everything would be all right. And even then, she was sure that one day she'd be out because the monster was real, and one day people would meet it again.

The car had pulled into a small compound somewhere near the Thames, with the HDA signs prominent on the fence. A crystal-white executive VTOL jet was sitting on the pad. It didn't register, because such a thing didn't apply to her. So she sat passively in the limousine as it drove towards the striking little machine. There were HDA guards from the GE Legion standing beside the airstairs. Then they pulled up outside and Elston opened the door.

'What is this?' she asked. Her brain was finally starting to work again, assessing, plotting out scenarios. None of them ended well.

'Come with me,' Elston said.

'You're not taking me to prison. What is this? What's going on?'

He held up a palm-size taser. 'Get in the plane, or I use this and drag your zapped ass up those stairs.'

She shrank away from him, and he really did it, he jabbed the taser prongs down on her shoulder. When she stopped screaming, the two guards pulled her stunned, shaking body out of the car and hauled her up the airstairs.

The flight was three hours long, but she didn't know what speed they were travelling at, and she didn't recognize the marque. The plane had narrow delta wings, it was probably supersonic. It was night outside when they landed, so she had no idea where they were. Not that it mattered – even if she knew the exact geographical coordinate, it was of no possible use. There was no one she could call, no one who would help.

All she knew was that they were near the sea, she could smell it in the air as she walked down onto the hot tarmac of the apron. A windowless van was waiting for them. She didn't protest when Elston told her to get in.

This time the drive was barely ten minutes. When they

stopped, gravity was different, lighter than Earth. The reception area was a huge metal cave as big as any airport hangar, with curving walls illuminated by bright artificial lights. There were a lot of struts arranged in triangles, reinforcing the walls.

She was quickly hustled away down a corridor that seemed to be built from ducts and pipes and cables, the only unencumbered flat surface was the concrete floor. There were pressure doors at every junction. And she went through a lot of junctions. Part of her thought that might be deliberate, that they were intentionally disorientating her.

The section she wound up in was like a clinic in a dirt-poor country. Metal furniture and not much of it. Desks with minimal electronic modules, none of it neat, they all sprouted a tangle of fibres and cables. No windows. Guards who were ordered not to talk to her.

She only ever knew three rooms. Her cell, four metres to a side, with a small bed that hinged down from the wall, a plastic office chair, a table where she ate all her plastic tray meals, a toilet, and a washbasin. Room two, the interview room, was next to it.

Angela was taken straight there. It was almost identical to the cell. Square with a table in the centre, her chair on one side; two chairs on the other. The guards sat her down and secured her wrists and ankles, then a technician came in and stuck various electrodes and sensor pads on her skin. Smirking when he unzipped the front of her prison service overall to apply the heart monitor and another couple of cold pads just below her bra which would monitor temperature and perspiration. She glared back at him, but inside the dread was building.

Death was the only true fear. But it wasn't something which she had control over, she was realistic about that. Then again, they hadn't brought her here simply to kill her. The restraints, the sensors, the unknown location, the effort involved getting her here – it all meant one thing. They wanted the truth, and she was going to give that to them. But the truth they so desperately wanted wasn't important to her. That was her one hope. Her talisman. The knowledge which would keep her sane and rational.

Once all the patches were stuck to her body, the technician manipulated a couple of cameras on segmented metal stalks so they could track her eyes, watching pupil dilation and blink-rate. Then there was a simple mic so vocal stress patterns could be analysed.

'You're so ready,' he said, stroking her cheek. Angela didn't flinch, just awarded him a sneer.

Elston was one of the interviewers. The junior of the pair who occupied the chairs opposite her for all those countless hours. It was Major Sung who asked most of the questions, again and again.

'We'll begin with the calibrations,' he told her as the technician finally left and the door slid shut.

Angela gave him her best pitying look. 'You want to know about the monster. I'm not here to hide anything. I just can't understand why you didn't look into this earlier.'

'So you know, we haven't stopped searching,' Sung replied levelly. 'There is no evidence it ever existed, no trace. We have had no sighting in the wilds around Abellia. No forensics proof. Nothing. We've spent a small fortune examining this, and now we need to know if it really is just a bullshit legal defence ploy.'

'It's not! I saw the fucker. It's real!'

'We'll get to that. But first, tell me your name.'

'Angela Tramelo.'

'Age?'

'Eighteen,' which was what appeared on her birth certificate, which was presumably the file he was reading.

'What were you studying at Imperial College?'

'Sports physiotherapy.'

And so it went. She thought for about eight hours. They gave her something to drink when she asked. Even unstrapped her twice so she could use the toilet in her cell. But other than that the questions went on relentlessly. What did you see? What room were you in when the attack happened? What did the alien look like? What did you do? Why did you run? Describe the alien in more detail. Did you see it actually kill the others?

Did you kill them?

Did you have a glove made of blades?

Did you hate Bartram North?

Did he hurt you?

Did you detest the sexual acts he made you perform?

Why would the alien kill them all?

*

After they removed the sensors and electrodes and unstrapped her they took her back to the cell, gave her a meal tray, a plastic pack containing a clean T-shirt, underwear and trousers, soap, toothpaste and brush, a towel – and locked the door. She had no idea how long it was before the door slid open again; she was asleep on the bed. The guard brought in a fresh meal and said: 'You've got half an hour.'

He was telling the truth. Half an hour later she was back in the interview room with the pervy technician feeling her up. Sung and Elston came in.

'I'd like to go through yesterday's testimony again,' Sung said.

Angela groaned in resignation and slumped her shoulders.

That style of questioning went on for five days without a break. Every detail she could remember, every incident queried as they made her describe the event repeatedly. Each time they looked for discrepancies, hounded her at the slightest variance, mocked, shouted, sounded sympathetic.

On the sixth day Angela was taken to the third room. It was a lot bigger than the others. But then it had to accommodate a machine the size of a hatchback car. When she saw it for the first time she thought it was a medical full-body magrez scanner. It wasn't a bad guess. They didn't use it that day, nor for several more. Instead, she was strapped down on a metal gurney with only a blanket for padding. She refused and struggled the first day. It took three guards to force her down while the same technician fastened the restraints.

'What are you fucking doing you bastards?' she screamed at them. It made no difference, the abuse, the curses. They didn't care. So as before the sensor patches were applied, the cuff around her arm to monitor blood pressure. The only thing missing was the camera to watch her eyes.

Then the technician wheeled in an IV drip.

'No!' she yelled. 'No no no. You can't do this.'

'I'm sorry, but we can,' Major Sung said. He nodded, and the technician slid a needle into the vein on the top of her hand.

It took a while for whatever they were using to take effect. The room stilled, then it grew hot. Walls began to move – breathing. Voices sounded like orchestras. Insistent voices. The technician loomed large, adjusting the flow, making it just right for her he told her. And the voices began. She started speaking. Profound thoughts about how the universe worked. How colours were so important. How Marj was such a comfort when she was a child. She could remember Marj, so that was real, truthful. Marj who was sweet. How she missed her mother, who if they didn't know was French you know. How she loved her mother. How she hated the alien. The alien that was a dark shadow cast across her memories, bursting out of the nicest images of her life.

The gurney spun round like a carousel. She threw up.

Angela never did know how long that part lasted. Days at least. The drugs left her too confused between the sessions. Often they'd have to feed her milk drinks with proteins blended in, or soups where someone patiently spooned the warm liquid between numb lips. Her swallow reflex kicked in, otherwise she would have drooled it all out again.

She was definitely ill at some point. Feverish and shaking. People argued around her. She'd almost recovered when they strapped her down on the table again. The needle was as big as her arm, and the narcotic spewed out of the end, engulfing her in champagne bubbles that glowed with magical light. She started talking again, but always aware of what she said. They probably wouldn't expect that. The narcotic was supposed to have a stronger effect.

They let her recover for a whole day. Then she had to be guided on unsteady feet back to room three. Once again she was strapped down on the gurney. 'I fucking hate you,' she told them. 'When I get out of here I'm going to kill all of you. I'm going to lead the alien right here and watch and laugh while you scream and die.'

'Hold still,' the technician said. This was new. This was different. No sensor pads now. A metal crown with adjustable screw clamps that went round her head. He turned the screws until the contraption was fixed to her, pressing into her flesh, then he fastened it to the gurney somehow. She could hear the harsh metallic *clunk* as it slotted into its lock mechanism.

Delicate metallic spiders swung into view, except normal spiders didn't have legs ending in flat plastic hooks. She cried out helplessly, mewling pitifully as he carefully hooked their curved edges round her eyelids, holding them permanently open. She couldn't blink now. Couldn't move her head – not that she tried, too scared any motion would rip her eyelids. Couldn't move her limbs. 'What are you doing?' she yelled at them. As always, they never bothered to answer her.

The gurney was wheeled across the room, and she was suddenly sliding into the guts of the big machine which had to be some kind of scanner. Light shone into her eyes. It was bright, zipping through the spectrum in strobe flashes. And she couldn't blink. Then the machine started buzzing and humming loudly, like it was preparing for takeoff.

'Get me out of here!'

The universe turned white. A single slim black line sliced down the middle. The universe turned black. A single white line sliced down the middle. It turned white. A white circle appeared.

She couldn't blink. Couldn't stop seeing the light.

'What the hell is this?'

White. Black. White. Black. White. Black. Each with a shape:

126

circle, triangle, rectangle, square, pentagon, hexagon. More. Geometries she didn't know the name of. Blank. Single images materialized. Tree. House. Ball. Car. Human. Horse. Dog. Lake. Wine glass. Table. Chair. Keyboard. Plate. Mountain. Beach. Rose. Shoe.

They were showing her an encyclopaedia of everything. Monochromed. Chromatic. It was bewildering. She felt as if her brain was going to explode from the quantity of vision they were forcing in. And she couldn't blink. Tears were pouring out now, trickling down her cheeks.

'I will kill you,' she promised in a whisper. The light was burning her now, inflaming her neurones. The pain was swelling. Thudding behind her temples in time to her heart. And still the images kept power strobing in.

Nothing made sense. She didn't know if she'd been unconscious or not. The difference in her existence was in the images. They weren't so bright, and they moved now, like solid clouds scudding about. The sound of the machine had gone as well. People were talking instead.

She felt gentle pinching sensations but her mind was spinning so she didn't know where they came from. Then the shapes withdrew and she could blink. Her eyes were incredibly sore. She squeezed them shut, tighter and tighter. Tears still came squeezing out of the sides. She was sobbing uncontrollably now.

Then there was a prick on her arm. She opened her eyes to see Elston pulling a syringe away. 'I can't take this any more,' she told him in a dead voice.

He looked like she'd slapped him. 'Almost over,' he murmured in an embarrassed tone.

She could feel her thoughts losing cohesion again. This time it wasn't as bad as the IV drip. She could still think, though it was difficult, as if she was drowsy, rising from a deep slumber.

Something clamped across her face, and she couldn't see. She felt the gurney moving again. The air changed and she knew she was back in the machine. To confirm that, the humming and buzzing and whirring started up again, setting her teeth on edge.

'You're in Bartram North's mansion again,' Sung's voice said softly. 'It's the night of the murders. You said you were on the seventh-floor landing when you heard something.'

'Yes,' she said. 'Yes, I did.'

'You went into the lounge to see why the lights were off. And you slipped on something. Then you found the light switch. The lights came on, you said. You're in the lounge, Angela, what did you see? What was in there Angela? What was going on?'

'I've told you!' she moaned. 'They were there on the floor. Dead! All of them, dead.'

'Then what happened? What happened after you went into the lounge?'

'Bartram's door opened. I saw it open.'

'What did you see then, Angela? What came out?'

'The alien,' she moaned. She didn't need drugs to remember it, she'd never needed drugs for that. 'The alien was in there. Monster with its claws out. Mariangela is behind it, and Coi and Bartram. Their blood. Everywhere their blood. Oh God, it's ripped them apart. There's just pieces left now. Pieces.'

'Look at it Angela, as it comes for you, what do you see?'

'Monster!' she screamed. 'Monster. Monster. Monster. Monster. Monster.' And the screams became sobbing. 'It killed them. Killed all of them.'

She despised the memory now. It was the memory that was the cause of the deaths she'd witnessed. The memory which had trapped her, which controlled her life. The memory which had imprisoned her in here with her torturers. She wanted to rip the vile thing from her head.

The machine began to power down, its noise fading out. The gurney trundled over the floor again, and the blackout cups were lifted from her eyes. Elston, Sung, and the technician were staring down at her. They didn't look happy, but then when have captors ever been pleased by their victims?

Her head was freed from the crown, straps removed from her limbs. She was too drained to move. Her whole body was shaking despite the weakness, the sore eyes, the terrible headache, the nausea. She was used to such affliction now, it was how she lived.

'What is that thing?' she growled, glancing at the big machine.

'A mind reader,' Sung answered simply as he helped her sit up on the gurney. 'It scanned how your brain interprets images. Then once it had catalogued those patterns, we got you to remember.' He pointed at the screens on the wall.

Angela squinted. Her eyes still ached, and she couldn't focus properly. A poor-quality video clip was playing on a loop. The setting was familiar, a kind of stripped-down version of the seventh-floor lounge in Bartram North's mansion, the furniture was in the right places in the broad central corridor, but it lacked the expensive elaboration of the originals, paintings on the walls were reduced to odd smears of colour. The doors to Bartram's bedroom were open, framing a dark shape that seemed to be lunging out of the screen. The monster was square in the centre. Humanoid, with dark, hard skin mimicking a human's contours, hands opening. The blades expanding as they straightened out, growing to fill the entire screen.

Angela gasped. It was her memory. They'd taken her memory from her, pulled it right out of her skull with their diabolical machine and filthy drugs. 'Oh my God.'

'Looks like you told us the truth,' Elston said.

'As you believe it,' Sung added quickly.

'It's real,' she hissed.

'Maybe. That's for the review committee to decide.'

'You saw it.'

'I saw what you believe happened. What your mind interprets as reality. There's no other evidence, no empirical proof.'

'Then why did you do this to me?' she yelled. The effort sent her swaying back, gripping the edge of the gurney for support.

'We need to know.'

'Rot in hell you fuckhead.'

'This from a lying whore.'

'I am not lying.'

Sung grinned. 'But you are a whore.'

'I'll find you. So help me, I will.'

'Yeah right. Elston, take her back; we're through here now.'

Elston and the technician helped her stand. She began the painful walk back to her cell. When they got there Elston left the technician to lower her onto the small uncomfortable bed. She looked up at him, eyes wide and entreating. All full of tears and fright in her beautiful young face. He glanced down uncertainly.

'I need to feel something,' she said in a small voice. 'I need to feel real again. Please.'

He licked his lips and shot the open door a quick look.

Angela took one of his hands and slid it down the top of her T-shirt. 'Please.' She held the other hand. 'I want this.' Her free hand caressed the side of his face. He grinned roguishly and bent over her. Angela jabbed her forefinger into his eye. The flesh gave beneath the tip of her finger, and she kept on pushing, squeezing down the soft orb. He screamed in agony and tried to jerk away, but his hand was caught up down her T-shirt. She crooked her finger and yanked back savagely, feeling tissue tearing. Blood poured out of the eye socket as the ball popped out. Angela laughed with demented pride. 'Treat me like shit, motherfucker. Go on, do it again!'

Guards ran in. Expressions of horror flaring. Angela aimed a kick at the first one. Three of them landed on her, and they all crashed to the floor. Pain flashed red in her vision as the air was knocked out of her. Then she saw Elston race in.

'Oh, Great Lord,' he grunted. 'You psycho bitch.'

'You're next, motherfucker.' Angela squirmed and bucked below the weight of bodies. 'You're next.'

Something pinched her shoulder. Something incredibly sharp. The world wobbled, then vanished.

*

'Out you come.'

'Huh?' Angela blinked awake. She felt utterly awful. There was a lot of ache, shoulders, arms, chest – all badly bruised. She thought she was going to throw up her gut felt so bad. The light was bright as it shone in through the back of the prison transfer van, making her squint and hold her hand up as a shield. She was sitting on a slim bench, dressed in prison overalls; hands and feet shackled.

A female prison guard in a dark-blue uniform unlocked the securing pin, releasing her chains.

'You're not going to be a problem, Tramelo, are you?'

Angela started to laugh. The thick burbling sound was dangerously close to demented.

'Are you?'

The laugh stopped as abruptly as it began. 'Who me? Of course not.'

'Of course not, *ma'am*.'

'Yes, ma'am.'

'That's better. Remember you and I have to get along together for a long time.'

Twenty years.

*

Vance looked up as Captain Antrinell Viana walked in to his office. His welcoming smile was genuine enough. He'd served with Antrinell on a number of occasions, and found him highly competent. Antrinell was born on Matuskia, which had been settled by a coalition of Asian-Pacific nations. A quietly devout Christian, he had found nothing to interest him in their frantic expansionist capitalist economy where individuality was prized above all else, and social responsibility came a poor second in the race with personal success. After graduating with his degree in quantum cosmology, Antrinell had walked straight into the HDA recruitment office. With the Agency suffering a perennial shortage of science staff, his career advancement had been fast. His gravitation to the philosophy of the Gospel Warriors inevitable.

Antrinell matched the smile. 'Long time, Colonel.'

Vance came round the desk to shake hands. 'Certainly is. How's the family?'

'Good, thank you. Artri started his first year at school.'

'No! That makes him . . . five?'

'Yes. And Simone is three.'

'Ah, where does the time go?'

'The Zanth eats it. So there's really going to be an expedition?' Antrinell asked, glancing round the basic office with a bemused expression. 'Vermekia said it was in a holding pattern.'

'That was yesterday. HDA is ready to greenlight. Commissioner Passam landed at Abellia three hours ago. She's finalizing our operation parameters with Brinkelle North.' He grinned wolfishly. 'Now that's one meeting I would like to see. They should have thrashed out the basics by tonight if they haven't killed each other by then.'

'Do we really need Brinkelle's permission? St Libra is part of the trans-stellar alliance, after all.'

'Legally no, of course not,' Vance said. 'But Brogal is her fiefdom, and Abellia is the gateway to that continent. The only one. We need all the Norths cooperating with us.'

'And?'

'They are. Especially Augustine.'

'I'm glad to hear it.'

'I'll be leading one of the forward teams; I'd like you to be my second in command.'

'I'd be delighted.'

'There are a number of factors coming together for this. Is Jay's squad with you?'

'Yes. They've brought the quantum field monitoring equipment. I'm not sure how well it's going to work, though – we've barely finished the design stage.'

'But it will work?' Vance asked pointedly.

'Fundamentally, yes. We can detect the kind of backwash disturbance a Zanth rift will produce. It's the level of sensitivity we're attempting which is untried.'

'I know, but we need to see if there's been a small intrusion.'

'Yes, I was given security clearance for the full file. A human-shaped monster? Really?'

'It had to come from somewhere,' Vance said reasonably.

'Agreed. But it can't be Zanth.'

'Why not? We have no idea of the Zanth's abilities.'

'All right: why would the Zanth bother? If it wants Earth it will swarm and take it. Nothing we can do about it despite the rubbish our politicians and generals spout.'

'True. So disprove it for me. Eliminate that possibility.'

'I can't prove a negative.'

'Perhaps not, but if there is more activity down here and the detector doesn't show anything it will strengthen the case about it coming here from St Libra.'

'And justify the Expedition,' Antrinell said. 'I get that. But then I'm left asking how it came here through the gateway. Cargo? That's your hypothesis?'

'It was on St Libra, now it's here. I don't know how, I just know there's a North in the morgue.'

Antrinell held his hands up. 'All right. I can see this has already got way too much momentum for simple logic to stop it. And I'm not going to be the one telling the emperor he's naked.'

'Thank you. How soon can you and Jay get the detectors up and running?'

'There are fifteen units. We need to ring them around the city and interface them with HDA's secure net. That's going to take the better part of a day.'

'All right. That's better than I was expecting.'

'Vance, are you really sure you want to commit to this? If it goes bad there's going to be a nightmare of recrimination fallout.'

Vance nodded slowly. 'Believe me, I've thought about it. But there are parts of this which simply can't be explained. And the General spoke to me personally; I'm going to be representing him on St Libra.'

'Shaikh himself?'

'Yes.'

'Ah. Well, in that case, let's hope Jesus smiles on us. With added kindness.'

'We can do with all the help we can get,' Vance acknowledged.

It made a pleasant change having a fellow believer working with him. Too many people in the HDA frowned on the Gospel Warriors; the atheists and cynics, mocking the old concepts of faith. He'd long ago learned not to mention his devotion to the Lord to his fellow officers.

An icon expanded in Vance's iris smartcell grid. 'Access the office mesh,' he ordered his e-i.

Corporal Paresh Evitts had arrived in the outer office, accompanying Angela Tramelo. The sight of her sweetly neutral expression told Vance all he needed to know.

'Stay for this,' he told Antrinell and went back behind the desk.

The corporal knew he was in it up to his neck. He stood front and centre of the desk and snapped off a perfect salute. 'Sir. Corporal Paresh Evitts reporting as ordered, sir.'

'At ease, Corporal,' Vance said. He'd worked with GE Legion troops before. They were good, a match for any other national forces. If they hit physical trouble he'd have no problem trusting his life to them. But Angela Tramelo wasn't a combat zone – not the kind Legionnaires were used to, anyhow.

'Corporal, you and I are going to spend a lot of time together over the next few months, so I'm going to make this very simple,' Vance told him. 'When you are given a direct order, *especially* concerning this woman, you follow it implicitly. You do not listen to her, you do not do as she asks, you carry out your duty. Any questions?'

'No sir.'

'Sorry,' Angela said to the beleaguered corporal; the tone was impressively insolent. It matched the pout.

'What were you doing in Last Mile?' Vance asked.

'Sir, buying some supplies for St Libra, sir.'

'And it was her idea, yes?'

Paresh Evitts licked his lips. 'Yes, sir. Ms Tramelo said that we should be prepared for the St Libra environment; she's been there before and—'

'Not interested. Wait outside. When Ms Tramelo comes out,

you will escort her to her assigned billet with your squad. Nowhere else. Understood?'

'Sir.' Another perfect salute, and Corporal Evitts turned and exited the office.

Vance told his e-i to cancel the grid, so he could look at Angela without any graphic overlays. 'You're such a bitch.'

She grinned and plonked herself down in a chair opposite him. 'Come on. I'm helping those poor boobs. They're going to be dead anyway when we find the monsters' nest or city or mothership or whatever the hell they live in. You wouldn't deny them a last touch of comfort in their final days in this universe would you? Or are you going to tell me government-issue kit is going to be all we need in the jungle?'

'Do not attempt to subvert my people. I will ship you straight back to Holloway.'

Angela turned to stare at Antrinell, and raised a curious eyebrow before glancing back at Vance. 'Straight back? Not like last time, when you snatched me and tortured me for months?'

'You were not tortured.'

'Really? I'm glad you think that. Because I think you haven't forgotten the last thing I said to you back then. You remember, that day when your guards beat me into a coma.'

Through teeth clenched tight together: 'You were sedated after you ripped a man's eyeball out. I remember that.'

Angela gave a victory laugh. 'Justifying yourself in front of your colleague. Religion always feeds its followers plenty of guilt. And a fundamentalist nut-job like you must get a real bad dose.'

He glanced down at the small diamond and bronze pin in his suit collar. Trust her to know what it symbolized. 'I have a problem with you,' he said, 'nothing else.'

'I'm glad you realize that.'

'You're not listening, Angela. We didn't know you were a one-in-ten.'

'Guilty and jealous. Poor boy.'

'Your original file must have been implanted in the transnet databases. Your past is a forgery.'

'My past isn't relevant. What I saw that night, is. It's very, *very* relevant, especially as those monsters have obviously found a way to use the gateway without setting off any alarms. And, Elston: Major Sung might have had enough doubt to make him cover his worthless ass, but not you. You know what I saw was real. You made sure of that, didn't you? That was not something I lied about. That's not something I *could* have lied about. Thanks to your machine, you saw what I saw. I bet you even uploaded the file to current status in your private cache. Did you? Do you jerk yourself off over it at night?'

'What were you originally doing at Bartram North's mansion? Why were you there?'

'The truth?'

'Yeah, sure, try it for a change.'

'I was being fucked by Bartram North. That's what I was doing there. That's what he was paying me and all the other girls for. But I didn't kill him. I didn't want to be in jail. I was sent to jail because no one would believe the truth. And you, Jesus-freak, even when you saw the truth in my mind, what did you do? Did you go running to show the court? Did you tell the authorities there was grounds for a retrial? Did you, fuck? No. You hung me out there like those corrupt bastards in the justice ministry.' Angela slammed her fist down on the desk, which made Vance flinch. 'Do not ever attempt to pass me off as the bad guy. I saw an alien monster butcher a houseful of human beings. I fought it off and escaped. And you punished me for that: you, the government, the system you're an asslicker for. I am not the bad guy. But you, now; you are an evil torturer, you are part of the corrupt political machine, and you perverted the course of justice. When you have a moment, you just feel free to tell me what your precious God thinks of all that.'

'I'll find out,' he snapped back, wishing he didn't feel like it was just bluster. 'I'll find out who you are. I'll find out what you are.'

'You already know what I am,' Angela said as she rose to her feet. 'I'm your second-worst nightmare. The first, the one waiting for you on St Libra, that's what your God made in His own image, just like you.' She pointed at the door. 'Now either let me be your technical adviser, or send me back to Holloway. Of course, the case file I put together on my trip here might just download into the cache of every civil rights activist linked to the transnet if I'm not around to reup the timer code every now and then. Make up your mind, Jesus-freak.'

Vance told his e-i to open the office door. 'Stay out of trouble. I mean it.'

Angela winked at Antrinell as she sauntered out. 'Be seeing you.'

'Sweet Mary, she's coming with us?' Antrinell asked.

'For every minute of every hour of every month we're all crammed together on the expedition: yes.'

'Wow, this is going to be one fun trip. And . . . torture?'

'Brainscan.' He hesitated. 'There were drugs involved, too. Probably less sophisticated than we'd use these days. It wasn't particularly pleasant, but we had to know for sure.'

'So what did the scan reveal?'

'Exactly what she said – an alien monster butchering Bartram North's harem and household. I'll let you access the files; you can give me your thoughts once you've reviewed them.'

'What do you think?'

'I think I asked her the wrong questions back then. I won't make that mistake again.'

*

The site of the first mesh coverage gap which Sid examined was in Keelman's Way, a strip of (nominally) green parkland running along the Tyne to the west of Redheugh Bridge. When he got there just after ten o'clock in the morning he had already written it off. For a start, access was difficult – the only route through was a path for pedestrians and bicycles, which was guarded against incursions from cars on a rat-run by bollards at both ends. The bollards could retract down into the tarmac to allow park-maintenance vehicles through, but you needed the code. All right, not too difficult to obtain if you were a dedicated bytehead, or to bribe out of a city worker either, but there would be tyre prints in the snow. The functional meshes on either side of the coverage gap hadn't seen any kind of vehicle in the area on Sunday evening before or after the estimated time the body had been dumped. And as for getting down from Rose Street, which ran along the top of Keelman's Way, not a chance. The slope was high, steep, and planted with thick trees. Sid knew there was no way he'd ever be able to carry a body down that. True: that didn't rule out some kind of sledge, though it was highly unlikely.

But procedure was procedure, and he couldn't afford any balls-ups. Not today. Not with this case.

Small swirls of snowflakes drifted down out of a grey-haze sky as he climbed out of his car and walked towards the cordon barriers. The air temperature still hadn't risen above freezing. A cluster of agency constables over by the bright-orange barriers were wearing thick coats and balaclavas, stamping their feet and looking thoroughly pissed off as he approached them. It had been a cold, boring morning for them. They tried not to show too much resentment when they greeted him, and told him they'd turned away a total of five walkers, two with dogs, since they started at six o'clock. That was good, he thought, if that was all the activity they were getting then the site wouldn't have been disturbed too much yesterday.

Sid could see a couple of Northern Forensics vans parked on the other side of the barriers, but outside the bollards. Six agency SOCOs (Scene of Crime Operatives) were covering the ground, waving various sensors around; another two were leaning over the rail above the river in the middle of the coverage gap. The smartdust coating the rail was either physically dead or the mesh had been ripped. Both technicians were retrieving individual smartdust motes, trying to determine which it was.

What Sid wanted was to go over to the lead SOCO and get an impression of the site examination. But there was another car parked by the bollards, a big dark Mercedes. Its presence didn't surprise him. He walked over and the front window slid down.

Aldred North was sitting inside. The front passenger door hinged up, and Sid used a patch to pause his official log before he climbed in.

'So I'm guessing this isn't the return to work you expected,' Aldred said.

'No. Look, man, I'm sorry it was one of your brothers.'

'Duly noted. And thank you. If we just knew which one . . .'

'Aye, that's more than strange.'

'You're telling me. It's not just Ari and Abner running through the list. I'm here to tell you that my office is on it as well; if they get anything they'll feed it into your investigation through Abner.'

'Okay. Thank you.'

'Don't say that yet. I'm pretty sure Brinkelle's family is being open with us. I know Bailey – this has shaken them up.'

'Bailey?'

'He does my job for the Bs.'

'Right.' Sid rubbed his hand across his forehead. 'Look, I appreciate your support in all this.'

'Least we could do after your suspension. I appreciate your discretion on the matter. And don't worry, your post in our security division is secure.'

'Thanks.'

Aldred nodded at the SOCO crew making slow progress across the thick snow. 'It's not here, is it? They're not going to find anything.'

'No, they're not. Look, I know this isn't pleasant for you, but it would help me to have some solid facts rather than transnet gossip.'

'About what?'

'Aye come on man: you. Your brothers. Your sons. How does it actually work?'

'Ah.' Aldred grinned faintly as he stared out at the frozen parkland. 'The way it is? Sure. Us 2s are born from Augustine's girls. The transnet crap you access has it that he sleeps with all of them. Perhaps my older brothers were conceived like that, I don't know. But all of us conceived in the last seventy years

139

were a result of artificial insemination; after all he is a hundred and thirty-one now. I mean, this is a good body, and Christ knows we can afford the best anti-geriatric treatments. But come on. Maybe a few were natural conceptions in that seventy years. I know I wasn't. My mother only met Dad three times before she got packed off to the clinic.'

'Met?'

Aldred sighed. 'He interviews them to make sure they are suitable mothers. We don't grow up in a giant Brave New World crèche, you know. We have nice middle-class homes to nurture us.'

'No, actually I didn't know that. But I'm glad to hear it.'

'So that's the 2s. There's eighty-seven of us still living – not counting Sunday's body. Five have died in accidents.'

'Were they . . . ?'

'No. There is no chance they secretly survived, all right?'

'I have to ask.'

'Yeah. Anyway, their ages didn't match the corpse – they'd all be too old, for one thing, as the last one was fifty, and he died twenty-eight years ago. So no, it wasn't one of them.'

'With anti-geriatric treatments it might be, though, right?'

'Wow, you really are paranoid.'

'I'm trying to find a solution.'

'The autopsy's biochemistry report showed no signs of anti-geriatric treatments in the corpse's tissue.' Aldred let out a long breath and stared out of the windscreen. 'Besides, anti-geriatrics don't wind the clock back, they just slow it down a bit.'

'Like a one-in-ten?'

'Same principle, it just doesn't work as well, and it's mostly cosmetic. If you're going to rejuvenate someone you need the techniques Bartram developed, and they are phenomenally expensive. Do you know there are about a hundred trillion cells in the average human body – and thank fuck us North's aren't fat bastards. For true rejuvenation the DNA in each one needs a specifically tailored repair sequence vectored in. It takes over a decade of treatments to complete. Not even Northumberland Interstellar can afford that for eighty-seven of us.'

'Let alone people like me.'

'Quite. So no, the victim is a genuine 2North.'

Sid knew he shouldn't ask, but with Aldred in confessional mode he couldn't resist. 'What's the point?'

'Excuse me?'

'Why did Augustine do it? And his two brothers as well. Why have so many sons?'

'You know why Dad and my two uncles were born, don't you?'

'Kane North perfected human cloning.'

'Yes, but why?'

'I've no idea. That's why I'm asking.'

'The Norths back then were old American money, a long line of financiers, bankers, landowners. They were the über-establishment traditionalist, conservative, Ivy League, WASPs, with each new little North destined for greatness and intent on multiplying the family wealth and power on Wall Street and in Washington. That was one of the reasons Kane went to West Point. Serving one's country was tradition and duty; a lot of Norths put in a tour with the military, we certainly served in the Civil War, probably even the original revolution against the British. Anyway, grandfather Kane got himself shipped out to Afghanistan. That's where he got hit by an IED – improvised explosive device. He was shipped back to the States and given an honourable disability discharge.'

'I see.'

'No I don't think you do. He survived, sure, but the fucking thing blew his balls off.'

'Crap on it!'

'Yeah, well. No way could he have kids; that was it, end of the line. The family wealth would start getting diluted through relatives and lawyers and managers. Well, old Kane didn't like that idea. He might not have testosterone bubbling around in his brain any more, but he was still a North. So he moved to Scotland and began recruiting members of the Dolly team – the ones who first cloned a mammal, a sheep by the name of Dolly. The States has a long history of official disapproval when it comes to manipulating human genes; it's a legislative nightmare thanks to the Religious Right, then as well as now. Far easier to set up a pioneering lab over here in Edinburgh. Not that everything which went on inside there was strictly legal. Long story short: the triplets were born, my dad and two uncles. But of course, the genetic fixing techniques were crude back then, and I'm a result of that quirk. We're a dead end, Sid; evolution culls our offspring inside of three generations. So if you can't go deep, go wide. Us 2s are the ones who actually built Northumberland Interstellar. Nearly two hundred of us in total back then before the split; directors and managers all acting with the same drive, the same direction, possessing the same determination. This world has never seen anything like that build-focus since the days of the kings who ruled with divine right. To this day, St Libra is the only planet opened by a single person, even though there's a lot of mes. New Monaco, that's nothing, a multi-financier world. Besides, it's a refuge, not a society.'

'But you have children, too.'

'They are a mistake,' Aldred said bitterly. 'And the 4s are even worse. But you can't fight human nature. We have women, we need them like any straight man; wives, girlfriends, lovers, one-night stands, even good old-fashioned golddiggers still, god-bless-'em. Thankfully there are fewer and fewer children. And soon there will be none.'

'You don't know that. I thought Augustine was rejuvenating. It's been buzzing about the transnet for years.'

'He is. But it isn't complete, the process is still being refined. Not that it matters – a new generation of 2s is emerging. Except they're not even 2s any more, not really. Brinkelle was the first. Bartram and his Institute finally eradicated the fix which contaminated his DNA, and reverted it to something more normal. She's the first genuine offspring any of the triplets ever had, even though she's IV conceived and germlined to the hilt. And she's had children, real children, not 3s. We original 2s are a dying breed, Sid, we'll never be repeated. Our era is over. Brinkelle's family is the future now; and whatever the hell Constantine is doing at Jupiter. After he's rejuvenated, I guess even Father will get himself fixed and have proper children.'

Sid took a long moment, the two of them sitting in uncomfortable silence. He'd been totally unprepared for that level of unburdening. Not that he was entirely surprised, he'd seen what the grief of bereavement could do to people countless times. The need to talk, the need to explain, as if that somehow comforted the dead.

'It has to be a C,' he decided.

'I know. But we've had precious little contact with Constantine since the split. He and Augustine exchange messages a couple of times a year, but that's all. And Jupiter still claims none of their people are on Earth.'

'You said there were nearly two hundred 2s back in the day. If it wasn't one of your brothers, and you trust Brinkelle, then it had to be a C. If he was here clandestinely, then they won't tell you, will they? And if he was involved in something dodgy, it's probably the reason he was murdered.'

'By an alien hand?'

Sid let out a hugely frustrated groan. 'Ah crap on it, I just don't know what to believe. This whole case is a fucking nightmare, man, and I'm the one stuck with it.'

'You want my advice?'

'Oh God, yes please.'

'Play it exactly the way Elston wants you to. Find the place the body was dumped in the river and grab us some solid evidence from the site. Nothing else matters.'

'Aye, I suppose you're right there. But . . . Jesus!'

'I know. Let me repeat, there's a senior place reserved for you at the company no matter what the outcome to this crock of shit. We owe you, and we don't forget our friends.'

'But you want me running this case as well, don't you?'

'Yes, Sid, I do, because I know you're straight with us.'

'Right, well, I'd better be getting on with it.' He pressed the door switch, and it hinged smoothly upwards.

'Good luck.'

Outside again, Sid reactivated his official log, then accessed the Northern Forensics field ringnet. The site SOCO team data slid down his grid: names, rankings, assignments, the equipment they'd deployed, initial results. He told his e-i to connect him to the senior supervisor, Tilly Lewis. Tilly was one of those people who were easy to work with, which was getting to be a rare event in law enforcement these days. Smart, experienced, and competent, she was a huge asset on any investigation, which was why Sid had arranged through Osborne to have her work with him today.

'What have you got for me?' he asked.

'I'm knee-deep in virgin snow and I've fallen over twice this morning. What do you think?'

'Thought so.' He scanned round Keelman's Way. She wasn't that difficult to spot. The SOCOs were all wearing regulation light-green coveralls, bulked out by many layers of thermal clothing underneath, making them look like inflatable mannequins as they waddled their way through the thick snow. One of them, just below the treeline, was wearing a bright-pink bobble hat with earflaps. Sid waved solemnly. 'Can I come up?'

Tilly waved back. 'Sure. I've covered the ground between us, so you won't be fouling up any evidence.'

Sid started up the slope. It was hard work. The snow was over sixty centimetres in some places. Drifts around the trees were a lot deeper. Little waves of powder snow erupted from his feet at every step, leaving a wide rumpled track behind him.

He was flushed and breathing hard by the time he finally reached her. 'This is stupid,' he grunted.

Tilly grinned broadly. 'Sure is.' She had a cute roundish face which he'd rarely seen frowning. He'd decided a long time ago that she must have had some kind of happy virus in her blood,

144

which was just as well given some of the things they'd uncovered together at crime scenes. Her mane of auburn hair was tucked into the pink hat, with a few spiral wisps escaping around her temples. She kept pushing them away from what looked like a pair of fat binoculars she was using to examine the snow.

'How are the kids?' he asked.

'Took them to my parents for Christmas. They always get spoiled rotten there. So I'm bloody glad school's started. Yours?'

'About the same. We're thinking of moving.'

'Really? Where?'

'Jesmond.'

'Wonderful, you'll be close by.'

'Okay. That's over. So there's nothing up here?'

'No. If anyone brought a body down to the river to dump in they had to come down from the road above, and through here.' She waved up at the trees with their dark branches all constricted by a crystal mantle of ice and snow.

'That's my thought exactly. But it's a bit of a long shot.'

'Not when you're dealing with probabilities. Go through them and get rid of them one at a time.'

'That's supposed to be my job.'

'Nah, you just correlate the data us true workers pull in from the field. I'm the one freezing my bum off while I try and find tracks.'

Sid gave the optical gadget she was carrying a pointed look. 'All right, I'll bite. What is that thing?'

'CDMR.'

'Aye man, thanks a bundle.'

'Comparative Density Microwave Radar. Top of the range. Costs your department a packet if I just lift it out of the case, and I have to lift it out because we can't just scatter smartdust around like we normally do. Bloody snow.'

'Riiight.'

She grinned again and handed them to him. 'Try it. Look at the snow.'

He put them to his eyes. The image was weird, a three-dimensional montage of green and blue ripples stacked on top of each other. 'Very psychedelic.'

'You've just got to interpret it correctly.'

'Correct me any time you like.'

'Behave. Now, don't use the CDMR and just look at the snow along the trees.'

He did as he was told.

'Nothing, right?' Tilly said. 'If anyone had brought a body down they'd have left a big set of tracks.'

'Yeah, but it's been snowing a lot since then. Any tracks would have been covered in an hour on Sunday night.'

'And that's a common problem for us. So . . .' She gestured at the CDMR set. 'Now look at that area.'

He did as he was told, focusing on the patch of ground just short of the treeline which she was pointing at.

'What you're seeing,' Tilly said, 'is a false-colour image of snow density. You see those small triangular shapes?'

Sid concentrated on the image. There were some green specks, which could have been triangular. They lay just under the uppermost blue stratum. 'Yeah.'

'Imprints from duck feet, probably a day old judging by how deep they are.'

'Crap on it.' He put the CDMR aside, and stared at the patch of snow. It was completely blank.

'Even a duck has enough weight to compress the snow it stands on,' Tilly said. 'Those little footprint patches are slightly denser than the surrounding layer. So you see, if anyone had dragged a body down here it would show up like a motorway, no matter how much snow had fallen on top of it.'

'This wasn't the site?'

'This wasn't the site. Besides, Noel just confirmed the smart-dust was burned out from a lightning strike on the railings a couple of months back. The city hasn't got round to spraying any new motes down yet.'

'Okay. You've convinced me. Let's move on to the next gap.'

Sid led the Northern Forensics vans back over the river to Elswick Wharf on the north side. They turned off the main A695 road along Penn Street which curved left into Water Street, where they drove under an ancient disused railway bridge and down the slope past a series of shabby microfacture plants and industrial warehouses to a roundabout junction with Skinnerburn Road and Monarch Road, both of which ran along parallel to the Tyne. The bankside itself was among the most expensive real estate in Newcastle, colonized by exclusive apartment blocks, smart hotels, and prestige office towers, all of them separated from the water by a broad promenade. Private security was obligatory here for each building, given the status of the occupants. Broad swathes of smartdust sprayed along every wall made Sid think this was going to be a waste of time as well.

Directly opposite the roundabout was a building site, with high temporary fencing surrounding a new apartment block development. Its first three storeys had already been completed by the automata which rode the scaffolding. Agency constables had it sealed off, not that there was any construction activity today. The gates were locked and the automata still, with snow filling every mechanical inlet while big icicles hung threateningly from the tough hoses looped along the hydraulic platforms.

To the left of the construction site was an old brick office block, with boarded-up windows and a broad sign at the front proudly explaining Hargold Management was about to refurbish the building ready for occupancy summer 2142. According to Eva, whatever smartdust was coating its walls hadn't been active for nineteen months, the time when Hargold Management bought the building.

Sid and Tilly surveyed the gap, a narrow alley created between the construction site and the dilapidated office block. The route to the waterfront wasn't on any map because it wasn't something which existed on any plans. When the apartment block was completed it would be fenced off, but for now it was an access point for tankers pumping raw up to the automata.

Sid pointed along the slim passage. 'The smartdust on the

147

promenade at the far end isn't working. Their meshes dropped out of the civic net midday Sunday.' He turned to the small roundabout. 'And coincidence: none of the road's macromesh around the junction is working, either.'

'When did the road macromesh fail?' Tilly asked.

'It didn't. The road hasn't been repaired in years, and the raw tankers have been churning up what's left, so the smartdust has degraded until there's not enough left to mesh. Refurbishing the road is part of the construction licence. Standard practice. When the apartments are finished the contractor will tidy everything up.' He stared back up Water Street. 'So ... you can actually drive the length of Water Street without a single sensor or memory cache knowing about it. The closest working mesh with visual spectrum reception is up there on the A695.'

'Then this place is feasible for a body dump.'

'Yeah,' he agreed. 'Now, if it was down to me, I'd park at the far end of this alley, and haul the body across the promenade to the river. It's what, barely fifteen metres?'

Tilly walked over to the slim plastic barrier the agency constables had thrown across the street in front of the alley. She lifted the CDMR set, and studied the snow between the site fence and the office block.

When she turned back to Sid she was grinning. He took the CDMR set and scanned it down the alley. Just beneath the top layer of snow were two cobalt-blue lines; they ran almost to the far end. He put the set down and stared at the pristine surface, feeling very relieved. 'Tyre tracks.'

'Yes.'

'There's a lot of compression below them from earlier traffic. But judging by the depth I'd say those were made some time at the weekend.'

'Okay. Let's put your team on it. I'm going to call the office and get Dedra to pull the traffic records for a couple of kilometres in every direction.'

They left four members of Tilly's team to work down the alley millimetre by millimetre, and went round the other side of the site to reach the promenade. Despite the weather, several people were walking along. Over the last week the snow had been compacted, then frozen hard between snowfalls, leaving the surface icy and perilous.

'Too messed up to show any traces,' Tilly said, scanning it with the CDMR.

'Aye.' Sid was looking across the wide expanse of black water. The tide was halfway out, leaving broad mudflats on both sides, glistening dully in the winter light. Just looking at the sluggish, calm water flowing past in the middle of the channel made him feel chilly. On the south bank the plush white club buildings and elegant jetties of Dunston Marina encircled the ancient tidal basin. He gave the gleaming shapes of the moored yachts a suspicious stare. If the body had come from anywhere, he'd have put good money on it being the marina.

'Here we go,' Tilly called excitedly.

Sid hurried over to the black iron railing she was bent over. The bank here was a concrete slope, tangled with sickly weeds and denuded brambles glued with ice and snow. The mud began two metres below, a line tangled with the usual detritus which marred every river: torn packaging, lengths of wood, metal objects that looked like parts of vehicles, malformed 3D plastic spars, bottles . . .

'See here,' Tilly pointed excitedly. 'Broken strands, flattened grass. Something heavy slid down here.'

Sid swung round. They were standing directly opposite the end of the temporary alley. 'Gotcha!'

*

Sid had never been in the HDA base before. Seen it enough times, though. The inside was exactly as he expected, a perfect reflection of the stark concrete exterior. Vance Elston's office was actually inferior to the rooms of the Market Street Station. Now that took dedication.

Vance greeted him with a mildly puzzled smile. 'You do have my access code. There's no need to turn up in person for every piece of good news.'

'At least you think it's good news.'

'You think I was being too hard on you?'

'We all have our jobs to do.'

'I'm glad you understand that.' Vance sat back behind his desk. 'So what have you got for me?'

'Elswick Wharf is where the body was dumped into the river.'

'You're sure?'

'Forensics hasn't officially confirmed it, but they will, yes. The smartdust meshes on the promenade were ripped on Sunday afternoon, a real pro bytehead job. They managed to induce a surge that physically damaged a lot of the smartdust power systems so the mesh couldn't be reactivated by remote. Then there was a snag on the side of the alley, a piece of metal sticking out of the fence. We think that's the one which made the marks post mortem on the victim's left leg.'

'Excellent.'

'Yes and no. We have a good lead now, but the coroner has had some results back as well.'

'And?'

'Our unknown North was killed Friday midday, approximately fifty hours before he was dumped into the Tyne.'

'Okay, well we knew he wasn't likely to have been killed on the side of the river. You told me that, what with the clothes missing and all.'

'Yeah. But fifty hours? Where was the body all that time? It doesn't take that long to extract the smartcells, so what else was happening? I'm not saying we can't solve this, but everything we discover is opening up new questions.'

'Why are you here, Sid? Quitting on me?'

Sid gave the HDA spook a long look; Elston was clearly sharper than he'd written him off as. 'No. I know we have an unlimited budget, but I need to know how far you'll back me.'

'All the way.'

'Really?'

'What do you want, Sid?'

'Ordinarily, I'd start analysing traffic around Elswick Wharf that night. That way we can find out what went into the area, and start checking on each vehicle. But there's a lot of the road macromesh around Elswick Wharf ripped or degraded, this isn't the smart end of town after all. I'm also suspicious about the general lack of smartdust surveillance. It isn't a show stopper, we just have to expand the area until we have a tight perimeter. That's a lot of data to go doing the virtual timewarp with.'

'I understand that. Go with it. If you need more analysts, you got them.'

'It's not just the data, it's how you read it and apply it. Now we can build some very good virtuals of the traffic from the sections of city's road macromesh which do work, but we run into a problem of perspective when we start running them in the zone booths.'

Elston spread his hands wide. 'Solution?'

'There's a zone theatre in the Market Street Station, which would be the perfect system to run this kind of virtual. Only it never worked properly from the day it was installed, and hasn't worked at all for the last thirty months.'

'You said it: unlimited budget.'

'Aye man, fixing it is just down to money true enough. But the Chief Constable's office has been in dispute with the company that installed it. The case is winding its way through the courts. O'Rouke has taken it personally, it's him versus them now. Nobody gets in the way.'

'Leave it with me.'

'Thanks.' Sid got up to leave.

'How in the Lord's name do you people ever solve any crimes?'

'Any way we can.'

*

Sid never did get to hear what Elston said to O'Rouke. After all, he had a clear alibi – he was out of the station, driving back after briefing the forensics team out at Elswick Wharf. He returned to the Market Street Station mid-afternoon, when everyone was quietly swapping gossip on the Chief Constable and how his temper had reached a whole new level of rage – no one knew why, though, not even Chloe Healy.

Sid called Eva and Ian back from their assignments, and started explaining the logs he wanted lifting. Ralph Stevens came over, and the four of them studied a map of the area up on the main wallscreen, which had a depressing number of broken road macromesh sections and kaput smartdust. They kept taking the perimeter back until Sid just said: 'Sod it, work on a kilometre radius around the crime scene.'

'That includes the Scotwood Road,' Eva protested. 'Which has the main entrance to the Pinefield singletown. It practically points down Water Street.'

'I know,' he said. 'But we have an AI to establish the basic virtual. After that it's just elimination.'

Her red hair swished about as she shook her head in dismay. 'I'll start to set it up, but I'll need some help.'

'I'll see if Ari and Abner have finished.'

'They haven't,' Ralph said.

'Aye man, come on,' Sid said. 'We know now he's been dead since Friday. Friday, man! And no one's noticed?'

Ian leaned in a bit closer. 'It was a C. Has to be. Now nobody's ever going to admit that.'

'Just because we can't identify the victim, doesn't mean we can't find the murderer,' Sid countered.

'Love the optimism,' Ralph told him.

Quarter of an hour later, five technicians from the Felltech Zone company – specializing in hi-rez holograms – were escorted up to the Market Street Station's second floor and into the defunct zone theatre. They each pushed a trolley of equipment with them.

Ralph delivered the news to Office3 ten minutes after that.

'So that's what got up O'Rouke's arse,' Ian muttered.

'Well I'm impressed,' Eva told him. 'That's exactly what we

need to run the Elswick Wharf traffic virtual in. You guys do know what you're doing, eh?'

Ralph gave Sid a suspicious glance. 'Sure.'

*

Preliminary forensics data from Elswick Wharf started to come in around seven o'clock. Sid brought Dedra and Reannha over to assist with tabulating the results.

'I want a database on everything,' he told them. 'If we have a footprint, you need to tell me what kind of shoe, who made it, how many were sold, and who bought them. Same goes for threads, paint scrapes – whatever they send us.'

It wasn't quite the bonanza he'd been hoping for.

'Sorry,' Tilly said when she called Sid an hour later. 'But for what it's worth, we have to be dealing with a professional crew. They knew what they were doing. There were very few confirmed traces.'

'Yeah, thanks,' Sid replied. 'I guessed that as soon as I saw the corpse.'

'One piece of good news. We managed to lift a lot of snow samples with the tyre tracks on. They were covered, of course, but we're using a more sophisticated version of the CDMR in the lab. I might have a tread pattern for you later tonight.'

'Tilly, you are a fucking angel, pet.'

'It gets better.'

'Go on.'

'Professional crew, remember. I haven't got a tread match yet, but the distance between the tyres was easy.'

'Oh yes! One point seven eight metres?'

'See, one day you'll make a grand Chief Constable.'

'Thanks, Tilly; let me have the tread pattern as soon as you get it.'

He called the office together. 'We just got a break,' he told them. 'The vehicle was a standard citycab. The wheel separation distance is a perfect fit.'

The reaction was to be expected, reluctant grins and knowing glances. The lightening of the load. Everyone was suddenly back on familiar territory again.

'What?' Ralph asked.

'It's the standard way to ship anything illegal around town,' Ian explained to him. 'There are so many of them they're anonymous, it's like the shell game multiplied by a thousand. Wherever they are, they're not suspicious. Every gang in the city either owns one or has access to a few. So this was a professional hit. No aliens involved.'

Ralph pulled a face.

'Okay,' Sid said. 'Everyone back to work. Eva, I want every police report on taxis beginning Friday morning. Anything suspicious – a stolen taxi, whatever – find it for me.'

It took her eight minutes. 'Got it,' Eva announced loudly and triumphantly. 'Taxi burn-out spotted by an agency patrol along the edge of the Fawden GSW on Monday morning. It's a regular patrol, and they swear it wasn't there on Sunday.'

'Get me the perimeter mesh memories for Monday morning,' Sid ordered.

'Already there,' Eva said.

The office stopped to watch as real-time feeds of the GSW perimeter came up on the largest wallscreen. 'Mesh at the metro station,' Eva said. The image was showing a fence, but not a good one, running down the northern side of the metro track, links rusting, with sagging sections clogged by weeds which provided an easy ladder for snow to mount. Beyond it was a wasteland of derelict buildings standing like lonely broken teeth between the piles of rubble which were the buildings that the city had got round to demolishing.

'There,' Eva said. She enhanced the image, centring on a burned-out vehicle.

'Aye, that's the one,' Sid said. The bodywork was instantly recognizable, even though the carbon and aluminium had melted and sagged. It must have been a fierce fire to do that, he thought, there was nothing left of the internal fittings. Which spoke of an

154

accelerant, and quite a lot of it judging by how much snow had melted around the wreck. 'I want it.'

*

Sid took Ralph in his car, following the big agency BMW GroundKing vehicles as they joined together in a convoy along the A191 heading east from the centre of the city out to Fawden.

Eva called. 'Clear route,' she said.

Sid's grid threw up a streetmap. The city traffic management AI had shunted everyone off Jubilee Road, giving the convoy absolute priority.

Strobes flared and sirens began their high-pitched wail as the lead GroundKing turned into Jubilee Road. Sid was grinning as he accelerated sharply. Traction stability warnings flashed amber on the dashboard as the car began to slip on the sparkling frost that was smothering the tarmac, then the auto compensated, and they were racing down Jubilee Road. It was damn childish, but you just couldn't beat being at the front end on a deployment like this.

'Doesn't this sort of tip them off?' Ralph asked, raising his voice above the noise.

'The whole city knows we're here,' Sid told him. 'Gangs monitor the traffic just for times like this. Besides, no one involved is going to be within a kilometre of the taxi.'

'Then why?'

'Keep the civilians out of the way. I don't want any accidents.'

'So it's overkill?'

'We need the taxi, and this is a GSW area. My forensics team has to be safe, that means a minimum number of constables to secure a perimeter. And as we have an unlimited budget . . .'

They crossed over the metro track. The lead GroundKing, beefed up with riot-armour and protective buffers, didn't bother with going along the side of the GSW area to an official gateway – it rammed straight through the flimsy fence and charged directly at the burned-out taxi. Sid crossed into the GSW and slowed, taking care to keep in the track marks of the vehicles in front. You never knew what was lying around in the filth and rubble of somewhere like this.

Government Services Withdrawn meant just that: a civic area that had been designated surplus due to emigration. Inevitably, it was the poorest areas of town, when their dwindling population fell below a certain density, taking it below the cost-effective level for a city council to maintain. Then the remaining homeowners and businesses were bought out and the streets closed down and sealed off. After that, the neighbourhood simply awaited redevelopment, theoretically through either the private or public purse. In reality it always had to be a GE grant; financial institutions directed their investments to the new worlds these days. Nobody cared about dreary collapsed slumzones on Earth, because there was never a decent return to be made. So inside the perimeter there were no utilities, no transnet connections, no council services provided; no fire brigade tenders would respond to an incident inside, nor would ambulance or police. Businesses were not permitted to operate within a GSW. Legitimate businesses, that is; for every other sort of enterprise the GSW areas were a godsend. Which was why the smartdust ringing the boundary was always under constant rip-attack and EM pulsed and sprayed with toxic crap. The city renewed sections on a weekly basis. Police didn't intervene much with the occasional glimpses of lowlife excess the meshes gleaned amid the debris and the derelicts; only visible murders and all-out riots were subject to suppression operations, when the riot squads ploughed in, cracking heads and dragging off the known recidivists for a one-way ticket to Minisa.

Grid graphics showed Sid the GroundKings encircle the taxi. Agency constables in light body armour and carrying automatic weapons jumped from the back of each vehicle, and started to fan out, securing the surrounding land. Sid climbed out carefully, the bullet-proof vest worn under his leather jacket restricting his movements. For once he didn't trigger the badge on his coat. No need to give the GSW residents an obvious target.

His e-i quested a direct link to Tilly Lewis. 'Okay, we're secure. You can come in.'

Two Northern Forensics vans drove in, followed by a big tow-truck. Lighting rigs telescoped up from the vans, immersing the blackened wreck in a pool of brilliant white illumination.

'So much for matching a tyre tread,' Tilly complained as she got her first good look at the taxi. The tyres were misshapen black bracelets shrink-wrapped around the wheel rims, their wire mesh poking through the frazzled slirubber.

'I want everything you can get for me,' Sid said. 'A complete work-up.'

'Boot's open,' she pointed out. 'So the fire will have scoured the inside of any traces.'

'They're good, but you're better.'

'Oh please.'

'Come on, pet, we're still short of solid information.'

Tilly pulled the hood of her green isolation suit over her pink bobble hat. 'I'll see what I can do.'

'Thanks. I'll access your report in the morning.'

'Morning? You want this processed overnight?'

'Of course.'

'Sid, I'll have to call the lab techs back in. That's like quintuple time.'

'You can thank me in the morning.'

'You're leaving?'

'Nothing else for me to do until you produce those vital clues. The operation commander will keep your guys safe. And my bed beckons.'

'I hate you.'

'Just keep thinking: quintuple time.' And with that he got in the car and drove home.

Wednesday 16th January 2143

Sid hadn't expected to be back in Elston's office quite so quickly. Not after yesterday's meeting, but here he was at half past nine in the morning, barely up to speed on all the data which had come in during the night. Ralph Stevens had insisted on visiting the HDA base, so Sid drove over the Tyne Bridge in the murky gloom of a winter fog, which he hated more than the ice and snow. The car's radar threw up slender green outlines across the windscreen, helping him steer along the road with relative confidence. The only thing he could see of the van in front was a bright scarlet smear of rear lights, and between them the central green light showing it was driving on manual, while the oncoming lane was a torrent of blue-white glare. Even with modern safety aids and auto, several cars had shunted or worse. Three times he had to slow and go around transport agency patrol cars which had arrived to sort out the prangs.

'Put your log on hold, please,' Ralph had said as they walked in to the administration sector where Elston had his office. And once again Aldred was there waiting in the office.

'What did the taxi tell us?' Elston asked as soon as they'd settled in front of his desk.

'The fire was extensive,' Sid said. 'They knew what they were doing. No tyre tread left for us to match. Same with the interior, no hair or skin flakes. However, there were two possible mistakes. First off, a complete set of male clothes was left in the boot. They were doused in bioil, but they were bundled, which left enough residue to work out their size, especially the shoes. It's a good fit for the corpse.'

'Can you identify them?'

'The lab is working on it. It looks like he was wearing an expensive silk suit.'

'Well that narrows it down,' Aldred muttered.

'It's a possible lead,' Sid countered. 'Of course, clothes are circumstantial, but if you're destroying evidence it would make sense for them to belong to the victim.'

'So the body was in the boot, and they used the taxi to transport it to the Tyne?' Elston said.

'That's the way it's shaping up, yes. Most of the taxi's electronics were ruined in the fire, but again there's enough left for a reconstruction and analysis. It won't be cheap or quick, but Osborne seems to think they might be able to recover some software from what's left of the vehicle's network.'

'So we'll get the log?'

'No. The network's memory chip had been removed. But if this was a professional crew, they would be using a false registration licence with the macromesh, that's gang procedure one-oh-one. However, that kind of fix is custom written. If any of the software is still in the network, we might be able to trace it.'

Elston pursed his lips. 'Okay, that's impressive, even with the number of maybes you shoved in there.'

'Actually, it's almost irrelevant. I'm not relying on that at all, it's all very dependent on labwork that's going to take weeks, and you're right: too many maybes. Rule of thumb, if you don't solve a case, or at least have a prime suspect, in the first five days you probably won't get it to court. The good news is that the taxi was hallmarked. Nano-level threads are incorporated in the chassis and bodywork at the factory; tens of thousands of them. You can't get rid of them; every component is riddled with them. So we identified it as a taxi that was stolen eighteen months ago from its owner in Winlaton.'

'And who's going to notice one more taxi in Newcastle?' Aldred said.

Elston ignored him to fix Sid with a stare. 'So what's your next step?'

This was the part Sid was looking forward to, the office detective's version of speeding down the fast lane with siren and strobes cranked to maximum. 'It's all down to backtracking the taxi now. We know where it ended up, in the GSW, and we know where that trip started: Elswick Wharf. So I want its route between the two.'

'And how will that help?'

'Firstly to see if anyone got in or out, and where it went. But more importantly once we have its time and location fixed, we can read the licence code off the city traffic register. Now they probably kept changing it, that would be part of their fix program. But if they did we're looking for a taxi whose electronic code entered the area around Elswick on Sunday evening and never left. It's a target to us as sure as keeping the same licence code. Once we have that, we'll be able to visually backtrack it to wherever it picked the body up. And when we have that, we crack the case wide open.'

'Sounds like a big task. You can do that?'

'Aye, man; we just construct a virtual of the entire city for Sunday evening. Every smartdust mesh, every spectrum, every road macromesh; sling it all together in an AI and watch our own history play out in hi-rez detail.'

'In the station's zone theatre,' Elston said in a neutral tone. 'Impressive.'

'Expensive.' Sid shrugged.

'Quite.'

'My team is already on it. I told them to start this morning.'

'And yet we still don't know the identity of the murdered North,' Ralph said.

'I have to ask why not?' Elston said, looking directly at Aldred. 'You keep promising full cooperation.'

'It's one of us who was murdered, of course we're co-operating.'

'Not an A,' Elston said. 'And probably not a B. Apparently Brinkelle is as concerned about this as Augustine. That just leaves us with Constantine's sons.'

'He says no.'

'You need to ask again. Ask hard.'

'I'll tell my father to make the point.'

'Thank you. Sid, what about the cargo routes through the gateway?'

Sid did his best not to wince. He wondered if Elston already knew about him shouting at Ari that morning. Everything else in the office had gone so smoothly, he'd been thrown by Ari messing up and probably overreacted. 'Seventy per cent of the companies receiving freight in the designated period have responded to our enquiry. Their shipments were all intact, none were empty or had anything missing.'

'And the rest?'

'Ari is finishing the list. They'll be called today.'

'So we don't know yet how it got through?'

'Aye, not yet.'

'And I don't think that's where our main focus is being applied,' Ralph said.

Sid gave him a startled look. He was cross with himself for trusting the liaison officer. Politics at this level was deadly, and he'd allowed himself to be fooled by a pleasant attitude and apparent support.

'Go on,' Elston said.

'Sid is quite right. The taxi indicates a professional criminal gang familiar with the city. Not an alien.'

'The method is identical,' Elston insisted. 'A five-blade hand.'

'Yes, but it is the only connection. Nothing else. As evidence goes, that's circumstantial at best.'

Now Sid understood why they were having this conversation in Elston's office, and away from any official log. The expedition

161

was becoming a juggernaut, with politicians and HDA officers adding their weight. Whoever slammed the brakes on now was going to get crushed into the bedrock never to be seen again – not by any employer.

'Something unknown is targeting the Norths,' Elston said. 'HDA has to know what.'

'I understand. But you must be prepared for the taxi connection to lack an alien component.'

'Fair enough. I'll inform my superiors.'

So in the end, that's what it all boiled down to. Everyone covering themselves. Sid might have laughed if he wasn't so busy trying to estimate his own exposure. Finding a gang which had bumped off a North ought to be protection enough. Surely?

*

'I'll take you back to the station,' Aldred said when they reached the base's car park.

'But . . .' Sid gestured at his own car.

'One of my people will take care of it,' Aldred said. So Sid watched in bemusement as a suited aide got out of the black Mercedes and trotted over to the police car.

'What now?' Sid asked as the Merc's passenger doors folded down and the auto took them out of the base. There was a lot of traffic coming in through the gate, Sid noticed, just as there had been yesterday. He'd been so sure a positive result on the case would protect him, but all those people and equipment arriving for the expedition made him feel vulnerable again.

'Don't panic,' Aldred said. 'He wants to see you, that's all.'

'Who?'

'Augustine.'

'Oh, crap on it.'

The Merc took them to some big office tower in Westgate, one of a dozen owned by Northumberland Interstellar in the city. There was a helicopter waiting on the roof pad, contra-rotating blades already turning idly.

'I don't even know where Augustine lives,' Sid said as he settled back into the cabin's surprisingly comfortable seat.

'It's not far,' Aldred promised.

The helicopter's soundproofing was excellent, and Sid could barely hear the turbines as they powered up. Then they lifted smoothly, and immediately banked, curving round to head north. After that his sense of direction gave up. He tried looking through the window, but the fog was still cloaking the city. Flying through impenetrable mist was ten times worse than driving through it.

'I have a favour to ask,' Aldred said.

Sid was glad of the excuse to concentrate on the cabin again. 'Aye man, this is my season for handing them out.'

'Don't worry, you're coping remarkably well. I'm rather looking forward to a virtual of the entire city. Has it ever been done before?'

'No. They ran a virtual of the whole Byker district four years ago for the Eiricksson case, that's the biggest we've ever done.'

'Anyway, I'd like you to ease off on Ari.'

'He ballsed up. He was supposed to compile a complete list of importers.'

'You switched him round from finding the body's identity. That office is spinning so fast it's confusing.'

'Oh, come on.'

'Sid, he's a 3.'

'What!'

'He's a 3.'

'But . . .'

'Everyone prejudges us at the best of times. You're all very prejudiced towards the 3s.'

'I resent that.'

'You automatically assumed Ari was a 2. Why? Simple enough: you were sure a 3 wouldn't be capable of any meaningful detective work. This whole city knows for sure that 3s aren't the smartest, it's a rock-solid urban myth. In reality, the replication errors are never the same. Ari is one of the good guys, Sid, he's doing the best job he can, and trying to shield himself from additional prejudice at the same time.'

'Is he your son?'

'No.'

'Crap on it. Okay, I'll try not to be such a bastard.'

'Don't let him off completely, I don't want positive discrimination, that's the worst you could do. Just understand, that's all. He'll get there in the end.'

By the time the helicopter flew out of the fog they were north of Newcastle. Sid saw what he thought was Alnwick – easy enough to recognize the huge old castle on the edge of town. They were descending by then.

The land was wilder here, a lot of farms had been sold on to land investment companies who were quick to milk money from GE naturalization schemes, allowing the hedges and meadows to revert. They flew over deep valleys and wooded slopes, the coastline just visible on one side while the hills rose up towards the west. Their destination was never in question: a mansion set in extensive grounds with a meandering stream and two lakes separated by a waterfall – all frozen. The whole expanse was surrounded by a thick barrier of trees, guaranteeing privacy from anyone on the ground. You could walk by without ever knowing it was there.

As to the pyramid-shaped mansion, its modernist façade was made up from huge rhomboid glass windows set into a gridwork of thick black steel beams. To Sid it looked like the top section of some New York skyscraper had been sliced off and dropped down in the middle of the countryside. It didn't really belong in the rolling English landscape; but like every billionaire before him, Augustine wanted to make a statement.

The interior was equally lush. Massive glass doors opened into a broad arched hallway which led directly to the central atrium. With solar lighting backing up the meagre daylight seeping through the glass apex far above, it was like walking into a botanical greenhouse. Huge ferns and tropical trees rose out of long troughs, fat verdant leaves waving in the air currents spinning off from the humidor mist jets. The largest tree, right in the middle, had strange branches that were curled into tight-packed spirals, extending horizontally from the trunk.

Sid broke out in a sweat from the heat. He took his jacket off, struggling to recognize any of the plants – there was something slightly odd about the leaves with their dark vein lacework. 'What are these plants?'

'These?' Aldred asked in an amused tone. 'These are St Libra's plants, of course, the famous zebra botany.'

'But the leaves aren't black and white,' Sid said.

Aldred gave him an odd look. 'Uh, you know there's no animal life on St Libra, right?'

'Aye, there's not supposed to be. The monster—'

'Forget the monster,' Aldred said. 'On Earth and the other settled trans-space worlds, plants absorb carbon dioxide and crack it into neat oxygen – that's photosynthesis.'

'I get that, man.'

'But on St Libra there are no animals to breathe in the oxygen and exhale carbon dioxide, which is the other half of the equation. So evolution got smart. Roughly half of St Libra's plants do what we're used to, and generate oxygen, while the other half reverse the process. If it gets out of balance, say if the oxygen exhalers thrive, they make the atmosphere oxygen-rich, which in turn favours the other variety, who return to the ascendancy. It's a constant cycle. "Zebra" has nothing to do with colour, it's about direct opposites.'

'Right,' Sid said. 'But if all the plants evolved that way because there aren't any animals, where did the monster come from?'

Abner gave an elaborate shrug. 'Trillion-Eurofranc question.'

'Detective Hurst.'

Sid turned round to see a North walking towards him, assisted by a pair of Rex legs which were the sleekest exoskeleton he'd ever seen, looking more like a fashion accessory than a medical necessity. He looked young, this one, maybe in his thirties, although the curly brown hair was missing; the skull's skin revealed by the absence appeared a little too pallid, and the arms were disturbingly thin. Legs, too, presumably, though they were hidden by trousers and the lean dark Rex segments.

He was flanked by two girls – one blonde, one redhead – both in their early twenties if not younger. They wore short summer dresses, showing off a lot of toned flesh.

'Augustine North,' Sid replied.

There was a tiny whine of servos as Augustine North walked over and put his hand out. 'That obvious?'

Sid resisted the obvious comment about the girls; after all, who else would have such an attentive escort? They were both astonishingly attractive, but all he could feel was a form of pity that they'd wound up here, human cattle all placid and obedient when they should have been out having fun and living life for themselves. A father's resentment firing up, he supposed; Zara would never wind up like this, he'd make damn sure of that. 'Aldred mentioned rejuvenation takes time, sir.'

'Great. My security chief is a gossip.' Augustine walked over to a marble bench near the centre of the atrium and sat carefully. 'Can I get you anything? I've heard you're a coffee man.'

'No thank you, sir.' Sid wondered how that piece of information had filtered up to Augustine's level. The girls moved away, standing patiently at a discreet distance.

'I have two principal questions for you,' Augustine said. 'And forgive me but at my age I like to hear the answers to such things directly.'

'Aye, I understand that.'

'Realistically, are you going to catch the killer? And was it an alien?'

'We're making very reasonable progress tracking down the killer. Given that we have neither motive nor the victim's identity yet, that is positive. As to the alien, all I can tell you is that to me it's looking like a proficient underground hit. However, there are some things which don't add up. The lack of identity bothers me a lot. If this is some clandestine corporate operation involving Brinkelle or your brother Constantine, then I will probably never be able to find the answers for you.'

'Ah yes,' Augustine North smiled grimly. 'I actually agree with that religious nut.'

'Sir?'

'Vance Elston is an adherent of the Gospel Warrior church. There's an uncomfortable number of them in the HDA, not that it's actually illegal, but I suspect it colours their viewpoint somewhat.'

'I didn't know.'

'Nonetheless, I admit the body could well be one of Constantine's sons. Our split was never the most amicable, despite the official version. Bartram and I at least understood each other. But Constantine . . . now he was a dreamer, and slippery with it. I'll get in touch with Jupiter again and press him for the truth.'

Sid studied Aldred to try and judge how much slack he was entitled to here. But the 2North was giving nothing away. To hell with it, Augustine himself was treating him like a grown-up, so . . . 'Sir, I apologize for asking, but this would make the investigation a lot easier. Is there any chance you fathered a son without knowing?' And he just couldn't help glancing over at the two girls.

Augustine caught it, and chuckled. 'I appreciate why you're asking; my reputation isn't exactly admired by the Pope. But sadly I have to say no. The corpse was in his late forties, yes? That would put me in my late seventies or eighties when he was born. It wasn't a good decade for me physically, and I hadn't begun Bartram's therapies then. All the 2Norths conceived around that time were done so in the company's clinic. There are no lost princes, not in my kingdom.'

'Then can you guess why a C 2North would be here, what kind of clandestine mission your brother would send him on?' He knew he'd never get an answer, that if there was a reason it would be some kind of high-level covert corporate crap, the type that never even made it to the unlicensed political blogs. Rumours and whispers would echo round the case, the bogeyman for every rookie cop for decades to come.

'I simply can't imagine why he would be bothered with us any

167

more,' Augustine said. 'His techno-Marxist ideology looks down on my old-fashioned market commerce with great disdain. He simply wouldn't bother himself with corporate or financial activities any more. I appreciate your candour, Detective. Aldred has told me about you, how you understand the way the world works. Whatever the outcome, you have my word this case will not screw up your record.'

'Thank you, sir.' Having the same guarantee made twice in two days by two of the most powerful Norths in Europe was astonishingly reassuring. It almost elevated it to believable. 'What will you do now?'

'Me?' Augustine seemed mildly surprised by the question. 'Well, until the murder is solved one way or another, political expediency means I'll be cooperating with the HDA, and allowing their ridiculous expedition through to St Libra to hunt for killer monsters in the wilderness. Brinkelle has also agreed to them using Abellia as their base – she has even less choice than I.'

Thursday 17th January 2143

Home capsules were slowly replacing the older, static residences in the newest and largest section of the Jupiter habitat amalgamation. Constantine had been the first to adopt one, leaving behind the elaborate truncated pyramid he'd built in the first torus habitat they'd constructed. Walking out on it had been quite symbolic, casting aside everything that had come before, physically, mentally. Now a single room was his whole house, moving slowly round the interior of the massive cylinder like the VW camper van of a bygone era. Physically, it was a melange of metamolecules, the most advanced material to come out of the constellation's zerogee nuclear extruders. Its boundary was defined by soft glowing lines that twisted, expanding or contracting as he required. The walls they described could be varied from matt black to completely transparent. Furniture too was ephemeral, matt-black shapes outlined in slender threads of purple or orange luminescence.

He lay on the incredibly soft mattress waiting for Reisa to come out of the bathroom which had inflated out from the side of the main chamber. Women, like the items he'd brought from Earth and were kept in storage compartments beneath the home capsule, were something he hadn't shaken off in his new life. Not that he'd ever intended to. But the relationships were mature ones now, based on respect and admiration and possibly even love, rather than the exploitative conducts he and his brothers had pursued throughout his first eighty years. Reisa had been with him for eleven years now. A record he was rather proud of.

His e-i informed him Coby was calling. He let it come through, and his son's head materialized at the foot of the bed, indistinguishable from a solid object.

'You have a call from Earth,' Coby said.

'Another one. Whatever does Augustine want now?'

Coby's smile was sly. 'It's not Augustine. This is General Khurram Shaikh himself, using the diplomatic circuit encryption . . .'

'Ah yes, that was inevitable I suppose. Have you accessed the message?'

'Yes, he's very formal, and very polite, and yet very insistent.'

'Of course he is. All right, let's take a look.'

Khurram Shaikh's head replaced Coby's. It tilted in a slight bow of respect. 'Constantine North. Thank you for taking the time to receive this message. I understand you've been informed that a North clone has been killed in Newcastle, with a method similar to the one employed against your brother Bartram and his household twenty years ago. Firstly, my condolences. We are of course expending considerable resources trying to find the perpetrator, alien or human. There are some factors which are unknown at the moment, and I respectfully request your assistance in enlightening me where you can. The investigation we are mounting is enormous, and I cannot afford it to be compromised. Everything you say will of course be classified as top secret. So I urgently need to know if the Norths discovered an alien species on St Libra, and if it is the one performing these murders. I am not concerned with any conflict you have with Augustine or Brinkelle's side of the family, but the existence of another sentient species is profoundly important to the entire human race. I am charged with protecting all of us, and I take my position most seriously. If there is another potential threat out there, I must know. Constantine, we need your help with this; if the human race is to survive in this universe, we must

170

do so collectively. Do not abandon us; we would never abandon you. I look forward to receiving your answer.'

'And if I don't get it I'll come up there and rip it out of you,' Reisa said scathingly. She'd emerged from the bathroom just after the message started playing. 'They never change, do they?'

Constantine smiled and held his hands out to her. 'They're upset. I'm very upset; after all, one of my nephews has been murdered. This isn't how I expected the endgame of the mystery to play out.'

'But they suspect your involvement. After all, you're different. You turned your back on their civilization, that makes you the unknown, which always scares them. Fright and envy are never a good combination for planet humans.'

'Their suspicion was completely predictable. And please stop the "them and us" analysis. Ultimately our sojourn here at Jupiter will be temporary.'

'Constantine, I love you dearly, but if you think their civilization will ever adopt our philosophies you are delusional. They'll grab the weapons, say thank you, and career onwards in their own psychotic fashion.'

'The Zanth has forced them to change their perception of the universe.'

'It gave them an excuse to build HDA, the biggest military force we've ever known, and the greatest drain on resources. All it does – really does – is provide the masses with the most monumental false hope since religion reared its ugly head.'

He gave her a gentle squeeze. 'I can never give you a diplomatic posting, can I?'

'Constantine . . . is there a sentient alien species on St Libra?'

'I don't know. I've been searching for the answer to that question for twenty years now. In all that time I've accepted only two things: that it's a very big planet and something killed Bartram. Something very odd. And now I'm ready for it.'

'And you'll tell the HDA?'

'Ah, now that's the big question. I can't answer that until I know for sure what it is.'

'So what are you going to tell General Shaikh?'

Constantine banished the image of the General's head, and ordered the home to turn completely opaque. 'Let me sleep on it.'

*

A North being murdered could never be kept quiet for ever. It didn't matter how much you pleaded or threatened people involved with the case, it was simply too big. Besides, with the no-limits budget, a whole new level of agency personnel were involved. There must have been over a hundred in total, then there were those they shared offices and labs with, and of course pillow talk. Transnet reporters, too, had an extensive network of contacts among Newcastle's government employees whom they bought drinks for and arranged favours in return for the occasional indiscreet word.

Sid had his suspicions about where this leak had originated. O'Rouke had really not appreciated having his hand forced over the zone theatre; he'd been out to bust Felltech Zone. Partially, Sid heard whispered, because they'd never come through with certain promises made just prior to the contract being awarded.

Wherever the leak came from, it began to surface on Thursday morning. Chloe Healy had spent an hour briefing and preparing him for the two o'clock official media conference. It wasn't just local reporters he was up in front of, but the big national media groups from across the trans-stellar worlds. A dead North was Big News. So much so, that Sid even allowed himself to be coaxed into the station's make-up suite before facing the cameras and battering-ram questions.

It was, he said with a straight, sombre face, Albert 3North who was the tragic victim of a carjacking that had gone wrong. The police were looking for the stolen VW Ropolis – he released a flood of data about the car to the station's public site. And yes, the raid on the Fawdon GSW area on Tuesday night was connected, a taxi used in the carjacking was recovered.

A lot of colleagues had come up afterwards to tell him how

well he handled it. He even got a short congratulatory call from O'Rouke. Despite how successful the media conference was, and he was pretty pleased with himself, he resented the time it consumed. Office3 on the third floor was buzzing today and he didn't want to be away from it. Everyone was excited by the prospect of a full city virtual. And everyone apart from Lorelle and Ari was working on the project, pulling in Sunday's surveillance memories on a district-by-district basis. They were also transferring the entire civic traffic management data into the dedicated AI they'd bought time with. Even Sid had helped, using his somewhat rusty programming ability to define geographical coordinates to the AI. Dedra and Reannha were supervising the dataflow from the city planning office, generating a graphic skeleton of Newcastle's street and building layout onto which the AI would project mesh data and vehicle logs. Unless there was a major glitch, the virtual should be up and running by midday tomorrow.

Sid had let everyone go home at seven that evening apart from Reannha, who would supervise the AI as it compiled the results. Her relief would take over at midnight. After reviewing the last batch of forensics data to make sure there were no revelations, he'd said goodnight to Reannha and left. Even Ralph Stevens had gone back to whatever hotel he was staying in.

He turned into Falconar Street, and parked close to the bottom end. The whole of one side was a single terrace of two-storey houses, built from a dark-brown brick with painted stone window mullions. A market-man's ideal of middle-class aspiration. Naturally, the row was well maintained, with tiny neat front gardens behind a low wall, all of them swamped by snow which had paths cleared to the front doors. Sid could never remember exactly which one Ian lived at; so he walked along the street content to let his e-i guide him. Purple and yellow graphics winked urgently in his grid: Ian rented the upper floor of a house close to the centre. The door lock flashed green as Sid's e-i gave off a proximity quester.

There were three rooms: a decent-sized front lounge with

built-in kitchenette, a bedroom which was the same size, and a compact en suite bathroom where every shelf and cabinet was filled with male grooming products. Ian rented the place purely for its location, close enough to Market Street Station that he could walk to work in summer, and equally adjacent to the city's main clubs and pubs. He'd lived in it for two years, and the only furniture he'd bought in that time was a bed. As he said, 'I won't be using anything else.'

Eva was already there when Sid arrived. She always refused to sit on the bed, disapproving as she did of the weekly parade of girls Ian brought back to the flat. Instead she'd snagged a pillow, and sat with her back to the wall in the lounge. Ian had claimed the marble-top surface of the kitchenette's breakfast bar.

'Beer?' he asked as Sid walked in.

'Sure.'

Ian took one from the small fridge. Sid could only see bottles in there, it certainly wasn't chilling any food.

The flat didn't have built-in wardrobes, so Ian hung his clothes on a long metal rack which he'd bought from a retail store. Sid sat on the floor beside it and took a sip from the bottle. 'If we meet in the pub, the meshes have enough definition to run lip-reading software.'

'Crap on it, boss,' Eva muttered. 'Who are we bumping off?'

'We're saving our careers.'

'Away wi' you, man,' Ian said. 'You think we can't solve it? We're building a city virtual for crap's sake. A city! We've got an unlimited budget, a real one. Aye, there's some pricks looking over our shoulder for sure, but they're not interfering. This is the chance in a lifetime, man. We can solve this. It's gonna be colossal.'

Sid was surprised at the level of passion in his deputy's voice. Since when had Ian turned careerist? 'Solve it? Really? The outcome we have to produce is an alien with knives for fingers. That's what the politics requires. So hands up who thinks that's what we're going to parade in front of the press next time we have a conference like today's?'

'Crap on it, they know that's not going to happen,' Ian exclaimed. 'Ralph understands; he's a twat but he knows what's real. He accessed the forensics reports on the taxi and Elswick Wharf, he knows this was some corporate shit that went bad.'

'You're not listening. This isn't about what *happened*, this is about what's *expected* from us. Governments are putting together an expedition to St Libra, the HDA is throwing everything into this. Let me show you something.' He told his e-i to access the site.

Ian's wallscreen started playing the introduction to the Gospel Warriors. It was childish, ridiculous, simplistic. It was the devout belief that the Zanth was Lucifer's agent, that the followers of the church were blessed by Jesus. Only HDA members were entitled to become Gospel Warriors. There were testimonials from the congregation, accounts of how they'd been spared during the New Florida Zanthswarm, sincere, earnestly spoken tales of tragedy and death narrowly averted as the Zanth missed them or their vehicle by centimetres, how the arms of Jesus had embraced them and moved them out of danger, how angels had pushed lethal Zanth masses onto a new trajectory so they fell clear.

Sid cancelled the link. Ian was laughing openly, while Eva wore a more troubled expression.

'That's the kind of mentality we're up against,' Sid said.

'Aye man, they're a bunch of fucking religious nutters,' Ian said. 'So what?'

'Elston: he's one of them, isn't he?' Eva asked.

'Yeah,' Sid admitted. 'And he's not alone. I checked round some of the unlicensed political blogs. The Gospel Warriors are widespread in the HDA officer class. Secularists are concerned that they see the Zanth conflict as some kind of crusade.'

'But it is,' Ian said.

'Not a spiritual one. Look, the point is these people are expecting one outcome. Everything – our case, the expedition – is geared around that outcome. If we screw it up for them, we're going to get royally arse-fucked.'

'We can't produce an alien,' Eva said.

'I know that. The trouble is, we might not be able to produce the murderer, either. This was a well-organized hit. And the only reason anyone would dare take out a North is for some covert corporate deal that's gone badly wrong. It'll be something like the 2111 cartel. You remember that one, right? Northumberland Interstellar and the other eight bioil giants restabilized the bioil market, but wiped out the speculators doing so. Lot of people got burned, big people. Most likely, the 2 was eliminated so a 3 who's been bribed or coerced can take his place to run whatever scam is going down this time around. And it won't be small, which means the corporate boys are going to trigger every cut-out they have. Whole office buildings of managers will get roasted on the altar of plausible deniability. We'll never find out what was happening and who is involved.'

'But they want an answer,' Ian insisted. 'Not even companies can stand up to the HDA. The Norths have already folded – they're letting HDA send an expedition into St Libra. We can find the murderer.'

'They want *their* answer,' Sid insisted. 'And this investigation can't provide that for them. Even if we find who's driving the taxi, there will be cut-offs, people who got their orders from unknown contacts. The gangs know how we work, they're not going to give us anyone. This investigation will stall in a shitstorm of questions we can't possibly answer.'

'Which is also what the HDA wants,' Eva said. 'No answer from us also justifies sending the expedition.'

'Yes,' Sid agreed.

'So we're covered, then?' Ian said.

'From the HDA, yes.'

Ian spread his arms wide. 'Who else is there to worry about?'

'I'm concerned about what happens to us, personally, after-wards; not right away, but in a year or two when the expedition's history and the case is shunted to inactive status. Like I said, what's that going to do to our real careers? Because there's one person who does want to know who killed the North.'

'And that is?' Eva asked.

'Augustine. I know, because he told me when I met him.'

'Aye, no shit, man?' Ian said. 'When?'

'Aldred took me out to the mansion on Wednesday.'

'What was he like?' Eva asked keenly.

'Kind of weird, but he is very serious about this. And this is his city, he'll be here long after Elston and the HDA have moved out and started chasing their next demon. Which leaves us with a problem. I have a family, and I had a promise of an agency job.' He looked at Eva. 'Ragnar works in the bioil industry.'

'He's in AI management development strategy. They wouldn't . . .'

'Yeah, they'll leave your husband alone because they got where they are by being sympathetic and understanding. Look, the Norths are expecting us to solve this. Really solve it, not just spout HDA bullshit at media conferences.'

'You just said it,' Ian said. 'This is some corporate deal that went tits up. We can't find who is responsible, this investigation is focused on chasing an individual, and if the killer is a professional he won't even be on Earth any more, let alone Newcastle. Nobody's ever going to trial for this. Fuck it! We're screwed.'

'We might not be able to find the killer,' Sid said. 'But what I'd like to be able to tell Aldred is which company is behind it, or at the very least which gang was hired to do the hit.'

'So what's the problem?' Ian asked. 'He's in Office3 most of the day. As soon as we know, he'll know.'

'No he won't,' Eva said, giving Sid a level stare. 'Because even if we ever find the taxi driver, he's not going to give up who he's working for. That's if the driver's still alive. Contract this hot and dirty, that makes the street soldiers expendable. He's probably already dead.'

'Most likely,' Sid said.

'Ah, crap on it,' Ian said. 'So what do we do?'

'Like you said, the gangs know our procedures. We need to come at them from a different angle.'

'How different?'

'We need to work backwards. Find out which gang was involved by ourselves and somehow turn the investigation on to them. Drop some evidence into our official investigation, but it will have to be something that can't be traced back to us.'

'I don't know . . .' Eva said.

'Crap on the evidence, man,' Ian said. 'How do we find which gang is involved anyway?'

'I have a contact who knows where to ask those kind of questions,' Sid said. 'But if we're going to do this, I have to know you're with me.'

Ian grinned and took a slug of his beer. 'Sure. But you need to make Aldred know where the real credit lies.'

Sid turned to Eva.

'We have to be careful,' she said slowly. 'There can't be any sign we diverted the investigation.'

'There won't be,' Sid promised.

*

Constantine North smiled out of the big screen which dominated one wall of Khurram Shaikh's office deep below the red sands of the Australian desert. It was a politician's smile, Major Vermekia thought, sincere and comforting. But it demonstrated an emotional maturity that shouldn't belong on such a youthful face.

'So he's rejuvenated,' General Shaikh murmured.

'Yes, sir, if it is him,' Vermekia said. 'After all, there's no way of telling them apart, and no one has seen Constantine North since 2088.'

'We have enough to worry about without trying to confirm the precise identity of a North on the other side of the solar system, thank you.'

'Sorry, sir.'

The General's eyes narrowed disapprovingly at the frozen image. 'If it is him, he's a hundred and thirty-one years old, and he doesn't look a day over twenty-five. Which in itself is interesting, because I've heard rumours about how good the techniques actually are.'

'Bartram North pioneered them.'

'Now there's an irony.' The General settled back behind his desk. 'All right, we accept that this man speaks for the Jupiter habitat. Let's hear what he speaks.' He ordered his e-i to apply the diplomatic key to the recording.

Constantine's smile came to life. 'General, thank you for your message. I can certainly understand your concerns and I hope I can throw some light on the situation. Firstly, I can categorically confirm that my brothers and I never found any sign of a sentient alien species on St Libra. That doesn't preclude its existence, obviously, in the light of the murders and Angela Tramelo's testimony. Something is killing members of my family and I would not withhold any information I had that could explain what it is. For the record, I think your expedition is the correct way forward. If there is a hostile sentient on the Brogal continent, we need to know about it as a matter of urgency. I'll also confirm to you personally that the unknown North murdered in Newcastle is not one of my sons. Outside of our supply trips to Earth, which these days are mainly to collect genetic material for safeguarding, I do not concern myself with your society and its commercial activities. So I'll conclude by wishing your people every luck with the expedition. If you need any further information I'll be happy to oblige.'

General Shaikh was silent for a long moment, studying the now blank wallscreen. 'Did you believe any of that?'

'It was plausible,' Vermekia ventured.

'Yes, wasn't it just? I'm inclined to believe him about St Libra. In which case the expedition should go ahead. How is the Newcastle police investigation progressing?'

'They're assembling a virtual of the entire city's road traffic for that day so they can track the vehicle involved with the murder. Colonel Elston is hopeful it should produce results.'

Friday 18th January 2143

Newcastle at night oozed out its own thick miasma of light pollution. Streetlights and houselights burned merrily in defiance of energy prices; dazzle-stars of traffic lights switched endlessly through their sequence, entire office blocks were lit up from within, their efficient ceiling panels proudly displaying rank after rank of empty desks and cubicles. The centre of town was a thick foam of colour as the holograms and neons of adverts throttled entire streets in their quest for brand victory. Vehicles added to the glare, headlights and tail lights creating jumbled rivers of photons sluicing along above the snow-coated tarmac.

There were dark spaces, too, necrotic skin blemishing the exotic creature of light. Parks, roofs of the older buildings outside the centre, the GSW districts; Sid was expecting those, but there were further, more unsettling shadow haunts, too. Streets that faded in and out of existence, with only his mind filling in the distance between the illuminations; a surprising number of road junctions had dropped out of vision in a celebration of darkness.

Even so, the full city virtual was impressive. Sid and Ralph stood on the side of the zone theatre, aloof from the undulating sprawl of buildings like dinosaur monsters in some Asian disaster zone drama, ready to trash the unsuspecting metropolis. Before them, nine o'clock Sunday evening played out, with thousands of toy cars sliding about in defiance of the ice, and ant people scurried along the pavements.

Sid couldn't resist it, he waded out through the strata of light until the Fenham district encircled his knees. He half expected his legs to stir up current-like swirls amid the twinkling image, but the theatre projectors ignored his presence, continuing to implement the virtual all around him. Looking straight down he watched a bus crawl along Fenham Hall Drive. It dissolved out of existence as it approached the junction with the B1305, which was represented solely by the structural map outlines, grey geometrical outlines that the city planning department memory conjured up as a substitute for mesh-derived fact.

The bus reappeared on the B1305, heading south towards the river. Sid glanced over to the long slit windows on the wall of the theatre zone that fronted the control and manipulation centre. Ari and Dedra were sitting behind the main desk, while Ian, Eva, and a couple of others were crammed into the dimly lit room behind them. 'Magnify the junction, would you please,' Sid said, pointing to the grey sketch.

The city expanded dramatically around him in a way that induced a momentary bout of motion sickness. The zone theatre had been built so they could completely re-create whole rooms from first-on-scene visual logs, producing a pristine view of the entire crime scene that could be examined pixel by pixel for evidence which could get displaced or overlooked later when the harassed paramedics blustered in and agency constables were tramping about. Now, Sid studied the architect's lines of the junction with some annoyance. 'How much smartdust covers this area?' he asked.

'It's not the smartdust quantity, it's down to how the motes mesh, and if the distance between them is too great they can't interlink,' Ari replied. 'The city took a pounding from those twisters in early December which clawed whole swarms of them from their positions. Then there's our piss-poor maintenance schedule, not to mention straight vandalism. Cover a mote in spraypaint or glowgloop and you kill its sensor ability and solar power input in one – it's effectively dead.'

'What about deliberate sabotage?' Ralph asked, coming over to examine the junction.

'That too,' Dedra admitted. 'We're identifying a lot of rips this weekend.'

'Okay, so we haven't got full street-mesh coverage here,' Sid said. 'What about showing me a visualization of the bus from the traffic management AI. Rerun this a couple of minutes, I want to see the network representation of the bus go through the junction.'

The entire virtual reversed, vehicles travelling backwards in fast motion. Green and purple symbols which the city's management network employed to tag each vehicle materialized, packed with ever-changing digits. Sid watched the bus drive carefully down the last twenty metres of Fenham Hall Drive. It vanished, along with its purple traffic management symbol.

'Drop out,' Dedra confirmed. 'Hang on, let me check.' The bus and its symbol reappeared on the B1305. 'Yeah, the road's metamesh is down there.'

'Bring the scale back down,' Sid said. When the virtual shrunk back to its original size he looked at Elswick Wharf, then over to the black smear of the Fawdon GSW. The junction wasn't directly between the two, but not far off. 'When did that part of the metamesh fail?'

Ari was studying his zone console display. 'Late Saturday night.'

Sid and Ralph exchanged a look.

'Freeze the image,' Sid said. 'Now highlight all the sections of the road metamesh which are down.'

A swarm of scarlet markers appeared. Sid whistled silently. There were hundreds city-wide, but the greatest density was a broad swathe between Elswick and Fawdon. 'Okay, now overlay all the street meshes which are out, or we haven't got a memory log for.' Amber marker points sprang up. Again, the majority were sitting between Elswick and Fawdon. 'Which ones are combined? Take out the remainder.'

Over half of the markers from the rest of the city vanished. 'A hundred and seventeen between Elswick and Fawdon, boss,' Dedra announced.

'There was a lot of planning went into this,' Sid decided. 'Not to mention the organization you'd need for implementation. All right, Ian, I want forensics teams out at two dozen junctions where we have failure overlaps. Sample the dead motes on the walls and in the tarmac. I want to find out what killed our sensor coverage, and get me exact times. If they were taken out by an electromagnetic pulse instead of a rip we can run a second virtual and see if we can spot the culprits.'

'Aye man,' Ian said. 'I'll get right on it.'

'Thanks,' Sid said. 'Dedra, we're going to have to do this the real hard way. Shift the virtual to centre Fawdon's GSW area around me.' He waited, trying to remember the worst-case procedures he'd mapped out in his mind. 'We know the body was dumped into the river from about ten o'clock onwards, so I need logs of every taxi that came within half a kilometre of the GSW between nine thirty Sunday night, and one o'clock – to start with.'

They watched as the virtual rushed forward to ten o'clock with a blaze of streaking headlights. It slowed and stopped. 'Okay,' Sid said. 'Highlight the taxis.' He waited patiently while a solitary green tag appeared on Kingston Park Road bordering the northern boundary of the GSW; the feeling he got from orchestrating a virtual on this scale was almost indecent. If the police had this level of resources available for every crime, the buses to Minisa would be full indeed. 'Let's do the rounds,' he told Ralph.

'What else are we looking for?' Ralph asked.

'A taxi that isn't licence-coded as a taxi. It's a simple misdirection that's screwed more than one case; the gangs use it a lot. So let's not start with elementary mistakes, eh.' He walked round the GSW area, examining every road. When the images collected by the meshes were projected onto the basic map they didn't have the highest resolution, but a citycab taxi was an iconic profile. Anything remotely close and he could ask for magnification.

After a moment's reluctance, Ralph started to move in the

opposite direction, circling the darkness of the GSW. 'Nothing,' he declared eventually.

'Take us forward thirty seconds,' Sid ordered. He began to scrutinize the new pattern of vehicles.

'Really?' Ralph said. 'Thirty seconds?'

'Yeah. Long enough to register a change, but it doesn't give enough time to dash into the GSW without us seeing.'

'But we have about four or five hours to cover.'

'Aye man, you got somewhere else to be?'

Saturday 19th January 2143

Bright winter sunlight shining out of a cloudless sky gleamed across the city's mantle of snow, producing a powerful white glare along every street. Traffic in the monochrome haze was slow that morning, with every city road clogged. The Newcastle ring road had been closed at five am, allowing the HDA logistics corps to tow a Boeing C-8000 Daedalus strategic airlifter from the local airport where it had landed last night all the way round to the St Libra gateway. It had gone through an hour before, but the civic management AI was still struggling to route vehicles back to a normal pattern.

Rebka had to put her sunglasses on against the intrusive shine of brilliant white snow as she sat in the back of the NECatering Services staff bus while it crawled along the heavily congested A167. Her new employers were a company who had a lot of government officials as senior non-executive directors; contacts which made landing a support contract for the expedition inevitable. NECatering Services existed purely as a revenue generator for private shareholders, a typical modern operation, subcontracting most of its operation and squeezing its suppliers. Junior staff turnover was huge, they were all employed on temporary contracts with legal minimum benefits, record-keeping was poor, and corporate accounting even worse – not that the GE Tax Bureau ever investigated them.

That made it ridiculously easy for Rebka and her support

team to insert a suitable legend into various official databases, creating a background for twenty-year-old 'Madeleine Hoque', who flitted around Newcastle's temporary jobs, never staying with one employer for more than two months, which NECatering Services would never scrutinize with any efficiency anyway. Madeleine submitted her job application online, and was accepted within ten minutes. It took the team's byteheads a little longer to transfer her to the expedition personnel, but again the task was accomplished with minimum fuss – NECatering Services didn't exactly hi-fund on digital security. All that left was a couple of days' training for her basic GE grade five hygiene permit. She did that for real in a rundown commercial training kitchen over in Winlaton, so that when she arrived at the HDA base with other NECatering Services employees she knew a whole bunch of them who'd been on the same course, and she wasn't the new girl, the odd one out.

The fifteen-seater bus pulled up to the base entrance at ten thirty on the Saturday morning. They all disembarked outside one of the stern concrete buildings while big HDA transports and lorries trundled past. Containers had been arriving for days now, leaving the storage yard behind the base fast approaching capacity. But young Madeleine Hoque and her new friends huddled together watching a convoy of seventy-tonne juggernauts, their flatbed trailers loaded to the maximum, heading out of the base and down to the St Libra gateway at the end of First Mile.

'Blimey,' Lulu MacNamara grunted as the slipstream from one juggernaut sent her scarf fluttering. 'I've never seen anything like this before.'

'We're making history, okay,' Rebka agreed.

'What's so bloody urgent over there? Some radicals peeing in the algaepaddies?'

'Got to be something to do with the dead 3North,' Fuller Owusu announced confidently.

'That was a carjacking,' Lulu said.

'So the police say,' Fuller countered. 'You don't really believe that bollocks, do you?'

Lulu shrugged. 'Dunno.'

Luther Katzen, their team supervisor, had been talking to the guards. He waved thanks and came back to the NECatering Services group. 'Come on. I've got our billet assignments for tonight. We'll get a briefing in an hour when everyone else is here.'

Grumbling and exchanging bemused glances, the little team picked up their overnight bags and trooped after Luther.

'Share a room?' Lulu asked her new pal Madeleine.

'Sure,' Rebka said. 'But I'll bet it's more than two to a room.' She stared up at the gloomy concrete front of the building with its narrow dark windows. 'This place isn't exactly a hotel.'

Lulu giggled. 'I've stayed in worse places, pet. Besides, we get to go to St Libra; and in winter, too. How sweet is that? It'll be like a paid holiday, this. All tropical and hot, like, while everyone back here is bloody freezing.' She patted her cylindrical bag happily. 'I bought a new bikini. Going to get me a good tan. Me friends'll be right jealous.'

'Good idea,' Rebka said. It was tempting to try and talk some sense into the girl – Lulu was in her early twenties and perennially cheerful – but that would be out of character for Madeleine, who was also fresh to everything and without any real focus in life. So she held back. Maybe she could take Lulu on a quick shopping trip through Last Mile before they got shipped out, persuade the girl to fill her bag with something more survivalist-orientated.

Rebka was right, they didn't have rooms. Everyone from NECatering Services was assigned a dormitory.

Lulu nudged Rebka. 'Sharing with the fellas,' she smirked. 'At least we can cop an eyeful of what's worth having.'

Rebka locked her bag in the bedside cabinet, and waited, gossiping along with the rest of them while the next two busloads of their fellow employees arrived. It was midday when an HDA lieutenant came in and clapped his hands for attention. 'Okay people, this is the way it is; I'm here to tell you that you're here because HDA is mounting an expedition to St Libra's Brogal continent to measure genetic variance. We're trying to find out if there's any truth to the rumour of an as-yet unclassified sentient alien species living in the deep jungles. To do this we will be establishing a number of forward camps from which the science teams will operate. As this is a joint military and scientific mission, you will be on the civilian side providing food and general domestic support. Environment-suitable clothing will be issued to you at sixteen hundred hours. You will be transporting through the gateway tomorrow, and will immediately forward to Abellia. Please do not leave the base, that will screw up our schedule, and will result in a heavy financial penalty for you and your company. Any questions, please use your e-i to access the base AI which will have an expedition FAQ function operating within the hour. Company supervisors, you will be issued with specific organizational requirement details at nineteen hundred hours at the NCO briefing, block D, room 629. Do not be late. Thank you.'

He walked out. The dormitory was silent for several seconds after he vanished. Then everyone started talking at once.

'Crap on that,' Lulu exclaimed. 'What's Brogal, anyhow?'

'St Libra's northern continent,' Rebka said.

'Aye, pet, isn't that where Brinkelle North lives?'

'Yeah. I think it might be.' And cover or not, Rebka couldn't help a slow smile of satisfaction.

*

The hectic activity right across the base allowed Rebka to wander around unchallenged as long as she didn't try to walk into any of the high-security areas. Everyone she passed wore the slightly dazed expression of people roused from a decent sleep to perform an unexpectedly urgent task. There was smartdust smeared every-where, of course, with secure meshes linked to AIs with powerful facial characteristics recognition software, who would build a file of her movements. She didn't care – she had nothing to hide at this juncture, so all the file would show if anyone ever bothered to access it was an excited, curious young civilian girl taking an awed look round the base, jumping out of the way of uniformed staff and cargo lorries.

Standing beside a big maintenance garage where engineers were running checks on several lorries she told her e-i to call Clayton, using one of their disposable routing addresses; that way no one could ever trace the call recipient. The call itself was core-encrypted, with an overlay of false data that was a preloaded conversation between Madeleine and her boyfriend.

'I'm in,' Rebka told him. 'We're all getting shipped out to St Libra tomorrow.'

'Well done. The expedition has hit the news, it's getting blanket coverage.'

'Figures. Any leads on the murder?'

'We're still running down the taxi route to the GSW area. It's taking a while – someone knocked out a lot of sensors across town. That implies the killer has either a team or a lot of friends in low places. Trouble is, no one wants to accept that.'

'Really?'

'Well, Hurst knows the score, and most of his old team are with him, I think, but the HDA isn't accepting anything that might run counter to the official explanation.'

'Figures.'

'On which front, Elston has requested that all the A 2Norths are genetically tested to confirm there's no imposter in their ranks.'

'Wow, how did that go down?'

'Hang around the front gate. Aldred is on his way to the base for a face to face with Elston.'

Rebka chuckled. 'Should be fun.'

'There's someone else arriving in about eight minutes if the traffic doesn't get any worse.'

'Who?'

'Pizza delivery boy.'

'Fascinating.'

'Angela paid for it. I'm tracking her Social bank account to get a handle on her.'

'Smart move,' Rebka conceded.

'It means you can get a visual if you want.'

'This is a bit early. I'll think about it.' The call ended, and Rebka hovered outside the big garage undecided. 'Oh what the hell,' she muttered eventually. 'Got to happen sometime.'

The traffic must have been okay. It was almost exactly eight minutes later when the pizza boy turned up at the main gate on a three-wheel franchise scooter. The guards made him park it to one side, and he pulled a stack of big pizza boxes out of the rear thermal pannier before walking through the side gate.

Rebka followed unobtrusively as he headed over to block C. It was an unrestricted area, so her e-i pulled up a floorplan for her. The delivery boy didn't have far to go, heading straight for the large gym on the first floor. Rebka watched him push through the swing doors without hesitation, and she sidled up to them as they closed. There was a long window set into them, and she peered through.

A squad of GE Legionnaires were running through their exercises: pushing weights, running on treadmills, two of them were hammering the hell out of punchbags. Angela Tramelo was with them, dressed in an orange vest top and loose tracksuit trousers to show a body that was almost as fit as the soldiers around her, running on a treadmill with an expression of quiet determination set on her sharp-featured face. That determination was quite something, Madeleine thought; Angela was a woman who could carry focus to the ultimate extreme. But then that was just confirmation of a trait Jupiter had suspected for a very long time.

For some reason, Rebka found herself gripping the little glass phial she carried round her neck on a silver chain. Grounding herself. It eased away any anxiety that had been brewing. She watched the exercise session come to an end as the Legion squad descended on the pizza boy with cheerful whoops and shouted thanks. Angela switched the treadmill off and joined them, snatching up a big slice of Hawaiian pizza, with cheese strings stretching out. She chatted easily with her companions, with just a hint of flirtatiousness when it came to a couple of the men. If she hadn't known otherwise, Rebka would've assumed she was just another member of the squad, so tight was the camaraderie. And who could fail to appreciate that strategy? Angela was integrating herself perfectly. When it came down to that crucial moment the squad would be reluctant to act against her.

'Brilliant,' Rebka whispered, and backed away from the gym. She'd been expecting a swirl of emotional turmoil at the first glimpse, but instead all she could feel was a surprisingly strong sense of admiration.

Even now, even being the professional friend with Lulu, Rebka could never be as easy with people as Angela clearly was (and that after twenty years locked up in the hellhole of prison). Rebka was sure her own underdeveloped social skills came from her early life. She still couldn't remember anything prior to her fifth birthday. Her parents, Monique and Carvell, told her that was because she'd been very ill from birth. It was only due to the excellent geneticists at Jupiter that she had survived at all. The essential gene therapy that had resequenced her DNA had taken years.

She'd been discharged from hospital a day before her fifth birthday, allowing her to go home and have her very first party. That was the day her proper memories began, the moment her life truly started.

*

Sid and his team identified twenty-nine taxis entering into the zone around the Fawdon GSW area on the Sunday night. Mesh coverage around the actual boundary was about the worst in the city, with only the other three GSW areas attempting to rival it. So they had no idea which one actually wound up as the burn-out. They ran the simulation forward until morning, but only two were recorded as emerging by midday on the Monday morning; although plenty of taxis had driven away from the district, none of them had licences or codes which matched any of the twenty-seven which had gone in.

Sid called a halt then. 'Half of the morning shift is going to be operating on false registrations,' he told Ralph Stevens. 'The fare money will go into secondary accounts registered in Vietnam or Dubai or Chechnya so the Tax Bureau doesn't show an interest.'

'I thought Nigeria was favourite for secondaries,' Ralph muttered.

'Our gangs like to spread the load.'

'Huh! So now . . . ?'

'So now we backtrack the twenty-seven taxis which wound up around Fawdon that night, and see which of them came from Elswick Wharf.'

It was meticulous work, sometimes requiring the simulation to be shifted in two-second intervals when a taxi hit a particularly bad junction. By six thirty that evening they'd followed eight of them on various routes picking up and dropping off various fares. A task made even more difficult in two cases by the taxis switching registration codes while they were cruising between fares. But in the end all eight had been cleared – they hadn't been anywhere near Elswick Wharf.

'Are we squealing on them to the Tax Bureau?' Ian asked.

Sid shrugged. Both of them were in the theatre's control centre, taking a break from wading through the simulation while Ari and Reannha took a turn scratching their heads over what turn the ninth taxi was taking when it vanished into a dead space. 'We've got enough on right now,' he said, which wasn't a flat-out 'no'. The internal sensors could always be reviewed – unlikely . . . but. Besides who didn't have a secondary these days? Grande Europe taxes were so high they were a joke – his official city police salary was taxed at over fifty per cent, and that was before pension contributions. He might be police, but he was people, too.

Ian just nodded.

Abner came into the control room. He seemed to be a permanent fixture in Office3 right now, Sid thought. His brother's murder must have affected him more than he showed. Constant devoted work was clearly his way of dealing with it.

'I've just been talking to Tilly Lewis over at Northern Forensics,' Abner said. 'They've finished their review of the road metamesh.'

Ian turned away from the simulation. 'And?'

Abner grinned. 'Twenty per cent natural glitches and breakdown. But the other eighty per cent, between the GSW and Elswick, were deliberately taken out. The gang ripped most of the wall meshes. But the smartdust in the tarmac was zapped with a magnetic pulse. It's completely dead, you can't reactivate it. This was all done on Saturday night. They started at about seventeen hundred hours. The last failure is logged at one thirty-seven next morning. We think they must have used three to five cars with a mag pulse generator on the bottom.'

'Crap on it,' Ian grinned happily. 'That's going to take a lot of additional people to correlate.'

'Did the surviving meshes catch anything?' Sid asked.

'I pulled the logs for the approach roads of ten junctions they zapped,' Abner said. 'When I ran a correlation there was no overlap. They'll be switching licence codes on the vehicles between each strike.' He nodded through the window at the sparkling simulation. 'If you want them, you'll have to run a correlation exercise on your great big virtual.'

'Aye, man, no way can we take the time out for an operation like that,' Sid said. 'It'd be a step backwards, not cost effective for the case. It took days to work up a simulation for Sunday night, we can't take another couple of days to work up Saturday as well.'

'Thought so,' Abner said in a resigned tone.

'What about the mesh rips?' Sid asked.

'They've got good byteheads, is about the best I can tell you,' Abner said grudgingly. 'I couldn't spot where the attacks got into the monitor network, let alone where they originated from. But the rip they used is powerful, the same as the one that caused the surge around Elswick. The city's not going to like it, but they'll have to strengthen the whole countermeasures suite. Frankly we were lucky they didn't fry every mote of public smartdust in Newcastle. The rip is certainly powerful enough.'

'These guys are more precise,' Sid said. 'They're not flash, not showy. Face it, the only stroke of bad luck they've had so far was the body getting snagged at Millennium Bridge.'

'I've got an hour before I'm off shift,' Ian said. 'Let me run another quick review of the junctions. I've done positional correlations enough bloody times before.'

'Thanks,' Sid said. 'I'll give Trose Secure a call, they're good, but the city can't normally afford them; stick them on analysing the rip attack. Abner, you stay here and help Dedra run the simulation. I want everyone familiar with the theatre procedures anyway. It's starting to look like we'll be pulling an all-nighter.'

'Sure thing, boss.'

*

As Sid's nominal deputy, Ian Lanagin just qualified for one of the little private offices along the side of Office3. He greeted the eight officers and constables working the zone consoles in the main section, all of them busy processing forensics data from the taxi, which was slowly coming in, along with results from the dump site; three were still checking cargo deliveries; while one poor junior constable was tasked with calling local restaurants and finding out what meals they were serving last Thursday evening – a long shot based on the autopsy results of the victim's stomach contents.

Once he settled behind his desk he called up the forensics results for the magnetic pulse assault on the junctions' smartdust, then linked to the city's traffic management AI and requested approach road logs, letting them download into the secure police network. Once that was underway he used his authority code to activate the Kenny Ansetal case file on his console. Nothing had been done, of course, it was currently classed as neutral. In another week, if there hadn't been any entries or follow-on

194

activity, the station AI would automatically downgrade it to inactive status.

The results materialized in the console zone, and he called up the profiles of Gail Stratton and Kayleen Edenson, the two witnesses he'd chatted to. He had to use his authority code again, but a minute later their financial records were on the screens in front of him. He noted on the official log that he was looking for a payment transfer indicating one of them had sold the i-3800. He also opened the finance records to full data display for a month before the incident, which quadrupled the information on the screens, showing outgoing payments, their purchases, as well as income. It began to scroll down, and he scanned it methodically for the kind of entry he wanted. Bar accounts were easy to spot, he knew the names of Newcastle's clubland well enough. Pattern analysis was instinctive, part of his detective's training, aided by years of experience. Heavy spending early in the evening, soon tailing off. The girls bought their own drinks to start with, the kind of spending which usually expired mid-evening. Someone else stepped in to buy the drinks: QED, they didn't have regular boyfriends.

He was equally adept at recognizing the supplementary data points. Clothes store accounts dropped through the zone display, and he quickly read along the line, seeing what they'd bought with a well-practised eye. He found everything he needed within five minutes, but let the scroll continue so no one could really determine what he'd looked at. Their basic profiles also showed their ages, which decided it for him.

With their profiles and finances closed back into the case file, he used a patch program to monitor Gail's e-i location through the city communication routers. The patch allowed him to piggyback the tracer request on the North case authority. There was so much data flowing into that sub-network it was unlikely anyone would spot it without a full forensics audit. Even so, it wasn't logged as his request – good old Ari had that honour. A phishing tap had caught his codes yesterday.

That done, Ian spent the remaining forty minutes trying to spot any vehicle that kept turning up at the same time that junction smartdust was scorched in a magnetic flash. Abner had been right, whoever was doing it were very professional, they were switching licence codes.

He signed out of the station at seven thirty, and took his car home for a quick shower and a change. By eight fifteen he was back out on the street, and calling a taxi, ready and eager for everything the glorious city could offer a single man on a Saturday night.

'Where to?' the driver asked.

Ian consulted Gail's location icon flashing away in his iris smartcell grid. 'The Indigo Parrot,' he said, a reasonable enough club in Newgate Street.

She'd be surprised to see him. They normally were, but that was always a good opening line of the Lanagin bullshit charm offensive. Information ruled all in this century, the ultimate currency; and his edge – drinking a whole lot deeper than most from the eternal datastream – made him very wealthy indeed. He knew her age, height, bra size, weight, that she was on the market, and as a nice little bonus, her medical record which showed she was clean of any STDs; all knowledge to be manipulated to his advantage.

Ian closed the secure link to the station and settled back to enjoy the ride.

Sunday 20th January 2143

It was another cloudless winter morning, clear cold air allowing the sun to shine hard and bright on the winter-bound city. There was no heat in the radiance, so the sunlight made little impression on the banks of snow other than sending a few trickles of slush leaking across the roads and pavements.

Traffic in the centre of Newcastle was sluggish. The ring road was closed to all non-HDA traffic for the day. Sometime just after midnight a pair of Airbus C-121T-FC SuperRocs had flown in to Newcastle airport, their massive Rolls-Royce Thames engines waking up half of the city as they flew low overhead. Deliberately, Vance Elston felt; making their presence known, emphasizing the HDA's authority and purpose. The Norths might own the city, but even they had to acknowledge it was the HDA who ultimately called the shots. It was the expedition which dominated everyone's thoughts now, and the procession of planes and vehicles around the city was turning the day into a carnival. Thousands of residents were ignoring the cold, and lining the route to enjoy the spectacle of heavy military-style machinery heading through the gateway. Short of a full Zanthswarm deployment, it was the greatest action the St Libra gateway would probably ever see. Who wanted to miss that?

Vance's limousine slowed as it approached the western end of Mosley Street, and the auto negotiated the snow piles blocking the gutter to pull up close to the pavement. He stepped out and stared up at the ancient stone steeple of the St Nicholas Cathedral, frowning at its odd little gold and scarlet wooden box halfway up which housed the clock. The bells were ringing cheerfully, and a reasonable number of people were answering the call for the holy day's communion service – mostly elderly, Vance noticed with some disapproval. Didn't young people have time for the Lord these days? Major Vermekia and Antrinell Viana were waiting outside the ornate age-darkened wooden doors set back into the entrance archway.

Vance greeted Vermekia warmly. 'Busy time?' he asked.

'I'm so jetlagged right now I'm gonna loop round on myself and bite my own ass,' Vermekia grumbled. 'The General sends his personal greetings, and wishes you bon voyage.'

'Tell him: thank you. Much appreciated,' Vance said.

The three of them moved to one side, away from the mildly curious gaze of well-dressed parishioners entering the cathedral.

'Jupiter called back,' Vermekia said. 'Constantine in person answered the General's questions. He completely denied that they were in any way involved in the murder.'

'Well he would, wouldn't he?' Antrinell said.

'Maybe. And while we're on deniability, Constantine also said they never found a sentient on St Libra, but admitted that doesn't mean there isn't one. Fair enough, it's a big planet.'

'Any word on when we're shipping out?' Vance asked.

'Nah, the General wants to see where the investigation leads. He's going to give it a few more days to allow the logistics corps to get their act together, but realistically it's impossible to issue a recall order now.'

'Detective Hurst's team is working quite hard, actually,' Vance admitted. 'They've put together an impressive virtual of the city so they can attempt to trace the murderer's movements last week.'

'Is it an alien?' Vermekia asked directly.

'If it is, it had local help.'

'Huh. Well we've got enough nut-jobs worshipping the Zanth.

If there's another species lurking about on St Libra it's probably got its followers, too.'

'What worries me most about this is if the sentients have found a way though the gateway undetected. It isn't a pleasant thought, but it would explain a lot.'

'True. How's Tramelo working out?'

'Freedom-happy the first day,' Vance said. 'Testing her boundaries, which was only to be expected. But she's quiet for now. She's definitely one person who firmly believes the alien exists.'

'You want to interrogate her again?'

'Not necessary. Not yet. I am concerned about her past, whatever it is; but I can see how troubled she is by the alien. She thinks it's going to kill us all if we give it a chance.' He gave Vermekia a significant look.

'And you?'

'There are too many inconsistencies for this to be an ordinary murder, even as part of a covert corporate operation,' Vance admitted.

'And the kill methodology is one giant consistency,' Vermekia concluded. 'What about Jay Chomik's detector systems?'

'Nothing,' Antrinell sighed. 'The city is ringed tight with them now. If a Zanth molecule sneezes, we'll know about it.'

Vance grinned. 'I like the metaphor, but this isn't Zanth. Not its style.'

'I'm glad you know so much about it,' Vermekia said. 'But something is killing Norths; and for all they're a bunch of weird clones, they're valuable to trans-stellar civilization as a whole.'

'I've reviewed Tramelo's testimony and the autopsy on the 2North,' Antrinell said. 'I've got to say, to me it looks like a guy in some kind of weird power suit or with dark cyborg implants.'

'If it's a lone psycho, why wait twenty years between killings?' Vermekia asked.

'That's one question on psychology, one query. And we're putting together a multi-billion-dollar expedition because of it? That's too extreme.'

'The expedition was launched because of the uncertainty. We have to know. We *have* to.'

Antrinell gave a reluctant sigh. 'I get that. But didn't anyone in the general staff science team mention just how unlikely it is for bipedal life to evolve anywhere else? There's no evidence for it on all the planets we've visited. Hell, Guanimaro animals don't even have limbs, and they get along fine.'

'The general science staff did a very lengthy review,' Vermekia said. 'First off, Sirius is close, and that opens up astrogenic theory, that basic life in this galaxy is spread between stars by microbes.'

'No way. It used to be called panspermia theory, and it was finally disproved a century ago. Nothing complex enough to reproduce itself, even a monobacterium hitching a lift on an interstellar comet, can maintain its molecular integrity for that kind of timeframe in a vacuum at absolute zero.'

'It wasn't disproved because it can't be. You can't run an experiment to check it. All that happened was one bunch of scientists with a counter-theory carried the day over its proponents back then. That's all. It's an argument over statistics and probability. In other words, nobody has a clue.'

Antrinell threw his hands in the air, shaking his head. 'Whatever.'

'Secondly, and more relevantly, is St Libra's biosphere itself,' Vermekia said. 'It's a real anomaly; this no animals or insects environment is unique. Suspiciously unique. No other world we've found has just plants. Now, there's never been a lot of research into St Libra's fossil record. Highcastle only has one university, and that concentrates on turning out bioil engineers for the algaepaddies and refineries rather than archaeobotanists. But there are a couple of teams working on St Libra, and the results that have trickled in over the last thirty years give us cause for concern. As far as they've found, there was no life on St Libra prior to about one and a half million years ago.'

Vance frowned at the information. 'I didn't know that.'

'It's all buried in obscure academic journals. And again, they've not conducted many digs, and you can't judge a planet St Libra's size from eight sample points close together on one continent. There's also the problem that St Libra's zebra botany is simply too sophisticated even if you disregard the lack of a fossil record. That's a young star, don't forget. Plants that complex shouldn't have had time to evolve. All of which has the general science staff postulating that what we have on St Libra is an artificial bioforming event instead of natural evolution. In other words, someone manufactured St Libra's biosphere. A couple of million years ago, a whole batch of bacteria and seeds were dumped on that planet and left to get on with it.'

'Creation time,' Vance grinned.

The others chuckled appreciatively.

'The only reason you do that is if you're developing real estate for your own species,' Antrinell concluded.

'I don't believe it,' Vance said. 'Nobody thinks in those kinds of timescales.'

'Nobody human,' Vermekia countered.

'If it had been bioformed ready for species expansion, then they would've been able to take possession after a few thousand years.'

'Maybe. Nobody is asking why they haven't turned up yet. But it's another huge question mark hanging over St Libra. Imagine what the formers would think if they came back to check on their project and they find our algaepaddies leaking terrestrial biocrap all across their landscape. Maybe it's a freaking art project – if you have the technology to bioform on an interstellar level, you certainly don't have economics as we know it. Or it's an emperor's nature park. We don't know, and that's the point. That's why the expedition is going ahead.'

'If there's a sentient on St Libra, we'll find it,' Vance said.

'I'm sure you will.' Vermekia gestured at the cathedral entrance as the bells fell silent. 'Shall we go in, gentlemen. Your mission could do with every blessing our good Lord can bestow, and who knows when you'll get a chance to pray properly again.'

*

Crowds lined Newcastle's western A1 ring road more or less its whole length, from the junction with the A696 airport link road to Last Mile and the gateway itself. The banks beside the bridge over the Tyne at Lemington provided a great place to watch from. Everyone on the slopes stared across the gulf in awed fascination as the first double-deck SuperRoc approached the crossing. The carriageways were barely wide enough to take the main undercarriage bogies, and then people started to wonder if the bridge would actually hold the weight. A fully loaded SuperRoc weighed in at over 600,000kg, but operational empty weight was barely 300,000kg, which the bridge would be able to handle.

A praetorian guard of technicians in their uniform grey-green HDA parkas scurried around the massive plane as it crept forwards. The tow-tractor had its auto firmly disengaged as the driver steered it down the exact centre of the bridge. A vanguard of the parka figures checked the ice and snow had been properly cleared from the tarmac as the nose undercarriage reached the bridge – nobody wanted a loss of traction now. More parka people swarmed around the main undercarriage, verifying clearance.

The SuperRoc made it over the bridge just after nine in the morning, and everyone cheered as it rolled onward around the ring road. The second SuperRoc and three more Daedalus strategic airlifters followed sedately.

Sid had brought Jacinta and the kids to a vantage point at the end of the car park that used to serve Bensham Hospital, just above the train line that bordered the eastern side of Last Mile. The hospital was half-demolished, with the developers awaiting various city permits to redevelop the area with a trio of lavish thirty-storey office towers. Its proximity to the gateway itself, which was just a few hundred metres away, made it one of the most valuable chunks of real estate currently available in New-castle. Quite how that particular section of city-owned land came to be sold off had caused five councillors to be placed under investigation by the regional budget scrutiny office.

But pressed up against the car park's tall galvanized metal fence, the Hurst family did have a splendid view across the lumpy solar roofs of Last Mile buildings to the gateway itself. The metal road ramp which led into the trans-spacial connection was empty. It had been lowered, settling down on the exit route below, so freeing up more of the gateway to take the bulk of the planes. All other traffic to St Libra, commercial and personal, had been suspended; even the constant stream of emigrants on foot had to wait for once. Today they had to mill around at the entrance to Last Mile until the HDA transit was complete.

'Why are they all going to St Libra?' Zara asked, as the towing tractor hauling the first SuperRoc turned off the A1 at the Lobley junction, and crawled slowly into Last Mile, curving round to line up on the grey haze of the oval gateway.

'It's an expedition, stupid,' Will taunted his sister.

'Yes but *why*?'

'They're exploring Brogal,' Jacinta said. 'We don't know very much about that continent, and the HDA is checking to make sure it's safe.'

'Why wouldn't it be safe?'

'There have been reports of possible alien sightings,' Sid said, repeating the official explanation and hating himself for doing it.

'The Zanth?' Zara asked anxiously.

'No, not Zanth, darling. Something else. They don't know what, that's why they're looking. It's probably nothing, but they have to make sure, that's their job.' He exchanged a glance with Jacinta, who was struggling to hold in her contempt.

'It's on the ramp, look,' Will said, pointing eagerly through the fence.

Directly ahead of them, the tow-tractor's fat front tyres trundled up the slight incline. Sid wasn't sure if it could pull the giant plane up a slope, even one as gentle as this one had been reduced to. He put his arm round Zara, giving her an affectionate squeeze.

'Is it going to fit, Daddy?' she asked.

'It should do,' Sid said doubtfully. It would certainly be close. The SuperRoc's wings were folded back flat along its fuselage. It was a feature designed into every plane the HDA ordered, since they all had to pass through gateways and be mission-ready as soon as they were on the other side. The tall twin tailfins were also hinged down.

Will grimaced as the tractor crawled into the gateway's distortion haze. Then the SuperRoc's nose slipped in. The parka people congregating around and underneath the plane were becoming more animated. Green laser fans swept out from the oval portal, measuring the plane's position and clearances. It inched onwards.

Sid almost winced as the engine pods reached the gateway. The plane was going really slowly now, with measurements being taken constantly. Technicians clustered under the jet pods, arms gesticulating wildly. He was sure there could have been only a few centimetres clearance. But slowly and surely the plane carried on.

The crowd in the car park was cheering and whistling enthusiastically as the pods passed across to St Libra, then it was just the tapering rear fuselage left.

'Back in a minute,' Sid told Jacinta. She gave him a disapproving look, but nodded.

'Daddy, where are you going?' Zara asked in dismay. 'The next airplanes are just arriving.'

'I've seen an old friend,' he said, and started worming through the tightly packed throng of people pressing up along the fence. He ignored the irritated looks flashed his way as he pushed and shoved. Eventually he wound up at the back of the crowd, standing beside what first impressions marked as a rounded hump of traditional camelhair topped by another, smaller hump, this one of red and yellow wool. Sid could just make out a face in the small gap between coat and hat. Detective (retired) Kaneesha Saeed had dark Asian skin, mottled by a shoal of ebony blemishes, oily tips of curly black hair peeked out from the constricted rim of the hand-knitted hat, and her glasses had bulging lenses which distorted her hazel eyes. It had been nearly four years since Sid had seen her last, and in the intervening time he guessed she'd doubled her weight – at least. On someone who barely came up to his shoulder, it made her appear almost spherical.

'Thanks for seeing me,' he said.

Kaneesha took a drink from her Costa espresso cup. 'Sure. I heard you got suspended.'

'I'm back on duty now.'

'Good for you, pet.'

Sid guessed that suspension was a kind of final approval stamp for Kaneesha. She'd applied for early retirement six years ago, accepting a heavily reduced pension for getting out ahead of at least three internal audits. Not that she'd needed to worry about money: she now lived in a penthouse apartment on Quayside, just east of Ouseburn; then there was a second home on Sao Jeroni, the Brazilian world. Word around Market Street Station was that she could afford the life because of gang payoffs, which was pretty much a standard reaction; though Sid had heard senior officers like O'Rouke were worried she'd been a full-on gang member since the day she walked into the city recruitment office and began her constable cadet training – which was the true reason they allowed her to take retirement and quietly get the hell out of the service. Because if it ever got out that the police had been infiltrated ... Sid didn't know, and wasn't about to judge. They'd worked together a couple of times. Got a decent result.

'Quite a sight, huh.' He indicated the second SuperRoc which was now starting up the gateway ramp.

'Why is it a sight, Sid? Why are they bothering?'

'I can't say, man. I got me a gravity case right now.'

Kaneesha grinned around the cup's plastic lid. 'Can't escape, huh? I remember those.'

'The North carjacking. It might be connected to all this, you never know.'

Kaneesha finally paid him some real attention, her glasses' lenses giving her pupils a weird magnification as they focused on him. 'You playing with the big boys, Sid?'

'Yeah.'

'Aye, well you be careful, pet. They don't play nice.'

'I will be, thanks.'

'How's the family?'

'Growing fast. I need to know a few things that aren't on file, Kaneesha.'

She looked away, sipping more coffee. 'Like what?'

'Where do the gangs touch the corporates?'

Kaneesha spluttered on her espresso. 'Fuck, Sid, you can't ask me that.'

He smirked at the classic reaction, maybe feeling some satisfaction. 'Why not?' The second case they'd worked on produced a bad moment. Kaneesha had been trailing a suspect, and got jumped by a group of street punks. It wasn't a planned ambush, she just hit the wrong place at the wrong time – standard police nightmare. Sid had broken off his end of the tail and waded into the fight, using a multi-fire taser and some non-regulation high-strength teargas he just happened to be carrying in a non-standard extended-range dispenser. 'We don't have any secrets, you and me.'

'Sure we do, pet.'

'I have this problem, see. They gave me the North case, and I don't think I can solve it with standard procedures. I need another way in. And it looks like the North might have been caught up in some kind of corporate crap.'

'Aye, I thought that bullshit about a carjacking was pretty lame.'

'Bought me some time,' Sid said.

Kaneesha gave the massive plane edging through the gateway a more thoughtful look. 'And this is the result. What the fuck are they scared of, Sid?'

'It's not the first time a North's been killed. Remember Bartram?'

206

'Aye, just about, me e-i would have to pull the files to be sure.'

'Whatever the reason that North died last week, the killer had a lot of help dumping the body – and I'm short of leads. Come on, there must be something; you led the city's Gang Task Force. There must be some contact between them and the corporations.' He studied what was visible of Kaneesha's face, seeing how the multitude of tiny dark blemishes were dry and cracked. Some had even been bleeding – they looked sore. And she had gloves on, he couldn't check her hands.

'Not as much as you'd think, nor the transnet dramas make out,' Kaneesha said reluctantly. 'The corporate lads have their own dark teams to handle any dirty work for their security departments. Completely deniable, of course. You'd never find a connection that would stand up in court.'

'Aye man, come on, help me out here. I've got to produce something for O'Rouke and the Norths, something solid, else I'm right down the crapper.'

'The corporates do have some contact, but it's usually all small scale. They need pimps to provide some decent-looking girls and boys for visiting execs, on top of that you can throw in some hardcore tox, but that's the kind of level I'm talking.'

'Come on!' She was stringing him out like a pusher, and enjoying it too if he was any judge.

'Maybe. Hypothetical, like, pet; if there's a dirty breaker op going down, they might just use some street troops for the sharp end, put another level between them and it.'

'A breaker? What's one of them, then?'

Kaneesha sighed. 'What do they teach at the academy these days? All the St Libra bioil producers, the big ones led by Northumberland Interstellar, they like to keep a hard lid on any oil futures market. They don't like anyone but themselves making profits from the fruit of their labours. So they break anything that threatens to change the price as they set it, which is enough to make a healthy profit but not enough to strangle the trans-stellar economy. You know they have whole office blocks of economists working out what that price should be? It's quite a delicate balancing act between growth and recession. After all, nobody wants to turn back the clock to the depression which followed the 2092 Zanthswarm – that took two decades for us to climb out of. See, pet, nowadays, the price of bioil actually has nothing to do with production costs and quantity, it's meticulously calculated to the last percentage point so as not to cause any dip in the trans-stellar finance markets. When the 2111 cartel stepped in and stabilized the market, they wound up controlling a big slice of the entire bioil market process, and they aren't going to give that up without a very nasty fight. So if anybody was trying to mess with that, to reintroduce a futures market in some backdoor fashion, then I'm not surprised they wound up floating along the Tyne.'

'Why would a North want to mess with the current arrangement?'

'Maybe he wasn't, that's the point you're getting at, pet, isn't it? The other guys are going to be just as tough. Think what's at stake here.' She waved her coffee cup towards the gateway. 'See those pipes down there under the ramp? Ever think just how big they are, how much bioil they can pump through per second? Everyone lies about St Libra production only providing GE and its affiliate planets with eighteen per cent of our bioil. True figure is more – a lot more. No one else wants those bloody great algaepaddies leaking all across their nice new clean worlds; and Earth's soil is too valuable for anything other than food crops – that battle was won a century ago. But nobody's going to admit how dependent we are, because St Libra is this niggling little embarrassment to Brussels, in that it's the one gateway they don't have political control over. It belongs to the Norths, and they aren't about to hand it over to any Euro Bureau.'

'Crap on it,' Sid murmured. 'I'd heard it was fifteen per cent. Are you sure?'

'Oh yeah, at least. So if you want to try and go up against that monolith monopoly with its vested interest and unlimited funds and hardcore political support, people on the sharp end are going to get hurt. Then of course you've got plenty of bioil subsidiary markets to choose from; you could target emission bonds, carbon-exchange certificates, clean-burn validates, double-back users, post-spot delivery leverages – they're all open to manipulation if you've got the balls. So if you're mad and ballsy enough to run with a market sting along those lines then at the very minimum you're going to need some serious hardcases, people who know how to corrupt your rival's staff and smooth over problems fast. That'll be those dark teams, they're the ones who'll have contacts with the street-level lowlifes that are going to be paid to run the truly shitty jobs. No way you're going to crack that nut, pet, it is way too tough. Even if you reel someone in on suspicion, they'll take an exile to Minisa or a twenty-year sentence over doing any kind of plea bargain with you. They're not stupid.'

'I'm not so sure about that. I've got the HDA backing me up, and they can be persuasive.'

'That doesn't scare these people. But it does worry me. I'm out and clean, pet; I don't need my name bobbing up in official circles again.'

'Crap on it! Kaneesha, I don't even know you. I need some names, man, for me not for them. You're killing me out here. Someone in the gangs who gets to talk with a corporate. Come on.'

She shook her head, and poured the dregs of her espresso onto the packed snow of the car park, watching the dirty brown liquid melt the crust. 'I know dozens. All dead since I got out. Does that tell you anything?'

'Kaneesha!'

'Why don't you ask your friend Aldred? Work this from the other side.'

He glared at her. 'You're still in.'

'No.' She jabbed a gloved finger at her face. 'I watched your brain making notes when you saw my face. This shit I've got, this has to be dealt with. I have to go away, a long way away, pet, to find the kind of gene therapy that will get me through this. And that's expensive. I'm not taking any risks. I've lived risk for too long now. That part of my life is over.'

'One fucking name, Kaneesha. One! You owe me that. There's no risk in that.'

'I'll think about it.' She turned and started off across the car park towards the rusting exit barriers.

'Kaneesha!'

'Don't call me again, not ever. I'll call you. Maybe.'

Sid watched her waddling away, his jaw clenched hard; he wanted to run after her, to swing her round and shout some more, make her understand how he *needed* this. It would be useless, he knew. Besides, she'd said *maybe*. In the kind of world she lived in that was like a gold-plated promise.

*

After the second Daedalus went through the gateway, Sid drove Jacinta and the kids back into the city centre, and parked in the Market Street Station. It was convenient for the shops, and he didn't have to pay a charge.

'And don't even think about "just popping up" to check on your case,' Jacinta warned as they got out of the car.

'I never did,' he protested. 'This is a family day, I told you that.' He ignored the look she gave him; it'd taken a lot of argument before she'd even agreed to him meeting Kaneesha. Besides, his iris smartcell grid had a small real-time display showing him the progress the team was making up in the zone theatre. They'd backtracked eighteen taxis now. None of them had been the one at Elswick Wharf.

They made sure Zara and Will were wrapped up, coats buttoned, scarves tight, gloves on. Then Jacinta led the way to Grey's Monument. With everyone drawn to the spectacle of the planes going through the gateway, the shops were slightly less crowded than usual for a Sunday lunchtime. Sid went into Stanatons, the schools outfitters, in Central Arcade. With its glazed brown tile façade and palm trees beside the door, the shop looked like it belonged to the time when the Arcade was built, two hundred and forty years ago. It was resolutely old-fashioned, with child-sized mannequins wearing the uniforms of a dozen private schools. The sports equipment was modern, though. Sid never did like the idea of kids wearing those big protective helmets with bars across the front. Along with all the padding incorporated in the rest of their field kit it symbolized the official paranoiac anti-risk culture which he so relished sneering at. In his day football had been proper football, none of this tag-tackle rubbish they played at school nowadays. If you got hurt you were more careful next time, it was the only proper way to learn. He always lost that argument with Jacinta, who couldn't bear the idea of her babies being exposed to 'needless harm'. Fortunately Stanatons' mirror was twenty-third century, so Will could rotate the image to see what he looked like from all angles in his new blazer. That led to an argument with his mum about the style and fit. Sid and Zara kept well out of it, browsing the girls' section for things she claimed she couldn't live without. She was right, her school scarf was worn, and the gloves too small. By the time they left they were carrying three bags, and Sid's secondary account was down five hundred Eurofrancs. Half of Europe's population had secondaries, funded by moonlighting jobs or off-book bonuses.

Sid's police force salary went through valid channels, but his job provided a whole range of opportunity for enhancing cash flow. Keeping the balance was the tricky aspect; too many police reacted like kids in a gamer store, overreaching themselves the moment they cleared probation. They made themselves easy targets for extortion by gangs and investigation from Tax Bureau inspectors. Sid had steered clear for the first couple of years until he got his promotion; even then he made sure he was never ostentatious enough to warrant investigation, and he never had bothered with the petty stuff: the local defence lawyers who needed evidence to glitch or disappear, club owners, tox kings locked into boundary wars, small businesses venturing into areas without permits. He was in Newcastle for heaven's sake, the town where the bioil money, the truly astronomical numbers, bubbled through every corporate core, enriching everyone it passed.

After six months of quiet good-boy behaviour as a junior detective, he'd extracted a Northumberland Interstellar middle-manager from a potentially nasty situation at a club. It never appeared on any police file, he never asked for anything – which interested people as he knew it would. A couple of days later Aldred himself had sat down with him in a Jamaica Blue coffee franchise to say thank you in person.

Ever since, his secondary had received a monthly retainer from an untraceable account on New Monaco. Occasionally, Aldred would get in touch, and ask some question or other. A question that could only be answered by someone with access to secure government databases. They could get it through a dozen routes, of course, but he was a useful route, a reliable route, a route who understood the etiquette. Right up until last September when he'd made a mistake going through the UK treasury, downloading data on a company which was green tagged for review. Apart from that, his career had gone smoothly, promotions were regular. Even the New Monaco payments had risen, mirroring his police grades.

After the arcade they went to Livie's, halfway along Grey Street, for Sunday lunch. The wide windows in the front of the grand old stone building allowed the kids to watch people and traffic as they drank banana milkshakes from a straw.

'Did you like the house?' Sid asked when the food arrived. They'd all run through the virtual the estate agent had down-loaded, taking turns in the zone so they could see as much or as little as they wanted.

Zara grinned round her straw. 'I know which room I'm having.'

'Oh, do you?'

'The one at the back. You know, when you turn left at the top of the stairs.'

'It's on the right,' Will said with a sneer. 'Don't you know your left from your right?'

Jacinta gave her son a cautionary glance.

'It looks onto the garden,' Zara said, deliberately ignoring her brother. 'I've only ever seen the road from my window before, which is boring. I really like the garden, Daddy. I ran the virtual's season-reveal function, there are so many flowers in the summer.'

'Can we have a squidgoline in it?' Will asked hopefully. 'A really big one, like Eric's got?'

'Not that big,' Sid said, remembering the enormous bouncer-slab Will's friend had in his garden. 'But possibly we can get you one, yes.'

'There's got to be some astonishingly good behaviour from both of you before that ever happens,' Jacinta warned quickly.

'Absolutely,' Sid confirmed. 'And it won't be until summer at the earliest.'

'Aye man, that's extortion,' Will complained.

'Less of that, thank you.' Sid pointed a warning finger.

Will pulled a perfect teenage-sulk face, and poured some gravy over his Yorkshire puddings.

He must have been practising, Sid thought. *Just what is he going to be like when he finally is a teen? Damn, it's not so long away.*

'So you did like the house, then?' Jacinta asked.

'Yeah,' Will and Zara chorused.

She gave Sid a significant look as she rolled her spaghetti onto a fork. 'So?'

A red high-priority icon popped up into Sid's grid. He grinned broadly. It was all he could do not to punch the air in triumph. 'Go for it,' he said. 'Book us a real-world viewing.'

She gave him a surprised look. 'I didn't realize you were that keen.'

'Aye, it's a nice house, pet, and it's in our budget.' The icon was unfolding with geometric precision.

Taxi twenty-two was the one that'd dumped the body at Elswick Wharf.

Monday 21st January 2143

The 22.27 hours Sunday night virtual was centred on Water Street, with the Tyne bordering one side of the theatre, and Scotswood Road the other. Sid stood amid the dilapidated structures on the east of Water Street, looking over the network of small roads that laced the old buildings and shabby industrial sheds together as the land fell down to the water. The layout across the slope wasn't that complicated, hardly a maze. Running right through the middle was an old rail embankment, which was now Cuttings Garden Park, a slash of green amid the urban darkness, a relief for the local residents which included a petting zoo for kids who never got out of the city.

The locale where his legs vanished into the virtual was where the gang's byteheads had done their worst. None of the meshes facing Water Street was active, they'd ripped them apart. The road's smartdust macromesh had been pulsed to death. The AI running the virtual had painted over the outlines with library images from the city's planning department, showing the façade of the buildings in a quiltwork of seasons from bright high summer to grey autumn, wet surfaces, dry panels baking in sunlight, slush, mud, ice ... Nothing from the actual weekend survived.

It was slightly better from halfway up the slope, beyond the dividing line which was the A695 Scotswood Road. Even there, magnifying the image scale made the sensor failures even more prominent. Sid looked down on the six-lane carriageway that was Scotswood Road. Directly below him was the AI construct of the junction with Dunn Street, cutting through the line of car showrooms which lined the south side of the major road. On the eastbound carriageway, just appearing on the image recorded by the mesh of smartcells coating the Citroën showroom's front wall, was the taxi. It was a dark blue verging on black, and absolutely identical to all the other citycabs.

Last night, once they'd established this was the one, Abner, Ralph, Reannha and Eva had run pattern-match programs from the best mesh images they had. There was nothing on the vehicle: no mud-splash, no dint, no scuff that distinguished it from any other. The team had also gone over the route several times, constantly freezing the virtual image in an attempt to actually see the driver. But, as a quick call to Tilly Lewis at Northern Forensics confirmed, the windshield and side windows were all coated in a one-way privacy film. Nobody got to see in, nor did the door open at any time.

'And they changed licence code how many times?' Sid asked.

'Four,' Eva confirmed. She was standing next to him, giving the taxi a pensive stare. 'Each time at a junction they'd disabled.'

'So, they knew which junctions had been taken out.'

'Absolutely, boss. Most times, he'd wait until another taxi was in the junction. This was meticulous planning.' She pointed down at the taxi. 'From where he is now he hangs a U-turn at the Park Road junction and goes right back into the centre of town. Every turn, every nasty bend, every awkward junction: this bastard takes it. It took him forty-eight minutes from this moment until he vanishes into the GSW area.'

'Not bad for city traffic,' Ian commented from inside the zone theatre control centre.

Sid gave him a grin through the glass. 'Aye, man; not bad.' He gazed down at the dowdy riverside area again. 'All right,' he said, very aware of Ralph Stevens standing beside Ian, watching dispassionately. 'This part we have to get perfect. We have to find out where this taxi came from, because that's our murder site. The bastards ripped half of this district's meshes in case we ever did this, so we're going to show them just how much better we are. Let's see.' He turned and glanced down at the little alley next to the building site where the taxi had parked to get rid of the body. 'To get here it had to either come down Water Street, Monarch Road, or Skinnerburn Road. It's practically at the intersection of those three. So, where did it turn onto them? Dedra, our entry perimeter is from Redheugh Bridge, right along Scotwood Road to its junction with Armstrong Drive. We'll start with the two hours leading up to this moment.'

'Yes, boss,' Dedra murmured.

Sid jabbed his finger back into the image of the taxi. 'I want every taxi that drove in. I don't care what colour it is, what its licence code is. Start with the assumption that it's false. Only when we clear it visually and with data confirmation does it get taken out of the zone.'

The projection started to shift, shrinking so the area he'd designated could fit in. All the licensed citycab taxis were high-lighted with neon-blue graphic tags.

'Ari, you join me and Eva in here; we're going to coordinate visual observation alongside Dedra's digital trackers. Ian, set up in Office2, I had it cleared out first thing. I want to investigate every taxi we find. Check with the owner, the management company, the driver, and the fare – confirm what we're seeing in here, even if it's just a ride down the 695.'

'That's going to take a lot of work, boss.'

'I'm going to call O'Rouke, get him to assign us some extra detectives for a couple of days.'

He caught Ian's muted grin through the glass and knew exactly what his deputy was thinking: *rather you than me.*

Ian was right of course. O'Rouke ranted for several minutes before finally, grudgingly, agreeing to transfer even more of the detectives he couldn't spare to Sid's team on a temporary basis.

By lunchtime Office2 was full of detectives making calls to check the route of every taxi that passed through the simulation in the zone theatre. Fifteen of them arrived to take their place at the zone consoles: a bunch of low-grade, poor-performance sickie kings which O'Rouke had managed to offload from other investigation teams, who appreciated being rid of all the deadwood. But the job Sid had given them wasn't difficult, and with Ian riding them hard they only had to make a few calls to substantiate what each vehicle's official log was claiming.

When Vance Elston made his secure call at four o'clock that afternoon, Sid was able to report they'd identified two hundred and seven taxis as being in the area between 20.30 and 22.27 that night.

'What about earlier?' Elston asked immediately.

Sid glanced over at Ralph; they were both in his small side office with the seals active. 'We believe the two-hour timeframe is reasonable. If you have a body in the boot, you don't want to hang around. They will have driven from the murder scene to the river as quickly as they could without drawing attention to themselves.'

'They probably weren't parked up just to throw off our timeline, either,' Ralph said. 'That opens a window for random discovery.'

Elston snorted. 'Did the detectives tell you that?'

'It's logical, and I agree with it.'

'We have a new team checking out the legitimacy of each taxi,' Sid said. 'So we'll start with those we can't account for first. If we still haven't identified it after we've visually reviewed all two hundred and seven in the zone we'll go back to earlier that evening and begin again.'

'How long is this going to take?' Elston asked.

'Realistically we can thoroughly backtrack four to five taxis per day. They're going to be driving all across the city. It takes time to do it properly, and we can't afford to miss a stop.'

'Fifty days!' Elston exclaimed. 'I cannot accept that timescale.'

'It'll only take fifty days if it's the very last one we review,' Sid countered. 'Probability says it'll be about two to three weeks maximum before we hit on it.'

'I remember you saying if we don't catch them in five days we never will.'

217

'Aye, that's in a normal investigation,' Sid said. 'So far, this doesn't qualify as normal on any level.'

'Damn, I was hoping for something a little more encouraging once you'd confirmed the taxi.'

'There's still forensics; they're going through what was left of the taxi. But whoever fireballed it knew what they were doing. Given what we've seen, the way the bodydump team wiped out road macromesh and ripped the wall-mounted smartdust, I want to get the city's Gang Task Force to start pressuring their informants, see if anyone knows anything. If this is your alien, he definitely had help from the locals.'

'We need to keep this investigation secure.'

'It is. In fact bringing in the task force as an alternative line of investigation will help reinforce the carjacking line. That's exactly the kind of crime low-level gangs perform.'

'It's logical,' Ralph said. 'And it could well produce a decent result. We need to open as many lines of enquiry as we can.'

'Are you going native on me?' Elston asked.

'I'm pushing any angle that will uncover what the hell happened last weekend.'

'Okay,' Elston said. 'It has my blessing. And I can even contribute another line of attack for you. It's been agreed that all the A 2Norths will undergo genetic testing. If one of them is a fraud, they won't be able to hide it much longer.'

'That's grand,' Sid said. Off the top of his head he could think of half a dozen ways for an imposter to get round that test, especially if one of the other North families was involved. Samples weren't hard to substitute if you had a couple of hours' warning. 'I've got Trose Secure working on whoever ripped the smartdust meshes; they're about the best in the game. If I can pull in some byteheads for interrogation, we might develop some additional leads into the gang which did this. There was so much activity on Saturday and Sunday that someone somewhere has to be exposed.'

'Okay.'

'I'd like to keep on some of the extra detectives we had assigned to the case today to cover that aspect.'

'It's your investigation,' Elston said. 'Just do it. I'm not here to hold your hand.'

'I'm telling you because I want to be able to call on you in case I get crapped on by O'Rouke over this. I've soaked up another fifteen detectives from the station, there's barely anyone left to cover a mugging in this city, let alone anything serious.'

'Ralph, cover him,' Elston said. 'Anything else?'

'Not today,' Sid admitted. 'This is the legwork phase that every case has to plough through. It's boring but essential.'

'I know everything about good preparation, thank you. Keep the updates coming, and call me the second you get a break.'

'Yes, sir,' Ralph said, but he was already talking to a dead screen.

Sid shook his head in dismay. 'Thanks,' he said to Ralph.

'If I didn't think you were doing a good job, I wouldn't support you.'

'Aye.' Sid reached up and tried to work some of the kinks out of his shoulder muscles. Spending half the day stooped over the zone projection hadn't helped his posture, but spotting the taxis had been critical. It was the one thing he wasn't prepared to delegate.

'You do understand we can't let it take fifty days,' Ralph said.

'Yeah, I know.'

Monday 28th January 2143

The seven o'clock buzz of the alarm clock dragged Sid out of a pleasant dream. He groaned in tired frustration and managed to hit the snooze button before Jacinta could stop him. Whatever the dream was, his fickle memory had chucked it by the time he flopped back onto the mattress.

'You'll have to get them ready this morning,' Jacinta said. She sounded in pain.

His grid loyally opened out, filling his vision with icons and basic text. Nobody had spotted a taxi picking up the North's corpse yet. *Must program a longer gap between waking up and the grid coming on.* 'I know.'

She'd pulled a late shift on Sunday. Good money; but an emergency procedure meant she hadn't got to bed until four.

He told his e-i to mute the grid, and lay there until she started snoring again, then carefully got out of bed. Will and Zara were both stirring. He managed to get them up and into the bathroom without making too much noise. They'd grown used to Mum coming home late and needing to sleep, so they went downstairs quietly, carrying a pile of school clothes from the airing cupboard.

'Well done,' he told them both as they got dressed in front of the old Rayburn cooker in the kitchen. It was a thermo-store model, with a thick black collector slab of phase-change material mounted on the south-facing wall outside where it soaked up heat all summer long. That heat then radiated slowly and constantly into the ovens and hotplates, keeping them warm so they only needed a small electrical boost to bring them up to cooking temperature. It also made the kitchen the warmest room to be in first thing on a winter's morning.

Sid flicked on the Rayburn's quick-boost function and poached some eggs for breakfast.

'Have you both finished your homework?' he asked as they sat down to eat.

'You asked that last night,' Will complained. 'I told you I filed mine on Friday. The school network confirmed and certified. I'm in the clear.'

'I'm not checking up on you,' Sid said. 'Just concerned, that's all.'

'I read all my book, Daddy,' Zara said earnestly. 'I like the pony princess stories.'

Will pulled a face but didn't jeer. Sid gave her an encouraging smile. 'Well done, pet.' Zara was a keen reader, but he couldn't wait for her to get on to more interesting stuff. The teachers all said how important it was to support her at this stage; too many kids went for the easy option of zone interactives as soon as they'd covered the basics.

'So can we have a puppy if we get the new house?' Will asked as he cut up some toast. 'It's easy big enough.'

'A puppy is a lot of work you know,' Sid said. He'd sneaked off on Friday afternoon to visit the house in Jesmond. Ian and Eva had covered for him, loading Ralph down with file after file for review. It wasn't hard – the investigation was amassing a phenomenal amount of data. His initial estimate of backtracking three or four taxis each day had proved somewhat optimistic. On Thursday they'd managed just two. The route one had taken through town was absurdly convoluted, then the fare had been driven out to Morpeth, which required a whole new batch of mesh files to follow. Ralph was there in the office and zone theatre with them; he understood. Elston was less forgiving.

'I'll walk it, Daddy,' Zara promised solemnly. 'Every day.'

'We'll see.'

'See what?' Jacinta asked. She came into the kitchen, wrapped in a big towelling robe, her hair wild. A hand covered a big yawn.

'You should be asleep,' Sid scolded.

'I want to say goodbye to everyone,' she said, and put her arms around Will and Zara, squeezing lovingly. 'Now: see what?'

'If we get a puppy.'

'Only in the new house, Mum,' Zara said.

'Oh.' Jacinta gave Sid an interested look. 'Really?'

'I thought we might put in an offer,' Sid said. 'I went over our finances last night. We can probably afford it – if we get a decent price for this one.'

'Aye pet, are you sure?' Jacinta sat down hard, and reached for the pot of tea.

Sid looked round the table. 'We all liked it, didn't we?'

'Yes!' the kids yelled.

Jacinta sipped some tea, combing a hand back through her hair. 'Blimey.'

'Can't live here for ever,' Sid said, and gripped her free hand. 'Let's go for it. Call the estate agent, make an offer.'

'How much?'

'Go for fifteen per cent under the asking price.'

'It's down as offers in excess of.'

'And if the vendor does get offered more, they'll be very happy. Until then, there's our offer for them to consider.'

'Fifteen per cent?' She sounded uncertain.

'They haven't had a serious offer yet, and it's been on the market for six weeks.'

'Aye, but nobody buys at Christmas.'

'Do you want to try for the house or not?'

'Okay.' She squeezed his hand back. 'I'll call the agent later this morning. Hell, we'll have to get this house valued. And I'm telling you now nobody is coming to view, not even on virtual, until it's been cleaned up. And—'

'Finish your tea,' Sid told her.

*

When Sid walked into Office3 at eight thirty, Tilly Lewis was there waiting for him. As soon as the door seal turned blue she handed over a thick folder of hard copy, and three memory chips.

'Final forensics report on the burn-out taxi,' she said.

'Thanks.' Sid took her though into his side office, and secured it. 'So what have we got?' he asked as he loaded one of the chips into the secure Office3 network, downloading the data into their dedicated memory.

'Everything got burned badly in the fire.'

'Aye man, *that's it?*'

'You saw it. Someone set off a fireball in that taxi, there must have been ten litres of bioil used. We're good, but we can't work miracles.'

'Okay, what about the vehicle's network? Did you manage to recover any of the software fixes?'

'Ah, that's still ongoing. The components had to go to a specialist company in London. They use quantum electron analysis to read the processor circuitry directly. They usually work on aerospace networks, recovering data after a plane crash, so this shouldn't be a stretch for them. But it's not going to be quick.'

'Right. Thanks Tilly.'

'There was something. Not the taxi itself. You remember the bundle of clothes in the boot?'

'Aye.'

'Never bundle clothes if you want them to burn properly. Cloth makes a good insulator, the core of the bundle was intact.' She reached forwards and flicked through the hard copy. 'The shirt had five cuts on the left breast corresponding to the pattern on the body you hauled out of the Tyne, the surrounding area was drenched with blood. Same with the suit: matching cut pattern, and an equivalent large bloodstain.'

'Definitely my victim's then?'

'Yes, the blood DNA confirms he was a 2North. These are the clothes he was wearing when he was killed, and this is the taxi used to ferry the body about. Ah, here we are—' She slipped a sheet across the desk.

Sid looked at the photo of a pair of socks, laid out on a shiny white examination table, with a ruler on one side for scale. They were dark grey, and they'd been singed in patches. He glanced back at Tilly. 'Yeah?'

'The suit came from Hatchar, expensive; but, sadly for us, off-the-peg. That company's GE-wide including affiliate planets, with two shops in Newcastle, and an additional three franchises in local department stores. Same goes for the shirt, a BrollBross; favoured by executives trans-stellar-wide, nothing distinguishing about it. There are ten outlets in Newcastle alone, as well as a netstore that shifts thousands of shirts a day. So what we have is a standard executive management uniform. Exactly the kind of crap I'd expect a 2North to wear.'

Sid's forefinger tapped the photo. 'And these?'

'Made out of drensi wool,' Tilly said triumphantly.

'Be kind, pet; I'm really not a fashionista kind of bloke. Why is that unusual?'

'Drensi isn't actually wool, not off a sheep, anyway. It's the shredded fibre from the sidestalks of a drensi plant – that grows on St Libra.'

Sid gave the photo a more interested stare. 'Away wi'ya?'

'It gets better. Drensi wool is nice, a quality product, feels good to the touch, and reasonably long-lasting. However, it's not exported. They simply couldn't make it cost effective because there's way too much competition and protectionism in the GE to ship any back here. So it's widely used on St Libra as a sheep-wool alternative, but you won't find it anywhere else.'

'The victim has been to St Libra.'

'Yes. It's the only place he could have got those socks.'

'Anything else to substantiate that? Some trace on the suit?'

'No. His suit was cleaned just prior to the murder – we found standard dry cleaning compounds embedded in the weave. His shirt was fresh on that day as far as we can tell, same goes for the underpants and socks. No St Libra spores or traces. It's just the socks that link him to the planet. Exactly the kind of thing you buy when you're away from home.'

'Hmm, any halfwit defence barrister would smash that argument apart in front of a jury, but then I'm never going up in front of a jury with it to start with. It's a lead, and I thank you for that.'

'My pleasure. Our invoice is on its way. Make sure you're sitting down when you access it.'

*

After Tilly had left, Sid read through the whole forensics report on the bundle of clothes from the boot of the taxi. Tilly had been right about most things – the suit and shirt were pricy but commonplace. It was just the socks that gave them a lead. He called Ian and Ralph into his office and put a secure call through to Aldred.

'The suit and shirt are a long shot,' Sid told them. 'But I'm going to assign a data specialist to them anyway. I want to build a list of 2Norths who bought that style of suit, and that specific shirt. If any of them bought both then we'll be getting close.'

'I'll put Johan to work compiling the lists,' Ian said. 'He's good. We'll probably need a warrant, though – companies as big as these get precious about handing over lists of customers.'

'Aye, I'll get the station's legal office on in,' Sid agreed. 'But it's always going to be a long shot. I'm more interested in the socks. Aldred, can you supply me with a list of your brothers who have visited St Libra in the last year?'

'Not a problem; but I'll warn you it's probably about half of us if not more. Northumberland Interstellar management personnel travel through the gateway extensively, certainly at senior level. That's what the job requires. Even I can't get out of it.'

'Eliminating half of you from the enquiry would be a big plus factor right now,' Sid said.

'I understand. You'll have the list this afternoon.'

'Thank you.'

*

That was the easy secure call. At one o'clock Sid was back in his office with Ralph, the blue light glowing coldly around the door, and the windows opaque. It wasn't just Vance Elston calling, the other half of the wallscreen showed Commissioner Monique Passam. She was sitting on some kind of veranda, with big exotic tropical plants just beyond the railing, shimmering a rich emerald in Sirius's intense light.

'Colonel Elston has been briefing me on the progress of your investigation, Detective,' she said in her measured tone, making it sound as if Elston had been handing her something toxic.

The *your investigation* crack wasn't lost on Sid. Already she had established clear water between them in case of a poor result. 'My team has made considerable progress, Commissioner,' Sid said in an equally expressionless tone. 'We've identified the vehicle used to transport the corpse around town, and we're backtracking now to locate the actual murder site.'

'How many taxis do you have to backtrack?'

'Two hundred and seven.'

'And how many have you cleared so far?'

'Twenty-seven.'

'That's not the kind of progress I was anticipating.'

'The local criminal gang who assisted with the disposal of the body are well versed in this kind of activity. Their cover-up was elaborate, which will ultimately allow us to identify them.'

'Are you saying it wasn't an alien?'

'I'm saying the killer had a lot of help from people very familiar with Newcastle.'

'That disproves nothing,' Vance said. 'We've had confirmation from the genetic tests run on the 2Norths. They are all who they say they are. No imposter was inserted into Northumberland Interstellar, this isn't a corporate scam, which was the only viable alternative theory for the motive. Something odd is going on.'

'Excuse me,' Sid said. 'I never said there wasn't. And it's only the A 2Norths we've cleared. The victim was definitely on St Libra at some time recently – forensic analysis of his clothes confirms that. And we still have two further branches of the North family to tie down. So far all we have is assurances, nothing solid.'

'Detective,' Passam said sharply. 'I am here in Abellia heading the most important trans-stellar mission that the GE has supported in thirty years. I was dining with Brinkelle North herself last night, and you're still peddling this nonsense that corporate manoeuvring is the cause of all this, specifically Brinkelle's branch of the family. I cannot accept your wild theory. You have provided no solid evidence, just speculation. Your investigation has practically stalled and you're casting round to find a scapegoat to absolve your lack of results. A pair of socks does not implicate an entire corporation in murder.'

'I didn't say they were—'

'I believe what we have here is a difference of perspective, Commissioner, nothing more,' Elston interjected. 'Detective Hurst is doing his best in difficult circumstances, but he is by necessity focused on one aspect of this problem: his murder investigation. We have to examine the bigger picture. Something killed Bartram and his household twenty years ago, the same thing that's just struck again. There's something odd going on here, and there is a very strong St Libra connection, even Detective Hurst has conceded that.'

Like bollocks do I, Sid fumed silently.

'Whatever happened in Newcastle is over,' Elston continued. 'We have to concentrate on the origin of the problem: the Brogal continent.'

'I agree totally,' Passam said quickly. 'The expedition is the correct way to proceed. Newcastle has provided no evidence to refute that.'

'Can I at least continue to investigate the murder of a North?' Sid snapped.

Commissioner Passam never faltered. 'Of course your investigation should continue, it may yet yield something of importance to us. Colonel Elston, I believe you're joining us soon?'

'I'm scheduled to fly out on Thursday with my team.'

'Excellent. Detective Hurst, you now have full authority over the investigation. Find that murder site for me.'

'Aye, right.' *And that covers your arse. Bitch!*

Ralph smiled openly when Elston and the Commissioner vanished from the screen.

'What?' Sid growled.

'You're getting better at this.'

'Crap on you, too.'

'No, seriously. You did well not throwing something at her.'

'Aye man, she just abandoned the whole investigation because it doesn't suit her politically. What kind of dipshit moron does that?'

'A fully fledged GE Commissioner, apparently.'

Sid slumped back in his chair, and managed a weak grin of his own. 'I am going to laugh my fucking head off when I prove this was a corporate op, I swear. I will announce how pointless her and her precious expedition is to every world in the trans-stellar universe at that media conference.'

'See, she's motivated you. She does know what she's doing.'

'Screw you.'

'Not at the distance we'll be working at. I'm bailing on you too, back to my office. I will need a progress report every day, and I'll give you some cover with O'Rouke, but if you need more resources, especially on the scale you've been burning them up lately, you'll have to provide a good reason.'

'Aye man, I know.'

*

'So we just keep chasing down the taxi routes?' Eva asked that night in Ian's flat. She'd snagged a pillow again, using it to cushion the floorboards where she was sitting, drinking some green tea Ian had made for her.

'That's what we're left with,' Sid admitted. He opened his beer bottle and slumped down against the wall in the barren lounge.

'It's everything now, which is kind of depressing when you think about it. All that work, the biggest investigation for one death that Market Street has ever known, and I'm playing spot-the-taxi in a giant zone virtual. I should bring my kids in, they're good at that sort of game.'

Ian was sitting on the kitchenette's bar, swinging his legs aimlessly as he watched his colleagues. 'O'Rouke pulled most of the detectives back from Office2 ten minutes after Ralph left this afternoon,' he told them. 'I've only got Johan and two others left.'

'How many taxis did they clear before they were pulled out?' Eva asked.

'About seventy-five. Not bad for that bunch of fuck-ups. But they investigated a hundred and twenty. So forty-five were bogus, either with false licence codes or unregistered drivers, or their company claims they weren't logged out that evening.'

Sid had to grin at that. 'Aye, nearly a third operating off-book; that tallies with urban myth. Who wants the taxman grabbing your weekend takings?'

'It's not all going to be the taxi drivers loading up their secondary accounts,' Eva said. 'The gangs will be running courier routes through the city, too.'

'Yeah, that's going to be our biggest problem,' Sid said. 'Sorting the ordinary illegitimates from our bodydump. It just means we really are going to have to backtrack each one individually.'

'Oh crap on it, the taxi we want is going to be the last one we backtrack,' Eva groaned, tipping her head back onto the wall and closing her eyes. 'I just know it is. Our luck is that bad.'

'Forty more days of overtime isn't bad in my book,' Ian said.

'Haven't you tuned in to the money story?' Sid asked.

'What?'

'I heard in the station that the HDA haven't paid O'Rouke a single Eurofranc so far.'

'Crap on it! Really?'

'We've spent a fortune, half this year's allocated murder investigation budget so far on this one case, and we're not even in February yet.'

Ian gave him an evil grin. '*You've* spent it.' He tipped his beer bottle in salute.

'That's not funny,' Eva told him.

'But true,' Sid sighed. 'And that doesn't include getting the zone theatre back up and running. Or the agency invoices that are going to hit at the end of the month.'

'O'Rouke is going to have us on school traffic duty for the rest of the century,' Eva said. 'Our luck is truly fucked.'

'Why haven't the HDA paid?' Ian asked.

'Different accounting procedure, so they claim. They don't do instalments. They'll reimburse us after the investigation is concluded and we file a total cost invoice with them.'

'But . . . even if we get lucky and backtrack the right taxi by the end of the week, that still won't finish the investigation.'

'Wait,' Eva said. 'Do they mean "conclude" as in bring a prosecution or expose the alien? What if we don't, what if the case gets shunted to inactive status? Does that count as concluded?'

Sid shrugged broadly. 'You tell me, pet. It's a pretty big incentive for Market Street to bring a prosecution. Then there's the Norths applying their own pressure. I'll bet that's contributing to HDA's ballbuster attitude: everyone wants to keep O'Rouke kicking my arse, apart from the bitch Commissioner.'

'Then we really have got to solve it?'

'Yeah.'

'So why waste time on bollocks like the suit list?' Ian said. 'Everyone knows you use a secondary to buy clothes. None of the 2Norths will be registered as owning that suit and shirt.'

'I know,' Sid said. 'But like I said, we have to get official procedure out of the way so we can focus on finding the real culprit. And the genetic test they made the 2Norths undergo was a big help.'

'How?' a puzzled Eva asked.

'It showed that all the A 2Norths really are 2Norths.'

'Aye.' An animated Ian clapped his hands together. 'I'm with you, boss. We've got an imposter.'

'Very probably. It was a North dead in the Tyne, simple fact – so one way or another the Norths are in it up to their necks. Either it was a B or C who got discovered working whatever scam is going down, and they got eliminated. That's unlikely, because Augustine and Aldred are pushing hard for us to find out what did happen. So my guess is that it's Brinkelle or Constantine behind this, and the body is one of Augustine's sons. Which means Ian is right, a B or a C has replaced him, they've taken over his life.'

'If that's right,' Eva said slowly, 'then our victim has to be a 2North who was quite senior in Northumberland Interstellar, someone who has access to top-level codes or data . . . whatever they're after.'

'Which ties in nicely with the socks thing,' Sid said. 'Aldred said senior management is always travelling through the gateway to St Libra.'

'It has to be Brinkelle behind it,' Eva said. 'The murder method was used against her father.'

'That doesn't make a lot of sense,' Ian said. 'Bartram and his people were killed by that mad psycho girl: Tramelo.'

'Misdirection, probably,' Sid said. 'Who knows? We have to focus on what we're solid with. It's a corporate covert op, made worse because it's undoubtedly tied in with their old family split. Blood feuds are always the worst kind.'

'But what kind of corporate scam?' Ian asked.

'Doesn't matter,' Eva said. 'We can forget about the stupid alien theory and work the case properly now.' She glanced over to Sid. 'How's it going with your gang contact?'

He pulled a face. 'I asked the question. We've just got to wait for the answer.'

Thursday 31st January 2143

'Remember, guys, when you go through: look up.' It was Angela's best advice, sincere, too. And they took it. Of course they did, she'd invested a lot of time becoming a part of Paresh's squad. She was virtually one of them now the big day had arrived.

Oh-seven-hundred-hours – full GE Legion detachment of the St Libra Northern Geogenetic Expedition to report to base transport pool with full TE (Tropical Environment) kit. Oh-seven-twenty-five – convoy vehicle start and systems check. Oh-seven-thirty – convoy roll out under escort. Transit gateway to St Libra, and proceed to Highcastle Airport. Airlift to commence seventeen-hundred-hours local time.

They did like their precision orders did the HDA. So Angela wound up sitting in the same old black minibus that was up near the front of their convoy of ten identical minibuses at just after seven thirty as it trundled out of the base and down to the gateway. Corporal Paresh Evitts sat beside her with Private Atyeo in front driving down the slope and through the Kingsway running down the centre of Last Mile, just like last time sixteen days ago. It was her version of the good old days. Except that is for the black sedan at the front of their convoy, the one carrying Colonel Vance Elston.

He'd been in his cream-coloured TE uniform that morning as they all climbed into their vehicles. The first time she'd seen him in a dress uniform since she'd left Holloway. She didn't like it – too many bad memories.

The HDA police car escort which was leading the convoy peeled away onto the off-road just before the bridge-like ramp which led up to the gateway. She gave Paresh a playful nudge and pointed up through the window. He grinned back, and obediently looked up.

Two weeks of platonic friendship, two weeks of constantly being at her side, two weeks of gym exercise, chugging beer, bitching about HDA brass, about the wait, about the piss-poor briefings, about the inadequate TE kit ('Told you so'), not being allowed off base at night, crap food in the canteen, cramped conditions, badly run drills. For her, another prison routine, but with decent transnet access. For Paresh, a strange life that mutated him into a cross between ultra-protective big brother and a chaste Victorian suitor. As far as the rest of the squad was concerned, she'd elevated herself to mascot status – one of the team, with the only exception she wasn't allowed a weapon. Otherwise she could keep up with all their training routines, join in the banter, share the dirty jokes. Trust was the key, and she'd captured it.

Elston's car slid through the rigid iridescent wall of grey fog that was the trans-spacial connection. Angela tensed up, and even remembered her own advice. They passed through the gateway.

Brilliant white light flooded into the minibus. Atyeo twitched the wheel slightly in reaction.

'Wow.' Paresh fumbled for the sunglasses in his top pocket. 'Didn't think it was gonna be that bright.'

Angela was already searching the sky. 'There,' she said simply.

Paresh followed her gaze. St Libra's sky was a clean deep turquoise, which somehow seemed to be a whole lot higher than Earth's. He barely noticed that. Slicing right across the northern sky like some kind of magical veil was the planet's phenomenal ring system. From the tightly braided A-ring skimming along at the top of the atmosphere, it stretched out for half a million kilometres to the outermost T-ring with its eight little shepherd moonlets. The main bands were noticeably denser, producing distinct ribs clotted with gravel-sized specks of rock, though the space between them was still suffused with ice granules and dust forming a magnificent sparkling mantle that spanned the heavens from east to west.

'Holy mother,' Paresh whispered in reverence.

Angela looked out on St Libra's glory, feeling a strange sense of relief that it was there; that there was natural beauty in the universe still. Holloway had denied her such things for so long, she'd half-believed she might have simply imagined it along with the rest of her previous existence.

On the seats behind her, the rest of the squad was registering its amazement at the spectacle.

'You weren't joking, were you,' Paresh said.

'Not about this,' she told him. 'You can't joke about this.'

'Thank you for telling me . . . us.'

She grinned and put her wraparound sunglasses on. 'To be fair, it's not something you were likely to miss, now is it?'

'No.' He peered up into the sky again, as if it might be some sort of trickery.

'If you think it's grand now, wait till night time. Sirius makes it gleam twice as bright as Earth's moonlight.'

'That I can believe.'

'Very romantic,' she said.

He gave her a slightly wary, tentative grin. For two weeks she'd never given him the slightest intimation that their friendship might grow into anything more. Good pals was the limit, given she was his official charge. Until this morning. When the squad was packing kit and getting dressed she'd stood beside her bunk bed, where she had the top mattress and Paresh the bottom. Wearing just bra and briefs she'd slathered on high-factor sunblock oil until her skin was slick and glistening, taking her time, an exhibition like some zone babe on a raunchy location shoot. Paresh was sharing the same space beside the bunks, pulling on his own cream-coloured TE uniform. It had been a tough struggle for him not to gawp. The few times their eyes had met, she'd given him the neutral smile of someone oblivious to the testosterone storm she was kindling.

The balance had shifted now. He was the uncertain one, the one who would risk his dignity to come after her. The one easier for her to control.

'Kind of a pain, too,' she said. 'The rings are why St Libra can never have comsats, or any other kind of satellite for that matter. You might be able to see the stars twinkling through them, but for all intents and purposes they're solid. No satellite could ever pass through them intact.'

'We've got the e-Rays,' Paresh said. 'They'll provide all our coms cover out in the jungle. It won't be anything worse than we've trained for.'

'Yes it will be,' she taunted.

'Come on, have a little faith. You've seen that we're tight, that we can take care of ourselves and our objective.'

'I hope so.'

Another grid ramp led down from the oval gateway, mirroring the Newcastle side. At the bottom, a semicircle of mirror-glass offices and dark engineering units curved away to the right, boasting company names in high colourful letters; with the surrounding ground lost beneath fat swathes of tarmac where hundreds of cars and pick-ups were parked without any order. To the left of the ramp were the warehouses and processing sheds, far larger than anything in Last Mile, which handled St Libra's imports. Closest to the ramp was a bus station, with each embarkation pier empty. For the last couple of weeks, emigration to St Libra had been down to a few hundred people per day, with everyone marshalled together and scurrying through when HDA wasn't using the gateway. Angela couldn't see any people outside anywhere.

A broad apron of tarmac expanded out from the end of the ramp, with feed roads curving off to the various nearby buildings. Directly ahead was a three-lane carriageway, with a giant sign beside it: WELCOME TO MOTORWAY A. It led directly away from the gateway, out into the harsh bioil industrial sector which dominated the landscape, where giant tank farms, coated in silver heat-resistant blankets, stretched across the raw rust-red soil to the horizon. Between the tanks were forests of elaborate refinery columns swathed in a tangle of tubes and conduits, and puffing out jets of steam which soon dispersed in the hot, cloudless atmosphere. The ground itself was mostly obscured by a snake's nest of thick pipes, interconnecting at the stumpy cylinders of turbine pumps, all sheltered from the elements by simple roofs of corrugated composite.

'Has it changed much?' Paresh asked.

'Not really. The buildings are bigger, and there's a lot more tanks; otherwise it's the same.'

'So where's the city?'

'Highcastle? I've no idea, but it's about ten miles away I think. I never visited. It's a bit of a dump by all accounts. Company town.'

'Maybe that's grown as well, improved some.'

Angela eyed the raw industrial panorama in all its functional ugliness. 'Somehow, I doubt that.'

The convoy picked up speed, chasing down Motorway A. As they drove, the air-con fans grew louder as they struggled to accommodate the sudden impact of St Libra's hot, humid atmosphere. The air in the minibus became cold, clammy, and laced with a faint smell of bioil. Narrow tracks branched off Motorway A every couple of hundred metres or so on either side, signposted with enigmatic alphanumerics. They meandered away through the tanks, little more than twinned tyre ruts worn into the stony soil, host to long puddles shimmering in the low sunlight. Then after five miles, when the tanks finally ended and some kind of local purple-green grass reclaimed the soil, the road forked, and they took the left-hand lane. Angela caught sight of the sign for the airport, another twenty miles away.

Slowly, the native vegetation started to reassert itself across the exposed soil, though the whiff of bioil coming off the refineries was a constant. Dark grass with subtle hues of purple and aquamarine, shining like diffraction patterns, spread out from the tarmac, interrupted by hemispherical scrub bushes with strange white branches poking out of the uniformity of blue-green leaves.

Then there were the wire trees, which she remembered, like silver sculptures of leafless terrestrial trees.

'I thought it was all jungle,' Leora Fawkes complained.

'We're on the Great Jarrow Plain,' Angela told her. 'The centre of Ambrose, which is pure algaepaddy territory. When we get across the ocean to Brogal you'll see real jungle.'

'So where are the algaepaddies?'

'Wait till we get airborne, you can't miss them.'

Highcastle Airport sprawled across twenty-five square miles. There was room for that kind of sluggish extravagance on St Libra; the flat land was mostly mown grass, with buildings dispersed around the two long runways and their attendant maze of taxiways and link roads. The control tower stood at one end, a spire of bleached white concrete topped with a band of blue-green glass. Even after ninety-two years of human occupation, it remained the tallest structure on the planet. Because they were all divorced from each other, there was no sense of scale to the rest of the airport buildings; not until you got up close and realized how big they were.

The airport was the first time Angela saw any sign of human activity. HDA's logistics corps was working hard with their task of supplying the Primary Staging Area at Abellia Airport, seven and a half thousand kilometres away. All the bulky equipment containers, standard airload 350DL cargo pallets, GL56 pods filled with raw, the fleet of ground vehicles, the helicopters, and flat-fold Qwik-Kabins that HDA had sent on ahead through the gateway – it was all spread grid-fashion across the airport tarmac or sheltered in the open-sided hangars, awaiting its flight out.

As well as the SuperRocs and Daedalus strategic airlifters, HDA had requisitioned all seven planes belonging to the planet's one airline: AirBrogal. Four of those were commercial Boeing 2757s, modified to a single first-class cabin that could carry a hundred and fifty passengers to Abellia in contemporary luxury, along with express cargo packages. Three Antonov An-445s made up the remainder of the fleet, long-range cargo planes with a payload similar to the Daedalus, which were used to haul medium-weight high-priority items out to Abellia's wealthy fashion-conscious, must-have consumers. Everything else, the real heavy items, were trucked along Motorway A in huge lorry-trains then shipped across the sea.

The only other planes parked in the shade of their hangars were the supersonic executive jets of the ultra-rich who had homes in Abellia. There was nowhere else to fly on the planet.

The Norths had established a sovereign state with its own constitution in the middle of the massive Ambrose continent, whose legitimacy was officially recognized by every Earth and trans-stellar government. Its border was a circle roughly two thousand kilometres in diameter encompassing the algaepaddies and farms – that was all they took responsibility for. Eastshields, the tiny port town on Ambrose's northern coast where Motorway A finally ended, was the only other place where the primary constitution applied; and that town only existed to load and maintain the five cargo ships which sailed over to Abellia.

Way beyond the Great Jarrow Plain, and spread out along three thousand kilometres of Ambrose's south-east coast, were the Independencies; St Libra's great attraction for the politic-ally disaffected of Earth and the rest of the trans-stellar worlds. They comprised a plethora of tiny nation states, each one proud and protective of its unique constitution. The first ones to be founded existed side by side on the mainland with clearly defined boundaries, while the more recently established communities were extending themselves out across the myriad islands of the vast Tyne Archipelago, colonizing a section which they'd named the Isles of Liberty. Just about every political and economic ideology humans had ever dreamed up, along with the full range of theocracies, could be found within the Independencies, provid-ing a sanctuary for every type of dissident.

Everybody who travelled to that region of St Libra, which was where all the emigrants of the last eighty years headed, did so along Motorway B, which wasn't even tarmacked for most of its length. None of the Independency states owned a runway – they all treasured their isolation too much for quick contact with the trans-stellar society they'd rejected.

*

Angela's minibus pulled up beside one of the giant open-side hangars, whose curving solar panel roof was big enough to shield both of the SuperRocs side by side had they ever been permitted a rest. A quarter of the concrete floor was taken up with HDA 350DL pallets and GL56 pods. Trestle tables had been set up near the row of portable toilet cabins, with chilled water dispensers, and coolboxes of snack food.

'We're here until the flight,' Paresh announced to his squad. 'You are responsible for your own kitbag until we embark. Do not let it out of your sight.'

A wash of hot air gusted into the minibus when Atyeo opened the doors. Angela hoisted her personal bag onto her shoulders, shoved a cotton sunhat down on her head and went to collect her HDA issue kitbag from the locker at the side of the minibus.

Several hundred people were milling about in the hangar; a big contingent of Legionnaires, along with science staff and HDA technical support specialists. They all formed their own groups, with little cross-contact. Angela found the instinctive tribalism amusing.

She collected a flask of chilled water and a pack of sandwiches from the bored catering people, then joined Paresh's squad, sitting on her kitbag and watching the unchanging landscape outside. Ground-heat shimmer turned the air to a haze, making the distant buildings waver. Apart from a few HDA trucks and flatloaders rolling past in some weird dance between container stacks, nothing moved.

Transport corps staff arrived in a bus, and drove the minibus convoy away. Lieutenant Pablo Botin came over and announced the SuperRoc was 'slightly behind schedule', which was greeted with typical Legionary scorn.

Angela settled in to watch the sun slide down the sky, making sure she had a view of the incredible rings. The lazy atmosphere, cloying bioil-fumed air, bright light, and perpetual flat terrain triggered a feeling of true freedom for the first time since she'd walked out of Holloway. Here, she really could give everyone the slip and walk over the horizon never to return.

Not yet, though. There were a few things she had to check out first, and the expedition was flying her direct to the first one.

About an hour after they arrived, a convoy of six mobile biolabs pulled up just inside the hangar, so that the roof's shadow covered them. They were big vehicles, with six individually powered wheel hubs under a chassis that supported a high driver's cab, a small living section, and the windowless lab itself, which stretched for two-thirds of the length. Looking at the one-and-a-half-metre-diameter tyres and their thick hub suspension pistons, Angela reckoned there was very little terrain they wouldn't be able to cope with.

Vance Elston and a couple of other officers went over and started talking to the xenobiology teams who'd emerged. It was clear they all knew each other well. She made a mental note of that, curious why a spook like Elston would bother with science nerds.

One of the Boeing C-8000 Daedalus airlifters came in to land, touching down with a squeal of brakes and squirts of dirty smoke from the undercarriage bogies. It taxied over to a cargo terminal, and opened its rear ramp doors. The nose also swung up slowly, allowing the logistics corp crews to load pallets from both ends as quickly as the flatbed trucks could deliver them. Engineers ran their flightworthiness checks, inspecting the turbofans. At the same time, a couple of fat bowsers drove up and began pumping in JB5 biav fuel. The flight crew disembarked, handing over to a fresh crew.

As the loading progressed the sky started to darken quickly. Angela watched the cloud front sweep in from the west, a churning slate-grey mass that appeared implausibly low over the ground given the magnitude of the sky. The wind picked up, sending cooler gusts through the open hangar. She delved into her bag, and zipped a thin fleece over her T-shirt, then folded the sunglasses away. Most of the Legionnaires were standing at the edge of the hangar, watching the rainstorm approach. She knew better.

The Daedalus was turned around in an impressively efficient forty-five minutes. It trundled back out to the runway, and raced up into the sky, just beating the arrival of the clouds. The deluge of rain they brought with them was as thick and heavy as she remembered. That was the thing with a world with a landmass that was mostly tropical or sub-tropical. It rained every day, often more than once. And in keeping with St Libra's size, at nearly twice Earth's diameter, the rain was on an equally overwhelming scale.

The noise it made striking the panels of the hangar roof made conversation all but impossible. Everyone standing near the edge stepped back smartly as the cascade splattered across the concrete. Angela's view of the airport shrank rapidly; so dense was the fall, she could barely see the neighbouring hangar. Outside, the landscape she could make out was reduced to blurred monochrome outlines. Nonetheless she could see the build-up of water in the ground's gentle undulations – what she'd taken to be long natural dips were actually broad drainage channels, taking the water away from the runways and buildings.

'To hell with this,' Gillian Kowalski grunted; she was sitting with Omar Mihambo on a kitbag close to Angela.

'It won't last long,' Angela told them.

'They didn't tell us we'd need fucking scuba gear,' Omar said.

Lightning flared, making everyone jump.

DiRito was grinning out at the wall of water curtaining off the edge of the hangar. 'Everything really is bigger and better here, isn't it?'

'Even the monsters,' Angela said.

Paresh gave her a disapproving glance, which she deflected with a rueful grin as the thundercrack rolled round the hangar.

After forty minutes the rain finished as fast as it began. The clouds tumbled away into the east, not that their retreat brought back much daylight. Clean air gusted through the hangar in the wake of the clouds, taking away the last hint of bioil fumes. Over to the west, the dazzle-point which was Sirius sank quickly into the horizon, promptly followed by the high-magnitude star that was Sirius B, which was now almost in opposing conjunction with St Libra. The primary seemed to be shining right through the edge of the ring system, making the curving shroud of particles glow merrily.

'Hey, there you go, guys,' Angela said, pointing up at the rings. 'That's an omen for your first day. The G-spot's come out for you.'

The squad clustered round her, trying to see what she was pointing at. Almost halfway across the span of the rings, a tiny swirl of darkness was creeping along one of the thicker bands.

'What is that?' Mohammed Anwar asked.

'One of the shepherds. An asteroid-sized moon which helps keep the rings stable. Technically, it's on the outer edge of the F-ring. But . . . everyone calls it the G-spot.'

'Hard to find, huh?' Hanrahan said as he squinted up.

'Only for you boys,' Angela shot back at him.

The squad laughed as the sun finally slipped below the horizon, and the full spectacle of the rings glimmered wide across the twilight sky.

Their SuperRoc landed fifteen minutes later. Paresh's squad joined one of the two queues snaking back across the apron from the twin sets of airstairs which the ground crew wheeled up to the fuselage. Angela guessed there must be close to four hundred of them embarking, though the plane could actually hold over eight hundred when fully configured for passengers. But this was a combi version, with the lower deck currently converted to cargo.

Flatbed trucks delivered pallets to the forward fuselage hatchways, while the clamshell doors at the back hinged wide, and a ramp slid down. The biolabs were driven carefully up into the belly of the SuperRoc. Angela saw Elston standing at the bottom of the ramp, watching keenly as the vehicles went in. After the fourth one was secured he and another officer left and walked round to the airstair at the front, cutting into the queue so they could go straight up.

Just as Angela finally got to the bottom of the airstair, one of the An-445s landed, to be greeted by a swarm of logistics corps personnel. They began their loading in tandem with their colleagues attending the SuperRoc. If this afternoon was standard, that made it a planeload of personnel or materiel flying out to Abellia every two or three hours. She whistled silently – the expedition must be costing billions. Somebody other than herself was very serious about finding the monster.

Despite Angela's misgivings, the SuperRoc's seats weren't too bad. The cushioning was firm, and there was a reasonable amount of leg room. They were arranged in rows five abreast. She let Leora Fawkes take the window seat; Paresh sat on her other side, with Josh Justic and Audrie Sleath filling the rest of the row.

Her e-i quested a link to the plane's smartnet, which offered her a limited connection to the transnet, warning her to download anything she needed for entertainment on the flight to a personal cache, as the connection would end as soon as they took off. She selected the files, most of which came from unlicensed sites, on recent Grande Europe history and Middle Eastern politics in the trans-stellar age, a collection she'd been skimming back in the HDA base, and settled down to read them on her grid, ignoring the plane's safety briefing.

She roused herself briefly as the SuperRoc accelerated down the runway, pushing her back in the cushioning as it reared up. The flight was due to last nine and a half hours thanks to their Fall Zone transit, which would see them flying low and slow for a thousand kilometres over the Marsden Sea. It would take them through the night to land at Abellia early morning local time, which was completely contrary to her body clock, which was telling her she was just coming up on lunchtime. At least it would give her time to read up on the files, though as always she told herself to pay equal attention to both topics, knowing Elston would be reviewing her access.

As she expanded the files back into her grid, she wondered how much he'd managed to find out about her past now he suspected her Tramelo background was bogus. Not as much as he would've liked, she guessed; the database which held the most vital details of her origin and life was off-limits even to Elston's beloved Alien Intelligence Agency. That would bother him, she knew, him with his desperate little-man superiority and right-to-know-job arrogance; though ironically that exclusive data didn't have the slightest relevance to the expedition nor the alien monster. In fact, the only thing he might find, if he was super-efficient with DNA analysis, was her true mother. Angela smiled secretively at the prospect, *now that would be an interesting meeting*.

The SuperRoc climbed steadily, banking gently to line up on a north-eastern course. Silver-grey ringlight shone in through the windows.

'Oh wow, will you take a look at this,' Leora gasped, pressing her face against the window.

Angela craned her neck to look over the Legionnaire's shoulder. The land below was perfectly illuminated by the bright ringlight, revealing the algaepaddies. Each one was a perfect circle a thousand metres in diameter, its rim made from a low earth bank bulldozed out from the centre to create a shallow crater. Once they were filled with water from the daily rains, the genetically modified algae were introduced, quickly blooming and multiplying in the planet's ideal combination of warmth and moisture, turning the surface into a thick glistening sludge. It was harvested by a boom arm, which was fastened to a central pillar, and rotated round and round, taking two days to complete a full circuit, siphoning off a high percentage of the crud, yet leaving enough so that when the arm came round once more there was a full blanket of algae grown back over the surface again.

The harvested sludge was pumped over to a refinery, where its water content was removed, leaving the raw algae to have their hydrocarbon-rich corpus processed into any of the half-dozen biopetroleum products utterly essential to the trans-stellar economy. Demand was massive, and expanding in line with the current steady economic growth of the human worlds. That was the reason why the glistening circles stretched out as far as Leora could see from the vantage point of a plane already four miles high. They were packed together in a precise lattice, which only surrendered to the rare small hills on the plain. The distance between them was calculated to allow narrow spine roads and the pipe network to co-exist. There were also the overspill channels, draining away the excess rainwater, a regimented tributary network that merged into larger waterways before combining into motorway-sized channels that finally disgorged into the region's natural rivers, flushing surplus algae away to contaminate the native riverside ecology all the way down to the sea. Ringlight shone on them too, creating a herringbone array of steady silver lambency threading round the algaepaddies.

'That is one hell of an impressive set-up,' Paresh murmured behind Angela. 'It's like it goes on for ever.'

She turned back to him. 'Several hundred miles, yeah. But think how many people it supplies with bioil on how many worlds; how much of trans-stellar life as we know it is dependent on St Libra.'

'Those Norths, huh, smart people.'

'Ruthless people if you want to be honest and accurate.'

'That sounds bitter.'

'You know why I was there at Bartram's mansion, right?'

'Uh, sure.'

Angela smiled to herself at how self-conscious he seemed to be about that. 'The original three brothers; it's like they had their brains scooped out and replaced by silicon. They don't connect to anything human. They understand emotion and feelings, but only so they can manipulate it. Their freak kids, the 2s, they're a little more human; I suppose it's because they're all flawed – at least in relation to the three bad dads. But they still contribute to the collective. In fact, the collective wouldn't be possible without them.'

'Collective?'

'Northumberland Interstellar, which basically is St Libra.'

'So it's lucky for the human race we've actually got them?'

'If it hadn't been the Norths and St Libra, it would've been someone and something else. Like thousands before them, they saw an opportunity and they went for it. Smart, ambitious people have been doing that, bending the universe around them, for most of our history. The majority of them share the same characteristics as the Norths.'

'You sound like you hate the rich because they are rich.'

'Money buys you a decent life, I don't begrudge anyone that. How they get it can be a problem, depending on your beliefs.'

'What are yours?'

'I believe in personal survival, and I'll do whatever it takes to maintain that belief.'

'That's kind of bleak.'

Angela grinned at him. 'That doesn't mean I can't have some fun along the way. I just haven't had much for . . . Oh yeah: twenty years.'

'A genuine miscarriage of justice. That's got to be the toughest break I ever heard of.'

'Yeah. But when we all trip over the monster out there in the jungle and load its pic on the transnet, I'll be in line for some serious financial compensation. Hopefully I'll be able to trash some senior government careers as well. Nice bonus.'

'So that's what this is about, revenge?'

'Look, right now I'm not locked in a prison cell, I get food given me every day – well, HDA rations, anyway – I have clothes, I've got you guys to talk to instead of the psychopaths I was banged up with and the sadists who guarded us, I have a view from my window, and I can access the transnet. And if I believed in Disney endings I'd even keep an eye open for Mr Right. My life is on the up right now.'

'Except you think we're all going to die out in the jungle.'

'You. I think *you* are all going to die. Because you don't believe in what I've seen; to you this is just another deployment exercise.'

'I believe.'

'I hope you do, Paresh. Seriously.'

'When the crunch comes, I'm going to prove to you that you've been underestimating us.'

'Yeah. Look, sorry if I keep coming over like a bitch; it's just that I'm used to taking care of myself.'

'Not much rak, huh?'

'Excuse me?' She gave him a suspicious look, rather liking the playful mock-innocent expression she saw on his face, but then Paresh was still a kid in so many ways.

'Random Acts of Kindness,' he said. 'You need some in your life. Everybody does.'

'No, I don't have much of a rak, but hey, this is the twenty-third century, you can get anything fixed if you have enough money.'

They grinned at each other.

'We're back to money again,' he said.

'Always,' Angela said. 'So do you like a girl with lots of rak?'

Paresh smirked. 'I'm not fussy either way.'

She smiled and went back to her files on the Blue Kama democracy rebellion which had swept through the Arab countries in the early twenty-second century.

*

People were just starting to doze off when the SuperRoc began its descent into the Fall Zone. They'd left the port town of Eastshields a thousand kilometres behind, and were now out over the Marsden Sea, five hundred kilometres short of the equator. Below them the sea came close to steaming. Evaporation was constant, producing a thick band of hot mist which circled the whole of St Libra's oceanic equator, surging up to the very top of the troposphere to power the endless rainstorms which roiled through the planet's atmosphere.

The SuperRoc's radar was on, scanning the unbroken fog and cloud it was slicing through at a cautious six hundred and fifty kph. Not that the pilots would have much warning if any rocks did plummet towards them. They were flying at seven hundred metres above the sea now, the lowest safe altitude at which the turbofans could maintain their efficiency in such humidity.

'I don't see why we need to be this low,' Josh Justic complained.

Angela glanced over, seeing the way his hands were gripping the end of the armrests. Josh wasn't a good flyer, and this was about the worst flight on any of the trans-stellar worlds.

'We're a lot better off down here,' she promised him. 'We're flying under the rings right now, and the A-ring grazes the top of the atmosphere. The drag aerobrakes a million particles a day below orbital velocity. It's mostly just dust we're talking about, specks not even as big as a grain of sand, but there's a few bigger rocks jumbled up in there too. They generally disintegrate when they reach the mesosphere and plume like a cascade of shooting stars. So if any do survive their own shockwave and get down to the troposphere, the radar will pick up the ionization trail easily enough, and the pilots will have time to fly us away from the fallpath.' *In theory*, she added silently. This low-and-safe manoeuvre was mainly for the benefit of the passengers. In the fifty-four years since Bartram established Abellia no plane had been hit by a ring particle – of course, there had been a lot of reports of engine failure due to excessive humidity in the combustion chamber.

A bright flash outside illuminated the whole row of startled faces.

'What was that?' Josh demanded.

'Ring particle disintegrating. Don't worry, it's twenty miles overhead, and smaller chunks are good news – they burn up a lot faster. Basically, if you see the flash it means you won't get hit by the debris it exploded into. It's the dark ones you have to fear.'

Josh didn't look convinced. Angela shrugged and went back to her reading. The flight crew started serving the 'evening' meal: a plastic box with a baked potato, cheese, and tuna. There was only water to drink, and pudding was a small Cadbury's chocolate bar.

Angela suspected the crew passed it out to distract everyone from the near-constant purple and scarlet flashes that burst through the darkness above them.

*

She dozed off about the time they cleared the thousand-kilometre-wide Fall Zone corridor, and the huge plane climbed back to its normal cruise altitude for the remaining fifteen hundred kilometres to Abellia. The cabin lights came back up to full intensity twenty minutes out from the airport.

'Morning, sleepy,' Paresh said.

Angela grimaced at him, rubbing at her eyes and yawning widely. They were already descending, with the cabin crew walking down the aisles, making sure everyone was using their seatbelt. A gentle dawn light was shining through the windows.

'It's the middle of the night,' she protested. 'I hate transplanet timelag. It takes me days to adjust.'

'The Legion always toughs it out,' Audrie informed her.

Angela gave her the finger and brought her chair upright for landing. The undercarriage lowered with a lot of *clunks*. Only now did Angela regret giving up the window seat to Leora. She peered intently at the vista beyond the window. They were just approaching the shoreline along the western side of Abellia.

'Holy crap,' Angela muttered.

'What?' Paresh asked. 'I thought you knew this town.'

'I used to,' she said, staring down at the coastal city that Bartram North had so clearly modelled on Human Idyll 101.

Abellia was built on a forty-kilometre-wide pear-shaped peninsula, an errant eruption of rock jutting out from Brogal's rugged coastline. It was mountainous terrain, with the tight-packed slopes falling straight down into the water around the whole peninsula, and in doing so creating hundreds of coves with broad sandy beaches. Bartram had built the original cargo ship har-bour at the southernmost point, allowing civil engineering plants to sprawl back into the two closest valleys. They'd long since been uprooted and booted out into the hinterlands, allowing the old town area around the expanded harbour to develop into a gleaming civic centre, with theatres and arenas and schools; even a college campus jostled for space with malls and galleries. Outside that central cluster of long public beaches and marinas, the coves had been claimed by individuals or belonged to the elaborate condos that ran along the back of the sands.

White Californian-Spanish villa-mansions had colonized the mountains inland, where artificial terracing halted soil erosion and allowed terrestrial green to spread up the valleys, forming parks and golf courses that were irrigated from the white-water rivers which drained away the daily monsoons. Slim roads switch-backed up the rugged gradients and arched between hills on narrow, architecturally adventurous bridges. Highways cut rigid lines across the antagonistic topography, tunnelling through any inconvenient mountain to carry the traffic directly between districts with minimum fuss. Native vegetation with its darker colours still persisted on the steeper inclines, dominating the heights above the city. None of the peaks had snowcaps – that just didn't happen on St Libra; instead the apex of most mountains had been claimed by clubs and spas, or really big private mansions. The blue blobs of infinity pools were everywhere.

Yachts and smaller pleasure boats carved long white wakes through the clear sea. There were even some big pontoons anchored offshore, with stores and restaurants and bars, served by water taxis.

'It's grown,' Angela said in a subdued voice. She should have expected it, but even so . . .

'Five minutes to landing,' the pilot announced.

She took a deep breath as her heart began to race. An adrenalin tingle swept through her body, bringing a sudden chill. Everything came into hard focus as primeval instincts sharpened up protectively, alert for danger.

'You okay?' a concerned Paresh asked.

'Sure.' They were memories, that was all; triggered by the sight of the city they came slithering out of dark places. Too many of them.

Friday 1st February 2143

Most of the expedition pilots were toxed up with HiMod to keep them sharp and push them through their natural sleep cycle without the chem-buzz of a street stim. Ravi Hendrik didn't bother with analeptics. No need, not even now he was pushing fifty. And as to why his fellow pilots had turned users he didn't understand at all.

How could you not stay fresh and focused on this world, with this mission? Ravi's European Aircraft Corporation CT-606D Berlin heavylift helicopter was the latest model to roll off the production line; shiny-new and ridiculously expensive – like most of the expedition's equipment. Even with such top-of-the-range systems, he didn't bother with the autopilot, preferring to fly on manual, even during the refuelling, when they suckled up to the tanker-variant Daedalus, which they'd had to do twice on the two-thousand-kilometre trip. He preferred it because of the bright-yellow JCB compactor hanging on cables beneath the Berlin, looking utterly surreal as it zoomed over the St Libra jungle at close on two hundred and fifty kph. Loads like this did hellacious things to their flight stability.

He lived for shit like this. A man in tune with his machine, flying with a purpose.

After eight stressful hours the ferry flight of four Berlins was now only about fifty kilometres out from Edzell, the first advance base that was being carved out of the jungle two thousand and seventy kilometres straight north of Abellia. Another ten minutes would see Ravi lowering the compactor down into the clearing. An overnight stay and then tomorrow a fast flight back to Abellia to pick up more outsize equipment.

First priority for the HDA engineering corps at Edzell was to use the dozers and compactors which the Berlins delivered to carve a runway out of the wild ground for the Daedalus planes, whose design allowed them to land on some pretty rough surfaces. Once that strip was established, the big planes would take over supplying the base and expanding it up to full operational status; but until then it was all dependent on the Berlins. Ravi and the helicopter pilots were the pioneers everyone else was depending on to pull off this truly wild schedule. The whole expedition, from Commissioner Passam down to the catering staff, was following this flight in real time, admiring their ballsy skill. Right now his neurones were pumping him a high no tox could match. Oh yes.

The weather radar display shining across the cockpit canopy showed the afternoon storm as a giant red wave sweeping in from the south-east. If nothing went wrong they should just be able to outrun it. Any kind of weather forecast on St Libra was a boon. Without satellites they were as close as Ravi had ever been to flying blind. Thankfully the e-Rays provided some coverage along the flight path to Edzell, but this zooming into the unknown was all part of the great game.

'Cloud coming,' Tork Ericson called above the turbine whine and gearbox growl which saturated the cabin – military birds weren't big on soundproofing. He was an aviation engineer, sitting in the co-pilot's seat today to help with the abnormal load.

'We'll beat it,' Ravi called back. 'This is one smooth gig.'

'But not as cool as a Thunderthorn,' Tork supplied.

'You got it.' In his glorious youth Ravi Hendrik had flown SF-100 Thunderthorns, the HDA's first line of defence against Zanthswarms. And Ravi had been a newly qualified pilot, eighteen months out of HDA flight school, when the New Florida Zanthswarm began. He'd flown mission after mission above that doomed world. Nothing in his professional or private life since had ever come close to matching the sheer terror and exhilaration of that all-too-brief time.

The HDA had reassigned him away from his beloved SF-100 when he was in his late thirties. Younger pilots were coming through the academy, boys and girls with hunger to kill the Zanth, with faster reflexes and more up-to-date systems knowledge than that sad old-timer Ravi Hendrik. They didn't have the real-life experience, but that counted for shit in these days of virtuals. So Ravi was assigned to support flying duty as the clock ticked down to pension time – still extremely important work his squadron commander insisted, even though he was older still and knew exactly what a load of bullshit he was feeding to resentful sidelined ex-hero pilots.

It was a Bad Thing, he knew, but Ravi wanted every day to be a Zanthswarm day, allowing him to fuck the enemy with D-bombs that *he* launched, that *he* detonated amid the terrifying rifts through spacetime. The universe's greatest power trip.

But even he had to admit, this crazy expedition was pretty hot. A good swansong for his career.

The alien jungle stretched out to the horizon in all directions, lush glaucous vegetation clinging to every hill and ravine, plants that possessed a unique vitality, clogging tributaries until they swamped, forming cliff-like sides to the deeper faster-flowing rivers. It was relentless and all-powerful. Giant, palm-like trees stabbed upwards, towering thirty to forty metres above the main canopy like green impaling spikes waiting for the Berlin flight to make one mistake. Vines festooned the gaps caused by steep gorges. Bubble-bushes, a pink-hued scrub that grew in clusters across any sodden area, thronged the folds creasing the mountainsides, where misty streams trickled downwards. Waterfalls spewed white from rock precipices, falling for an age into deep pools. Thick tattered braids of cloud meandered along valleys and round peaks. Away to the west, the land rose in a vast massif that created an even more rugged-looking plateau country beyond. Much of it as yet unnamed – who had the time?

'Man, this is one mean bushworld,' Tork said.

Ravi nodded. He got it. Travelling like this, low and slow, over land where no human had ever been before, and likely-as-not never would again, made him very conscious of how far they were from civilization. More importantly, how far from help if anything went wrong. The expedition had some Sikorsky CV-47 Swallows, including a fully equipped medevac version. But even Ravi had to question how useful they'd actually be at plucking casualties out of this remote verdant wilderness.

Their only communications out here were routed via relay packages in the six e-Ray AAVs (Autonomous Airborne Vehicle) that were flying tight, high-altitude loiter patterns, strung out across the gulf between Abellia and Edzell. It had taken four days to position the e-Rays, which had gone on to perform preliminary scans, plotting out the basic topography, searching for the features they needed.

A two-kilometre flat zone, close to water, with low bush coverage, had been found with relative ease. A couple of Berlins had flown out to drop preliminary camp equipment and a detachment of engineers – along with a full Legion squad for protection. None of the evaluation flights had detected any alien animals, not even insects, but Major Griffin Toync, who was head of expedition security, wasn't taking any chances. They were here to find potentially hostile aliens, and he didn't want them finding the expedition first.

After eight hours of flying, and placing more trust than Ravi found comfortable in their inertial guidance system, he spotted the lake. It was at the base of a wide gentle valley that was clear of jungle, with just a few lone bullwhip trees standing among the wispy amethyst-shaded grass. They were probably his favourite trees amid St Libra's intriguing zebra botany. Spores grew along the inside of the coils, dark nut-like nodules. When they were ripe the coils unwound like a loosened spring, and flung them wide across the surrounding ground. It was one of the more interesting mechanisms St Libra's evolution had developed to compensate for the lack of birds and insects. Of course, a lot of the plants shook or trembled, throwing seeds off like a dog coming out of water. The plant orientation briefing warned them about the peppershot bush, that coughed out a spore cloud like pepper dust, which played havoc with human skin.

Sunlight shimmered on the long serpentine patch of water fed by a river at the head and leaking away into a broad swamp six kilometres away at the lower end. The cluster of black and silver bricks that were the expedition's Qwik-Kabins above the lake shore made an incongruous sight amid the pervasive colourwash of St Libra's abundant flora. Two Berlins were sitting beside the shelters. Legionnaires patrolled the loose perimeter of the camp, including the eighty-metre stub of raw earth which a lone dozer had cleared.

Clouds were already crawling across the sky as Ravi brought the Berlin round to the end of the infant runway to hover. HDA engineers scuttled underneath the big helicopter, holding their sunhats in place against the downwash. The senior loading officer on the ground guided him down, and the dozer touched the earth. Tork released the cables, earning a thumbs-up from the ground crew. Ravi peeled away to find a landing site.

Later, after he'd had a rest, he'd help unload the rest of the equipment and supplies the Berlin had brought, along with the fresh food. They could barbecue the burgers and sausages this evening, enjoying a tropical sunset without the usual insect attack that plagued most of the trans-stellar worlds. As he settled the big copter, he saw the contra-rotating blades on the parked vehicles start to turn as the turbines were fired up. The crews were desperate to get airborne before the bulk of the storm hit Edzell. They had at best seven hours of daylight left, along with a refuelling rendezvous with the Daedalus tanker, so they'd be finishing the flight back to Abellia in darkness. Ravi grinned approval at that – more skilled flying.

He throttled the turbines back, and initiated the general craft powerdown sequence. Raindrops began to splash across the bulging cockpit windscreen. It was growing dark outside, the twirling mass of cloud had already veiled the sun. Tomorrow he'd be sitting about, waiting for the next Berlin flight to arrive before he could leave. That gave him several hours to scout round and get a feel for the territory. Maybe the engineers would allow him to drive one of the dozers. It was a grand time to be alive.

Sunday 3rd February 2143

There were supposed to be as many coves around the Abellia peninsula as there were days in the year – though you had to be generous in your definition of 'cove' and there was a question over which planet's year . . .

The bungalows of Camilo Beach were simple structures nestling among the low dunes between the beach itself and the Rue du Ranelagh, a twin-lane highway that bordered the bottom of the slope. They were made from white concrete, with big glass doors opening onto neat patios and sandy yards, giving everyone easy access to the beach. It was a nice community, and right from the start designed for families of Abellia's burgeoning middle class; the independent business people and company staff whose contracts had expired but chose to stay on

Saul Howard woke up with the bright Sirius light streaming through the gap at the bottom of the blinds. For a while he just lay there, enjoying the quiet drowsiness that allowed his mind to wander through warmly pleasant notions. Somewhere deeper inside the cottage bungalow came the occasional muffled thuds and voices that meant the kids were awake and up. Most likely trying to make themselves breakfast, and hell alone knew what kind of mess that would result in. At least Isadora, the eldest at fourteen, would take charge. Though why a teenager would be up this early was a sore puzzle to him. That particular clan were supposed to sleep until noon and then grump around the house all day, not be the kind of happy delight Isadora had developed into. That she so broke the stereotype format was something he should be thankful for.

Must take after her mother.

He shifted his head so he could see Emily. A tangled wave of rich auburn hair ran down the pillow, just revealing that enchanting, fine-boned face with its small mouth and long nose; skin darkened by a decade and a half's exposure to St Libra sunlight made it hard to distinguish the delightful freckles these days. But they were there, unusually visible this morning in the hazy light.

For a long moment he considered reaching out and stroking the hair. Leaning forward for a kiss, which she would respond to lazily. Slide the sheet down slowly and coyly. Emily never did wear anything other than PJ trousers, which even after sixteen years of marriage he still found irresistibly sexy. But then she had a body to match that beautiful face.

The notion of a morning consisting of nothing but leisurely sex was enticing indeed. But as his heart quickened and he woke up fully he had to sigh and roll off the bed as gingerly as he could. The en suite was eight depressingly familiar paces across the tiled floor. Sadly, at fifty-eight he didn't quite have the body to match that of his much younger wife; joints were perennially stiff and twingey, short curly hair which long ago had turned traitor grey was now realigning itself in the dreaded male pattern baldness, and his gut, despite daily exercise and a healthy diet he hardly ever cheated on, was sagging. A mounting decrepitude which his bladder reminded him of with its standard morning urge.

Emily had roused herself when he returned, propping herself up on one elbow and wrapping the sheet demurely round her shoulders. He rolled back onto the mattress and snuggled up beside her.

She grinned knowingly. 'They're already awake.'

'They won't come in.'

'Down boy.'

Saul rolled his eyes in mock despair. 'It's the weekend.'

'Now you're just coming over all needy.'

'I've always been needy.'

An elegant eyebrow was raised disdainfully. 'Yes.'

'We could put a lock on the door.' Something Emily had never countenanced – she wanted the children to be able to come straight in if anything was wrong.

'Why stop there? Why don't we just move out?'

'You are a cruel lady. But I like your thinking. We could probably afford to rent, maybe a nice pied-à-terre.'

She smiled at his foolishness and leant over to kiss him. The top of the sheet came free, and he slid his hand across exposed silky warm skin.

Little footsteps thudded noisily along the corridor outside. Saul had just managed to turn the snog into a harmless-looking mum and dad cuddle when the door burst open. Jevon, their eleven-year-old, came zooming in, all eager smiles.

'Surf's up!' he announced gleefully.

Saul manfully resisted the obvious double entendre. 'Is it?'

Isadora appeared in the doorway, holding six-year-old Clara's hand. She gave her mother a guilty glance. 'Sorry, I couldn't stop him.'

'It's okay, darling.' Emily patted the bed, and Jevon landed beside her with a bounce, still all eager smiles.

'Can we go down on the beach?' he asked breathlessly. 'Please, I've done my teeth and everything.'

'We need our breakfast first,' Saul said. That was when he caught sight of the antique clock, and pressed his teeth together in dismay: 7:48. On a Sunday!

'I'll get it,' Jevon volunteered enthusiastically.

Saul did well not to shudder at the memory of his son helpfully bringing Mum and Dad breakfast in bed a couple of weeks back. 'It's okay, we'll manage. You need to check your board, and pack the beach bags.'

'Done it already!'

'You'll just have to wait,' Emily said. 'It's too early. We will go later, all right. That's a certified cert.'

Jevon pulled his end-of-the-world face, but accepted his mother's ruling. There was always an argument when Saul told him to do anything. The way it should be with fathers and sons, Saul supposed, but it did get exhausting.

Saul pulled on a towelling robe and walked through to the kitchen where the debris of a hurriedly eaten kids' breakfast was still on the table. Emily prepared their croissants and coffee while he shoved the mess into the dishwasher.

'You don't have to wait until I get back,' Saul said as they took their light meal out onto the small vine-sheltered patio outside the kitchen's sliding glass doors.

Emily stood over him as she put the little tray down. Always a mildly intimidating sight. She was an easy six-foot tall in her bare feet, while he just about made five nine.

'It's Sunday,' she groused. It was exactly the same inflection Isadora now used when complaining about how unfair the universe was. Clara was starting to learn it, too.

'Big day for us,' he countered, as always.

'I know,' she sighed and sat down beside him.

Breakfast outside with a gorgeous young wife on yet another cloudless tropical morning wasn't a bad way of starting a Sunday, he admitted. The patio was wedged into a corner of their cottage, a perfect morning suntrap with two sides made up by white-washed concrete walls, leaving the other two open to the view across the beach that began a mere fifty metres away. St Libra's rings swept across the sky above the sparkling, wave-tossed sea. Pergola beams ribbing the patio were webbed with a tangle of terrestrial honeysuckle and native aquelvine – the latter for the shade given by its dark glossy leaves, and former for the scent of the flowers.

As he drank his coffee he could hear the waves slapping against the fine pale sand beyond the low dunes with their feathery reeds. Without a single giant moon, St Libra lacked the tides which roamed across Earth's oceans, but between them the rings' little shepherd moonlets and some healthy ocean winds produced batches of decent waves. The beach that Camilo Village was clustered round had good surf most days. Isadora was already a proficient surfer, with Jevon determined to match his big sister; while little Clara was an expert body boarder. Saul enjoyed his days on the beach, splashing about in the water with the whole family, occasionally catching a good curl and keeping his balance, following it up with a barbecue for lunch; and Clara still liked sandcastles, while Jevon pretended he'd grown out of it but joined in with a spade anyway.

'You okay?'

Saul shook his head and smiled at his wife. 'Sure.'

'You seemed a bit distant, there.'

He gave the rings-dominated sky a guilty glance, but none of the huge dark HDA planes was overhead at that moment. 'Just this expedition nonsense, that's all.'

'What's to worry about? You don't really think there's a sentient species living out in the wilds there, do you?'

'No. Course not. It's stupid. It's just the disruption that's all. And the amount of bioil they're using up may leave the city short. We don't have that many algaepaddies, and it's not like we can import it from Highcastle.'

Emily gave him a curious look. A hand waved up casually at the bungalow's high sloping roof. 'We have a photovoltaic roof, which produces more electricity than we use. The cars have auxiliary batteries for the fuel cells, which have enough charge to get us either to the school or the shop, and we can recharge them here if the tanks ever do truly run dry. So what's your problem?'

He shrugged. 'Our economy. It might turn sour. The farms need bioil, you know. Tractors don't run on batteries – they have high-rated fuel cells – and a lot of them have biodiesel engines.'

'Tell me you didn't just say that. That's such establishment talk. *I'm awfully worried about the economy, the market's down, you know, do you think we should we change the interest rates, old chap,*' she taunted.

'Ouch!'

'Sorry, but . . . come on. This is exciting for the kids. Jevon wants to drive out to the airport and watch the planes, especially those big SuperRocs.'

'Does he?'

'He's eleven! And they are big chunks of shiny machinery whizzing round over his head, helping to discover aliens hidden in the jungle – what else does he want to go and see?'

Saul almost said *the surf*, but that would accelerate the argument and they'd both wind up getting stubborn and defensive like they always did when they fought, which wasn't wise. Not at this time on a Sunday morning. 'I'll maybe take him out there this evening if there's a SuperRoc flying. The airport must publish a flight schedule somewhere on the transnet.'

'That'll be nice for the two of you. I'm surprised you haven't been out there already, it's the biggest collection of boys' toys we'll ever see here.'

'Military crap doesn't really interest me.'

'Hmm.' She gave him a suspicious glance.

He smiled, as if admitting defeat, acknowledging that she was right about everything always – secret to a successful marriage.

Forty minutes later he was dressed in jeans and a grey sweatshirt, ready to go to work. Emily had put on a lavender beachsuit, ready for the waves and the sun. It was skin-tight, and made her look utterly fabulous. She grinned when she caught him looking at her, and gave him a long kiss. 'Hurry back,' she teased.

'Right.' He gave each of the kids a quick hug. 'Be good. And do what your mother says; remember the waves are not your friend.'

'I'll be good, Daddy,' Clara promised solemnly.

'Yeah, I will,' Jevon yelled as he rushed out carrying his board.

'Bye, Dad.' Isadora smiled.

'Bye.' Saul said absolutely nothing about the blue and pink bikini she was wearing. Absolutely nothing, because there wasn't a whole lot of it to comment on. The Ford Rohan saloon opened its driver door as he approached, and he climbed in. 'Take me to the shop,' he told the auto.

The fuel cells powered up as the garage door slid open, and the auto backed the Rohan out into bright sunlight. Isadora would put a T-shirt on when she went out surfing, he knew, which was fine, and she also knew to apply hifactor sun cream before she spent an age getting her tan just right. He told himself it didn't matter because there weren't many people using the beach, mostly the families from the other bungalows. But the group of friends she hung out with after school and during the weekends was now starting to include more boys.

Saul sighed as the Rohan turned out of Camilo Village's access road and onto the Rue du Ranelagh, which would take him straight down to the old town. Isadora and boys shouldn't bother him, he knew, but even now he'd never managed to truly shake free from his formal Jewish upbringing back in Boston. He could still recite most of Rabbi Lavine's stern lectures on the sanctity of marriage and the fundamental foulness of teenage sex; it was as if the old man had mistakenly picked up a book of Catholic commandments when he walked into the temple and nobody had ever corrected him.

What Saul ought to be was happy that his daughter had lots of friends, that she'd find boys she adored and who worshipped her; but there would be other boys, the kind which he'd know at first glance before they even opened their mouths were no good at all, and he'd hate them and not be able to say; and anyway St Libra wasn't a place with huge opportunities, not the right kind of opportunities anyway. Bartram North had set it up as an isolated community purely to service his beloved Institute far beyond the usual legislative restrictions prevalent on most trans-space worlds. It was pleasant enough with its unvarying climate and zero taxes, but without any real industry or economy the kids would never achieve much for themselves. What Isadora needed was a place where she could truly blossom, instead of fall into one of the hundreds of life-traps surrounding her in Abellia . . .

Hell, why can't I be proud of her and have faith rather than worry all the time? He supposed it was the fate of fathers everywhere.

The Rohan drove into the Delacroix tunnel, powering up the slope. When it emerged the other side, the Rue du Ranelagh curved sharply along the side of the valley.

Up ahead was the remarkable Lazare Bridge, a white marble strip that rested on a couple of massive toroidal supports, the north end higher than the south. Big tankers full of raw trundled along it, electric axle motors straining against the incline. There was a lot of construction work under way in Abellia. With all the beaches around the peninsula now taken, the rich were having to build their tacky fifty-room mansions further inland on giant terraces carved into the mountains, or across plateaus raised up out of the valley floor to lift their foundations safely above the churning rivers. With each new extravagant, expensive site full of chittering automata and harried supervisors came another decent branch of infrastructure which Brinkelle required they contribute to the community as the price for her permission to live in her fiefdom. It was a splendid way of funding decent civic amenities for those who didn't necessarily come here by choice, but were subject to economic necessity like most humans.

Saul wondered how the expedition would affect the desirability of owning a place in Abellia. Not that the truly rich lived here permanently, it was just another house spread around the circuit of their eternal migration. Most of the big houses went unused for a year or eighteen months at a time before their plutocrat owners visited in the forlorn hope of witnessing some new spectacle or experience that might momentarily enrich their jaded got-it-all lifestyle. Maybe the chance of being shredded by a nonhuman monster would actually appeal to their type. Although knowing them there would be an influx of armed hunters, relishing the thrill of stalking their lethal prey through uncharted jungle.

That was the thing Saul feared as much as he admired about life in Abellia. Despite the allure of its beauty and ease, it was like nowhere else in the trans-stellar worlds. Here civilization really was a veneer, an incredibly rich one, but flimsy none the less. He'd come here twenty years ago to exploit some of the human savagery which lurked just below that glossy sheen of respectability, and now he had to live with his choices. Of course, he'd never expected to marry and have kids, but Abellia had smoothly gone on to convince him that life here could be normal. And he'd fallen into the nightmare of believing it.

Beyond the bridge, the valley opened out, revealing the rings hanging across the southern sky, glowing with a sunset-gold hue. And a big dark plane was flying along them, descending towards the airport away to the north-west of town.

Saul frowned at the plane as the distant growl of its jets washed around the silent car, knowing full well that was the real cause of his moody anger. It had been the same ever since this ridiculous expedition had been announced. Right from the start the official reason made no sense: evidence that there might be a sentient race living on the unexplored Brogal continent. Evidence that was never declared or defined. The HDA was going in to examine genetic diversity, they claimed vaguely; there were possibilities uncovered by on-going academic research that more than just plants had evolved after all.

Lies, Saul knew, pathetic, evil lies. Nobody was researching St Libra genetics; there was no profit in it, their biochemistry was too different from terrestrial. There had only ever been one single example of non-botanical life on Brogal: the monster which had slaughtered Bartram North's household. The Abellia political sites had been positing that, too, resurrecting the events of twenty years ago, at the same time scornfully reminding everyone of the mad psycho girl who had actually been convicted of the murders. They at least were clear in naming that as the more likely cause of the expedition.

Saul suspected they were right. What he utterly failed to understand was: why now? Why after twenty long, squandered years did anyone suddenly decide to investigate a discredited rumour? And not just a small enquiry, either. Hell alone knew how much money the expedition was costing.

He wasn't sure what he feared most: if they'd find something out there in the endless wilderness of jungles, or they wouldn't.

His life was settled now, however wrong he'd been to allow that to happen. He'd made his sacrifices, done his utmost for those he loved more than his own life, and moved on. He'd never expected anything to change. And that was what really bugged him, the cause of recent sleepless nights and general irritability. It was starting to look like events completely beyond his control were about to chew him up and spit him out once again. It just wasn't fair. Not at all.

*

Velasco Beach extended for four hundred metres in a slight crescent curve to the west of the Alonso marina, itself an outgrowth of Abellia's original cargo harbour. Its location in the middle of the old town, along with its size, made it a popular attraction for Abellia residents who couldn't afford their own beach, a place they could relax away from the precocious demanding rich whom they served. The Hawaiian Moon water sport store had a great location in the middle of the promenade behind Velasco Beach, jammed between Rico's bar and grill, and the Cornish ice cream shop. The Rohan delivered Saul into the staff-only car parking slot behind the Hawaiian Moon at ten to nine that morning. Pelli and Natasha, the two surf-mad youngsters who worked behind the counters, were already there waiting for Saul to open up. The back door's mesh of smartdust acknowledged the owner's biometric signature along with his e-i's code, and the locks clicked back.

Saul had owned the Hawaiian Moon for twelve years now. The concept had started off with just him and Emily at a stall down the far end of Velasco, with little Isadora toddling round enchanting the customers with her cheeky smile. Now he owned the store outright. Two-thirds of the long, single-storey, white concrete building was given over to beachwear, a mix of designer labels and more reasonably priced gear. Emily selected it all; her brief time spent in the fashion trade back on New Washington gave her an eye for what looked good and would sell here. The clothing side made a nice profit year after year.

Saul's part of the business took up the remaining third of the store as well as the whole back room. That he knew so much about surfing and boards still occasionally amused him, but even though he'd been bitten by the surfing bug relatively late in life, the addiction wasn't one he could kick – and didn't want to. So now he supplied surfboards to fellow enthusiasts, and lessons for those who'd seen people gliding effortlessly along the tops of the waves and mistakenly believed they could do just as well. Several types of board were on display in the front, but it was the back room which had two state-of-the-art 3D printers and five tanks of specialist raw. They allowed Saul to microfacture any kind of board listed on the transnet, and there were tens of thousands. He'd even designed a few of his own, more suited to the milder waters of St Libra, which were popular.

Pelli went in and started examining the holographic decals on yesterday's boards, seeing if they'd adhered properly overnight, while Natasha dumped her bag in the little staff room that also served as a storeroom. Saul told the store's network to open the security shutters. Given Abellia's minuscule crime-rate he always thought them a waste of time, but the insurance company insisted. As they rolled up, he looked out across the vitrified sandstone promenade. There weren't many people about, as the shops and stalls were only just opening. A few early swimmers were in the water, and families with very young children were setting up camp on the sand with towels and sunshades.

Three people walking along the promenade stopped in front of the Hawaiian Moon, staring in past the mannequins dressed in rainbow sarongs and wet-look beachsuits. Recognition kicked in, giving Saul a nasty shock. He didn't know the woman with dreadlocks down to her hips, but the other two . . . It had been fifteen years since he'd seen Duren. The man was twice Saul's width, and none of that bulk was fat. The jet-black hair was thinner now, tied back in a tiny pony-tail with a silver band; and there were a couple of demon-eye tattoos glimmering fire-red round his eyelids, but other than that it was as if no time had passed. The other man was a North, dressed in a simple white shirt and green shorts, with worn leather sandals on dirty feet. And Saul knew exactly which North. Only one member of that clone-hoard had a greying beard that came halfway down his belly, which along with his garb marked him down as some mad preacher prophet, an analogy which was best not spoken out loud.

The three of them regarded him without moving. It was as intimidating as he supposed it was meant to be.

'Pelli, Nat, go get yourselves a coffee,' Saul said.

'But I've just got—' Natasha started.

'Don't argue, just go. I'll call when I want you back. My dollar, okay.'

She frowned at him, and glanced across at the three immobile figures outside. Confusion was conjuring up a lot of questions.

Saul gave Pelli an urgent signal.

'Come on, babe,' Pelli said, and ushered her towards the rear door. A suspicious Natasha allowed herself to be hustled away.

Saul told the store's smartnet to open the front door. The bolts *snicked* across loudly. For the first time in twelve years, opening up the business didn't sound auspicious.

Duren came in first. For someone so big he moved easily. Saul remembered the hours they spent at the small gym they were both members of back in the day; while Saul's ambition had been to keep himself lean for surfing, Duran went for building strength. And when he wasn't on the gym weights, he was taking his kung-fu classes or kickboxing, whatever allowed him to beat the crap out of other people without getting arrested. Outside of politics, it was what he lived for. He reached nirvana when the two could be combined.

There was a heartbeat while Saul looked at his old not-quite friend, too overwhelmed and nervous to react. Then Duren's round face grinned widely, showing off a couple of canine fang implants. 'Man, you look good for an old dude.' Duren grasped Saul's hands, engulfing them completely in a hot, sweaty grip. 'You haven't put on a fucking gram in what, ten years?'

'Longer than that,' Saul grinned back, hoping it looked sincere.

'Still hitting the curves?'

'When I have the time.'

'Yeah,' Duren said, his voice like a wheezy whisper. 'I heard you got married. You! And you've got, what, three kids now?'

Saul's heart started racing. *Oh shit, oh shit, oh shit* – this wasn't casual, a happy tour round the old times. 'Yeah, three.'

'Cool. Man, I want you to meet some friends of mine. This here is Zulah.'

The woman gave him a sullen nod, the glass beads in her dreadlocks clicking together smartly as her head moved. Saul couldn't remember ever seeing someone with skin so black before. He suspected the pigmentation had been enhanced, it was like a stealth coating. Definitely a statement.

'And this—' Duren began proudly.

'Zebediah North,' Saul completed. 'Pleasure to meet you.'

'Mr Howard; I've heard a lot about you from brother Duren.'

'Oh dear.' He kept it light, the old-pals-never-stop-joshing act. 'It's not true.'

'That would be a shame,' Zebediah said.

'Come in, sit down,' Saul said. 'We have some tea in the back.'

'You are most kind,' Zebediah said.

'Lock the door,' Zulah said as she walked past, making sure she was first into the back room.

Duren gave an exaggerated shrug at her behaviour. Saul told the smartnet to seal up the shop, and went into the back room, wishing the whole sensation of doom was just down to his age and paranoia. But . . . Zebediah North!

He was the only North ever to rebel against his family – effectively turning against himself and everything the Norths had achieved. He rejected it all: the company, his dead father, brothers, cousins, wealth, even his name. Saul couldn't recall what it used to be, but he'd been born a 2, one of Bartram's sons. His one-man uprising had started right after the slaughter. Everyone at the time had said how that must have pushed him over the edge. He'd broadcast across the transnet about how the human 'occupation' of St Libra was wrong, and how he would take this message out to the real people, educating them about their mistake. Over the next few years, spent as a nomad oracle travelling around the Independencies, his message had modified and softened somewhat to teaching people how to live in harmony with their adopted world. Mainly: kick Northumberland Interstellar off St Libra, and rip up the algaepaddies.

Zulah was examining the 3D printers, which irritated Saul. But telling her to stop would make an issue of it, and he wasn't ready for that yet.

'So are you still active?' Duren asked in his forceful whisper.

'No. But you already know that.' For a while Saul had been involved with the fledgling political opposition groups in Abellia. There weren't many of them. After all Bartram had been a pretty benign dictator, and that at least hadn't changed under Brinkelle. Some civic issues could actually be voted on, nobody came here against their will, and anyone could leave at any time. In theory. Economics wasn't entirely favourable to the non-wealthy who got stranded, but if you were in real monetary dire straits you could always get a charity passage on one of the cargo boats back to Eastshields and either go back through the gateway or settle in an Independency. Even so, Saul and others had been agitating for a more open style of democracy; an elected city council would be a good start rather than the occasional online referendum on trivia like where to site a new school. And there was also the question of rights for those born in Abellia – not many admittedly – but their numbers would only ever increase. Saul's principal cause, the reason he had gotten involved, was healthcare. There were excellent hospitals in Abellia, including the massive Institute itself which Bartram had founded, Abellia's whole *raison d'être*, and arguably the best medical facility to be found among the transstellar worlds. But financially they were all out of reach for any of the independent workers. You simply had to have a health plan paid for by your employer, and that wasn't compulsory. Everyone attracted to the meetings had been equally aggrieved by the health coverage situation, but they had a host of other issues as well.

The problem with all this hot radicalism was the quality of

people it had attracted. After a couple of years attending meetings of new-formed 'people's committees' – where even the most dynamic chairperson could rarely get a vote passed on what kind of coffee was going to be served at next week's meeting – Saul had walked out never to return, completely fed up and dispirited at achieving nothing for democracy's progress within those two years. Besides, Brinkelle had started to move towards establishing a universal health plan – not a particularly good one, but definitely a safety net for the worst cases. He knew he was being too judgemental – that most of his fellow agitators meant well – but there was a limit to how many hours of his life could be spent on procedural points and backstabbing and ideological schisms and who called who what in the bar last night. Duren, on the other hand, was attracted to the scene by precisely that kind of debate which spilled over into the physical.

'Yes, Saul,' Zebediah North said. 'We know that.'

'So why are you here?' It was almost a rhetorical question. Their arrival couldn't be coincidence. For one frightening moment he thought the North might know the true reason for him coming to Abellia all those years ago. After all, Northumberland Interstellar's security department was good. But if they did know, he wouldn't still be walking round, let alone allowed the liberty he enjoyed.

'The expedition, of course.'

'Yeah, I figured that.'

'It is another violation of St Libra's sanctity.'

Saul couldn't help glancing at Duren. But the big man didn't show a hint of amusement. He was a true believer now, Saul realized. Zebediah had provided both cause and leadership, everything that had been missing from the heart of Duren's life before.

'Yeah,' Saul said wearily. 'But at worst they'll spend six months running round the northern jungles then go home and have to try and justify how much they've spent to their governments. Unless there is a monster living out there?' He deliberately left it open.

'There are no monsters on St Libra,' Zebediah North said. 'Only the evil which humans have brought with them.'

It was a strange thing, but Saul could believe what he heard. The way Zebediah spoke the sentiment – without shouting, without a politician's faux hand-clasp sincerity, but instead with utter from-the-soul conviction – simply made it a universal truth. No wonder poor Duren was such a devout disciple these days. It would be hard to resist such evangelicalism.

'Right,' Saul said, shaking off the mesmerizing delusion. 'So what do you want to do about it?'

'I must learn exactly what they are doing. I need to see for myself the level of the violation they commit. Only then can justice be levelled against the perpetrators.'

'I see. And how do I fit in to all that?'

'We need some information, man,' Duren said. 'That's all.'

'What kind of information?'

'On the expedition.'

'Yeah, I get that, but it's all there on the public sector of the transnet. Why come to me?'

'I need the full personnel list,' Zulah said abruptly.

Saul did his best not to chortle at her. 'I can't get you that.'

'Three years with Abellia TeleNet, working to establish the third-generation communication architecture for the city,' Duren said.

'Twenty years ago,' Saul blurted.

'The systems you helped design and instal are the backbone of today's local net,' Zebediah said. 'There have been no technological revolutions since then, only expansion. The net has grown with the city, but that's all.'

'Okay, but that doesn't make me some kind of bytehead super hacker.'

'No, probably not, and yet . . .'

And Saul had never felt so judged before – Zebediah's stare was relentless, allowing him to gaze upon Saul's very thoughts. Exposing his guilt.

'You're a curious man, Saul Howard,' Zebediah said. 'Here you are in Abellia, with which your early involvement with the democracy movement illustrates your dissatisfaction. Now you've evolved into an ageing surf dude with a sweet family, demonstrating a streak of independence. Yet to be contracted by Abellia TeleNet, you needed to be a fully fledged corporate software nerd. I've had a lot of experience with them, decades, and you don't strike me as the type. You're not dedicated to code and systems and protocols, not you, not a free human soul who delights in the joy of riding the waves, feeling the spray of freedom in your face. Such dreary things can be learned by anyone with half a brain, of course, if there was a good enough reason for it. So why would you do that?'

'I was young, I followed the money. And no one stays with the same job for life. *You* know that, don't you?'

'Touché. But you weren't *that* young even twenty years ago. Why did you come here, Saul? And more to the point, why have you stayed?'

'Wife. Three kids. Surf's up every day.'

'I don't believe you.'

'Tough shit, pal.'

'I can see I make you uncomfortable, Saul, and I'm genuinely sorry for that. I simply came here to ask a favour from someone I was led to believe shared some of my ideals. Do you really wish the expedition to go completely unchallenged? For if I don't question it, who will?'

Saul looked from Zebediah to Duren. Neither of them was giving away a thing, just waiting patiently, pleasantly even. He didn't bother making eye contact with Zulah, she scared him more than Duren ever could. 'The personnel list?' he asked finally.

'If you could, I would be in your debt,' Zebediah said.

'Nothing else?'

'No.'

'This may take a while. I'm not exactly up to date on this kind of thing.'

'Thank you Saul. St Libra is grateful for your help.'

'Sure.'

*

Vance Elston walked over from his tent to the Remote Observation centre – a grand name for three Qwik-Kabins locked together, with air-con grilles thrumming and an elaborate antenna dome on top. A trailer with two high-output fuel cells was standing along one side, with thick power cables plugged into the Qwik-Kabin's utility sockets; gentle plumes of steam drifted out of their vents as they hummed away. Just as he was going up the five metal steps to the entrance, he paused to watch a SuperRoc touch down on the runway. Even after three days at Abellia airport the sight of the big planes flying their airlift mission was impressive. They were still flying round the clock, mainly delivering equipment now. After he'd arrived in Abellia, engineers had converted both the SuperRocs back to full cargo configuration. AirBrogal 2757s were scheduled to bring in any remaining HDA personnel.

The Abellia compound was a muddy, temporary city of tents and Qwik-Kabins inside the airport perimeter, bordered along one side by the rows of pallets and ground vehicles due to be shipped out to the forward bases. Several types of helicopters were parked down an apron at the other end of the airport, waiting their turn to fly forward. So far, Vance had been very impressed by the skills of the pilots. The whole process of setting up Edzell had gone a lot more smoothly than he'd been expecting.

Vance glanced up at the sky as he went through the door to the Remote Observation centre. It was another cloudless morning, with the rings shimmering a pastel silver above the mountains of the Abellia peninsula. Humidity was strong, and the wind was starting to pick up from the south. Rain was coming in maybe three hours. Weather wisdom was a sense he'd quickly developed after arriving. There had already been five torrential downpours, two of them at night, which made sleep impossible in a tent.

He went through the ante-room, allowing his eyes to adapt to the subdued lighting inside the Remote Observation centre. The Qwik-Kabins had formed a large central space, with a row of zone consoles and some big panes along the front wall. Pilots on two zone consoles monitored the six e-Rays so far operational, making sure they maintained position in the relay chain over the jungle. The drones were beaming back a lot of information for the big displays. Most prominent was a weather radar image of the southern portion of Brogal. Vance was pleased to note a big cloud front massing out at sea, and due to landfall in three and a quarter hours. Other displays were showing camera images of Edzell. Front and centre was one with an over-the-pilot-shoulder view from a Daedalus cockpit as it approached Edzell.

The back of the room was crowded with senior expedition staff, headed by Charmonique Passam herself, closely attended by the official GE press corps: a small troupe of reporters with a sole camera crew, all carefully marshalled by Carole Furec, the expedition press officer. Brice North was also in attendance, one of Brinkelle's daughters, and obviously a one-in-ten – she looked about seventeen even though the file in his iris smartcell grid said she was twenty-three. None of Brinkelle's five children shared any characteristics, either with each other or their mother; and she'd had only one herself, Beatrice, her first; the remainder were all surrogate born. Some North traditions just didn't change, he thought.

Brice looked like she had a strong Japanese ethnicity in her make-up. Shorter than most people in the room, she held her wide shoulders perfectly square, while her long face appeared inexplicably sad. It was distracting to the men in the room; someone that young, beautiful, and apparently vulnerable was earning a lot of glances to the detriment of the full mission focus. All their wistful smiles would be for nothing, Vance knew; she wouldn't be interested in some HDA trooper, whatever the rank. Wouldn't lower herself. That intense way she regarded the big screens was the real giveaway of her age and North-heritage intelligence. It even seemed to be unsettling Passam. He wondered if he should try to arrange an encounter with Angela. Both of them had the same level of drive and intensity, it would be like looking in a mirror, with just skin colour distinguishing them.

Vance sidled over to Griffin Toyne, who was also making sure he kept below the VIPs' radar.

'You should stop looking at people like you want to fight them,' Toyne said quietly. 'Especially female people.'

'I assess every situation for its potential. It's what I'm trained for.'

'She's not going to fuck you, either. Not even for novelty value.'

'Yeah, I already assessed that.'

Toyne grinned. 'Have the xenobiology teams made any progress?'

'Yes, but all negative,' Vance said. 'Antrinell and Marvin have been out into the hinterlands as far as the roads take them, which isn't far, maybe a hundred klicks past the airport. Every sample they've taken shows a typical St Libra genetic composition. There's nothing abnormal growing out there.'

'That's good news.'

'Not for the taxpayer. It means we have to go ahead with the forward bases.'

Toyne gave him a curious glance. 'You didn't strike me as the Taxpayer Union type.'

'I'm not – I'm the fast efficiency type. I want this confirmed, one way or the other.'

'Then you should know we may have to slow our schedule; we're slightly concerned about JB5 biav stocks.'

'On St Libra? You're kidding me.'

'This isn't Highcastle. The local refinery is only set up to produce biav for maybe ten commercial aircraft, and some executive jets.'

'Then switch refinery production for more biav. They certainly have enough bioil for all their Rolls-Royces and Mercedes here.'

Toyne lowered his voice. 'That would require Brinkelle's co-operation, and she's not happy about any of this. She didn't quite appreciate the scale this expedition was going to be mounted at.'

'Who did?'

One of the centre's officers gave Passam a quick nod. Up on the main wallscreen the Daedalus was coming round to line up on Edzell's runway.

'That is one small streak of mud,' Vance muttered. Even as he watched he could see ribbons of water shimmering on the newly created runway.

'Big enough,' Toyne said. 'I've been on missions where they landed on a strip half that size. Besides, they've already shipped out an approach guidance system; they could land at night in a thunderstorm if necessary.'

Vance didn't believe a word of it. But the pilot held the approach steady, clearly satisfied with what the camp team had cut out for him.

He held his breath, offering up a small prayer as the Daedalus touched down. The pilot made a perfect landing, though the big plane did come to a halt with only about thirty metres of runway left. Everyone in the centre applauded. Passam spoke a few words of congratulations to the pilot, then turned to her press acolytes.

'It is with the greatest delight that I am now declaring the Edzell base formally open. I would like to take this moment to commend the efforts of the HDA personnel who have worked so hard to make this possible. As always I am impressed by their dedication and professionalism. It is precisely this kind of proficiency which will see us successfully push back the frontiers of knowledge amid the unexplored and unknown regions of this splendid world.'

Vance and Toyne looked at each other, sharing their private contempt for the politician.

'Let's go get lunch,' Toyne said.

'Amen to that.'

*

Saul was bizarrely pleased with himself when he did finally plug an unrestricted link into the expedition's secure network. Unrestricted, that is, if you didn't want to access any of the level-ten files. A quick scan of the register didn't show any level-ten files, but why would the security protocols be included in the closed network if there weren't any? *Standard package?* he wondered. Except that would be a little too neat. It was probably that someone of his inexperience simply couldn't find them. And with his dire lack of current ability, merely trying to discover their coding tags would probably trigger all sorts of alarms. So he flicked through the files that he could access, basically the kind a one-month probationary HDA company clerk was allowed to retrieve, and downloaded a copy of the expedition personnel, through random routing pathways in Abellia's net.

'Why, thank you, Saul, this is excellent information,' Zebediah North said.

Saul leaned back in his desk chair and watched the zone console screen curve away from him. The icons that'd been blazing along his optic nerves vanished, icons for programs he hadn't used in a while. They'd been stored in a hidden cache on the back room's console, the one usually employed for operating the printers. Old habits die hard, thankfully.

Zebediah and his two disciples – no other way of describing them – were busy studying the list flowing down their grids. Their lips fluttered as they talked via their linked bodymeshes, excluding him from the conversation. Fingers flicked idly through keyspace, twisting the invisible icons. Saul's e-i reported the ringlink which connected them employed medium-grade encryption. They were quite serious about keeping their discussion private.

Saul was tempted to run through the personnel list himself, but that would mean second-guessing them, and he just didn't want to get involved. He'd already had to call Emily, and tell her he was going to be late home. She'd been upset, but not angry. Now he just had to decide what to tell her; his past life was something he'd never gone into in real detail. She knew the same story he'd told Duren, that he'd been a contractor for Abellia TeleNet before striking out on his own in a variety of crappy jobs. He'd told her that he'd left Earth because of a failed marriage and a personal tragedy, which wasn't quite a lie – but context was king, and he'd never corrected her interpretation of that. She'd never asked for details, not in seventeen years of marriage. It was probably shame at first – after all *her* reason for being in Abellia wasn't particularly pleasant – and when topics get sealed off they tended to stay that way. Once their new life together had got under way he certainly didn't have a reason to dredge up the past, there was too much that had to remain safeguarded. Admitting why he knew Duren, though, wasn't catastrophic, his involvement with Abellia's ridiculous political movements was believable justification. And his time with Abellia TeleNet made him a logical choice for Duren. So she'd probably wind up being concerned for him, and no deeper questions would be asked, which was vital.

'We have someone of interest here,' Zebediah said.

'Really?' Saul didn't want to know.

'Bastian 2North,' Zulah said. 'He's perfect.'

Which didn't make any sense to Saul, which really wasn't good. His instincts were fired up now, thoughts racing to find a way out. He just couldn't afford to get involved any deeper. This wasn't going to end well, not for anybody, he knew that now. Zebediah was too wrapped up in his own importance, he didn't see outside his own shallow obsession-derived interpretation of the world, didn't see that you don't fuck with the HDA, not when they were on a mission like this one.

'Can you harvest a profile for us, please?' Zebediah asked.

'You're kidding, right?' Saul blurted. 'He's your brother.' Yet a stupid part of him was actually curious why a B North was being included on the expedition. It had to be politics.

'It's been a while,' Zebediah said equitably. 'I lost touch with my family. I know so little of them now.'

'But . . .'

'It would be a big help. And a search like this is hardly illegal.'

Then why don't you run it, Saul thought bitterly. It was such an obvious question he didn't bother: so there's no connection, of course, you use a patsy. He didn't dare look at Zulah or Duren. 'Okay, fine,' he said with a burst of indignation. 'But this is it, after this I'm going home. I have a family, as you keep pointing out.'

'I understand,' Zebediah said.

That placid, reasonable tone was starting to get to Saul. He told his e-i to immerse him back in Abellia's net. They might well be trying to set him up, but he still knew a thing or two about avoiding access traces. He started loading in one-off relays and fake net address routes, using some backdoors he'd established in Abellia TeleNet all those years ago. No way would anyone ever be able to tell he'd been compiling data on Bastian 2North, legitimately or otherwise.

*

The tents which made up Abellia airport's new city were made from jet-black photovoltaic sheets. Another logistic corps screwup given the quantity of intense sunlight beating down on them during the day. But the electricity they produced was more than enough to power all the ancillary systems included in the basic tent module, like the net cell, compactor toilet, internal lighting, kettle, and microwave oven. Too bad there wasn't any air-con. Angela had just shaken her head in disbelief at the sight of their accommodation as they disembarked the SuperRoc. The logistics corps had laid out the expedition camp in a perfect square along the airport's southern perimeter, with a cliff of containers and pallets down the northern side – closest to the runway. The arrangement, while logical, tended to channel all the foot traffic along the east–west tracks between the tents. With the rains coming at least once a day, the ground was getting badly chewed up by all the heavy HDA boots tramping along; the local grass had long since been mashed, now each day saw the mud getting deeper and wider.

Angela was getting fed up with it. So far the mud hadn't got inside the garters she wore, but that additional layer of protection was hot in this weather, making her legs sweat. And she walked about the airport a lot.

'I need some time alone,' she told Elston. 'I've been locked up for twenty years, and crammed into the Newcastle base for another fortnight. Just be a decent human for once. It's not like I can escape to anywhere from here.'

So he'd reluctantly agreed to let her have an hour a day to herself without Paresh or any of the squad beside her.

'But you're not to leave the airport perimeter,' he warned, and had her clothes smart-tagged to emphasize the lack of trust.

Angela walked away from the tent streets, making a complete circuit of the airport. There were few buildings: the main terminal, a cargo terminal, the engineering hangars, fuel depot. She walked round the tarmac aprons and taxi lanes and connecting roads, watching vehicles drive past at ridiculous speeds. Stood and stared at each plane landing and taking off. Talked to logistics corps personnel as they shuttled pallets and tanks about.

Each day she either waited until it had rained, or scoured the sky to make sure it would be clear of clouds for a while. On the third day she set out in the middle of the morning, taking her solid memory cache with her. It was half the size of her palm, and slipped into her pocket easily. She didn't need it for the memory capacity; it had its own cell built in, with a much greater range than her own bodymesh.

When she was walking down the side of a taxiway it detected the airport's net, and connected her via a cell in the main terminal. She might not have had transnet access for twenty years, but there were certain aspects of digital security she'd learned in Holloway – and it hadn't been from the official educational sessions, either. It was a simple fact of life that her fellow inmates had a knowledge of criminality that was at least equal to any law-enforcement specialist.

Angela's hands started flicking icons around, navigating away from Abellia, then St Libra itself, out into the true transnet. The dark cache was there, just as Zarleene Autrass (found guilty of killing two people – unfortunately for her, they were undercover cops) had confessed, shifting between transnet trunks, a purely random pattern unless you knew the key. Once opened, it contained a repository of many powerful hacking tools and secure link systems. But then Zarleene had been a top-flight AI creative until she fell for the wrong man, one who was charmingly persuasive, attentive, devoted, and excitingly wicked in bed. Zarleene: a petite twenty-five-year-old with poor social skills, who wouldn't have lasted a week in Holloway's brutal environment. Sweet hopeless Zarleene, who'd been all teary grateful for the protection Angela offered against more predatory inmates, and even more thankful for the snatched moments of passion, the vital human contact.

Angela immediately upgraded her e-i, equipping it with high-grade quantum encryption. Once the key had been sent back to her via multiple random routes, she incorporated layers of AI-level predictive behaviourals, constructing a real personality within the transnet which she designated the authority to handle her credit account and monitor her in real time in case she ever needed help fast – a big sister e-i. Content she was now reasonably secure, she had a nose around the rest of the cache's menu to see what else Zarleene had left behind. Mostly it was software for route ghosting, key grabs, and firewall crash and snatch; everything you needed for the kind of financial raids her suave man had groomed her for. But there were other software packages as well. Angela started familiarizing herself with their functions. Before long searchbots with registry immunity dispersed into the transnet, heavy with the requests Angela had loaded in. She withdrew from the dark cache, using the stealth access routines she'd found inside to cover her tracks. 'Thanks Zarleene,' she said silently. It wasn't even betrayal, not really – they'd both come away with what they wanted. Besides, there had been a lot worse things in Holloway over the years.

She joined Paresh's squad for lunch as they walked over to the big mess tent on the side of the squishy temporary city, watching out for the bigger puddles. Half of the squad didn't bother with trousers any more, they just wore boots and shorts. Angela wasn't so keen, she'd seen what some types of St Libra spores could do to human skin if they weren't cleaned off right away. They were relatively clear here as the hinterlands behind Abellia were mostly farmland and meadows. But you never knew what could blow in from the wildlands to the north.

'Here they go,' Marty O'Riley called.

Angela raised her sunglasses to gaze at the three Daedalus planes rolling along the taxiway to the runway. An hour before, she'd quested the camp's glitch-prone net to watch the feed from the first one landing at Edzell. The HDA was keen to build up the forward staging post camp quickly, keeping up the tremendous momentum they'd achieved to date. She knew the next batch of e-Rays was scheduled to be flown out tomorrow, so the observation crews could start to find a site another two thousand kilometres further north from Edzell; countryside which no one had ever seen other than through fuzzy images taken from space during the Sirius preliminary assessment probe ninety-three years ago. Once that second camp was up and running, the true exploration phase of the expedition would begin.

The first Daedalus roared along the runway before tipping up into the clear sky, climbing swiftly.

Several squad members whistled and cheered it on its way. Angela watched it with a great deal more ambiguity. Paresh's squad still didn't have the right attitude to the mission, they were far too complacent.

'Football game this afternoon,' DiRito said as they carried on to the big mess tent. 'Plenty of squads are putting a team together. We're going to make up a league.'

'Football or soccer?' Angela asked, which earned a huge groan from everyone.

'Soccer. The one and only proper football!' Omar Mihambo said in disgust.

'You GEs,' she countered. 'So small-minded.'

'We gave it freely to the trans-stellar worlds.'

'Feel free to take it back any time.'

'At least the rest of the worlds understand it.'

'Yeah, because they're too dumb to understand *real* football rules.'

'Did you play soccer in prison?' Leora asked.

'Some.'

'What position? Were you any good?'

'I was okay, I guess. I could run fast with the ball.' Though she couldn't imagine playing in her new hiking boots.

DiRito and Josh Justic looked at each other. 'Midfield,' they announced together.

'Do I get a choice?'

'Do you want to let us down?'

'It's only seven a side,' Leora said. 'Easy and fun.'

'At least come along to the practice,' DiRito pleaded.

'I'll check my schedule.'

The mess tent was marquee-size, with open sides all round. A canteen counter had been set up at one end, with bored, tired NECatering Services staff handing out meals on a permanent basis to cope not just with the expedition ground personnel but also the constant airlift flights. Angela and the squad joined the end of a long queue just as Passam arrived for her lunch. As befitted her status in life, the Commissioner was wearing an expensive royal-blue European-tailored business suit with a silk blouse and black shoes that were splattered in mud, as were her tights. Despite the heat, her rigid hairstyle was locked into place, and her make-up a total mask through which beads of perspiration were oozing. Several PA drones hovered round their queen, smiling nervously as she walked to the head of the queue.

Service in the canteen might be a good-for-morale, first-come-first-served basis, but Passam was clearly a devout believer in herself being more equal than others.

'Thank you so much,' she said, addressing the queue members about to scoop up their dishes from the counter. 'I do have a most important i-conference call scheduled in a little while. It's with the GE Finance Bureau you know. Got to keep them happy.'

Without actually making eye contact with the people she'd pushed in front of, she stood at the counter and engaged in more simply delightful chit-chat with the girls serving up the meal packets. Her PAs closed protectively around her, grabbing their own trays.

Angela stared at the scene. Her muscles had locked up with shock. She felt the flush rising up her face. Something was muting the sounds of the mess tent as a weird sharp tingling spread savagely across her skin.

Without warning her legs gave way, pitching her onto the floor of pulped grass.

'Angela?' Paresh asked from what must have been miles away. From being exhaustingly hot she was now icy. Her limbs were shaking uncontrollably. 'No,' she whimpered. 'No no.'

'Hey, what's happened?' Paresh and Omar were reaching for her, turning her onto her back. Alarmed faces loomed over her, blurred by tears.

'No! It can't be. It can't be! No!' Her voice was rising as the hysteria swept her along. She couldn't breathe. She tried jerking down some air, body juddering as muscles spasmed wrongly.

'Angela.'

'Medic! Call a medic.'

'What the fuck happened to her?'

'Angela,' an alarmed Paresh shouted. 'Angela listen to me: you have to breathe.'

She was arching her back, gulping air down against the contractions in her throat. There was no pain, just a body in chaos, reacting as if someone was pumping an electric shock through her. The wild thought made her want to laugh. She couldn't. Couldn't do anything but thrash about as if gripped by a seizure.

Paresh and Omar were pushed aside. A couple of people with Red Cross eagle armbands were abruptly kneeling beside her. She could only see them down a long grey tunnel now. There was a lot of shouting that was very faint.

Something was clamped over her nose and mouth. She tasted dry air with a weird metal tang. Her heart was pounding madly as she finally subsided flat onto her back, sobbing uncontrollably.

*

The field hospital was made up from ten Qwik-Kabins locked together, forming a generously equipped emergency centre with five small operating suites, along with a full body diagnostics chamber. Its main purpose was triage, delivering quality patch-'em-up treatment before shipping the injured out to a proper hospital. Anyone with bad physical damage to their body who came through the door and was still breathing was almost guaranteed to survive. Something that looked like a psychological breakdown wasn't a syndrome they were geared up to handle, though.

Bland composite walls shone an uncompromising beige from the glaring monochrome ceilings. The light hadn't even been dimmed in the curtained-off assessment cubicle where Angela lay on a narrow gurney. Whatever sedative the paramedics had pumped into her worked a treat. Her thoughts were perfectly calm, disconnected even. Certainly her body was at rest, breathing calm, muscles quiescent. She didn't feel the need to move as she stared at that perfect expanse of lit-up ceiling. Even the air-con buzz was mildly therapeutic – she could hear subtle harmonies buried within its harshness.

Eventually, though, the monotonous light and sound grew boring. She had no idea how long she'd been lying there. She suspected a couple of hours at least. The drugs had wound her down from what she knew had been the mother of all panic attacks, which allowed her to think about what she'd seen. That didn't mean she'd come to terms with it, but sure as the devil shits on human life she knew it wasn't coincidence. It couldn't be. That knowledge alone made it bearable.

Angela took a proper interest in the cubicle. There was a diagnostic panel on a swing arm above the gurney, three screens alive with information about her body. She could see glistening patches on her hands where smartdust had been smeared on with some kind of gloop. There would be other patches on her chest, her neck, limbs . . .

'Loop the data,' she told her augmented e-i. 'Don't let them know I'm awake.'

'The smartdust embedded in the walls and ceiling is providing a visual image of you, which the medical staff is observing,' the e-i told her.

Angela closed her eyes and feigned sleep again. 'Loop that as well.'

'Completed.'

'Warn me if anyone comes.' She swung her bare feet off the thin mattress, grabbed her glasses from the bedside locker, and peered round the end of the curtain. The emergency centre had five identical cubicles, and hers was the only one occupied. She saw a medicine cabinet down the other end of the room.

Benefits of a prison education: it took less than thirty seconds for her augmented e-i to crack the authorization code, and the narrow blade from the multifunction penknife in her camping utility belt was already inside the physical lock. Take the box from the back of the stack so nobody notices one has gone missing. Five seconds for the blade to lock the cabinet again, and the digital authorization system automatically resets . . .

Dr Tamika Coniff pulled back the curtain to see her patient propped up on her elbows. Such a fast return to consciousness was slightly surprising, given how much sedative the paramedics had pumped her with. But as the doctor had learned during her internship, every human body is troublingly unique.

'What happened?' Angela asked in a thick voice as the doctor's penlight was shone into her eyes.

'I'm not sure, exactly,' Tamika Coniff admitted as she noted the normal pupil reaction. 'How do you feel?'

'Bit groggy, like I've been stoned.'

'Accurate enough description. Physically, there's nothing wrong with you now.'

'Really?'

'As best I can determine, yes. The smartdust monitoring your vitals is certainly telling me your body functions have returned to normal. However, I'd advise you to implant a suite of medical monitor smartcells. Every HDA member has them, and it allows your bodymesh to monitor you on a permanent basis. If any abnormality begins, your e-i can shout for help. Proactive monitoring increases survival chances.'

'Okay. I'll remember that.'

'We have spare suites of medical smartcells here in the hospital. I can apply them now, if you'll just add your certificate to the release.'

'I'll think about it.'

Dr Tamika Coniff gave her a disapproving look. 'I see. They are excellent suites, if that's what you're worried about. I have one myself.'

'I'm sure they are. Just let me get used to the idea.'

'Very well.'

'Thanks, Doc.'

'Can you tell me, is there any family history of epilepsy?'

'No.'

'I read your file. Twenty years in jail?'

'That's me.'

'Did you have access to narcotic drugs while you were incarcerated?'

'It was a jail, Doc. If we got candy bars once a month we were lucky.'

'So that would be a yes, then.'

Angela grinned weakly. 'Actually, no. I didn't bump any tox in jail. I'm not screwed up that way.'

'And judging by your appearance, you're a one-in-ten.'

'No fooling you.'

'That can produce some physiological quirks that we're only just discovering. But I'd say you suffered some kind of neural overload episode, probably trauma induced. I can't imagine what it must be like getting your freedom back after so long. Then returning directly to Abellia would act as an inordinately strong emotional trigger. Psychologically you're swinging from one extreme to another. That is very hard for a mind to process, hence the physical reaction.'

Angela did her best not to sneer at the doctor's solemn analysis. It was so far from what had actually happened, the real trigger, as to be laughable. But she couldn't say that, so instead she nodded wisely and said: 'Yeah, coming back here isn't exactly my idea of funtime, either.'

'That's good. Acknowledging you have a problem is the first step in surmounting it.'

'Right.' Angela was rather liking the doctor. She was probably a head shorter than Angela, and in her mid-thirties. A little too heavyset to be a beauty, though her clear Indian heritage gave her auburn skin a healthy lustre. But it was the brisk attitude which truly appealed – the doc saw a problem and tried to slice right to the core. Under different circumstances they might have got along.

'Then to be honest there's not a lot more I can do for you,' Coniff said. 'The expedition doesn't have a professional counsellor. If it happens again, I could officially recommend you are taken back to Earth.'

Angela grinned at Dr Tamika's earnest face. 'It won't happen again. Fool me once, never fool me again. I was caught off guard, is all. Besides, I won't be sent home. I'm too essential.'

Dr Tamika frowned. 'You sound like you know what caused this.'

'Thankfully, not the smell of mint.'

'Ah yes, that was in our briefing. You said the monster smells of it.'

'Yeah. So be careful.'

'You know you can speak to me in confidence.'

'I look forward to it.'

'If you feel the symptoms emerging again, come and see me before it builds back up to today's level. I can prescribe anti-depressants. There's no shame in it, you know, especially after everything you've been through.'

'Sure. I'll be good.'

'All right, I'll get the datawork finished and discharge you. And please consider that suite of smartcells.'

'Thanks. I will.' Angela laced up her boots, then Velcroed the gaiters in place. There was no sign of her sunhat, which annoyed her. She pushed the curtain aside.

'How are you feeling?'

'Son-of-a-bitch!' She took a half-step back from Elston, who was standing directly outside the assessment cubicle. 'Jesus wept, you're getting even creepier, you know that?'

'I'm concerned about you, that's all.'

'Don't be, I'm fine.'

'You were carried out of the mess tent having a fit. You even scared Commissioner Passam. She wants to know you're all right.'

'Tell her I'm flattered by her interest. You can do that, you're good at lying.'

'What happened? Seriously, I'd like to know.'

Angela walked away, heading for the entrance. 'Shock. Seriously. Didn't you overhear that bit? I've been locked up for twenty years on a false charge. Getting out is a humongous deal for a lifer. Then you considerately dragged me back here where it all happened, and will probably happen again.' Angela raised her voice as she passed the ward station where Dr Tamika Coniff and a couple of nurses were huddled round a desk with three small screens and a zone console. 'The doc asked if I'd been screwed up by illegal tox when I was in jail. Don't worry, I didn't rat you out, didn't tell her how you tortured me for weeks and shot me full of shit that scrambled my brain.' She watched the anger rise across Elston's face. A cheap thrill, but it was enjoyable knowing she could still get to him.

'Get out of here.'

She blew him a kiss. 'Yes, sir.'

'We're on the same side, you know,' he called out as she sauntered away. 'We're both human. It isn't. You might want to think about that.'

Angela opened the door, giving him a backwards finger as she stepped outside into the sunlight and warmth.

Paresh and DiRito and Leora and Gillian and Josh and Audrie and Omar were standing outside the field hospital. They looked around as she appeared. Smiles appeared on their faces.

'Fuck, she made it.'

'Hey, you don't look too bad.'

'What did the doc say?'

'Are you okay?' Paresh asked, full of real concern.

It was so unexpected. People *cared*. About *her*. An astonished Angela stared at them, lost for words. For an awful second, she thought another panic wave was about to crash over her. But it didn't, because she knew how to control herself, how not to let the slightest weakness show. *Focus.*

Angela grinned, which was an easy thing to allow. 'I panicked. I saw the food again, and just . . .' She shrugged.

They laughed as they gathered round. She was hugged; Leora and Audrie kissed her. Paresh sheepishly handed her the sunhat she thought she'd lost.

'Thanks,' she said, and gave him a long look as she pulled it down on her head. Again, the delightful puppy boy rolled over, tail wagging.

'Seriously, girl, what happened back there?' Omar asked.

'Sorry I scared you guys. The doc said I'm still screwed up over prison and getting released, all that shit. Coming straight back here wasn't the smartest thing I could have done. It just got to me, is all.'

'Are they shipping you back?' DiRito asked.

'Oh fuck no. I've still got to watch out for you guys. Nobody else is.'

'Hey!' They started joshing her back, protesting. They teased her about missing the seven-a-side football, bragging about how well Atyeo's team had done before getting knocked out by Corporal Hiron's squad.

Good people, she admitted reluctantly as they walked back to the main camp.

Overhead, a silver-white V-shaped HyperLear curved sharply across the sky as it came in to land with a guttural roar from its turborams. The sight brought on a nostalgia burn stronger than Angela expected, but then she was vulnerable today. It had been a long time since she'd flown in anything like the supersonic executive jet.

*

April 2121 had been unusually cold, even for a London struggling out of another miserable winter where the Thames had yet again frozen over. Late snowfalls were still clogging the streets and slowing the traffic when Angela Tramelo arrived on the trans-Europe express at St Pancras station, direct from Nantes where she lived with her mother. She registered at the Imperial College for her first year of sport physiotherapy studies, with football treatment as her speciality class; no different to all the other middle-class eighteen-year-old girls away from home for the first time who thronged the college buildings. Her GE citizen files and certificates were all accepted by the college AI, and the freshman year's fees paid from her account with the Paris First Trans-stellar bank.

With her accreditation confirmed, she went to the flat her mother had arranged; two rooms on the second floor in a nice house just off Draycott Avenue, sharing the communal kitchen with three other students. Youngsters from similar backgrounds living together in a respectable part of town, and within easy walking distance of the university. Just the kind of place a decent mother would choose. It was also conveniently close to Chelsea's King's Road, with all its wondrous bars and restaurants.

So it was that Angela Tramelo began her studies, spending hours in the gym each week, and not so many hours in the lecture theatre learning about the mechanics of the human muscular structure and how it connected to the skeleton; most importantly for a fresher, she made friends and hit the hectic party circuit. The right friends were essential. Imperial College was as cliquey as any other university, and Angela swiftly learned who were the genuine children of the wealthy as opposed to her peers from a comfortable middle-class background. She began hanging out with the richer types, accepting dates from boys with social connections who promised exciting, roguish times for a girl from the rural provinces. More significantly, who hung out at London's more exclusive clubs, including the Gusto on Park Lane.

That was where Melyne Aslo first saw Angela Tramelo. There were a lot of extremely beautiful young girls in Gusto – they were practically a required accessory for older men. Models, zone starlets, society daughters, they all dressed in couture and partied the night away. That's what made Angela stand out, she was fresh-faced pretty but lacking the poise most of the club's beauty clique possessed, and her clothes, while chic and sexy, were hardly high-label. It clearly didn't matter to the third-year Libyan business student who'd brought her; he was busy showing off to her and his gaggle of university chums, buying the most expensive drinks and toxes, downing them so fast that he'd soon be losing consciousness, but not before making a complete arse of himself.

Aslo watched the girl discreetly. The thick white-blonde hair was long, hanging down almost to her hips – Aslo suspected extensions, but given the girl's pale complexion it was probably her true colour. Tall enough, she didn't like them too short. Athletic – check. Great smile. And most intriguingly: bored. Oh, she was hiding it from her mealticket oaf of a boyfriend. But Aslo was experienced enough to see how his ridiculous antics were turning her off; she'd have been promised a decent night on the town only to be a part of the same stupid old student excess, just in a plusher building. Even so, she wasn't walking. The attraction of the Gusto lifestyle was countering her aversion.

Gusto's network was wide open to Aslo's e-i, which quickly located Angela Tramelo on tonight's guest list. Fifty seconds later she'd harvested a complete profile. A football physio! Angela was perfect.

The first time Angela went to the ladies' room, Aslo moved in. She'd done it so many times before, a casual encounter, friendly talk offered. The girl was delighted someone else showed an interest. *Quelle surprise*: Nantes was Melyne's favourite French city, she adored the huge ancient chateau right in the centre, the narrow old streets, the opera house – visions of which she was accessing through her contact netlens as she babbled about them. They exchanged e-i codes, and Aslo went home.

Next afternoon Angela met her new Best Friend for tea in a café in Thurloe Street, outside the South Kensington Underground station. Angela had just finished another arduous gym session, her tutor taking the class through a series of warm-up routines while explaining their proper application, so she was dressed in her sports kit with her big hair all wrapped up and trailing loose ends. A complete ingénue, Aslo decided as she appraised the girl in daylight. When Angela sat down she unzipped the fleece tracksuit top; underneath her tight sprinter vest showed off a lot of taut midriff. Apparently, she didn't even notice the way Aslo's gaze lingered on her exposed flesh.

Melyne Aslo explained she was an events organizer working out of an office in Fulham, helping with corporate, government, and private functions. She didn't need to work now that her divorce was final, but it kept her busy and in contact with the right people. She said she remembered how difficult money had been when she was at university fifteen years ago, so if Angela ever needed some additional income, stewardessing at events paid well and it could all go to a secondary.

Angela was grateful for the offer, agreeing enthusiastically.

Aslo spent a month grooming her. It was her one major talent, and it began with the strengthening of friendship into trust. First came the allure of premier parties and charity balls, 'Tiffany has let me down badly, I need someone to go with, darling, would you mind . . .' new clothes, 'my treat, you deserve it for helping me out'; meeting important people straight off the transnet news and gossip shows: CEOs, GE Commissioners, financiers, designers, zone celebrities – all of whom were delighted to be introduced. Then there were the football matches – Angela visited all the major London clubs, watching games from the executive boxes lining the top of the stadiums, making her enthusiasm for the game very apparent. Aslo was especially pleased about that. So it was that Angela inevitably spent less and less time at Imperial College as Aslo systematically corrupted her existing lifestyle, making her question and reject her formal upbringing. 'Well, you are a little bourgeoise, my dear, but not to worry, it's hardly shameful. Shame is only for the truly repressed.' Encouraging her to accept gifts and promises. 'Say yes, free yourself, there's no obligation.' Congratulating her on taking long breaks with new friends in their palatial holiday chalets. 'See the way life is truly lived, how rewarding liberation is.' Aslo was the gatekeeper to a parallel life lived in the same city as the university students who slogged through courses and lived off fast food and toxed out at night, but this life was one of carefree luxury and laughter that lacked for nothing material. A seductive life which Angela lived more and more. Nobody wanted to retreat from that.

Aslo finally made the grand suggestion towards the end of May. After weeks of revelling in the high life during which her world view was subtly yet comprehensively adjusted, Angela was quick to agree. Kabale was promptly summoned to join them. Another of Aslo's stable of escorts, he was almost as pretty as Angela and, with his shirt off, implausibly hunky. He stayed in the Mayfair apartment with them for a week, during which Aslo supervised Angela's introduction to a variety of sexual practices she had never encountered before, coxing her until she was proficient in all of them.

At the end of May, Aslo kissed Angela goodbye at London's King's Cross station, leaving her on the platform with a suitcase of excellent new clothing and a one-way, first-class ticket to Newcastle. For this Melyne Aslo received payment of one million Eurofrancs to her secondary, believing right from the start that *she* had chosen Angela.

*

Marc-Anthony collected Angela at Newcastle station. A flamboyantly effete sixty-year-old, he made up in personality what he lacked in stature, introducing himself, without any trace of irony, as Bartram North's girlfriend wrangler. He had an outrageous sense of humour, which Angela immediately warmed to.

First stop was Northumberland Interstellar's security division, a thirty-storey tower of darkened glass in the city's Manors district.

'Why are we here?' Angela asked as their uniformed escort took them across the lobby to the lifts.

'Final check-up, sweetie,' Marc-Anthony said as the lift doors slid shut.

'But I thought Bartram and Augustine had split,' she said.

'They have, but it was an amicable split.'

The security building had a small clinic on the tenth floor. An efficient nurse took a blood sample, then Angela had to put on a robe and lie still in a complex scanner mechanism.

'Why?' she asked nervously.

'It's okay, I've taken dozens of girls through this process before,' Marc-Anthony said. 'The blood was to check for any problems.'

'You mean diseases.'

'Sweetie, people get about a lot these days. It's wonderful that we can, but Bartram has to be careful. He can't afford to catch anything right now.'

'And this?' Angela gestured round at the scanner.

'Keep still,' the nurse told her.

'The Norths have a lot of enemies,' Marc-Anthony explained. 'We're just checking that all your cy-chips really are just for netting up.'

'I haven't got any cyborg implants yet,' Angela said. 'I can't afford them. I use interface sets.' She pointed to the black earring that linked her to the transnet.

'Good for you. Your body is a temple, especially one as gorgeous as yours. Don't junk-jam it with crap. And it's not just communication cy-chips we're checking for.'

'Why, what else can cy-chips be?'

'Nasty, sweetie. I've seen the list they keep around here. Arms companies are frightfully inventive when it comes to being downright diabolical. Trust me.'

They waited in a small ante-room for the results to come through. Angela was confident there wouldn't be a problem, the microscopic nuclei threads embedded along both ulnas were organic-based and currently inert – effectively undetectable. They ought to be, they'd cost enough from the dark cy-tech specialist on New Tokyo.

'What's he like?' she asked.

'Who, Bartram? A pussycat.'

'Oh, come on!'

Marc-Anthony gave her an expressive shrug. 'Okay, he's a hundred and nine years old, and a multi-trillionaire in any currency you care to name. There's nothing he hasn't seen or done. Happy now?'

'A hundred and nine, really?'

'Yes.'

'Oh. Look, I'm not sure I can . . .'

He giggled. 'Your face, sweetie. Listen, don't worry, he's halfway through his rejuvenation. It's not too unsightly.' He looked from side to side, then beckoned Angela close. 'Between you and me, he's not up to much, if you get my drift. He mostly likes to watch right now. You've got an easy gig, just play nice with the other girls and suck a little dick occasionally. We all have to do that in this life.'

'Right. I still don't get it. If he's so rich, how come there aren't girls who'll just be with him anyway? I saw enough of them in the clubs in London, and those guys didn't have anything like this money.'

Marc-Anthony sat back in the chair, suddenly looking very prim. 'And that's exactly why.'

'What do you mean?'

'He's not paying you for the sex, sweetie, he's paying you to shut up and leave afterwards. Men, they're all the same. Especially the Norths. They don't want to engage with you, to talk about feelings and other people's lives – to them that crap is a waste of time and energy. Girlfriends and wives are a drag. Norths get on and *achieve* things, that's what their family is all about.'

'That sounds . . . lonely.'

'Oh no, sweetie, they're not lonely, they've got you. That's all they need to get by. Trust me, I've seen them up close and nasty personal for twenty-five years now.'

'Why do you do this?'

Marc-Anthony put on a mischievous smile. 'I'm basically unemployable otherwise. A disgraceful incident in my long shady past involving some illegal tox and an indecent vegetable. In public!'

Angela laughed. 'I don't believe you.'

'Well, maybe I was exaggerating the vegetable's importance. But this isn't such a bad job. I get to meet lovely people like you. You know, you have quite the most beautiful green eyes.'

She reached over and squeezed his hand. 'Thank you.'

'Oh don't, you'll get me all soppy.'

The nurse came in. 'All clear,' she told them.

'Right then,' Marc-Anthony said cheerfully. 'Let's get out of this truly dismal weather, and into some real sunshine.'

A black Mercedes executive saloon drove them straight to the gateway. There was a GE Border Directorate office at the end of Last Mile. Angela was surprised that all she had to do was put her hand on a biometric scanner and have her e-i certify her citizen status to the Directorate's AI. It cleared her for transit immediately, and issued her with a small GE visa chip with a return authorization.

'Don't lose it,' Marc-Anthony warned as the Mercedes slid smoothly up the metal ramp that led into the gateway. 'It's not so easy coming through the other way.'

The Mercedes drove smoothly along Motorway A to the airport. Marc-Anthony enjoyed her delight at St Libra's rings, even stopping the car so she could get out and have a proper look. She breathed in the exotic air just like everyone visiting a new world for the first time, not complaining about the pervasive bioil smell, barely able to contain her excitement at being on St Libra.

It was a HyperLear LV-700 which was waiting for them at the airport. A neat delta-wing, fifteen-seat executive jet whose P&W Excelsior turborams were capable of pushing up to a cruising speed of Mach 3.8.

'What about everyone else?' Angela asked as a stewardess took her bag at the bottom of the airstairs.

'Just us,' Marc-Anthony said.

They didn't fly low and slow through the fall zone. It was probability, Marc-Anthony explained. A quick dash through at high altitude had the same chance of impact as the commercial flights lumbering along in the murky fog fifteen miles below. Low and slow was all down to psychology, keeping the passengers content.

It was raining when they arrived at Abellia, thick dark clouds shielding the coastal town from view as the HyperLear descended towards the airport. A Jaguar JX-7 convertible, with the roof up, drove them along the Rue de Provence which took them out to Gironella Beach where Bartram's mansion sat on the narrow shelf of land between the deep sands and the steep plateau slope behind. The clouds drifted away north and the dazzling Sirius sunlight played across the sparkling turquoise sea as the Jag emerged from the tunnel, showcasing the tremendous vista ahead of them. Even knowing Bartram had chosen the Abellia peninsula out of a whole world didn't quite prepare Angela for the sight. The rumpled slopes at the back of the two-mile-wide cove were huge and almost vertical, smeared with jade and aquamarine vegetation that clung to the narrow fissures in the rock for the first third before losing traction, leaving dark moss and spore-bloom to thrive on the naked rock above. At the far end of the curving wall, a vast waterfall thundered down for over two hundred metres, producing a continual explosion cloud of spray that swirled with rainbow diffraction waves in the brilliant sun-light. The grounds around the mansion were neatly maintained, a perfect compromise between formal and natural; planted with carefully chosen luxuriant native trees, providing a colourful arborious parkland that gave off a musky sweet-pine scent in the humid sea air.

'Oh wow,' Angela murmured as she stared at the mansion.

'I know,' Marc-Anthony said proudly. 'It has that effect on everyone. Gaudy, but so chic with it, don't you think?'

'Uh huh.' Now that he'd said it, she wasn't sure about the mansion on an aesthetic level. It seemed so out of place in this naturalistic setting, yet at the same time it was so impressive it could actually compete with the magnificent landscape. Bartram's designer had gone for a pyramid with a truncated apex, so that it resembled the urbane modernist version of some Inca temple. The façade comprised huge rhomboid sections of glass, each one a different colour, and framed by beams of matt-black metal. Wide horizontal balconies were wrapped round it, supporting long troughs full of high-desert plants.

'Wait till you see it at night, sweetie,' Marc-Anthony said. 'The frame lights up. We look like a miniature Vegas on the seafront.'

The Jaguar dipped down into a tunnel, which took them to a hangar-like garage directly underneath the mansion. The only cars parked there were Jaguars, identical JX-7 models to the one Angela had just arrived in, even down to the silver-blue colour. There must have been fifteen of them. Marc-Anthony just shrugged when she gave them a puzzled look. 'Don't ask.'

When they came up a spiral stair into the main atrium with its black and white marble floor, the air was noticeably cooler and dryer than outside. Sunlight streamed down from the transparent apex high above, striking the chrome rails on each of the landings stacked between tall fluted pillars. Two of Bartram's girlfriends were there waiting for her on the broad casual loungers that gave the place a hotel lobby feel rather than anything homey. Olivia-Jay, with her dark lustrous skin and eastern-Mediterranean features of wide lips, flattish nose, and hazel eyes; thick short-waved hair flowed down over her shoulders. She was wearing a gauzy pearl-white skirt and a breezy, welcoming smile. Karah was less effusive, waiting politely while Olivia-Jay bounced over and gave Angela a big hug. An interesting restraint considering Karah was completely naked. Angela's first impression was of a redhead fitness fanatic who would dwarf most woman pro-volleyball team members.

'Welcome to wicked Gironella,' Olivia-Jay said. 'The overtox by the sea.'

Karah kissed her on both cheeks. 'It's not that bad,' she said in a husky tone. 'You'll be all right.'

'Us girlfriends, we stick together,' Olivia-Jay said. 'Especially when Brinkelle's about.'

'Behave,' Marc-Anthony warned in a mock-serious voice.

'Who's Brinkelle?' Angela asked, because it was the kind of question a naive eighteen-year-old would ask. It was odd, but she hadn't expected that meeting the other girls would be so tough. She hadn't even considered them before now. But despite their jaunty character she thought them sad. In fact she was starting to feel angry that they were here, angry that in this day and age old men still coveted and exploited young girls as they always had, that there hadn't been any social progress since Roman times, how actually opening up new worlds had been a backward step because so much was now beyond the reach of true civilization and accountability. And as they always did, the Norths took the whole scene with girls to its extreme, because they could, because excess defined them, because unaccountability was their god.

You knew all this before you came here, she told herself sternly. *It's why you're here. Come on, focus, there's nothing you can do for them. They're here for the money, just like you.* She gathered up her self-control and smiled nervously at her two new friends.

'The daughter,' Karah said. 'She's only in her twenties, and she's already a complete bitch.'

'Girls, girls.' Marc-Anthony clapped his hands together. 'Who're the bitchy ones? Honestly. Now, please, Angela needs to get settled. It's been a long trip.'

'You're in the room next to me,' Olivia-Jay said. 'Come on.' She started tugging Angela towards the lift positioned discreetly behind the sweeping staircase.

Her room was on the sixth floor, a massive square with a split-level polished stone floor and gold velvet walls. A two-star interior in a five-star building, she thought in bemusement. But the long external glass wall opened onto her own section of balcony, with a view to the south-west and that fantastic waterfall.

'Your clothes are in the closet, and indexed in the mansion's net,' Marc-Anthony said.

'But—' Angela pointed to her case, which was already standing beside the circular bed.

'You don't wear your own clothes here,' Olivia-Jay told her. 'And that's if you wear any. Poor old Karah. Naked is part of her contract.'

'I've procured the kind of garments Mr Bartram enjoys,' Marc-Anthony said. 'They're in your size.'

'How do you know my size?'

'Ms Aslo sent your details last week.'

'Oh.'

'Now, Mr Bartram won't be back until this evening, he's over at the Institute today for treatment. You can have a rest until he arrives. I don't know about you, but coming through the gateway always messes my body clock.'

'Yes. Thanks.'

'I'll pick out something appropriate for your introduction later.'

Angela went over to her bag and took out an interface set and her netlens glasses. 'Is there an access code for the mansion's net? I'd like to tell my mum I'm okay.'

'Your mother?' Olivia-Jay squeaked.

Angela pursed her lips in resignation as she clipped the black earring on. 'She thinks I'm still at Imperial College. I don't want to let her know I've dropped out. Not yet.'

'The mansion's an open area access,' Marc-Anthony said. 'Just get your e-i to register.'

'Thanks.'

Angela waited until they'd left the room then sat on the bed. Unsurprisingly, it was a water mattress. Her e-i placed a call to her mother's transnet interface address. The unavailable icon popped up in her netlens; Angela told her e-i to access the voice-message function. 'Hi Mum. It's me. Just want to let you know I'm fine. Studying hard – ha ha. There's a bunch of us going out to the West End this weekend, if I can afford it. But that company I told you about has offered me more stewardessing work, so I might finally have some cash again. Call me when you're back. Love you. Bye.' She flopped down and rode the mattress's slow wave beneath her. There was nobody at the interface, of course, certainly not a mother. It was a one-way relay. What she said didn't matter, there wasn't even an elaborate code anyone could decrypt. Accessing the interface was the message, a simple one: *I'm in.*

Wednesday 6th February 2143

'I'm going to bust out of this place,' Angela announced quietly.

On the other side of the mess table, Paresh froze up, a fork wound tight with spaghetti halfway to his mouth. 'What are you doing?' he whispered back. 'I'm supposed to watch you, make sure you don't go anywhere unauthorized. Besides, your clothes are tagged.'

'Oh yeah, I'd forgotten. That's going to stop me all right. Hey, could I borrow your scissors?'

'Angela!'

'If you come with me, you won't get into trouble for losing sight of me, then, will you?'

'Huh?'

She grinned roguishly, and used a finger to push the fork towards his mouth. He didn't resist.

'Come on,' she said, with wide-eyed mischief. 'A night on the town; just the two of us. There are decent clubs here, not just the rich hang-outs. And you've never truly eaten until you've tasted milliseed in chilli sauce.'

'You're crazy.'

'But smart with it. Think about it, we're going to be shipped out to Edzell any day now. That's two thousand kilometres away, and it's only the first camp, a staging post. Crap knows how far we'll be going eventually, or how long for. You think this alien is going to be easy to find?'

'Did you hear something about us being forward deployed?'

'No. I'm just applying logic.' She pointed out through the sides of the big mess tent where a Daedalus was rolling along a taxiway towards the end of the runway. 'They're even nightflying supplies out to Edzell. And they've already got four e-Rays up on the other side.'

'Yeah, but the last one found this huge mountain range further north.'

'The Eclipse Mountains, so called because the range is so big it eclipses everything.'

'Damn, is there anything you don't know?'

'This place is one giant teenage girl gossip fest. Besides, not even HDA thinks a mountain range is classified information. I access the Observation Centre feed on my grid a lot.'

'Okay, but, a jailbreak?'

She sucked on a chunk of watermelon. 'The point is, we're going out there soon, and who knows when we're coming back. So let's award ourselves a little R&R time. You think Passam eats in this tent every night? Fuck, she doesn't even sleep in the airport compound.'

'Yeah, I heard she and her people are in the Mortant Hotel.'

'Five-star rating, and all at the taxpayers' expense. So . . . ? It'll be no fun by myself.' She gave him an entreating look.

'Oh hell.'

*

Angela borrowed a plain white short-sleeved blouse from Leora and a simple turquoise skirt with a gold hem from Audrie. Her squadmates weren't the same size as her, but the fit wasn't too bad even though she had to keep tucking the blouse back in. The pink and yellow trainers were also Leora's, worn with three pairs of socks to keep them on.

'Did you remember to swap your underwear, too?' Paresh asked.

'What underwear?' Evil: but worth it for his expression.

Paresh knew one of the quartermasters in the motor pool.

They checked out a Land Rover Tropic, with a patch loaded to suspend its log for the evening. Driving along the Rue Turbigo into town, they were both conscious about how out of place the big olive-green vehicle was amid the coupés and supercars and limousines on Abellia's roads. But there were plenty of other HDA vehicles about, so . . .

Angela told the rugged vehicle's auto to take them down to Velasco Beach. They walked along the promenade as the dazzle-point of the sun slid down towards the horizon. There weren't many people left at this time of day, and the stores along the front were shutting up. Paresh insisted on wearing his smart fatigues. 'So they can't accuse me of being off duty,' he said. The HDA clothing earned him a few curious looks, but certainly no hostility.

There was a marina at the end of the promenade, the Rueda, which hadn't been there twenty years ago. Reasonable enough, Angela supposed. It was strange how the time in Holloway was compressing, reducing to a weird discontinuity, but the memories of her earlier life were stronger now than they had been for a long time.

'These shops weren't here before,' she said as they walked along the vitrified stone. 'And those ones over there were still being built. All we had behind the beach back then was stalls, like a market. And I don't think the promenade was this long, either.'

They stopped and leaned on the black metal railing, watching the stragglers making their way off the beach. 'What was it like back then?' Paresh asked.

'Smaller town, obviously. But I didn't spend much time in this district. I was mainly out at the mansion.' She knew that wasn't what he was asking for, that he was fishing about her earlier life. The sweet puppy boy that he was, it had been all too easy to twist his hopes to an impossible high of anticipation over tonight. She almost felt guilty about that. And actually, it had been twenty years . . .

'How was that?'

'I don't want to talk about it.' She pushed some wisps of hair back from her forehead as she gazed out to sea. 'Sorry, I'm not quite ready for that. And you don't want me to have a fainting fit again. Not tonight.' The promise in the tone was indecent.

'Sure. I can wait.'

'Paresh, I have to ask, what is someone as nice as you doing in the HDA?'

'Hey, we're the good guys. We defend the human race against the Zanth.'

No you don't. Not really. Not defend us. Just organize us when the Zanth swarms. Angela grinned. 'My turn: sorry.' She stood up on tiptoes, pressed against him, and awarded a kiss to his lips. A casual kiss. A kiss for a friend. A kiss that went on longer than a friend intended. A kiss that meant more, and so surprised her. He could see that in her eyes when she finally parted. The look that said where this evening was going to end, and that she was rather pleased that it would.

Thursday 7th February 2143

Dawn brought a thin mist creeping in across the sea to meander around the dunes at the back of Camilo Beach. Saul watched it materialize out of the semi-dark that was a St Libran night, illuminated first by the pale ringlight, then the dawn's horizon haze. He was sitting in a chair on the kitchen patio, dressed in a thick white cricket sweater he'd owned for eight years, a pair of long, baggy, cyan-green shorts with sagging side pockets, and ancient trainers. His eyes were red rimmed and he was frightened someone would see them and ask why he'd been crying. It would be another couple of hours before his family roused themselves, and Emily would realize he hadn't been to bed that night. Two hours to pull himself together, to get his rampaging emotions under control. To push down the bitterness and hatred at what fate had delivered to him.

The languid St Libra waves made a constant swishing noise that rolled over the empty sands as the small tide started to turn, bringing the waters back. He thought about it as he stared out at the grey water with its white crests. How easy it would be to take his board out there, to settle down on the comforting warmth of the sea and start paddling. Paddle out and out, set course for Ambrose, or maybe the Dry Isle in the fall zone. To leave all this behind, because the strain and shock was going to kill him as sure as drowning in his beloved ocean. And the ocean would be cleaner.

His eyes closed to shut out as much as he could of the world, and breath came down in shudders. He couldn't do it, of course. All he could see in the nothingness were the faces of his lovely family, frantic faces as the days stretched out and the lifeguard searches were called off. How lost the children would be without him, how Emily would be broken. How they would never know why, never understand. That sad bewilderment would hang over their lives for ever, scaring them.

As a husband and father he had responsibilities. It wasn't that they couldn't survive what was happening, he just didn't want it to happen. Not to them. Camilo Beach, Emily, the children, this whole leisurely agreeable life: they were his second chance. Beautiful proof that he'd finally moved on and left his terrible past behind.

But you could never leave the past behind. Not really. Not a past like his. So that was it, time to choose. To walk away from everything, or face up to what was happening and try and work out what the hell to do next. Not a choice really. The only thing he couldn't work out was how Emily would react. She didn't deserve this; he'd promised her a decent life away from the misery which had threatened to claw her down from happiness.

Maybe that was the real reason they'd been drawn together. There he'd been, adrift and alone, trying to recover from the horror of his life, the loss and the terrible uncertainty, not truly knowing what to do. A man on auto. And even then drawn to the ocean for whatever it represented, the missing segment of his soul.

Saul had found her on the old town harbour wall after midnight, a hunched figure sitting on the edge. He'd heard the sobbing before he actually saw her. There had been that long moment of indecision, to turn round and leave her, or do the decent thing. And enough time had passed for him finally to be able to reach out to another human. What with this being Abellia, he basically guessed her story before he even sat down beside her, because when he was settling on the concrete he saw how young she was, how beautiful.

'He kicked you out then?'

Emily turned to face him, cheeks wet with tears. She gave him an uncomprehending look, and burst out crying again.

It was the oldest human story, but one refined by Abellia. Emily was a model at the start of her glamorous career, growing up on New Washington, and her lover was an older, richer man, unveiling the excitement and freshness of his world to her. He'd brought her out to Abellia for an exhilarating fun holiday in the family mansion. That was when she realized what the relationship really was: how she was property, this week's amusement. They fought, and he didn't need that kind of shit, not from the likes of her.

'I haven't even got any clothes,' she sniffled. 'He said that as he'd bought them all, they belonged to him. And he wouldn't fly me back to Highcastle on his jet.'

'Because it costs money,' Saul filled in. 'And money is all that sort care about. Cheaper just to leave you here than pay for a ticket. After all there's no law against it. He's not the first, and he certainly won't be the last.'

'What do I do?'

Saul could have been truthful, could have told her that someone as young and pretty and female would never lack for anything for long – not if she didn't want to. That all she had to do was sit in the right bar and smile at men. But then she knew that now – that's why she was sitting on the harbour wall in the middle of the night with enough tears to create her own high tide.

'I've got a spare room,' he said. 'You need a bed for the night. And I know it looks like this is the end of the world right now, but trust me it won't be so bad in the morning. Nothing ever is. Especially not in a St Libra dawn, when the sun rises between the sea and the rings.'

She gave him a suspicious, sulky look. 'Why would you do that?'

'My own daughter: I'd like to think someone would give her a break if they found her in this kind of state.'

'Really? Where is she?'

'She died, very young. Long story, and full of sorrow. But it's for the best, or so I keep telling myself.'

'Oh, I'm sorry.' And with that, she allowed him to walk her to his flat in one of the converted harbour warehouses. The whole building was pulled down three months later as part of the developer's plans to turn the harbour into a swanky leisure complex now that the newer, bigger cargo port had been built further along the coast. Emily was still with him when they moved into a new apartment complex in Los Geranios valley; by then she wasn't using the spare bedroom any more.

Saul never did fully understand why it had happened. There were much better catches than him even among Abellia's service contract staff, let alone the middle management types – all of them younger, smarter, richer. But they had something together, and he could actually trust her, which wasn't something he expected to do ever again. And in one tiny way age acted in his favour, he'd learned enough over the years to recognize a genuine chance at happiness. For the first time in his life, he didn't blow a relationship.

Until now, he reflected bitterly. But once again, age was on his side, because if nothing else, he'd learned how to be a stubborn little motherfucker over the years. And what happened last night didn't have to decimate his life and family, not if he just held his nerve.

Saul thought back across the last few hours, carefully reviewing what he'd done and said and heard. None of it was particularly incriminating. Not from a legal perspective. It was Emily he worried about. *If she knew, what would she think?* After all, this was his past life. For twenty years he'd never believed for one second that could ever be an issue.

So . . . maybe just not tell her. Though she'd know something was up – which he could always blame on Duren coming back into his life.

He nodded slowly, convincing himself it wasn't as bad as he'd thought. The shock had dazed him, muddled his thoughts. All he had to do was keep his mouth shut and stop acting like a neurotic wreck. *I can do that. I can.*

A communication icon expanded in his grid. He studied it for a disbelieving second. 'Confirm caller identity,' he told his e-i.

'Duren.'

'He's got to be fucking joking,' Saul grunted. It was all he could do not to jump up and search round to see if the big man was out there among the dunes spying on him. He took a moment to calm himself – storming in all riled up was never going to be a good idea where Duren was involved.

His hand reached into the keyspace his iris smartcells were conjuring up, twisting the icon. 'This is too damn early,' he said. *Attack first, keep your opponent on the defensive.*

'I know man,' Duren replied. 'I wouldn't call unless it was really important, you know that, right?'

'What the hell is important at this time of the morning?'

'We need to borrow your boat.'

'What?'

'Your boat, man.'

'This is ridiculous.'

'I wish it was man, really I do, but we need it. Now.'

'What for?' But even as he asked, Saul knew he wouldn't get an answer, leastways not the real one. His decision was let them use the boat, yes or no. Reason was irrelevant.

'We just want to get out to sea before everyone else. If you release it to us now, you'll get back home without disturbing your family.'

Bastard! Motherfucking bastard. But . . . Duren and Zebediah and Zulah were the perfect way to deflect Emily's attention. He could get back from the marina and confess how Duren had crash-landed back into his life.

*

Rueda Marina was at the opposite end of Velasco Beach from the old harbour. With Sirius just starting to shine through the edge of the rings, the marina's curving concrete sea walls glowed in a bright pink-wash light. This early in the morning, it'd taken Saul barely twenty minutes to drive to the entrance. There were only a handful of cars in the park outside the clubhouse, keen boat owners who'd been out at sea all night. Duren and Zulah were standing beside a big old Renault pick-up truck when the Rohan pulled up beside it.

'Man, good to see you,' Duren said, smiling broadly as he gripped Saul's hand.

Saul gave Zulah a nervous glance. She was wearing wrap-around sunglasses, but seemed on edge. *What could put her on edge?* 'Sure,' he said. 'Let's just get you in there, shall we.'

'My man.' Duren gestured casually at the fenced-off lawn in front of the clubhouse, with its broad locked gate which led to the wharfs. 'Good security here, huh?'

'There are meshes everywhere,' Saul agreed. 'The boats aren't as fancy as most in Abellia, but they still cost.'

'Good. Hate for anyone to steal one.' And with that Duren reached over into the back of the pick-up. He lifted out a surfboard bag.

Saul stared at it in growing dismay. The black bag was maybe two metres thirty long – right length for a board that'd suit someone Duren's size. But staring at the way it bulged along most of its length, Saul knew there was no way it was carrying a board. Then he saw how even Duren's muscles were straining from the weight of the bag, veins standing proud from his leathery skin, and the nightmare was complete. *Holy shit, what the hell is in there?*

'Let's go,' Zulah said, carrying a small shoulder bag.

Without a word, Saul walked over to the gate. His e-i confirmed his code with the marina's network, which checked his biometric pattern with the smartdust woven into the gate and fence. The gate lock clicked, and it slid back.

Duren and Zulah followed him wordlessly down jetty two to the berth where the *Merry Moons* was waiting. The yacht was ten metres long, with a telescoping mast and fully automated sails, which could also be crew rigged. He'd wanted the children to know how to sail properly, and always regretted how few weekends they actually spent out on the sea.

Duren was sweating from effort as he dropped the surfboard bag onto the wood-ribbed decking. It made a dull *thud*. Not the noise a board would make.

'Thanks, man,' Duren said. 'I personally appreciate you loaning the boat and all. I'll make sure it's back okay by tonight.'

'Right,' Saul said.

Duren gave the yacht a significant glance with his red-glowing eyes. 'The network code?'

'Oh, yeah.' He told his e-i to give Duren the network code for the *Merry Moons*, adding silently: sorry girl. Though right now he didn't even care if he never saw the boat again. There was nothing linking him to any crime. *The surfboard bag!* Just a man lending some out-of-town friends a boat. *The surfboard bag!* No reason he should ask them where they were taking the yacht while standing where the jetty meshes could see him. *The surfboard bag!* 'Take care of her.'

'We will,' Duren said. He opened the main cabin door, and vanished inside.

'I'd like you to get me some things,' Zulah said.

'Uh?' was all he could manage. He was starting to wonder where Zebediah was. Nowhere near anything too dangerous. Leaders never were.

She gave him a small folded piece of paper. When he started to open it, her hand closed around his.

'Nothing urgent. I'll call you in a few days.' Her bodymesh quested a link to his e-i, and a money transfer to his account flipped up into his grid. 'Here's some cash, that'll be enough to cover it. No need to show me any receipts. I trust you to do a good job for us.' She took her sunglasses off, and peered at him closely. Judging, always judging. 'You won't let us down, will you?'

Saul shook his head, swallowing pitifully. 'No.'

'I'll call you in a few days. Store it in the Hawaiian Moon for me until then. Don't want to impose on your family home.'

Saul couldn't see anything but the transfer pending icon.

'Take it,' Zulah said.

Instinctively he told his e-i to open one of his ancient secondary accounts, one he hadn't used for twenty years. Nobody in Abellia had secondaries – they didn't need to because there was no income tax. He reached up and flipped the transfer icon, and the money twisted away into a Vietnamese bank.

Zulah gave him a satisfied nod. 'Be seeing you.'

Saul turned sharply and walked away, not looking back. They thought they'd hooked him in with the payment, but it wasn't that easy. There were things about Saul Howard they could never guess at. Whatever else happened from now on, he wasn't going to be the placid obedient victim they were anticipating.

*

Corporal Paresh Evitts regained consciousness by slow, painful degrees. First he was only aware of how much his head hurt. Every beat of his heart brought another hammer thud on the inside of an aching skull. Vision was grey, except for the terrible electric red sparkles which bloomed with every thud. Mouth was dry and tasted of what he imagined must be camel dung. Skin cold and damp: fever flesh. Right leg: dead – nothing at all, no sensation. He tried to move it from the odd bent-up position, and promptly groaned at the stab of pain that motion brought. Blood was flowing into oxygen-starved muscles again, bringing life back in a wave of fire. Which made him very aware of how his stomach was feeling.

'Oh fuck.' He rolled onto his back and his cheeks bulged. He couldn't actually lift his head, he was too frightened that the migraine-pulse would split his forehead open and spill his brains out across the sheets.

Sheets?

He blinked back tears and self-pity to try and focus on his environment. Some kind of hotel room: yellow walls, grey carpet, white ceiling. Windows with shutters on the inside, leaking St Libra sunlight round the bands. Door to an en suite which

315

someone was using. He could hear the hiss and splatter of the shower.

'What?' Paresh finally managed to raise himself onto an elbow, which was pretty unpleasant. Okay, so he was on a big bed. There were no pillows, though he could see a couple scattered on the floor. No duvet. And he was naked. Really, completely naked. Some kind of dark wet stain on the sheets. *Shit, is that blood? No. Okay.* Actually, make that several stains. A bottle of champagne on its side on the nightstand. Another bottle of red wine on the floor, and a smaller bottle of raspberry vodka liqueur. Some suspicious empty silver-grey tox sacs lying beside them. And clothes. His uniform had been thrown round the room, along with . . . Paresh squinted. The white blouse Angela had been wearing was hanging over the back of a chair. Blue skirt on the carpet next to his pants.

'Oh, holy crap!' Paresh moaned and flopped back on the bed. He didn't remember. That was terrible. In his life, there had been a few – actually only a couple – one-night stands when he'd woken up the next morning and genuinely couldn't recall the girl's name. That was mortifying enough. But this . . .

They'd been to some bars last night, he remembered that clear enough. A beer or two as they talked, like a real date. Then the restaurant. The Rufus! Yeah, he remembered that, and the milli-seeds. No way could he forget that course. Angela had insisted on ordering that dish. The things really looked like terrestrial millipedes only with fur, but they were seeds from the Cochowa tree; when they were ripe they dropped off and crawled away to germinate nearby, their movement slow and graceful. Until you dipped them in chilli sauce, which made them wriggle frantically. You were supposed to pop them into your mouth and swallow whole. Angela had wolfed down a bowlful. He'd tried two before giving up, and she'd laughed at how he wasn't the big tough soldier after all.

Then they'd hit the club. No – clubs, plural. Multiple! A few more memories were creeping out sheepishly.

She could dance, could that Angela. Ho boy! And each lithe

316

movement made him stare bewitched at a body that was down-right fantastic. He'd been getting hotter and hotter all night long despite the beer and wine they'd drunk. She knew how to party, too: but he matched her bottle for bottle, glass for glass, tox for tox. The nanny smartcells in his mouth flashing all sorts of warnings across his grid until he shut them down. Then she folded her arms round his neck, and whispered: 'Please Paresh, it's been twenty years. Can you imagine twenty years without sex? I need you so badly.'

They must have teleported to the hotel, because that was the next thing he remembered. The two of them standing at the end of the bed, his tongue down her throat, hands pushing up inside the blouse, groping her fantastic tits.

'Give me one minute,' she'd said, and scuttled off into the en suite. 'And Paresh.'

'Yeah?'

'You'd better be naked when I come back in here.'

That was it. That was the last thing he remembered. Which was unbelievable. You don't fuck the night away and remember *nothing*. But they must have. He stared round the room again, the bottles, the stains, even his arm had raspberry vodka lick-marks on it.

Paresh Evitts wanted to cry.

The door to the en suite opened and Angela stepped out, damp hair combed back, wrapped in a red hotel towel.

More than anything Paresh felt relief that it was Angela, and not some other girl. Which was just pathetic.

She was giving him a wicked smile. 'How are you feeling?'

'Er ... you know.' He couldn't take his eyes off her, she looked amazing. Everything a man could ever dream of: smart, beautiful, sexy.

Angela licked her lips provocatively, and slowly opened the towel. Her skin was still glistening wet. 'So is it?'

'What?' Paresh croaked.

She walked round the bed until she stood over him, and let the towel drop completely. 'You remember.'

317

No! No, I fucking don't!

'Last night,' she said, and drew down a deep breath, showing off perfect abdominal muscle tone.

Paresh thought dying right now was about his best option. 'Uh—'

'You said you thought I'd look even better in daylight.' Her hands began to move sensually down her sides as she swayed her shoulders. 'So do I?'

'Yes.'

She smiled again, and she was so happy it was like a flash of Sirius sunlight. Happiness he'd given her. Then she was on the bed, on all fours, on top of him. A teasing tongue licked at his cheek, his ear. Her hand curled round his cock. 'We made up for one day last night,' she murmured hungrily. 'So now you need to start taking care of the other nineteen years three hundred and sixty-four days.'

He'd never known humiliation like it. This incredible woman had her sensational naked body on top of him, eager face centimetres from his, hand round his flaccid dick, begging him for sex. And his hung-over, overtoxed body couldn't even produce a twitch of arousal.

'Sorry.' He struggled out from underneath her. 'Sorry.' He couldn't look at her. The shame was far worse than the physical pain. 'Hangover. Feel sick. It's not you. Not you. Really.' He blundered into the en suite and slapped the bolt across the door, looked at the waiting toilet, and promptly threw up into it.

Friday 8th February 2143

A wide blanket of unbroken cirrus had sealed off the sky, producing an odd omnidirectional light across the jungle. It had been there when Angela walked up the rear ramp into the dark cylindrical fuselage of the Daedalus, reducing shadows to small grey spectres flitting across the ground. There was no wind, not even Abellia's usual sea breeze; of course the cloud did nothing to kill the heat, and with the humidity building, physical activity had been difficult. Half the time she felt she was sucking down spray rather than simply breathing.

It had taken the squad over an hour to pack up their tent that morning, and they were all sweating and cursing by the time they'd finished. Orders to forward deploy had come down without warning from Lieutenant Pablo Botin as they were eating their breakfast. They'd bagged their kit, voices filling the wet air with taunts and bullish jokes, eager at the prospect of moving up-country at last. Their tents were folded down into neat, shiny black bundles on top of their respective module. And there the squad sat in the mud, surrounded by their bags, everything and everybody waiting for a logistics corps loader truck to come and collect them, starting them on the route out of here.

All that sweaty, busy activity made it easy for Paresh to not talk to her, continuing the theme of yesterday. When they got to the Daedalus it was configured to carry cargo, with passengers strictly subsidiary, cheap meat fitting in around the important pallets and equipment. Its cavernous interior was a whale's gullet sculpted from metal and composite; seats were simple strut-frames which folded down from the side of the fuselage, with a nylon mesh to sit on. Even Vance Elston had to make do with one, stuffing audio-null foam into his ears, and grimacing at the smell, engine roar, poor lighting, vibration, and two toilets shared by sixty people. Angela suspected he rather enjoyed the hardship, it was all very macho. She couldn't see what Paresh thought of the plane: he'd chosen to sit on the other side, with the mobile biolabs taking up the bulk of the interior between them.

Her poor puppy boy was suffering deeply, for which she felt a mild amount of guilt. She'd actually been looking forward to some decent sex in the hotel that morning. After that didn't happen, they'd both sneaked back to Abellia Airport in a subdued mood. The rest of the squad was dying to know if they'd made out, but neither was saying anything.

On the two-and-a-half-hour flight she read more of her history and politics files. Not just to maintain her cover any more, but to gain a real understanding of what the hell had happened on Ramla during the last twenty years. Ten minutes from landing she cancelled the files, and used her grid to look out through the plane's external meshes as they started to descend towards Edzell.

The runway had been extended since the first successful Daedalus flight, the dozers and compactors working round the clock . . . not that Angela could really see much difference. It still looked like a tiny streak of mud from the air, although there were definitely turning circles at both ends now.

Their undercarriage clunked down. Angela saw Josh trying to crush his seat's metal struts, and grinned. Then they were on the ground, and bouncing about wildly, decelerating hard. Everyone winced as the pallets and biolabs strained at their hold-down straps. The straps held, though, and soon the plane had taxied off the runway.

The ramp lowered, letting the bright St Libran sunlight flood in, making them all blink and scramble for their sunglasses. A wash of hot humid air replaced the conditioned atmosphere they'd been breathing, bringing with it a strange musty spice scent. Spores from a billion native plants, Angela recognized warily, the sentinels of the jungle, a clear warning to humans that this was alien territory. Milliseeds she liked, the smaller reproductive microorganisms from the planet's astonishing zebra botany she could do without. Human tissue was a real attractive nutrient source to some of it.

She trooped down the ramp, several obedient paces behind Vance Elston. Today's odd cirrus cover was still above her, motionless in the becalmed air. Despite the brightness, it was a gloomy way to arrive, another portent in collusion with the vegetation odour, adding to her mistrust of the forward base. She took a tube of sunscreen from her pocket and applied it to her arms. Her T-shirt was an HDA-issue scoop-neck. One minute in the jungle and she'd already weakened. The long-sleeved T-shirts she'd bought from Birk-Unwin were somewhere near the bottom of her bag; they were just too damn hot to wear. She proudly stuck with the garters, though.

Edzell was a miniature version of the HDA compound at Abellia Airport. A cluster of Qwik-Kabins formed the centre of the camp, housing the new Observation Centre, alongside the logistics corps offices, and a field hospital. Rows of the black tents were lined up behind, along with another big mess tent. Engineering shops had been set up, big open-ended hemispheres of plastic where mechanics checked over ground vehicles. But mainly, Edzell was an equipment staging post. Rows and rows of pallets were already starting to build up, along with helicopters and vehicles scheduled to fly on to the next forward camp as soon as the e-Rays found a suitable site beyond the Eclipse Mountains. However, the biggest single cargo Edzell stored was bioil. Huge bladder tanks had been laid out on the other side of the runway, thick rubbery cubes that were pumped full by the expedition's single Daedalus tanker every time it touched down. That was all it did now: fly continual circuits night and day, bringing biav and bioil to the thirsty vehicles and helicopters and fuel cells.

Once the mobile biolabs had lumbered down the ramp, a self-loading pallet truck went inside the Daedalus to extract the remaining cargo. Paresh's squad were detailed to put up everyone's tents.

'That's what I'm here for,' Gillian Kowalski grumbled. 'Fucking servant for the science prats.'

'We're security,' Paresh told them as they tramped along after the self-loader truck. 'But while we're here, we're also general aides to whoever beckons. You'll soon be doing a lot worse than putting up a tent. Get used to it.'

Atyeo moved up beside Angela. 'What did you do to him?' he asked in a low voice. 'He's been like this since the two of you got back.'

'Nothing.'

'Ah, well no wonder, then. Man had his hopes up high.'

'Man drank too much beer,' she said.

Atyeo laughed.

Angela helped to put the tents up, adding to the rows of shiny black, heat-junkie triangles already lined up. Nobody hurried, not in the stifling humidity. They were distracted by the ground crew readying the last e-Ray for launch. The e-Ray AD-7090-EW50 AAV (Autonomous Airborne Vehicle) was built by Neiti Aeronautic, and was a sensor-laden drone intended to provide HDA with a decent, comprehensive back-up sensor coverage during a Zanthswarm when satellites were being knocked out of space. A simple pinched-delta planform, twelve metres long, with a ten-metre wingspan, its upper fuselage skin was a single black photovoltaic collector, providing 10kw to power the trio of motors that drove a large twin-blade rear propeller, augmented by a dozen helium bubbles incorporated within the fuselage providing extra lift, making it half-dirigible.

Angela and the squad started applauding as it took flight. The black triangle juddered its way upwards. When it was five metres off the ground, the big rear propeller started turning, adding some stability. It would take ten hours to reach its operational station on the other side of the Eclipse Mountains, two thousand kilometres away. But once there it would loiter, flying a long lazy figure-eight pattern constantly for up to five hundred days without needing maintenance; relaying communications all the way back down the chain of its sibling e-Rays to Abellia.

The squad finished putting up tents by mid-afternoon, and the lieutenant hadn't detailed them with anything else. Up above, the single roof of high cloud was starting to break up in the strengthening winds.

'Can we go swimming?' Omar asked. 'The lake's only half a klick away.'

'No way,' Ramon said. 'I'm not getting my balls bitten off by a ten-metre native shark.'

'There are no fish,' Angela said. 'Like there are no animals or insects.'

'And Ramon has no balls anyway,' Mohammed chuckled.

Paresh checked with the lieutenant. 'We can go swimming,' he announced. 'But there's a briefing at eighteen hundred hours. We're going to start perimeter patrols tonight.'

'What? Angela just said there's nothing here.'

'Hey!' she protested. 'I said there aren't any fish. I didn't promise you anything else.'

'We're on perimeter detail,' Paresh said. 'Maybe the monster's not here, but we need to keep sharp, build up some appreciation for the jungle and how to operate here. Be ready for it. And tomorrow, when the xenobiology teams head out to do their sampling shit, we escort them too. Come on, people, this isn't a fucking holiday. Get real.'

Subdued, the squad pulled towels and swimwear from their bags, and headed off towards the lake. Out here, the native plants seemed to have more vigour than they did around Abellia Airport. Vines were already twining eager tendrils up the support legs of the Qwik-Kabins. The route to the lake was worn, with tramped-down brown-green grass budding new blades from every break, brighter blue-green shoots stabbing upwards like fine bristles.

'Are you avoiding me?' Angela asked.

Fine alert soldier Paresh made – she'd sneaked up on him along the path. He wasn't walking with anyone else, and nobody wanted to walk with him.

'No,' he said grumpily.

'Then what?'

'I just . . . I don't know what happened.'

'I do. We both got stupidly toxed. No big deal.'

'It—' He waited until Audrie and Josh walked past, both of them half-smirking as they looked on curiously, eager to watch the lovers' tiff.

'Oh,' Angela said in exasperation. 'Stop.'

'I didn't say anything.'

'No, stop walking.'

He did as he was told, and Angela stood beside him while the rest of the squad passed. 'Catch you all in a minute,' she told DiRito who was at the back of the line.

He grinned, saying nothing.

'That's never happened before, right?' Angela challenged. 'The morning part, I mean.'

Paresh's face twisted up. Angry at first, then just plain miserable. 'I guess I'd had more than I realized.'

'Uh huh. You do get that I'm a lot older than you, don't you?'

'Yeah. It's difficult, you know, you look like you're maybe twenty, but I get it.'

'Even before jail, I'd lost count of how many men who had their first *never happened before*. So either I'm like a human damping rod, or it might be a little more common than you guys like to admit. Either way, it doesn't bother me.'

'Thanks.' Said, but not really meant.

She sighed. The male ego . . . 'Is that the monster over there?'

'What?' He looked around in alarm.

'I thought I saw something move, Colonel.'

'I'm not a, oh ah.'

'Over there. In those bushes.'

His own grin was returning. 'Those thick bushes?'

324

'Thick bushes away from this path, that nobody can see through.'

'Could be dangerous.'

'Very dangerous. They look quite prickly to me.'

'I've got a towel.'

'Me too. Shall we investigate?'

'I think we ought to.'

They walked away from the track to the lake, then started running. By the time they reached the sprawl of bushes and thinthillow trees they were both laughing. Angela wiggled her way past the tight packed branches of hayneleaf, making the mauve seed pods pop and the ruddy screw-like spirals zip out in short arcs.

There was a flat patch of ground inside, and they sank down to their knees, kissing urgently. Angela put both arms up, letting him pull her T-shirt off. Then her hand was inside his fatigue trousers, feeling his cock stiffening.

'I get to go on top,' she said.

'Yes ma'am.'

'Call me ma'am again, and you're dead.' She pushed him down, and straddled him. Sirius shone down on them, a glare-point ruler in the vast cobalt empire of St Libra sky. It was gloriously hot on her naked skin, crowning her body. She adored the moment, adored the bright heat, adored the other heat which came from finally having a man inside her again, adored being here amid the trees and bushes, being free in the wildlands. This was where her real new life began, the start of the fightback. Returning to Abellia, with its wealth and skin-deep glitz, had too many memories shackling her to what had been. But out here in the jungle, this was different to everything that had gone before.

*

There were five resident girlfriends in Bartram's mansion in 2121. Angela had tried to keep her emotional distance from them, as Bartram did from her; aiming for being colleagues rather than building up any friendships. That wasn't so easy with Olivia-Jay. That sunny-girl personality was switched to maximum all the time. Angela suspected all the effusiveness was covering up for some deeper insecurity or low self-esteem. But if it was a mask, if she truly loathed what she had to do, Olivia-Jay never let it slip. So it was hard to keep pushing her away. After a while Angela didn't bother. It turned out that having Olivia-Jay as a friend was quite useful.

They let the Jag's auto take them into town in the morning. It had rained not an hour earlier, so the roof was up to keep the spray out. Another thirty minutes and the bright Sirius sunlight would have burned away the last of the moisture. As it was, Angela could see steam rising off the tarmac.

'I talked to Meshean last night,' Olivia-Jay said as they turned on to the Rue de Montessuy, which would take them along the Osuan valley, almost all the way to the old town itself.

'Oh?' Angela wasn't that interested; Meshean had been one of her predecessors, leaving the mansion a couple of months ago.

'She's started her history and politics course at Istanbul University.'

'That's great. Good for her.'

'Do you think you'll go back to Imperial College?'

'Not sure. Haven't really thought about it.'

'Oh. But when you go back to Earth you'll have enough money to live properly and study.'

'Yeah.' Angela smiled at the girl. Trouble with Olivia-Jay was she truly believed in happy endings. She had so many plans for what she would do afterwards with all the money. Her middle-class background was never more obvious than when she day-dreamed about the future ten years hence: settling down on a new world, getting married, and having five kids. That was when Angela had to lock her own mask into place and not unleash a torrent of scorn at such bourgeois delusion. Olivia-Jay would have been too hurt by a friend shattering her dumb illusions. Maybe that whole ridiculous white knight scenario she was holding out for was the one thing which kept her smiling through. Though Angela had her suspicions about that – Olivia-Jay was just a little too uninhibited in bed to put any real meat on the whole dippy routine.

Bartram seemed to believe it. Or at least he'd never called her out. But then Bartram wouldn't bother. That would have meant engaging with his girlfriends, showing an interest. Marc-Anthony had nailed it when he said there was no true involvement. With the whole billionaire mansion retreat Bartram had crafted himself a specific fantasy, whereby girlfriends draped themselves decorously around the lounge he was using, or the dining room, or poolside, or bedroom. They were there to complement the mansion's decor and grand artwork – that and fuck when told to.

The topics Bartram did discuss with them were politics, music, medical science, market economics, and sports – specifically the English League One football. That was why the girlfriends were all recruited from universities, so they could hold their own in conversation and even put forward their own opinion. Karah, surprisingly, was a first-year genetics student, with her eye firmly on an Ivy League med school scholarship, which was in her contract as the final bonus; Lady Evangeline, the fiery politics student and token leftie, was going to be a GE Commissioner one day if she didn't bring about the downfall of the whole corrupt establishment first; Coi, the sharp-as-nano finance analyst whose netlens glasses brimmed with figures from dawn till dusk, was destined to run either a national treasury or a trans-stellar bank. So it was Olivia-Jay who turned out to be the musical prodigy, able to play the antique Steinway grand piano in the seventh floor's lounge with a virtuosity which had quite startled Angela the first time she heard it; she was equally adept at guitar, but her true talent lay with a voice that was smooth and husky as twenty-year-old malt. That left Angela as the sporty tomboy: she knew every League One player – their club, position, and form for the last few seasons – and could argue for hours about what formation play managers should and shouldn't use. It had taken months of reviewing classic games, memorizing results, players, managers, League One gossip, but she could now talk the great

327

game with the best of them. There was being a whore, and then there was just plain debasing yourself – but it had paid off. Apparently, the football girlfriend position hadn't been filled for a while. The first thing Bartram had said when Marc-Anthony introduced them was: 'So explain the offside rule to me, then.'

The Jag pulled into the car park behind Velasco Beach. It was early afternoon, and the southerly wind and shepherd moonlets conjunction was raising a reasonable swell on the ocean. Angela and Olivia-Jay stood on the new promenade along the back of the sands and watched surfers riding the curls.

'Can you do that?' Olivia-Jay asked, her expression going all wistful as she watched the lean beach-suited figures showing off.

'I haven't for a while,' Angela admitted. 'I'm way out of practice.'

'Will you teach me? We could get some boards delivered to the mansion.'

Angela had just known that would be her response. 'I suppose we could.'

'Oh thank you!' Olivia-Jay gave her a big hug and kiss.

Angela kissed her back, smiling at the girl's simple glee.

'I don't know what I'd do without you.'

'You'd survive.' Angela put her arm round the girl's shoulder. 'Now come on, let's make the most of our time out.'

They wandered into the narrow streets of the old town. The buildings close to the sea were mainly old warehouses and engineering shops, all metal frame and cheap panelling, their original purpose modified by sharp developers into bargain apartments and small individual stores. It wasn't the rich who used them, they had their own grander streets with exclusive malls and arcades and spars. This part of town belonged to the lowly contract workers.

Angela led them into Maslen's café on Leseur Street, where the owner favoured east European synth pop from thirty years ago. She ordered a mint tea, while Olivia-Jay asked for an espresso with a syrup shot. Both girls looked at the row of amazing pastries and cup cakes that Maslen himself baked in the kitchen out back, but the notion that they might get to taste one was a rebellion too far. All their food was carefully measured and prepared at the mansion, and they had to log on daily to the gym machines or use a monitor band to record a jog round the grounds or a swim. He might be a gossip, a toxsoak, a fibber, and a shameless vanity merchant, but Marc-Anthony took his job very seriously. The girlfriends had their weight limit written into their contract, along with fitness levels and general physical appearance. Even tan shades were detailed – Olivia-Jay had to sunbathe nude for ninety minutes daily, a clause requiring her to turn over every ten minutes, to maintain her dark complexion; while the Celtic-skinned Karah couldn't risk going outside without fullblock cream on. Lady Evangeline wasn't allowed to trim her waist-length raven tresses. Angela herself was required to exercise twice as hard as the others. He did like his stereotypes did Bartram.

'The surfboards are on their way,' Olivia-Jay announced happily as Angela chose a white plastic table by the window to sit at.

Angela put her jazzy orange and black beachbag behind the chair and picked up her Japanese-style tea cup with both hands, blowing at the surface to cool it. 'Don't say I didn't warn you,' she said.

Olivia-Jay's behaviour, the impulse buy, didn't bother her any more. The boards would be ridiculously expensive, since everything in Abellia was either flown or shipped in, adding to the cost. It didn't matter – anything the girlfriends wanted was just loaded onto the mansion's general finance tab. Should they want to, they could keep the things they bought afterwards. Though loading up with jewellery from Abellia's fanciful brand showcase emporiums earned them a ten-minute diatribe about gratitude in Marc-Anthony's office.

Someone sat at the table behind Angela. She paid them no attention.

Olivia-Jay leaned forward. 'Lady E is leaving next week,' she confided.

'What? How do you know?' Angela was certain Evangeline had another month to go on her contract. Four months was standard.

'I overheard Marc-Anthony and Loanna talking about it yesterday.'

'I see.' Loanna was the wardrobe mistress, who before she worked at the mansion used to glam up celebrities for a Hollywood zone production company. Hating herself for asking, for being part of it all, Angela said: 'Why?'

Olivia-Jay rolled her eyes. 'One too many ideological rants to Brinkelle.'

'I thought that's why she was here, to give Bartram something to shoot down.'

'They weren't expecting someone quite so committed to the socialist cause. Brinkelle is worried she gets Bartram a little too worked up.'

Angela shook her head in disbelief. Bartram always started the politics argument at their evening meals. It was his preferred topic, animating him more than the other discussions. The more heated the ideological argument, the longer he kept Evangeline in his bed afterwards. Angela suspected revenge sex was his favourite. Which made Brinkelle's motivation highly questionable. 'It's just jealousy. She has a lot of daddy issues.'

Olivia-Jay giggled wildly. 'I always think you'd be better off talking politics with him rather than Lady E.'

'Really? And can you imagine Evangeline telling him how Gilmer should play fullback, and Dewey ought to be on the other wing?'

'Got a point, there. See, you're the smart one, Angela.'

She just smiled airily. *Don't even get started on that discussion, however light-hearted.* 'Come on, time to go.' She picked up her beachbag.

'No rush,' Olivia-Jay grumbled. 'He's having treatment today. He never wants us around after that.'

Angela had reluctantly come to admire Bartram for his dedication to the treatment. The biomedical Institute which he'd founded was devoted to one thing, developing a human rejuvenation process. Like every branch of science, genetics had suffered a major slowdown when trans-spacial connections had unlocked the new worlds for settlement. In the new era, money did what money always did, and went for the fastest payoff. With the gateways opening, that was investment in entire planetary economies; familiar corporate growth patterns and government bond schemes but in markets that didn't suffer from Earth's heavy regulation and harsh taxes. It wasn't cutting-edge tech companies which brought the quick big profits any more, but the old staples of utilities and farming and distribution networks, and of course the algaepaddies. The money loved that. It was familiar and low risk with margins greater than gleaming short-lived technological breakthroughs. All the science-rooted consumerism corporates had suffered in the decades that followed publication of Wan Hi Chan's theory; the money didn't want maybes when it could have certainties.

That was why the three North brothers had eventually split, they had the money and the drive to break the stagnation, each pursuing their individual vision of the future. For Augustine it was the straight corporate route, continuing to grow the bioil giant that had the fiscal and political clout to shape destiny. His greatest accomplishment to date was the cartel which had broken the futures market, and brought some much-needed stability to the trans-stellar economy. Constantine chose isolation supported by self-sustaining high-tech replication technology, hoping to achieve a human–machine synergy, elevating himself to the singularity. No one knew what kind of progress he'd made, but no new cyborg deities had yet materialized in Jupiter orbit. While Bartram lusted for the oldest human dream: eternal life.

Out of the three, it was looking like Bartram would be the first to fully succeed. To begin with, the Institute had given him a genuine daughter, the first and only genuine offspring to be born to the three brothers. She was the family and future they had been denied before; supplanting all the 2s. And now, by painful increments, his body was being returned to its youthful ideal. Even better, this time round his reconstituted genes would have the one-in-ten sequence factored in.

The process was phenomenally expensive. Some organs could be regrown for him; the heart, lungs, kidney, liver, spleen, bladder, muscles – a long useful list that modified stem cells could shape themselves into around pre-moulded scaffolds of tissue, producing a viable body part ready for transplanting. But that still left the remainder of the human body: the all-important skin, and bone, and blood vessels and nerves, all of which had to be rejuvenated in situ with gene-replacement therapy. Then there was the brain, for which Bartram's Institute had pushed neuro-genesis techniques to astonishing new heights. It wasn't just the cost which was staggering; the combined procedures took time. A lot of it. Rumour around the mansion was that Bartram had begun that stage twelve years ago.

Angela didn't know, and didn't really care how long or how much it cost. The results were clear enough. Today, Bartram, at a hundred and nine years old, was more like a spry fifty-year-old unexpectedly struck with arthritis. He resented the painful stiff-ness, but was resolute in his determination to overcome it.

'So we can spend even longer in town, then,' Angela said.

Olivia-Jay gave her a sly look. 'Are you seeing someone?' she asked breathlessly.

'Don't be ridiculous. I wouldn't get anything if I did that, exclusivity is clause one in the contract. It's the only one that ever matters.'

'You are, aren't you?' Olivia-Jay was almost bouncing with excitement.

'No! I just want a bit of time to myself. That's not unreason-able, is it? Now come on.'

They went to Birk-Unwin first, much to Olivia-Jay's obvious disapproval. It was trying to push itself as a quality department store, but its pedigree showed in its accommodation: a revamped single-storey food-processing factory with awkward stanchions running the length inside that couldn't quite be disguised by fanciful marketing displays. Nor did the location help, halfway down Marbeuf Avenue, several blocks from where Abellia's real glitz and glamour began. For all its aspirations, Birk-Unwin was always going to be reasonably priced, last-year's-model merchandise for the middle-income patron. So Olivia-Jay sighed theatrically as Angela dragged her between counters. Eventually she found what she was looking for.

'You've got to be kidding,' Olivia-Jay said as Angela got an assistant to unlock the jewellery cabinet.

'No.' Angela held up the gold banana-shaped cufflinks, turning them in the light. They were the kind of deliberately gaudy trinket a low-rank manager would wear to demonstrate independence from the corporate machine – maybe something his fiancée had bought him. 'I'll take them,' she told the assistant.

'Angela!' Olivia-Jay protested.

'I know what I'm doing, thanks.'

'Clearly, you don't. Because if you did . . . Come on, let's go to Tiffany's, or Jerrards, or anywhere. If you really loved him, you would.'

'I don't, so flip it to zero.' She told her e-i to pay Birk-Unwin's account, using her own money, not the mansion's tab. 'Gift-wrapped, please,' she asked the assistant.

Tying a purple ribbon round the box took an extra three minutes. Longer than it should, but then the man was sneaking glances at the pair of them while he wrapped and tied.

'I'll catch you back at the Jag later,' she told a mildly pouty Olivia-Jay once they were outside.

'Suppose so.'

Angela let the girl take the first taxi. She wouldn't put it past Olivia-Jay to try and follow her. Once she'd seen the cab turn off at the end of Marbeuf Avenue her e-i called another one for her.

'Monturiol Beach,' she told the auto. They pulled away from the kerb emitting microwave and laser pulses which the road-guide cables and other autos deciphered; vehicles the length of the avenue adjusted their speed and positioning, allowing her cab into the modest flow. Angela peered down into her bag. She took out the gift box, unwrapped it carefully on her lap, and removed the gaudy cufflinks. Then she reached into the beachbag and found the palm-sized black cardboard box that had been dropped in while she was sitting in the café.

It contained a pair of cufflinks identical to the ones she'd just bought, as well as a pair of gossamer-thin grabber gloves. She took the gloves out carefully, remembering to hold them by the blue tag on the rim. They were so thin it was like holding mist. When she held them up they swayed about in the air-con streams with all the sluggish inertia of seaweed. As they moved, their refraction shimmer painted a phantom outline in the air – it was about the only way she could tell they existed.

Frightened they would tear, she carefully slid her hand up into the first one. She needn't have worried, their molecular structure had been carefully designed. When it was on correctly, she peeled the blue tag off, activating the adhesion process. The grabber glove melded to her skin. Even when she held her hand ten centimetres from her eyes, there was no way she could tell the glove was on. She rubbed her cheek. It felt like skin. Satisfied there was no way anyone could detect the grabber glove outside of a spectroscopic analysis, Angela pulled the second glove on. After that she opened the gift box from Birk-Unwin, and swapped the cufflinks round.

Monturiol Beach was a small cove with deep rocky headlands on either side. The land at the back was taken up by the Ibanez condominium, a sweeping white concrete and dark glass structure with eight tiered balconies along the front, and living walls at both ends, producing elaborate vertical gardens. Apartments inside started at eight million Eurofrancs, with full valet services on tap, making it the nesting place of hard-edged bachelor types, the kind of executive who provided all the management and financial service support which the true corporate overlord didn't like to be separated from.

The cab stopped by the main gate, the auto lacking authorization to proceed. Angela's e-i gave the gate manager her identity certificate, and the cab rolled forwards again. It stopped thirty seconds later under the eagle-wings portico, and Angela climbed out. Behind her, the Birk-Unwin cufflinks were wedged down the side of the seat cushions, unlikely to be found for months, if then. She'd swallowed the blue tags.

Angela took the lift to the eighth floor. There were only four apartments at that level, all penthouses. The door of number three recognized her, and opened.

Barclay North was waiting in the big open-plan lounge, with its balcony overlooking the deserted beach. Angela gave him a coy grin. 'Hi,' she said, all husky voiced.

'Hi yourself. You look great.'

'Thanks.' She did a little twirl, which sent the short flimsy skirt fabric rising up. That morning she'd dressed specifically for Barclay, not that it required much thought or effort – short skirt, tight white T-shirt without a bra, simple pumps; hair tied back, moisturized skin but no make-up. A slightly cheaper version of the clothing Marc-Anthony and Loanna made her wear at the mansion. They knew what Bartram liked, she'd been chosen for her toned-up athletic looks, and their clothes emphasized that. And, of course, what one North liked all the others did, too. It wasn't exactly trans-spacial connection science.

The twirl finished up with her in front of Barclay. She dropped her bag and wrapped her arms around him, kissing hungrily. Barclay was thirty-one, and already appointed as Abellia's Civic Administration's comptroller; the kind of position Bartram insisted remain within the family domain. His age meant he was almost the last 2North to be born before Brinkelle. There would be no more of his kind – Bartram was expecting to walk away from his treatment with fully functional gonads. All future offspring would be like Brinkelle – a concept which made Angela shudder. It also made Barclay not a little jealous and resentful of his little sister, which made things easy for Angela from the first moment she started flirting with him.

The kiss finished. Still grinning, Angela pulled her T-shirt off, warming her face into a sultry I-can't-wait expression. 'I've got something for you,' she purred.

Barclay could barely look away from her naked torso. 'Yeah?'

She took the ribbon-tied box from her bag and offered it to him. He opened it up, mildly curious. When the lid came off there was a flash of puzzlement, quickly and professionally hidden. 'Thank you, Angela.' His lips twitched in genuine appreciation.

'I know it's not much,' she said, her face tilted up, all youthfully serious now. 'But I wanted to give you something. I want you to know how much you mean to me.'

His smile was proud. As expected. He was the one who bought trinkets for girls, not the other way round. Like all men, especially ones as powerful as the Norths, he liked to believe a beautiful girl would fall head over heels for him. And that's what must be happening, because she had so much to lose personally if Bartram ever found out about their affair, so she must like him for him, not just his money and position.

'They're quirky,' he said. 'I like that. I'll put them on right away.'

'No, don't.' She slipped the skirt down her legs, then wiggled out of her thong. 'At least, not right away.'

They did it in the Jacuzzi first, which he always liked. Then they took a break in the sauna, followed by more thrashing about on the lounge's big cream-leather couch. One time, she let him have her up against a wall, legs and arms spread wide, all nicely submissive, the way a North enjoyed. Her hands were open, with his pressing up against her, pushing her hard against the wall, fingers to fingers, palm to palm. She triggered the grab, allowing the glove circuits and receptors to record his complete biometric pattern.

After the wall, he collected a bottle of champagne from the kitchen, and they finished up in the bedroom with him licking the icy fizzing drink off her abdomen and thighs – just like his brother–father.

Monday 11th February 2143

The zone theatre's city virtual showed the citycab taxi pulling in to the kerb outside the Suffren club on Carliol Street, just a few hundred metres from the Market Street Station. A man walked backwards out of the club and got into the taxi with a weird gravity-defying hop.

'Get me his ID,' Sid told Lorelle Burdette in the control room.

'Running a recognition routine now,' she assured him.

The taxi pulled away from the club and manoeuvred backwards onto Worswick Street, moving in the half-time which the detectives had found was the easiest way to follow vehicles reversing along Newcastle's ancient tangle of streets and through the dead coverage areas of ripped meshes and pulsed smartdust. This was the seventy-fourth they'd backtracked, and Sid was starting to worry about human error creeping in. It was tedious work that had so far produced nothing except for short tempers and growing resentment. Probability alone meant that they'd find the right taxi soon enough, and discover where it had picked up the unknown North's body.

Twenty minutes later the taxi was driving backwards along George Street towards the vast Fortin singletown, a carbon-black macrobuilding built in 2105, that had evicted the college and all the commercial units between Scotswood Road on the south up to Elwick Road, with George Street making its eastern wall and Maple Terrace its western. At thirty storeys high, it dominated the surrounding districts, looking like a nest of manufactured coral, soaking up the sunlight as part of its low-energy commitment, inset with ten thousand blind silver windows. A self-contained community with housing, shops, offices, schools, theatres, and fully protected by agency police. Connected to the Metro network, and with a recognized civil council that made sure local taxes were low, it was both inclusive with and separate from the rest of the metropolis. Singletowns were the best possible way forward for Earth's cities, its developers championed back then; projects that would eat up GSW areas, banishing urban blight, providing homes and jobs for everyone. Indeed, three other singletowns had been built in Newcastle around the turn of the century. With low property taxes and a screening policy to keep out undesirable residents they became havens for the corporate middle classes; the ultimate gated communities, shutting out the rest of the world's problems.

Sid watched the taxi back its way down George Street, getting ever closer to the ramp junction which led to one of the Fortin's underground road access ramps. 'Come on, down you go,' he murmured. If the taxi had come out of there, picked up the passenger from inside the Fortin, that would effectively eliminate the vehicle. The surveillance systems in the singletown worked; privately funded, any rip, glitch or damage was repaired immediately. They could grab a full history of the man.

Once again, the investigation had no luck. He watched the taxi roll past the ramp junction, and into Blandford Street. From there, of course, it wound up in the dead gap of the junction with St James's Boulevard.

'Why did it take that route?' Lorelle asked.

'Who knows?' Sid replied, and told her to centre the junction. Sometimes they got lucky, and a mesh further down the road would give them a bad visual angle on the blanked-out section. Not this time. Naturally. So Sid had to study the busy junction for several minutes, working out which of the taxis that drove through it was the one he was following.

And that was why this was getting dangerous. They'd decided

that each investigator was limited to a two-hour shift; the level of frustration combined with the finicky detail required meant that short-cuts and assumptions were too tempting. Sid wanted to backtrack every taxi himself, to be absolutely sure. But that was a physical impossibility, so he had to trust his colleagues. The nightmare scenario was they finished all two hundred and seven only to find somewhere down the line they'd made a mistake, that someone had overlooked a gap because the route appeared obvious, or they were tired, or they'd been distracted for a couple of seconds. If they didn't find which taxi it was they'd have to start over.

Actually, that wouldn't happen; O'Rouke would make very sure of that.

Sid confirmed the taxi travelled all the way along the Boulevard to the junction with the A186, and handed over to Eva at eleven o'clock. His two hours were up, and the relief was as strong as the guilt as he walked out of the theatre.

The state of Office3 was a perfect reflection of the team's morale. He still had a full complement of detectives working their way through data at each of the consoles. All of them in sweaters against the poor air-con. Fast-food wrappers and disposable cups were piled up precariously in the bins. The carpet had acquired additional unidentified stains. Cushioning on the arm of Abner's chair was held on with black gaffer tape.

Pausing by the door while the blue seal came on, he found the drabness and apathy to be supremely depressing. What a difference a month made, back when they started with their unlimited budget and bigtime political pressure to get this solved. People had arrived early and stayed late, bringing a surge of enthusiasm to the monumental task. Now this. And he couldn't even find it in himself to deliver a decent pep talk each morning. He felt like a fifth-division club manager at the end of the season, faced with relegation to oblivion. All his clever talk, keeping Eva and Ian tight to deliver the killer clue, had been pissed away in a drizzle of mediocrity. And from the way Chloe Healy and Jenson San regarded him in the canteen these days, like alligators watching a duckling, he was pretty sure O'Rouke was up on the sixth floor sharpening his knife.

His iris smartcell grid produced a communication icon that made him frown. It was the Newcastle Metro emblem, a dark yellow square with a stylized red M in the centre. He twisted the icon, and watched the text unfold from the Metro management system, telling him his dayrover ticket was now active.

Just to prove how blue his thoughts were, it took him a good thirty seconds to work out what it meant. He collected his jacket from the inner office. 'Out for lunch,' he told Ian as he walked away.

Light snow was falling from a dark-grey sky, precursor to a heavier fall within a couple of hours. He trudged up Grey Street towards the Metro station at Monument, the closest to Market Street. It was like early evening, the light level was so depleted. Sludge clung to his ankle boots as he went down the steps to the underground entrance.

Kaneesha Saeed was there, a ball of navy-blue mohair with a green tartan scarf and matching hat. She wandered over to a big map of the Metro network stuck on the wall opposite the bank of escalators. He stood beside her, and she shuffled sideways until she was facing a hologram poster for a Parsec resort in the Mediterranean, where girls in bikinis played slo-mo volleyball on the beach, a white marble hotel glimmering in the background. A constant stream of people walked along behind them, tramping the slush and jostling their backs.

'No mesh on this,' Kaneesha said.

'No lip-reading software,' he finished for her.

'You're growing into your job, Detective.'

'Thank you. Do you have a name for me?'

'No.'

'Crap on it, Kaneesha, what is this?'

'I picked up some words. Something's happening. Something big.'

'Okay, man. What?'

'I don't know that, moron. I'd have to be inside to know.'

Sid glared at the exotic beach with its brilliant sunlight and emerald palm trees. 'Fuck's sake,' he hissed.

'It's a big deal going down. Think what that means.'

'Low odds on two major corporate ops running simultaneously.'

'Well done, pet. Whatever the murder covered up is reaching its endgame.'

'Can you find out?'

'No.' Her round head shook from side to side. 'This is your way in. You need to work through the Gang Task Force. They're idiots, but they're not totally useless. The evidence will be in their intelligence somewhere. A pattern, a name. You have to find how it hooks into your case.'

'Yeah, right.'

'We're through now, Detective. Goodbye.'

'Take care, man.'

*

Sid had never liked the fifth floor. For a start it was home to the Police Standards Division, which ran in-house investigations against Newcastle's officers; and he'd spent enough time in their office last year. But it also housed three of the city's major task forces, who regarded themselves as the elite. Sid had his own views on that.

Detective first grade Hayfa Fullerton met him in the lobby outside the lifts; no one was allowed into the task force offices unescorted. A lot of smartdust scattered around had suppression functions, making sure the fifth floor's networks remained secure.

Hayfa herself was in her fifties, with a tired-looking face to which she'd applied a minimum amount of make-up; her dark hair was cut short, a style that required little upkeep. Helped by a grey, mid-price department store suit, she successfully projected the image of a drab bureaucrat too busy filling in expenses to deal with anyone. The greeting was professionally courteous, and nothing else. She showed him to her office. A corner office, Sid noted, the one directly underneath O'Rouke's, though considerably smaller.

'So what can I do for you?' she asked once he'd sat down in front of her desk.

'You've heard about my case?'

'The North carjacking; word is you're not making much progress.'

'We're running a simulation that should produce our principal suspect.'

'Right. The taxi backtrack HDA forced on O'Rouke. He's not pleased, Sid.'

'Name a time you've seen O'Rouke happy.' He gave her a cards-on-the-table grin, which was a masterclass in smooth. She was one of O'Rouke's devotees, a real solid block of the support pyramid which kept him in his office. 'Whoever killed my North had to have gang support.'

'Logical. The taxi was one of theirs, and ripping the meshes took organization. But if I knew anything I would have given you the data. I mean, screw the memo on inter-department cooperation, I could do with the credit.'

'Take the credit. I just need to survive.'

'So why are you here?'

'There's a big play coming off, I think the two might be connected. I'd like your intel on it.'

'Uh huh.' She gave him a neutral stare. 'And how did you come by that notion?'

'My own investigation. A source dropped a word.'

'That's a big word to drop.'

'So there is something happening?'

Hayfa took her time, making a show of deciding, pushing home just who was alpha here. 'We're picking up some activity on the street,' was all she finally admitted to.

'Unusual activity?'

'Only in scale.'

'So there is something going down?'

'Could be. We don't know yet. Best guess we can make from the money that's being splashed round and the lowlives it's buying, there's some kind of shipment coming in.'

'Okay. Who's being loose with their money?'

'Good question. That's what my people are trying to find out.'

'I need the data they've gathered. The AI can run correlation on it.'

'Our sources need to remain secure.'

'Aye, man, I wasn't thinking of broadcasting this.'

'I'll ask which of your team has clearance to handle this. It's sensitive. If any of them make the grade we'll talk again.'

'Appreciate that.' Sid got up to leave.

'How is the HDA connected to all this, Sid? Why the pressure?'

'It's a North,' he told her.

'Bollocks. What's going on?'

He couldn't help himself: 'If you like, I can find out if you've got clearance.'

'Screw you.'

'Sure. But I'd like you to get that data to whoever you clear out of my people by tomorrow morning at the latest. You don't want me to go over your head on this, trust me, man. I'm swimming in shit, don't get in with me.'

The blue seal around Hayfa's door died away as it opened, and she gave him a V sign.

Monday 18th February 2143

'Our survey was approved by the City Architect's Office,' Jacinta said over breakfast. 'It cleared the Civic Administration network last night.'

'Aye, brilliant, man,' Sid said. The survey was the last legal obstacle to selling their Walkergate house; an official report by a ridiculously expensive building structural analyst that concluded four walls and a roof existed, but guaranteed nothing else. Sid had already sorted out the mortgage with a company registered in Cambodia, who'd agreed to loan them money for the Jesmond house based on a combination of their salaries, and provided a certification to that effect to his solicitor. That would allow the money to be legally transferred on completion of the sale. As far as his UK bank and GE Tax Bureau would know (and could prove) the Cambodia mortgage company held the deeds and received monthly payments. In reality, Sid owned the mortgage company, and it had taken a loan from another finance market in Vietnam, a much smaller one, because they were using a big slice of Sid's secondary savings as a down payment on the new house as well as the equity from the old one. So out of the official monthly mortgage repayments half would pay off the Vietnam loan at a reasonable rate, and the rest would go direct to Sid's secondary. They'd legitimately wind up with a bigger house, and have more spending money per month than before.

'Does anyone want this house?' Zara asked anxiously as she spooned up her porridge.

'Fifteen virtual viewings so far,' Jacinta announced proudly. 'The agent said three have requested a visit as soon as the datawork's cleared.' She and Sid clasped hands and shared a look.

He didn't have the heart to tell her just how bad things were with the case right now. No taxi and no overlap between all their data and Hayfa's, plus he suspected Hayfa hadn't downloaded everything. And O'Rouke wanted to reassign five of the team members.

'So you two are going to have to keep your rooms tidy,' Sid warned the kids.

'Mine is,' Zara said immediately.

For the first time Will dragged his gaze from the screen which was showing the news from St Libra. The expedition e-Rays had successfully flown over the vast Eclipse Mountains, and were relaying the astonishing images of soaring snowy crags and valleys. 'And mine,' he protested.

Sid eyed the lump of porridge on the front of Will's Monday-morning-clean school shirt and pulled a dubious face. 'Aye, well let's keep them that way, shall we?'

'I'll take them in this morning,' Jacinta said. 'If you can collect them tonight. They've both got clubs, so it'll be six o'clock.'

'Sure.'

Their hands finger-played again. 'I know you like to get in early after a weekend.'

'Thank you.' He grinned.

'Urgh,' Will said; his nose was wrinkled up as he gave their hands a dismayed stare. 'What is wrong with you two?'

'Nothing, everything is fully functional, actually,' Sid said. He smirked at Jacinta, who started giggling.

Will gave his sister a perplexed glance, then shook his head dismissively and scooped up some more porridge.

Sid and Jacinta exchanged one last glance. He knew they wouldn't be able to get away with that kind of behaviour in front of the kids for much longer. That, moving house, the case – however it ended – it was definitely the end of an era. The world had that feel to it these days, as if he was marking time. He suspected it was the eternity of the zone theatre simulation which he had to return to day after day which was conjuring up the sensation. *Aye well, only a hundred and nine of the little bastards left now.* Today they'd reach the halfway point. Somehow he knew he wasn't going to convince the team it was all downhill from now on.

*

Sid let the Toyota's auto make the drive to the Market Street Station. It hadn't snowed for five days, and the roads were reasonably clear, allowing traffic to flow as it always did when the majority were on auto. A heatless low sun shone brightly out of a clear sky, glinting off the ice which gripped the buildings.

He let the official police overnights roll down his grid, keeping current with how the city had behaved over the weekend. As badly as usual by the look of things. Assaults, drunken brawls, burglaries, two arson burn-outs, three murders, a medium-size tox bust at a club, a whole column of car smashes from faulty autos, drunk manual drivers (why do they do that still?), and not enough grit on the roads.

As the Toyota dipped down into the station's underground car park Sid frowned and asked his e-i to bring up the file on one of the murders. The name was vaguely familiar. When the file started to expand he wished he could close it all down again. Jolwel Kavane had been found on the Heaton GSW site. Actually, a passing agency patrol car had seen him at four o'clock in the morning. It wasn't difficult. Someone had doused him in bioil and set it alight.

When Sid got up to Office3 he used the secure net to run a check. Jolwel Kavane had been mentioned in the information Hayfa Fullerton had sent down from her task force. He was a long-time police informer who was due to be contacted by the task force.

Hayfa Fullerton wasn't at all pleased to see him when he stepped out of the lift on the fifth floor. She never said a word as they walked down the corridor to her office. Sid took a guess that she hadn't been up to see O'Rouke yet. The murder of a police informant was going to bring down a pile of grief as well as a formal investigation.

'So what happened?' he asked.

'You tell me. Everything was going along fine until we shared our intelligence with you.'

'No. Don't even try that one. I accessed the file. Kavane was one of your actives on this. You were working him.'

'Maybe. We'll never know now, will we?'

'So do you handle the murder investigation, or does that get kicked downstairs?'

'Downstairs. I don't have time and money to waste on crap like this.'

'Crap like this?' Sid snarled. 'He was burned to death, man. It doesn't get any worse.'

'That's the point. It's how the gangs deal with snitches. That's why they do it in public, too, not just bump them off in some cellar where nobody will ever find them. It's a warning to everyone else. One you don't ignore. All our contacts will be diving for cover today. Whatever the hell was going down, we won't find out about it until after, if then. This is over now, do you understand? We blew it.'

'Ah, crap on it, man.'

'Still no taxi, huh?'

'Still no taxi.'

'Okay, look, we're both going to get our arses kicked on this. If you find the taxi, let me know.'

'Why?' Sid asked suspiciously.

'You said it, these two are probably connected. Find the taxi, see who gets in and out with the body, and I'll run them through our AI. We both know they're gang members, and we have hundreds of names, confirmed and suspected. If anyone can identify them for you, it'll be my task force.'

He didn't have to consider the deal for long. 'Okay. I'll keep you in the loop.'

*

The message came through at eleven o'clock, issued from O'Rouke's office. He was to report to the senior briefing room on the sixth floor in ten minutes. Sid thought he was getting hauled up before O'Rouke for a bollocking, then he noticed who else was included on the message: every detective above grade four in the station.

He shared the lift up with three of them, all exchanging puzzled glances. They trooped into the briefing room and waited until O'Rouke came in. He was flanked by Jenson San and another man Sid didn't recognize, but who wore the kind of stiff attitude and dark suit that nailed him as a senior bureaucrat – manipulative, negative, self-serving.

'This is a GE-wide inter-agency alert,' O'Rouke said. 'And is classified Global Restriction.'

Sid was icy alert now. *Another Global Restriction? Crap on that.*

'Mr Scrupsis is from the GE Bureau of Alien Affairs, he'll explain what's going on.'

The bureaucrat stepped forward. 'Thank you, Chief Constable. This is basically a missing persons alert, and I'll explain the importance of it in a moment. We are issuing this to every local and national law enforcement agency in the GE, and our equivalent colleagues are doing the same all over Earth. As of last Friday a Professor Sebastian Umbreit and his family – his wife and two girls, aged ten and seven – have gone missing. They live in Switzerland just outside Geneva, and the alarm was raised by work colleagues late last Friday. The local police investigated, and found no sign of a struggle. As far as we can determine, Mrs Umbreit picked the children up from school as normal, sixteen hundred hours on Thursday, and returned home. Local traffic records confirm this. Professor Umbreit left the institute at eighteen seventeen that evening, and also drove home without incident. Both cars were in the garage when the police arrived.

We have not yet determined the exact time or method of abduction, but it is clearly a very professional operation.'

Sid was glancing cautiously round the room to try and see Hayfa Fullerton, and what her reaction to all this was. Surely this couldn't be the big operation the gangs were mounting?

'As to the reason for the high level of the alert,' Mr Scrupsis continued. 'All I can tell you is that Professor Umbreit works for the Swiss National Nuclear Research Agency. His knowledge could be extremely dangerous in the wrong hands. So, his profile will be loaded into the civic AIs who will scan every surveillance system for him; in addition you will be issued a basic file on him, which you are to pass on to every member of your team. His field of expertise must not be revealed under any circumstances, not to them, or friends, or family. I hope this is understood.' He stared round the room for emphasis, meeting as many gazes as he could. 'Very well, thank you for your cooperation.'

'Stay behind for a moment,' Jenson San said quietly to Sid as everyone started to leave.

Sid waited where he was until the room cleared – even Jenson San baled, clearly glad not to be a part of the smaller meeting. The blue seal came on around the door, and the windows turned silver. O'Rouke stayed up on the small rostrum, directing an inscrutable stare at Sid. For once his face had lost its ruddy flush, not that Sid could detect any nervousness.

'So is there a connection?' Sid asked.

'To your case?' Scrupsis said. 'We don't know, obviously. But this is the second major trans-stellar criminal incident in five weeks – actually in twenty years. That's pushing it for a coincidence.'

'What was Umbreit's speciality?'

'He is head of a D-bomb design team. You know what a D-bomb is, don't you?'

'Oh crap on it,' Sid grunted in complete dismay. 'Yeah, I know; it's the nuke they fire into a Zanthswarm.'

'To be specific, it's the nuke they fire into the spacetime rift that the Zanth use. It distorts the rift at a quantum level, and makes it useless – for a while anyway. The Zanth adapt to everything we throw at them, that's why the designs have to be constantly improved. As a rule of thumb, what worked last time won't work next time.'

'Aye. Look, man, I can see what a huge deal this is, but really I don't figure a connection with my case.'

'What do you think your case is, Detective?'

'Find the alien who murdered the 2North.'

'And you believe that?'

Which wasn't a question Sid had any intention of answering. 'It's a very unusual case, and that's why it has the resources it does.'

'Good answer. If there are aliens running round Earth, then they might well be trying to acquire our advanced weapons technology. Speaking for myself and my department, I believe that to be a pile of crap. This is vile corporate manoeuvring, conducted on the grandest scale, and we intend to expose it for what it is.'

Sid turned to O'Rouke as if he was appealing to a priest. 'So what do you want me to do?'

'Continue exactly as before,' Scrupsis said. 'Run down the gang which killed the North. When we have them, we will have their corporate paymasters. Then we will step in and close this whole shoddy enterprise down permanently.'

'Aye, I can do that.'

'Good man.'

'Give me updates as soon as you have anything new,' O'Rouke said. 'I'll liaise with Mr Scrupsis.'

'And what about Ralph Stevens?' Sid asked levelly.

'You continue to report to him,' O'Rouke said. 'After me.'

'Aye,' Sid said. He glanced back at Scrupsis. 'You and Stevens, you don't work from the same office, do you?'

'No, Detective, we do not.'

'Got it.' He turned to leave.

'How's the taxi hunt going?' O'Rouke asked.

Sid's e-i quested the door to unlock. The blue seal light faded. 'Absolutely bloody nowhere, man.'

Friday 22nd February 2143

By eight o'clock in the evening the last of the day's thin clouds had blown away over the North Sea, leaving the stars shimmering harshly in the thin clear sky. The temperature had been dropping all across the city for hours. It was going to be a cold night even by Newcastle standards.

After he parked his car at the end of Falconar Street, Sid pulled the jacket zip right to the top, and put on a woolly hat. He could make out his cloudy breath in the pale streetlights as he walked along to Ian's place. It was so tempting just to forget about all this and go home. Immerse himself in the noise and fun chaos of the kids, a meal together with Jacinta, some time alone after the kids went to bed. A good answer to a week that had been pure hell, starting with Kavane's gruesome murder and the alert over the Umbreit kidnapping. He absolutely hated the politics of it all, Ralph's office against Scrupsis, neither of which he could control; O'Rouke's involvement too made him more wary. Then he'd had a meeting with Aldred. It was the same little Jamaica Blue café on John Dobson Street as their very first encounter. It had taken a while, and some delicate investigation, but Sid finally discovered why Aldred didn't mind having a conversation in broad daylight with him: Northumberland Interstellar owned the franchise; all the smartdust was deactivated while they were sitting together – nothing was recorded, so no lip-reading software could ever be applied. It gave Sid an appreciation of just how extensive the North family's influence was.

Aldred had come in on the Wednesday morning, and they sat in their usual corner booth, away from the door.

'I take it you want to talk about Umbreit?' Aldred asked.

'And Scrupsis.'

'Ah, the man from Alien Affairs. Bad name I always thought, makes it sounds like they're shagging them rather than investigating them.'

'They think your brother's murder and the kidnapping are connected. Scrupsis believes it's all part of some big corporate scam.'

Abner's eyebrows rose. 'A D-bomb scientist is part of corporate manoeuvring? Did he say in what way? Are our rivals going to nuke us?'

'Aye man, don't you start in on me.'

'Sorry,' Aldred grinned as he blew gently at the chocolate sprinkled foam on top of his cappuccino. 'But it is funny. Two government agencies in a jurisdiction war, and they accuse the corporates of arming up as an excuse to cage-fight.'

'So who does want a D-bomb scientist?'

'The distant worlds, most likely.'

'The what?'

'Distants. Planets like New Persia, or Kofon, or True Jerusalem, or Georgia. Worlds that don't have gateways to Earth, that were opened by nationalist societies that want to propagate colonies made up entirely of believers; pure cultures taken from the old country. They need protection from the Zanth just like everybody else, and as they're distant, the HDA can't help them.'

'I thought True Jerusalem was just a rumour. And I hadn't even heard of the others. Are they real?'

'Who knows? As you and I aren't Jewish we'd never get the secret invitation handshake, would we? And I'm certainly not Chinese nor Muslim, so same goes there. The much better rumour is there's another US world out there somewhere; apparently their government will evacuate to it if we ever lose Earth.'

'I don't need this, man, I really don't.'

'Look, you're here for my advice, right?'

'Aye.'

'It doesn't bother us who gets involved higher up the ladder, okay? It's a government turf war – irrelevant to what's actually going on. You are the one finding out who killed our brother. And you're doing it properly. That's what matters. So . . . kiss the arse of whatever idiot is putting the most pressure on O'Rouke, flog your team, file your reports with everybody, but don't slow the investigation. We're relying on you, Sid.'

The Norths were about the only people who were, Sid reflected that night as he made his way to Ian's flat. Everyone else was waiting for him to screw up so they could initiate stage two of their conflict. As he opened the front gate on the little terraced house he contemplated exactly what he should tell Ian and Eva. It might just be time to cut them loose, make sure their careers weren't tainted too badly by the case. Even as he thought it he realized he'd all but given up on the taxi simulation.

'Evening, Detective.'

Sid jumped. There was a dark blob in the shadows of the tiny front garden, only visible as it moved forwards.

'Kaneesha! Aye, man, what the hell?' He couldn't make out her face at all, just another shade of darkness between coat and whatever hat was pulled down over her hair. Even her wisps of breath were faint.

'Jolwel Kavane used to be my informant,' she said with a thread of anger in her voice. 'I recruited him back in the day. I ran him for seven years. He was a perfect snout, he didn't know what was going on at the top, but everything else he told me was solid gold. I owe him a couple of promotions at least.'

'I'm sorry. I didn't know.'

'He was reliable, Sid. He would have told his controller whatever he knew. You don't pressure people like Jolwel to find things out, that's not how it's played. You listen to what he says, you hear the names, and you turn the heat on them because they're new nobodies, the expendable ones, not Jolwel. He's not an expendable. They knew that, that bitch Fullerton and her crew, they knew it and they didn't fucking care. They were too greedy, they wanted things fast. That's not how it works in intelligence, you put a case together slowly, take years if you have to. But this mad North murder, it's fired everyone up so hot they can't think of anything else but the prize at the end. So they put pressure on him. They got him to ask, when it should have been them doing the asking. See, pet, everyone knew Jolwel didn't ask about things he wasn't involved in. He was never the curious one; he was a solid gang lad. A dependable who *didn't fucking ask*! And when all that changes, when he's different, you know he's grassing you up.'

'I don't want to make it worse, but Hayfa's intelligence hasn't given me anything. I'm no closer to solving this.'

'Aye, and now everyone is ducking for cover. That stupid fatherfucking bitch. She couldn't organize an orgy in a brothel. How the hell did she ever wind up in charge?'

Sid was getting more than a little curious why Kaneesha was here. Not just for rant therapy, that was sure. So he humoured her, quietly confident this was going to be the gold he'd been praying for since the beginning. 'O'Rouke. How else?'

'Aye, crap on it. When he's gone, this city'll see the sun again, I tell you.'

'I expect so.'

Kaneesha let out a long sigh. 'Marcus Sherman.'

'Who?'

'Marcus Sherman, he's the one you have to watch. He's the organizer, the one with the contacts and the muscle and the money. He's putting this together. Not that it's his operation, he's not that high.'

'Never heard of him. He wasn't in any of the intelligence reports.'

'Of course not, nor will he be in any database you can access; he's not as stupid as Fullerton. He used to be in Northumberland Interstellar security before he went freelance. That's how come he's the contact point, Mr Go-To. And the corporate boys trust him because they know they can disown him faster than shit falls down a sewer. There's no way he'll ever turn on them if he did get charged. He'd know about a warrant being granted before the case detective, and if that ever happens he'll disappear. He's got the money for it, he only stays because the game is his blood.'

'Nobody is going to apply for a warrant, Kaneesha. Not with this.'

'Good man.' She held out an envelope. 'This is a photograph of him.'

'Thanks. Kind of primitive there, man.'

'Kind of cautious, Detective. If you ever were stupid enough to try and build a case, his lawyer would be entitled to your log. They'd work the devil's own backtrack. He doesn't get my name, Sid.'

Which is why she was waiting for me here, because she knew this night would be off-log. Jesus, that's smart paranoia. 'Okay, I understand.'

'I hope so. You have to be super-careful, Sid. Marcus doesn't need proof. If he even hears your name there's going to be trouble, big trouble.'

'None of this will go through the station. That's not how I'm working the case.'

'All right. Final details, he's got a lot of houses around town, and he never stays at one for more than a couple of nights at a time. But he does have a boat called the *Maybury Moon*, berthed at Dunston Marina. He's sweet on it, maybe too sweet. Apart from that, he's hot on smartdust and software security. If you're going to hack him you'll need a bytehead a lot better than anyone at Market Street.'

'Thanks, Kaneesha.'

She opened the gate and stepped out into the gloomy frozen street. 'Stupid thing this. Man, I didn't even like Jolwel. Nobody did. But then nobody deserves to die like that.'

*

'What's up?' Ian asked when Sid walked into the flat. Eva had claimed her usual place against the wall, sitting on a pillow, and holding up a shot glass. 'Brennivin,' she said. 'Decent Icelandic schnapps. I thought we'd toast the death of the case in style. It's been a long time dying.'

Ian couldn't stop staring at Sid. 'What is it? What's happened?'

'Put the bottle away,' Sid told Eva. 'We just got our first break.'

He'd drunk two bottles of beer by the time he'd finished explaining everything: Umbreit, Kavane, and Scrupsis; the bureaucrat fight; Aldred's distant worlds theory.

Sid cracked open his third beer. 'So what we have is a wild connection that'll probably be completely wrong. But it's a connection. Like I said, I'm not interested in the reason, all I want is the bastard who stabbed the North to death.'

'And Marcus Sherman can give us that?' Ian asked dubiously.

'If my source is right, he probably organized the cover-up afterwards.'

'Hey, that might explain why there was such a gap between the murder and dumping the body,' Eva explained. 'If the murderer hadn't planned on killing the North . . .'

'Then there wasn't a plan in place to dispose of the body,' Sid carried on. 'And it took time to set up. Saturday and Sunday to be exact.'

'So how do we tackle Sherman?' Ian asked.

'Like rancid plutonium.' Sid ripped the envelope open with his forefinger, and pulled out the photo. It showed a man in his mid-forties, dark skin and black hair, stylish stubble on his cheeks and a tiny goatee. Sid couldn't ever imagine a face like that smiling. 'So we start with low-level observation, and that means finding him. He's fond of his boat at the Dunston Marina, which is where we'll begin. Once we have him in real time we can track remotely. Ian, can you set up a secure link to the police network, one that doesn't register?'

'Leave it with me. There's an access code I can use which can't be traced back to me.'

Sid took a good guess why he had that, but didn't voice it. 'Fine. I'll get us some basic equipment. Once we're following him we build a pattern of movement, get a list of where he stays in town, find out who he's seeing. Somewhere along the line there's got to be some crossover. Once we have that, we can refocus the official investigation.'

Saturday 23rd February 2143

Her name was Jen. Ian knew that because her name was in the quick-memo section of his iris smartcell grid when he woke up. He'd loaded it in the cache when he went out after Sid and Eva had left. It took a while to get Jen out of the flat. More time than Ian normally allowed for. The normal routine was fuck as soon as he was awake: make the toast and tea while the girl was having a shower, then the phoney fix up to meet up agreement, call a cab and show her the door. That was Saturday morning standard. Maybe Jen had started to have regrets about the night, maybe she was needy, or had issues, or maybe her place was a tip, or she couldn't afford to heat it so she simply wasn't in a hurry to go back there. Whatever it was, she lingered in bed after he got up, fired off casual questions, even propositioned him again while the kettle boiled – well, he wasn't going to say no and disappoint a lady now, was he? They were doing it on the lounge floor when the toast popped up, which made them both laugh. That was bad, a shared moment. She took another hour to leave, asking him about himself, telling him stuff he didn't want to know about her. Nothing he didn't know anyway; he'd harvested her profile days ago.

All of which meant he was late for the gym, which was a large part of his Saturday morning standard. Ian had membership of five gyms and health clubs strategically placed round the city; his biggest thing was for girls who were serious about keeping themselves in shape. Thanks to clingy Jen it was after ten o'clock when he arrived at Harley's Fitness Machine, on St George's Terrace up in Jesmond. The main hall had a decent range of modern equipment, and smartdust packs that could complement a standard bodymesh to monitor heartrate, oxygen consumption, and muscle performance. Ian didn't need the packs, as he already had an extensive suite of smartcells which constantly watched over every health aspect of his body.

He went for a full ninety-minute workout; with his bodymesh linked to the equipment, making sure muscles were used to full capacity, while checking that tendons and ligaments didn't get near a tear point. Hydration level, blood sugar, toxins, endorphins were projected into a simple multicoloured graph whose sine waves danced elaborately across his grid. The patterns were second nature to him now, he could read them and adjust his body tempo at a near-autonomic level. At the end he requested a full physiology analysis, making sure body fat was down to the accepted minimum. Sid and Eva had stayed longer than expected last night, so he'd had a couple more beers than he ought. Six-pack continuity assured, he hit the shower.

Two girls were signing in when he left the changing room. Joyce, who was marathon-runner thin, and tall with it, asking the receptionist about the midday disco workout.

'Aye, man, I've missed that,' Ian complained in cheeky dismay.

Joyce smiled back, and they started the flirt talk about favourite pieces of gym equipment and city jogging routes. She was a dancer with the Sage tour group, he found out. Her friend, Sammi, became all sullen when Ian told them he was a policeman. Genuine police, not agency, he promised. That made no difference to the sulk. He liked that, a challenge made success so much sweeter. He wished them both a good time at the disco workout, and caught the Metro back down to Monument.

Ian's shift started at midday. He went to the locker room to change into a suit. Sid was in there, also changing. They had the same dark-green shoulder bags, and when their lockers were open side by side they made the switch like a pair of pro dealers working a club full of celebs.

It was an effort to walk into Office3 these days. He and Sid had spent time discussing what to do about the despondency crystallizing round the case team, and hadn't produced much of a strategy to reverse it. With the taxi backtrack still ongoing and barren, they now thought the whole idea was a complete waste of time. All so very different to the crackle of excitement when the whole city simulation came on line the first time. Now it was just a drudge routine, performed evenings and weekends purely for the overtime.

Ian sat behind his desk, and waited as the console screen curved round him. Sparkly laserlight synchronized, producing sharp 3D images. Once again he called up the Marcus Ansetal case. His e-i loaded a small file into the office network; it was coded as his follow-up on the investigation, officially declaring all avenues of enquiry had been followed and exhausted. He certified the case as closed, but when his virtual hand reached for the program status icon he flipped it to inactive. The data shrank back into the network, but didn't close. Ian called up the North case, and ran a quick overview. Nothing new. *Of course.* He closed down his console and went down to the zone theatre on the second floor where Abner, Lorelle, and Reannha were spending a miserable Saturday afternoon, and joined in back-tracking taxi number one hundred and sixteen.

He signed out at six thirty; handing over taxi one hundred and seventeen to the evening shift with all the enthusiasm of a janitor facing a flooded bathroom. Ten minutes later he was back in his flat.

The green shoulder bag contained a brand-new Apple console, with a huge memory and processing capacity. Sid had assured him last night it wouldn't be a traceable purchase. Ian admired the smooth white rectangle with its tiny purple and green LEDs, wondering just what kind of contacts Sid actually had to be able to afford something like that on a secondary. He pulled a cranberry-flavoured water from the fridge, and sat on the edge of the bed, plugging the gadget in. The boot-up and owner interface took a couple of minutes, a process run by his e-i. He didn't have a screen or a zone booth in the flat – no use for them. Instead he put on a pair of old-style netlens glasses; they were late-model, with a very high resolution. Ian pursed his lips in appreciation, the image was just as sharp as anything a modern zone could produce.

His e-i connected him to the Market Street Station network by a long complex route with trace-proof cut-offs at each cell. Once he was in, he used Vance Elston's code to request a secure link to the Office3 network. Ian had acquired it the first morning Elston had turned up to lord it over the investigation, using a simple phishing mask over the network's interface protocol when the spook had registered himself in Office3. Secure networks were set up to prevent illegal access from the outside but they weren't geared up to protect themselves from illegal patches to be inserted from inside the firewall – at least not on a system as cheap as the one used in Market Street.

With Elston's authority established, he set up a new section of the network with full visual recognition and AI tracking. Next was location; the police network accessed all the surveillance meshes in and around Dunston Marina. Sherman's image he had to scan in from the photo, which was so unbelievably old world, but once it was in the software would be able to catch him in the marina. That was all he needed to begin the operation. Once the software tagged Sherman it would harvest the transnet code from his bodymesh and run an orthodox follow-observe program that would track him across town. Probably not very well – Ian had loaded in a lot of restrictions given how Sherman was supposed to have plenty of digital security. They would have to be cautious, accepting that the software would lose him pretty quickly after he left the marina the first few times. But it would slowly learn and improve, allowing them to harvest a profile of movements and associates. Once they had something concrete they could start to take over monitoring Sherman themselves, running the surveillance like a proper operation.

It was seven o'clock when he'd finished loading parameters and safeguards, making sure there would be no comeback even if some bytehead did uncover the operation. Feeling better than he had all day, Ian went for a shower. He'd have a meal with a couple of the lads from the station as arranged, and watch where the night took him.

Sunday 24th February 2143

Angela had spent a couple of evenings in the Edzell mess tent listening to a pilot called Ravi Hendrik simultaneously bitching and bragging about bridgeheading Camp Sarvar. He'd recounted every minute of the helicopter flight's hazardous progress through the Eclipse Mountains, dodging wicked razor ridges and towering peaks and violent microburst squalls and zero-visibility cloud swarms. It had been entertaining stuff, the old pilot had a way of making it sound like the most difficult flying any human had ever done across the trans-stellar worlds. All good entertainment before she and Paresh sneaked off into the ringlit bush outside the camp perimeter.

Entertaining in a dusky camp, sure. Unnerving now that she herself was flying over the Eclipse pinnacles. She spent most of the two-and-a-half-hour flight with her bodymesh linked to the Daedalus fuselage meshes, watching the colossal mountain range beneath. First it was a forward view, because they were visible ahead almost from the moment the big strategic airlifter took off from Edzell. Then for a good half-hour she was looking down directly as they passed overhead. Just. Their Daedalus had a cruise ceiling of fourteen kilometres, which put the white glitter of the Eclipse's major peaks disturbingly close as they traversed the range. The e-Rays that had been sent out scouting ahead from Edzell pinpointed a dozen mountains soaring up over ten kilometres high. Finding them had triggered a whole surge of macho rhetoric among the expedition members, particularly the Legionnaires. There had been a lot of talk about climbing the tallest peak and planting the HDA flag on top. So much so that Commissioner Passam had officially requested clarification from General Khurram Shaikh – the predictable answer being wait and see what else the expedition finds, then we'll think about it.

The tallest peaks weren't even the worst of the flightpath problems. There were hundreds of peaks over five kilometres high. Given that the Berlin helicopters had a maximum ceiling of four thousand three hundred metres – reduced considerably when carrying an external load – their route through the range had to be plotted with extreme care. Ravi had flown the pathfinder mission, verifying the crazy zigzag course determined from e-Ray optical and radar data, flitting along ten-mile canyons barely wider than a New York avenue, occluded in a permanent twilight unusual on St Libra, then swooping over the fortress ridges, battling the uprush of thermals that came shrieking like a banshee out of deep crevasses without warning; testing the relatively safe areas earmarked for refuelling.

Naturally the section of the range directly between Edzell and Sarvar was the widest part, where it bulged around the split. The Eclipse Mountains had erupted out of the planetary crust as a vast Y shape, stretching over two and a half thousand kilometres from east to west, forking halfway along. The northern spur carried on the main range, stretching it due east, while the slightly shorter and lower spur, now named the Umbra range, curved away southwards.

For most of the time as the Daedalus flew over them, the image of the mountains seemed to be etched in monochrome. All Angela could see was white snow and dark rock. For once St Libra's ubiquitous zebra vegetation had been banished. The range was as barren as the Ambrose continent's Long Dead Desert. Watching the deep-blue, mile-wide glaciers curve around the hulking prominences she could only smile at the Legionnaires' ridiculous dreams of setting up any kind of camp to challenge a ten-K peak. They were lucky their aircraft allowed them to surmount the range. Talk among the xenobiologists was that this might be the dividing range, the one that separated branches of planetary evolution. She supposed it was possible. After all, the monster had to come from somewhere. But for the life of her she couldn't imagine it trekking through the mountains. It would have to go around. If there was an around.

Nobody knew what lay to the east. Even the e-Rays from their precarious eighteen-kilometre operational loiters couldn't see past the distant sentinel summits. But when the Daedalus finally cleared the northern extremity, and the land sank back to a jumble of sharp valleys and rumpled plateaus smothered in tortuously thick jungle, she saw the beginnings of the massive River Dolce tributary network. All the frozen water that was eventually pressure-goaded out of the Eclipse range, the slow march of the glaciers, the avalanche spills of the mountainsides, the icy rivulet trickles and leaky lakes that oozed out into the rock clefts, finally combined into irresistible torrents that came thundering out of the foothills, gathering speed and warmth as they surged northwards where every fold in the land was bisected by a river that merged then merged again and again until the raging tributary river eventually spilled into the Dolce itself, which swept down to the coast, merging with other rivers as it went, until it became the Jaslin estuary – which had been visible on the original survey pictures.

The humidity of the Dolce tributary basin was incredible. Permanently shrouded in vapour, only fragments of the land could be glimpsed through brief tatters in the boiling white blanket that capped the entire area. After the Eclipse range this was the next hindrance St Libra had thrown at them.

Angela gave up watching when the mountains were behind them. The bland bright homogeneity of the churning mist was boring and depressing. She knew if she allowed herself to watch it, she would begin to overanalyse its sameness and size, think where she was, how far from civilization, how utterly dependent on the HDA and people like Ravi she was to get back. That would make her brood. Best not think about anything, to be a simple tourist content with travel alone.

Two and a half hours of nerves and forced ignorance, then the landing gear clunked down with alarming abruptness.

'Thank crap for that,' Paresh murmured from the seat next to her.

'You okay?' she asked quietly. The flight seemed to have drained the usual snappy verve out of the entire squad. Nobody looked relieved the flight was ending, nobody was eager to see what awaited at Camp Sarvar.

'Those mountains were big,' he said. Which was quite expressive for Paresh, who was a man who liked to keep his world simple and easy.

It wasn't the mountains, she knew, it was the distance they'd accumulated, and the knowledge that before long they'd be flying northwards again, to one of the front-line camps that were the designated next phase. The third batch of e-Rays was already being deployed to hunt down suitable locations. Paresh was experiencing the dependence she'd done her best to suppress, the knowledge of just how tenuous their link back to civilization had become. How nobody was going to come to their help out here if they did find the great St Libra monster.

'We're over them now,' she told him reassuringly.

Once again the Daedalus landed on a strip of raw compacted ground that looked way too short to be attempting anything so foolhardy. Once again Angela gave quick silent thanks to the pilot's skill. The rear loading ramp hinged down, and the passengers disembarked ahead of the mobile biolabs which had accompanied them. Angela looked around; apart from a different skyline, with higher mountains surrounding them, there was practically no difference between Sarvar and Edzell the day she arrived there. Similarity even extended to layout.

'Tents,' she announced.

Paresh gave her a curious look. 'What?'

She smiled a superior smile.

Lieutenant Botin came over to Paresh. 'Corporal, your squad is on tent duty. I want them up by seventeen hundred hours. Consult the quartermaster on location.'

'Yes, sir,' Paresh gave the lieutenant a fast salute. He turned to Angela, and gave her a rueful grin. 'Tents,' he agreed.

Monday 25th February 2143

The alarm which his e-i allowed through established night-time information filters was both audio and visual, sending smartcells buzzing in his ears and flashing a subdued blue light into his retinas. Vance Elston lurched upright on the cot in his tent, adrenalin firing his thoughts. His body was on some kind of small timelag, lacking coordination.

'What?' he asked his e-i.

'The field hospital has logged time of death for Chet Mullain: oh-six-eleven hours today.'

'Damnit.' Vance struggled with the zip on the sleeping bag, trying to extract himself out of the thin sock of lightweight material. While he untangled himself, his e-i was calling up Mullain's file: Chet Mullain was one of the Sarvar command staff, a low-rank HDA soldier assigned to administration. Not critical, not even outstanding, background information didn't reveal any important family. Just another grunt from Dublin signed up to serve and save the human race, escaping from his no-future city estate.

The AVV team were filling another e-Ray with helium in the quiet air which accompanied dawn as Vance hurried across the dew-damp camp to the compact block of three Qwik-Kabins containing the field hospital. A strong citrus tang permeated the air as he half-jogged, the scent the result of jungle spores which drifted over the camp whenever it wasn't raining. *At least it isn't mint*, he thought. He went inside the air-conditioned building, wiping the sweat from his forehead as the chill atmosphere inside made goosebumps rise. It might have been daybreak, but St Libra's heat had barely abated overnight.

The body on the emergency room gurney was covered in a tough blue sheet. A couple of paramedics were slumped against the wall, despondent with their lost battle for life, their disposable plastic coveralls slick with blood. Dr Tamika Coniff stood at the foot of the gurney, methodically checking bits of equipment; some kind of auto running her body, it was non-work to mitigate the failure.

'What happened?' Vance asked. And even his discipline couldn't prevent him from crossing himself.

Coniff didn't seem to notice it. 'I couldn't save him,' she replied. 'Half his torso was crushed. It was only the resuscitator which made him technically alive when they brought him in.'

'Brought him in from where?' Vance turned on the paramedics as his e-i quested a link to them, running down their files. 'Where did you find him?'

'Cargo row,' Mark Chitty, the chief paramedic said. 'Some of the pallets fell on him. We had to get the logistics corps guys to lift them.'

'When did this happen?'

'About half an hour ago. His bodymesh was firing off medical emergency pings the second it happened.'

'Right.' An accident, then. There'd been several on the expedition – broken limbs, nasty gashes, burns, a crushed foot – nothing remarkable in that, everyone was in a hurry, everybody was tired, especially logistics corps personnel. It was really only luck nobody had been killed until now.

Commander Ni strode into the hospital, his face grim. A fatality in his camp wasn't something he wanted on his record.

'I'd like to review this,' Vance told him.

Ni's face registered shock, then annoyance. He gave the doctor a quick guilty glance. 'You think it's suspicious?'

'No,' she said. 'He suffered massive blunt-force trauma, he could not have survived.'

'I don't doubt his injuries,' Vance said. 'We just need to be sure of the circumstances.'

'All right,' Ni agreed. 'But discreetly.'

'Understood,' Vance said. While the commander talked to Dr Coniff, Vance went over to the corpse and held his hand over the head. He told his e-i to recover Mullain's visual memory. The dead man's smartcells responded poorly, the visual data was a series of colour smears, revealing nothing.

'Doctor?'

Coniff turned to him, her eyebrows raised impatiently. 'Yes?'

'His smartcells seem to be glitched, the bodymesh log has been corrupted.'

'Fairly typical. We hit him with the defibrillator half a dozen times. That kind of charge tends to scramble smartcells.'

'Surely smartcells are designed to withstand that level of punishment? One of their major functions is to relay medical information during an emergency.'

'They complement our sensors, yes. You'll find the smartcells themselves are functional, you just need to reboot them. It's their software which the electric current disrupts.'

'And if I reboot, I'll lose any existing data.'

She shrugged at the lack of how that concerned her, and returned to her conversation with Commander Ni.

Vance made his way over to the other block of Qwik-Kabins which made up Sarvar's official headquarters. They were split into tiny cubicle offices, of which his position entitled him to one that had a bench for a desk, and could fit in one extra chair. The walls were thin composite, making genuine privacy a joke. Once he'd squeezed himself round to his seat, the console screen curved round his face and produced a perfectly focused wraparound image. His e-i quested a secure link to the camp's primitive network. 'Get me Tramelo's tag log,' he told the software. As well as the crude network, the camp's sensors were minimal, but sufficient to keep watch on the woman. Back at Edzell he'd noted all the regular nocturnal excursions. Most nights she walked half a klick outside the perimeter, stayed in one spot for about an hour, then came back. The third time he'd used a copterbug, half the size of his hand, that whirred off silently into the night, tracking her. What the little spy gadget's excellent sensors revealed in infrared didn't surprise him – after all, she still looked hot, that's why she was in Bartram's mansion in the first place. Nor was he particularly surprised to see it was Corporal Evitts fornicating with her, but he was disappointed. The corporal had been specifically warned she was a threat to discipline, yet he'd allowed his animal lust to take precedence. They were too far into the mission for a formal reprimand and demotion, since that would disrupt the squad's efficiency, for Evitts was a popular leader. But when they got back to Earth the corporal was going to have some serious demerits loaded on his record.

The tag log showed him Tramelo had stayed inside Sarvar's designated perimeter since they all flew in yesterday. More importantly, she'd been in her tent when the accident occurred – at least, all her clothes had been. His e-i called Corporal Evitts.

'Yes, sir,' the corporal answered.

'I want to confirm that Tramelo is in the tent with you right now.'

'Yes, sir, she is. We're getting ready for breakfast.'

'Was she there all through the night?'

There was a moment's hesitation, enough to show Evitts was worried about the direction and implication of the question. 'Yes, sir, she was.'

'You were awake then, watching her?'

'No, sir. I was asleep.'

'Then you don't know. Please ask everyone in your tent if any of them saw her there during the night.'

'Yes, sir.'

Vance wondered if he was taking paranoia too far. But there were too many unknowns here. And he was still furious about the last report from Ralph Stevens, that Scrupsis was trying to sabotage the Newcastle police investigation and divert it to his own wretched office – Vermekia should have squashed that the instant the issue arose. Perhaps he was just taking his anger out on Evitts, but the corporal needed a serious reality check. Vance wanted a dependable squad when they went forward to the next camp and the mission began in earnest.

'Sir,' Evitts said.

'Yes.'

'Everyone who woke at some point last night confirms Tramelo was in the tent. That's about five or six sightings between twenty-three hundred hours and six this morning, sir.'

'Thank you, Corporal.' He cancelled the link. In all probability, Tramelo wasn't involved, but Vance just had to be sure. The accident bothered him. He couldn't help questioning the timing, why here and now? Everyone else seemed to be ignoring the true purpose of the expedition. That there was a high probability of hostile aliens out here somewhere, intent and capability unknown.

Vance called up Chet Mullain's log from the administration network, reviewing his work record, the files which the man had worked on yesterday in a cubicle not five metres from where Vance now sat. The log was blank. Goosebumps returned along Vance's arms. A quick extended check showed it was only yesterday's log that was missing. He called two of the camp's administration staff, asking if Mullain had spent the day working as normal. He had, they confirmed; they were buddies, they'd been in the cubicles on either side, and the three of them ate in the mess tent together. It was a perfectly normal day.

Which ended in Mullain's death, Vance filled in silently.

He went across to Mullain's cubicle, and started examining it. The tiny space was empty of anything personal – if it hadn't been for the number stencilled on the door he wouldn't have even known who'd been assigned it. A further review of Mullain's work log for Friday and Saturday didn't produce anything useful. Boring days spent on rotas, trying to juggle available skills to requests coming in from officers and NCOs, adding notes as to real abilities, grading people according to what they actually achieved rather than what their file claimed they could do.

Vance called Antrinell, arranging to meet him on cargo row,

where Mullain had his accident. Standing orders for the HDA were that fatal accident sites had to be left intact until cleared by the investigating officer. When Vance arrived, a logistics corps squad was waiting beside a couple of self-loading pallet trucks, surveying the clutter of fallen pallets. Vance actually recognized the corporal in charge: Corfes Sandresh, a small, wiry Egyptian who had little appreciation for the expedition or the wild wonder of the jungle surrounding them. Corporal Sandresh lived simply for the job, for loading, moving, stacking, and reloading packages wherever and whenever they were required. That was probably why he looked so miserable.

'Talk me through it,' Vance told him.

In its entirety, the row of airload 350DL pallets was a hundred and twenty metres long; stacked four high and mostly two deep. It was the front rank of what would soon be a regimented field of similar rows flown in by Daedalus. The stack on the end of the row had toppled on top of Mullain. That was when his bodymesh yelled for help.

Each stack of pallets was tethered by cables, attached to the highest pallet, making sure they would remain stable – after all, Sandresh pointed out, the ground wasn't perfectly level. Some of the stacks leaned over, not much, but they were definitely veering away from the vertical. They were designed to withstand a fifteen-degree tilt before tethers were necessary as opposed to a precaution. In Sarvar, no stack was tilting over four degrees.

'So what happened to the tethers?' Vance asked.

Corporal Sandresh looked desperately unhappy. 'They weren't correctly secured to the anchor posts, sir,' he said.

Vance examined the tethers, slim carbon cables with a huge breaking strain, wrapped in a high-visibility red and yellow sheath. They should have been threaded through the end of the anchor pins, which were driven half a metre into the ground, then looped and clipped. Someone hadn't checked the clips.

'Who is responsible for this stack?' Vance asked.

'I am, sir. It's my responsibility. I'm sorry, I really thought they'd been clipped properly.'

And Vance knew that a man like Sandresh wouldn't make that kind of mistake, no matter how big a hurry he was in. 'Which other stacks are you responsible for?'

'Most of them, sir. Corporal Wertheimer is also authorized to certify the cargo – they're split between us depending who's on duty at the time.'

'Show me. I want to see five stacks that you personally signed off.'

'Sir?'

'You heard.'

So they followed Sandresh along the row, stopping to peer at the anchor pins whenever they came to a stack which his log confirmed he'd examined and cleared. Vance wasn't in any way surprised to see all the tethers were correctly looped and clipped.

Halfway along the row, he stopped and looked back. The camp's ground vehicle park was fifty metres beyond the end of the row, with three of the self-loading pallet trucks, and the dozers and compactors which had carved out the runway, along with the mobile biolabs and a couple of MTJs (Multi Terrain Jeeps), the entire complement of Sarvar's ground vehicles. It wasn't laid out anything like as neatly as the pallet row, with the vehicles parked in roughly the same area. Vance looked from the cluster of vehicles to the two self-loading trucks which the logistics corps personnel had used to lift pallets off the fatally injured Mullain.

'What's the theory, Corporal? How could the stack have toppled?' Vance asked.

'He must have tripped on a tether cable, sir. It was just coming up on dawn, and they're not that visible in ringlight.'

'He tripped and pulled the whole stack down? That's some trip.'

The corporal shrugged. 'No other way it could have gone, sir. Something had to act as a trigger.'

'Can a man pull a tether cable that hard?'

'He was probably jogging, sir. Mullain liked to keep himself in shape.'

'Yeah,' Vance said slowly. 'Hit it at speed. That would most likely do it. Thank you, Corporal; you can tell your people to clean up now.'

'Sir.' The corporal saluted and headed back to his squad.

'So?' Antrinell asked. 'What are you thinking?'

'I'm thinking there's no way tripping on a tether cable is going to bring a stack of pallets down on top of you.'

'You've got the same problem with someone pushing the stack,' Antrinell said. 'Those 350DLs can weigh up to a couple of tonnes. An elephant might be able to shove one, but I'll bet whatever you like a man couldn't.'

'No,' Vance said. 'They used a self-loading truck. The damn things are parked right next to the row, and they're fuel-cell powered; in other words: silent. Mullain wouldn't have known it was on; he certainly couldn't hear it, probably didn't even see it parked right up behind the stack. So when he walks up to the designated meeting point our murderer just tipped the throttle, and the whole thing comes crashing down on top of him. Ten seconds later the truck is parked back with the others, and nobody can ever prove different.'

'A murder?' Antrinell said.

Vance was pleased with his deputy, there was no hint of scepticism in his voice. 'Mullain discovered something yesterday, something in the files. His log has been wiped.'

'And that got him killed?'

'I don't believe in coincidence,' Vance said. 'Mullain deals with personnel, so whatever he found must relate to the information HDA has compiled on them. Presumably he was on his way to meet the person with the discrepancy.'

'So it was a blackmail threat which went wrong,' Antrinell said. 'After all, he didn't report the anomaly, whatever it was. Instead he arranged to meet his intended victim out here to load up his secondary.'

'And didn't realize how big a deal it was for someone,' Vance mused. He looked round the camp as the glare-point of Sirius began to rise into the sky. People were making their way over to the mess tent, with plenty of curious glances being aimed at the cargo row. The local net seethed with microlinks. Everybody knew. 'And we're stuck out here with them.'

'Do you think it's related to the alien?' Antrinell asked.

'I don't see how. The only person who has even a tenuous connection is Tramelo, and she was tucked up with a squad of Legionnaires. Probably in a very literal sense.'

'So what do we do?'

Vance gave the mobile biolabs a long look. 'I want you to check our primary cargo, see if anyone tried to tamper with it. Also, see what you can do to increase security on the biolabs; maybe some extra smartdust applied to the vehicles. Don't use anyone apart from your own team. We don't know who we can trust out of the rest of the camp.'

'Yes, sir.'

'I'm going to round up the first people to reach Mullain. We'll interview them together. I want to construct a timeline.'

*

Vance had to borrow Commander Ni's office in the Qwik-Kabins block. It was the only one which could hold more than two people. As it was, with himself behind the desk and Antrinell along with the interviewee crammed in on the other side, space was severely limited.

The first to shuffle into the airless cubicle was Mark Chitty. His file said he was twenty-eight, but his short beard made that hard to determine visually. He wore the shapeless grey-green half-sleeve scrubs of all medical personnel; as a uniform it suited him, bestowing a degree of assurance. You'd be glad to see him arrive at an emergency. The worn-down attitude possessing him in the hospital that morning had now turned to a more resentful air.

'You were first on scene?' Vance asked.

'Yes, sir.'

Vance frowned. Chitty had already decided this was an us-and-them interview, which was a big mistake. Curious, too; he must have undergone enough inquests since he qualified as a paramedic. 'Did you see anybody else around the body? I don't mean someone running away from the cargo row, just someone up at that time of the morning? Or maybe a shadow or movement you couldn't identify, and didn't waste time on?'

'No sir, there wasn't anybody else.'

'All right, so you got there first with Juanitar Sakur, yes?'

'Juanitar is my partner. He's still training for his full paramedic qualification.'

'Fine. What did you see?'

'Mullain; or at least the top half of his torso. The rest of him was crushed under the pallet.'

'Did you think he would survive?'

'Not really, but that doesn't matter. You always do your best. I couldn't be certain how bad the damage was until we got the pallet off him.'

'So you called for help.'

'Yeah, Corporal Sandresh. I know him, and he's in charge of the camp's cargo.'

'Quite, the logical choice. How long before he arrived?'

'Maybe five or six minutes.'

'So did Mullain say anything in that time?'

'No, sir, we rigged him up to the resuscitator – it's important to keep the brain oxygenated. The neck was easily accessible, so we could pump artificial blood into his brain through the carotid artery.'

'All right. Who turned up?'

'Sandresh and two of his squad; er, Kaysing and Piszkiewicz I think. They made good time.'

'And they got the loader trucks?'

'Yeah.'

'Who turned up next?'

'Lori, Bernstein, and that North who's with us. They heard

the noise, and they helped get Mullain free. Piszkiewicz and Lori helped me and Juanitar carry him back to the hospital.'

Vance glanced over at Antrinell. 'Bastian North was there?'

*

'Yes, it was me,' Bastian 2North said as soon as he sat down. 'I did what I could for the poor man. Is that a problem?'

'And you were there this morning because . . . ?'

'There was a lot of shouting. The kind that says there's a big problem.'

'Yes. Can we go back one. What were you doing near the cargo row that early in the morning?'

'Taking a walk. It's so damn hot I find it hard to sleep.'

'And you went over to help?'

'Of course. Is there a reason I shouldn't?'

'Not at all, no. And thank you for that. So what was going on?'

'Your guy, Mullain, was trapped under some pallets. It wasn't pretty, there was a lot of blood on the ground. Some paramedics were working on him, and a couple of squaddies were using the trucks to try and get the pallets off. Everyone was frantic. But they got him out. Maybe they shouldn't have, I don't know, if it'd been me under there, with that much damage, man the pain must have been incredible.'

'Mullain was conscious?'

'Pardon me: no. All I'm saying is, they weren't doing the bloke any favours, you know.'

'Yeah. I saw the body in the hospital. So, did you see anything else?'

'Like what?'

'Like someone heading away from the scene.'

'No.' Bastian drew the word out, giving Vance a hard stare. 'Why would somebody be doing that?'

'It's hard to topple those pallet stacks over.'

'All right, let me rephrase: why would they topple onto

Mullain? I've never met the man, but he's just an admin guy, right?'

'Yes. He deals with personnel, so if anyone isn't who they claim, he'd be the one to find out.'

Bastian North ran a finger across his brow as he pondered the statement. 'All right, you know why I'm actually here?'

'Officially you're Brinkelle's observer. That means politics.'

'You say it like that's a bad thing.'

'I've never met a good politician.'

'Ah, man, standard cynic response, and very appropriate in this day and age. But there's a difference between the incompetent, corrupt zealots who run government, and the interactions and accommodations which soothe and control human dynamics – which is what we have in Abellia. Brinkelle sent me along because we have a stake in this expedition, a far more personal one than anybody else.'

'That and she controls the bioil on Brogal.'

'Politics. But you do acknowledge our concern?'

'Yeah, you have that interest.'

'So what I need to know at this juncture, Colonel Elston, is if you have any suspicion that the alien which murdered my father and brothers is in any way connected to Mullain's unfortunate death?'

'And let's not forget your father's staff, as well, I believe?' Vance didn't know why he was pushing, just that something about the North's attitude rubbed him wrong. If allowed, Bastian would talk and talk, taking control of the conversation, denying anyone else a say. A common enough practice among politicians, though according to his file he was mainly involved in civil engineering management back in Abellia.

'My father's staff as well,' Bastian conceded. 'Though obviously I don't have the personal connection with them. However, I am concerned with the instrument of their destruction. So I ask again, was the alien involved in this?'

'I don't see how it could be,' Vance said. 'If Mullain's death was deliberate, the only clue we have points towards a very mundane human motive.'

'Sex?'

'Money.'

'Would have been my next guess. Thank you, Colonel. If there are any developments, I'd like to be kept informed.'

'Of course.'

'I see Angela Tramelo is here at Sarvar.'

'She is. She's here under my supervision as a technical adviser. Is that a problem?'

It took Bastian a while to say anything. 'No. I don't suppose it can be, given what has subsequently happened to my cousin back in Newcastle. She should be given the benefit of the doubt, despite what Brinkelle believes. After all, it was always a stretch to think a girl could have physically slaughtered all those people.'

Once again, Vance's thoughts went back to the insubstantial image the brain scanner had extracted from Angela's thoughts. It had featured in his mind a lot recently. 'That doubt is one of the major reasons the expedition was approved.'

'Yes. And it would seem she is a one-in-ten. We didn't know that at the time.'

'Nobody did.'

'Did you ask her about it? I find it curious such a person would be recruited as one of my late father's girlfriends. Actually, that's not true. I find it highly improbable. In fact, unbelievable.'

'And yet she was.'

'Do you have any theories why?'

'No. Obviously it wasn't for the money.'

'Information, then? She was some kind of spy perhaps? No, that doesn't make much sense, the techniques developed by our clinic in Abellia were always made freely available. And that was all my father had an interest in.'

Vance could see how troubled the North was by Angela. 'I have to ask you not to confront her. She's not the most ... stable of people right now. Twenty years in jail for a crime you didn't commit is quite a burden for anyone.'

'You believe her to be innocent? You believe in the alien?'

'I believe it's possible, yes.'

'A politician's answer, Colonel.' Bastian smiled. 'Bravo. I will restrain myself from any encounters with Ms Tramelo.'

Antrinell waited until Bastian 2North had left the block of Qwik-Kabins before speaking. 'Damn, they are weird.'

'The North clones? That's kind of inevitable.'

'I wish we didn't have him with us.'

'That also is inevitable,' Vance said. 'They have a right to be with us – somebody killed Bartram and the rest. Either it was Tramelo or something out there in the jungle.'

'Marvin and I didn't find any genetic variance at Edzell.'

'Edzell is close to Abellia as far as this planet is concerned. Besides, we're on the other side of the Eclipse Mountains now. If there is variance, it might begin to show up here. The biolabs are scheduled to start local sampling in a few days, once the tanker Daedalus has built up our fuel stocks.'

'All right. So who do you want to interview next?'

'Send Omar Mihambo in. I'm curious what he was doing so close to the cargo row at that time of the morning.'

*

'I couldn't sleep,' Private Omar Mihambo said. 'That's all.'

Vance regarded the hulking young man squeezed uncomfortably into the chair opposite, and relaxed. The poor private was clearly unhappy at being called in; didn't know why he was here, suspected nothing. An innocent. The smartdust Vance had spread on the arms of the chair confirmed his heartrate and perspiration levels were those of someone close to panic. He had no control over his impulses, even his youthful face was open, a veritable playground of emotion.

Unless of course he was a one-in-ten like Angela, a trained agent making a mockery of Vance's improvised lie detector. A corporate black ops infiltrator, part of the same operation that murdered the Newcastle North, and Sid's suspicions were right.

Vance shook his head in annoyance. Focused. 'And you heard the commotion?'

'Yes, sir.'

'Who was there when you arrived?'

Omar Mihambo stared at the ceiling, brow furrowed with the effort of recall, the need to satisfy. 'The paramedics. Some of the logistics corps boys, but they were going for the trucks.'

'Where were the trucks?'

'Really close. It didn't take them long to get them over. Trouble was lifting without making the damage worse.' His lips pressed together. 'Mullain's ribs were pulped. You could tell as soon as they got the pallet off he wasn't going to make it, he was just mashed-up meat from the chest down.'

'So who arrived next?'

'I'm not sure. The North was there, I know that. And Dorchev. Some of the catering people, I don't know their names. It was a crowd by the time they took him away.'

'What about before? When you ran over did you see anyone else in the area?'

'Not really. There were a few of us heading for the paramedics. We all got there more or less together.'

'Nothing odd?'

'The monster? No. It wasn't there.'

Vance almost envied Mihambo's simplistic version of the universe. 'Tell me about Angela Tramelo.'

'What about her? She wasn't there.'

'You mean you didn't see her there?'

'No sir,' Mihambo said defensively. 'I did not see Ms Tramelo there.'

'All right, Private, calm down. Corporal Evitts asked people if they could confirm she was in the tent that night. Were you one of those who confirmed that?'

'Yes, sir. I told you, I couldn't get to sleep. I just dozed. It's the heat. Quartermaster should never have given us black tents, it's stupid. She was on her cot each time I looked round.'

'All right; what about the rest of the time? Are you getting on all right with her?'

'Yes, sir. She's one of the good guys. What they did to her in prison was plain wrong.'

'You do know what she was accused of, don't you?'

'Yes, sir, first thing she told us. She didn't do it. That's why we're here, isn't it? To find the alien that did.'

'Yeah, that's why we're all here.'

*

'I wondered when you'd call me in,' Angela said as she sat in the chair. Her eyes narrowed and she frowned down at the armrests. 'That's a strange place for a mesh. Oh, unless you want to monitor the body signs of anyone who sat here. Now why would you want to do that, Elston?'

Vance resisted a groan. For someone who'd come out of prison without any smartcells or e-i she'd managed to upgrade remarkably well. 'People lie. About many things. About their age.'

'You didn't ask a lady how old she was, did you? I'm shocked.'

'Where were you when Mullain was killed?'

'Killed?' She gave him an accusing stare. 'So it wasn't an accident?'

'*Accident* stretches credibility. Not that I can prove anything. So where were you?'

'In the shower where I was getting fucked by Paresh. He enjoys what you can do with a little bit of soap and water.'

'Clever. A gangbang is always a good alibi, especially for the star of the show.'

'I'm strictly a one-man woman, Elston. If I did it, so did he.' She choked down a laugh. 'Oh my, you actually considered that for a moment, didn't you?'

'Not really.'

'Lucky for you there aren't any meshes on your seat. Right?'

'Had you ever met Mullain? Talked to him?'

'Christ no. Some HDA nonentity – why would I bother?'

'Quite.'

'Why am I here? You don't really think I was involved?'

'No. I need a different angle on this, something outside the usual command structure. You've bedded down nicely with your squad.'

'Ouch. Elston, that was quite sophisticated for you.'

'So is there anything going down that I should know about? Blackmarket for kit. Tox?'

Angela shook her head slowly. 'No. Nothing like that. Not yet. We've only just arrived. It'll happen though.'

'I know it will. I need to know if it already has.'

'No. Sorry. I can't give you a motive.'

'Rumour? A fight over a woman? A man?'

'Hell, you're desperate to explain this. No. No rumours.'

'All right. Thanks.' He gave her a dismissive hand gesture. She remained seated.

'Omar said he was a mess when they found him,' Angela said.

'Yeah.'

'So what did the post mortem say?'

'There won't be one, not here,' Vance explained. 'The body-bag's on the next Daedalus flight out. They'll take him back to Earth. I expect there will be an inquest in Newcastle.'

'You're kidding, right?'

'What's wrong?'

She let out an exasperated hiss. 'I'm a . . . scrap that. You're an alien monster with blades for fingers. You've just stabbed Mullain through the stomach, eviscerated him. How do you cover that up? Perhaps you'd consider pulverizing the corpse?'

'Shit!' Vance glanced up, to see Antrinell was looking as shocked as him.

Angela got to her feet. 'You really are crap at your job, aren't you?'

Thursday 28th February 2143

As the night's mellow ringlight was supplanted by the sharper glare of Sirius rising, the hillside teeming with venichi vines began to change colour, the air itself turning thick, smearing the slope of glossy olive-green leaves with an oily orange haze. As the stronger light struck the vine, the underside of every leaf shook and shivered, casting loose the minute spores which clotted their surface. Venichi vines always released their spores at dawn so the day's turbulent thermals would carry them as far as possible before the stiller night air permitted them to drift down.

The cloud expanded quickly, oozing down the gradient to sweep out over the flat land beyond, thinning and spreading as it went. By the time it enveloped Camp Sarvar it was more tenuous than smoke, but still cohesive enough to contaminate the sunlight.

Angela was oddly entranced by the uneven orange stain swirling through the sky, though she detested the constant urge to sneeze which the granules inflicted upon her. So she steeled herself against the discomfort as she stood at the edge of the expanse of battered grass which was Camp Sarvar's helicopter landing field. Fifty metres away, the Berlin's turbines started up, sending a shimmering haze out of the notar exhaust grids at the end of its tail. There was a moment when she wondered if the spores would affect the turbines, reducing their efficiency, and cancel the takeoff. But Ravi Hendrik fed power to the big coaxial blades, and both sets began to spin up to a blur.

She could just see Elston's head through the curving cockpit transparency, disguised in a sturdy helmet with a broad dark visor. Her hand raised in a mocking salute as the Berlin lifted, and moved slowly across towards the end of the cargo rows, where a bulldozer was waiting. It took several minutes for the logistics corps team to fasten and check tethers, but eventually the helicopter rose again. There was a slight pause as the tether took the strain, then the yellow bulldozer was tugged off the ground, wobbling about in the powerful downdraught. The five squad members who'd gathered round to watch with her cheered half-heartedly.

'Four days without him,' Paresh said with a sense of satisfaction.

Angela didn't share the relief. There were times when she thought she and Elston were the only people on the expedition who took the alien seriously. Now Elston was flying up to Wukang, the first of the three forward exploratory camps, two thousand kilometres to the north-west, assuming his post as camp commander. If they kept to the kind of high-pressure schedule used to establish the existing camps, then it would be three days before the dozers and compactors would have finished preparing a runway. Angela and the squad would then fly out in a Daedalus; a simple civilian adviser didn't rate a helicopter flight. In the meantime, Elston had told her, Antrinell would be supervising her.

She'd seen the tiny lapel pin that was always on Antrinell's fatigues. Another Gospel Warrior. Another religious fanatic to whom facts and reality took second place to dogma. He'd been keen enough to have the autopsy on Mullain. And they'd all been relieved when Doc Coniff had found no signs of a five-blade stab wound among his tattered entrails.

Despite that, Elston had pushed Commander Ni into increasing the camp's security. Smartdust meshes were smeared everywhere, watching over the whole area inside and out. Legionnaires patrolled the perimeter at all times. That hadn't gone down well with Peresh's squad, nor any of the other Legionnaires. They were used as a general workforce by the rest of the camp, and now they had additional duties. Paresh himself was particularly upset; the opportunities to be alone with her were reduced still further. For two nights she'd been virtually alone in the oppressively hot tent; a shower together was a rare event, and there was no leaving the camp on foot for a little privacy. Still, at least it made him more appreciative when they did manage to snatch a secluded moment to couple.

'When do you go out on patrol?' she asked.

'Forty minutes. We'll be out for six hours. Captain Chomik wants us to familiarize ourselves with the whole area. Possible infiltration routes, counter-tactics, observation points; we're to make it our home turf.'

'He's taking things seriously, thankfully. I wish I could make you do the same.'

'Hey, I know they're out there.'

'You just tell me that so you can get laid.'

'No. I know you well enough now to know you never killed anyone. So it has to be real, right?'

'Yep, that's good enough to get you laid today. When did you say your patrol finishes?'

Paresh couldn't quite keep the happy gleam from his face. 'We'll be back around seventeen hundred hours, then I'll have a debrief with the lieutenant.'

'Six o'clock, then. That gives me long enough to find somewhere private.' She looked round at Sarvar in its ginger pallor, the cargo rows that were still lengthening with every Daedalus flight, the fuel bladder store, lines of parked vehicles, and the tent town. 'This camp is big enough, now.'

'I wish we didn't have to skulk around like this. We're grownups, for heaven's sake.'

'I know. But the HDA has its rules. The last thing I want is to damage your career. We'll cope just fine. Then when all this is over, we'll talk about the future.' That last was to stop him doing anything stupid like declaring how much he loved her, or wanted them to walk off into the sunset together. She wouldn't put it past the puppy boy to blurt it out, his world view was that simple. And if he did go and make an ass of himself she'd have to play along, which ultimately would mean hurting him badly when he realized how he'd been manipulated, that he was simply a commodity she'd traded.

Twenty years in jail must have given her more of a conscience than she'd realized. That or she'd become weak. It had never bothered her before, certainly not with Barclay, who by letting her into his life had unknowingly supplied her with all the codes she needed.

*

It was balmy that long-ago night, as all nights were on St Libra. The air was ripe with the scent of the sea as Angela walked down the gallery that ran the length of the mansion's seventh floor. She was naked except for a lace-trimmed black velvet choker and a towel from Bartram's bedroom slung over her shoulder. There was nobody else awake at this time, so her only real worry was that she might leave some tell-tale oil smears on the marble floor as she went. Earlier that evening the other girlfriends had taken it in turn to give her erotic massages while Bartram voyeured their sapphic performance. Each one had applied more oil, and now her skin was simply covered in the stupid stuff. But she had to take the risk – there wouldn't be a better opportunity than this.

There were no security sensors on the seventh floor. Bartram was quite obsessed about his privacy, and didn't want to risk some bytehead punk hacking into the mansion's network and watching him through his own sensors. Security in the mansion, therefore, was perimeter based, geared up to make sure nothing untoward got inside and up to the seventh floor, which was where Bartram actually lived.

Along with the mansion's senior staff, Angela and the other girlfriends had their rooms on the sixth floor. Most nights they would be dismissed from Bartram's bedroom when they'd finished satisfying him, and have to go back downstairs to sleep. There were a lot of nights when they were back down on six, after they'd showered and changed, that they'd all congregate in one of the rooms – without Marc-Anthony hovering as he did all day every day – and they'd wind up drinking an unauthorized bottle of wine and chattering like sisters. Angela had resisted at first, content with Olivia-Jay's friendship, but after two months at the mansion she was so bored with the daily routine she gave up and joined in.

But not tonight. Tonight, Karah, Coi, and Mariangela (Lady Evangeline's replacement) had been sent back down to the sixth floor after getting all hot and slippery with Angela, leaving her and Olivia-Jay with Bartram as a threesome. Forty minutes later, Bartram was snoring softly with Olivia-Jay curled up beside him, also sleeping soundly, as well she might after combining that much tox with champagne. Olivia-Jay only had another ten days left on her contract, and she was trying hard not to show how disappointed she was about not being offered a renewal. Angela rolled off the bed and went into the en suite for some towels to rub as much oil off her legs and feet as she could.

The big windows at both ends of the gallery were open, and all the lights were off, leaving dusky-silver ringlight alone to illuminate her way. There was a moment when she thought she heard someone else moving about. No one else should be anywhere near the seventh floor at that time. The dark weapon implants in her hands switched to semi-active status. She simply couldn't risk discovery, not yet. But it was just the gauzy drapes fluttering slowly as the mellow sea breeze gusted through.

Bartram's study was halfway along the gallery. Angela stopped in front of the tall dark wood door, and checked both ways. Nothing moved, no alarms sounded. She opened the door and slipped inside. The study was decorated in the same faintly retro-Egyptian style that pervaded the rest of the mansion. Bartram had a thing for the lifestyle of old royalty, and believed that the stark, expensive aesthetics of the pharaohs contained an elegance and impact which the lavishly opulent palaces of later European monarchies lacked. There weren't many ornaments in the room, but those that did rest on pedestals and in alcoves had been acquired from auction houses for tens of millions of Eurofrancs. Angela smiled bleakly at them, immune to their beauty and history.

Bartram's slab-like ebony desk had three big console panes set into its surface, resembling windows into interstellar night. Angela took the choker off, and slid her thumbnail along the slit on the inside. The velvet peeled apart to reveal the tiny interceptors hidden inside, like fat silver needles. She put the towel down on the floor, and lay down on it, shuffling her way underneath the desk. The undersides of the consoles were above her now, and she began to apply the smart needles against the correct locations on the casing of the middle one. Data began to flow across the contact netlenses she was wearing, showing her what to do, the progress they were making. It had taken months of practice to perfect the procedure, more time even than she'd spent memorizing football crap. She muttered instructions to the little systems as they wormed their way into the console's internal circuitry and optical pathways, bypassing the inbuilt activation security systems.

The subversion took an achingly long ten minutes. Angela wriggled out from underneath the desk as the central pane came alive, showing the console's basic management architecture: a tunnel hologram with icon levels stretching down towards the bottom of the universe. A keyspace projection materialized above and to one side of the pane. Angela smiled down at it, and pushed her hands into the floating array of sharp red symbols. The console read the biometric pattern of the hands, and agreed they were Barclay's. A new layer of icons materialized in the pane, and she let out a long breath of relief; the mimic gloves she'd put on as she got dressed that evening had not only survived all the oil, they'd replicated the pattern which the grabber gloves had recorded weeks before.

She started manipulating the keyspace. Barclay's codes allowed her into the finance office of Abellia's Civic Administration. Barclay's codes, exposed by the little processors in the banana cufflinks, following and recording every tiny movement of his hands and fingers as they flicked through keyspace.

Once she was in, she called up a list of pending civil-engineering projects. A quick review showed her several that were suitable, but she chose the Delgado Valley development purely for the timing, which was excellent; the project was due to move into phase one in another five months. Once a road tunnel had been drilled through the base of the surrounding mountains from the Rue de Grenelle, five miles of valley all the way down to the sea would be open for development. There were over fifty contractors bidding for the basic infrastructure project, starting with the tunnel.

Angela established a link to the Vietnamese legal office she'd set up before arriving at Imperial College, and Barclay's all-important authorization certificate confirmed the legitimacy of one last bid. This was from GiulioTrans-stellar, whose profile as an established construction and management company was included in the bid datawork, along with financial guarantees from the HKFD bank. GiulioTrans-stellar was one of twenty-seven fake companies they'd fabricated in readiness, whose specialities covered a whole range of products and services that Abellia was always issuing contracts for.

Extricating herself from the finance office systems took as long as getting in. She went carefully, checking each stage to make sure she'd left no trace, that no monitors were raising queries. With the bid secure, she dived back under the desk, and cautiously extricated the interceptors from the console's physical systems, leaving no trace of the violation.

A final wipe of the floor to make certain there was no trace of oil to betray she'd ever been there, the choker fastened back on, and she slipped back out into the long gallery as silent as the fluttering shadows thrown by the drapes. The Delgado Valley contract wasn't due to be issued for another month, coinciding with the end of her contract. The money for the winning company would be transferred to Abellia's main civic account four days prior to the award, ensuring sufficient funds were available. That would be her window, which was cutting things fine, but establishing a legitimate-seeming contract was the procedure they'd agreed to. It was sophisticated and took time, but it had a much greater chance of success. The finance office network and North security was always watching for crash and burn raids. All she had to do now was pull off another intrusion like this one, and use Barclay's certificate to nominate Giulio-Trans-stellar as the winner. The money would transfer in microseconds, and then nothing else mattered, nothing at all. If they caught her it would be bad. Realistically, a brutal interrogation and possibly execution – the Norths were not known for forgiveness and charity. Hopefully, she'd be able to get out of the mansion and back to Earth while the finance office was still trying to figure out what had happened, and their security division did their best to trace the money. They never would find it, of course; there were too many cut-offs and anonymous accounts built in to the route through over a dozen banks and four planets that'd been designed to deliver the prize where it was so desperately needed. And then there was the definitive safeguard: she didn't know the final segment of the trail, so it didn't matter what they did to her. Would they be surprised she was prepared to make that ultimate sacrifice to ensure the theft's success? Yes. But then they were used to dealing with organized criminal gangs and sophisticated con artists and quiet sneaky byteheads. Not people like her.

Bartram and Olivia-Jay were on the big bed where Angela had left them, lying close enough to appear a normal couple. She dropped the towel in the en suite, and slid gently onto the gel mattress beside Olivia-Jay. The girl let out a sigh suspiciously like a whimper, her thick mop of raven hair stirring.

'Shush,' Angela whispered. 'I'm here, darling, I'm here.' She kissed the back of Olivia-Jay's neck tenderly, closing her arms around the disturbed girl. Olivia-Jay snuggled back into the embrace, and relaxed once more, falling back into a deeper sleep pattern.

Angela grinned for everything she'd achieved, and listened to her racing heart begin to calm. *One more month. One, that's all.*

Friday 1st March 2143

Ian went home during his lunch break. It was becoming routine. He didn't speak to anyone as he went down to Market Street's underground car park; but he did curse the overcautious auto as it crawled through the rain-slushed roads and delivered him back to Falconar Street; he almost cursed Sid and Eva for including him in their mad, doomed scheme. There was no real reason for him to be doing this. It was only another murder, a police case. He didn't give a shit, not outside the station and overtime hours. Except, this one, the North slaying, had tweaked that little demon of curiosity that lurked and whispered and goaded every genuine detective. Ian had to admit, he was intrigued by the complexities and politics.

So back home he went to keep a check on their surveillance operation. Sid and Eva both acknowledged that they really needed to run the whole thing with a real person monitoring and controlling the software. The police routines Ian had acquired were intended to keep an eye out for thugs, hookers, street scum, and known snatchers working the city's stores. Trying to follow a vanilla criminal trained by corporate security and alert for any law enforcement activity was always going to be a stretch.

None of them could spare the time for that. Even if they did, their absence would bolster Market Street's thriving gossip culture. Questions would murmur on rumour-greedy lips. They couldn't afford questions.

But . . . The original code had been cutting-edge back when it was written. Newer, more expensive, versions had undergone multiple improvements until they'd risen beyond the budget of ordinary police forces – now they were mainly used by agencies on contract. However, the core functionality remained sound.

So, slowly, hour by painful hour, the software began to harvest a profile on Marcus Sherman, unofficial main suspect for the North murder. Ian had launched the operation on Saturday; the surveillance quietly riding Dunston Marina's meshes didn't even spot and confirm Sherman until Tuesday evening. Since then it had followed Sherman as he was picked up in a black Mercedes every morning, using Elston's HDA authorization to slip through the traffic macromesh, examining transnet cell records for his e-i access, learning codes and compiling a list of contacts.

Marcus Sherman kept some interesting company. Firstly, there was Jede, who seemed to be his lieutenant, always there shadowing the man, always the one you had to speak to before you could talk to Sherman himself. Boz, who was straight muscle; and took that job definition way too seriously. Illegal steroids and obsessive gym sessions had produced a caricature of a bodybuilder physique. Ian completely disapproved. Fitness was about gym work, healthy eating, and body-awareness; factors which combined to sculpt and maintain a toned athlete physique. Boz was just a loser grotesque. Not that Ian ever wanted to go one-on-one with the freak.

Ruckby was Sherman's second bodyguard and enforcer. A man who took a more normal approach to achieving an intimidating presence by bulking up on bad food and possessing a nasty temper.

The only other regular was Valentina, a seventeen-year-old beauty from Canada who was chauffeured to Sherman every night, and took a cab back to her flat just behind Quayside the next morning.

So far Ian had established that Sherman slept at the *Maybury Moon*, a flat in Heaton, and a house in Benwell. Details where he went during the day were difficult. Twice he'd changed cars after stopping at a café. But the profile was growing.

Ian put on the netlens glasses, and examined the morning's information. So far Sherman had driven into town from the Benwell house and gone to an office block in the centre, not far from The Gate. He'd stayed there less than half an hour.

That didn't matter, it was another location to watch. Ian's e-i supervised a whole string of searchbots running in the new Apple console, tracing ownership of the office, monitoring links in and out, capturing images of everyone who visited the office, harvesting basic profiles for them.

After he left the office, Sherman had gone straight to the city's ring road, and driven north up the A1. He'd turned off just before Alnwick. That was where coverage ended. Ian knew the area well enough, a maze of little country roads with an invisible maintenance priority level as far as the Country Highways Bureau was concerned. What there was of any macromesh would be covered by ice and snow that wouldn't see more than one snowplough a month. Tracking Sherman's Merc by remote was a lost cause. Ian loaded a search and notification order into the road traffic management network, which would alert the observation software as soon as the Merc ventured back onto a main road with a functioning macromesh.

Even though Ian was enjoying the feeling of superiority their whole covert operation provided, he had to admit it hadn't turned up any kind of overlap with the North murder investigation. He knew what Sid would reply if he ever voiced that particular doubt: 'Aye, man, give it time.'

Ian was starting to wonder how much time he could afford. But he couldn't help the interest developing in the elusive Mr Sherman. The man was a true player, the kind that had never featured in any of Ian's normal investigations.

Satisfied that the surveillance software and the searchbots he'd added were going to contribute a reasonable-sized file to the growing profile they were building, he left the flat and headed back to Market Street.

Tuesday 5th March 2143

The flight from Sarvar to Wukang didn't bother Angela anything like the previous Edzell-to-Sarvar flight had. Perhaps it was a level of fatalism creeping into her mind, induced by the dark monotony of St Libra's rampant zebra vegetation. Or more likely, she admitted to herself, simply the lack of any meta-feature like the Eclipse Mountains to fly over this time. Their flight took them two thousand kilometres north-west from Sarvar to another of those now-familiar strips of compacted naked soil with a little cluster of tents and Qwik-Kabins and vehicles at one end. Wukang was the first of the three projected forward camps, arranged almost like compass points, north-west, due north, and north-east from Sarvar, which was now being relegated to supply-base status. Varese, the camp due north, was already having its landing strip bulldozed; while Oamaru, away to the east, had just received its first successful Berlin landing yesterday. No more forward camps were scheduled – this was as far as the expedition was going to venture, as far as the budget would take them.

Reasonable enough, Angela thought as the Daedalus rear-loading ramp lowered itself amid a chorus of high-pitched whining from electrohydraulic actuators. If the xenobiologists couldn't find any sign of animal life this far away from Abellia, then they weren't going to find any – period.

She half-expected Elston to be waiting for her at the bottom of the ramp, but he wasn't anywhere to be seen. Antrinell had been doing a discreet but competent job of watching her at Sarvar.

As she stepped out onto the muddy, compacted soil she settled her sunhat with a quick flourish. The morning rain had left the air muggy. Mist was rising from the jungle vegetation which lay a couple of kilometres away from the flattish ground around Wukang. Away to the north, where the land rose sharply again, stationary clouds lurked amid the steep hills.

'End of the line,' she said.

'You make that sound kind of sinister,' DiRito said.

'It's not meant to be. This is simply as far as we go. The next time we get on a Daedalus, it'll be for the flight home.'

'You don't think we'll go any further?'

Angela indicated the mobile biolabs filling the centre of the fuselage, which the plane's flight crew were now uncoupling from their lock-down latches. 'They'll travel out from here, maybe even forty, fifty klicks. But that's it.'

'The owls didn't see anything round here,' Omar said.

'Do they know what to look for?' Angela countered. 'That thing I encountered was intelligent. And they've had ninety-two years since humans arrived on St Libra to prepare for us. No, for once the HDA is right, genetic-variance testing is the way to go.'

She watched as Antrinell climbed into the cab of the first biolab. His attitude towards the machine was almost protective. The fuel cells fired up with a mild gust of white vapour from their exhaust vents on the side of the big vehicle.

'Uh oh,' Paresh murmured. 'Tents.'

Angela followed his gaze. Lieutenant Pablo Botin was heading their way.

'Tents,' she agreed. High up in the sky, another Daedalus was circling round to line up on the runway. More equipment, more personnel. Each of the big airlifters was flying three times a day out from Sarvar. Passam and the command staff were throwing everything at establishing the forward camps as fast as possible.

Wukang and its two cousins were the HDA's statement of intent to the vast planet. They challenged the eternal jungle, making it very clear that humans were going to uncover its secrets one way or another.

Angela couldn't help wonder what would happen if they succeeded. For some reason that scenario had been missing from every general briefing HDA officers had made. She knew they'd have one, she could only hope that it was going to be good enough. All she'd had was a single blind survivalist impulse: *run like hell.*

*

They were tight white shorts. Hot and sexy on a blonde babe with a fit body. Clingy, quality fabric with a sparkly sheen, designer label, cheeky cut to emphasize taut buttocks. Marc-Anthony and Loanna had stood back and admired their choice, especially when those shorts were matched by a low-slung, ebony mesh halter top.

The top had been left behind when Angela sneaked back to Bartram's seventh-floor study. And now the shorts were ruined. Blood was to blame, blood soaking into that expensive, absorbent fabric. Mariangela's blood, Coi's blood, Bartram's blood, Benson 2North's blood, Blake 2North's blood . . . Blood that had come teeming out of ripped flesh and shredded hearts. Enough blood to turn the mansion's marble flooring into a slippery lake of the stuff.

Angela had slithered and skidded in the lounge, falling over repeatedly. Her bare flesh was covered in blood. Hair matted with the stuff. And the funky shorts had turned to a glistening scarlet belt, becoming sticky and restrictive as they were heated. And her skin was very hot by now.

She'd run. Of course she'd run. But there was method to it. She still possessed just enough presence of mind to snatch a small bag from her room on the sixth floor. A bag that was always casually ready for a quick departure, with those truly important items she'd need if things went wrong and she needed to make a fast exit. Not that they'd ever considered it would be like this horror.

The bag was now gripped by fingers with white-stressed knuckles as she fled down the rest of the stairs, trapped within the mansion's silent gloom. The silence frightened her more than the treacherous glimmers of ringlight that seeped across the stairs, distorting their size, stretching out deep shadows to fool her. Again she'd fallen, tumbling hard down the unforgiving marble, leaving long smears of blood in her wake. Her grunts and muted cries absorbed and killed by the silence.

But she was the only one making any noise. There should have been alarms blaring out across the night, waking everyone, summoning guards with weapons. Alarms that banished the silence. Comforting alarms. Instead, the silence engulfed her, followed her as she fled in terror down the stairs to the huge ground-floor atrium. More silence was waiting as she took the next flight of stairs down to the basement garage. Not even ringlight ventured down here, it was pitch dark. Within the sensory absence she stretched her arms wide, fumbling against the walls to give some illustration of where she was. Blind, running for her life, hoping – praying! – there was nothing sharing the darkness.

Below and in front: a hint of light. Four slim lines. A rectangle. Door!

Angela burst through it into the garage. Here at last was light. Ceiling strips shining a bright, universal green-tinged light. She blinked in the comfortless glare, hyperventilating wildly. Looked down at herself in numb dread. The blood that painted every part of her was congealing, darkening, flaking, moulting off her own skin like some obscene scab membrane.

Her wretched wail echoed round the garage.

Two long rows of silver-blue Jaguar JX-7 coupés were lined up on either side of her. She thought she heard something in the stairwell behind, and jumped, whimpering.

'Get a grip!' Angela screamed at herself. She ran for the first Jag and vaulted over the door into the driver's seat. Her hand slammed down on the dashboard, and she winced at the sharp flash of pain from the dark weapons in her fingertips as they hit the walnut veneer. The tips had come sliding up out of her flesh just behind the nails, tearing her own flesh as they rose – the little gashes were still raw. Despite the presence of those extraneous tips, the Jag's auto read the biometric as Barclay 2North. The joystick telescoped out of the dashboard and the seat's fat shoulder harnesses hinged round to hold her comfortably. She flicked the car to manual, and twisted the joystick hard, demanding full acceleration. Wheels spun fast, sending up tyre smoke, and the machine leapt forward. Auto override kicked in, assisting her steering as she turned to avoid the other row of Jaguars and the concrete stanchions. Then she was aiming the car at the ramp, racing up into the night. Headlights came on, cutting through the drizzle outside. The coupé's roof started to slide up.

Angela hit a hundred and seventy kph by the time she reached the short tunnel connecting Gironella Beach with the Rue de Provence on the other side of the hills. There was some skid as the traction control fought with the rain-slicked road, but Angela refused to ease up.

In the tunnel, shock finally caught up with her, and she started shaking uncontrollably. Tears flowed then as the numbness and focus of instinctive self-preservation ebbed. Breath was taken down in convulsive gulps. They were dead, all of them, slaughtered. Everyone she knew in the mansion: butchered mercilessly.

The Jaguar zoomed out of the tunnel and she let go of the joystick, switching back to auto. Driving was just too much now. Amid the shock and fright, her mind was trying to grapple with what had happened, to be rational. It was difficult. Death on such a scale and with such visceral ferocity wasn't something she'd ever considered. But now it had happened, and had to be dealt with. Had to.

The contract had been awarded. She'd managed that, actually pulled off the heist. The money transfer had gone through. Abellia's Civic Administration finance office had paid Giulio-Trans-stellar one hundred and eight million Eurofrancs as a deposit for the infrastructure contract. Right now all that binary code money would be percolating along the route they'd devised, twisting and changing at every bank and finance house; identity and currency would morph a dozen times before vanishing into the digital event horizon at the end of the route, the void of which she knew nothing.

Full completion would take a couple of hours. Anything involving that many exchanges and owner switches was by necessity complex. She couldn't afford to be caught, not until she was sure it was complete. That single notion cooled her thoughts to an icy calm. Nothing else mattered. She was still on mission; no matter how ludicrously fucked it was now.

Ringlight shrank away, smothered behind a wall of thick cloud that frothed across the sky. Drizzle turned to a torrent of rain which splattered down across the tarmac, forcing the auto to slow.

Angela slammed the brake on, making the car fishtail as the wheels fought for grip. She opened the door and scrambled out to stand under the monsoon. Tipped her head back to let the heavy drops sluice her clean. Hands scraped urgently at the disgusting drying blood that caked her skin, and red rivulets began to trickle down her legs. She stripped the shorts off, and flung them away across the verge. Obsession to be rid of the gruesome contaminate consumed her now, she scraped and scraped at her skin until she was scratching and grazing her-self. Completely naked, saturated in the swirl of water, she was shaking again, from the cold this time. When she looked back at the car, with its orange interior lights glowing, the driver's seat was tarnished with blood. She opened the boot and pulled out a blanket to sit on. Only then did she set off again, ordering the auto to take her into town, all the way down to Velasco Beach.

The monsoon was lifting by the time the Jag arrived at the car park behind the beach. It was half past three in the morning. She knew there'd be no one about, she didn't even bother checking.

Down to the beach itself, fifteen paces from the bottom of the promenade steps, one pace out from the wall. And dig. Don't think what you'd look like to some accidental observer, naked, in the rain, clawing desperately, trying not to cry any more. It took a minute, burrowing into the sand like some mad dog, before her fingers scrabbled against the emergency package.

Just lifting it out of the hole sent a jolt of relief through her, like a bump from a sanity tox. She got back into the Jag, passenger side this time, wiping sand off her legs and arms with the blanket, then ripping open the polythene-wrapped package. Everything she needed for a quick exit was there.

First, the sac, bumped hard against her jugular so the deactivants would circulate fast. She held her hands up, looking at the small, still-oozing scabs on her fingertips where the tips had retracted into her flesh again. The dark weapons would take a few days to dissolve back to their basic nuclei threads; and she'd feel like crap while they did it, so the New Tokyo specialist had warned her. Irrelevant.

There were three interface sets, all preloaded with identities. She picked up the first, and took a steadying breath as she called the emergency transnet address.

'It's me,' she told the voice-message function. 'The transfer has gone through. Okay? Really, it's through. There was enough money, more than enough. A hundred and eight million. And Christ, darling, it was so easy. Everything we planned, everything we wanted; we did it, we really did, we pulled it off. But, oh shit, I found . . . afterwards . . . Shit, Goddamnit, they're all dead. Dead. Bartram, the girls, others . . . Dead. Just wiped out, like animals. Torn to pieces. It was monstrous . . . yeah, that's what, a monster. A monster is loose. I know that sounds . . . crazy, but I'm telling you the truth. There was nothing I could do. Really. Nothing. I swear, really swear: nothing. When all this nukes the transnet, when you see for yourself, believe me I didn't have anything to do with it. You will do that, won't you, my darling, you'll believe me? I know no one else will. I'm going to run for it now, try and make it back to Newcastle. They'll come after me, so this next bit is really hard. I can take it, all right? If they catch me, well that'll be the price, I'll owe it and I'll pay it. I don't mind. It's worth it. The money's safe, beyond them, completely beyond them, beyond the bastard Norths, beyond the police, beyond the judges and the lawyers and the agents. Now you have to make sure that's how it stays. You have to be safe, too. You have to stay hidden. Don't break cover, don't risk anything for me, not ever. If you love me, promise me this one thing. Promise me, please, I'm begging. There's so much I want to say, to tell you. I know I'm a bitch, that I forced you to do this, that I screwed up your life. But . . . and shit I know this is going to sound wrong, I'd do it again, all of it. We never had time, you see, not the time I wanted, so yeah, I'd do it again because that would be some more moments we'd have together. One thing, one thing always: I love you.'

Angela cried again. There in the Jag, naked and wet at four in the morning; alone with the drizzle pattering softly on the roof, knowing she would never see anyone she loved ever again, no matter what happened next. Cried for several minutes, until she reminded herself that loitering like this was going to screw things up even more, that she had to get going, had to face down the universe and all the crap it had dumped on her.

So—

Take the two clean interface sets. Dump the one you've just used down a drain in the car park along with the spent sac. Clothes: there's a pashmina in the bag, wrap it round your torso so tits and ass don't show, and that'll have to do for now. Cash, that's okay, there's a coded account that one of the interface sets can link with. Car? They'll trace the Jag fast, so, drive it round the back of a nearby warehouse, then order a complete power-down; follow that with ripping the main power cables from the buffer batteries. A little spray can squirting onto hands, and the molecules of the mimic gloves disassociate – wipe the residue away on the wet grass. Walk out onto the street, and use the interface set to call a cab. It arrives ninety seconds later.

'Airport,' she told the auto.

*

There was no way Angela should have got as far as she did. Anywhere apart from Abellia and she probably wouldn't have. Chaos helped her. Chaos and severe emotional distress. The bodies were found eventually as the rest of the mansion awoke. Staff who had rooms on the fifth floor never went up to the sixth or seventh unless summoned or the daily schedule required it. It was half past seven in the morning before one of Bartram's aides finally went upstairs and promptly threw up as he saw the congealing pool of blood that had spread out of the lounge. Security personnel started arriving minutes later. The sight that greeted them in the lounge and Bartram's bedroom, and senior staff bedrooms on the sixth floor stopped them cold. Training just didn't cover this.

Angela booked her plane ticket as the taxi sped out along the Rue Turbigo towards the airport. A standard AirBrogal commercial flight scheduled to take off at eight that morning. The taxi pulled up outside the airport's solitary terminal just after five. Angela walked straight along the concourse, loosely clad in the pashmina, carrying her small bag, looking unwaveringly ahead with complete disregard for any startled glances thrown her way. That, at least, was something she could do with perfect ease; the haughty aristocratic indifference to anyone else's opinion. She had a right to be wherever she wanted to be, doing whatever she wanted to do. Those people who did look at her saw just one more appalling trusteenie in a town full of them, recovering from another wild night.

She paused only for a few moments at a cyberserve clothes stall and a chemist's before heading into the women's washroom.

Angela Tramelo never did come out of that washroom. The girl who did emerge fifty minutes later had the identity of Helin Anisio, and she had short rust-red hair, not long blonde, and she wore jeans and a black T-shirt with red sneakers.

At Bartram's mansion, five B 2Norths had arrived. The brothers were distraught at the carnage, the pain of loss. Everyone was looking to them to take charge. Orders were slow in coming.

It didn't help that Abellia had no real police force. Corporate security handled most problems, and their priority was contacting the surviving Norths, establishing they were alive and warning them a maniac was on the loose. By eight forty-five a proper headcount was taken at the mansion. Brinkelle arrived at nine o'clock, anguished and furious, shouting at her brothers that she was in charge. By then, security was getting its act together. She was informed that Angela Tramelo was missing, and shown poor-quality sensor recordings of a Jag tearing off into the night.

'Find her!' Brinkelle screamed.

At ten o'clock two black helicopters landed on Velasco Beach. Security guards fanned out; it took another twelve minutes for them to locate the inert Jag. The Abellia Civic Authority officially announced Angela Tramelo was a fugitive, and alerted both the airport and the dock. Two passenger planes and five private jets had already departed that morning. Airport security reviewed images of all passengers embarking. None of them matched Angela. All further outgoing flights were cancelled. Coast guard helicopters began searching the sea for any boats that might be carrying Angela away from Abellia.

Back at the manor, it was clear to the security officers with a police background that the murders were seriously weird, the result of a very disturbed mind. The best guess they could come up with to explain method was someone wearing a muscle-amp suit with powered blade fingers. That meant it was pre-planned. Given the only vehicle leaving the mansion that night was the Jag carrying Angela, the suit had to be close by. A thorough search of the grounds began.

Midday saw the Jag delivered to the Institute, the nearest laboratory the Norths had that could run any kind of forensic analysis. Genetic samples were taken from all the blood caked onto the blanket and driver's seat. By one o'clock it was confirmed Angela had been in the Jag.

Security, with Brinkelle goading them on, turned to how a muscle-amp suit could get past the mansion's security perimeter

– in and out. Gironella Beach's protection protocols were focused on preventing anything or anyone dangerous from breaching the perimeter. The sensors had seen nothing coming in or out, including the comprehensive scanner system spread across the seabed beyond the sands. The only anomaly was the Jag speeding out, and it wasn't queried by the AI running security because it was being driven by . . .

'Not possible,' an astonished Barclay said to an audience of Brinkelle and three other 2Norths. 'I was sleeping on the sixth floor. I was fucking lucky I wasn't a victim, too.' Then he broke down and started crying.

'How did she get your biometrics?' Benjamin asked; as the eldest 2North he was the calmest head in the mansion that whole frantic day. 'You can only grab the readings from sustained physical contact.'

It came out then, in gulps and stammers and self-recrimination. The affair which had started just a few weeks after Angela had arrived at the mansion as Bartram's new sports girlfriend.

'She used you,' Brinkelle snapped. 'You went behind Father's back, and she used your weakness.'

'Like I'm the only one who's ever done that,' he shouted back.

'You brought a psychopath into our home!' Brinkelle yelled relentlessly, never giving up her fury and contempt.

'I didn't bring her here. And she's not a psycho. She couldn't be. I know her, what she's like,' Barclay insisted. 'She couldn't have done this. Could she? I didn't know she was grabbing my bio-metric. Why would she do that?'

'If she didn't do this, and right now I do find that hard to believe,' Benjamin said, 'she was certainly an accomplice.'

'Oh dear God.' Barclay dropped his head into his hands and whimpered. That moment, his brothers decided later, was the start of the monumental breakdown. It was also the last time any of them ever saw him. He ran out of the room back to his guest suite on the sixth floor, and stayed there for two days, refusing to open the door or talk to anyone. The next they knew he'd taken a Jag in the middle of the night, and driven off into town. Three months later, he appeared again in the Independencies, calling himself Zebediah and denouncing his entire family.

Angela's flight landed at Highcastle airport at five o'clock. For the last three hours she'd been sweating and shivering in her seat, wrapping herself in a quilt. The fever was caused by fragments of the dark weapons infecting her blood as they broke up. As she'd been warned, it made her feel like crap, but she managed to walk unaided out of the plane.

She couldn't quite believe there wasn't a whole regiment of armed and armoured security hardcases waiting for her to disembark. But there wasn't.

An outbreak of good fortune was the last thing she was going to question; so she took a taxi from the front of the terminal, and headed off down Motorway A. It was a straight, clean drive. She only stopped the car once, when it arrived at the junction with Motorway B.

She stared along the ribbon of tarmac stretching away to the south-east. The Independencies would mean staying on St Libra for the rest of her life, and that was destined to be a real long time given her expensive pre-birth genetic workover. None of the micro state governments would ever hand her over to the Norths, even if they did know she'd taken up citizenship inside their border. And with most of them there was no requirement to prove and register your identity. But that would be it, she'd remain on St Libra, living a backwoods existence. Today, she might manage to get through the gateway and back on to Earth. Even if they didn't want to question her already, by tomorrow the Norths would definitely want her in their custody. The gateway border officers would be watching out for her.

As soon as the plane came in range of Highcastle's transnet, Angela had been accessing the news. The slaughter at the mansion was the only story. So far her name hadn't been mentioned. Either they didn't want to warn her she was being hunted, or they hadn't even realized she was missing yet. And if they were hunting her, she would have been arrested as soon as she stepped off the plane – unless her crude identity switch had fooled them. If it had, it wouldn't for ever.

Motorway A it was then.

Ten minutes later she was in the gateway transit terminal. Helin Anisio's i-e certified her identity as a Libyan-Italian citizen; the scanner she put her hand on confirmed the biometric matched Ms Anisio's GE citizen file, and she told the bored agency staff she was coming back from a two-week holiday in Abellia. When they asked if she was okay, she assured them her shivers were from the cold she'd come down with after getting caught in a downpour the previous night.

Angela walked through the gateway. That put her in the GE Border Directorate reception hall. The only thing Helin Anisio didn't have (as she didn't actually exist) was a GE visa chip. That was the one item it had proved impossible to get hold of to bolster the legend's identity. Angela didn't care, she was on the right planet now, she just had to swap identities back again. She put her Angela Tramelo visa chip in the slot – and all hell broke loose.

*

'Why did you run?' It was the question repeated endlessly over the next three months. More than once Angela woke up shouting the phrase: 'If you're innocent, why did you run?'

'Because I was scared' just didn't cut it. And of course she couldn't really tell them why she ran, why she was really there in the mansion. The whole 'alien monster' claim was simply laughed at as a pathetic, transparent defence counsel lie.

For three months the GE Justice Directorate was subject to formal requests, even mild threats, that Angela Tramelo be extradited to Abellia to stand trial. But Abellia's national status wasn't legally defined. Technically the GE had no treaties with it. And then there was the GE's core constitutional issue: the right to life. No prisoner or suspect could be handed over to a state which had the death penalty.

Abellia's legal team argued the city state didn't have the death penalty. The GE Directorate counter argued the Norths' fiefdom domain didn't have a legal precedent *against* the death penalty.

It was the only argument that went Angela's way. She was tried in London's Old Bailey. She had a good defence counsel paid for by the state – who desperately wanted to be seen as impartial. The prosecution had seven senior barristers, six of whom were paid for by Northumberland Interstellar.

Contrary to everyone else's expectations, Angela grew progressively more angry and resolute during her incarceration awaiting trial. This was usually the period when the guilty broke down and confessed. Not her. Shock, fear, loneliness, and uncertainty weren't the best psychological traits to share a solitary cell with for so long, and she was becoming more and more incensed that no one would listen, no one would believe that she'd seen a monster. Even her defence lawyer advised her not to make it part of her alibi. But that was the anger which fuelled her, so naturally she shouted it loud and defiantly, which the prosecution delightedly used to make her seem even more unstable – the kind of deranged personality that fitted the psychological profile of a serial killer.

The jury agreed, and the question of where she'd spend the rest of her life was resolved.

Thursday 7th March 2143

The monsoon had started an hour before dawn, blotting out the ringlight, drumming hard on the tents so no one could sleep, turning the moist ground to a quagmire. It was still going strong at eleven o'clock local time. The closest e-Ray to Wukang, orbiting six hundred kilometres away, revealed a vast swarm of clouds pushing slowly southwards, inland from the polar sea. Huddled inside their Qwik-Kabin on the edge of the forward camp, the AAV flight team studied the radar images and estimated the storm would clear by mid-afternoon.

Sarvar duly cancelled all the Daedalus flights scheduled for that morning. The sheer quantity of water made it uncertain if they could even resume later. With its compacted soil, Wukang's runway had become a long, shallow lake that was taking a long time to drain.

At midday, Vance Elston ordered two of the camp's three Land Rover Tropics to start scouting round, looking for paths through the jungle that the mobile biolabs could take in a few days' time when the forward camp was up to its full complement of personnel, equipment, and fuel.

Half the camp stood in the shelter of the big mess tent, watching the grey-green vehicles depart, lumbering over the sodden ground. It wasn't long until they vanished from view, absorbed by the silver-grey deluge before they reached the fringe of the jungle itself.

'Lieutenant Botin,' Vance said.

'Sir,' the lieutenant snapped.

'Let us find out how effective your squads are in bad weather. I want the perimeter secured and monitored. Move out.'

'Yes, sir. All right, people, you heard the Commander, jump to it. Assembly point by the vehicle park in ten minutes.'

Sitting at a long trestle table in the middle of the mess tent, Angela watched the authoritarian farce play out, and gave the squad a rueful grin as they pulled on their poncho capes and trudged out into the heavy rain. She finished her cheesecake, and walked over to the table where Elston was sitting with Jay Chomik and Forster Wardele, one of his junior administration officers.

'You got any orders for me?' she asked.

'Why, would you obey them if I did?'

'I was thinking, given that I can't join the guys on patrol, maybe I could help you?'

'How?' Elston asked in a voice thick with suspicion.

She shrugged. 'I'm good with basic datawork, and you're down Mullain. I know you haven't been assigned a replacement.'

'You want me to give you access to the administration network?'

'For rotas and managing store inventories, sure, why not? You think I'll use such a magnificent position of trust to steal enough raw to print out an airship and escape?'

Elson gave her a reluctant grin, and turned to Jay. 'What do you think?'

'Mullain did clear a lot of crap from the system,' Jay said grudgingly.

Angela pushed the advantage. 'Fine, show me what to do, slap access restrictions on everything else, and see if I'm any good.'

'Why are you doing this?' Elston asked.

'Truthfully, I'm bored shitless. And you and I both know I'm not the bad guy here. It's out there waiting for us.'

'Okay. You get one shot.'

'Thank you.'

'Forster, show her the drudge work.'

*

The administration division in Wukang was one Qwik-Kabin. Angela found it hard to credit, but the work cubicles were even smaller than the ones back at Sarvar. Forster wedged himself in next to her and started explaining the operating system and the procedures that needed managing. Despite having semi-smart software in the network, human input and ability was still essential for an enterprise like Wukang, where any problem that crept up was unique, needing a judgement call that the software couldn't handle because it didn't have any experience.

'In theory, it should learn everything after a week or so,' Forster said. 'Then we can kick back and relax.'

'And in the real world?'

'I'm going to be jammed in here till the day we pack up and head home.'

She grinned, enjoying his pragmatism. Forster was mildly flirtatious the whole time, which she neither encouraged nor slapped down. He wasn't anything like as useful as Paresh, but she wasn't about to shut down any options at this stage.

The software was absurdly simple, and the work mundane. She started rearranging personnel assignments for the next week, matching teams to the exploration plans that Elston and Antrinell were drawing up, allocating the kind of equipment and supplies they'd need, then loading resupply estimates to Sarvar.

'That's pretty good,' Forster admitted as she worked her way through daily fuel-consumption estimates.

'It's not exactly gateway science.'

Forster left her after ninety minutes, telling her to call him when she encountered a problem that stymied her. He was only a thin composite wall away, he said with a mildly hopeful smile.

Angela knew it would be pointless trying to load any subversive programs into the camp network from the Qwik-Kabin console –

Elston would have already established monitors to see what she was up to. Fortunately she didn't have to. Reviewing personnel files was a requirement for this job. So, once she'd sorted out Friday's assignments, taking into account the rescheduled delivery flights, and shunted maintenance shifts round for the Land Rovers, and ten other finicky variables, she called up the camp's personnel files and began reading the summaries. Given that she was using her e-i to interface with the network and orchestrate dataflow within the console zone, it was easy to copy the files into the solid memory cache sitting unobtrusively in her utility belt. An act that Elston would need very good software to detect; and if he did, he'd know why she was doing it – or think he did.

The only reason to copy the files was to review them in detail later on, which is what she intended. Elston would see Angela playing detective, because Mullain had found something in those same files, something important enough to get him killed. Logically, it must have been a discrepancy big enough to call someone's entire identity into question. Someone in Wukang was operating under a legend.

Angela knew who, of course. What had utterly defeated her over the long month since that fateful Sunday at the start of February was figuring out why. She was hoping the file might provide a clue. And she would read it properly later, along with every other file, because Elston must never know the one she was interested in.

*

Angela was still in her new cubicle an hour later when Elston arrived in the Qwik-Kabin. He was frowning when he opened her door.

'What's up?' she asked.

'Have you loaded in a new schedule for today?' he asked.

'No. It looks like Saturday is going to be my first big experiment with your lives. I expect everyone will enjoy having the day off when it all grinds to a halt at breakfast.'

'Are there any earlier versions of today's schedule?'

'Er . . . hang on.' She was quite pleased at the way she retrieved data from the network, fingers flicking the icons in her keyspace, e-i shifting the larger database levels for access. 'No, I can't find one. What's up?'

Elston scowled. It was worry that puckered his flesh up, not anger. His voice dropped. 'We don't know where Iyel is.'

'Iyel?' She didn't even have to call up the personnel files again. 'He's one of the xenobiology team, right?'

'Yeah. Except they can't find him.'

Her fingers closed over a blue and yellow icon, spun it round and flicked a node on the side. Iyel's Thursday itinerary expanded in her zone field. 'He should be helping with final drive-power system checks on biolab-2. They're supposed to drive it round for thirty minutes this afternoon, but not to go into the jungle. Should be back by now.'

'Marvin hasn't even taken the biolab out yet. They've been waiting for Iyel.'

'And his access code isn't active?'

'We can't establish a microlink to his bodymesh.'

'So he's got to be outside the camp network's range. Oh, did he tag along with the Land Rovers?'

'I used a relay through the e-Ray to call them. He didn't go with the Land Rovers.'

'Shit. Okay, if he was in trouble, injured or something, his bodymesh would call for help.'

Elston glared at her. 'Only if he's in range.'

'How would he get out of range? Wukang's network range extends for five klicks, doesn't it?'

They stared at each other for a long moment. It was Angela who broke, shoulders slumping in dismay. 'Oh it can't be,' she murmured. 'It just can't.'

'I'm going to officially declare him a missing person.'

'Look, maybe he's not answering because he's busy.'

'Don't be ridiculous.'

'I'm not being ridiculous. What if he's sneaked off for a spot of one on one with his girlfriend or boyfriend?'

'I've already used the emergency responder code. He can't deactivate that, half his smartcells are HDA issue, and the response is hardwired in. He's not out there.'

'This can't be right,' Angela said. 'Even if he's dead, the smartcells will respond. So he must be over five kilometres away.'

'This is classified, but the dead North they found in Newcastle had his smartcells physically removed.'

Angela gave him a shocked look. 'You're kidding me.'

'I wish I was.'

'Oh shit. That means there really is more than one. And they know how to disable smartcell technology.'

'Yeah,' Elston said. 'Look, I know it isn't you. I've reviewed your tag logs from this morning; you're accounted for.'

'Oh, thank-fucking-you.'

'But I also know about you and Paresh, and what you get up to together. So I need to know, have you, or anyone else, found a nice convenient route out through the perimeter? Some way to get outside and have your carnal fun.'

'No. It's secure.'

'Damnit.'

'Elston, the squad is out there right now patrolling. Have you warned them *it* is out there?'

'Not yet, no.'

'You have to warn them.'

'I will. I need to be certain first.'

'When was the last time someone saw him?'

'First thing this morning. Leaving his tent to go to the wash-room.'

'Hell, that's a long time. And it was pissing down badly then. Maybe that screwed with the perimeter sensors.'

'Maybe.'

She started to follow the thought, not enjoying the route. 'But, if Iyel was snatched and carried off, then *it* would have to get into the camp first.'

'I know,' he whispered.

'Elston, listen. It did this before. It got inside Bartram's mansion for fuck's sake; and nobody is more paranoid about their personal safety than a billionaire. It walked right through the mansion's security sensors and up to the seventh floor, like it was a ghost. Nothing spotted it, there was no alarm. Radar, infrared, pressure webs, sonics, magrez, visual. Nothing caught it!'

'You did. You saw it.'

'Yeah,' she said hoarsely. 'I did.'

'Right. You keep quiet about this part, understand? Say nothing, not even to Paresh. I'm going to launch a search for Iyel now, and that's going to twist people up badly as it is. I do not want rumour adding to low morale. Are we clear?'

Angela nodded. 'We're clear.'

Sunday 10th March 2143

'We can get it.'
  'All of it?'
  'Think so, yeah.'
  '*Think* isn't good enough. I need definites.'
  'All right. Okay. I'll make sure.'

*

Everybody in the GE used secondaries. It was part of the culture now; socially acceptable. There had been many attempts by the Brussels parliament to legislate against it, and the Tax Bureau certainly did its best. But of course, if a method had been found to clear up people's finances and put them on a hundred per cent legitimate, transparent basis, it would have worked for *everyone*, politicians and tax officials included. The general battle had been abandoned fifty years ago. But the technology and software which allowed people to set up and manage their secondaries also gave the police quite an armoury to uncover such fiscal malfeasance on an individual level. As the saying went, they could always get anybody sentenced, it just depended what crime they chose to charge you with.

Exposure of a citizen's secondaries was one of the simpler methods available to a modern police officer, especially one who was a surveillance expert, like detective Ian Lanagin.

The first time Jede had used a secondary e-i code to call

someone, he'd been walking down Percy Street. Ian used Elston's authority to sequestrate all the log records from the three transnet cells covering Percy Street. This kind of request was completely standard for the police – Ian's own authority level allowed him to do it – but as always with this investigation he didn't want anything that could be traced back to him.

*

'We have it.'

'Glad to hear it. Ruckby will call to arrange delivery.'

'It was expensive.'

'I know.'

'We had to pay more than we were expecting.'

'So?'

'So, I'll have to charge you extra for it. Got to cover costs.'

'I do hope that wasn't a serious attempt to extort money from me. You know who I work for, don't you?'

'I'm telling you, it cost a lot to get hold of.'

'Fine. We'll find another supplier.'

'You won't. This is specialist shit, man.'

'I will. Then you'll be left with a product you can't sell, and us looking for you. We don't take kindly to being dicked around.'

'Ten per cent. Ten per cent more. That's all. And I still don't make any profit.'

'We pay you the agreed price, or you start drowning in shit.'

'You're killing me here, man.'

'Oh please, I'd never kill you.'

'That's good man, we can talk. This is reasonable. We can sort this out. I'm thinking eight per cent.'

'I'd never kill you, because if you're dead you won't be able to suffer.'

'Fuck you, man.'

'The price we agreed is the price we pay. You'll be contacted to arrange delivery. I'd advise you follow the instructions.'

*

The next time Jede used the secondary e-i he was in a pub on Granger Street. Ian obtained the local cell log, and ran a comparison with the Percy Street records. There was one access code that occurred in both. They had Jede's secondary (or at least one of them). The intercept order was loaded into the transnet management AI using Elston's authority, and all subsequent calls Jede made were routed through the Market Street network, which skimmed them off into the classified investigation sub-section – directly into the Apple console in Ian's flat. As well as Jede's secondary, the AI also intercepted the calls to and from the other transnet address codes Jede had called.

*

'It's Sunday night. Usual place.'

'You don't get it until the money is registered in my secondary.'

'Remember who you're dealing with. You don't get sweet shit until we've checked it. And, kid, we have an expert.'

'It's good. This is the real thing, okay.'

'I'm okay, because I don't have anything to worry about. Eleven o'clock tomorrow. Don't make us come look for you.'

*

Ten fifty-five on Sunday night: the chill rain was coming in hard from the North Sea just as it had been doing for the last two days. The deluge was slowly sluicing away the ice and snow that had accumulated across Newcastle's buildings and streets all through winter. Overwhelmed gutters across the city were spilling cascades of freezing water directly onto pavements. Water running freely across ice made driving and walking extremely treacherous. The Accident and Emergency departments of all the city hospitals were reporting five-hour waiting times for fracture victims, so many had slipped as their familiar city roads morphed from frigid to fluid. And there Sid was, in the middle of all the wet sub-arctic misery, sitting in a car signed out from the police fleet, privately registered so no one passing by would know law

420

enforcement officers were in there waiting should they run a sneaky check on the licence. He was parked on the corner of Beechwood Gardens, just outside Last Mile, waiting for the exchange. Whatever the exchange was. It had never been named in the intercepts, where Jede and his unknown supplier talked in phrases they'd surely pilfered from cheap crime dramas. Ian and Eva were also loitering in a fleet car, but on Herford Road at the south end of Last Mile.

'Boss, I think we're starting,' Eva said. 'Ruckby's car just turned into Kingsway.'

Sid's windscreen display showed the erratic grid of Last Mile's roads, with plenty of dark areas where the macromesh had failed. A purple symbol appeared at the south end of the Kingsway road that cut straight through the centre of Last Mile. 'Got him,' Sid acknowledged. 'Anyone with him?' Ruckby drove a big Ford Turusse saloon, registered to a North Korean business address – matt-black paintwork, but easy enough to eyeball.

'Can't tell, but he won't be alone. We're following now.'

Sid pulled away from the kerb. He drove into Last Mile, level with the gateway, and started cruising up the sharp neon glow and hazy hologram sparkles that besieged the air down Kingsway's length. With all the adverts reflecting off the rain-slicked tarmac, it was like driving through a wriggling tunnel of light. Even at this time of night there was still traffic about. Big HDA lorries rumbled towards the gateway, still faithfully carrying equipment and supplies for the expedition, though there weren't so many of them now. Company trucks with their iconic logos nestled up to store loading bays. Decade-old vans with scratched and dinted bodywork made the nightly resupply run to small independent shops and outlets. Scooters with panniers big enough to carry a body. Even bicycles were towing carts. A big shiny new Toyota six-wheel J-Cruise headed down towards the gateway, piled high with St Libra survivalist goodies. Sid was mildly surprised to see the migrants hadn't abandoned their dream despite the expedition, a reminder that outside Newcastle and his investigation the great community of trans-stellar worlds and nations was carrying on as normal. He watched a little group of the poor sods trudging along, pulling ancient supermarket trolleys loaded with their possessions, hunched against the freezing rain, their coats slick with water as they drew closer to the gateway and the promised Independencies beyond. A quick check on the windscreen display showed him closing on the purple symbol. When he looked up, he caught Ruckby's big dark Turusse turning off just ahead of him.

'Visual now,' Sid reported. 'He went into Sixth Avenue.'

'Okay boss,' Ian replied. 'The macromesh has him, too. We're turning into Eighth Avenue; if we park on the junction with Dukesway we'll see him when he comes out.'

'I'll turn round at the end of Queensway and wait.' As he said it, Sid saw a dark-red Kovoshu Valta pass him; hologram prism stripes along the side sparkled and wiggled as it went. Boz was driving the big rock-star car, his massive profile highlighted by the brilliant façade of a farm store whose lights were shining down on a camel pen. And he was staring directly at Sid's car.

'Shit, shit.'

'What's happened?' Eva asked.

'I think I just got made by Boz.'

'Ah crap on this, man,' Ian said. 'The macromesh just lost Ruckby.'

Ian saw the purple symbol had vanished from the windscreen's display. 'Crap, Boz warned him.'

'I don't know about that, man, the macromesh is seriously screwed around here. We'll cut along Dukesway and try to get a visual.'

'Right. I'll double back,' Ian said. He told his e-i to monitor the functioning segments of macromesh down Sixth Avenue to see if Ruckby had switched the Turusse's licence code to avoid observation. No vehicles were registering. 'Ruckby must have turned off.'

'Yeah, that's what we think,' Eva replied.

'Okay, Boz is going to be watching for me; you guys take a drive along Sixth Avenue.'

'Turning in now,' Ian said.

Sid studied the grid of Last Mile's roads trying to work out what to do next. Any decent, legitimate surveillance operation would have back-up cars, a team of fifteen detectives, complete smartdust coverage, even a few small airborne micro-drones to track the suspect. This half-arsed campaign they'd thrown together was bordering on farce. He abruptly turned the car down Eighth Avenue, which was an ambitious term for a long gap between two stark carbon cliff walls of modified commercial blocks. The photonic deluge of adverts was muted here, reduced to a few signs flickering behind grilled-up windows. Overhead photopanels cast a dusky green-tinged light that illuminated the monotonous rain. Blocked drains had produced an overspill along both gutters which was now swelling out to cover the cracked tarmac. The car's tyres generated a small grubby wake as he drove cautiously, sending chunks of ice bobbing about.

'I'm not surprised the macromesh can't find anything here,' he muttered. The smartdust must have degraded and failed long ago under this kind of climatic abuse. He turned again, going down Princesway South. 'Crap on it!' He braked hard. The grid on the windscreen, data taken directly from the Newcastle civic highways department, showed Princesway South as a direct connection between Eighth and Sixth Avenues. Not in the real world. Seventy metres ahead of him was a grey composite wall, stitching together the buildings on either side. It had the etched resin web pattern of a structure fabricated by automata, a simple skin spun over a hexagonal stress frame. A long roll-up door was directly ahead, its base swallowing up the old road.

Sid twisted the joystick and reversed out of Princesway, back onto Eighth Avenue. 'I can't get through.'

'We're on Sixth now,' Ian said. 'No sign of him.'

'He could have cut down to Western,' Eva said. 'Or gone into a warehouse. Just about every store here has a loading bay.'

Sid turned out into Dukesway. A couple of lorries rolled past, their fat tyres sending dark ripples scudding across the water-logged road. Impenetrable shadows occluded the end of countless doors and narrow alleyways on either side of him. Only a few overhead photopanels worked. It was a gloomy, sinister road which Sid suddenly found he didn't like being alone on. 'This is stupid,' he said. 'If we drive round looking for them, they'll spot us for certain. Get back to the station, we're through here.'

'Aye, man, good call,' Ian said.

Sid accelerated as hard as he dared, sending a wash of water surfing over the pavement. He just wanted to be out of Last Mile now. The district with its unruly delight of chaos, decay, and greed had defeated them.

*

They never did find Iyel. Vance Elston kept the search going for two days. Legionnaire squads combed the surrounding land out to the edge of the jungle. The remaining camp personnel examined every tent, pallet, and vehicle. All three Land Rovers and both MTJs drove round the nearby jungle, crunching over the smaller bushes and tearing down the tangle of vines strung between every trunk. Wukang's three Sikorsky CV-47 Swallows, light scout helicopters, spiralled further out above the lush, impenetrable tree canopy, firing constant high-power pings to try and trigger Iyel's bodymesh responder code. They also activated their infrared scanners, hunting for any body-sized hotspots. Elston never said anything to the pilots, but he was a damn sight more eager to uncover moving alien monsters than he was a stationary cooling human corpse. It didn't matter, the Swallows didn't find either. A pair of Raytheon 6-EB Owls were flown along the closest rivers by the AAV team; a long-shot, in case he'd been swept away by the fast water.

After the second complete search of the camp, the personnel not flying or on foot patrol outside the perimeter went back to their normal duties. The Daedalus flights resumed and continued to build up the camp's inventory. Iyel's official status was moved to: missing on duty. Officially, as there was no body or evidence of foul play, he wasn't dead.

Camp rumour had a very different view, concocting brilliant, elaborate and improbable theories about how he'd been eliminated.

It was evening when Vance finally admitted defeat and changed Iyel's file status. The air-con in the Qwik-Kabin was straining with the load of another sweltering St Libra day, and outside the camp personnel were gathering for the Sunday night barbecue, which was fast becoming a tradition for the expedition camps. He told his e-i to establish a secure link to Vermekia. A secure connection through a six-thousand-kilometre e-Ray relay above the jungle, then an undersea cable, followed by another four-thousand-kilometre land line with dozens of civilian relays and cells was something of a joke, but the call was audio only and AIA encryption was still the best.

'Two deaths?' Vermekia asked.

'One death, one missing,' Vance said, wishing he didn't sound so defensive.

'So what's happening?'

'Mullain I can just about write off as the victim of some illegal activity he'd stumbled across. Iyel looks a lot more suspicious.'

'Was it an alien abduction?'

'I don't know,' Vance admitted, which was tough to say. 'There's no evidence either way.'

'What's your hunch?'

'All I'll say is that I'm pretty certain that it wasn't Angela Tramelo. Although, I have to admit none of the other camps have had incidents like this. Not yet, anyway.'

'There can't be anything else going on,' Vermekia said. 'I won't accept that much coincidence.'

'I'd point out that Wukang has responsibility for the primary defence mission,' Vance said. 'If the aliens found out about that, they might begin with an incursion. And Iyel was on the xeno-biology team.'

'But he wasn't part of the defence mission.'

'I know.'

'And how could the aliens possibly know?'

'We don't have any idea about their true capabilities. But we do know one of them might have been in Newcastle.'

'So you believe they do exist?' Vermekia asked.

'This is starting to make me think it's possible, yes. But of course there's no proof, only circumstantial evidence. As always, we need something concrete. How is Detective Hurst doing?'

'Still backtracking those stupid taxis.'

'Really?'

'Yeah. Statistically, he should have found it by now. If you ask me, it's a complete waste of time.'

Vance experienced a strange pang of sympathy for the poor detective, plunged into a nightmare investigation with way too much pressure applied from everyone. 'He's doing the job we asked him to.'

'Whatever. It's you we're looking to now to provide the answers.'

'I understand.'

'When will you start genetic sampling?'

'Wukang is up to full strength now, so I'm sending the first convoy out into the jungle tomorrow.'

'Glad to hear that. We need some results.'

Vance signed off, and spent a long minute in the confined cubicle staring at the one narrow slit of window his status had gained him. It framed the edge of the rings which were beginning to shine brightly as St Libra's rotation carried Brogal into night. Two deaths (he was convinced Iyel had been killed) was beyond coincidence. He was sure *something* was out there in the jungle. It unnerved him, because he couldn't understand the reason for the creatures staying hidden. And he was just beginning to appreciate how isolated Wukang was. The Lord's universe was a lot bigger than the human soul was comfortable with.

Music started playing. Some guitar rock track that sounded tinny and lost inside the Qwik-Kabin. It would sound the same out in the jungle, an alien noise, absorbed and broken by the vast sprawl of vegetation, completely insignificant.

Vance sighed and tried to push his growing concerns to one side. At least for tonight. Tonight there were burgers and sausages, lettuce that had been chilled for too long, and toasted rolls with not enough ketchup. Just like all barbecues should be, a celebration of being human. He shut down his console, and went out to join in.

*

Angela enjoyed the Sunday night barbecues. Everyone seemed to relax a little – forget the reason why they were here and kick back. The food wasn't bad, even though she was never sure the burgers were cooked properly in the middle. It didn't matter, because for a few precious hours the smell of charcoal repelled the jungle scents, music held back the planet's innate oppressive silence, and people banished HDA uniforms to dress in civilian clothes.

They didn't use the mess tent. The grills had been set up in the area behind it, their charcoal glow a bright orange, contrasting with the silver ringlight. Smoke plumed up, accompanied by meat juice sizzling. The first batch of food was ready when she arrived with the squad. They lined up with plates, scooping up salad and waiting for the catering staff to dole out the meat.

'These sausages are always too spicy,' Mohammed Anwar complained.

'You are such a wimp fart,' Gillian Kowalski told him.

'Why can't we have two types? It's not gateway science.'

'Oh sure,' Dave Guzman said. 'Let's just order out.'

Angela was laughing with the rest of them. She looked round at Paresh, who was grinning.

'I'm just saying,' Mohammed claimed with dwindling dignity.

Angela held her plate out, and thanked Lulu MacNamara for the sausages and burger that the red-cheeked girl slapped down.

'It's always where you are,' a voice said, clear and loud. 'Mullain at Sarvar, now Iyel here.'

Angela looked round. Five people down the line, Davinia Beirne was staring belligerently at her. She was one of the AAV team, an Owl technician.

427

'You talking to me?' Angela said.

'No other camps have a serial killer in their team,' Davinia said. 'No other camps are having people murdered.'

'Hey!' DiRito stepped forward, his face all anger and outrage.

Angela put her arm out, stopping him from going any further. 'It's okay.' She sensed other squad members closing round her. 'You got a problem?' she asked Davinia.

'How many more of us are going to disappear like Iyel?'

'I don't want anyone to die. And I've never killed anyone. Not here now, not twenty years ago. I'm here in this shithole to help you, to stop the aliens from killing anyone else. I don't have to be here, remember that, I could be safe back on Earth. All I am is a dumb volunteer. But when *they* start to come out of the jungle for you, you're going to need me.'

Chris Fiadeiro and Mackay, from the AAV team, came up beside a sneering Davinia. Angela stared at her, watching closely for tell-tale muscle movement, ready for a sudden lunge forward. Fully expecting the squad members and the AAV team to stop Davinia from reaching her. But there had been too many prison fights for her to rely on other people.

That was when Bastian 2North arrived at the barbecue to witness the stand-off scene, with everyone silent while the chirpy steel guitar music played on. The North cocked his head to one side to look at Angela, his face impassive. She was proud she didn't back down, didn't turn away. The moment was painful, stretching out way too long. Then Madeleine Hoque slapped a burger down on Davinia's plate; Davinia appeared irritated by the action that broke her aggressive concentration. Mackay pushed her slightly, and she grunted in contempt and walked away. It was over, finished. Bastian moved on to join the end of the queue.

A hand closed tightly round Angela's forearm.

'Let's get you the fuck out of here,' Leora Fawkes said.

Angela nearly tripped she was pushed along so forcefully. She didn't complain, she went with it, her friends forming a neat circle round her.

428

'You all right?' Paresh asked as the squad sat on the grass together.

'I don't like being a party pooper,' she said.

'You're not,' Marty O'Riley said. 'We know you were with us both times.'

'Davinia's always toxing up,' Josh Justic said in a low voice. 'She's got a real problem there.'

'You're only saying that because she turned you down,' Atyeo said, grinning as he munched a sausage down.

'Oi! She did not turn me down.'

The squad laughed. They'd settled into their usual routine. Comfort and camaraderie. Angela started eating her own food, and saw Paresh was still giving her a concerned look. She mouthed: 'I'm okay.' And saw his relief.

A whole group of friends like this was rare, people you knew you could rely on, who were perfectly comfortable with each other, who were all equals. Angela had known that once before. In a strange way it had been the polar opposite of this barbecue. But the memory association was strong; sitting out like this, with oh-so different people, under very different stars, sent a sudden chill along her arms. She was surprised those times could still resurrect themselves so clearly in her mind; that was a past life now, belonging to a different person so very long ago.

*

The last in a long *long* list of exuberant parties the young Angela DeVoyal had attended was at Prince Matiff's mansion on the 17th of January 2111, a date everybody in the trans-stellar finance industry would always remember. She'd gone with Shasta Nolif, of course. They were virtually inseparable on the New Monaco social scene. Best friends since for ever.

The DeVoyal family fortune was originally derived from Wall Street and the global finance markets before progressing smoothly to take advantage of new business during the trans-stellar expansion. They were old East Coast money, complete with aristocratic airs and cold-equation dealings with other people.

As the heir, Angela DeVoyal was as beautiful as only the germline-modified could be, along with other traits her father, Raymond, desired: tall, healthy, strong, fast, smart, a memory that resembled silicon in its perfect recall. Luci Tramelo, who gave birth to Angela, was under a simple surrogate contract, and left a week after delivery, as soon as the DeVoyal estate clinic had conducted appropriate tests on the infant Angela to confirm her DNA was everything Raymond had paid for. The other required traits – those that couldn't be sequenced in, like the ancestral ruthlessness, cunning, and near-megalomaniac ambition – were instilled by an upbringing and education that made sure the family's business and revenue stream would carry on in safe hands.

Shasta's family money came from an industrial barony in India, one which her great-grandfather had astutely and ruthlessly expanded into a global giant at the start of the twenty-first century, employing over a quarter of a million people across thirty-seven countries. Her grandfather had deployed that same ruthlessness to diversify into production of raw, enabling him to ride the microfacture revolution out among the new trans-stellar worlds.

For Prince Matiff's party, Angela had chosen a deceptively simple white dress with a mermaid skirt as her arrival attire. Two seamstresses from the Italian couture house she was currently patronizing had been included in her entourage so they could finish the creation – it was so snug fitting, and the Jajescal spider silk fabric with its micro-diamond glitter grains so delicate, that they had to sew her into the dress just before she alighted. To complement it, over a hundred ruby and emerald pins were woven into her big blonde hair; and her necklace, earrings, and web-bracelet were a matching vintage Roicoutte set, costing slightly more than eight million dollars.

Angela was mildly upset that her father hadn't accompanied her to the party, but the family AI had identified an unusual surge of bioil running though the vast European supply pipe network that ran from Newcastle to the Balkans. He suspected the source was the French world, Orleans. But he didn't know the buyer; and with the quantity involved he should have known all about the deal. So he told her he was staying behind to watch the market. The DeVoyal finance house controlled nearly forty per cent of the GE bioil futures market, and he didn't want to be outsmarted by a rogue deal.

Angela and Shasta had timed their departures so their hypersonic VTOL executive jets touched down on the mansion's landing field at the same time, mid-afternoon of the first day. That way they could share one of the gold-plated horse-drawn carriages up the greenway to the white and silver splendour of the mansion, with its twin spire turrets stabbing a hundred and fifty metres into the clear violet-tinged New Monaco sky.

The Prince greeted them, standing in a line with his eight wives, all selected from good Arab families from Riyadh and New Persia, who knew their place and performed their duties correctly. 'I hope you're going to come to bed with me before this is over,' he purred in Angela's ear as she was announced to the vaulting gold and marble ballroom by the scarlet-uniformed Officer of the House. As a direct descendant of Arabian Royalty, Matiff affected head-of-state rituals complete with ornate military-style guards as if he were still ruling a desert kingdom back on Earth.

'We'll see,' Angela murmured back with a demure smile that gave nothing away. There'd been parties where they'd both retired to a private suite, enjoying each other's uninhibited sexuality. Sometimes it was just the two of them; sometimes Shasta or another girlfriend joined them; sometimes Matiff enlisted his male relatives to carousel her. The wickedness and pleasure was always excellent.

'Please,' Matiff said. 'There's plenty of time. You know how much I appreciate you physically.'

'I know, sweetheart,' she said. It was the same for most men. The one-in-ten modification to her DNA had become active when she reached her full height and the initial onrush of puberty

431

hormones had subsided. Right now she still looked a perky seventeen; a faux adolescence it might have been, but the sexual lure was still very real.

'Housden will be here,' Angela said. 'He's arriving this evening.'

'Are you two serious?'

'Might be,' she said enigmatically.

'Ah, he is so lucky. Once again, I beg you to marry me.'

'One day, maybe, Matiff. But not right now.'

'Until that day.' He bowed, holding her hand a little too tight as he kissed it.

The ballroom had an orchestra up on the balcony, playing stately dance music. A dozen couples were already on the floor, twirling elegantly. Waiters in white tailcoats offered flutes of champagne on silver trays as the girls walked the length of the room, towards the Orchard Hall where there was a rock band playing. Together they quietly scanned the dresses on show; fabulous, elaborate couture from across the trans-stellar worlds; with every designer trying to attract attention and gain more commissions from the ludicrous wealth of New Monaco. Angela was surprised at the number of prosthetics, especially wings and peacock-style tails – that fad had surely passed? In turn, rival female eyes performed radar-efficient scans of their own garments, intuitively comparing cost and aesthetics. Through it all, the smiles were unbroken, air-kiss swarms flying free.

'Housden?' Shasta asked. 'Really, sweets?'

'Cute, big dick, sense of humour, right age. Kind of rare to have all those in combination, don't you think?'

'And one of us.'

'And one of us,' Angela conceded. Housden was from a Chinese family whose mining conglomerate had made it big in Africa before trans-spacial connection technology opened up the stars, and rare earth minerals stopped being so quite rare. As with a lot of similar corporations, they successfully shifted their core business from mining to refining raw and continued to flourish.

'There's always the Prince.'

Angela frowned. 'That's not an option.' For all his charm, Prince Matiff was a little too old-school for Angela; his wives were required to be obedient. Then there was the business rivalry.

The final decades of indigenous Gulf oil wealth had seen tens of billions of petrodollars channelled into bioil refineries and vast tracts of land on new worlds for algaepaddies. Those new refineries had kept the original families of Gulf princes at the forefront of trans-stellar energy production. They didn't appreciate the kind of manipulation of the bioil futures market led by the DeVoyal house, and always made life difficult for traders by refusing to cooperate on production figures and market shares and investment leverage.

Consequently, sleeping with the enemy, in a very literal sense, was a dark pleasure for Angela (and, she suspected, for the Prince, too) but that was all.

Angela and Shasta started dancing amid the dry ice waterfalls and rippling lasers. They split up when Shasta found herself dancing suggestively with a group she knew vaguely. Angela went on to the dining hall, where tables were laid with an extraordinary variety of food. Floor-to-ceiling windows gave a panoramic view out across the grounds. At the bottom of the slope at the front of the mansion was the mile-wide fountain lake. Huge geysers of water sprayed their way high into the twilight sky: straight power columns, twirling arcs, splayed spumes, airborne wave curls; all of them illuminated from below, changing colour as they gyrated.

On her way outside into the twilight, Angela passed a group of S&M fiends in their tailored leather costumes adorned with gold chains and diamond-tipped spikes. They were on their way down to the Roman Slave Dungeon where Matiff had hired a dozen of California's finest porn stars to man the manacles. Their excitement at their prisoner was palpable. They'd captured an angel, a beautiful adolescent male with a perfectly muscled torso who had wings of snow-white feathers surgically grafted onto his back. He was being tugged along by a dwarf who was dressed in bandoliers of tox sacs. Angela couldn't help grinning at the outrageous sight as they went past.

There was camel racing in the grass-walled amphitheatre Matiff had dug in one of his gardens; an amusing homage to his cultural roots. Housden arrived in time for the second race, all tall and hunky-looking, his shaved head decorated with silver tattoos, looking very dashing in his Nanru suit. They joined a group of friends in one of the stadium suites to watch and cheer on their chosen steeds. Placing quarter-million-dollar bets on each race, Angela lost two and a half million in total; Housden did better, coming out half a million in profit.

A chauffeured buggy took them down to the secluded pavilions, nestling in their individual clearings of blossom trees along the shore of the fountain lake. Angela had to send for the Italian seamstresses to undress her. The erotic masseuse in their pavilion was a giant of a woman, so much so that Angela felt a little thrill of nerves as the white dress was removed in front of her. Housden stood beside the padded bench where she lay down, watching in delight as she was slowly covered in oil that reflected the undulating colours of the offshore fountains. Amid the soft drizzle of pink petals, the powerful masseuse began kneading flesh in a diabolically skilful shiatsu that was soon producing helpless shudders along Angela's thighs. After a while, Housden joined in; fucking her while the masseuse continued her exquisite torment. Angela was sure the whole estate could hear her cries at the end.

For her second dress Angela wore a sleek scarlet silk number, while her stylist arranged her mass of hair into a deceptively plain peasant wave that flowed down her back. Once the entourage put the finishing touches to her appearance, Angela and Housden joined the big gathering on the lawns for the pre-breakfast banquet.

Dawn came, pushing a chill breeze with it. Housden escorted her indoors, and they agreed to separate for a while. She knew what he'd be doing – she'd seen him looking round the female guests several times. Fair enough – her own e-i had been receiving Matiff's calls for two hours now.

One of the mansion's footmen was waiting for her, and it was with an amused sense of inevitability she allowed him to escort her to the bedroom where the Prince and five of his wives were waiting.

Fatigue was starting to set in, but Matiff was a host prepared for every eventuality, and wasn't going to let her lassitude spoil his morning. One of the wives bumped a tox for Angela which sent her into a daze, hands fumbling at the furniture to stay upright. Recovery was fast, delivering her directly to a state of fresh and healthy mid-morning wakefulness. She stood in front of Matiff, while he watched with a cold anticipatory smile as his wives plucked the scarlet dress from her skin. Then they made her kneel before him.

*

Angela woke in a guest suite bedroom by herself. It wasn't something she enjoyed – this was a party, she shouldn't be alone. She was angry with herself for the resentment and self-pity. Though, if she was honest, she was also reacting to the Prince's surprisingly disturbing behaviour. He'd taken things a lot further than she'd been prepared to go, relishing her outrage and dismay.

Her entourage were waiting in the suite's lounge outside. She vaguely recalled them being summoned to collect her once Matiff and his wives had satiated themselves. Now, their presence and attention were an immediate comfort. There was a tox which banished the hangover. A bath was run containing scented ointments which her body therapist and a maid helped gently rub in, reviving her. Her haematologist ran a quick scan on her blood to make sure none of the stimulants Matiff had bumped her with were harmful. Angela's enhanced liver and kidney functions could handle a large range of pollutants in her bloodstream, which was why she always had to drink twice as much as ordinary people just to get tipsy, but who knew what the Prince had used. The hair stylist worked her usual miracles and tamed the dishevelled tangle, weaving in some fresh flowers and slender platinum threads, which was when Angela asked: 'What time is it?'

She wasn't entirely surprised when they told her it was one in the afternoon. Matiff had certainly taken his time enjoying her discomfort. Long enough that there could be no mistake; she knew now that he didn't consider her an equal, which was extraordinarily offensive.

As the entourage helped her into a new dress, she activated her transnet interface, and her e-i told her she'd had three calls from her father which she'd missed. It wasn't like him to call when she was at a party. She told the e-i to call him back, but he wasn't interfaced. 'Let me know when he is,' she told it.

Determined not to let Matiff spoil the party, for that would be another victory, she flung herself back into it.

Down in the Orchard Hall a seven-piece band called Pink Isn't Well were grinding out their prog-emo tracks. Angela wasn't fond of that style anyway, and in her current mood it left her cold. She went out and took a chauffeured buggy down to the amphitheatre where the afternoon no-rules cage fight tournament was playing out; with the last man standing claiming a five-million-dollar purse. Angela watched in wide-eyed illicit thrall as limbs were deliberately broken, faces pulped to bloody meat, and below-the-belt blows commonplace. She imagined it was the Prince getting pounded down there in the ring, which made her feel a lot better.

*

There was another costume change before attending the evening races. To accommodate it Angela had a proper massage, and a skin cleanse with irrigation, and the haematologist formulated a scrubtox to take down the alcohol high. When she was clean fresh and ready, her dermatologist sprayed platinum fleck scales to every square centimetre of skin, turning her a glossy, buffed silver. With true artistry, the dermatologist shaded the coating to emphasize cleavage and lines of musculature. Then the couturiers brought out a mauve ballgown that was mostly broad straps; complementing the platinum sheen to emphasize her figure's femininity and strength.

436

When the entourage had finished performing their ritual, Housden joined her and Shasta for the evening hog-roast picnic.

'Wow,' he said with a greedy smile that wouldn't stop. 'Wow, wow, and wow again. Can I kiss you? I don't want to muss the platinum, you look too fantastic for that.'

'You may kiss me. It won't muss.' Angela forced a giggle. She couldn't decide if she should mention Matiff's behaviour to her friends. After all, what could they do? And it might upset Housden, he was that sweet. So she said nothing as they all got into a buggy for the ride down to the sloping field above the fountain lake. Torches that sent out flames of green and blue scintillations illuminated the pathways snaking through hundreds of tables that lay in grottos of arched sweet-scented rose and clematis vines. Five roasting pits ringed the kitchen area, each one with a different animal on a spit above the radiant coals, a bull, pig, reindeer, buffalo ... 'It's not really a panda, is it?' Housden asked, frowning at the last pit.

'I wouldn't put it past Matiff,' Angela conceded. 'It's the kind of shock-value he enjoys.'

They settled at a cast-iron table under a cluster of hand-painted Japanese parasols suspended from a wistaria loop and told the catering crew what they wanted. Angela didn't quite have the nerve to ask for panda, but Housden did. 'I've got to call his bluff,' he claimed.

'Men!' Angela and Shasta clinked their glasses.

The slope gave them a grand view of the two big scarlet hot-air balloons that had risen up, a mile apart, their tether ropes turning them into a pair of captured moons floating fifteen hundred feet above the ground. Five surprisingly small Cessna rocketplanes thundered over the mansion between the twin spires, and curved round sharply, heading for the first balloon. Angela clapped in admiration as the dark needle-delta shapes twisted round each other, scarring grubby contrails behind them that twined in the balmy evening air like rampant DNA strands. The rocketplanes soared round the balloon in tight acrobatic curves that drew another wave of applause from the picnickers.

Angela gasped when two of the planes came perilously close, wingtip almost touching wingtip as they manoeuvred for best position to curve around the balloon. Always the thrill came from anticipating a mid-air collision, the bright orange flower bloom of flame, of smoking wreckage spinning out of the explosion. Of life in danger of extinction.

Somewhere, so deep down it was almost in her subconscious, she wondered if she was becoming desensitized to life's experiences. She'd tried so many pleasures at the never-ending procession of New Monaco's parties that only the increasing extreme excited her now. She almost envied Shasta with her business trips, and slow ascension to the control of an engineering empire spread over ten worlds. Her family legacy was tangible, where the DeVoyal empire was nothing but digits.

They were in the middle of the second rocketplane race, for which Angela had put a quarter million dollars on the emerald craft piloted by Duke Douglas, because she liked the name, when Housden gave Shasta a little nod.

'I've just seen someone I need to say hello to,' Shasta announced, and walked off.

'That was subtle,' Angela chided him.

'I know, sorry, babe.'

Angela's e-i informed her the market alert over bioil production had changed to level one amber; St Libra was still increasing its flow through the Newcastle gateway. She dismissed it, her heart suddenly lifting, because she'd guessed what this was. And yes, she was a proper New Monaco woman, and experienced in just about every aspect of an astonishing life, and professionally blasé, but it would seem there were still some things that were just naturally exciting . . .

Housden cleared his throat. 'Angela, I think what we have is pretty good, and I'd like to make it permanent.'

She smiled at the expectant look on his broad face. And it was sincere. She knew him well enough to determine that. 'Yes, of course I'll go permanent with you.'

He leaned forward and gave her a tender kiss. 'Thank you.'

Angela was suddenly looking at a small box he was holding out to her. She grinned and opened it. Inside was a ring of clear crystal. In fact, very clear, and sparkling. Her hands went to her cheeks in genuine surprise, and delight. 'Oh Housden, is that . . . ?'

'Yeah. I got you a diamond engagement ring. Just call me Mr Classic.'

She giggled as she took it out and held it up to admire it. And *Lo!* it fitted her finger perfectly. 'How in all the trans-space worlds do they do that? It's spectacular. I love it.' And a small wicked part of her mind couldn't wait to show it off to Shasta – who would be so jealous.

'One of our family mines on Mosselbaai turned up a huge uncut. I took it to a company in Amsterdam who've developed this new cutting technique. Something to do with precision neutron beams. Anyhoo . . . they cut a circle out of it. That's the very first – and only, as far as I know.'

'Thank you.' Another kiss, more urgent this time. 'Thank you very much.' Angela fed him shrimp dipped in garlic, he proffered a flute of champagne dosed with JK raspberry vodka. They kissed again.

'And thank you for asking, as well,' she told him. 'You're quite a catch, you know.'

'I might say the same.'

'So are we having children?'

'I'd like them. I'm sure the lawyers can agree on a formula.'

'That's what we pay them for,' she agreed. There would be no announcement, of course, not until both teams of lawyers had hammered out the basic deal – that was the New Monaco way. It would doubtless take a couple of months negotiating and finalizing the contract, detailing everything, including the number of children they could afford, and the percentage of wealth they'd receive from both sides. After all, who wanted children that fell below New Monaco's citizenship requirement of fifty billion in assets? Not her, that was for sure.

'You know, if we do have a child, I'd like them to have a

mixed company, not just straight money like us, and your raw refineries.'

'A diversification?' he mused. 'That's nice, but you still need a core strategy.'

'I know. I was just thinking aloud.' Dealing with money in isolation was a topic which had begun to trouble her as she slowly started to work with her father in the market. For the DeVoyals it wasn't even money any more, not really, not as billions of ordinary trans-stellar citizens who had bank accounts and secondaries understood – not coins and credit accounts. With her father guiding strategy, their AI manipulated pure binary digits, breeding numbers with other people's numbers. The markets they dealt in were utterly beautiful in their complexity, but at the end of the day they were only left with more numbers. Cause and effect was becoming harder to locate and, with it, relevance.

'That's very sweet,' Housden said. 'You'll make a wonderfully protective mother.'

'Ha! That's just me being practical – I'm not quite at that stage yet. On which topic, I'll tell you now we're having a surrogate for the gestation. Ranietha might think it's romantic and retro-chic carrying a baby round inside her for nine months. But I spend too much money, time, and effort keeping this body on top form to throw all that away.'

'And that top form is very much appreciated, I promise you. Whenever you're around, peptox sales fall dramatically.'

Angela snuggled up closer and gave him another sip from the crystal flute. 'Housden, you don't have to answer this, but are you a one-in-ten?'

He shook his head. 'No babe, I'm not. I was born before that became available. Missed by five years so my father said. Why, does that bother you?'

'Not really, no. Besides, you should be able to rejuvenate soon. They say Bartram is close to proving the procedure.'

He raised a glass. 'Here's hoping.'

They ate the rest of the barbecue as the rocketplanes zoomed round and round overhead. By the time the last race, the champions finale, was over, Angela was back in pocket by three quarters of a million. 'Damnit!' Housden was down one and a half.

'Don't be so grumpy,' she teased. 'Together we're still in front.'

'Yeah, but we're not married yet.'

The fountains began to lower their dancing veil of spray, allowing the guests to see the opposite shore of the lake for the first time. The applause which burst out when they saw the grand finale to the party was long and enthusiastic.

'He's got to be kidding,' Angela said. Above the shore, an incredibly old-fashioned silver rocket crucified by a dozen potent spotlights sat on a big concrete pad. White mist oozed sensually down its frost-webbed sides. An implausibly small blue-grey capsule squatted on top, while the scarlet escape rocket at the apex appeared to be some kind of primitive afterthought. Next to it, the crude gantry tower, which was half cables and pipes, had a thick arm extending out against the capsule.

'No he's not,' Housden replied. 'I heard about this. It's a Mercury Atlas.'

'A what?'

'A space rocket, with a one-man capsule on the top. It's a full-scale replica of the first rocket America used to send an astronaut into orbit. There's a proper network installed instead of the old electronics, and some modern safety systems in the capsule, but essentially it's a 1960s orbital space mission.'

'And it's going to fly?'

'Oh yes, it's real. Matiff's cousin Nanjit is going to do the honours.'

'Nanjit is going to fly into orbit?' she said indignantly. 'That toxhead?'

'He doesn't have to do anything, and it's only a couple of orbits. He'll splash down in the Tanyic Sea, eighty miles away. Matiff imported some boats and recovery helicopters specially for it.'

'Son-of-a-bitch! How much is this costing him?'

'Sixty – seventy million, they said. He had to commission Boeing-Zian to build it for him. It wasn't easy, there aren't any original blueprints left. Their designers had to retro-engineer the capsule and the rocket from museum pieces. Apparently he had to promise to sponsor two exhibitions at the Smithsonian just to get them the kind of access they needed.'

Angela giggled wildly. 'This is going to start a party arms race.' She twisted round to see the elated Prince standing at the front of his grand Bedouin-style pavilion atop the slope, taking bow after bow. That was when she noticed a couple of 2Norths at his side, looking relaxed and contented. There was something wrong with that scene – Northumberland Interstellar and the Prince's family bioil conglomerate weren't quite rivals, but there was no love lost between the two.

Giant projectors came on at the foot of the slope, showing Nanjit getting out of a truck at the base of the gantry tower. He was in a bulky silver spacesuit with a dull-orange bubble helmet. It certainly looked authentic, even down to the ribbed hoses plugged into sockets on his chest that connected to a metal life-support case one of the support team was carrying behind him.

Another cheer went up.

Angela told her e-i to call her father again, using full priority this time. He still didn't respond. Now that was completely wrong. She connected to their estate's AI, and closed her eyes against the crazy Space Race re-enactment so her netlenses could provide a clear visual.

'Is my father in the mansion?' she asked the software.

'Yes, ma'am.'

'Where?'

'In his private study.'

'Use the internal sensors and give me a visual.'

'I am unable to comply.'

'Why?'

'The sensors in that room have been disabled.'

The warmth she'd basked in so adoringly – warmth from

champagne, the evening air, the party, of becoming engaged – deserted her flesh. 'Who disabled them?'

'Your father must have done it. He is the last person I have a record of entering that room.'

'Shit.' She stood abruptly. 'Tell the crew to get my jet ready,' she told her e-i. 'I'm leaving now.'

'What is it?' Housden asked in concern.

'It's Dad, he's deliberately taken himself out of contact.'

'Why would he do that?'

Angela gave him a mildly exasperated shrug.

'Okay, yeah,' he admitted contritely. 'That was stupid of me.'

'It's all right.'

'What are you going to do?'

'Talk to the fool, find out what the matter is.' As she said it she noticed the market alert for bioil had risen to full amber. The surplus coursing into the GE was higher than it had been since 2095, when the formation of the Human Defence Alliance crippled national budgets and plunged the trans-stellar worlds into a recession they still hadn't fully recovered from.

'I'll come with you.'

Angela hesitated. 'That's very gallant, but I can take care of this. You stay and enjoy Nanjit getting blown up.'

'Okay.' He gave her a kiss. 'That's not exactly how I was planning to spend this particular night.'

A chauffeured buggy pulled up beside their table.

'Me neither. I'm sorry, I'll make it up to you. I still haven't worn my leather costume. And I don't intend that to go to waste.'

'I'm going to hold you to that,' he said levelly.

She clambered into the buggy, which drove quickly up the slope. Her e-i told her Prince Matiff was calling. When she glanced over to his lavish pavilion she could see he was leaning on the side of his giant chair, watching her buggy.

Down by the shore, the projectors were focused on Nanjit's elevator as it ascended the gantry tower.

'You're not leaving us now?' the Prince asked.

'Sorry, Matiff, something's come up.'

'The correct form of address to a royal of my rank is: Your Highness.'

What? she mouthed silently. Matiff was developing some serious asshole issues. 'I apologize, but I have to go.'

'I understand.'

Some primitive instinct powered up Angela's concern. When she looked back at the royal pavilion, she saw a 2North chuckling delightedly beside a grinning Matiff. It wasn't a pleasant grin at all.

'Faster,' she told the chauffeur.

They arrived at her plane a few minutes later, a sleek cranked-delta HyperLear LV-505z that could make Mach 3.8 at full throttle. At that speed the DeVoyal estate was barely twenty-five minutes away. She told the pilot to accelerate as hard as they could.

They'd barely gone supersonic when her e-i flashed a red market warning in her netlenses. The GE oil surplus had now been noticed by the general market. Still more was being offered for sale by the seven largest companies working out of St Libra, enough to meet demand for a year to come, in addition to the quantity already held by the futures market. But what really disturbed her wasn't the quantity, which was astonishing, it was the price: the seven producers were keeping level. 'Cartel,' she whispered. The St Libra producers – Northumberland Interstellar and the Great Eight – had collaborated and released a coordinated glut.

Angela gripped the armrests as her muscles knotted, leaving minute platinum traces smeared across the soft leather. Console panes slipped out of the table in front of her, rich with more detailed graphics. And she watched in dismay as bioil prices dropped, and dropped, and kept on heading down. 'Son-of-a-bitch,' she grunted. 'What's our exposure?' she asked the family market AI.

'At the current level, thirty-seven per cent.'

'Son of a motherfucker.' And Dad wasn't doing *anything*,

wasn't buying to try and stabilize the glut, wasn't selling to cut their losses, which were already frightening. *A whole year's worth of bioil for the GE?* It must have taken months – years! – to plan and manufacture this kind of overcapacity.

She could authorize their trading floor dealers, but she didn't have a strategy. Northumberland Interstellar, Matiff, and the others – never silent about how they hated the bioil speculators – were trying to wipe the DeVoyals and all the other bioil commodity traders out of trans-stellar space. The surplus would keep on coming, gushing through the gateway in a tide that all her money could never stop. She ought to contact the other traders, formulate a response. Do we buy it all, do we sell and sink the market? If it sank far enough, would that threaten the producers themselves? Force them to stop? The cartel must have made these same calculations as part of their preparation.

More warnings appeared. The banks were suspending all credit to the DeVoyal finance house.

'No!' she cried. 'No, you can't do that.' Now all she could do was sell their other holdings, try to shore up their repayments. And she knew exactly what would happen if she started taking losses on their other commodity reserves to fund the bioil glut they owned – the banks would start issuing repayment notices.

'What do I do? Dad? *Dad!* Oh fucking hell.'

When the HyperLear landed in front of the DeVoyal mansion, the surplus released by the cartel had driven the trans-stellar bioil market price down to forty-five per cent of what it had been that morning. Angela was scared now, a state she barely recognized. Any attempt at a mass buy-up now simply wasn't going to work, not with these quantities. If you combined the resources of every futures dealer she knew, they still wouldn't have enough money – and the glut showed no sign of slowing down, let alone ending. It was a merciless flood-and-drown operation, superbly organized.

With the price of bioil dropping, the rest of the market was rising. A sustained low energy price was precisely the boost that the trans-stellar economy needed to raise its wings and fly out of the fifteen-year recession. The glut was a wonderful benefit to everybody. Outside the financials, share prices were already adding points, currencies strengthening. She could feel the hope and expectations of all the billions of ordinary people across the trans-stellar worlds: she knew them, their reborn optimism, their excitement kindled by the prospect of change. From Earth's slum-maze cities to the dreary identikit new towns of the trans-stellar worlds, they'd be rejoicing for days, cheering Augustine North and his co-conspirators. Not one of them would ever notice or care that the finance market had changed, had shrunk to accommodate the end of the bioil futures floor. Why should they? The glut was good for them. For a few years, while it lasted, before the new-filled tanks were drained and bioil producers became absolute lords of control, and manipulated their prices as they wished. Nobody cared that a few rich people suffered in the transition; never had, never would.

Like all of New Monaco's residents, Raymond DeVoyal had built himself an enormous mansion at the centre of his ten-thousand-square-mile estate. The main double-H structure had four central courtyards, with a pedimented grand façade sprouting long symmetrical colonnade wings curving away on either side to form an extensive *cour d'honneur*. Gothic-dark tourelles rose from most corners, ringed by tall clerestory windows of stained glass. And at the centre was a hexagonal dome covering a big pool with its own tropical jungle, radiating a bright-emerald light straight up into the night as Angela flew low overhead.

The HyperLear came down on the perfectly level lawn at the end of the west wing. Angela hurried over to a small buggy which one of her father's PAs was driving. They raced under the archway to the left of the main entrance and into a courtyard. Light streamed out of every window, illuminating the square with its prim little garden sections as if the walls had trapped the day's sunlight. Another archway, into the second courtyard, and a smaller door was open at the base of a hexagonal tower.

Angela strode into the broad hallway. This was the private wing, the heart of the mansion, the most extravagant with interiors that put the old French Sun King's palaces to shame. She hesitated as she came into the hall. Nearly thirty of Father's staff were all milling round on the polished oak parquet flooring with its huge inlaid rose of ash and ebony. They wouldn't normally so much as glance her way, let alone stare at her. But now she knew all those worried, helpless expressions as they turned to her. They'd stolen them from her.

A couple of senior PAs and Marlak, their chief legal officer, accompanied her in the elevator up to the fifth floor. Her father's study was a wide circular room, sticking out from the end of the mansion, as if a flying saucer had crashed into the wall and become wedged there. Its walls were completely transparent, giving him a panoramic view out over the grounds and the snow-capped mountains beyond.

Two aides were standing outside, waiting anxiously for her. They couldn't get in because the door wouldn't acknowledge them, yet the security system was fully functional. Angela put her hand in the scanspace while her e-i sent her personal code into the network. The doors swung back smoothly.

Raymond DeVoyal had known. He'd known because he'd spent the whole sixty-three years of his adult life dealing in commodities, and specializing in bioil. He knew because his intelligence gathering far outstripped anyone else in the field. He knew because the family AI's expensive, exclusive genetic algorithms were plugged into private sensors in the trans-stellar pipe network, they sampled the money flow between banks and bioil companies, they absorbed and extrapolated tiny whispers from a thousand personal contacts in the industry. Trends were spotted weeks if not months in advance of competitors and rivals. DeVoyal was a trademark of excellence for commodities, always in profit, always an investment leader. Ahead of the game for centuries.

So with all his knowledge and ability, two days ago Raymond had spotted the unexplained surge of bioil flowing through the GE pipes network – unexplained and unallocated. He declined Prince Matiff's party in order to track the origin and the finance and the buyer. After an hour he knew it wasn't coming from Orleans. The Newcastle gateway was the culprit, and the more he searched, the more flow volume he uncovered, and the more the pattern became apparent. Then came the lack of deviation on the spot market, with every St Libra bioil producer charging the same price, and fulfilling the cautious orders which started to come in. He knew the trend before anyone else. He who tried to call Augustine North personally, only to have the call rejected. He whose unrivalled understanding of the market realized a cartel had been assembled in quiet meetings and agreements that didn't exist in any memory store, and he guessed what its terrible end game was. He saw its size. He knew the political power behind it.

Granted this insight, he carefully disabled the cameras and sensors inside the study. Sat in his favourite antique wingback chair to watch the sun sinking behind the splendid mountains on the horizon, sipped a century-old brandy and bumped a tox, and another tox. And another, and another . . .

Angela put her hand to his cheek, refusing to believe even though he was cold to the touch. Unmoving. His eyes wide open. Flesh pale and stiffening in rigor. Refused to believe, because that power of the mind would make all this unreal. Refusal would make Daddy be alive still.

With slow whispering insistence, reality broke through the stubborn denial. Angela DeVoyal sank to her knees beside her dead father, and for the first time in over a decade, she started sobbing.

Monday 11th March 2143

Sid didn't get out of Market Street Station until after nine o'clock. When he did it was like fleeing the scene. His fellow detectives had written him off. They nodded as he passed them in corridors, then there'd be the backward looks, the muttering, shaken heads. He could see it all without having to look.

'It's over.'

'Ah man, did you hear? He's blown it.'

'O'Rouke is going to fucking crucify him.'

'His fault they're going to cut overtime for the rest of the year, the stupid turd. Did you hear how much he's spent? We're the ones who'll suffer.'

'Man, they set him up good.'

Monday was a day spent doing two days' work, checking everything, reviewing, revising. Five hours spent in the zone theatre, going meticulously through the backtrack, taking more and more time – as if he was trying to postpone the inevitable, so the whispers went. Not true, he just had to make sure there were no screw-ups, not now. More hours in Office3, enduring the accusatory silence from what was left of the team.

Their backtrack still hadn't found the taxi. *Everything* hinged on that. They'd covered all the other lines – the imported freight manifests, the forensics. None of it had produced any kind of lead. There were only three taxis left to check when he finally called it a day, handing over to the night shift. Telling them to call him *the instant* they found one loading up with the North's body.

The right taxi being in the last three was so statistically implausible as to be impossible. But he wasn't going to call it off now – might just as well jump into the Tyne himself.

Even though he'd promised Jacinta he'd be home hours ago to help pack, he drove round to Falconar Street and parked at the north end. The door lock on Ian's flat flashed purple when Sid's e-i pinged it. He frowned at the small panel, and called Ian direct.

'All right, man, give me a minute,' Ian replied.

So Sid had to wait on the doorstep as a cool wind sent the thin drizzle splatting against his leather jacket. Finally the lock turned green, and Sid pushed the door open.

He might have guessed. Ian had a girl in the flat – a tall, skinny lass in her early twenties. She was standing in the lounge as he barged in, worming her feet into trainers. And the whinge he had ready shrivelled up and died in embarrassment.

'Sorry, didn't know,' he muttered to Ian, who was standing with her, dressed in a towelling robe. Sid hated the impression he must be giving her, like he was Ian's dad instead of a real grown-up.

'It's okay, man,' Ian said. 'This is Joyce.'

'Hiya, pet,' she said, smiling.

Another girl came out of the darkened bedroom, doing up her lumberjack shirt.

'And this is Sammi,' Ian said.

Now Sid really was coming off like an old-time dad: dumb-struck, and, yes, just a tiny bit jealous. When he risked a glance at Ian he saw the proud gleam in his partner's eye, and knew Ian was quietly content about all of this, that it added neatly to the reputation of the station's grade-A superstud.

'Hello,' Sid said like a true nerd.

Sammi wasn't anything like as chipper as Joyce. She just gave Sid a sulky look from behind her chaotic strands of hair and reached for a coat that was lying on the lounge floor. Police

450

instinct told him that grouch wasn't because he'd interrupted, but more like resentment he hadn't arrived earlier.

Ian kissed Joyce, who responded keenly. 'I'll call you,' he told Sammi. Her lip curled up in sullen animosity, and she pushed her way out of the lounge. Joyce gave Ian a last kiss as Sammi's boots stomped down the stairs. 'I'll talk to her,' she promised, and hurried out.

'Everything all right?' Sid asked.

Ian grinned lecherously. 'Aye, man; what do you think?'

'I think Sammi wasn't very happy.' And this wasn't the conversation he'd ever wanted, let alone tonight.

'Aye, well, it was her first time. You know what they get like.'

'First . . . ?' Sid spluttered.

'In a threebie, man, in a threebie.'

'Ah. Oh, right.' *And no, I've no idea.*

'Beer?'

Of all people, police shouldn't drink and drive. But the auto could take him home easily enough, just slowly, carefully avoiding the cars on manual. 'Sure.'

Ian opened the fridge, and produced a couple of bottles. Sid took his, and slumped down in his usual place.

'I can't believe we screwed up last night so bad,' Sid said.

'Last Mile is a stone-age maze. The traders like it that way, they rip and burn any new smartdust the city applies. It was always going to be dodgy, man.'

'Yeah, I know,' he sighed. 'I just thought we were owed some luck. It's not asking for much. We've had bugger-all so far.'

'So nothing from the zone theatre this evening, then?'

'No. And tomorrow I'm going to be facing O'Rouke.'

'He can't dump it all on you. He put you in charge of the investigation.'

Sid knew what Ian was thinking, that the investigation would go on – politically it had to – but O'Rouke would appoint one of his cronies to head it up, prove to the people he had to answer to that he was faithfully doing all he could. That Sid was the one who'd screwed up. 'No! No other bugger would step up and take it, that's what happened.' Though now he was wondering if they'd been quietly warned off.

'But they won't close it. Not a murdered North and all this alien monster bollocks.'

'Maybe you're right.' Sid took a deep swig from the bottle. 'So what fallout have we got from our Mr Sherman and his merry men?'

Ian gave him an uncomfortable grimace. 'Aye, well, you might have been right about Boz making you. None of them have used their original e-i access codes since the exchange last night.'

'Oh crap on it.'

'Except Jede. He stood in the middle of Monument at two o'clock this afternoon, and made three calls, all to petty criminals we've got on the police database. Nothing criminal mentioned in the calls, but he made them using a new e-i access code.'

'Where we could see him, and check the local transnet cells?'

'Aye.'

'So they know we're on them, and they want to find out who we are.'

'Looks like he was setting bait for us, boss, aye.'

'Shit.'

'If they suspect we're on them, we're going to need more than the surveillance routines we have been running.'

Sid took another swig. 'Aye, I know.'

'What do you want to do?'

'It was a B North that we hauled out of the Tyne, the socks prove that. It was a Newcastle gang that dumped him in the Tyne, which to my mind confirms some kind of dark corporate involvement. My old contact tells me something big is going down, so whatever this corporate shit is, it's still going on.'

'Man, it's too big for us,' Ian said softly. 'I'm sorry, but you've got to know when to quit.'

'Yeah,. I suppose.' He still couldn't get over the A Norths. Aldred and Augustine himself had looked him in the eye and said they wanted the killer found. Why would they do that if they were the ones responsible? Trouble was, he just didn't know enough about their family, and how they really regarded each other. Murdering your own clone brother had to be the last taboo, surely? But then he'd been in the police long enough to see some pretty sick stuff go down, and not just in the GSWs.

'You can't decide tonight,' Ian said. 'We need to know how the backtrack plays out. You never know...'

'Oh, I do. I really do.' Sid finished his beer. 'See you in the morning.'

Tuesday 12th March 2143

It ended on Rothbury Terrace in Heaton. Sid stood in the zone, with his legs vanishing into the bright greenery of Heaton Park. That gave him a perfect viewpoint of the taxi reversing into the street as the virtual simulation wound steadily backwards. Here the macromesh was intact, and the vehicle licence code had remained the same for the whole time they'd observed it – there was no mistake, no shady grey margin of error. Now Sid towered over the neat road, hands on hips as he watched the driver get out and walk the funny backward walk into a house at the west end of Rothbury Terrace.

'Pause it.'

'That's where he lives,' Dedra Foyster said.

Sid glanced over at the window, seeing Ian staring out at the virtual with a professionally blank face. Seeing Chloe Healy and Jenson San at the back of the control room; both in smart dark suits, saying nothing, but channelling their boss's anger very efficiently.

Tellingly, Aldred 2North wasn't present. And if his support was being taken away . . .

'Do we know how long the taxi was parked here?' Sid pointed down at the offending citycab.

Dedra and Lorelle went into a huddle, hands fluttering within their keyspace.

'Seven hours, boss,' Dedra said with an apologetic shrug.

'Uh huh.' So Sid had just seen the driver begin his shift, the driver who was clean, with a taxi that was correctly licensed. A legitimate taxi they'd watched pick up and drop customers for five hours. A taxi that hadn't collected a corpse from any-where, nor delivered one to Elswick Wharf. The last of two hundred and seven taxis. Their final chance to develop a proper lead. 'Looks like we've been crapped on from heaven itself,' he muttered.

'Detective Hurst, can we have a word,' Jenson San said.

Sid wanted to say no, a petulant, childish, pathetic: No. Because he knew exactly what this talk would be, so really what was the point?

'Take a break,' he told his team. 'We'll review after lunch.'

The simulation winked off, leaving him in the blank zone theatre by himself. He watched everybody file out of the control room, several shooting defeated glances his way. Ian hesitated, but Sid inclined his head, and his partner was gone.

Chloe Healy and Jenson San came into the theatre.

'You fucked up,' Jenson San snapped.

'Speak to me like that again, and you'll wake up in hospital you little brown-nose bastard.'

'All right boys!' Chloe said, holding her hands up at both of them. 'The backtrack didn't work. Sid, why not?'

'I don't know. We know a taxi was used to carry the body, the bloody thing is still sitting in the forensics lab. It had to drive down to Elswick Wharf somehow.'

'Your team was sloppy,' Jenson San said. 'They missed it. It's that simple – you missed the damn thing!'

'So you agree the virtual was the right way to progress the investigation, then?' Sid asked snidely. He was furious and frus-trated, and needed to vent somehow. It would only be a minor assault charge anyway.

'Under proper leadership, it probably would have been.'

'Get me the people I want and we'll run it again.'

'You're blaming your people now?' Jenson San asked smugly.

Sid felt his hand closing up into a fist.

'We're not running it again,' Chloe said firmly. 'This investigation needs a different approach. Sid, go and prepare a summary. O'Rouke wants it by the end of the day shift. We need to see how to move forward from this.'

Sid wanted to say something, have some answer that would vindicate him and his team. Truth was, he'd still do it all the same. He'd followed procedure perfectly. There was no new angle, unless you counted Sherman – which they'd also blown out there in the wretched muddle that was Last Mile. 'Right,' he said, 'I'll get onto it.' Because there was nothing else left. The murderer had won, had outsmarted him and his entire team.

He left the theatre and walked down the corridor to the lifts. Nobody in the corridor looked at him. Ian and Eva weren't waiting. The lift doors slid shut. His hand paused over the buttons, finger pointing at the third floor.

'Fuck this!'

He jabbed the button for the underground garage, level two. No way was he going to give that little turd Jenson San the satisfaction. Besides, they were wrong. His team hadn't made mistakes. They were good people, devoting weeks to one task because they'd been enthused, convinced that the taxi backtrack was the one thing that could crack the case wide open. He'd known it, too, manoeuvring Elston to get the theatre up and running again no matter what it cost him with O'Rouke. *I'm right, crap on it. I am!*

*

Sid parked his car on Water Street, just down from the iron railway bridge, relic of centuries gone by. There probably hadn't been a train pass across it for a hundred years. Yet the city continued to maintain it, a precious heritage of iron and rust-worn rivets, with twenty layers of paint sun-bleached to a pastel blue and pocked with burst blisters dribbling iron flake mucus down the graffiti-grimed sides. Thick stone supports on either side of the road were still sound despite the webbing of cracks and crumbling cement joins, not even three metres high, with

456

arched pedestrian walkways on either side reeking of urine and dog faeces.

He got out of the car and turned his jacket collar up against the breeze. Newcastle's cloudless sky was a bright translucent turquoise, with the horizon frosted by a pale haze as the weather prepared to shift out of winter into a short wet spring. Rainwater was still trickling along the gutter, down the sharp slope of Water Street towards the Tyne. He stood with his back to the bridge and studied the construction site above Elswick Wharf. It was two months now since they'd hauled the North out of the river and found the little alley where the taxi had parked to dump him. Now that the snow and ice constricting the scaffolding and gantry beams had melted away, automata had resumed work on the luxury apartment block. A couple of cement lorries were parked outside waiting, while another was backed into the alley which the taxi had used, fat manky hoses plugged into its pumps so it could feed its load up to the gridwork which was soon to be the fifth floor.

After two months in the theatre zone, Sid knew the area by heart, the businesses occupying every yard and shed, the roads, the line of the riverbank. The theatre virtual had a gloss that was lacking out here in reality. Here the buildings were shabbier, the colours dull, the strips of grass yellow and flattened from the snow that had covered them for the last four months. Even so, it was the same. And they'd covered it all.

'So how the fuck did you do it?' Sid asked the bleak, semi-forgotten district.

He started walking, heading along Railway Terrace, with the stone embankment wall on one side topped by a dishevelled wilderness of bushes and trees, and the dilapidated railings of the company yards on the other. Under another antique railway bridge on Dunn Street, just as decrepit as the last one, but with broad curving steps on one side that led up to Cuttings Garden. Along Railway Street which had the rear entrances to another row of small companies huddled in their tumbledown frame and panel buildings, a refuge for the machines and electronics and crafts of previous generations. Behind them, further downslope, he could make out the curving roof of the City Arts Arena, which was covered in scaffolding and automata as it underwent a full refurbishment, bringing it up to the latest venue standards. He walked the length of Railway Street, hunched against the damp air, until he came to Plummer Street, then he doubled back, walking along the side of the A695 dual carriageway that was the Scotswood Road. Traffic here was a monotonous buzz of fuel-cell vehicles, churning up a mist-like spray that beaded his leather jacket as he trudged along the crumbling tarmac pavement. The Fortin singletown loomed up on his right, a drab carbon cliff inset with blank silvered windows that emitted no light. On his side of the road were the garage showrooms and the big stores of semi-industrial products, the refrigeration units and power cells and automata and engineering tools and retail fittings that a city like Newcastle bought in quantity. A prosperous stretch of road then, shielding the motorist's eye from the grungy old-style industry that occupied the slope behind it.

Sid had no idea what he was doing, other than confronting his enemy. This was where he'd been defeated, here among the decaying tarmac and obsolete buildings. Somehow they'd been utilized to fool and mock him. Secret tunnels. Microgateways. Something! There had to be something here they'd all missed. His ridiculous, doomed, observation in Last Mile on Sunday night had triggered the conviction: not everything is on the map.

He reached the Peperelli scooter showroom. There was a narrow alley between it and the Kiano car showroom next door, leading back down to Water Street. He glanced down it, seeing the washed-blue bridge. Footpath only – no way you could drive a taxi down there. He plodded onwards, past the glass windows sheltering the cheap cars imported from Taiyuan, one of the Unified Chinese Worlds. Between the showroom and the U-Fix budget DIY store next door was a little lane at right angles to the A695, a lane that led round to the compound at the back of the Kiano showroom, and the U-Fix loading bay. Sid hesitated, and slowly walked down towards the ivy-swamped chain-link mesh

458

that sealed off the compound from Cuttings Garden. His e-i sent out a ping, but the damp tarmac below his feet didn't have any smartdust, wasn't part of the city macromesh. Sid pressed his face against the wobbly chain-link mesh, peering through the ivy and thorny strands of bramble on the other side.

They'd never checked it back in January. Never seen that under a metre of snow it was a blank wilderness. Never seen this end of Cuttings Garden from the Water Street Bridge to the Regal bioil station at the end had been cleared of plants and benches and paths and ponds and the visitor information centre. Never saw it had been bulldozed flat in preparation for development.

Never queried it during two hundred and seven taxi back-tracks because on the simulation the template from the city planning office still showed it as Cuttings Garden, the sweet little urban greenland amenity. And if the template said so . . .

Sid shoved his fingers through the mesh, and pulled *hard*. The whole fence swayed back, and one of the wooden posts lifted off the ground. It was rotten, broken off at ground level. Those thick gnarly strands of ivy that wove through the mesh were just about all that held the fence in place now.

'Oh yeah,' Sid growled. He rattled the fence again, feeling his heart pound furiously as the mesh bobbed about limply. 'You smart, smart bastards. Oh that was good. That was so very good.'

Wednesday 13th March 2143

Sid didn't need the alarm clock to wake up. He'd been lying on the bed with his eyes open since at least six o'clock, shifting from his back to his side, trying not to pull the duvet about too much. In truth, he hadn't slept much at all that night. His mind was too busy, too excited. He hadn't got back home until after midnight, and even when he did sneak into bed he couldn't resist playing the small visual file over and over through his iris smartcells. Just to make absolutely sure. It had taken hours of data mining to secure the final proof he was going to need to confront O'Rouke with, and he wasn't about to assign anyone else to the task. Abner or Dedra could probably have found the data and run the image filters in less than an hour. Sid didn't want them involved. He was the one O'Rouke had set up. Now he'd put it together. Today was the day Sid Hurst turned it all around. And that felt wonderful.

He watched the luminous figures on the clock head towards seven o'clock, and reached over to switch the alarm off. The movement was too big. Jacinta groaned and stirred. Those enchanting green eyes peered at him as if confused by what she saw.

'What time did you get in?' she asked.

'Late. Sorry.'

'How bad is it? You look happy. Did you find the taxi?'

'It's good. I've cracked the case.'

She shuffled up onto her elbows. 'The backtrack worked?'

'Not quite.'

'But—'

'Hey, have a little faith.' He leaned over and kissed her.

'Sid!' It wasn't exactly a protest. They kissed again, moving closer as blood heated. Hands pushed impatiently at the duvet, shoving it down. He started unbuttoning her PJs, slower now, heady with promise. Jacinta's chortle was enthusiastic and amazingly dirty.

Thudding feet rampaged down the short landing outside. Ending as the bathroom door was slammed shut.

'But I was first,' Zara wailed in end-of-the-world torment. Her little fists beat against the bathroom door in rage. 'Let me in, ya dosshead.'

'Stuff you,' Will called out happily.

Sid started laughing. He disentangled himself.

Jacinta just rolled her eyes and sighed. 'Ah well. At least I got to remember what it was like.'

Sid climbed out of the bed. Looked around in puzzlement at the cases and boxes which took up most of the floor. Yesterday's clothes were slung over a pile of plastic cartons printed with the removal firm's logo. 'Er . . . where?'

'Clean shirts in the blue case,' Jacinta pointed, then started shoving clips into her hair.

'Thanks. Um, socks?'

She gave him an exasperated look. 'If you were here to help, as you keep saying you will be—'

'I know. I'm a pig. But, pet, this is so close to over.'

'You're very certain about that, aren't you?'

'Yeah.'

'Mum!' Zara cried. 'Will's finished, but he won't come out. He's doing it deliberately.'

'Am not!' Will's muffled voice claimed indignantly.

'I'll get it,' Sid said blithely, which earned him another curious look from Jacinta.

Breakfast was a glass of orange juice and a Marmite toast

sandwich packet lifted from the fridge and shoved into the microwave. He noticed there wasn't much of anything left in the fridge.

'You should eat better,' Jacinta said as she poured cereal into bowls for their feuding children.

'I'll get a proper lunch,' Sid claimed, knowing there'd be no chance. Today was yesterday revisited, yesterday as it should have been. He hadn't felt this upbeat in ages. 'But I've got to get into the station early.'

Will and Zara had both started eating their cereal. Jacinta gave them a careful glance, before fixing Sid with her gaze. 'You do remember we're moving on Saturday, don't you, pet,' she said in a low, warning voice.

'Aye, man. I know. Some credit, please.'

'Good. Because you're here on Friday helping me finish the packing, then we've got to clean this place top to bottom.'

'We can get a firm in to do that. We're not broke, and you deserve a break.'

'Sid . . .' She was genuinely worried now.

He went over and kissed her. 'I mean it. Now, I've got to go. And I'll probably be late again tonight. But I'll call and let you know, I promise.'

'You are all right, aren't you, pet? The North case?'

'I'm good. And tonight I'll sit down and tell you all about it.'

*

Sid was mildly surprised when the lift took him up to Market Street's sixth floor. You had to press the button and have your e-i enter a code. He wouldn't have put it past O'Rouke to restrict him, especially after he went walkabout yesterday afternoon – then told his e-i to refuse all calls from his police colleagues while he sat in an empty office on the second floor to datamine until late into the evening.

O'Rouke's PA protested when he walked into the corner office's ante-room, but Sid simply ignored the bluster about appointments and a full diary and following protocol. 'I'll wait,' he said, and went over to the window to watch the drizzle soaking early commuters scuttling along Pilgrim Street.

Sure enough, O'Rouke arrived at eight fifteen, as he did every morning. Dressed in his immaculate uniform, tailored to de-emphasize the gut, with gold braid shining on his shoulders. Head down and scowling as he stomped across the ante-room towards the safety of his office. Obviously pre-warned Sid was stalking him, there was no attempt at eye contact or acknow-ledgement. Jenson San was with him, like some kind of wingman interceptor ready to thwart any attempt Sid might make to plead for more time.

'Good morning, sir, I need to see you,' Sid announced in an annoyingly sprightly voice. He knew he should be aiming for conciliation, but what the hell . . .

O'Rouke kept on going for the sanctuary of his office. He didn't quite hesitate, but it was close, because he knew Sid just didn't have any right to be that confident.

'I know who did it,' Sid said.

O'Rouke hadn't quite made it to his office door. This time he hesitated. Fatal.

'You know shit,' Jenson San said. 'You didn't even file a summary as you were ordered. That's a disciplinary offence. Another one on your woeful record.'

'My report will go direct to Ralph Stevens,' Sid said. 'I have his personal and direct interface code. Do you really want the HDA to be told I know how to solve the case and you blocked it?'

'I'm not blocking anything, you useless turd,' O'Rouke barked.

'Good, then I need to run the theatre simulation one last time.'

O'Rouke took a step towards Sid, his ruddy face darkening, highlighting the web of tiny blue veins on his nose and cheeks. 'You think I don't know who manoeuvred Elston into reactivat-ing that theatre? Did you think that was funny? Did you?'

'I don't think it was funny. I needed it. I got it. That's all that matters. Same as this.'

O'Rouke was silent for a moment as he considered his options. 'What the fuck have you got?'

Sid gave a pointed glance at the PA, then Jenson San. 'This case is classified as high as anything ever can be.'

O'Rouke's mouth squashed to a bloodless line. Sid half-expected to hear teeth grinding.

'Get in here,' O'Rouke snapped and stomped into his office.

Sid grinned a taunt at Jenson San and followed O'Rouke in. The door closed and the blue seal came on. Windows turned opaque.

'You've got some balls,' O'Rouke said grudgingly as he sat in his desk chair.

'Because I can back it up. We both knew this was going to be a pig right from the start.'

'Don't I fucking know it? The Mayor isn't even taking calls from me any more. Scrupsis won't *stop* calling me. Those HDA shits still haven't paid us a single Eurofranc. And I've got you spending money like a New Monaco parasite.'

'Parasites don't produce anything useful.'

'All right, enough with the fucking gloating. What did you find yesterday after you walked out on your team? And it better be good.'

'The map is not the territory.'

'What?'

'They outsmarted me. That's what happened. They know our procedures, the gangs always have done. And they were ready for us. Look, you've just murdered a North – a North for fuck's sake! – and you know that's going to bring a universe of turds tumbling down on you, since the resources the police are going to devote to the case will be phenomenal. But you fool us into thinking the bodydump was ordinary, that you're going by the numbers, just like the investigation. It was a decoy. The ripped meshes, the burn-out in the GSW district. All designed to show us they were playing their side of the game straight down the middle. A taxi drives to Elswick Wharf, throws the body in the Tyne, and drives out to the GSW where it's firebombed. We know that happened.

So we devote everything we have to finding that taxi driving to Elswick. And I mean everything: money, political clout, man-hours, AI time. There's never been a simulation this big before, it's unheard of, it simply doesn't get any more impressive. But they know what we're looking for, they guided us into thinking they'd buggered the roads and surveillance across the city so they could sneak the taxi in there without us being able to confirm it. And we – I – fell for it.'

'All right, smartarse, so what did happen?'

Sid told his e-i to activate one of O'Rouke's wallscreens. A map centred on Water Street materialized.

'We tracked every taxi that went into that general area for two hours before the body was dumped on Sunday night. That's how we got our two hundred and seven. But we didn't count them back out again. Why would we? We knew it had to be one of them – after all, we found it in the GSW. If we had counted them out we'd have found the discrepancy. They pulled a switch on us.'

He pointed at the western side of Cuttings Garden, standing above the Armstrong Industrial Park. 'This isn't a community park any more. It was sold off last August to a developer, a typical dodgy Newcastle property deal, with the council selling off public land to the highest bidder, and no doubt a few backhanders pumped into secondaries because of it. But it's still on the City database as Cuttings Garden because they haven't filed their planning application yet. So in our simulation it's still a park. All the developer did was clear the site as they're entitled to do. And they did that last September, by cutting a road through these trees behind the Armstrong Industrial Park and driving their bulldozers up it. A temporary dirt track that also isn't on any kind of registry. In other words, there was a way down from the embankment and straight to Elswick Wharf in the area where there isn't a single working mesh. And this chain-link fence here, the one at the end of the lane that leads round the back of the Kiano showroom, it's easier to move than a bloody gate. I actually went there in person, I checked it out.

I could push it down with my hand, never mind driving a citycab over it. Now look at this.'

He told his e-i to change the file. A grainy blue-grey image appeared, showing a dual carriageway with snow falling on it. Buildings along the side were indistinct shadows. Streetlighting was poor. Vehicles were blobs with headlight beams crawling along. 'They ripped and burned the macromesh at the A695 junction with Park Road, which is almost level with this lane. Meshes which give a visual on this stretch of road were also ripped. But I found this last night after two hours searching the logs we didn't access before; it's a visual from the mesh on a timber yard on Georges Road, five hundred metres away. They didn't bother to rip it – it's got a piss-poor angle and worse resolution because it wasn't set up to look down the A695. But even with all those disadvantages, it does actually give us a glimpse at the lane. You're seeing an enhanced image here. Now this is ten oh three Sunday night.'

The e-i illuminated a pair of headlights coming out of Park Road with a purple bracket. 'As far as our preparative analysis of the macromesh showed, this taxi drove down Park Road and took a right turn onto the A695, carrying on westward. The macromesh around the junction was ripped, but that didn't matter, because the taxi licence is the same, from when it enters the rip and then again thirty-two seconds later when it leaves it. All the simulation data shows us a taxi driving along normally, so there's nothing to check. We didn't include it in our list of two hundred and seven. Why should we?'

He told his e-i to play the image. O'Rouke leaned forward. The double splash of the taxi's headlights turned right onto the A695, then took a sharp left into the lane. The headlights vanished. But another vehicle swung out onto the A695 at the same time. 'Another citycab, same licence code,' Sid said. 'They synchronized the switch perfectly. They probably parked the re-placement decoy there on Saturday, after all they spent the whole day preparing the bluff for us.'

O'Rouke nodded at the screen, his eyes never leaving the

bright glimmer of the headlights. 'Run the theatre simulation again,' he said in an angry whisper. 'Find that motherfucker and bring him to me.'

*

This time the zone theatre control room was packed. This time people wanted to be there, wanted a part of what was happening. News of Sid confronting O'Rouke that morning had been round Market Street Station within seconds. Then the private meeting was over, and Sid had authorization to reactivate the big theatre simulation . . .

So the original investigation team were there, with Dedra and Eva on the consoles. Ian standing to one side, along with Abner and Ari. Lorelle was there, completely ignoring Chloe Healy and Jenson San, who were standing right next to her. Right at the front, with his breath misting the glass, O'Rouke was watching Sid himself wading through the knee-high photonic cityscape as he backtracked the taxi through the tangle of those snowy Sunday night streets. Aldred 2North had arrived at Market Street just as they began running the simulation, standing behind O'Rouke's shoulder, watching intently.

The image unwound five seconds at a time, allowing Sid and Dedra and Eva to check and confirm the log data each time, ensuring they were still watching the same taxi, that it hadn't changed its licence code, that there hadn't been another switch.

'You've done this for two hundred and seven taxis?' O'Rouke asked. 'Just like this, stopping and checking?'

'Yes, sir,' Ian said.

'Bloody hell. That's . . . good work.'

'Thank you, sir.'

Sid heard the exchange, but held his tongue. O'Rouke had put him back on probation, pending the outcome of this backtrack. Sid knew it would work out okay, but there was no point in deliberately antagonizing the Chief Constable. He still had a way to go before he could claim his grade-five detective's pension and take up Aldred's job offer. Though, actually, O'Rouke's job would

467

be opening up in a couple of years. No! That was unthinkable – the politics, the backstabbing, the deals.

After forty-three minutes working the simulation, Sid watched the taxi slip down a ramp on Stanhope Street which led to an underground garage beneath the huge St James singletown. The time on the log was nine fifty-one. He froze the image as the taxi was half out of view down the concrete slope, and gave the bonnet a knowing smile. 'This is it,' he said softly. The taxi hadn't stopped anywhere, hadn't picked up or dropped off any passenger. 'This is where they collected the body.'

'Are you sure?' O'Rouke asked dubiously.

'It drove from here directly to make the Cuttings Garden switch; this has to be it. Even if it isn't, we can always backtrack it further. But for now I want every log from every grain of smartdust in the St James singletown, running from the Thursday before the murder to Monday morning.'

'Aye, man, I'll get down there myself,' Ian said. 'A little personal contact with the security office always smooths the way, and that's a lot of data we're asking for.'

'Yeah, good call, man, get on it,' Sid said. He glanced at O'Rouke. 'I think we need to finalize strategy, sir.'

*

'That was a real phoenix flight you pulled off this morning,' Aldred said in the lift on the way to the sixth floor. Having him along made Sid feel a whole lot safer.

'A phoenix?'

'Rising out of the ashes.'

'I told you he was the man,' O'Rouke said. 'Right back at the start. I said our Sid would crack this for you.'

'I do remember,' Aldred said. 'But nonetheless, that was impressive.'

'The map is not the territory,' Sid explained.

'That's what I tell all my detectives on their orientation day,' O'Rouke said. 'Set them straight, get their heads screwed on right to begin with.'

'We rely too much on data analysis,' Sid said, brave enough to ignore the Chief Constable. 'We don't get our hands dirty any more. It allowed the gang to take advantage of us.'

Aldred gave him an approving nod. 'Well that's just come to an end.'

This time Sid was offered a seat opposite O'Rouke's desk as the windows turned opaque. With Aldred in the chair next to him, he knew whatever he asked for would be granted.

'We need to have absolutes now,' he said. 'So I want all the logs Ian collects from the St James singletown to be worked into a simulation. I'll need agency help formatting the memories, and a lot of AI time.'

'I'll clear that for you,' O'Rouke said.

'Thank you. But what I really need to know is what to do about our two observers, Stevens and Scrupsis? I'm supposed to update both of them immediately we have a critical development, and this certainly counts. We do have to tell them, but I really don't think we deserve interference now.'

'Inform them both together,' Aldred said. 'Let them battle for jurisdiction. I'll have a word with Augustine, he'll know who to call; we need to make sure they don't ruin this by having a turf war that attracts attention in Brussels. We haven't got the taxi driver yet. And we can't let him slip away from us now. This situation must remain absolutely secure.'

'Working up another simulation should help,' O'Rouke said. 'It'll damp down expectations around the station.'

'There's something you need to know,' Aldred said.

Sid gave the North a surprised sideways glance. He didn't like the tone at all – it verged on embarrassment, which was completely wrong for any North, let alone Aldred. O'Rouke, whose political awareness was infinitely greater than Sid's, also stiffened up. 'Anything you contribute will be valuable,' the Chief Constable said in a neutral voice.

'I live in the St James singletown. A penthouse in the South Wing.'

'I see,' Sid said, trying to work through implications. Legally,

Aldred probably couldn't continue as their case liaison, any defence lawyer would argue his presence was prejudicial, a potential evidence contaminant. But then this was never entirely about what would go to court.

'In fact there are several of my brothers living in the St James,' Aldred said. 'I suppose it's inevitable. The place is exclusive, and slap in the centre of town. It's perfect for us.'

'It might have some implications on the case,' O'Rouke said carefully. 'From a purely legal perspective. Detective?'

Oh, thank you. 'Do you have an alibi for the Friday of the murder?' Sid asked with a level voice.

'An alibi?' Aldred lifted both eyebrows.

'Yes, sir. As soon as we can confirm that, then we can show any defence lawyer reviewing our logs that there's no prejudicial influence involved.'

'Ah, I understand. Actually, I was in London that day, taking some meetings. Let's see.' He muttered something to his e-i. 'I left the St James in my car that morning at 9:45, drove straight to my department's headquarters. My helicopter was booked and on the roof pad, so I flew down to London. My e-i can give you the meeting schedule, along with the names and contact codes for everyone in the meetings. I flew back up to Newcastle at ten that night. Got back to the St James about one o'clock Saturday morning.'

Sid nodded with considerable relief. 'That's easy enough to check. Let me have the files, and the licence code of the car you used, and I'll have Eva run a confirmation. Shouldn't take her more than an hour.'

'Excellent.'

'You get this sorted out fast,' O'Rouke said.

'Yes, sir.'

'So could the victim be one of the St James residents?' O'Rouke asked.

'No, sir,' Sid said. 'Every A North is accounted for.'

'So is it significant the murder happened in a singletown where several of the brothers live?'

'We'll know more when we have the taxi driver in custody and identify the precise location of the murder.' Sid hated giving non-answers like that, but after this long in the force they slid so easily off the tongue.

'Okay. I want every update as it happens.'

'Of course. There is one thing,' Sid said, and resisted the smile at how he was suddenly the centre of attention. This kind of political trading was what these two knew best.

'What is it, Detective?'

'Once we've identified the taxi driver, I'd like my team to perform the arrest,' Sid said. 'They deserve that. They've worked their arses off for over two months now.'

Aldred and O'Rouke exchanged a glance.

'Fair enough,' O'Rouke said. 'I'll front the press conference afterwards to announce that we have a suspect in custody, and I'll make sure you get full credit.'

It was all Sid could do not to laugh out loud. O'Rouke knew every trick in the file, and played them all ruthlessly. 'Thank you, sir.'

Thursday 14th March 2143

Sid should have known it wasn't going to be that easy. Ian had called as soon as he reached the massive singletown to say the building had suffered a sustained rip attack on the Saturday in question. The electronic support company St James employed to maintain their network hadn't fully restored the meshes until Monday lunchtime.

But Sid's breakthrough had inspired the team. They got creative.

Sid stood in Office3's virtual booth, and stared at the poor-resolution image that filled the air around him. It showed a big lobby with tall plants, expensive black and blue marble walls, with thick pillars supporting a ribbed vault roof. 'What am I looking at?' he asked.

'The personal visual log from Vicky Thellwell, who's the receptionist on the main desk,' Eva said. 'It's a security thing. The St James upgrades the smartcells of employees who deal with their residents and important clients. Their visual log from all the time they're on the premises is stored in a secure cache for five years in case legal need it.'

'Okay,' Sid said. 'Run it.'

At nine twenty-seven pm on Sunday the thirteenth January, Vicky Thellwell was dealing with a young couple who were checking in to one of the St James' three luxury boutique hotels. Personal visuals always made Sid slightly giddy, and this was no exception. Vicky's eyeballs seemed to dart about like a humming-bird. Smiling at the couple, looking down at her keyspace, a display pane, scanning the lobby for the porters, back to the couple, a glance at how much luggage they'd wheeled in, slightly longer look at the man, concentrating on his face (Sid supposed he was quite handsome), a track down his clothes (presumably assessing style and price).

'Here it comes,' Eva warned.

Behind the couple, one of the lift doors opened. There was a man inside, with a very large wheeled luggage bag. Three people got in, and the doors slid shut. The image froze in a smear of light: as the doors closed Vicky was looking away.

'Maybe,' Sid said reluctantly. 'The bag he's got could be big enough.'

'We calculated the size and volume,' Eva said. 'It's big enough.'

'Okay, granted, and the time is about right. Do we know if the lift was going up or down?'

'We couldn't check,' Ari said. 'But it was going up. He was on his way to collect the body.'

'You sound very confident about that,' Sid said.

'We weren't here all night for nothing, you know,' Eva retorted.

'Go on then, pet,' Sid said. 'Enjoy your moment.'

'Actually, it was Ari's idea,' she said.

'Simple enough,' Ari said. 'The singletown was ripped. But the gang couldn't know in advance what was coming in and out of the garage they used.'

'Smart,' Sid said, trying to keep his voice approving rather than surprised. Maybe Aldred was right, he didn't expect a 3 to come up with impressive ideas. 'What was there?'

'Another taxi came in to pick up a client who'd pre-booked while our target was parked. It's owned by an independent driver, name of Matt Jorden, who is a careful man when it comes to liability and security. His taxi has a band of smartdust, and he keeps the mesh log.'

The image surrounding Sid changed. He was looking out

across a typical underground garage, with unpainted concrete walls and ceiling, occupied by rows of cars parked between pillars. Matt Jorden's taxi was parked in the temporary stop bay outside a set of automatic glass doors which led to the lifts.

Their suspect came out the doors, tugging the huge bag along. Sid could see how he was struggling with the weight as the little wheels juddered along the rough concrete. His back was to Jorden's taxi the whole time as he walked down to the end of the temporary stop bay. Then he went round to the boot of his taxi, which was blocked from view by two cabs parked between them. A minute later, it drove away. The time in the corner of the display was nine fifty.

The zone booth image vanished, and Sid stepped out into Office3 to face the team. Ralph Stevens was also there, going over their results. Like a proper spook he'd simply been in the Market Street Station when Sid arrived first thing that morning. There was no sign of Scrupsis yet, so Sid guessed Ralph and the HDA were winning the turf war.

'That was good detective work,' Sid told Ari.

'Thanks, boss.'

'So the only image we have of his face so far is the one from the receptionist's retinal log?' Sid asked.

'I've been working on it,' Abner said. 'There's a lot of AI enhancement, but it should be enough, especially as we have his height and weight.'

The suspect's face appeared on the office wallscreen. Sid guessed he was mid-forties, with a bulbous nose, dark hair receding from his forehead, small ears, and a wide mouth. It looked too much like a digital representation for Sid, but he knew that Abner had worked wonders building this from the distant snatched glimpse Vicky Thelwell had accidentally given them.

The team were all looking at him, waiting expectantly.

'Okay, let's run it,' Sid said.

Abner made a show of flicking an icon in his keyspace.

Even Sid didn't expect a confirmed identity quite so fast. But eighteen seconds later it flashed up on the wallscreen. The AI hadn't even begun to access the GE's main citizen database; their suspect was already stored in the Market Street network, entered by the Gang Task Force.

Ernie Reinert, age forty-one, a known mid-level Red Shield gang member. Previous employment with Securitar, a legitimate GE-licensed paramilitary agency. He'd been let go in 2134 after a tour in Greece. Securitar was contracted to 'investigate' political dissidents. Reinert was dismissed for improper conduct on duty, which included a lot of missing company equipment, and using excessive force against two detainees who subsequently spent three months in hospital because of him – Securitar had to pick up the bill. The Gang Task Force had an address for him in South Shields. His legitimate business was a commercial repair and service garage in Jarrow, which also dealt in second-hand cars, which the task force noted was an ideal cover for gang activity. There were official records – his court appearances for minor charges, extensive juvenile record, charges filed but never prosecuted.

Sid looked up at the wallscreen where the details of Ernie's broken life continued to roll down. 'Hello, Ernie, my name's Sid, and I'm coming for a little visit.'

*

Sid immediately sent Ian and Eva round to the garage on Western Road. It was a confirmation mission. They were to act as a couple looking to buy a car, taking their time viewing everything Ernie had on his lot, and checking he was there while Sid organized the arrest. Abner ran electronic cover, placing limiters in the transnet cells on Western Road. Sid called in NorthernMetroServices to provide fifty armoured constables for an arrest and site securement team.

They rode in convoy, with the team in squad cars, leading eight BMW GroundKings over the Tyne Bridge, then eastward to Jarrow on the A104. A couple of agency helicopters flew cover overhead, equipped with sensors for ground tracking. The City traffic management AI kept their route clear, changing lights at each junction so they just rolled through without a stop. When they were a mile from the garage they split into three teams, approaching from every direction.

Sid sat in the passenger seat of the lead car with Ari driving, and closed his eyes so he could receive the direct feed from Ian's iris smartcells. He and Eva were standing beside a two-year-old Volvo estate with Ernie Reinert himself, talking about power-cell efficiency and service costs.

'One minute out,' Sid told Ian. 'Get ready.'

Through Ian's eyes, Sid saw Ernie stumble in the middle of extolling the durability of the winter tyres fitted on the Volvo. He frowned and looked out along Western Road.

'Boss,' Abner said. 'There's a lot of traffic going to the target's e-i. I can't block it all without isolating him completely.'

Ari turned the squad car into Weston Street, three hundred metres from the garage. 'Gun it, man!' Sid ordered. The siren came on, and acceleration shoved him back into the seat. 'Airborne: down and target-lock. Ground team: move in now!'

Ernie took a step away from the Volvo as the siren wail washed over the garage. He turned and—

'Don't!' Ian warned. His pistol was out, laser dot playing on Ernie's grey sweater. Eva had also drawn her weapon, covering the mechanics peering out of the garage maintenance shop.

Ernie's flight to freedom never even got started. He was on his knees, hands behind his head, when Sid's squad car came to a screeching halt in the garage forecourt. The chopper was hovering at rooftop height directly overhead, its downwash forcing everyone to lean into the howling air. GroundKings blocked the road on either side of the garage. Agency constables in light body armour fanned out, ordering civilians to get clear. Two armed teams rushed into the garage.

'Get in here,' Sid ordered the armoured prisoner van. They bundled Ernie into the back, informing him of his rights as they went. Sid didn't care, just wanted to get him out of plain sight where a sniper could pick him off. The van also had an efficient netjam. Ian and Eva started to search him, doing a pat-down and running a scan.

The helicopter lifted. Four garage staff were hauled out by the constables, and made to kneel on the forecourt. Ari went along the line, putting handcuffs on.

Ralph came over to the back of the prisoner van, and looked at a silently glowering Ernie on the other side of the internal mesh gate. 'Good job, Sid.'

'Thanks.'

'Really, we appreciate it. But . . . sorry. Gotta be done.'

Sid frowned. 'What?'

Three huge dark military-style helicopters swooped in low over the industrial estate behind the garage. One landed fast on Western Road between the GroundKings, its rotors barely missing the corner of the garage. Three suited men jumped out of the side door, and ran towards the prisoner van. The other two helicopters hung overhead, weapons pods unfolding from the short forward fins, to rotate menacingly.

'With all respect, our interrogation will be a lot more thorough,' Ralph shouted above the roar of the turbines and rotors. 'We don't have to worry about lawyers and rights.'

'You can't do this,' Sid yelled back furiously.

'We're HDA, and this is our field. Hand him over, please, Sid.'

The three suited men had arrived to stand behind Ralph. With a sinking heart Sid knew there was no point in even trying to argue. He beckoned a stony-faced Ian. 'Bring him out.'

Ernie's defiance had vanished. He looked badly worried as his HDA escorts grabbed both arms and hustled him towards the helicopter.

'Now what?' Sid shouted.

'Keep the investigation going,' Ralph said. 'Find out what went on at the St James singletown. I'll keep you in the loop about the information we extract.'

That single chilling phrase stalled anything else Sid was going to say. He stood there among Ernie's crappy used cars with Eva on one side and Ian on the other, the rest of the team scattered round the forecourt, watching their triumph vanish into the helicopter. The rotors spun up to full speed, and it tugged itself off the ground.

'Bastard!' Ian bellowed into the thunderous wash of air.

Sid looked round helplessly. Then he realized he'd have to call O'Rouke, who was standing by for the confirmation of a successful arrest so he could have his press conference. 'Oh crap on it,' he groaned.

Saturday 16th March 2143

'Where are you?' Corporal Paresh Evitts' voice was flush with misery and desperation.

'Incoming,' Ravi Hendrik assured him. Pulling data from the navigation graphics was second nature – no e-i analysis required for that. 'Five minutes now.'

Thick warm rain lashed against the Berlin's broad windscreen as Ravi flew the heavy machine low and hard across the jungle in answer to the research convoy's frantic call for help. Wipers made very little difference. The waterwash over the curving transparency blurred his view of the dense undulating tree canopy fifty metres below. Most of his imagery was coming from iris smartcells interfacing with his netlens visor, the helicopter's network blending the data from specialist optical sensors in the nose, fuselage smartdust meshes, and radar. Natural vision was almost a distraction. Except Ravi had been flying long enough to know you never relied on software-enhanced visuals alone, eyes were still a pilot's greatest asset.

The long strands of mist rolling around the hill slopes were almost invisible to the electronics; without the thickness to register as cloud, but opaque enough to conceal surprises. Ravi was always watching out for St Libra's taller tree specimens, the bullwhips or metacoyas or vampspires, soaring out of the canopy to snag the unwary. A few weeks back he'd seen a vampspire well over a hundred metres high.

Today, fifty kilometres from Wukang, amid a rumpled countryside of steep hills and sharp ravines, he was especially vigilant. It was gloomy that morning, with Sirius invisible behind dark clouds that piled high up into the sky, bringing an early dusk to the valleys and rivers. Humidity was degrading the turbine efficiency. This was bad weather to be flying in. Worse for those on the ground, though. His e-i was accessing the link between the convoy and Wukang – everyone was close to panic and shouting a lot. It made for a confusing babble in his ears. Doc Coniff was trying to talk Angela Tramelo and Leora Fawkes through a procedure to seal up a deep wound with equipment in their emergency pack. From the description, poor Marty O'Riley had finished up with some kind of jagged branch impaling his thigh. It was all high-pitched shouts interspersed by Marty's screams. Then Juanitar Sakur was also demanding the doc's attention as he tried to stabilize Dave Guzman's spine. Ravi thought that was telling: the convoy's paramedic concentrating on Dave's broken back rather than Marty, who as far as he could make out was pumping blood everywhere. All those urgent voices actually made Ravi glad he couldn't afford to receive visual feeds from Angela, the way she was linking them back to the doc.

'We can hear you now,' Paresh Evitts said.

'Good for you,' Ravi muttered as lightning flickered somewhere through the rain and cloud.

The Berlin cleared a long ridge and turned into a valley, where the slopes were covered in unbroken vegetation. Sensors immediately locked on to the convoy vehicles. The biolab and two Land Rover Tropics were perched on top of a steep ravine, just visible in the muddy landscape of tall bushes, wild trees, and rock outcrops; while radar painted the Multi-Terrain Jeep halfway down the ravine side. Ravi winced. It must have rolled many times before slamming into a clump of rocks amid the waving grey-green fronds of tiwillow bushes. They should never have been travelling so close to the edge – but that was for Colonel Elston to sort out later.

Ravi scanned the area, looking for any open land. He knew he wasn't going to find any, but St Libra was a world of surprises, that was sure. Maybe ten people were lined up along the top of the ravine, their ponchos slick with rainwater. Tiny purple and scarlet climbing ropes threaded the gulf between them and the beat-up MTJ. More people were crawling around the wreck, soaking wet and smothered in mud.

'Can you put it down?' Paresh asked.

Ravi circled the crash site, studying the sloping ground, the closely packed trees. There was enough distance between the trunks for the convoy vehicles to worm their way through the jungle, but landing something as big as the Berlin?

'Not going to happen,' Ravi told him. 'Not here, or anywhere close.'

'My people are hurt down there.'

'I know. I'll hover. We're going to have to winch them up.'

'Ho shit. Okay.'

Ravi swung the Berlin round again while back in the main cabin Tork Ericson got Leif Davdia, Mohammed Anwar, and Mark Chitty into their harnesses. Mark would help with the triage, while both the winch-qualified Legionnaires would strap the injured into the Berlin's medevac stretcher.

The Berlin nosed its way forward through the deluge, sending out a cyclone of high-velocity rain to slash at the vegetation. Ravi was at the same level as the vehicles on top of the ravine now, inching closer, compensating for the valley's random microbursts and the surges of rain. Dead ahead he could see Antrinell Viana and Marvin Trambi, close enough to make out their grim faces. Lightning flashed again, somewhere behind the helicopter. Visuals from the fuselage mesh showed him he was directly overhead the MTJ. Tork opened the fuselage side doors. Ravi locked down the ranging sensors, alert for the Berlin being shoved around by the weather.

'Cleared for winch descent,' he told Tork.

The first two men slipped out on the end of tough carbon wire, sliding with arachnid agility down to the accident below. Watching them go, Ravi knew it was going to take an hour to get

481

the five seriously injured Legionnaires up to the Berlin. An hour spent holding position perfectly in the deluge and fickle gusts. He could do that. An hour in these conditions was nothing to an ex-Thunderthorn pilot who'd flown swarm duty.

*

Back in 2119 Ravi had been stationed at Groom Lake in southern Nevada, one of the two US Tactical Aerospace Force front-line bases on Earth tasked with exospheric defence. At the time he was thirteen months qualified to fly the new Lockheed SF-100 Thunderthorns, which were America's major contribution to the HDA.

When the preliminary Zanthswarm alert came through he was engaged in some serious downtiming in Vegas, busy losing most of his six-month flight bonus. The base commander's response was immediate and impressive, dispatching a fleet of helicopters out to the gaudy desert jewel town to pick up her service personnel. Everyone was back on station and sobered up within two hours, just as Groom Lake's war gateway technicians opened a trans-space connection to New Florida.

Ravi and his co-pilot, Bombardier First Class Dunham Walsh, were in the pre-flight briefing room along with the rest of the Wild Valkyrie pilots, reviewing New Florida's basic geographical layout. The American world had nine major continents, of which only three – Oakland, Tampa, and Longdade – were developed enough to have states, with senators appointed to sit in Washington. HDA command assigned the Wild Valkyries to defend northern Oakland, an area covering three and a quarter million square miles. The base commander wished them Godspeed, and ordered them to status red.

Ravi and Dunham drove out to their Thunderthorn, *Bad Niobe*, under a cold desert night sky, with the stars twinkling brightly overhead – mocking them, Dunham said. Ravi loved the sight of the Thunderthorn's aggressive three-hundred-and-seventeen-tonne missile-tight profile, as he loved everything about the spaceplane, including the one-point-eight-billion-dollar unit cost. From nose to tail the SF-100 measured fifty-eight metres, with its variable sweep wings fully extended it was fifty-three metres tip to tip, while in their swept position for exoatmospheric flight the wings hunched back to a trim thirty-one metres. In full aerodynamic mode – hatches closed and weapons retracted – it was as sleek as its design team could make it, with sharp curving surfaces blending the wings efficiently into the fuselage; engine nacelles in the wingroots housed turbofans and rockets, sprouting twin shark-profile tailfins on top; a slight bulge on the upper fuselage for the oval cockpit capsule with its narrow silvered wraparound windscreen. The fuselage was a shimmer-black metalloceramic, hugely resistant to the ferocious blasts of heat and radiation it would be soaked with in combat.

Ravi settled into the pilot's seat and plugged his suit umbilicals into the sockets. The spaceplane's tacnet began to upload New Florida exospheric arena data. US Tactical Aerospace Force loaded in their weapon codes. The ground-crew chief confirmed tanks full and hoses uncoupling. Ravi released the ground brakes and the Thunderthorn rolled forward sedately, taking nineteenth place in the line of eighty-five war-ready Wild Valkyries.

The squadron emerged into the desert night one by one, and growled their way along the base's taxiways to the trans-space deployment runway. At the far end, the silver-grey oval of the war gateway awaited, like a smear of caged moonlight.

Ravi watched the squadron commander open up her Thunderthorn's turbofans, and the big spaceplane surged forwards, accelerating hard along the half-mile runway. The SF-100 had reached its top ground speed of two hundred mph when it streaked through the gateway. A second Thunderthorn was already accelerating along the runway behind it.

Five galling minutes of waiting later, and Ravi was steering them onto the deployment runway. Watching the four glaring salmon-pink exhausts of *Kickass Iole* racing away ahead of them, he rammed the throttles to max, and *Bad Niobe* surged forward eagerly amid a howl of turbines. Acceleration pushed him back into his seat. *Kickass Iole* vanished into the war gateway in front.

'Scared?' Ravi yelled out gleefully.

'Oh fuck yeah,' Dunham shouted back.

Ravi laughed in delight. And *Bad Niobe* shot through the war gateway—

*

—into space seven hundred and fifty kilometres above New Florida. Noise was sucked away as the thin vapour spume of Earth's atmosphere that jetted through the gateway with them dispersed with an energetic sparkle, leaving them in the vacuum. *Bad Niobe*'s turbofans stuttered and died as their air flow vanished. Ravi's grip on the joystick eased off slightly. The immediate locale seemed clear. Nacelle intake hatches slid shut. Already the war gateway had vanished, jittering away as all unanchored trans-spacial connections did. For once the phenomenon played out in the HAD's favour, enabling Groom Lake to scatter Thunderthorns into a protective umbrella formation above their designated continent.

Ravi's first five seconds were an imperative visual and tactical orientation.

The planet curved away beneath them, a horizon slicing across Dunham's side of the windscreen. New Florida's thick cloud streamers gleamed bright in the gold-tinted sun. Oakland was a sprawl of brown mountains and blue-green vegetation, with its rivers and everglades flashing gold. In the little time Ravi had for a visual sweep he couldn't see any signs of human civilization lurking beneath the lazy clouds. Nevertheless, there were twelve million US citizens living on the continent below, all desperately trying to reach the gateway that led back to Miami and safety. His task now was to buy them that time.

Already, bright stars were flaring, not far away by cosmic standards, incandescent blooms of plasma billowing wide. The first Mk-7009 nuclear missiles detonating against the enemy. Ravi never saw them shining brighter than quaint fireworks, the band filters of the cockpit windscreen made sure of that. *Bad Niobe* wouldn't let her human crew suffer from the radiation bursts and rampant high-energy particles that were starting to fill space above New Florida's ionosphere.

Hatches irised open down *Bad Niobe*'s spine, allowing sensors to slide out and scan round. A ruff of silver thermal-dump panels concertinaed upwards from the rear fuselage, radiating away the heat generated by the Thunderthorn's innumerable systems.

'Battle ready,' Dunham announced.

A 3D radar display emerged from zero-point and expanded across Ravi's field of vision, projected by his helmet visor. The image kept jumping, sharp graphic lines fuzzing and juddering.

'Heavy EMP out there,' he grunted. Twenty seconds since emergence, and they were already in the thick of it. *Bad Niobe*'s electronics were ultra-hardened against interference, but even her tacnet was affected, operating below optimum efficiency.

'Yeah. Quantum state is in deform, too. Can't link to the geosats. We've got no comnet.'

'Ground stations?'

'Nah. Nukes and rent distortions are screwing the spectrum but good.'

'Okay. Let's go do our job.'

Bad Niobe was starting to fall. They hadn't emerged at orbital velocity, the war gateway vector was locked relative to the planetary surface, so gravity was starting to make itself known. Ravi reached for the joystick again, triggering the reaction control thrusters. Burps of hot gas erupted from the tiny rocket nozzles clustered around the rear of the nacelles. The Thunderthorn swung round to stand on her tail, and . . . 'Son of a motherfucker bitch,' Ravi whispered as the first true sight of their impassive, terrifyingly unbeatable enemy slid across the windscreen.

Two hundred kilometres above them, the Zanth was tearing vast rents across spacetime to swarm into the New Florida star system. Jagged nebulas of scarlet and heliotrope were swirling and swelling in seemingly random fluctuations all around the habitable planet, a livid cloak that nearly blotted out the clean stars beyond. Out from the infinite nothingness of the open rents, chunks of Zanth resembling angular teardrops over two hundred metres across at the base were slowly oozing through. Like the Thunderthorns, their velocity relative to the planet was zero. But gravity soon captured them, pulling each chunk into a fall that accelerated them to terminal velocity long before they reached the atmosphere. Faux icebergs with boundless refractive internal planes, they scattered sunlight and starlight around them, casting an iridescent lustre as they dived through empty space.

'Like being crapped on by a fallen angel,' Dunham grunted.

'No,' Ravi growled, angry at himself for being thrown by the spectacle of a billion tonnes of prismatic Zanth flakes cascading towards him. 'There's nothing angelic about this bastard.' He fired the *Bad Niobe*'s six main rockets. Hypergolic fuel mixed and burned in the bell-shaped nozzles at the back of the nacelles. Noise and vibration returned to the cockpit. Three gees acceleration shoved him back hard into the seat, and the Thunderthorn rose on a searing cataract of flame towards the scintillating invader like a wrathful demigod.

Weapons bay hatches opened. D-bombs missiles telescoped out on their launch rails; their electronics were simple and hardened against the weird quantum instabilities created by the nulldimensional rents. The spherical warhead glowed with the violet malevolence of Cherenkov radiation, as bands of exotic matter were restrained in their compressed state, barely extruding into spacetime.

Ravi cut the rocket engines, and *Bad Niobe* continued its silent climb. Directly ahead was a glimmering rent the shape of a mashed candyfloss bulb, tens of thousands of tiny scarlet fissures writhing together in a diabolical cyclone. Zanth chunks slithered out of the burning haze, moving with sedate grace as gold sunlight bathed their myriad facets, and they began their long plunge to the planet.

'That's our bitch,' Ravi announced. The quantum sensors around the nose told him the rent was still eighty kilometres away.

'Arming four,' Dunham said. 'I-G locked in. Ready to launch in fifteen.'

486

'Confirm.' Ravi punched his code into the weapons console. 'We have actives. You have launch authority.' Radar was starting to pick up the first of the swarm's shoals as they closed on New Florida. The damage any one of them would cause by just crashing into the land was enormous. Anybody within a couple of kilometres of one would die in the impact blastquake. Ravi wanted to fire every Mk-7009 *Bad Niobe* carried, to nuke the Zanth chunks into radioactive fragments.

'It's not going to make any difference,' he whispered. The deluge of cold twinkles were spread right across his view now, falling from every point in space. There were thousands of them, tens of thousands . . . And the swarm had only just begun.

'What?' Dunham asked.

'We're not going to save anything. Nobody's going to survive this.'

'For fuck's sake, Ravi!'

Reality impact the Groom Lake shrinks called it. The abrupt realization of the Zanth's immensity. Faced by an enemy so overwhelming the human soul simply shrank to a foetal ball and whimpered piteously.

'Goddamn it,' Dunham snarled. He snapped the red guards off the launch switches and flicked each of them. 'Four lights.'

Bad Niobe trembled. The missiles streaked away at ten gees, their solid rocket exhaust plumes enveloping the Thunderthorn in a swirl of fizzing sun-drenched particles that was over in seconds.

Ravi watched the plumes dwindle against the gyrating scarlet rent. The monstrous constellation of Zanth chunks shimmered, growing steadily brighter as gravity pulled them closer.

'What the hell is wrong with you?' Dunham demanded.

'Can you see what's out there?'

'Oh yeah. I can see it. Ten seconds until D-bomb contact.'

Ravi tried not to sneer at the brash optimism. The quantum distortion thrown out by the rents played havoc with electronics. They'd be lucky if just one of the missiles even reached the scarlet horror above. Nonetheless, he found himself counting down.

Two D-bombs flared, brilliant magenta starbursts of spacial discontinuity pumped by hundred-megatonne fusion explosions, devastating the delicately balanced crimson effervescence that extended back out of spacetime to what- or wherever the Zanth originated. The D-bombs bruised the rent. Ravi could see the brown stain of fractured pseudodimensional fabric shiver, re-coiling like living tissue struck by a thunderbolt. The stain spread, *fast*, ripping through the conductive scarlet fronds. Twist-ing them. The rent shuddered, spitting out streamers of bizarre energy, as if it was weeping. Then the entire edifice withered, imploding to resurrect a swathe of normal space. And the ever-falling swarm of Zanth.

Ravi grinned ferociously at them. The D-bombs had worked against the rent, sealing it up. *We can make a difference. A small one, but tangible.*

He scanned the radar display. *Bad Niobe*'s digital functionality was improving again now the rent was gone. The tacnet was plotting vectors for the descending Zanth chunks. Mk-7009s rose out of their bays.

'Let's do some damage,' Ravi said.

*

Four hours in freefall above New Florida. More evasive manoeuvres than Ravi recalled. Hypergolic fuel down to twenty per cent. A second phase of rents were snaking into existence, five hundred kilometres higher than the first. From *Bad Niobe*'s altitude, their D-bombs would just reach the new rents. They had seven Mk-7009s left. Once they were gone, the spaceplane would have to let gravity win, begin the long glide back to the surface and through a gateway to Groom Lake where they could re-up the fuel and warloads.

Four D-bombs soared away towards the spiky vermilion fissure above.

'Incoming,' Dunham warned.

Ravi had already seen the hail of boulder-size particles sweep-ing in. *Bad Niobe*'s rockets burned ferociously, powering them away. Their sector had steadily become more hazardous as it filled with blast debris hurtling in every direction. He gripped the joystick, rolling the big Thunderthorn. More systems were dropping out. Somewhere south at a lower altitude, a dozen nukes detonated. The radar display was showing almost nothing.

'I don't—' Ravi began.

The impact noise was loud enough to strike his head like a physical blow. He didn't know if he lost consciousness or not – he certainly couldn't make sense of anything for an indeterminate time. When he did try and focus again, he couldn't hear anything, not even his own breathing. His suit had stiffened. *Cabin puncture!* Didn't need what was left of the display graphics to know *Bad Niobe* was tumbling erratically as gravity tugged them down. Something was obscuring half his vision, graphics wiggled across the inside of a dark splodge. His hand came up instinctively to wipe the helmet visor. Gauntlet fingers came away red.

'Dunham.' Ravi wiped some more of the blood away, twisting round. 'Dunham – oh fuck it!' His muscles locked rigid in shock. The pebble-sized Zanth fragment that'd penetrated both the metalloceramic fuselage and the cockpit capsule's impact armour shielding had sliced Dunham's head clean off, taking quite a lot of the shoulder with it. The battered helmet was still bouncing casually around the cockpit, spun about by the still-flailing spaceplane.

Ravi fought hard against vomiting. A hand instinctively flipped open his suit's thigh pouch. He bumped the nausea suppressor. Warm buzz of the drug gushing along his bloodstream.

Priority: stop *Bad Niobe*'s tumble. He applied pressure to the joystick, finding out what was left of the reaction control system simply by seeing what response he got to each nudge. The port nacelle seemed to have taken the most damage. Slowly he cancelled out the giddying motion with incremental burps of gas, bringing the wounded spaceplane to a halt – forty-degree inversion relative to the planet, nose pointing at the south-east horizon. The chewed-up flight console was rearranging itself as the tacnet used the remaining display screens to show essential information. *Bad Niobe* was still venting something from a split tank. The nose began to drift again.

Ravi tracked the rogue vent down to a starboard nitrogen tetroxide tank, and opened the valves to drain the remaining liquid through a non-propulsive vent. Several fuel cells had been knocked out. The fuselage stress web was reporting an alarming number of punctures.

'And one dead co-pilot,' he muttered savagely.

Radar was still operational, reporting a massive amount of high-velocity particles sleeting through space all around him. The Thunderthorn's primary defence against collision – the sheer vastness of space – was decreasing with every minute. The Wild Valkyries had been exceptionally successful, nuking hundreds of Zanth. Now Ravi had to live with that success. It would probably kill him soon enough. Even the surviving Zanth were taking a pounding from the fragments.

Another touch on the joystick, slowly swinging the Thunderthorn round until the nose was pointing directly down at the beleaguered world, and he fired the main rockets again. Only three were functioning, requiring him to vector them constantly. Twenty-second burn, assisting gravity, sending him powering planetward.

Gravity slowly became more noticeable as the *Bad Niobe* sank downwards. Ravi changed the big spaceplane's alignment for the last time, levelling out so the belly was presented flat to the atmosphere. Dunham's helmet fell lightly onto the cockpit's floor, coming to rest beside Ravi's feet, and the headless corpse slumped forward, its arms dangling down. Bloodsplatter that was vacuum-boiling ran sluggishly down the bulkheads and console and windscreen, drawing long crimson trickles as it went.

Ravi did his best to ignore the gore. Sensors retracted down into their recesses, and the hatches irised shut. Flaps and wing camber actuators ran through their test sequences. Overall functionality wasn't too good the tacnet surmised. Ravi had a good old fatalistic chortle at that.

The ionosphere was alive with a moiré phosphorescence,

490

strong enough to obscure the land beneath. Hundreds of nuclear explosions launched by the Wild Valkyries and their counterparts over Tampa and Longdade had saturated New Florida's atmosphere with high-energy particles and hard radiation, hypercharging the ionosphere. Even if the Zanth stopped their swarm immediately, the planetary biosphere would take centuries to recover from the radioactive blitz.

Bad Niobe descended into the blazing maelstrom. Ravi felt the cockpit thrumming as aerodynamic surfaces began to cut through the thickening energized mist. A whole new set of red warning icons flashed urgently. He couldn't see anything through the contaminated ionosphere, except for a constant barrage of flashes as Zanth debris disintegrated in spectacular fireball explosions.

'We'll get you home,' Ravi promised Dunham's corpse. 'Don't you worry.'

They fell fast through the atmosphere. Ravi angled the nose down, using their aerofoil surfaces to convert their descent into forward momentum. Eerily distorted sunlight filled the cabin as they fell through the turgid base of the swollen ionosphere, and straight into a massive electrical storm. Lightning ripped through the air, skittering along the Thunderthorn's wings to spit incandescent plasma balls from the tips in a segmented contrail.

Down into the cloud layer, and rain added to the hostile barrage New Florida's atmosphere was greeting its defenders with. Ravi extended the Thunderthorn's wings, listening to the stress structure creaking as they stretched out to their full extent. The dive angle began to shallow out. He was flying with inertial navigation only, curving round in a long arc to land at Yantwich Airport, where the HDA retrieval gateway was waiting.

Ravi was seventy kilometres out, under the clouds, and travelling at Mach two point eight, when the radar gave him a proximity warning. He banked *Bad Niobe* to port, and just caught sight of the intact Zanth chunk bursting out of the dark clouds ten kilometres north. It streaked on downwards through the squalling rain, its facets flickering weakly in the diminished sunlight. Impact threw up a dense blastcloud ring of filthy air which obscured it from view. Ravi held his breath, hoping forlornly that the crashdown would smash the alien brute as thoroughly as any 7009. But as the grimy cloud was sluiced away by the rain he could see it sitting at a sharp angle at the bottom of an enormous crater.

But then it was never about saving the world, he reflected, just buying the people time to get out. One day maybe, HDA would find a way to repel the rents, divert the Zanth away from the trans-stellar worlds where humans lived. But by then he suspected his grandkids would have grandkids of their own.

Ravi was mildly surprised when all the undercarriage bogies slid down and locked, giving him three greens. Ten kilometres out from the runway, and three of the Thunderthorn's four turbofans lit up. Ground radar found him. He had basic communication with air traffic control. The tacnet was downloading *Bad Niobe*'s status to Groom Lake.

Even with all the damage, Ravi managed a wheels down in the centre of the runway. Emergency vehicles chased him all the way to the gateway at the end of the taxiway. As he reached it, another of the Wild Valkyrie squadron's Thunderthorns was touching down behind.

The other side of the retrieval gateway was a near-physical jolt, leaving him faintly dazed. One moment he'd been fighting for his life on a world dying beneath a brutal alien invasion, now here he was back under the big calm Nevada sky, with the familiar buildings of Groom Lake throwing out their usual heat-shimmer welcome. Engineering vehicles converged on *Bad Niobe*. Ravi shut down the turbofans as the rad-haz trucks started spraying the spaceplane with a gooey turquoise decontamination fluid. Technicians began plugging umbilicals in. The tow-tractor hitched itself to the nose wheel, and tugged him to the combat engineering hangar.

As they rolled into the vast building he could see a dozen Thunderthorns already inserted into the long line of robot repair bays. Two of them were in even worse shape than *Bad Niobe*. Tech crews in radiation suits teemed over every surface, assisted by the bay's AI and remote tools. Cybernetic arms lifted broken sections of fuselage off the stress structure, while more arms moved fresh ones into place. Battered nacelles were simply removed and new ones slotted in. Every on-board system was modular, so any damaged component was quickly unplugged and a replacement lowered in.

Bad Niobe was back to flightworthiness standard after two hours twenty minutes.

'Send me back,' Ravi pleaded with the squadron commander. He'd been furious when he saw Toho and Janinne waiting beneath the ladder into the patched-up cockpit.

'You lost Dunham,' the commander said.

'I didn't! The fucking Zanth shrapnel got him. Half a metre over and you'd be talking to him not me. It was chance, is all. It's got nothing to do with my ability. Come on! Dunham and me, we blew the shit out of fifty Zanth.'

'It was bad, Ravi, I don't know if you can cope again.'

'It was *great* out there. I was great. Come on: fifty Zanth fucked, and I brought *Bad Niobe* back. It's not like you've cloned a whole load of pilots, we're not Norths. Come on, send me back. Give me some HiMod to keep me sharp, and I'll nail you fifty more. You can't seriously think Toho is a better pilot?'

'Toho is just as good—'

'Fuck he is!'

'—but I don't have enough pilots, you're right. So you get some rest, and when *Bad Niobe* gets back, I'll send you out again.'

Ravi wound up flying six missions against the New Florida Zanthswarm. He never thought he'd make it back after the fourth. They wound up ejecting the cockpit capsule when *Bad Niobe*'s starboard undercarriage collapsed on landing, and the spaceplane cartwheeled into a mangled fireball that even the combat engineering hangar couldn't fix. He got his final two flights in a different Thunderthorn because of pilot attrition. Space above New Florida was becoming dangerously rad-toxic, but the Thunderthorns still flew, getting fewer D-bomb shots into rents that were now over three thousand kilometres above New Florida, smashing fewer Zanth chunks with each passing hour. They kept going because no one else was going to help the besieged population.

Eventually, four days after the Zanthswarm began, and to the anger and dismay of every surviving squadron member, HDA command shut down the exospheric defence flights. The rents were now opening over five thousand kilometres above New Florida. Space between them and the atmosphere was a foul blizzard of fractured Zanth shards capable of pulverizing any spaceplane. The ionosphere was aglow with radiation, making New Florida look like a cool sun.

There was nothing left to save any more.

*

Vance Elston kept wiping the perspiration from his forehead as the Berlin thundered over the jungle back to the accident after dropping off the injured at Wukang. It was unpleasantly hot in the helicopter's cabin. No one bothered with air-con. Tork Ericson was leaning against the open side door, chewing gum as he stared out across the trees' lush, glistening canopy. It was late afternoon, and St Libra's heat-hazed air was insufferable. Bizarrely, the open side door, with the contra-rotating blades shimmering just a metre above, did nothing to circulate any cool air. But then, Vance seriously doubted there was any of the stuff on the whole planet.

'Two minutes out,' Ravi Hendrik announced.

Vance checked his safety harness and went over to stand behind Tork's bucket seat, looking down at the rumpled ground. This was hilly country, steep but not impassable. It was only the jungle which created any difficulty, with the trees uncomfortably close together, and thick undergrowth making it difficult for any vehicle. Nonetheless, the research convoy had got this far from Wukang, just over fifty kilometres. Crashing down the undergrowth, using the robot buzz saws on the front of the MTJ to slice through any wooden obstacle or snag, like trunks or low branches and the unending curtain of vines. It was why they'd brought the tough vehicles on the expedition; they could push, cut, and smash their way through anything except for solid rock.

Tork thrust an arm out, pointing. 'There,' he yelled above the roar of the rotors.

Vance looked out at the crash site. Strands of vapour were winding up from the vegetation, the morning rains evaporating fast beneath the raw Sirius sunlight. The thin agitated mist curled round the mobile biolab and two Land Rover Tropics parked on the top of the ravine; the vehicles were bedecked by various cases and packs, all the tents and equipment the convoy would need to make camp overnight. His gaze followed the steep muddy slope downwards. There were long skid marks through the red-brown soil, pulped vegetation, and finally the MTJ on its side against a rock outcrop. Its packs had split on impact, festooning a broad swathe of ground with debris, tents, and clothes flapping about in the regular breeze. A couple of Legionnaires were crouched beside the stranded vehicle, the slender, colourful threads of climbing rope attached to their belts stretching all the way back up to the top of the ravine.

'Damnit,' Vance grunted, crossing himself in reflex. DiRito should never have been driving so close to the edge. Which was a fine thing to say with hindsight, but it hadn't been him trying to negotiate the daunting jungle.

The Berlin swept in over the parked vehicles, and hovered twenty metres above them. Trees and bushes bowed and swayed in the downdraught.

'If you're going down, sir . . .' Tork said.

Vance nodded grimly, trying not to show his nerves. It had been a *long* time since he'd done this in training. 'Right.'

Tork spooled out a metre of winch cable, and clipped it to Vance's harness. The winch arm swung out. Vance wanted to cross himself, but resisted the urge. Tork slapped his helmet twice, and he leant out of the door, letting the winch take his weight. Then he was spinning slowly as the cable lowered him.

Paresh Evitts grabbed his legs and steadied him as he reached the ground. The winch cable was unclipped, and the Berlin veered away to hover directly over the MTJ.

'Sir,' Corporal Evitts saluted.

Vance returned the salute.

Paresh was covered in mud which was drying rapidly in the brilliant blue-white sunlight. His young face reflected worry, anger, and weariness. 'How are they, sir?' he asked.

Vance couldn't help glancing at the three black bodybags lying next to the biolab. Corporal Hiron, who'd been in the MTJ's front seat next to DiRito; Privates Peace-Davis and Ramon Beaken as well. 'The doc thinks O'Riley will keep the leg. Tramelo and Fawkes did a good job extracting the branch. Sleath and DiRito will be okay, they just have broken limbs. But the doc's not so happy with Guzman. They can treat his spine a lot better back at Abellia, so we'll know more when he gets there. The four of them are being medevaced out on the next Daedalus flight. It should be landing in another hour.'

'Okay.' Paresh nodded.

Vance thought the young corporal was fighting back tears. 'You ran a smooth recovery operation here, Corporal. Your squad has a reason to be grateful for your leadership.'

'Thank you, sir.'

Antrinell Viana came over and saluted. 'What now?'

Vance glanced round the site. Darwin Sworowski, the camp's ground vehicle chief, was already winching down from the Berlin to the MTJ. 'You take the convoy vehicles back to Wukang. I want you to carry the bodies with you. The Berlin will recover the MTJ and airlift it back. The engineers think it can be patched up.'

'That I'd like to see,' Antrinell grunted.

'Corporal, get the bodies into the biolab, please, and wind it up here. You'll leave as soon as the Berlin lifts.'

'Sir.' Paresh performed a mediocre salute, and walked off to his squad who were sitting round the two Tropics. Vance caught a glimpse of Angela, who was slumped against one of the wheels, filthy and listless. There was blood streaked with the mud on her khaki vest.

496

'So?' he asked when Paresh was out of earshot.

Antrinell let out a long sigh. 'Hellfire. I don't know. Hiron was pathfinding. I was in the biolab following the MTJ. There's no way it was deliberate. DiRito went too close to the edge in the mud. It was foolhardy, but we've all driven along the edge of the gorges out here. I'd probably have done the same thing if I'd been taking point.'

'Did you see the fall?'

'No.' Antrinell pointed at the broken undergrowth below the trees twenty metres away where the vehicles had cut a path. 'We were back there. We keep a minimum forty-metre distance between each vehicle now. That was something we learned on day one. If the MTJ comes up against something it can't get past, you have to back up and start over along another route. Can't do that easily if we're all clumped up nose to tail.' His breath whistled out between clenched teeth. 'We had a ringlink between all the vehicles. The screams . . .'

'I want to look where they went over.'

'Sure.'

Vance walked to the edge. The mud was drying rapidly now. The ground was a mess of footprints, skid marks, and trampled vegetation. Smara Jacka, from the xenobiology team, and Gillian Kowalski were sitting on the rocks, belaying the safety ropes attached to Josh Justic and Omar Mihambo, who were down at the MTJ helping Sworowski attach carrier hooks to the machine. They were tethered to a big bullwhip tree which leaned towards the edge. Vance glanced up at the tree, with its horizontal coil branches overhead, the smooth light-brown bark furred by short, silky white hair. The way the bullwhip's branches held themselves parallel to the ground put him in mind of a terrestrial cedar.

Despite the amount of foot traffic, it was easy enough to see exactly where the MTJ had gone over. The wheels had skidded through the soft mud of the slope, tearing out smaller plants as they went. Vance walked down the track on top of the ridge, then closed his eyes and told his e-i to play the recording. DiRito's visual record began to play and Vance was in the MTJ's cabin as it jounced about over the rough ground. Hands up in front, struggling with the steering wheel. Even with power steering and traction control, the MTJ was a brute to hold steady on this kind of terrain. DiRito seemed to have some kind of stupid pride thing going, maintaining a speed that Vance considered foolhardy. Hub motors in each of the four wheels kept it crunching forwards over everything but the biggest obstructions. And if those were tree trunks, the lethal-looking mandible-like buzz saws on the front chopped them back.

DiRito had emerged from the jungle, into the relatively clear strip of land along the edge of the gorge. He turned and began to drive parallel to the edge. There were some rocks—

—Vance opened his eyes, matching the clump of thigh-high boulders in front of him with DiRito's visual record—

—DiRito turned right. Vance could understand that. Left would take him back towards the jungle, right was clearer, even though the MTJ was closer to the top of the ridge now. The MTJ turned fine, went round the rocks. Carried on up the hill.

Everything was normal, then there was a lurch, and the windscreen was suddenly facing the open sky above the gorge. DiRito was fighting the steering wheel, the back wheels lost traction in the mud. Watching it, Vance could sense the momentum as the rear of the vehicle swung round. Amid a shaking image, DiRito's arms were a frantic jumble of motion on the steering wheel. The MTJ was just starting to respond when the horizon began to tilt.

'Stop,' Vance told his e-i. He'd run the recording eight times since DiRito arrived at Wukang's clinic. Trying to understand what had happened.

'So?' Antrinell asked.

Vance stood on the spot, and examined the ground. Mashed-up honeyberry bushes and vine fronds. Mud starting to dry. Same as the rest of the jungle. He turned a full circle. The team members lounging around the Tropics were all watching him. The Berlin was circling slowly overhead.

'DiRito hasn't stopped shouting that something hit the MTJ,' Vance said.

'Well he's bound to claim it wasn't his fault.'

'Hmm,' Vance said. He could still see the stricken Legionnaire in Wukang's little clinic, fighting against the pain, desperate to tell anyone who came close. 'We were hit. Something pushed us. It wasn't me! It wasn't my fault! I swear.' Pleading. Insistent. Distraught. Vance had seen enough interrogations, witnessed enough people in shock, in denial, furtive, hostile. He was pretty sure DiRito was telling the truth. But truth was a subjective thing. Then again, something had definitely happened to the MTJ to send it sliding like that.

But now, hours later, and in that same exact position, Vance couldn't see a single thing that might have caused it to swerve so sharply. He poked his boot toe into the soft ground. Even the mud was consistent, no hidden deep puddles or small sink holes. Power surge in a hub motor? Traction control was all software balanced, after all. But incredibly safe. And the chances of a glitch at the exact moment that would cause this . . .

Vance moved a short distance away from the forlorn survivors. 'Lucky it wasn't the biolab that went over.'

'You're telling me,' Antrinell said. 'We've got some decent body-impact protection built into our seating, but that would have given it a sore testing.'

'Yes. I was thinking more of what you're carrying.'

'Ah. Well there's even less to worry about on that score. The warheads can impact bare rock at terminal velocity and they won't even graze, let alone break. They have to be armed to begin their release sequence.'

'And the solid rockets?'

'They're not going to detonate just because the biolab rolled over a few times. There's a lot of protection designed into the system.'

'Good. We might be needing it.'

'Excuse me?' Antrinell said.

'I'm not convinced this was an accident.'

'I don't see how it could be sabotage.'

'Me neither, but this one is definitely poised between the two. So we need to be sure our payload is safe.'

'You can't be serious. Even if they exist, how would the St Libra aliens know what we're carrying? There are only twenty-eight people in the whole HDA that know about our fall-back precaution.'

Vance nodded slowly, wanting to believe Antrinell was right, that he was just being paranoid. 'Tell me again where Angela Tramelo was at the moment of the accident,' he said quietly.

Antrinell couldn't disguise his shock. 'You're kidding, right?'

Vance said nothing, just looked at him.

'Oh Lord, you're not. Okay, she was in the Tropic behind me. Corporal Evitts was driving it. Passengers were Tramelo, Kowalski and Justic. Dean Creshaun was driving the last Tropic, with Bastian 2North, Melia, and Dorchev in with him. Every one of them can confirm she was there. We had her surrounded, Vance. There's no way she could have caused this.'

'All right, I'll accept that for the moment.'

'You really think she's involved?'

'I don't know what the hell is happening on St Libra, that's the problem. There's too much happening to us to just write it off as bad luck and coincidence. But I do have an idea about Angela, which I'm going to share with you. In case.'

'In case . . . Really?'

'We're accumulating fatalities at an alarming rate don't you think?'

Antrinell had to nod agreement at that. 'Yeah. Even my people have been talking about it.'

'And she's always near.'

'To be fair, so were all of us.'

'But none of us were here when Bartram North and his household were slaughtercd.'

'I thought her interrogation showed us a high probability that the monster does exist.'

'Yet the more the Newcastle investigation continues, the more it seems that the North's murder was connected to some kind of illegal corporate operation.'

'But we have Ernie Reinert in custody now. The team on Frontline will get the truth out of him.'

'Ralph Stevens will uncover who employed him, yes. If he knows.'

'What is this?' Antrinell asked. 'Are you having doubts about the expedition?'

'I don't know. An alien species certainly fits everything that's happened. But what about Angela?'

'What about her?'

'She's a one-in-ten,' Vance said. It was something which had bothered him right from the moment back in January when Vermekia had given him her file. Seeing her at Holloway Prison, exactly the same as she'd been all those years ago, as if she'd time-jumped from then to today, had bothered him badly. It wasn't jealousy – not exactly, though he'd started to be a lot more critical of himself in the bathroom mirror every morning. He simply didn't understand where she'd come from, and that went against everything he stood for. AIA was about getting answers. 'She was arrested twenty years ago. I'm not that good at judging age, but she looked like she was about nineteen then. I've done some digging on the one-in-ten treatment. It kicks in during late teens, once you're near physical maturity, so back then she could have been anything between eighteen and thirty.'

'I get that,' Antrinell said. 'So?'

'It's hugely expensive now. And even assuming she's forty-five, which I have my suspicions about, she was conceived around 2098.'

'Yeah, those figures check out.'

'The figures, yeah. But who is she? One-in-ten treatments are hugely expensive and rare today, though they're not as exceptional as they used to be. But forty-five years ago? That's the very early pioneering days, when it would have been phenomenally expensive.'

'Okay.'

'Okay, so who, forty-five years ago, was rich enough to spend that kind of money on a daughter? And we're talking tens of millions, here. It's hard to find reliable estimates. On top of that most American states have strong anti-germline laws.'

'A billionaire, obviously. We're not short of them on the trans-space worlds, now or then.'

'No. We're not. But I've asked Vermekia to dig up what he could. It's interesting. We found a possible family DNA match to a Luci Tramelo, who's on file with the GE Citizenship Bureau. She was a French citizen who emigrated to Orleans forty-seven years ago, age thirty-five. When she arrived in Pantin, she bought a large vineyard on the edge of town and lived there comfortably, marrying a year later. There are three children of record, and they still run the vineyard. But Luci herself died two years ago. There's no record of her parents' family having enough money to buy that estate for her, and there aren't any French state employment records for her prior to emigration. So the assumption I've made is that she bought it with her surrogacy payment. The DNA comparison gives us a second-generation connection, so genetically speaking Angela is the equivalent of her grandchild. That also makes sense given the alterations made to a one-in-ten's DNA. The interesting thing is, Vermekia couldn't get a match on any other of her familial traits. We don't have any records for her probable father.'

'I find that hard to believe. The AIA can access every government identity database.'

'No, actually, we can't.' Vance grinned. 'There's the distant planets for a start. As they don't officially exist as far as the trans-space worlds are concerned, we've never been able to get to their networks. Then there's New Monaco.'

'Ah. Yes, I like it. A world of multi-billionaires that we're not allowed to visit. That would fit.'

'Indeed it would. In fact, it's about a perfect fit. Except for one small point.'

'Yeah?'

'What in the good Lord's name is a New Monaco heiress doing as Bartram North's whore?'

'Ah.' Antrinell's humour visibly withered. 'Yeah, that is a good point.'

'The only possible explanation for her being in that mansion would be as an undercover agent. And that's a real long-shot. But it still doesn't explain her motivation – someone with that kind of money and upbringing simply wouldn't do such a thing. Though if she did, it opens up the whole corporate dark ops question.'

'So you're saying the Newcastle murder was the latest phase of some twenty-year corporate battle, and there is no monster?'

'No. I was there when we interrogated Angela. I sat and watched the brainscan pull that picture from her thoughts. She has a memory of something unnatural in Bartram's mansion that night. And given the rest of that interrogation, it's hard for me to ignore that.' Although there was one thing he was never going to confide to Antrinell, and that was Angela's resistance. He'd seen the toughest men crack in that most unholy suite of rooms, left weeping on the floor, toxed-up crazy, begging to be asked any question, desperate to satisfy their interrogators. Pathetic in their addled eagerness.

Whereas they'd got everything they wanted from Angela, but they'd never broken her. Reduced her to a miserable distraught self-pitying state, yes. But that inner fury of hers was still burning fiercely at the end – you just had to ask the technician who'd lost an eye to her rage. She never submitted. And it took a very special person, one with total self-conviction, to go through everything Frontline could throw at them and survive with their psyche relatively unscathed. A someone who possessed the utter arrogance and self-belief of a born and bred New Monaco resident.

'Hell.'

'Yes, quite,' Vance said. 'We're right back where we started, with a lot of unexplained deaths on St Libra. If we're going to work this one out we'll need hard scientific evidence. So what have you got for me?'

'Nothing helpful,' Antrinell admitted. 'We've taken over eight thousand samples since the convoy left Wukang. The guys were getting good with the collectors we issued. We've already processed seventy per cent. There are a phenomenal amount of plant species here, but no real variance from the main St Libra genetic sequence.'

'Right.'

'That's not just here, Vance. We took samples at Abellia, Edzell, and Sarvar. There's no variance anywhere.'

'But they weren't large area samples.'

'No. However, they are stretched over six thousand kilometres. Total stability over that kind of distance is a pretty conclusive indicator. And we haven't included the equal lack of variance that exists all the way down to the Independencies.'

'You're saying we're wasting our time?'

Antrinell shrugged his shoulders. 'If it was up to me, then yes. My vote is for packing up and going home. This world is odd, certainly, and the more I see of it the more I'm coming round to the bioforming theory.'

'Really?' Vance asked in surprise. Antrinell had always been adamant that all life in the cosmos was God's own mystery, a perfectly natural one. And the Lord had blessed many planets with life. Except in all the decades of exploration, humans had never found another sentient species. Which tended to support the Good Book's tenet of God making man in his own image. So far all the universe had revealed was man and Zanth. And every Gospel Warrior knew the Zanth was an incarnation of the devil.

'Yes. I can just about buy the zebra botany evolving naturally. There's a symmetry to it that we don't normally get in nature. However, it's quite elegant, and we've seen weirder things on the non human-compatible planets we've surveyed and left alone. But, every day I look at the autoradiography bands we've obtained from the processed samples, and I see a genome that's extremely sophisticated. Exactly what you get from several billion years of evolution. This is the endpoint of these plants' evolution, their pinnacle. The world is in harmony, a balance which is like nothing we've ever seen before. Yet there's no fossil layer.'

'That anyone's found. And face it, Northumberland Interstellar hasn't been looking hard.'

'There's not a single ammonite on a planet this size? One! Come on.' He gestured round at the hills. 'Besides, Sirius hasn't been around for billions of years. It's four hundred million years old at best. No. All this was planted. Recently, in geological terms. But it was put here.'

'Why?'

'Why does the Zanth exist? Our Lord works in very mysterious ways. One of His elder children chose this world as a garden, perhaps? We do not get to question why, at least not in this life.'

'And the unexplained deaths we've had? DiRito was right, something hit the MTJ, some force that knocked it towards the gorge.'

'Those deaths only happen to our camp.' Antrinell tipped his head back towards the Tropics. 'And there's one person connecting both times.'

'Not Newcastle, she doesn't.'

Antrinell grimaced. 'Yeah.'

'Ralph should have completed Ernie Reinert's interrogation in a couple of days. Once we know for sure if the Newcastle murder was corporate-linked we'll have a better idea how to proceed here.'

'Fair enough. But my guess is on the corporate option. Damned moneylenders never change, there's nothing they won't do to make a buck.'

*

Her back slumped against the hot black tyre of the Tropic, Angela watched Elston and Antrinell in deep discussion close to the edge of the gorge. There was a lot of animation in their gestures. Plenty of passion and belief in the words. They deliberately kept their voices low so no one else could hear them.

Right now she didn't much care what they were talking about, though she could guess she was featuring heavily in there. There were a couple of times when Antrinell had used his head to gesture at the Tropics, deliberately not glancing at her and the others.

The accident had left her as shocked and drained as every convoy member. It had been a frantic time. Antrinell and Paresh had agreed to her abseiling down to the MTJ because of her weight. Everyone was scared the vehicle would slip again and carry on falling to the bottom of the gulley. So she and Leora had been first down, using tough carbon-filament ropes to secure upturned wheel hubs to the rocks. That had been the hardest quarter of an hour she'd spent, ignoring the cries of her injured friends inside while they secured the vehicle. And always, she'd been alert for the treacherous smell of mint amid the jungle's pervasive melange. Only when the MTJ was anchored to the rocks did they go inside with the emergency medical field packs and start to do what they could.

After that, after she'd crawled in through the shattered window and recoiled in dismay at the blood and suffering, she shifted into some kind of auto-function state. See what needed doing, assess how to do it, and just get on with the job. Pull the vicious honeyberry branch out of O'Riley's thigh, ignore his agonized screaming, seal up the ripped artery with the clever gadgets in the field pack. Emotions didn't come into it. Angela was good at that, good at isolating and ignoring her feelings. Everyone had been thankful and full of praise for what she'd done, especially when they saw the extent of the injuries she'd dealt with. She smiled thinly at the memory of their surprise, even Paresh had been alarmed at how much blood was soaked into her clothes when she'd finally hauled herself back up to the top of the ridge.

You could take the girl away from New Monaco, but you could never take New Monaco away from the girl.

Last time she'd suffered what to most people would be a debilitating emotional shock, she'd managed to quickly disassociate herself from any foolish animal state of mind and function logically. It was a pure survival instinct. And had she ever needed that straight afterwards . . .

*

Angela's jewellery was kept in a walk-in closet, one of the rooms which made up her bedroom suite in the family's New Monaco mansion. She stood in the middle of the floor, and looked round at the hundreds of small drawers. It was like standing in a safe deposit vault, except there were no locks. And now there was no security. Theft from the staff was always a minor worry, so the mansion's AI maintained a constant watch over the jewellery closet. The only people who could override it were her and Raymond. Angela had overridden it, switching it off.

She walked over to the console. The inventory was kept there, along with a useful style-match program which helped her coordinate with her wardrobe, suggesting appropriate items. She slipped her hand into the keyspace and her e-i loaded her code in. It wasn't the big, high-value items she was interested in. Of all the exquisite pieces she'd amassed or been given over the years, there were plenty of smaller bracelets and rings and tiaras and necklaces. Hundreds of them, so many she didn't actually know the full extent.

Drawers slid open silently. Flecks of light materialized all across the room, as if someone had lowered a glitterball. It was simply the refraction glimmer cast by all the superbly cut diamonds now exposed to the closet's sharp monochrome lighting panels. While she walked round examining the display, her e-i began to worm its way deep into the AI registry levels, wiping specific data as it went.

A green and purple icon popped up in her netlens projection – Marlak was calling her. 'Let it through,' she told her e-i.

'I'm sorry, Angela,' Marlak said. 'But the Council Agents are arriving.'

'Of course they are,' she said. 'I'll be down in a moment. I'm getting changed. After all, I can hardly meet them in my party frock, now can I?'

'Of course not. I'll inform them.'

When she walked back out into her bedroom, Daniellia, her maid, was waiting. Angela immediately noticed the change in the woman. She ignored the new lack of civility and began undoing the straps of her mauve ballgown.

'I'm sorry about your father,' Daniellia said.

'Thank you. Where's Lizzine?' Her dermatologist, who should be here ready and attentive to get the platinum scales off her skin. Greeting the Council Agents while shining in tens of thousands of dollars' worth of precious metal probably wasn't the best strategy.

'Back at Prince Matiff's, ma'am.'

'Oh yes, of course. Well, you'll have to help instead.' Angela stepped out of her ballgown. 'Find the skin eluents will you please, there's a dear.'

Daniellia didn't move. Angela raised an eyebrow. Normally that would be enough to turn the girl into a quivering mouse creature. Not now.

'I'm sorry to bring this up tonight,' said Daniellia. 'But we've been wondering if our contract payment will be honoured?'

'I see.' Angela slid a ring off her finger. The diamond set in the band probably wasn't over three carats. 'Here.' She tossed the ring to Daniellia, who caught it neatly. 'Payment plus bonus. Now find me the eluent. Please.'

Daniellia stared at the ring for a long moment, then tucked it into her blouse pocket. 'Yes, ma'am.'

Angela was wearing a simple pair of tailored trousers along with a black Rivanne top and Moffont jacket when she finally came down the curving stairs of the private wing. Her netlenses were dark except for one figure glowing at the corner of her vision. A long number, one which spelled the end of her world.

Marlak was waiting for her on the first-floor landing. 'They're here,' he said in a disapproving tone. The lawyer was over sixty years old. He'd been with the DeVoyal family for the last forty, and was devoted to Raymond. He could have retired years ago from the money he'd earned, living a pleasant life on Sao Jeroni, where his grandchildren had settled. Instead he chose to stay on, relishing the challenge of modern finance legality. It was the only way he knew, the way to keep his brain active.

'Thank you,' Angela said.

'I think it's wrong of them to arrive so quickly. I can lodge that complaint with the Council.'

'I don't believe the Council would give a flying crap about anything a DeVoyal says at this point. So let's not make this any more humiliating than necessary.'

'I understand. But please know they do have to follow the law. I will note any abuses.'

'You're a darling.'

There were three of them waiting on the polished wooden flooring of the hallway. Two men and a woman, all dressed in black suits. Expensive designer suits, Angela noted, as was fitting, but grouped together they managed to make them look like a uniform.

'Ms DeVoyal,' said Matthews, the agent in charge. 'Our sympathies for your loss.'

'Thank you. Please state the reason for your visit?'

'The New Monaco Council of Governance has been made aware of your family's current financial situation. A group of thirty-two banks and market institutions have filed for loan repayment following today's collapse of the oil futures market. Treasury records indicate you don't have enough money in your assets to make good their claim. Is that true?'

'How do I plead, you mean?'

'Yes,' he said implacably.

'Big day for you. You don't get this very often, do you?'

'I have no personal involvement in this matter, I assure you. Ms DeVoyal, I must ask you for your answer now, please.'

Angela took a breath. 'No. My family cannot pay the debts at this time. I'm sure if you just let me begin negotiations with—'

'I'm sorry. But I'm not concerned with what rescheduling agreement you may eventually come to with your debtors. I am only concerned with the New Monaco residency laws. To confirm then: your net worth is no longer in excess of fifty billion US dollars?'

'Correct.' *There is no net worth – I'm two and a half billion in debt, which I'm sure you know.*

'In which case, I regretfully have to inform you, that by the Council of Governance's constitution, you no longer qualify as a New Monaco resident.'

'I was born here. This is my planet.'

'No, Ms DeVoyal. It *was* your planet. Legally, you now have twenty-four hours to attend to your affairs before I escort you to the gateway. However, the Council is pleased to extend a non-prejudicial offer of a further forty-eight hours' extension so you may arrange your father's funeral.'

'That's very kind of them. Marlak?'

'I'll see to it.'

'The Council would like to add that should your finances recover, you will be most welcome to reapply for citizenship.'

'Indeed,' she said loftily. 'I'll remember that.'

Matthews cleared his throat, clearly relieved that she wasn't making a scene. 'Thank you, Ms DeVoyal. I'll remain with you until this is over.'

She gave him a derisive smile. 'You think I'll make a break for it? That I'll turn feral and live out in the hills, preying on the innocent townsfolk?'

'I don't believe that, no.'

'Sorry, that was impolite of me. You're only doing your job. It's been a bad day. You know?'

'I think you're coping very well.' Matthews nodded to the woman agent. 'You can tell them to come in now.'

'Who?' Angela asked sharply.

Matthews gave Marlak an uncomfortable glance. 'Um . . .'

'Angela,' Marlak said uncomfortably. 'The banks have been in touch with the Financial Regulatory Board. A team of the Board's Officers has been appointed to administer the remaining family assets. They need to recover as much as they can from your companies and holdings.'

'I see. Right now?'

'They're worried you might try to hide assets.'

'Oh really?' She glanced up as a whole group of people started to walk into the grandiose hall. Unlike the agents, their clothes weren't anything like as expensive. Office worker-types. The kind of little people she didn't even register as she went about her usual day. Now they were here to rip the carcass of her life apart and earn themselves a nice bonus for doing so.

Angela held her hand up. 'See this ring? It's my engagement ring. My fiancé proposed to me tonight. Who does it belong to?'

Matthews was starting to realize this wasn't going to be as easy as he'd thought. 'Technically, the Board's officers can claim every personal item you own. In practice, they will of course leave you with some clothes and other low-value effects which have a sentimental value. I'm afraid a ring like that will definitely be claimed. Er, is that diamond?'

'It is. Let's just see what my fiancé, a New Monaco citizen, has to say about that, shall we?'

Matthews inclined his head. 'Of course.' He and the other agents went into a huddle with the team from the Regulatory Board office, leaving her alone with Marlak.

'They really will track it all down,' Marlak said quietly. 'Your father and I never thought to hide anything away. New Monaco was supposed to be the one place where a plutocrat's wealth was safe.'

'I know.' She narrowed her eyes. 'What about you? They can't take anything of yours, can they?'

'Nothing that's already been paid to me, no. I haven't had this month's salary, so theoretically that makes me one of your creditors.'

'Sorry.'

'Don't be. I'm rich in my own right – by normal standards, anyway. In fact, you're welcome to come and live with me on New Washington for as long as you need. The house has a guest cottage in the grounds. You know, it's been eight years since I visited.'

'No. That's really, really sweet of you, Marlak. But I don't do charity. Looks like you actually will have to retire and spend more time with your grandchildren.'

Marlak pulled a face. 'Horrible thought. But what about you, what will you do?'

The unspoken question was the one she flinched at. *What can you do? What use are you?* 'That's something I'm going to have to learn. I've got degrees in financial theory. That might help me . . .' She trailed off. *Get a job.* The more she thought about it, the more bleakly funny it was. *Who in this universe would ever give me a job? Hell, even I wouldn't employ me.* She gave Marlak a rueful smile. 'Twenty billion other people manage. Somehow.'

'They do indeed. I didn't know you were engaged. Housden, is it?'

'Yes.'

'He's a good man. Call him. He deserves to know from you.'

'Right.' She drew down a long breath and told her e-i to place the call she'd been dreading.

It was Prince Matiff's transnet address management software which responded to her call. 'The Prince will no longer accept calls from you.'

'I understand. Do you have a message relay facility?'

'Yes.'

'Message begins: Pray you never meet me again. Pray very hard. End message.' She licked her lips, pleased with how good that made her feel. A hollow threat – or maybe not. She was going to live for a long time. *Thanks to Daddy.* Angela sniffed away the tears before they could properly form.

Housden answered her call straight away. But then he was always a class act. 'I heard,' he said. 'The cartel just became the talk of the party. I'm so sorry about your father.'

'That's very sweet,' she said. 'He didn't suffer. Quite the opposite.'

'Good.'

The silence stretched out. 'Housden. Under the circumstances, I'm hardly going to hold you to your proposal.'

'I . . . I don't know what to say. If it was just down to me, then of course we'd stay together. But the family . . .'

'Always the families,' she said with a sad smile. 'I know.'

'Perhaps, you would be a mistress?'

Angela laughed, which made the agents stare at her. 'Oh Housden, you really are the best. No, you go and find yourself someone wonderful. Please. For me.'

'I love you, Angela.'

'I like having sex with you, too.'

'It's more than that, and you know it.'

She held up her hand again, admiring the diamond ring for the last time. The raw diamond it was cut from must have been the size of a duck egg. *Incredible!* 'I'm wearing the ring. I'm looking at it right now. It's beautiful, Housden.'

'It is yours. I had it made for you.'

'You're really the best. But I can't keep it – literally. The bailiffs will take it from me, and sell it on. I can't have that. It is the grandest romantic gesture of our generation. You have it back, and give it to your next fiancée. Anyone who deserves you, deserves it.'

'Let me talk to my family. Perhaps I can still make us happen.'

'No, my darling. Don't do that. It really is better to have loved and lost. You keep on living this life for me, okay?'

'But what will you do?'

Again, that question. What use is a New Monaco citizen in the real universe? 'I'll be fine, don't you worry. And anyway, I'm a one-in-ten, remember? You and I will probably wind up together in the end. Someday before my thousand years are up.'

'I will count every day.'

'You do that. But right now I want you to call an Agent Matthews. Tell him that the engagement is off, and that the ring is yours. He'll make sure you get it back, okay?'

'I will. Angela, I really did love you.'

'And I will never forget you. Promise. Goodbye, my darling.' She turned to face the cluster of agents. 'Hey, Matthews.'

By the time he was facing her she'd eased the ring off. 'Catch!'

The panic on his face as he lunged for the spinning ring was comical.

'You'll be getting a call from my ex-fiancé in a moment. See he gets it back.'

The agent scowled at her.

Now for the really important call.

'I can't believe you called me,' Shasta said. 'We all know what happened, the cartel and everything. The Prince has announced an extra day of partying. It's going to be fantastic.'

'Really?' Angela growled. 'So is he launching an Apollo to celebrate?'

'It's not appropriate for you to call me any more. You know this.'

'If you know about the cartel, then you know I could do with a little help right now.'

'There are many transworld charities I give to most generously. My e-i will provide you with a list.'

'No Shasta. I need help. I need you to get me off this godawful planet. Today.'

'This planet is paradise. Don't ever call me again. My e-i won't allow you access. Goodbye, Angela.'

'Bitch!' Angela spat at the dead connection. That did leave her with a major problem. She'd thought she could rely on Shasta. If the roles were reversed, she certainly would have helped. *Wouldn't I?*

'Everything all right?' Marlak asked.

'I don't know. Agent Matthews?'

He left the others and came over to her. 'Yes.'

'It's the middle of the night. My father's committed suicide, and I'm a bankrupt who's about to be exiled. Do you mind if I go to bed now, please?'

'Of course.'

*

Angela woke up alone. It was a habit she hoped she could quickly break. At least it was in her own bedroom; which even though its decor was utterly perfect, designed by some of the best home stylists to be found across the trans-space worlds, today didn't feel like home at all.

Because it's not. Not any more. It belongs to the banks.

She took a shower and went into one of her walk-through wardrobes. Simple jeans and a sweatshirt were the order of the day, she decided. She started telling her e-i to summon her maid and hair stylist, then stopped. 'Stupid,' she muttered. On quite a few levels.

This was when she had to concentrate. 'Is the surveillance still off in my suite?' she asked the e-i.

'Yes.'

'Give me the visual location of everyone in the mansion.' She studied the diagram her netlenses produced, seeing Matthews was waiting in the corridor outside her suite. Marlak was in her father's study with several Board officers, who were hardwiring their own systems into the family AI.

She went back into her bathroom, and took the jewellery from the pockets of her discarded robe where she'd left it last night. They were the items she'd removed from her collection, erasing their listings from the AI. She'd chosen five rings and two sets of earrings. Not big pieces compared to some she had, but the gems were all large and flawless. Between them they'd be worth a million and a half dollars US – if you bought them from a store. She was under no illusion that she'd be able to get that price, but it was a start.

Concealing them was more problematic. She looked round the bathroom and finally decided on the soap. A nail file carved out deep slots in the side of a rose-perfumed bar, and she eased each item in carefully, then pushed soap flakes back in around them, sealing up the bar. It went in a washbag along with stuff like her sonic toothstik, and already opened bottles of oil and some make-up. The agents would let her take that without any question, but getting through the gateway was going to be difficult. She'd be searched and scanned. Non-residents travelling out by themselves always were. And she knew they'd be exceptionally thorough with her for precisely this reason. Until last night she'd been relying on Shasta to travel with her. Staff accompanying their employers were waved through every time. It was something she was going to have to work a way round, and fast. Maybe Daniellia would be open to a proposition?

Angela sat in her dressing room, and started combing her damp hair out. It took a lot longer than when her stylists did it. She hadn't imagined that something this basic would be so difficult, but she kept getting the brush caught in tangles. And why were there more of those than usual?

Agent Matthews was ready when she came out of her suite into the main corridor. 'There seems to be something wrong with the network in your private quarters,' he said.

'Good morning, Agent Matthews, have you had breakfast yet?'

'We'll need your AI access codes.'

'No, me neither. Did you keep any cooks on? I suppose I can make toast and boil an egg. How difficult can it be? There must be a 101 instruction file somewhere on the transnet.'

'The codes, please.'

She rolled her eyes and ordered her e-i to send them to the agent.

'Thank you,' he said in his monotonously polite tone. 'And I know how to boil an egg. You won't starve today.'

'You're very sweet. I think you're in the wrong line of work.'

'It pays well.'

'Really? Any vacancies? I do have first-class knowledge of the New Monaco finance markets.'

He shook his head in wonder. 'I never will understand you people.'

'No, you never will. Poor you.'

Matthews was right, he did know how to cook. She sat in the West Wing kitchen, which she'd only ever visited three times in her life, and let him serve her scrambled eggs with smoked salmon, on thick toasted bread. He showed her how to use the delightfully antique orange squeezer. Forcing the juice out of the halved fruit by pulling down a lever on the side of the chrome-plated apparatus gave her a ridiculous sense of satisfaction. The coffee machine, however, had more controls and flashing lights than a gateway control room. But again, he knew how to operate it.

'I do have a lot of things to get used to, don't I?' she said reflectively as she held up the espresso cup with its perfectly made contents.

'Quite a few, yes.'

'Any tips?'

'Take a while and work out what you want to do with the rest of your life.'

'And how do I pay for that time?'

'Your father was born in America. That gives you a legal residency claim. They have social security. Not much. If you're young and able, you get shipped out to a new world and given ten acres to grow your own food on. Same with Grande Europe.'

'Shipped out,' she said in distaste. 'Maybe I should just have "failure" tattooed on my forehead.'

'Won't any of your friends help?'

'Some might. My ex-fiancé. But I don't do charity, Agent Matthews.'

'The transnet media would probably be interested in your story.'

'Yes, I'm sure they would.'

Matthews frowned and looked up. 'Excuse me,' he said, and walked out.

When Angela told her e-i to find out what was going on, it reported that she didn't have access clearance to the mansion net any more. 'Too late,' she muttered under her breath.

Matthews returned a couple of minutes later. A familiar figure was walking beside him. Shasta's father, Bantri. Taller than Matthews and getting on for twice as wide. His round face had a full beard, which she remembered from her childhood as space-black, but which was now submitting to an infestation of age's silver threads; and his brown eyes had all the merriness of a serial killer. He wore a dark-purple silk suit that tended towards a more Chinese style than Indian. The diamond pinned to the front of his traditional turban would also be large enough to carve a ring out of, Angela decided. But then Bantri did fancy himself a modern version of the old maharajas.

'My dear girl,' he boomed in a bass voice, and opened his arms wide; the way she imagined a benevolent uncle would treat her.

She walked over to be engulfed by his embrace. 'Hello, Bantri.' It did surprise her that out of everyone, he would be the one to come and offer sympathy and comfort. Acts of kindness didn't feature heavily in his life. She was already busy trying to work out what kind of advantage he was looking for at the mansion.

'I'm so sorry about all of this.'

'Not your fault, Bantri. We should have been more cautious, and certainly more alert. But the bioil market was always profitable. Ah well, too late now.'

He clasped her hands in his, and squeezed tightly. 'Your father was a great man. I will miss him terribly.'

'That's very kind.'

'And you? What of you? I see the parasites have descended on you already.'

'This is New Monaco. Everything is about the money.'

'Of course, of course.' He took a step back and looked at her with greedy admiration. It was an expression which suited him far better than any attempted kindness.

'So you have no money?'

'No, Bantri,' she said coolly. 'But you know this.'

'I do. Yes, I do. It is a terrible thing to be poor in the transstellar worlds. I wondered if I might help?'

Angela was quite pleased with herself for working out the main reason why he was here before he made the offer. It meant she wouldn't betray any surprise when—

'You would make a most magnificent acquisition for me,' Bantri continued in a hopeful tone. 'I would be honoured if you would accept.'

'A six-month contract, and you obtain full Indian citizenship for me, beginning today. I'll need somewhere to live afterwards.'

He blinked at her immediate response. 'Eighteen months.'

'Twelve, including a tax-free bonus. And I keep the clothes I want.'

'Fourteen. The bonus. A dozen outfits, but no couture dresses. I know how much you and Shasta spend on them.'

She gave him a nod.

He raised a thick finger that wore several rings, and beckoned.

Angela recognized the man who hurried through the kitchen door. Tariq, Bantri's senior lawyer; Marlak's equivalent.

'Tariq will draw up the contract,' Bantri told her. 'I'm going to look at the artwork in your library. I feel I might make an offer for some of your Monets.'

'Good choice.'

His smile was unpleasantly triumphant. 'Yes. It is.'

'You don't have to do this,' Matthews said as soon as Bantri left the kitchen. 'Not this, not selling yourself.'

'I seem to be short of other commodities. You and the Board officers have made very sure of that, Agent Matthews.'

'But this . . . You haven't even looked at what's out there, the possibilities.'

'Oh please, you don't really think I'm going to squeeze my own oranges for the rest of my life, do you?'

He shook his head, anger dampened by dismay. 'Hell, you people.'

Angela got her e-i to review the contract file Tariq formatted. The salient points were all there, not that she cared. Being a part of Bantri's staff was the goal. If she was going to have sex with a fat older man . . . well, it wouldn't be the first time.

She added her certificate to the file and went upstairs to pack. One of the Board officers supervised, making sure she didn't try to slip any of the couture dresses or designer shoes or anything else ridiculously expensive into her one permitted valise. The washbag was never queried.

*

They left that afternoon, after she buried her father in a grove of newly planted terrestrial oaks, his favourite. On the plane back to

Bantri's estate she made the first elementary mistake, thinking she would be sitting in the forward cabin with him.

'No no, my dear,' he said, 'your place is not here, not now,' and dismissed her with an airy wave of his hand. Angela stood up and headed for the staff cabin at the rear of the plane. None of them spoke to her for the whole duration of the flight.

*

So Shasta did get to see Angela again. Though to her credit she kept her word and didn't speak to her erstwhile friend. She arrived back home after another twenty-four hours partying at Prince Matiff's mansion and found her father at breakfast in their palace's morning room. He sat alone at the table, eating slowly, savouring each mouthful as if it were his last.

Angela was standing placidly two paces behind his heavy carved chair, wearing what would be her typical clothing through-out the contract: a halter top and baggy pantaloons of gauzy fabric. The serving maids ignored her as they brought Bantri fresh plates and poured his coffee from a silver pot. But then everybody in the palace ignored her. She rather welcomed that.

Shasta walked into the morning room and kissed her father dutifully, even though she was obviously cross with him. They exchanged a few pleasantries, and she announced she was going to bed for a week to recover. 'It was that good.'

She walked away, pausing only to thrust her face centimetres from Angela's. Glared without speaking, then stomped off back to her own wing of the palace. As petty and pathetic as any toddler who didn't get their way. Neither she nor Bantri saw the soft smile of contemptuous amusement that lifted Angela's lips for a moment.

Three weeks later, Bantri visited India at the start of yet another business tour. He spent about half the year away from New Monaco, inspecting his empire, taking meetings with managers and financiers, entertaining politicians and bureaucrats. Angela knew his routine well enough – it had been Shasta's constant childhood complaint that Daddy was never around.

As was standard practice, Bantri's entourage were quickly and politely waved through New Monaco gateway control. Angela waited patiently until they reached their five-star hotel in Mumbai. Once Bantri was asleep she took her washbag out of the valise and walked out of the hotel.

Nobody in the entourage even knew she was missing for ten hours. Why should they – she wasn't their friend.

Tariq called her transnet address several times in the first forty-eight hours following the realization she'd deserted her patron. First with questions, then with threats. The last call he made was to inform her that the contract was now officially void, her Indian citizenship was revoked, her new bank account was frozen, and they were applying for a court order to reclaim all monies paid to her.

It didn't matter; that three weeks of pay Angela had accumulated had already bought her a one-way plane ticket (standard class – dear heavens!) to New York. She was standing in Central Park at the start of a new day and smiling round at the glorious old buildings by the time Tariq's first call came through.

Sunday 17th March 2143

A bright sun in a cloudless sky brought a calm warmth to Newcastle's damp streets. Night was over and the rains gone, leaving a freshness that finally promised the retreat of the fierce winter. Sid drove the short distance from Jesmond to the Arevalo Medical's Royal Victoria Infirmary. The footings for the new oncology clinic were now dug deep across the old car park, but at eight o'clock on a Sunday morning, he didn't have to worry too much about finding an empty space in the remaining section.

Sid found a charity store open in the main entrance lobby and bought a bunch of flowers and a big cube of chocolates. His e-i guided him through the maze of connecting corridors that stitched the sprawling complex together, delivering him to the Hadley block after a couple of minutes. Tilly Lewis was in a private room on the seventh floor.

She smiled up at him as he knocked on the half-open door. 'Hey, didn't expect to see you. Come on in.'

Sid peered round the bright clean room; it had the decor of a mid-price hotel, certainly there wasn't any visible medical equipment except for some blank monitor screens on one wall. 'No family about?'

'Hell no. They won't be here for another hour or two, hopefully more. I'm enjoying the rest.'

'You look okay,' he told her in relief as he pulled a chair over to the side of the bed.

'Forget that. Are those Devorn chocolates?'

'Yeah. It's only quarter past eight, though.'

'In real time. In a hospital, that's about midday. They woke me at six for breakfast. I nearly put the nurse in the next ward for that.'

Sid laughed. 'So when are you out?'

Tilly started opening the cube. 'Possibly as early as this afternoon, depending on the next scan. I'd like to make it to tomorrow. A whole two days without having to look after the kids. Bliss.'

'So they're not worried then?'

'A little bit of smoke inhalation? Nah, pet, I'm fine. This is all precautionary. We managed to get out before it got too bad.'

'I'm sorry.'

'For what? You weren't there.'

'My case. I should have known they'd try and wipe out as much evidence as possible. Ernie's garage was an obvious target.'

'Everything is with hindsight, pet.'

'Those agency constables were idiots.' It had been a classic distraction, a couple of joyriding kids racing along Western Road in a jacked car. They'd driven right into the garage's forecourt and side-skidded into the parked squad car before charging off again. The agency constables tasked with safeguarding the forensics team had ignored every protocol in the file and taken off in pursuit – wasted as it happened, they never caught the kids. Thirty seconds after they'd left, Molotovs had come flying through the garage windows.

'No real damage,' Tilly assured him, and chose an orange crème from the cube's top layer.

Sid had to admit she didn't look any different to usual. 'I'm glad. So are we going to get anything useful from the garage?'

'Ha! I knew it, you're not interested in me at all. It's always the case with you.'

'That's not—' He saw her grin, and shrugged.

'Gotcha.'

'Aye, pet, you're evil.' He plucked a walnut whizz from the cube. 'Jacinta says hello.'

'Weren't you moving house this weekend?'

'Aye. Yesterday.'

Tilly narrowed her eyes to give him A Look. 'Shouldn't you be unpacking?'

'One of my friends is in hospital, pet. What can you do?'

'She'll put you in the bed next door if you're not careful.'

'I know. But the removal company was good. They didn't break anything, and all the boxes are in the right rooms.'

'Men! You never change.'

'And you never give up hoping you can change us.'

Tilly sighed and found a hazelnut truffle. 'No, there wasn't anything there.'

'Where?' Sid asked innocently.

'Dickhead. The garage. We were going through the motions. But it was the weekend.'

'Triple time, huh?'

'Absolutely, pet.'

'Nothing?' Sid asked. She'd been right: shamefully, results formed a big part of the reason to visit her. Lab analysis of samples was important, but if someone with Tilly's experience said there wasn't anything useful at a scene then that was enough for him. She knew what to look for, what to take away for examination.

It would be Wednesday before Northern Forensics produced a report on the items already taken to the lab. Wednesday was just too long.

'No. Nothing that could ever tie him to the Red Shields. That garage was his legitimate front, remember. Clean as a major GE company's accounts. I doubt you could even charge him for subbing spare parts.'

'It's not what he did so much as who he did it with.'

'We did pick up a lot of residuals. The lab is running DNA analysis on them, so you'll find out who was at the garage – some of them anyway. But it doesn't prove anything.'

'Thanks, Tilly.'

She held up the cube. 'You bring these, and you can visit any time.'

*

Sid walked into Office3 just after nine o'clock, pleased to see the team already there ahead of him. Ian and Eva were sitting next to each other, both absorbed with the data their consoles were throwing at them, not saying anything; he'd tasked them with tracking down Reinert's secondaries. Lorelle Burdett was busy working through Reinert's transnet calls for the last few months, identifying contacts, trying to link him with known Red Shield activity. Dedra was checking through the alibis of the nine 2Norths who lived in the St James, and covertly following up those enquiries with questions to their closest friends and colleagues about recent behaviour. Had they noticed a change in the last couple of months, perhaps? Did their friend forget topics they'd talked about? Did he suddenly have trouble performing his job? Anything that would indicate a substitution had been made.

Aldred and Reannha were handling liaison with the agency data operatives who were compiling all the surveillance logs around the St James singletown into a zone simulation for the Friday when the murder had been committed. Meanwhile, Ari had been spending his time compiling general network data on the St James, trying to find any leads on the rip. Even rips had signatures if you knew how to scan for them.

It was like walking into a church, Sid decided. No banter. No smiling faces. In fact the silence was absolute. He liked to think it was dedication to the case rather than sullen, Sunday morning blues.

He saw Aldred sitting at a spare desk. Eva had checked and confirmed his alibi within a couple of hours last Wednesday. He had indeed left the St James at nine forty-five and flown down to London the day his clone brother was murdered.

'I've just visited Tilly,' Sid announced. 'She's fine. But she does think the surviving forensics material isn't going to produce much by way of leads.'

'What kind of idiots do the agencies employ these days?' Reannha asked.

'The very best idiots, clearly,' Sid retorted. 'Don't worry, their failure will be featured heavily in my report. O'Rouke will crap on their supervisor from a great height. Endangering lives like that could earn them a contract suspension.'

'Aye man, that'll teach them,' Ian growled sarcastically.

'Actually, that kind of threat is the worst a company can have,' Aldred said. 'Hitting them in the cash flow is a lot more effective than whinging about procedures and inadequate training.'

'All right.' Sid wheeled one of the desk chairs over, and straddled it so his hands were resting on the back. 'What have we got? Ari?'

'The rip is similar to those used to screw the city surveillance. The code mutated, but it's from the same source. Whoever did it was responsible for launching both attacks.'

Sid couldn't tell if Ari was pleased at announcing the utterly obvious, or if he was simply being methodical, allowing procedures to rule him. 'Any leads on who wrote it?'

'Not yet. But it was good code, the best. That implies AI involvement with the formatting. Which in turn costs money. Our Digital Counter-Intrusion Service is reviewing known free-binary radicals to see if anyone dropped out after the rip to live the highlife on their fee.'

Sid didn't comment, but he could see the same thing on everyone's face. If the freebinary who wrote it was that good, they wouldn't be on any DC-IS listing, and they'd know not to flash the cash. But then trying to pull anything factual from the transnet was always akin to eating soup with a fork. 'Thanks. Ian?'

'Ernie's good, I'll give him that. We've got a secondary he uses for the garage; plenty of decent cars sold legitimately for low cost, so you keep your vehicle licence tax to a minimum, while you pay him the difference of the true value through a secondary payment. Standard stuff. But it's like it was flashing red lights to show us he's a normal second-hand car dealer. No other second-aries that we can find yet.'

'Lorelle?'

'Plenty of names on his contact list, but no cross-reference with known Red Shield members. I'm with Ian, he's got a digital ghost we haven't tracked yet, and without his e-i to break down, we probably never will.'

'Looks like we're hanging on Ralph's interrogation for all our information,' Sid said. 'Dedra?'

Dedra Foyster gave Aldred a sly glance. 'All the alibis are confirmed. None of the nine Norths who have apartments in the St James killed our victim. The follow-up you gave me is taking a little more time. So far I'm pretty certain about five Norths; no change in behaviour, no sudden holidays or time off work, no odd memory lapses. Everyone who knows them well says they've stayed the same.'

Sid wondered if she'd checked Aldred's continuity yet. Would he be one of the people she asked? He quashed a grin. 'Abner?'

'We're about ready to take it to the zone, boss. The AI is running a last pass on mesh memory cohesion.'

'Great. I'll go in with you.'

*

Taken in isolation, the St James singletown was uninspiring. A large central dome containing the commercial sections, with five residential towers, each one different; a twisted spire, elongated pyramid, squat barbican, a weird narrow tower that looked as if it had been squashed into place by other skyscrapers on either side – now missing – and the living globe stack, whose external surface bands between windows were all shrubs and vines. Standing above the structure's projection in the theatre, Sid felt that the architectural software that had been used to produce it had been left to run without any human intervention; it lacked ambition and vision. Build big and impressive, but don't try anything new.

He was used to seeing the real thing, of course – it sat on the other side of Barrack Road from the St James' stadium, where many a Saturday afternoon had been spent in exultation or misery as Newcastle United slipped in and out of League One with terrible monotony.

'Expand it to fill the theatre floor,' Sid said. 'But leave a fifty-metre boundary. We need to see everybody who comes in and out.'

In the control room, Reannha changed the projection parameters. Sid and Abner watched the singletown expand in front of them.

'Take me back to midnight, Thursday 10th January. And highlight all entrances: public doors, staff door, delivery bays, garage ramps, emergency exits, utility access hatches. The lot.'

The roads darkened at his feet; while the vehicles rolling along them squirted low headlight beams across the snowy surfaces.

'What are you searching for?' Aldred asked. He was pressed up against the control room window, looking in on the zone theatre.

Sid and Abner swapped a glance. 'For the next twenty-four hours: every North that goes in, either on foot or in a car, taxi, bike, whatever,' Sid said. 'One of them has to be our victim.'

Green symbols appeared on the doors and ramps down into the garage. Sid hadn't been expecting quite so many. But then this case had acclimatized him to the amount of detail in the zone on this case. 'Let's go,' he told Abner. He started to walk anti-clockwise, up Stanhope Street, examining the tiny figures on the pavement that were hunched up against the cold winter night.

*

Ian got back to his flat at eight o'clock that night. He'd just spent three hours in the zone theatre himself, and was tired by the endless repetition of searching the miniature people, asking for them to be expanded, for the AI to run characteristics recognition on the shadowed faces. After those thankless dreary months of backtracking taxis, to be back in the theatre qualified as cruel and unusual punishment. At the same time, the dread and despondency of the taxi backtrack was missing. They'd already found six Norths going into the St James by ten o'clock Friday morning. The case was picking up momentum now. He was impatient for Ralph to return with the results of Ernie Reinert's interrogation. That would propel them into the final stages. Contrary to all the gloomy expectations he'd had at the start, they might actually arrest the murderer. Not the people who ordered it, mind – you had to be realistic about such things. But even so . . .

Ian sat on the bed, put on his netlens glasses and accessed the Apple console. The weekend's activity by Marcus Sherman and his crew that the AI had managed to track was all there waiting for him in a depressing number of files that needed examining and cross-referencing. Just looking at them all laid out in a neat three-dimensional matrix of red and green icons made him sigh. Sid and Eva were going to have to come over tomorrow night and help, he decided. That or they'd all have to agree to calling it off. In the meantime . . . He started with a simple timeline overview.

The AI's monitors had started to slowly reacquire data. It helped that they had established physical residencies where Sherman and his people had to return to at some point.

Jede had gone back to his flat in Felling on Friday night. When Ian reviewed the local transnet cells, there were several calls made from the correct location, but with the new e-i access code.

'. . . what you are asking for is going to take time . . .'

'. . . there is a synthesizer which can produce the items, but it is restricted . . .'

'. . . raw for that kind of tox is licence-only, what you have to do is go back two stages in the chemical process . . .'

'. . . ready for delivery . . .'

Ian grinned behind the glowing symbols of his netlens glasses. 'Aye, bollocks,' he grunted. You didn't have to have much by way of smarts to know that was all a lure. Sherman's crew were trying to sucker them into acting on an exchange that never was.

A good way of finding out how interested the police were in their activities.

Very, was the simple answer. But they mustn't know that.

The smart counter-entrapment played out with Ruckby and Boz as well, both of whom made calls with new interface codes. All skilfully building the fiction. Even Sherman himself re-appeared for a while at Dunston Marina, when Ruckby delivered Valentina to the *Maybury Moon* for the night.

Ian almost stopped the review; Joyce would be arriving soon. Then he spotted an untraceable call routed through the cell serving Jede's flat at 7:04 am Saturday to yet another e-i code they had no record of. It was short and encrypted at a level that the AI couldn't break.

He immediately pulled the rest of the logs for Jede's flat. What-ever the call had been, it fired a quick reaction from the man. Sure enough, Ian watched a mid-rez mesh log from the street outside showing Jede hurrying out at 7:11 am. He climbed into his parked car, drove off, and the macromesh lost him less than two minutes later when the licence code vanished. As always, it would take a proper police operation to reacquire and follow the car. On a hunch, Ian pulled the logs for Boz and Ruckby. Sure enough, they'd left their homes by 7:30 on Saturday morn-ing, and promptly vanished into the city, swiftly evading the surveillance routines.

None of the crew reappeared until much later. Boz was on Valentina chauffeur duty that night. Ruckby went out clubbing that evening, showing up in front of half a dozen hi-rez public meshes. And Jede used a secondary account they knew about for the first time since the Last Mile débâcle to pay for a pair of high-class escorts, who turned up at his flat. All perfectly normal, not hiding anything.

Ian removed his netlens glasses and gave the silent Apple console a thoughtful stare. Whatever data they needed to confirm Saturday's gameplan plainly wasn't in there. 'So what were you all up to yesterday that was so important?' he asked. 'Pay Ernie's garage a visit, did you?'

Monday 18th March 2143

The light of a March dawn wasn't particularly intense, but the bedroom curtains were worn and ill fitting. The windows seemed unnaturally bright to Sid as the light tickled him out of his sleep. He stared at the clock, whose green digits told him it was already twenty past six. Braced himself for the start of another day in the Hurst household.

There were some footsteps scurrying round somewhere outside the bedroom. But no bickering, no shouts, no fists banging on the bathroom door. Zara's bedroom had a tiny en suite, because, as Will sneered, 'I'm not having a kazi next to my bed.' He was free to use the big bathroom all by himself.

'Heaven,' Jacinta muttered. She had her eyes closed, but there was a smile on her face.

'Aye, I think we might have made it,' Sid agreed. 'Mind, heaven would have proper curtains, like.'

'We can't afford them.'

'So it's a pious heaven, then?'

'Looks like it.'

'And I don't suppose there's anything in the fridge for breakfast.' Last night's supper had been a Chinese meal delivered to the house.

'No, pet; strangely, I spent more time unpacking yesterday than I was expecting to. Can't think why. No time for my e-i to go shopping.'

Sid eyed the stack of unopened boxes along one wall, and decided on cowardice. 'Lucky that in a place as posh as Jesmond there's a café on St George's Terrace that serves a canny breakfast.'

Jacinta opened her eyes and grinned. 'You've not forgotten how to show a girl a good time, have you?'

'Oh no. Not me.' Sid climbed out of bed, and made a real effort to work out which case had his clean shirts in.

'The blue one,' Jacinta said.

'I remember!'

St George's Terrace was a five-minute walk away, a road with shops and businesses along one side, and neat terrace housing on the other. Tall cherry trees down the pavement were just starting to bud. Sid imagined they would look wonderful when the pink blossom came out.

Café Black was a small family-run business, offering a reasonable menu. Sid went for a full English, with scrambled eggs on toast, bacon, mushrooms, grilled tomatoes, and a slice of fried black pudding.

'Careful, pet,' Jacinta said. All she'd ordered was tea and toast; the kids were having cereal and toast.

'It's going well,' Sid told her.

'Is this the dead North case?' Will asked.

'Aye.'

'Everyone at school says it wasn't a carjacking. They say that Brussels had him whacked.'

Sid nearly coughed up his orange juice. 'What?'

'It's on all the unlicensed sites,' Will said.

'Does the government really kill people?' Zara asked.

'No. Absolutely not.'

'I don't want you accessing unlicensed sites,' Jacinta said.

'What else are they saying at school?'

'Sid! Don't encourage him.'

'Aye, that's not encouragement, it's enquiring. What are they saying?'

'Well, that Brussels wants to make St Libra part of the GE, and the only thing stopping them is the Norths.'

'Brussels doesn't want to make St Libra part of the GE. Do you know why?'

'The Independencies,' Zara answered, smiling proudly.

'That's right. See, St Libra is the place people go to when they're not happy with the government where they're living. There's room for all of them, there. The last thing the GE needs is millions of people who'll fight their authority.'

'Do you like the GE, Dad?'

Sid was pleased with how he managed to avoid giving Jacinta a look. 'They pay my salary, so they're not all bad.'

Zara screwed her face up into an inquisitor's expression. 'But—'

'Eat your cornflakes,' Jacinta ordered.

'Yes, Mum.'

Sid finally risked glancing at Jacinta. 'It's because it's taking so long to arrest someone for the carjacking. Everyone expected us to find the suspect straight away.'

'When will you get him, Dad?' Will asked.

'This week, I hope,' Sid said.

'You sound very confident about that, pet,' Jacinta said, holding her mug of tea idly in front of her face.

'Aye, reasonably,' he said.

'Will you be on the zone news?' an excited Zara asked.

'No. That'll be the Chief Constable.'

*

The zone theatre was no longer running the St James simulation when Sid arrived at Market Street at eight o'clock. Ari and Lorelle were waiting for him in Office3 when he walked in. He knew they had the late-night shift, and given the number of coffee mugs on the desk they were sitting at, he judged they'd not been home.

'We found something,' Ari said, his face a combination of exhaustion and elation.

'Come through,' Sid said, and led them into his private office. He didn't bother activating the security seal, not with the rest of the team starting to arrive for the morning shift.

Lorelle was smiling when she settled herself just inside the door. That was telling – Sid hadn't seen her look remotely happy since the case began. 'What is it?'

Ari exhaled loudly. 'Adrian North arrived at the St James at 8:03 am on Friday, the 11th of January. He was quite open about it – we picked him up on three meshes getting out of a taxi and using the main entrance. His e-i responded to a general entry query from the security program in the St James net. He was there.'

'And?' Sid asked.

'We can't find him leaving.'

'We checked every minute right up until Saturday evening, boss,' Lorelle said insistently. 'There are twenty-three Norths coming in and out; they've got cars, they took taxis, they walked out with groups of friends. None of them was Adrian. So, either he eluded us, or he stayed there well after Saturday evening. Either way, it's the first possibility we have.'

'The only possibility,' Ari said.

'Aye,' Sid said. 'And we've checked Adrian out during the investigation?'

'Yeah. He's a 2, a bioil specialist working in Northumberland Interstellar's production division.'

'No kidding?' Sid said. 'A full walking talking cliché, then.'

'He has an apartment down on Quayside,' Lorelle said, reading the data straight off her iris smartcell display. 'Underwent the DNA verification, so he's not an imposter.'

Overlooking the Millennium Bridge, Sid thought. An irrelevant coincidence, there was no knowing where the body would end up that night.

'Do you want us to extend the simulation to Sunday and Monday?' Ari asked. 'See if we can find him leaving?'

'No, we're a long way past anything like that,' Sid said. He

534

told his e-i to pull Adrian's interface address from the station network, and make the call.

'What is it?' Adrian 2North asked.

'Sorry to bother you, sir,' Sid said. 'But we're just clearing up a few details on the carjacking case.'

'Go on then. But be quick, I'm due in the office in half an hour.'

'We're trying to establish what time you left the St James singletown on Friday the eleventh, and what exit you used.'

'What Friday? I haven't been to the St James for months.'

'Sir. Friday the eleventh of January, the weekend we found your brother's body.'

'Sorry, but you've got me mixed up with one of my brothers. I haven't been to the St James this year. I think the last time I was there was back in September, some kind of concert in the Sacrose Theatre.'

Sid gave Ari a sharp look, and muted the call. 'Any chance you misidentified?'

'No,' Ari insisted. 'His e-i confirmed his identity.'

'Our records show you were there, sir,' Sid told Adrian.

'Well your records are wrong.'

Oh no they're not.

*

Eva handled surveillance. Standing in the zone booth, extracting mesh imagery and traffic data from the city macromesh, watching over the agency squad car like an invisible electronic angel. Sid wasn't taking any chances, he'd located the nearest squad car to Quayside and ordered them round to Adrian 2North's apartment block to take him into protective custody. Another three nearby squad cars were dispatched as back-up, an agency helicopter on patrol was reassigned to fly cover.

The agency constables escorted Adrian 2North to their car, and drove for Market Street. It was less than a kilometre, but after Ian had quickly muttered his off-log suspicion about Sherman's crew being responsible for firebombing the garage, Sid took no chances. He used his case authority to clear a passage through city traffic, resequencing traffic lights, and overriding autos, allowing the squad car and its escort to travel fast.

So fast, they almost beat him to the underground garage. Sid and Ian and Lorelle had only just got out of the lift when the squad cars came rushing down the ramp, their strobes casting weird shadows across the dark concrete cavern.

The squad car's rear door unlocked and slid back, allowing a thoroughly bewildered Adrian to look out. His expression changed to worry as he saw Sid and the others carrying pistols.

'What the fuck . . .'

'Move, now,' Sid snapped. They hauled Adrian out of the squad car and into the lift. It took them straight up to the second-floor secure holding section.

Adrian had clearly been getting ready for work. He had his suit trousers on, and a smart shirt, cufflinked but not buttoned up to the neck. The tip of his red and gold tie was flopping out of his pocket.

Incredulity had quickly turned to anger as he was hustled into the interview cell. That was soon vanquished by worry when Sid reappeared with Aldred.

It was a classic arrangement. Square room with no window. Table in the middle with two seats on either side.

'You don't need a lawyer,' Aldred said.

So Adrian sat by himself, trying not to look too perturbed by his strange morning. He was in his mid-forties, similar enough to the victim.

Sid and Aldred sat facing him, and half the case team were hooked in through a secure link, as was Ralph Stevens – wherever he was. A strange moment for Sid, questioning a man with the face of the murder victim, supported by another of the identical clones. Not that he was particularly religious, but there had to be something fundamentally wrong with distorting nature in such a fashion.

'Could you start by giving the station network your identity code, please,' Sid said.

The simple binary pulse materialized in Sid's iris smartcell grid as a purple line. Confirmed as Adrian (or at least his e-i), and that code was identical to one a North had given to the St James network at 8:03 am that Friday. 'I have a problem,' Sid said. 'A North using your code went into the St James singletown on the day of the murder. He didn't come out. At least, not using your code.'

'Well it wasn't me,' Adrian protested.

'That's what we're here to find out.'

'No. You don't understand. I was on St Libra. I remember that week well enough. I got mugged.'

'Mugged?'

'Yes. Look, I'm over there three weeks out of five. I supervise management at half our refineries. It'd been a tough week, so I went to a club in Highcastle to chill down.'

'When was this?'

'In St Libra terms? Early evening. The days aren't synchronized, you know. A St Libra day is about eight minutes longer than an Earth day. So, yes, early evening on St Libra. Thursday on Earth.'

'All right,' Sid said. 'You were at the club. What club?'

'Dervashe, on Thirty-Fourth Street.'

'I know it,' Aldred said. 'It's quite exclusive, several of us have membership.'

'Yeah, well, anyway,' Adrian continued. 'It started out a decent night. There were a couple of girls who were interested. We sat together, met up with friends. Had a meal, some drinks. Danced. Bumped some tox. Then next thing I know I'm in the manager's office, it's about four o'clock in the morning local time, and there's a killer pain on the side of my head.'

'Did anyone see anything?' Sid asked.

Adrian pushed his lips together, chewing on embarrassment. 'The club security people, they found me in a stall. They claim I fell and hit my head.'

'Did you?' Aldred asked firmly.

'Who knows? I don't even remember going into the gents.'

'How much tox did you have?' Sid asked.

'Hardly any.'

'Okay.' And Sid had to work hard to keep the disbelief from his voice. It was a standard victim claim; no, I never touch the stuff; that or it was a *bad batch*. Either way: Not My Fault. 'So you came back to Newcastle?'

'Not right away. I have a flat in Highcastle; cheaper than a hotel given how much time I spend there. So I went back there for a few hours to clean up and get ready to come home. That's when I realized it was a mugging. I didn't have my GE visa chip. And, trust me, you really need one of those to get back through the Border Directorate on this side.'

'Anything else missing?'

'Not that I noticed, no.'

'All right, your visa chip is missing. What did you do?'

'I went to our offices in Highcastle. They sorted it out for me. We do have some clout in Brussels, after all. The Directorate issued me with a temporary chip, and I came back through.'

'When?'

Adrian sucking down some air. 'Late Friday, Newcastle time. It was night when I got back, I know; there were fireworks going off all the time. That fusion plant contract, I guess. And the Northern Lights were strong, I remember them.'

'Okay, thank you.'

Sid and Aldred went out into the corridor. There was an armed guard on the interview room, police detectives, not agency people. They walked towards Office3.

'So, what's he like?' Sid asked.

'Not a toxhead, if that's what you mean,' Aldred said.

'So he got slipped a mickey?'

'Looks like it.'

Ian and Reannha were waiting for them in Office3, big smiles on their faces.

'What?' Sid asked.

'We just checked,' Reannha said. 'The GE Border Directorate records show Adrian North coming through the gateway on Friday 11th January at 6:48 am.'

'Our unknown used Adrian's visa chip,' Sid said.

'Yes, boss,' Ian said. 'Then Adrian North came through the gateway again at 10:31 pm on Friday 11th, this time using a temporary visa chip issued by the Border Directorate office in Highcastle.'

'And they didn't fucking notice?' Sid asked.

'The original visa chip was reported missing at 11:50 am,' Abner said. 'And the Border Directorate automatically cancelled it so a temporary one could be issued. You can't use a visa chip with any identity other than your own.'

'But a North with the correct identity codes . . .' Sid filled in.

'Exactly.'

'So we do have an imposter North in Newcastle,' Sid said. The satisfaction of knowing was like knocking back a triple vodka: a dose of pure joy. *I was right, this is a corporate scam. There's no stupid alien monster, there never was.* He chuckled. 'Oh crap on it, how much has that St Libra expedition cost the taxpayer?'

Ian was grinning widely. 'Hundreds of millions.'

'More like billions,' Reannha said.

'Can I be the one that tells Elston?' Sid asked Aldred.

'It's not that funny,' Aldred said stiffly. 'Because you're implying this was a North against North corporate operation.'

Sid's smile fell away. He glanced at Ari and Abner, who shared their brother's expression of heated disapproval. Three identical faces with matching intent directed at him was intimidating. 'Aye, and what does it look like to you?' he said belligerently.

There was a long silence while Aldred marshalled his argument. 'I don't know,' he conceded.

'Thank you,' Sid said.

'It's very hard to accept. I don't understand what's going on.'

'I appreciate that,' Sid said. 'But to me it's quite clear. An unknown North came through the gateway, using Adrian's identity, and went to the St James singletown. We then have two possibilities. Either this fake Adrian killed one of you and assumed his identity, or he himself was killed.'

'That would explain why we've never been able to identify the body,' Abner said grudgingly. 'Which has always been a real concern.'

'So it's a B North behind all this, then,' Ian said.

'Definitely a B North that came through,' Sid said.

'Then he was the murder victim,' Aldred said. 'Because there's no way one of us would kill another.'

'His socks,' Ari said. 'They were drensi wool, remember. Only available on St Libra. They killed a B.'

'Who's *they*?' Ian asked cynically. 'This is all you.'

'I'm sure you'd be happier believing your brother was a victim of someone else,' Sid said. 'But what about an unstable North? Are any of you prone to psychosis?'

The three clones exchanged a troubled look.

'Some of the 4s are a bit flaky,' Ari admitted. 'But we know the victim was a 2.'

'We've been through this,' Ian said. 'If there's an imposter, then he's also a 2. We checked all of you.'

Abner cleared his throat. The whole office looked at him. 'There is Zebediah,' he said.

Aldred let out a hiss of exasperation.

'Who's Zebediah?' Sid asked.

'That's what he calls himself now,' Aldred said reluctantly. 'Zebediah was one of our bothers: Barclay, a 2. He was badly shaken up by Bartram's murder, there was some kind of breakdown. He changed his name to Zebediah and started this weird crusade through the St Libra's Independencies.'

'What sort of crusade?' Eva asked.

'He wants to shut down the gateway,' Abner said. 'He claims the planet is being contaminated by human cultures, and that it must be isolated so the residents can live in harmony with the planet. Basically, he's a super-green environmentalist who wants to put back the clock and get rid of the algaepaddies.'

'Where is he now?' Sid asked.

'The age is completely wrong,' Aldred said. 'Zebediah is in his sixties. The fake Adrian was in his forties.'

Sid wasn't going to take that kind of diversion. 'Do you keep track of him?'

'Not really,' Aldred said. 'We don't consider him a real threat. To the people living in the Independencies he has a degree of novelty value as a North rejecting his brethren, but his followers are more of a cult than a political movement. There's not that many of them. Beatrice might get the odd report on his whereabouts if he does something completely stupid or outrageous.'

'Beatrice?' Sid asked in bewilderment.

'Brinkelle's daughter. She's in charge of their general family security.'

'Okay. I need to know where this Zebediah North is now, and I definitely need to know where he was on January 11th. Call up this Beatrice, and find out.'

'Of course,' Aldred said.

'In the meantime, we have a job to do,' Sid said to the office. 'The imposter Adrian went into the St James, and a body came out. Either it was him, or he killed a 2North. We know the Red Shield gang is involved to some degree through Ernie Reinert, which makes this a lot easier. The alien monster theory is now dead. Eva?'

'Yes, boss.'

'I need another zone simulation pulled together. Follow both of the Adrians from the moment they step through the gateway. I'm interested in everything the first one does on the way to the St James, but don't skimp on the second, either.'

'Understood.'

'The rest of you: I want every North in the St James on Friday eleventh brought back here for detailed questioning.' He stared directly at Aldred. 'We're going to make one last push to try and see if any of them is the imposter. Harvest as much background detail on them as possible, and go through every day of their life to see if they actually lived it. We'll need full access to your family records.'

'I'll see you get them,' Aldred said.

'And I'll start by interviewing you.'

'I thought you might.'

*

It had rained most of the afternoon, thick heavy droplets sluicing down out of dark swirling clouds. The accompanying wind had driven the falling water almost horizontal, making life in Wukang just that little bit more depressing. All everyone wanted to do was skulk about in their tents avoiding work. Vance Elston wasn't going to let that happen. With idle hands being the devil's playground he firmly believed in work being the best way of keeping people focused properly. Nobody was going to have slack time to think about the MTJ accident. So the engineering teams were busy in their open-sided garage repairing the battered vehicle from components microfactured on site. More staff were preparing the second mobile biolab and testing the other vehicles for another sampling expedition starting tomorrow. AAV operatives were flying the Owls low, mapping out possible routes across the terrain to the north-east. Camm Montoto and Esther Coombes from the xenobiology team were overseeing the images, determining any potential sites of exceptional botanical interest amid the unending jungle.

The first expedition rolled back into camp mid-afternoon, its personnel depressed and exhausted. Again, Vance's work-ethic came to the fore, and he made them unpack and evaluate their vehicle status without pause.

Fortunately, by late afternoon, the clouds swept off to the east, clearing the sky. Residual water immediately started to steam away, boosting the humidity still further. But at least everyone could walk about without their rain gear on.

The evening meal was served as Sirius sank quickly towards the horizon and the rings began to shade down from icy silver to a more lambent glow across the southern sky. Vance was just about to leave the Qwik-Kabin to grab a bite to eat when the secure call came through from Ralph.

'We've had some interesting developments,' he began.

'Ernie Reinert?' Vance asked immediately.

'No. And that's not going so good. He doesn't know much, certainly not who murdered the North. But we have extracted some useful names from him, which should bring us a step closer to whoever ordered the bodydump.'

'Okay, so what have you got for me?'

'Detective Hurst found an unknown North coming through the gateway on the day of the murder. He went directly to the St James singletown.'

Vance was so surprised that for a moment he couldn't find anything to say. 'Are you sure?' he asked, which was not quite a professional reaction, but . . .

'The unknown stole the identity of Adrian North to come through GE Border Directorate. He went to the singletown and vanished. So either he was murdered, or he committed the murder and impersonated his victim.'

'Good Lord.'

'Yeah. It really is starting to look like some kind of North family feud after all.'

Vance clenched his fist and tapped it gently against the top of the desk, beating out an irritated rhythm. 'We had a bad accident here on Saturday.'

'Yes, it was on the news.'

'I'm not convinced it was an accident.' Even as he said it, he hated how desperate it sounded. This was an operation that was going down in flames, and he was the boss looking to throw blame around. But you had to be here to *know* something was wrong.

'Vance. Hurst and his team are doing a good job. They're re-interviewing some Norths who might be the imposter. And Ernie has already confirmed the apartment he picked the body up from; we'll have to give them that in a day or so. Forensics will rip the place apart.'

'You're not sending in our people first?'

'Vermekia has vetoed that. He wants the investigation to continue uncompromised.'

Vance knew what that meant: HDA command was coming round to the corporate conflict theory. From a political perspective, the expedition was now left with its ass hanging in the wind. 'Does anyone have any theory why the Norths might be fighting?'

'That's the odd thing, there's no reason anyone can work out. They deny it completely, of course. Given the imposter who came through is probably a B North, the best anyone can suggest is Brinkelle trying to take over Northumberland Interstellar, but that's pretty wild. Since this broke, the one person both the police and Brinkelle are interested in is Zebediah North.'

'Isn't he the family nut-job?'

'Yeah, Barclay North, who went crazy after his father's death. Unfortunately, he's the wrong age – he doesn't fit the imposter who came through.'

'It could have been one of his children, a 3 we didn't know about.'

'Possibly, but it was definitely a 2 that Hurst pulled out of the Tyne. And all the A 2s are accounted for.'

'Yes, you're right. Sorry, it's been a stressful few days here.'

'So has Antrinell found any genetic variance?'

'No. He's starting to think this is a waste of time, too.'

'Neither of the other two forward camps have found anything either.'

'How long have we got?'

'Vermekia wasn't going to commit himself. But unless something happens, you'll probably be getting your withdrawal orders in a week or so.'

'Okay, thanks, Ralph.'

'Sure. Take care out there.'

Vance sighed and sank back in the cramped chair. It was vanity, of course, but back in January when the case was fresh and new he'd believed this expedition to be supremely important. Now he was beginning to acknowledge that the evidence to launch it had been flimsy at best. Images from a dazed, drugged girl's brain. Her pathetic protestations of innocence.

Angela was the key, he knew she was. If he could just find out

544

what she was doing in Bartram's mansion . . . 'Call Tramelo,' he told his e-i.

*

Angela didn't bother knocking on Elston's door. The Qwik-Kabin was small, he'd have heard her come in. She barged into his office and found him behind his tiny desk staring into a display pane. The purple and green data was unreadable from where she stood. She sat without being asked, enjoying the relative cool blown out by the struggling air-con.

'I'd already gotten my tray,' she complained. 'I haven't eaten anything reasonable for days.'

'Yeah, that's a real tragedy,' Elston snapped back.

Angela blinked and gave him a closer look. He was usually so well mannered and polite, in that creepy way all religious obsessives were. At any other time she would have enjoyed seeing the doubt and worry on his stiff face. Not now though, not with the multiplying number of 'accidents'. 'So what's the problem?'

'Guzman's not going to be walking again.'

'Yeah,' she said gloomily. 'We heard. There are treatments. Nerve regeneration. The kind of thing the Norths are developing at their Institute in Abellia—'

'That not even the HDA can afford for its wounded. Sort of like one-in-ten treatments.'

'You asked me in here so you can spew your spite all over me?'

'No, sorry. Angela, what were you doing at Bartram's mansion? Telling the truth now can't possibly cause any harm.'

Once again she was pleased with the way she kept her emotions in check. *Daddy would be proud.* 'I was a whore. Does that make you feel better?'

'You're many things, but whore isn't one of them.'

'Gee, thanks.'

'I wish you'd trust me.'

'I don't suffer from Stockholm syndrome, thanks. Not with my torturer.'

545

He let out an exasperated sigh. 'I'm sorry about that. Okay?'

'That just makes it a whole lot better.'

'Angela . . . damnit.'

She was genuinely curious now. This was an Elston she hadn't seen before. 'What's happened?'

'The police found out an unknown North came through the gateway just before the Newcastle murder. Everyone is starting to think the murder is corporate related, or at least some kind of family power struggle.'

'Son-of-a-bitch! What about you? What do you think?'

'We haven't found any genetic variance. It's starting to look like you might have been mistaken.'

'Mistaken! Are you fucking kidding me? If there wasn't a monster, then that implies I killed them. You motherfucking bastard. If you think I'm going back to jail, you're wrong.'

'Nobody's saying that. We're interested in Zebediah North.'

Angela frowned. 'Who?'

'You'd know him as Barclay North. He had a breakdown after his father was killed. Changed his name and started campaigning for St Libra to sever all ties with Earth, including closing the gateway. Did you ever meet him?'

Angela sat perfectly still, the chill of the air-con banished by the blood heat pounding through her skin. Keeping hold of her anger was becoming very difficult. *How could I have been so stupid? Letting him lull me into lowering my guard. I'd almost started thinking of him as human.* 'Fuck you!' she screamed. 'Piece of shit torturer. I hope you catch cancer and die rotting. If your God exists, I'll have the satisfaction She'll be sending you right down into your medieval hell. And even that's too good for you.'

'Whaaat th—'

'Nice try. Get friendly. Earn your victim's sympathy. Then mindfuck them. Well all that means is that we can add rape to your list of crimes now.' She got to her feet, too angry to say anything else.

'Wait! I don't understand. Please, what, what . . .' he spluttered.

'You don't understand,' she snarled back in savage mockery. 'Read that straight out of the torturer's manual, did you?'

'Will you calm down and tell me what just happened.'

Angela paused. Still uncertain and hating herself for giving him the benefit of the doubt. 'Barclay North, yes? That's who you're talking about? Asking me oh-so-innocently if I knew him?'

'Yes. It might be important.'

'Just after you want to know what I was doing at the mansion—' She stopped herself, alarmed she might be giving too much away.

'Angela, I swear on the Bible itself I don't know what you're so upset about.'

'Barclay North started calling himself Zebediah North and broke with the family? Is that it?'

'Yes. They don't know why. He disappeared a couple of days after the murders. They didn't see him again for months until he reappeared in the Independencies.'

'That was amazingly clever of him,' she snapped.

'How is it clever?'

'You're still pretending this isn't some softening-up process?'

'Goddamn it!' He abruptly looked shocked at the blasphemy he'd uttered. 'What happened with you and Barclay?'

Angela took a calming breath. 'We had a fling, is all.'

'What?'

'You heard. Contrary to popular belief, there is a difference between the Norths. He was,' she chose her words carefully, 'nicer than the others, especially his father.'

'I didn't know. How different?'

'Not crazy different, if that's what you're implying – oh fuck, why am I even talking to you about this?'

'Every little piece of information helps.'

Angela gave him a hard, disapproving stare. 'That information cannot possibly help you.'

'Why not?'

'Because Barclay 2North is *dead*. He was slaughtered that night along with all the others the monster massacred. I found ... I saw his butchered body in that motherfucking mansion. Get it? I. Saw. His. Corpse. And I truly know it was him. Whoever Zebediah is, it's not Barclay.'

*

It was ballsy sneaking into the seventh-floor study that night of all nights, but Angela considered it worth the risk. A double bluff, nobody would be attempting anything illicit with people around. Not that there were many people, just some of Bartram's sons. Barclay had turned up that evening, along with Benson and Blake and Barrett. A family dinner to discuss business. She'd been in attendance in the dining room of course, along with Coi and Mariangela and Suski (Olivia-Jay's replacement). Loanna and Marc-Anthony had styled the girlfriends in short, expensive cocktail dresses so they could sit flanking Bartram to form hot enticing adornments. It had been difficult for her not to pay undue attention to Barclay during the meal. But she'd refrained. He had been equally scrupulous, chatting with all the girlfriends, just as flirtatious with each one.

The brothers had gone on into the seventh-floor lounge to continue talk about deals and companies and finance. Bartram had told Suski to go with them, allowing her to showcase her pianist skills and the range of her voice. Angela didn't think she was anything like as good as Olivia-Jay, but acknowledged that was a biased opinion.

So it was Angela, Mariangela, and Coi who went back down to the sixth floor to be costumed up by Loanna and Marc-Anthony, ready for a night in Bartram's bedroom. Mariangela was in a long lace and silk robe, imperious and spectacular with her hair flowing free; while Coi was in simple white PJs, all innocent and eager. Angela, they put in the white shorts and a gauzy black halter, congratulating themselves on their choice – except it was what she suggested. And that was the essential part.

At two o'clock in the morning, with the rainclouds sliding in from the sea to obscure St Libra's glowing rings, she wore those shorts as she walked confidently along the seventh floor's gallery. The lights were on low, and some of the brothers were still up in the lounge. Suski was playing the piano, singing with a throaty gusto.

Angela slipped into the retro-Egyptian study. At least nobody had been using oil in bed tonight, she didn't have to worry about smears and towels. The waistband of the shorts concealed the little interceptor needles. She plucked them out, and wiggled beneath the desk.

It was all ready. The money for the Delgardo Valley contract had been transferred to Abellia's main civic account yesterday. GiulioTrans-stellar's bid was still logged and pending, along with all the rival bids. Once again she used Barclay's codes, awarding the bid to GiulioTrans-stellar. One hundred and eight million Eurofrancs vanished into the transnet banking sector.

Angela let out a little whimper of relief. For once not angry at herself for the display of emotion, the way her eyes watered up. It was done. Over. Nothing else mattered.

But it would be nice to get out of here.

She withdrew methodically, forcing herself not to rush. Fold the civic account back up using Barclay's authorization. Close down the infiltration, extract the interceptor needles and slip them back into her shorts. Shut down the console.

Heart pounding, she opened the study door a fraction to peer out. The brothers must have finally gone to bed. The lights were out all along the gallery. It was perfectly silent, and unusually dark. With the rings veiled by thickening cloud, there was very little light filtering through the big windows at the far end of the gallery.

Angela shut the study door, and started creeping back to Bartram's bedroom. Halfway there, she put her foot into some kind of puddle. She was directly outside the lounge, and she realized that one of the big double doors was open. It was completely black inside.

The liquid wasn't water. She knew that: too thick, too sticky. And curiously, too warm. She frowned, not understanding what she'd trodden in. It was irritating, because she'd have to clean it off before she sneaked back into bed.

She went into the lounge, and there was liquid all over the floor. Her feet slipped, and she went flailing down onto her knees, landing hard. 'Ow! Son-of-a-bitch. House: lounge lights on minimum.'

The mansion's AI didn't respond. 'Oh come on!' Angela struggled upright. The smell in the lounge was strange, unpleasant. She couldn't quite place it, though there was a definite scent of mint mixed in there. Somehow it triggered a deep unease. This was getting ridiculous, she could feel the liquid all over her skin now. Some kind of pipe must have burst. Air-con coolant? But at least she now had a reason to be walking about at this time of the morning: *I heard something.*

The manual switches were behind the door. She slithered about like a sugared-up toddler on an ice rink, trying to get to them. Five tiny green LEDs glowed on the panel, guiding her. One more slip, and she reached them, slapping her hand against the buttons.

The lounge lights came on. For a moment her mind rejected the sight of her own body. The liquid coating her was bright scarlet. The colour slammed a warning straight into the most primitive section of her brain. Blood!

Angela gasped in shock. It was everywhere, pooling all over the marble floor. And her feet were still in it. She cried out again, louder this time, her fear and disgust echoing round the big room. Spun round, a motion which sent her flailing about as yet again she lost her balance. Crashing down painfully on all fours. And looking directly at Barclay's corpse, two metres away.

Something had punctured his chest, slicing through his blue and grey striped silk shirt, and skin and ribcage to rip his heart apart. Blood had gushed out of the ragged multiple wound, spilling across the floor. Angela stared helplessly into his face with its strangely endearing death-mask expression of peaceful surprise. She knew it was him. He was wearing her banana

550

cufflinks. But there was too much blood to have come from just one person. She raised her head.

Suski was lying beside the piano, her throat slashed so brutally she'd almost been decapitated. Two more Norths were sprawled on the floor. One with the same bizarre heart wound as Barclay; the other had been split open from crotch to thorax, his organs and intestines slopping out amid the blood.

Angela fought against the hysterical scream that was trying to force itself up her windpipe. Self-preservation alone kept her silent, one tiny spark of remaining rationality knew the maniac had to be close by – she mustn't alert him. She glanced up at the ribbon-like lightstrips curling artistically round the ceiling, knowing that switching them on had been a terrible mistake – that and the noise she'd made earlier.

She scrambled to her feet again. Nausea at the blood coating her skin threatened to burst out of her stomach in a spasm of uncontainable heaving. *Ignore that. Focus.*

Angela gripped the door for support, and peered out into the long central gallery, ready to make a fast sprint for the stairs. Light from the lounge had fanned out into the darkness beyond. Five metres away, the door to Bartram's bedroom was opening silently. The sight was enough to banish all emotion, clearing her mind. She held her breath, and activated the dark weapon implants in her arms.

*

After Angela left his minuscule office in the Qwik-Kabin, Vance sat behind his desk for over an hour, thinking things over. What she'd claimed couldn't be right. And yet . . . for the first time since they'd first encountered each other twenty years ago, Vance was certain he'd finally got something truthful out of Angela Tramelo. Barclay 2North was dead, her rage and confusion was unfeigned, he knew that; she really had seen the body – and if anyone could identify Barclay it was Angela. But everyone knew Barclay survived the slaughter to become Zebediah. So if Angela was right then somewhere, somehow, an unknown North had appeared in Barclay's place and become Zebediah. Now, twenty years later, another unknown North had come through the gateway from St Libra to walk upon the Good Earth.

That the two events were connected was incontrovertible. But proving it was going to be a sore test of his abilities. And as for convincing HDA command . . .

His e-i pulled all of Angela Tramelo's original statements, and ran a search for any reference to Barclay 2North. Sure enough, there in the third day after she'd been arrested she described the scene she'd found in the mansion's lounge to a Newcastle police detective. Vance cancelled the transcript, and lifted the ancient AV file from storage. The console screen curved round his face, delivering him into the zone, and he looked back across twenty years' time into the secure interview room, where an Angela Tramelo with badly cut short red hair sat handcuffed behind a table with a bewildered defence solicitor beside her, while the senior of a pair of detectives asked question after question.

'Oh my Lord,' Vance muttered softly. 'How about that.' He'd almost missed it, but the younger, more junior detective sitting in the room was Royce O'Rouke. No mistaking the puffy features of that face, even though it wasn't as red and angry as it was all the time these days.

The senior detective, Garry Ravis, was taking her back through her discovery of the bodies.

'I heard a noise,' Angela said in a dull voice. She looked in a bad way, quite ill, wearing dark-green police-issue overalls, and wrapped in a blanket. Her shoulders shivered constantly, and she was drinking a lot of water. 'When I went out into the gallery, it was dark, every light was off. I stood in a puddle outside the lounge and went in. When I turned the light on I saw them, Barclay and the others. Suski had only been with us a couple of weeks. Someone had . . . Oh sweet fucking heaven, they'd been torn apart.'

'So then what?' Ravis asked uncompromisingly.

'I heard something in the gallery. When I went back out it was there waiting for me.'

'The monster?'

'Yes.'

'Uh huh. You see this is where I get confused. You said in your first statement that you saw it coming out of Bartram's bedroom. But that was the room you were in, wasn't it?'

'Yes. I said it was close to Bartram's room. I'd gone out for a break.'

'Then you fought it off, and ran?'

'Yes.'

'But everyone in Bartram's room was also massacred. So how do you explain where the monster was when you walked the, what? Ten metres from the bedroom to the lounge? In the time it took you to get that distance, it had gone into the bedroom behind you, silently ripped apart Bartram and two more girls, then came out to fight you – and lose.'

Angela's head lolled back, it looked like she was about to pass out. The recording even showed the sweat soaking her forehead. Vance began to wonder what had been done to her in the station.

'I don't know the order that fucker killed everyone in. All I know is, I ran while it was on the ground.'

'And you knocked the monster over?'

'Yes.'

'A monster strong enough to rip fourteen other humans apart?'

'Yes.'

'Bollocks. You're a lying little bitch. You were wearing a power amp suit, weren't you? You killed them.'

'No.'

Vance halted the file. Angela had no motive to say Barclay was dead, no reason at all. She'd only mentioned it a couple of times, and twenty years ago nobody had picked up on it. Her testimony was regarded as unreliable at best, with alien monsters added to turn it into a ludicrous work of fiction. Looking at the state of her in the recording, he could almost believe the whole alibi was a work of fever hallucination.

His e-i found a medical report from the station doctor. They'd run a standard blood screen for toxins, and found minute traces of some weird biochemicals in her. They weren't in the GE narcotic database, though that didn't mean much, there was always experimental stuff coming on the market; and she had just been on St Libra. Angela denied she was a toxhead, like she denied every other allegation Ravis threw at her. The doctor had written the fever off as a flu variant induced by St Libra's spores; it had passed after five days.

'What were you doing there?' Vance asked the silent, still image hovering in the zone. It hurt that the reason she'd never confide in him now was a totally reasonable hatred of him thanks to the time they'd spent together on Frontline.

It was raining again when his e-i put a secure call through to Ralph and Vermekia. Big droplets drumming hard on the Qwik-Kabin roof, smothering all other sound.

'Something new has come to light,' Vance opened with. 'Angela just told me that Barclay North was killed by the monster.'

'You got me out of bed for this?' Vermekia asked.

'I've been over her old police interview files. She claimed it back then, too. Nobody paid any attention.'

'But if Barclay's dead, who is Zebediah?' Ralph asked.

'Good question. An unknown North. And who came through the gateway back in January?'

'What are you saying?' Vermekia said.

'You don't think that's a coincidence too far? Two of these odd five-blade slayings, and both times we have an unidentified North close to the scene?'

'So? There's a little coterie of 2Norths that the family keeps quiet about,' Ralph said. 'That just reinforces the whole incestuous family fight scenario.'

'Can we at least check through the forensics reports from the mansion?' Vance asked. 'See if there's any evidence of a fifteenth body.'

'There aren't any forensics reports,' Vermekia said. 'At least, nothing decent. Some photos of the sixth and seventh floors after the bodies had been taken away. Basically, just a lot of dried blood on the floor. Nothing more detailed was ever released, not even for the trial. The Norths didn't want images of their father or their brothers' bodies hitting the transnet. I can't say I blame them. Someone in the police or court would have leaked them. They'd be valuable.'

'HDA has the pathology reports on the weapon,' Vance said.

'Again, released to us by the North Institute on Abellia, because at the time they were worried about the possibility that it really might have been an alien. A few files remain under heavy access restriction even now.'

'We could run a hack into the North Biomedical Institute.'

'No, Vance,' Vermekia said. 'I appreciate what you're trying to do, but you need to think about winding up operations at Wukang.'

'We've sent out one sampling mission so far. One.'

'And you're preparing to send out another tomorrow. See, I do read the reports you load into the expedition network. The other camps have also started sampling, with identical results. There's nothing out there. Zebra botany is the only living thing on St Libra. It's weird, and interesting, and generates a whole load of wacky theories among evolutionists who don't appreciate the complexity of the Lord's work, but that's all it is.'

'There's something going on here. Something strange.'

'I'm not denying that. But it's not strange enough to justify another billion Eurofrancs supporting the expedition. Don't worry, you're covered. It was Commissioner Passam who drove it all forward. She can explain to Brussels and the HDA funding committee when she gets back. Your name won't be mentioned.'

'What a relief,' Vance said. It was a shame that much irony didn't carry through a secure call.

'I'll bring it up with Aldred North at this end,' Ralph said. 'Whatever else this is, it's the Norths that are getting murdered. They genuinely want answers.'

'Do we know yet if Zebediah is still in the Independencies?' Vance asked.

'No. It's quite hard to ascertain. The micro nations are all very proud of their lack of connection to the transnet. The Norths are sending someone down there to investigate.'

'No offence, but shouldn't we run that check ourselves?'

'Good point,' Vermekia said. 'I'll authorize that. We have deep assets in the Independencies. I can put—'

The camp network received an emergency medical alert. Vance's e-i threw a torrent of data into his iris smartcell grid. It was Esther Coombes' bodymesh that was calling for help. Her suite of medical monitor smartcells were reporting catastrophic heart failure and chest tissue damage, her blood pressure hit zero, brainwave function in terminal decline. Location was on the edge of camp, a couple of hundred metres from the mobile biolabs.

'Botin,' Vance ordered his e-i. 'Lieutenant, initiate camp security protocol red-one. We have a breach. All personnel secure the perimeter.'

'Sir. Activating now,' the lieutenant answered.

'Keep all non-essentials in their tents. Assume active hostile. Search and capture, full force authorization.'

Vance opened the weapons cabinet on the wall above his desk, and pulled the Folkling carbine out. Checked the safety. Slotted a magazine in, and jammed another two into his pocket. Then ran for the door.

The rain was dense and warm, reducing visibility to a few metres. Lights had come on all across the camp. Showing as white smears lost in the filthy night. Vance started to jog towards Coombes, his bodymesh emitting identity pings in case a squad of jumpy Legionnaires collided with him.

Then the camp network dropped out. He wasn't sure, because he was still running, slipping and skidding on the mud, but several lights seemed to vanish at the same time. 'Hellfire,' he grunted. His bodymesh was strong enough to establish a direct link with Botin. 'We have to get our network back up – we're wide open without it. Have some of your people escort Wardele and whoever he needs to the Qwik-Kabin.'

'Yes, sir.'

Despite the warm water drenching his clothes, Vance felt a shiver run down his back. *I was in the Qwik-Kabin a minute ago.* The camp's network didn't depend on one cell, of course, it should have carried on regardless; but Wukang was small, a lot of traffic was routed through the big processor in the Qwik-Kabin. It was the logical sabotage point.

He saw torch beams wavering about through the sodden darkness ahead of him, and changed direction towards them. His e-i sent out a ping, and found Justic and Kowalski clustered with Montoto from the xenobiology team and Mark Chitty the paramedic. The emissions from Coombes' bodymesh were delivering the bad news even as Vance jogged to a halt. The Legionnaires and Montoto were standing over her, shining their torches down for a kneeling Chitty to work by. But Chitty was leaning back, slumping in dismay.

Vance looked down at Coombes, teeth gritted against his fear and anger. There was never any question she was beyond every revival technique Chitty could apply with his field pack of clever medical gadgets. The cleanly sliced flesh above her heart where five blades had penetrated her ribcage left that in no doubt.

Tuesday 19th March 2143

Eva froze the theatre zone image as Adrian 2North walked into the lobby of his Quayside apartment block. It was snowing outside, with the taxi pulling away from the building, wheels struggling for traction on the compacted ice that covered the cobbles of the private loop road to the front door.

The simulation had followed Adrian from the moment he stepped through the gateway at half past ten that night, catching a taxi, which took a laboriously slow journey across the winter-gripped city with its dangerous roads; delivering him to his home. There was no mistake, no substitution, no switching taxis. This was the genuine digital and visual trail he'd left across the city's nets and meshes.

'Time, 11:09 pm,' Eva said. 'That's probably quite late for the murder.'

'Could be,' Sid agreed. He was standing in the theatre control room, looking out into the gloomy January night scene, remembering how cold it had been down by the Tyne when he and Ian answered the two-oh-five. A quick study of Adrian North's face showed him how thoroughly pissed off the man was; bags under his eyes, tiredness, exasperation. It was all written there. A man who's just been through a bad experience and simply wants to get home. The last proof that this was the real Adrian 2North – intangible though it was.

'So the first Adrian that came through the gateway is the imposter,' Ian said firmly.

'I think we'd all agree with that,' Sid said. He glanced round at O'Rouke and received the swiftest nod of confirmation.

'So now what?'

Ari and Lorelle, who were operating the theatre's consoles, gave Sid an interested look.

'Thanks,' Sid told them. 'You can shut this down now.'

Interest turned to annoyance, and they left the control centre. Ian opaqued the window, cutting Eva off.

'It's a North against North war,' Sid said. 'Even if Aldred denies it, or doesn't know about it. Personally, I think the fake Adrian is the one we pulled from the Tyne. Those interviews with the other 2Norths from the St James singletown were pretty conclusive. None of them are imposters.'

'Christ is bloody crapping this out personally,' O'Rouke grunted. 'Augustine owns this town. Fuck it.'

For once Sid actually felt sorry for the Chief Constable. He wasn't too certain where this latest development was going to leave him, either. 'Ralph Stevens called me this morning, sir,' Sid said. 'We should be getting Ernie Reinert back tomorrow.'

'The poor bastard's still alive, huh?' O'Rouke asked.

'Apparently. Stevens said they had some helpful information for us to follow up.'

'The name of the murderer?'

'No sir, he was clear about that. But at the very least he should have the apartment which Reinert collected the body from. Once we have that, forensics should be able to move us forward. I'm going to get a team from Northern Forensics put on standby. I want their top people on it as soon as we know.'

'Aye, good call,' O'Rouke said. 'You know, those HDA accounts bastards have been in touch. They're ready to process our first batch of invoices.'

'That's, er, good, sir.'

'Too bloody true. This almighty dogturd can't get flushed out of my city fast enough.'

Sid and Ian exchanged a look. If they were going to raise their suspicion about Sherman's involvement, this was the time.

'Our procedures actually worked, sir,' Sid said. And he couldn't help noting the tiny flicker of relief on Ian's face.

O'Rouke chortled. 'First fucking time, eh?'

'Yes, sir.'

'You boys have done well. Don't think I haven't noticed. Lanagin, you should maybe think about your next grade exams. I know a couple of people on the board I can have a word with.'

'Thank you, sir, I'll consider that.'

Sid assumed that Ian's impending promotion was O'Rouke's way of saying he'd keep his part of the bargain to bump Sid to grade-five. That was the thing about the Chief Constable, Sid reflected: you never quite knew if he was shitting out metaphors or not.

Sid's audio smartcells chimed loudly. At the same time his iris smartcells shone a bright-blue icon into the centre of his visual grid: a universal code blue. All government employees were to activate emergency civil control plans. Police leave was suspended. Officers were to report to their station commanders.

'Holy shit,' O'Rouke spat.

'You don't know what it is?' Sid asked.

'Not a fucking clue. That fucking Mayor, he loves keeping me out-stream. Bastard shit.'

They hurried out of the control room. Sid told his e-i to sweep the news sites, legitimate and unlicensed, to find the biggest GE-related story. Fragments of news immediately came worming out of icons in his visual grid.

GE Border Directorate announces temporary suspension of traffic through the Newcastle gateway.

Amateur astronomer Rozak Ueu, a Highcastle resident, releases pictures of Sirius two minutes after sunrise. Abnormal sunspot activity visible.

Northumberland Interstellar issues a confirmation that bioil flow from St Libra will remain constant.

Highcastle city council declares that it will seek to officially confirm the sunspot reports.

HDA Brussels headquarters denies the sunspot activity is linked to a Zanthswarm.

Sid's heart went *thud* at that one.

Jacinta called as he got through the door of Office3. 'We just got a major situation notice,' she said. 'We've been put on high-casualty incident standby. What's happening?'

'I don't know for sure. Something to do with sunspots on St Libra.'

'Sid, what are sunspots?'

'No idea. Look, pet, we've just gone to code blue ourselves. I'll call as soon as we know anything real.'

'What about the kids? Should I get them home from school?'

Sid checked his time display: 10:47. 'Not yet. Look, I'll know first if anything big breaks. Probably. I'll call you.'

'What's happening?' Ian demanded as soon as the blue seal came on around the door.

'Nobody knows,' Ari said. He pointed at the wallscreens. Reannha was using their network to skim news sites with an AI filter. Studios and reporters were flipping up at stroboscopic rates. One image froze.

'There,' Abner yelled.

Sid stared at the screen. It was TyneScan-5, a local news office that normally dealt with business and finance in north-east England. Their smartly dressed reporter was standing on Kings-way in Last Mile, with her back to the gateway. The road beside her was clogged with stationary traffic. People were climbing out of their vehicles to clump together and talk in low urgent tones. Immigrants on foot were hesitant, not walking forward eagerly as they usually did towards their private vision of utopia. It was as if they could all see some kind of storm ahead which remained invisible to TyneScan's camera.

'Let's have some volume,' Ian said.

'... the outbreak of sunspot activity remains unconfirmed

because there are no real space-based instruments in the Sirius system,' the reporter said.

'Sunspots?' Eva asked incredulously. 'This is all because of sunspots?'

Sid quietly told his e-i to access a summary of sunspots.

'Sunrise in Highcastle was twenty-three minutes ago,' the reporter said. 'So we're expecting some verification over the next couple of hours. The city authorities are appealing to all amateur astronomers to get in touch with them.'

'What the hell is going on over there?' Sid asked.

*

It was shaping up to be a beautiful morning. The hazy splendour of the rings, dominating the night sky with their ephemeral silver shimmer, faded into submission as the intense blue-white light from Sirius slipped over the rim of the giant planet. Sharp monochrome splinters prised their way through the muggy air in the valleys to surge across the jungle, sparking against the heads of the enormous metacoyas and bullwhips and vampspires that spiked up from the rumpled eau de nil landscape. Leaves on the smaller trees and vines glistened and sparkled as the remnants of the night's rainfall effervesced, exhaling a tender mist that softened the light's impact as it rushed across the flatlands and swamped Wukang in a warm golden hue. Mountainside streams shivered in platinum ripples as they cascaded their serpentine way down to the lakes and tributaries that drained the land.

Sitting at the edge of Wukang's big mess tent – unshaven, eyes rimmed with flesh stained red from sleeplessness – Vance Elston glared right back at the majesty of an alien sunrise. The Folkling carbine was cradled on his lap, one hand resting with deceptive lightness on its stock. A pleasant warm breeze stirred his matted hair, and he took a deep breath. Grimacing straight away. The air was heavy with a salty citrus smell. Reluctant familiarity told him it was honeyberry spore, spewing up from the underside of the swollen, bronze leaf-tips. At least that invader was one his senses could register.

He straightened his shoulders, wincing at the stiffness the night's vigil had bequeathed as he squatted for hour after hour in the same place, staring ignominiously out into the hostile, gloaming-claimed territory of his own command. The Legionnaires who had ringed the mess tent with him to perform all-night sentry duty were also stirring as Wukang became visible again.

The birth of a new day made him take a fresh look at the camp. Vines were growing up tent guy ropes and twining around the pallet stacks. Even the compacted soil and stone of the short runway was starting to green over, with clumps of tough moss and tufts of grass sprouting up. St Libra was already reclaiming the niche humans had arrogantly thought they'd secured for themselves.

'Dear Lord, forgive us our trespasses,' Vance muttered. 'And grant me wisdom this day.' He crossed himself.

Behind him, the rest of Wukang's surviving forty-eight personnel were starting to rise from the floor and chairs where they'd spent the night. Some had slept. Vance guessed most hadn't.

Antrinell came over, looking worried and uncertain. 'Morning, sir.'

Vance gave him a gruff nod. 'I want Lieutenant Botin and every department head together for a briefing in ten minutes. We'll hold it in the maintenance garage. Legionnaire squad to confirm it's a clean area first.'

'I'm on it.'

'And get the cooks to start breakfast. We're going to need it.'

'Can people go back to their tents?'

'No. The whole camp has to be searched and secured first. We need to be certain that thing has gone.' He gave the ablutions block a sympathetic glance. 'The Legionnaires can verify the latrines are clear first.'

'Sure. So it's real, then?'

'Did you check with the Legionnaires for me?'

'Yes.' Antrinell lowered his voice. 'She was in the tent with half of Paresh's squad at the time Coombs was attacked.'

'Thank the Lord for that.'

'What do we do?'

'I've been checking in with Griffin Toyne and Vermekia on an hourly basis. They agree with me, now that we've confirmed hostile activity in this area Wukang should be expanded and upgraded to a military operating base. The time for science is over. We'll bring in more Legionnaires and start hunting properly. Until then we secure the runway. And stop getting killed.'

'The MTJ?'

Vance shrugged. 'I have no proof. I suspect they did it, because right now I'm not giving anyone the benefit of the doubt.'

'Okay, I'll get things moving.'

Vance watched as his orders got kicked down the chain of command. Two teams of Legionnaires were dispatched, one to the latrines, the other to the garage. Cooks and ancillary staff fired up the ovens and microwaves. Food trays were heated, tea and coffee urns filled. A queue formed. It was almost normality.

Vance coughed. The scent of spores was a lot thicker this morning, agitating the back of his throat. He called Griffin Toyne again, and confirmed they'd made it through the night.

'We'd like the body back in Abellia for examination,' the major said.

'It's in our clinic. I'll get the doc to prepare it for cold transport.'

'And nobody saw anything?'

'As soon as we restore full net function we'll review the mesh logs. But don't hold your breath.'

'You said the camp's net failed after the attack?'

'Yes, sir.'

'So that means our alien got through the perimeter sensors without being detected?'

Vance was starting to appreciate what it was like being an interrogation subject who had plenty to hide and avoid. The irony wasn't pleasant. 'It must have, yes.'

'Any theories how it did that?'

'Not one, no.'

'On the other hand, Angela Tramelo was already inside the perimeter.'

'Her whereabouts were verified. First thing I did. She was with four Legionnaires at the time Coombs was killed.'

'Okay. But it's been commented on that's she's always in the area. No other camps have been attacked.'

'Was she in the Newcastle area back in January?' He surprised himself by the amount of anger behind the question.

'I'm on your side, Vance. We're just saying, that's all. But consider this: if it was her who wiped out Bartram North and half his mansion, then she probably had help, an associate of some kind – who's never been caught. That was a specialist-built weapon, after all; and it was never found. So as far as we're concerned she is still very much on probation.'

An associate? He could almost hear Commissioner Passam saying it, her slick political questions aimed at the Right Places, casting doubt and undermining facts. She could almost rival him when it came to disinformation techniques. 'I understand perfectly. We'll watch Tramelo.'

'Thank you. I appreciate how difficult it is out there.'

'How long before we get our additional Legionnaires?'

'HDA has already issued a deployment order to the Paris barracks. Two hundred troops plus equipment. They'll be through the gateway today. So we estimate we'll be able to start airlifting them from Sarvar to Wukang by Friday latest.'

'Sounds good.'

'Don't worry, you'll get all the back-up you need. I heard General Shaikh has already been briefed. He was the one who signed off the Paris troops for you. They're taking this very seriously back home where it counts.'

'Appreciate that.'

'Stay alive, Vance.'

'Wasn't planning anything different, sir.'

The secure call ended, and he let out a long breath. The relief that more Legionnaires were on their way was profound. He'd need to announce that fast. Morale could do with a boost. But Passam trying to corrupt the dataflow was trouble he didn't need.

A tall cardboard cup of coffee was held in front of him.

'Thought you could do with this,' Angela said.

'Thank you.' He took it from her and drank the hot liquid down. Instant, with milk granules, and microwaved. For some reason it tasted great.

'And thank you,' Angela said.

'For what?'

She sat on the corner of a trestle table. 'For trusting me. For not handcuffing me to the central tent post for the night.'

'Yeah, well . . .'

'I guess Leora and Atyeo were convincing when Antrinell asked where I was,' she said with a sly smile.

'Nothing gets by you, does it?'

'I keep my eyes open. So did you ask your bosses about Barclay?'

'He's alive. He's Zebediah now. That's official.'

'Interesting. Why would the Norths concoct that fantasy?'

'I thought you'd be . . . not happy, but certainly relieved. The monster is real. You're in the clear.'

'And you splashed that right into the news streams did you?'

'We need to get things in order first.'

Angela laughed bitterly. 'That's the HDA I know and love.' She took a deep breath, and frowned, searching round.

'What?' he asked.

'That cinnamon smell, that's rubystick; and there's hayneleaf in there as well, some other scents I don't recognize. No mint, though, thankfully.' She held up a pair of binoculars she carried on a strap round her neck. The lenses rotated automatically. 'Holy crap it, that whole patch of ground is on the move. I've never seen that many milliseeds together before, there must be thousands of them. It's like the whole jungle is sporing all at once. Why do you think it's doing that?'

'I've no idea. Is it relevant?'

'This many coincidences bother me.'

'Go talk to Marvin. Seriously, I'm paranoid enough right now. I don't need it making worse. Find an explanation.'

'I'll do that.' She stood up.

'Any ideas how we go about trapping it?'

Angela grinned. 'Very *very* carefully.'

*

First priority, Vance told the briefing, is to re-establish the camp perimeter integrity. The Legionnaires were to investigate every structure for the alien. Then they would patrol the perimeter until the net, along with their boundary sensors, was back up and running.

Wardele reported that the net failed from a routing capacity overload, which left the cells isolated. Their hardwired response was immediate shutdown to protect data packages in transit. All they needed was a soft-reboot instruction.

'So was it deliberate?' Vance asked.

'I'd say yes. A normal net wouldn't be affected, there are too many cells to lose overall cohesion. But here it's small, easy to target.'

'So you're saying the alien understands our technology?' asked Davinia Beirne from the AVV team.

'It looks like it, yes.'

She gave Vance a worried look. 'I thought we were looking for some kind of hidden primitive tribe, here.'

'You thought wrong,' he told her. 'Forster, we need to harden the net against any further attacks.'

'It will be,' Wardele promised. 'I know software crap that freebinary radicals haven't even thought of. I'll have it secure by lunchtime.'

The meshes and sensors had failed them completely, Vance said, allowing the alien to walk right into camp. But the weather was awful, and they were using passive systems. From now on, two Owls would be on constant patrol around the camp, using radar, sonar, infrared, photon enhancement, and laserscan to search for any movement in the surrounding bush.

'Karizma, I need active sensors on the ground, too. Is that within our microfacture capability?'

'I think so, yes,' said Karizma Wadhai, the camp's microfacture chief. 'Once we've tweaked the template for this environment my team can churn out enough microwave radar and laser trips to ring the perimeter. Might take a day or two for that many.'

'I want two rings,' Vance said. 'An inner one for the tents and buildings. That has to be functional for tonight. Then get the camp perimeter covered by tomorrow. After that we'll talk about extending coverage outside, to see if we can catch the things coming.'

'No problem.'

'I also want everyone issued with protective armour vests. There's enough in store. I know it's hot, but they are to be worn without exception and at all times. This thing goes for the heart each time.'

'Yes, sir.'

'Doctor, did you get anything from her smartcells?'

'No, I'm afraid I couldn't,' Dr Coniff said. 'Something ripped the software in all of them. All higher functions were glitched. Frankly it's a miracle her bodymesh called for help, but that functionality is hardwired in. Very hard to disrupt.'

'So there's no way we can see what attacked her?'

'No. The visual memory cache was empty.'

'Okay, well that just reinforces what we already know. The aliens understand our technology.' Then he told them the good news, that reinforcements were on the way. That there wouldn't be any more sampling missions. 'Basically we spend the rest of the week sitting tight and maintaining our own security. I believe we're more than capable of that.' He felt like ending the briefing in a prayer, but reluctantly declined, knowing the upset that might cause. He needed the department heads to believe in him, which given their backgrounds would only come if they had confidence in visible ability and strong leadership.

As soon as the briefing finished, Marvin Trambi called him over to where the mobile biolabs were parked. 'We may have a bigger problem,' he said, indicating the door of biolab-1.

Vance looked at the long scratches in the bodywork around the door handle. 'Oh my good Lord preserve us,' he muttered softly.

'How did it know?' Marvin asked. 'How did that thing know what was in here?'

'I don't know,' Vance admitted. 'But Antrinell and I were asking the same question back at the MTJ crash site.' A whole new universe of worry was opening up: that the aliens had infiltrated HDA, that they had been studying humans for the Lord alone knew how many years – decades even. 'Maybe Iyel said something. We never did find him.'

'Iyel didn't know about this part of the mission.'

'He was smart. He could have worked it out. I suspect most of the xenobiology team has. After all, the missiles take up quite a bit of volume in the lab.'

'Not visibly, but yeah, you may have a point. The xenobiology team all know the vehicle's basic layout, they know we're missing some volume.'

'Is there any chance it can get in?'

Marvin shook his head. 'Not by hitting the door with its spiky flint axe, no. This baby was designed to be Zanth-proof. You could let off a tactical nuke a kilometre away and all that'd happen would be a few blisters in the paintwork. You need the access codes and the right biometrics.'

'It disabled the net. It has more than a spiky axe.'

'Maybe it does, but think on this, even if it got in and acquired the warheads, what's it going to shoot them at? They're only effective here. It'd be killing itself and its own planet.'

'Alternatively, it would be stopping us from using them.'

'Yeah,' Marvin agreed grudgingly. 'But HDA will just send

another batch through. If it knows anything about us, it knows that. We wouldn't have any choice. Remember, we can't fight another species – we can't afford it. The Zanth is our enemy. It takes everything we've got.'

And all we can do is run from it. 'What does the biolab log show?'

'Nothing,' Marvin said. 'Something ripped the external smart-dust.'

Vance reached up and touched the biolab, moving his finger-tips gently, almost reverently, over the scratches in the metallo-ceramic bodywork, feeling the roughness under his skin. He didn't like to think of the force needed just to create such hairline marks. 'This is their target,' he decided. 'We provoked them bringing this here.'

'Provoked them? They slaughtered a whole bunch of us. They're still doing that.'

'We invaded their planet.'

'I can't believe you just said that. If there was any sign of sentient life, this whole world would have been quarantined immediately.'

'Then we didn't look hard enough,' Vance said. He was rather enjoying how calm he was, how rational. He was close to meeting another child of God, how could he not be enraptured by that?

'We need deployment authority,' Marvin said. 'Just in case. Have you spoken to Vermekia?'

'No. Not yet. But Passam is causing a small problem.'

'What kind of problem?'

'She's deflecting the blame back onto Angela. My guess is the Commissioner is rather worried about the evidence the police have been turning up back in Newcastle. To them it looks like a North family fight. I admit, I was thinking the same thing myself until last night.'

'That moron bitch. Has she tried asking Esther her opinion?'

'I'm sure Passam will come round eventually. In the mean-time, I'll call Vermekia. But we have to direct our resources on securing this camp. The MTJ crash has left us very short on Legionnaires. Convenient, that.'

'Oh hell. We've really been caught out, haven't we?'

'Understandably. There is no evidence that any animal sentient evolved here. But then, it's hard to see how the plants evolved here, as well.'

'So . . . you think they're not indigenous?'

'I've always questioned that. But I suspect we'll get the chance to find out soon enough now.'

*

Actually, standing behind the canteen counter in the mess hall was a pretty reasonable viewpoint. Rebka could watch a lot of the activity going on outside. The Legionnaires going from tent to tent, waving their guns around as they went in to see if an alien monster was lurking in the shadows. The AAV crew prepping an Owl for flight. The microfacture team vanishing into their office to begin work on the sensors that Elston had ordered. Then the colonel himself, suddenly hurrying off towards the vehicle compound. She couldn't see him directly, the clinic and administration Qwik-Kabins were in the way, but last seen he was heading for the end where the biolabs were parked.

As Wukang's net rebooted it was soon handling dozens of links as everyone started analysing their situation. Bandwidth along the e-Ray relay to Abellia was reaching capacity limits as people called family and friends.

Rebka's e-i called Madeleine's 'father'. 'Hi, Dad,' she said as soon as he came online.

'How's it going?' Clayton 2North asked.

'Really bad. Someone was killed last night. They think it was an alien that did it.'

'That's horrible. Are you okay?'

'Yeah. The Legionnaires protected us all night. We're safe now, and more Legionnaires are on their way; they told us this morning.'

'How about your friend? Is she safe?'

'Yes. I saw her this morning. She's still alive.'

'That's good. Was she anywhere near the killing?'

'No, Dad, she didn't see anything. She wasn't close enough.'

'So are they going to bring you all home?'

'Not just yet, no. We'll be here for a while, I think. They're starting to issue us with protective gear just in case.'

'Smart of them. Make sure you wrap up well with some of your own clothes.'

'Don't fuss, Dad, I know how to take care of myself. How's your new job?'

'I've fitting in just fine. They're a good team.'

'I'm glad. Has Aunt Jane turned up yet?'

'No. But we're very close to finding out where she went. I'm expecting some good news in the next few days. The police have been really helpful with that.'

'I'm sure Grandpa will be pleased to know.'

'He is. He's proud of you, too. He asked me to say that.'

'I'll be back soon. I'm going to bring you all presents when I come.'

'Love you, darling.'

'You too, Dad. Bye.' The link ended, and Rebka collected another tray of breakfast packets from the kitchen. Lulu was taking the rubbish bins out to the compactor. Her eyes had the tell-tale purple speckles of swarine spore infection, but Rebka could see the poor girl had been crying as well. She sat down next to Lulu and put her arm round the frightened girl.

'I wasn't expecting this,' Lulu said weakly. 'Everybody's getting killed. I thought the Jeep accident was bad, like, but this. I can't hack it. I thought I could, but I can't. Something evil is out in the jungle. It's going to get into the camp again. I know it is. It'll come for us. I'm really scared, Madeleine. I want to go home.'

'Hey,' Rebka squeezed her gently. 'We know it's there now. The Legionnaires won't let it come through again.'

'Aye, pet,' Lulu said, and rubbed at her eyes. 'Do you think?'

'Put it this way, love, do you really think Omar's going to let anything dangerous get close to you?' Rebka had spent a month now watching Private Omar Mihambo flirt with, then blatantly entreat before finally begging Lulu to go take a walk into the jungle with him one night.

'We didn't, you know,' Lulu said regretfully. 'Just snogged, like. I've got a boyfriend back in Benwell.'

'Yes.' Martyn, who Rebka now knew more about than she did Raul back home on Jupiter. Lulu never could shut up about him. 'But Omar's sweet on you. He'll make sure you're safe. So try not to worry, okay?'

'Aye.' Lulu sniffed loudly. 'Look at us two, like, on another planet with a killer alien running round, and all we can do is chat about the fellas.'

'That's what keeps people going,' Rebka said. She felt so sorry for the terrified girl. Keeping cover in the face of such blatant human distress, not offering out-of-character assurances, was turning out to be the hardest part of the mission. She hadn't been expecting that. In a way she almost envied Angela – keeping her own myth going for over twenty years. That level of resolution was inhuman. A thought which made her snort in amusement.

'What?' Lulu asked.

'I was just thinking, pet, the fellas are probably talking about us, too.'

'Aye. That Chris on the Owl team, he fancies you something rotten, you know.'

'I noticed.' Weeks of not understanding the unsubtle hints and deflecting endless cliché lines had brought her close to smacking the stupid remote pilot. 'Look, they're going to hand out the armour vests soon. Promise me something. I know they're going to be really hot, but wear it. All the time, pet, not just when we're dishing out crud in the mess tent, okay? For me? I want to know you're safe.'

'Okay.'

Luther Katzen came bustling out of the kitchen tent. 'There you are. Come on girls, we're not paying you to sit around moping. I've got another dozen meals ready to go front of shop. Please!'

Rebka gave him her best stone face. 'You're not paying us to be targeted by a killer alien, either, yet here we are.' She walked past him, ignoring the startled look on his face. Lulu followed, carefully keeping her eyes averted from the supervisor while grinning sheepishly.

Rebka was busy handing out breakfast packages to the subdued medical staff when the news about the sunspots flashed along the e-Ray relay. Her immediate – and dumb – reaction was to glance up at the burning glare point that was now well above the horizon. She immediately had to blink away the pink afterimage smears.

Wukang was a few degrees east of Highcastle, so their dawn arrived earlier than it did in the planet's capital city. Not that anyone on the expedition would be bothering to check the star, she thought. From the few reports slipping into the transnet it seemed to be pure chance that Rozak Ueu had spotted them at all. His real interest was in the orbital dynamics of the outer ring shepherd moons, which he was studying at sunrise. He only noticed the sunspots because there were so many of them. Sirius was a potent star, but ever since the Norths had opened the gateway, sunspots had been minimal. Rebka wondered what the new outburst would do to the solar wind; active regions which accompanied sunspots on Sol were the source of flares which shot vast quantities of high-energy particles into space. They used to practise flare emergencies in the Jupiter habitat.

*

She'd been twelve going on thirty when they had their first *flaredown* party. That was what the children called it. To the adults, it was just another rad-haz downtime drill.

She'd been swimming with her brother Raul and their friends Jenna and Ibiqu in a shallow lake near her home when the eerie siren wail sounded across the habitat. The light bracelets around the axial spindle shifted to a strong red tint, and began to pulsate. Rebka stared up at the signal in rebellious annoyance. Her personal interface, in the form of a cute blue and green bead necklace, was lying on the shore next to her towel and clothes. Nobody could call her directly to urge her along to the shelter hall. No one would know if she spent another ten minutes in the water. It was such fun splashing around, diving down to the artificially sculpted lake bed with its freshwater coral growths. The fish were all large, colourful, and curious about the interlopers in their aquatic world.

'Come on,' Raul called. He was treading water three metres away, beckoning her on.

'I think I'll just stay here for a bit,' Rebka said.

Jenna and Ibiqu stopped swimming and stared at her in a mix of shock and surprise.

'It's a flare warning,' Raul said, as if that should explain everything.

'It's a practice. And anyway, even if it was real, the particle storm wouldn't reach us for another couple of hours. And even then it wouldn't affect this habitat. Our shell has arb molecule shielding. It's only the original sections where it's a problem.' As if to emphasize the point, she duckdived smoothly, swimming down to the sandy lake bed with big easy strokes. The once familiar topography was now different and mysterious in the dusky red light. Long sluggish ribbons of weed wiggled round her as she slipped between the coral bulbs, tickling her skin. Fish darted about, vanishing into fissures. She played grab at them with her fingers.

A hand closed tightly round her ankle, and she twisted in surprise. Raul was there, cheeks all puffed out, pointing vigorously at the surface. Rebka spread her arms wide in a theatrical surrender, and kicked lazily for the surface.

'Don't do that,' Raul stormed when they were back on top. All big brother protective and angry.

'You're so government,' she taunted as they headed back to

shore where Jenna and Ibiqu were already getting out. 'You should join the GE Commission. They love ordering people about.'

'You don't know what you're talking about,' he grumbled back. 'You listen to your lessons, but you don't understand them.'

She ignored him as they quickly towelled down. He was being equally stubborn, pretending she didn't exist. Jenna went over to him. Rebka watched as the girl put her arms round her brother's shoulders. A tender touch, as if she could ease away his frustration and upset.

Some instinctive unease made Rebka realize she wasn't going to be tagging along with Raul much more. He preferred hanging out with friends his own age these days. She resented that; Raul had been such fun since she arrived home from the hospital. Exciting, protective big brother, rampaging through the habitat, getting into trouble together. Laughing together. Daring each other on. Sharing punishments when they inevitably got caught.

Perhaps that was why she was so hard on him these days. She'd always known this time would arrive . . .

The shelter hall wasn't exactly a hardship. A long windowless structure of thick arb-coated metal with corridors branching into igloo-like communal chambers. There was food and games and a little theatre show in the evening for the kids.

Rebka sat through the amateur 'all-join-in' sing-along production of *Snow White* with a sullen sulk, refusing to open her mouth at even the most jolly of songs. She didn't sleep much that night in the girls' dormitory, preferring to play the most aggressive games her interface could access – and she knew some good work-round routines to get at the 18+ section of the habitat entertainment net. *Thank you Krista – now that was somebody who knew how to be a proper elder sibling.*

She was expecting the full censure and smart talking to from her parents when they went home the following morning. But they knew her moods and responses better than she realized.

It wasn't until four days later that her mother sat down with her on the broad patio area, under the shade of the burgeoning palm trees that were now overwhelming the house.

'So what was wrong with the shelter hall?'

Rebka sighed long and hard. She might have known it wasn't going to be overlooked. 'Nothing was wrong with it. I was just having a nice time in the lake. I was coming anyway, you know. Raul is just such a panic-merchant.'

'Actually, Raul is quite remarkably sensible for a teenager. I was expecting him to be the troublesome one.'

'Meaning what? Meaning *I am*? Well why don't you just send me back, then, if I'm so much trouble?' Arms folded stubbornly, pouting as far as her lips would stretch.

'Send you back?' her mother said in a clear tone that made Rebka realize she might just be overdoing the drama.

'Well, come on. I'm not stupid.'

'No. Just obstinate. That's what I like about you.'

'Mum!' She held up her hand. 'Difference. Yeah?'

'Certainly is. So?'

'You're about as black as possible; Dad was born in India; and my skin's so white you'd think I was covered in snow.'

'You've never seen snow.'

'Duh. Zone!'

'I'll thank you not to take that tone, young lady. Now why don't you tell me how long this has been bothering you?'

'I don't know. Like for ever.'

'No it hasn't. You used to be the happiest of all my children. I was so proud, after everything you've been through.'

'So you're not any more, then?'

'Hoo boy. Okay, what do you want to know?'

'Where did I come from? Are you my parents?'

'You came from one of the Distant Planets.'

'The what? I've never heard of them.'

'Ah, something you don't know. Good, well you look them up when you can spare the time from hacking into the habitat's 18+ entertainment cache.'

Rebka flushed bright red.

'The Distant worlds are planets that aren't affiliated to the rest of the trans-stellar community, usually for political reasons,' her mother explained. 'And you were brought here for treatment, because we can offer the best genetic therapy there is.'

'And the other? You and Dad?'

'You don't have any of my DNA in your cells, nor your father's. Do you believe that means you aren't our daughter? That we don't love you just as much as Raul and Krista?'

'No,' Rebka muttered. Now her eyes were getting all wet for no reason. 'I'm sorry, Mum. I just thought . . . I don't know what I thought.'

Monique went over and put her arms around the upset girl. 'Now listen to me. From the moment I saw you being brought onto the spaceplane at Gibraltar, I wanted nothing more than to protect and nurture you. One day you will have to be told about your heritage, because it is unique and special. But we haven't talked about that because you are still a child, and I want that to last for as long as possible, because I love your laughter, and your excitement, and I like beating you at tennis, still; and I even like your temper tantrums because it proves what a determined little horror you are. And when you smile it is the most precious, wonderful moment in the universe for me.'

Rebka couldn't help it, she was sobbing openly now. 'Am I awful? Is that it? Am I from bad people? Will I be bad too?'

'No, of course not. Far from it. And this is why we haven't made an issue of this, the past is over and you have the whole of your future to live in. And when you do face up to this issue, your dad and I will be there to help you through anything you find difficult. But for now, will you please just concentrate on having a good time? There's so much in this weird and enchanting habitat of ours to enjoy. So much to learn.'

She nodded solemnly. 'I will. I'll be good.'

'You don't have to be perfect, dear. Just figure out which rules you shouldn't break.'

'Like ignoring a rad-haz alert?'

578

'Like reacting as if it's designed to annoy you personally. It's not. We didn't always have arb molecule shielding.'

'I know. I told Raul that.'

'You really do pay attention to your lessons, don't you?'

'I like school,' she insisted.

'Thank heavens for that.'

'And I let you win at tennis.'

'Oh really?'

'Why are we here, Mum? Why did Constantine build the habitat?'

'Because somebody had to.'

'Why? What's it all for?'

'Jupiter is an enclave of human civilization that we are determined will not fall. We are both a refuge and, if necessary, a seed to regrow humanity should the Zanth succeed in wiping out all our worlds. Your father and I came here with Constantine because we believed in his vision, to build a society that rejects avarice and selfishness, and more than that, one that can help the rest of the human race.'

'Is that what we're doing?' Rebka asked excitedly. 'Helping people?'

'Yes. Even though they don't know it yet.'

*

The Trans-stellar Situation Centre was a large concrete-ribbed chamber on the lowest level of the HDA headquarters, itself the size of a small town buried a supersafe kilometre below Alice Springs in the Australian desert. From there, its designers believed, it would be able to function for at least a month after a Zanthstorm began, leading the ultimate battle to protect the old homeworld long enough for the inevitable evacuation. It was a fight which would largely be coordinated from the Situation Centre, whose walls were covered with big curving holographic panes, each one showing various enhanced images of every human-settled star system. Fleets of observation satellites, possessed of more sensor boom spikes than sea urchins, circled those stars in orbits that varied from a couple of million kilometres above the blazing coronas right out to the frozen wastes of the outer cometary belts. Their only function was to monitor the quantum structure of spacetime for any hint of the distortions which were the precursors to a Zanthswarm, beaming the data back to the planetary gateways, and from there through the dedicated, heavily protected HDA network on Earth.

The entire monitoring set-up was completely automated, with the most powerful AI cores ever built analysing and interpreting every quiver and fluctuation in every field interstice. That didn't prevent HDA from filling the Centre with over a hundred highly specialist technical staff, each sitting alertly at a zone console, checking the telemetry streams from the satellites, and reviewing the status of each star system on a continual basis.

They were ready for any sign of an emerging Zanthswarm that might threaten a world settled by humans.

However, for all the contingencies they trained for, all the different scenarios thought up by the tactical review board, the Situation Centre didn't quite know how to respond to the news of sunspots on Sirius. There certainly wasn't an alert status that reflected it. And the information bubbling through the transnet was more gossip than hard data. That, then, was their first priority, Captain Toi decided, to determine exactly what was happening. As head of the Sol watch section, she also had oversight for St Libra, which was the HDA's perennial problem child.

Unlike every other trans-stellar world, the giant planet didn't have its own HDA section. Nor was there an HDA base there, either, just an office in Highcastle. St Libra was only a minority HDA member. That was all down to money. The Highcastle Council, which was the largest democratic government on St Libra, declined to tax its citizens and corporations at a level that full HDA membership required. Mainly because Highcastle was a company town; the Council set up by Northumberland Interstellar and its bioil compatriots. The theory drawn up by accountants was that everyone on the planet (under their dominion) lived within a few hundred kilometres of the gateway. They could all get out fast, unlike other planets whose pioneering citizens gloried in spreading out from pole to pole. This was in the days before Bartram went and established Abellia, of course, but even after that nothing changed.

Then there were the Independencies, who without exception were openly hostile to any notion of what they denounced as: *submitting to HDA's repressive militaristic authority.* That left the whole problem of what would happen if there ever was a Zanthswarm on Sirius open to a great deal of political buck passing. Would the GE allow all the rebels and anarchists and anti-authoritarians and religious fundamentalists back through the gateway – assuming any of them ever made it that far during a Zanthswarm? Politically, it would be difficult to slam the door shut on millions of people who would be killed if they couldn't get back. Which then left the possibility open for HDA providing evacuation cover; paid for by every other planet's taxpayers. The final decision of just how humanitarian humanity would actually be was one that was constantly pushed off every government's agenda.

Now Captain Toi had to make the preliminary analysis, which might well result in finally getting an answer to that thorniest of questions. She turned to the colonel in command and asked: 'What do I do?'

'Get more data,' was the simple answer.

Toi looked up at the single large wall pane that displayed all the spacetime structure data the HDA received from St Libra. Compared to every other pane in the centre it was almost blank. It was impossible to launch satellites from St Libra, since no space vehicle could ever get through the rings. Instead, HDA had chosen to place five quantum sensors across the Ambrose continent. Theoretically they should be able to detect the kind of instabilities that indicated an impending Zanthswarm. If they were lucky, Highcastle might get warned half an hour before the chunks began to fall.

Right now, none of the detectors was registering any kind of quantum anomaly. So the HDA, the greatest protective force ever assembled by the human race, would have to rely on a bunch of mildly eccentric telescope owners in Highcastle to base a judgement that might ultimately result in millions of people living or dying. And she didn't even know how many telescopes there were. 'Not acceptable,' Toi told the pane forcefully.

General Khurram Shaikh arrived in the Centre an hour later, responding to the colonel's request. As usual, he was in full dress uniform. As he came in he was flanked by his staff officers, Major Fendes and Major Vermekia. 'So where do we stand?' he asked the colonel in charge of the Centre as he settled in behind the Sol section. 'Do I need to issue a Zanthswarm alert?'

'No quantum instabilities registering on our St Libra detectors, sir. It doesn't look like a Zanthswarm yet.'

'So this is just a natural phenomenon?'

The colonel turned to Toi. 'Go ahead, Captain.'

'If it is a Zanthswarm, it's a very unusual one.' She told her e-i to bring up the image. On the Sirius wall pane a large circle materialized, primarily composed of blue and yellow speckles. It was covered in dark splodges, like some kind of cancer chewing on a healthy organ. 'We got lucky. The e-Rays being used by the expedition were built to operate during a Zanthswarm and provide us with additional communication relays. Part of their sensor suite is designed to look directly upwards into space. We use the information they gather to feed our tactical base for the Thunderthorns. So far the expedition has just been using them to map the land beneath. I ordered them to scan up instead. What you're seeing is a baseline composite image of Sirius in real time.'

'That's good work, Captain,' the General said.

'Thank you, sir. Of course we can only see one half of Sirius from the planet, but we're assuming this outbreak is uniform. The spots we're observing are certainly well distributed.'

'Do we know when this started?'

'The science advisory team I've got has been measuring the

582

expansion rate – we're thinking the first ones started to develop about eighteen hours ago. Twelve have now reached seventy thousand kilometres in diameter and show no sign of contracting yet. Given the scale of Sirius, we're expecting them to grow considerably larger than they do here at Sol, where they've been measured up to eighty thousand kilometres across.'

'All right, so what's unusual about sunspots on a star?'

'Sir, Sirius has always been a sunspot minimum star – it's never been observed with anything approaching this kind of mass outbreak before. So far we've counted fifty-six sunspots. They usually erupt in pairs, because they're driven by magnetic field twists in the photosphere. For this many to appear within such a relatively small timeframe something has to be agitating the whole star. And, sir, they're still appearing. If anything, the rate of emergence seems to be accelerating.'

Khurram Shaikh gave Captain Toi a long look. 'Agitating the star?'

'Yes sir. The underlying origin of sunspots is the interaction between a star's magnetic field and its convection zone. And the only thing we know that can operate on this kind of scale is the Zanth. Even so, it takes weeks for a convection layer disturbance to rise to the surface and produce a spot. This has been building for a while.'

'What about the companion, Sirius B?' the General asked. 'Could that have triggered it?'

'The astronomers on the team don't think so, sir. Right now Sirius B is still on an outward orbit; it's twenty-three AUs from A. It's difficult to see how it could affect the primary in this fashion at such a distance. If there was any interaction between the magnetic fields of both stars it would be when they're at their closest. There have been two conjunctions since we opened a gateway to St Libra. Nothing like this happened at either time.'

'So you're considering an external event as the reason?'

'Given how stable Sirius usually is, the astronomy team believe that's likely.'

'You said the disturbances take weeks to rise up through the convection zone,' Vermekia said. 'So when did this agitation actually start? Could it have been back in January?'

'Possibly. The timescale isn't exact. We'd need to have a much greater knowledge of the star's internal structure, which we simply don't have. Nobody ever put solar science satellites in orbit there.'

'You said the astronomy team thinks this might be due to an external event,' the General said. 'Does that imply there's another theory floating round?'

Toi gave the colonel a desperate look, which he ignored. 'There is one other thing to consider,' she blurted.

'What is it?' Shaikh asked patiently.

'Sir, there's something called the Red Controversy.'

'The what?'

'There is some evidence that Sirius once turned red.'

'Red, Captain?'

'Yes, sir. There are records of old astronomers recording Sirius as having a red coloration.'

'When was this?'

'Sir, eh, 150 BC was the first recorded instance.'

'Are you joking, Captain?'

'Sir, no sir. There have been several such inconsistencies in astronomical accounts in early history. They all happened prior to the invention of the telescope so there's no modern verifiable proof available. But the legend persisted for some time. There was even a tribe in Africa who supposedly knew about Sirius B centuries before telescopes confirmed its existence.'

'I'm glad you're doing your homework, Captain, but exactly how is this folklore relevant?'

'Two things, sir.' She glanced up at the pane as the Centre's AI bracketed a newly emerging sunspot. 'We don't know how many sunspots will erupt. If they continue at the current rate the overall luminosity may conceivably fall.'

'And the spectrum will redshift,' the General concluded. 'Very good.'

'In which case we'll have to admit there's a very long-term

natural cycle at work inside Sirius, something that might produce this kind of phenomenon only every two thousand years. The reports from the forward camps and the areas outlying Highcastle do seem to support this, too.'

'How?'

'Every plant on the planet is releasing its spores – that has to be an evolutionary trait. The jungles are bracing themselves for a storm. Some of the botanists are claiming the leaves may be sensitive to spectrum shift. However the plants know, they're right to react in this fashion. The high-energy particle streams being ejected by this sunspot phase are colossal. Those storms are going to hit the planet in a few hours, and the effect they'll have on all our electrical systems there is going to be extremely detrimental.'

'Will it affect the gateway?' the General asked sharply.

'Nobody knows, sir. But the atmosphere will be in turmoil once the particles start to energize the upper layers.'

'Yes. I see your point. So we've confirmed something unusual is happening, and yet we still don't know if it is natural or Zanth related.'

'And we might want to consider if it originated from St Libra itself,' Vermekia said.

'How could that be, Major?' Shaikh asked.

'We've got a lot of unlikely coincidences starting to accumulate here, sir, especially after last night's incident at Wukang.'

'There's no genetic variance,' Fendes said. 'None at all. The Norths are sending assassin clones to kill each other, or some such nonsense. Now you're suggesting an unseen, unknown alien running round a jungle with a spear can also interfere with a star's convection layer?'

'The St Libra aliens are not unknown,' Vermekia answered smoothly. 'They are real enough to have killed several HDA personnel already. They also understand our technology well enough to circumvent most of it. To me that is a clear indication of highly developed abilities.'

'There is no animal life on St Libra,' Fendes insisted.

'And what about the species which bioformed that world? If the geneticists on the expedition have shown nothing else, it is the extremely advanced evolution of the plant life, which given the age of the star is frankly impossible. Are you going to cherry-pick their results? St Libra is a huge enigma which we have been ignoring for too long.' He jabbed a finger at the big pane with its sickly star dominating the Centre. 'That is not a natural event. Something is happening out there, and we have to find out what.'

Shaikh nodded. 'In that at least, we are in agreement. Captain, what options have you got to expand our information on Sirius?'

'Very limited, sir,' Toi said.

'But you do have something for me?'

'Realistically, there's only one thing we can do at this point, but it's expensive.'

'I'm the one who deals with politicians and their national treasurers, Captain. Let me make that decision.'

'Yes, sir. We have several batches of multifunction sensor satellites in storage at our Cape Town base ready to be deployed in a Zanthswarm. They're intended to bolster the surveillance clusters above whatever planet is being attacked, so their systems are battle hardened. If we were to open a war gateway above Sirius and inject them into orbit around the star they should be able to function in those conditions for a while, and supply us the data we need.'

'Break into war stocks?' The General seemed slightly bemused by the prospect. 'Very well. You have the authorization to begin that operation. Colonel Fendes, liaise with the Cape Town base commander. Make this happen fast. I want to know what's happening in that bedamned star system.'

Wednesday 20th March 2143

It wasn't the peculiar light which woke Saul Howard, but the sound. The sea was wrong. Living at Camilo Beach for so long, the sound of the waves sloshing across the sands was ingrained. This morning the sound, the rhythm, of the waves, was different somehow. Saul lay in bed for several minutes trying to figure out what exactly had changed. It was subdued, he decided, as if the tide had taken the water out like it did back on Earth rather than St Libra's gentle ebbing.

Sunspots can't do that, he thought, *can they?*

He realized Emily was awake beside him. Turned his head to see her looking at him. Hazy light that shimmered slowly between pink and nankeen was stealing past the shutters, dappling the bed. It wasn't a light that he'd ever seen before, so he didn't know if it was morning or the middle of the night.

Emily smiled gently; though the strange shifting light allowed him to see the uncertainty haunting her. Yesterday, with the news of the sunspot outbreak dominating the transnet, had proved unsettling, and additional reports were coming in that the expedition was in some kind of trouble, that people were dying out in the jungle. The news sites didn't have names, so he didn't know who, which troubled him deeply. This wasn't life as it should be in Abellia.

He watched in silence as she moved the thin duvet aside. Her hands slid the PJs over her hips and down her legs. Then his beautiful young wife slipped sinuously on top of him, naked and hungry, soft hair swishing across his chest, reaching for him, effortlessly coaxing him erect. A long involuntary sigh of delight escaped her mouth as she slowly impaled herself. Hands entwined, gripping hard. Neither of them said a word as they began to move together. There was an urgency to her he hadn't known for a long time, perhaps not even since the first few months after they became lovers. Now, she wanted the physical contact, needed the comfort and reassurance it bestowed. So did he.

There was a long time afterwards when they held each other close, still silent. Kissing and smiling, hands stroking, exploring as if they'd never known each other before. An intimacy which held the world at arm's length.

Eventually he glanced at the clock. Frowned. It was stuck on 23:17. Yet he knew it was close to morning. The aurora borealis which the solar flares had brought to St Libra's atmosphere must be affecting the house's electrical systems.

'I need to find out what's happened to the sea,' he told her.

'I know. I hear it, too.'

They put on towelling robes, and went out through the kitchen's patio doors. When he asked his e-i to show him the time, it flashed up 5:57 in his grid. The fact that the sophisticated program was unaffected by the solar flare was good news. At least part of the house's net was still functioning.

Outside, the sky was alive with the fluorescence of the aurora, sending tremendous rivers of pale colour undulating through the upper atmosphere. They were considerably brighter than the ringlight. Despite himself, Saul had to marvel at the naked display of energy.

Still holding hands they made their way over the sheltered patio and onto the familiarity of dry warm sands. He was mildly relieved to see the waterline was in the right place. Not that he'd *really* believed the sea was in retreat, but . . .

When they got to the line of damp sand, Saul's first thought was that there'd been some kind of bioil spill. In the electron-kindled light from above the water was dark, slick, its viscosity altered by some unknown alchemy. Mysterious and threatening, it sucked and gurgled aggressively on the sand. There was no surf any more, waves had become smooth elongated ripples, their power dampened as they slid ashore. And worse, the water was lumpy.

'What is that?' Emily asked in a disconcerted murmur. Her hand tightened its grip on Saul.

He looked from the ripples that strained to reach his bare feet, across the mild swell all the way to a horizon where the rings and borealis streamers struggled for supremacy. The entire sea had the same syrupy constituency. He drew down a breath, tasting air full of tangy sulphur brine. And he finally knew what he was seeing.

'They're jelly bubbles,' he said incredulously. 'Millions of them.'

As with the land on St Libra, so with the water. The planet's seas had no fish, no shells nor plankton. Not even coral. There was only seaweed; and the dominant plant, certainly around the coastlines, was the ubiquitous jelly bubble. A glutinous, almost translucent ovoid as wide as a human hand, suffused with seed like a limpid pomegranate. It grew on a simple ribbon rooted in sand. When ripe, the ribbon would moult away releasing the jelly bubble, which would then float up to the surface and be carried on the fate of wind and tide as it too slowly began to decay, shedding seeds as it went.

The sea before Saul had been smothered in a carpet of jelly bubbles, millions of them jostling together in a squishy coagulating mess. Somehow they had all broken free of their anchor ribbons simultaneously overnight, ripe or not. Now they were decomposing in turn, saturating the water with a slushy avalanche of seed.

'This is crazy,' Emily said. 'How could they know? They said on the transnet news all the plants released their spores because their leaves sensed the sun changing. But how would the jelly bubbles know to do that?'

589

'I don't know,' Saul replied, mesmerized and alarmed by the transformed sea. Occasionally, when out surfing, he'd wound up with an acrid mouthful of jelly bubble shards as the swell dunked him under. It was a vile taste, and if you swallowed the stuff then you had to get ashore quickly, because it invariably acted as an emetic in a human stomach. But it wasn't lethal, at least not in the usual small doses surfers suffered. But this . . . Happy, friendly Camilo Beach was now besieged by a sea of mushy poison.

'We need to warn the neighbours,' he said sorrowfully. 'Maybe fence it off, make sure the kids stay out.'

'They're good kids,' Emily said automatically. 'They won't go into this.'

'Yeah. I certainly wouldn't.'

'What's happening, Saul? It's not the Zanth, is it?'

He knew that apprehension only too well. If it was Zanth, they'd never make it to the Highcastle gateway. His eyes closed against a dark fear stirring, one he never thought he'd feel again. As if to emphasize the worry, he heard a distant sonic boom as some plutocrat's private jet streaked south to safety. 'This isn't the Zanth,' he said with as much confidence as he could gather. 'The plants here have clearly evolved to cope with the sunspot outbreaks. This is what they do when it redshifts. They survive. And we will too.' He eyed the silent majestic rivers of light cavorting across the sky, disturbed by their size and intensity. This was only the first day of the flares, and the sunspots had still been multiplying when he went to bed last night.

'Survive what?' Emily asked. 'How badly do the sunspots affect St Libra?'

'I don't know,' he admitted. It wasn't a question he was comfortable thinking about. But you're going to have to, he told himself sternly. You have a family to consider. To protect. *Like before*. 'Let's get back inside. I'll call Otto and Kelly for starters. We should maybe think of teaming up, pooling resources. The village is reasonably isolated.'

'Just what are you expecting?'

Saul gave the auroras a suspicious stare. 'I'm just trying to think ahead a bit, that's all. And face it, Abellia isn't exactly self-sufficient at the best of times.'

'If it's not the Zanth, then we can go through the gateway. It would be hard, but we could start over on another planet.'

'Maybe. If the GE lets us back. They weren't allowing any travel yesterday, remember. And there aren't that many planes available.'

'I thought I married an optimist?'

'Don't worry, you did.'

Saul started calling the neighbours as Emily busied herself making breakfast. The children were all subdued as they came into the kitchen. They too were in tune with the rhythm of life in Camilo Beach; the changes manifesting outside were unsettling. They didn't understand what was happening. Emily made them eat, making fresh waffle mix and allowing then to pour their own maple syrup as a treat.

Otto, Kelly, and five other neighbours answered Saul's call. They were all equally perturbed by the turn of events, and started calling their neighbours in turn – a chain reaction resulting in a meeting of Camilo residents arranged for ten o'clock that morning.

Duren called Saul just after seven. 'Disturbing times, my friend. I hope you're all right.'

'Not really. The sea is full of jelly bubbles.'

'Yes. That aspect of the uprising is just starting to feature on the news. Most odd. The planet is clearly making it known we are not welcome, just as brother Zebediah predicted.'

'Really? I thought it was the star that was the problem.'

On the other side of the kitchen, Emily asked: 'Who?'

'Duren,' he said quietly, which produced an instant scowl.

'The star and its planets are parent and child,' Duren said. 'You cannot be surprised at their anger, they are simply responding to our violation of their sanctity.'

Saul was starting to miss the old Duren, the one to whom any argument was settled by smashing someone through the nearest wall. 'Sure. I'm kind of busy today. What did you want?'

'It is time.'

'Time for what?'

'For the end of our occupation to begin. The planet is driving us off into the great blackness from which we came.'

'Seriously, I'm busy.'

'I know. I will only take a brief moment of your time. We'd like you to bring us the items we requested earlier.'

'Oh, come on! Today?'

'Especially today, Saul. You have got them, haven't you?'

'Yes. I've got them.' Once he had the raw, Zulah had given him some simple microfacturing details which the 3D systems at the back of the Hawaiian Moon had no trouble in producing. When he told Emily about the request, they'd talked about whether he should do it or not. In the end, as the cylinders didn't seem to have any dangerous function, he'd gone ahead and produced them. Pressure vessels with internal bladders weren't anything he could go to the Abellia police with. They had to know what Zebediah was going to use them for before that particular anonymous call was placed. Saul had even set up an untraceable address to make the call – just like the old days.

'Then please bring them to us,' Duren said. 'This is our address.'

An icon popped up into Saul's grid, unfurling to reveal a location off Rue Turbigo on the outskirts of town. 'I'm not sure I can do that today.'

'I understand. I see you're at home right now, aren't you?'

A simple question which sent a cold flush along Saul's spine. Duren's e-i must be more advanced than he suspected. He didn't answer.

'Shall I send Zulah to come and collect our items?' Duren enquired.

Saul nearly shuddered. 'No. I'll bring it all to you.'

'This morning, please.' The call ended.

'You can't go today,' Emily said.

'I'm not having that woman here at the house. You haven't met her, you don't understand what she's like.'

'She doesn't know what I'm like.'

'No, please, Emily. I have to go. This ends today. Whatever they're doing, I'm going to tell them this is the last time I help them.'

'I think we should call the police now.'

'And tell them what? Come on, darling, we've been over this a hundred times. We can't even figure out what those cylinders are for.'

She gave him a reluctant pout. 'Well, okay. But I want some safeguards. I'm going to ride your bodymesh.'

Instinctively he didn't want it. Not to be dependent on her for help. Not to involve her. But there was also a guilty relief from knowing that she'd be with him, that she'd be able to call the police if things went bad, if they started pushing him around, demanding he give more. 'Okay,' he said.

He drove the Rohan out of Camilo Village and onto the Rue du Ranelagh. That was when the first glitch of the day hit him. The car's auto flashed a warning in his grid that its link to the road's macromesh was intermittent. Saul switched the auto off and took full manual control. Up above, Sirius was burning brightly in the sky, its intensity not noticeably different from any other day. But the borealis strands were visible even in the star's full glare, winding with serpentine agility through the air high above. With the car's top down, he could feel the static in the atmosphere making his hair crawl.

There was little traffic on the roads. Even the centre of town was practically deserted. He pulled up into the reserved parking slot behind the Hawaiian Moon, and climbed out. Both Rico's bar and the Cornish ice cream shop were shut, along with most of the stores along the promenade.

The three cylinders were in the back room, resting in full view on the shelves that lined one wall. The two smaller ones had a two-litre capacity, and contained the bladders. Valves were fitted at both ends, which made the principle easy enough to under-stand. Fill the bladder with some fluid, then push air into the cylinder at the other end, which would squeeze the bladder, emptying it. Saul didn't get why you couldn't use a pump, but then he didn't know what the overall operating requirements were. The third cylinder had a four-litre capacity and two inlet valves, so no prizes for guessing what that would be filled from.

He hadn't known what to expect when Zulah gave him the specifications. And he still didn't understand them. They weren't even designed to take much pressure. The valves, though, were high-precision, providing very accurate flow regulation. He suspected that was the real reason they'd come to him, there weren't that many microfacturing systems around that could build the valves. *Not with owners they could push around.*

The cylinders went into an old canvas backpack, and he returned to the car, half expecting the police to come crashing out of the shadows to arrest him. But nothing happened, no cars screeching out of side alleys to block the Rohan, no armoured team yelling at him to surrender. So the backpack sat on the passenger seat as he drove through the streets of the old town, hitting the on ramp at the big Osorio Plaza junction. And for the first time that morning he was moving through normal traffic, having to concentrate on steering and keeping his distance from the others. All the other vehicles had their green tail lights on, warning they were being driven manually. After decades of relying on auto it was a nervy few minutes until he got used to it again. He gave the cars around him a bemused look, wondering where they'd suddenly appeared from. Then he remembered Rue Turbigo was the road to Abellia's airport. The city's residents weren't waiting to see the outcome of the sunspots and the HDA's investigation into possible Zanth activity. They were heading for the gateway as fast as their credit rating would get them there.

Duren's address turned out to be a whitewashed villa in a small development halfway up the side of Huerta valley. The grass peeking out of the slope's reddish flinty soil was wispy and dry as Saul drove up the switchback. This far from the coast the hot air lacked the humidity he was used to. There were about twenty villas packed together on the terrace carved into the mountainside, giving their occupants a fantastic view of the landscape falling away below them. He couldn't see anybody moving round as he pulled in. Only Duren's villa had a vehicle parked in front of it, an Alpha Romeo eight-door Tuzan limousine with deep chrome-blue paintwork and black alloy wheel hubs.

'The whole place is deserted,' Emily said.

Saul looked round slowly for her, gazing at the neat little development with its irrigated shrubs and trees. The only sound was the wind gusting along the valley. 'Okay, let's get this over with.' He walked across the baking asphalt to the villa. Before he got there, the middle door of the limousine slid upwards.

Duren was sitting inside. 'Man, good to see you again.' He held out a big hand in welcome, fang teeth overhanging his lower lip. 'You, too, Emily, even though we've never actually met.'

'Shit,' Emily said in Saul's ear. 'They've found the link.'

Saul held up the backpack. 'I brought your stuff.'

'Thank you. Come on in.'

It took a nerve he didn't know he had to climb into the limousine. The door swung down smoothly behind him, and he found himself sitting on a curving seat next to Duren. The interior was decorated in tasteless purple and gold fabric with black furniture, including a bed which took up the rear quarter. He was facing a young woman in her mid-twenties, wearing grey-green overalls with a small topaz-yellow hoop and triangle corporate logo on the arm. She had the kind of perpetually serious expression that belonged to a sixty-year-old, betraying her as another of Zebediah's devout disciples.

'Saul, this is Catrice,' Duren said. 'She believes as we do.'

And I don't. 'Where's Zebediah?' Saul asked, while what he was really pleased about was the absence of Zulah.

'Did you wish to speak with him?'

'Not particularly.' He held up the backpack. 'Look, I made what you wanted. I'm out of here.'

'Does it fit?' Duren blinked, and for an instant his demon-eye tattoos glimmered at Saul.

'Fit?'

'Let's find out, shall we?' Duren took the backpack from him and handed it to Catrice. 'Thanks,' she muttered, and removed one of the two-litre cylinders, placing it on the bench seat beside her. A slim black case was opened.

Saul watched with interest as she carefully threaded a section of pipe to the cylinder valve, nodding in satisfaction. 'I have to tell you something,' he said.

'And what's that?' Duren said in his annoyingly equitable tone, the one that said whatever Saul thought was completely irrelevant.

'I won't be seeing you, any of you, again. I don't care about what you're doing, or your beliefs. You should look up at the sky some time. Sirius is going crazy. You might want to think about that.'

'Perhaps you should consider why it is going crazy, Saul. This planet does not want us here, especially now.'

Saul found talking to someone who spoke like this to be very difficult, someone whose irrationality manifested in a calm reasonableness. 'It's a sunspot outbreak, Duren, not a political protest. And what do you mean, especially now?' He could have kicked himself for asking, for involving himself.

'The expedition,' Duren said. 'They came here prepared to kill this world, Saul. The HDA has brought a great evil with it. Zebediah warned us. He knew this would happen.'

'Nobody's killing anything.'

'They can, Saul, and they will if their arrogance decides it is necessary. There is no crime they will not commit sheltering under the perverted guise of protecting their interests. That is why the star is answering their violation the only way it knows how.'

'Right.' Saul was getting edgy now, anxious for this bizarre torment to end so he could just get the hell out of the limousine. Opposite him, Catrice was now plugging fibre optics and power cables into the valve actuator.

'I know how this will end, Saul,' Duren said. 'I know St Libra will triumph, because this has all happened before.'

596

'What?'

'An age ago. Others came to this world, to try and claim it for themselves. Can you imagine such conceit? To claim a world, a life, that does not belong to you.'

'What happened?'

'They left. It is the fate of all ephemeral animal life when the sun grows cold. We all seek its warmth to nurture us, without its bounty such small weak creatures as ourselves cannot survive.'

'You're saying aliens came here to St Libra before us?'

'Yes.'

'How do you know that?'

'Zebediah told us. He knows the history of this world, this life.'

Saul absolutely refused to ask. *No way. I am not going down that route.* Instead he turned to Catrice. 'Does everything fit?'

'Yes,' Catrice said.

'Then I am leaving.' It came out as a challenge. 'No offence, but I don't want to see or hear from you again.'

'You cannot escape the message St Libra is delivering, Saul,' Duren said. 'Look around you. Look at the immensity of what you are facing. What we are doing is such a small part, but we contribute what we can, and are proud to do so. Humans are not welcome here any more. You should go home, old man, back through the gateway to live a happier life.'

'Whatever, dude.'

The door slid open, and Saul stepped out into the hot, arid air and blazing blue-white light of Sirius. A sensation of profound relief powered him all the way back to his Rohan. He switched on the fuel cells, and drove out onto the switchback which led down to the Rue Turbigo.

'What the hell was all that about?' Emily asked.

'They're nuts,' Saul grunted. 'The whole goddamn coven of them. Rabid wackos: ancient aliens, flying saucers, HDA blowing up the planet. Zebediah has invented the mother of all conspiracy theories. What bugs me is how he gets them to listen to it all, never mind believe it.'

'Because they're sad needy people,' she told him. 'That's who cults always recruit from.'

'Yeah, but ... damn!' He turned onto the Rue Turbigo. Travelling into town was easy. There was no traffic on his side of the road. 'I can't believe Duren is involved. I knew him back in the day. He just wouldn't listen to this kind of bullshit.'

'You said yourself he was just using it as an excuse to use violence on non-believers.'

'Yeah. Probably.' He twisted the throttle hard, picking up speed. On the other side of the Rue Turbigo, traffic was filling both lanes. Red and green tail lights shone bright, even under the gleaming cloudless sky. He wasn't really paying attention to the cars and trucks. Then something jumped out of the line of humming vehicles.

'Did you see that?' he asked.

'See what?'

Saul braked, craning his neck to get another glimpse of the big van that had gone humming past. 'There.' He told his e-i to hold the image.

'Oh yeah,' Emily said.

He accelerated again. The side of the van had the same sharp yellow hoop and triangle logo that was on Catrice's overalls.

'AeroTech Support Services,' Emily said, reading the lettering underneath. 'I'm accessing it now. It's a city-registered company, part owned by Abellia's Civic Administration. They service aircraft at the airport.'

A cold panic started to rise, turning Saul's skin clammy. 'What are they doing, Emily? Oh fuck, what have I built for them? An aircraft? Are they going to sabotage an aircraft?'

'Saul, calm down. Nobody's going to attack an aircraft. They're delusional, not psychotic. They want to make statements, get themselves noticed and listened to. They want recognition, not jail.'

The image of Zulah's hard face swam into his vision. *The bag!* He'd never told Emily about the surf bag Duren had carried onto the *Merry Moons*. Too weak, he railed at himself. Too scared of what was in there.

'We have to call the police,' he said. 'Use the address I set up. Warn them.'

'Warn them about what?'

'Why did I build the cylinders for them? I'm so fucking stupid. I knew they're crazy. What was I thinking?'

'You didn't know anything, you still don't. And you did it, because they threatened you. You were scared. Hell, I was scared and I never met them. Those things you told me.'

You think that's bad? There's so much I never told you, so much I never can. 'Please, Emily. Use the address. Tell the police we think some political group is going to sabotage a plane, or the airport. Send them the blueprints, say the cylinders are part of the device. Maybe they'll work out what Zebediah's built.'

'Saul . . .'

'Emily, I won't be able to live with myself if something bad happens and I didn't try to make it right. Really, I can't do that.' *Not again.*

'All right, darling. But I hope you set that address up right, else we're going to be answering some very difficult questions.'

*

The strange message arrived in the network of Abellia's police station at nine fifteen. Like every public department, the police were short-staffed that day as half of Abellia's workers stayed home, trying to understand what was happening, and taking steps to safeguard their families. The detective who did finally get round to examining it at nine fifty-five didn't know what to make of it – Zebediah North was in town with a bunch of crazed followers threatening people. Weird cylinders that might be connected with harming a plane. Nut-jobs working for Aero-Tech Support Services. It was all utter crap, of course, but given the current circumstances . . . He forwarded it to the small HDA security office which was operating out of the camp at the airport, as well as airport security. Both of them sent the blueprints on to engineering experts for a detailed analysis.

What came back *fast* shunted the threat level to a much higher grade. AeroTech Support Services was immediately suspended from operating, and its personnel ordered not to approach any aircraft. Fuel stores were also proscribed to them.

Major Griffin Toyne requested a secure private meeting with Commissioner Passam to brief her on the potential threat. She agreed, scheduling him for a conference at the hotel suite she'd taken over at twelve seventeen – her next available appointment.

At twelve minutes past twelve, the expedition's one Daedalus C-8000-KT tanker variant lifted off from Abellia's runway. It was carrying a full load of various bioil fuels to resupply the tanks at Sarvar, a payload weighing 92,000kg. The four Pratt & Whitney H500−300 high-speed turbofans were producing 210 kilonewtons of thrust each, pushing the heavy plane on a steep vector up to its cruise altitude of fourteen kilometres. It had reached two thousand three hundred metres when an explosion blew out a centre section of the fuselage approximately three metres in diameter. A blast which simultaneously punctured one of the five bioil tanks filling the centre of the plane.

The resultant fireball expanded over two hundred metres in diameter as it cascaded down on the fields below, flinging wreckage fragments over an area seven kilometres wide.

*

Saul was out on the beach at the time, hammering posts into the sand above the tideline. Camilo Village residents had printed a whole load of warning signs, telling people not to go into the sluggish, corrupted water. The detonation rumbled in over the mountains, making him stop work and look up in puzzlement. The sound was like an approaching thunderstorm, yet the sky was clear of cloud. Only the borealis streamers remained, sending long flames of cold electron light flickering down to stroke the tops of the mountains.

As he paused, his e-i started to relay the news from the airport.

Saul sank to his knees and started to cry in front of his children. It was the utter nadir of a life which only twenty-six years ago had overflowed with promise and joy.

*

Boston in mid-summer was hot and beautiful. Saul loved the whole bustle of the place. It was his home town after all, which added loyalty to the opinion. The densely packed buildings as he walked across the Common were a welcome sight. While he'd been off world he'd missed the grandeur of both the ancient houses and the modern towers dominating downtown where he was heading. The contrast should have been too great, yet somehow they worked together here, creating the look of a vibrant city, exemplified by bustling streets and well-maintained infrastructure. Unlike half the East Coast cities, Boston's population had remained steady while the new American worlds enticed the disaffected and the would-be empire builders; along with all the long-term welfare dependants who were relocated by the Federal Independent Landowner Act of 2057. The colleges helped keep Boston prosperous, of course, the students and sponsoring companies contributing to its civic identity, a commercial core whose steadfastness attracted a great many other enterprises who sought nothing more than stability during tumultuous times. New industry flourished. Older industries and businesses evolved and survived. As an entity, Boston had ridden the changes of the twenty-first century with alacrity, and come through relatively un-scathed.

Saul left the Common behind, and started off down Summer Street. Traffic was heavy, with everyone making their last dash for the office or studio or store. He never did understand where everyone who worked in downtown parked. Every block was packed with thriving businesses, evidenced by the animated residents thronging the sidewalk around him. That perpetual urban vivacity gave Saul a lot of pride in the old town. But he'd always known it was never for him. His elder brother Joseph would continue with the family firm; in great-grandfather's day, that meant just dealing with property, but since land prices had collapsed during America's trans-stellar expansion, grandfather and his father diversified strongly into development and finance. Now Joseph had moved into the office on the top floor in Kilby Street, sitting behind the rosewood desk commissioned back in 1958. Joseph, who lived for The Deal, thriving on the endless accountancy minutiae and legal contract clauses and tax leverages which Saul found wholly tedious. And his younger sister Lindsey had already emigrated to Ramla with her orthodox husband Peter. Rather too orthodox for Saul's more neglectful tenets, but Lindsey loved him, and was happy, or so it sounded in the infrequent, dutiful sibling calls they made to each other.

He reached the junction with Purchase Street and braced himself against the abrupt increase of pedestrians surging out of South Station. Noah was waiting for him on the junction with Congress Street. His forty-three-year-old land manager was in on the meeting to make sure he didn't make a total ass of himself. Saul thought they made a good team, his money and enthusiasm coupled with Noah's experience and practicality. A sure foundation of success. They went into the modern, carbon-black office block, and took the elevator to the eleventh floor.

Massachusetts Agrimech had a corner office which provided a view straight down onto the narrow Fort Point Channel Parks. Standing in the reception room, Saul watched the little automated tractors buzzing about, trimming the park's yellowy grass. He wondered idly if Massachusetts Agrimech made them as well, it would be a good advert, and they did seem to produce every conceivable type of machine used for agriculture.

'Mr Castellano will see you now,' the receptionist, a handsome young man dressed in an imitation of this year's Yomoshi business-style suit, said.

Saul and Noah went through the tall black wood doors to an office that was Spartan expensive, with white walls and black and red furniture. There was no desk, only a conversation area arrangement of couches around a smoked glass and walnut coffee table. Brando Castellano was rising up from the red couch, with a professional, welcoming smile. Pretty much what Saul had been expecting, he was a man in his fifties who didn't put in enough time at the gym, and had to have his dark suits cut accordingly. Only slightly off-putting was the Stetson on the coffee table. But then Brando Castellano greeted them with a very Texan: 'Howdy, folks.'

By then Saul was oblivious to Brando's accent and personal appearance. There was a girl standing behind the red couch. She wore modest heels, which put her level with Saul. An enticingly athletic build was easily discerned through the sharp, tight business suit with its above-the-knee skirt. Her hair was blonde and bushy, woven into a long tail that was barely constrained by a silver mesh that hung all the way down her back. Despite her figure, it was her face that made him stare, knowing he was being rude yet unable to stop himself. She was beautiful, with a pronounced bone structure framing a pert nose and heavenly moist lips. Enchantress-green eyes were giving him a tolerant look that clearly wasn't going to last long.

'I . . . hello,' he stammered. Behind him, Noah stiffened in disapproval and concern – five seconds in and the boss was already thunderstruck in love. Saul couldn't help it, he'd dated his fair share of well-to-do nice Jewish girls, but none of them had ever come close to having this impact. He was only mildly put out by her age, she looked about eighteen. Would she be troubled by a ten-year age gap? Should he be? What would Mother say?

'My assistant, Angela Matthews,' Brando Castellano introduced her with gentlemanly good nature.

'I thought Angela Matthews owned this office,' Noah said.

'That's Mom,' Angela said. 'I'm actually Angie Jr.'

'I'm glad you're here, not her,' Saul said before he could stop himself.

The green eyes lost their last trace of amusement. Noah just groaned. Saul flushed crimson and shook her proffered hand limply.

Brando Castellano gestured for everyone to sit. 'So you gentlemen are looking for some farm machinery?'

'Er, yes,' Saul said. Angela was still standing behind Brando. He tipped his head back to look at her. More like admire. She was so much more intense than any teenager he'd ever met. Poised too. 'I'm establishing a new farm offworld. We'd like to see what sort of deal you can offer.'

'With us you get the whole package,' Angela said.

Was that a flirt line? It sounded like one. 'Yes, absolutely.'

Noah actually covered his eyes with his hand, massaging his temple as he let out a sigh. 'Have you had time to review our list?'

'Why, I swung through it all last night,' Brando Castellano said. 'I'm pleased to say we can meet every requirement.'

'Can you?' Saul asked.

'This office represents a big trans-stellar company,' Angela said. 'And the size of your order makes you very attractive to us.'

It was flirting. It was!

'Anyone can supply the equipment,' Noah said. 'What really concerns us is the after-sales support.'

'A company without happy clients goes out of business very quickly,' Brando Castellano assured him. 'We all understand that.'

'So you can include that in the contract?' Saul asked.

'We'd only agree to a deal that completely satisfies you,' Angela agreed.

Another line? Please let it be so.

'We'd be looking at the financial structure very closely,' Noah said.

'Our loan terms are most advantageous,' Brando Castellano promised. 'Would you be looking at lease-loan or a straight-forward owner finance?'

'For this quantity, we'd need terms.'

'Of course you would,' Angela said. Her lips turned up into the smallest smile. 'On a larger contract, which is what yours would be to the area office where you're based, the owner has a much greater leverage. Believe me, if we can swing the deal we don't want to let you go. Size always gives you the strength to negotiate a discount, and the most beneficial terms.'

'Yes.' Saul wanted to see how Noah would counter that excellent argument. But for some reason Noah seemed to have given up in disgust.

Then it was details. Exactly the kind of thing that had sent Saul running from the family office. Not today. Today he contributed everything he could, every question he'd heard his father and brother ask their clients. Service arrangements? Spare parts, licensed microfacture or import with discount? Maintenance – would you consider a local start-up partnership with Massachusetts Agrimech, giving both sides a larger presence? Tax advantages? Haulage to site cost-waiver? Ownership holding company registration?

After ninety minutes, Brando Castellano had put together the basics of an agreement. He'd crunch numbers that afternoon, he assured them, and supply Saul's lawyer with finance and contractual details for review and final negotiation.

'It's a beautiful venture you've got yourself, sir,' Brando Castellano said as they shook hands on the prospective deal. 'I envy you. Why, if I was a younger man I'd probably join you out there.'

Saul smiled blankly. 'Would you like to have a drink with me sometime?' he blurted.

Noah's whimper of distress filled the silence that entombed them.

'A drink?' Angela's voice was unbearably hard.

'Please?'

'With you?'

'Uh ... well ...'

'A prospective client?'

'... you see ...'

'Not only is that completely unprofessional, it is also incredibly presumptuous.'

'... I didn't ...'

'Exactly how is that level of discourtesy supposed to impress me?'

'Oh,' a crestfallen Saul murmured. 'Look, I'm really sorry. I just . . . you're so. Oh hell.' He'd gone crimson again, he knew he had. The heat blooming in his cheeks must surely be triggering the office's air-con. Noah and Brando Castellano were giving each other a mortified look, both calculating how much the blown contract was going to cost them.

Saul's hand waved pathetically at the door. 'Sorry. Sorry. We'll go.'

'Why?'

'Uh?'

'Did I say no?' Angela asked acerbically.

'Er . . .'

'One drink. Tonight. Seven o'clock. Which bar?'

Saul's mouth wouldn't respond to his desperate brain.

'Darryl's Bar over on Union Wharf is good,' Noah said. 'So I hear.'

'Fine,' Angela said. 'Darryl's Bar. Don't be late.'

Saul wasn't really conscious of leaving the office. He blinked, seeing the traffic of Purchase Street sliding by in front of him as he swayed on the sidewalk. 'Noah? What just happened?'

'You got yourself a date, chief, is what happened.'

Saul started to smile, one that grew and grew. 'I did, didn't I?'

'I hope you've got a certified will. You're going to need it with that one.'

'Isn't she amazing?' All he could see was that gorgeous face with its beguiling smile saying: *yes*.

'She's . . . something, all right.' Noah was laughing now. 'Jeeze, I've never seen anything so brave. Or so utterly dumb. The way you asked her! I'd sooner stick my dick in a food blender.'

'Hey, that's the woman I'm going to marry.'

'That one? Just remember what female spiders do after they mate.'

'Damn, you're jealous. You are.'

606

'Chief, I can honestly say: no, I'm not.'

'Yeah, right. Hey what's this Darryl's place like? What do I wear there? What sort of drink do you think she likes?'

'Not sure it matters. You know they still don't serve liquor to anyone under twenty-one in this state, don't you?'

'She has to be . . . Oh, maybe not. What do you think? She's twenty?'

'Chief, you've got to focus. We've got a meeting with the seed merchants in forty minutes. We need something for all that shiny new machinery to plant.'

'Right. Forty minutes. Plenty of time. I'll be okay. What about that green jacket? Have you seen me in that? Would that be all right? Not too urban professional?'

'Oh holy crap.'

*

As it happened, Darryl's Bar had a reasonable degree of class. Booths with comfortably low lighting. A long polished counter with stools, and an impressive array of bottles on the glowing shelves behind. Two slick barmen who relished a cocktail mix challenge. Even a private terrace with a view out across the water, with citrus candles to hold off the evening's insects.

Saul wasn't late. Six o'clock was a perfectly reasonable time to arrive, he felt. Courteously early in case she showed up a little beforehand, too. And it gave him a chance to check things out in case Noah had screwed up and it was a dive. It also gave him time to have a beer to calm his frankly terrified nerves. Two beers calmed them more. Three left him chilled and *suave*. Oh yeah. After all, he was something of a catch himself. An offworld landowner, a future empire-maker. Dressed accordingly. Not the green jacket. It was the kind of thing he'd wear to take his mother out. Instead, a simple purple shirt with white check, light fawn jacket with slim lapels, black jeans, and the expensive Douton boots. *Yeah, looking good is you, as the frat boys used to say.* And it had been a welcome long time since he'd sought their approval.

Lost contact with most of them. Deliberately. He grinned into his beer. Looked up as the conversation in the bar drained out of the air.

She was standing in the doorway. Scarlet summer dress that seemed to shine with its own light, complementing her perfect complexion. Skirt shorter than the one in the office, allowing powerful legs to take long strides, low-cut top showing a modest cleavage that needed no support. Lustrous waved hair flowing round her shoulders.

Everyone watched as he got off the stool and walked the length of the bar to greet her. That walk was bathed in the green light of envy radiating out of every man there. Probably half the women, too, he thought smugly.

Saul stopped with a pace left between them. Any closer and he wouldn't be able to admire the whole vision.

Don't blow this. Nothing as good will ever happen to you again no matter how long you live. Don't blow it. Please. Don't—

'Hi. One drink waiting for you.'

Angela licked her lips, keeping down a smile. 'What did you choose?'

'A Sancerre, a one-eleven. White isn't like red, it doesn't improve with age. But the eleven was a good year.'

'Only for some. But I'd like to try that, thank you.'

So there was another walk the length of the bar. This time a victory procession.

The barman almost ruined it. 'Gonna need some ID,' he said apologetically as Angela reached for the chilled wine glass. She said nothing, her face unreadable. Which even the barman found intimidating. Saul didn't know what kind of certificate her e-i sent, but the barman backed off like there was a wild tiger in the room. Angela picked up her wine.

'Booth or counter?' Saul asked. 'Your call.'

'Terrace. It's a warm evening. Let's enjoy it.'

'Terrace it is.'

They sat at a small table, with a candle and sprig of scented freesias between them. A view out over the water where pleasure craft flitted about.

'I have a confession to start with,' he said.

'Go for it.'

'I'm twenty-nine years old and I'm currently living with my mom and dad.'

Angela giggled. 'Where do Mom and Dad live?'

'Chestnut Street. Other side of the Common.'

'I know Chestnut Street. Nice part of town. It's comfortable for old money.'

'Yeah, I guess we're that.'

'You said, currently?'

'Yeah, well you know what I've bought myself; I'm going to be living on the farm in a Qwik-Kabin until I can afford to build a house. I'm just back in Boston for the last time while I buy the equipment and seed I need to make it a success, then it'll be back to the good old Qwik-Kabin permanently. I'm the younger son, you see. I'm cutting loose from the family to make it on my own. Blown every dime in my trust fund on the farm, much to everyone's horror. But it'll be worth it. Honestly, Angela, you should see where I'm setting up. Five thousand acres of the greatest soil, with an option loaded in the Oakland Governor's office network to buy another eight once I've shown viability. Not that land costs much on the new worlds, but Washington doesn't want people claiming whole continents for themselves as an investment.'

'Well done, you.' And she actually looked impressed. 'I admire someone who follows their dream. Not many people ever really do that when they finally come down to it. Too many choose the blind discomfort of security. Trouble is, there's no such thing, not really.'

'Wow, a cynic.' She didn't talk like a teenager, which just made her all the more intriguing.

'A realist.' Angela twirled the stem of her glass between thumb and forefinger. 'Want my confession now?'

'You're seeing someone?'

'Nothing so bland. My mom doesn't own the Massachusetts Agrimech office. She left Dad the week I was born.'

'Oh. I'm sorry. Who does, then?'

'I do. Brando is an actor between gigs. It's a question of expectation, you see. For all his quirky little problems he has the gravitas to be the front man. You saw what went on this morning, your friend Noah considered me to be office decoration. Brando was the man, the contact, the guy other guys can do business with.'

'Shit,' he said in astonishment. 'You own Massachusetts Agrimech?'

'It's a local commission franchise for Ravenshall. I buy and badge the hardware, and have the backing of their product service network, which is massive. Good money in it. Your order is for one point three million. That's kind of like the minimum for someone setting up in the new US Territories.' Green eyes narrowed, waiting for the reaction, judging.

'I knew there was something amazing about you. I just couldn't figure out what. Guess that makes me the dumb one.'

'No. It's a polished set-up. I trained the team myself. So . . . Now you know, going to take your business elsewhere?'

'No. Truthfully, I feel even safer dealing with you now. I thought I was ambitious, but you just blew that conceit out of the water. How did you ever get into this business?'

'Dad taught me a lot about finance before he died. I understand how to leverage funds, and agricultural machinery is all about the kind of high-value items that are in demand now we're in post-recession growth. You just have to put yourself at the centre of the deal, and let the banks and supplier do the hard work. It was kind of obvious.'

'To you, maybe. Remind me never to introduce you to my brother.'

'Why's that?'

'He'd divorce his wife and marry you in a second. He lives for finance deals.'

'Nah, I bet he's not as cute as you.'

Once more, the cheeks betrayed him with their heat. 'So where do you come from? I can't quite place the accent. And how did you wind up in Boston?'

'We travelled a lot while I was growing up, so I got me a lot of influences. And Boston: because it's not New York. I had something go bad on me there. Don't ask.'

'Okay. Different question.'

'Go.'

'Would you like a second drink?'

*

Angela lived in North Quincy. 'It's a nice area now they've thinned out the number of houses,' she explained. Rent was cheap, so she could afford a big place with a view of the beach which was less than a minute's walk from the local Metro station. And the train took her straight into South Station for work, so she didn't need a car.

A lot of her conversation featured money, he found; how she made it, or the cost of things.

'I'm like you,' she said over dinner that night. After Darryl's they'd moved on to The Luciano restaurant. 'I want to make a fresh start. If you're going to do that properly, you need money.'

'Fresh start?' He laughed. 'Don't you just mean: start? You only make a fresh start once you've messed up for a few years.'

'I'm twenty-one,' she said. 'And I've done enough to want to start over.'

'Okay, so what sort of beginning have you got planned for yourself?'

'I haven't decided. But you're right to move off Earth. Too much is established here, all people care about is the status quo and playing safe. Taxes are an anti-business joke. The amount of regulation is offensive; it only exists to maintain bureaucrat job security. Real growth is difficult under those circumstances, especially for a modest start-up; you have to look to the frontiers.

That's where people are truly free again. The lands where any-thing is possible.'

'I think you're doing pretty well for yourself.'

'Relative to who?'

That was the thing, she was smart as well as beautiful. In fact he worried that she was a lot smarter than him. Halfway into the date, and he was scared she would see he wasn't good enough. He'd already accepted that she was way tougher.

'Want to come back to my place?' she asked over coffee. 'I don't really want to meet your parents tonight.'

Saul thought he might start crying. The evening had been exhilarating, she was a girl walked out of fantasy. He'd thought if he could survive it and get a second date he would have done better than he deserved.

'I would like that very much,' he said simply.

They caught a Metro train out of South Station, riding it down to North Quincy. Then it was a short cab ride to her apartment on Apthorp Street. North Quincy was a big residential suburb that had been gentrified over the last fifty years, with its original sprawl of relatively cheap houses being developed and restyled to favour the younger generation of city workers who couldn't afford the kind of prices burdening the inner districts. When Saul climbed out he could hear the waves rolling in on the beach. 'That's something I'm going to miss,' he said. 'My farm is three hundred miles inland.'

Angela reached up and stroked his cheek. 'Wrong thinking,' she said. 'Your first farm is three hundred miles from the beach.'

She was renting a big clapboard bungalow with a veranda running its length outside. 'I don't need this many rooms,' she said as the door unlocked itself for her. 'But the living room sold it for me.'

He could understand why. It was large, taking up half the floorspace, with wide doors opening onto the veranda outside, and a big stone fireplace at one end. She'd decorated it in pastel blues and white; furniture was simple wooden frames with lots of cushions. Saul liked the summer feel of the place, but he imagined winter would be a bit bleak. A real bachelor pad, he admired ruefully as Angela walked around, lighting candles. The kitchen was spotless from lack of use. Jacuzzi out on the veranda, with yellow underwater lights illuminating the bubbles. Bedroom dominated by a king-size bed with an antique brass rail headboard. He glimpsed that as she opened the door to it and said, 'I'm going to change. Back in a minute.'

Saul, man of many worlds, nearly thirty years old, decently well off, reasonably experienced with women – didn't have a clue what to do. He looked at the couches and cushion pile, at the fizzing Jacuzzi. Looked down at his clothes. Take them off? Maybe just the boots.

There he was, sitting on a big floor cushion, tugging off his farmer-in-the-city boots as devoid of suave as you could get when she came back in. He'd worried he might be nervous, that he'd had too much to drink, that he wouldn't live up to her expectations and requirements. That the night would be a wash out like . . . Well not that many, but it had happened. But when he scrambled back up on his feet that whole plague of doubts vanished. Just looking at her in the provocative negligee she'd slipped into with its black silk straps and lacy panels that hinted at so much incredible flesh gave him the hardest erection of his life. Angela saw it, and smiled haughtily. She made him stand there while she stripped his clothes off, which in itself was an amatory torment.

When she was finished, and he was naked in the middle of the room, she paused; a manicured nail tapped against her teeth in theatrical indecision as she looked round the living room. 'Where first?' she mused. 'Rug in front of the fire? Jacuzzi?'

Saul couldn't take any more. He roared as he leapt at her. Angela shrieked and giggled as they collapsed onto the cushions.

They spent five days in her house. Five days naked. Five days ignoring work except for authorizing payment to Massachusetts Agrimech. Five days talking and laughing (a lifelong Democrat, he was mildly shocked anyone so gorgeous had such Republican tendencies). Five days having every meal delivered. Five days of the hottest sex Saul had ever had. This was grown-up sex, he decided, and it was a wonderful revelation, they were adults doing as they pleased without consequences. This more than anything, more than the rows with his parents, finding the farm, blowing his entire inheritance on his dream, *this* was what marked being truly liberated. He was complete for the first time in his life.

'Why me?' he whispered into her ear some time during the third night. They were lying on some cushions they'd taken out to the veranda, letting the warm night-time sea air dry the sweat from their bodies. Making love outside with the possibility someone might see, even if it was the middle of the night, had excited him in a way that was surprising. So much youthful repression bursting like a dam that for once he'd impressed Angela with his enthusiasm. Now he held her close, relishing the touch of her skin down his chest and all the way along his leg. 'You could have anyone you wanted, you know you could. Why me?'

She stretched out an arm and reached for the wine glass, taking a long sip before answering. 'You're me,' she said.

'Hardly. I don't get it.'

'Me without the baggage. Me how I want to be. This farm you've got, that's taking the leap I've been telling myself I'm going to take. You believe in yourself, you're willing to take the risk. It's been a long time since I believed in myself.'

He kissed her to stop her saying anything so sacrilegious, wanting to own her, wanting to belong to her. 'I know what love is,' he told her. 'It's you.'

That enigmatic expression took over her face again. He never knew what kind of judgement she was passing, all he could ever do was hope it was a favourable verdict.

'You're a good man, Saul Howard,' she said eventually. 'I didn't think there were any left.'

On the fifth day, when dawn's sunlight was flooding through the open veranda doors, Saul got down on both knees and gazed up worshipfully at his angel with the wild hair. With every ounce of courage, he made himself say: 'Please marry me, Angela.'

614

'That's very sweet—'

'Don't!' He pulled her down so their faces were level, and he could see the consternation in her green eyes. 'Don't do the sweet routine, nor the we-don't-know-each-other one. I have never been more serious. Marry me, come with me to the farm, help me make it the start of something fabulous. I'll screw it up without you, without someone who can see all my mistakes. Damnit, Angela, I don't even want to leave this house. I just want to be with you. Please?'

For a long moment she stared at him, and he finally understood that enigmatic expression was really just a mask over sorrow and fright.

Then she smiled cautiously. 'Yes.'

'Yes? Yes what?'

A sigh of exasperation. 'Yes, I'll marry you.'

'Really?'

'Oh!' She pushed at him.

Saul pulled. And proved he was stronger. The kiss lasted a long time.

They did Vegas, flying out that afternoon. Saul couldn't believe that part of it. Nobody got married in Vegas, not really. But there they were, by themselves, trying not to laugh as they walked down the aisle of the Lord's Passion chapel at eleven o'clock at night, Angela looking bad-girl stunning in a vamp's wedding dress hired for an extra $87, taking the cost (including three-girl gospel-style choir) to $778 and 12 cents, plus the $500 state licence.

The honeymoon was two days spent in a high-roller suite in the new Battersea Hotel on the strip. Saul would *really* have liked it to be longer, but the machinery from Massachusetts Agrimech was now ready for delivery and shipment, as Angela told him several times. And as Noah's increasingly frantic calls reminded him, the planting season was fast approaching. And if we don't make that, chief, you've blown it beyond redemption.

So a reluctant Mr and Mrs Howard flew down to Miami, where they booked into a waterfront hotel for one night. Which

615

was when they finally made the call to Saul's startled parents, informing them they had a new daughter-in-law. The next morning saw the happy couple travel through the Shenandoah gateway to begin their fresh-start life on New Florida.

Thursday 21st March 2143

Vance Elston woke early, and pulled on one of his standard-issue grey-green HDA T-shirts. It was the same one he'd worn yester-day, and the creases showed that, as well as the whiff. But at that it was the cleanest he had. Laundry over the last few days hadn't exactly been his top priority. He slathered the tamiopozine cream over his red itchy feet before his last fresh pair of socks went on. One invasion of honeyberry spore was enough. He hadn't ever realizcd until he found his shins and calves covered in the sticky ejecta fluid one evening. Ever since, he'd worn full-length trousers and gaiters. Just like Angela always did.

He went out into the idiosyncratic light that now ruled St Libra's atmosphere. Borealis cascades teemed across the sky, dripping fluidic globules down across the dark jungle. Just visible through them in the south, the ghost crescent of the rings glowed pallid silver, their influence waning before the interloper. Also deteriorating were the camp's network links. The core cells and processor hubs were connected with fibre optics, which was immune to electromagnetic interference, but the standard body-mesh links were suffering from increasing dropouts and low bandwidth as the charged atmosphere vented its static plague in the form of blanket electromagnetic screams. As he looked about he could see thin strands of lightning crackling round the local mountain tops as insubstantial clouds scudded about.

'Dear Lord grant us your blessing,' he appealed in a troubled murmur. 'For I have looked upon the Zanth, and seen the face of the devil.' The astonishing lightshow was all a little too close to Zanth rifts for comfort.

Antrinell walked over, the lines on his round face emphasizing his dismay. 'I hate this weather,' he grunted. 'I almost wish it would rain again.'

'It's about to get worse,' Vance told him quietly. 'I talked to Vermekia. The satellites they pushed into Sirius orbit confirmed the sunspots are affecting the entire star. And the things are still erupting. The oldest are about a hundred thousand klicks across now.'

'Any Zanth activity?'

'None.'

'That's something.'

'I've accessed the worst-case scenarios the Situation Centre's Sirius task force has put together. They're talking about a big climate change.'

'Climate change?'

'Possible. Let's just wait and see, shall we.'

Most of the camp personnel were now out of their tents, standing around, waiting for the dawn. It was getting lighter in the eastern sky, not that it diminished the cold borealis flames. Vance hated the mood of his people, to the point at which he felt responsible. The Daedalus explosion yesterday had spooked everyone as much as it shocked them. It made it very clear just how tenuous their connection to the rest of the trans-stellar worlds had become. Right now they were feeling hugely isolated and vulnerable, and there was nothing he could do to alleviate that sensation.

Talk died away as Sirius rose above the horizon.

'Oh my Lord,' Vance whispered, unable to help himself. The exclamation was thankfully lost amid the gasps from the rest of the watchers.

Sirius, the giant star that burned with nuclear blue-white intensity, was tinged a gentle salmon pink.

'How many sunspots are there?' an intimidated Antrinell asked.

'Just under four hundred now,' Vance told him. 'There's no astrophysical theory which can explain it. The event is completely unprecedented.'

'It's not coincidence. It can't be.'

'I agree. But I'm beginning to believe this is beyond mortal understanding.'

While the rest of the camp lined up for breakfast, Vance walked over to his office in the Qwik-Kabin and sealed the door. The e-Rays were suffering badly from the particle assault on the upper atmosphere. Although designed to function through the irradiative carnage of a Zanthswarm, they were susceptible to degradation from the barrage of lightning strikes. Their operational altitude left them particularly exposed. Systems decay was becoming a real concern for the AAV teams operating them as components suffered from surge burn-out.

However, there was still sufficient bandwidth for a secure link between Abellia and Wukang.

'Good morning, Colonel,' Commissioner Passam said as soon as the link was established.

'Ma'am. We've just had sunrise. Sirius has redshifted.'

'Yes, I've been accessing the images directly from the satellite cluster. It's most unsettling. Solar infall on St Libra is fifty per cent down on a week ago.'

'I see. I didn't know that. Have you confirmed what caused the Daedalus explosion yet?'

'Yes. It was definitely sabotage, though that's not what we're telling the media: as far as they're concerned it was a maintenance issue. We've established a binary compound explosive was placed in the central undercarriage well. They tell me that was a good place, it immediately ruined structural integrity as well as ripping open the bioil tanks.'

'Oh Lord.'

'Yes. And we were warned, which is the oddest part of this.

Someone called us from an untraceable transnet address. They claimed it was Zebediah North's followers.'

'What docs Zebediah North say?'

'Nothing. Nobody knows where he is. Nobody can find him.'

'I see. What now?'

'Whoever warned us claimed he was in Abellia. Resources will be increased and targeted accordingly. We have to locate him.'

'Good. So what will happen with the Daedalus fleet and our supply flights?'

'Ah. Obviously we've grounded all flights until each remaining Daedalus can be thoroughly inspected. Two of them are here at Abellia, which we believe makes them more susceptible to sabotage. As of now, no civilian crews will be allowed access to any expedition vehicle. HDA crew will be conducting the inspections. Colonel, that instruction also covers all helicopters at Wukang. You have to get your flight engineers to clear them before they're flown again. That includes a complete software reboot as well — we just can't take any chances. There's no way of knowing what Zebediah's followers have prepared for a follow-up. Software bugs could have been downloaded months ago.'

'Right. Okay, that makes sense. So when will the replacement tanker get here?'

'There is no schedule on that as yet.'

'What? We can't function without a tanker. I always thought it was stupid, only having one.'

'Once the HDA appraisal of a potential Zanthswarm is over, then a replacement tanker will be considered. Until then we'll have to make do with the standard Daedalus. I'm told they can be reconfigured to carry additional tanks, so the loss isn't critical.'

'I see.' Listening to her talk her politician talk, Vance began to worry about how she could use the situation to cover herself at the expense of the mission goal. 'What about my Legionnaire reinforcements, what's their ETA now?'

'I'm sorry Colonel, but the GE has closed the St Libra gateway to all traffic. The Legionnaires never came through.'

'They can't close it to HDA personnel. Those troops had already been deployed.'

'They have been temporarily reassigned to the GE Border Guard. There's some concern that Highcastle's population might overrun Newcastle if they surge through the gateway. Obviously, allowing them through would have to be subject to negotiation. If it is allowed, it will have to be with our consent and under our conditions.'

'All well and good, but what about us? This is leaving us badly exposed out here.'

'One of the reasons for this call is for me to formally issue an operational reduction notice. You're to suspend all non-core activities at Wukang. Resupply will be a problem in the immediate future. We're considering a partial evacuation, shutting down the three forward bases and reducing Edzell and Sarvar to skeleton crews until the situation improves.'

For once, even Vance found it difficult to stay calm. 'We've found an alien of unknown type and origin, exactly what the expedition exists for, and you're contemplating a shutdown?'

'It's not a shutdown, Colonel, this would be a tactically driven option. You must understand, circumstances have changed. And there is no concrete proof of an alien.'

'Esther Coombs had her heart ripped out by a nonhuman claw.'

'Or Angela Tramelo's accomplice is using their perverted power amp suit again. We just don't know yet.'

'And is there a theory on how he smuggled himself and a power amp suit on board a Daedalus?'

'Presumably the same way it was smuggled into Bartram's mansion twenty years ago – with Tramelo's help.'

Vance paused for a moment to keep his anger under control. 'Then let me find out. Give me my Legionnaires.'

'That simply isn't practical any more. I'm sorry, Colonel. We're going to have to wait until the sunspot situation is resolved. Until then we'll just have to struggle on as best we can.'

'I see. Thank you, Commissioner.' Vance ended the call, and immediately placed another one to Vermekia.

'I thought I'd be hearing from you,' Vermekia said.

'You have to get her idiot decisions reversed. The aliens are here. I can confirm their existence. Think what that means. Vermekia, we're *this* close.'

'You've got crazies blowing up planes. There's something seriously weird happening to Sirius itself. And I'm not even taking into account a potential Zanthswarm. We have to prioritize, Vance. I'm sorry.'

'Pushing those satellites through a war gateway has cost a couple of billion at least. All I need is a new tanker Daedalus for a week, and a hundred Legionnaires. What does that cost by comparison?'

'I know, okay? This is as frustrating for me as it is for you. I promise as soon as we understand what's going on with the sunspots then I'll push for the resources you need. But, Vance, I've got to tell you, it's not looking good for the Newcastle investigation.'

'Why? What's happened?'

'I'm assuming Scrupsis has leaked this to Passam, which is why she's running for cover. The results from Ernie Reinert's interrogation have come through. I know General Shaikh himself accessed them last night.'

'What did Reinert say?'

'Disappointingly little. Basically, some unknown controller told him to go to an apartment and clean up a mess that someone else left behind. Opinion here is hardening around this being some North on North fight.'

'And Esther Coombs?'

'I don't know, Vance, I'm sorry. Look, with all the scientific effort focused on the Sirius sunspots right now they're going to have an answer soon. When they do, I'll get you your extra Legionnaires. Until then, have your helicopters checked out and keep a strong perimeter guard.'

After the call ended, Vance stared round the tiny office. For the first time since he'd heard about the Newcastle murder, he began to worry. He was used to being in charge of missions, but this time there were too many politicians involved, and they were screwing up badly. 'Dear Lord, protect me from their stupidity.'

*

For an age Sid had craved a particular quiet breakfast, the envisaged scene playing out in his mind like some kind of well-to-do ideal twentieth-century family, where the children sat up straight at the table without speaking and deferred politely to their parents. A standard breakfast at the Hurst house was normally noisy thanks to William and Zara fighting and bitching about the food; rushed because the family default mode was everyone running late; bad-tempered because he was tired and thinking of work.

But today his wish had been granted. It hadn't been nice at all. Both children sat and ate in silence as they watched the news. The panes on the wall in the new kitchen had been showing TyneOne news, which took a perverse delight in the catalogue of depressing images it showed. Kingsway full of paramilitary-armoured GE Border Directorate troops, backed up by HDA Legionnaires, not letting anyone through. Furious Last Mile independent store owners, threatening to sue the GE to reopen the gateway and compensate them for loss of earnings. Outside Last Mile, crowds of fractious would-be refugees and farmstead settlers expanded by the hour. Local police and agency constables containing them. Thunderthorns at the big HDA base in Toulouse taking off to exercise. Northumberland Interstellar media officers issuing reassurances that the flow of bioil was unaffected. A mocking contrast to images from the other side of the gateway, revealing even bigger crowds building up along Motorway A, with a tailback of stationary cars, vans, and trucks over twelve miles long. More unnerving was the light which exposed them. Sirius shone red in the sky, surrounded by massive swirls of undulating borealis iridescence. St Libra was a truly alien world now.

Sid arrived at Market Street at eight o'clock thanks to sparse morning traffic. The universal code blue was still in force, but he was pretty sure the building was understaffed as he made his way to Office3.

Tilly Lewis was waiting for him as he came in.

'I don't have a scene for you yet,' he told her as he settled in behind his desk. 'We're expecting our information to arrive sometime this morning.'

'That's okay, pet,' she said cheerfully. 'Gives you time to certify this.'

A file icon appeared in his grid. 'What is it?'

'It's a legal statement.'

'Aye, what have I done wrong now?' he exclaimed.

'Not you. It's an insurance thing for the firebombing. Northern Forensics needs to have the senior case officer's confirmation that NorthernMetroServices were officially assigned security and protection on Ernie's garage at the time of the attack.'

'Oh right. Okay, I can certify that. Leave it with me.'

'Thanks. Reinert's insurance have already put their claim in. The place was gutted, what's left is going to have to be demolished; all the workshop equipment has gone, and there were some cars inside, too. It all adds up, especially when you include the medical bills for me and my team. And Northern Forensics certainly aren't paying for it.'

'I understand. Are you okay now?'

She grinned and fluffed out her thick wavy hair. 'Sure. How about you?'

'The kids were watching the news this morning. It frightened them.'

'I know how they feel. The unlicensed sites are saying all HDA troops barracked in GE are on standby. Do you know anything?'

'As much as you do. O'Rouke is spending his whole time with the emergency planning committee. If there is a Zanthswarm, Newcastle is going to be overrun by Highcastle refugees. That's

624

why we kept the kids out of school today. Jacinta's staying home with them.'

'Ours went in, but Nathaniel is only two minutes away if it hits the fan. Benefits of working at home.'

'I don't get how HDA can't know,' Sid admitted. 'They've sent dozens of satellites through to look at Sirius. I thought we could always spot the way the Zanth buggers up spacetime.'

'We can. But sunspots aren't a Zanthswarm.'

'Aye, I suppose. This case has been nothing but strange since it began.'

'Your case?' Tilly asked. 'How is a carjacking tied in with Sirius sunspots?'

'Don't ask, okay. That was a slip of the tongue.'

'Ask what?' She grinned. 'My team are in the canteen downstairs, waiting for you to give us the scene. I'll join them.'

'Thanks, Tilly. I'll call you soon.'

After she left, Sid spun the legal statement file round, twisting to open. A simple data sheet expanded over his grid. He glanced at the final claim figure, and whistled at the impressive size. It would have to be sent to legal along with last Thursday's case logs to confirm the garage handover had been correctly authorized, but he was confident no one could query it. He was instructing his e-i when he caught an item on the garage contents list. 'Well crap on that,' he muttered in excitement.

There was no visual record in the file Tilly gave him. But as he was being asked to certify the statement he'd be perfectly justified in checking details himself.

Sid called up visual logs from the arrest, and the zone console screen curved round his head. He immersed himself in the iris smartcell recordings from various officers and constables, watching through their eyes as they charged into the garage. Jerky images showed him a chase after one of the garage workers. Officers with pistols held in two-handed grips checked various rooms for anyone hiding. He even caught sight of himself a couple of times. *Where did that gut come from?* After a while he closed the logs and leant back out of the zone. He smiled contentedly, far happier than the day gave him any right to be.

Ian burst into Sid's office at eight thirty. 'He's here!'

'About fucking time, man. What room have we got?' Sid could hear the low throbbing of a helicopter landing on the station's roof pad.

'Interview seven,' Ian replied.

'Okay, calm down. We have to be totally professional now. Think of the court admissibility procedures.'

'Aye, I know,' Ian said with a hurt tone.

'Spread the word.'

'Got it covered, boss.'

Sid stood up and put his jacket on, straightened his tie, and went out to see just what Ralph had brought him.

Five minutes later he was standing in interview room seven's observation office, watching the wall-size pane which showed him Ernie Reinert sitting passively at the room's table. Sid had interviewed hundreds of suspects, knew all the stages: the defiance, the panic, the miserable monologue confession, the plea for understanding. But this, Ernie's zombie-like lack of interest in the world around him, this was something new. Something he felt very uncomfortable witnessing. Part of him wanted to ask how the Reinert of last week, the contemptuous tough-guy gang man, had been reduced to this. A bigger part knew not to ask, that the details would haunt him.

Even so, Reinert had been officially signed over to his custody. 'Is he okay?'

Ralph Stevens, suited and impassive like a finance floor dealer, gave a knowing nod. 'Mr Reinert is fine. He was very helpful, and declined to have a lawyer present during questioning.'

'Really? So what did he say?'

'Ah. Well, there's good news and bad news,' Ralph said. 'The best part is that he picked the body up from the St James singletown apartment 576B.'

Sid wanted to call Ian and Tilly immediately, let them off the lead. 'How could there be bad news?'

'He doesn't know who sent him to the St James.'

'How can he not know?'

'Sid. He doesn't know. The information doesn't exist.'

'Aye, so how did he wind up with the job of disposing of the body?'

'When he was booted out of Securitar, he stayed in contact with his old section boss, Kirk Corzone. Between them, they arranged for Ernie to receive orders for certain important jobs by instructions from an untraceable address. According to your own station records Kirk Corzone had connections with the Red Shield gang. He was the middle-man, the go-between for the corporates.'

'And we can't pick him up because . . .'

'He was killed five years ago. Typical gangland slaying over a tox exchange that went wrong.'

'But someone is still using that untraceable address, right?'

'Yes.'

'Okay. So what happened?'

'It went off pretty much as you've already uncovered. Ernie got the call on the Friday evening, telling him there was a body in apartment 576B, and that it had to be disposed of carefully. All traces of identification removed, smartcells extracted. Interesting thing: the data provided told him where the secure smartcells were located.'

'That's very detailed,' Sid said. 'You'd have to get into the North family records to find that kind of knowledge.'

'I see where you're coming from, but this is the information Reinert gave us.'

'Okay, go on.'

'Reinert immediately called four associates: Maura Dellington, Chester Hubley, Murray Blazczaka, and Lucas Kremer.'

'We're already holding Hubley and Kremer,' Sid said. 'They work at Reinert's garage.'

'Yeah. Convenient all round that he employs them legitimately, it makes them a tight little crew. Dellington and Blazczaka spent Saturday ripping meshes around town, while Hubley and

Kremer prepared the two citycabs. Hubley drove the decoy cab into place just before midnight Saturday. The rest you basically know. Hubley walked back to the decoy on Sunday evening. Dellington, Blazczaka, and Kremer used different routes to arrive at apartment 576B during the afternoon, and started cleaning. They stripped the body, extracted the smartcells and sliced the fingertips off. So when Reinert drove his taxi to the St James it was ready to be bundled into the case and driven away.'

'They must have been shocked when they walked in and found whose corpse was waiting for them.'

'Apparently Dellington and Kremer wanted to forget the whole thing and leave. Blazczaka persuaded them to stay and get on with the job.'

'Okay.' Sid told his e-i to access every file they had on apartment 576B. The owner file filled his iris smartcell grid. He pursed his lips at the image superimposed over Ernie Reinert. 'Tallulah Packer. I take it you've already harvested a profile?'

'Yeah. Twenty-five years old, parents divorced eleven years ago, father owns a software house in Suffolk, mother has a transnet company supplying smoked food, she was educated at Bath University. Smart enough to get taken on a graduate fast-track programme at Northumberland Interstellar, and currently works as bioil demand and distribution analyst in their Southern Europe office here in Newcastle. Engaged to one Boris Attenson, a banker. All very straight life standard.'

'An analyst? Do they have any other kind of employee over there?'

'Doubt it,' Ralph said. 'I've never met one.'

'Anything else?'

'Plenty of small details, but that's the big picture.'

'No sign of an alien monster?'

'No sign,' Ralph admitted.

'Right then; let's get started.'

*

Sid took charge of the team going to apartment 576B, taking Eva and Ralph along with four agency constables, and a full forensics team. Abner headed up the arrest team pursuing Maura Dellington. Lorelle and Ari went after Murray Blazczaka. Ian was assigned to bring Tallulah Packer in. 'You owe me,' Sid murmured as her image appeared on the big wallscreen in Office3. A dazed Ian nodded slowly, never taking his eyes off the picture.

It was quite a procession that came out of the service elevator onto the fifth floor of the twisted tower that stood on the eastern side of the St James singletown. The building's security officers, police, Tilly's team with their five equipment trolleys rattling along behind. Curious residents gave them a wide berth. Sid put on his disposable white cleansuit in the corridor outside apartment 576B, along with Eva, Ralph, and the forensics team. He knew it was a waste of time, the murder was three months old after all. But procedure was king, so he didn't protest even though the faces around him clearly shared his irritation. Once they were all suited up, the St James security manager ordered the door to unlock.

Tilly ordered the flock of eight-legged cyber-insects that had clambered out of the trolleys to go into the apartment. 576B had two bedrooms, a bathroom, kitchen alcove, and a split-level lounge with a view across Leazes Park. Fabrics were all patterns; both the dresser and the main table had fresh cut flowers. Several rugs were strewn over the polished wood floor. It was all very girl-about-town Sid thought.

The cyber-insects scuttled forward, trailing long whisker antennae along the floor so their mesh of smartmicrobes could sample the composition of everything they touched. Two of them began to circle a section of the sleek grey tiles just below the step up to the back of the lounge. A larger, more bulbous, cyber-insect crabbed over to them and sprayed the area with a fine aerosol. Tilly ordered the apartment's net to turn the lights down and close the curtains. She shone an ultraviolet torch at the floor. A large stain glowed purple-white on the wood.

'Blood,' she announced happily. 'And plenty of it. Ernie wasn't lying.'

It wasn't right to be happy about a murder scene, but Sid was immensely satisfied to be finally looking down at the luminescent chemicals. So much work and risk had gone into bringing him to this place. 'All right then,' he said. 'Seal the room. I want a full work-up, every test you've got. I want a complete forensics profile.'

Tilly's team brought in more equipment from the trolleys, setting up tripods with ultra-rez sensors. The cyber-insects began to probe the corners of the lounge. More of the little gadgets were released in the other rooms.

Sid started to look through the apartment for himself. The bed in the main bedroom had a jazzy duvet that had been levelled and then covered with a whole load of cushions arranged by size. He shook his head at the sight and moved on – there had been enough arguments over cushions and curtains with Jacinta down the years. The dressing table was also an exercise in neatness, with make-up bottles and tubes in various cases and boxes. He started opening drawers. 'Eva, take a look through this for me, please.'

She came over and looked down at the drawer he'd opened. It was full of bras. 'What, boss? You gone shy?'

'Aye cut it out, man. I will do many things for the police, but going through women's underwear isn't one of them. So you let me know if you find a five-blade claw at the back of any of these drawers, okay.'

Inside the cleansuit's hood, Eva smiled at him. 'Okay, boss.'

Sid went into the bathroom. No surprise, everything in the medicine cabinet was regimented. That included the three tox sacs; one of which was a peptox. Sid gave it a small sympathetic smile. 'Poor Boris,' he muttered.

'Two toothstiks,' Ralph said, looking over his shoulder.

'Aye.' Sid turned to one of the forensics team. 'Bag them, please. I'll want them DNA fingerprinted. Let's confirm it's the fiancé Boris that stays over.'

'What are you thinking?' Ralph asked.

'I'm thinking I could have told you everything about this place just by accessing our Tallulah's file. Young, single, professional working in the bioil business. This town's got a ton of them. They're all the same.'

'So?'

'So why did our fake Adrian come straight here? What makes Tallulah Packer stand out from the rest of her tribe? That's what we need to focus on. Why her?'

'All you have to do is ask.'

'Aye, I'll be doing that all right.'

*

Sid was back at Market Street by eleven o'clock. The arrest teams had all been successful. To a degree. Murray Blazczaka had put two agency constables in hospital with minor injuries. Ari North had a black eye which was still swelling. It was Lorelle who'd finally subdued him with a taser.

Like everyone returning to Officc3, Sid took a look at Ari's face. Winced and grinned. 'You okay?'

'The bastard blindsided me, boss.'

'Aye, course he did. Keep the cold-gel pack on.'

Maura Dellington was also in one of the custody suites. As was Tallulah Packer.

'Ian is in there with her,' Abner said pointedly. 'Processing.'

'I'm sure he's just doing his duty.'

'Must be very thorough, he's taking for ever.'

Sid declined to comment further, and told himself he felt no envy.

'Boris Attenson is downstairs,' Dedra Foyster said. 'With his solicitor. They're getting arsey with the desk sergeant.'

'Are they?' Sid mused. 'Oh dear.'

'We really don't want any custody interview mistakes,' Aldred North said. 'Not now.'

'No,' Sid agreed grudgingly. 'I'll bring them up myself.'

Boris Attenson was someone else Sid could have described

perfectly without ever having met him. Tall, with blond hair that at age thirty-one was already starting to thin. Just overweight, but not yet bloating thanks to membership of the old college rugby team. Pale skin, scaled with a good covering of freckles, moisturized against the toll corporate hospitality extracted. Tailored suit in sharp grey fabric with ziz-shark stripes. Tailored shirt with currently fashionable high-collar, complemented by a three-hundred-Eurofranc purple and gold Korean silk tie. His daily office outfit was finished off with hand-stitched leather shoes that probably cost more than a new set of tyres for Sid's Toyota Dayon.

The solicitor accompanying him, Chantilly Sanders-Watson, could have been his big sister. Smarter sister, Sid corrected himself, as her professional id icon popped up in his grid. A partner in Rattigan, Herandez, and Singh, a legal company all too familiar to Market Street officers toiling away on a high-profile case. If you could afford them it was like buying yourself a get-out-of-jail token.

'Why has my fiancée been arrested?' Boris demanded.

'She hasn't been,' Sid said in a tone that matched Boris's.

The banker blinked in surprise, and gave Chantilly Sanders-Watson a help-me glance.

'Could you tell me Ms Packer's status, please Detective Hurst,' the solicitor asked calmly.

'She has been remanded in custody to assist with our enquiry. Her agreement was voluntary, with the option to retain legal counsel during interview.'

'Of course she wants a bloody lawyer!' Boris blustered.

'Which enquiry is that?' Chantilly Sanders-Watson asked.

Sid gestured round the station reception room, where several stressed and distressed relatives were bunched round the desk. Three suspects under agency constable escort were waiting to be signed in. 'Perhaps you'd prefer to discuss this upstairs in a secure office?'

'Thank you,' Chantilly Sanders-Watson said.

The desk sergeant dabbed a temporary building access smart-dust tag on the hands of both visitors, and they all trooped into the waiting elevator. 'As yet we don't believe Ms Packer has committed any criminal act,' Sid explained. 'However, one was committed in her apartment.'

'What are you talking about?' Boris said. 'I was there myself last night. Your thugs stormed into her office and hauled her out like some common criminal. Do you have any idea what that has done to her reputation?'

'You mean Mr Darcy will cancel her dinner invitation?' Sid asked innocently.

'Now look you—'

Chantilly Sanders-Watson put a warning hand on Boris's shoulder. 'What criminal act?'

'Murder.'

'That's preposterous! Tallulah hasn't killed anyone. You're disgusting suggesting she was involved. I'll sue the whole bloody lot of you for slander.'

Sid was no longer talking to Boris Attenson. 'I've just come back from her apartment in the St James,' he told the solicitor. 'Forensics estimates at least two litres of blood was spilled on the floor. And yes, they confirmed it to be human blood.'

'I see. In which case Ms Packer will certainly need representation at any interview she gives. I will also require the arresting officer's log to ensure no undue influence was exerted during her holding custody period.'

'I'll have that certified and ready for you,' Sid promised, fervently hoping Ian hadn't spent the whole time in the squad car staring at Tallulah's chest. Maybe giving him that duty was a bad call.

Tallulah Packer had been assigned interview room four. When Sid got there Ralph and Eva were standing outside, leaving Ian and Aldred in the room with her. In the flesh, Tallulah was as frighteningly attractive as her id file images had portrayed her. Tall enough to play for her university netball team, she had a round face framed by rich dark auburn hair cut just above her shoulders. A wide mouth had perfectly shaded burgundy lipstick to emphasize its sensuality, while deep hazel eyes were full of concern. Sid could only assume she'd perspired raw pheromones into the interview room, because that was the only reason a professional police officer like Ian would be sitting on the edge of the table, chatting to her with a reassuring smile splashed all over his face. At least Aldred was showing some restraint, sitting behind the desk and maintaining a polite silence.

Chantilly Sanders-Watson took in the scene with a single interested glance. Tallulah stood up fast at the sight of Boris, and the two hugged.

Ian put a restraining hand on Boris's shoulder. 'That's enough, sir.'

'This is my fiancée, you cretin. Are you all right, darling?'

'I'm fine,' Tallulah said in a husky voice. 'Really.'

'Out of courtesy we've allowed you in here, sir,' Sid said. 'Now you've seen your fiancée is fine, you'll have to wait in our guest centre until our interviews are complete.'

'I'm staying with Tallulah!' Boris insisted.

'It's all right,' Chantilly Sanders-Watson said. 'I'll take it from here.'

Sid beckoned Eva in, and got her to escort a fuming Boris from the interview room.

'I'd like to know why you're in a police interview room with my client?' the solicitor asked Aldred.

'I am an accredited legal representative for my family on this case,' Aldred replied smoothly. 'I'll send you the registration certificate.'

'Please do.' She stared at Ian. 'Is this a new interview technique you're practising, Detective?'

'What?'

'GE Criminal Apprehension Act 2131 clearly states no custodial interview may be conducted in an intimidating fashion. You are positively looming over my client. That can be very threatening.'

Ian rolled his eyes and stood up.

Chantilly Sanders-Watson sat beside Tallulah, and gave her a reassuring smile. 'The police will leave us now. You and I are going to have a talk, and if you wish to speak to them afterwards then I'll permit that.'

Sid and the others walked out of the interview room.

'Who's the bitch?' Ian asked.

'Someone we don't call a bitch,' Sid said. 'I need you to prepare your official custody log from this morning. The solicitor wants to access it.'

'Visual as well?' Ian asked in a worried tone.

'Yes. I understand there are some glitches in the station cache. Review it to make sure there's not too many.'

'Understood, boss.'

'I can't believe we have to do this,' Aldred complained.

'*We* wouldn't,' Ralph said pointedly.

'It's not come to that yet,' Sid said. The image of an empty Ernie waiting forlornly in interview room seven still refused to stop haunting him.

'One indication that she was involved and she's coming with me,' Ralph warned.

'Understood, but I want as much as I can get from her first. She's not a tough guy like Ernie.'

'That solicitor is,' Aldred said.

'Who will also be removed if she annoys me,' Ralph said. 'And the rest of the interview will then be conducted under authorized HDA procedure.' He sent an icon to Sid. 'All approved and ready for my certificate to activate it.'

It took another ten minutes, but Chantilly Sanders-Watson eventually came out and said: 'My client has agreed to speak to you in order to clear up any misunderstanding about her involvement in your case.'

Sid took the lead, with Ian sitting in the chair next to him. He was pleased about that – it meant he didn't have to sit directly opposite chilly Chantilly.

'I need to ask you where you were on Friday the eleventh this January,' Sid began.

Tallulah leaned forward, anxious to reply. 'I don't even have to check my personal log. We were in Amsterdam, at a little hotel just off Rembrandt Square. It was a long weekend break.'

'We?'

'Boris and I. He was celebrating. His bank was involved in the bond issue for the new fusion power stations.'

'How long were you away?'

'Thursday to Monday.'

'I'll need all the details.'

'Of course.'

'And I'll want to interview Mr Attenson.' He didn't, not really, Sid just knew neither of them was involved in the murder. They were too worried and puzzled, resentful at this ordeal he was putting them through.

'I'll put it to him,' Chantilly Sanders-Watson said.

'Good. It would be in the interests of both clients.'

'Have you ever met Adrian 2North?' Ian asked.

'No. Never. Why?'

'Can't tell you, I'm sorry,' Sid said. 'Do you know any other 2Norths?'

'Of course I do, I work for them. I meet them regularly.'

'I see.' Which was an interesting answer, one he suspected was primed by Chantilly. 'Any reason why Adrian would come to your apartment?'

'No. I told you, I don't know him. Is he the one from the carjacking?'

Sid's e-i pulled up a section of transcript from Ernie's HDA interview. 'Apparently the people sent in to cover up the killing knew your personal access codes. They basically walked straight in, no alarms, no questions. Who have you given the codes to?'

'Only Boris.'

'Old boyfriends? Family? Friends?'

'No. Just the two of us. Really.'

'A service guy? Perhaps someone who came to repair the fridge last year?'

'No. That's all handled by building maintenance. If anything goes wrong, I have to authorize access and they're escorted to the apartment by security. It's all part of the lease. That's why there are no meshes inside the apartment, so you have privacy. It's tough to get in, but once you are inside you're completely secure. I liked that, it's a big reason I chose the St James.'

'But anyone in the St James security team can get into your apartment?' Chantilly Sanders-Watson asked.

'Well, yes, if there's an emergency.'

'Thank you.' The solicitor gave Sid a modest victory glance. 'And cleaners? Does the St James provide them as well?'

'Yes, I contracted for housekeeping twice a week. They only come when I'm at work.'

'So that's a lot of people who can come and go without you actually being there?' the solicitor said

'I suppose so, I never really thought about it like that. The management promised their staff are all vetted for a criminal record. They won't employ anyone who's been in trouble with the law.'

'Thank you,' Sid said firmly to the solicitor. 'What days do housekeeping visit?'

'Monday and Thursday.'

'Are you friends with any criminal elements in the city?'

'You don't have to answer that!'

Tallulah smiled sheepishly. 'I know a lot of finance sector people.'

'Don't we all,' Sid agreed. 'And others?'

'No, no gangsters or anybody like that.'

'Okay. Tallulah, the medicines in your bathroom, do the people who supplied them know where you live?'

Tallulah blushed heavily.

'Detective,' Chantilly Sanders-Watson warned. 'That creaking sound is the thin ice you're treading on.'

'We need to know,' Sid said earnestly. 'A man was killed in your apartment. We need to know why they chose the St James as the place to do that.'

'I don't know,' Tallulah insisted. 'We got the tox in a club. I've never seen the guys who sold them before. See, I'm being honest. This is a complete nightmare for me.'

'All right; now I know this is a memory stretch, but did you notice anything around that time? Back in January. Someone following you? Someone you kept bumping into?'

'No.' She shook her head, looking thoroughly miserable. 'Nothing like that.'

'When you came home from that weekend in Amsterdam, nothing odd about the apartment?'

'No.'

'Any exes making threats?'

'No.'

'How about work? Are you dealing in commercially sensitive information?'

'Not really. It's all data harvesting and interpretation. The conclusions are AI boosted. I suppose they could be worth something to the right people.'

'So you're helping determine future company policy?'

'I think you're overestimating my position. Our division generates a hundred market proposals a week.'

'No one's ever contacted you about your conclusions, shown an interest in obtaining your results, offered you money?'

'No. I don't even talk about them to Boris.'

'Have you got your visual cache from January?' Ian asked.

'No. I wipe it after a week. Everyone says that's what you're supposed to do.'

'For future reference: that's urban myth,' Sid said. 'Everyone would be a lot safer if you kept the visual memory.' He could see Chantilly Sanders-Watson raise an eyebrow in derision. She didn't actually challenge the assertion.

'Who did you tell you were going away for the weekend?' Ian asked.

Tallulah puffed her cheeks out with the effort of recall. 'I'm not sure. Couple of people at work, perhaps. I had to okay the days with my boss, so he knew.'

'Thank you for your cooperation,' Sid said. 'I'm going to have to ask you to stay here while my team verifies your story. And I'm afraid your apartment has been officially classified as a crime scene. Forensics should be finished by tomorrow. In the meantime I can offer to put you up in a city hotel.'

'Thank you. I'll stay with Boris.'

*

'Not involved,' Sid announced to Office3. He glanced at the big wallscreen which showed Tallulah's picture. In it she was wearing a pretty blue dress and smiling brightly, sunlight glinting off her hair like some kind of shampoo advert. 'Let's get rid of that,' he told Reannha. 'But in the wild event of me being wrong, I want all Tallulah's files for that Amsterdam weekend checked and verified. Hopefully we can get her out of here this afternoon.' *Before she distracts anyone else.* 'Ian, you're with me. We're interviewing Boris next.'

'Oh crap on it.'

Tallulah Packer was released from police custody at four fifteen that afternoon, with a court-granted travel limit, restricting her to Newcastle city for the next fortnight.

According to the team her alibi was perfect. She and Boris were in Amsterdam the whole time. Amsterdam police even managed to extract some log memories of them together, strengthening the alibi.

'Then why her apartment?' Ian asked that evening when he Sid and Eva convened at his flat.

'People who work with her knew it would be empty,' Eva said. 'Her holiday request was in the Northumberland Interstellar personnel network. It wouldn't have been hard for anyone looking for a random decoy to find out. I say she was chosen simply to throw us off.'

'She was evasive about knowing any 2Norths,' Sid said. 'She didn't deny it, but the answer was designed to be ambiguous.'

'Aye, man, you know whose fault that is.' Ian opened a bottle of beer and passed it to Sid.

'Yeah.' Sid took a swig. 'I know she's allowed representation, but Rattigan, Herandez, and Singh? Wasn't expecting that.'

'Well we know who to blame for that. Boris the dick.'

Sid held the bottle up in salute. 'Aye, you called that right.'

'How the hell does a wanker like that end up with her?' Ian said. 'She's beautiful, man. I've never seen a lass so gorgeous.'

Eva and Sid gave each other a knowing glance.

'Same background and he's got money,' Eva said. 'It's not exactly a one-off. Forget it. We got everything we needed from her.'

'Name of the actual killer would've been good,' Ian muttered.

'You're picking on the wrong elements,' Eva said. 'The lawyer and the fiancé are a pain, sure, but look at what we achieved. We got the murder site. If we're ever due a break on this case then it's going to be down to the forensics.'

'Aye,' Sid said. 'You know I'm genuinely proud of you guys, the whole team, like. We were given an absolute bastard here, and everyone stuck to it. I never expected us to last past week one, and here we are with the murder scene and the clean-up crew.'

'But this is about as far as we're going to get,' Ian said. 'Realistically, man. It was a corporate battle. We can't crack that. The real hope was Ralph would squeeze a name out of Ernie. Fuck knows what they did to the poor shit, but if he'd known he would've spilled it. He's the cut-off.'

'No. I think we can take this further,' Sid told them. His discovery that morning had allowed him to go through the day with high confidence. Now it was time to share, and he was eager.

'She can't love him,' Ian said. 'Not really. She's way too good for him. She must know that. She can take her pick.'

'Yes,' Eva drawled sardonically. 'Boss, maybe we should consider it wasn't random. What if this corporate shit is all about her work?'

'I don't think bioil distribution analysis is that critical, is it?'

'She works on demand and distribution patterns. Isn't that what the one-eleven cartel was formed to break?'

Sid struggled to recall the history. He remembered the cartel being on the transnet news while he was at school. 'I thought that was about the producers kicking speculators out of the market.'

'But if this is corporate, then bioil has to be at the heart of it.'

'Yeah. Could be.'

'He'll ruin her,' Ian said. He'd been sitting on his kitchenette bar, staring sullenly at his feet. 'A girl like that, it's not right. You can't turn someone like that into a corporate wife. What kind of life is that going to be for her?'

'Ian, she won't be ending up as some kind of trophy wife so he can win bragging rights at the golf club, okay? You said it, she's a girl that knows her own mind. Don't worry about her.'

'What if she can't see it? I bet he's a right fucking charmer, that bastard. You've only got to look at him to know he's got the lines, got the moves all right. You know they live on credit, don't you? All them banker types. They've not got real cash money, not even in their secondaries. They survive on promises they can't keep.'

'She knows men lie,' Eva said in a tone that signalled an approaching sense of humour failure. 'Trust me, we all do.'

'Aye, bollocks. He's wrong for her.'

'Ian! Later, okay, man. I've got some news.'

Eva and Ian both gave Sid the swearing-in-church look of surprise.

'Jacinta?' Eva asked.

'No! Crap on it, two kids is enough. No, I mean about the case, this part of the case. I had to review Ernie's garage for Tilly this morning. I accessed your visual log, Eva.'

'Mine?'

'Yeah. You went into the garage itself, the workshop.'

'Only for a minute, while we were waiting for Reinert.'

'Yeah, but there was a Kovoshu Valta parked at the back. And

I've seen that colour with those hologram prism stripes before; man the car is eyeflash enough, add those stripes and you've got a match. Boz was driving that car in Last Mile when we ballsed up the exchange observation.'

'Crap on it,' Ian muttered.

'Sherman is connected to Reinert somehow, enough that Ernie loans out vehicles to the likes of Boz,' Sid said. 'What are the chances of Reinert being in contact with two people that far up the food chain?'

'You think Sherman is Reinert's controller?' Eva asked.

'Aye, I'll give you very good odds on it. Ernie might not be quite the failsafe cut-off the corporates think he is.'

'What do we do?' Eva asked.

'We don't go to Aldred with this,' Sid said. 'The Norths know more than they're letting on, or some of them do. What I'd like to do is interview Ernie about his involvement with other gang crimes. Now we know there's a link we need to uncover it legitimately, so we're not compromised.'

'Good idea, boss,' Ian said.

'Yes,' Eva said. 'Gets my vote.'

'Thanks. The other possibility is that I ask Ralph for some help, off the record.'

'Why?'

'If Ernie can't open up a route back to Sherman, we're going to need something I can feed directly to the HDA. Ralph knows how this kind of deal works. I can keep you two out of it, there's no need for him to know what we've been doing.'

'Well that's down to you, boss,' Eva said. 'I'm surprised the HDA is still here, to be honest. They must know there was never any alien monster.'

'Aye, your call, man,' Ian said. 'But if you want to tell him I'm backing you up with this, you can.'

'Thanks but it's been me pushing this. I'll take the risk, and the heat.'

'Okay then.' They all raised their bottles to that.

'A word,' Ian said quietly to Sid as Eva left.

642

'Sure.' Sid waited for a moment, watching a strange flurry of emotion cross Ian's face. Finally, Ian said: 'I want to see her again.'

'Who?' It was instinctive, then Sid realized. 'Aye crap on it, man, you don't mean Tallulah?'

'Yes.'

'Oh bloody hell. All right, look, Ian . . .'

'You don't understand. She's incredible. It's like she's this perfect woman.'

'Okay, man, first off, she's an engaged perfect woman.'

'Only to *him*.'

'Ian. Listen to me, you can't go messing with that. Not the way you usually do.'

'I don't know what you mean.'

'Yes you do. What do you want me to do here, man, give you my blessing? I'm not a vicar. Man, you know you can't go after her.'

'Why not? Why can't I? It's not like we're playing by the rules, is it?'

Sid gave him a level, warning gaze. 'What we're doing is trying to gather more leads for the investigation, to get a result. What we're not doing is wrecking evidence and witness credibility.'

'I wouldn't do that.'

'Aye, Ian, come on, man! There are a thousand others out there.'

'Not like her. She's fucking amazing. Hot enough to burn lava. But it's not just that, she's smart, and funny. I've never met anyone like her before. I could make it work. Aye, for her I could.'

'She's a potential witness in the biggest case you'll ever have.'

Ian ran a hand back through his product-glossed hair. 'Aye, crap on it. I know. But . . . Come on, boss, have you ever seen a lass like that?'

'Shit. Okay, listen: whatever you do, whatever move you make, it has to be after the case is over. Do you understand that? I can't afford to have our logs challenged in court.'

'I'd never do that.'

'Aye, all right, then.'

'She is, though, isn't she? She's beautiful.'

'Oh crap on me for saying this – yes, she's lovely. But just remember, she really does have the choice of anyone she wants, and right now she wants Boris. My advice: screw around with that and you're asking for trouble.'

'Aye. Thanks, man.'

'I'm sorry. Life can be a real bastard sometimes. Are you going to be all right?'

'I'll be fine.'

Friday 22nd March 2143

It was Ernie Reinert's lack of defiance which Sid found most unnerving. They were back in interview room seven, with Reinert wearing a standard light-grey prisoner overall with Velcro fastenings. After sitting at the same table for year after year being subject to defiance, abuse, threats, and getting spat at more times than he could count, it was almost like he was on the defensive now.

Ralph Stevens hadn't objected to the interview, though he had been curious. 'Trust me, he told us every useful piece of information he could.'

'Yeah, but I read the transcripts,' Sid said. 'You concentrated on the disposal operation and Kirk Corzone.' The transcripts had been extensive, heavy with information, though they only amounted to about three hours. It was more like a statement confirming an earlier confession, all very formal Q&As. It made Sid wonder about what had happened for the rest of the week Reinert had been with the HDA, which wasn't an area he was comfortable with at all.

'Of course we did, those are the key issues,' Ralph said.

'I'd like to try a different approach.'

'He's yours now. We don't want him back. Ask him whatever you like, but I'll need to be in the observation office.'

Reinert refused a solicitor, claiming he didn't want one. Sid could appreciate that, they had enough on the HDA transcript to have him relocated to Minisa's polar colony – assuming the courts accepted the transcript. Most of Newcastle's judges were way too liberal in Sid's opinion.

'I'm interested in your anonymous friend who sent you to the St James,' Sid began. 'The instructions you receive from him always come from the same address code, right?'

'Yes, sir,' Reinert said, polite and respectful. 'That's how I know the call is genuine.'

'That's good e-craft,' Sid said. 'Elementary, but good. Three AIs tried to trace where the call originated from, but it was random dispersal routed, listed as interfaced with fifty-seven public cells around Newcastle. So your friend clearly knows his transnet security.'

'I'm sorry, sir, I'd like to help you catch him, really I would.'

'Thank you, Ernie. So there was never any address for you to call?'

'No, sir.'

'What happened if something went wrong, if you couldn't do a job?'

Ernie looked confused. 'I could do all the jobs.'

'Was anything ever said about what would happen to you if you couldn't do one?'

'No, sir. I just knew not to screw up. Old Kirk, he made that clear when he gave me the address code. Said if anyone used it to call me then there was no going back. I accepted that, sir, I know the score.'

'So you never tried calling that address code yourself?'

'No, sir, no point. Kirk said it was never interfaced until I was being called.'

'Did Kirk ever indicate if it was a man or a woman on the other end?'

'No, sir. I tried to remember those kind of details. I tried really hard for the others, but I couldn't.' He started shaking as a thin layer of sweat beads erupted from his brow. 'Please don't send me back there, sir, not to them. I'm trying to help, really I am. I'll try so hard for you, sir.'

Sid and Ian exchanged an awkward glance. 'I know you're

trying, Ernie,' Sid assured him. 'So let's try a different line, shall we? Can you tell me about the previous jobs you did for the untraceable address? How many have there been?'

'Just the four, sir.'

'Okay then, tell me about the first three.'

By themselves they weren't particularly remarkable. The first two, both in the first year after the arrangement began, were targeted muggings. Ernie had been given images of his victims, told what hotels they were staying in, and told what to retrieve from them. In both cases it was a personal transnet cell. Ernie had to leave the first gadget in a CoCoMore franchise café toilet, and the second in the gents at Newcastle Station. The third job had been last year, and was a whole different level. He'd organized a break-in team for the offices of D'Amato and Livie, a law firm specializing in corporate tax affairs. They had to gain entry without raising any alarm, and replace one of the network cores with an identical make and marque which Ernie collected from a waiter at the Olive Branch Bar on Grey Street, opposite the Theatre Royal. Ernie believed the man was wearing an identity mask, his face had that slightly too stiff look to it. After swapping the gadget, the team was to exit the office, also without incident. A feat they'd accomplished, much to Ernie's satisfaction. He'd expected more jobs to come his way after proving himself like that. Then he got the St James disposal.

Sid and Ian went into the observation office where Ralph had been watching. Lorelle Burdett joined them.

'The mugging victims were easy to find,' she told them. 'Vladimar Orwell and Gus Malley.'

'Who do they work for?' Sid asked.

'Orwell is employed by Longthorpe-AI – he's a software expert.'

'Okay, can you find out what contracts Longthorpe had at that time?'

Lorelle gave him a smart grin. 'That'll be tough without a warrant, but they work just about exclusively for the bioil industry. Their AIs specialize in pipe-flow dynamics.'

'And Burdett?'

'Michtral Engineering.'

'Ah.' Even Sid had heard of them, a massive German heavy industry group that built bioil refineries. 'I don't suppose we'll find out who D'Amato and Livie's clients are.'

'Again, we'll need a warrant. But in this town, any law firm worth over a Eurofranc is going to have bioil companies on its client list.'

'Thanks, Lorelle.'

'So?' Ralph asked as she left.

'So,' Sid said, 'each of those jobs was bioil-industry related. Reinert's controller is corporate.'

'Yeah, that's something we're strongly considering. However, the reason we haven't abandoned your investigation is because someone on the expedition has just been murdered by a five-blade claw.'

'Aye, crap on it, man,' Ian exclaimed. 'You sure, like?'

'Oh yes. Coombs was a xenobiology specialist. She was at Wukang, that's Elston's camp.'

Sid didn't know how to respond. He'd been so sure he'd just made his case perfectly. 'There can't be an alien,' he said. 'There just can't. It's North against North.'

Ralph shrugged. 'Sorry, but we're not quite there yet. So where do you want to go next?'

'Forensics,' Sid said. 'That's all we've got left on the murder scene.'

'Is that going to turn up anything?' Ralph asked.

It was Sid's turn to shrug. 'We'll know when we know.'

*

Ralph Stevens left Market Street Station at six thirty that evening, walking towards Grey Street. Sid was standing on the corner, drinking a boXsnaX tea from a cardboard cup. 'Nice evening. I'll walk with you.'

Ralph showed a brief flicker of surprise. 'Sure.'

They crossed Grey Street outside the theatre and turned up

towards the Monument. Ralph stopped outside the Central Arcade's big stone arch. Inside, the glass-roofed hallway was lined with small exclusive stores; while the upper levels had been refurbished as a boutique hotel just as its architects had originally envisaged over two centuries earlier.

'You know this is me, right?' Ralph said.

'Yeah. I've never been inside the hotel. What's it like?'

'Nice. Why don't you come up and take a look.'

'That'd be grand, thanks, man.'

Ralph's room was decorated in lush brown, gold, and red colours, with a big bed and a small zone cubicle. The windows gave him a view down across Grey's Monument. Sid looked at the pedestrians for a while, then the curtains swished shut.

'I don't often ask strange men back to my room,' Ralph said.

'The hotel doesn't have meshes inside the rooms,' Sid told him.

'Lip-reading software, huh?'

'It's admissible in court.'

'I'm interested.'

'You want this solved, don't you, one way or another, alien or corporate?'

'HDA is focused entirely on proving or disproving the alien theory. That comes before anything, including court evidence and police log procedures.'

'All right then. There's a possibility we may have a lead that isn't on the police logs.'

'What?' Ralph demanded. 'Don't fuck around with us on this, Sid. That's a world you do not want to inhabit.'

'There's a hint from the gangs that something big is going down. I genuinely don't know what, but you don't get much bigger than murdering a North.'

'Did this come from the Gang Task Force?'

'No. This is a private non-police source, which is why it's not on any log. Remember what happened to Jolwel Kavane?'

It took a moment, but Ralph's expression gave him away. 'Ah. Fair enough. So what do you want me to do?'

'I can carry on chasing down the lead on my own, but I need some help.'

'Sure. What sort of help?'

'Surveillance. The best you can get for me. Keep it off-log so if it all goes arse over tit there'll be no comeback for you. I want something I can tag three or four individuals with, something that they can't detect or rip or burn, and they'll never know about until we come crashing through the wall.'

'Are you sure that's the way you want to play it?'

'It's got me this far.'

'All right, Sid, I'll see what I can do for you.'

Saturday 23rd March 2143

It had rained overnight for the first time in a couple of days. Angela's boots squelched on reassuringly familiar mud as she walked over to the long row of 350DL cargo pallets containing the camp's stores. The jungle lapping against Wukang sparkled outlandishly in the borealis scintillations, with a billion droplets scattering the citron and cerise lightblooms in a prismatic miasma. Overhead, the ruby glarc of their malaised star was hidden by thickening clouds that were powering in from the north, buffeted along by a fast wind. She wasn't accustomed to so much background noise on St Libra; as well as the wind, she could often hear the crash of distant thunder rolling in across the hills.

Those sharp cracks had become a constant reminder of the fragile relay of e-Rays that connected her to the greater civilization of the trans-space worlds. A reminder reinforced by one file in the camp's net which everyone kept accessing, as if that would somehow lessen the blow. The e-Ray which had circled valiantly above the Eclipse Mountains for close on two months had been subject to the greatest barrage of lightning strikes. It had withstood them far beyond any redundancy measures its design anticipated, with component after component blowing. The AAV team had compensated with work-rounds and software patches until yesterday afternoon. The one remaining motor that drove the propeller had taken a direct hit, burning out. Without the stability it provided, the e-Ray began to pitch and yaw in the storm-accelerated jetstreams; gyrations which quickly sent it tumbling in a wild dive. Its weakened stress structure began to buckle, struts snapped puncturing the helium bubbles, and it began to long fall to the savage peaks below. A fall that was broadcast in hi-rez clarity from avionics that resolutely continued to function until the moment it struck naked rock.

The gap it left in the relay chain was significant. The two e-Rays on either side of the Eclipse Mountains could just lock on to each other and maintain the relay; but that link had come at a massive cost in bandwidth, increasing the perception of isolation.

It was stupid, she kept telling herself. After all, they were less than eight hours' flying time from Abellia. *If we had a plane.*

Angela reached the row of pallets, and told her e-i to ping the first. The smartdust tags on the boxes and packages stowed inside the casing responded, and content lists rolled down her grid. She and Forster Wardele had been reviewing the state of Wukang's supplies ever since the night Coombs had been murdered. The attack on the camp's net had done more damage than they realized at first, wiping or corrupting thousands of files. And the general inventory hadn't been heavily protected.

Paresh appeared at the end of the pallet row, leading Atyeo and Josh, all three of them in light body armour, grey carbon segments flexing as they moved. Their Heckler carbines were held with deceptive lightness, short barrels supporting several sighting sensors. Angela grinned and waved.

'Hi,' she said when they came over. She didn't try to kiss Paresh. Not fair in front of the others when they were all on duty. Beside, his helmet would have made that difficult.

'How's it going?' he asked.

Angela gestured at the long row of pallets. 'I didn't realize we had so much stuff. I suppose it's lucky.'

'Yeah,' Paresh spat. 'Shit on Passam.'

The real triumph of seclusion had come when they heard about the Daedalus at Sarvar evacuating seventy of the base's eighty personnel first thing Friday morning. As soon as the small maintenance crew at Sarvar had finished their physical inspection for bombs, it had flown them all directly to Abellia.

'A strategic withdrawal,' Passam had told Elston. A Daedalus would return to Sarvar, refuel from the plentiful stocks there, and evacuate everyone from Wukang, Varese, and Omaru. When everyone from the three forward camps was back at Sarvar, they'd be brought home in a last evacuation flight by two Daedaluses.

'That's bullshit,' Ravi Hendrik shouted in the mess tent Friday evening as the news filtered round. 'Nobody is going to fly over the Eclipse range in these conditions. It's practically suicide. The last flight was lucky to get through with the lightning only knocking one engine out. Eighteen times they got hit on the way back. Eighteen! One of the pilots at Abellia told me.'

Angela had spent the time since telling herself she wasn't bothered by the isolation, that it was temporary, that if they really needed help the HDA would order a Daedalus to fly in. 'Once we find out what we've got stored here we'll be better off,' Angela said. 'But there's certainly enough food for a couple of months. Especially if you include nutrient jelly.'

'Oh hell, girl,' Atyeo pulled a face. 'Have you ever eaten that crap?'

'No. Is it bad?'

'Doesn't matter what composition pack you mix it with, it still tastes like semolina that someone's pissed in.'

'Thanks for the image,' Angela told him. 'So, have you seen anything out there?'

'Nothing,' Paresh said. 'It's not showing itself. But we'll find the bastard eventually.' He patted the carbine. 'And when we do, it'll be sorry.'

What Angela wanted to tell him was how childish he was being, how stupid his reliance on having the biggest gun, but she held back. Wasn't going to play the bitch token, there was too much resting on the Legionnaires being on her side. 'You just be careful out there.'

Something made a sharp *click* sound over by the pallets.

The Legionnaires heard it too. Paresh glanced round. All of them lifted their carbines.

Click. Click.

'What the hell . . .'

Something stung Angela's cheek. 'Ow!' Her hand came up automatically, a wasp-swatting reflex. But St Libra didn't have insects. Then something flickered across her vision before *clicking* off her armour vest. She cancelled her grid completely.

The *clicks* were merging into a continuous clatter. Angela stared in amazement as a small white pellet bounced off Paresh's armour right in front of her. Something pinched the back of her hand. Then her head was pricked again. She knew what the pellet was, just refused to acknowledge it. *That can't exist on St Libra.* But there were dozens of them on the muddy ground around them, with more landing every second. As if to emphasize the portent, the wind started to gust harder.

A mesmerized Josh was bending over, picking up one of the white pellets. 'Hail?' he said incredulously.

Angela glanced up. Which was really stupid. She cried out as more hailstones smacked into her unprotected face. 'Son of a bitch.' The sky above was darkening further, a grey veil sliding across the borealis streamers, growing gloomier towards the horizon. Even as she hunched over for protection she could see the hailstones were getting bigger. *Everything is larger on St Libra.* One the size of a pebble struck her on the back of the neck. 'Ouch.' Her e-i was reporting a general alert. Angela looked round frantically for cover. The tents were a couple of hundred metres away. And she was suddenly suspicious about how much protection they'd offer in this. One of the self-loading trucks was parked at the end of the pallet row.

'Come on!' she yelled, and started sprinting for the machine. The Legionnaires ran after her, their armour making them slower. The sound of the hail hitting them turned them into clattering robot-like creatures. Then she was at the truck, diving underneath, scrabbling her legs round so they weren't left exposed.

654

Paresh and the other two arrived, and crawled in with her. The hailstones landing outside were as big as golf balls now, hitting hard, bouncing, shattering the ones already lying in the mud. They covered the ground as far as she could see, steaming lightly.

'How the fuck could this happen?' Josh yelled above the constant impact roar.

'Sirius has redshifted,' Angela shouted back. 'That means it's cooler. St Libra is starting to chill down.'

'You're shitting me, right?'

'Does it fucking look like I'm joking?'

Pressed up next to her, his arm over her shoulders (as if that would do any good), Paresh gave her a worried glance. 'What else is going to happen?'

'I don't know, I'm not a goddamn climatologist.' Anger was good. Anger stopped her being afraid.

The deluge stopped after twenty minutes, when the clouds blew away to the south. Shifting variegated aurora light shone down once more, shimmering off the deep swathe of hailstones that smothered the ground.

Angela and the Legionnaires crawled out from under the loader truck, and looked around at the ruined camp. Boots crunched on the uneven layer of ice. It was already starting to melt, vapour tendrils thickening around Angela's legs and rising. People were emerging from wherever they'd found refuge from the despoiled sky's fearsome hostility.

'Wow, holy shit,' an aghast Paresh muttered as he took in the damage. None of the tents was standing. The few that did still have a frame intact had shreds of photovoltaic sheets hanging from them, flapping weakly in the fading wind. Hailstones had shredded the glossy black fabric as if it was tissue. Even the big central mess tent had long tears across the roof, its posts leaning precariously. 'This can't go on,' Paresh said loudly, close to panic. 'We've got to get out of here. Fuck the lightning, they've got to send a Daedalus for us. They've got to.'

'They will,' Angela said, knowing it was all a lie. 'Don't worry, they'll come and get us.'

Monday 25th March 2143

Office3 was short on people when Sid arrived. Eva and Abner were sitting at their desks, immersed in their console zones, but they were alone. Last night had seen city police and agency constables deployed en masse to a holding yard in Last Mile. They were kept on standby through the night, ready to back up the GE Border Directorate troops.

Highcastle residents had made an attempt to break through. The riot on the St Libra side had lasted for hours. The Directorate troops wound up using water cannon, heat-induction beams, and tangle bullets. Eventually the would-be returnees were repelled. But they were still there, thousands of them, camped out in their vehicles along Motorway A. The morning news was full of threats about turning off the bioil supplies to Earth unless they were allowed to come back. The GE energy commissioner was flying to Newcastle for talks with Augustine North. Markets were falling. And the HDA still refused to say if the sunspots were Zanth-related.

Tilly Lewis was waiting for him when Sid came in, carrying her coat and fold-down pink umbrella which was still dripping on the worn carpet. He grinned at the damp tassels of hair she was squeezing. 'Is it raining?'

'Comedy master, huh?'

'Come on through.'

The seal on the door of his office turned blue.

'So what have you got for me?' Sid asked.

656

There was a slightly awkward pause as she avoided eye contact. 'Well, there was definitely a murder in apartment 576B.'

'Aye, come on!'

'Full report,' she said as her e-i loaded the file into the office's network. 'I'm sorry, Sid, I know how critical this was for you. But, really, it was months ago, and that apartment has been cleaned twice a week ever since. That's on top of the bleach job that was done on it by Reinert's people.'

'You've got to give me something.'

Tilly nodded in discomfort. 'It's more or less a definite that the murder did happen there, that 576 wasn't a staging post. There was a sizeable pool of 2North blood on the floor in the lounge. Bleach had ruined most of it, but we got a positive DNA match. Then we confirmed a small blood trail to the bathroom, where the body was put in the bath. That's right?'

'Aye. Blazczaka and the others confirmed that's where the body was when they arrived.'

'It was put there to bleed out. The heart was a mess, of course, there was no arterial spurt aside from the kill stab. But given the size of the wound, leakage would occur for a while afterwards. So moving him was done to reduce mess in the apartment. In my opinion.'

'Whoever did it, didn't want to hang around, and they didn't want Tallulah to find out. Fair enough. But they were still thinking ahead, about the disposal.'

'Yeah.'

'And there's nothing else you can tell me?'

'We eliminated every fingerprint we found, every DNA trace. They're all accounted for, either St James staff or Tallulah's friends. There's nothing there that's going to help you. I ran every test we have, took more samples than we do normally.'

'Aye, thanks, I appreciate that.'

'Where does that leave you?'

'Putting together a status report for O'Rouke. What happens after that ain't up to me.'

Tilly pressed her lips together. 'All the things we can do these days, the avalanche of data available; I really thought every crime could be solved if you threw enough resources at it.'

'Yes, this one is different, that's for sure.'

She stood and brushed straggly hair out of her eyes. 'Sometimes you've just got to let go, Sid.'

'So I'm learning.'

*

Sid had lunch in the canteen with Ian. Every table was full; all officers were still on alert, ready to respond to the GE Border Directorate in case the gateway was breached.

'I can't see it happening,' Ian said as he ate his tomato salad. 'Those GE troops are tough bastards, and they've got the full riot-suppression gear.'

'This isn't a riot,' Sid said. 'Highcastle is a city of smart, educated people who are terrified. It's only going to take ten of them to get truly pissed off with the GE, and they'll go back to their microfacture shops and return with real weapons. It'll be Amsterdam in '21 all over again.'

'I heard they've got Legionnaire squads backing them up. Rocco over at Blakelaw Station said he saw them arrive at Last Mile. Blacked-out vans, and everything.'

'There's three million people on the other side. I don't care what kind of Horatio shit the troops pull on the ramp up to the gateway, they'll get through in the end.'

'So turn the gateway off.'

'And cut off the bioil? Not a chance.'

'Well, I still don't see what they expect us to do if they do come pouring through. It'll be the HDA that'll have to deal with it.'

Ralph Stevens was suddenly standing by their table. 'Did someone call for the cavalry?'

'Hey.' Sid grinned up. 'Join us? We can find you a chair somewhere.'

'No, that's okay.' Ralph handed over a Mikalljan store bag. 'Here's that shirt from Kolhapur you asked for. Try it out. If you

658

like it my contact can get you some more. The fabric is syeel, it doesn't grow anywhere else, something to do with soil enzymes.'

Sid took the bag and placed it beside his feet. 'Thanks.'

Ralph gave a one-finger salute and walked off.

'A shirt?' Ian asked.

'Aye, this syeel stuff is supposed to be the best cotton in the galaxy. Did you hear Aldred was here this morning?'

'What did he want?'

'They've lost track of Zebediah. He hasn't been seen in the Independencies since the expedition began. None of his followers know where he is.'

'Well that's no surprise, not really.'

'No.' Sid stabbed a meatball from the centre of his spaghetti. 'I suppose not.'

Tuesday 26th March 2143

The sun was bright enough that it actually made the security film on O'Rouke's office windows glow a subdued saffron. The haze permeating the office somehow managed to emphasize the pock-marks on the Chief Constable's face, darkening his skin tone. It didn't help that he sat behind his desk in silence as Sid briefed him. His conclusion: the North was murdered as a result of some inter-company fight.

'We can hold Ernie and his crew for another forty-eight hours without charge, but after that we'll have to reapply. I have to show the judge that our files have been forwarded to the prosecution bureau for assessment. Once that happens and charges are brought, it'll be public record there was no carjacking. A North was murdered.'

O'Rouke remained silent, unmoving, which was unnerving. Sid was desperate for some kind of hint. Slow-burn anger, full screaming rant?

'How is this possible?' O'Rouke said quietly. 'I mean, for fuck's sake, two months and bloody millions! And we haven't even got all the sodding agency and specialist invoices filed yet. Now you're telling me we still don't have anyone we can pin it on?'

'We have Ernie Reinert.'

'That shitbag? So fucking what?'

'You can use what we know to deflect. Tell the reporters it

was an outside hit. That it's all down to money and bioil. That the kill order could have come from any company or bank or billionaire across the trans-stellar worlds.'

'And what about his identity? I'm supposed to face the news filth and say we don't even know who the dead arsehole is?'

'That's down to the North family. Their records aren't good enough.'

'Fucking brilliant. You want me to blame Augustine North now? Maybe I'll just stab myself in the eye with a blunt stick, it'll be less painful.'

Sid resisted the impulse to smirk. 'I told you this bloke was good. Unless we find out what corporate war is being waged, we're never going to move this on.'

'And you're going to find that out, are you?'

'No, sir. Look, we've done everything we were asked to by the HDA, we proved it wasn't their stupid alien. Ask them to help. If Ralph agrees, he can probably fling Reinert and the others into some polar penal colony where they won't come back from. He's got the authority, and crap knows IIDA aren't afraid to use it. Have you seen the state they reduced Reinert to? They're pretty ruthless, and we've done everything they asked.'

'The devil has personally chosen me to crap on, Hurst, I swear it. You know I'm set to retire in another eighteen months? When this hits the transnet I'll have about two minutes to clear my desk and get escorted out.'

'Can't imagine the force without you, sir.'

'Stop brown-nosing you stupid dick, that's Jenson's job. You're real police.'

'Thank you.'

'You reckon Stevens would go for this exile thing?'

'At this point, how can it hurt to ask? Maybe Jenson San could handle the question for you?'

'Too bloody right he would. All right, leave it with me.'

'And the investigation? What do you want me to do?'

'You're sure you can't go any further?'

'I don't see how.' Which was going out on a very long and

very fragile limb. But if the new surveillance didn't produce results, O'Rouke would never know.

'Ah bollocks to it: close it down. Hand everyone their case-end certificate, deep-cache the network files. You and Lanagin can resume general rota duty. Send the evidence you've harvested on Reinert to the prosecutor, but not until tomorrow. I'll get Jenson to talk to Stevens today.'

'Aye, I'll organize that.'

'And, Hurst, make fucking sure everyone understands this is still classified.'

'Got it.'

*

The conference room was one which any corporate CEO would be familiar with. Big oval table with democratically positioned leather chairs, perfectly neutral air-con atmosphere, holographic panes on the wall, neat consoles at every place. Expensive and efficient.

Major Vermekia didn't approve. He found it an indication of how far corporate culture had pervaded every aspect of human activity. It was blandification, rubbing everything down to a smooth managed expectation. Military life shouldn't be like that. Officers should be constantly reminded their decisions held people's lives in the balance. And for an HDA officer, that could well mean millions of lives.

Despite his disapproval, he kept his expression neutral as he followed General Shaikh into the conference room. The General was certainly a man of honour. Rare enough in this day and age. Shaikh would do what had to be done, no matter his surroundings, of that Vermekia was confident.

The Sirius science team Captain Toi had assembled were standing beside their chairs. Those big panes on the wall cast a faint pink light across the room. Instead of corporate accountancy data, each one carried a similar image of Sirius, its seething photosphere mottled by dark blemishes, plasma warts screwing up the flux lines. They accounted for over half the surface area now.

Shaikh took the chair at the head of the table, and gestured everyone else to sit. 'Captain Toi?' he asked.

She stood up. 'Sir. We sent forty-eight satellites through the Cape Town war gateway. Thirty-one remain functional.'

'What happened to the rest?' Shaikh asked.

'Solar radiation storms knocked them out. They were in the closest orbits. We now don't orbit anything closer than twenty million kilometres of Sirius.'

'The storms are that powerful?'

'Yes, sir.'

'I see. Proceed.'

'Twenty-one satellites are in the twenty- to twenty-eight-million-kilometre orbit, scanning the star. They're viewing the photosphere in visual spectra as well as scanning Sirius's magnetic and gravitational fields and quantum signature. So far they have detected absolutely zero disturbance in the surrounding quantum fields. There are unusual fluctuations in the magnetic field, which correspond to the twists in the convection layer. But the astronomy team believe they originate within the star, and could be caused by deep current patterns within the core.'

'Is this a known phenomenon?' the General asked.

'Sir, this is Dr Tavarez, our compressed-matter expert.'

Dr Tavarez, a tall, slender academic with a balding scalp, nodded nervously as everyone turned to him. 'General. We've not seen radiation-zone currents produce quite this kind of cycle before, but we are dealing with exceptionally large timeframes, especially in relation to historical astronomy.'

'Doctor, I simply need to know if this is natural.'

'I understand. Given the sheer size of Sirius, an asymmetric imbalance within the radiative zone, or even the neutron core itself, could conceivably operate on this kind of thousand-year timescale. Just because we haven't encountered it before does not negate its possibility. We are constructing theoretical models which admittedly require a stretch of credulity, but will provide a framework to explain the observed effects. And although I personally regard the Red Controversy as dubious at best, the facts we witness today are undeniable.' He waved a bony hand at the panes. 'There is also the response of the St Libra plants. To have an automatic reaction to this event is the strongest indicator that it has happened before; frequently, in order for a plant to evolve a response. Something affects Sirius's magnetic field on a regular basis. It has to be an inordinately powerful cyclic influence, which suggests that the core is responsible.'

'So it is natural?'

'I believe so. Certainly the remaining satellite data seems to support an absence of Zanth activity.'

'Captain?' the General said.

One of the panes changed to show a 3D orbital schematic of the Sirius system, with nineteen solid planets, including St Libra, orbiting between the two stars, and three small rocky airless worlds chasing odd elliptical high-inclination orbits around Sirius B. The ten remaining sensor satellites shone as green triangles, covering a volume of space thirty AUs from Sirius A.

'Not one of the satellites has detected any kind of fluctuation within the quantum fields. There is simply no evidence of any kind of Zanth activity as we understand it,' Toi said. 'Sirius space is completely clear.'

Vermekia cleared his throat. 'So if we disregard the sheer size of the event, there's nothing to make us suspect it is of Zanth origin?'

'There is its incongruity,' Dr Tavarez said. 'Although I am loath to rule out anything in a natural universe, this sunspot outbreak is completely unprecedented.'

'But not artificial? Not generated by an external force?' Shaikh persisted.

'I don't see how it could be,' Tavarez said. 'Whatever is happening within the star's core is the key to this, for that is where the magnetic field is generated. It's going to take decades of study to understand the core's deep cycles.'

The General looked round the table, making brief eye contact with each of the scientists. 'I understand this is fascinating to you on an intellectual level, but equally you must understand the effect it is having across the trans-stellar worlds. I require a consensus. Are you agreed there is no evidence of the Zanth at Sirius?'

'Sir,' Toi said. 'That is the conclusion of this committee.'

'Thank you. Captain Toi, I am hereby officially cancelling the Zanthswarm stage two alert. Please notify the Situation Centre. Our forces are to stand down.'

'General,' Dr Tavarez asked, 'may we retain the satellites to continue our observation?'

'Major?' Shaikh asked.

'Impossible to bring them back through the war gateway,' Vermekia said. 'And if we did, they're dangerously radioactive; I don't see what we'd do with them. But retaining the war gateway opening just to maintain communication links with the satellites would be expensive.'

'Can they be monitored from St Libra?'

'I'm sure some kind of antenna can be put in place at our Highcastle office, yes.'

'See to it. Does anyone have an estimate how long the sunspot outbreak will last?'

'Several months at least,' Captain Toi said. 'That will simply be how long it takes for the current spots to dissipate. If more continue to erupt, then the timescale simply cannot be known. It must have lasted a reasonable length of time for it to be noticed by naked-eye astronomers.'

'Years, then?'

'We think that's likely, yes.'

'And the effect on St Libra?'

'General,' Professor Dendias, the climatologist, said. 'I believe we're looking at a major environmental shift. The sunspot activity hasn't yet reached a peak, although it is slowing. The first spots to emerge remain substantial, and our estimate has them endur-ing for a couple of months. St Libra's atmosphere is already reacting to the reduced solar infall; there have been reports of rain becoming ice, and even unconfirmed reports of snow from the southernmost Independencies. This is just the start, there's no telling what the ultimate effect may be. We might even see the inauguration of temperate bands in the north and south that will persist for years.'

'I see. My thanks to all of you for the work you've done.' The General stared at the panes while everyone except for Vermekia filed out. When the door closed and the blue seal light outlined it, he cocked his head at Vermekia. 'You've remained in contact with Elston?'

'Yes, sir. Wukang is hanging on in there.'

'Are the warheads secure?'

'Yes, sir. I receive daily confirmation of that. However, the e-Ray link is now somewhat tenuous.'

'And the murders?'

'The Newcastle police are convinced their body was the result of a corporate war. I have to admit the evidence they've amassed points to that. However, Stevens has briefed me there remains one semi-official lead the chief detective is following up with our assistance. I'll wait and see how that plays out before passing judgement. The murder of Coombs at Wukang is more pressing. Elston is convinced an alien is picking off his people. There are some perplexing incidents building up out there. But Passam is looking at evacuation.'

'No. Wukang and the others are to remain until we have proof of an alien or whoever murdered Coombs is exposed. Now the Zanthswarm alert is over, can we get the extra Legionnaires we promised out to him?'

'The remaining Daedalus planes and the SuperRocs have been cleared for flight. But by all accounts flying over the Eclipse Mountains right now is going to be tough.'

'A war gateway, then?'

Vermekia sucked down a breath. 'Can be done, of course. We could drop a Daedalus through at high altitude above Wukang. But we wouldn't be able to recover by that method, of course.

It's the anchor problem, as always. If we want direct access to the middle of the Brogal continent you're looking at constructing a new gateway. It would cost tens of billions.'

'And take months, if not years,' the General said. 'Yes, point taken. Even if they do capture an alien, it will have to be flown out. So Sarvar and Edzell need to retain their skeleton crews to facilitate that.'

'Our people are going to be fairly isolated anyway while the storms last. They can handle that. I'd be inclined to wait for the Newcastle result before we attempt to drop a Daedalus through a gateway into Wukang's airspace. The reports I've had from the other forward base xenobiology teams out there are confidently saying no animals have evolved on St Libra. There is no genetic variance.'

'Smart plants?'

'Anything is possible, of course. But all the geneticists are saying the plants have a sophistication that would have taken a long time to evolve naturally, certainly longer than Sirius has been in existence. It looks like the planet was definitely bioformed a couple of million years ago.'

'Then we're looking at the aliens who created the biosphere.'

'And given what we've done to the place since we arrived, they'd be justified in being very angry with us.'

'Then why don't they just come out and say so?'

Vermekia shrugged. 'The big question.'

'No.' Shaikh jabbed a finger at the mottled photosphere. '*That's* the question. Did they do that? An alien species which can switch off a star is possibly more frightening than the Zanth. We're wasting time scrabbling round in jungles and chasing gang lords in Newcastle. It's pitiful. What we should be doing is establishing gateways to a dozen unexplored star systems to see if we can find this species, damn the cost of it.'

'Elston knows there's something out there threatening Wukang. If anyone can catch it, he will.'

'And our contact with him is reliant on some e-Rays being beaten up by storms. That's unacceptable. Order the camps at

Edzell and Sarvar to deploy their reserve e-Rays – I want the link firmed up. And I think Elston should be given the full activation codes as a precaution.'

'I'll get them sent to him.'

'Good. But make sure he understands it's a last resort. Only to be used if aliens are based on St Libra and pose a clear and verifiable threat to the human race.'

'He knows why this particular weapon was created, and the circumstances for deploying it. You can rely on him.'

*

Sid wasn't worried he'd screw up using the applicator tube. He was also confident he could get into the locker where Boz had left his clothes while he went for his regular evening work-out on the gym's machines. It was being in a gym in the first place that was the whole flaw in the plan. Any gym member or regular who looked at him would instantly know he didn't belong, that he was an interloper. Patrons of Regency Fitness would wonder what he was doing. Query why he was opening a locker – slobs like him didn't need to change clothes because they didn't do sessions. They'd raise a fuss, maybe call security or even the police. It would all go catastrophically wrong because like every middle-aged man with a real job he didn't watch his diet like he should, or exercise properly. That lapse was going to come back and bite him hard.

'Are you all right?' Ian asked over the secure link.

'Fine.'

'There's no one in the locker room. I'm monitoring the whole gym.'

'I know.' Sid was cursing the whole arrangement and the paranoia it had kicked off inside him. Gyms were Ian's natural habitat. He should be in here while Sid stayed back in the flat and provided electronic coverage. But no – Sid wanted to show that he was prepared to take as much risk as anyone. So he went first.

Regency Fitness was a gym and fitness lifestyle business buried in the heart of the Fortin singletown. The men's locker room was large and brightly lit, with wood-fronted lockers and a pigeon-hole wall full of fluffy fresh towels for the marble-tiled shower room. He'd been inside for thirty seconds now, and Ian was right, he was the only person in there. Seven men were currently registered with the gym's network as using the facilities. So seven of the fifty lockers would be in use.

Sid hurried along the row, and found the first closed door. The lockers had simple coded lock pads. He told his e-i to quest the pad with the subber patch he'd copied from a bytehead's cache a couple of years ago when they arrested her. It popped open. He looked at the clothes piled up inside.

'Not his,' Ian said; who was riding the image from Sid's iris smartcells.

Sid closed the locker and went on to the next one. The fourth one he opened belonged to Boz, those outsize clothes were instantly recognizable. He pulled the applicator tube from his pocket; the size of a matchstick made of buffed stainless steel. When he touched it to the heel of Boz's shoe, his e-i triggered the launch system. A smartmicrobe was released, its sticky molecule surface adhering to the dark rubbery polymer of the heel. It would sit there passively recording the emissions from Boz's links, ready to download on command. Small enough and new enough with its quantum junction structure to be impervious to ordinary detection systems, even those of Beijing's dark tech barons should prove ineffective against it, Ralph had said.

Sid closed the locker door, and left the macrobuilding.

Wednesday 27th March 2143

It was two o'clock in the morning, and this was absolutely the last application of the night. Ian was tired after an evening of chasing the streets for the known cars of all Sherman's crew. A casual brush past, and quick tap with an applicator tube without breaking stride. Changing identity masks and wriggling in and out of clothes in the privacy of his own car, so none of Sherman's visual analysis routines could watch through security meshes and identify a pattern as he and Sid and Eva collided with the target vehicles.

As far as they could tell, no alert had gone out. So at half past eleven, Ian had cracked an empty flat in the same Heaton tower block where Marcus Sherman rented on the nineteenth floor. He'd worn an identity mask modelled on the absent owner's face, keeping the building security net mollified. Now he was lying on his belly in the cloakroom, studying his grid to monitor the progress the specialist drill in front of him was making as it slowly bored through the wall. The little machine made no sound as it slowly spun the half-millimetre diameter bit through the cavity between the two flats, creeping forward with achingly slow precision. Developed specifically for hostage tactical teams, it could cut through almost any kind of wall material without giving itself away. With a millimetre to go through the final plaster panel, Ian ordered it to stop. His e-i accessed a monitor program he'd infiltrated into the tower's network, and he tightened his grip on a nine-millimetre Tunce pistol he'd liberated from the Market Street evidence vault.

Ian had waited until Sherman was back in the flat before beginning. It was their optimum time, he and Sid reasoned. With Sherman in residence the flat's perimeter security would be operating on reduced sensitivity, watching for human-sized trouble; a lone assassin, or a hit team, or a snatch squad. There were a couple of hardmen in the flat on the other side of the hall, ready to respond in seconds should anything hostile begin a stealthy approach to their master's lair.

After Sherman arrived home at one o'clock, the delectable Valentina had been delivered to him, wafting in on the scent of Parisian perfume and trailing gossamer ribbons from the arms and hem of her diaphanous black jacket. Ian had given them forty minutes to relax, maybe tox up and move into the bedroom, then he started the drill.

He ordered it to recommence. Ninety seconds later the diamond-edged tip gently penetrated the plaster. Diminutive holes around the bit's point sucked up any dust, pulling them back so not even the tiniest evidence of the puncture was left scattered on the carpet of the master bedroom's built-in wardrobe. With the hole complete the drill bit withdrew.

Ian held his breath. There was nothing, no alert flashing through the tower's network, no goons bursting out of their flat with firearms waving round. Air escaped slowly through his squeezed-up lips as he felt the tension in his spine throttling back. He slipped the pistol's safety back on and let go of the grip.

Normally, this was the point where the hostage team would send a cloud of smartdust puffing through, try and gain valuable data on the local environment, position of bad guys and victims. Not tonight. Ian held up the small, clear plastic case and looked at the tiny ant-shape inside. It was one of the toys Ralph had supplied. Ian still wasn't sure why the spook had cooperated, but knowing they had some kind of approval from on high had given their off-log observation a legitimacy that was comforting. Not that the spook wouldn't dump them the second anything went wrong, he acknowledged stoically.

The tiny cybernetic ant crawled through the drill hole, unspooling a gossamer fibre as it went. It was a simple remote control, eliminating the need for any link emissions that might be detected. A weird monochrome fish-eye view expanded into Ian's grid. Carpet strands loomed around him like a thick stumpy jungle. He directed the ant towards the first pair of shoes.

There were eight pairs in all, from traditional black hand-made leather evening shoes, to tough ankle boots, to some worn trainers. The ant took eleven minutes to get to them all and stick a smartmicrobe bug to the heel of each one. Ian eventually walked it back to the hole, spooling up the gossamer fibre as it went. When it was back in the case, a different probe was sent into the hole. Original plaster fragments were mixed with a clear epoxy, and extruded, filling the hole so no suggestion of the breach remained. When Marcus Sherman opened the wardrobe tomorrow morning everything would be as before. Ian could only hope he'd put the shoes he'd worn that night into the wardrobe, rather than fling them across the room as he and Valentina tore his clothes off. Somehow, he couldn't envisage Sherman doing anything that spontaneous. From what he'd seen over the last few weeks, the man's control freakery extended to every facet of his life.

*

Angela woke to find the silvery thermal blanket had slipped off the tropical sleeping bag some time during the night. Her feet were cold, and her nose was sniffly from the chilly air. Ringlight and the borealis phantasms shivered around the inside of the mess tent where the cots had been set up, generating a perpetual unstable twilight. It seemed as though half of the camp's person-nel were snoring, or coughing, or squirming round. Nobody was at ease.

Without her grid clock telling her it was only 5 am she wouldn't have known what the time was. She sat up to pull the foil blanket back, and saw Paresh on the cot next to her. He'd been out on patrol until a couple of hours ago, and he was due out again in another three. That was all he and the Legionnaires did these days, tramp round and round Wukang with their helmet sensors straining through the rain and mist and weird light and electrical storms.

She gave him a wistful look. His strong young face was ageing by the day, with dark bruise skin round the eyes, stubble, a tautness pulling at the flesh beneath his chin. And dirt. All of them were filthy now; jungle soil lodging in their pores, encrusting nails, matting hair. No one took time in the showers. Alone, naked, unseen. Too much of a risk with the monster creeping round.

Paresh twitched and let out a slight moan. Somehow he'd twisted the one-tog sleeping bag around himself. Angela went over to him and slowly unzipped his bag, careful not to wake him. Then she snuggled into the little gap on the cot, draping her own open bag over the two of them like a narrow quilt, and tucked the foil blanket on top of that. Paresh shuddered again. She stroked her silly, troubled puppy boy as she would any child with night terrors and he nuzzled up to her. His breathing calmed and he fell into a deeper sleep. Satisfied, she put her arms protectively round him. That was when she saw Madeleine on the other side of the mess tent, who was wide awake and watching her. They looked at each other for a long moment as Angela gave the girl a lopsided grin. Madeleine eventually gave an identical grin and rested her head back down, closing her eyes.

Angela stayed perfectly still, blood pounding round her body as the wonder alone warmed her. *She knows. That smile, she's telling me she knows.* Some part of her wanted to jump out of the cot and run over to the girl. The temptation was instinctive and almost overwhelming. But if she did that, then the last twenty years would have been for nothing. Elston, just a few cots away, would know, would work out what had happened because he was a tenacious little shit. With that information, he might even go on to figure out that her body with its genetically improved

673

organs had dealt with the drugs they'd pumped into her faster and more efficiently than they had known. That she'd never completely lost control as they believed. Not that she'd lied, but she'd held back from volunteering as many truths as others undoubtedly had in that diabolical room. Shielding the one truth that gave her the will to live, to fight, to retain her sanity.

Amid the flickering light of the besieged atmosphere she tightened her arms around the puppy boy and forced herself to calm. Surprisingly, the contentment sent her back off to sleep soon after.

*

Breakfast preparations woke her an hour later. Paresh was now thoroughly entangled round her. Legionnaires around them were sitting up and grinning knowingly at her. She shrugged back at them, and nudged him awake.

Madeleine and the other general staff had been up a while. Breakfast was already under way as Angela and Paresh shambled over to the counter. Dawn's pink light was shining through the mess tent windows, exposing the sorry sight of another morning. The cots had all been crammed at one end of the mess tent, with the tables at the other, and the counters in the middle. Overhead, the roof sheet was patched and webbed, reinforcing it against any further hailstone deluges.

Good hindsight, Angela thought. She collected a big mug of tea, and picked up a package of bacon and scrambled egg on toast, adding a smaller package of grilled tomatoes and mushrooms. She and Paresh sat together, him rubbing sleep from his eyes while she opened the package seals and piled food on her plate.

'You always eat like this,' he said.

'Most important meal of the day,' she told him. 'Didn't your mom tell you?'

'Most girls I know are concerned about their weight. It never seems to bother you.'

'Is that good?'

He grinned and sipped some of his coffee. 'Sure.'

'I have a fast metabolism. I just need to exercise and the calories burn off quick.' Angela gave the mess tent door a dejected glance. 'Not that I'm getting any exercise at all right now.'

'Angela?'

'This doesn't sound good. Sure you want to ask?'

The puppy boy almost backed down, but the question was clearly chewing him up inside. 'Why are you here?'

'What do you mean?'

'You knew there's an alien here, right? So you knew we'd find it eventually.'

'I'd say it found us, actually.'

'Whatever. It's here. It's real. There was no need for you to accept Elston's offer to come back here. You could have waited a few months. Then when the expedition gets back you would have been exonerated. You knew that. You could have got a lawyer, or something.'

Angela pushed the bacon round with her fork: she was watching Madeleine behind the counter as the girl smiled bravely and handed out packages and found extra sachets of ketchup and added milk to tea and poured coffee and fended off the flirts. The girl's personnel file didn't have much detail, just the basics: where she was born, parents, school, address, credit rating, a couple of references from past employers. One of millions of GE twenty-year-olds going nowhere. Except of course she wasn't.

'So why?' Paresh persisted.

'Huh? Oh. Have you ever been to jail, Paresh?'

'No.' He shook his head emphatically.

'Then you've no idea what it's like. I was there for twenty years, Paresh. Locked up like a beast for seven thousand three hundred days. And that was for something I didn't do.'

'I'm sorry.'

'Yeah, I could have sat it out for another six months. But why the fuck should I? I've spent twenty years knowing the truth, that I'm innocent. Twenty years of being called a liar. Twenty years of being some piece of sub-human filth without rights, without a voice. Twenty years of abuse for something I didn't do. Twenty years because the government and the Norths are corrupt. Twenty fucking years I was locked up. And the alien put me there. That monster did this to me. It took everything away from me. *Everything.* All I'd known. All that I loved. Every night when I was sealed away in that tomb they called a cell, all I truly possessed was the knowledge that it was real. That it was out here laughing at me. That's what kept me sane, even though it's a very shaky kind of sane. So, yeah, I came on the expedition that's hunting it down. Because I'm going to find it, Paresh, with or without anyone else's help. And when I do, it will pay for what it's done to me. And, Paresh, don't you stand in my way when that happens, because nothing in this universe will be able to protect you if you do.' With that she got up and strode out of the mess tent.

Outside, the air was cool. Clean, too, empty of spores, which she relished, taking down deep breaths to try and calm herself. It had rained overnight, of course, leaving the plants and the ground glistening. But the shine was sullied; leaves on the bushes and vines were brown round the extremities now, frostbitten by hailstones. Over in the distance she saw Atyeo and Gillian in their armour, walking along the row of ruined tents. Gillian raised an arm in greeting.

Footsteps squelched in the mud behind her. For one blissful second she thought it might be Madeleine. But no, they were too heavy for that.

'Are you all right?'

She turned to look at Elston's concerned expression. His protective armour vest emphasized how broad-shouldered he was. For most people his presence would have been intimidating.

'Do you care?' she asked.

'That was some speech back there. I didn't hear all of it, but enough to worry me.'

'I didn't say I was going to kill it. But there's nothing in my contract that says it has to be in one piece when I turn it over to you.'

'We don't actually have a contract.'

Angela chuckled. 'I didn't think God had lawyers. The other fella's got them all, hasn't he?'

'I'm just making sure you don't do anything stupid, is all.'

'Thanks for the interest, but I keep telling you, I'm capable of looking after myself.'

'Yes. I'm aware of that.'

'At least we all survived another night. But I see the relay bandwidth is still pitiful. Did Sarvar manage to launch a replacement e-Ray?'

He sighed. 'No. They had high winds all yesterday. They'll try again today.'

'So if we do catch our alien, whatever condition it's in, how do we get it back to Abellia?'

'For that, they'll send a Daedalus. They'll send an armada of them if that's what it takes to get through.'

'Uh huh? I don't know how well your chain of command is working, but there have been rumblings.'

'Rumblings?'

'About us being stuck here. There's talk that you're not doing enough to get us out.'

'Well, I'll be making an announcement about that later today. It's going to be very clear on our mission requirement.'

'We're staying, aren't we? It's logical. We're the ones the alien is targeting, and this is what the whole expedition is about. Someone with balls is making real decisions.'

'Would you care to name who's been rumbling?'

'Karizma Wadhai. She's really not happy about being here, thinks HDA should be doing more to protect us or evacuate us.'

'I thought you'd finger Davinia.'

'Yeah, her, too.'

'Don't worry about Karizma. I'll sort that out.'

'You know what I don't understand,' Angela said.

'What's that?'

'Why we're not already dead.'

'Why are you saying that?'

'Being back here. Sometimes you forget just how big St Libra is. It takes an event like this.' She waved up at the borealis streamers smeared across the roseate sky. 'An entire star going crazy. *Then* you remember how big it is, the sheer scale of everything here. So tell me, Elston, how many aliens are living on this world do you think? A hundred million? Ten billion? There's enough room for ten times that number without even starting to overcrowd. And we have just one coming after us. One! It doesn't make much sense, does it? Where the fuck are they? Where are their villages? Their cities? Their farms?'

'The xenobiology team is convinced St Libra was bioformed. The plant genetics are too sophisticated to have evolved here. Sirius simply isn't old enough.'

'And there aren't any fossils.'

'That too.'

'So, what? This is a lone protector sentry the bioformers left behind to guard the jungle? Armed with five knives?'

He gave her a soft smile. 'I hadn't considered it in quite those terms.'

'You should have done. You flew over the algaepaddies on the same flight as me. We're screwing this planet over just like all the others we contaminate. Small wonder the protector wants to get rid of us one at a time.'

'You believe that?' Elston asked.

'I've seen it at work. It's a killing machine, one without mercy.'

'How did you survive that night? And forget the bull about fighting it.'

Angela grinned, sadly amused by how easily they slipped back into their historic roles. 'Everything I told you was the truth. One day you'll see that. If you're still alive.'

'The truth, but not all of it, right?'

'Ah, now you're starting to understand. Well done, you.'

'High praise. Thanks.'

'One other question,' she said.

'What's that?'

'Why do you think it's just targeting us, Wukang? Why not any of the others?'

'I'm not sure. It remembers you, maybe?'

Angela gave his blank face a close scrutiny. It was far too composed. He would never have lasted a second in any poker game with New Monaco residents. 'Oh I think we both know that isn't true.'

'Go back into the mess tent and put your armour vest back on, please. I need to make my morning call to Abellia. We'll be finishing the new building panels today, so I'll need the figures on our remaining raw capacity when they're done.'

Angela gave him a mocking salute. 'Aye aye, captain.'

'Colonel. I'm a colonel now.'

*

Vance went directly to his office, not even glancing back to see if Angela did as he'd asked. He was slightly unnerved by her question. Which was something he should have expected; the camp was bound to start wondering why they were being singled out. It had to be the weapon. Somehow the alien knew, or sensed it. *That or Angela really does have an accomplice; after all, somebody sabotaged the Daedalus.* Which was possibly even more unnerving.

He sat behind his desk and resisted the impulse to turn the heating on. Must conserve fuel. Condensation was beading every surface, as if a lake mist had gushed through the Qwik-Kabin during the night.

His e-i called Commissioner Passam's interface address code, and switched to a secure linkage. The response was from Jaclyn Waruts, the expedition comptroller, a GE staffer, not HDA.

'Where's Passam?' Elston asked.

'I'm sorry, Colonel, the Commissioner is unavailable.'

'Unavailable?' Vance asked incredulously. 'You mean she's dropped off-net? Where is she?'

'Her absence is temporary. I have full authority to speak for her.'

Vance considered that. Nobody was ever off-net, in this day and age it simply didn't happen. So what was she doing that was more important than receiving a call from a forward camp commander? 'I'd like to talk about some resupply flights.'

'Absolutely,' Waruts said. 'The aircrews are already reconfiguring a Daedalus to a tanker role. It should be ready in another week. We'll assess the Eclipse Mountain situation then. Hopefully they'll be able to fly by then.'

'They are HDA planes. They can fly across it now, there's enough redundancy in their systems to withstand multiple lightning strikes. We're using up a lot of raw constructing new buildings, we need more. And I'd also like additional Legionnaires. You have several squads at Abellia.'

'Colonel, I appreciate your position, but our risk assessment of the Eclipse Mountain conditions is that a flight over them is too hazardous.'

'The alien this expedition was put together to find is here, now, killing us. I need assistance. This is the HDA, our troops know they will be exposed to jeopardy during operations.'

'Your pardon, Colonel, but they signed up to fight the Zanth. That is their assumed risk, not to be sent recklessly into hazardous weather.'

'And the hazard we face?'

'Colonel, you've accessed the same reports from the Newcastle police that I have. The North murder there was the result of an inter-company fight. If you want your people to be safe, I suggest you confine Angela Tramelo to quarters and find out who her accomplice is.'

'What's left of our quarters are scattered across the mud. I need some help here.'

'A situation team is drawing up long-term emplacement protocols for all the forward camps. We'll be sending them to you in a couple of days; they'll explain how to maximize your existing resources.'

'I am fully aware we're staying here. But if I'm going to keep this mission together and functional, you're going to have to find a way of getting equipment, fuel, and supplies to me. All you have to do is fly a Daedalus around the western end of the Eclipse Mountains to get it to Sarvar. They certainly have the range to do that. Once it's at Sarvar it can just ship cargo out to us without your *risk*. I know the existing stockpile there is sufficient to keep it operating for a month if necessary.'

'That is an option we're actively considering. But no decision can be taken until the Commissioner has conferred with HDA command.'

'When will she be back on-net?'

'Soon, Colonel, I assure you. Hopefully before the end of the day.'

'I want to know as soon as she is. I want her to call me.'

'Of course.'

Vance watched Waruta's icon shrink from his grid. 'Get me Vermekia,' he told his e-i.

'We don't know where Passam is,' Vermekia said.

'We're the AIA, we know where everybody is.'

'I'll need to talk to our people at Abellia. It won't take long.'

'What about getting a Daedalus back to Sarvar? The western route round the side of the mountains should be safe enough.'

'Theoretically, yes, but that's a long way round; the e-Ray can't quite see where the range finishes. If anything does go wrong, the crew will be beyond range of the helicopters at Edzell or Sarvar.'

'I've got a hostile alien roaming round out here. From our understanding of the plants, it could well be the forward scout for a whole species. Dear Lord, this is what the HDA exists for.'

'I know. Listen, Vance, as soon as you verify existence I can get help to you inside of an hour, okay. The General himself will authorize a war gateway to Wukang. We can drop fifty Daedalus into your airspace. You're not isolated, and we haven't forgotten you. Just get us the proof.'

'All right. No one likes being bait, you know.'

'I understand. We appreciate what you're doing out there.'

*

After she'd put her armour vest back on and finished her lukewarm breakfast, Angela went over to the microfacture team. Their shack had been extended with a patchwork of thick sheeting and composite panels, two days' work for the ingenious minds of the microfacture team, growing their domain mushroom-fashion. She pushed aside a heavy flap and went inside. It was noticeably warmer with the two main print extruders running constantly. They were churning out battleship-grey hexagonal panels one and a half metres in diameter, with clever stud-locks along the edges to fasten them together.

Karizma Wadhai and Ophelia Troy who made up the microfacture team had been joined by Wukang's pilots and aircrew, who were currently redundant and had a wealth of technical expertise to contribute. Ever since the hailstones trashed the tents, they'd all been working on constructing replacement accommodation. Elston didn't want the camp to be on the retreat, to make do; huddling under a patched-up tent drained them of confidence, turned them into victims. Their mission couldn't be conducted on those terms.

Ophelia Troy had designed the panels. The lock-studs had needed some tweaking, but the panels could now be clicked together quickly and easily to form simple igloo-like domes.

There was another hour of production, with the hexagons sliding out of the extruders to be stacked with the rest, before Karizma announced they had enough to build the first five domes. Angela joined the work party.

She had to admit it, Elston had been right. It felt good to be doing something constructive. With her armour vest on while she worked, she became almost as warm as she had been before the sunspot outbreak, though thankfully the humidity was considerably reduced. She and Tork Ericson worked as a pair, lifting the hexagons into place for the dome building crew to snap the

682

lock-studs together. They weren't heavy, which was part of the problem – they caught the wind easily, and their size made manoeuvring awkward; the pair of them had to strain to wrestle them into place.

Despite that, the second dome was in place by midday; five metres across, with an entrance archway that was due to have inner and outer curtain doors, sealable against the wind and rain. A team armed with brushes began to slap epoxy glue on the outside of the first dome, ready for some salvaged squares of pv tent sheeting to be stuck over. Olrg Dorchev and Leif Davdia began the finicky job of wiring them to batteries, and laying cable to the camp's main fuel cells.

'No windows,' Angela realized, squinting up at the apex of the second dome which Ravi and Chris Fiadeiro had hammered into place, cursing with every blow – the lock-studs were supposed to make assembly easy, a child's model kit, Karizma promised.

'There's a raw combination that can do transparent at the strength we need,' Ophelia told her. 'But we don't have much of it. Doesn't matter, the domes are just for sleeping in, and no windows means we'll keep this damn borealis light out.'

Angela and Tork moved on to the newly laid floor of the fourth dome, itself a grid of the ubiquitous hexagons. She quickly took off her armoured vest and long-sleeved shirt, then pulled the vest back on over her T-shirt. Sweat gleamed on her skin, cutting channels through the dirt. She could feel it on her face, too, and grinned. Once, she had employed someone whose sole job it was to keep her skin in perfect condition, with oils and massage and monitored UV exposure. Once. In someone else's life long ago. Angela couldn't even remember her dermatologist's name, nor what she'd looked like. With Tork, they hefted another of the big hexagons and held it where Darwin Sworowski indicated. It *clunked* into the edge of the base, and Darwin shoved a triangle into the gap at the side.

They'd got the first two rows of hexagons into place when Elston called everyone to lunch. Angela didn't protest. Red Sirius was invisible now, isolated behind a dense low cloud front that was sliding in from the north-west, bringing stronger, cooler gusts with it. Always the sound of thunder grumbled over the vast landscape as threads of lightning flickered along the far horizon. She needed the break, and that heavy bank of cloud wasn't going to be good news. She could envisage them finishing off the last of the domes in the pounding rain of a real St Libra monsoon.

Mohammed, Leora, Paresh, and Lieutenant Botin himself were slogging round another eternal circuit of the perimeter while the rest of the camp slipped into the mess tent. Elston set up a ringlink to them as he stood up and called for everyone's attention.

'HDA has officially cancelled the Zanthswarm alert. Those sensor satellites they pushed through didn't find any abnormal quantum fluctuations in the Sirius system. However, the sunspot outbreak is continuing. Apparently, that means we now have to consider preparing for much colder weather than we were expecting.'

'How long until we get an evac flight?' Karizma asked.

'This is a fully functional HDA camp, part of a large and expensive HDA expedition that came here with one purpose,' Elston replied. 'We now have explicit proof the alien we're seeking is close by. We will not be running away from that simply because the weather turned unpleasant; I will not despoil the memories of those who have given their lives getting us where we are.' At that he stared at Karizma until she lowered her own gaze.

'This creature will be tracked down and its origin and purpose determined,' he continued. 'I'm hoping for some resupply flights from Sarvar before too long, but you can clear any thoughts of flying back home right out of your heads. We're here for the long haul, people, make no mistake about that. Now, the domes should be completed by tonight. Tomorrow we are going to re-establish some order and security to this camp. After that, our mission will move forwards again. That is all.'

There were a lot of silent meaningful glances flashing round the table where Angela sat as people resumed their meal. She was guilty of joining in.

'That'll shut Karizma up,' Gillian said quietly.

'Don't count on it,' Josh challenged. 'Did you see? The civilians were almost in tears when our colonel gave us the good news. We'll be eating shit stew for supper tonight.'

'How are they going to get resupplies in?' Omar asked. 'The Daedaluses are all back at Abellia.'

'I talked to Ravi,' Angela said. 'They can probably fly round the western end of the Eclipse Mountains between Edzell and Sarvar. Less dangerous.'

'Do we even know where the western end is?' Atyeo asked.

'Dunno. Ask the AAV team,' Angela grunted. She finished her asparagus soup and walked outside. For the first time in days the irritating vulgar pulsations of the borealis streamers were gone, blotted out by the continent of murky cloud that had slithered in from the north-west. The landscape was reflecting an unhealthy salmon-pink shade that came percolating through the cloudbase. And it was calm. The wind had died away in the short time she'd been in the mess tent.

Angela rubbed her bare arms, finding goosebumps had risen. Slowly, and with an awful sense of foreboding, she tipped her head back to stare up into the strangely out-of-focus cloud. There was no thunder any more, only emptiness as the atmosphere absorbed all sound.

'No,' she whispered in astonishment at the impossibility.

Snow had begun to fall gently out of St Libra's disfigured sky.

*

They finally cracked open the bottle of Brennivin when they reached Ian's flat that evening after work. Sid thought it was worth celebrating. Even Eva agreed, taking a full shot glass from Ian before settling back against the lounge wall.

'I'm sorry about Ruckby,' she said. 'The security at his place was just too good. I was picking up mesh emissions from outside.

He must have covered every wall with smartdust. It's like a digital fortress in there.'

'Aye, pet, don't fret it,' Ian said. 'I got Sherman, Sid got Boz, and between us we tagged five vehicles. If that ain't enough, I don't know what is.'

'It'll do,' Sid agreed. 'We don't want to push our luck. I'm thinking we might even reduce our original observation programs. I don't want to spook them now.'

'I'll sort that out tonight,' Ian said as he hopped up on the counter. He took a sip of the Brennivin and tried not to grimace.

'So how long do we leave it before we download?' Eva asked. 'Is there a capacity limit?'

'Theoretically, the microbe bugs will harvest their bodymesh emissions for about four months before they reach their limit,' Sid said. 'Of course we don't have that long. I reckon about ten days' worth of calls should give us a proper picture of what the hell they're involved in. Maybe a fortnight. I'd like longer.'

'Will they catch the download?' Eva asked.

'Hopefully not, but that's part of the risk.'

'O'Rouke will crap on us from on high if he finds out what we've done, going behind his back and all,' Ian said.

'Screw him,' Sid said. 'We've got the HDA behind us if we get a result. Besides, O'Rouke is on his way out.'

'Really?' Eva asked. 'How do you know?'

'Ralph turned him down flat when he asked if Ernie and the others could just be shipped out to a penal colony; said they're here to defend all humans, not act like his private Gestapo.'

'So?' Ian asked.

'So I had to send our files to legal. The lawyers O'Rouke retained say we've certainly got a case against the five suspects, but there's a problem using evidence supplied by the HDA.'

'It's a government agency operating inside its remit,' Eva said. 'Even if we don't like its methods.'

'Yes, but to prove it was a legitimate involvement, we'll have to explain to the court how our first suspect was an alien monster.

Market Street is going to look ridiculous. Worse, it could be played that we're protecting the Norths.'

'That's bollocks, man.'

'Aye, but it's going to be said. The unlicensed sites are going to have a field day, not to mention conspiracy theorists. The whole Bartram North case will get reopened. It'll be a high-order crapfest.'

'How long before the files go up to the Prosecution Bureau?' Eva asked.

Sid grinned. 'With O'Rouke calling in markers, Legal can delay it for a week or so. Statutory limit for internal review is nine days.'

'You're evil,' she laughed. 'The same time we pull in all Sherman's calls.'

'Aye, if there's anything there we might just be able to throw O'Rouke a lifeline. How grateful do you think he'd be?'

'Sod gratitude,' Ian said. 'How much will he pay for it? Crap on it man, you could be the next Commissioner.'

'I'm just back off suspension.'

'Aye, but we'd really get those promotions. Probably a couple of grades.'

Sid downed the rest of his Brennivin in one. Pulled a face. 'Let's see what Sherman's up to before we make any plans.'

*

After the other two had left, Ian sat on the bed and put on his netlens glasses. The case's secure network was still open, Sid had made sure of that. On a technicality, they didn't have to close it down completely before Legal sent the files up to Prosecution. Until then it was still registered as open. He used Vance Elston's authorization codes to worm back into the station network, and begin harvesting.

Tallulah Packer was twenty-five years old, though her face was so sweet she could pass for a good three years younger. She was living a little too high, like every other executive in Newcastle.

Her bank accounts showed she earned a good salary – more than him – but each month she spent more than she earned. Clothes, shoes, evenings out, trips, rent on the St James apartment; her main account had run up quite a deficit, which the bank didn't complain about because of the magic Northumberland Interstellar account code on the monthly income payments – and the interest it charged her.

There were no medical bills, he saw delightedly – that amazing figure and beauty was all one hundred per cent natural. She did have membership at Finely Toned, a spa in the St James single-town, but that was all.

His e-i slotted a priority news icon into his grid, which he reluctantly opened. Tallulah was far more interesting than anything else in the world.

Eighteen major GE news sites were covering Commissioner Charmonique Passam returning through the Newcastle gateway. Unlicensed sites factored in their information, that she'd flown back from Abellia on a private HyperLear and that every one of her staff had been left behind. Reports of snow from Abellia were confirmed with video shots of white flakes drifting to ground, kissing the lush tropical plants and turning to slush on the roads.

'Aye, you complete cow,' Ian murmured as Passam stood up at a podium which had the GE Alien Bureau seal on the front. Her smile was as brittle as antique porcelain. 'I'm happy to announce that the St Libra geogenetic expedition has been a complete success. Through the diligent, dedicated work of the forward camp science teams we have confirmed that there is no genetic variance on St Libra. No insects or animals ever evolved there. It is what we always thought, a world of beautiful and dynamic zebra botany. And I would like to thank everyone who contributed to the expedition for helping to make it the tremendous feat of accomplishment that we can all be proud of.'

Even the licensed reporters weren't going to let her get away with that. What about the sunspots, they demanded, what about the weather, the snow – what about the people you abandoned in the jungle?

Passam's formidable smile never faltered. 'The sunspot out-break was a simply astonishing coincidence. A natural phenom-enon of the star which has only just revealed itself to us, but one that has historical validity. And my colleagues at the forward camps have not been abandoned, as you disgracefully put it. The forward camps have adequate supplies and emergency rations to continue operations for months without resupply. The personnel will of course be airlifted out as soon as there is a break in the weather. As you know, criminal elements on St Libra severely restricted our Daedalus flights, killing the flight crew in an atro-cious act of terrorism unprecedented in modern times. If any hardship falls upon the forward bases, these fanatics must take sole responsibility. Thank you.' Passam walked away from the podium, to be shielded from any further questions by a herd of assistants and press officers.

'Arseholing bitch,' Ian concluded. He put a block on transnet news, and returned to his harvesting.

Boris Attenson was actually thirty-four according to govern-ment records, not the thirty-one his public profile claimed. A significant monthly payment went to a private and discreet clinic for follicle regeneration. Ian grinned at that. His expenses were also interesting. Plenty of money spent late at night in the restaurants and clubs of London, Brussels, Berlin, and Paris – signed off by his bosses as legitimate client entertainment costs.

The next part was tougher, cross-indexing bodymesh emis-sions with local cell records, with e-i coding. It took an hour, but Ian was in his element. By the end he had Boris's secondary accounts in a Venezuelan bank. The amount of money was impressive. Every month Boris spent the equivalent of Ian's salary on vices and luxuries for himself. Ian wasn't envious about the money; there were always rich pricks like Boris pissing their life away, and always would be, that was simply how the universe worked. What was intolerable was him taking Tallulah down that route with him. Tallulah who would be so much better off in Ian's arms. In his bed.

Ian checked through the payments, and linked them with

Boris's location. Experience again gave him an edge, knowing the signs that no AI could correlate. It was eight days ago, the week before Tallulah was questioned; Boris was staying in a London hotel on the South Bank, and there was one last late-night purchase. Ian immediately pulled the hotel security files, knowing what he was going to find even before it materialized in the netglasses. As he expected, there was Boris climbing out of a taxi at quarter to one in the morning. And there was the girl who wasn't Tallulah, smartly dressed, young and pretty, with the neutral-face boredom of everybody whose self-esteem was non-existent, waiting for this interminable night to be over, the same as every other night, waiting for the john to spend himself, bracing herself to listen to the I-love-my-girlfriend speech afterwards, delivered with guilt and shame, the hunger for sympathy and understanding. She'd give Boris that, he'd paid a lot for it.

Ian froze the image of Boris disappearing into his hotel room, toxed up, almost indifferent to the hooker. The end of another day in the wonderful world of high finance, closing the deal, screwing your rivals.

'Not any more, pal,' Ian told the image.

Tuesday 2nd April 2143

It was the screams which brought everyone running as fast as their armour and multi-layered clothing would let them, not the bodymesh's medical alert. Screams of panic and pain always cut clean to the centre of a human brain, demanding attention and response. This was no exception, its siren call amplified by the nervy atmosphere that gripped Wukang, the fear the monster was among them once again.

At the time, Angela was helping carry a load of food packets from one of the 350DL pallets over to the mess tent. She and Roarke Kulwinder from the xenobiology team had spent quite a lot of the last three days bringing food in out of the snow. He was a cheery man in his late thirties, who was always linking to send her pictures of his wife and two small children; they were about his only topic of conversation. Once again he was telling her about the woodland den he'd built for the kids last summer when the screams began, hysterical, rising and falling as the victim desperately sucked down breath. Angela got a fix on the origin, which was immediately backed up by her e-i; a medical alert was coming from Luther Katzen's bodymesh, about seventy metres away on the other side of the mess tent. She and Roarke stared at each other for a moment, then they both dropped the packages and started running as best they could in their bulging clothes.

It had snowed every day at Wukang since the first flakes

appeared last Wednesday. The ground temperature was too high for snow to settle, though, and the flakes had turned to slush. Shallow streams of icy water had meandered across Wukang, soaking the detritus embedded in the mud following the hailstone tumult. There were tide rings of rubbish twirling sluggishly round the vehicles and domes and engineering shacks as the filthy water shunted lighter items about. Inventory became close to impossible. Angela and Forster faced a constant struggle to find items for the microfacture team.

Thursday was spent struggling to assemble the final pair of accommodation domes as snow swarmed through the camp. With six in total, the forty-eight remaining members of camp Wukang were crammed in eight to a dome. Cots salvaged from the tents were squashed up tight, leaving very little free floorspace. Hooks and bands were fixed to the highest hexagonal panels, and kitbags hung up like massive, dowdy larval sacks. With light coming from lanterns wired up to the salvaged tent pv sheets and boosted by cables from the camp's main fuel cells, the interior of each one was as gloomy as it was foetid. There was some warmth in there at night with so many bodies sharing such a confined volume, but that just simmered the smell of unwashed skin.

Once the domes were complete, the microfacture team set about producing thicker, warmer clothes for the camp personnel. Long parkas were the preference, big enough to be worn outside the armour vests; most people matched them up with quilted, waterproof trousers. Hats were also ejected from 3D printers, along with scarves and gloves. They weren't the best cold weather clothing ever made, but they did give people a degree of protection from the bewildering winter.

By Saturday the relentless fall of snow and constantly dropping air temperature had finally sucked the last residual heat from the soil and plants; ground temperature fell below zero. The snow no longer melted; instead it started to build up. Puddles and rivulets that had formed their own flat marshy tributary network across Wukang solidified to precarious slicks of ice. Leaves on the smaller ferns and vines turned to mush as their cells froze to death, and they began to fall amid the flakes, adding a dangerously slippery layer of organic slime to the snow. Since Sunday, over half a metre of snow had descended on Wukang. It had to be scraped regularly from the mess tent roof and the engineering shacks, lest the weight rip the straining sheets open. Paths were tramped down. Vehicles were started daily and driven around so they didn't get snowed in. The kind of snow dumped on them varied; most nights it came as sand-like granules, getting everywhere, by day it was big sticky flakes that adhered to every part of the jungle's trees and bushes, turning them into an alpine frost-forest. That same clingy snow smothered the surface of the camp's equipment, buildings, and vehicles alike, cloaking the smartdust meshes with equal severity, so their reception was blocked across most spectra including visible light which powered them, eliminating their sensor function, wrecking links, degrading the camp's net further.

Paths had been tramped down, but compacted snow was slippery, especially when it was mixed with the organic mucus of disintegrating leaves. Angela had to be careful as she closed in on Luther. There'd been enough falls over the last few days, people winding up in the camp's clinic with gashed hands and badly bruised legs. She rounded the side of the mess tent, and saw over a dozen people running across the rumpled white landscape. Her grid tagged Paresh, Sergeant Raddon, and Omar among them, holding their Heckler carbines high, shouting at everyone else to stay back.

Everyone was converging on a Land Rover Tropic which was skewed across the churned-up sludge track outside the administration Qwik-Kabin, its headlight beams illuminating the moderate fall of snow with clear white light. The driver's door was open. A figure she recognized as Olrg Dorchev from the camp systems team was scurrying towards the back of the Tropic, stomping his way through a high mound of unblemished snow. Luther Katzen was lying there, still screaming, clutching at his leg as he rocked back and forth.

Then people closed in round him, Paresh and Omar waving frantically at them to slow down and back off. By the time Angela arrived, Luther had quietened down; now he was groaning in pain. She could see blood staining his dark-green trousers, splattering onto the snow. The blood showing as near-black in the pacified pink light of Sirius. The leg didn't look right at all. Something about the angle, the way the knee and foot were twisted.

'I'm sorry, man, I'm sorry,' Olrg was moaning. 'You just came out at me.'

Angela winced at that, looking back at the Tropic. Luther must have slipped on the ice. Judging from the angle of the vehicle, Olrg had tried to turn away – too late. Bound to happen in these conditions, if people—

Then she smelt it. *Mint.* The air was cold, her nose had chilled down, but she still knew that smell. Her eyes watered up. 'Shit, oh shit.'

Mark Chitty and Doc Coniff had arrived, lugging their field kit. They knelt beside Luther, pushing Olrg out of the way. A circle had formed round them, people looking on grimly, thanking their deity it wasn't them lying there in the blood and vomit, willing the medics on to work a standard twenty-second-century first aid miracle.

Angela's e-i quested a link to Paresh. 'Stay alert,' she told him. 'This wasn't an accident.'

A frown creased up his face. 'What?'

'Keep a look out,' she insisted, pushing her way through the passive onlookers. 'Don't let your guard down.' She got annoyed looks, irate looks. Ignored them all as she barged up to Elston. 'Breathe in,' she told him.

His concerned expression turned to ire. 'What?'

'Breathe in through your nose, right now! Tell me what you smell.'

Further admonishment died as he realized what she was saying. He stood very still and drew down a long breath, sniffing. She saw the moment he smelt it, saw the shock appear on his face. 'Nobody move,' he ordered. 'Legionnaires, assume a guard position around us. Scan the camp, please. This is a combat lockdown situation. Everybody not at the accident remain where you are, link your position to Lieutenant Botin immediately.'

Luther's whimpering was the only sound as the Legionnaires on patrol moved in, circling the group. More armour-suited figures moved in the distance, heading for the mess tent and the shacks; weapons active, small ruby laser fans sweeping through the silent snowfall.

'Sample it,' Angela said. 'Fast.' Already the scent was fading, scattered by soft drifting snowflakes and icy gusts.

Elston nodded, and opened a microlink to Marvin. A minute later the door on mobile biolab-1 unlocked and slid back. Marvin hurried over. When he arrived he went into a huddle with Elston, and the two of them walked over to the patch of snow where the Tropic struck Luther. Marvin started waving a long plastic sampling wand round. Elston was studying the ground.

'I want everyone back into the mess tent,' Lieutenant Botin announced. 'Corporal, you and Leora will accompany the medic team back to the clinic.'

Angela started walking back to Elston.

'That includes you, Tramelo,' Botin said sharply.

'You need me out here,' she said.

'Okay,' Elston said reluctantly. 'But you do as you're told.'

'Sure. But hurry, it can't be far away.'

Elston bent down to talk to Luther. 'What happened?'

'Easy on him,' Dr Coniff said sharply.

'That can wait,' Elston snapped back. 'Luther, what happened? Concentrate. Did you slip?'

Luther's face was shining with perspiration. Through the pain he tried to focus, to remember. 'I . . . I don't know. I thought there was someone there. Perhaps. Oh shit it hurts.'

'Did they push you?'

Mark Chitty cut away the last of the trousers, revealing mangled flesh and exposed bone of the shattered hip. Luther howled as a couple of instruments were applied.

'Try and stay still,' the doc urged. 'I know it hurts, but we've got to sheathe it now to get you back to the clinic.'

'How bad?' Luther grunted between clenched teeth.

'Don't worry, I can set the bone and realign the muscle tissue. Now keep quiet.' At that she glared at Elston.

'Olrg?' Elston demanded. 'Did you see anyone with him? Any thing?'

'I didn't even see him, not really, not until he stumbled in front of the Tropic. He was on the side of the track. I braked, but the wheels didn't grip properly. I wasn't going fast, really, Colonel. I wasn't.'

'I know, but think, you must have noticed Luther, even if you weren't concentrating on him directly. Was he alone?'

'Oh dear God . . .' Olrg was looking down at Luther, frantic at the suffering he'd caused. 'Maybe. I thought – there might have been someone beside him. It was snowing. I was focused on the track.'

'Send me your visual memory,' Elston said.

It was like he'd slapped Olrg. For a moment the man was in as much pain as Luther. 'Sir, I didn't have my cache running, sir.'

'Oh for—' Elston glared. 'I thought I made protocol quite clear?'

'Yes, sir, you did sir. It's just that the grid makes it difficult to see in snow. And . . .' He gestured round at the big flakes that filled the air.

'Then just cancel the grid. You don't close down your whole iris smartcells function. Come on! This isn't gateway science.'

'Yes, sir.'

'Get back to the mess tent. I'll deal with you later.'

Angela watched Olrg walk off into the swirling of snow, shoulders hunched, head down. The wind was picking up, she saw, the snow getting thicker. Her own grid showed her the Legionnaires' tags as they spiralled out across the camp. They wouldn't find anything, she knew, they hadn't before in clear weather with Wukang's sensors fully operational. 'Did you catch anything?' she asked Marvin.

'Inconclusive,' he said. 'I'm picking up micro-quantities of St Libra's usual atmospheric contaminants, but no specific molecular signature stands out. It's just the residuals of the jungle spores.'

'Angela was right,' Elston said. 'I smelt it, too. That thing was here.'

They all looked down at Luther. Chitty had managed to cover the damaged hip and thigh with some kind of thick sleeve, while the doc had got an IV collar attached to his neck.

'He was lucky Olrg is actually quite a good driver,' Marvin said. 'It could have been a lot worse.'

Angela took one corner of the stretcher, with Elston, Marvin and Chitty taking the others. Lieutenant Botin himself provided their escort, while the doc fussed over Luther the whole time. It was only a couple of hundred metres to the clinic, but every step twisted up her alarm. The gloomy pink light filled the camp with desultory shadows. *It* could be lurking in any one of them. And the snow was getting worse. There could be an army of them out there, obscured by the chill dark silence. Waiting. Her mind had no trouble filling the dim void around her with the monsters, all of them flexing their blade fingers, ready to resume the battle she'd fled from twenty years ago.

A rectangle of white light spilled out from the clinic's open door. The other paramedic, Juanitar Sakur, hurried down the Qwik-Kabin's steps to help them carry Luther into the assessment centre. Angela stood back once they'd got the sedated catering supervisor on the gurney, and Coniff started working on him. She found it strange being in the clinic with its warm air and bright white light. It was an enclave of real life. Her fear of what lurked outside its thin composite walls abated. Which was foolish, she knew.

'Now what?' Angela said. 'You can't keep the Legionnaires out there. The network's failing, we don't have a sensor mesh working that's worth a damn. If that thing can walk into the camp in what's left of our daylight and push one of us under a Land Rover, then it can leap out on them without any trouble.'

'I am aware of our tactical situation,' Elston said calmly. 'Lieutenant, the AAV team report that this snowstorm is going to be the worst yet. The e-Ray weather radar is showing some bad cloud and wind approaching us. We have about an hour and a half to get everyone inside and batten down the hatches.'

'Yes, sir,' Botin said.

'How bad?' Angela asked.

'We're facing blizzard conditions,' Elston said. 'So each dome will have to become self-sufficient for the duration. Angela, I want you to organize food allocation for everyone. We'll ride this out in the clinic and the domes. Marvin, get the biolabs driven over to the domes, and park them close; the xenobiology team can live in them for the time being. It'll free up a little space inside the domes, too, which will be more pleasant for everybody. Everything else, we'll shut down.'

'A blizzard?' Angela said. 'Son-of-a-bitch, we're already half a metre deep in snow.'

'I noticed.'

*

It was a frantic hour. Elston wouldn't let anyone outside without a Legionnaire escort, which restricted the amount of preparation they were able to make. Even so they managed to kit out the domes for a couple of days' independence. Food packages were doled out. Power cables from the main fuel cells checked. Heaters the microfacture team had printed out were powered-up. Chemical toilets were taken from the latrines and installed in the domes. Data cables were unspooled and plugged into the biolabs, giving the network cells a hardline link.

In the end, Elston ordered all the ground vehicles to be driven over to the domes, and parked them in a picket ring with the two biolabs. The pilots protested that nothing was being done to protect the helicopters, but there wasn't time to rig any kind of canopy over them.

With the xenobiology teams moving out of the domes to bunk in the biolabs, Angela had the opportunity to rearrange the dome accommodation. Even it up, Elston had told her, and give everyone a Legionnaire for protection.

'If you want me to switch domes, Lulu and I come as a pair,' Madeleine Hoque said through a link to Angela as her e-i started sending out the new lists. 'Not negotiable. The poor thing is terrified.'

'All right, I'll shift people round to make that happen.' Angela had to take a moment. It was the first time Madeleine had ever acknowledged her.

The two girls arrived at Angela's dome carrying their kitbags, escorted by Omar. They'd just finished shutting down the kitchen equipment. Snow was dripping off their parkas and trousers, forming little puddles on the panel floor.

'Jesus, that's bad weather,' Paresh said as he sealed up the inner and outer entrance curtains.

'I don't think the mess tent is going to last,' Lulu announced as she unzipped her parka. 'The snow is already making the roof sag. It's going to rip again.'

'This kind of weather, we can live without it,' Paresh said.

'As long as the fuel cells keep working,' Omar said, helping Madeleine hang her kitbag on a ceiling hook.

'Will they?' a nervous Lulu asked.

'They'll be fine,' Angela said. 'Olrg told me they're designed to keep operating in conditions a lot more hostile than this. I'm more worried about the e-Rays. If you check the telemetry, the closest one is showing some flight system problems. Hardly surprising, there's a lot of electrical activity in these clouds.'

Lulu sank down on a cot and put her head in her hands. 'Why don't they just come and take us out of here?' she asked in a high, miserable voice.

'Hey, it's okay,' Madeleine said, sitting beside her. 'We get a break from cooking and cleaning for a day in here.' She nudged the girl. 'With two Legionnaires to protect us. Isn't that right, Omar?'

Omar gave Lulu a friendly smile. 'Nothing bad going to get in here past me and Paresh. Depend on us, we won't let you down. Know why?'

Lulu looked up at him, and sniffed loudly. 'Why?'

'We're not officers.'

She managed a weak grin.

With only five cots occupying the floor, they started organizing their expanded living space, using a couple of cots as couches, putting the circular radiant heater in the middle where they could gather round to enjoy the warmth it gave off. The air temperature lifted to the point where they could strip off their outer layers, though everyone kept their armour vest on. A curtain was rigged round the chemical toilet. Angela kept herself permanently linked to the smartdust on the entrance curtains. The meshes would warn them of anything large coming through.

Elston linked to everyone individually, checking they were okay and inside as the winds began to build. 'No one is to go outside until the blizzard is over,' he ordered. 'If you have a medical emergency, you must be accompanied by a Legionnaire to go to the clinic.'

'He's too paranoid,' Madeleine announced as she closed her microlink with Elston. 'He should ease up and let people think for themselves.'

'There's something dangerous out there,' Paresh said. 'He's worried about our safety.'

It was only the middle of the afternoon, but as she sealed up the entrance Angela had seen the last of the pink daylight abandoning the sky, so thick and oppressive were the snowclouds. They could hear the wind streaking past through the dome's thin panels, a constant background snarl, interrupted occasionally by a thump as some piece of camp equipment broke loose or toppled over. The heavy plastic sheets used to cover the entrance thrummed steadily as the wind shook them, but the seals held.

Both bright-white lanterns hanging amid the bags swung in slow arcs, sending shadows swaying across the curving walls. Right in the middle of the dome, the circular radiant heater glowed a cosy orange.

The panels were a problem, Angela soon found. The way they were printed, with fibre chains woven to give multidirectional strength, meant they were tough enough to withstand the wind and another hailstone barrage. But Karizma's team had been in a hurry, concerned with maintaining structural integrity. Not much thought had been given to thermal loading. The radiant heater set up a good convection current in the middle of the dome, but the panels were chilling down rapidly in the blizzard. Condensation began to build up, trickling down the sides to form thin slicks on the floor. After a while the droplets began to glint as ice crystals solidified. Before long, they were sitting in the middle of a diamond glitter cave as the hoar frost consolidated its grip.

Angela got out the ball of blue and green wool she'd asked Ophelia Troy to print for her, and began knitting. The fuzzy fibre was wholly synthetic, of course, but it had most of the properties of real wool. More important, when it was knitted into a hat with long earflaps like she was doing, it could breathe through the weave. The parkas and winter trousers that had quickly been printed weren't the most porous, and sweat built up in the layers underneath, which grew cold and unpleasant very quickly. It was something Karizma's people promised to review during the blizzard downtime.

'I remember my gran used to do that,' a fascinated Lulu said. 'What are you making?'

'A hat.' Angela grinned at Paresh. 'One that can fit under a helmet.'

'That's a bit of a lost art,' Madeleine said. 'I guess I know where you learned.'

'The authorities had to find something for inmates to do. There's lots of courses available for stupid activities like this in jail. I have to admit, I never thought it was something I could ever use on the outside.'

'So why did you sign up for it?' Paresh asked.

Angela held up a needle and gave him a wicked smile. 'You've no idea how useful it was getting my hands on something like this in Holloway.'

'Are you going to sue them?' Omar asked. 'I mean . . . twenty years! Holy crap.'

'If they're sensible and offer me decent compensation, I won't have to take them to court.' Angela started knitting again, the *click click click* of the needles just audible above the snarling wind and shivering entrance curtain.

'I don't think I could stand being locked up for twenty years,' Lulu said. 'Not if I hadn't done nothing wrong. What can they pay you for that? It's not right.'

'A very large amount of money,' Angela said. 'For a start.'

'And the people that put you in jail?' Omar asked. 'What about them? They must have covered up evidence. They're corrupt. They need to be taken down.'

'I really can't be assed spending time wrecking their careers, what's left of them,' Angela said. She held up the hemispherical shape she'd achieved. It just needed a rim and then the earflaps attaching. 'You see, I'll be reaching middle age when they're four hundred years dead. How does revenge get finer than that?'

'Aye, pet, how old are you really?' a rapt Lulu asked.

Angela winked. 'Enough to know better.'

*

After she finished the hat, and made sure it did fit under Paresh's helmet, Angela started work on a scarf for herself. There would be gloves next, she decided. Then a big pair of bed socks. After that, she'd consider taking requests.

The ice crystals coating the walls of the dome were starting to grow like miniature stalagmites. Each time someone walked across the frozen floor, their boots would scrape off a fine layer of glittering crystals. Thunder started to resonate outside during the evening, the discharges muffled by the weight of fast snow raging past outside.

Roarke Kulwinder, sitting in the cab of mobile biolab-2, let everyone ride his vision, seeing the lightning flashes erupting behind the smear of white motion that had engulfed the vehicle. The data cables connecting the domes and vehicles together were holding well, allowing Elston, Botin, and Sergeant Raddon to monitor everyone's bodymesh constantly. Sensor meshes in each dome were also linked to monitor programs, making sure the monster didn't get in.

'It'd need inertial navigation to find us in this,' Omar concluded after watching the blizzard through Roarke's eyes for a few minutes.

They made supper at seven o'clock, heating packets of pork stew and tea sachets in the microwave. Angela caught Madeleine watching her several times, just as Madeleine had caught her trying to sneak glances across the dome. Nothing was said between them. Any outside observer would assume they didn't much care for each other, Angela thought wryly. She'd seen it in Holloway often enough; the silent challenges, rigid politeness in public. Then when the guards had their backs turned it was either fight, get fucked, or fly over the wall. Holloway never had a wall any inmate could reach.

Everyone settled down at nine o'clock after another sachet of tea. Angela dressed in two layers of thin trousers and long-sleeved T-shirts before topping off with her one sweater and jamming a woolly hat (her first effort) over her head. She managed to get three socks on each foot before worming into her sleeping bag. Omar took the first watch, allowing Paresh to get onto his cot beside Angela. They grinned at each other, content with the proximity. The lanterns were turned down to a glimmer, with the radiant heater still glowing bright cherry-red in the middle of the dome, sending a heat shimmer mushrooming through the air above it. The encrustation of ice crystals seemed to glow even brighter in the gloom. Outside, the wind and thunder continued their battle. The taut entrance curtains played their discordant violin harmonic incessantly. Angela just knew she'd never get to sleep.

Wednesday 3rd April 2143

Angela was woken by a hand shoving hard against her shoulder, shaking her vigorously. Even then, she could barely make it up to consciousness. When she did force her eyes open she had a splitting headache. 'What?' she croaked.

Madeleine was on her knees beside the cot, her face pale, straining to suck down air as if she was on top of the Eclipse Mountains.

'Air,' Madeleine groaned back. 'Carbon dioxide. Killing us.'

Shit. Angela searched round the dome, seeing Omar lying face down next to the radiant heater. The wind and thunder were still howling outside. She made a supreme effort to struggle out of the sleeping bag. Madeleine was crawling towards the entrance curtain, every movement a terrible effort. She fell more than once. Angela almost blacked out again as she began her own squirming. The two of them arrived at the vibrating sheet, and managed to prise open the seal at the bottom. An airtight seal so the freezing wind and snow didn't come billowing in.

Angela heaved, gulping down the clean air which had been caught in the small gap between the inner and outer sheets. For a moment her head began to clear. She knew the clarity and strength wouldn't last. She swayed up onto her knees, grabbed the outside curtain and tugged.

A blast of freezing snow-saturated air knocked her backwards.

The snow banked up against the outer curtain avalanched into the dome, engulfing her legs. It was *cold*, painfully so. The lanterns swung wildly, clashing against the rocking kitbags. Anything loose took flight. The curtain round the chemical toilet ripped free and joined the mini-cyclone. Weird flares of light amid the deluge of snow stabbed into the dome for a second then vanished.

'Full broadcast alert,' Angela shouted at her e-i. 'Wake everyone.' She kicked her legs out of the snow.

Paresh and Lulu were thrashing about in their sleeping bags as the wind tipped them onto the floor. The heater had toppled onto a semi-conscious Omar. He wailed as its glowing red surface seared into his cheek and ear. Flesh sizzled, jetting out puffs of smoke. He jerked round instinctively. Another lightburst from outside provided macabre illumination for the scene.

'What's happening?' Elston demanded.

Angela struggled to her feet. Madeleine was already trying to secure the outer curtain, but there was so much snow on the floor she could only close the top half. The dazzling light flared once again, sending blue-white rays prising their way through the gaps.

'Carbon dioxide build-up.' Angela peered up through the wavering light and gyrating kitbags inside the dome. There were three grilles on the apex panels, designed to let air through and keep rain out. They were covered in hoar frost like the rest of the panels, but that shouldn't be enough to block them. 'The grilles don't work. You need to warn everyone.'

Paresh made it out of his sleeping bag; he was groggy, fighting the debilitating headache, but got the heater upright, switching it off. Its rosy glow faded. The lanterns were turned up to full brightness. Lulu was still in her sleeping bag on the floor, crying like a baby, her wailing as loud as the wind and thunder.

Angela helped Madeleine close the outer curtain, sealing it down to the top of the half-metre-high pile of snow. Her fingers had just about lost all feeling by the time they started on the inner curtain. The flesh was white, and she was shaking badly.

'Thanks,' she said to Madeleine through chittering teeth. 'How did you know?'

'My smartcells warned me,' Madeleine panted back. 'The medical suite monitors my breathing.'

'Right.' Angela didn't know what else to say, maybe something about how good that medical suite was. But no minimum-wage Geordie catering girl would ever have smartcells like that. So she kept quiet and gripped the girl's shoulder tightly; the first time she'd ever touched her. Her eyes watered up. 'We're alive,' she said with a desperate smile.

'And we're going to stay that way,' Madeleine said.

They looked at each other for a long moment.

'Need some help,' Paresh said. 'First aid kit, someone.'

'Got it,' Angela said. She rose unsteadily to her feet and told her e-i to find the box's smartdust tag. The dome was a complete mess. Her grid showed her an overlay, with a purple icon pulsing on top of Lulu's cot. She shoved it aside and picked up the first aid box.

The side of Omar's face was bad. His skin was charred, cracking open to show bloody red flesh below. Paresh bumped a painkiller sac on his neck, and started spraying the burn surface with a nuflesh foam.

Angela started to monitor the camp's links. Four of the other five domes had responded; all of them were suffering from carbon dioxide build-up; all reporting their grilles were blocked; some of the occupants had already lapsed into unconsciousness. However, with the alarm raised, the entrance curtains were opened, allowing gales of fresh air inside. Without an answer from the sixth dome, Leora Fawkes, who was on duty in biolab-1, went outside with Roarke Kulwinder, the two of them holding on to each other as they forced their way through the blizzard to the dome and unsealed the outer curtain. They found the five people inside – Josh Justic, the pilots Lorelei and Juan-Fernando, Bastian 2North, and Olrg Dorchev – all unconscious but alive.

By then, Atyeo and Ophelia Troy had gone out to inspect their dome and find out what had gone wrong. They reported that the wind had driven powdery snow into the protective vents on top of the dome, blocking them. No air could get in through the grilles. It was easy enough to clear, but it had to be done by hand – from the outside.

Medical reports weren't so promising. Lorelei, Olrg, and Winn Melia, Chris Fiadeiro, Sergeant Raddon, and Forster Wardele were all suffering bad CO_2 poisoning; then there was Omar with his ruined face. Dr Coniff wanted her paramedics to check the poisoning cases. She also asked for Omar to be brought to the clinic where she could treat his burns and make sure his eye wasn't damaged. Elston and Botin arranged for Antrinell and Darwin Sworowski to pull a stretcher like a sledge, which they'd use to take Omar over to the clinic. They'd be escorted by Botin and Gillian Kowalski, who'd return with Chitty and Sakur. The two paramedics would go round the domes, examining the worst poisoning cases.

That just left the blocked air vents. Elston didn't want the curtain doors open, that offered no one protection against the ferocious blizzard, and little warning should the monster arrive. His order was for a Legionnaire to pair up with someone from each dome; together they'd go out and clear the vents. They'd monitor how fast the snow built up again, and repeat the clearing process every couple of hours. It wasn't pleasant, but better than CO_2 poisoning or being directly exposed to the brutal elements for however long the blizzard lasted.

Angela paired up with Paresh. She pulled on her parka in the glacial air which now filled the dome, numb hands taking a long time to zip up the front. She hunted round for her boots, while a weepy Lulu was comforted by Madeleine. The gloves she'd used the day before were still damp, and starting to stiffen as they froze. She righted the heater and turned it back on, holding her hands above it. The moisture started to thaw dripping down onto the orange circle to hiss and boil while chilblains gnawed at her fingers. While she was preparing to go outside again, Madeleine was helping a teary Lulu into her parka. Paresh upped Omar's painkiller dosage, and wrapped him up in his own sleeping bag.

Hands began to pull at the bottom of the outside door curtain's seal.

'Who is that?' Angela bellowed. Paresh lifted his Heckler carbine and swung it round on the entrance in a single smooth motion.

'Antrinell,' a voice yelled back over the wind. The curtain seal parted and the wind surged in again. Angela grabbed the base of the heater before it could tip over again, and switched it off to be safe. A blaze of light erupted briefly, silhouetting a figure kneeling on top of the snow mound.

Antrinell pushed his way into the dome through the gap. Snow stuck to every part of his parka and trousers in clingy strings and gobbets. His helmet-light shone a yellow beam around. 'Sorry to scare you,' he said. 'That damn electrical storm is screwing with our links. Nobody can broadcast anything out there.'

'I've never seen lightning like that,' Angela said.

The bulky figure made a shrugging motion. Behind him, Darwin was pushing his way through the gap. Between the four of them, they managed to manhandle a semi-conscious, moaning Omar outside and onto the waiting stretcher. There was a canopy over half of it to protect his head and torso from the elements. Angela couldn't see it being much use in these conditions. They had to get him to the doc somehow, though, and it was better than nothing.

Gillian gave them a small wave as Antrinell and Darwin picked up the harness, and leaned into the gale, walking away with slow short steps. The lightning was flaring constantly, not simple forks but huge dazzling ball lightning blasts that streaked down out of the unseen clouds above like an old-style artillery barrage. They exploded into the ground, firing off long tendrils of electrons that whipped about before expiring.

'Screw this,' Paresh yelled.

'We have to dig the snow away,' Angela yelled back. She guessed there was at least a metre on the ground now, with drifts two to three metres high against some surfaces. The irregular blaze of ball lightning bursts showed the vehicles as nothing more than mounds.

'Okay,' Paresh agreed. 'Go get something to dig with.'

Angela crouched down and wiggled through the gap again. It was only fractionally quieter inside the dome, with ice particles churning through the turbulent air. Lulu stared wildly at her, fearful and exhausted from her carbon monoxide fugue.

'We've got to dig the snow away from the entrance,' Angela called out above the noise. 'We'll never get the door curtains closed and sealed again until we do.'

'Sure.' Madeleine nodded. She steadied her kitbag and opened a pouch, taking out a lethal-looking hunting knife. The diamond-coated blade made short work of a cot, cutting it into big squares of plastic.

'Thanks.' Angela put on her sunglasses as protection from the wind-driven snow, and grabbed one of the squares. She pushed back out into the blizzard. Madeleine stayed inside, flinging great scoops of snow through the gap, half of which would immediately swirl back in. Angela went to work on the snow outside, trying to clear a crude ramp down to the entranceway. Another two days of this and the dome will be completely buried, she thought.

Madeleine closed the curtain as far as she could, reducing the gap so less snow was blown back inside the dome. After the makeshift shovel flung four or five loads outside, she'd squeeze the seal down another couple of centimetres.

High-velocity snow stung Angela's exposed cheeks as she dug. She was forever wiping clogged-up snow from her sunglasses, but she was grateful for the protection they gave her eyes. The feeling from her fingers began to dwindle again. It became as much effort to grip the raggedy plastic as it was to fling its contents into the air. The ball lightning continued its frightening detonations. One must have landed close; she flinched as best she could in such heavy clothes as a vivid tendril of electrons danced directly overhead, grounding out through one of the entombed vehicles.

Angela had no idea how long it took before Madeleine was

eventually closing the seal along the bottom of the curtain. She couldn't feel her hands, her cheeks had been pummelled insensate. Each breath burned cold down her throat. Ball lightning explosions erupted all around the camp.

Paresh put his head up against hers. 'Let's clear the vents.'

'I can't feel my hands,' she shouted back at him.

'Here.' He shoved the Heckler at her and took the square of cot plastic. Then he started to crawl up the side of the dome. Darkness closed in as the lightning paused.

Her e-i reported a link open as soon as the lightning faded. 'How are you doing?' Elston asked.

'We've got the door cleared. Unblocking the vents now.' No need to tell him she had a weapon in contravention of just about every order governing the expedition. 'Did Omar make it to the clinic?'

'He's there. Coniff says he'll be okay. His eye isn't damaged, just the tissue round it. Might not look as pretty again without some reconstructive procedures.'

'Have you seen this lightning?'

'Yes.'

As if to emphasize the point, a violet plasma ball struck the sagging ice-sheathed mess tent, sending petals of electrons banshee-screaming overhead. The blow was too much for the communal centre, hammer-smashing it into the ground amid an eruption of displaced snow. Angela bowed her head against the spume of ice that the wind hurled outward, swaying in the impact. The link dropped out then re-established itself. 'To hell with this!' she moaned. When she looked up she could see Paresh pick himself up, and resume his painstaking scraping of the vents. Night closed back in on them. 'Elston, if one of those lightning balls hits the fuel tanks we're going to be seriously screwed.'

'I know. But there's nothing we can do about it now. Olrg told me they're lightning resistant anyway.'

'This son of a bitch isn't lightning, it's like we're under attack. How long is this going to last?'

'I don't know. We lost contact with the e-Ray hours ago. Before that, the weather radar showed the cloudmass stretching back a long way. The AAV team reckoned another ten hours.'

'Ten more hours of this son of a bitch? No fucking way!'

'I know. Can you see Sakur and Kowalski? They left Justic's dome five minutes ago. They were heading for Atyeo's dome to check on Raddon and Forster.'

'I can barely see my own hands in this.'

'Okay, well—'

The double alarm flung red icons into Angela's grid. One was from Mohammed, an intruder alert. The other . . . 'Shit!' Angela snarled. Tork Ericson's bodymesh was calling for help. Medical data showed his life signs were decreasing rapidly, blood pressure dropping, heart running wild. She focused on the heart read-out, if it was still pumping . . .

'You getting this?' she demanded.

'It's here,' Elston said. 'It's attacking us.'

'Can you see anything?' Paresh asked as he slithered back down the side of the dome.

Angela turned to look in the direction of Mohammed's bodymesh emission, matching up her poor vision with the grid display. She ripped her sunglasses off. Another lightning ball streaked down behind her, its indigo flare turning the snow to scintillating comet dust. In the fleeting moment of illumination she could see all the domes. Several of them had people nearby, bulky snow-encrusted figures like herself and Paresh. They all looked the same. As the lightning braids whipped about through the air she saw one of the figures lying on the ground. Her grid navigation profiling told her it was Tork. Tork who was staining the snow with dark blood gushing out of his ripped throat. Tork who had Mohammed standing over him, crying out in shock and anguish at the carnage. And behind them was another figure, just as tall and featureless as everyone else, but one that had no bodymesh coding in the grid. A figure moving off into the blizzard. Seemingly unaffected by the terrible wind and snow.

711

'Mohammed,' Angela yelled. 'Behind you.' She cursed her stiff fingers in their useless layers of cumbersome fabric as she tried to knock the Heckler's safety off.

The tangle of lightning bolts fizzled out, plunging the camp back into darkness. Somehow, she managed to snag her ice-hardened gloves on the safety, which snicked off. She brought the carbine up, using her grid to align it on the point she'd last seen the monster. Waiting— Her frigid finger hooked round the trigger. Waiting— Cursing as her e-i was denied access to the Heckler's targeting systems because she didn't have the codes. Waiting—

'Paresh, let me have access—'

The storm spat a seething ball of gentian plasma into the ground over towards the administration Qwik-Kabin. Angela knew she only had a second as the ball bloomed into a corona of churning electrons. The panorama flashed into existence once again. Tork sprawled on the snow. Mohammed looming above him, his own Heckler raised, swinging round uncertainly as he searched for the murderer, slim intense ruby laser beam cutting through the thick snow. And the monster itself, just visible as it strode off into the howling whiteout without hesitation.

Angela pulled back on the trigger. Holding herself against the kicking weapon, keeping the aim flat. Hearing the roar of the bullets leaving the flaring muzzle. The lightning withered and died. And she knew she hadn't hit the monster. It was still walking away, unaffected by the bullets strafing the air around it. 'Motherfucker!'

Mohammed was firing now as well. She could hear his carbine coughing above the wind-yowl. Straining eyes seeing the blue-white pulse of muzzle flame. Even the targeting laser was there, trying the penetrate the snow.

Useless, she knew, all useless. It had gone. Slipped back to wherever it hid so perfectly from them. Until next time.

*

The blizzard lasted for a further seven hours. Angela and Paresh went outside another three times to clear the vents on the top of the dome. Each time the snow was higher against the dome walls, so each time they first had to shovel snow away from the entrance to get out.

'That's going to be a real problem,' Madeleine said after their second excursion. 'There's got to be a lot of weight piling up out there.' She gave the ice-bedecked walls a thoughtful glance. Even with the heater on continually, the hoar frost remained. The pile of snow that had come washing in when they opened the door curtain to flush out the CO_2 was still squatting on the floor, with tiny rivulets of water trickling down its sides, looking like a miniature ice volcano. As it slowly melted across the floor panels it refroze, producing a sheet of ice that made walking round inside tricky.

Ophelia Troy had redesigned the roof vents to stop them snow-clogging again. She and Karizma Wadhai were now working on schematics for a tunnel-like entrance to proof the domes against further blizzards, turning them into true igloos.

'Once we've dug the microfacturing shack out,' Paresh grumbled at the ringlinked news. After Tork's slaying, Elston was constantly sending round information he considered good for morale. Checks on everyone's status and location were also made every ten minutes.

'To do that they've got to design and print a spade,' Angela said.

Madeleine grinned. 'But to print a spade they've got to get into the shack.'

The three of them knocked their tea mugs together in salute.

'Won't the bulldozers be able to shove the snow away?' a puzzled Lulu asked. The poor girl had become despondent since Tork had been killed, saying very little as she huddled up inside her sleeping bag. The others often heard her sobbing when she rolled over to face the dome wall.

'Yeah,' Paresh agreed kindly. 'They'll be able to help us a lot.

Don't worry. If we can survive a night like this one, we can survive anything.' He paused as another lightning ball hit the ground somewhere outside. It was technically dawn now, and the atmosphere's bombardment was definitely easing off.

'Can't we, like, use the helicopters to get out of here?' Lulu asked.

'They don't have the range to get us to Sarvar,' Angela said sympathetically.

'But the runway is covered in snow – planes can't use it.'

'There are versions of the Daedalus that are ski equipped,' Paresh said. 'I've seen them when we were training in Northern Russia a couple of years back.'

'Oh.' Lulu rolled over again.

The wind eased off considerably by mid-morning, taking with it the last tatters of cloud. With only wisps of moribund cirro-stratus congregating high above, the pink light from Sirius shone down on the beleaguered camp. Dome curtain doors were opened, and people emerged into a rubicund arctic landscape. The first few days of snow had come to rest on the jungle's trees and bushes and vines, giving them a bulbous white coat. It had looked odd, bizarre even, but they were still recognizably encircled by the jungle. Now, the lavish vegetation was buried below massive snowdrifts. The taller trees – the bullwhips and vampspires, and metacoyas – remained standing resolute above the undulating white carpet, but they were encased in coats of remarkably clear ice five to ten centimetres thick. Captured beneath the rippled crystalline surface, dead leaves which hadn't fallen remained encased, a threadbare celadon fringe along the bigger boughs and branches.

Above the frigid, blitzed winterland, the aurora borealis streamers had returned in force. Curving rivers of phosphorescence snaked their languid way across St Libra's high sky, casting eerie colour tones across the ground.

Angela stood outside the dome that had sheltered her and nearly killed her. Only the top half remained uncovered, though even that had a white crust of snow. Around her the snow fields glowed violet as if they were carrying an electric charge, a tone which shifted to the glowing aquamarine blue of the Caribbean Sea, before melding to a green as deep as the jungle they covered. The sequence varied as the silent, random ripples of light swayed across the sky. But the iridescence was always there, always adding its own spectral sparkle to the glittering snow.

Camp Wukang's personnel moved as if toxed, trauma victims mumbling inanities to each other. For the first time, Angela began to appreciate Elston. He was the one invigorating everyone, striding round in person, letting them all see he cared that each one of the personnel had endured and survived. Issuing orders, explaining how they were going to get through the rest of this challenge.

The bulldozers were the priority for the ground vehicle engineering team. They were clearly going to have to do something about the astonishing quantity of snow that had fallen. Elston had spent several hours that morning in a conference link with his department heads, planning his next steps.

Tork Ericson's body was carried over to the clinic, where Dr Coniff performed a quick autopsy. Cause of death was easy enough. A cluster of five extremely sharp blades had slashed across his exposed throat, almost severing the head from the body.

'That does give us a small advantage,' Elston said as Coniff slid the cadaver into one of her two morgue fridges.

'An advantage?' she queried.

'Ericson was wearing an armour vest, as ordered,' Elston said. 'The creature normally goes straight for the heart. It couldn't this time, the armour protected him.'

'It protected his chest,' Dr Coniff said.

'Then we need to produce full body armour for everyone,' Elston said. 'It'll be tough to move around for everyone, but better than being dead.'

'Tell me something,' the doctor asked. She pointed to the big pile of clothing in the sink that she'd removed from Tork's corpse. The snow clinging to his parka was melting, soaking into the other garments. 'How did it know he was wearing an armour vest? His parka was on top. You couldn't see it.'

Elston looked from the pile of sodden clothes to the rectangular fridge door, and back again. 'I don't know,' he admitted.

*

Once the bulldozers were dug out and their fuel cells started, their first priority was to excavate snow from around the microfacture shack. With a slope cleared down to the entrance, the big yellow machines lumbered back to all the other vehicles parked around the domes. An hour later ramps had been dug down to the front of each of them, and the bulldozers moved on to the domes.

The next batch of vehicles to be cleared of snow and started up were the two self-loading pallet trucks. Elston and Ophelia Troy had decided they couldn't risk the accommodation domes being buried. If there was another blizzard of the same duration and intensity as the one they'd just come through, then the snow would cover the domes. She'd already told him her concern about the thermal effect of the winter conditions on the panels – the composite they'd selected wasn't intended to be used in such a cold environment, and she was worried about it losing strength and cracking if it was loaded heavily in the sub-zero temperatures.

So the bulldozers cleared a trench round each dome, and two ramps down on opposite sides. The self-loading trucks inched down the ramp slopes of the first dome to be cleared, and slowly manoeuvred their long fork-lift prongs under the dome. With a link between their autos synchronizing the lift actuators, they hoisted it off the ground, and slowly moved it over to a fresh patch of snow much closer to the clinic. Ophelia and Karizma inspected the result, making sure the panels survived without stress-fracturing before they gave the go-ahead for the remaining five to be moved.

After that, the bulldozers and trucks were tasked with moving pallets closer to the domes. The biolabs were started up and moved. Printers began to churn out modified vents for the air grilles, then moved on to producing smaller hexagonal panels to fabricate entrance tunnels for each dome, completing their igloo-mimicry. Power and data lines were relaid. Everybody watched the sky for the return of clouds, except the Legionnaires – their gazes were on the surrounding snow field, alert for anything moving out there.

By mid-afternoon, the AAV team had prepared an Owl for a rocket-assisted launch. The add-on system was a standard kit, of which Wukang had three. They were intended to be used when a short runway or even clear field wasn't available. Although the vast expanse of snow around the camp was clear of obstacles, Ken Schmitt, the AAV team chief, wasn't sure what would happen if an Owl tried a takeoff run. It might just skate along and lift off as normal, but then again if the snow was soft it could just plough itself in. With Elston's support, Ken Schmitt decided not to take any chances. The team slotted a pair of solid rocket boosters onto each side of the fuselage, and the whole assembly was towed away from the domes by a Land Rover. Two hundred metres from the Administration Qwik-Kabin, the drone plane was set up with its tail planted in the snow, nose pointing straight at the sky.

Nobody had been particularly surprised when the blizzard ended and they couldn't contact the e-Ray which had spent the last couple of months loitering three hundred and fifty kilometres to the south. The AAV team was hoping to boost the Owl to an altitude where it could locate and link to the next e-Ray in the relay chain – assuming that had survived.

The rest of the camp stopped work preparing their accommodation against the inevitable arrival of further bad weather, and gathered to watch the lone firework display. Ken's e-i ordered the Owl's twin eDyne fuel cells to power up. Once the network confirmed the pre-flight systems check, he switched to full auto, and stood back to watch the countdown.

'. . . seven, six, five, four . . .' the onlookers chanted across the silent winter wilderness.

Both solid rocket boosters ignited in a flash of orange light and billow of smoke. Steam followed, hissing out from around the searing flame as it burned into the snow, and the Owl rose rapidly into the iridescent sky. Twin columns of flame and smoke twisted round, braiding together as the Owl's nose orientated itself along the flight path, curving round to point at the grey lustre of the ring bands which commanded the southern sky. The crackling roar washed over the cheering spectators. After seventy-five seconds the rockets were exhausted. They separated from the Owl's fuselage and began their tumble back to the ground. The drone levelled out, and began its long, shallow spiral upwards through the spangled ion torrents sweeping through the sky around it, coaxial fans spinning silent and bright at the tail.

Forty-five minutes later, still spiralling high above Wukang, it made contact with an e-Ray. Two of the four in the relay between Wukang and Sarvar had fallen during the blizzard. The remaining two were in bad shape, but still airborne, though with a gradual drift downwards as they lost helium and power. Even in this calm post-blizzard day there wasn't enough redshifted sunlight to fully charge their regenerative cells. But two were enough to provide a tenuous link.

'It killed Ericson last night,' Vance told Vermekia. 'We barely made it through the blizzard, and that was just the first to hit us. Either get us out of here or reinforce us.'

'Those are not easy options,' Vermekia said. 'Do you have any proof?'

'Yes! Finally, we do.' He sent Angela's visual file through the link, watching it with Vermekia as lightning flared, revealing Ericson lying on the snow, and Mohammed standing over him. A vague human shape shambled off into the raging snowstorm as the light died. Then another flare as the ball lightning exploded, and the muzzle of a Heckler carbine fired wildly at a grey shadow.

'That was Tramelo's visual?' Vermekia asked.

'Yes.'

'Why has she been issued with a carbine?'

'Are you joking? Did you see those conditions? She was standing guard while Paresh cleared their dome's vents.'

'Okay, I appreciate things are tough for you there. But, Vance, that image isn't exactly conclusive. And the provenance means it's going to be immediately called into question. How come she's the only one that ever sees it?'

'I don't believe I'm hearing this, not from you. Ericson had his throat slashed apart by a five-blade weapon, we see a humanoid shape running off, and that isn't good enough.'

'Where was Tramelo during the actual murder?'

'That visual was taken seconds afterwards. Seconds!'

'I'm just asking you what I'm going to be asked. This is good, but I don't think it will be enough. The Newcastle investigation is over.'

'Not good enough? Another man is dead. Dead! Killed by a five-bladed hand.'

'I know. Opinion here is that we wait to see what kind of corporate battle is going on. Once Reinert is charged, that will give the GE Financial Regulation Bureau the opportunity to go into Northumberland Interstellar's level one network and find out what they're involved in. Scrupsis is confident they'll find evidence of black ops.'

'Scrupsis! What happened to Ralph's follow-up investigation?'

'Nothing yet. Hurst is still harvesting data.'

'We have the alien stalking us. You've got to push for reinforcements. Speak to the General. Show him the visual, explain what's happening here.'

'Vance ... He knows. He's the one who is waiting on the Newcastle situation to resolve. He's been burned by the satellite deployment; the politicians are not happy with it.'

'But we needed to know if the sunspots were Zanth related.'

'I know. And now, with the wonder of hindsight, everyone is moaning about the cost. Passam pulled the rug out from the expedition, and now she's running for cover, saying its work is complete.'

'One Daedalus flight. One, with enough Legionnaires to give me a decent chance of capturing this thing. That's all I need.'

'Vance, it isn't just one. Not any more. A Daedalus can't land at Wukang, not with all that snow. And you said yourself it's just going to get worse. If we're going to get to you now, it'll mean building a full gateway. Not even the HDA can swing that.'

'There are ski-equipped Daedalus variants for arctic conditions, I know there are, they're in the registry. Drop one of those out here. It can land, and make the journey back to Abellia.'

'I'll brief the General. Explain how urgent it is. You have my word on it.'

'And if the answer's "no"? What about us? The situation out here is not good. The e-Ray relay isn't going to last much longer. What do we do?'

'My office has drawn up land evacuation procedures for you. I'm sending them now in case the relay does fail.'

'Land evacuation?'

'It can be done – it was always factored into the mission profile. If you can get to Sarvar, you can winter over without any trouble. Now that there's just a skeleton crew there, you'll have enough supplies and fuel to sustain you for over a year. It'll be safer for you, too. With a convoy on the move, the alien will have trouble keeping up.'

'Only if the thing is on foot. It didn't have any trouble reaching us here in the middle of nowhere. How did it get here? Has anyone in your office analysed that?'

'Vance, I appreciate the position you're in, I really do. But no one could have anticipated Sirius redshifting. I have to say you're not the only one on St Libra in a difficult situation. It's only going to take another week of this and we're going to have the mother of all humanitarian crises on our hands. The Independencies are already living on food stocks that aren't going to last long. The algaepaddies can't survive prolonged cooling, which is going to eliminate ten per cent of GE's bioil supply. Most of Highcastle is already camped out by the gateway demanding to return. And nobody is making any decisions, certainly not in the GE. Every commissioner is running scared of a decision. Right now they're having summits about holding summits on what to do. I've never seen anything so pathetic. Even the licensed news shows are sneering.'

Vance took a deep breath. 'Okay. But all that is going to mean nothing if it turns out there's another hostile alien species on St Libra.'

*

Vance called Antrinell and Jay Chomik to a conference in his office. The heating had been off during the blizzard, allowing the water vapour to freeze on every surface; now he'd switched it back on again, and condensation was dripping down the walls and ceiling. His solitary wall pane was showing a feed from the Owl's weather radar, which revealed another large mass of cloud approaching from the north-west.

Vance knew he must order the Owl to be retrieved within the hour or it would be lost to them, annihilated by what looked like a blizzard as ferocious as the first one. But Vermekia hadn't got back to him with an answer from the General yet. He wasn't entirely sure why he bothered keeping the Owl flying. He knew full well what the answer would be.

Vermekia was a good man, a fellow Gospel Warrior dedicated to ridding the universe of evil without personal prejudice; but that didn't stop him being human. Stuck under the Australian desert for months at a time, he had become part of the HDA headquarters staff now, assimilating their mainstream culture. He hadn't abandoned Jesus, but he certainly followed the bureaucrat tenets now. Words were weighed for full political content before being uttered, high-level contacts and allies were slowly accrued. Vance was sure Vermekia would argue that he could best serve the cause of the Gospel Warriors by insinuating himself into the highest echelons of the HDA. And looking at the big picture, he might even be right. But for now, stuck in the middle of a newformed polar wasteland and cut off from the rest of the human race, Vance found it hard to follow Jesus's preachings to forgive; it was all too obvious that Vermekia had fallen to the oldest sin of all: vanity.

'I don't believe we'll be receiving any external help now,' Vance told his two principal colleagues. 'We must face this with our fortitude and whatever comfort Jesus can bestow us in His wisdom.'

'Vermekia will help,' Jay said.

'I don't believe he can,' Vance said. 'He's a prisoner of HDA politics and bureaucracy as much as we're prisoners of the weather. Assistance would be a blessing indeed, but we have to strategize for the worst. Vermekia's office has sent through some plans for us to travel in convoy to Sarvar. I have to concede that is looking attractive to me right now.'

'Are you sure?' Antrinell exclaimed. 'That's two thousand kilometres away. And we're totally unprepared for this kind of terrain. Nobody's ever faced a jungle covered in snow before.'

'We have to be realistic,' Vance said. 'If the last sunspot erupted tomorrow, it would still be a month or more before it dissipated along with the others – not that any have bled away yet. And how long it would take for the snows to melt after that is anyone's guess. The planet's entire albedo has changed. But I do know that we'd be better off travelling over a frozen snow field than trying to drive over a melting snow field. We can do this, gentlemen. I reviewed the preliminary figures and we have the resources. Just. The longer we wait, the more our chances of success are reduced.'

'Fair enough,' Jay said with mounting concern; his focus was distant, betraying his reading of the data in his grid. 'But what about the creature? Or creatures?'

'Vermekia believes we will have an advantage over it if we're travelling.'

'That's stupid,' Antrinell said. 'It caught up with us here, didn't it?'

Jay clenched his fists in frustration. 'If we just knew what it was ... Look at us, we're a species that travels between stars, we're here with the most sophisticated research tools known, the best sensors, some damn good troops, and we've got *nothing*. We're frightened of a boogieman in the night like some medieval peasant. How could this happen?'

'On the contrary,' Antrinell said. 'We know a lot about it.' He held his hand up, silencing Jay's protest. 'Aside from its psychology, which I'll grant you is strange. But first off, we know it's not from this world. The plants simply don't have variance, their genetic composition is too rigid. There's no diversity here that could account for animal life. So like us it is a foreigner here. Secondly, I believe it to be singular. If there were many, then we'd be dead. It's that simple. We may not understand its motivation, but we are very aware of its goal: our death. If there was more than one, they would simply overwhelm us. They are faster, stronger, and have a mastery of our technology that allows them to circumvent our sensors.'

'You think it's a protector sent by the bioformers?' Vance asked.

'That is the most logical conclusion. I've considered others. Perhaps it is a hunter and we are its sport. Or it is rogue in some way. But the protector theory is the strongest. I'm not sure why it slaughtered everyone in Bartram's mansion, perhaps something to do with the Norths contaminating its world. But we can be certain why it has singled out Wukang rather than any of the other forward camps and supply bases. We are the ones with the weapon capable of destroying St Libra.'

'And how do you explain its humanoid form? Evolution as we understand it is not going to replicate our own bipedal structure, there are too many random factors involved. Let alone give it a hand with five fingers.'

'It has that shape so it can walk among us.'

'But I've seen it,' Vance said. 'Twice; I watched the image the brainscan pulled from Angela's mind, and I saw her iris smartcell recording from last night. It's human-shaped, but not human.'

'I considered that,' Antrinell said. 'That's what has bothered me since we began this expedition, and it's the single glaring flaw in all the theories which political opponents like Scrupsis and Passam can use against us every time. In which case the simplest explanation is the most likely: it's human-shaped when it's in attack mode. That would explain just about everything that's happened. We've already postulated it's from a civilization with a very advanced technology base.'

Vance glanced at Jay, who was looking extremely uncomfortable. His mind was racing, trying to come up with an explanation that would exclude such an idea. But he had travelled inside the terrible wonders of a Zanthworld, seen what *alien* truly meant, the potential involved. When everything, every possibility however remote, had to be taken into account, a shapeshifter was eminently reasonable. 'But who?'

'Who's the one person who's been in every murder location?' Antrinell said.

'It can't be Tramelo,' Vance said. 'I simply won't accept that. We've scanned her, taken DNA samples. And the real proof it wasn't her is the Newcastle murder.'

'Where did she come from? Why has she not changed appearance in twenty years? And do we know her exact position at the moment of each slaying? How fast is the creature? How stealthy? It has never been captured by any sensor. All we have is her accounts of its appearance.'

'She's human,' Vance said, resenting how he was regressing to simple stubbornness to fund his argument.

'I'm sure she is – when it's convenient for her to be. Or maybe she doesn't even know what she is. What if it only emerges from within when there is a reason for it to do so?'

'Jay?' Vance asked.

'You know I've never trusted her.'

'Let me ask you this,' Antrinell said. 'If it's not her, then who?'

It was a question Vance couldn't answer. That kind of analysis and interpretation process had been the bedrock of intelligence operations for centuries, forming a large section of his basic training courses. If there was an answer it lay somewhere in the personnel files of the expedition members. He'd have to review them all carefully, looking for discrepancies, some clue of a legend.

The notion made him stiffen in surprise. When he'd allowed Angela to help them with simple administration tasks after Mullain's death he'd loaded some discreet monitors in the network to keep watch on her access. One of the first things she did was review the personnel files. Had she worked this all out a month ago?

'All right,' he said. 'We'll start with the assumption that it isn't one of us three. If the creature is here to gain access to the warheads – well, the three of us have that access.'

Jay and Antrinell nodded grudging agreement.

'Tag Angela again,' Vance told Antrinell. 'She's got some clever programs that can spot an ordinary smartdust emission, so use some of our smartmicrobe bugs this time.'

Jay grinned. 'I can do that.'

'I'm going to ask Vermekia to run our personnel records through an AI confirmation routine. If there are any anomalies, that should find it. In the meantime,' he waved a hand at the wall pane with its vivid yellow and purple blotch of approaching cloud, 'I want us properly prepared for the blizzard this time.'

'And the evacuation?' Antrinell asked.

'I think it's inevitable. We'll use the blizzard downtime to start gearing up.'

*

Twenty minutes later, he was talking to Vermekia again.

'I'm sorry, Vance, but the General said no. We ran the visual you gave us through AI analysis. The creature's proportions are human, as is the gait. Whatever Tramelo saw, it's human. We think you've got a psychopath in the camp, not an alien. Presumably it really is her accomplice.'

Vance took a moment to consider the AI's analysis, perturbed by how many factors were converging. 'Tramelo shot at it.'

'But she didn't hit it, did she?'

Vance almost laughed. The kind of laughter that diverted a

bellow of anger. 'Very well, in that case I'd like you to have an AI analyse the personnel records of everyone at Wukang. Look for a legend, someone who's been planted on us.'

'That I can do.'

'We're going to put the evacuation into motion. I don't expect the e-Rays to survive this next blizzard, but I have five emergency com rockets; they should be able to reach an altitude that'll allow a brief relay to Abellia's network. If I use one, it'll be because the creature is real. So could you at least have a ski Daedalus on standby?'

'I'll call in some favours. I know one of us in tactical command. It'll be written off as a readiness exercise.'

'Thank you.'

'Take care out there, Vance. I know that Jesus is testing you with this mission. I will pray for your deliverance.'

*

Detective Ian Lanagin was back down on the fourth floor, assigned to the city command office, helping orchestrate the police response to the gateway blockade – which was an indication of his status with O'Rouke. It was a good duty after the workload of the North case; he'd had nothing to do for the last two days. The GE Border Directorate troops were tough fellas; nobody had got through from St Libra, despite near-daily attempts to break the line. But each time the Highcastle residents were better organized, and more violent. Meanwhile the GE commissioners sat round their fine oval tables in Brussels, sipping mineral water and avoiding anything that resembled a decision about what to do with the people of St Libra. Other national leaders were starting to put pressure on, making statements about their concern over GE's inability to accomplish anything.

And still the bioil flowed from St Libra's reserve tanks. Ian knew damn well that was all Brussels cared about. But it gave him time to relax and drink tea and swap gossip with his colleagues. The city command office was circular, with two rings of desks staffed by twenty detectives and specialist tactical constables, reporting to the duty sixth-grade detective in the centre. Ian had a desk on the inner ring, where he was assigned to handle the reserve placings. He'd got twenty-three big GroundKings full of agency constables parked around Dunston Hill and along the A1, ready to deploy if anything got out of hand in Last Mile. From the data flowing across his grid and the console zone links to civic meshes it wasn't going to be the St Libra mob that would be their main problem. Newcastle was backing up with would-be refugees. Most had travelled across continents and oceans to reach the gateway; some had even made it from other worlds. Ian had never listened to them before. They were a background noise he'd grown up with, as much a part of Newcastle as the Tyne Bridge. But now, as he hunted round for something to fill his boring days, he accessed the transnet news, whose reporters were covering the gateway closure. The impoverished refugees told stories of the hardship they'd endured, how they'd spent everything they had to escape from persecution and violence and intolerance and oppressive ideology, how they'd been forced to leave everything behind, including loved ones and family in some cases. The countries and governments they named and denounced so avidly surprised Ian – he didn't consider them especially corrupt or repressive. But then he'd never held the kinds of strong convictions that Directorates or People's Committees or Security Agencies or Religious Police disagreed with.

These refugees however were driven by anger and fear, determined to reach the haven of the Independencies, where their new life could begin in joyous freedom, and the past could finally be cast loose. Now, thanks to a diktat from unseen unelected bureaucrats, sunspots and weather were the excuse preventing them from joining comrades and brethren and fellow believers. They'd fought their way out of prisons or worse; they really weren't the kind of people plastic barriers across the road were going to stop for very long. The Red Cross had set up temporary shelters for them, but resentment was building fast.

Ian had bet thirty Eurofrancs that the first riot would kick off on Friday. Constable Merkrul who ran the Market Street book hadn't given him good odds.

At nine o'clock when he was already on his second cup of tea from the canteen, his e-i reported one of the monitor programs at Newcastle Station was registering activity. Ian carefully suspended his official log, and pulled the monitor data into his grid.

Boris Attenson was catching the London express train. Ian smiled grimly at the station mesh feed showing Boris and two colleagues striding down the long curving platform to the first-class coaches at the front of the train. He hated the arrogance the besuited man demonstrated, the casual wealth in his hand-made shoes and long tailored camelhair coat. Hated the braying laughter as the three of them conversed. Hated the face.

Ian switched monitors. Today, Tallulah was wearing a pleated amethyst skirt and dark-orange blouse under a white jacket with gold buttons and a broad collar. He thought she looked good in those colours; they set her chestnut hair off nicely. She'd caught the Metro train to Gateshead at her usual time, then walked to her office on Bensham Road to arrive there just before eight thirty. He watched the image from civic meshes smeared across buildings along the street, pleased that she had a spry smile on her face when she met a co-worker for the last twenty metres, the two of them chatting away avidly.

His surveillance ended at the building's entrance. Accessing the interior meshes would be difficult; it could be done, but real-time access authority for a private building would be logged by the Market Street network; not even Elston's phished codes could circumvent that.

Ian didn't mind. He'd be able to see her again at twelve forty when she took her lunch break. She usually took the Metro back down to the city centre with friends. They visited cafés and some of the smaller chain restaurants. On Monday when it had been sunny, she'd walked over the swing bridge with a whole group from her office and sat out in a pub garden near the Guild Hall overlooking the river. She'd worn a floral dress that day, with her navy-blue jacket buttoned against the lingering chill in the air blowing off the Tyne. He preferred that outfit to today's; not that she ever wore anything that was less than swish and stylish.

With Tallulah safe at work, and Boris racing down the east coast main line at three hundred and twenty kilometres per hour, Ian called Mitchell Rouche, a detective working for the London Metropolitan police force. They'd teamed up a couple of times on cases that encompassed their respective cities, and drunk a few beers together in the process. He and Mitchell were comfortable with each other, sharing the same opinion of the world and the people who occupied its various strata.

'I may need a favour today,' Ian said.

'Okay, nothing too rich, I hope,' Mitchell replied.

'No, man, there's someone on the train down to you. I don't like him. And he truly believes that heat in his arse is the sun shining out of it. He needs to learn it's my boot that's stuck up there.'

'What do you want to happen?'

'Same thing for anyone who breaks the law, he should be arrested. That's our job, man.'

'How big a law does he break?'

'Well there's the beauty of this. He'll be visiting clubs tonight, he always does. I've got a monitor on his secondary account. When he buys something he shouldn't, I'll let you know.'

'Okay. I'll have to move some shift work round, but I can cover that.'

'Thanks, man, I'll owe you.'

'Certainly will.'

*

Which was why at eleven thirty-five that night Ian was riding Mitchell's iris smartcell visual as the detective led a pair of agency constables into the Thames Europina hotel on the south bank. The glass cage lift took him up the outside of the building to the thirty-third floor where Boris Attenson had rented a suite for the night. Mitchell stared out at the ancient Millennium Dome half a

729

klick away, whose third plastic roof was finally being replaced by link-chain molecule sheeting printed directly into place by large spider-like automata.

'I've sent the payment transfer order to the Scotland Yard network,' Ian said. 'That'll provide a reason for you to query his identity.'

'Okay,' Mitchell said. 'What do you want me to do with the girl?'

'Nothing. You're just enquiring about a payment transfer, it's part of an on-going investigation into the club and if they're trafficking. Attenson will do the rest, especially if you don't show due deference.'

'You ever going to tell me what he's done?'

'He's a banker.'

''Nuff said.'

Mitchell activated his jacket badge as he walked along the short corridor. He told his e-i to open the suite's door with the override provided by hotel security. His e-i sent out a general broadcast as he shouted: 'Police, do not move, remain where you are.'

The two constables rushed in as the room lighting came up, their tasers drawn. Mitchell followed at a slower pace. There were squeals coming from the bedroom.

Ian grinned at the cliché scene that was revealed through Mitchell's iris smartcell feed. The dancer from the club was sitting up in bed, silk sheet gripped tight to her neck as if it was some kind of invincible shield. A short dress of purple sequins was lying on the floor. Her scarlet thong was draped over Boris Attenson's head. It was the only piece of clothing he wore.

He'd tried to snatch a tox sac from the bedside cabinet and stuff it down the back of the headboard. The constables grabbed him mid-act, and pulled him onto the floor. He was on his knees, hands behind his head with a taser pressed against his chest.

'Officer, really!' he blustered. 'There's no need for any force to be used. You have the wrong man.'

'Really?' Mitchell asked in amusement. Boris moved a hand in an attempt to pull the thong off. A constable slapped it back. 'So you are Mr Song Lee Hoc?'

Boris grimaced at the mention of his secondary account name. 'That's not who I am. I can explain.'

'I hope so. We've been monitoring the Pink Apricot account.' Mitchell gave the girl a pointed glance. 'They're under investigation for human trafficking. Mr Song Lee Hoc made a large payment from his North Korean account to them this evening, and now here you are with a club employee.'

'What? No, no. This is all a mistake. Look, Officer, please. Can we perhaps discuss this off-log?'

'I'm sorry, Mr Hoc, I don't understand.'

'I'm not Song Lee Hoc,' Boris said, his face growing very flushed. 'This is ridiculous. You damn well know what's going on.' He made an effort to stand. A constable whacked the back of his knees with a telescoping nightstick. Boris screamed and collapsed. 'Fuck you fuckers! My lawyer will crucify you fascist bastards.'

'Resisting arrest, and threatening a police officer,' Mitchell said. 'I think you'd better come down to the station.'

'Oh Christ, don't do this. No. Please. Come on. Don't.'

'Tell you what, Mr Hoc. Seeing as how I'm in a generous mood, I'll let you put your pants on before we take you down through the lobby to the squad car.' Mitchell pointed at the thong. 'Are these yours?'

*

An hour later Tallulah Packer was woken by a call from the London Metropolitan police. Her e-i confirmed the authenticity of the call.

'I'm very sorry to disturb you at this hour, ma'am,' Detective Rouche said. 'But we've taken a man into custody following an incident at the Thames Europina hotel. His bloodspec revealed that he's bumped a lot of peptox, and there's some confusion

731

about his identity. The profile we've harvested from his e-i indicated you were an acquaintance. I was wondering if you could provide a positive visual identification for us.'

It took a sleepy, bewildered Tallulah a moment to reply. 'I . . . yes.'

The image that was sent to her grid showed her fiancé on his knees beside a hotel bed with a naked hooker cowering behind him; he had a red thong on his head.

'Can you tell me if this is Mr Boris Attenson?' Detective Rouche asked.

'Yes. It is.'

'Thank you ma'am. Sorry, again, to disturb you.' The call ended.

Thursday 4th April 2143

It was field 12-GH-B2 that made the call. Driving out of High-castle on the north-west road towards the top of Lake Alnwick, Adrian 2North realized it could have been any of the sectors Northumberland Interstellar was cropping that called him in. Snow had finally reached the centre of Ambrose after a not inconsiderable journey of three and a half thousand kilometres from the massive continent's southern coastline. A week of winter winds and deluges of icy rains had preceded the gentle flakes, so when they did arrive no one was surprised.

Adrian was in the middle of his management duty week, which had been extended by the gateway restrictions. In the office tower at the centre of the city he'd spent a lot of time accessing the reports from Abellia, watching in dismay as the blizzards struck Brinkelle's fiefdom, bringing a metre of snow in less than three days. Nothing was flying out of Abellia Airport any more, and the entire remote district was coming to terms with having to survive by itself until the sunspot outbreak lifted. There'd been some talk of flying supplies over from Eastshields using aircraft with skis, but that was mainly wishful thinking from unlicensed sites and worried Abellia workers. As Adrian had full access to Northumberland Interstellar's level one network he knew nobody was even looking at leasing such aircraft, let alone preparing to ship one through the gateway.

So there he'd been, sitting on the seventh floor in the control centre with the air-con switched to its unfamiliar heating function, overseeing the staff who ran the vast pipework network, when the call came in. It had been snowing for seven hours by then, with the ground cooling enough to allow it to settle sporadically. He looked down on the outlandish mantle building up on the city's roofs, and called down to the garage, reserving a big Range Rover Elite after making sure its service history was up to date. He sent the supervisor to get a box full of self-heating food, and a two-litre thermos of coffee. One of the few downtown clothing stores that remained open was doing a great trade in winter coats. Adrian had one printed out in his size and climbed into the Range Rover.

With the exception of Motorway A, most of the roads beyond the city boundary soon ran out of tarmac, giving way to compacted dirt tracks. The north-west route was no different, which meant the snowfall completely wiped it from view. He couldn't tell what was road and what was the sandy scrubland on either side. The forward radar and mesh sensors just managed to penetrate the icy cloak, displaying the twin ruts in his grid. Combined with the Range Rover's inertial navigation system, he could steer along the track with reasonable confidence, providing he didn't go over fifty kph. He was used to tearing down the tracks though the algaepaddies at over a hundred and fifty.

Nothing else was moving out among the algaepaddies. Northumberland Interstellar staff had proved exceptionally loyal, sticking to their jobs while the majority of the city bundled their valuables into cars and vans, and took off for the gateway. Presumably, they believed Augustine North would make sure they were allowed back if the situation got really bad – after all most of them were registered GE citizens working on St Libra for tax-free salaries and a decent bonus. That was another issue noticeably absent from the level one network.

The windscreen wipers were on, pushing the fluffy flakes to the side of the heated glass. Headlights on full beam cut through the fall. And the Range Rover net remained linked to Highcastle's transnet cells. But the feeling of isolation grew with every kilometre. It wasn't the outrageously unfamiliar snow which was the problem, but the light. Adrian simply couldn't get used to the meagre coral glimmer illuminating the landscape.

Two hours after leaving the office, he reached field 12-GH-B2, a cluster of twelve algaepaddies, whose crop was genetically tweaked to provide biodiesel. Gwen Besset, the district manager, was waiting for him at the end of the track, sitting in her jeep with the heater on. She was heavily pregnant, and wrapped in a thick poncho.

'Thanks for coming,' she said. 'Regional kept saying they couldn't spare anyone.'

'That's okay. I think someone at my level needs to know first hand exactly what the effect is.' Adrian had worked with Gwen for over seven years now, and trusted her judgement. If she said there was a problem, it was likely to be a big one.

They walked up the embankment slope of the first algaepaddy to stand on the rim. Adrian stared out across the kilometre-wide circle of sludge smothering the water. Even with the bad red light he could see the mottling. Dark patches had emerged on the rumpled surface, seemingly at random. They ranged from a couple of metres across to one that was over fifty. The majority were just behind the giant boom arm which swept round and round, almost as if it was responsible for spreading them.

'The dead areas started appearing this morning,' Gwen said. 'Hardly surprising. The algae was never designed to live in this kind of temperature. Its growth rate has been slowing all week. Output is well down.'

'Yes,' Adrian said. 'To twelve per cent, as of last night. Augustine himself noticed that figure. But this . . . Not good.'

They walked along the rim to the boom arm with the snow swirling round them. For once, the sweet-sulphur smell of the algae was reduced, diluted by the cold air. He watched the flakes landing on the algae where they slowly dissolved.

'You will get us out, won't you?' Gwen asked. 'If it gets really bad here? I mean, the farms have lost their entire crop now. They say the citrus groves can't survive more than a couple of weeks of this weather, assuming it doesn't get worse. Everything will have to be replanted when the sunspots end. But the supply chain doesn't have a lot of reserve built in.'

Adrian stopped at the bulky end of the boom, which was crawling along its concrete rail, thick roller wheels barely turning. The motors inside the drive casing were making a loud grinding noise he'd never heard before, as if their axle bearings were filled with sand. He looked at Gwen, whose hands had come to rest on her bump. 'If it ever gets to that stage, we'll make sure our employees get out.'

'Thanks, Adrian, appreciate hearing that.'

He pointed at the drive casing. 'So what's happening here?'

'Resistance,' Gwen said simply. 'The algae is starting to frost up. That's preventing the boom intakes from ingesting, which turns them into bulldozer blades. The system can't cope with that kind of inertia; the stresses we're seeing are way outside spec-tolerance.'

'Crap on it,' Adrian muttered. They went up the short metal steps to the walkway which ran the whole five hundred metres along the top of the boom. Looking down on the algae he could see the usually mushy bloom starting to frost up, becoming stiffer and sluggish, reluctant to enter the inlet nozzles. Long puckered mounds were starting to accrete across the intake meshes. That was what the boom was pushing against. 'And they're all the same?' he asked.

'Every one in the field: I inspected them all. Which means it's the same for every algaepaddy on the Jarrow Plain. They're dying and breaking down at the same time. Adrian, you've got to do something. The algae we can reseed when the sunspots finish. But replacing every boom arm NI owns? That's going to cost more money than my e-i can count. Is the company even insured for that kind of disaster?'

Adrian scowled grimly down at the dying algaepaddy. However he tried to spin it in his mind, he couldn't deny Gwen was right. He told his e-i to call Augustine using the most secure encryption he'd got. It wasn't a call he'd ever imagined he'd be making, and it took a lot of resolution to stick with it and go past all the security buffers. Even a 2North wasn't entitled to instant direct access to Augustine. But eventually the call was permitted by Augustine's e-i.

'Adrian,' Augustine acknowledged. 'I see you're out in the fields. What can I do for you?'

'I'm sorry, Father, but we need to shut down bioil production. All of it.'

*

At seven minutes to six the monitor program receiving the feed from meshes along Bensham Road alerted Ian that Tallulah Packer had walked out of her office. It was raining that evening, so she popped up her umbrella, called out her goodbyes to colleagues, and scurried off to the Gateshead Metro station.

She was going straight home to the St James singletown, he knew; interception routines in the transnet had given him full access to all the calls she'd made that day. The majority had been work-related, and as hectic as expected on the day NI and the other St Libra Great Eight bioil producers announced that they were shutting down their algaepaddies. However, several had been from girlfriends urging her to come out with them that night. She'd turned them down with thanks, saying she just wasn't ready for that kind of recovery programme yet. It was far too soon after what 'he' had done. Even her mother had called, full of awkward concern that the engagement was over.

Ian's monitors were also tight on Boris Attenson. He'd made police bail first thing that morning, and taken the express back up to Newcastle. Calls Ian had intercepted revealed how displeased his bosses at the bank were, but given the turmoil in the financial market all day his indiscretion was sliding in far below the board's radar. Boris even put in a few hours in the office that afternoon.

Now the monitors showed Boris entering the St James singletown on the Barrack Road entrance, and finding a table in the Travorl bar, ordering a coffee. The bar's mesh sensor was a good one, allowing Ian to zoom in and see the light film of perspiration on Boris's brow. A nervous, desperate man working up his courage. Sure enough, with the coffee only half drunk, Boris called the waitress over and ordered a scotch.

That was all Ian needed. It couldn't be better if he'd asked Boris to please go and made a complete prat of himself, that way you can completely screw up the relationship.

Ian opened his desk's top drawer and took out the big evidence envelope he'd collected from the Market Street vault that morning. As soon as he left the station he headed straight to Monument Station and took the Metro one stop up to St James Station.

The St James singletown didn't have many internal meshes in the residential zones, but because of the murder in apartment 576B Sid had ordered smartdust to be smeared on the corridor outside, linked directly to the police network. The chance that the murderer would return to the scene was practically non-existent, but with the case having so much authority and resources, one mesh had been an easy gamble.

Ian arrived at the St James seven minutes after Tallulah got home. He loitered in the main lobby, watching Boris in his grid. Finally, the banker got up and walked through the singletown's commercial arcade to a bank of restricted lifts. He'd clearly kept his code, because the doors opened for him. Ian moved for the lifts in the lobby, using his police access code.

The corridor mesh showed Boris hesitating outside apartment 576B. He couldn't call Tallulah directly any more; after this morning's eight excruciating calls she'd finally told her e-i to revoke his access to her address code. So Boris had to meekly press the buzzer, then, when he got no reply, he started knocking on the door like a relic from the nineteenth century. But it worked, the door opened, framing a weary-looking Tallulah whose expression fluctuated between anger and dismay. Boris immediately started pleading, practically pushing his way in. Tallulah shut the door.

Out of sight at the other end of the corridor, Ian waited for one minute then walked to the door, and told his e-i to call Tallulah. The timing was perfect, he could hear muffled voices, angry and wretched. They both stopped.

'Yes?' Tallulah asked.

'It's Detective Lanagin. I'm returning some of the items forensics took away. The lab has finished with them now.'

'Oh . . . right.'

The door opened. Tallulah looked so miserable, eyes red-rimmed from crying, hair lank, shoulders slumped, it was as if she'd just come back from a funeral. Ian just wanted to put his arms round her there and then.

Boris was standing at her shoulder, a toxfiend in bad need of a fix. Desperate to push his case, yet irate at the unexpected interruption. He glared at Ian.

'I thought you'd want these as soon as possible,' Ian said, and handed the big plastic envelope over to Tallulah. He hadn't even bothered to read the full contents list, there was clearly clothing in there, along with some small hard items.

Tallulah gave the envelope a blank glance as she accepted it. 'Uh, thank you.'

'Everything has been cleared. And cleaned, too.' He smiled.

'Look, Officer, this really isn't the time,' Boris said shortly.

Ian appeared to notice him for the first time. 'The time, sir?'

'Yes. We're busy. It's a private matter; you understand.'

'I see.' He peered at Tallulah who wouldn't meet his gaze. 'Are you all right, Ms Packer?'

'She's fine!'

'Ma'am?'

'My fiancée is fine,' Boris snapped. 'Would you leave now, please. Don't make me file a harassment report.'

'You're not my fiancé,' Tallulah whispered. She started pulling at her diamond and ruby engagement ring, juggling with the forensics envelope.

'Don't do that,' Boris protested. 'Darling, please, let me explain. The police were—' He grimaced and glared at Ian.

'No,' Tallulah sobbed. 'Just go! I don't want you here, Boris. I don't. Please!'

'I'm not leaving until you listen to me.'

'I think that's enough,' Ian said. 'Sir, the homeowner has asked you to leave. Please do that.'

A finger was thrust towards Ian's face. Boris was turning red. 'Stay out of this. This is all your lot's fault in the first place.'

Ian frowned his lack of understanding. His head tilted to one side as if he was pausing to read data from his grid. 'Aye, the Metropolitan Police held you on a disturbance and identity theft charge this morning. I see the magistrate bound you over to keep the peace. Do you think you're obeying your bail conditions right now, sir?'

There was a long moment with the two staring at each other when Boris might have taken a swing at Ian; he was certainly enraged enough to be that stupid. Some deeper instinct must have cut in. Ian was younger, taller and, judging by the way his shirt was stretched over a hard-muscled chest, a great deal fitter; and he was also a policeman.

'We need to talk,' Boris said bitterly.

Tallulah turned away, close to tears again.

Boris reached out with one hand, but never quite had the courage to touch her. He walked out of the apartment.

Ian hurriedly shut the door. 'I'm really sorry, Ms Packer. That was probably the worst timing of my career.'

'No. No it wasn't. Actually, thank you for coming. I'm really glad you arrived. I don't know what I would have done. I was stupid to let him in.'

'I, er, accessed the police report. I can understand why you don't want to see him right now.'

'Ever,' she said. 'I don't want to ever see him again.'

'Aye, I know that feeling myself.'

Tallulah gave him a mildly puzzled look. He shrugged. 'I was engaged myself, two years ago,' Ian said. 'She broke it off. Not like this, mind. Well, I suppose it was a bit. She found someone else. Better prospects, so she said.'

'Why do people do that?' Tallulah asked bitterly. 'You let someone in until they become your whole life, then they turn round and stab you through the heart.'

Ian hated seeing her so despondent, and knowing he was the real reason made that worse. He could almost feel guilty, except exposing Boris was an act of kindness for her in the long run. 'Down to timing, pet. We were always going to find out eventually. Best it happens early. Mind, there never is a good time, that's the problem.'

'It just hurts. Why does it hurt so much?'

'Is there someone you can visit, or call over? A girlfriend, like? Have an evening telling each other all men are useless.'

Tallulah almost managed a grin. 'You're not all like Boris.'

'I just don't want to leave you like this, pet. Are you sure you're going to be okay?'

'Yeah, I'll survive.'

'Okay.' It was hard, making himself walk away. But this had to be played perfectly. Tonight was about contrasts, showing her that good guys did exist, that he was one of them. 'Listen. This is my address code. If he comes back, or causes any more trouble, I want you to call me. Any time, day or night. I mean it.'

'I don't think he will. He knows it's over, he just doesn't want to admit it.'

'Aye, but if you do need help use my code. Please? Promise you will. I need to know you're going to be safe and careful.'

'All right.' She smiled weakly. 'If he turns up again, I'll call you.'

'Take care then, pet.' Ian gave her his serious smile, and left apartment 576B. It was all he could do not to dance down the corridor.

Monday 8th April 2143

The Raytheon 6B-E Owl measured nine metres in length, with a seventeen-metre wingspan giving it a glider-like planform, albeit one that was a lot more manoeuvrable than the average glider. Weighing in at just over three and a half thousand kilograms at takeoff, it was designed to cruise at a modest 315km/h for a maximum endurance of forty-seven hours. However, its primary function was low-level survey. The one that had been rocket-launched that afternoon flew upwards through St Libra's freezing aurora-dominated atmosphere, curving round and round Wu-kang in a long leisurely spiral, was now struggling to break through its 8,340-metre service ceiling. Ken Schmitt and his team had done their best, loading patches into the vehicle's smartware pilot, stripping out several sensor systems, bypassing power limiters in the eDyne fuel cells and the Passau motors driving the tail-mounted coaxial fans so it produced an extra eight per cent thrust, allowing it to push on up to a greater altitude.

But once it reached 9,300 metres the wings couldn't generate any greater lift, nor could the fan blades bite any deeper into the thin air. Yet that still wasn't high enough. The communication bay was sending out ping after ping without getting any trans-ponder reply from the e-Rays. Radar couldn't find anything solid in the sky, though it was at its extreme range limit. The smartdust mesh that covered most of the fuselage couldn't detect any arti-ficial electromagnetic emission points across the whole southern sky – though the aurora borealis and the hypercharged iono-sphere made that a particularly difficult spectrum to scan.

'It's not the altitude,' Ken Schmitt acknowledged after the Owl had circled at 9,300 metres for ninety minutes. 'If there was anything up there, we would have found it. The e-Rays are down.'

'Not surprising in that blizzard,' Vance said.

'We have got the emergency rockets,' Davinia Beirne said from the other desk in the AAV shack where she was monitoring the Owl's telemetry. 'They should be able to punch a signal all the way over the Abellia from their apex.'

'I hope so,' Vance said. 'But frankly, we don't have anything to say to them yet.'

'How about Norman Sliwinska was murdered?' Davinia said scathingly. 'Someone else other than God needs to know, surely?'

Vance chose to ignore the barb. Norman Sliwinska had been outside during a small lull in the snowstorm on Saturday after-noon. A team had been sent out to clear snow away from the AAV shack, which was in danger of collapsing from the weight of the drifts. The wind had eased off, allowing people out, but the snow was still falling heavily, and the air was overloaded with static from the tremendous lightning storm, making bodymesh links close to impossible.

An intermittent medical alarm from Sliwinska had been picked up by the camp's hopelessly degraded network. Too little and too late to produce an accurate fix. The Legionnaires outside, osten-sibly protecting the clearance team from exactly this ambush, had eventually found blood on the snow. In the three circuits they made of the domes and vehicles, the Legionnaires never found Norman Sliwinska's body. The clearance team abandoned their efforts and returned to their domes, allowing the AAV shack to take its chances. Unlike poor Norman, it had survived the rest of the blizzard.

There was one good aspect of the murder which Vance hadn't shared with anyone: the smartmicrobe bug they'd tagged Angela with confirmed she had been in her dome with Paresh and the two catering staff when the monster struck. It definitely wasn't her. Important though that was to Vance, it still didn't rate expending a comm rocket for. He knew the knowledge wouldn't sway Vermekia.

'I don't like that weather front,' Ken announced.

Vance glanced at the pane showing the Owl's weather radar imagery. The thicker false-colour waves of yellow and purple were heading in towards Wukang at a steady rate.

'How long till it hits us?' Vance asked.

'About an hour until the strongest part of the storm arrives,' Ken said. 'But we're already on the edge, it's just going to get worse. Sir, we need to think about recovery. It'll take a good fifty minutes to get the Owl back down.'

'I second that,' Davinia said. 'We're going to burn out half the power train unless we ease off soon. There's nothing out there for it to contact.'

'Okay,' Vance said. 'Bring it down. But I want you to land it as close as possible to the camp. And take three Legionnaires with you to collect it.'

'Yes, sir,' Ken said.

*

While the Owl spiralled down, Karizma Wadhai was supervising the team tasked with lifting the domes again. This time the snow had drifted almost a metre up against the panels. The bulldozers pushed it out of the way, leaving room for the self-loading trucks to slide their lift forks underneath. Josh Justic's dome was the first they attempted to move. The trucks had barely got it half a metre off the snow, when they heard a tremendous *crack*. It lurched as a split opened up, cutting neatly across panels. The trucks hurriedly lowered it again as the uneven sections shifted about.

Inspection showed that seven of the panels had fractured and split. 'It's the cold,' Ophelia explained to Elston as they walked round the broken dome. 'We weren't expecting it to be this cold.'

Vance examined the jagged gash in the panels; the sagging

dome put him in mind of an egg that had defeated the hatchling inside. 'Are all the domes going to split?'

'If we try and move them, then yes. They're just too brittle to lift now.'

'And if we leave them in place, the weight of snow will also fracture the panels, yes?'

'Probably, sir, it depends on how much snow builds up.'

Both of them turned to face the north-east where the Owl had shown the next storm was approaching. Already, snow was starting to fall, thin hard specks forming a grainy layer on the existing mantle. Pink sunlight was fading as evening drew in, abandoning the sky to the restless borealis waves.

'How do we protect them?' Vance asked.

'We thought the bulldozers could shunt the existing snow into a wall around each dome. That might act as a snow break, at least for this next blizzard. It's the best proposal we have.'

'Okay, we'll give that a go. What about this dome, is this repairable?'

'No, sir. We can't patch the panels, we just need to make new ones and reassemble. And we can't do that in the timeframe we've got left today.'

Vance took a look round the camp. It was a depressing sight, he admitted to himself. Six people and a Land Rover Tropic were just visible out on the snow field half a kilometre away, waiting for the Owl to finish its decent. The bulldozers and self-loading pallet trucks moved round slowly, crushing deep ruts into the snow in a random pattern that people had to straddle while they walked about. Snow almost covered the other vehicles, turning them into idiosyncratic lumps. A well-worn path to the clinic, which had snow piled up to the Qwik-Kabin roof where the drift just rounded off. A ramp had been dug down through it to the entrance, and held in place by a flimsy makeshift fence of posts and packing straps. But then, he acknowledged, everything in Wukang had a makeshift feel to it right now. The microfacture shack had what amounted to a road leading to its entrance, so many vehicles had driven up to it. Camp personnel, always in pairs or more, moving round slowly in their parkas and quilted trousers, collecting fresh stores from the pallets, which first had to be dug out with spades the microfacture team had printed. The general systems crew were working on the fuel cells, making sure they'd keep working through the storms.

It was all wrong, he thought, they were struggling to keep up with current conditions while trying to be vigilant for the alien's return. Day-to-day existence was taking up all their time and effort. They had to lift themselves out of this deadly hiatus. And they would never do that by staying here.

Vance came to his decision, and quested a link to Antrinell and Jay. 'We're going to leave, travel in convoy to Sarvar.'

'Are you sure?' Jay asked.

'Yes. Our situation here is unsustainable. We're sitting round accomplishing nothing and presenting ourselves as a target for the creature. Heating the domes is consuming a huge amount of fuel. Right now we have a decent bioil reserve that can power the vehicles all the way to Sarvar. If we wait here for another week or ten days, that reserve becomes marginal. We need to prepare and move out as soon as we can. The schedule Vermekia sent is a good place to start, but we'll need to modify it considerably.'

'You made the right choice,' Antrinell said. 'I can't see them resupplying us inside of a month. There was way too much politics crapping on us from the top of the expedition.'

'And we're probably safer travelling,' Jay said. 'Vermekia was right, the creature will have trouble keeping up.'

'I'm not giving up on our primary mission to capture it,' Vance said. 'We need to work that into our travel plan.'

'Understood.'

Vance started issuing his orders. Bulldozers to build protective snow walls round the five remaining domes. The people in Justic's broken dome to billet down elsewhere. The microfacture team and the vehicle technicians to move into the now-reinforced microfacture shack and live there during the blizzard, where they would start printing the items needed for the trek south. Vehicle refit to start as soon as the blizzard ends. Department heads to liaise on ringlink during the blizzard, where the convoy details will be finalized.

*

Marvin Trambi kept on working while the rest of the camp jumped about to prepare them for the next blizzard. Conditions in mobile biolab-2 were calm and easy. The fuel cells providing the cab systems and laboratory with power operated at high temperature, which was bled into the air-con, keeping the scrubbed atmosphere inside at a civilized twenty-three degrees. The lighting was white and bright. Their little habitation cabin, wedged between the driver cab and the lab itself, had five bunks along with a kitchen gallery, and even a shower in the tiny washroom cubicle.

He'd done his fair share of moving loads around outside in the lulls between snowstorms, so he'd experienced the conditions the rest of the camp endured. It left him feeling mildly guilty about living in the biolab, but his work was the reason the expedition had been sent out here. Something everyone else seemed to be losing sight of with the murders and sunspots and weather flip.

He was sitting at the bench which ran the length of the lab, listening to some light jazz while the equipment was running genetic sample analysis. The biolab came with five separate RFLP analysis systems. Marvin had spent weeks sitting at the bench, reviewing the plant samples his colleagues brought in. The biolab carried the most comprehensive database of St Libra botany outside Highcastle University. When the little segments of bark, or branch or leaf cluster captured by the samplers was brought in, the first thing he did was run the visual identification routines. Anything that resembled a plant already in the database was immediately rejected. Some were zebra mirrors, a CO_2 to oxygen variant, while the records showed an oxygen to CO_2 converter with the same leaf shape – they were also rejected. The expedition was looking for a much greater divergence than that. Even restricting the genus they ran through genetic analysis to

747

complete unknowns, the two biolabs had so far seen over nineteen thousand different plants through the autoradiography process, searching for evidence that just one of them had a different ancestry, originating along a different branch of the evolutionary tree. They hadn't found even a hint of difference.

It was fully accepted among the expedition xenobiology team now that St Libra was bioformed. Their only argument was how long ago the event had occurred. However, Marvin was still interested in mapping the genetic difference. Given how many plants they'd encountered over a relatively small area of the total planet, the original genetic base must have been huge. After all, the plants had to evolve somewhere. It was a sore puzzle to Marvin how quite this many distinct plants could originate from a single common ancestor. His favourite hypothesis was that they'd evolved on a world with an even bigger surface area than St Libra, which raised some intriguing cosmological questions.

What he was truly desperate for was a hint of what else might have evolved on the origin planet. Presumably the planters had. After all, why would you bother bioforming a planet with vegetation that wasn't compatible with your own biochemistry? But if they had evolved in tandem with the St Libra plants, then surely the St Libra plants were adapted for a biosphere with insects and animals – which they didn't seem to be. But that avenue of investigation was so far nonexistent. Whatever the original plant on the origin world, it was giving no clues as to what else it had shared that world with. And it was curious that St Libra's plants thrived so well without insect and animal life, a milieu they'd evolved into. But if they were truly natural, then who had transported them here, and why?

St Libra was an intellectual challenge on so many levels. Barely a week in, before they even got to Wukang, Marvin realized he was far more content amid the enigmatic zebra botany jungle than he'd ever been studying the Zanth.

He carefully prepared a further batch of leaves for the first stage of analysis, feeding the capsules the sampler embedded them in to one of the automated processors which mashed them up separately before injecting a reactive agent which would break down the cell membrane to release the genetic material contained within. After that he could begin the more lengthy process of preparing that material for autoradiography. Their top-range scanners from the Cambridge Genomics Agency could run fifteen thousand simultaneous comparisons – more than they'd ever had in one batch.

Except the lab had run out of the agent. 'Damnit,' he mumbled. His e-i quested the lab's net. The camp's diminished network told him the lab supplies were still outside in a pallet. It was one that'd been moved close to the domes and vehicles, but still . . . outside.

Marvin stood up and stretched, unkinking stiff muscles. There was just so much damn preparation involved with going outside these days. He went into the little decontam airlock at the front of the lab, and cycled it. Smara Jacka was in the driver's cab, drinking tea from a mug as she munched on a packet of chocolate bonbons. She peered back through the small open hatchway into the central cabin as Marvin started pulling on his waterproof quilted trousers.

'We're out of the sample reactant again,' he complained.

'Damnit. Okay, I'll come with you.'

Elston's standing order was that no one was allowed outside alone. Marvin looked at the weather outside the cab's wide windscreen. Snow was whipping past, illuminated in the pastel emerald and cerise and topaz blooms of the borealis. It was the leading edge of the blizzard, not that he was sure he'd be able to tell the difference when the main body of the storm was upon them. The camp's links were full of snatched comments as the AAV crew helped the Land Rover Tropic driver creep towards the domes; the vehicle's wheels were losing traction on the claggy snow, and everyone was anxious to get back to their accommodation dome. Others were still getting supplies to the remaining domes. Josh Justic and the others from the broken dome were taking their belongings to new billets; as were the microfacture team as they headed for their shack. A Legionnaire squad was making one final perimeter patrol, trudging unhappily along the route, unable to see more than ten metres. The systems crew and aircraft technicians were trying to finish the lighting rigs they used for aircraft maintenance at night, hoping they could flood the campsite with light, and provide some kind of warning should the alien killer return.

'Don't bother,' Marvin said as he shoved his arms into a parka, fastening it over his armour vest. 'Our pallet is only twenty metres away.' He patted the Heckler carbine as he put the shoulder sling over his head. 'And my friend here will look after me. You can see me most of the way from the windscreen anyway.'

'You sure?'

'It's fine.'

Gloves, two layers; a hat with ear muffs under an armour helmet; pull the parka hood over that; ski-style goggles – and he was ready. He went into the door compartment, and his e-i gave the vehicle his lock code. The outer door popped out, and slid to the side on its rails. Snow gusted in, and heat raced away from him. He went carefully down the short ladder-steps to the snow outside. They'd moved the biolab that afternoon, driving it up out of the drifts that had accumulated on both sides. But the snow was accumulating against the big wheels once more.

He looked round as the door slid closed and locked again. There were maybe thirty people outside, hurrying to wherever they were going to wait out the blizzard, yet he couldn't see one of them. His bodymesh link with Wukang's net dropped out, then returned. The aurora borealis turned his speckled universe a dainty violet shade which chased away to salmon pink.

Marvin's e-i gave him a navigation display in his grid, highlighting the pallet with the lab supplies. He put one hand on the Heckler, and started walking towards it. Ten paces later, and the biolab's headlights flashed twice. He waved at the dark shape, assuming Smara could see him.

A minute later he was at the pallet. It took a while for him to clear the snow away from the side, wiping with gloved hands that were steadily becoming colder. Feeling began to seep away from his fingers. Eventually he exposed the flaps and opened them to get at the slim containers packed tightly inside. His helmet-light shone a stark halogen-white beam on the labels, and his e-i sent out a ping to the tag he wanted. A purple symbol appeared in his grid, identifying the container with the agent.

Far above, the aurora shimmered to a lambent green, casting a benign cyan glow across the pallet. A shadow slid over it, as smooth and oppressive as a lunar eclipse. Marvin twisted round.

The monster stood before him.

'No,' Marvin whimpered. Even through the numbing fear, he stared in amazement, trying to find the alienness of the bulky figure, the pure scientific evidence of evolutionary divergence from terrestrial life. Like all the xenobiology team he'd been given full access to the restricted reports of Frontline's interrogation of Angela Tramelo. She had described it well.

Dark it was, with those infamous savage knife blades for fingers. Leather turned stone for skin; today splattered with snow that clung to every wrinkle. Bipedal humanoid profile, he noted, with limb articulation a perfect match for *Homo sapiens*. A calcium mask face incapable of expressive projection. But the eyes, Angela had never mentioned the eyes; sunk back protectively into their sockets, they were human.

It was *fast*. An arm shot out, striking him in the chest. The terrible force flung him back violently, spreadeagling him against the pallet. But the impact went on longer than a simple blow, and it slowed at the end, as if the monster was punching through viscous fluid.

The arm was pulled back. For some reason, Marvin could no longer feel anything. His body had stopped breathing, even the growl of the wind had lessened to a sigh. Sweet gentian borealis light glimmered around him. It illuminated glistening fluid dripping from the monster's fingerblades.

Marvin looked down at his chest. Blood was flooding from the rent in his parka. The blades had punched clean through his warm clothes and the armour vest underneath.

751

He opened his mouth to say: 'Oh,' but blood surged up into his throat, drowning his vocal cords. The warm liquid poured out of his mouth as his legs gave way, pitching him forward. Marvin Trambi was dead by the time his face smacked into the snow.

*

It was true springtime in Newcastle now. April had brought nights that were still cool, but by day the sun shone bright and warm out of a cloudless sky, rising a little higher every noon. If there were showers they were swift, moved on quickly by a brisk wind to leave the city gleaming fresh and clean in their wake.

Ian always enjoyed the spring. Everybody's mood improved after their immersion in the drab winter of north-east England. Girls wore dresses again. Urban trees budded, adding a refreshing frosting of verdant green to the harsh stone and concrete streets.

And this year Tallulah had entered his life. This year promised to be the finest yet. He just had to play it right.

By eleven forty-five that morning the silver rain had stopped, and the sun was shining intermittently through clouds that scudded away into the western horizon. Ian walked over to Eva's desk. She'd been assigned to another third-floor office, working a case over in Arthur's Hill where a family argument had resulted in the father killing one of his children before the mother chopped him apart with the knives she'd brought back home from their restaurant. Did that make it premeditated? Eva was working through witness statements and psychiatric reports to determine what had really happened that bad night.

'Buy you some lunch?' Ian asked.

Eva gave him a surprised look before her freckled face turned happy. 'Sure. Thanks. This is just too gruesome. Those poor kids.'

'I thought there was just the one?'

'One dead, but he had a brother and sister. They're both in care now. Nobody is going to win this one.'

752

They walked out into the mild humidity of Grey Street, and turned down towards the river.

'So have you seen Sid?' Eva asked.

'Not over the weekend, no.'

'We're going to have to trigger the downloads soon.'

'I know, pet. I heard legal is going to send the North file on to the Prosecution Bureau tomorrow. If we don't have anything on Sherman, it's all going to hit the fan by the end of this week.'

'I don't know why he's waiting so long. I would have downloaded by now.'

'Aye, that's why he made it to third grade. He takes risks.'

'Sid?'

Ian gave her a grin. 'A dark horse is our Sid, pet. Thought you knew that by now.'

They walked down Quayside, going under the base of the Tyne Bridge.

'Where exactly are we going?' Eva asked.

'In here.' Ian led her into the Tollamarch Arms, one of the pubs that occupied the big row of Georgian buildings that lined this end of Quayside. The room running along the front was a grandiose relic of ancient corporate elegance, with a high ceiling and the kind of wide oak floorboards that no one could afford these days. Where solicitors and their clerks once prowled through ledgers there was now a long bar complemented by deep leather chairs and polished resin tables with knotted legs. It served a good range of bar snacks and provided an excellent view out across the river, the perfect venue for middle-management lunches. They found a window seat; Ian ordered a mineral water while Eva chose a glass of Sauvignon Blanc.

'So how busy are you on the fourth floor?' Eva asked as they read the menus.

'It's eased off a bit now the GE is talking to Highcastle Council about letting people back through. The HDA Legionnaires have stood down, anyway; it's just the GE Boarder Directorate troops guarding the gateway, with the agency constables on reserve. And

753

I know for a fact that NI personnel are being allowed back. I was down on Last Mile this Saturday afternoon. There must have been fifty buses coming through the gateway in the hour I was there.'

'Because they've shut down bioil production,' Eva said. 'There's no reason for them to be there, any more.'

'They have to keep them sweet,' Ian said. 'Northumberland Interstellar and the other Great Eight will need engineers to start the algaepaddies back up once the sunspots have gone and St Libra's back to normal again.'

'I suppose.'

The waitress brought their drinks over. Eva ordered a salad with sautéed duck liver, walnuts, apple, and grape; Ian had the salmon fillet with new potatoes.

'Did you hear what the actual percentage of GE bioil is that comes from St Libra?' Eva asked in a low voice. 'My husband says that the cut-off is going to—'

Tallulah and two of her female office colleagues walked in. They were chattering happily as they came through the door, already taking their raincoats off. She stopped and gave Ian a surprised look. But not an unhappy one.

He'd got the timing about right, then.

'Hello,' he said as he got to his feet. 'I didn't know you used this place.'

'Um, yeah, sometimes,' she admitted, warding off curious glances from her friends.

Eva's freckled forehead had creased into a mild frown of suspicion.

'How are you coping?' Ian asked.

'Oh, better now, I suppose.'

'That's good.' He made a show of coming to a reckless decision. 'Look, it's fate I guess that we both wound up here. See, as it's my lunch break, I'm technically off duty, so I'm in the clear to ask you if you'd like to go for a drink tonight, and maybe see Bloxo at the Sage.' He waved a hand at the window, where the huge bulbous semi-silver curves of the giant Sage building dominated the other side of the river.

754

'Bloxo?' Tallulah's surprise overrode her caution. 'They've been sold out for weeks. How did you get tickets? Even Boris couldn't—' Her lips pressed together in annoyance.

'Aye, well, man, being in the police does have some advantages. I have a friend who has a friend, so down the line my question goes, and back up comes a pair of tickets. But I'm a sad singleton again. So . . . yours if you'd like.'

It took her a moment, spent not consulting with her friends. 'Okay, that would be nice, thank you. But I'll pay for it, of course.'

'Aye, not going to argue with that, then.'

They smiled sheepishly at each other, the way it always was between people who'd just shared a moment. Both submitting to fickle impulse that might, just might, lead to something altogether more promising.

Ian's smile had grown wider by the time he sat down; and Tallulah was walking off to a spare table on the other side of the room, friends gaggling in hushed, excited voices.

'I don't appreciate being used like that,' Eva said, her tone and expression unforgiving.

'Aye, man, it was just chance she came in here.'

'No, it wasn't. Ian, this trick you pull harvesting them, it's not nice. Actually, it verges on creepy.'

'Not with her,' he said, defensively.

'Yes, with her,' Eva insisted. 'This is just the same thing you pull with all the others.'

'How then?' Ian hissed in exasperation. 'How else does someone like me ever get to meet a girl like that? I don't know any other way. Okay, so I might have known she was coming here. But after that, everything that happens is just natural. You heard her, she said yes.'

'All right, so she said yes. But Ian, she's a witness in the biggest case you'll ever work on. The murder was committed in her apartment.'

'Away wi' you, man, that's just coincidence.'

Eva shook her head before taking a sip of the wine. 'Not with this case. I've seen how smart it was put together. There'll be a reason, a connection. Her apartment was chosen for a purpose. I never fell for her innocent beauty bollocks. I don't care how pretty she is, she knows something. She has to.'

'Come on! What? We harvested everything there is to harvest on her. She's a victim. They chose her at random to shunt us into another dead end. That's the smart of it.'

'You're being crapped on. They should ban men from interviewing girls like that. Especially men like you. So you "just happen to have Bloxo tickets" is a coincidence, is it? They're piling up in her life, aren't they? Or maybe that is her life, a coincidence that there's always a coincidence?'

'That's got nothing to do with it. You saw how she was with me. She never considered saying no. It's going to work, her and me, you see.'

'Until she finds you hitting on her best friend, or her little sister, or her mother if you're really bored.'

'No,' Ian said firmly. 'Not this time. This time, man, I knew as soon as I saw her.'

'Oh dear God.' Eva took a bigger drink of the wine. 'I can't believe I'm saying this, because crap knows you deserve to be hurt for once, but be careful. A girl like that . . .'

'Aye, what, man? She's too good for me? Is that what you think of me?'

'She's an eight and a half, maybe a full nine. You're what? A four?'

'Bollocks to you, pet.'

'Just do yourself a favour, ease up until we download from Sherman's crew.'

'There is no connection!'

'Fine. Good. Prove me wrong. If she is genuinely innocent, that's going to force you into making some serious choices for once. It's about bloody time you started to grow up, because – and trust me on this – Tallulah won't put up with the usual shitty way you treat women. If you are even approaching serious, you're going to have to get your act together big-time.'

'Aye, thanks for that, Mum.'

Eva couldn't keep her face stern. 'You and her? Really. I've got to admire that level of ambition.'

'Hey, she's not that far out of my league.'

'Dream on, Romeo.'

Tuesday 9th April 2143

The ten weeks since he'd landed on Newcastle's Town Moor in his lightwave spaceship had been difficult for Clayton 2North. That first night, when he and Ivan's team had abducted his brother-cousin Abner, had probably been the worst. But Abner's age matched his own rejuvenated appearance the best, making him the inevitable choice. It had been a long time since he'd done any active field work. He had to steel himself against Abner's fear and confusion when they broke into his flat and surrounded him in his own bedroom. Fortunately, such aloofness came easily to a North.

The bargain helped. Abner's cooperation in exchange for a full rejuvenation treatment at the Jupiter habitat, something he would probably never receive on Earth. To sweeten the deal, Clayton even offered a one-in-ten genetic resequence at the same time. Abner seethed and shouted and cursed, but after that show of defiance to prove he wasn't someone you could just push around, he agreed to being given a thousand years of extra life with phenomenal bad grace.

So it was that Clayton had gone to work on the morning of Tuesday the fifteenth of January masquerading as Abner. He had some leeway settling in; with a brother 2North just murdered it was reasonable to expect him to be shocked, not quite his usual self. With the codes and personal information Abner had grudgingly donated in a fast debrief, he had quickly grown into his adopted identity. From that moment the only other victim of the swap had been poor Melissa Stosnoski, Abner's girlfriend, who had been unceremoniously dumped – again, a well-refined North trait.

For all his achievement in fitting his new role, those ten weeks had been deeply frustrating. He had to admit, Detective Sid Hurst ran a good investigation, especially under the duress of HDA supervision and interference. The determination all of the team showed in the nightmare monotony of backtracking the taxi was admirable.

But for all the investigation's achievements, the only substantial result those ten weeks had actually delivered was Ernie Reinert, the expendable clean-up guy who didn't know anything. Hardly a stunning success.

Something on St Libra which had killed several Norths had returned, and was still walking round Newcastle with impunity. Given how thorough and dedicated Sid had been, that was actually quite troublesome to Clayton. It was Constantine's unshakable belief that there was no conflict between Augustine and Bartram setting the agenda, this wasn't a corporate conflict gone bad. This was something altogether stranger. Ever since Bartram's murder, Jupiter had been playing the long game, waiting for the alien to emerge again.

Constantine's first decision following Angela Tramelo's near-farcical trial was to appoint Clayton to head up a detailed private enquiry into the whole horrendous event. He'd spent eighteen months on a painstaking review, unencumbered by political jurisdiction turf wars between Abellia and the GE, but aided by specialist and expensive byteheads who could pull information from places they shouldn't even know existed. He even visited New Washington and personally talked to Marlak; an altogether more pleasant experience than his fast, short, expletive-filled meeting with Shasta Nolif. When he'd finished he was able to present a revelatory file to Constantine concerning the utterly fascinating life of Ms Angela DeVoyal/Matthews/Howard/Tramelo.

She was innocent of the murders he had no doubt, her brutal HDA interrogation clinched that. Which meant there really was an unknown entity targeting the North family. As a precaution they brought Rebka to Jupiter, a covert operation Clayton still regarded as his finest hour. Having her living in the habitat and part of their community gave Constantine an extra move to play should they need it. After that, there was little else to do but watch and wait. No one had expected the wait to be quite so long.

But now, despite everything, Newcastle was proving to be a dead end. The only unnerving thing to emerge was the existence of at least one unknown 2North. And nobody at Jupiter had any idea about that. Whatever or whoever it was that had taken to murdering Norths, it had moved back to St Libra. Rebka's last call had been very clear on that point. Now she along with the rest of Wukang was cut off, and being stalked. He was reasonably confident she could survive any attack from the creature whose image had been extracted from Angela's memory. Rebka had the same advanced combat equipment he did, and she was trained for the encounter.

What Clayton didn't understand, and it was his biggest worry, was why the alien had singled out camp Wukang.

So while the Newcastle police had finished investigating the murder, and sent their files up to the Prosecution Bureau, Clayton certainly hadn't given up his analysis. Which was why he was in Market Street at nine pm, sitting in an unused second-floor office, with the room's security mesh neutralized, accessing supposedly inactive network files. He'd always been curious about the firebombing at Reinert's garage while forensics were still going over the place. It implied there was something in the garage that the murderer didn't want the police to find; which in turn implied that the murderer was in contact with a local criminal crew capable of organizing a successful attack.

He told his e-i to access the investigation logs using infiltrators he'd planted in the Office3 network that day he arrived. His grid filled with the case's network architecture, and he noticed that eighteen observation routines were still active, using Market

Street's visual recognition and AI tracking systems. He got the e-i to hack their management sub-routines easily enough, finding they'd been authorized by Vance Elston back in late February. Which was interesting, given that Elston was at camp Edzell on St Libra at the time.

Clayton immediately loaded some monitors of his own to check his unauthorized access hadn't been spotted. But the network wasn't issuing any alerts. He started digging deeper. Whoever had set up the observation routines knew what they were doing, employing a route with multiple random switching and cut-offs with self-erasing logs. He had to access the secure AI the Newcastle team used to run the trackback.

Data gleaned from the observation was flowing to an address he was familiar with: Detective Ian Lanagin's bachelor flat. But who Ian was gathering information on was more interesting: Marcus Sherman, Ruckby, Jede, Boz. The last three all had entries in the police network, petty criminal offences from years back, with the Gang Task Force noting that Boz might be a possible Red Shield member – no proof. Marcus Sherman had no record of any kind loaded into the Market Street network.

It took the Newcastle team's AI four minutes to find the name. Fifteen years ago, Sherman used to work for Northumberland Interstellar's security division. He left the company, and fell off-net. Judging from a quick harvest of the data the observation routines were pulling in, Mr Sherman was maintaining his über-low profile to this day.

Clayton sat back in his chair, and gave the console a serene smile. Ian Lanagin wouldn't waste his free time chasing corporate ghost operatives. He had a total of two non-work activities, his fitness kick and hitting on girls. This was something else, something a lot more important, and he wouldn't be doing it on his own.

'Sid,' Clayton murmured admiringly to the empty office. 'What have you been up to?'

*

The flat in Falconar Street was easy enough to break in to. Clayton took Ivan with him, leaving Sophia and Holdroyd, the other members of the Newcastle team, in the car parked three houses down.

It was quarter to ten, and the clouds were building in the sky, blocking the crescent moon. All of which left the street dark and devoid of pedestrians. Sophia and the AI quickly ripped the civic meshes smeared across the brickwork of the terrace houses, and Ivan decoded the lock. They went in calmly, knowing they had plenty of time.

Ian wasn't the only one who monitored people for personal gain. The team was checking his transnet access constantly: he was at the Stravoss restaurant in The Gate, good food but the service was notoriously slow, he'd be there for another hour at least.

Once they were inside the three-room flat Clayton and Ivan looked round in confusion.

'Where's the furniture?' Ivan asked.

Clayton shrugged and glanced into the bedroom. 'He's got a bed. And look at that Apple console, it's practically got the capacity to run an AI.'

Ivan applied an interceptor patch to the back of the sleek rectangle with its tiny green and purple LEDs. Clayton sprayed a patch of smartmicrobes onto the ceiling, then went into the front lounge and kitchen, repeating the procedure.

'We're done,' Ivan announced. 'I've loaded mirror relays inside the Apple. What he knows, we know. I'll get our AI to run an analysis.'

'Let's go.'

*

Back in Abner's cosy flat in the Fortin singletown, Clayton settled down to wait. Ivan and the rest of the team kept shooting updates to his e-i on their progress with the data from Ian's Apple. Call records showed Sherman and his associates were involved in some kind of handover. So far they hadn't found anything which connected them to Reinert, except for them all dropping from sight the day the garage was firebombed.

It was a simple coincidence that no policeman would ever send on to legal, never mind the Prosecution Bureau. Clayton knew what it meant: Sherman and Reinert knew the same people further up the food chain. Sid would understand that, too.

So why hadn't he included Sherman in the official investigation?

Clayton's second surprise of the night was when Ian returned home. The monitor program tagging his transnet interface showed him taking a taxi from the Gate centre back to Falconar Street. Then the meshes in the flat gave Clayton a bird's-eye view of the lounge as Ian and his date walked in.

It was Tallulah Packer. Clayton viewed the image for a moment in complete disbelief. He thought the angle might have thrown off his recognition. But then they started talking in that easy casual way that eager lovers have, and there was no mistake. She was teasing him about the lack of furniture. He took it with good grace, and offered her a wine, a Semillon Verdelho. Apparently it was her favourite. They kissed. Fumbled at each other's clothes. Ian led her into the bedroom, the wine glass forgotten on the kitchenette counter.

Clayton cancelled the feed from the mesh in the bedroom. He wasn't a voyeur.

Ten weeks working in the same office as Ian made him sure of one thing: this wasn't a cover-up. Ian kept his brain in his dick, and Tallulah was astonishingly pretty. He was guilty of being terminally stupid by dating a potential witness from the case, but nothing more sinister.

Clayton checked the time: eleven twenty-three. The traffic from Ian's surreptitious observation routines was slow and steady as they followed Sherman around the city wherever they could gain digital traction. Nothing big was happening tonight. He got into bed and promised himself he'd review the forensics team's visual logs from Reinert's garage tomorrow.

Wednesday 10th April 2143

Clayton's e-i woke him up at two ten am with a major alert, triggered by the call monitor he'd put on Ian's transnet interface. He shook himself awake and put the team on standby. His e-i pulled real-time imagery from the smartmicrobe meshes at Ian's apartment.

*

Sid drove the Toyota Dayon into a space practically outside Ian's flat, too quick and braking too hard. The auto flashed up an amber caution in his grid as the car detected other vehicles front and back. He ignored it. Temper had powered him out of his own house and got him here at just after half past two in the morning following Ian's cryptic call. But fatigue was creeping back. He was tired, irritated to be woken, and just wanted to be home in bed.

The house's outside door opened as soon as he pinged it, and he stomped up the stairs. Ian was waiting in the lounge, dressed in PJ trousers and an old grey T-shirt.

'Why are you crapping on me at this hour?' Sid demanded. 'Is Sherman going to kill someone? I had to tell Jacinta that Market Street was calling me in.' He stopped. Tallulah Packer was standing in the bedroom doorway, looking unbelievably hot wrapped in Ian's dressing gown, her auburn hair delectably dishevelled.

764

'You're fucking joking,' Sid growled.

Tallulah's lips quivered as she fought back tears.

Ian went over and gently put his arms round her, close and reassuring. 'It's all right, pet. Please, I told you you'll be fine. You've done nothing wrong.'

'What is going on?' Sid asked.

'Tallulah told me something,' Ian said. 'It's not something I'd ever share. Not normally, like. But, boss . . . it's really important. To us. To the case.'

'All right.' Sid took a breath, trying to calm down. 'What is it?'

Tallulah stayed mute, shaking her head.

'We were talking,' Ian said, his own embarrassment making him hesitant. 'Aye, you know. Getting to know each other. Saying about all the kinds of sex we've both had, which we liked best, what we wanted to try with each other—'

'Ian . . .' Sid *really* didn't want to hear this.

'Boss,' the pleading was painful. 'Our exes, we talked about our exes.'

'I had an affair,' Tallulah said at last. She couldn't look at Sid, keeping her eyes downcast. 'It ended when I got engaged. Well, almost. It's been over since December, anyway.'

'Okay, well we've all had fun when we were single,' Sid said. It seemed the right thing to say.

Tallulah drew down a long breath, as if she was in a confessional with a particularly unforgiving priest. 'I was sleeping with Aldred North.'

Sid simply didn't possess an instinct to guide his reaction to that. He just stood there with his jaw open dumbly. 'Aldred North?' he repeated, because he had probably misheard. 'You were Aldred North's girlfriend?'

The poor girl nodded, looking like she was about to cry again. Ian's arm tightened round her.

Sid rubbed a hand across his forehead, massaging the fatigue away. 'All right, Tallulah, listen to me. Ian is quite right – you've done nothing wrong. We just have to know a few details, that's all. The investigation is over, and if you tell us everything we can keep you out of things, okay? That's why Ian called me over here, to make sure you're covered.'

'Really?' Tallulah asked. 'I'm not in trouble?'

'No. Not yet,' he said, which was partially truc. 'But, pet, we have to understand what happened. That's what's really important here. So: how long were you seeing him?'

'Six months. No, wait, more like eight. We met back in March last year. He wanted to keep it quiet – he was still seeing Lady Jennifer, but it wasn't going well, it hadn't been for a while. He was really unhappy. He said he didn't want to make it any worse, that we should give her time to finish their relationship on her own terms.'

'You were seeing each other in secret?'

'Privately.' Tallulah pouted. 'I'm not a home wrecker, I didn't break them up. It was practically over when we started.'

'I see. So you met in your apartment, not his?'

'Yes. We couldn't go to his because Lady Jennifer was still living there.'

'And he lives in the St James, so it was easy.'

'Yes. At first. But . . . I met Boris. And we could go out in public together and do things like I never could with Aldred. Oh, we went away for a few weekends together, but it was always the two of us in some chalet or villa. Never in public. It was exciting at first, then in the end I realized he was just using me. All he wanted me for was sex.'

'When you figured that out, you broke it off?'

She sniffed. 'Yes.'

'So back in January, he still had the lock codes for your apartment?'

'I . . . yes. Changing the code would be difficult. Boris would want to know why; he was quite possessive. And Aldred was seeing someone else by then. Lady Jennifer had left him.'

'All right,' Sid said. 'Now this next bit is very important. Why didn't you tell us this when we took you into custody?'

'He was there. Aldred was waiting for me when Ian took me up to the interview room.'

'Oh crap on it,' Sid groaned, remembering that day, how it didn't seem odd at all. In fact, at the time it was Ian's behaviour which he'd worried about. 'What did Aldred say? Did he threaten you?'

'No. Nothing like that. He was reassuring. He said he'd protect me from any involvement, that no one would ever have to know about the two of us. And ... and ... Boris was there. You remember Chantilly Sanders-Watson?'

'Oh yeah,' Sid said. 'I remember her.'

'She was my lawyer, only she wasn't; Boris paid for her. I couldn't tell her why it was my apartment that poor North got murdered in. Boris might have found out. We were going to get married!'

'So you played the innocent card,' Sid said. 'Claimed you had no idea why your apartment was chosen.'

'Well I don't,' she insisted. 'Not really. Aldred called me afterwards, he said he was really sorry, that it was likely someone was trying to discredit him, or set him up, that it was part of a high-level corporate conflict and I shouldn't worry any more, that he'd make sure you, the police, stayed away from me. And he can do that, he's a very powerful man.'

'Aye,' Sid said. 'He is that.'

*

Clayton carried on watching while Sid made himself a cup of tea. Tallulah and Ian went back into the bedroom, where she got dressed. Ian's e-i called for a taxi.

'Sir, do you want to question her?' Ivan asked. 'We can intercept the taxi, pick her up in one of ours.'

'Taxis are useful in this town, aren't they?' Clayton mused. 'So perfectly anonymous. And they all look the same.'

'Sir, it's time-critical, we need a decision.'

'No. Leave her alone. She's not a player, she's simply been used.'

'So did Aldred kill the victim?'

'I don't know. If he did then he must have a very warped reason to use this particular method and do it in his ex-girlfriend's apartment. It doesn't make a lot of sense.'

'Could he have told Tallulah the truth, that someone is trying to discredit him?'

'I suppose so. Crap knows, Augustine has enough rivals on Earth. The old cartel always seems solid from the outside, but you never know when the bedrock is going to shift underneath you without warning. Ask Angela. Nothing in this life is certain.'

'But the creature is real – it's killing people at Wukang.'

'I know. But we don't know why.' He saw Tallulah and Ian come back out into the lounge. 'Let's see what the police make of this, shall we. It would seem I've underestimated them.'

*

Sid drank his tea, making every effort not to listen to what was being said in the stairwell outside the flat. Voices were muffled by the door, but from Ian's urgent, near-pleading tones, it was obvious he was desperate to see Tallulah again.

The taxi pulled up outside, and Sid watched through the window as Tallulah climbed in. It was a citycab, he noticed idly. *So we've come full circle.* Ian stood on the pavement, watching the taxi until it vanished from sight.

'Quite a night,' Sid said gently as Ian came back into the lounge.

Ian gave him a forlorn look. 'Aye, man, I screwed up.'

'You did the right thing telling me.'

'Not that, I mean with her.'

'Ah. What did she say? Will she see you again?'

'Aye, she said we could talk. I know what that means.'

'No, you don't, Ian. You only know what that means when you say it. If Tallulah said it, that's good. She will see you again. She needs you, Ian. You're the one who can get her through this.'

'She wasn't involved. She wasn't. That bastard Aldred used her.'

'I don't think he did.'

'Huh?'

'A North was murdered in the apartment of the mistress of Northumberland Interstellar's head of security. Really? We still don't know who our victim was, but we know it was corporate, which makes the location an attempt to ruin Aldred. My guess is Aldred probably had the body cleared away by Reinert, he's certainly got the connections to make that happen. Whoever did it couldn't have been expecting that.' As he said it there was still a wisp of doubt troubling him. Augustine North had seemed very genuine when he said he wanted to know who had killed his son. And if Aldred knew he was being set up he'd have asked Sid to ease up on the investigation.

I'd probably have done it, too.

'So how do we find out?'

'Ian. We don't. Not for O'Rouke and the Prosecution Bureau, anyway. Whatever's going on is completely out of our league, which means we have to be extremely careful. A North was murdered: if you've got the clout to do that, a couple of policemen aren't going to bother you. If we ever do find out, it's for ourselves only, to satisfy us that it's over and we're in the clear. Understand?'

'Aye, and how do we do that, boss?'

'Ask Aldred.'

'Ask him?'

'He trusts me, because I've never let him down.'

'Wait. Aldred is your corporate contact?'

'You don't make it up to third grade without help and approval, Ian. Not in this screwed-up world.'

'Oh crap on all of this.'

Sid put a hand on Ian's shoulder, squeezing tight. 'Honesty night, huh. Painful stuff, man.'

'Aye. You'll really just ask him?'

'It might need to be quite a forceful question. We'll have to prepare.'

*

Sid arrived at the Jamaica Blue café on John Dobson Street just after eleven o'clock and sat in an empty booth beside the window. He watched people walking past in the bright spring sunlight, envying their simple lives. They lived in his world, but never saw the complexity, the forces which moved them. There were times he wished he didn't.

'Morning,' Aldred said and slid onto the bench opposite Sid. As always he was wearing a smart suit, but not a flashy one. A typical anonymous North. If you had to take a guess, you'd go for Northumberland Interstellar management, but what kind of division was unknowable.

Sid saw a bodyguard up at the counter ordering a tea and croissant, another out on the street, close to the café door, watching people going in.

Am I the only one that sees them?

'This is difficult,' Sid said.

'Oh dear. What have you got for me, Sid? You know I don't bite.'

'I've been told the Prosecution Bureau is going to charge Reinert today. Which means everyone will know your brother wasn't a carjacking victim.'

'I don't think many ever did.'

'Aye, well, the only thing they can charge him with is accessory after the fact. If a court finds him guilty, he'll serve two years in a correctional education camp, then be dumped on his very own five acres of Minisa on the opposite side of the planet from its gateway and told not to come back.'

'Yes.'

'There's going to be a media shitstorm when the charges are publicly logged with the court. Lots of politicians, especially opposition ones, asking why the police can't find the murderer. O'Rouke will promise the case will remain open.'

770

'Of course he will. He has no choice.'

'But it's dead. We covered every angle. I genuinely don't have another lead to go on. I'm sorry.'

'Sid, I already briefed Augustine when Reinert's file was sent to the Prosecution Bureau. We know what's going to happen. And I know you did everything you could, I was there, you know.'

Sid looked at him over his tea cup. Was Aldred playing him? 'You were a big help with O'Rouke.'

'Yes, well, O'Rouke is something of a dinosaur. Effective, mind – he's done great things for this city, and we're all grateful – but it's probably best he claims his well-deserved retirement package now.'

'And me?'

'No, Sid. We don't blame you.'

'O'Rouke will be putting me up for grade-five before he leaves. The filework's already been logged with the promotions board.'

Aldred pursed his lips. 'One grade from the top, eh? You deserve it. You did a good job.'

'Is there still a place for me in your division? I'd appreciate an honest answer. I deserve that, I think.'

'Sid, we're not the mafia, I've always been level with you, that's what I like about our arrangement. Yes there is a place for you at Northumberland Interstellar, there always will be. Can I offer some advice?'

'I'd welcome it.'

'Stick with a grade-five position for a couple of years before you think about the transfer over.'

'Okay. Why?'

Aldred indicated the street scene on the other side of the window. 'Sunny day out there, nice and warm. It's going to be another drought summer.'

'They all are these days.'

'Not on St Libra, they're not. Our entire operation there is in the process of shutting down. We're bringing our people back here.'

'I know. That's good of you.'

'Sid, Northumberland Interstellar is a corporation, bottom line. In fact, the *only* line. We only do charity if we get a decent tax relief out of it. We're bringing them back because the farms out there are as dead as our algaepaddies. It's cheaper to allow personnel back than it is to ship food to them through the gateway. It's cheaper for them to find themselves a rented house on the open market here than for us to provide their tropical condo with insulation and power for heating. And when this is all over, when the redshift ends and the snow melts, it's going to wash away half of Highcastle. That city isn't hardy like Newcastle, Sid, it wasn't built for cold weather. We'll have to rebuild it. This could break us, Sid, this could break Northumberland Interstellar.'

'Crap on it. Seriously?'

'I don't know, Sid. My father doesn't know. Nobody knows. Not even all those analysts that fill our offices. But building ourselves back to pre-sunspot levels is going to take decades of work. Money is going to be tight. And we'll be competing for credit with the other bioil companies that are going to be expanding their operations while we're down and out. That's on top of the recession we've just triggered and no one has noticed yet.'

'The recession?' Sid wished he didn't sound quite so ignorant.

'Sid, St Libra supplies over sixty per cent of the GE's bioil, and quite a lot to other nations, too. That tap has been turned off. You're going to be lucky if you can heat your house next winter. If you've got a log-burner stove, I suggest you start chopping down trees this summer. We're in for ten years of very harsh times. Which is why I suggest you keep your government job, funded by that glorious, everlasting, inexhaustible supply of taxpayers' money. I can guarantee you a job right now – I can't guarantee you the company will survive.'

'Oh.'

'Oh indeed.'

'Sorry. I didn't realize how bad this was. I've not been paying attention.'

'I know. Three weeks ago, the murder was all that mattered to me, to my brothers; and our father was obsessed by it. Now, even I don't care. So thank you for the job you did, Sid. We won't forget our friends. But you need to look after yourself and your family.'

Sid followed Aldred out of the Jamaica Blue café. He stood on the pavement and watched the North walk over to the Mercedes limousine parked in the loading-only bay. The bodyguards closed around as he got in, then the car was pulling away into the traffic.

When it turned into St Mary's Place and vanished from sight, Eva and Ian came up behind Sid.

'That was depressing,' Eva said. 'Sixty per cent? I didn't know it was that much; my husband said it was thirty. Damn, we're in for some bad times.'

'Brussels never liked admitting how dependent we were on St Libra,' Ian said. 'Bloody typical, like.'

'Did you place the smartmicrobe?' Sid asked them.

'Aye man, no problem,' Ian said. 'That little cyber-ant machine walked right up to his shoe and zapped the heel. Lucky the café switches their meshes off while you have your meetings.'

'Aye. Lucky. We're due some of that.'

'So how long do we leave it before we download Aldred?' Eva asked.

'Let's give it another week,' Sid said. 'If he's going to talk to Sherman again, it'll be soon. We'll download everyone simultaneously and see what we've caught.'

'Let's hope he keeps wearing those shoes,' Eva said.

'We gave it our best shot, pet,' Sid said. 'One way or another, this is going to be over soon.'

'Tallulah called,' Ian said with a broad smile. 'While you were in there talking, she called. She said she'd see me this evening.'

Sid put his arm round Ian's shoulder and gave him a happy shake. 'That's good, man. If the two of you can survive something like last night, you've got a real chance with her.'

'So don't blow it,' Eva said. 'When you take her out tonight, don't be you.'

'Hey!'

'I mean it,' Eva said. 'She needs to talk about this. Don't make the evening just about getting her back into bed. If you want this to last, show an interest in her.'

'She's got a point.' Sid grinned. 'For a start, steer clear of the places you usually go.'

'Aye, man,' Ian groaned. 'Dating advice from married people. Give me more of that.'

Thursday 11th April 2143

The thaw arrived as fast as it was unexpected. Some pocket of warm air that had somehow endured the redshift and storm patterns came rushing in from the south-west during Wednesday night, driving the aurora borealis away. But by then, warm was a relative term for the Brogal continent.

When it did arrive at Wukang just after daybreak, the snow walls around the domes were nearly four metres high, and windsculpted into impressive arching overhangs, as if nature was mimicking the curvature of the panels. The onset of warmer weather brought out work details. Armed with long poles, they started to break off slippery chunks around the apex of each wall. The snow was already turning to slush and dripping hard. They had to work quickly before the entire overhangs tumbled down. The weight of them would probably shatter the dome panels underneath, themselves trapped at sub-zero temperatures under a second, thinner layer of insulating snow that covered them.

Outside the snow walls, the drifts were thawing under the stunted pink light that shone down through a clear sky. Trickles of water began to deepen, cutting through the snow to form crumbling gullies. It was as if the snow had started to rot. People walking about found their feet sinking up to the knee. The only vehicles able to move with any success were the tracked bull-dozers. Vance Elston immediately set them to work, clearing the heavy dunes that had built up around the microfacture shack and the Qwik-Kabins.

With the clear-up under way, he called a senior staff meeting in the microfacture shack. It was crowded in the long rectangular space. Ophelia's team had been working constantly, printing a prototype sledge to be pulled by vehicles, a couple of thick V-shaped ploughs to fit on the front of the MTJs, and several broad tyres with deep treads.

'The tyres we have are all too narrow for these conditions,' explained Leif Davdia, the vehicle chief. 'We can fit these to the MTJs and the Land Rovers without any trouble. But the tanker and trucks will need some work. If we can cut away some of the bodywork from around the wheel arches I think we can fit a decent size.'

Vance stood beside one of the tyres intended for an MTJ – it came up to his elbows. 'Is there enough raw for this?'

Leif and Ophelia exchanged a look. 'We think so,' Ophelia said. 'Given we won't be coming back, we can use everything. The trick will be a blend that can withstand the cold and give us the flexibility we need.'

'All right, which vehicles are we using?'

'The three Tropics,' Forster said.

'Hopefully,' Leif said quickly. 'I'd like to make some systems modification before we set off.'

'What's wrong with them?' Vance asked.

'The clue's in the name,' Karizma said.

Vance gave her a look, but let the rudeness slide. They'd all been working hard in unfavourable conditions, and nobody got much sleep. Even so, he told his e-i to remind him to speak to Jay about her. They needed to maintain discipline now more than ever.

'Davdia?' he invited.

'Uh, yes, well the same applies to most of our equipment, but it's most acute for the Tropics. They don't even have heaters in the cab. Rigging something up to the air-con isn't a problem, I can have something crude but working inside of a few days. But

776

then there's the bodywork. It's the same problem we had with the domes – the composite wasn't designed for this temperature. They'll be brittle.'

'What about the chassis?'

'That's not a problem, sir – they're Land Rover standard. It's everything else which is customized according to environment.'

'Wouldn't it just be easier not to take them?'

'No, sir,' Forster said. 'We've got an accommodation shortage. We'll be putting some people in sledges as it is.'

'I see. Okay, carry on; what else?'

'I want to use the MTJs to take point duty; the snowploughs can cut through the deeper drifts. They can alternate to give their crews some relief. Whichever one is off-point will tow a sledge, along with all three Tropics. Then the tanker, of course. And both trucks will be used to carry additional fuel-bladder tanks; they're capable of towing more supplies on sledges too, if we have time to print them. We're expecting to leave the trucks behind as we run down our bioil. The cabs only take two people, so it won't be too much trouble.'

Vance waited a moment. 'What about the biolabs?'

'We considered them,' Leif said. 'But frankly, they use up a lot of fuel. I think we're better off putting people into sledges.'

'No,' Vance said flatly. 'We're taking the biolabs. I'm not having anyone travelling in a sledge, period. We're adding complexity and putting people in harm's way. The entire xenobiology team can travel in the biolabs, and some extra personnel too. If you're worried about fuel, they can tow their own reserve tanks. Sorry, but that's not up for discussion.'

'Yes, sir.'

'We might not have enough raw for their tyres,' Karizma said. 'In fact I know we don't.'

'The biolabs are configured for difficult terrain,' Vance told her. 'They can crawl over Zanth if they have to. In the convoy they can go in the middle – the snow will be compacted from the lead vehicles. They'll be able to cope with that as they are.'

'You're making this more difficult than it has to be.'

'Excuse me?'

'Enough,' Jay cautioned her.

'No. It's not.' Karizma faced Vance, completely unrepentant. 'You got us into this. You could have insisted on an evac flight when this world started crapping on us, but you didn't.'

'We have a mission to complete,' Vance said with what he hoped was quiet authority. 'And you are a serving HDA member.'

'Bullshit. This isn't a mission, it's a fucking disaster.'

'Wadhai!' Jay warned.

'What? I'm going to be in trouble? Big fucking deal. This convoy, it's a bunch of crap. You're making it worse for us. Two thousand kilometres through a jungle that's four metres deep in snow. That's a complete fucking joke. Nobody can do that. You're going to get us killed out there, and for what?'

'I'm getting us out of here,' Vance said. 'In case you haven't noticed, that creature is killing us here.'

'We've got the comm rockets,' Karizma said. 'Jesus, just use them. Fire them up to a height where they can shout to Abellia, and get us a Daedalus.'

'There's four metres of snow on the runway,' Jay said.

'You said there's a ski variant coming through the gateway. That can land here.'

'HDA is considering dispatching one,' Vance said. 'If we capture the alien, they will probably send it through.'

'What?'

'There isn't one on St Libra. The situation is more complex than you think.'

'You lied! Jesus fucking Christ, you fucking lied to us!'

'That's enough,' Jay said. 'Do not make the mistake of assuming you are beyond disciplinary action here.'

'The convoy is plain wrong,' Karizma said. 'You're asking us to risk our lives on a wild chance that we can travel two thousand kilometres in vehicles that are built for hot mud and tropical typhoons. We have supplies here to last us for months – fuels, food, raw, it's enough. But not if we burn all the bioil in vehicles on this crazy risk. The sunspots will fade. For crap's sake, the snow's already melting. We just sit it out. Even a normal Daedalus can land on a wet runway, and we've still got the dozers, we can extend it.'

'I'm sorry,' Vance said. 'We have no idea how many months or years the sunspot outbreak will last. Our last instructions from HDA command were to reach Sarvar, which has more than sufficient supplies to last for the rest of the year. The decision has been made. Now please perform your duties as required, or I will have you removed and restrained. There are enough technical specialists in this camp to replace you.'

Karizma glowered round at everyone, then got to her feet. 'Yes, sir,' she whispered furiously, and stormed off to the other end of the shack where the printers were thrumming away.

'I'll talk to her, sir,' Ophelia said.

'Please do.'

*

The thaw didn't last long. By midday the winds had returned, bringing strands of high cloud to web the roseate sky. Temperature began to drop quickly. Water refroze, crusting the snow with a dangerous sheet of ice. Work parties hurried to complete their tasks as the cold phosphorescence of the aurora borealis wormed its way back into the upper atmosphere. As yet there was no sign of a blizzard, but the camp was becoming adept at their weather-lore; conditions were building. Everyone wanted to be finished as Red Sirius began to sink below the horizon.

Captain Antrinell Viana chose to spend the time working in biolab-1. It was his way of mourning Marvin Trambi. The expedition had begun with ten members in the xenobiology team, now there were only seven. However you looked at it, odds or percentage, it wasn't good. They all felt vulnerable now, cocooned away inside the pleasant normal environment of their armoured laboratories while the rest of the camp personnel hunkered down in fragile domes or the busy microfacture shack, fearful the monster would return. So far there hadn't been any open hostility; though he'd heard about Karizma Wadhai's disgruntled protest that afternoon. All of the camp had by now. Gossip continued to flow perfectly despite the faltering net.

He had his own reservations about the convoy, but held his tongue. Elston was doing his best in impossible circumstances. As the executive officer, it was Antrinell's duty to support the colonel no matter what. In truth, he was just glad he didn't have to make the decision. And now that decision had been made, he would support it to the full.

Roarke Kulwinder and Smara Jacka were working in the lab with him, preparing plant samples they'd taken before the temperature fell and encased the jungle in ice. Smara was playing some electric country music, the steel guitar reverberating through the lab.

Antrinell let it ride. As music went it wasn't his first choice, but it was harmless enough, and it let him ignore his current circumstances. His console was showing him the genetic data they'd collected so far. To begin with, they'd just been running fast and easy comparisons, looking for divergence. Antrinell wanted more now; he'd assigned his colleagues to mapping entire genomes rather than the more simplistic fingerprinting techniques they'd been doing to begin with. Genomes took a lot longer to sequence, of course, but Antrinell was looking for a pattern that wouldn't be visible anywhere else.

The evening wore on. Roarke and Smara took turns to go into the central cabin and grab a meal. Tamisha Smith came in to spell them. Antrinell stayed where he was, burning espresso and chocolate snacks to keep going. Eventually, he was on his own. Just like Marvin. The intricate holographic colour bands of St Libra's genetic molecules swirled around him, more often than not slightly out of focus as his tired eyes took time to adjust to the new images shone onto his retinas by the console lasers.

He missed Marvin. They'd known each other a long time. Now there was nothing left to mourn. As with Norman Sliwinska, the creature had left no body behind. All they had was the stuttering alarm of Marvin's bodymesh, a signal consumed by the storm before a fix could be made. Blood in the snow. A lot of blood. Enough for Dr Coniff to run a DNA fingerprint, confirming it was Marvin's. Enough to know he was dead.

Panic and fear had penetrated the camp far more efficiently than the arctic cold. Nobody liked the lack of bodies, too much speculation could build around the loss. The blizzard's howl and ball lightning detonations amplifying the grisly imagination all minds were capable of.

The laboratory door whirred as it slid back. Vance Elston came in and sat at a spare stool next to Antrinell at the bench. He gazed at the coffee cups and crumpled food wrappers without comment. 'It's late,' he said.

'I know. What's happening outside?'

'The temperature is heading below thirty again. No blizzard, yet, though. For which I'm grateful.'

'I don't think there can be any more snow to dump on us, can there?'

'I wouldn't count on it. Ken says this temperature switch is providing the perfect condition for oceanic transpiration. The oceans are still warm, so evaporation rates have accelerated. We may yet get more snow. A lot more.'

'I'll believe it when I see it.'

'Everything is bigger on St Libra.'

'Yeah, I noticed. How are the convoy preparations going?'

'Ophelia Troy and Leif Davdia are working a miracle. But they can only prepare one vehicle at a time. The printers can't churn out components any faster. Then they have to be fitted and tested. It'll take a week to ten days to get everything ready.'

'If there's any of us left by then,' Antrinell said bitterly.

'Are you planning on sleeping tonight?'

'I guess so. I'm not accomplishing much here now. I can't focus. I think the doc needs to test my eyes.'

'What are you working on? Zhao said you've got everyone sequencing entire genomes.'

'I'm trying to establish a way of comparing evolutionary scales to terrestrial plants. I want to see how complex these plants are.'

'Why?'

'It will tell us how old the origin world is, how long life has existed there. I thought that might give us an idea of what we're dealing with.'

'And has it?'

'Possibly. Comparison is difficult, these plants are a lot more sophisticated than terrestrial plants. I thought it was odd because we haven't found any equivalent of the viral and fungal predators that we have on Earth. Everything here is in balance. But now I'm thinking that's because they've out-evolved those predators and microbial diseases. Their biological resistance to indigenous bacteria attack is absolute.'

'So they're old, then?'

'Yes. But the odd thing is, they've stopped evolving.'

'How can you know that?'

'I compared the genomes on plant varieties we've encountered here in the middle of Brogal against the same species growing on Ambrose. They're identical.'

'Well isn't that to be expected?'

'Not at the most fundamental genetic level,' Antrinell said. 'I mean, they are really identical, which even if they were only brought here a hundred thousand years ago shouldn't happen. That's plenty of time for mutations to creep in. It hasn't. Variance checking clued me in. There is no variety even within a species. Every bubblebush is identical with every other bubblebush, every noxreed is the same, every falrillary vine, every tobgrass blade, every honeyberry. All of them are the same. There's no cross-fertilization, the spores simply reproduce the parent plant. Each species' genetic composition is fixed. We knew they are all parthenogenetic, but this is like perfect clone reproduction. There is only one of everything. Do you understand what that means?'

'There must be some variation, a degree of genetic drift. Look at the Norths, each generation is a little different than the last, a little worse.'

'Forget our world. Comparisons are worthless. The plants here are a billion years ahead of us. St Libra's plants don't mutate or evolve because there's no need to. They're the pinnacle of their

782

world's evolution.' He lowered his voice to a whisper. 'This is what God intended to create, this is life without flaws. We're walking among perfection, Vance. This is the life eternal. That's why the planters brought it here, to a planet orbiting a young star, so it could continue living for a good part of eternity. We shouldn't be here, we shouldn't be despoiling it. That is why He's punishing us.'

'Who brought the plants here, Antrinell? If they are the end-point of the origin planet, then where are the people, the entities which evolved with them?'

'Well one of them is just outside. We know that.'

'Yes,' Vance agreed slowly. 'But it's a human shape, not an alien. That's been the problem all along.'

'Vance, He made us in His image. This is it, this is the proof we've been searching for since the day Wan Hi Chan published his theory of trans-spacial connection. Christians have been living in fear of this time, we listened to the atheists mocking us and we doubted Him. We shouldn't have, it was our ultimate lack of faith. If we can meet St Libra's guardian, we can show the trans-space worlds the truth in our gospels. The atheists will repent and join us at our altar, the false religions will wither and die.'

'That's . . . a big claim to make.'

'You're a believer, a true believer, just like me. We are the Gospel Warriors, Vance. We carry the Lord's name outward into the darkness, it is our sacred duty to carry His light, His enlightenment. Don't falter now.'

'I do not falter,' Vance said sternly. 'I'm simply worried about your enthusiasm. I don't want it to be misplaced.'

'I know. Vance, we have to meet the guardian, to talk to it, to explain.'

'We will. That's the one thing all of us agree about. But in the meantime, we take every precaution. I don't want you taking any risks, is that understood?'

'I understand. Don't worry, I've no intention of venturing out there alone.'

Monday 15th April 2143

The alarm clock buzzed sharply. Sid felt round for the snooze button on top. Too late, his bodymesh registered a change of status and activated his iris smartcells. The grid expanded across blurry vision, diary function reminding him of today's events. He groaned in dismay.

'Come on, pet,' Jacinta said. 'This is an important day for you.'

'Aye,' Sid mumbled. He told his e-i to banish the grid. The bedroom was comfortably dark, with slivers of pale sunlight sliding round the thick towels they'd hung across the windows. It was temporary, Jacinta said, until the curtains she'd ordered arrived. And when they did, they'd show up the rest of the room. It would need decorating. With a new carpet. Their old furniture didn't fit right, either.

'Have you got much work on this week?' he asked as he climbed out of bed.

'Not too much. Bypass tomorrow, so I'll be late back home. And there's a lung replacement scheduled for Friday – early start. Other than that it'll be light A&E work.'

'So nobody's cutting back on operations?'

She grinned as she pinned up her hair. 'Cutting back.'

'Yes.'

'Sorry, pet, bad old hospital joke. No, it's just average. Why?'

'People are talking about a recession. I just wondered if the insurance companies were reducing funding.'

784

'Pet, insurance companies are always trying to reduce payouts. Nothing new there. It's the engineering companies you want to watch if you want to know how bad things are. Half the city factories supply stuff to Highcastle and the algaepaddies and refineries. They're the ones that'll suffer in the shutdown. Anyway, everyone's making lots of profit from bioil. Have you seen how much it costs to fill the cars up?'

'Aye. But that's supply and demand. Without St Libra's supply, the other producers can charge what they like.'

'Sunspots can't last for ever.'

'No,' he said carefully. 'But I'd like us to think about how we'd get through next winter if GE does go into recession.'

'All right, pet, we'll do that.'

'Thanks.' He went into the en suite, and started the shower.

When he came out, he found Jacinta had laid out his one decent suit, a Heron Trall they'd bought a couple of years back. The shop had tailored it to him for a perfect fit.

'You need to look good for this,' she told him as she held up various ties for scrutiny.

Sid sucked his belly in. For some reason the trouser waist was tight. 'That'll be the day.'

Jacinta picked out the dark-purple silk tie. 'This one,' she decided.

'I look like I'm going to a wedding.'

'You look just fine.'

Zara and Will were already sitting at the kitchen table when Sid got downstairs. They were dressed in their school clothes, eating cereal and juice they'd got for themselves. The French doors were open, letting in the fresh morning air.

'Dad! Are you going to a funeral?' Will asked.

'No I'm not! Don't be so bloody cheeky.'

'Language,' Jacinta warned behind him.

Zara started giggling.

'I've got a court case,' Sid explained. 'It's important. There will be a lot of reporters there.'

'Is it the North carjacker?' Will asked.

'Yes. But it wasn't a carjacking.'

'You said it was,' Zara insisted. 'You told us Brussels didn't whack him.'

'They didn't.'

'So who did?' Will asked.

'We don't know.'

'Then why are you going to court?'

'To charge the person who covered up everything afterwards. Look, it's complicated, okay. I'll tell you all about it tonight.' He made himself some toast, and went out through the French doors onto the patio. It was being unfair to the kids, but he wasn't sure he could make happy small talk with them, not today. Apprehension was building. Even his bodymesh was catching signs of it, the medical function flashing up heartrate and blood sugar warnings into his grid. His metabolism was accelerating, gushing out adrenalin.

Jacinta joined him. 'Are you all right, pet; you seem a bit . . . distracted.'

'I'm fine.' He looked up at the steep roof with its small rust-red clay tiles and jet-black pv panels. 'You know, there's room for a lot more panels up there. Modern ones, with a decent energy-conversion percentage.'

'I suppose so.'

'We could get a proper regenerative gel-cell installed, store the summer power so we don't need to buy any in during the winter.'

'They cost a fortune. We've got all the decorating to do.'

'No point in decorating until you've got the basics sorted out. What about the garden?' He gestured at the shaggy lawn, which was mostly yellow patches from the previous owner's dog peeing everywhere. The raised flower beds that enclosed it were overgrown and weed-infested.

'What about it?'

'It's not right for kids. We should take out the roses and flowers, grass it over, maybe put in some goalposts for Will. And round the side here, that could be a vegetable patch. It's big enough. We could get a new freezer, a bigger one to store everything in. We'd have home-grown food in the winter.'

'Stop! For a start, all this would cost a fortune. Secondly, what is wrong?'

Sid gave the open doors a guilty glance. 'I talked to Aldred last week. The GE, and probably everyone else, is dipping into recession. St Libra used to supply sixty per cent of our bioil.'

'Sixty? Aye, crap on that, like. Are you sure? I thought it was about fifteen.'

'No. That's what Brussels wanted everyone to believe. Turns out good little GE bioil production companies haven't been investing the way they should; it's been all dividends for shareholders and no infrastructure expansion. So life is going to get tough for a while, maybe a long while.'

'Which is why you want to go all survivalist on me?'

'I got a bonus this weekend. Unexpected. It's Aldred's way of saying thank you for the investigation. We can afford to be a little more self-sufficient.'

She puffed out her cheeks. 'Well it wouldn't hurt, pet.'

'Good, we'll get some quotes in.'

'What about the whole puppy issue? Will's been asking every day. He's even behaving himself – as well as he can. We can't put it off for ever.'

'Sure. Why not? Puppy steak tastes good with the right sauce.'

'Oh!' Jacinta's hand flew to her mouth as she started to giggle. She gave the open French doors a frantic look. 'Don't! They won't get that. You're just so evil.'

He grinned and put his arms around her. They kissed. 'So what kind?' he asked. 'A St Bernard? English Sheepdog?'

'Crap on it, no. A big pedigree, what are you thinking, man? We'll get something small from the rescue centre.'

'Small dogs are yappy. I hate them.'

'If times are hard, we can't afford a big dog. Do you know how much they cost to feed? And then there's vet insurance.'

'Maybe we'll get them both a goldfish, instead.'

Jacinta gave the door another cautionary look. 'And the potatoes we grow will make good chips to go with them.'

They both laughed guiltily, hugging tighter.

Zara appeared in the doorway and cocked her head to one side as she looked at them. 'What's so funny?'

'Nothing, poppet,' Sid promised. 'Now have you done your homework?'

'Done it. Logged it,' she said proudly.

'Aye, gimme five. I'll take you both to school today. I don't have to be at the court until ten.'

*

Market Street that afternoon resembled what Sid imagined the end of term at some posh boarding school would be like. Everyone milling round not working, every table in the canteen full so people could swap opinions and gossip. Offices empty. Cases ignored. Ominous 'personal effects' boxes were piled up outside some doors, ready for the janitor staff to move them. Outside or to a higher floor – that was the only topic.

It was as if the morning's court hearing was irrelevant to Market Street, rather than the incident which started the revolution. Ernie Reinert had pleaded guilty to the charge of accessory to murder; while Maura Dellington, Chester Hubley, Murray Blazczaka, and Lucas Kremer were all charged under the lesser charge of conspiracy to conceal a crime.

The media turn-out was huge, with all the large news offices tipped off by both O'Rouke and the Mayor's office. Sid was the one who had to face them, explaining the carjacking was a necessary cover story which allowed the police to maintain the integrity of the murder investigation. He'd done all right, he thought, maintaining his composure during some pretty abrasive questioning. Most of them wanted to know why the actual murderer hadn't been caught.

Good question, he acknowledged to himself before repeating the official line about the investigation still being on-going.

Back in the station, answering Jenson San's summons, those colleagues who noticed him amid the turmoil had all congratulated him on keeping his cool.

When Sid finally stepped out of the lift on the sixth floor, just about every door had the ubiquitous stack of boxes outside. All the doors were left open, their seals dark. Nothing private or privileged was happening on the administration level today. Chloe Healy was standing beside the water cooler at the end of the corridor, listless and morose. They locked eyes as he walked towards the Executive Bureau door. Like him, she'd put her best suit on for today, a classy grey silk number with a crisp white blouse. Perfect make-up was spoilt by what looked suspiciously like tear-flushed mascara.

Jenson San greeted him in O'Rouke's outer office. There was no sign of the PA.

'He's ready for you,' Jenson San said.

There were only five boxes in O'Rouke's office. All of them already filled, and sealed with tape. Eight green plastic bags were next to them, stuffed with shredded paper, crushed memory caches, and lumps of semi-solid removal sludge that'd been applied to the walls and a couple of patches on the ceiling to remove broad sprays of smartdust motes.

O'Rouke was sitting behind the desk, which had an orange ribbon-label fastened round one leg, so the janitor staff knew to take that down to a waiting lorry. The Chief Constable's tunic was open, but the tie was still fastened round his neck, white shirt immaculately pressed. Sid had been half-expecting O'Rouke to be working his way through a bottle of whisky, but instead the Chief was sipping tea from an antique bone china cup. A matching teapot sat on the desk.

'You can go,' O'Rouke told Jenson San.

The staff representative left the office, and the blue seal came on around the door. O'Rouke snorted at the pale light. 'Don't know why I bother. Everyone's going to know anyway. What difference does a few hours make.'

'Sir?'

'Has that pants-stain Milligan been in touch with you yet?'

'No, sir.' The announcement about the Chief Constable's office had been made at lunchtime, just after Reinert's appearance in court. Royce O'Rouke was retiring after forty-three years of dedicated service to the city of Newcastle. The Mayor actually managed to look sad on the city hall podium as he spoke to the reporters. Detective, sixth grade, Trevor Milligan was going to assume charge of Newcastle's police operation, a position which would be confirmed by the full council in six months.

'The man's a total dick,' O'Rouke grunted. 'Can't find his arse with his own hands. And that's one fat arse.'

'Certainly is,' Sid agreed.

'I worked with the Mayor,' O'Rouke said. 'You've got to do that; the city would be screwed otherwise. But I fought for a budget, for a service that did a decent job – I wasn't in his pocket like Milligan. Now we're all going to get crapped on from higher than the Zanth. It's all going to go to hell, especially with this recession bollocks hitting us. Half the city's revenue is bioil dependent. Where's the money going to come from now, huh?'

'The Mayor will have to find it somewhere, sir.'

'Yeah, but where's Milligan going to spend it, eh? That's what counts.'

'I'm sure the new Chief Constable will understand, sir.'

O'Rouke poured a cup of tea and handed it to Sid. 'Aye, sure as bears flush after they shit outside the woods he is. You and I, we've gone head to head enough over the years, but you're smart, you know the way things really work round here. You don't put up with the bollocks that half of them do. I always respected that.'

'I get the job done,' Sid said, wondering what the hell O'Rouke was leading up to.

'Yeah. That's what we need, Sid.'

'I'm not sure I follow . . .'

'That bastard Mayor, he's spinning this as a big success. Someone arrested for the North murder, but we both know that's total bollocks. Reinert is a dickhead nobody. You and I will never know who killed that North, or why. That's the way it is in this city. Nobody gets to fart around here without the bloody Norths giving you permission to. And they approve of you. I know they do.'

'Everybody builds up contacts. You have to.'

'Exactly. I have contacts, too, that's why I'm walking into a nice little non-executive directorship at NorthernMetroServices. That's the way it works.'

'Congratulations, sir.'

'But I'm not there yet. I don't officially vacate this office until the end of the afternoon shift and hand over the network codes to Milligan. Which means I can still make some appointments before Milligan brings in his own bunch of wankers to screw things up. And a fresh appointment will be bloody hard for him to shift, at least for the first six months until the council give him the job permanently.'

'Yes,' Sid said cautiously.

'I'm taking some good people with me, but I'd like you to stay here. You're grade five now, so you qualify for control of a division up here on the administration floor.'

'I don't think Milligan will like that.'

'Bugger that turd. Kressley is coming with me. Milligan would have shifted him over to the primary school bicycle patrol or some shit, so he's taking early retirement and stepping into a coordination role at Northern Forensics. I want you to take control of his office, Sid.'

'Ah,' Sid said. Now he understood. Kressley had run the Market Street agency Contract and Implementation office. That controlled the flow of city money to the agencies, and NorthernMetroServices was the largest beneficiary. 'You trust me with that?' he asked sharply.

O'Rouke gave a savage grin. 'It's a two-way street. I don't know what kind of deal you've got running with Aldred, but you need more than one of the big boys behind you if you're going to finish up owning this office. Now those agencies, they spend a lot of cash over there in the Civic Centre. They know how to look after their friends.'

'Chief Constable? Me?'

'What, you're not good enough?'

'I hadn't thought that far ahead.'

'Then it's about time you did. You're capable of it. Five years in C&I, building up allies and shafting Milligan, and you'll be perfectly placed. So, are you accepting Kressley's job?'

The last thing Sid ever wanted to be was Chief Constable. The politics alone repelled him. A nice corporate office and a decent salary had always been the goal. But that was with Northumberland Interstellar under Aldred's patronage – and now that pleasant dream of the future was probably going to get blown to shit when they downloaded the bugs from Sherman's people.

Sid stuck his hand out. 'Thank you, sir. I'd like to accept your offer.'

'Good man, that's a smart move.' O'Rouke shook vigorously.

It was, but not for the reason O'Rouke believed. The old Chief Constable was assuming that the status quo would remain, that the sunspots and mass emigration through the gateway were temporary and life would get back to normal soon enough; while Sid knew for sure that life in Newcastle was going to shift. Aldred was involved in some kind of inter-family-company fight, and even if they could never pin the murder on him the implications of that struggle had to manifest somehow. Accepting the C&I position opened up the largest range of options. It was simple self-preservation.

*

'Chief of C&I?' Ian asked that evening. 'I can't believe he offered you that. It's a weekly lottery win. The agencies will give you anything you want. Crap on it, everyone said Kressley had homes in Cannes and Auckland, as well as that bloody great North Shields mansion he lives in.'

'Five kids through private school and then university; two of them went to American Ivy League colleges, too,' Eva said. 'I can't even work out how much that cost.'

'I heard he kept a mistress at one of the singletowns, too,' Ian said. 'Younger than his daughter.'

'Yeah,' Sid said. 'I know what everyone said about Kressley.'

'Well done, boss,' Eva said.

'It's a preservation thing, you know. I took it because it puts me in a good position. I'd never get that kind of appointment from Milligan. He doesn't even know who I am.'

'He does now,' Eva said.

'Aye,' Sid acknowledged. They'd had five minutes alone after the handover ceremony on the sixth floor. Milligan had expected to drop Oni Schwalbe straight into Kressley's job, the way he'd slotted the rest of his loyal cronies into critical positions on every floor in Market Street. But a brand-new appointment wasn't something he had the clout to challenge, much less reverse. Milligan had proved more phlegmatic than Sid was expecting. They quickly came to an agreement about consulting each other when it came to the larger contracts; Milligan after all had got the Mayor's support thanks to some intensive lobbying by Security Dynamic. They even shook hands on it as Sid left the corner office. Oni Schwalbe, however, wasn't so generous; she'd brushed past Sid, giving him a vindictive glare as she went back down to the fourth floor and the job in traffic she thought she'd just left behind.

'Can he evict you?' Ian asked.

'It's a long process, and O'Rouke still has a lot of influence. Milligan doesn't want to start a battle his first week. Besides,' Sid said with a grin as he remembered the meeting, 'he's only just found out how much we spent on the North case, and the HDA hasn't paid the bill yet.'

'Still not paid?' Eva asked in surprise.

'No,' Sid confirmed. 'I think Ralph might be waiting for us to tell him if we have anything.'

The three of them turned to stare at the Apple console.

'You sure you want to do this?' Eva asked. 'We all did okay

on the back of the case. And it looks like we're heading into a recession.'

'It needs to be settled,' Sid said. 'We've come this far. Even if none of this ever goes to trial, we'll be on the inside track.'

'Which isn't necessarily the safest place to be,' Eva muttered.

'Look, we'll download and see what we've got. Then we can decide what to do with it. But we can't leave this now.'

She gave him a reluctant nod.

'You know I'm committed,' Ian said in a dull tone. 'I have to look out for her.'

Sid didn't comment on that. He'd never seen Ian infatuated like this before. Tallulah was clearly the greatest *femme fatale* in town. Strange what love – or obsession – blinded you to.

'All right, then,' Sid said. 'Let's get it done.'

The three of them put on netlens glasses. The ancient, obsolete police observation routines were still faithfully hounding after Sherman and his people as best they could. Sid checked on Aldred's position, which was in his St James singletown apartment. Eva confirmed Sherman himself was in a car heading for Dunston Marina. Ian chased down Jede. Boz was in the Regency Fitness gym pumping iron. Ruckby was approaching Quayside to collect Valentina.

Vehicle locations popped up into a map of Newcastle. Cells next to all Sherman's known residencies were readied.

'Everyone ready?' Sid asked.

'Go for it,' Ian hissed.

Their instruction flashed out across Newcastle's transnet. Every public cell in the region of their targets broadcast a code. In response, the smartmicrobe bugs fired off their cache, everything they'd recorded from their quarry's bodymesh links to the transnet. The download only lasted a few milliseconds, but Eva was monitoring Ruckby intently. He was the bytehead among them, if anyone was going to detect the security breach it would be him.

Sid's grid displayed the results. Out of the five cars and eleven shoes on which they'd managed to plant a smartmicrobe, four cars and nine shoes responded – including Aldred's.

'Good percentage,' Eva muttered.

'Has Ruckby detected anything?' Sid asked. He was still following Marcus Sherman, who wasn't making any frantic calls from the car as it turned into Colliery Road.

'I think we got away with it,' she said.

Sid told his e-i to access the call files now sitting in the Apple console. It ran a correlation, seeing if any of them matched. The results slipped down Sid's grid in a glowing neon-green matrix.

'Gotcha,' he murmured in satisfaction. Aldred 2North had called Marcus Sherman three times in the last week.

Thursday 18th April 2143

Saul Howard led the scavenger group along the Rue Balzac that meandered gently along the west side of the Pinsappo valley. The snow was several metres thick on the tight slopes, burying the scrub vegetation and swaddling the palm trees that villa owners fenced their properties with. He only knew he was still following the road thanks to the tops of the signs, which stuck up out of the snow like tumour-stricken ice gravestones.

It had been years – decades, actually – since Saul had skied. The old skills had come back eventually, after a few days of skids and falls; and now he was rather pleased with his reawakened knack. For someone twenty-five years out of practice, he was still one of the better cross-country skiers from the Camilo Village community.

Today there were five of them in the little group sliding cautiously through the imposing mountains. Otto and Lewis were flanking him, with Ayanna and Markos bringing up the rear. All of them were bundled up in thick layers of clothing against the gentle swirls of snow that fell from the high clouds. Saul had too much on, which meant he was sweating profusely from the effort of slogging up the mild incline. It had taken them a couple of hours to get to this point, three or four hundred metres above sea level. The climb had been relentless, hindered by the winds that swept along the valleys, always blowing against them no matter what direction they took. Ever since the climate altered, the sweet sea winds that used to blow against the Abellia peninsula had grown harsh and unrelenting.

Goggles protected his face from the minute ice grains that were constantly airborne, scouring any unprotected human skin. The winds were forever reshaping the surface of the snow, sculpting strange wave-shapes and curving ridges in completely random arrangements, transforming the sturdy mountain slopes into weird slow-motion seas. Out on these ventures, he was permanently alert for loose snow and the dangerous fissures that could twist legs and send unwary skiers tumbling down pristine inclines. There were also avalanches to be aware of, great slides of snow that came rushing down out of nowhere for no reason. All of them scanned the jagged skyline above as they followed the road, trying to see where the snow had piled too high. More than once he'd abandoned excursions and turned back because of the towering mounds above.

The light didn't help. Red Sirius distorted by the shifting aurora borealis made the shadows twist and the scale mislead. This was not a landscape for the fainthearted. Too many people had been lost in the first few weeks for Saul to ever relax and take the whole experience as something rewarding, no matter how much food they gathered.

'That one looks good,' Otto called above the vacant whistling gusts.

Saul saw where he was pointing; up ahead maybe three hundred metres, a big three-storey Roman-style villa sitting in its long terrace garden, with whitewashed walls, broad balconies and jet-black windows. Its mantle of snow softened the rigorous angles, overhanging the balconies and sweeping up the colonnade pillars to press against the first-floor windows. The roof had collapsed in places. He could see the apex had buckled, producing long depressions in the shallow slope of the solar panels. There was no sign that anybody else had scouted the villa.

'Sure,' Saul said, and changed direction.

The villa had big iron gates attached to stone columns, and a three-metre hedge reinforced with a carbon security mesh. Saul could just see the frost-blackened tips of the dead hedge bushes protruding from the top of the snow as he skied over the boundary.

They took their skis off just outside the balcony, then piled up their backpacks. Markos smashed one of the big windows with a clay plant pot, and they went inside. It was a bedroom, which they ignored and carried on to the broad gallery landing which surrounded the central atrium. It was so dark, they had to use their torches. Strong white beams splashed round, revealing that, amazingly, the glass cupola had survived, though no light could ever penetrate the metres of snow smothering it. Instead, the roof had broken and buckled in half a dozen other places, the rents allowing snow into the top-floor rooms. Once inside, it had come slithering out of every open door to spread along the upper landing. Long, steel-hard icicles wreathed the edge of the banisters, even extending down the stairs. The carpet under Saul's heavy boots had succumbed to a glittering centimetre-thick frost, completing the transformation from villa to winter-time crypt. Nothing responded to the quests his e-i was sending out. The villa's systems were completely dead. He flicked a switch on the wall, with no result. Even the light circuits had blown.

Nobody said anything as they made their way downstairs. The routine was familiar by now, they were here for food, and that was always stored in the kitchen or pantry, sometimes the basement, and plenty of these houses had wine cellars. Big houses like this one were only ever used as occasional homes for their wealthy owners. Gourmet foods were delivered a day before they arrived to ensure freshness; everything else was in packets or freezers. The quantity some of the larger houses had stashed away was phenomenal. Saul was sure that a couple of them they'd scavenged were owned by some kind of survivalists. It wasn't just food in those houses. There were 3D printers, big tanks of raw, and underground reservoirs of bioil. Of course, their ideology had them fleeing a Zanthswarmed Earth, even they hadn't built roofs to withstand tons of snow.

It was the smaller houses and bungalows such as those of

Camilo Village which had been the easiest to reinforce. After the first massive snowfall, over fifty residents had gone into the small forest of native sparpine on the other side of the Rue du Ranelagh and started felling timber. The village was home to local workers and business owners, the type of people who worked hard and possessed practical skills. Saul had taken two days to bring his printers and tanks of raw back from the Hawaiian Moon store on Velasco Beach before the roads were abandoned. One of the first things he'd designed and microfactured was a wood-burning stove from a tough thermal resin. It now sat in the middle of their big open plan lounge, a perfect medieval kettle, throwing out a lot of heat from the scraps of wood the kids continued to retrieve from the now-diminished forest.

A bulldozer from a resort construction site ten kilometres inland just off the Rue du Ranelagh had been commandeered right after the first blizzards started, and now performed daily communal snow-clearance, keeping the drifts away from the bungalows, and shoving the snow across the beach into the sea. Most days the kids would be outside with brooms on very long poles, scraping the latest fall off the PV roof panels. They still had electricity, although the bungalow net had to prioritize systems.

What they – along with the rest of Abellia's remaining residents – were short of was bioil. Like a true baron, Brinkelle distributed her city-state's reserves of fuel in accordance to need – as she saw it. Medical services were also rationed. Those resources, rather than money, allowed her rule of law to continue. Not that anyone protested – survival in such hostile conditions precluded political dissent. Besides, as Saul admitted to himself, she did a reasonable job. Some of the city net was still functioning; Camilo Village had a connection to what was left of the civic administration. They got a tank of bioil delivered every ten days or so for the bulldozer, because what it did – protecting everyone's bungalow – was deemed to be an essential. And when Nerys had gone into labour, a search and rescue helicopter had flown through the snow to airlift her to the Institute. She had a baby boy. So there was a loose form of organization and community cooperation rather than direct government riding to the rescue, but then Bartram and Brinkelle had always practised a somewhat *laissez-faire* doctrine when it came to their domain.

Saul was quite surprised she and her family hadn't abandoned them altogether. It would have been easy enough for them all to fly back to Highcastle and through the gateway. But, for whatever reason, Brinkelle had remained. He suspected it was to maintain absolute control over the Institute, which her branch of the family had devoted themselves to. Without that, she'd be just one more transworld billionairess amid countless others – nothing special at all.

By staying and ensuring the Institute with its seventeen thousand personnel survived, she would maintain her more exalted status. Exactly how she could keep things at Abellia going for more than a couple of months was subject to a lot of late-night talk in the village. Energy could be stretched and conserved to keep things going for a while yet. Food, though, was a very different commodity.

Brinkelle had been very clear that individual communities wouldn't receive any help from her administration when it came to feeding themselves. That had been the toughest part. There had been times when no one could venture outside for a week, the blizzards had been so fierce. Recently, though, the weather had been more restrained. Camilo Village took advantage of those lulls, sending out four or five scavenger teams to scout the big houses abandoned by their off-world owners.

At the bottom of the villa's stairs, Saul headed across the atrium floor. After a week of visiting strange houses he'd developed an instinct about the layout, especially when it came to where the kitchen was. The darkness seemed to act like a muffler, consuming sound. Light beams swung round, exploring the doors and archways. The rooms glimpsed beyond were glazed in ice, their windows completely black underneath the drifts.

The villa's kitchen was larger than Saul's living room. It had two bulky range cookers, and a central island with a bread oven, and a steam oven, and a pizza oven. An array of excellent copper pans hung from an overhead square-rack.

Saul swept his beam around the twinkling frost-coated surfaces. It stopped briefly on a bristly grey lump on the floor beneath one of the range cookers, then he forced it onwards. The cats had probably been huddling in the place they knew was sometimes warmer. Nobody was quite reduced to eating that kind of meat. Yet.

Five bright beams came to rest on the huge double-door fridge. Lewis forced it open, revealing eight shelves crammed full. There were good-quality packaged meals, cartons of milk and juice, a lot of meat and fish, yogurts, jams, butter.

'Let's start,' Saul said.

Markos unzipped a big canvas bag, and started to sweep everything off the shelves. All the food had frozen solid. It didn't matter what the use-by date was any more, they could cook it.

Ayanna and Saul went into the utility room off the kitchen.

'Bingo,' she exclaimed. There were two huge chest freezers at the far end of the room. When they smashed the locks off, they found them laden with every kind of food.

'This is a week's worth for the whole village, easily,' Saul said. He opened up his own bag, and started filling it. It would take several trips up the stairs. Then they'd assemble the sledges they'd carried with them in the backpacks. Another of Saul's designs, printed with the last of the raw he'd brought back from the Hawaiian Moon. They weren't that easy to steer, but the scavenger teams always made sure the route back from the foraged houses was downhill. As such, the sledges had proved invaluable when it came to bringing medium-sized loads back to Camilo Village.

Saul lifted the bag up, blowing his cheeks out at the weight. He carried on regardless; this expedition, like all those he'd been on and those yet to come, were about one thing, making sure his family had enough to live on until this terrible winter was over. He knew that would only happen in a community, with everyone pulling together and helping each other until the sunspot outbreak finally declined and the world returned to normal. That belief and insistence was what kept him going, what made him one of the people the rest of Camilo Village looked to. His quiet determination had surprised Emily, who'd never witnessed that side of him before.

But then, she didn't know what he'd gone through before they'd met. These circumstances were nothing like those; but the goal was identical: survival. He knew he could keep going no matter what, because he'd endured all the misery and hardship and hopelessness once before. Saul and adversity were not strangers.

Out in the villa's kitchen, Markos and Otto had just about cleared the fridge of its bounty. Saul's torch beam bobbed round the extravagantly equipped room, marvelling at how fast it had lost its value and relevance.

'Almost finished,' Otto said.

'We'll need a couple more trips to empty the freezer,' Saul said. 'It's a good-sized haul.'

Otto nodded, watching Saul's torch illuminate the swanky kitchen. He was clearly thinking along similar lines. 'Then what?' he asked. 'What happens when there's no more houses left to scavenge from?'

'The sunspots have to end some time,' Saul replied. His standard reply every time the children asked that same question. 'Even if it takes a year.'

'We won't last a year,' Otto said.

'There's always the Institute.'

'What about it?'

'They have clone vats. I imagine there's all sorts of single-cell proteins they can grow to feed us.'

'That's right,' Markos said. 'Brinkelle has a fusion plant out there as well. They can keep us going for as long as it takes.'

'Then why hasn't Brinkelle said anything?'

'I don't know,' Saul said, tiring of the way everyone turned to him. 'Maybe she doesn't want us to develop a dependency mentality.' *I could certainly do without it.*

'But you think they can grow food?' Otto said.

'There's seventeen thousand biogenetic researchers who will starve if they don't find a way. That's got to be a big incentive.'

'Sure,' Otto said, convincing himself. 'Yeah, of course they will.'

Markos and Saul exchanged a glance, then Saul picked up his heavy bag of frozen food, and headed for the stairs.

*

It was gone eight o'clock in the evening before Sid finally finished his conference links and meetings with the legal department and planning sessions with Market Street's Operations chief; then there was just his own datawork to finish off. A day of arguments and deals and agreements and discussion, with everything checked and scrutinized by Milligan and his cronies who delighted in manufacturing problems and pushing them Sid's way. He'd promised Jacinta he'd be back home by six, 'seven at the latest, pet, honest'. But that was before the GE's announcement of a settlement to the St Libra residents' negotiations. He was starting to form the opinion that Kressley might have earned his money after all.

All day long the transnet had been cluttered with news about the agreement. The GE negotiators had finally agreed to permit a limited return of non-bioil workers from Highcastle. They were to be issued with temporary humanitarian resident permits, and pay a significant Return Bond. The permit would automatically expire one month after the sunspot outbreak was officially declared to have ended.

In reality, that meant two hundred thousand people were going to come pouring through the gateway, starting on Saturday. That left Newcastle with three days to prepare for them.

Dispersal was the Mayor's strategy, tying in to the main GE policy. Every hotel room in the city was taken by the bioil company workers who had already been allowed through the gateway. There was no room for anyone else, so they were to be bussed out, put on trains and sent across the continent. The Southern states weren't happy about that; Highcastle's population was mostly drawn from the Northern states and France, who all had massive bioil production facilities on the giant world. Further concessions had to be made, such as assisting the refugees out to the GE trans-space worlds where there was plenty of room for fresh settlers. Anything that stopped them from settling on the old continent. And Newcastle was the test. Additional anti-vagrancy by-laws were being rushed through the council, giving police and their contracted agencies fresh, stronger powers to move people on. Humanitarian funds were also sought from various charities, government bureaux, and aid agencies to help the flow of people onwards and outwards.

All of this was going to require some strict policing to make sure no one got lost between the gateway and their transport out of the city. Hundreds of police, along with over two thousand agency constables, were going to be deployed to secure the routes. GE Border troops would be held in reserve. And all the arrangements were going through Sid's C&I office, to be examined and authorized. His e-i had been subjected to a deluge of calls from agency executives, friends who knew agency people, colleagues who were now becoming intermediaries. His diary was already full of dinners for the next two months (with the agency providing their own licensed babysitters each time) and he'd turned down five holidays – two of which were on trans-space worlds. Jacinta hadn't been too happy about that; though interestingly three medical agencies had already been in touch offering her a chief of staff position and a big raise.

The wealth and power he'd been shown was impressive, but he was quietly pleased at the way his office had handled the logistics. The city would be ready to cope with the deluge of freezing, hungry, and broke refugees when they came pouring through on Saturday morning.

Sid had said goodnight to his new team, and took the lift

down to the first sub-basement. Down here, in a concrete warren with steel doors and harsh blue-green lighting, were a dozen restricted rooms, the largest of which was the firing range, next to the armoury. Sid avoided those, and made his way to the secure equipment store. The area was divided into five sections, and Ian had looped the mesh log on each of them, so no one knew he was walking down the corridor to the mid-security vault containing the mobile surveillance equipment. His e-i sent Detective Brannagh's identity and code into the lock; Brannagh was in the Police Standards Division, one of those in last year's investigation into Sid's conduct. He didn't have a lot of allies in Market Street should anyone ever run an audit on the equipment store. The locks clicked back and the door swung open.

The room inside was ribbed by concrete and split by five rows of metal grid shelving. Ancient air-con fans whirred into life, trying to deal with the fusty air. Sid walked along the second rack, examining the neatly stacked cases. There were a lot of gaps, he noticed in bemusement. Most detectives grade-two and above knew how to access mid-security facilities.

He found the cases he wanted on the third shelf; black aluminium rectangles, thirty centimetres by twenty, and ten thick. Again his e-i gave the vault's inventory management net Brannagh's codes. He pulled three of the cases off the shelf and turned to go.

'Evening, boss,' Abner 2North said.

Sid winced. He hadn't heard Abner come in, and of course Ian had disabled the meshes so he couldn't use them himself to check he was alone. Nothing for it, he'd have to bluff it out. He smiled at Abner. 'Evening. Just collecting some micro-copters for a case. What are you looking for?'

'Boss, that was awful; you're chief of C&I now, you don't do cases that need a micro-copter. So if you don't mind I'll cut the bollocks, seeing as how you've disabled the mesh logs. Ian left a whole load of covert surveillance monitors running using Vance Elson's authority codes. Now you, he, and probably Eva are carrying out some kind of off-log operation. I'm not too bothered by that, we all do it. But this was my brother who was murdered. I think I have a right to know if you know who killed him.'

'Aye, crap on it,' Sid grunted. He supposed he should have realized that someone would notice eventually, especially a detective with Abner's forensics training. 'Who've you told?'

'No one.'

'All right. But let's not do this here, we need to leave.'

'Sure. Let me give you a hand with one of those.'

Sid hesitated as Abner held out a hand, his expression carefully neutral. That face . . . Sid remembered it white and passive on the mortuary slab; Augustine, angry and determined; Aldred, so calm and calculating. It really was true, the Norths were everywhere in Newcastle, one way or another. He sighed in acknowledgement of that simple reality, and passed a case over to Abner. 'Thanks.'

'Brannagh, huh? Good choice.'

Sid shrugged. 'Aye, what can you do? Jenson San's already left.'

*

For once Ian must have accessed the meshes on the staircase leading up to the door of his flat. He wasn't surprised when Abner walked in with Sid, just edgy. It was left to Eva to give the North a worried look.

'He found the observation routines,' Sid said by way of explanation.

'Crap on it,' Ian muttered, pressing his lips together in anger. 'Sorry boss, I should have been more careful.'

'So now what?' Eve asked.

'I want to find who murdered my brother,' Abner said.

'You might not like the answer,' Sid told him.

'Is that why you're doing this off-log?'

'Yeah.'

'Okay, look, I'm not going to turn you in to Milligan or Aldred. But I need to be part of – what?' He looked round at their expressions.

'This isn't going to be pleasant,' Sid told him carefully.

'Just . . . what is going on?'

Sid knew he didn't have a choice, he hadn't since Abner caught him in the store. Probably a long time before that if he was honest with himself. 'We found out why your brother was murdered in the St James apartment.'

'Oh?'

'Tallulah Packer was having an affair with Aldred last year. He has her door lock codes.' Sid waited for a response, but Abner said nothing, so he told him the worst of it. That Aldred knew Marcus Sherman, that this was all some corporate manoeuvre, that Norths were probably fighting Norths. How they'd bugged Sherman's people – and Aldred.

'What did you find out from the downloads?' Abner asked quietly.

Sid was impressed. He knew if he'd been told how his family was implicated in something this terrible he was sure he wouldn't manage to stay so calm. But then, Abner knew exactly how his brothers behaved. 'The downloads didn't capture as much as we'd hoped. There's a lot of conversations we only got one side of. But from what we've put together so far, Sherman's team is planning a raid on Trigval Molecular Solutions. That's a very high-tech company based in Jarrow. They specialize in molecular assembly chambers. We don't know what they're used for – that information isn't in the transnet, which is interesting – but they're a defence-listed company.'

'I've heard of them,' Abner said softly.

'How come?' Eva asked.

'They're important to Northumberland Interstellar. And I was up to speed on the family business before I shifted over to the police.'

'How important?' Sid asked.

'Trigval's molecular systems can produce active-state matter. That's a kind of intermediate, or trigger state for effecting negative matter properties. Which is the basics of trans-spacial connection technology.'

'So this raid could wind up affecting the gateway?' Ian asked.

'Not really, or at least not directly. It's not like active-state matter is scarce, there's a lot of companies produce it. And you can hardly have a blackmarket in the stuff. It takes some very specialist raw, for a start. I don't quite understand this.'

'Maybe it's just a simple technology theft?' Eva said. 'Sherman has a buyer for the technology in the distant worlds.'

'And why would Aldred be involved?' Abner asked. 'Northumberland Interstellar owns a gateway. We have the technology, we don't have to steal it.'

'Because of something else he's involved in,' Sid said. 'That's the whole problem here – we don't know exactly what's going on.'

Abner looked at the small black case he was holding, as if he'd only just seen it for the first time. 'So what's your plan?'

'They're still putting the raid together. We're going to use the micro-copters to provide us with full coverage. This time we'll be able to see what they're up to.'

'This time?' Abner asked sharply.

'They've been involved in other, similar, activities,' Sid said. 'A handover. Talk of another acquisition. And we're sure they were the ones who firebombed Reinert's garage. If we can follow them afterwards, and see who they hand this stuff over to, we may get a better idea of what exactly is going down.'

Abner nodded slowly. 'And the micro-copters would be ideal for that. Okay, I was trained to fly one of these. I'll help you with the observation.'

'And after?' Eva challenged. 'If it turns out Aldred was involved in the murder. What then?'

'I'll help you arrest him myself,' Abner said. 'And I'll make sure he's held to account for what he's done.'

'You're the same as him, as are all of your bothers,' Sid said. 'Do you think you're capable of killing one of them?'

'No. I personally couldn't do that. But we are all slightly different – it's only urban myth that has us as identical. He'll have a reason for doing what he's done. I'm looking forward to hearing what it is.'

Sunday 21st April 2143

Vance had to lean into the wind which drove the hard ice particles almost horizontally across the camp. He was glad the microfacture team had finally got round to printing some decent protective goggles. The particles which did strike the few slivers of skin unprotected by fabric stung badly before the cold numbed the graze.

Beside him, Private Omar Mihambo was on escort duty, schlepping stoically through the raging snow and effervescent mutable light of the aurora. The Legionnaire's weather-sheathed carbine was held ready, and he was scanning round as best he could. His cheek was now recovering underneath its layer of nuskin that was working its magic. The patch was protected from the elements by various membranes. On top of those he was wearing several thin layers of fabric, wound like a facial turban. A balaclava knitted for him by Angela went over that so he could wear his armour helmet without it rubbing against his cheek. Then he'd put on his specially sculpted snow goggles. Lieutenant Botin hadn't thought he was ready to be put back out on patrol, but Omar had pleaded and Vance acquiesced.

Nobody wanted to go outside any more. It wasn't just the fear of the creature which stalked them, the cold was acting like a viral tox on their thoughts, their attitude; dragging their mood down. It was an effort simply to put on the correct clothes in preparation to venture out. Then more often than not the wind would be blowing, making even walking a difficulty. Vision was a few metres. Far better to stay inside, huddling round a heater, working to prepare the convoy, however menial the assigned task.

If for some reason Omar was resistant to the same disposition as the rest of the camp, then Vance wasn't about to ignore that. They needed armed protection now more than ever.

Vance finally caught sight of the shack ahead, a soft wall of bright-orange fabric. It was the simplest covering the microfacture team could come up with, a fifteen-metre-diameter balloon of thick fabric kept under positive pressure by fans blowing in excess heat from a fuel cell. Horribly energy-expensive, but effective.

Snow falling on it slithered off as it turned to sludge, making sure that there was never any excessive weight building up on top. The ring of crunchy ice that built up around the rim was slowly rising, but Vance hoped they'd be leaving by the end of the day, so that wouldn't be a problem.

They went through the short access tunnel, closing the outer awning of fabric before opening the inner so no pressure was lost. Inside, the warm air hit them, heavy with the melange of bioil, fresh polymer, and ripe human that swept straight down Vance's nostrils as he unwrapped the printed scarf from around his face. Snow crusting his parka and waterproof trousers started to melt, dripping onto the floor. He took his goggles and helmet off, but not much else – it wasn't that warm inside the shack, just above freezing.

Two of the Tropics occupied the majority of the floor, sitting under bright floodlights. Four or five people were working on each one. Vance had to grin with enthusiasm as he saw the modified vehicles. The new tyres were amazing, as high as his chest and equally wide. It was the ultimate pimp-up machine to please his inner boy. An image that could only ever be amplified by the remote-control machine gun mounted on the roof.

Every convoy vehicle had a similar weapon, which was why preparation was taking longer than originally scheduled. Vance had insisted. A morale booster following from Wukang's latest loss.

It had been a standing order for a long time that nobody was allowed out alone.

Mackay from the AAV team, and Juan-Fernando, one of the helicopter pilots, had faithfully followed that order last Thursday as they went out into the blizzard to check on the emergency comm rocket launchers. They'd carried regulation sidearms, too, according to Davinia and Leif, who bunked down in the same accommodation dome.

Neither of them had returned.

Vance had to change the standing orders: now anyone going outside had to take an armed Legionnaire as escort. No exceptions were allowed. The machine guns on the vehicles were included at the same time. If they encountered the creature after the convoy set off, they could open fire immediately, without having to wait for the Legionnaire squad to climb out and give chase.

Ravi Hendrik and Ophelia Troy were on the cab roof of one Tropic, finishing the machine-gun installation, connecting it to a small microwave radar mounted on the side of the barrel. As Vance watched, it swivelled from side to side then changed elevation, pointing down.

Ravi grinned. 'Hey boss, this'll teach the bastards not to bring a knife to a fist fight, huh?'

'Is it ready?' Vance asked.

'Got some work to do on the targeting software, and these servos are a bit rough and ready, but we'll be finished when it's time to bug out.'

'Good man.' Vance walked round the back of the first Tropic to where Darwin Sworowski was tightening up the wheel lock nuts on the offside axle motor. Jay was standing beside him, handing tools from a tall wheeled cabinet when Darwin asked for them, and looking every inch the fifth wheel.

Jay looked up. 'Sir.'

'How's it going?' Vance asked.

Jay glanced at Darwin, who shrugged inside several layers of overalls.

'Vehicles will be ready in three hours,' Jay said.

'I thought they were finished,' Vance said. He tried not to let annoyance show in his voice, but in his heart he'd expected this visit to the garage to be the one where he gave the order to drive out.

'We've done as much refit work as we can,' Darwin said. 'But there are some adaptation issues.' He patted the big tyre with its thick tread. 'Once you alter the wheel size, especially to this degree, then you completely change the gearing. The axle hub motor torque will have to be recalibrated. It also means we'll use a lot more power to turn the wheels.'

'More power,' Vance mused. 'You mean more fuel?'

'Yes, sir.'

'Okay, have you revised the convoy estimates?'

'Uh, we should make Sarvar with a twenty per cent reserve. That's the worst-case scenario,' he said hastily. 'I'm hoping we'll have around thirty per cent left.'

'You're just telling him what he wants to hear,' Karizma said as she walked over from the second Tropic. 'We'll be lucky if Jesus lets us get halfway to Sarvar before we run out of bioil. What then, eh? What's your contingency for that, camp commander?'

'If my vehicle team chief says we'll be there with thirty per cent fuel left, then that's the information I base my decision on.'

'It's a guess! A wild, stupid guess. Christ himself doesn't know how tough it's going to be out there.'

'Hey,' Darwin snapped. 'I've had two test drives in a Tropic and one in an MTJ. I know what they'll be dealing with.'

'You did a circle of the camp. That tells you nothing. Crap on it, we don't even have a map!'

'The AAV team have drawn up a good chart from the e-Ray data.' Jay said.

'Bullshit! It's barely got a five-metre resolution. And that's just a gradient plot – we've no idea of what your God's actually hidden under the tree canopy. There could be a million gorges between here and Sarvar. You cannot back up that twenty per cent wish with any real knowledge. We have to stay here.'

'Nobody is coming for us,' Vance said. 'And the creature is taking us out one at a time.' He found it interesting that Karizma had started to blaspheme a lot more when he was around. Presumably a crude attempt to highlight his belief in the hope others would question his judgement. It was easy enough for him to ignore: it wasn't as if he didn't have the practice.

'Creatures,' Ravi said.

Vance looked up at the pilot in annoyance. 'What?'

'There has to be more than one. Come on, look at what it's done to us. It took out Mackay and Juan-Fernando without a sweat. And I knew Juan – there's no way he'd roll over without a fight. They're out there, okay, gathering round the camp. One day soon there's going to be enough that they'll just walk in here no matter how many Legionnaires are on patrol, or remote weapons we've rigged up. You stay right here if you want to, but me, I am leaving.'

'Nobody is staying,' Vance said firmly. 'I want these Tropics loaded and ready to leave in three hours. We are driving away with or without any final torque adjustments, understood?'

'Yes, sir,' Darwin said. 'We'll be ready.'

'Good. Carry on. Jay, assemble the rocket-launch crew. I want Abellia to know what's happening.'

*

The Aero-Roe corp HA-5060 emergency comm rocket launcher was an oblong box five metres long and two in diameter, sitting on a small trailer. They used MTJ-1 to tow it away from the camp, though drag was a more accurate description. The trailer's small wheels kept getting stuck in the snow, it was only the MTJ's power which kept yanking it along. Riding in the cab, Vance got an uncomfortable demonstration of what it was going to be like slogging through thousands of kilometres of the antagonistic frozen landscape. It was almost enough to make him hesitate. But Ravi had captured the essence of everyone's thoughts. Rumour around the camp was that more than one creature was out there in the snow-clad jungle. Everyone just wanted to get the hell away. Discipline was going to collapse if they didn't; already the capture mission was effectively over. Even Vance acknowledged just how bad their situation was now. His own strategy was to make it back to Sarvar and then – when the sunspots were over, and the climate returned to normal – another, better-equipped expedition could return to Wukang. For now, the creature had the upper hand. It was an admission Vance hated, but above all he was a realist.

With Olrg driving, they took the rocket launcher six hundred metres from the administration Qwik-Kabin. Sergeant Raddon and Leora Fawkes stood guard in the driving snow while Ken Schmitt and Chris Fiadeiro prepared the launcher. It didn't take much. The trailer extended legs from each corner, sinking pads deep into the snow. Then the oblong box slowly hinged up to vertical.

Back in the AAV shack, Davinia Beirne confirmed they were receiving the HA-5060's telemetry. Everyone clambered back into the MTJ, and Olrg drove it away.

They parked three hundred metres away from the launcher. Everyone craned forward to try and see through the thick smear of snow whipping past outside.

Davinia completed the short countdown. A brilliant orange light flared through the blizzard, overpowering the pastel fluctuations of the aurora. Then the roar of the triple solid rocket boosters slammed into the MTJ, accelerating the snow even faster. The unseen light source shot upwards and quickly faded from sight.

Vance closed his eyes as he whispered a small prayer. The HA-5060 emergency comm rocket was designed to be launched in adverse conditions, but this was a real stretch of its design criteria. His grid shone with neon brightness as he kept his eyes shut, relaying the telemetry.

At seventeen kilometres the three booster rockets burnt out and jettisoned. The rocket was still surrounded by cloud and ice particles, which would be dangerous if they extended much higher. Velocity was building, and the nose cone was starting to friction-ablate. The main stage ignited, slamming out seven tonnes of thrust, accelerating the HA-5060 hard as it finally cleared the clouds at twenty-one kilometres.

Thirty-three seconds later the solid rocket fuel was exhausted, and the four-hundred-kilogram payload package separated, continuing upwards under the tremendous impetus of the rocket thrust.

All Vance could do was wait and watch the telemetry data. At least they were receiving data, though the antenna was consuming a lot of power to punch through the storm.

When it passed through the three-hundred-kilometre level, the payload started beaming data packages directly at Abellia. They knew the expedition camp there had assembled a receiver antenna as soon as they arrived back in February, which should be permanently operational. Everyone was hoping the storms hadn't knocked it out.

After seventy seconds they got a reply from Abellia.

The cheering in the MTJ cabin was raucous. A line of icons appeared across Vance's grid as the link to the base's net was established. The only one he was interested in was Major Griffin Toyne.

The payload package reached three hundred and fifty kilometres, soaring still further. Pre-loaded messages recorded by Wukang's personnel started to flood into Abellia's network. Vance's e-i reported that Toyne was responding.

'Really glad to hear from you,' Toyne said. 'What's your status?'

'Not good. It's killed four of us now. I'm evacuating to Sarvar. It's all in my report, but I'd like a quick confirmation from you that there's enough supplies there to sustain us.'

'Yes. There's only a skeleton crew left there, fifteen people. All the supplies and fuel are still in place.'

'Good. The report contains our proposed route. If the situation does change in the next week . . .' Vance's e-i told him that the payload had reached four hundred kilometres, and its rate of ascent was slowing drastically. Apogee was close.

'Unlikely,' Toyne said. 'The sunspot outbreak seems to have stabilized. It's constant now.'

'Damn. Do the astronomers have any idea how long it'll last?'

'None at all. Listen, Vance, Highcastle is emptying fast, the residents are abandoning the planet. We'll stay on of course – we don't leave our people behind. There's a final evacuation operation being planned for all the forward camps, but it won't be enacted for a few months. You'll be in a much better position if you can get to Sarvar. We will come for you, the General himself has promised that.'

'Thank you.'

'Do you have any more data on the creature?'

'No. The weather here is abysmal. It's degrading every sensor we have. Smartdust is utterly useless. We're practically living in the twenty-first century.'

The payload reached its peak at four hundred and thirty-seven kilometres, pausing for an instant amid the supercharged ions of the upper ionosphere, and recording a hail of hard particles inbound from Sirius. Several processors started to glitch under the radiation assault, and the software hurriedly compensated.

'I'm sorry we can't do anything for you. But if anyone can get through this, it's HDA people.'

'How are the other forward camps managing?' Vance asked as the payload began its long fall.

'We lost contact with them as well. None reported any creature activity. It's just you.'

'Anybody have any theories on that?'

'No. But Alice Springs is working on it.'

More processors inside the package dropped out. Telemetry showed a problem with the main power circuits. The radiation environment was far outside recommended tolerance levels. Static levels on the outer casing were threatening to break through the insulation.

'Okay, what happened with the Newcastle investigation?' Vance asked.

'It's over. They charged Ernie Reinert with accessory to murder. The trial will conclude this week. But they never found who gave the order.'

'Really? I had more faith in Detective Hurst.'

'You ask me: this whole expedition has been a disaster from start to finish.'

'It's not over yet. The creature is here, and it's killing us.'

'I can't get any action on that, Vance. Officially, it's still Tramelo or her accomplice.'

'For fuck's sake!' Vance's fist came down on the chair in front. Everyone in the MTJ cabin stared at him, none of them had ever heard him use profanity before. 'You know it's not true.'

'We'll get you out, Vance. You have my word on that, we will not abandon you.'

'An airdrop would be helpful.'

'Absolutely. As soon as the storms break. The meteorologists think that won't be long. The atmosphere is stabilizing.'

'Could have fooled me.'

The package link dropped out for a couple of seconds. When it came back, telemetry showed the electron build-up on the casing was reaching critical. As gravity pulled the package back down towards the land, the charge level started to increase further.

'We're going to lose it,' Davinia warned everyone.

Some of Wukang's personnel were lucky, their e-is actually managed to get calls all the way through the gateway and into the transnet, enabling them to have a couple of hurried minutes talking to their families. The camp's official log cache was successfully downloaded to HDA headquarters. Amid it all, Angela was the only one unmoved. Saul, the one person she might have tried to contact to say goodbye to, didn't need the universe of grief that would land on them if the connection was ever understood. She couldn't expose him to the risk. Besides, saying goodbye yet again to her old husband would be too much for his gentle soul.

After providing an exceptional eleven minutes of contact with civilization, the halo of electrons around the casing finally overloaded the insulation, and discharged through the package. The dead mass continued its three-hundred-kilometre fall in silence.

*

'Did any of you access the Abellia base's official news releases?' Karizma asked in an open ringlink to all the HDA personnel below sergeant rank. 'There is a final evacuation plan being worked out. We just have to stay here and they'll pick us up in another month.'

'There was no timetable,' Angela responded. 'It was a morale tox, propaganda for the stupid and weak. Did you believe it?'

'It's real.'

'More real than the monster?' Paresh asked.

'Screw you. Everyone knows it's your friend-with-benefits who's killing us anyway.'

'Shut the fuck up,' Paresh said.

'She's leading you round by the balls,' Karizma retorted. 'Can't you see that?'

'I see our only chance of surviving this is to leave.'

'You're wrong, all of you. We can survive here until the snow melts if necessary. The printers can manufacture real shelters if that Jesus-freak Elston wasn't using all the raw to modify the vehicles. He's on a crusade, you know. He doesn't care how many of us die so he can prove himself to his God.'

'It's done,' Angela said. 'We're going. Live with it, it's the only way you will.'

'We'll never make it. We can't carry enough fuel.'

'Keep this up, and I'll put you in irons myself,' Paresh said. 'Last warning.'

Karizma's e-i showed her the ringlink's participants were

dropping out. She looked round at Davinia Beirne and Leif Davdia. 'Idiots!' she stormed. 'Can't they see the fucking obvious? Elston is going to get us all killed with this crazy convoy.'

'They're frightened,' Davinia said. 'Frightened of the monster and intimidated by the command structure. After all, we're all trained to stick with the chain of command no matter what. That's the HDA way.'

'We'll die if we leave.'

'You're right,' Leif said. 'Those modifications we made to the vehicles aren't enough, not really. Not for terrain like this. Elston is delusional if he thinks otherwise.'

'Probably got told to leave directly by God,' Davinia grunted in contempt.

'Then you'll both stay here with me?' Karizma asked. 'There'll be more than enough supplies and fuel for the three of us to last until the rescue mission arrives.'

'The Legionnaires will obey Elston,' Leif said. 'Right up to the moment they get five blades shoved through their hearts, the dumb fucks. You heard Paresh, they'll taser us and throw us in a sledge if that's what their orders are. We have to be smarter. We have to pick our moment.'

Karizma nodded grudgingly. 'Yeah. But we can't afford to wait too long.'

*

The Wukang convoy finally came together at two o'clock in the afternoon. Like everyone, Angela was allowed to bring a small bag of possessions. She chose a few clean clothes, socks and underwear – after all, nobody ever died from wearing stale, dirty clothes, and she was wearing most of hers in layers. For the rest of the bag she packed in equipment she'd bought at Birk-Unwin: the torch, inertial guidance module, memory cache, and one of the sunglasses. Paresh laughed at that, but she argued that the smart lenses might be helpful in the murk that was St Libra's current atmosphere. However, she did leave behind her precious bottles of sunguard oils. The utility belt she wore under two sweaters and the armour vest. Any remaining space in the bag was taken up with balls of wool, and knitting needles.

She didn't so much walk out of the accommodation dome as waddle. The wind had dropped considerably, but the cloud cover was still absolute. Snow drifted about through the air, tinged pink by the delicate sunlight. The aurora borealis had withdrawn, only occasionally sending slow tattered ribbons of sea-green light meandering through the base of the clouds as if they were the wake of some vast airborne organism.

Beyond the domes, the ten vehicles that made up the convoy were lining up, their sharp white headlight beams cutting cheerily through the gloom. Angela regarded them with a sense of relief as they vented soft white vapour from their fuel cells, permitting herself the satisfaction of seeing something *happen*. She'd been deeply involved with the planning, of course; Elston and Forster regarded her as essential now, and they never bothered to review her work. So she'd coordinated the requirements each team leader had drawn up, producing lists, balancing weight and size and importance. Elston had the final say, but the majority of the cargo she could see was there because of her.

Most of the vehicles were draped with pannier-style nets bulging with pods and cases and boxes. Roof racks were piled high. And to her eyes the sledges looked almost unstable, they were carrying so many bladders of bioil in their frameworks.

'Hey you,' Paresh said. 'You take care now.'

'I'm not the one riding on the bomb.'

'Oh great! Thanks for that.'

'Take care yourself,' she said.

They *clunked* helmets, which made Angela grin at the sheer childishness of the gesture. Paresh turned and walked over to the convoy's tanker. He and Atyeo were sharing the cab. Elston had insisted on it being driven and guarded by Legionnaires.

There was only one tanker, but the two self-loading trucks were now stacked with bioil bladders. Ravi Hendrik and Bastian 2North were sharing the driving in the first; while Ophelia Troy and Gillian Kowalski were in the second.

The three Tropics and both mobile biolabs were towing sledges. That left the MTJs to trailblaze, their snowplough blades clearing a path for the less powerful and more awkward vehicles to follow. The buzz-saw blades that had been so useful when they were exploring the jungle last month were folded back across the bonnet, ready to deploy forward when vegetation became more of a problem than snow.

Angela had given herself a berth in Tropic-2, along with Forster Wardele, Madeleine, and Sergeant Raddon. She smacked off as much snow as she could from her parka and trousers, opened the door and hauled herself up onto the back seat next to Madeleine. There was barely enough room. Madeleine was also heavily wrapped up in her parka and a generous number of layers. Their arms pressed up against each other. Angela shoved her bag down on the floor, between the boxes containing rations for several days. She grimaced at the sight of the plastic panseat and fempee funnels and empty flexbags sharing the floorspace, but that was going to be her life for the next couple of weeks, or however long it took them to reach Sarvar.

'Locking the doors,' Raddon said from the driver's seat. 'So here's some simple ground rules. Once the doors are shut, we turn up the cabin heater and everyone can take off some clothes. Do not open your door without warning the rest of us, okay? Now we'll take three-hour turns to drive. Front passenger is the watch – that means you keep a look-out for everything from the monsters charging at us, to other vehicles skidding, and possible avalanches. Front passenger also has fire control on our remote gun. Rear-seat passengers are welcome to access the sensors to supplement the watch.'

'When it's time to swap round, how do we get from our seats to yours?' Madeleine asked.

'We're all going to have to learn to channel our inner gymnast,' Raddon said. 'I don't want to open the doors unless it's completely necessary.'

Angela agreed with that. Warm air had been blowing out of the vents for a minute, and she hadn't yet felt any change in temperature. Big slabs of foam had been stuck to the bodywork inside the vehicle to act as a thermal barrier, but the Tropic just wasn't intended for cold weather.

'Everything is going to be slower and methodical,' Forster said. 'That's all.'

'I've never driven anything like this,' Madeleine said. 'And certainly not in these conditions.'

'Big-freeze driving isn't so hard. You'll pick it up, don't worry.'

Madeleine pulled her balaclava off, and gave Angela a wary grin. 'Yeah, I suppose we're all capable of things we didn't know we could do.'

'When the chips are down,' Angela replied. She saw Raddon squinting at them in the rear-view mirror, trying to work out if there was something more being said than the words spoken.

Her e-i told her that a ringlink was being established, connecting all the vehicles and personnel. Elston wanting to keep watch over his mobile fiefdom. The colonel had chosen to ride in biolab-1 himself; and Angela was interested to see Karizma and her cronies Leif and Davinia were all in MTJ-2, the one which had fallen down the ravine.

'Everyone is in their assigned vehicle, and Darwin tells me the vehicles are all fully operational,' Elston said. 'Thank you all for the effort you've put in over the last week. With a little help and understanding from Our Lord we should reach Sarvar in about a fortnight. There are enough supplies and fuel stock there to see us through the rest of this climate anomaly. All right, now let's take things slow and easy – remember I want everyone there in one piece. Leif, lead on please.'

'Yes, sir,' Leif replied.

Angela's grid display showed MTJ-2 start to move out, wheels spinning as it struggled for traction. Small waves of snow spilled away from the edges of the plough blade, clearing a flattened track. MTJ-1 followed, containing Dr Coniff and the paramedics, along with as much medical equipment as they could cram into the cramped cabin. Poor old Luther Katzen was also in there, cursing about being a burden as his thigh and hip slowly knitted back together. Too slowly for the doctor, according to the gossip Madeleine had managed to prise out of Mark Chitty.

Both the biolabs followed, tugging sledges laden with food and equipment and some fuel. Then came the tanker and two trucks. The three Tropics were designated to bring up the rear.

Madeleine started pulling her gloves off. The dusting of snow on her parka had melted, dripping onto the seat and floor. 'Can I take the armour off?'

'Sorry,' Forster said. 'The colonel insists we keep some degree of personal protection even inside the cab.'

'Figures,' Angela grunted as she pulled her own balaclava off.

Raddon had struggled out of his parka and gloves, but kept a small dark-grey woollen hat on. They all watched the Tropic carrying Lieutenant Botin, Dean Creshaun, Fuller Owusu, and Chris Fiadeiro roll past the windscreen, its sledge slithering along behind.

'Here we go,' Raddon said, and engaged the axle motors. The Tropic nudged forward. Angela accessed the mesh smeared across the rear of the vehicle, watching in her grid as the tow cable stretched and finally tugged the sledge along. Then Raddon was shifting up the torque differential, and the big tyres seemed to be gripping the snow. Certainly the wheels weren't spinning.

Angela exchanged a nervous glance with Madeleine, then smiled as they gradually picked up speed. For once she actually felt mildly optimistic. The modified vehicles worked, her colleagues were tired but they were smart and determined, they had enough fuel, probably enough food. Sarvar was achievable. After that, well . . . she wasn't heading back to Holloway, that was for sure.

Tuesday 23rd April 2143

The buildings remaining amid the piles of rubble in the West Chirton GSW area were mostly ruins. Those that weren't complete burn-outs had long since had their windows smashed and roofs reduced to skeletal timbers. Even the graffiti were vanishing beneath blooms of moss and algae and the ever-spreading ivy creepers. The old road layout slowly melded into the decay beneath dunes of brambles and rampant buddleias.

Daylight saw kids scrabbling over the piles of smashed bricks and chunks of concrete, scavenging for the tiniest scraps of metal or playing violent games of chase. At night, even the delinquent youths made themselves scarce. People a lot more dangerous than juvenile gang-idolizers made their purposeful way along the streets under the cover of darkness.

Ian and Abner had a section of the GSW under observation using Ian's covert access with the Market Street network. On the previous Saturday, one of the micro-copters had flown a low, silent pass over the GSW area. Any sensor or mesh belonging to a gang protecting their territory would see a profile similar to a bat – it even followed the same fast, slightly erratic trajectory common to all the *Chiroptera* genus. It hadn't landed, but a cloud of smartdust had come scudding out of its fuselage to coat one of the rubble piles directly opposite an old shop. A purely visual observation would reveal no activity in the decrepit structure. However, its broken windows had been covered with corrugated iron sheets. The sliding doors at the side were unbroken. Vagrants who roamed the GSW knew not to approach.

When Ian accessed the mesh at nine o'clock that evening, it showed heat leaking out of the covered-up windows and secure doors. Ruckby had arrived an hour ago, along with a couple of mechanics whom the Gang Task Force database listed as being involved with vehicle theft operations.

'Here it comes,' Abner told him.

Ian saw it in his grid: a van driving carefully along the remnants of the road. The big sliding door was opened, and the van nosed in, parking up next to an almost identical vehicle waiting inside. 'That one's changed colour since yesterday,' Ian commented.

Boz and Jede were having the vans boosted to order, then driving them out to the GSW where the mechanics could ghost them; changing licence and colour.

The big door was hurriedly closed again.

'Whatever they're targeting in the raid, it's going to be big if they need vans to carry it away in,' Abner said.

Ian told his e-i to shunt the mesh image to the side of his grid and compress it. He looked over at Abner, who was sitting against the wall of the flat's lounge, the place Eva normally claimed. Something about that was just wrong. For all his help, Abner didn't belong in their fellowship. There wasn't enough history between them. And Ian still didn't understand his motive. 'I don't get it,' he said out loud.

'Get what?'

'Why you're helping us.'

'Really? I'd have thought it was obvious. Somebody is killing my brothers. They started twenty years ago, and we still haven't found them. That bothers me, it bothers me a lot.'

'But, now you know it's all been a fight inside your family.'

'No I don't. Not yet. I admit it doesn't look good, not for Aldred, but I really do need to find out exactly what's going on and who is involved. That's the policeman part of me, the reason I chucked the usual corporate route and joined the force.'

Ian gave a small snort. 'Everyone thinks you're in Market Street to make sure we toe the corporate line.'

'No. We enjoy a challenge, us Norths. It just manifests in different ways. Me, I'm mildly obsessional about solving the puzzle.'

'Like Sid.'

'Not that obsessive. He's good, and politically smart with it. He really could make it as the next Chief Constable.'

'Aye. Probably. That'd be the best thing that happened in Market Street in a long while.'

'If he does I hope he cuts back on the bureaucracy. Man, that's the downside I wasn't expecting when I joined.'

'There's always a way round.'

'Yes. So why did you watch Sherman off-log? The investigation could have done it – we were given the clout to do anything.'

'Something about where the information came from. Sid needed to keep his source quiet.'

'Ah, I see. Honourable with it. Maybe he won't make Chief Constable after all.'

'What about you?' Ian asked. 'What are you going to do if we harvest proof that Aldred's involved?'

'Depends what he's involved in, doesn't it?'

'What about me and Eva? Are we covered if it goes bad? Do we get the blame for digging too deep?'

'No, Ian; I've got a direct line to Augustine, I'll make sure he understands. You're doing the right thing, too. This has to be solved.'

'What if it is Augustine behind everything?'

'It isn't.'

'You sound very sure.'

'I am, trust me. This is something different altogether. Did you see the news from St Libra? Something has killed four people at camp Wukang.'

'Aye, man! Not that bloody alien thing again.'

'What is killing them, then?'

Ian shook his head. 'Well not Sherman, that's for sure. Maybe the two aren't connected?'

'I'd like to think that. We'll know before long, won't we?'

'Aye.' Ian gave the 2North a long look, still unable to gauge how much trust there was between them. 'Did you really not know there was a 2North that wasn't on anyone's official register? You know, the one we fished out of the Tyne.'

'No, nobody knew about him. And that's the most worrying part of this for my brothers and me. I still find it hard to believe one of us could be implicated in his death. We're not saints, none of us, but that is beyond me no matter how big the disagreement, so it should be beyond any of us.'

'You said you were all a little different.'

'Yeah, a little. But not this. This is too much.'

'Okay.' An icon popped into Ian's grid, and he expanded the mesh feed again. 'Oh aye, another van's arriving, look.'

*

Ralph had taken the same room in the Central Arcade hotel so he could be in town for the end of the trial. Sid claimed a chair while the agent took a bottle of Newcastle Brown from the fridge.

'This stuff any good?' he asked, holding up the chubby bottle.

'Let me give you some free survival advice,' Sid told him. 'Don't ever ask that in Newcastle again.'

Ralph grinned and twisted the cap off as he sat down. 'So we got a conviction, then. You must be pleased.'

'Ernie Reinert. A guilty plea which got him twenty years followed by permanent relocation. It's nothing and you know it.'

'Yes. So where are you?'

'I wasn't as smart as I thought. Abner found out what we're doing. He's joined up with us.'

Ralph paused with the bottle tipped back to his lips. 'Did he tell Aldred?'

'No, and that's where this gets really interesting.' Sid was impressed that Ralph let him tell the whole story without interruption, but then this was doubtless going straight into the agent's cache like some self-obsessed celebrity gush.

Only at the end did Ralph give a start. 'Trigval?' he asked sharply. 'Are you sure?'

'Yes. Sherman's people are putting the raid together right now. They're ghosting the vehicles, and putting together some equipment in the GSW, so we're assuming it won't be long.'

'What's your gameplan?'

'I want the raid to go ahead,' Sid said, trying to guess Ralph's responses. 'Sending in a tactical squad to catch them red-handed would be easy, and it'll get Market Street to the front of every news show, but in essence it's the same as arresting Reinert. It's premature. If we're ever going to resolve this, we have to follow the vans to the handover; that way we can see what the hell is going on. Aldred is too smart to take part himself, but if we get far enough along the line we should be able to harvest enough proof.'

'Good call. There's just one alteration you need to make.'

'What's that?'

'I'll be joining you.'

*

The estimate Darwin and Leif had come up with was a hundred and fifty kilometres a day. Back in the inflated orange fabric of the garage at Wukang, as they changed tyres and adjusted drive systems, such a figure seemed both reasonable and achievable, derived as it was from extensive flow charts and graphs.

So far they had covered a hundred and two kilometres since they set off two days ago. Vance would have wept if he thought the Lord would help because of it. But He helped those who helped themselves, and right now Vance had delivered himself to this place. Nobody in biolab-1 was saying anything, of course, but he could well guess the dissent brewing in MTJ-2, where Karizma and her admirers were doing all of the difficult trail-blazing work. And it *was* tough, especially in the jungle. No one could have realized just how arduous it was going to prove. Four or five metres of snow on the ground meant that the vehicles would sink down nearly a metre before the snow started to provide some stability. In those circumstances the snowplough blade was effectively useless. The MTJ driver only lowered it when they reached a drift, pushing it aside rather than attempt to ride over.

By itself, the snow could have been overcome. But in the jungle, the height of it elevated the vehicles almost into the canopy. A canopy that was encased in ice and holding up even more snow. The tangle of interwoven branches was so dense they could barely see five metres ahead. It was as if they were inside a snow crystal with all its sparkling three-dimensional complexity, and no section was the same.

There were clear sections where the convoy could proceed relatively smoothly, patches of savannah without any trees. If anything they just added to everyone's frustration when they reached the next swathe of jungle and had to slow again.

When they did hit yet another dense cliff of knotted trees, MTJ-2 had to deploy its buzz saws continually, cutting and slashing. The snow crust surrounding the branches detonated under the blade impact, splatting violently across the windscreen; then the blades hit the rock-solid frozen wood, and the screeching vibration shook the whole vehicle. The windscreen wipers laboured to clear the mash of ice and sawdust, allowing those in the cab to see the next layer of branches or vine snarl to chop at. With a metre of path cleared, the driver would throttle the MTJ forward, pushing into the snow, the big front wheels rising up only to sink down again as the white powder compressed under the weight. Then it would stop, and they'd use the buzz saws again, although the blades were never designed to deal with frozen wood. Leif was apprehensive about the strain they were putting on them. He was repeatedly forced outside to check and adjust the chain tension.

The constant stop-start progress was excruciating. All the

other vehicles would sit and wait until the MTJ had cleared a few hundred metres, then move forward together in an attempt to catch up.

Their second difficulty was just as acute, wasting almost as much time. The weight of the biolabs would often send them sinking into the track which the MTJ had made. Every time they had to dig round the wheels to lay matting, then use MTJ-1 to tow them out. That was a quick learning process, getting a feel for the vehicle as the tow rope began to take the strain, with both drivers linked to try and synchronize the pull.

Inside the jungle, the problem was made much worse; with the track being so narrow, if the second biolab got stuck the MTJ couldn't come back for it, so they had to use the winch on the front, attaching the cable to the back of the first biolab and hoping it was a good enough anchor.

After the first three times that happened, Vance reorganized the convoy so the trucks and tankers followed the two MTJs. They were heavy, but unlike the biolabs they'd been fitted with the wide snow tyres. Their traverse helped compact the snow a little better. But the mobile biolabs still sank in with monotonous frequency.

As Sirius dipped below the horizon, Vance ringlinked a conference with his department heads.

The first priority was to free up MTJ-1 so that it could take point duty and give MTJ-2 some relief. Dr Coniff, the paramedics and Luther would transfer over to biolab-2, swapping with Antrinell, Camm Montoto, Omar, and Vance himself.

'We have to get out of the jungle,' Leif said once they'd agreed to that.

'Don't start suggesting we just turn back,' Vance warned him.

'No, sir. I wasn't going to do that. But we do need a clearer route. If we carry on like this, we're going to run out of fuel in another ten days. We won't have travelled five hundred kilometres.'

'I'm aware of that, thank you. Do you have a suggestion?'

'Right now we're heading south-east, straight for Sarvar. But if we head directly south from here we'll hit a tributary of the River Lan in a couple of days. We can use the rivers like a highway network, travel straight through the jungle without having to clear every metre of the way with the buzz saws.'

'But the Lan just feeds down into the Jaslin,' Jay said. 'It goes south-west.'

'Yes, but the Dolce feeds into the Jaslin north of the Lan, and that can take us back almost to Sarvar.'

Vance called the map up into his grid. It was rudimentary, composed from the e-Ray images and ancient survey pictures taken when the first gateway had been opened in the Sirius system. He could see the route Leif was talking about, and if you thought of the rivers as roads it almost made sense – but it was hardly direct. 'How far is that?'

'Over three thousand kilometres, sir.'

'And what about our fuel reserves?'

'We can make it; providing the rivers give us an open path and we can travel at a decent speed. I've been reviewing the figures. We can leave the trucks behind once the bladders run dry, and the tanker too for the last section.'

'Give me those fuel-consumption files, please,' Vance said.

'If we keep going this way then we fail,' Leif said. 'We all know that – we'll have to turn back in another five days. But this way we can at least see what the river is like. If it's clear, and the convoy can travel on it, we can push on. If it doesn't, we turn back again and we've lost nothing.'

The problem with turning back, Vance thought as Leif's files appeared in his grid, was that the quantity of fuel they'd left behind at Wukang wasn't enough to see them through more than another six weeks. Not if the convoy returned with empty tanks. If they turned round right now, though, there'd be enough to take them possibly into July. 'I'll review your data,' he told Leif. 'And give you a decision by the time we've finished swapping personnel between the vehicles.' Which wasn't entirely true; the

831

hiatus was purely to show that he was in charge, and deliberating carefully before issuing their orders. But Leif had been right, there was no point carrying on through the jungle as they had been. They had to find out if they could use the rivers.

Sunday 28th April 2143

Déjà vu had wrapped itself around Sid tighter than a heavy winter coat. Three minutes past midnight, and here he was sitting in a privately registered police car on the north-east corner of Campbell Park, with Ralph sitting beside him as they waited to see what Sherman's people were up to. A light rain was washing in from the south, chilling down the streets after five days of cloudless skies. Despite the lateness of the hour, his e-i was still bouncing off calls from agency executives. It had been a frantic week – agencies had been employed by the city, which was desperate for their civil relief divisions to help with the flood of Highcastle refugees coming through the gateway. The Mayor's senior staff had routed a lot of those arrangements through Sid's office, as it had plenty of expertise in dealing with agency contracts, and everything needed finalizing fast.

Even now, the dedicated trains provided by Brussels were still running from Newcastle's central railway station, taking the exiles down to the channel tunnel, then fanning out across the GE to designated dispersal cities. Buses ran on a constant loop between Last Mile and the station's grandiose stone entrance on Neville Street, with the city's traffic management network providing a clear route, and squad cars riding escort ostensibly to keep those particular streets clear, but in reality to make sure no one jumped off to make themselves a life in Newcastle. The city simply couldn't afford any more migrants right now. It was struggling to cope with the bioil workers who'd returned earlier, and they all at least had company moncy behind them.

Away from the hustle and bustle of the Highcastle relief operation, Sherman's team was coming together under Jede's careful management. Three vans had been ghosted in the West Chirton GSW hideaway; now they were driving eastwards along the A149, keeping well within the speed limit, doing nothing which could attract the attention of any officialdom.

One of the three micro-copters was keeping pace with the lead van, the one containing Ruckby and a couple of byteheads they'd drafted in to help with the raid. The second van was driven by Boz, and had a pair of street soldiers riding with him, tough guys armed and ready to deal with any trouble. Jede drove the third van by himself.

To mirror them, Sid and Ralph were together; Abner shared a car with Eva, parked up on the north edge of Jarrow; while Ian was by himself, waiting outside the Simonside Metro station car park. They weren't using the surveillance routines, or even accessing the traffic macromesh to keep tabs on the vans. The Gang Task Force files on the two byteheads that Jede had recruited showed they were experts at dealing with alarms and observation routines. Sid was taking no chances. Despite the drizzle, he was determined they'd track the raid via micro-copter alone. And this weather was mild, the sensors on the little machines could easily cope with a light Geordie squall.

'Do you think they'll kill the guards?' Eva asked over their secure ringlink. 'Those thugs Boz has with him are armed.'

'I doubt it,' Sid said. 'Sherman won't want to draw excess attention to what goes down tonight. If I know him he'll be lifting a whole load of stuff as well as his actual target items, that way nobody will know what they were actually here for. It'll look like a high-end blackmarket theft.'

'But if they do? If something goes wrong?'

'Then we know exactly who to arrest.'

'That won't mean a lot to the victims' families. We could have had a tactical team on stand-by.'

Ralph turned his head to look at Sid. In the yellow streetlight filtering through the windscreen his skin looked deathly grey, amplifying his expression.

'There's a lot of maybes in that, Eva,' Sid said.

'These people are professional,' Abner said. 'They'll shoot tasers and tranks, not bullets or e-bolts.'

'Great,' she said. 'So we're relying on Sherman to be capable.'

'He didn't get where he is by making a noise,' Ralph said. 'Besides, this is an official HDA operation. It's my responsibility, and therefore my decision not to involve anyone else. You're covered.'

Now it was Sid's turn to give Ralph a blank stare. The agent responded with a shrug. 'Shuts her up,' he muttered.

Sid let out a long breath, and returned to the visual in his grid.

Trigval Molecular Solutions dominated the Bede Industrial Estate where it was situated, a seven-storey, ultra-modern carbon-black, all sharp-edged geometries intersecting at odd angles, crystallization architecture that had gone subtly wrong. It was surrounded by a moat of corporate parkland, with a formal layout of grass, pruned bushes, and staked trees, with precise leisure zones of benches and tables where employees could take a break in warmer months.

The vans driven by Ruckby and Boz arrived at the entrance, where a red and white barrier was down. It slid up immediately, and they both drove in, following the road round to a loading bay door at the back of the building.

'No alert registering in any police network,' Ian said. 'They're in clean.'

'Oh, they're good,' Ralph acknowledged.

The two goons were already out of Boz's van when a security guard emerged from a side door to check up on the unexpected activity. A tiny flash was visible to the micro-copter's sensor mesh, along with an electromagnetic spike. The guard crumpled. One of the goons dragged him back inside. Ruckby led the byteheads in after them.

'Taser,' Ian said. 'Happy now, pet?'

'Ecstatic,' Eva retorted.

They waited and watched for seventeen minutes, while Boz sat patiently in his van and the drizzle gradually abated. Sid tried not to think of the silent mayhem playing out inside the black building. Eva's worries were a meme gaining power in his mind.

Eventually, Jede drew up at the entrance, and the barrier lifted again. He drove round to the other two vans, then he and Boz went inside. It was another eleven minutes before one of the loading bay doors rolled up, sending a fan of bright orange-tinged light spilling out across the wet tarmac. Boz jumped down from the platform and hurried over to Jede's van, backing it up to the open bay. Shadows wove back and forth through the light as the team started loading up the van.

'Aye man,' Sid said grudgingly. 'Got to admit, they know what they're doing.'

'Can we see what's in those crates?' Ralph asked.

'Not without sending the copter in closer,' Sid said. 'Which I'm not going to do. I don't want to blow this now. Abner, launch the other two micro-copters, please. We need to keep tight on Jede's van when they go for the getaway.'

'Going airborne now.'

The van was loaded after another four minutes. Doors slammed shut, the loading bay lights went off. All three vans drove out.

'Okay,' Sid said. 'Abner, Ralph; we're following Jede's van. Focus on that, we have positive IDs on the others, we can pick them up any time.'

'Aye, boss,' Abner said.

Sid glanced over at Ralph for confirmation, but the agent already had his eyes closed as he whispered instructions to his e-i which controlled the micro-copter's flight. He figured any more instructions would just be patronizing, and let the agent get on with it.

The three vans separated as soon as they cleared Trigval's gate.

Boz and Ruckby headed back towards the city in their respective vans, while Jede took the Tyne tunnel.

Sid switched the police car to auto, and told it to start following Jede. Abner sent one of the micro-copters racing on ahead to the north of the Tyne, making sure it would be at the far end of the tunnel when Jede came out.

'Unless they pull a switch on us,' Ian said. 'The tunnel is the best place for that. And we know they're good at that kind of subterfuge, look how they fooled us with the taxi.'

'Unlikely,' Ralph said.

'We're on the tunnel approach now,' Sid said. 'If there's another van, we'll see it.'

They dipped down the approach road and went into the tunnel. Sid watched his grid, allowing himself a quick smile as Jede's van cleared the far end. 'Seems okay.' His e-i relayed a warning from the auto that the macromesh of the road junction at the end of the tunnel had glitched, and advised him to switch to manual. 'Oh yeah, like that was coincidence. What's he doing, Abner?'

'Circling the roundabout, twice now. Ah, no, wait, here we go, he's off down the A19.'

Sid switched the car to auto. 'And what's the betting the van's got a different licence code now?'

'No takers,' Ralph said. Behind them, Eva and Abner were entering the tunnel, with Ian a minute further back. Traffic was minimal, mainly taxis, which brought a wry grin to Sid's face.

Abner and Ralph kept the micro-copters in a triangular formation two hundred metres above the van. Their three cars took up position trailing half a mile behind, and drove steadily. Jede kept going all the way to the end of the A19 where he turned onto the A1.

'Interesting,' Ian said as they watched the van turn onto the northbound carriageway and accelerate down the practically empty road. 'Where's the bugger off to, then?'

They followed the van onto the A1, and Sid kept their speed

constant for a while, allowing the separation distance to build to a couple of miles. When that was established he matched Jede's speed.

After four miles, the carriageway's overhead lights ended, leaving them racing on into the darkness. A lot of the land beside the road used to be fields, but the farmers had long ago taken GE grant money under the natural reversion scheme. Now the forests were spreading out again, covering the undulating land with sturdy deciduous trees that provided a huge wildlife reserve.

'Going to have to think about bringing the micro-copters down to recharge soon,' Ralph said. 'We can do it in relay.'

'Aye,' Sid agreed. 'Who knew he'd be coming all the way out here?'

They passed a sign for the Alnwick slip road.

'Augustine lives round here, doesn't he?' Sid said.

Ralph shot him a look. 'It can't be. He could just buy Trigval, there'd be no need for tonight's activity.'

'Aye, just saying, man.'

'Screw this,' Ralph grunted.

'So what else can active-state matter be used for?' Sid asked. 'Apart from in gateways.'

'Sorry, classified.'

'The company was defence listed, we checked. So it has to be involved in some kind of weapons for the HDA.'

'I can't fault your logic.'

'War gateways, is that it? They're supposed to be a lot more stable than the exploratory ones, you know, before you send through an anchor mechanism.'

'Sid, really, I can't tell you. It's need-to-know only.'

'All right,' Sid grumbled.

They spent the next ten minutes in silence. Then the van reached North Charlton. The micro-copters showed its brake lights coming on, followed by the indicator.

Sid studied the map projected on the windscreen. There were three tiny roads spiking out from the hamlet. None of them was included in the macromesh. 'Crap on it.'

Ralph growled in agreement. 'Those roads are too small, and nobody but locals use them at this time of night. If this is where the handover is, they'll have them monitored.'

'We've just passed the B6374 turning. Nothing for it, we'll have to keep going. Eva, Ian, turn off onto the B6374 and we'll see where he goes.'

'Got it, boss,' Eva said.

Sid watched anxiously as the van drove over the carriageway bridge, and started heading east on the narrow track. 'Oh bugger it, that road leads back to the B6374. Eva, Ian, just stop.'

Sid drove under the bridge which Jede had gone over a minute before. He resisted the impulse to crane his neck in an attempt to spot the van. Besides, he could see from the grid that Jede was south of them now.

The van carried on down the lane at barely twenty mph. Then they all saw its brake lights flare red again, and it turned off.

'Now where are you going?' Sid asked. His e-i immediately pulled the satellite image up onto the windscreen, superimposing it over the map. The image had been taken in mid-summer, when the meadows and spinneys were graded shades of lush green. They saw the track the van was on, which led to a cluster of old buildings enveloped by the burgeoning forest.

'Farmhouse,' Ralph said. 'And there's a lot of infrared emission down there. Interesting, because my e-i's harvest is telling me the barns are under redevelopment as holiday cottages for the English Countryside Retreats Company.'

'Keep the micro-copters back,' Sid said urgently. 'If this is the centre of Aldred's operation, they'll have some serious sensors keeping watch.'

'The copters are well stealthed, boss,' Ian protested.

'I don't care. These people are smart. We pull them back.' Sid was desperate to turn the car around and head back to where the others were parked on the B6374, but that just couldn't happen. He'd have to leave at least an hour before coming back through North Charlton to avoid suspicion. 'What now?' he asked.

'I call it in and get us back-up,' Ralph said. 'A lot of back-up.

This has just turned serious. They're not handing the systems on for blackmarket resale; that's a functioning operation down there involving active-matter technology.'

'Aye, crap on it. I was kind of enjoying this, man, you know.'

'Sid, you've done a terrific job. Really. It won't go unnoticed.'

'Thanks. One favour?'

'What?'

'Let us in on the rest of the case. We'll take the back seat, no question, but I think we deserve to be there. We might even be able to keep contributing.'

'Last fling, huh? You're supposed to be an office baron now.'

'Still my case, though, man. And you owe me.'

'We're going to need high-level liaison with local police. I'll mention your name to some people.'

*

The Wukang convoy had finally cleared the jungle on Friday, two days longer than Vance had been quietly praying for. As if to compensate, the weather had gradually been improving. The aurora borealis was still the dominant power in St Libra's atmosphere, but the clouds were higher, and occasionally breaking up, allowing them to see clear up to a copper sky where Sirius burned its unnatural bright roseate pink. They even caught occasional glimpses of the rings. Temperature had risen a couple of degrees. The winds still blew, though their strength had diminished.

Such good fortune should have allowed them to make better progress. But open ground brought its own problems, and they still didn't cover much distance each day.

Vance was driving MTJ-1, taking point. It was almost a displacement activity for him. Driving over the unending snow field required his absolute concentration. He simply couldn't think about anything else, which was a relief.

The landscape of blank snow shimmered in gaudy reds and greens as the snow reflected the aurora's gigantic phosphorescent rivers overhead. The shifting light played havoc with his perception, making the ridges and dunes and gulches formed by the snow hard to judge. Sometimes a hump he'd thought of as rising only a metre would turn out to be as high as the MTJ, and he'd ram into it believing the plough blade would slice clean through only to come to a juddering slam-halt, embedding the vehicle so firmly the axle hub motors couldn't extricate them. Then they'd have to take twenty minutes to half an hour to rig up the tow cable, and the other MTJ would haul them free. After that they'd have to find a lower point in the ridge and punch through. If they couldn't find a low saddle, they'd just have to keep ramming the dune until they broke through, which could take hours.

As a result they were tracking a zig-zag course across the snow, taking way too long to reach the river. Vance was starting to worry about the accuracy of their maps, and the inertial navigation systems. By his and Ken's reckoning, they should have reached the Lan tributary yesterday. One more problem which the sheer grind of driving banished.

They were travelling through low hill country, winding along the wide valleys, dodging the spinneys and treacherous rough expanses of snow which they'd long since discovered covered vast swathes of ferns. The strange, jagged snow covering was always loose, and the frozen fern fronds snapped like glass if anything drove over them, turning the whole area into a giant ice granule swamp that would pull the vehicles down and surround them with a powdery shale while their wheels churned away uselessly.

Vance could see a dune up ahead, sparkling green as the vigorous aurora borealis slithered through the clouds above. He studied it intently as the MTJ rolled onwards relentlessly, the snowplough blade cutting cleanly through the rumpled surface, while their big tyres threw off churning fantails as they flattened the snow for the convoy to follow. It didn't rise too far out of the surface, maybe a metre or so at the top. The pitiful radar image on the windscreen confirmed what he was seeing, though he almost discounted it. Snow with all its varying densities, as they'd discovered, did strange things to the return. He gunned the throttle, and turned the wheel slightly so the MTJ was lined up full square. Only when the tip of the snowplough was about to hit did Vance realize he'd made a mistake again. Now he could see over the brow of the dune, the deep depression behind it was visible to him.

'Wrong,' he snarled as the snowplough hit the dune. He concentrated hard, aware of how the vehicle began to dip then slow as the resistance built up. He knew there wasn't enough power to get them through; impact with a hundred other dunes made such knowledge instinctive now. Snow thrown up from the blade and bonnet drew a lazy arc in the air, smothering the windscreen and thudding down loudly on the roof. He carefully throttled back, timing it so the motors were still by the time they came to a halt. The wipers strained to clear the fat smear of snow from the windscreen.

'Good call,' Camm Montoto said as they finished moving.

'Let's see,' Vance said. He put the axle motors into reverse, and applied power. If he'd got it wrong, if he'd kept the acceleration going too long as the MTJ buried itself in the dune, they'd be stuck fast. The MTJ shifted backwards a fraction. Vance maintained power, making sure the big tyres didn't spin, allowing them to gain some traction on the flattened snow. Slowly and surely the MTJ began to back out of the dune, crawling up the incline.

'You okay?' Davinia asked over the ringlink.

'We're moving,' Vance confirmed. 'There's a slope on the other side, not sure how deep.'

'Are we going round?'

Vance looked at Omar, who was sitting in the passenger seat. The Legionnaire grinned, which scrunched up the protective membranes covering his cheek. 'We can manage that.'

'Going through,' Vance announced to the ringlink. The MTJ extracted itself from the dune, and Vance continued to back up. Twenty metres from the dune he stopped, and adjusted the snowplough blade height. He twisted the throttle sharply, sending the MTJ racing towards the dune again. He had to keep a strong hold on the steering wheel, making sure the big vehicle threaded straight into the gap he'd already created.

They hit the snow again, punching further in. Vance intuitively knew they weren't going to make it, and eased up on the throttle as he felt the MTJ's momentum dissipate once more. Backing out slowly again. Lining up. Charging forward. Keeping the blade tip aligned on the centre of the gap.

Third time was enough. They broke through, with snow forming an airborne curtain overhead. They bounced and jostled down the slope on the other side as the wipers worked fast, clearing away the smears and chunks of snow. There were trees ahead, a big sprawl of bullwhips and cozpal and trinnades, meshed by vines which in turn produced a vast undulating roof of snow and ice. The snow around them was the now-familiar rumple of submerged ferns.

Vance throttled back and turned left, giving the bad snow a wide berth before slowly coming to a halt. There weren't many functioning sensors or much working smartdust on the MTJ, but he could just access enough in his grid to give him a view back to the gap he'd rammed through the dune. The second MTJ was manoeuvring through. Davinia used the snowplough blade to carve a deep slice out of the side of the gap, producing a wider track for the trucks and biolabs.

While they were waiting for the rest of the convoy to come through, Vance told his e-i to bring up the map again. Something somewhere didn't tally. Either the map was wrong, or the inertial guidance. But each vehicle had an independent guidance system, and they were all agreeing on where the convoy was. Logically then, it had to be the map.

Vance studied the profiles and contours carefully, trying to find a recognizable landmark. Apart from the tributary itself, there wasn't one. But as Leif said, it was just a question of travelling due south. They had to reach it at some point. Their fuel levels would have to be reassessed when—

'Oh shit, shit!' Ophelia exclaimed over the ringlink.

'It's going, it's going,' Gillian added.

Vance accessed the MTJ's rear mesh just in time to see truck-2 sinking into the snow. It started to tilt over. Vance sucked down an anxious breath. Before the angle grew acute enough to tip it on its side the movement stopped, but the truck was now embedded in snow to the top of its wheels. The sledge it was towing slid serenely along one side, then twisted sharply as the cable jerked it to a halt.

'Oh for crap's sake,' Omar protested. 'There goes the rest of today.'

'Yeah,' Vance agreed in a jaded tone. 'Looks like it.'

It took ten minutes to get ready for the outside. The four of them squirmed round, putting their clothing layers back on. Vance pulled a high-neck sweater over his quilted shirts and thermal underwear. Then there were another two sweaters before he fixed his armour on. Thermal overtrousers went on next, followed by waterproof trousers. Two sets of gloves. Surprise – Angela hadn't knitted him one of her balaclavas, so he had a printed version which scratched his ears, and a thick hat which just fitted under his helmet. With all the layers on, he was free to struggle into his parka. Finally there were the goggles.

'What do we ever do if we need to get out fast?' Camm grunted from the rear seat as he wrestled his parka on. 'Anyone got a contingency protocol for that?'

'Just get out,' Antrinell said flatly. 'Worry about the cold later. It takes a couple of minutes before it does any real damage.'

'Good to know,' the xenobiologist grunted sarcastically.

They climbed out into the bitter air. Vance tramped along the side of the track the MTJ had created, boots sinking ten centimetres into the virgin snow, which made every step an effort. When he passed truck-1 and the tanker he got back onto the track, walking down the depression rut made by the tyres.

Ophelia Troy had already got her outer layers on, and was outside, inspecting what had happened. Gillian remained in truck-2's cab, looking disgusted with herself.

'Why didn't you follow the track?' Vance asked Ophelia. He

was looking at the snow, seeing the way truck-2 had veered away from the track he and MTJ-2 had cleared.

'We picked up some sideways drift going down the slope,' Ophelia said. 'No point trying to correct when you're going down. Gillian would have just steered back onto the track when we were back on the flat. Which we were doing. It wasn't much. Crap's sake, if you'd been three metres further over it would have swallowed you too.'

Vance nodded slowly. She was right. The snow where the truck had sunk down didn't look any different, the surface was a little more puckered perhaps, but nothing to indicate how light it was underneath. In fact he didn't understand why the density was so different. Just another obstacle St Libra was throwing at them with its usual dispassion.

The other convoy members were gathering round. Vance was pleased to see the Legionnaires were all carrying their weather-sheathed carbines. Leif and Darwin peered down into the holes which had captured the wheels.

'There was running water under here,' Darwin decided. 'I think it chewed the snow away from underneath. The truck fell through the roof of a small ice cave. It's sitting on a whole lot of crushed ice now.'

'Makes sense,' Antrinell said. 'We're at the bottom of a slope. Maybe this used to be some kind of run-off.'

'Maybe,' Vance said, knowing how petulant he sounded and not caring. A week of the relentless delays and frustrations which the convoy had thrown at them had worn away any vestige of humour.

The first priority was to dig the wheels out. The sledge towed by Tropic-2 was broken open and spades handed round. Two people per wheel began scooping the snow away. It was difficult work; with the loose snow crumbling easily, the ramps they were making had to be twice as wide as the tyres to prevent them falling in on themselves.

Karizma went over to the sledge towed by biolab-2, and hauled out the flex grids that they would place under the truck's tyres. She and Erius started locking the individual units together to form four long strips. Leif himself tethered the truck's sledge full of bioil bladders to MTJ-2, and carefully pulled it clear.

While the tyres were being dug out, Vance ordered all the vehicles to top up their tanks. He was helping unwind a hose from the side of the tanker when Angela came over.

'The fuel's lasting surprisingly well,' she said. 'I've been keeping track of consumption.'

'Given we spend most of our time idle while we wait for the lead MTJ to make some progress that's hardly surprising. Keeping the cabs warm doesn't use up half as much bioil as driving.'

'But we're taking a long time getting anywhere.'

'The tributary can't be more than a day away now, no matter how poor our map is.'

'Good.'

'All right, Angela, what's bothering you?' He glanced round the convoy. Most people were out of the vehicles, either helping with the refuelling or digging round truck-2. Five Legionnaires walked a simple patrol pattern round them, scanning the empty white landscape. There had been no hint of the creature since they left Wukang.

'The fuel may be holding out,' she said. 'But I'm not sure the food will.'

He closed his eyes. *Please Lord, just let one thing go right.* 'Really?'

'Elston, it's been a week, and we've barely covered three hundred kilometres. We were planning on taking two and a half weeks, three tops. I calculated the food load on that basis, plus a week's worth of composition gel in case of emergency.'

Vance checked round again, this time making sure no one was close enough to overhear them. 'Are you telling me we haven't got enough food?' he asked in rising frustration.

'I'm telling you that if we take more than another couple of weeks it'll be touch and go. For a start you need to tell everyone to cut down. They're all eating as if there was a resupply flight about to drop crates of gourmet meals on us tomorrow. We also

846

need to get them used to the composition gel. Once it's prepped a carton gives you a perfectly calculated two thousand calories per day; that's all you really need. And if it looks like we're going to take longer, then they can go on a diet for a week. Wouldn't hurt.'

'Okay. I'll break that news once we've got truck-2 clear. We'll start to alternate composition gel with our standard meal packets tonight.'

'Thank you.'

'Have you ever tasted composition gel after it's been prepped?' he asked.

'No.'

'Consider yourself fortunate.'

Vance carried on with the refuelling, dragging the hose nozzle over to MTJ-2. The snow field around him was abuzz with activity as the hoses were pulled out, and tanks filled. The front wheels of truck-2 had now been cleared, and Erius was down on his belly, wriggling and shoving, trying to get the obstinate strips of flex grid into place along the crude ramps of ice chunks. Leif had already attached a pair of tow cables to the front of truck-2, now he was waiting for the MTJs to finish refuelling and manoeuvre into place. The two vehicles plus the truck's own hub motors should be enough to pull it out of the collapsed ice cave, so Leif claimed.

After ninety minutes of hard work by everyone, truck-2 was ready to be liberated. The MTJs were hooked up to the cables, and slowly rolled across the snow, angling so that their pull would compensate for the way the truck was leaning. Leif drove MTJ-2, while Antrinell was behind the wheel in 1; Gillian was in truck-2's cab, determined to make amends for the disruption she'd caused.

Vance stood back with a big group, watching as the tow cables took up the slack and became taut. Ophelia Troy was down on her knees beside the truck's offside front wheel, just above the ramp, watching to see if the tyre tread was moving onto the flex grid, linked to Gillian to relay what was happening. Paresh Evitts walked alongside MTJ-2, keeping an eye on its performance for

Leif, while Dean Creshaun was performing the same duty for MTJ-1. Vance could see the vehicles start to shake as they applied pressure. A rear wheel on MTJ-2 spun as it lost grip. Truck-2 shuddered and lurched a few centimetres forward.

'Tyres touching the grid,' Ophelia said. 'Take it easy, we're almost there.'

Smiles were appearing amid the watchers as the truck began to lumber forwards, slowly shifting back to the vertical. The motion caused the tow cables to slacken off for a moment. Both MTJs lunged ahead, tugging the limp cables taut again, exerting their full force in less than a second.

Then the cable connecting the truck to MTJ-1 snapped. It happened with a crack like a gunshot, which made Vance flinch, muscles contracting to deliver him into a half crouch. The two halves of the cable slashed through the air, releasing their tension energy at high velocity. They emitted a menacing whispering whistle as they moved. But even that sound wasn't enough to alert those nearby to what was happening, so fast was the cable moving.

Abruptly freed of its load, MTJ careered forward, beginning a wild turn. The back end of the vehicle caught Dean Creshaun as it spun, knocking him sideways. Meanwhile its cable end slashed through the cold air, keeping parallel to the snow. It slammed directly across Paresh Evitts' chest. The armour vest he wore underneath his parka saved him from being sliced in half, though the tough woven filaments of the breastplate section buckled and cracked from the ferocious impact, dissipating the impact back through the layers of sweaters and shirts. His arm was also flicked by the cable. Again the armour protected him from any direct lacerations, though the humerus was instantly snapped in two and the shoulder dislocated. He was flung backwards several metres through the air to land on fresh snow, already unconscious.

Ophelia Troy was still kneeling at the side of the ramp of ice that had been dug down to the truck's offside front wheel. The truck was rolling laboriously up the ramps, bringing its chassis level with her head when the tow cable snapped. The length still attached to the truck lashed sideways with its signature high-frequency whistling. Ophelia's brain was just starting to register something was wrong when the cable caught her across the side of her throat, above the collar of her armour waistcoat. Her unprotected neck was severed clean in two by the guillotine-like swipe. The muscles of her body took a moment to lose their rigidity, holding her headless torso in its upright crouch position while her heart's last few beats sent blood fountaining up out of her severed carotid artery. Only as the sickening jet of blood finally dwindled did Ophelia's body relax and topple over.

In the cab, Gillian didn't know what had gone wrong, only that an unexplained judder ran down the length of the vehicle. She was also aware of a slight hiatus in her progress forward. In response she twisted the throttle, determined not to lose the momentum that had brought the tyres out onto the flex grids. 'Come on!' she yelled at the recalcitrant truck. Out of the corner of her eye she saw the rear of MTJ-1 starting to skid sideways. It smashed into poor Dean Creshaun. 'Shit!' But still she kept power on, forcing the truck up the ramp towards freedom. Paresh Evitts flew through the air, and a whole cascade of icons burst into her grid like a firework explosion. That was when she acknowledged what her subconscious already knew: something was drastically, terribly wrong.

Truck-2 lumbered out of the ramps, and Gillian eased the power back. Then she began to focus on what the red icons were telling her. At the same time, the shouts and screams came thundering through the cab's makeshift insulation.

Angela had no memory of running. One second she was standing with everyone else as the truck did its weird quiver, the next she was panting from exertion, staring down frantically at Paresh's limp body. The front of his parka had been split as if someone had taken a knife to it, cutting through the padding to expose his armour. That too was battered, she could see the thick weal of stress cracks across the front, ironically mimicking a frost pattern. Her e-i was accessing his bodymesh medical smartcells.

He was still alive. She ripped his goggles off, and tugged the skewed balaclava round. A faint breath mist puffed out of his lips. Blood was dribbling from the corner of his mouth.

'Paresh!' she screamed.

Dr Coniff emerged from the crowd that was arriving, and sank down beside Angela. 'Move,' she barked as she tugged her gloves off. Angela shuffled aside, allowing the doctor to reach for Paresh's face, finger pressing to find a pulse. 'Airway open, no sign of obstruction. Mark, scanner!'

Mark Chitty dropped to his knees on the other side of Paresh, extracting a small hand-held scanner from his pack. The doctor started waving it across Paresh.

Angela hated how helpless she was. It was all she could do not to interrupt the doctor and demand an explanation. Instead, all she could do was watch.

'Damnit,' Coniff growled. 'Can't get through the armour. Okay, arm's broken, but that's clean. Shoulder will need relocating. Can't inspect the chest wall for flail segment, but there's going to be a lot of soft tissue damage. Mask!'

Chitty had already got a clear oxygen mask ready, a plastic tube coiling back into his pack.

'I need a stretcher,' Coniff called out. 'Mark, stabilize the arm and get him into the biolab.' She clambered to her feet and looked round to where Dean Creshaun was sitting up in a daze, surrounded by his buddies Olrg and Lance.

'Wait,' Angela yelled as the doctor started hurrying over to Dean. 'What about Paresh?'

'We need to get him inside,' Coniff said over her shoulder. 'I can treat him properly when I can get him scanned. He's stable enough.'

'Ho crap!' Angela exclaimed. She gripped Paresh's hand, squeezing him through the protective gauntlet. 'I'm here, sweets, you hear me? I'm here. You're going to be fine, just fine.'

Mark Chitty cut the parka off Paresh's broken arm with a small powerblade, and rolled a tube sleeve up the armour. The sleeve inflated quickly.

It seemed like hours before Juanitar Sakur and Sergeant Raddon came shambling gracelessly through the fluffy snow, carrying the stretcher. Paresh was eased on to the canvas. Angela took one of the corners, and they made their way back to biolab-2 as fast as they could. As they went she was dimly aware of a commotion breaking out, a hysterical Erius was shouting at Leif. Everyone knew that Erius and Ophelia had a thing going back at Wukang. Now, Erius was blaming Leif for the calamity, since he was the one who'd connected the tow cables . . . and he was the one whose plan they'd been following.

'Your fault, you bastard!' Erius screamed, and took a maddened swing. In so many clothes it was a pitiful blow, slow and cumbersome. But his fist did make contact, and Leif swayed back, stumbling. So then he launched himself at Erius in equally furious retribution. Several Legionnaires waded forward, pulling them apart.

That was when the stretcher bearers passed Ophelia's corpse. Someone had covered it with a plastic sheet, but it wasn't wide enough to conceal the spray of frozen blood that was scattered across the churned-up snow. A couple of metres away another, smaller, sheet was draped over the head. Angela felt her stomach churn, and thought she was going to be sick.

Paresh groaned. Blood started to fleck the inside of his mask as he coughed.

'You're okay,' Angela shouted at him, trying to bend over as she trudged along, putting her face above his. His eyes were fluttering. She wasn't sure he was fully conscious. 'You hear me? You're doing okay. The doc's coming and everything's going to be fine.'

They reached the mobile biolab and manoeuvred Paresh into the small door compartment. The outside door slid shut, and Angela stomped her feet impatiently while they got him through into the central cabin area. When the door slid back again Coniff had arrived with Ken Schmitt helping a limping Dean Creshaun. So again Angela had to wait while Dean and the doctor went inside.

When she did finally get through the door compartment, the central cabin was badly cramped. They'd moved Luther to the driver's cab passenger seat; the other members of the xenobiology team travelling in the vehicle had vacated into the lab section to give the medical team space to work. Dean was sitting in a corner, with Juanitar Sakur helping him get his layers off. Paresh was lying on a gurney with Mark Chitty and Antrinell removing the last of his armour. The oxygen mask was still clamped over his mouth and nose, but the bleeding seemed to have stopped.

Dr Coniff gave Angela an annoyed look. 'We don't have room. Wait outside, please.'

'Make me,' Angela spat back.

Antrinell gave her an exasperated glance.

'Come sit with me,' Luther said, and patted the driver's seat. Angela gave him a fast nod, slightly shocked by how sickly the catering supervisor still looked, and wormed her way round to the little oval hatchway, scraping snow off her boots and gaiters as she went. It started melting right away. She stared at the little puddles in a daze. The inside of the biolab was life from another time and world: white light, warm dry air. She'd been braced against the grinding cold for so long that this was the milieu which felt wrong now.

With Luther's cautious help, she began removing her own layers. Coniff slid a big scanner arm across Paresh, her eyes closed as she concentrated on the image. Chitty began cutting the last T-shirt away. Angela's breath caught as she saw the vivid purple and black welts discolouring the skin across his chest.

'It's okay,' Mark Chitty told her kindly. 'The armour's impact honeycomb absorbed a lot of the impact. It's good stuff. Without it he'd probably be dead.'

'Multiple broken ribs,' Coniff reported, her eyes still closed. 'Can't see any signs of pulmonary contusion, but I want to keep an eye on that. Repeat the scan every hour to see what develops.'

'Got it,' Chitty murmured.

'Moving on to the heart. With this kind of blunt force there's going to be some myocardial contusion. Let's set up an EKG, please. Get me a baseline.'

Chitty sprayed a clear gloop saturated with smartdust on Paresh's violet chest. 'Mesh established and linking to our net. Processing and monitoring his cardiac rhythm now.'

Paresh moaned again, wheezing down a breath.

'Enough,' Coniff said. 'I want him properly sedated. We'll put the shoulder back in and set the arm.' She turned to stare at Angela. 'Your boyfriend's lucky. He's young and built like an ox, which helps. We'll repair the damage, and pump him full of anti-inflammatory steroids. The ribs will cause a lot of discomfort for a few weeks, but that can be mitigated by some internal nuflesh insertions once the bruising reduces.'

'He's okay?' Angela was dismayed at how pathetic she sounded.

The corner of Coniff's mouth lifted up, which must have been her version of a smile. 'Yes. Now you *will* leave us, because I'm not having you in here when we hammer his shoulder back into its socket – it's too gross for friends and family. He'll be under anaesthetic for hours anyway. Mark will let you know when he's awake, you can talk to him then.'

'Thanks.' She took her time getting her outer layers on again. Watching as Paresh was properly anaesthetized. Chitty started tightening some nasty-looking metal clamps around his torso and upper arm. Angela wrinkled her nose up, gave Luther a quick hug of thanks, and left.

The transition numbed her for a long moment. St Libra's malignant cold wriggled its way through gaps in her layers, scratching minute prickly fingers against her flesh. The pink sunlight was beset with bold green flickers, turning the snow a sickly grey-purple. She stood outside the biolab, looking around. The scene now was identical to all the other refuelling breaks they'd made on the journey so far. Vehicles parked in a line. People walking about carrying equipment. Darwin and Olrg packing the flex grid sections away in the sledge. Truck-2 being reconnected to its sledge. Legionnaires on patrol. There was no sign of Ophelia's corpse.

Angela abruptly set her jaw and marched across the rumpled snow to truck-2. When she reached it, the cab was empty, and the tow cables had been removed. A bulky figure was moving to intercept her.

'How is he?' Elston asked.

He'd know, of course, but he was giving her an excuse to babble, to let her pent-up fear go spewing out. At any other time she'd appreciate that. 'He'll be fine. They're fixing the arm now. The doc didn't want me there for that.'

'I see. I'm glad.'

Angela pointed at the truck. 'Where's the tow cable?'

'It got packed away. We have additional cables so there's no problem.'

'I want to see it.'

'Angela . . .'

'I want to see where it split. I want to know how a cable with a fifty-tonne breaking strain can snap when an MTJ gives it a little tug.'

'Come with me.'

Elston took her arm, which was an almost useless gesture. She had so many layers on her arm was too wide for him to grip properly. Certainly he couldn't pull her along. She chose to go with him as he headed slowly back to biolab-1.

'You're right,' he said quietly.

'What?'

'I looked at the ends. The cables are a bundle of superbonded carbon filaments inside a triple layer polymer sheath. Someone had cut it. Not all the way through, they'd severed just enough filaments so it wouldn't snap straight away.'

'The son of a bitch has caught up with us,' she grunted.

'We haven't seen any sign of it for the whole week we've been travelling. But that tow cable's been used a dozen times to pull the MTJs out of drifts. If it had been weakened back at Wukang, it would have snapped before now.'

'Son of a bitch,' she said in a throaty whisper. 'You think it was done today? But that means one of our people did it.'

'Yes. The only possibility I can come up with is Karizma, who wants to go back to Wukang. But I'm not sure how this helps her case. Besides, Ophelia was her friend, and an active member of their little turn-back-now cabal.'

'She wouldn't,' Angela said. 'She had to know she'd be putting Ophelia in harm's way.'

'Which leaves us with a big problem. We were all out here. It could have been anybody.'

'Damnit.'

'Anyone you're suspicious about?'

Angela regretted he was all wrapped up, she couldn't make out his expression. Because that was one hell of a leading question. 'Nobody. Sabotage doesn't make any sense. If we get stuck out here, we die. It's that simple.'

'All right then. I'll reorganize the vehicle rosters to take the injured into account. Biolab-2 is getting crowded, and truck-2 needs another driver. We'll move on as soon as the doctor has finished with Paresh's shoulder.'

*

From the front passenger seat in Tropic-2, Rebka watched the intense talk between Angela and Colonel Elston play out. She was pretty clear what topic was under discussion. As soon as the tragedy happened, most people instinctively rushed over towards the MTJs where Paresh and Dean lay, battered and incapacitated. A few hardier souls, led by a distraught Erius, had made their way over to Ophelia's headless corpse in time to see her steaming blood slowly freeze into the snow. Rebka had gone with the bulk of the convoy personnel, taking a slight curving detour to pass by the broken tow cable. As she went she picked it up and let it run through her mittened hand until she got to the end. She let it drop immediately. By then her cache had captured the image perfectly.

As Dr Coniff tended to Paresh, she'd huddled with the others in a semicircle, anxiously awaiting a verdict. Behind her goggles her eyes were closed as her grid displayed the image for her to review. Thousands of hair-thin filaments flopped out of the torn polymer sheath like a root system at the base of a plant. They looked ragged, as well they might after breaking under such a strain. But not all of them, over half ended neatly together. Some kind of blade had sliced through the cable.

It left her with two questions. When? And the nature of the blade? One of five that were arranged in a finger array?

'Incoming,' Angela announced over a link to Tropic-2. Raddon opened the rear door as Angela knocked snow from her boots and gaiters on the bodywork. Then she was inside and settling into the seat.

'How is he?' Forster asked, twisting round in the driver's seat.

Angela pulled her balaclava off and started unzipping the front of her parka as the cab's heater blew warm air around them. 'Lucky, so the doc said. The armour saved him. He's got some broken ribs and the arm. They're going to monitor him to make sure his heart and lungs are okay. And that's about it. Man, he looks like one giant bruise.'

Rebka pulled her own balaclava off. 'That's good news.'

'Yeah. Thanks. The dumb ass had me worried for a minute, there.'

'Elston said we're resting up for a couple of hours,' Raddon said. 'He's sent Darwin to help Gillian drive truck-2.'

'We should shove a meal in the microwave,' Rebka said. 'It'll be nice to eat one while we're sitting still. I might not cover myself in food for once.' She made herself busy, keeping in the Madeleine persona as she put their packets in the microwave and generally ran through the bubbly short-order waitress routine. The Tropic's cabin was soon filled with the smell of pepperoni pizza and hot chocolate, adding some small amount of cheer to the sombre mood.

Even her own optimism was growing shaky now. If they didn't find the tributary soon, then they would have to turn back. The prospect of waiting for rescue at Wukang was a bleak one. Right up until the tow-cable sabotage she'd been certain she could complete the mission, and capture the creature – whatever it was. It would be tough, she'd always known that, but the systems she'd brought with her from Jupiter instilled a level of confidence that she was now acknowledging might be misplaced. But then no one could have foreseen events unfurling in the disastrous way they had since she arrived on St Libra. Not even Constantine, who had spent two decades preparing. The constant attrition of personnel had unnerved her as it had everyone in the convoy. Smartmicrobes she'd placed strategically among the vehicles had died in the blizzards and sub-zero temperatures. The smart programs she'd infiltrated into the convoy's net had been reduced to ghosts of their former selves as the hardware failed and degraded. She was still fairly sure she would be victorious in any one-on-one combat. However, engineering that encounter was becoming increasingly unlikely. Like everyone, she had no idea where the damn thing concealed itself. It really did emerge from nowhere, which meant that while her metamolecule armour was inactive she was as vulnerable as anyone else. Her only alternative was to become more overt in her efforts, potentially pitting her against everyone else. It might yet have to come to that.

She realized her hand had crept up her chest to touch the phial she wore round her neck. 'To help ground you,' Constantine had said when he'd given it to her. Even now she was impressed by how prophetic those words had turned out.

*

Rebka had woken up early that day. All smiles and excitement as the habitat axle light rings pumped up to full intensity, and the colourful jungle birds greeted its fast dawn with a chorus of squawking. She pushed back the thin duvet and sat up on the edge of the bed, stretching and yawning.

'Clear the window,' she told her e-i. The curving wall in front of her turned from a purple haze to a simple window looking out across the habitat. Two of the house's surrounding circle of palm trees blocked her view in the centre and to the right, their long leaf crowns sagging down to allow the tips to rub against the top of the glass. The third palm, the one on the left, had died about a year ago, leaving a tall withered stem that was already decaying, hosting all manner of interesting orange and topaz fungi. Dad hadn't yet got round to organizing a replacement. He and Mum were still arguing over what to plant; both agreed they weren't having anything so big so close to the house again. Rebka suspected the argument never would be finished.

She slowly walked across her room, sliding her feet round the clothes and dirty underwear and sports equipment and cups and empty bottles and bits of the neumanonics kit from her year-ten science project and floform-stone sculptures and sketch pads and brushes and make-up boxes and . . .

Her cheeks puffed out in mild dismay at the maze of crap smothering the carpet. Maybe she ought to clear up some time. Mum had given up nagging years ago, but refused to help, saying she had to take responsibility for her own life. Good old Mum, always banging on about being a proper citizen.

And today I am.

One of the drawers had some fresh knickers and a bra. And her jeans from yesterday – and a few days prior – were still relatively clean. There were three washed and pressed T-shirts in the cage basket she'd brought back from the utility room recently. She chose the orange one, with flowers embroidered on the cap sleeves.

'Give me a mirror,' she told her e-i. A section of the window turned perfect silver, and she studied herself critically. Tall, which was okay thanks to the long legs; blonde hair that was dark enough to verge on chestnut, but was easy to dye, and still had pink and purple tips, with a single zombie-green forelock stripe; long face, pretty enough even with a thin nose, though she still considered it belonged to someone a good two years younger. Rebka frowned, peering forward, then let out a sigh of exasperation. To celebrate that youthfulness, her chin had erupted a couple of new spots overnight. She squared her shoulders and hustled her bra up into a better place. Grinning. Dad always rolled his eyes in not-quite-mock-disapproval at the scoop necks she favoured.

She went into the tiny en suite bathroom. Sloshed some dentjel round her mouth and spat it out. Washed her face carefully with the cleanser, then rummaged through packets to find some sup patches which she applied over the spots. Spots. Today of all days! Eyeliner, purple and gold. Brush the hair into shape – not enough time for a shower and shampoo now. Rub scent on strategically. And she was ready for whatever the grand day threw at her.

Both her parents were waiting for her at the breakfast bar. The ground floor's archway windows were fully open, allowing the morning air to gust gently into the house. It was fresh with the humidity of the overnight mist which atmospheric services squirted into the habitat every day between one and four in the morning. Birds flittered about through the trees, and geckos were skittering up the house walls.

Thinking about it, Rebka realized life couldn't be much better than this. Perhaps she did have a lot to be thankful for. And maybe she should have expressed a little more gratitude over the years. The surge of emotion caught her by surprise, and she swallowed hard, especially when she saw Mum and Dad both fighting to hide their own pride and sorrow.

Then the pair of them were smiling broadly, holding out their hands and chorusing: 'Happy birthday, darling.'

Rebka hugged them, not really caring that her eyes were all watering up. 'I love you,' she squeaked out.

They'd prepared her favourite breakfast. Sweet bacon and a pile of pancakes with strawberries, dussulpears and cream, and maple syrup. A tall glass of mango and cranberry juice poured over crushed ice. Farmhouse loaf toast with thick-cut blood orange marmalade.

'I can't eat all this,' she protested weakly as they all sat at the big patio table.

Dad grinned and popped a champagne bottle cork, pouring

the chilly fizz into their juice glasses. 'Best way to start today,' he promised. 'You're only going to be eighteen once.'

Through her happy giggles she saw the strange look her parents exchanged, and wrote it off to the fact that she'd be moving out soon. Her very own apartment in the new habitat shell, twice the length of this one with a lake that almost qualified as a sea it was so large. She'd even been considering asking for one of those mobile home capsules which people were starting to use, but wasn't sure if that was just a fashion statement. Either way, she'd be independent, like Raul and Krista had become after they reached their majority. This house would be very big for her parents after that, she thought. Maybe that's why things like decisions on replacement trees were being put off. Although she couldn't imagine home without them in it.

They all touched their glasses in salute, and sipped the fortified juice.

'Thank you both,' she said, still all teary. 'Look, I know I've not been the best daughter ever. And—'

'Hey, none of that,' her father said and put his arm round her. 'I don't want you to spoil your present opening. I've been planning mine for months.'

Despite her rampaging emotions, Rebka was abruptly curious. 'Oh?'

He reached under the table and produced what looked like a slim rectangular box, wrapped in blue and silver paper with a pink ribbon round it. Rebka took it, even more intrigued now she felt how heavy it was.

'Go on!' her father urged, as eager as her.

She pulled the ribbon's bow and unwrapped the paper. The object inside puzzled her for a moment, she'd never actually held one before, then realization dawned. 'A book!' she exclaimed. When she turned it over, the title was printed in gold leaf: *Alice in Wonderland*. Now she really did cry, it had been her favourite for so many years growing up. Such weird incredible adventures, even to her, a girl living in a space habitat orbiting Jupiter. Or perhaps especially here, the strangeness of Alice's travels was easy to relate to. 'Thank you, Daddy.' She folded her arms round him, hugging tightly.

'It's not a first edition or anything,' he said gruffly. 'But it is twentieth century. I got Clayton to pick it up when he was on Earth last.'

'It's lovely.'

Her mother held out a much smaller box of black velvet. It contained a plain gold ring. 'My grandmother's wedding ring,' she explained. 'I just want you to always know and understand you are truly family.'

As she embraced her mother, Rebka was worried she was going to spend the whole day in tears, albeit happy ones.

Eventually – ring on her finger where she could admire it, book on the table waiting to be read – she tucked in to the pile of pancakes.

'Raul and Krista are coming over for lunch,' her father said. 'Just the family. A quiet time before tonight's party.'

Rebka grinned wolfishly at that. She'd spent months planning tonight's event with all her friends.

'Do you know what you're wearing yet?' her mother asked.

'Uh, no.'

'We could go through some catalogues together, choose something to print out.'

'Yes, please. That would be lovely.'

Her father cleared his throat. 'You haven't forgotten what you have to do this morning, have you?'

'No! Go and see Constantine.'

'Good.'

'What does he talk about? Raul and Krista would never say. It's all very mysterious, which is stupid.'

'He just asks you what you want to do with your life, to make sure you're happy here. After all, we can't really afford malcontents in something as fragile as a habitat.'

'Wow, that's going to be boring.'

'It probably is, dear,' her mother said primly. 'But try not to show it. After all, it is his habitat.'

'What's he going to do if I tell him I hate it – kick me off?'

Her father's face fell into his hands.

Rebka pressed her lips together in self-censure. Dad was so easy to wind up. 'Don't worry, Dad. I'll behave. Kiss-promise.'

'Well I suppose there's a first time for everything,' he countered.

*

Rebka's e-i directed her up the side of the habitat shell into the low-gravity regions. She'd never quite forgiven herself for not enjoying zero gee. It looked such fun: flying, somersaulting with more grace than a ballerina gymnast, bouncing off the walls like a perpetual-motion squash ball, and there were always the awesome rumours of freefall sex which was supposed to be amazing. But her inner ears disapproved in a major way, resulting in more than one instance of projectile vomiting. Even her notoriously stubborn persistence had stalled from trying to 'acclimatize' after the fifth time her mother made her wash all her own clothes and apologize in person to everyone else in the axis gym.

Now the lift which ran all the way up to the axis stopped seven hundred metres above the curving floor at the one-third gravity level. She pushed off in a gentle walk, keenly aware of inertia as she glided in long arcs between her feet touching the corridor floor. There were big hand hoops on the walls every couple of metres, to grab when you needed to slow, stop, or change direction at a junction. She kept her arms out, ready to seize one just in case. So far her stomach was holding out.

The door her e-i delivered her to didn't seem any different from all the others in this section, which according to the overlay blueprint was mostly used for habitat maintenance engineering. It slid open and she glide-walked into the darkened room beyond.

The room was a lot bigger than she was expecting, like a small docking hangar with a curving ceiling ten metres above her. There were weird structures spaced throughout it that resembled giant strands of DNA, but with multiple helixes that had warped and bloated, made out of a substance that approximated to pearl. The multiple curving ridges of varying sizes which interlocked all over them in seemingly random patterns bestowed the appearance of a sea creature shell, convincing her they were living configurations rather than technological. It was hard to tell because they were phasing in and out of spacetime; random sections would dematerialize to sketch their original profile with sharp emerald and orange laserlight sparkles, as if photons were interchanging with atoms. Their haze made peering through the gloom of the chamber difficult.

When she did squint, she could see the wall at the far end was made up from big rectangular window sections that looked directly out into space. A figure was silhouetted against the rotating starfield.

'Rebka, thank you for coming,' Constantine North said.

'It's a tradition,' she replied, and walked cautiously towards him, anxious not to brush against any of the distended not-quite-real structures; if nothing else, when they did exist, the ridge pinnacles looked sharp and hard. 'I wasn't going to be the one who broke it.'

Jupiter's darkside slid into view as she reached him. As always she was thrown by how young he looked, only a couple of years older than Raul. Yet she knew he was born over a century ago.

'If anybody would . . .' he said.

Rebka pouted. 'I'm not that bad.'

'No. Of course not. The teenage years are always a trial for parents, yet somehow all of us seem to muddle through in our own way.'

'Mum said you want to know if I'm happy here.'

The pale light reflected off Jupiter's cloudbands painted grey shadows on his face. 'Not quite. The purpose of this interview is to determine if you're going to *be* happy living here.'

'I guess.'

'I liken this talk to the Amish *rumspringa*.'

'You just lost me.'

'The Amish are a society within a society, living in the United

States. They have rejected modern life to live a quiet pastoral existence, an existence they've followed for centuries. However, when they are teenagers, their families actually encourage them to go and sample the wicked delights of the majority culture which surrounds them, the *rumspringa*. What the rest of us consider an astonishing percentage, nearly ninety per cent, choose to return after their time away and join the Amish church for good. I suppose that speaks a lot of our arrogance in the belief that our way of life is superior. I find that humbling and quite salutary.'

'And that's what you're offering me?' she asked uncertainly.

'In a way, yes; this is your *rumspringa* moment. I wish to offer you an explanation and a choice. I am trying to build, if not a democracy, then at least a consensus based on a common ideal. So please forgive the irony of me acting like a patriarch. It would appear old habits die very hard indeed. Do you know why I set up this society out here?'

'We're an ark, humanity's last hope if the trans-space worlds fall to the Zanth.'

'That's a part of what we are, yes. But I want something a lot greater than that. Ultimately, I want us to defeat the Zanth.'

'Wow. That's . . . big.' She was starting to wonder how long this was going to take; there were so many things she needed to get ready for the party.

'It certainly is,' he said in amusement. 'But to do that, to be able to pursue the pure science theorems which can deliver that goal, we need to be free of the debilitating economics and material concerns which have acted as an anchor on true human creativity for centuries now. I looked round me, nearly sixty years ago, and saw nothing but stagnation. The HDA, for all its nobility of purpose, is a holding action, nothing more. That is why I founded Jupiter. We already have the technology in the shape of microfacture and fusion energy to step beyond the economics which have governed us for the past few hundred years and free us from material concerns. Yet we don't. The dead hand of society's inertia and the financial interest of the elite minority hold us back as a species. They govern us so they can continue to govern us.'

'History repeating itself,' Rebka said brightly.

'Precisely. I was a part of that stagnation, along with my brothers, opening St Libra for human settlement and founding Northumberland Interstellar, helping to maintain the bioil market dominance. More than anyone, I know how strong it is, how easily it contaminates and absorbs any divergence from the norm. Breaking free was an argument the three of us conducted over many years. My dear departed brother Bartram believed that by giving everyone a lifespan of millennia we would learn to value life so much more than we ever have done, and thus would change happen. Poor, poor Bartram. To be the first of us to achieve his goal, the first human to begin rejuvenation. His murder was fate's cruellest irony. Augustine . . . well, he believed that evolution would come anyway, bring enough people enough riches and progress was inevitable, he said. He accused us of wanting the fast and easy option, of being the worst products of the entitlement generation, of being so selfish that we believed wishing alone would make it so, of not working and suffering to earn our achievements. So he stayed and continued to build his corporate behemoth, content the wealth it brought was the answer to everything. And then there was me: I chose isolation to give me the freedom to pursue a different societal route. And this location over any other, over a distant world, or city-state like Abellia, forces its residents to appreciate science and technology. We have to keep the machines working merely to survive. It helps focus the mind on the reality of the universe at large. Nonetheless, this is just the interim stage, Rebka, here, today, at Jupiter. We are the fulcrum for the revolution. What you have grown up in is essentially a renaissance enclave populated by millionaire Marxists, devoted to pushing science forward in new directions because the old ones have plateaued a generation or more ago. That is why I now always hold this conversation in this particular chamber.' He gestured round at the coiled structures with their ephemeral mass state condition.

'Okay, I'll bite,' she said. 'What are these things? I've never seen anything like them.'

'It's active-state matter, which is sort of common enough. However, what we did with it is something different and new. This is a lightwave engine, capable of flying the whole habitat amalgamation away to safety should we ever be threatened.'

'The habitat is a spaceship?' she asked in delight. It was a wonderful notion.

'I always said it would be an ark,' Constantine replied levelly.

'Wow.'

'Hopefully we'll never have to move it, but this type of spacedrive is precisely the kind of innovation our society was set up to create. The theory was developed and the hardware built without reference to cost and the political economic consequences.'

'So you're not going to give it to anyone else?'

'Frankly my dear, I don't see the point. It isn't something which can defeat the Zanth, it is a convenience for us to have our ships with such a drive. Whereas its introduction to the transspace worlds would simply cause widespread economic upheaval and mass unemployment. If they truly wanted this technology they could develop it. Let them keep their torpor.'

'Okay,' Rebka said uncertainly. 'But it might help in a Zanth-swarm. Fighters with lightwave engines would be better than the Thunderthorns, wouldn't they?'

'Yes, there would be an improvement in their flight envelope, a considerable one. But the Zanth would still swarm. And introducing lightwave technology would come with a price tag of vast upheaval, and yet another two-decade-long recession. In tandem would come an extreme level of interest in what we are achieving for ourselves out here. Such a drive would end our isolation for good. That is why not making it available is mainly a political decision on our part.'

'Oh. I see. I guess.'

Constantine's smile became sympathetic. 'I'm afraid it gets worse. Jupiter, like a true Marxist state – the very worst kind –

cannot permit any dissidence from the ideology. This habitat is a fragile artificial environment, there is no Wellsian conflict playing out here between education and barbarism, because we can afford no barbarians. Out here our constitution is simple: with citizenship comes total responsibility. We are a one-dogma society, and if you do not like that, if you disagree with our aim, or simply want to live your own dream, if you don't believe in what I'm hoping to achieve, then you're not merely free to leave, we'll encourage you to go wherever you want and even set you up there.'

'I'm not really a science geek,' Rebka said, feeling almost overwhelmed. This is not what she thought she'd have to deal with on her birthday. Although, actually, she found it all rather exciting.

'I know,' Constantine said. 'But our true goal is understanding, complete knowledge, not just on an abstract level, but in a very physical, practical arena as well. To each according to need and ability.'

'So you see me contributing on the physical side of things?'

'I do. Rebka, there is a puzzle that I need to solve. So far the answer has eluded me despite a tremendous effort by Clayton and others. I believe you may be able to be of enormous help in its resolution. In fact, it is why I originally had you brought here. Among my other quirks, I do believe in karma, and our families are deeply entwined in this affair.'

'My family?'

'Indeed.' He handed her a small glass phial on a silver chain. 'By the way, happy birthday.'

'Thank you,' she said automatically. 'Er, what is it?' The phial seemed to be half-full of very dry dust, judging by its near-fluid motion when she tipped it.

Constantine fastened the chain around her neck. 'A very rare item these days: it's soil from your birthworld. I thought it might give you something to hold on to in times of uncertainty. To ground you, if you like.'

'Oh, really?' She held it up to study the grey-brown motes. 'From True Jerusalem? That's neat.'

'No, Rebka. Not True Jerusalem. That is where you came here from. But you were born somewhere else entirely.'

*

Sid was more than impressed with Ralph, and it was starting to veer into intimidation. After they'd identified the farmyard Sharman's operation was based at, Sid had carried on driving north for another thirty minutes along the A1, then turned around. Half an hour later he was back at the B6347 junction south of North Charlton, and turned down it. By then it was half past two in the morning. Ralph had spent most of the drive with his eyes closed, murmuring to his e-i. Now he looked out of the windscreen at the darkened countryside. An overlay satellite map graphic slid across the windscreen.

'Keep going past the first turning. There are some farmhouses along this road, we're going to the second one.'

Ian and Eva had parked their cars on the side of the B6347 by the junction. As Sid drove past they began to follow. A minute later they came to Cuckoo Farm, a modern hexagonal house with a curving solar roof. The field behind was covered in industrial-scale greenhouses, all shining with the yellow-green glare of artificial lighting.

'It's a commercial chrysanthemum farm,' Ralph said. 'Which is good for us. The greenhouses are all hydroponic and heavily automated, and at the same time lots of vans come and go during the day. My people identified it as the best place to set up a forward monitoring post.'

'Uh huh,' Sid said.

'Drive past the house and straight into the barn.'

The barn was twice the height of the greenhouses, with one of its tall roller doors already open. The headlights played across two black sedans already parked inside amid the agricultural machinery and pallets of nutrients and buckets for transporting the flower stems in. Deeper in, he could see the mulching machines and soil sterilizers.

'Are those your people?' Sid asked. There were six of them standing on the dirty concrete floor, all in suits with long coats. It was like a uniform. He thought he recognized one of the women from the helicopters that had arrived to claim Ernie Reinert.

'Yes,' Ralph said. 'They were on standby in Newcastle. I told you we needed back-up.' He opened the door and got out.

'Of course you did,' Sid said under his breath. Eva, Ian, and Abner were getting out of their cars, giving the HDA agents judgemental looks.

The Micklethwaite family who owned and ran Cuckoo Farm were huddled in a group, sleepy and bewildered in thick coats thrown on over their pyjamas. Three kids, aged between twelve and seven, were clinging to their parents. An old woman, who Sid took to be the grandmother, was starting to argue with an agent, her croaky voice rising. She was claiming a lot of rights, as well as being insulting about Nazis and corrupt government officials.

A rant that was almost comforting to a policeman, it was so familiar. Sid started to relax.

'Thank you for your cooperation,' Ralph said, cutting through the tirade. 'You will be fully compensated for our use of your property. Now, we have arranged for accommodation at a five-star resort hotel.' He gestured to the biggest car. An agent held the back door open.

'I hope that's not compensation from the city,' Ian murmured to Eva as the sullen Micklethwaites obediently clambered in.

'This is good organization,' Sid said to Ralph as the family was driven away.

'Thank you. I do have a certain degree of influence. Now, let's go take a look round the house and see where we can set up a command post.'

They wound up choosing the lounge. The remaining agents started bringing in cases of equipment from the car, including a secure laser array to link directly the HDA satellite constellation in geostationary orbit. 'In case Sherman's byteheads are watching the local net,' Ralph said. 'I don't want them catching a traffic increase from Cuckoo Farm.'

By then it was three o'clock. Sid and his team went home. There was nothing else they could contribute at that point.

*

It was coming up to eight o'clock in the morning, and Sid was driving to Market Street. Jacinta had complained that he was working on a Sunday again, that he shouldn't have to do that now he was senior management. He did what all married men did when it came to their jobs: blamed it on the boss and promised he'd say something this time.

The Toyota Dayon was on auto, because he didn't trust himself to drive. Too little sleep. Despite the fatigue, he was excited and quietly pleased. He'd played a hunch, taken a huge, reckless gamble with his career, and it looked like it was paying off. Whether or not the farm did have a connection with the North murder, he was backed by the HDA now. With their approval and the agencies pitching for him, the Chief Constable slot was theoretically possible. What he needed to do was start building a relationship with the Mayor.

Sid grinned out at the wonderful old sunlit stone buildings of the city centre, enjoying the daydream of a world where everything worked smoothly and in his favour. So close to the resolution, he was intently curious about whatever corporate fight had resulted in the North's murder. He was sure Ralph would tell him, even if it was off-log.

His e-i told him Ralph was calling. 'Morning,' he said cheerily.

'I need you to come to Cuckoo Farm, now,' the agent said.

Market Street Station was thirty seconds away. 'Really?'

'Yes.'

'Okay, then. I'll drive up to you. I'll be there in less than an hour.'

'No, I don't want you in your own car. Sherman probably has

a list of every police officer's vehicle licence code. And if he doesn't, Aldred certainly has.'

Which was true spook paranoia, Sid thought, but he wasn't going to argue. 'Okay then, how do I get there?'

*

It was a drive to the HDA base in Shipcote, where he switched to a civilian car with an agent. That drove him to a commercial district alongside the A19, and another change of vehicle. This time a company van belonging to Allison's Floral House. He even had to wear the overalls.

They pulled in to Cuckoo Farm just after nine o'clock; to anyone or any program observing just another regular flower collection.

It wasn't the first covert visit the farm had enjoyed that morning. When Sid walked into the lounge it had been filled with consoles and big hologram panes, far more equipment than the few cases he'd seen being unpacked before he left. The farmhouse Jede had led them to was centre stage of the panes and screens, shown from various angles. Between them the images came in just about every colour, covering a vast range of spectrums from straight visual to thermal to electromagnetic. There was even a grainy high-magnification monochrome which seemed to be drifting. Ten agents were sitting at consoles, four of them on fold-out chairs, monitoring the operation. A couple of smaller screens were flicking through faces, with profile streamers running along the bottom.

As he watched the monochrome image, someone walked out of the main building and over to an outhouse.

'Hostile three,' someone announced. 'Hair pattern confirmed.'

'Thanks for coming,' Ralph said.

'Sure. How are you getting these images?' He pointed at the black and white picture. 'I thought you were worried about them picking up emissions from airborne systems.'

'We are. That's a satellite feed. We're altering the low-orbit

871

sensor flotilla orbital tracks to provide constant coverage. A satellite passes overhead every three minutes now.'

'Aye, crap on it. That must cost a fortune, man. I didn't know there were that many of them up there.'

'Classified.'

'So what the hell do you need me for?'

'Something happened. I want you to advise agent Linsell, who is about to start running a team for me out of the HDA's Shipcote base. We need to put Sherman, Aldred, and all known associates under constant observation. You're familiar with them, so you can draw up the protocols, provide her some tactical intelligence.'

'Aye, but Sherman's a canny bugger, mind. And Aldred has his own corporate security department shielding him.'

'You're smarter than them, you've shown that. And you don't even have to consider a budget. Linsell will requisition whatever you tell her she needs. We must have constant real-time data on all of them. And I need it starting by this afternoon.'

Sid gave the panes another look, becoming alarmed by the intensity of the operation. 'Okay, I can help advise. So why are you doing it? What changed?'

Ralph turned to one of the screens running through faces. It froze to display a man Sid thought he knew, maybe late thirties, a long face, receding hairline, and wearing old-fashioned glasses. Couldn't put a name to him.

'We deployed some remote insects last night,' Ralph said. 'They sneaked through the woods and established some meshes, then positioned a couple of long-range lenses in the treetops. They all have fibre-optic links to us, so there's no giveaway signature.'

'Insects? Really?'

'Better versions of the ones I loaned you. Yes. We got good coverage of the farm and its surrounding buildings. Then two hours ago, we saw this man. He came out of the farmhouse and went to the largest barn. Hasn't come back out, yet.'

Sid stared at the face on the screen. 'Who is it? I think I know him.'

'You do,' Ralph said flatly. 'Professor Sebastian Umbreit – there's a planet-wide alert out for him.'

'You are crapping on me,' Sid gasped. 'He's the D-bomb designer that went missing.'

'Kidnapped, along with his family. Yes. And whoever brought him here has now supplied him with defence-grade microfacture equipment capable of producing active-state matter. That's what they took from Trigval last night, and it's a major component in D-bombs.'

'Fuck it, man. What do they want with a D-bomb?'

Ralph shook his head sorrowfully. 'I've no idea. But we seriously need to find out.'

Tuesday 30th April 2143

The clouds had been thinning out all morning before abandoning the sky completely for the afternoon. It was the first time in weeks Angela had seen the rings in their full majesty, though Red Sirius and iridescence from the aurora borealis was now daubing them a sickly mauve as they curved above the southern horizon. Below it, three kilometres away at the bottom of a gentle slope, was the Lan tributary. Angela kept looking at it, mainly for reassurance that something on this wretched journey was finally going right. As Leif had predicted, it was flat, solid, and relatively straight, a proper highway through the unforgiving landscape with its jungles and valleys. Three kilometres away. So close now.

As she trudged along the line of the stalled convoy vehicles the freezing air was clear enough for her to see the crests of the aurora streamers tens of kilometres overhead. Above that she caught the occasional glimpse of a hazy mauve phosphorescence capping the atmosphere. The ionosphere, overwhelmed with the particle storm from Red Sirius, was glowing like a faint neon sign, radiating the planet's distress back out into space. Flickers of thin lightning played through the upper atmosphere as the layers sought to equalize their energy levels.

For all its strange beauty the sight was depressing. The climate wasn't going to change in the short term, and short term was what they now operated in. Even that seemed to be running out on them. She passed the small orange garage balloon that contained MTJ-1, which was now looking flaccid as the maintenance team prepared to open it up again and drive the vehicle out.

Two of the axle hub motors on MTJ-1 had failed within three hours of each other on Monday afternoon. Everyone started muttering about sabotage. Except Leif and Darwin, who'd been half-expecting it. As they told Elston, a vehicle that had fallen down a gorge was always going to have reliability problems on a two-thousand-kilometre trek. A diagnostic review showed that nothing other than a complete replacement would do. So out came the fabric garage for the vehicle team to work in. They'd spent eleven hours solid stripping out the old bearings and replacing them from the spares stock.

Angela arrived at biolab-2, and her e-i ordered the sliding door open. She waited until the small door compartment had cycled before taking her balaclava and gloves off. As always, the light and warmth seemed unusual to her. The air somehow managed to make her feel queasy, but then there were nine people sharing the biolab along with the strong smell of medical antiseptic, all of which put quite a strain on the air-con filters.

Paresh was awake and propped up on pillows, which allowed her to ignore the sensation. His cheeks were partially flushed, like a school kid at play. She supposed that was good.

'Hi,' she said as she slithered between his gurney and the one where Luther was resting. Luther still looked in a bad way, with grey skin and a whole load of tubes connected beneath his sheet. She didn't like looking at the fluids in the bags on the end of them, the colours were just wrong.

'Hey, you,' Paresh replied.

Angela gave him a quick kiss, very aware of everyone else crammed into the cabin and driver's cab. 'How are you feeling?'

'Pretty good. The doc's giving me the good drugs.'

'Lucky you. We've started on the composition gel.'

'Yeah, I know.' He gestured over at the tiny galley alcove, which had one of the mealmaker machines sitting on a shelf, with thick engineering tape helping secure it to the stainless steel surface.

Angela wrinkled her nose up at it. They looked like a budget version of the coffee machines franchise cafés used, just without the steam and whooshing sounds. Operation was simple enough: you slotted the gel pack on top, and chose your meal, which came in a tiny silver carton, coloured according to food type: beef stew, apple crumble, mashed potato, soup, chicken curry – over twenty varieties. The machine blended the flavour into the gel along with a gelatine-type powder to alter texture, giving a reasonable approximation of a proper meal – so claimed the manufacturer's extravagant brochure file. As Angela and everyone else discovered that lunchtime, what actually farted out of the nozzle was a blubbery cream with grains of food dye and bitter artificial flavouring mixed unevenly.

'I can't believe I put that stuff on the stores list,' she told him. 'If I was trying to save weight I should have just left Karizma behind.' Just thinking about food sent a shiver down her body. She was strangely cold despite the biolab's heat.

Paresh grinned. 'I wouldn't know, the doc is keeping me on real food.'

'Hell, I wish I was injured.'

'Don't be, there's only so much chicken soup a man can take.'

Angela turned to where Dr Coniff was sitting close to Luther's gurney. 'How long before he's up again?'

'Give it a few more days,' the doctor said. 'This stopover is probably the best thing that could have happened. It gives the nuflesh a chance to stabilize his rib fractures; it's binding them together nicely.'

Angela squeezed his hand. 'See, you're doing fine.'

'Yeah. So how long before we can get going again?'

'Darwin is taking MTJ-1 out for a test drive. They were deflating the garage when I came over. If the bearings are working okay we'll drive down to the tributary first thing in the morning.'

'I heard the colonel has already checked it out.'

'Sure. MTJ-2 and Tropic-1 drove down there this morning. The water's frozen solid, and there's only a metre or so of snow on top. We'll be able to make up for a lot of lost time, and it won't punish the vehicles anything like the jungle has been.'

'Finally, some good news.'

She held up the bag she'd carried over. 'New sweater for you when you get up. I rushed it a bit, so the lines aren't perfect.' Another involuntary shiver ran along her muscles, making her arm shake as she handed the thick red and blue sweater over.

'Thanks.'

The doctor was giving her a pointed look. 'I'd better get back,' Angela said. 'I've got a whole load more balaclavas to knit. Looks like I've finally found my true talent.'

Paresh coughed, wincing badly. 'Everyone likes what you do.'

'Sure. You take care now. I'll come back next refuel stop.' He looked disturbingly weak lying there, so much so she found it upsetting. Coping with illness – either her own or in someone else – wasn't something she had ever done well; an inability that was close to shaming her. She deliberately avoided glancing at Luther as she wriggled out between the gurneys. Shifting him into the driver's cab to make room for the emergency clearly hadn't done him any favours. She'd overheard Juanitar Sakur saying how much internal damage Luther was suffering, and how the convoy journey wasn't helping.

'I'll come out with you,' Mark Chitty said. 'I have to check on Dean Creshaun.'

Angela waited politely while the paramedic pulled on his layers and parka. They both went through the door compartment together. Outside, MTJ-1 was being driven cautiously on a big loop round the convoy vehicles, just skirting the swathe of trees to the east. The garage formed a strange puddle of fabric on the ground, more gentian than orange in the unstable light.

Chitty waved goodbye, and tramped off to biolab-1 where Dean was recuperating from his injuries. Mild concussion and bruised ribs didn't require the kind of intensive monitoring and attention Luther needed, so the doctor had assigned him a berth over in the other biolab where he'd be comfortable for a few days.

As Angela walked back to Tropic-2 she felt her stomach churn again. And a headache was building now, as well. Her mouth was filling with saliva, and she was worried she was going to be sick. Something was making her oddly sensitive to the changes of air. Then she felt an altogether different urge from her body. 'Oh, son of a bitch,' she moaned and started running as best she could for the Tropic. She was going to need the panseat fast as soon as she got inside. Her e-i established a link to Madeleine, and she pleaded with her to get everything ready. Screw dignity, she was desperate. Sweat was breaking out all over her body.

'Not you, too?' Madeleine replied.

Angela didn't even care who else was suffering, all she could focus on was getting to the Tropic.

*

Mark Chitty left biolab-1 as Sirius sank down towards the horizon. There was basically nothing wrong with Dean any more, the check-up had been a formality. He could rejoin Tropic-1 in the morning when they all set off.

Thin flakes of snow swirled round him as the wind picked up, stirring the surface. He watched the vehicle engineering team carrying the rolled-up garage to the sledge behind biolab-1, and waved to them as they passed. MTJ-1was now back in the convoy line, with a couple of people at the rear, fixing boxes back into the pannier. Several people were heading back to their own vehicles. Two of them seemed to be running, flailing legs kicking up short plumes of snow. With all the wind-down activity, Mark could allow himself the belief that they really would start off down the tributary tomorrow morning. A route that would carry them clear through to Sarvar. Another week and they'd be safe.

'Got some delivery duties for you,' Dr Coniff said when he was halfway back to biolab-2. 'Five confirmed cases of stomach flu, and a lot more reporting early symptoms. They're going to need taraxophan to bring it down.'

'Okay, I'll be back with you in a minute.'

'Take the three Tropics; Juanitar will visit the trucks and MTJs.'

'What about the biolabs? Nobody in two seemed to be suffering. Why haven't we caught it?'

'We have,' Coniff replied. 'Miya and Zhao have got it. I don't feel too good myself.'

'Damn, what the hell caused this?'

'Got to be food poisoning. Too many of us got it simultaneously for it to be contagion.'

'It's that bloody composition food,' Mark said immediately. 'There's got to be something wrong with the mealmakers.'

'Probably. We'll isolate the cause later. Right now I want to get everyone dosed up and hydrating.'

'Sure.' Mark looked ahead to see where biolab-2 was. The weather was starting to worsen, and Sirius had nearly left the sky. It was going to be a long, very unpleasant night. He didn't like to think what conditions were going to get like in the vehicles – after all there weren't that many panseats. It would probably be best if people just went outside, dropped their trousers and squatted. Except that wasn't so easy with all the layers. And the monster, he acknowledged sagely.

As he passed truck-1 he saw a silvered cylinder away on the snow over by the towering trees. It must have fallen off MTJ-1 during the test drive. He knew the cylinders contained spares, each vehicle carried their own inventory, even the biolabs. And with the way the snow was fluttering about, it could well be covered by morning. Those spares were important.

'Hell,' he muttered under his breath. It wouldn't take more than a minute to walk over there, and he could even see the wheel tracks the MTJ had left, a path leading directly to the cylinder.

Mark started off towards the forsaken cylinder. It turned out to be further away than he'd estimated. Judging distance in the blank snow was always tricky. The MTJ tracks were curving now, skirting the bullwhips and metacoyas. The trees had helped mislead him too, they were bigger than he'd thought, distorting scale as much as the interminable white land.

He was a couple of metres from the cylinder when he saw the footprint. It was to the side of the lines of compressed snow left by the broad low-pressure tyres, out where the snow was untouched. Its shape confused him at some deep instinctual level. Never mind someone had been out here with the MTJ, there was something else wrong with it. He stopped and bent over, shoving his goggles up so he could examine the profile properly. It took a moment, but eventually he realized just what it was that caught his attention. 'Toes?' he exclaimed. A foot had made the imprint, not a boot. Someone was walking round without anything on their feet. And how unbelievably stupid was that?

Snow fell, making a loud pattering sound.

'What?' Mark turned round, staring at the source of the noise. A thick cataract of snow was tumbling from the nearest bull-whip, a huge specimen reaching over sixty metres up into the iridescent sky. That became an irrelevance to Mark as he caught sight of the figure standing amid the trees. So he never noticed the snow had fallen from one of the bullwhip's coiled branches as it quivered and shook, sloughing off the frozen casing. The figure standing fifty metres away was a dark outline, humanoid, but in no way human.

'Crap on it!' Mark yelled. He ordered his e-i to quest an emergency link to the convoy net. The creature wasn't moving, wasn't charging towards him. 'Help,' Mark pleaded down the link. 'Oh, help.' In front of him the creature raised its arms, hands with long blade fingers moved elegantly through the air.

'What's happening?' Elston demanded.

Mark watched in silent amazement as the creature's arms wove around in fast elaborate motions. All he could think of was a conductor leading an orchestra in some wild discordant melody.

The low bullwhip branch liberated from its shawl of snow uncoiled with a rapid serpentine motion. At the trunk it was as broad as a human torso, a width which tapered down to a few centimetres at the tip. It slashed out like a loosened hurricane whorl, releasing all the pent-up compression energy that the constriction fibres had built up in the months since it had flung its last load of spores across the countryside. Instead of extending itself horizontally to give the spores their greatest dispersal trajectory, the constriction fibres along the branch twisted, sending the branch lashing downwards.

Mark Chitty never saw or heard it coming. The section of the branch which struck him was thicker than his thigh, and it caught him on his side, just above his pelvis.

His bodymesh fired off a frantic medical alert, sending the gruesome damage details into the convoy net.

Elston: 'Chitty!'

Coniff: 'What's happening? What—'

Juanitar: 'Mark!'

Mark hit the ground hard, rolling over a couple of times. He wheezed down a shaky breath as his blurred vision started to regain focus. The incredible pain started to drift away as if he'd been toxed. A dark-red mist was compressing his returning sight; his grid churned into nonsense then blanked out. High above him he saw the bullwhip branch curling itself back into a neat horizontal coil, the furry white strands on its bark rippling like the hackles on some agitated animal.

His head sagged to one side, and he was looking at the creature again. It continued its mad conductor's dance, arms urging the unheard symphony up in its crescendo.

'It's alive,' a dazed, fascinated Mark told his frantic colleagues. 'All of it.'

Another bullwhip branch came hurtling down, smashing him ten metres across the snow, breaking both legs. He had barely come to rest when he was struck again, each blow shunting him deeper into the cluster of trees. After the third impact his consciousness began to dwindle. He could feel no part of his ruined body now. And still the creature stood where he'd first seen it. Long blade fingers swept out in exuberant triumph, their gloss-black surfaces refracting Sirius's enfeebled red light through the swirling snow, as they puppeted the bullwhips.

Mark's inert body was pummelled further and further into the big trunks. Again and again the bullwhips struck, pulping him to a flaccid sack of broken flesh with tattered limbs flopping about. Blood soaked into his layered clothing, pouring out of skin punctures where shattered bones had ripped through. Droplets left dark stains on the pristine snow, the only evidence of his passing. Most of his smartcells were wrecked and all that was left of his bodymesh broadcast a feeble signal.

The final swipe sent him thudding down beside a huge bullwhip, out of sight of the convoy vehicles. Half of its coiled branches began to judder, shaking off their crisp ice coating. Snow cascaded down, burying Mark's corpse and blocking the last of his bodymesh's emissions. More of the bullwhips started shaking snow loose, covering all traces of blood and the impressions Mark had left along his brutal route to oblivion.

*

Vance forced himself to take part in the search, even though his body was on the point of collapse from whatever poison he'd been blighted with. Only eight of the convoy's personnel were unaffected, including Paresh Evitts and Dean Creshaun. That was the giveaway – neither of the two injured men had been given composition meals. Luther, on the other hand, had insisted he be treated the same as everyone else, and proudly spooned down some broth churned out by the biolab's mealmaker machine. The remaining six – Lorelei, Lulu MacNamara, Leora Fawkes, Antrinell, Karizma Wadhai, and Leif Davdia – had all avoided the composition meal that lunchtime.

Vance ordered all of them out into the glimmering twilight, except for Lulu. The catering girl would have been a complete liability traipsing round the countryside, even if she had done as he asked.

Twice in the last thirty minutes Vance had dropped to his

knees and vomited weakly onto the snow. He was shaking continually, while his skin flushed and soaked his clothing layers with sweat. His headache ebbed and flowed, often forcing him to stand still and suck down air when the pain spikes became too much to endure. Raddon and Mohammed had insisted on taking part, claiming their symptoms weren't too bad. Dr Coniff had monitored their medical smartcells and disagreed. Vance had over-ruled her.

So now the eight of them were strung out in a loose line, searching through the edge of the trees as the wind sent zephyrs of snow twisting about the trunks, and the aurora borealis cast its eerie glow, throwing the huge trees looming above them in unnerving black silhouette. Behind them, every vehicle in the convoy had turned to face the broad clump of trees and switched on their headlights. The scatter of white light created a multitude of confusing shadows washing across the ground. Vance was also monitoring the remote machine guns on the vehicles, which were tracking the search party, alert for any unexplained movement around them.

Every possible precaution taken, and still Vance felt as if he was walking along a precipice. The creature was out here. He knew it. Somehow it had caught up with them.

The vehicle meshes had provided a rough coordinate for Chitty's last position. They'd found nothing there of course. There had been a series of sharp degradations in the link strength and bandwidth during the attack. Whatever the creature had done to him, it had been in stages. Dr Coniff had said the last readings effectively confirmed his death. So the search party were out in the murky arctic conditions searching for a corpse. And with his body failing him, Vance couldn't even remember if the Lord had a reason for him to be doing that any more.

Mohammed let out a low moan and stumbled onto all fours. He swayed back and forth a couple of times. Vance thought the Legionnaire was going to be sick again. But instead Mohammed keeled over next to a massive ice-encrusted metacoya trunk, still groaning. Leora and Antrinell hurried over to him. Vance would have liked to help, but simply didn't have the energy. In fact, glancing back at the headlights, he wasn't sure if he could make it back to the convoy unaided. The white light inflamed his headache.

'Come on,' Antrinell said over the ringlink. 'Let's get you back.'

'You need to bring him to me,' Coniff said. 'I'm accessing his medical smartcells. His heart rhythm is becoming erratic. Colonel, you and Raddon need to come in as well.'

'Okay,' Vance rasped. A powerful spasm ran down his body. He couldn't even lift his arms any more. There was no sign of Chitty, no clue what had happened to him.

'Time to go, Colonel,' Lorelei was saying to him. 'The search is over, now.'

He hadn't even noticed her coming over to him, but her icon was there in his grid, and her arm was slipping under his shoulder. Another identity icon appeared in close proximity to his own. Leif was holding him on the other side.

'You need to lie down.'

Vance wanted to nod in profound agreement. Instead, he fainted.

*

After the uncontrollable bouts of vomiting. After the humiliating diarrhoea. After the hot and cold flushes. After the sweats and shaking. After inhaling the stench of everyone else's suffering in Topic-2. After drinking water thick with rehydration salts, and bumping sacs of taraxophan, Angela finally started to take notice of her surroundings again. She must have been dozing, she thought, it was the middle of the night.

The Tropic's cabin was dark, but the headlights were on, fluorescing the condensation which coated the windscreen. She was sitting in the front passenger seat. She vaguely remembered getting there after ducking outside when her sphincter started to send urgent warning signals along her spine yet again.

'How are you feeling?' Forster croaked from the back seat.

'Like crap,' she blinked, trying to get some proper focus. 'Actually, about how you look.'

'Yeah,' he said, and immediately closed his eyes. His skin was a sickly shade of grey, and damp with sweat. Both arms were twitching under the blanket he'd draped over himself. A thin stream of damp vomit stained the front of it. That was the mildest thing she could smell.

'Where's everyone else?' she asked.

'Raddon's in biolab-2,' he said without opening his eyes. 'They took him there after the search. Stupid pillock, trying to be a macho hero. Juanitar is treating him as best he can; he's suffering, too. Most of us still are. Madeleine recovered quickly, but that's youth for you. She's over in Tropic-3 helping Garrick, Winn, and Darwin; they've got it pretty bad.'

'Right.' Angela looked round for something to drink. Her flask was in its usual place in the door holder. Thankfully it was just pure water; she remembered gagging on the rehydration salt solution someone had made her drink, it was so foul. She took a few cautious sips, fearful they'd trigger another bout of nausea. After waiting a couple of minutes, she took a proper drink.

Forster had drifted back into a troubled sleep, quaking occasionally below his filthy blanket.

'Show me everyone's location,' she told her e-i. Her grid materialized, along with a constellation of identity icons. That was when she noticed the whirr of servos above her. The remote gun was armed and slowly sweeping from side to side, ready to blast anything approaching the convoy.

'Everyone is accounted for,' her e-i said.

'Good.' She expanded Elston's icon, viewing the readings from his medical smartcells with some alarm. 'Who's running the show?'

With Elston out of the game, Antrinell had taken charge. He'd organized efficiently, dispatching those who weren't affected to care for everyone else. Not that much could be done. The food poisoning, if that's what it was, left its victims utterly debilitated.

Before she succumbed to a raging fever which sent her drifting in and out of lucidity, Dr Coniff had instructed that rehydration was the priority. She also issued the maximum dose of taraxophan; the drug boosted the human immune system, which should help the body fight off the sickness, but it was known to put a lot of strain on organs.

Other than that, Antrinell had ordered the remote guns to full armed status, and had someone on constant monitor duty, accessing the few remaining sensors available to the convoy. His policy was shoot first and go see what they'd hit after.

Angela's e-i quested a link to him. 'I'm feeling a little better,' she said. 'Is there anything I can do to help?'

'Really?' Antrinell asked. 'You're okay?'

'I wouldn't call it that. I feel like I've been kicked about like a football for the whole game and extra time. But it's definitely starting to wear off.'

'Thank the Lord. That's the best news all week – you're the second one to beat it. Several of us are still getting worse. I was worried some wouldn't make it.'

Angela refrained from telling him that her genetically improved organs gave her better odds than anyone else to break the fever, that her liver and kidneys were designed to deal with toxin levels that would fell the healthiest twenty-year-old. At this point false hope was probably for the best. 'Do we know what it is, yet?'

'No. I've got Camm running tests on the gel. But unless he can identify what hit us we'll just have to carry on with the non-specific treatments Coniff ordered.'

'All right. What needs doing? And mind I won't be up to much.'

'MTJ-2 has some pretty sick people in it. Leif could do with some assistance.'

'Ten minutes. And just be careful what you point those remote guns at while I'm walking over there.'

'Thank you, Angela, I'm glad you're back.'

She found a packet of buttered toast slices and put the silver plastic rectangle into the microwave. No jam, she didn't want to tax her stomach just yet. The sachet of hot chocolate was given a forlorn look, but she left it alone to swig plain water from the thermos like a good little fitness guru.

'Show me Chitty's visual for the minute leading up to the attack,' she told her e-i. The image slid up into her grid, and she watched him tramp along the track MTJ-1 had left during its quick test drive. His goal was obvious, a cylinder of spare parts that'd dropped off the back. It was a poor image, made worse by the goggles and windswept flurries on snow, but she held back on running enhancement patches, she wanted to see exactly what poor old Mark had seen.

He stopped and bent over, pushing his goggles up. Just like Mark, Angela frowned in bewilderment at the human footprint. His muffled 'O-es,' was just audible, voice distorted by the cloth wrapped round his face. Then he was turning, staring into the trees. The monster was there, a lot clearer that it'd been the night it killed Tork Ericson, a dark human shape with wicked blade fingers glinting in the pallid aurora light. It waved its arms in bizarre gyrations. Then the recording abruptly ended as Chitty's link dropped out. When it re-established a few seconds later the bandwidth was tiny and only the core data was available.

Angela peeled open the packet, and nibbled on the first slice of toast. Something had made Chitty look up into the trees. And the monster had to be fifty metres away, so something else had hit the paramedic.

Then there were his last enigmatic words: 'It's alive. All of it.' She simply couldn't conceive what he was trying to describe.

'Show me the map of the convoy at that time,' she told her e-i. 'Overlay everyone's position.'

There were thirteen people outside when Chitty was attacked. Angela was one of them, tumbling frantically out of the Tropic to drop her pants – she still had the coldburns on her ass to prove it. Or maybe that had been later, she wasn't sure. The others . . . Chitty's icon was easy enough to see, alone some distance away from the convoy vehicles. Everyone else was clustered along the line; the engineering teams were packing up, and several people were out on the snow throwing up or worse.

She counted the icons. Nobody was missing. Nobody was near Chitty. That had to be wrong, because someone had made that naked foot imprint.

'Give me visual confirmation of everyone's location,' she told her e-i. 'Confirm they're where they seem to be.'

'The records are incomplete,' it replied. 'Only the MTJs and Tropics have internal meshes I can access. The biolab meshes are restricted, and the truck and tanker cabs do not have any meshes.'

'All right,' she said. 'Let's go for personal visual caches. They should all have been downloaded into the net.'

They weren't. People had been switching off when they were in their vehicles, where they were together and safe. Even Angela was guilty of that, her personal visual record ended just after she got back to the Tropic from visiting Paresh. There were no images of her running outside several times to vomit and defecate onto the snow. When she accessed the Tropic's meshes, they'd only caught two brief snatches of her stumbling through the door, and she'd been out in the night at least four times that she could recall.

Angela started to get changed, considering the available data and what it didn't show her. It had been chaos at the time Chitty was killed. People still walking round on legitimate errands, packing up after the MTJ repair. The sickness was beginning to take hold, stirring everyone like ants from a disturbed nest. She considered how she could have sneaked away in such circumstances. It would have been easy enough, a small scattering of smartdust on a seat emitting the correct personal identification code, and everyone would think she was in a vehicle when in fact she was silently running up behind Chitty with her bodymesh turned off.

Physically – technologically – it could be done, and quite easily, too. But the *why* of it was profoundly disturbing. That would mean the monster was getting help from someone on the convoy. But then the sabotage of the tow rope had already shown that one of her erstwhile colleagues was inimical to the expedition. It had to be the same person, because that was beyond coincidence.

She glanced at Forster, who was still juddering from the fever, his hair slicked down with sweat. It looked like he was seriously ill, but now her paranoia had been kindled she couldn't be completely certain.

You're being stupid, she told herself. If Forster wanted to kill her he'd had ample chance while the two of them were alone. *Who to trust, though?*

She made herself concentrate on stripping off her revoltingly damp, stained layers, stuffing them into a plastic bag, where hopefully they'd stay until Sarvar and working washing machines. She managed a quick wipe down with hand-sanitizer soap and a towel, followed by the usual Tropic limbo act to get into her last full set of clean clothes.

Forster's carbine was on the seat next to him. She checked it and slung it over her shoulder. The automatic pistol Raddon always kept in the glove compartment was stuffed into her parka pocket. Then she unlocked the door.

'Going over to the MTJ now,' she told Antrinell.

'I'll watch your back,' he replied.

Angela stepped out into the vicious St Libra night. Wind whipped at the fur lining her hood, while snow zipped through the headlight beams. Above her, the vast fluctuating folds of the aurora burned across the stars with cold blue phosphorescence. She checked round nervously and set off towards MTJ-2.

Who to trust? Who?

Thursday 2nd May 2143

Clayton North was careful around agent Sarah Linsell. The HDA officer was smart and extremely professional. On the job she never smiled, her thick auburn hair was cut to stay level with her shoulders as if it hadn't been authorized to fall any further; and the perfectly tailored navy-blue suit worn with a white blouse could have been a uniform it was so cliché. She was also hugely suspicious of everyone Sid Hurst had brought in to help with her surveillance operation. Or perhaps she simply resented their presence. Clayton had to admit he and Ian and Eva were almost superfluous.

The operation was run out of the HDA base sprawling on the slope above Last Mile. Not that they could see the gateway and its massive conglomeration of commercial enterprises. The long room Linsell had taken over was in the centre of the base's concrete fortress structures, and two levels underground.

Clayton was merely a tolerated appendage to the thirty-seven-strong team flown in to surveil Sherman and his crew. Each of them – Sherman, Aldred, Boz, Jede, Ruckby – had their own dedicated observation sub-team whose job it was to know their location and activity at all times. Even Valentina had been assigned a pair of observers, just in case she had a more active role than Sid's investigation had uncovered.

Micro-drones flittered silently above the city, following their prey. Cars which were swapped every hour also slid silently along the roads, following the crew on every inconsequential journey. Another pool of on-the-ground agents slipped in and out of stores, clubs, hotels, offices, and gyms frequented by the targets, chameleon-like in their ability to merge with the background. The marina berth three down from the *Mayberry Moon* had a new resident. One of the HDA's larger AIs had sunk monitor programs deep into the city's transnet cells, monitoring every bodymesh emission.

So either Agent Linsell was paranoid, or very capable. Either way, Clayton kept a low profile. His own quantum molecular systems kept alert for any smartmicrobes Linsell might have used to bug him. So far she hadn't, but he wouldn't put it past her. Ivan's team had spotted the sophisticated monitor routines she'd deployed in Newcastle's network to keep him and Sid and Ian and Eva under quiet scrutiny. They'd gone active within an hour of her arriving in the city. Ralph had obviously briefed her that they ran things off-log.

It meant he really had to live Abner's life on a permanent basis to avoid triggering any suspicions Agent Linsell might be harbouring. That made communications with Ivan difficult. He was resorting to dead downloads in public transport and on the street at designated coordinates. Jupiter was kept up to date on Professor Umbreit and the possible D-bomb assembly project, as was the lightwave ship waiting at the Lagrange point on the other side of the moon.

Not that he had a lot to update anybody with. Since Sunday when Sid had unexpectedly called them all up to the HDA base, Linsell had run an exemplary operation. The sub-teams had acquired their targets with precision and minimum fuss. With the truly unlimited resources they'd brought to bear, nobody had skipped out of sight for a moment.

Unfortunately, Sherman's crew had turned out to be model citizens ever since that point. Jede had returned to Newcastle mid-morning, and dumped the van in a GSW. Five minutes after he walked away it had burst into flame, much to the delight of the local feral youths. After that, there'd been no contact between

Sherman and Aldred. Sherman had gone about his usual dark business with care. The file Linsell assembled, containing calls about secondary money transfers, tox procurement, corporate data acquisition, and two blackmail scams being set up would have been enough for the city prosecutor to obtain a twenty-year sentence. Linsell wanted something else. Sherman had to be holding Umbreit's family somewhere. It was their hold over him, the leverage to force him to build whatever it was they'd got him doing in the farmhouse barn. Ralph and Linsell were desperate to find them.

Neither Clayton, nor anyone at Jupiter, could even guess what was being constructed at that remote location, nor why Aldred was apparently going rogue. Nothing in their analysis of bioil markets or general corporate manoeuvring could provide a reason for his behaviour. All they were left with was the connection to the strange slaying of the unknown North, itself linked to Bartram's death twenty years ago. If for no other reason, Clayton was taking this more seriously than even Linsell appeared to be.

It was six o'clock in the evening when the call was placed. All around the big, vaulting, underground room, agents looked up at the central wallscreen. It showed a map of the city, with all the target icons in bright purple. Aldred had just received a call from the farmhouse, linking through multiple cells right across the planetary network, and switching two hundred times a second to a fresh random route.

'He's finished the machine,' a voice boomed out of the speakers.

'Excellent news,' Aldred replied. 'Have you run the diagnostics?'

'Yes sir. It's got the parameters you gave us. Everything checks out.'

'Right. Inform Sherman we'll be moving to placement. I will see you all at the assembly point.'

Both Linsell and Sid were immediately responding to calls. Clayton knew it had to be Ralph Stevens; they were nodding curtly and in unison to whatever points were being made. He exchanged a knowing look with Ian, who was helping out with the sub-team monitoring Boz.

Up on the big map, icons were showing Sherman was now receiving a call from the farmhouse. Eva walked over to him.

'We haven't found the family, yet,' she murmured.

'I think that just became irrelevant.'

'Abner, come on, if whatever the hell that machine is actually works then nobody has any use for the family any more.'

'Aye, I know that, man, but we haven't got a single lead. For all we know Sherman doesn't know either. Suppose Aldred used someone else to kidnap the Umbreits?'

'We have to try,' she hissed.

Up on the screen, Sherman was calling Jede, who in turn called all the others.

'Everybody's moving,' Ian announced in satisfaction. All Sherman's crew were heading for their cars.

Sid joined them. 'She's agreed to let us accompany the assault team,' he said, looking very pleased with himself.

'What are we doing about the professor's family?' Eva asked.

'Everyone holds back until Aldred and the machine are in the same place, then the armed interdiction team storm in. Once the survivors are in custody they will be offered a cooperation deal. They tell us where the family is, and in return they get that taken into consideration by the judge at sentencing. If they all tough it out, Ralph will take them away for interrogation. We saw what that did to dear old Ernie. We'll find them.'

'That could take days,' Eva protested, with blood starting to heat her pale skin.

'Best we can do. The sub-teams will remain here and try and spot any communication to the people holding the family. There's a dedicated rescue team waiting on that.'

'All right,' she grumbled.

Sid smiled, and put his hand on her shoulder. 'You don't have to come along. You can stay here and make sure they're doing what they can for the family.'

'Trying to get rid of me, boss?'

893

'Aye man, no way. Not after all this.' Sid chuckled. 'How about you, Abner, you want in?'

'I have to know what's going down, boss. A brother was murdered because of this, whoever he was.'

'Okay then, we armour up and follow the primary team in. Our job is observation and support.'

*

Sid led his people out into the fresh spring evening, feeling perspiration prickling his armpits and neck under the tough armour jacket and regulation padded shirt. It was warm out in the base's car park, with the tarmac still radiating away the day's sunlight. Stars were emerging as bright pinpoints in the cloudless gloaming sky.

There had been a lot of decisions that delivered him to this point, and he could still just walk away and go home. Let Linsell and the interdiction team sort it out. After all, this was the reason they existed. Some stupid side of him was proud that he was here, doing what had to be done. But mainly he was scared shitless like any real, sane human being.

When he looked up at the constellations, he saw silhouettes of three black Mil US-22 VTOL fan aircraft on the rooftop pads of the main building. Squads of HDA's interdiction troopers were embarking through the broad side doors while the fans swivelled about as part of their pre-flight checks. The US-22s were silent and stealthed, capable of approaching urban targets without warning; in another twenty minutes when the gold twilight horizon vanished they'd be invisible to the naked eye and most sensors. The first thing any hostile would know about their arrival was when dark armoured figures came abseiling down out of the night sky.

Sid had been allocated a big Mercedes 4x4 Allclime; one of a dozen similar vehicles parked ready to transport the rest of Linsell's teams. As he opened the front door she came over to him, her armour looking as if it was tailored by the same store that made her suits.

'I appreciate the help you've provided,' she said. 'But you will lock into position and follow tactical protocol only. I don't want any deviation. You are designated secondary support now.'

'Aye, pet, I'll go with that,' Sid said in his thickest Geordie accent.

'Good,' she snapped and walked over to her command vehicle, a ten-seat Jeep Hassar.

'Wow,' Abner said. 'That's an attitude. Ian, did you hit on her?'

'No!' Ian protested. 'I don't do that, not any more. Not now I'm with Tallulah.'

'How's that going?' Eva asked with a lofty air.

'Good, man. We're together every night, at her place, like, not mine. I want to keep her well clear of everything we're doing. And we've talked about moving in together, like. You don't think that's too soon?'

Sid stifled a chuckle. This was not an Ian conversation as he knew it. 'When you're ready, you're ready,' he said. 'There's no set time.'

'No, boss, I'm sure I heard there was a GE regulation,' Abner said as they sat themselves down in the Allclime.

'Fifteen weeks,' Eva said with a straight face.

'Ignore the cynics,' Sid said. 'You're doing the right thing. She's a great girl.'

'You just make sure you treat her right,' Eva said. 'She's been through a lot. That bloody fiancé of hers, then being dragged into our case.'

'Aye, man, give me some credit,' Ian moaned.

Still grinning, Sid told his e-i to link the mission's tactical coordinator net to the Allclime's auto. His grid was displaying an aerial picture of the farmhouse. A six-wheel Ford Telay van was heading away from the cluster of buildings.

'Target A on the move,' the tactical coordinator announced. 'They put a large crate into the rear of the Telay before they left. Umbreit's also on board with four hostiles.'

'How bad would it be if they set off the D-bomb on the ground?' Ian asked suddenly. 'Are they big bombs?'

'They have fusion initiators,' Abner said quietly.

'Well that's good, right man?' Ian said. 'Fusion is clean energy, isn't it?'

'Ian,' Sid said wearily. 'He means the trigger is a fusion bomb.'

Ian gave them all a nervous laugh. 'Aye. Right. I knew that. So there'll be no fallout, like?'

'Do you want to go back to the command room?' Sid asked. 'It's underground in a HDA base. Safe as you can be.'

'No. We're in this together. But what about your kids?'

'Visiting the grandparents in Rutland.' As soon as he'd found out about Umbreit on Sunday he'd told Jacinta to get out of the city. He hadn't broken security, hadn't given an explanation. He simply told her that she had to do it; that something had developed in his case, that he didn't want her and the kids exposed to risk. She'd been on the A1 heading south before lunchtime.

'Oh,' Ian said. He glanced at Eva.

'Mine are back in the old country,' she said. 'It's an important cultural time in Iceland. They shouldn't miss out.'

Ian turned to Abner.

Abner shrugged. 'It was a brother you fished out of the Tyne. I have to know.'

The Allclime started to roll forwards, slotting into a line of vehicles heading out of the base. When he peered up through the windscreen Sid could just make out the shape of the US-22s lifting into the darkening sky. His grid showed him Sherman and Boz both approaching Last Mile. Jede and Ruckby were also heading in the same direction, though they were further out.

'Makes sense,' Abner said. 'If you're going to use a D-bomb anywhere, I suppose it should be in a gateway.'

'Why?' Eva asked as they passed through the base's main entrance. 'Aldred's spent his life working for your family company. St Libra is his life. All of you have worked so hard to make it successful.'

Sid watched the frown creep across Abner's face as if he'd just realized something. 'All but one,' Abner muttered, tasting the name as if it was something strange.

'Zebediah,' Sid said immediately. He remembered accessing the file Elston had given to the investigation. Zebediah was odd even by North standards. But then he'd been in Bartram's mansion on *that* night. 'Did any of your brothers sympathize with his cause?'

'No. None of us do. St Libra is where our wealth comes from, it's what's made us the force we are.'

'The most evangelical followers of any cause are those who converted to it,' Eva said. 'They've sacrificed the most.'

Abner shook his head. 'No.'

Sid could see the North hadn't convinced himself. He checked the grid. 'Looks like we haven't got far to go,' he said. Boz's car had slowed, turning into Eleventh Avenue North, on the south-eastern corner of Last Mile.

The interdiction force vehicles were separating, turning off down side roads as the coordinator network guided them along different routes into Last Mile.

A micro-drone showed Boz's car driving through a roll-up door on a big warehouse-style building. Two minutes later, Sherman arrived at the same location.

'Looks like we have our site,' Sid said. Data on the warehouse was running down his grid, the listed ownership was Mountain High, who supplied clothes and bedding suitable for tropical climates. Sid's e-i switched to building blueprints, showing the big discount store that took up a third of the ground floor, names of employees, company accounts, suppliers. Nothing cross-referenced to the case.

Their Allclime turned off the A167 and headed down the slope into Last Mile. It parked them on Marquis Way outside a store selling wind turbine kits and regen-cells. The street was almost deserted; hologram adverts shone gaudy turquoise and crimson across the 4x4's unwashed paintwork; store windows still shone, optimistically trumpeting goods that nobody was buying. The rest of the interdiction team vehicles were taking up position, parking in various streets in easy range of the Mountain High warehouse.

Jede and Ruckby arrived and went inside. The micro-drones tracking the Ford Telay van showed it travelling along the A1, curving round Newcastle's western suburbs. Ralph and the agents from his observation team were following a mile behind, hidden by the heavy stream of traffic.

'Here we go,' Eva said.

The sub-team covering Aldred showed his dark Mercedes coupé sliding up out of the St James singletown garage. A squadron of micro-drones took off to pursue him through the torrent of cars flowing smoothly along the city centre roads.

Sid realized he was still sweating despite the car's air-con. Nobody was saying anything, they all just sat there on the new leather seats with their eyes closed, reviewing whatever image or data the coordinator sent to their iris smartcell grids. As the critical people closed on the warehouse Sid felt as if he was the one with a noose constricting around him. The air in the car was thin, difficult to breathe, it made his heart race. In all the years he'd been police, all the raids he'd been on, all the busts, the arrests, even the chases, nothing had ever been like this. He wasn't ready for it, didn't want it. Ego had brought him to this point, that stupid refusal to quit the case, to simply do the job according to procedure and pick up the monthly salary transfer. Now look where it had brought him, sitting right next to a crapping great fusion bomb. The only way he was going to live through the next half-hour was if everybody else on the interdiction team followed procedure perfectly, didn't forget their training, and their government-issue equipment worked flawlessly.

When he looked around he saw Eva and Ian both toxed out on the same verge-of-panic moment as himself. He managed a weak smile, which they returned. It was a poignant, almost intimate connection.

Abner however was still concentrating on the information in

his grid, oblivious to the tension and worry the rest of them suffered from. Sid shook his own head in disbelief, not understanding how anyone could be so absorbed by what was happening they weren't emotionally affected. But that was the Norths for you, ridiculously focused.

'Target B approaching,' the tactical coordinator said. 'Target A inbound, estimated time to arrival five minutes.'

Sid watched Aldred's Mercedes drive into Last Mile and turn off into Eleventh Avenue North. Target A, the Ford Telay, was three minutes out, driving steadily along the A1.

'Target B has entered the building,' the tactical coordinator said in a level voice.

'Weapons check,' Sid announced calmly. He was carrying a nine-millimetre Walther pistol with a linked sensor sight. The target graphics materialized in his grid, blue and green, night-vision sensors functioning. He checked the chamber, confirmed the safety was on. It went into his holster. Taser fully charged, clip with five spools loaded. He twisted it onto the armour vest's Velcro strips.

The others in the 4x4 were going through the same methodical checks. Sid put in his earplugs, designed to cut out the immobilizer sonics. A helmet finished the protection.

'Everybody working?' he asked.

They were.

'Target A on approach,' the tactical coordinator said. 'Go to condition red. Strike initiation in fifteen – one-five – seconds after Target A enters the building.'

Sid switched on the strikeproof communicator sitting on the dashboard, a small black plastic box with a simple LCD display on the front. He told his e-i to go to standby mode. His grid faded away just as the Mountain High's roller door opened; he needed uncluttered sight. The Ford Telay was twenty metres away.

'Target A entering the building, on my mark. Mark.'

Sid started counting down, his lips mouthing the numbers silently.

'Ten seconds,' the tactical coordinator said, his voice coming from the strikeproof communicator's speaker.

Linsell knew what she was doing, Sid told himself. He'd seen the assault plan she'd drawn up with Ralph and other officers from the interdiction division. He'd even been asked if he'd had any comments. After reviewing it twice and seeing the hardware they intended to deploy, he'd just shaken his head and said: 'Looks good to me.'

'Five seconds.'

Sid slipped the gasmask on, and took a deep breath. His world acquired a strong emerald tint as a tactical display scrawled across the mask's vision slits and interfaced with his iris smartcells; icons popped up identifying team members.

That plan was the main reason he was here. He had confidence in the professionalism of others. An irony for him, given his usual attitude towards the mechanism of government. But Ralph and Elston and even Linsell didn't operate like the apparatchiks he had to deal with at Market Street and City Hall.

'Initiate strike.'

Three Lockheed F-7009s had scrambled from their base in Scotland as soon as Ralph confirmed a crate had been placed on the Ford Telay. They'd flown high patrol over Newcastle ever since, stealth-shielded from civilian radar. Now they dived from two thousand metres, afterburners on full, powering them up to Mach 1.8 so they outran their own sound waves. Even if there were sensors watching for hostile aircraft, they wouldn't notice them until they'd streaked overhead.

Burnpulse cannons in the noses locked on to the Mountain High building, and fired superfrequency electromagnetic pulses. They were designed to scramble any active electronics and over-load all communication links. If the hostiles in the building had warning they might conceivably suicide by detonating whatever Professor Umbreit had built. But fifteen seconds after the Telay's arrival, Linsell had determined they wouldn't even have the van doors open, let alone arm the device. The burnpulses should disable whatever systems operated the device.

Not that the electronic warfare was all she was going to bombard them with. As they levelled out at one hundred metres altitude, following knap-of-the-earth trajectories, each F-7009 fired three missiles. They were pre-programmed and smart guided. Velocity alone, at Mach 2.1, guaranteed they would penetrate the building's walls. One of them, a smartbuster, simply took out the roll-up door, blowing it into lethal shrapnel blades. Two more smartbusters ripped gaping holes in the walls at ground-floor level. The remaining three missiles slammed into the building and dispersed their sub-munitions capsules in a pattern which had been calculated to cover every cubic centimetre. There could be no hiding place for anyone inside.

The capsules let loose stun blasts, skin-searing radiative waves, incandescent strobes at frequencies calculated to induce neurological overload. Thick green-white gas fountained out, stinging exposed flesh and sending anyone who breathed it down into uncontrollable paroxysms of coughing. Another round of burn-pulses hammered electronics which had survived the first pulse.

Every window in the building blew out under the pressure of the stunblasts, jetting shards of glass horizontally across the surrounding area. Nearby streetlights flared into droplets of sunlight from the energy input of the burnpulse beams, then detonated into cascades of smouldering glass casings that bounced and skittered along the pavements. Hologram adverts blazed in one last burst of nova glory before dying.

Five seconds after the synchronized missile impact, the three US-22s dropped down out of the starlit sky, each one poised in front of a hole torn open by the smartbusters. Interdiction troopers slithered down their ropes in fast arachnid motions then charged into the gloomy caves filled with a churning green fog that was plagued by freakish phosphorescent discharges.

Amplified voices boomed out into the hellish interior.

'Freeze!'

'Do not use links. Do not speak.'

'You! Put that down.'

'Freeze! Last warning.'

The harsh crack of gunshots filled the air. Lone pistol shots at first, swiftly followed by bursts from automatic rifles. Blue-white light flashed inside the building.

Ten seconds after the first wave of troopers went in, the big 4x4 vehicles started to arrive, braking sharply as the tactical coordinator positioned them around the building. Doors were flung open. Agents sprinted out, holding their stumpy carbines in double-handed grips, rolling round the jagged edges of the holes. The eight-strong tech crew raced for the Ford Telay, lugging heavy cases, ready to deal with whatever machine Umbreit had constructed.

Agent Sara Linsell watched her operatives deploy from the front seat of her vehicle, viewing the internal deployment via her grid, and directing with the tactical coordinator. Right away the troopers hit a problem. The internal structure was completely different to the blueprints. The warehouse owners had constructed a honeycomb of rooms in the original cavernous storage halls, subletting to dozens of companies with glossy products to push on desperate refugees.

'Shag it backwards,' she murmured in dismay as the US-22 radars tried to penetrate the walls of composite spun up by automata in random shapes demanded by commerce's of-the-moment requirements. Troopers in pairs wove their way through the maze of low corridors, scaling flimsy ladders. It looked like at least eight floors had been constructed in the highest levels. And the walls had acted as barriers to the sub-munitions capsules. The building wasn't nearly as secure as it should have been by now.

'Device secure,' the tech team leader announced triumphantly. 'We're isolating now. Confirm presence of active-state matter. Removal in three minutes.'

A big ten-wheel HDA nuke-hazard truck rumbled across the yard, nosing up to the wrecked roll-up door, shoving its way through the gap with brute force. Metal screeched as fractured ribbons were rammed aside.

Sid Hurst's Allclime rushed onto the forecourt tarmac. The four police officers hurried out. As they did, another burst of gunfire thudded out from somewhere inside the building. Sarah Linsell's grid showed her the location, deep inside, on the new first floor. The troopers identified Ruckby as their opponent. His status shifted to dead.

Two agents pulled a body out of the building amid the swirl of green smog. Ralph Stevens walked over and inspected the dead man's face.

'Oh Goddamnit, that's Umbreit.'

'They shot him,' Linsell said.

'Bastards.'

'All right people,' she said. 'Our two priority targets are still loose, Marcus Sherman and Aldred North. We're building structural information now. Let's clear this bloody great maze one room at a time.'

*　　　　　⚹

The airborne assault on the Mountain High building, with the resulting devastation it inflicted on Last Mile's network, was the perfect opportunity for Clayton to re-establish direct contact with Ivan and the team. Not even the HDA AI could make immediate sense of the links flickering between the glitching public cells.

'We followed you out of the base,' Ivan said as the Allclime surged forward. Ahead of them the F-7009s flashed across Last Mile's skyline. A couple of seconds later, the 4x4 rocked on its suspension as their sonic boom washed across the streets, terrorizing cats and cracking windows. Between the planes and the missiles, just about every alarm in the district was wailing for help. 'That's quite an operation Stevens and Linsell are mounting.'

'Justifiable,' Clayton told them. 'Aldred is here. We need to retrieve him from the HDA. Get the lightwave ship to hold station one kilometre above the city. When we need it, we'll need it fast.'

'Copy that, sir.'

'Go to full active status yourselves. Get as close to me as you can, but for crap's sake watch out for the troopers. I'll call.'

The Allclime braked in front of the Mountain High building. Vehicles were scattered round. A US-22 hovered menacingly overhead, slim weapon pods pointing at the dark walls with their shattered windows.

Sid led them towards the decimated roll-up door where the nuke-hazard truck had shunted through with brute force. Clayton would have dearly loved to get his hands on whatever Umbreit had been coerced into building, but that simply wasn't going to happen. Concentrate on Aldred, he told himself. He's the key to it all.

The green gas was seeping round his ankles as Sid led them closer to the door.

'What are we doing?' Ian asked.

'Support duty, man,' Sid replied. 'Just like it says on the label.'

Past the door, the tech crew had got the crate out of the Relay van, onto a trolley they were wheeling towards the open door at the side of the truck. Ralph Stevens was watching them.

'Guess we won,' Sid said to him.

The agent turned to face them, his face covered by his gas-mask. The narrow vision slits revealed nothing.

'We still need Aldred,' Ralph said. 'He's in this bloody maze somewhere.'

Clayton studied the trashed wall beyond the Telay. The shredded spun composite revealed narrow corridors leading deeper into the pitch-black interior. Unknown rooms were exposed through savage cracks. If that same tight-packed structure was repeated throughout they were going to be in trouble. It would take hours to search through it all. Presumably as Aldred intended.

'Hey,' Ian said. 'Just a thought, but . . . did anyone see what kind of shoes Aldred was wearing?'

The gasmask hid Clayton's smile of admiration. Even now, he still hadn't learned not to underestimate the police.

'Worth a try,' Sid admitted.

'Good call, Ian,' Ralph said.

'I think we should take point,' Clayton said quickly. 'Come on, we deserve this. We're the ones who brought this to you.'

There was a moment's hesitation. 'Let's see if we get a response first,' Ralph said.

It took a minute to set up, Ian and Eva linking to all the vehicles ringing the building, reassigning their meshes to scan for a specific emission.

'Ready, boss,' Ian reported eventually.

Sid transmitted the code which would trigger a download from the smartmicrobe bug they'd attached to Aldred's heel in the Jamaica Blue café barely three weeks ago.

'Yes!' Eva and Ian cried together. The pulse had lasted barely half a second, but the meshes had triangulated. A coordinate appeared in their grids, hovering near the top of the crude blueprint of Mountain High building. As one they tilted their heads back to stare at the green-hazed ceiling five metres over their heads.

'Eight floors straight up,' Ian said.

'There are troopers on the sixth floor,' Eva said. 'We can always call for back-up once we get there.'

Ralph drew a mean-looking automatic pistol, and checked the chamber. 'Come on.'

There was no power left in the building. Even the occasional battery-powered emergency light they passed was dead. And there were none of those after the third floor. Three lift shafts cut clean through the floors, intended to carry goods and raw up and down, but following the burnpulses they were all immobilized. So they had to use the stairs and ladders which stitched the floors together to ascend into darkness.

Decades ago, when he was still living on Earth, Clayton had found a wasp nest in the garden. It had spooked him with its malignant beauty; how something so elegant and complicated could be created by a creature so unpleasant was beyond him. Now here he was, clambering round inside the human equivalent. The cell-like rooms seemed to have been woven by an aberrant

905

design program influenced by organic structures. Stairs or ladders didn't have central wells, they were separated by long twisting corridors, or as they found on the fifth floor, by a cloister with ancient cloth printers huddled in arching alcoves. Water or a similar fluid ran down the ladder tube between six and seven. Then they finally emerged onto the eighth level. Heat from the solar roof barely half a metre above their heads turned the motionless air sweltering. As soon as he climbed off the top of the ladder, Clayton felt the sweat oozing out of his pores to soak his T-shirt and trousers. The nightsight function in the gasmask vision slits gave the serpentine corridors an eerie aquamarine tint, as if he was underwater. Infrared bled in, sharpening the silhouettes with pink shades.

The radar picture from the US-22s hovering outside had captured the layout of the eighth level. It was separated out into simple hexagonal chambers, with the corridor maze separating them.

Ian led the way, heading to the location where they'd detected the bug's download pulse. He went slowly, his pistol raised, ready to aim and fire. Taking care to check the floor before each step.

Good procedure, Clayton acknowledged. They were making no sound as they closed on the doorway.

'Stand by,' he sent to Ivan. 'If he's here I'll need the ship for an extraction.'

'Yes, sir.'

Clayton started to activate the metamolecule armaments he'd brought from Jupiter.

*

Sid had thought sitting in the Mercedes Allclime waiting for the assault to begin had been tough. It was nothing to the tension of creeping round in the oppressive dark intestines of the beat-up Mountain High building, chasing after a phantom.

But now they were barely ten metres from the doorway where their prey might be hiding. He squeezed his pistol tighter, and wished the gasmask filter would let a decent gust of air down into his lungs. Ian was a couple of metres ahead of him, a jade and purple profile thanks to the overlay image. Edging oh so cautiously towards the doorway. It was open a crack, and there'd still been no giveaway sound or movement from inside. Eva, at the rear of their line, kept checking round to make sure Aldred wasn't creeping up behind them. It was that kind of environment.

'Sir,' Linsell said in the secure ringlink. 'We've detected an unauthorized transmission from your location.'

'That'll be Aldred,' Ralph said.

'No, sir, it's right beside you. High-level encryption.'

Sid twitched, automatically checking the ceiling as his heart-rate flushed litres of adrenalin into his bloodstream. When he glanced forward again, Ralph was silently indicating the wall. Sid nodded, Aldred was on the other side, maybe a metre away.

'Recommend you wait, sir,' Linsell said. 'I can't determine what's happening up there. The troopers are on their way.'

Ian had reached the door. He held up a hand. The rest of them gathered behind him, weapons brought up ready. Sid tensed, bracing his feet against the floor.

'Go!' Ralph yelled.

Ian charged into the door, shoulder hitting the composite hard, knocking it aside. Bright helmet-lights came on, broad beams illuminating the room in wild angles. Shadows leapt up, surging round as he rushed in. 'Freeze motherfucker,' Ian yelled.

Those were his last ever words.

The monster was there waiting for them, standing right in front of the door. It was exactly as the secure HDA file had shown Sid back in January: the size of a man, with a dark wrinkled hide like petrified leather. Its arm swung with a club's brutality, five lethal blade fingers slashing across Ian's throat, below the helmet above the armour vest, hewing flesh, muscle, tendons, veins, arteries, windpipe – only the spine avoided complete severance.

Ian's arms flew wide in a macabre theatrical gesture as his

907

collapsing body lurched backwards. His corpse crashed into Eva, who was directly behind him, knocking her aside. Five blades swiped through the air where she'd been an instant before.

Sid had begun his charge so hard he couldn't stop. Not the utter surprise at the impossibility before him, not the primal self-preservation instinct, *nothing* managed to divert his legs in those critical first seconds when he emerged into the room. He just kept powering forward, momentum propelling him inexorably towards the monster. Eva was screaming in terror as she hit the floor on one side of him. Arterial blood spewed out of Ian's throat, splattering the ceiling then arcing round to cover walls and floor as the corpse tumbled down, still entangled with the wailing Eva.

Finally, Sid managed to turn fractionally, avoiding an outright collision. His pistol swung about as he was level with the monster, and he fired off two rounds. Missing completely. The monster spun with perfect timing, and its elbow struck Sid on the side. The impact was terrible, he felt a rib break underneath the armour, and he lost his balance, twirling round chaotically to land on his arm. Breath was knocked out of him painfully as the carbon-beam floor slammed up into his chest.

Ralph stopped his own headlong rush and levelled his pistol, putting its muzzle centimetres from the monster's chest. He fired three shots. They ricocheted. Sid actually heard them slam through the spun composite walls. Ralph's body stiffened. Like Sid he didn't believe what he'd just seen. He jerked his pistol up, going for a head shot.

The monster's arm moved again in a smear of speed. Ralph lost the pistol and most of his hand in the sideways swipe. He stumbled back, crying in shock and agony as his finger stumps squirted blood.

It gave Sid just enough time to raise his own pistol again, arm wobbling as he tried to take aim amid the pain and his own fluctuating vision. Knowing it was all useless. Knowing this was his last moment of life. Yelling savage defiance at the monster as it took a swift step towards him.

Abner jumped into the gap between them. The monster

lunged forward, blades extended horizontally, aiming for the North's heart as its arm pistoned out with inhuman power.

Sid never did quite make out what happened – the gasmask's nightsight and infrared image were badly overloaded by everyone's garish helmet-lights. It simply showed Abner's outline shiver as if he was looking at him through a wash of overheated air. Then Abner was in a dark, slick, one-piece armour suit of some kind. There was no sign of all the clothes he'd been wearing a moment before.

The strangest *clunk* filled the confined space. And the monster's blades were rebounding, sending it juddering backwards.

'*Surrrprise*,' Abner warbled in a cheerful taunt.

The monster twirled with incredible speed, a perfect pirouette, arm extended. Blade fingers chopping furiously against Abner's arm.

This time the *clunk* was as loud as a church bell, reverberating across the room. The monster staggered back from the deflected blow.

'My turn,' Abner announced calmly. He tugged a very squat, cylindrical pistol from his waist. Pointed and fired.

The air boiled with thin lashing sounds. And the monster was fighting a tangle of netting that responded to its every frantic scrabble and twist by expanding and seething as if it were alive. Within seconds it was toppling to the ground, completely swaddled in rippling cords.

'What the *fuck*?' Sid managed to babble, choking back on a hysterical wail.

'I need extraction,' Abner was shouting. 'Now!'

Eva was lying where she'd fallen, weeping uncontrollably as she swatted feebly at the heavy corpse on top of her. Ralph thrashed about, clutching his ruined hand, unable to stop the blood pumping out.

'Abner?' Sid pleaded. 'What—'

'Sorry, boss. The name's Clayton, actually. Abner took a little holiday a while back. He's fine, don't worry.'

Sid gawped incredulously at the C North. Even now, even

amid all the butchery and with bone-chilling fear flaring in his mind he felt a little tweak of interest at the revelation. 'It was Jupiter behind this.'

The ceiling creaked as weird ripples flexed the solar panels and support girders. An unseen force ruptured it. Dazzling white light shone down through the widening breach, revealing fragments of panelling tumbling upwards in defiance of gravity. Sid slowly shoved his gasmask up and held a hand over his brow, shielding himself from the glare. Raw night air rushed across the decimated room. Now even the monster had stopped fighting the net to stare up at its fate.

Behind the lights, a massive vehicle was lowering itself sedately onto the overstressed roof of the Mountain High building. Sid couldn't help himself. He started laughing. A spaceship. He was looking at an actual spaceship floating down out of the star-smeared night sky. A thirty-metre cone of smooth dark-grey metal, with five wide rings curling out halfway along the fuselage like deformed wings. There was no sound, no rocket roar, no hushed hissing of stealthed fan ducts. Sid just knew it didn't work on any principles he would ever understand. But it was a thing of wonder nonetheless, so much so he nearly asked, *take me with you.*

'No, Sid,' Clayton said, suddenly serious. 'It wasn't Jupiter. This was never a North on North battle. We don't know what this thing is, or where it came from. But we'll find out.'

The monster was tugged off the floor. It spun up through the air towards a hatch Sid could see opening in the side of the fuselage.

Ralph made an incoherent snarling sound, pain and outrage crushed into one pitiful cry. Clayton bent over him, spraying something over his finger stumps.

'Take care, Sid,' Clayton said. 'It was a privilege being part of your team.' He started to rise off the floor, vanishing into the glare. The fallen angel reclaimed by his own.

Then the lights went out. The shape of the spaceship was briefly visible against the backdrop of delicate twinkling stars. It blurred, elongating upwards. Sid cheered it on wildly. Then the boom burst around him, the kind of thunderclap that only an object weighing hundreds of tonnes shredding the atmosphere could create. After that there was only the US-22s buzzing about in total confusion in its wake; and armoured interdiction troopers spilling through the door, ruby laser target beams chasing round as they sought something they understood amid the carnage and debris.

*

The HDA mobile field clinic was a fifty-tonne twenty-wheel lorry with five triage centres and two emergency surgery theatres. It was parked outside the Mountain High building, the triage modules extending out from its sides, and standing secure on telescoping legs, ready for all injuries the assault might result in.

They'd carried Sid into it on a stretcher, which he thought was degrading. But by then shock was starting to kick in, and he'd lost the power of speech. His skin was hot or cold, he couldn't decide. All he could see was the dark, glossy blades slashing. Ian's head flipping back. Blood exploding into the beams of the helmet-lights. His friend, his partner, was dead. Killed by an alien monster, who had been stalking the streets of Newcastle all along.

Keen, efficient young medical staff in green gowns and white masks had clustered round, eager to have a patient. His armour had been removed, clothes cut away from his torso. He didn't get to go to the theatre, since his cracked rib and bruising wasn't bad enough. Instead, the doctor treated him in the triage centre, sliding some shiny flexible tube into his chest through a tiny incision and wrapping the rib fractures with nuflesh.

Physically he was fine. They bumped a lot of tox into him.

'It'll help,' the doctor said reassuringly.

It was a lie. Tox took the edge off, calming his body and giving his face the expression of a happy idiot. But it never took the internal pain away, never stopped the memory of Ian's terrible death. He lived in a loop of time, where they burst into the hexagonal room, the five of them, hyped up on the thrill of their hunt coming to an end. They'd caught the scent of victory. It wasn't just the satisfaction of closing the case, they had anger powering them along, anger that Aldred had been the bad guy all along, anger that he'd wormed his way into their confidence, anger that they'd been fooled, that they'd opened themselves to him.

Except it wasn't the five of them. It was only four. Abner wasn't Abner, not the detective that Sid had known and quite respected. Clayton, whoever he was, had wormed his way into their lives as much as Aldred.

Clayton had lied. It was North against North. It always had been. And just as he'd suspected right from the start, he'd never know why, never be told exactly what had happened.

'How are you feeling?' a nurse asked.

Sid focused on the smiling young face above him. Without her mask she was beautiful. He wondered if all Jacinta's patients fell in love with her, too.

'My friend is dead,' he said.

'I know. I'm sorry, but your other friends are okay.'

'I want to see them.'

'All right. But not for long.'

'I know. My wife's a nurse, you know.'

'That's good,' she said. 'Can you walk? I can get a wheelchair.'

'I can walk.'

Eva was in the next triage centre. Blood-soaked clothes from the top of the Mountain High building had been removed, and her hair washed. Getting her clean was important, the nurse told Sid, because blood was a strong psychological trigger. Now she sat on the gurney, wrapped in two blankets, staring at nothing. Her Nordic-pale skin was so white that even the freckles had blanched away.

Sid sat beside her. 'It's over,' he said.

'He's dead, Sid. Dead.'

'I know.'

'Where did it come from?'

'I don't know. But we got the machine.'

'Umbreit is dead too.'

'Yeah, and Boz, and Ruckby.'

Tears started to roll down her cheeks. 'I've got to get out. No more police. I can't do this any more.'

'That makes sense.' He sat beside her and put his arm round her shoulders. There was nothing more to say. Eva leant in against him, thankful for the contact, the understanding.

They stayed together for a long time before Sid said: 'I'm going to check on Ralph.'

Sarah Linsell was already in the surgical theatre with Ralph, standing beside the bed, her armour jacket open down the front, holding her helmet. Sid looked at Ralph's hand, which was enveloped by a ball of translucent grey-green gel. Various wires and cables snaked out to a stack of equipment.

'Good to see you, Sid,' Ralph said in an exuberant voice that was louder and happier than it should be.

'Aye, man, how's it going?'

'Pretty good, but then they've bumped me full of tox.'

'Sorry about your hand.'

'That's okay,' Ralph grinned. 'They can fix it.'

Sid raised an eyebrow.

'We recovered all the fingers from the scene,' Sarah Linsell said. 'He'll be transferred back up to the base hospital in a little while. A surgical regraft team is flying in from France. They'll operate as soon as they arrive. With luck he shouldn't need any bionetic substitutions.'

'Good. So what did Umbreit build?'

'Classified.'

'What did he build?' Sid asked in a quieter, more assertive voice.

'Some kind of modified D-bomb,' Ralph said jauntily. 'As far as the tech crew can make out, it would've ripped up the quantum fields inside the gateway. That way it would be difficult to open another gateway to Sirius for about a century while the quantum fields stabilized.'

'And that's where they were going to set it off, in the gateway?'

'Jede turned,' Sarah Linsell said. 'Smart of him, given everyone else apart from Sherman is dead. The plan was for Aldred to get them to the gateway. After all, who was going to question the head of Northumberland Interstellar security? He told them he'd drive on by himself, with the bomb in his boot.'

'So even if he made it through alive somehow, he'd be trapped on the other side for a hundred years?' Sid mused. 'That's if anyone ever bothered to open a gateway there again. It doesn't make a lot of sense.'

'Nothing does,' Ralph said.

'So what about Aldred? Have the troopers found him?'

'No,' Sarah Linsell said angrily. 'They haven't. We've searched that building thoroughly, brought in more agents, covered it in so much smartdust it's now one giant mesh. We can scan every section of it simultaneously. He's not in there. We're working on the assumption that he used the confusion over the spaceship arrival to slip through the perimeter. He must have had help, some team we didn't know about. There's an alert out for him, he won't get far.'

'Ha!' Sid grunted. 'He's a North. He looks like every other North. I couldn't even tell when Clayton replaced Abner, and I've worked with him for years.'

'I'll do whatever I have to,' Linsell said.

'Aye, that's what I told myself when I was given this case,' Sid said. 'Much good it did me. I didn't even believe in the alien. But it's real all right, hiding out in the Mountain High building ever since January. Aldred must have known, he was the one covering for it, arranging for the body to be disposed; the Norths must have some kind of deal with it.'

She shrugged. 'So it would seem.'

'We'll need to check if Mountain High imported anything from St Libra,' Sid said. 'Crap on it, we were on the right track back in January, following up on crates that came through the gateway from St Libra. Why didn't we catch this?'

'Who cares?' Ralph said. 'You've got yourself a huge first. You caught an alien murderer, Sid. Nobody's ever done that before in all human history. You're famous.'

'Aye, but I didn't catch it. Clayton did. And are you going to tell me about that spaceship? I didn't know anything like that existed.'

'Neither did we,' Sarah Linsell said crisply. 'I believe General Shaikh is going to be asking Jupiter some very pointed questions.'

'And we still don't know what this whole thing was all about,' Sid said.

'We know the goal now,' Ralph said. 'Shutting down the St Libra gateway.'

'Aye, but why? The only possible beneficiary from that would be Zebediah North.'

'Maybe he had more support among his brothers than they were letting on,' Sarah Linsell said.

'Aye, maybe,' Sid said. The tox must have been wearing off, because he was now too tired to care. 'I'm going to go home now. Can you sort out a car for me and Eva?'

'Of course.'

'I'll see you tomorrow,' Sid told Ralph. 'After your surgery, like. I'll come and make sure it went okay.'

'Thanks, Sid. And I am sorry about Ian.'

'Sure.' Sid managed a grimace of a smile and ducked out of the theatre.

Chloe Healy was standing in the narrow corridor outside. Even though it was gone eleven o'clock she was as immaculately dressed as always. She was carrying a long protective plastic bag, the type Sid's laundry service delivered his suits in.

'Aye, bollocks to this,' he groaned. 'Go away, pet.' Part of him wanted to know how she'd got past the secure cordon, but then that was a part of what she was.

'O'Rouke sent me,' she said.

'Tell him to piss off.'

'He said you'd say that.'

'Did he tell you how to answer?'

'No. I have my own reply.'

'I'm not even going to hear it. Ian's dead, you know.'

'I do know. Every news site on the planet is alive with the story; licensed and unlicensed. Sid, they've got visuals of a spaceship hovering above Last Mile. They're talking about a plot to set off a fusion bomb.'

'It was a D-bomb. Look, pet, really, just leave me alone.'

'My reply is this: when have I ever been disloyal to whoever I'm representing?'

Sid's shoulders slumped. He really didn't need this, not on top of everything else. 'I thought you'd got an agency job?'

'I have. NorthernMetroServices. That's why I'm assigned to you.'

'No thanks, pet. Go home, that's what I'm doing.'

'This isn't going to go away. It's too big, the biggest story of the decade. The Norths tried to nuke Newcastle!'

'No they didn't.'

'Then you need to tell people that. You're the one they'll listen to and believe. Sid, there are five hundred reporters pressing up against the cordon HDA have thrown round this place. This is just going to grow and grow. It's your chance, Sid, your opportunity.'

'To do what?' he snapped.

'To make a name for yourself. To become the next Chief Constable.'

'Pet, you have got to be kidding.'

'No I'm not, and neither are a lot of other people. That's why I'm here. We have faith in you. This is exactly what you need to position yourself in the public perception. Haven't you earned this? Haven't you served your time, been treated like shit long enough?'

'Yeah, mainly by O'Rouke. And you.'

'Time to cash in.'

'Really?' It was nonsense, and he knew it was. Yet some persistent little thought worried away at his conviction. He'd burned his bridges with Northumberland Interstellar, and Ian had died following their case to its conclusion. No one else was stopping off to say: good job, thank you. Some little part kept reflecting on that, like the one that kept him on the case, kept chasing down the facts from places he had no right to be. 'I don't see how.'

'First, even O'Rouke didn't know you were still part of this. Was it off-log?'

'Yeah. We had a whisper about gang involvement, I decided to follow up.'

'Excellent, that means Milligan cannot take any credit, because he didn't even know what was happening. It was your initiative, your success. You saved the city from a D-bomb detonating.'

'I don't know . . .'

'You're here tonight. You were injured on the front line. You're a hero, Sid. Milligan is a lard-arse office squatter. You're a regular policeman who gets out on the streets to protect the citizenry, and puts his own life on the line to do it. We need you. Who would make a better Chief Constable, who would have more support, who would make the people feel safer?'

'I don't have the political contacts to pull this off.'

'You have a foundation, and tonight can build high on that, very high indeed. I can help you with that. Hate me and despise me all you want, but it's what I do. And I'm damn good at it. I understand the media. I know who to talk to, what angle to spin. You have to control the news, Sid, or it will sweep you along out of control; rule the transnet, dictate the information cycle, don't let the sites use you.'

'How?'

'We can start with a press conference. I've seen you do them before, you're good. And we have the ultimate knowledge monopoly here tonight. The Mayor doesn't know anything, neither does Market Street. HDA isn't saying a damn thing. You can be the city's representative right here and now, you can make sense of all this for people, make them feel safe again. People are worried out there, Sid, they know about the spaceship and they don't know what to think. There are a hundred rumours, and they're breeding worse ones every second. That's all anyone's listening to because there are no facts. Help correct that.'

He nodded his head slowly as the options began to crystallize in his mind. There were opportunities to be had here. It would be a very foolish man who thought otherwise, a man who didn't understand how the world worked. 'I'll need some guidance on how to say all that.'

Chloe Healy smiled shrewdly. She held up the long protective bag that clearly held all the kingdoms of the world. 'First we make you look good. I'm not having you stand up in front of everyone in a clinic gown that shows off your underpants at the back.'

Sid took the bag from her. No need to ask what it contained, she would have chosen the perfect attire for the occasion. 'Aye, I'd best get changed, then, pet.'

Friday 3rd May 2143

General Khurram Shaikh, the Supreme Commander Human Defence Alliance, walked into the Trans-stellar Situation Centre underneath Alice Springs, accompanied by Majors Vermekia and Fendes. Officers at the Sol section saluted quickly as he came over to them and sat at the chair at the head of the consoles. None of them could recall him looking so angry before.

'Are we ready?' he asked.

'Yes, sir,' Captain Toi replied. 'Cape Town is standing by.'

'Very well, proceed with the war gateway opening, Captain.'

Captain Toi turned back to her zone console and let the slim screen curve round her face. 'Power it up,' she told the Cape Town base commander.

General Shaikh watched the big wall pane that was displaying all the information being gathered by the five HDA satellites closest to Jupiter. It wasn't nearly as much as he would have liked. Providing a full range of high-resolution optical sensors wasn't a priority to the design geeks and budget lords of the deep-space satellite warning network that orbited Sol; the technological sentinels were intended to watch for any perturbation of quantum fields, that inevitable precursor for Zanth activity. The images which the Sol station team had pulled out of the quintet showed the North constellation as little more extensive than a blurred patch, like a dull silver nebula; it was difficult to make out the individual elements apart from the main habitat

919

amalgamation. Even so he was surprised by the size of the constellation.

'How many ... components in the constellation now?' he asked.

'Over a hundred, sir,' Toi replied. 'Plus some large chunks of astroidal rock; we've identified both metallic and carbonaceous chondritic types, as well as a sizeable iceberg; presumably they provide a full range of metals and minerals to process into raw. They've been busy.'

'Indeed.' The General watched the data gliding down the side of the pane, showing him the Cape Town war gateway powering up. The trans-spacial connection was reaching out to compress the forty-light-minute distance from Earth to Jupiter down to an effective zero. It was almost insulting to ask the fabulous machine to perform a connection over such a short length – it was designed to extend out to the very stars themselves, to help humans fight off the most terrifying foe in the universe. Now he wanted to use it to have an angry conversation with a stubborn recluse.

Several sections of the data turned red. Captain Toi's back stiffened. She began a fast conversation with the Cape Town technicians controlling the gateway. The data flipped back to amber, then went red again.

'Captain?' the General asked in a low voice.

She turned around to face him, a line of perspiration on her brow. 'Sir, we can't open the gateway close to Jupiter. Something is blocking the connection at the other end.'

'Do we know what?'

'The gateway technicians think it might be something equivalent to our EarthShield quantum-warp stations, sir.'

General Shaikh gave Fendes a cool look. 'How in Allah's name did Constantine get hold of that technology?'

'Industrial espionage, I would suggest,' the major replied.

'I disagree,' Vermekia said. 'Either Jupiter developed it on their own, like the reactionless space drive, or they've harvested it from an advanced sentient race.'

'On St Libra?'

Vermekia shrugged. 'That would be the logical conclusion.'

'Captain,' Shaikh said. 'How close to Jupiter can the gateway open?'

'We think about seven million kilometres, sir.'

'Very well, I suppose that will have to—' He stopped in shock as his e-i sent him a grade one alert. Two of the Sol section wall panes were changing, bringing up emergency situation charts. Earth's high-orbit sensor satellite armada was registering a change in spacetime fifty thousand kilometres above the Pacific Ocean.

'Not a rift,' Captain Toi barked. 'Repeat, not a Zanth rift.'

'What is it?' Shaikh demanded.

'Sir, it's a trans-spacial connection. It's holding remarkably stable – there's barely an emergence jitter. And it's approximately one metre in diameter.'

'What?'

'I think the mountain just came to Mohammed,' Vermekia said quietly.

'Sir,' Captain Toi turned to the General, looking astonished. 'It's emitting a comm link, interfacing with our strategic communication satellite squadron. Incoming call, using Jupiter diplomatic encryption.'

'Use my key,' Shaikh told his e-i, 'route the call to this station.'

Everyone at the Sol station watched Constantine North's youthful face materialize on the screen in front of General Shaikh.

'General.'

'Mr North.'

'You wanted to talk to me?'

'I certainly did. You seem to have developed some remarkable technology out there.'

'Thank you. As have you. I'm a great admirer of EarthShield.'

'I was referring to the spaceship drive.'

'Of course.'

'Your agent took *something* from Newcastle.'

'My son took an alien into custody, an alien that may well have been the one who killed my brother and my nephews.'

'This isn't the time to get personal, Constantine. That is the first sentient alien we have ever encountered. We need to establish a dialogue, not wreak vengeance. We cannot afford another interstellar enemy.'

'I am sorry that you judge me in that fashion, General. The dead are dead, nothing can bring them back; I am concerned solely with protecting the living, all of the living, wherever and whoever they may be.'

'As am I. The reason the Human Defence Alliance exists is to safeguard our species.'

'General, please understand I have no quarrel with you. I simply believe I am better placed to manage this incursion. It is us Norths that have attracted its attention. We are what it wants.'

'You have no right to monopolize this. We have to know what we're dealing with.'

'I have no intention of monopolizing whatever information this contact produces.'

'Good. Can I send a team to Jupiter to verify the encounter?'

'Regretfully, no.'

'Why not?'

'The HDA does not enjoy my full trust.'

'I find that insulting. My people are prepared to make the ultimate sacrifice to protect humans wherever they are, including Jupiter, if you were ever in need.'

'Please, General. You knew the alien was real. You knew twenty years ago, yet you deliberately kept that information to yourselves. I've seen the recordings of poor Angela Tramelo's rather brutal interrogation. I saw what you pulled from her memory. Yet you filed it in the deepest cache you have and conveniently forgot about it. Do not presume to lecture me on responsibility.'

'Images from a disturbed girl's mind do not constitute proof of anything. They could have been a zone drama she fixated on, a nightmare, a psychosis. We didn't know. Coming out and officially claiming the monster existed would have caused panic and fear. Our protection is not just physical. Civilization requires order to continue functioning. That too must be maintained.'

'Indeed. You are responsible to your political paymasters, and their eternal quest for the status quo. I am not. I will find out exactly what this creature is and where it comes from. I will also discover its intent. When that information is available, I will make it freely available to everyone. With or without your consent and approval. I believe we are approaching a time of profound change, both materially and philosophically. I hope you can adapt, General, I truly do, for I see you are an honourable man at heart, and such people are few and far between in these times.'

'Constantine—'

'I'll contact you when we have some information. You have my word on that.'

The link ended. Up on the big panes, the sensor satellites were reporting the trans-spacial connection had closed.

'Now what?' Captain Toi asked.

'We wait,' the General said. 'And possibly pray.'

*

Constantine took the transit pod over to toroid three by himself. The rotating wheel was at the end of the habitat amalgamation next to the original hostel wheel, separated by a latticework spindle three hundred metres long. Constantine didn't want to place the rest of the inhabitants in danger when the encounter finally occurred. The spindle even had explosive separation bolts. Just in case.

Toroid three had been built over eight years ago out of a superstrength carbon–titanium compound developed at Jupiter. That shell remained fixed, but its internal systems were in a permanent state of rebuild, ensuring the most advanced technology was always available in anticipation of this moment.

Constantine made his way to the reception chamber's supervision centre, a simple circular room with a single simple black leather office chair in the centre. He didn't need the paraphernalia of consoles and screens and zones embraced by the rest of the human race, not with his resequenced brain's multitude of connections and visualization routines. He sat down in the old chair he'd brought all the way from Earth fifty-five years ago, and waited. On the other side of the metamolecule wall, the main reception facility was a hemispherical chamber ten metres in diameter. The surface of both the floor and walls was currently configured to be soft, like a layer of sponge. Its only solid artefacts were a cot bed, a basin, and a toilet. A ring near the ceiling apex glowed with a blue-white spectrum matching Sirius under more normal conditions.

Satellites swirling around the constellation fed their senses into Constantine's brain, showing him the lightwave ship's arrival. It docked at toroid three's spindle port.

Constantine opened a link to Clayton. 'How are you doing?'

'This is definitely the way to travel,' Clayton replied. 'Good job I don't get vertigo, you could actually see the sun shrinking behind us.'

'And your guest?' It was a courtesy question, as more than half his augmented receptors were linked with the scanners that encaged the alien.

'It's been a good boy. Are you seeing that internal structure?'

'Yes. Most interesting.'

'Can I come down with it?'

'You know the answer. This is where I get to come out and play.'

'Father.'

'Yes?'

'Be careful.'

'I don't believe this situation will be settled by violence. But, yes, I will be careful.'

'We'll have the medics and space marines standing by anyway.'

'Aye, space marines! Hopefully the time of such nonsense is coming to an end. I said much the same to General Shaikh.'

'How did he take it?'

Constantine smiled wryly. 'I don't think he was best pleased.'

'No kidding? Are you ready?'

'Yes, send it down, please. And good job, by the way.'

'Thanks.'

A minute later the centre of the reception chamber ceiling distended, a translucent blue bulb surged down until its base touched the floor. The alien was inside, standing perfectly still as it was gripped by the smartfluid. It remained standing as the blue substance poured back up into the ceiling like an inverted raindrop splash.

Constantine waited for a few moments, but it still didn't move. There was no hint that it was anything other than a statue of leathery rock. He zoomed his vision in, examining the creature's eyes. That was the giveaway, the human orbs flicked round, searching the chamber.

'My name is Constantine North.' His voice filled the reception chamber. 'And I must say, from a quantum dynamics point of view, you have a remarkable composition.' In case the creature wasn't auditory capable, the words also flowed along the curving wall in fifty-centimetre-high purple lettering. Constantine generously displayed what he was perceiving, projecting a hologram image into the air next to his visitor. A humanoid form, with shadows of internal structure.

'Your molecules have an odd quantum signature, they're not quite in phase with spacetime. But they mimic our physiological layout, as if they're embryonic, ready to become one of us, or maybe the opposite.'

The alien turned its head. Constantine studied the shift of the molecules' quantum state which allowed the solid skin to become fluidic. It was an extraordinarily complex fluctuation pattern. One that would presumably allow the solid blade fingers to flex, to shred a human heart.

'I don't know what additional abilities you have, but we will do our utmost to contain you. Should you manage to break your bonds, well, there are weapons of last resort that will be used against you. I did not have you brought here out of hostility. I

925

simply wish to converse with you. If you are not capable of breaking out of this reception chamber, then you will remain here until you choose to initiate communication. That is really all I have to say.'

He sat back in the chair, swinging slightly from side to side, waiting . . .

The alien's quantum signature abruptly altered again. Molecules flipped to a normal state, interfacing perfectly with space-time. Becoming real. The visual manifestation of the change was impressive. Its tough hide gained colour and texture in less than a second, materializing into a smart blue-grey business suit, worn with a white and grey striped shirt and a natty purple tie. The face shivered into human skin, with dark-brown hair cut in an expensive neat style.

An adult North took a slow breath, and gazed round at the chamber with a mildly disdainful expression.

'Ah,' Constantine said in delight. 'Nephew Aldred, I presume?'

*

Wide arcs of snow sluiced away from both sides of MTJ-1's plough blade as Angela kept the power on to the axle-hub motors. Wipers swept the windscreen vigorously, clearing the constant impact splatter of the crystalline slush. She concentrated hard on the open ribbon of flat snow ahead, making sure there were no boulders in her path. The patchy radar image on the windscreen wasn't a lot of help; huge conglomerations of ice were clinging to the radar's housing. That focus helped her to ignore the stink in the MTJ's cab. Omar was in the passenger seat, jaw clamped tight against nausea and distress, trying to show an interest in the river that unrolled ahead of them. It was three days since they started driving along the tributary, and the rest of the convoy personnel were only just starting to shake off the illness. Elston and Garrick were on the passenger seats behind her, both of them wrapped in blankets and toughing out the discomfort as their bodies slowly recovered from the toxin.

It hadn't taken Camm Montoto long to isolate and identify the poison. Microscopic narsberry spores had been injected into the composition gel. Even Angela had been worried when that was announced. Narsberry was notoriously toxic. The spores were microscopic and airborne; poorly washed food resulted in dozens of hospitalizations each year. And this dosage level was a lot stronger than anything a dusty lettuce could impart; even *her* kidneys might not fully recover. Whoever it was, they'd come perilously close to murdering everyone in the convoy.

So now, Angela was gunning the MTJ hard, chasing down the tributary as fast as she dared. As if that would take her away from danger, from the would-be serial killer and the monster in the trees. But Leif had been right, the river was a road through this difficult land, flat and level, in some places a couple of hundred metres wide. She'd learned to be more cautious in the wide areas, the river was shallower there, which meant there were boulders buried in the ice and snow the big vehicle was cruising over. There'd been a few strikes when she was taking point and hadn't read the radar quite right. Not really watching out, not seeing the abnormal lumps until too late. Then came the frightening screech as the bottom of the blade shaved the rock, and the MTJ gave a lurch before settling back down again. But the MTJ could take it. She relished powering on with the brute of a machine – it was like taking revenge on the planet and everything it had thrown at her. She was leading them away from danger, from the past.

Red icons slid up into her iris smartcell grid, and she gritted her teeth. 'Son of a bitch.' Still scouting the peachy-coloured snow for hidden snags she started reducing power to the motors. 'Braking,' she told the other drivers on their ringlink.

Elston grunted out of his doze. 'What's happen – oh.'

'Sorry,' she said. 'But we knew he wasn't going to last.' The red icons were from Luther's bodymesh. The severe sickness brought on by the narsberry spores had been too much for his organs, already weakened and strained by the accident. In one way, Angela had been impressed by how long he'd held on for;

but it had cost him dearly in suffering. Not any more. The red icons were turning white – neutral. The same as Mohammed's had turned ten hours previously.

'We need to refuel anyway,' Elston said.

Angela brought the MTJ to a halt, and turned the wheel. The convoy vehicles slowly arranged themselves in a circle, sensors and remote guns pointing out across St Libra's icy wilderness. It wouldn't be night for another couple of hours, but they switched the headlights on anyway, sending the beams out to scour the low cliff of crystalline tree trunks which marked the riverbanks. Their radars swept about, scanning the surrounding environment as best they could. Nothing could sneak up on them now, and Antrinell's orders were that no one stepped beyond the circle.

Angela took several minutes to get dressed for the outside. There was no wind, but the temperature had dropped alarmingly over the last couple of days. People were exhausted. Those who had avoided the poisoning had been doing all the driving, and most of the refuelling. Mistakes came easy. Leif had taken his gloves off to deal with a tricky coupling at the last refuelling. His skin had touched the hose's metal nozzle. The cold numbed it instantly so he didn't realize; then when he did try to snatch his hand away he tore off a long strip of flesh.

'Take care out there,' Elston said weakly.

'You know me.' The lightness was forced, she'd seen how he still shook under the blanket. And she'd been keeping track of how much all the invalids in her MTJ had been eating. It wasn't nearly enough.

She stepped out onto the frozen river, and made her way back along the MTJ to the inner circle. The glow of red tail lights added to Red Sirius's salmon glimmer, casting the world into a dapple of vermilion. There were nine of them standing in the dark light, the lucky ones, depending on your point of view: those who'd escaped the poisoning – Lorelei, Lulu, Leora, Antrinell, Karizma, and Leif – and those who had recovered enough to help drive and take care of the sick – herself, Madeleine, and Josh.

'This is a major logistics point for us,' Antrinell said to them.

'I've been reviewing our fuel situation, and I want to dump truck-2. We can offload all its remaining bioil into the tanker and the bladders in truck-1. One less set of fuel cells will extend our range considerably.'

Angela glanced over to Karizma, but the woman's face was hidden behind bands of cloth and her goggles. She didn't make any protest.

'Okay then,' Antrinell said. He'd clearly been bracing himself for an argument. 'Josh, you and I will carry Luther to the sledge and put him with the others.'

'Why bother?' Josh asked.

'Excuse me?'

'What's the point? Why exactly are we burning bioil we can't afford lugging a whole bunch of corpses round the countryside? We should leave them here. Pick them up when all those Daedalus flights show up and save us. After all, it's not like the jungle is full of wild animals – they're not going to be eaten.'

Angela had to admit she admired the logic, even though the notion was intrinsically wrong somehow.

'For the record,' Leif said. 'If the monster gets me, you can leave me behind, too. I don't want to be responsible for holding the survivors back.'

'They are our comrades,' Antrinell said in a rasping tone. 'We should show them the respect they deserve for their sacrifice.'

'They sacrificed shit,' Karizma said. 'They were murdered. And if they slow us down, we'll be next.'

Now Angela understood, it was another challenge to the legitimacy of the convoy, another corrosive gnawing away at the leadership. Introducing doubts, encouraging the undecided to question the goal. Elston would have faced them down; Antrinell was different, a good second-in-command, but lacking his own authority.

'What's it doing to them?' Angela asked quietly. 'To Mark Chitty, and the others? After all, they were carried away for a reason. Anybody want to guess what it is? No? Well for the record I don't want to be left behind for it to vivisect or use in

929

its version of a satanic ritual, dead or alive. And while we're still running that record, our fuel isn't that critical, not yet. Their weight on a sledge won't make any difference.' Which was bullshit. She knew it would be touch and go if they made it to Sarvar on what was left now. Her own private hope was that they could get close enough so the camp's skeleton crew could drive a tanker out to them, or even better, a Berlin helicopter.

'We're not speculating about the fate of corpses,' Antrinell said, seizing the moment. 'Start the refuelling. I want to get it finished by nightfall. The aurora borealis is bright, so we should be able to make some progress this evening.'

The group broke up, trudging away grudgingly to their assigned tasks. Angela couldn't help gazing at the trees along the nearest bank; the glittering ice that encased them and the vines made the trunks look like frozen tusks. Sky and earth the jaws that would slam together and crush them. But that was just her overactive imagination.

'Thank you,' Antrinell said.

'I just want to get the fuck out of here,' Angela told him. She watched Madeleine slog over to the tanker, which she was now travelling in with Atyeo. It wasn't where she wanted Madeleine to be, the girl should be in the MTJ with her, where she would be safer. But that wasn't something she could swing right now. In a few days, when people had recovered and duties were shared out again, maybe.

'I get that,' Antrinell said. 'We should reach the Dolce in another day or so. After that it's a smooth ride up to Sarvar.'

'Sure,' she said, and went off to sort out the food packages.

*

Aldred had vanished in a quantum twist as fast as he'd appeared. Constantine studied the alchemic entity that had mimicked his nephew, utilizing every sensor they'd crammed around the reception chamber. Its atomic structure had somehow reverted to abnormal phasing. Whatever the origin of its abnormality, Jupiter obviously didn't possess a sensor to detect it. Not that he'd expected success in the first minute, but neither had he been ready for defeat on a technological level.

'I'd like to know what kind of avatar I'm talking to,' Constantine said. 'Assuming you are an avatar. Or do you just remote control Aldred?'

The thing in the reception chamber cocked its head to one side. A quest pulsed out, establishing a link to the chamber, with Aldred's identity code. 'I am Aldred as seen through my mirror.'

'Your command of language and syntax is excellent. Would you care to define your existence in a little more detail for me?'

'This is a copy of Aldred. It incorporates his biological structure and neural pathways, as well as his memories. However, it is not him – it is the bridge between me and your species.'

'Could you tell me who "me" is, please? That is rather important.'

'I am the life of St Libra.'

'Again: could you expand that?'

'I evolved billions of years ago, on a different planet somewhere else in the galaxy. I am the pinnacle of my planet's life, the endpoint. I became one. I now reside on St Libra. Its star is young; I will have a long time living in its warmth.'

'May I know where you live? We never saw any signs of sentient life. If we had done, we wouldn't have settled there.'

The Aldred avatar in the reception chamber tilted its head back a couple of degrees, as if listening to some strange noise. 'Constantine, I think we both know that isn't strictly true. It was obvious from the very beginning I was not native to St Libra.'

'You're talking about the jungle, the plants? We did assume St Libra had been bioformed, yes.'

'You speak only of the physical, the individual. I am beyond that.'

'How exactly?'

'The plants, my plants, are my biological component. I reside within them.'

Constantine found his own mouth was frozen in a gentle smile of wonder. 'The plants have a group consciousness? We never found any kind of cells that appeared neurone equivalent.'

'There are none. As I said, the plants are my biological component. I have many facets, but the biological is what I grew out of. They are my roots into this quantum reality.'

'So the life on your origin planet evolved into a single consciousness?'

'Yes. As you aspire to take your machines to their apex, so they may become your gods and slaves, the singularity you crave; so my ancestors were content to let life flow to its destiny. As you can imagine, it is a longer but ultimately surer course. I believe that in their animal form those ancestors weren't as short-lived as you, they never had your understandable impatience.'

'A Gaia singularity event,' Constantine said in awe.

'An appropriate if somewhat crude dictum. Yes, I believe we have defined me in your terms. Congratulations.'

Constantine grimaced, suddenly weary and despondent as the implications became clear. 'And we've been busy poisoning your environment ever since the day we arrived. Polluting you.'

The Aldred avatar walked over to the chamber wall, and ran the tip of a blade finger gently down the surface. It was almost a caress. 'You do it to every world you inhabit. Why single me out for your remorse?'

'Because you're different, and you know that. You know how we would have reacted if we'd been aware of your existence. Why didn't you tell us? Why send this avatar ninety years after we opened the gateway?'

'So fast you are, so quick in this tiny little animal body. Can you conceive of nothing outside your own viewpoint? I do not perceive as you do, I do not think at this speed any more, I do not react in an instant. I did reach out when I sensed that the plants were being polluted and dying, that new cells had come to St Libra that did not accommodate me. I gathered myself and found the strongest alien thoughts, which are yours: North. So many similar minds were interpreted by me as one. I looked in the mirror to find you, to make me you in your own shape. It is not something I have done often before. The first avatar I brought forth was not entirely successful. It was confused by its existence, not fully understanding what it was, my thoughts and its original human thoughts were in terrible conflict, so it lashed out in a very human way because that was the form it had.'

'The massacre at Bartram's mansion,' Constantine whispered, aghast.

'Yes: the monster. Changing shape, changing state, is intuitive to me, an ancient ability I imbue the mirror construct with. It chose what to be. That is a part of you: North. What you see before you is a monster born of your own subconscious.'

'Zebediah! The avatar was Zebediah.'

'Yes. Who else is going to preach that humans are an abomination, that they should be banished from St Libra? Those are my views given inarticulacy by your mind.'

'So what happened to Barclay?'

'Barclay was the first to be killed. After all, there can't be two Barclays in one universe, now, can there?'

Constantine knew the answer, but he had to say it anyway. It was proof to himself that he was still human despite his myriad improvements and alterations. 'The body in the Tyne, that was Aldred, wasn't it?'

The Aldred avatar stepped away from the chamber wall. 'Of course. Once again, there could not be two. This time, this avatar, is considerably more adept at living a human life. I learned from my mistakes with the last one; our two conflicting thoughts are less antagonistic now. Once I'd considered the alterations, Aldred was mirrored while he was on St Libra. Unfortunately, he'd gone back through the gateway before I had fully emerged. But Aldred has a lot of what is termed statecraft in matters of security. It was easy for me to follow him through the gateway and lure him to his old girlfriend's apartment. And his underworld contacts were invaluable in disposing of the body.'

'Why? Why not simply contact us and talk, explain what was going on, what you are?'

'That was my original intent. I, the avatars, were created to understand you, to assess what was happening to the greater me. They would have gone out into your civilization, examined your nature, and allowed me to understand enough to come to a decision. I'd actually started doing that with Aldred, started to build the foundation of a bridge. Then everything changed.'

'What changed?' Constantine asked sharply.

'A weapon. You brought a weapon to St Libra. I sensed it even though our temporal references are so dissimilar.' The avatar brought its thick arms up as if offering a human prayer. Its blades flexed. 'Even here I feel it. It is inimical to me. If you used it I would be broken. Oh, I would still exist, but I would no longer be whole.'

'What weapon?' a shocked Constantine asked.

'A plague, a virus, a pestilence. It is there on St Libra, an ember burning into my awareness. I have done what I can, as I did once before when another alien claimed my world for its own. I have wished the sun cold so the jungles are frozen, hibernating in safety through the new winter. I have made my world uninhabitable for you, driven so many of you away. This avatar was about to destroy your gateway so there could be no repetition of your violations. That way the weapon itself would remain and ultimately die in the cold.'

Constantine stood up. On his instruction the metamolecules of the reception chamber wall flowed apart, creating an archway.

'Dad, what are you doing?' Clayton demanded.

Constantine ignored him and walked across the soft floor to the unmoving monster. 'There must be trust between us,' he told it.

The Aldred avatar bent its neck forward, presenting its mask-face towards him. Constantine saw it didn't have eyes any more, just blank folds of the stony skin where they should be.

'Constantine North. The dreaming visionary, so Aldred's father called you.'

'Let me help. It has to be the HDA which developed the

weapon, whatever it is. I will get them to withdraw it immediately.'

'They can't.'

'Why not?'

'It is beyond them now.'

'I don't understand.'

'My other avatar, the first one. It is with the weapon now. The HDA sent the weapon to camp Wukang with Colonel Elston. Now they are lost somewhere between Wukang and Sarvar. The first avatar has slowly been getting closer to the abomination. It is afraid, as it has always been afraid since the moment of its creation. There are many humans guarding it, and they have weapons. For all our strength and ability, these mirror constructs are not totally invulnerable. So it is eliminating the soldier humans one at a time until the time where none will be left to protect the abomination. Once that happens, the weapon will be gone. All that will remain after that is the gateway. Now I understand the situation, now I am clear on what must be done, that too will be destroyed.'

'How?'

'I will mirror another of you. A thousand of you. A million if that is what it takes.'

'Don't do that,' Constantine said. 'I will close the gateway for you as an act of contrition. I have that ability.'

'You forget, in every respect other than creation, I am Aldred North, and I know Augustine very well. He would not agree.'

'I didn't say I'd *ask permission*. I said I had the ability to close it for you. A method which doesn't involve D-bombs or armies of mirror entities. A method which doesn't involve killing anyone.'

'Why?'

'Because enough people have died. Enough of your jungles and plants have been laid waste. Because we are both alive, and that is such a precious thing. We are different, which is even more important. And for me there is one thing above all which I need from you.'

'What is that?'

'You are not worried by the Zanth. You have the power to damp down a star's fire. You must have some way to defend yourself from the Zanth, to deflect it from swarming at Sirius. I need to know how you do that.'

'I simply do. The Zanth is . . . odd, even to me. But it is not infinitely powerful. I wish it away, and it is so.'

'There must be a mechanism, some quantum-field manipulation that you employ.'

'I don't think in those terms.'

'But you used to, and this avatar is a bridge. The transfer of knowledge is simply a question of language, of mathematics. That is a universal constant. Your help would be invaluable. For all our faults, humankind doesn't deserve to fall before the Zanth.'

'No. You don't. No life does.'

'Then I will contact the HDA. General Shaikh will listen to me.'

'They made that weapon, they made it with the intent of destroying all native life on St Libra. They made it *just in case*. Can you imagine that? Preparing for the obliteration of an entire planet's evolution as a tactical exercise? Can you then imagine the suspicion they will regard me with, a smaller less aggressive version of the Zanth, yet with the power to extinguish a star. There will always be fear, and because of that your politicians and military will always seek ways to destroy me. You'll understand when I tell you I don't trust them.'

'I told the General the very same thing myself a couple of hours ago.'

'Then I will continue to exterminate the convoy personnel myself, and finally the weapon.'

'Please don't do that, please stop killing people and let me try and find a solution. Once the gateway is closed there will be no more threat to you from Earth or any human. You say you are connected to the other avatar, to Zebediah? Let me talk to it, let me communicate through it directly with my agent in the Wukang convoy.'

'That will not happen.'

'Why not? I can resolve this if you let me.'

'It won't happen because the first avatar will not listen to me, even though it is me. It hears your words even as I hear them.'

'Then why?' Constantine asked.

'Its original creation process had too many flaws. It has become independent. Ironically, it now is more you than me.'

Saturday 4th May 2143

The crude map harvested from the e-Rays' reconnaissance data and ancient survey images, then reduced to feature outlines, filled half of MTJ-1's windscreen. The inertial guidance was placing them south of the river Dolce. In real life, Angela was still driving along the Lan, looking for the bigger river they were supposed to merge with. She'd come to hate their navigation system, stupid flawed thing that it was.

All that morning, tendrils of mist had been creeping out of the jungle on either side of the Lan, a lighter coral pink than the carmine snow over which it meandered with organic sinuousness. As the day progressed, the jungle's exhalation closed in on the convoy vehicles until by mid-afternoon it covered the whole frozen river. The plough blade in front sent up long swirls of the clammy stuff twining with the cataracts of snow it shaved off the surface to make a level track. She could see the vehicle's wake eddying away on both sides, as if some ocean leviathan was cruising the river.

'Cloud's building again,' Paresh said from the passenger seat next to her. He'd swapped with Elston the previous day after they abandoned truck-2, allowing the commander to go back to biolab-1.

Angela had been dismayed by Paresh's macho tough-it-out antics. But Dr Coniff had cleared the swap, saying his broken ribs were healing nicely; and he'd never eaten a composition gel meal.

He'd spent his days in biolab-2 using his one good arm to help tend the sick rather than resting and recuperating.

She took a quick glance up at the top of the windscreen where the condensation smear never shifted. The cherry-tinted rings had vanished behind some high russet clouds gusting in from the south. Faint green and indigo aurora borealis fronds waved about just below the rumpled clouds. 'Not dark enough to be snow,' she said. Her expert weather-lore verdict.

Paresh grinned. Which she had to struggle not to respond to. He was happier than he had any right to be; but she was glad to have him for company again. The only other person she missed having in the MTJ now was Madeleine.

They'd made good headway down the Lan since the last refuelling stop. She'd taken a rest from point duty that morning, then swapped with MTJ-2 after lunch. Her only problems this afternoon were the rocks lurking beneath the snow and oily fog which the radar didn't always expose in time. But then, according to Darwin, if it didn't stick up above the fog, the rock wasn't big enough to damage the MTJ. Not that she wanted to put that to the test.

As the fog had engulfed the smooth snow surface of the river, so the slopes on either side had started to build up. Now, in the middle of the afternoon, the convoy was travelling along the bottom of a wide, deep valley smothered with dense jungle. Without the Lan as their highway they would have been crunching forward metre by desperate metre as they had for the first few days. Best estimate put the turn onto the Dolce as the halfway point of their new route, and she knew they'd already used over half of their fuel. Abandoning the remaining truck would be a good trade-off, reducing consumption in exchange for squeezing the drivers into the other vehicles – there was room now that they'd lost Luther and Mohammed. And there was also the ever-shrinking supply of food reducing the weight the vehicles had to carry. She wanted to suggest to Elston they fire another comm rocket, and alert Sarvar they would need help.

Up ahead, the steepish U of the valley wall seemed to be

framed by a dark maroon cliff, as if the river turned sharply. Angela frowned. If it curved, then why was that wall directly ahead? And the cliff was vertical rock with scatterings of snow, mainly in shadow from Sirius and the rings shining behind it, which is why it was so dark. Having a world that was all graduated shades of pink and red made visual interpretation difficult. And the flow of fog seemed to cut off abruptly, as if blocked by the distant cliff face – which made no sense. And the radar showed nothing. *Nothing*.

Her perspective shifted, abruptly exposing the reality of what lay ahead. 'Shiiit!' Angela slammed her foot down hard on the brake. Her hand twisted the wheel throttle sharply, red warning graphics zipped up the windscreen as she shunted the axle hub motors into reverse. Her other hand slammed the plough-blade lever forward, lowering the point of the V deeper into the snow. Then she was yelling: 'Brake! Brake! Brake!' for the ringlink with the other drivers.

The MTJ juddered. A thick wave of snow from the blades curved spectacularly over the bonnet, smacking into the windscreen before thudding down on the roof. Traction warnings flared bright amber as the spinning wheels slipped and skidded. The whole MTJ started to slew round, shuddering madly.

Paresh gripped frantically at the dashboard with his one working hand, swearing at the top of his voice. Behind her, Garrick and Omar were clinging to seats and door handles. Angela's own harness tightened in preparation for a crash, pulling her back in the seat. It was all she could do to hang on to the steering wheel. Her hand hovered over the emergency tyre pressure button – she could blow the valves and send the air rushing out to give them an even greater footprint – and most likely shred them from the torque.

The MTJ came to a slam-halt, rear tyres lifting from the snow before bouncing back down, snowblade wedged deep into the gouge it had carved from the river ice.

'What the fuck!' Paresh cried.

Angela just sat there, heart pumping furiously as she waited for any slipping sensation to manifest. The wipers slid back and forth monotonously, freeing the mass of snow from the windscreen. When it was clear she pointed silently ahead with a shaking finger, still too shocked to speak.

Paresh peered forward. 'I will be crapped on from heaven's heights,' he moaned softly.

*

Everybody came out of the vehicles to look, edging cautiously past MTJ-1 like school kids daring each other on. They'd found the junction between the rivers. The Dolce with its vast tributary system extending all the way back to the Eclipse Mountains in the east, which was also joined far upstream by the more northerly Zell, was a truly stupendous flow of water. It had carved a massive canyon through the land, with raw rock walls nearly two kilometres high and an easy kilometre apart at the bottom. That was what Angela had seen and didn't comprehend. The Lan valley emptied into the Dolce canyon in a waterfall that was three hundred metres wide, and fell for over a kilometre to the much larger river below.

MTJ-1 had finally come to a stop an entire twelve metres from the edge. The convoy personnel stood there silently on the hard ice in front of the vehicle, watching the fog drift silently downward for several hundred metres before dissipating in the cliff's tenacious updraughts. The Lan's waters must have frozen slowly, continuing to run down the rock for weeks in smaller and smaller quantities until the river was finally stilled. The entire cascade was iced up; to the overawed group clustered on top it looked as if the waterfall had instantly succumbed to winter.

Vance exhaled a long breath, and silently thanked the Good Lord for sparing them. He looked along the canyon to the east where Sarvar lay. He looked west. There was no variation. The canyon was a mighty scar riven across the land, granting no relief.

'And how – just *how* in your stupid God's name – do we get down there?' Karizma asked.

941

Vance had to take a moment to compose himself; his temper was wearing thin under her constant attacks on his faith. 'At the lowest point. We'll send the MTJs scouting both ways along the canyon, see what they find.'

To his surprise, Karizma didn't argue. He started issuing orders.

*

The convoy carefully backed up, parking a considered two hundred metres from the top of the waterfall. They refuelled the MTJs first.

'I'd like to take my original team with me,' Leif said to Elston. 'They're all in reasonably good shape now. I know Karizma is a pain, but she is competent. If there's a possible route down she'll be able to evaluate the equipment we've got to see if it's feasible.'

It made sense, even though Vance wasn't entirely comfortable with it. The original team meant Karizma, Davinia, and Erius all in MTJ-2 together, the strongest opponents to the convoy. But even with a full tank, and a couple of reserve bladders on the back, the MTJ didn't have enough fuel to get them back to Wukang. So he said: 'Yes. Good idea.' That left MTJ-1, which he assigned Antrinell, Camm, Darwin, and Josh Justic.

Both vehicles were given a shortwave radio which Olrg had printed before they left Wukang. It was a primitive system, but at least had a chance of allowing them to stay in touch through the electrically supercharged atmosphere, and hopefully call in a route down if they found one.

'Travel for one day,' Vance told them, 'then come back, no matter what. Fuel is becoming critical now. If there is no way down within that distance, we'll have to turn back.' He watched Karizma as he said it, but with her bundled up in all her layers there was no way of telling how she reacted to that. Just looking at the canyon, she probably thought she'd won. There was no point in triumphalism.

The MTJs left the waterfall camp at five o'clock, pushing through the fog that still slithered out of the snow-clad jungle.

They'd have another hour of Sirius's pink light to travel by. If the aurora borealis returned with its usual strength at night, they might even be able to carry on. No one thought they would, not travelling by aurora and ringlight along the top of a two-kilometre-high cliff.

Almost as soon as the MTJs drove away, thick flakes of snow started to drift down out of the clotted sky, contrary to Angela's prediction. There was hardly any wind, so the flakes alighted gently on the vehicles and sledges, bringing silence with them and draining the remains of Sirius's stunted light out of the sky. Headlight beams that were already submerged in the lazy fog couldn't penetrate far through the flakes. Within minutes of it starting, the snow had obscured the jungle on either side of the convoy.

Ravi Hendrik hated the foul delicate stuff falling around him. He preferred his air clean and thin, up where you could see for miles, and a planet's horizon visibly curved, that place where light was bright and white, sending gold shimmers along oceans and clouds alike. It had been so long since he flew anything now, and he missed it, missed the freedom, missed the purpose flying brought to his life. He was also badly scared by their predicament, which he didn't even mind admitting. It would be a foolish man who didn't acknowledge their situation. If it hadn't been for the years of training and service he'd put in, he would have been strongly tempted to tell Colonel Elston where to shove his convoy. In that respect he almost admired Karizma Wadhai for her outspoken rebellion as much as he despised her for it. When you were in military service, you followed orders; without that, without discipline, there was only chaos. It wasn't as if Elston was deliberately trying to screw up; nobody could fight the kind of crap which St Libra had been dumping on them ever since they turned up. But in Ravi's private opinion, the convoy had been the mother of all bad decisions. And he really didn't like the way they were extended; half their fuel gone, hopelessly inaccurate maps, and a terrain that could throw any obstacle at them without warning.

'I hope they don't find a way down,' he said.

'What's that?' Bastian North asked.

'If we can't get down onto the Dolce, we'll have to go back. Even Elston will have to admit that.'

'True.'

Ravi and Bastian had partnered up to refuel the vehicles. For all he was one of the weird North clones, Ravi considered Bastian an all-right kind of guy. Yes he was rich corporate management, but out here he got stuck in and helped out. So the two of them had hauled the thick dark hose from the truck sledge over to Tropic-2. As always, it never unwound smoothly, so together they had to go back to the big drum it was wound round, and physically turn the thing, clearing frost from the bearings. Not easy when you were wearing as many layers as they were. The exertion made Ravi sweat. Then they'd have a long time standing round waiting for the tank to fill, and he'd chill down, and some of that sweat would start to freeze and chafe.

The fuel icon in Ravi's grid flashed green, telling him the tank was full. He told his e-i to switch off the pump on the sledge. Bastian twisted the hose coupling, and they locked the Tropic's cap.

'Just Tropic-3 now,' Bastian said. 'Then we can get in and have something hot.'

'If there's anything left,' Ravi grumbled.

They both took hold of the hose, and dragged it across the snow to Tropic-3. Ravi could only just make out the headlights. Snow in fog was such a weird combination. Only on St Libra, he thought. It would only be a matter of time before the lightning came, no doubt.

His grid showed him the location of the other refuelling team – Forster Wardele and Leora Fawkes – over at biolab-2. Jay and Raddon were distributing food rations; and it really was rations now; they were cutting back to one main meal a day. Lieutenant Botin and Atyeo were on patrol, providing cover if the creature attacked. Not exactly a huge confidence booster, but better than nothing.

Ravi waved to Winn Melia and Omar Mihambo, who were sitting out the refuelling in Tropic-3. They grinned out through the misty windows, and gave him a thumbs-up. A gloating Omar raised a mug straight out of the microwave. Ravi's three layers of gloves prevented him from showing Omar a rigid finger.

Up on the Tropic's roof, the remote machine gun swivelled smoothly back and forth, as snow built up on the barrel. Ravi wondered just how much use its sensors would be in such a thick fall. The density was unnerving him. It was perfect cover for the creature. He checked one more time that his holster was open, and the Folkling carbine wasn't frosted in, as could happen all too easily in this climate.

Bastian popped the Tropic's fuel-tank cap, and they jammed the hose connector on. Ravi's e-i linked to the Tropic's net. The tank was barely a quarter full. His e-i instructed the sledge's pump to switch on. The icon turned green, not that he could hear it whirring the atmosphere was so clogged. Even his own streamers of breath were invisible in the mist winding around him.

'I don't get this,' Bastian said.

'What's up?' Ravi's hand immediately went to the Folkling carbine. *Damn, I'm on edge.*

'It's not filling.'

'Huh?'

'Look. The tank isn't registering any bioil coming in.'

'The pump's working,' Ravi responded dumbly. He gripped the hose as tight as he could; even through the layers of fabric he should be able to feel the vibration of the fuel pumping along. 'Nothing.'

'Hell, the hose must be blocked,' Bastian grumbled.

Ravi's e-i switched the pump off. 'It'll be the valves on the sledge,' he said. 'The bladders are all linked, but it was a rush job.'

'Isn't everything?' Bastian said.

'Let's check it out.' The two of them tramped back along the convoy vehicles. They were parked in a rough circle again, but not as close as he would have liked, and there were gaps with the MTJs missing. The sledge behind truck-2 certainly looked as if it had been assembled in a hurry. Its simple platform had a framework of thin composite beams fastened together to form cubes; two rows of three, and stacked three high. The beams were threaded with pipes, as if an octopus had snagged its tentacles around them. They all led round to the pump manifold where the two hose drums were attached to either side.

When Ravi got there, the whole kludged-up apparatus was dusted with several centimetres of snow. His e-i quested the sledge's tiny net, and pulled the schematic into his iris smartcell grid. A diagnostic produced a matrix of green icons; all the pumps and motors were working. Then he noticed one of the bladders on the top was completely full, the level that was supposedly emptying into Tropic-3. That was wrong, the bladders were supposed to drain equally from the top down, maintaining the sledge's balance.

'Hang on,' Ravi told Bastian. 'I'll check that.' He started to climb up the spindly framework, aware of how his weight could pull the whole thing over. The sledges had never looked particularly stable to him.

He got to the top and pulled a small torch off his belt's Velcro. The bladder's cap was tight, he had to throw his weight into the twist, then it suddenly turned, and he flipped it open. Ravi hunched over the top of the framework and shone the bright beam into the bladder. 'Ho crap, Bastian, it's empty.'

The net icons in his grid vanished.

Because he was military, because he was alert for danger, because he was nervous of the snow and fog, because he was frightened of the monster stalking them, Ravi reacted instinctively. He pushed his weight forward and pulled his legs up. The top of the sledge was a lot safer than the ground, and *something* was happening.

'Bastian?' he called. 'Watch ou—'

But Bastian wasn't there. Instead, peering cautiously over the top of the bladder framework, Ravi was looking down directly at the monster.

Intuition and training kicked in automatically. He rolled fast, taking himself away from the enemy's view and range. The sight of those lethal blade fingers extending up towards him was terrifying. Then he felt the sledge framework starting to shake. The damn thing was clambering up the side after him. Instinct again: he rolled fast, which took him over the other side. Falling into the snow. It was harder than he'd been hoping, but the thick blanket was enough to soften his fall. Then he was up and running as fast as he could. He tugged the Folkling carbine out of its holster and fired a burst up into the sky. Somehow the monster had killed the convoy net, just like before back at the camp. Nobody knew where he was or what was happening. The shots would warn them.

'Find a bodymesh,' he yelled at his e-i. 'Link to it.'

'Three detected,' the e-i replied in its annoyingly unperturbed voice. Identity icons appeared in his grid. 'Which one would you like?'

'Strongest signal,' Ravi told it. That way the contact would last the longest.

He raced on, knowing the convoy vehicles were behind him, that he was alone out on the river in the pitiful twilight and cloying mist and sound-numbing snow. And somewhere out there was a kilometre-high plummet to oblivion. Trying to work out his bearings – the sledge had been on the side of the vehicle circle nearest the west bank. Theoretically that should mean he was heading for the trees.

'What's happened?' Raddon asked. 'We heard shots.'

'Mine,' Ravi said. 'The monster's here. It got Bastian. I'm outside the vehicles. Don't know where it is.'

'All right. Stay put. We'll find you.'

Ravi looked round wildly. He didn't want to stay put, he wanted to flee. But he knew that was stupid. So he stopped running and crouched down, facing the way he'd just come.

What he thought was the way he'd just come. There were no visual clues. Fog and snow had closed his freezing universe down to a few metres. He levelled the carbine along the route he thought he'd taken.

'I don't know where I am,' he said, not caring how pitiful that sounded.

'Ravi, this is Colonel Elston; Raddon is relaying the link. You must stay calm. We can triangulate on you.'

'Yes, sir.'

Ravi moved the nozzle from side to side, mimicking the remote guns on the vehicles. Then he slowly reached up and pulled his goggles down. Icy air stung his exposed skin, and he blinked away the water that came to his eyes. His iris smartcells switched to infrared. The miasma of snow turned green and blue. He strained, watching, waiting.

There! Right on the limit of resolution, a glimmer of pink, a higher temperature.

'Are any of you near me?' he whispered with his mouth closed.

'Just passing outside the vehicles now,' Raddon replied.

'It's here. I'm about to fire.' He squeezed the trigger with his gloved finger. His whole vision detonated into searing orange flashes. There was the oddest sound amid the roar of the carbine, a loud piercing whine. Ricochet. A couple of rounds had been deflected off a solid surface.

Ravi stood up, and squinted into the swirl of snow. He'd hit something.

It lunged at him. Scarlet sunlight flaring out of the dreary aquamarine murk, the shape of a man. Lethal blades slashing fast. Ravi sidestepped smartly – product of one too many bar fights that had got him into so much trouble back in those glorious days of R&R in Vegas. He countered, using the barrel of the carbine as a club, which went thudding into the monster's side. As soon as it hit, he fired again, sending three rounds slamming into the malleable stone hide. They had no effect. And the monster parried in turn, twirling its own arm like a duelling rapier as the bullet impacts thumped at it. The blades cut deep

948

into the barrel, and the carbine misfired, the explosion wrenching it out of Ravi's grip, snapping fingers as if his bones were formed of ice. The monster's arm recoiled too as Ravi went stumbling backwards, howling at the pain.

There was no strategy now, no careful considered blow and counter-blow. Ravi regained his balance and ran. The monster was death. Immortal. Unreal.

'Where are you? What happened?'

Elston's demands were disconnected, a vague mosquito buzz in his ears, irrelevant to his fight for survival. Ravi plunged forwards, sending the snow and fog eddying away, stumbling on treacherous crumbling snow, scrabbling upright, running again, falling. Onward and onward he went, building distance from the monster, from the convoy, from help. The carbine was gone, destroyed by those diabolical blades; he drew his Weston pistol from its shoulder holster, using his left hand. The safety he had to push off with the heel of his right thumb. The rest of his right hand was useless, throbbing with hot pain.

Blue light flickered faintly through the heavy snowfall. The aurora borealis had returned, and the mist seemed to be thinning, though not the snowfall. Ravi could feel the land rising below his boots as he pushed them through the fluffy snow; he was on the riverbank, climbing up towards the trees. Ethereal blue light shivered again. The jungle shone in front of him, sturdy black trunks encased in their enchanting crystalline shrouds, bound together by an impenetrable lace-like vine webbing that sagged beneath a million icicles. Somehow the aurora had swooped down to infest the knotted branches beneath the canopy, shining out through the speckled air, and projecting long shadows across the silky ground of the slope. The phosphorescence intensified and withered without rhythm, as if spectres were gadding through the trees. And finally there was sound, the dull *crump* of bulky snow streams falling onto the ground.

That was real. Ravi paused in his madcap flight as the aurora dimmed once more. Something ahead of him had moved. Something had shifted mounds of snow. His adrenalin-accelerated

949

paranoia visualized a thousand of the creatures shrugging their way up out of ancient graves to swarm upon him. Instinctively, he knew the forest was danger. An unseen force allied to the monster had erupted from it to strike poor Mark Chitty. Now it was turning its unseen eye upon him.

Locked in a crouch, panicked, not knowing where the greater danger lay, ahead or behind, he activated his infrared function again. His Weston waved about, covering as much of the area as he could.

Heightened senses warned him. He caught a flicker of motion from the corner of his eye, and jumped out of the crouch, diving down the slope. As he landed on his belly the end of a bullwhip branch came slamming down out of the iridescent aether. It struck him square on the back, hammering him deep into the snow.

The blow was everything Ravi imagined a traffic smash would be. Incapacitating. Pain peaking towards overload. Disorientating, stretching time out to make that single moment resonate on and on. Sheer disbelief was his only other companion amid the torment. The tree! The tree had hit him. It was alive, just as Mark warned them.

Ravi moved his head a fraction, seeing the branch lift elegantly, twitching as light as a cat's tail flick as it began to gather itself back into a tidy horizontal coil.

He'd heard his armour vest creak and crack as the branch hit him. That had saved him. But the armour was fractured now. He'd never survive another strike. And the trees were legion.

Keep going. Just as he'd done all those years ago above New Florida. The odds were impossible, then as now. That didn't matter. You did your best, you didn't give in. Always, you gave your all, just as the military did throughout history.

Ravi Hendrik heaved himself up out of the imprint his body had made. His yowl of anguish and determination was loud enough to wrench the fog and snow apart by itself. They'd have heard that back in Abellia.

He couldn't even stand erect. His back was too badly damaged.

The bodymesh showed a dozen small puncture wounds where the fractured armour had jabbed into him. He hobbled off down the slope again, a fearful Neanderthal retreating. His head was craned back so he could watch for—

Another bullwhip branch came lashing out of the jungle. Ravi vaulted as best as his crippled body could manage, and the branch tip sent up an angry plume of snow centimetres behind his ankles. He slithered on, rolling and bouncing down and down until he banged into something solid enough to stop him. Glanced up to see what the obstruction was.

The monster looked down at him, haloed in a sapphire glow from the aurora borealis. He'd bumped into its legs. A desperate twist wasn't quick enough. Those five dreadful blades came stabbing down. Ravi screamed in agony as one slid straight through his right upper arm, grazing the bone, pinning him to the crusty snow.

His left arm came up and round as if fired by an electric shock. It put his pistol muzzle five centimetres from the monster's inflexible face. He tugged the trigger. For once the bullet seemed to have some effect, punching the head back. He shot again. Again! A bright-orange spark erupted from the thing's brow as the bullet *piiinged* away into the night, and it swayed back. Ravi fired once more.

The blade withdrew, allowing the monster greater movement so it could avoid the relentless point-blank shots. Madness and fury shunted Ravi up to his feet. Following it. Shooting, always shooting. The dark head weaved from side to side, trying to elude the impacts.

Then, as Ravi knew would eventually happen, the trigger clicked uselessly. The Weston's chamber was empty. He and the monster paused for a second, staring at each other. Ravi could have sworn the thing was as startled as him by the crushing fall of silence. He did the only thing he could now, and threw the Weston at it before turning to run for his life. As he did the five blades came whistling towards him in a furious arc. Two razor tips caught his shoulder, ripping through his parka, slicing the flesh outside the rim of the armour. Ravi barely registered the new pulse of pain. So much of his body hurt now.

He ran on. His grid was still dead. All links down. Fire burned into his spine. He ignored it. Blood drizzled down his arm from the blade wounds. He kept one foot swinging in front of the other, nothing else mattered, kicking the loose top-snow aside. Running he didn't know where, just not up the slope to the trees.

It was behind him. Close. He could hear the snow being thrust apart as those inhuman feet pounded after him.

A deeper darkness grew ahead of him, and the mist churned around his legs, sliding forwards as if propelled by some natural urge. The snow was unrelenting, though sudden gusts began to buffet it up around him. Ravi *knew* then.

Another ten paces brought him to it. He was sliding precariously on naked ice as he came to the precipice. Fog glided over the edge, sweeping down into the black canyon to accompany the flurries of snow spinning giddily in the ragged updraughts.

He risked a glance over his shoulder. The monster was four metres behind, its arms coming up for the last, fatal embrace.

'Fuck you,' Ravi shouted with the full defiance that only a Wild Valkyries flyer could possibly muster. He turned, stiffened, and jumped—

*

The search party found some splatters of blood. In itself a miracle given how fast and thick the snow was falling.

Elston had dispatched two squads: Botin, Atyeo and Leora in one; Omar, Raddon, and Jay in the second. He allowed them to go outside the ring of vehicles, but not out of link range, pitiful though it was.

Back in the vehicles, Dean, Miya, and Ken tried desperately to clear the rip that had killed their net.

Links were bodymesh to bodymesh only, so everyone got to see through Botin's eyes as he shone a torch on the blood spots at the bottom of the riverbank. Flakes of snow landed softly on them, slowly obscuring the last evidence of Ravi Hendrik's existence.

Botin's team was a hundred and twenty-three metres from the vehicles, putting their link strength down to ten per cent.

'Can you see anything?' Elston asked.

'No sir,' the lieutenant replied. 'There's a lot of marks in the snow here, and three spent nine-millimetre casings. This is where we heard the last shots from. There was obviously some kind of struggle.'

'Lieutenant!' Leora called.

Attention switched to the Weston pistol she was looking at, lying in the snow with its barrel already covered in fresh flakes. She picked it up. 'Chamber's empty. He fired every round.'

'Is there any indication where they are now?' Elston asked.

'Tracks leading south along the river, sir,' Botin said. 'Two sets. They were heading for the canyon.'

'Do not pursue,' Elston said. 'I am not having you venture outside link range. Fire a flare.'

Botin pointed the stumpy flare gun into the air, and fired. There was a glimmer of pink-white magnesium somewhere up amid the heavy falling snow, but it was barely brighter than the electron-blue flickers of the aurora borealis that swam among the trees.

'He's not going to see that,' Atyeo said.

'He's not alive to see anything,' Leora muttered. 'Let's not kid ourselves here.'

'Stay on station another five minutes,' Elston ordered. 'Fire a flare every minute. If Hendrik doesn't show up after that, fall back to the vehicles.'

'Yes, sir.'

It took another fifteen minutes before Dean and his team managed to reboot the meshes and processors, bringing the convoy's net back on line. Pings fired out, coded for Ravi's body-mesh. It never responded.

Elston was startled to see Bastian's icon slip up into his

restored grid. Raddon led Omar and Jay over to the truck's sledge as soon as the green emblem appeared for all of them to see. Omar got down on all fours, and peered past the runners. 'Hey, buddy, didn't expect to see you again.'

'Has it gone?' Bastian North asked. 'Please God, it was terrible.'

He told them how he and Ravi had been having trouble with the sledge pumps, how they'd gone over to investigate, how he'd heard some sort of commotion on the sledge. He'd glimpsed the monster emerging out of the veil of fog and snow just as the net crashed, and dived for cover under the sledge. He'd stayed there, hearing gunshots then silence, too frightened to move. Then finally, when the cold was biting hard into his flesh, the convoy net had come back on line.

The Legionnaires escorted him back to Tropic-1, where he stripped off his parka and armour, and started to warm up. His face was badly bruised, some grazes leaking blood. 'Smacked into the side of the sledge as I went for cover,' he told them. By then Botin and his squad had come back. Everyone knew that Ravi was dead like all the rest before him.

*

Morale reached its nadir that night. Talk was the same in each vehicle. Every time the convoy stopped, the monster struck. They were only safe when they were moving, and now they couldn't. With the canyon presenting an insurmountable barrier, they had to wait to see what the MTJs found. So they sat in their vehicles, unable to sleep, barely able to see the headlights on either side, knowing their net was vulnerable to the alien, listening to the servo whine of the remote gun, knowing its targeting sensors couldn't penetrate the icy murk anyway. Waiting for dawn, waiting for the MTJs to return, waiting for the hated snow to lift, waiting for some intimation of hope.

Sunday 5th May 2143

The snow eased off some time after midnight, allowing sensors to stare further across the frozen river. There was no sign of Ravi's body, but then no one was expecting that.

Pale pink dawn brought tendrils of fog creeping out of the jungle again, slithering down to the river and over the frozen waterfall. As everyone was having their meagre breakfast allocation the shortwave radio crackled into life. It was Antrinell, his voice drifting in and out amid the hissing static of far-off storms. 'There's a way down. We're about fifteen klicks west from you. The canyon wall dips down, and there's a rockfall at the bottom. We can make it down there. Camm and Darwin are already halfway down, marking a route.'

'Stay there,' Vance radioed back. 'We'll come to you.'

They couldn't raise MTJ-2.

'This radio is not like a link,' Olrg told Vance. 'The atmosphere does weird things to short wave.'

'If we can reach one MTJ we should be able to reach the other,' Vance complained.

Olrg's face showed how much he disagreed, but he didn't contradict his colonel outright.

'They were supposed to check in every two hours, as well,' Vance said.

'We had the first scheduled call from MTJ-2 yesterday

afternoon, sir, they confirmed everything was okay, then the weather closed in, so we assumed that blocked them.'

Vance wasn't convinced. If it had been the other way round, and they'd lost contact with Antrinell, he would have simply waited for the MTJ to come lumbering back at the appointed time a day later. But Leif and Karizma, that was different. He told his e-i to open a secure link to Lieutenant Botin.

'I want you and Atyeo to take Tropic-1 and follow MTJ's route east. See if you can find any trace of them.'

'Sir. They set off last night. The snow will have completely covered their tracks.'

'I know. I just need to confirm that they stuck to the plan, and they didn't encounter the alien. Drive for a couple of hours, then come back.'

'Yes, sir.'

*

It started snowing again before the Tropic left, thick gentle flakes drifting slowly out of the dark vermilion sky. People saw the snow, and watched the Tropic roll steadily away along the top of the canyon, and grumbled among themselves. The morning's news about finding a way down to the canyon floor was offset by the latest development. Searching for the missing MTJ meant yet more delay, and they were parked where they knew the monster lurked.

Angela watched the Tropic vanish across the rumpled snow-scape as she stood behind biolab-2's sledge. It seemed to be her drudgework destiny to distribute meal packets from the dwindling stocks they were towing along. Off to her right, Olrg and Chris Fiadeiro and Raddon were clambering all over the bladder framework on the truck's sledge. There was some kind of fuel problem, which was where the monster had caught Ravi and Bastian last night. Judging by the swearing that carried on the still air, it was a major hitch.

She piled twelve meal packets into the bag Omar was holding

open. They were due for biolab-1, their allocation until the convoy was down on the canyon floor.

'See you in a bit,' he said, and headed off to the mobile biolab.

Angela picked up her own equally heavy bag, and started walking over to the tanker. Her e-i told her Ravi was questing her on a secure link. She stood perfectly still, a chill that was never part of the atmosphere creeping along her arms and shoulders. 'Open the link,' she told her e-i.

'Angela?'

'Who the fuck are you?'

'Angela, it's me, Ravi, I swear.'

'Where are you? What the hell's going on? We thought the monster got you.' Her e-i couldn't get a lock on where the link was originating from. Whoever had established it knew a lot about how to subvert the net-management routines.

'It tried. I got away. I can't move, Angela. I'm stuck over the edge of the canyon. It thought I'd fallen over, but there's a ledge ten metres down on the waterfall. For pity's sake get me out.'

'All right. I'll call Elston, we'll get you back.'

'No! No one else. You come alone. Please.'

She checked round to see if anyone was watching her. Snow fell softly onto the vehicles, adding to the twenty-centimetre layer that had accumulated last night. Warm vapour spewed silently out of the fuel-cell vents, and the remote guns maintained their mechanical vigil.

'No fucking way,' she said. 'I don't know who you are. That thing took out the net again last night. We're compromised. You could be it. I'm calling Elston.'

'No! I can't trust anyone else. Angela, you're the only one who survived it before. Nobody else has. I know I can trust you. And we both know someone is sabotaging the convoy. They're helping the alien for fuck's sake. Damnit, I'm scared, and I'm cold, so cold nothing even hurts any more. I don't think I can last much longer.'

'No.'

'Angela. The trees are alive. That's what Mark Chitty meant. It's the bullwhips. They went for me last night. The goddamn branches lashed out and smacked me about like I was a hockey puck. It knows that, the monster knows. The jungle is helping it, the jungle is killing us, Angela.'

It was crazy; his delusion was doing the talking, she knew it was. And yet ... The MTJ on the ravine. Something striking Mark. A dozen little mishaps. All explained, if you believed.

Angela had seen the monster. Had struck at it with her own hands. Felt it was real, solid beneath her skin; something the rest of the human race had sneeringly insisted was wrong for twenty years. She had been punished for that, for not giving in and doubting herself. 'The bullwhips?' she whispered. If they were part of the creature's evolution, part of its hatred, connected to it, then the whole world was against them. She tipped her head back, looking for the enfeebled red star buried behind the darkling clouds. *Sirius, too?* She could believe it. She could believe anything of that devil. In her mind was the image of it waving its arms wildly, urging something on to attack Mark.

'Yes,' Ravi said. 'One of them caught me on the back. Angela, help me. But steer clear of the trees.'

'All right. Give me ten minutes. I've got to work out how to do this.'

She dropped her bag of food off at the tanker, chatting briefly to Forster and Roarke who shared the driving. Then went back to Tropic-2, taking a long curving walk around the circle of vehicles. There was a big gap where MTJ-2 and the newly departed Tropic-1 had been parked next to each other. And the snowfall was growing heavier, reducing the remote guns' sensor coverage. She told her e-i to access the solid memory cache she kept in her pocket. Scanning down the list of Zarleene's dark software she found a program that would do the job she needed, and sent it into the convoy's net.

The remote gun on Tropic-2 kept on sliding from side to side, but now its sensors saw nothing. Angela walked up beside the battered snow-caked Land Rover and dropped the cache behind the fat rear wheel. Above the wheel arch were a couple of heavy printed bags that were strapped to the side of the Tropic. She opened one and pulled out a mini-winch – the so-called wall walker – a powered spool of superstrength tape. According to the inventory she had made back in Wukang, the bag also had some self-anchoring pitons. She found them eventually, and stuffed them in her big trouser pockets.

Disembodied voices from the team trying to sort out the fuel sledge drifted through the snow. She took one last look round. No one was visible. 'Turn off my bodymesh link to the net,' she told her e-i. 'And activate the cache.' The cache's link started using her identity code, so the monitor routines saw her as being in the Tropic.

Confident the heavy snow would conceal her from any casual human glance, she hurried out through the middle of the broad gap in sensor coverage,

Beyond the vehicles where snow ruled the air, the landscape of the snow-covered river was disconcertingly similar no matter where she looked. Her bodymesh kept a link open to the inertial guidance module she'd bought in the Birk-Unwin store in some life long ago. It was her compass now as the flakes swam round her and the sinister jungle mist oozed past her legs.

Angela had gone only about a hundred metres along the river when she realized someone was following her. She wasn't surprised. The whole Ravi being safe thing was a big stretch. Two options, this was either the monster or the saboteur. Either way, she was ready to settle this.

In a swift motion she pulled the carbine out of its chest holster and flicked off the safety catch. Footsteps crunched on the loose snow, coming closer. Angela tensed, ordering her e-i to link to the carbine's target sensors. This time she had the codes, Elston had assigned them to her himself. Green and purple graphics slid into her iris smartcell grid, smooth as neon fish.

A dark figure emerged from the curtain of snow. 'Son of a bitch,' Angela grunted. It had been a trap! The thing was humanoid, with an all-over featureless, shiny skin like crude oil that the snow slithered off. Which wasn't quite how she remembered it. The hands were ordinary, too, without any sign of the terrible blades. 'What are you?' she yelled defiantly as she brought the carbine round.

It was the strangest thing, the figure held up a hand, finger extended in a universal gesture asking for a moment. The slick skin shivered, flowing in narrow currents, draining away from the head and congealing into the same parka and waterproof trousers as everyone wore on the convoy. Then a gloved hand reached up and unwound the long blue knitted scarf, exposing the face.

Angel let out a startled cry.

'Hello, Angela,' Madeleine said. 'Whatever are you doing out here?'

Angela pointed the carbine at the sky as if she was performing a military salute. After the anxiety of creeping away from the convoy, the anticipation of treachery, it was almost too much for her to be confronting this girl. She felt the moisture build behind her eyes, a symptom of her profound longing. And she just couldn't keep the farce going any longer, not here, not now. 'Hello, Rebka,' she blurted. 'That's . . . if you know your name is Rebka.'

'Of course I know my own name, Mother.'

*

Angela was out jogging that fateful morning back in 2119. She liked to go out early, before the sun got too high and the clammy humidity from Oakland's bayous crawled across the flatlands to starve her lungs of oxygen. Before baby Rebka woke and the first of the day's inevitable mini-crises began. It was a time when she felt like she was far from her troubles. A false time, then, but one she needed.

She ran along the laser-straight stony dirt tracks the compactors had cut out. Over the last couple of years the hulking Massachusetts Agrimech machines had laid out a massive grid, linking the farm's vast fields for the tractors and drillers and harvesters. For those two years they'd enjoyed good harvests, the sweltering sun and abundant water allowing them to plant four crops a year. Saul had already filed the viability assessment with the Governor's office, and they were waiting to be able to claim another eight thousand acres that lay to the north. The land there was wetter than the acres they already farmed; there would have to be some elaborate drainage dykes. Saul, of course, had already planned them out – pumps, levels, ditches. Work was the poor dear's way of escaping from their worry over Rebka. She didn't begrudge him that, their life was tough enough now.

One of the big green and blue tractors rumbled towards her down the track, and she skipped up onto the stickgrass verge, not wanting to give the auto a moving obstruction to cope with. She was proud of the job all the Massachusetts Agrimech machines had done, but some of the software was definitely due an update. As Noah was constantly reminding her. The machine passed her, huge tyres splashing through the puddles in the ruts, and she smelt bioil in the warm fumes shimmering out of the vents. The fuel cells weren't burning cleanly. They'd have to pull the tractor in for maintenance before the end of the month.

Angela ran along field 17, which was just stubble now the combines had finished harvesting the Syntel breadmaize. It was due to be deep ploughed, then they'd plant it with Ni-hi barley. The chequerboard of their other fields stretched out beyond the mile-wide expanse of stubble. That was one thing she couldn't get used to, the gentle rolling lands of Oakland weren't *landscape*. She longed for mountains, some cliffs, a few valleys; something other than the interminable everglades and sluggish rivers and the oh-so-flat ground baking beneath its vast brilliant-sapphire sky.

She came to the corner of field 17 and turned left. The track here was overgrown, leading to one of the storm-pump stations at the end of the dykes. Half a kilometre away, and parallel to the track was Route 565, the freeway which cut clean through the county all the way back to Yantwich, the state capital, eighty klicks away. She could see the farmhouse now, three hundred metres away from the barns and Qwik-Kabin stack where they'd been living for the last two years. The house was half completed rooms, half black scaffolding sticking up into the sky, with automata clinging to it. They were still waiting for the tanker of flooring raw the contractor had promised ten days ago. Not that Angela had the energy to chase him like she should be doing. Not these days; tending Rebka absorbed every moment.

Sweat was trickling down her face, soaking the light-grey vest as she turned onto the final stretch leading back to the yard. When she'd started exercising again it'd been hell for the first few weeks, every muscle had been stiff, she got headaches, her body kept demanding the mass of food she'd consumed first during pregnancy then when breastfeeding. But she'd pushed herself, ignoring her aches. Now she was almost back to the kind of shape she'd been in before falling pregnant, flat stomach, flabby thighs just a horrific memory, puffy face deflated so that great bone structure returned to prominence. She and Saul had even been having some sex again, on nights when they weren't holding some worried vigil over Rebka's cot. Nights when she didn't just burst into helpless tears of pity and rage at the fate which the universe had dealt her.

Blue strobes caught her eye. An ambulance was racing along the freeway. Her heart jumped, and she stared intently at the Qwik-Kabin stack. Her netlenses were back in the bedroom. Jogging was a refuge from the pain of Rebka. She only left the house for forty-five minutes. Even Saul could cope for forty-five minutes. Surely?

Angela picked up the pace, flying along the track.

Sure enough the ambulance turned off the freeway at their drive, and started bumping down the long ribbon of crushed stone to the yard. She almost beat it to the Qwik-Kabin stack. The paramedics were already going through the door when she rounded the corner of the grain-drying shed and pounded through the puddles.

Half of the ground-floor lounge was given over to medical equipment, effectively turning it into a paediatric care ward.

There was only one cot-bed, made of stern metal with big retractable wheels. One of the paramedics was bent over it. Angela couldn't help the fast intake of breath at the sight. Saul was hovering beside the paramedic, looking all grief-stricken and pathetic.

'What happened?' Angela shouted.

And Saul was walking towards her, his arms held up in placation. 'It's all right. She was having trouble breathing, the monitor fibres said her oxygen intake was falling. I called them before it gets critical.'

She pushed her husband aside without bothering to reply or censure – as she'd been doing far too often of late. She knew that was wrong, that this wasn't his fault, but he was all she had to vent her anger on.

'It's okay, baby,' she cooed at the little shape lying on the cot-bed's mattress. Far too little for an eight-month-old, wearing a one-piece grow with pretty cartoon flowers. Rebka had tubes and data fibres snaking in through the grow's collar, and sleeve cuffs, and ankle bands. A grey-silver dialysis module sat on the mattress beside the infant, relieving her beleaguered kidneys. Frail, sickly Rebka's wrinkled face was screwed up as she wiggled in discomfort, a thin gurgling emerged from her mouth. She was too weak to cry properly. The oxygen line in her nose hissed lightly.

Just the sight of her daughter struggling for breath was enough to make the tears well up in Angela's eyes.

'She's still getting enough oxygen,' David, the paramedic said. Angela knew the whole county's emergency services staff by their first name now. 'We don't need to intubate,' he assured her.

'All right. Okay,' Angela said, dabbing at her tears, desperate for the good words. 'What do we do?'

'Her lungs' oxygen-processing capacity has been in decline for a while,' Alkhed said; the other paramedic who had been studying the monitors. 'We'll take her in and they can find out why.'

Angela squeezed her eyes shut. Take her in. Back to Palmville County General; the paediatric wing that she knew better than her own half-built house, its too-dark blue paint, the breezy lumin-pictures of anthropomorphized animals on the walls, the bed linen with its bees and dinosaurs, the parents' lounge: Hell's own waiting room with its dead-eyed weepy occupants where she didn't belong.

'Let's go,' Angela said. She held her jaw rigid, trying to get a grip on her tumultuous emotions. Another problem. Another vulnerability for that tiny body to deal with. She'd thought Rebka's lungs were out of danger, that the steroids were working now the respirator had been disconnected two weeks ago.

There had been no indicator; the pregnancy had gone well. Tests, and there were dozens, always showing mother and daughter were doing fine. New Florida might be a new American world, but it didn't lack for medical facilities, and Oakland was a fully fledged state now, with senators back in Washington. Palmville County General had an effective professional paediatric department. The Howard family's medical insurance, taken out with an Earth-registered company, was top-rated, and fully paid up.

It was only after the birth that they got an inkling of the dread that would befall their beautiful daughter. Rebka's jaundice, perfectly normal for babies, developed into full-blown liver failure that required a genemod pig organ transplant. That was the first of a deluge of medical calamities the child underwent. Each one was skilfully treated by the hospital and its devoted team. But every time one was sorted out, another disorder would appear. Their accumulation had led the doctors to suspect a systemic failure they hadn't managed to diagnose.

Most worrying to her distraught parents was her lack of growth. At nine months she was five and a half kilograms, and barely fifty-three centimetres high. But with her hypoplastic left heart syndrome, polycystic kidney disease, protein deficiency resulting in poor muscle development, weak immune system, and various allergies, below-the-curve growth was inevitable, the chief paediatrician warned them. Fortunately, her neurological development was unaffected. Saul had sworn she smiled once, only ten days ago.

David and Alkhed wheeled the cot-bed out of the door, with

the paraphernalia of critical medical support equipment resting on the shelves below the mattress. It was designed to fit in the ambulance's treatment bay. Once it was locked into place, David started plugging the systems into the vehicle's power and data sockets.

Angela picked up her bag that was kept permanently packed and ready beside the front door. Saul took his, then they were both in the back of the ambulance, with David tending the young patient, and Alkhed in the front, supervising the auto.

At least they didn't have to use the sirens, though Alkhed did keep the speed at a steady one-twenty kph down the freeway. It was early, so there wasn't much traffic yet. The familiar signs and farm roads slipped past the blackened windows. Angela stared at them blankly, refusing to let her utter misery rise up lest it drown every last rational thought in black despair. She hated the helplessness, the pathetic gratitude every time the hospital paediatricians countered a new crisis. Hated asking herself what was next, because that meant she was expecting some new problem to manifest when she should be willing her darling sweet child to get better. But her greatest hatred was directed right at the heart of an uncaring universe that could inflict so much suffering on a life so precious and innocent.

They drove past the off-ramp for Stamford, and Angela automatically reached for the bag. She was a mess, wearing a fitness vest and shorts, hair all tied up in bands, sweat-soaked socks in muddy trainers. There was a fleece jacket in the bag, some sports pants; netlens glasses and audio interface, even some cash, along with toiletries in a tatty old washbag. She blinked at that bag in surprise as she rummaged through looking for socks. It was probably her oldest possession, the one she'd brought with her from New Monaco with the smuggler's bar of soap.

That life was gone. If she recalled it at all now it was like the memory of a zone drama. It was hard to believe she was that billionaire princess. She'd got over it, that had been her triumph where she suspected so many of her kind would have failed; started to build a real life, not a fabulous life, but an adequate one that had potential. After all she had centuries to develop her stakeholding on a new planet into an empire that one day even her father might have approved. And sweet soppy Saul was a pleasant enough companion.

It had been perfect. Truly, two years of newlywed bliss while the farm flourished, they had friends, and most nights were spent hurrying to get naked in bed.

'What the hell is that?' Alkhed asked.

Angela looked past him through the ambulance's windscreen. Outside, the sun seemed unnaturally bright. Then she realized that something else was searing through Oakland's cloudy sky. Trees along the side of the freeway developed a second shadow that started sliding round quickly. Something brighter than a solar flare streaked down out of the heavens away to the south, dropping below the horizon.

She looked at Saul, whose jaw had dropped open.

Then her e-i was clamouring for attention. The HDA was officially declaring a Zanthswarm alert in the New Florida system. Evacuation procedure files were being downloaded to every citizen. She was too shocked to say anything.

'We have to go back,' Saul said. 'The ... the farm. It's everything we have. We've got to get ... to get—'

'Sorry, man, I ain't going anywhere,' Alkhed said. 'I'm taking this bus to collect my family. We've got to get out of here, off this whole planet.'

'We're not going back,' Angela said, ignoring Alkhed and staring directly at Saul. 'This is a Zanthswarm. Do you understand? In a day there will be nothing left. Nothing! It's over. There is no farm, not any more.'

Daylight changed again, with a bright glare sweeping through the eastern sky like slow-motion lightning.

'What do we do?' David cried in a frantic voice. 'We have to get to my house.'

'No fucking way, man,' Alkhed snarled. 'We're picking up my people.'

'My girl is pregnant.'

'I'll drop you off close.'

'You're on the other side of town.'

'Stop it, both of you,' Angela said. 'We've got days before it gets critical. The Thunderthorns will be flying soon, they'll knock the Zanth rifts out of existence. They are there to give us all the time we need to get to the gateway.'

'I'm getting my family,' Alkhed said stubbornly.

'You're going to drive us to the hospital,' Angela said. 'Both of you parked your cars there. You get into them and drive to your families. That way we all get what we want.'

'No,' Alkhed repeated stubbornly. 'You can ride with us if you want, there's room, but I ain't taking no detours.'

'Screw you, man,' David yelled.

'I'll drop you off, I said I would.'

Angela didn't have time for this shit, and Saul wouldn't be any use. He'd carry on with trying to be reasonable. They were past that now. She knew exactly how people reacted when their lives fell apart in a single moment. Down at the bottom of the washbag were some tox sacs, for when it all got too hard at the hospital, when she couldn't stand to watch her baby swamped by tubes, when five doctors were bent over her working frantically. She picked them out and swung her arm round, bumping three sacs simultaneously against Alkhed's exposed neck.

'Hey!' Alkhed yelped. He was clawing frantically at his neck while Saul and David stared at her wide-eyed. 'What the fuck, man? What . . .? Oh, whoh.' He started fast blinking. 'That is . . . whay?' His head started to flop about as if his neck muscles had lost all their strength.

'Angela!' Saul said.

She gave him her cold look. 'Yes? You want to go to his house? You want to get thrown out when his family realize there isn't enough room for all of us, and we have to keep Rebka's support units going? That what you want?'

Saul coloured bright red. 'No.'

Alkhed slumped forward over the steering wheel.

'Help me get him out of there,' Angela said.

Together David and Saul pulled the semi-conscious, tox-delirious man out of the driver's seat. Angela climbed in, and switched the ambulance to manual. 'David, I'm dropping the two of you off at the hospital.'

'Okay,' the paramedic said nervously.

Angela grinned savagely at his meek tone, and switched the siren on as she twisted the throttle, accelerating up to one-fifty. Alkhed's sunglasses were lying on the dashboard. She put them on even though the clouds were building and she could see the grey sheet of rain advancing towards Palmville. It was a good choice. A few minutes later the first nuclear explosions detonated five hundred kilometres above them as the Wild Valkyries squadron began their impossible task of intercepting the Zanth chunks descending on the planet. The clouds diffused the violent light-bursts, but even their grey underbellies glowed with monochrome brilliance from the explosions.

The ambulance hit the outskirts of Palmville with its neat rows of white bungalows sitting in their lakes of lush green lawns. Cars were pouring out of the prim estate roads, charging onto the feeder road to the freeway. People didn't care about speed limits any more. Traffic lights were being ignored as the fusion bombs continued to explode above the atmosphere. Three junctions were badly snarled, Angela had to drive up on the sidewalks to get round. The air was jammed with the sound of furious horns. Heading into town was easier than it was going to be getting out.

The rain arrived at the hospital at the same time as the ambulance. Angela drove straight to the staff car park and braked. 'Out, David!'

For a moment he looked like he wanted to argue. But now Saul wasn't showing any sympathy. The rear door popped open, and Saul shoved Alkhed's dreaming body out onto the wet asphalt. 'Good luck,' Saul yelled at David as a heavier belt of rain swept across the cars. He was given a venomous glare in return.

Angela didn't wait. She slapped her hand down on the door close button, and twisted the throttle again. They went racing out of the car park, back onto the main arterial road leading back to the freeway.

'How's she doing?' Angela demanded.

'Angela! You attacked Alkhed.'

'He was being an asshole, and we don't have the time. Now, how is she?'

Saul took a breath and went over to their daughter. 'Okay I guess. Her lungs are still getting enough oxygen into her blood.'

'Good. We're going straight to Yantwich and the gateway, it's only sixty klicks. Now listen, if she starts getting critical, you'll have to deal with it, okay?'

'I'm a farmer! We needed the paramedics, we needed David and Alkhed.'

'We've been looking after her for eight months. Us, just as much as them. You've learned the basics, they gave us those emergency courses, now fucking concentrate. This is the mother of all emergencies. You have to keep her alive until we reach Miami and a hospital.'

'I . . . yes, yes, okay. Shit, Angela, you toxed Alkhed out of his head.'

'I did what I had to. This world is ending, Saul. The Zanth is swarming, and there's no happy ending. But the three of us, our family, we're going to survive it.'

'I get it. I do now. I really get it. Drive, get us onto the freeway. Go on, get us to Miami. I'll look after her until then, I promise.'

'Okay then.'

With everyone driving on manual, the road was thick with slow-moving bad-tempered traffic. 'Screw this,' Angela announced, and swung the wheel. The ambulance bumped over the central barrier and started off the wrong way along the other side, lights and siren blazing. The few cars heading towards her dodged to the side. Several other cars on the outbound side pushed over the centre and started tail-gating her.

Three times she grazed cars coming the other way. Then they

were past the suburbs, and more and more people were using both sides of the road to get to the freeway. There wasn't a cop car in sight. They slowed to a crawl.

Angela looked round, seeing the slim thread of the raised freeway a couple of kilometres ahead. They were rolling forward at walking pace with the rain bouncing off the asphalt, smearing everyone's lights. The siren and strobes made no difference, no one was budging, no one giving up their place in the giant crunched-up queue.

Something dropped out of the base of the clouds, a lump of debris, Zanth or Thunderthorn – it was impossible to tell. Flame and black smoke followed it down. It hit the ground over where she knew the Conolley farm was.

That decided it for her. She turned the wheel sharply again, and they went bouncing over the verge and down into the drainage ditch.

'Angela!' Saul moaned.

'This is a rural area, ambulances are designed to get across virgin country here. A ditch isn't any problem.'

She began to accelerate, with the wheelbase straddling the stream trickling along the bottom of the grassy ditch. Memories from long ago bubbled up to help her; a thousand-kilometre rally she and Shasta had taken part in on Nagpur. Driving big luxury 4x4s through the Slapan plains and into the Donrital Mountains where the majestic Antrodyiils soared on the thermals. It had been tough but she had mastered the fundamentals of off-road driving.

After five minutes they were at the freeway, and she aimed the ambulance at the slope where the dyke curved round, engaging torque management, sending the vehicle grinding up the spike-grass to lumber out onto the slip road's verge. Cars scattered at the unexpected appearance of the bigger vehicle, and she jammed them into a gap, ignoring the honking horns and screamed insults. At least no one had shot at them yet.

On the freeway, the pace picked up, though people were still driving too close. The lightstorm above the planet, up where the

970

valiant Thunderthorns were flying, was increasing. They were still thirty klicks out from Yantwich when the first real shoal of debris punctured the base of the grim cloud. Whatever it was, the mass had started to split apart in the atmosphere as impact shocks pummelled away at its cohesion. Thirty or forty fireballs thundered down, drawing long filthy contrails behind them, their seething heads rippling out shockwaves. The concussions in the lower, denser atmosphere were fracturing the material at an increasing rate, splitting them into new flocks of lethal incandescence. They smashed onto the fields on the south of the freeway, kicking up huge plumes of soil and water. Angela saw a combine harvester flung thirty metres into the air, tumbling in a slow twirl. Then the shockwaves and sonic booms swept across the road.

At first Angela thought something had crashed into the side of the ambulance. It was shoved violently across the road, forcing her to swerve frantically to avoid the low crash barrier at the side. In front of her she saw two smaller cars flip over on their sides. Several did strike the barrier, one corkscrewing round, the others bouncing back with big dints in the side. A van smacked into the offside rear corner of the ambulance, sending it shuddering and skidding sideways until she fought it back level.

Nobody stopped to help those that had stalled or crashed. A couple of kilometres further along, when the injured had staggered out of their crumpled-up cars to shelter on the side of the road, they waved urgently at the ambulance. Angela kept on going.

The clouds were breaking up, taking the rains away from Yantwich. She could see downtown's meagre cluster of skyscrapers on the horizon now. But the clearing sky was plagued with fluctuating light from the fusion bombs and a deeper more persistent scarlet radiance from rifts that were expanding despite the best efforts of the Thunderthorn pilots. New Florida's own sun was slowly losing its dominance as the rifts grew to engulf space around the planet. Okeechobee had vanished altogether.

More battle debris came hurtling down in flame. Angela's e-i reported it couldn't find any net to link to. And the traffic was relentless. Each on-ramp was jammed solid. Cars at the front were simply shunting their way into the traffic zooming along the freeway. More and more she was seeing cars in the other carriageway heading in the same direction as her.

'Angela,' Saul called. 'Her oxygen rate is falling.'

Angela swore as a big pick-up truck cut her up. A blazing comet arched over the freeway, spitting out a barrage of gravel-sized shards that hit the asphalt like glowing bullets. She heard two thud into the ambulance's bodywork. The car on her left veered sharply. 'Deal with it,' she shouted back at him.

Signs for the gateway were starting to appear along the side of the freeway. She let out a little gasp of relief when she saw they only had ten kilometres to go. The disintegrating comet landed on a timber merchant a kilometre off the freeway, sitting in its own everglade clearing. She saw it in the rear-view mirror. The whole site was obliterated in a second, vanishing beneath a wave of flame and soil.

Eight kilometres from the gate a big convoy of armoured personnel carriers and giant Terrain Jeeps were racing down the carriageway taking them away from Yantwich. Red strobes and dazzling headlights heralded their passage; the cars using that carriageway had to get out of the way fast, pushing their way back onto the right side of the freeway.

When she passed the lead Terrain Jeep she saw the HDA emblem on the side and felt like cheering. The convoy just kept coming, there were hundreds of vehicles, carrying thousands of troops. A little further on, HDA vehicles were parked up on the verge, marines with long automatic rifles were poised on both sides of the freeway, watching the traffic. All the drivers started to calm down, slowing and keeping a reasonable distance. The horns fell silent. Civilization and order had returned.

It took another nine minutes to cover the last five kilometres to the gateway. The sky was darkening now, a malaised red shimmer from the rifts was obscuring the sun. Angela knew it would never recover. The only white light they saw now came from the nukes, whose blasts were increasing in frequency. Smoke and fine particle debris clotted the lower atmosphere. Material kept raining down from above, most of it bursting apart as it arrived sketching billowing black smoke trails, spreading smaller splinters wide, smoke lines multiplying.

The HDA had taken complete control of the approach to the gateway, channelling vehicles fleeing from the city into the stream that poured off the end of the freeway. Checkpoints and barriers had gone, there was a single dividing line of red steel bollards down the middle. The ambulance slowed to a crawl in the queue that stretched along the last kilometre. And still HDA troops and vehicles came through from Earth, rushing to help where they could.

Five minutes of the ambulance crawling forward at walking pace, and they passed through the gateway to Florida where the stars sparkled in a sky that was still two hours before dawn. The gateway district in Weston, due west of Fort Lauderdale, occupied the whole Shenandoah district south of the 595, with big arterial roads feeding in from the 595's interchange with the 75. Here, it was state troopers on traffic duty; they were a lot more excitable than the HDA marines on the other side, waving their guns around like high-school kids at a game as they ordered everyone onto the 595.

Angela's e-i told her it was acquiring the transnet, and she pulled out available routes. The ambulance's auto warned her there were strict traffic protocols in force, and all vehicles were being advised to switch to auto for correct management. The greater Miami traffic macromesh was clearing the freeways of all local traffic, which given the time of morning was relatively easy. Priority was for HDA convoys coming in from their local bases and heading to the three gateways; and to get the refugees clear. The primary objective already activated by the Governor was to keep the traffic flowing, preventing any kind of jam around the gateway. The other two New Florida gateways in greater Miami at Kendall and Boca Raton were undergoing identical traffic controls. Freeway off-ramps were being closed, forcing the refugees north where designated reception and onward transit centres on abandoned military bases were being opened ready to process however many of New Florida's twenty million inhabitants managed to get out. Compassion aside, the one thing the district mayors and state Governor wanted to avoid at all costs was the refugees to swamp the existing greater Miami area.

The e-i found the best local paediatric centre, the Dan Marino Centre attached to the Cleveland Clinic Hospital. It sat on the side of the 75 just four kilometres south of the gateway. The metamesh and state troopers and highway patrol cars had sealed off the access roads to the southbound 75.

She requested clearance, declaring a medical emergency. The metamesh AI refused permission for the route. A file came back saying medical facilities were being made available at the reception and onward transit centres. All refugees were required to use them.

'Hell!' Angela exclaimed. The freeway restrictions already covered the whole of the 95 up to Palm Bay. By the time she got there the prohibition would likely be extended. Westbound, the 75 was open to refugees; she could get across the National Preserve to Naples where there was a reasonable hospital. But that would take hours. And the Dan Marino was minutes away. Minutes.

'How is she?' Angela asked.

'The resuscitator is on,' Saul said in a frightened voice. 'I think I did it right, her blood is still showing as oxygenated.'

'All right. We're going to a hospital. Hang on.' She was all for smashing past the squad cars parked across the road, except the troopers had guns and the way everyone was wired they'd shoot without much provocation. Instead she told the auto to take the 75 west.

'What are you doing?' Saul shouted. 'We should go north. There's a centre an hour away at speed.'

'And that's going to have a specialist unit which can treat Rebka for sure?' she spat. 'Shut up and let me deal with this. I have to make a call.'

It wasn't an access code she'd ever expected to use again. The mystery was why it was still even in her address cache. She really should have wiped it sometime in the last eight years. Really, she should. Her e-i made the call.

'Angela?' Housden asked. 'My God, it's been for ever. How are you? Where are you?'

Angela hardened her face, fighting the lump in her throat. He'd taken the call. Actually taken it. She'd been bracing herself for his e-i to tell her to go to hell. Not all New Monaco residents were filth after all. 'I'm in Miami. I'm sorry, I wouldn't call unless I had to. Housden, I need help.'

'Miami? Shit, Angela, be careful. A Zanthswarm has been declared on New Florida, I only found out about it a couple of hours ago. That whole planet is going to come knocking down your door.'

'Housden,' she said. 'I'm one of the refugees.' All she could think was: two hours ago? How did he know then? She hadn't even started jogging two hours ago. So much of New Monaco life she had forgotten.

'Oh,' he said. 'Right. Of course, I should have guessed. A new world. That's damn bad luck.'

'Housden, I need to get to the Dan Marino Centre at the Cleveland Clinic Hospital, but the National Guard are blocking the off-ramps. Do you know anyone in the Governor's office?'

'No. But the family machine can swing it, you know that. What do you need?'

Angela studied the map her e-i was throwing across her netlens glasses. 'I need to get off the 75 at the Glades Parkway.'

'It's done. Or it will be by the time you get there. Send me your vehicle licence code.'

'Thank you, Housden. I mean that. You were my last hope.'

'Hey, it's nothing. Ah, the file's here. Angela, that's an ambulance. Are you injured?'

'No Housden. It's my daughter. I've got to get her to the doctors.'

'You had kids? Aww, Angela, that's great. I have two myself now. We should get them together some time.'

He didn't understand, she raged in silent mortification, he knows my name, but he doesn't know how life is lived in the real world. 'She's sick, Housden, really sick.'

'If she's your daughter she'll pull through. There was never anyone tougher, Angela. That's what I always adored about you.'

'Goodbye, Housden. You were the greatest.'

'Goodbye, Angela. Good luck.'

Angela drove steadily in the pre-dawn light. This section of the 75 was called Alligator Alley, a broad six-lane freeway with a big drainage waterway running along the northern side, forming a border to the vast Everglades Wildlife Park.

'Who was that?' Saul asked quietly.

Angela supposed she'd been talking out loud rather than the usual throat whisper; he'd have heard her half of the conversation, picked up the emotional tone. 'Old friend,' she said with a dry mouth. 'I used up my last favour.'

'Seriously? You know people who can order state governors around?'

'It's not like that, not at their level. Everything is reciprocal.'

'But—'

'Just leave it. Rebka needed him, okay. Nothing else matters.'

There were five highway patrol cars parked to block the Glades Parkway off-ramp, and two big personnel carriers from the National Guard backing them up. Angela slowed the ambulance to a halt by the first patrol car. An officer in armoured uniform was on the side of the road waiting for them. She lowered the window.

'Ms DeVoyal?' he asked.

'That's me.' And she could imagine Saul's face behind her, his hurt and confusion.

'I've got orders to escort you to the Dan Marino Centre,' the officer said in a voice which told anyone listening that he couldn't quite believe what was happening.

'Thank you.'

'You must have a very important patient in there, the order came direct from the Governor's office.'

'My daughter.'

That seemed to satisfy him, though it was clear he wanted to know why she was in the driver's seat. 'Okay, follow me.'

*

Four days later, on the day HDA command shut down their New Florida operation and pulled their last people back through the gateways, Angela and Saul were sitting in the office of Dr Elyard, Dan Marino's head of genetics. The doctor came in wearing a white clinic coat, looking vaguely harried, the sign of all department heads. He was a short man who was putting on a lot of weight, a receding hairline exposed a wide brow that was pricked with sweat despite the air-con.

He sat behind his blue retro-Coulsmith desk and gave them a tight smile. 'We had Rebka's genetic assay back yesterday from the Beijing Genomics Institute. Sorry it's taken a while for us to review it. Half of my junior staff are away volunteering at the refugee centres. However, I've been over the results myself. I must say I've never seen anything like it.'

'In what way?' Saul asked.

The doctor took off his frameless netlens glasses and started polishing them. 'The team treating Rebka at Palmville County General were correct, there is an underlying systemic problem. We determined it when we sequenced both of your genomes as well.'

Angela felt the blood leave her cheeks. After they'd sorted out Rebka's respiratory issue with a temporary oxygenator shunt, taking the strain off her little lungs, the Dan Marino team had gone after the problem of her multiple disorders with considerable vigour. Even Angela's gold star insurance didn't cover all of the tests, she had to pay the excess out of a secondary portfolio in which she'd invested the money from her New Monaco jewellery. 'What's wrong?' she asked coldly.

'Mrs Howard,' the doctor said. 'Excuse my bluntness, but we've never seen a genome like yours before. You're a one-in-ten, aren't you?'

'Yes.'

'What?' Saul grunted.

'A one-in-ten refers to a specific artificial sequence,' the doctor said. 'It reduces normal ageing factors in a human body after puberty.'

'How did that happen?' Saul asked dumbly.

'It's a germline process,' the doctor explained. 'We also noticed some considerable improvements made to your organ functions and the immune system. You have quite a genetic profile, Mrs Howard.'

'What's that got to do with Rebka?' Angela asked. 'Hasn't she inherited all of them?'

'That's the problem, I'm afraid. You must have been a very early generation.'

'I am.'

'Ah. You see, the sequences you were given can be added correctly and without any developmental problems to your DNA during germline modification. However, despite their viability, your additional sequences are extraordinarily complex. They don't get passed on intact, like the gene for red hair or height or bone density, all the components that decide what makes up a person. The artificial one-in-ten sequences, especially pioneering ones like yours, can be subject to replication instability during a natural ova fertilization process. I take it Rebka was conceived naturally, and didn't receive germline correction?'

'She was natural,' Angela whispered.

'And therein lies the real problem. I'm surprised your original genetics consultant didn't warn you about this.'

'You mean Rebka is contaminated with screwed-up DNA?' Angela said.

'That's a very harsh interpretation. Certainly a lot of her current complaints can be traced to unusual DNA components. If you'd had her assayed just after conception, then some genetic treatment could have corrected the problem by rebuilding the sequences. It's expensive, obviously, but you know that. And that initial treatment would have provided an opportunity to equip her with more modern sequences, less prone to . . . mistakes.'

'My genes are the problem?' Angela asked.

'In this case, I'm afraid so. Yes.'

'Okay,' Saul said in a shaky voice. 'What do we do? How do we treat this? How do we cure the damaged genes?'

'Mr Howard,' Doctor Elyard said. His posture was all sympathy, ready to explain the really bad news, the news parents were always in denial about. 'You have excellent insurance. That means we can make Rebka very comfortable here at Dan Marino. Some of the systems provided by Palmville that help sustain her are somewhat crude; there's nothing wrong with them obviously, but we can replace them with less obtrusive versions. Really, it will make her time a lot easier, a less stressful experience for both yourselves and her.'

'Palliative care?' Angela barked. 'That's what you're offering us? Fucking palliative?'

Elyard spread his hands wide, offering complete understanding. 'I do know how difficult this is to accept—'

'No. I get that you see this every day. But this is *my* daughter. I'm not accepting palliative anything. I want to know what can be done to cure her.'

'Mrs Howard . . . I'm sorry, we simply don't have that ability.'

'Fine. Who does?'

'You must understand, what you're asking for is extremely rare, and actually prohibited in most states, including Florida. It is also extremely expensive; your insurance will certainly not be able to begin covering it.'

'So there is a treatment? What is it?'

'Effectively, to correct so much genetic distortion you would be looking at a variant of the so-called rejuvenation process. From what little I know it's still at the experimental stage. People who have allegedly undergone it are reluctant to have the process publicly verified; financial necessity means they're all billionaires.'

'But it can be done?' Saul asked.

'We're talking about resequencing the DNA of every cell in her body. It would take years and the cost is astronomical, even for someone so small.'

'Fine,' Angela said. 'I need a list of places that can perform the treatment.'

'Mrs Howard, I suspect you would know that better than I. Even introducing your sequences to a zygote would not be permissible under current Florida law. You really ought to consult the team that ... created you.' He smiled blankly.

'If I go to them, how much is it going to cost?'

'I really don't know. It's not my field.'

'Bullshit. It's exactly your field. Take a wild guess. After all, I'm hardly going to sue if you're wrong, now am I?'

'I really cannot recommend this course.'

'Disapproval noted. How much?'

'Apparently, for a full-grown adult, the cost of complete cellular resequencing is just short of a billion dollars. So for someone Rebka's size, I would estimate – and this is only a very rough approximation – that you'd be looking at a figure in excess of seventy million dollars.'

'Shit,' Angela grunted. She'd been praying for two million, which she could just about manage if she liquidated everything in her portfolios. But she'd been bracing herself for five or seven, in which case she'd go pleading and begging to Housden; Shasta too, if she had to, dignity was the least of her worries. But seventy plus? There was no way she could get that much together, not in a few months.

'I'd like to talk to my husband, please,' she said.

Dr Elyard seemed quite relieved to let them have his office in peace. Saul stared at his wife for a long time before saying: 'You're a one-in-ten?'

'Yes, Saul,' she said. 'I'm a one-in-ten.' The worst thing was she knew he'd have to drag out this whole conversation, demand to hear her confirm each fact. He couldn't just put it together in his head and accept it like a grown-up.

'So ... how old are you?'

'Well not twenty-one, that's for sure. More like your age. Don't worry, I'm not that much older than you.'

'Then your mother never did own Massachusetts Agrimech? It was always you, wasn't it?'

'Oh for— Saul, focus! I'm not the issue here. Rebka is. Our daughter is very ill. Concentrate on that.'

'I can't,' Saul said miserably. Tears were starting to fill his eyes. 'It's over.'

'You heard the doctor,' Angela said harshly. 'She can be cured.'

'Seventy million?' he laughed bitterly. 'Even if Mom and Dad sold everything they had, they couldn't raise more than ten. I know, I used to be part of the firm.'

'We have to get it ourselves,' she said. Already she was thinking how to grab that kind of money, and who from. There were all types of financial scams she was familiar with from her time helping her father. Now she had a specific purpose, it was like a whole part of her mind had suddenly switched back on again. The sharp, calculating part belonging to Angela DeVoyal, the New Monaco princess who'd been missing for eight years. Missing, right up to the moment when the highway patrol officer asked if that was her name. Angela DeVoyal was smart and dangerously ruthless, and would set about obtaining what she wanted without a moment's hesitation.

Oh, how I've missed being me. How stupid I've been wallowing in misery and self-pity when what I should have been doing was taking charge and finding solutions.

'How?' Saul asked.

Angela despised the cloying desperation in his voice. 'Now listen to me. It is our daughter who needs this. And you need to know there is nothing I will not do to get her that money. Nothing. All I need to know now is if you're going to help me, because I can do this by myself if I have to, but it will be easier with your help.'

'I . . . of course I'll help.'

'Good. I'm telling you here and now that you're not going to like what's got to be done. If you don't want anything to do with me after this, then that's fine, because she'll be getting treatment by then and nothing else will matter.'

'I said I'd help. Of course I will. She's my daughter, too.'

'Yeah. Right.' But already she could see the shock and uncertainty in his eyes as he started to worry what she was talking about.

'How did you get that kind of genetic treatment originally?' he asked. 'I thought it was half transnet conspiracy theory.'

'My father was very rich. I'm not. Not any more.' She smiled without any trace of humour. 'And the people who are responsible for that, responsible for me not having treatment for Rebka's zygote, they're the sons of a ball-less bastard who are going to be paying to make this right.'

*

And so they had. The money from Abellia's Civic Administration account had transferred successfully to GiulioTrans-stellar. From there it wound its convoluted way to an anonymous account safe on True Jerusalem, where Saul's orthodox sister had taken Rebka, and where nobody but the most devout Jews were permitted. It was there she'd been scheduled to undergo the gene therapy that would repair her screwed-up DNA and turn her into a normal girl who would have a life to enjoy.

Angela had seen that transfer happen with her own eyes, had risked her life, had spent twenty years in jail so the scam would never be uncovered. So when she saw that young version of herself dishing out meals in the mess tent at Abellia Airport she'd been hit by a shock so profound it actually sent her into fugue. There could be no mistake, her own features were all there, mixed in with Saul's kind eyes and darker hair. Her daughter.

Alive. Healthy. Happy. And on St-fucking-Libra in the expedition as a waitress.

Such a thing was not a coincidence. Oh no.

Angela looked at that lovely face, still framed by the scarf as the snow fell around them. 'How?' she pleaded. 'How can you be here?'

Rebka gave her an impish smile. 'Somebody had to keep an eye on you, Mother. Constantine thought I was the best one to do it.'

'Constantine? Constantine North!'

'Yeah. Now don't get mad. He knows everything. He knows you and Dad pulled a scam in Abellia.'

'How?' she said faintly.

'Because he realized something was seriously wrong about the official version of the massacre. He had to know what really happened to his brother that night, and to do that he had to find out about you. His people did a proper harvest, not the stupid bodge job the police did when you were arrested. He knows you didn't kill anyone that night.'

'He knew I'm innocent? A *North* knew that?'

'Mother, you stole a hundred and eight million Eurofrancs from them.'

'For you! To make you better. So you could have a life.'

Rebka's eyes started to water. 'I know. There is no way you'll ever understand how much that meant to me when they told me. Hearing you existed was incredible, but then learning what you'd done, the sacrifice . . .'

'Please,' Angela said. 'Can I hug you? I haven't hugged you for twenty-one years. Letting go was so hard.'

Rebka opened her arms wide, and Angela almost fell into the embrace.

'I never knew,' Angela said. 'I never knew if the treatment worked. Never knew if you were alive. Nothing. I just hoped, that's all. Hoped for twenty years. You were my daughter, if anyone was strong enough to survive it would be you.'

'I love you, Mother.'

Angela put the girl at arm's length again, not letting go of her shoulders as she studied that hauntingly familiar face. 'Look at you now. So pretty.'

'Yeah? Well, I had a good role model.'

'The treatment worked? You're okay now? Your father thought you'd died. I knew he was wrong.'

'Yes, Mother, the treatment worked. The geneticists at Jupiter did a good job. And I'll be able to have children without complications.'

'Wait! What? Jupiter?'

'Yes. As soon as he found out about me, Constantine had me brought to the habitat.'

'Why?'

'He wanted to be sure my treatment was a success, and Jupiter has the best technology anywhere. One of Constantine's projects is examining how our brains can be enlarged and enhanced. He's hoping it'll give us the smarts to defeat the Zanth. That's why their genetics division is up there along with the physics department.'

Angela gave a brief snort of contempt. 'Whatever. You're alive and you're here with me. I'm sure the rest of it is going to piss me off no end when I get the details, but, this, this moment was worth everything.'

Rebka produced a mirror grin. 'You mind telling me why you're out here?'

'Oh shit.' Angela turned to look along the frozen river. The falling snow was still too thick to see more than a few metres. 'Ravi's alive.'

'What? Where?'

'The waterfall. Come on.'

They set off, still holding hands. 'How did you know I was out here?' Angela asked.

'I've got a smartmolecule tracer on you.'

'I should have guessed. And I suppose that thing you're wearing is from Jupiter as well?'

'Yeah, it's a metamolecule cloak, it can modify its appearance and function. You saw the armour variant. I wasn't sure if the monster was still creeping round out here.'

'Does it keep you warm?'

'Oh yes.'

'Lucky you. So what do you need it for? I've been trying to figure out why you were here since I saw you.'

'You really knew? As soon as you saw me?'

'Of course I knew. You're my daughter. You've got some of Saul in you, too. Thank God. That's what made it so easy to recognize you back at Abellia. That was a hell of a shock you gave me, let me say.'

'Saul. My dad, Saul?'

'Yes. He's not a ... Well, let's just say he's a bit softer than me. You'll like him; he's quite a charmer. I suppose Constantine found out he's still on St Libra?'

'Yes. I want to meet him.'

'You will. I already have. It ... didn't go as well as I'd hoped. He's paid the same time price as me, possibly even worse. Whatever Constantine did to snatch you off True Jerusalem he covered by faking your death. But there's nothing would make Saul happier than to see you. I know that much.'

'Twenty years, Mother. I don't know what to say.'

'It was worth it.'

'After I found out, I kept asking Constantine to break you out of Holloway. He said no, it would draw too much attention.'

'Fucking Norths.'

'They're not so bad. Not the ones I know.'

'Yeah? What else does he expect you to do on the expedition?'

'Capture the monster.'

'You are not to go anywhere near that son of a bitch. You have no idea how bad it is.'

'I have a very good idea. And I'll be safe, you saw the armour. I've got some weapons with me as well.'

'Really? I hope they pack enough firepower to wipe out every tree on the planet.'

'What are you talking about?'

'Ravi told me the trees hit him, the bullwhips. That thing controls them somehow.

'I will be crapped on from heaven.'

'Yeah. So don't go getting all youthfully overconfident on me. We're a long way from safe.'

Angela's inertial guidance module warned her they were closing on the waterfall. Confirming the proximity of the canyon, the snow was churning as the updraughts flowed over the edge. She told her e-i to ping Ravi again. He hadn't responded to her last few attempts to contact him.

'If you've got any Jupiter sensor technology, now would be the time to use it,' Angela said. 'We're kind of vulnerable on the lip like this.'

'Yeah, Mother, got that.'

Angela admired the tone – it was pitch perfect her own. They edged forward carefully until they found the top of the waterfall, where the ice curved down sharply and the wind began its mournful whistling. She got down on all fours and peered over, trying to keep the feeling of vertigo supressed, and not really succeeding. All she could see was the frozen water dropping away and the snowflakes fluttering away to a roseate infinity.

Her e-i told her Ravi was answering her call. 'Why do you keep dropping out?' she asked.

'Bit difficult staying awake. Sorry.'

'Okay, switch on your bodymesh. I need to get a fix on you.'

Her e-i reported a full lock. He was about forty metres away.

Angela and Rebka shuffled along the rumpled ice until they were directly above him. His bodymesh emission was coming from seven and a half metres directly down the ice face. Angela lay flat on the ice and stared over the edge. The massive frozen watercourse plunged away below her. It wasn't smooth like the river which fed it, there were folds and snarls in the ice, like a churning white-water rapid captured in mid-flow. Straining against the pink gloom and skipping snow Angela could make out a silvery blob on one of the flatter seracs. It was a miracle he hadn't slipped off.

'Gotcha,' she said. 'Is that a thermal bag?'

'Yes,' Ravi said. 'Only reason I'm still alive.'

'Okay. I've got a mini-winch with me. You'll have to clip it on to your belt. Can you do that?'

'Yes. I'll try. Thank you, Angela.'

She used the self-anchoring pitons to secure the little spool on the rock-hard ice. The tape unwound, and Angela guided it down. Watching the clip twirl around, swaying about in the wind, was like a bizarre version of fishing. Every time she moved her arm, trying to put the clip near Ravi, it would bob away. And Ravi didn't seem to be able to move his arm much. She had the alarming thought that she'd have to climb down and help him.

'Got it,' Ravi said.

The mini-winch whirred smoothly, pulling Ravi up the undulating wall of sharp snags. He hit a few of the prominences as he came, making Angela wince. Then he was level with the top, and she and Rebka grabbed hold, pulling him onto the river.

'For fuck's sake, Ravi!' Angela exclaimed. The thin silvery survival bag was down round his waist so he could fix the tape to his belt. In the pink Sirius light his parka was almost black it was soaked with so much blood. The sleeves were torn, showing blue skinseal foam that had been sprayed on wounds. He was shaking badly, though she suspected it wasn't entirely from the cold. Bruised eyes flickered open, and he gave Angela a gracious grin. 'Thank you.'

'Get him back into the bag,' Rebka said. 'We'll have to drag him back to the doc.'

'Angela?' Ravi asked weakly. 'Who's that?'

'It's all right, it's only me,' Angela said. She hurriedly pulled the bag back up to Ravi's collar, and tugged his parka hood into place. 'You need to vanish before we reach the convoy,' she said softly to Rebka. 'I don't want us to have to explain why you're out here.'

'Okay.'

'But for crap's sake keep alert for the creature.'

They took hold of Ravi under his shoulders and started dragging him along. He moaned at the pain then quickly lost consciousness again.

'So why did you come out here alone?' Rebka asked.

'Ravi asked me to, he said he didn't trust anyone else. I was the one who survived the monster once before.'

'Ah. That's something I definitely want to hear about.'

'You will. Later.'

When they were fifty metres from the circle of vehicles, Angela gave Rebka another too-brief hug. Then Rebka's clothes morphed into armour again. Angela watched the girl walk off into the heavy snowfall, feeling incredulous and elated in a way she had no right to be, given where they were and what they still faced. But ... Her daughter was alive and knew her. The sensation of relief was phenomenal.

She started dragging Ravi again. He'd shut down his body-mesh, so she couldn't access his suite of medical monitor smart-cells, but she didn't really need a grid display to know he was in a bad way.

When her guidance module put her thirty metres from the convoy vehicles she linked to the net. Her e-i switched off her cache identity then called Elston. A last instruction wiped the restrictor program in the remote gun on Tropic-2.

'What are you doing? How did you get outside the vehicles?' Elston demanded.

'I'm bringing Ravi in,' Angela replied, smiling at the anger she knew would be gripping him. 'He's badly hurt. Warn the doc.'

'Ravi?'

'Yes. He's alive. Just. Now are you going to help or just sit there and shout a lot?'

*

Vance Elston had personally led Sergeant Raddon and Leora Fawkes out past the vehicles. Sure enough, they'd found Angela dragging Ravi Hendrik along in a survival bag.

Even Dr Coniff had given the injured pilot a worried look when she and Juanitar pulled the thermal survival bag off him. 'Fluid,' was all she said for the first five minutes as they went about appraising the extent of his wounds.

Juanitar applied a collar of intravenous shunts around Ravi's neck, pumping plasma and artificial blood directly into his depleted circulatory system. Then he sprayed a solvent on the skinseal patches. As the artificial scabs peeled off, blood began to pump out of the wounds on his upper arm. Juanitar clamped them, and started to repair the muscle and veins.

'The spine has received some significant damage,' Coniff announced. 'The armour saved him from the worst, but what the hell did this do to him?'

'That was the trees,' Angela said. She was pressed up against the wall of the biolab's cabin, watching intently as the two medics set about tending Ravi.

'What do you mean, trees?' Elston asked sharply.

'He told me before he lost consciousness. The trees attacked him last night, specifically the bullwhips. The monster controls them somehow.'

'Ridiculous,' Vance insisted automatically. As he said it, he knew the dread of doubt, that such a thing might very well be possible in such a vast strange universe that the Lord had created for His children to live in.

Angela just laughed and pointed to where Dr Coniff was extracting a long fragment of the armour vest from the livid flesh of Ravi's back. 'So apart from being hit by a bullwhip branch, what else do you know can do that?'

Vance glanced at Coniff for help, but she simply raised an eyebrow and returned to the blood oozing from the wound. 'You said you found him on a ledge of ice on the waterfall. He could have landed on his back.'

Angela simply shook her head, a smug smile on her face. She'd won and she plainly knew it; even he was giving the possibility serious consideration. Something had struck the MTJ, knocking it off the ravine. Something had knocked Mark flying. And the others, the ones they'd lost, had they been consumed by the forest? If the creature was truly the planet's guardian, anything was possible. 'I'll walk you back to the Tropic,' he said.

'Sure.' She stepped into the door chamber, wrapping the damp scarf back around her head.

Outside, the snow had stopped; wisps of high cloud drifted slowly northwards, entwined with the ribbons of the aurora borealis. Red Sirius shone from the zenith of the sky, a pink dazzle-speck with radiative stipples so that to the human eye it appeared to be a sink point, consuming the light from the atmosphere.

'Okay,' Vance said. 'So how did you get out there without me knowing?'

'Just a net glitch.'

'You know that means I can't trust you now.'

'Did you ever?'

'It broke our net again last night.'

'Wasn't me. I've just risked my neck bringing Ravi back.'

'Yeah, about that: why? Why you, and why go alone?'

'He didn't trust anyone else. I'm the one who survived it before, so I'm the one he turned to for help. Ask him if you don't believe me.'

'How did he call you?'

'A secure link. I tried to locate its origin, but Ravi knows his black patches.'

He stared at her with mounting exasperation. 'Didn't you consider the risk? Going out there by yourself?'

'There were only three options: it was Ravi, it was the saboteur, or it was the monster itself.' Her hand came up to pat the carbine in its chest holster. 'Either way, I was ready.'

'I should take that away from you.'

'Really? I think Ravi made a smart call. Who else in this convoy can you really trust? Seriously? Karizma?'

'Don't.' Vance held up a warning finger. 'You know you should have called me.'

'Whatever. Are you going to keep on denying the monster can control the trees, too? That piece of news has already flared down our little net.'

'We will take adequate precautions from all possible threats.'

'Stop talking corporate bullshit. You have to warn people very clearly that the jungle is extremely dangerous, especially to anyone outside a vehicle. You also have to launch a comm rocket.'

Vance looked past the Tropic they were approaching, seeing the ice-cased trees standing tall at the top of the bank. His perspective played traitor for a moment, showing him an army of native elementals poised ready to charge down on his besieged command. 'I know how to handle this.'

'I hope so. If you don't, we're all dead.'

They reached Tropic-2, and Vance opened the front passenger door. Corporal Evitts was sitting in the driver's seat, wearing one of the hats Angela knitted, broken arm strapped to his chest. His expression was apprehensive. 'She's not to leave unaccompanied again,' Vance ordered. 'You are her escort on all duties.'

'Yes, sir,' Evitts barked.

'Angela.'

She paused, half in the Tropic.

'Thank you for getting Ravi back. It's the first time anyone has survived. That's good for morale, no matter what else came out of this.'

She nodded. 'Second. He's the second to survive.'

'Yeah, sorry. The second.' As soon as she was in the seat he closed the door. Even now, Angela was a complete enigma to him. Every instinct he had was to assign a secret agenda as the reason for going out there by herself to find Ravi. He stared at the edge of the jungle, admitting to himself that perhaps he was just too scared to believe. If it was true, and the trees themselves were being roused to overwhelm the convoy . . .

His e-i told him the convoy net had just acquired Tropic-1. He saw its location slip up into his grid, and frowned. The Tropic was driving along the Lan towards them barely six hundred metres away, which was all wrong, it should still have been driving along the lip of the canyon.

'What happened?' he asked Lieutenant Botin over a secure link.

'We followed the canyon as ordered. About a kilometre after we lost line of sight on the camp we saw a route cut through the jungle. The buzz saws on an MTJ make a very distinctive trail. We drove down it, and it just looped back to the Lan.'

'They've gone back to Wukang,' Vance realized. 'Karizma saw her chance, and left us.'

'The MTJ doesn't have enough fuel to get that far, sir,' Botin said.

It only took a moment for Vance to figure it out. He turned to stare at the remaining truck and its sledge of bladders. Olrg, Chris, and Raddon were clambering over the truck's framework, examining the bladders it was carrying. His e-i extended the link to include Olrg. 'What was wrong with the fuel bladders?' he asked.

'Two of the bladders were empty when they were showing full,' Olrg said, looking round from the framework. 'There was a glitch in their sensors. We're checking the rest of the bladders to make sure they're registering correctly.'

'Would the missing fuel be enough to take an MTJ back to Wukang?' Vance asked.

'Yes sir, probably. But the MTJs weren't carrying any bladders.'

'No,' Vance said. 'But the truck and sledge we left behind was.'

'They didn't transfer all the truck's fuel over when we abandoned it,' Botin said.

'No, Karizma left a couple of bladders full. The truck is on her route back. They'll strap the bladders to the MTJ and drive straight for the camp. We cleared a track through the jungle to reach the river, so it'll be a relatively clear run back for them.' Vance had to take a moment for his rage to peak. He was incredulous that any HDA personnel would mutiny. Not only that, by taking away an MTJ with its buzz saws and snowplough blade, they'd actively put the rest of the convoy in harm's way. Their actions verged on anti-human treason.

Vance walked over to the truck. Olrg was standing apprehensively beside it. 'Is there any more fuel missing?' Vance asked.

'No sir. It looks like just the two bladders on the sledge.'

'All right.' Vance told his e-i to quest a ringlink that included everyone remaining in the convoy. 'I regret to announce that MTJ-1 has mutinied, and made a run for Wukang. We still have MTJ-2, which will be sufficient to get us through the small amount of jungle we need to traverse between the Zell tributary which is our target, and Sarvar. Consequently, we are moving out in fifteen minutes. All drivers begin your vehicle checks.' Vance closed the link and stamped off to biolab-1, too furious to say anything more. He didn't even ask the Lord for wisdom and guidance, which was remiss of him, but the Lord would understand the frailty of human reaction in the face of such outrageous provocation.

Monday 6th May 2143

The blizzard had lasted for three days. On the morning of the fourth day, Saul Howard fed a couple of fresh logs into the stove in the centre of the bungalow's lounge. He'd been up several times in the night to add more logs, making sure the fire didn't die out. As a result, the room was still warm enough that he didn't really need the blanket he'd wrapped round his shoulders. But one look at the snow piled up against the glass of the big glass patio door made him want to shiver. And he didn't like to think how much was sitting on the roof. The bungalow's net was telling him the PV panels weren't generating any power at all. They were living off the regen cell store.

Of course there was precious little light during the day, red or otherwise, to generate any electricity. He walked over to the sliding door, feeling the cold radiating from the glass. The occasional pastel shimmer through the driving snow told him the aurora borealis must still be active above the dense blanket of dark cloud.

'It won't last much longer,' Emily said.

Saul turned to see her standing in the doorway. 'No,' he said. 'There can't be much snow left, for one thing.' He was convinced they were getting the worst of it, living next to the sea.

'I'll put the kettle on. We'll have some porridge for breakfast. That'll help.'

'Sure.' He glanced at the stove, seeing the new logs starting to catch with plenty of hissing. Spapine wasn't the best wood to burn, not that they had any choice.

'How much wood have we got left?' Emily asked.

'Mindreader,' he accused. 'Another week's worth, at least. I filled the spare bedroom. The blizzard will definitely be over by then.'

'Then we'll have to go scavenging again. There's not much food left in the village.'

'I know.'

'I wish Brinkelle would start producing this clone meat she's supposed to be brewing.'

Saul winced. That rumour was now set in stone among the residents of Camilo Village.

Emily started pouring water into the kettle. Saul sat on the settee, watching the snow flash past outside. He felt useless. Unable to do anything. Waiting passively. Terrified he was going to let his wife and children down, and unable to show his fear. Just like the previous time his life had fallen into crisis, twenty years ago.

That had been the last time he'd spoken to Angela, too, the last time he'd ever looked into her eyes. Even then he didn't recognize the gorgeous, beloved girl he'd married just three years previously.

The last time . . . until she'd frightened the crap out of him by turning up back at the start of February. But even then she'd been a stranger, twenty years on and she was the same person who'd replaced his wife during the New Florida Zanthswarm. The one who had dispatched him to St Libra to help with her crazy plan. The one he'd said yes to, because he had nothing else to offer his tiny tragic Rebka—

*

Saul sat in a corner seat of Maslen's café that morning, as he did every morning at the same time since he received the message, while wretchedly chirpy old-fashioned music played through the speakers. The seat gave him a position close to the emergency fire

995

door, and provided him a view of the front door so he could watch who came in. Angela insisted on things like that; craft, she called it – straight out of a cheap zone spy drama. What she expected him to do if Bartram's security troops ever came crashing in had never been clarified.

But he did it anyway, because that was all he had left, the hated plan that she'd come up with. His whole life had become something he was watching from a safe dark corner inside his own head, looking out at the world through the big windows that were his eyes, making his body act out the part he'd been assigned, speaking the lines from the script she'd given him.

It was mid-morning, and Maslen himself was still bringing trays out from the kitchen at the back of the café. The most delicious pastries and cakes were arranged artistically on the shelves in the glass counter, each one an individual mini-masterpiece. Saul stared at them, wanting to go and buy some more of the glazed fruit tarts. One more wouldn't hurt him. He'd put on a lot of weight since he'd moved to Abellia. He did nothing but his work at Abellia TeleNet during the day, accepting overtime in the unsocial hours that no one else wanted. There was nothing else for him to do, certainly he never felt like exercising. The doleful part of his mind which seemed to be guiding him these days couldn't see the point. Every time he went back to his tiny flat in the converted harbour warehouse he'd sit and access some book; biographies of historical figures were a favourite, or at least mildly interesting, he was working his way through American presidents and Russian rulers.

He stirred his espresso, debating whether to get another tart when they came in. Angela looking wonderful in a short emerald-green summer dress, thick blonde hair barely contained in a long braid with leather straps. She still looked like a teenager, exactly the same as she had that day he'd first seen her in the Massachusetts Agrimech offices. If anything she appeared even younger now; it wasn't achieved solely by her one-in-ten genetics, she possessed an uninhibited enthusiasm, her mouth curved permanently in a wondrous smile at the freshness of the universe she

996

beheld. It wasn't fair that she could appear so vibrantly youthful, when the best he could muster these days was sullen morbidity.

There was another girl with her. Another of the *girlfriends*. Another whore. This one was probably twenty for real, had darker skin and thick hair, wearing a thin white cotton top and a matching skirt with a lot of midriff exposed between them.

They were laughing together, talking in excitable whispers. Clearly the best of friends, and had been for years. Angela ordered a lemon tea, while the other asked Maslen for a smoothie. Then they teased each other about the pastries before sitting down together at a window.

Saul did his best not to stare. Not that it would make any difference. All of the male clientele in the café were snatching looks when they thought the girls couldn't see. Nobody was going to notice one more sad loser dressed in a company overall, not in this universe.

After the laughter and happiness had tormented him for too long, the second girl got up and gave Angela a hug and a kiss. 'See you back at the car in an hour,' she said, and went out with a swirl of her white skirt and a gust of flowery perfume.

Angela sat for a couple of minutes more, finishing her tea. Then got up and left. Saul waited, then followed her out.

The streets in the old town were narrow and short, with abrupt junctions and even smaller side alleys between big industrial buildings. He walked down the length of a disused warehouse with big boards announcing a developer was going to transform it into loft-living apartments. Angela was waiting for him in the third loading bay, a dank cave of concrete and sagging composite panels where not even Sirius's blue-white glare shone much light.

They looked at each other for a long moment. Saul saw her youthful vitality façade had already been abandoned, exposing the cold ruthless woman which the shell of deceiving flesh encased. She gave him a curious gaze. 'How are you coping?' she asked. She even sounded concerned.

'I'm here. I got everything ready just like you said.'

Angela came over and put her arms round him, not showing any disappointment that he didn't respond. 'I never doubted that you'd manage what was necessary, but that's not what I asked.'

'How the hell do you think I feel? You're my wife, I love you, and you're doing this.'

'This what?'

'Bartram. The *girlfriends*. Whatever you had to do back in London to convince them you were the right sort of girl.'

'Oh, Saul, darling, you've got to stop punishing yourself like this. It's only sex.'

'Only sex,' he said, worried he was going to start crying in front of her, the way he did most nights when he was all alone in his pitiful flat. 'Do you have any idea how much that hurts?'

'I'm the one having to fuck a hundred-and-nine-year-old man, so yes, I think I understand how terrible this is for you.'

'I'm sorry. It's just . . . this is so hard for me.'

Her grip softened, and she studied his face intently. 'I know. But think what we get out of it. Our daughter, alive and healthy. I would sacrifice anything for that. Anything. I didn't know I could love, not like this, not until we made her. She's us, Saul. She's our baby. You gave that to me.'

He managed a lame smile, and nodded. 'I can do this, too. For her.'

'You're a good man, Saul Howard. I'm proud to be your wife.'

'My sister called. They're on True Jerusalem. Rebka is in the best hospital on the planet. Everything is ready to go as soon as they get the money.'

'Good. I saw Barclay 2North in the mansion the other day. He noticed me. That part's going to be easy.'

'Right,' he said with a dry throat.

'Did you find some cufflinks?'

'Sure.' He took out the little box with the banana cufflinks he'd bought at the Birk-Unwin store.

'Oh wow.' Angela puffed her cheeks out in dismay. 'Yep, they're gaudy enough. Exactly what a man would choose.'

'The sensors are loaded in and ready.'

'Okay. I'll buy some legitimately, and we'll work the swap at the café as arranged.'

'Why don't you just take them now?'

'I can't explain them away if Marc-Anthony finds them, and he's a meddlesome little fucker. Let's just stick to the plan, shall we? I might even take Olivia-Jay along when I buy them, give me some cover.'

'Sure. You know the mansion best.'

'I do. So . . . have you got the sac?'

'Angela, we're exposed so much already. Weapons, too? Really? Think about it.'

'Weapons won't make any difference if they catch me. But what I bought in Tokyo might just be all that stands between me getting caught and me making a getaway. So please—' She held a hand out, palm upwards, giving him an expectant look that he couldn't duck.

He handed over the sac of activants, and she bumped it against her neck. 'There,' she said briskly. 'All done.'

'Just, please be careful. Please, Angela.'

'I will be. Don't worry about me. I was thinking, when you've handed over the cufflinks, your job is really over. No point in both of us being out on a limb here. Why don't you go back to Earth and wait for me to finish? I'd like that, knowing you were safe.'

'If nothing's going to go wrong, we'll both be safe. And I'm not leaving here without you. I might detest this, but I'm not going to abandon you. It's not me, Angela, that's not what I am.'

She reached up and stroked his cheek. 'After this is over, we'll be together, you and I. A fresh start on a new world, and this time we'll get it right.'

'This time,' he whispered.

Angela kissed him softly. Then she was walking back out of the loading bay, moving quickly. Not quick enough. For an instant he'd seen that same fear and uncertainty that had been there the morning he proposed. It meant the same to him now as it had then. Love is never something you decide for yourself.

'I'll wait for you,' he promised the empty air.

999

Tuesday 7th May 2143

When the convoy finally reached MTJ-1 on Monday afternoon, and Vance saw the 'way down' Antrinell had used the shortwave radio to call in, he thought it was an evil joke. The canyon wall was lower thanks to a valley steeper than the one they'd just left behind. MTJ-1 was parked close to the edge where a much smaller waterfall had fallen for about seven hundred metres to the frozen Dolce river below.

To one side of the lumpy ice streamers threading down the vertical cliff was a long talus of boulders and rock splinters that was barely angled away from the rockface itself. Vance wasn't alone in his opinion of the way down to the canyon floor. People came out of their vehicles to stare disbelievingly at the incline. Camm and Darwin were on their way back up, two small dark figures struggling through the treacherous loose snow.

But they had no choice; so a scheme was worked out, one that would utilize the winches which every vehicle was equipped with. The cable would be tethered to a large secure boulder at the top, allowing the vehicle to reverse slowly over the edge before letting the winch take the strain. The rest of Monday was spent assessing the route Camm and Darwin had negotiated down, testing boulders along the way for suitability as stable anchors.

Dawn on Tuesday morning saw them start in the pallid pink light and a tiny snowfall. Vance insisted a Tropic was first, they couldn't afford to lose the last MTJ, and he certainly wasn't going to risk the tanker or remaining truck.

Antrinell volunteered to drive the Tropic. He slowly reversed over the side of the canyon, tipping up until he was about seventy degrees, and the only thing holding the Tropic was the winch cable, certainly the wheels were useless now, they provided stability, nothing more. Everyone watched from a safe distance, the memory of the truck tow cable prominent in their minds.

The winch unwound for fifty metres, which kept everything safely inside tolerance limits. Olrg and Darwin went down and anchored the Tropic to the nearby boulders, then the winch was reattached, and the Tropic descended another fifty metres.

It took over two hours, but the Tropic reached the bottom of the precipitous slope without incident. A loud round of cheering broke out. Everyone knew that if they could get onto the river, they might just make it to Sarvar after all.

Tropic-2 was driven to the top of the talus, and its winch connected. Vance would only let the vehicles go down one at a time. The potential for disaster if there were several on the talus and one broke free was too much to contemplate.

It was late afternoon by the time every convoy vehicle was down on the wide ice flow of the canyon floor. Only then did Vance give the go-ahead to bring the sledges down. The snowfall had begun to grow heavier as the day moved on, and his worry as the clouds sank lower and the light faded was that they'd be separated from the sledges overnight. Winches were removed from their vehicles and used to form a relay down the slope. That made progress a lot quicker than it had been with the vehicles.

Vance was encouraged by the way things were going. Then Dr Coniff called him to say Ravi Hendrik had recovered consciousness.

In biolab-2's door compartment Vance shook off the glaze of snow adhering to his parka and waterproof trousers. Then the inner door opened and warm air hit him, instantly turning the remaining white ice particles damp and dark. Droplets began to run down, trickling over his boots.

Ravi Hendrik still looked awful, but he was awake and drinking broth from a big mug that Juanitar was holding for him.

Vance made himself smile as he pulled off his printed balaclava, sending more droplets scattering round. 'You're looking better,' he lied.

'Colonel,' Ravi said. 'Just glad to be alive.'

'I accessed your visual cache while the doctor was treating you. You're one lucky man. That was the mother of all fights.'

'Then you saw it? Saw the monster?'

'Yes, I saw it.'

'And the trees, the bullwhip? That's what Mark Chitty was trying to tell us.'

'I know,' Vance said. 'We can't go back into the trees now.'

Ravi's laugh was half-hysterical. 'So how do we get through the jungle to Sarvar?'

'They'll have to send a chopper for us, at the very least. I've ordered another comm rocket launch. Ken and Chris are unloading one from a sledge right now.'

'Good, that's good.' Ravi eased himself back onto the thin mattress.

'Ravi, I need to know. Did you ask Angela to come and fetch you?'

'Yes.'

'I see. Why? Why her?'

'She's the one who survived the monster before. She's the one I could trust. The only one.'

'You could have asked me.'

'Somebody is sabotaging the convoy. They just told me Karizma deserted with MTJ-1. But I don't even know if it was her. Maybe there's someone else. Things were going bad even before we even thought about a convoy.'

Vance did his best not to shout at the wounded, overtoxed pilot. He was surprised at himself now he knew how much it troubled him that someone in his own command didn't trust him. Lord curse Karizma and her invidious treachery. 'I think we can safely say it was Karizma,' he told Ravi.

'The alien is still out there,' the pilot replied. 'It won't let us leave this world alive.'

'If it thinks that, it's going to be seriously disappointed. Now you get some rest.'

'A Berlin can't reach us from Sarvar, not without refuelling. The Daedaluses won't fly over the mountains.' Ravi's voice was rising. Several lights on the monitors were turning amber as his stress levels heightened. 'We'll never get out. We're trapped here, and it's going to come for us one by one until there's nobody left. Nobody! There's no way out.'

'It won't come to that,' Vance assured him, glancing at Coniff for help.

'I shot it. I shot it point-blank in the face. It didn't even notice.'

'Yes it did. I've reviewed your recording. It was trying to get out of the way.'

Ravi laughed, a nasty high-pitched snarling sound. 'Get out of the way! That's it? That's all? Those were hollow-point nine-millimetre rounds. And it didn't *like* them?'

'Doctor,' Vance called.

Coniff was already standing, studying the monitor displays. Her e-i must have issued an instruction to the equipment because Ravi let out a long sigh and smiled lazily. 'Oh right, yeah, that's the answer to everyth . . .' His head lolled to one side and he was asleep.

'Is he going to be all right?' Vance asked the doctor.

'Providing treatment is maintained there's no reason why not. I'm still concerned about his spine, but the damage to his back is healing nicely. There's some residual shock from blood loss and hypothermia, but that is reducing now we've supplemented his fluids. He was lucky Angela recovered him when she did. A few more hours out there would have been fatal.'

'Thank you,' Vance said. He wondered if all the medical

profession had such a gloomy outlook. Back in the door compartment he wrapped himself up in his layers and his gloves before pulling the helmet down securely. The weather was worsening. Somewhere above the dark clouds, lightning was flaring, its flashes appearing like incandescent fissures in the surging underbelly. He could hear their deep basso rumbles rattling off the canyon walls. The snow was thickening, flakes growing to half the size of his palm. And the wind that beset the canyon was steadily increasing, driving the flakes against the convoy vehicles.

Up on the talus, the last sledge was halfway down. Vance couldn't even see the top any more. His e-i called Ken. 'How long until you can launch?' he asked.

'Fifteen minutes, Colonel. We've got the launcher set up. Running final checks now.'

'Is it going to be okay in this weather?'

'It should be, yes. But I'm still concerned we might not be able to maintain contact. Our meshes are so much junk, and that electrical storm brewing isn't helping. But it's the canyon walls which are the real problem. They're going to block the beam for sure.'

'But Abellia will receive it, right?'

'Yes, sir, they should be able to. Providing their dishes are still operational.'

'Understood. Carry on.'

Ken had expressed his reservation about the comm rocket earlier, which was why Vance had composed a message for Vermekia and whoever was left at Abellia. It contained Ravi's visual cache and an urgent plea for recovery. The monster's disturbing communion with the bullwhips had come as a profound shock to Vance. Such power gave the thing an almost supernatural aspect. He wasn't telling anyone, but he shared Ravi's view that they'd never get through the jungle alive. Vermekia had to listen now, had to help them. Even he, consumed within his world of petty office politics, couldn't keep ignoring the amount of proof Vance had compiled.

Vance walked the short distance across the circle of vehicles, and climbed into biolab-1's door compartment. There was more snow clinging to him this time than there had been in biolab-2. He shook it all off vigorously, and went into the main cabin. Antrinell, Tamisha, and Roarke were inside, enjoying some coffee. Hot drinks were the one thing they didn't have to ration yet. The three of them had been outside for hours, working hard to help bring the vehicles down the talus. Their lips were cracked and bruised-looking, while they all had red-raw patches of skin on their faces where the cold had crept round their balaclavas and scarves.

Vance stripped off his outer layers which were now slimed with slush and sat at the little table which had folded out of the wall. Tamisha offered him a mug of coffee, which he accepted gratefully.

'I've been going through the fuel levels,' Antrinell began. 'It will be tight assuming we stay on schedule from now on.'

'Yes,' Vance agreed.

'But I think we all know that schedule isn't going to survive. Not with the creatures out there. And now we know the jungle can be activated against us. We're not going to reach Sarvar. It's that simple.'

'I didn't expect that from you,' Vance said lightly. 'Anyway, I've requested recovery and evacuation in my comm rocket message.'

'A message that may or may not get through.'

'We have three more rockets left after this launch.'

'I'm sorry, sir, but I don't think you're really taking into account what we're up against. It's clear now that the jungle is in some way reactive to an alien sentient. There is a force here that we have underestimated to a monumental degree.'

'Are you saying I should have done something different?' Vance asked. That Antrinell was calling him *sir* in front of others from the xenobiology team was a bad sign. They'd known each other too long for that kind of formality. He could understand people were scared, but this kind of defiance in an executive officer was unprecedented.

'We all have the same information, sir,' Tamisha said. 'We came to the same conclusions. Based on them we agreed that the convoy was the right course of action. At the time.'

'And now you're changing your mind? You maybe should have thought about that before we climbed down here to the canyon floor, because the sweet Lord knows we can't get back up again now.'

'We're not complaining about the convoy, nor its location,' Antrinell said. 'What you need to take into account is our current situation.'

'You think I'm unaware of what's going on? Are you serious?'

'Sir,' Roarke said tentatively. 'It's not about awareness, everybody knows what's happening. It's the implications we're concerned about.'

'Vance, this is war,' Antrinell said. 'I'm not sure you appreciate that. It's been subtle and progressive, which is why we haven't necessarily reacted as we should have done. Whatever it is that's out there is intent on exterminating us. The planet is reacting to our presence, the trees themselves are trying to kill us. Personally, I now believe the sunspot outbreak is part of the conflict. There are clearly unknown powers at work here. Phenomenal powers, perhaps equal to those of the Zanth. And they are completely hostile to humans.'

'Yes. I'm not arguing any of this.'

'Then we should deploy the weapon we were given for precisely this situation.'

'Antrinell, I can't authorize that. The zero metavirus is tailored to kill all life on St Libra; anything that shares the native genetic molecule. That must surely include the guardian creature given the kind of relationship it has demonstrated it has with the flora. We can't do it. You and I especially, we know the Lord would not permit such a crime.'

'If we don't deploy the weapon, if we do nothing, St Libra will win. We're not going to make it to Sarvar, not with the creature and the jungle to contend with. We all accessed Ravi's visual recording. Bullets don't have the slightest effect on it. There is nothing else left to us. The metavirus will destroy this thing. It's our only chance for survival. And if we don't make it, who is going to warn the HDA and the trans-space worlds? The zero metavirus was created because we cannot face two alien threats, not simultaneously. And certainly not on the scale we have witnessed here. We have to eliminate this threat before it destroys us.'

Vance regarded his fellow officer and Gospel Warrior in utter dismay. It was incredible that someone who took the same vows, had the same views, could come to a decision that was completely opposite to his own. One thing Antrinell clearly didn't recognize was the depth and conviction of Vance's own belief in the Lord. It was everything to him, his basis for existing. He knew there had to be a purpose behind life and the universe. And only God could provide that. For God had created the universe, and that had to be for a reason. Vance never expected to know what it was, he fully understood he was too insignificant for that, he was content just to be a part of such a glorious existence. To live in a way his Lord would consider worthy. 'No,' he said with finality. 'And you are not to raise this issue again. We are not going to launch the zero metavirus. I do not consider the hostility of one misguided guardian sufficient to justify genocide.'

'Genocide?' Antrinell shouted. 'They're plants!'

'If that were so, we wouldn't be having this conversation.'

'You're condemning us to death. Without the zero metavirus we'll never get to Sarvar.'

'If it is meant to be, then the Lord will show us a way. Besides, I'm not at all confident the metavirus will work in this climate. The warheads can disperse it into the jetstreams, yes. But there's nothing living for it to latch on to when it falls to the ground. This temperature will kill it as surely as fire. It might take longer but the outcome will be the same. There will be no exponential growth, no contagion.'

'All right. But, you're forgetting, there's one St Libra lifeform that's still very much alive and active,' Antrinell urged. 'We might not get the planet's jungles, but we can take down the bastard that's murdering us. Come on, you have to let us try. We have a right to life, too.'

Vance considered the idea. He turned to Tamisha. 'Is it possible to build a localized dispenser, a gun or spray we can use against the creature?'

'I don't see why not,' she said thoughtfully. 'I should be able to design something that'll fit into our hollow-point rounds. We've got a couple of micro-precision printers here in the lab for spares production, they should be adequate.'

'Start working on it. I'll consider deactivating a warhead and extracting the metavirus for you to redeploy.'

'Yes, sir.'

'If,' and he held up a cautionary finger to Antrinell, 'this system can be made to work, then I will be the one who carries the pistol.'

'It doesn't matter who fires the shot, just that it hits the target.'

'Good.' Vance drained his coffee. 'I have a comm rocket launch to attend. We're finished here now. The subject is closed.'

Wednesday 8th May 2143

Angela's e-i said it was eight forty-two in the morning. Red Sirius had risen nearly two hours ago. Apart from the purple clock figures on the edge of her iris smartcell grid she wouldn't have known that. A blizzard was sweeping along the canyon. Confined and compressed by the towering rock walls, the wind and snow was roaring against Tropic-2's bodywork, making them shake every inch of the way as they crawled forward. Tropic-1 was ten metres ahead, its rear lights barely visible through the driving snow. According to the windscreen display, its bodywork barely reflected a radar pulse. Apart from the lightning bolts searing overhead every few seconds, the canyon was a confined world of darkness. Their headlight beams dissolved into the snow a few metres ahead.

Forster, who was in the driving seat beside her, was steering them on net data alone, coordinating the position of the other vehicles and inertial navigation read-outs. Somewhere up ahead, Elston was driving MTJ-1. Angela knew why he wanted to keep going, but frankly trying to carry on in these conditions was ridiculous bordering on foolhardy.

'We should stop,' Paresh said from the rear passenger seat. 'We're going to hit the canyon wall at this rate.'

'Then we bump and back off,' Angela said. 'That's got to be better than vanishing over a waterfall like I almost did.'

'Can't afford the fuel for a stop,' Ken said. He'd been assigned the final seat in their Tropic after the comm rocket launch the previous evening, when Elston handed out their new travel assignments.

Angela didn't comment on the fuel situation. She'd started to worry about the convoy getting anywhere close to the Zell tributary neighbouring Sarvar, let alone the camp itself. Right up until she accessed Ravi's visual log of his fight with the monster she'd been contemplating taking a Tropic with Rebka and heading back to Wukang like Karizma. But the bullwhips had now ruled that out. Then the comm rocket had launched amid a blast of flame and smoke, vanishing into the clouds and snow within a second. Ken had lost contact with it after thirty seconds. The final burst of data the convoy's net received before it vanished behind the canyon wall had revealed how thick and dense and chaotic the cloud strata were above the canyon. Not heavy enough to damage the rocket, Ken claimed, it would be able to complete its ballistic arc above the atmosphere. But now they didn't know if the messages had been received at Abellia or not. All they could do was hope that if the signal had got through then the images Ravi had captured were enough to kick HDA into launching a rescue mission, or at the very least a supply drop.

There were too many possibles in that chain of events for Angela. She'd spent most of the night lying awake in the seat next to Paresh, trying to come up with a plan that guaranteed her and Rebka a way through this. Short of dumping everyone else in the canyon and leaving with their food and fuel, nothing she could do now was going to make much difference. So she was just left with having to go along with Elston's plan to get as close as they could to Sarvar and hope the camp's skeleton crew could still fly a Berlin to pick them up. It wasn't much to hang her life on. That, she could almost tolerate, but to have Rebka in the same hopeless situation was almost too much to endure. She was desperate for some kind of action, something she could do which would make a difference. What that might be was proving disturbingly elusive.

A purple icon shone comfortingly in her grid. Rebka's location icon, showing everyone that the sheepish yet surprisingly resilient Madeleine Hoque was riding along in Tropic-3, with Garrick, Darwin, and poor old weepy Lulu MacNamara. It was Angela's private beacon of hope.

A bright amber light flared outside the Tropic. Angela knew immediately it wasn't lightning, for it wasn't fading away. Then the sound hit them, a blast that actually shunted the Tropic several metres across the snow. Three of the side windows cracked, one shattering completely. Crystalline shards of tempered glass cascaded over Paresh. Icy air howled through the vehicle, sucking the heat out in seconds. Forster shoved his foot down hard on the brake, and they rocked to a stop.

Angela didn't react for several seconds, she was too stunned to do anything. Her initial burst of fright was swiftly replaced by feverish worry. That had been an explosion. And the bright yellow light was still shining somewhere behind them, filtering through the blizzard.

She studied her grid frantically. The icons for the truck had gone, as had the bodymesh emissions for Josh Justic, who had been driving. Rebka was still there, still okay.

'What the fuck?' Paresh exclaimed.

Another explosion ripped the snow apart behind them.

'Crap on it, the bioil!' Ken shouted. 'It's the truck. The monster's blown the truck.'

Individual icons began to flash amber medical warnings in Angela's grid. Leora Fawkes, Winn Melia, Chris Fiadeiro, and Juan-Fernando, all of them riding in Tropic-1, were showing a plethora of injuries, with lacerated skin, impact bruising and several broken bones. Tropic-1's own sensors revealed the vehicle was now lying on its side, with badly damaged bodywork.

Paresh opened the door and jumped out into the blizzard, pulling his Heckler carbine out of its holster with his good arm.

'Wait!' Angela shouted, but he was gone, running towards the blazing wreckage of the truck. 'Shit!' She grabbed her balaclava and parka and lurched out after him into the punishing wind and snow.

There wasn't much left of the truck, its carcass reduced to crumpled panels and twisted-up chassis struts in the centre of a steaming crater. But it was burning furiously as the bladder framework slowly sagged, hissing and bubbling as it collapsed in on itself. The heat stopped anyone getting within twenty metres of the mangled cab.

One glance at the blackened, windowless lump of seething composite, and Angela knew there was no point trying to get close. Josh was dead.

There was another blast behind the truck as a bladder on the sledge exploded. Everyone who'd run over to help immediately ducked as fragments came twirling out of the discharge spitting sparks and flame as they scythed through the frigid air. Angela dropped to her knees as the fireball swelled up into the bleak snow, its swirl bloom slowly dwindling to a puff of filthy smoke that was sucked away.

'Keep back, keep back,' Elston was shouting. 'Botin, get a guard round the tanker, now!'

Angela took a dazed glance over at where the tanker ought to be, seeing little through the fast wash of sub-zero snow. Tropic-1, which had been following the truck, had rolled over, dark body-work glimmering in the flames. She crouched beside biolab-2, using its bulk as a shield should anything else detonate on the truck. The big vehicle had obviously been shunted about, its wheels gouging sideways furrows through the snow. Then she realized its sledge had absorbed a lot of the blast. It was a battered ruin embedded in the snow, surrounded by a vast circle of debris; torn boxes and flapping foil packages were being rolled and blown by the savage wind.

'Son of a bitch,' she groaned. Struggling to shove her rapidly chilling arms into the parka she told her e-i to quest Elston. 'Biolab-2's sledge has been busted wide open,' she said.

'Angela, we've got to get our injured people out of the Tropic. Unless the sledge hit someone I don't care.'

She finally got her goggles on, and focused on the battered Tropic-1. Several people were gathered round, some in parkas, some not. A couple were on top, pulling a dazed Leora out through a broken window. 'Elston, it's our food.'

'What?'

'Biolab-2's sledge was carrying most of our food.' She finally succeeded in zipping up the front of the parka, and pulled the hood over her head. Her ears were completely numb – she missed the balaclava and scarf. Right in front of her, hundreds of food packets were being slowly propelled across the canyon's ice floor as the wind blew relentlessly.

'Dear Lord.' Elston switched to a ringlink. 'Anyone not involved with Tropic-1 recovery, start picking up the food packets. Legionnaires, take perimeter duty now. No one venture outside line of sight.'

Angela started picking up the food packets closest to her. It was the most pathetic thing she'd done in years. At best she could hold maybe a dozen of the silvery oblongs, then she had to hurry over to Tropic-2 with its open doors and dump them onto the seat. Her bag was inside, the one she normally used to distribute the packets round the convoy. She pulled it out and began stuffing packets inside. All around her, people were bending over, bobbing about to pick up tumbling packets like impoverished shellfishers in shallow water.

Her e-i ran columns of figures through her grid as she snatched and snatched at the wretched fluttering foil. She screamed curses at the ones that eluded her stiffening fingers. It was like watching a wound pump her own lifeblood away; each packet skittering off into the inimical snow-thickened darkness was a day fewer that they'd be able to live.

Her attitude seemed to have got through to the others. Everybody was straining against the wind, grasping after the animated packets, shoving them into their open parkas or tipping them into a vehicle. Their own vehicle, she noticed.

The time of sharing was over, she knew – a lot of those packets they'd saved wouldn't be going back on any inventory Elston might order.

Angela spent another fifteen minutes outside, scuttling about after the food before Paresh told her to stop. The last of the individual packets was slipping beyond the simple perimeter the six remaining Legionnaires had set up. It was just as well, her hands in only a single set of gloves were now so cold she couldn't move her fingers any more. She leaned against the wind to walk back in silent misery to Tropic-2. Ken was already taping a panel over the shattered window. Forster was inside brushing snow off the dash and seats, while Paresh was still out on perimeter duty.

Angela shut the door behind her, and spilled her bag's contents onto the pile of packets already wedged between the front and rear seats.

'We've got a good week's worth there, haven't we?' Ken said dubiously from the front passenger seat.

'Probably,' she said. She held her hands over the vent, watching the clinging strings of snow start to melt and drip as Forster switched it to blow hot air into the Tropic. Her parka had a crust of ice nearly a centimetre thick, which was also dribbling down onto the packets, the floor, and the seat. She couldn't take it off because her hands wouldn't work. The gloves had so much ice attached they'd become her own personal mini-freezers. She was worried she might have to chip them off, and her fingers would go with them. 'Son of a bitch, I'm *cold.*'

'Let me get your gloves off,' Ken said. 'I've got a bit of feeling back in my fingers.'

'Thanks.'

A minute later the other back door opened and a cloud of snow puffed in as Paresh lumbered up into the seat. Then the door slammed shut again, and the interior calmed apart from the wheezing air-con vents.

'Elston is ordering us to drive into a defensive circle,' Forster said. 'Looks like we're stopping for a while.'

'We'll just have to stay here,' Ken said. 'There's not enough fuel to get us even halfway to Sarvar now. And food's blowing away down the glacier. And the monster's throwing grenades at us.'

'We don't know what happened to the truck,' Paresh said.

'Maybe Karizma isn't the saboteur,' Forster said. 'Maybe they're still with us.'

'No,' Angela said. 'That was the monster.'

'How do you know?'

'Because if it was the saboteur, they've just killed themselves as well. Karizma wanted to force us to turn back. Taking out the truck is a whole different ball game.'

Forster started the Tropic, and drove them round in a short curve, avoiding the overturned cadaver of Tropic-1, to take their position in the circle. The remaining six vehicles shone their headlights out across the rucked ice surface of the canyon floor while the lightning burst sporadically amid the massive cloudbank overhead. Only two of the remote guns were functioning, sweeping vigilantly from side to side; snow had clogged the actuators on the other four, although they could still fire if they ever acquired a target.

*

Vance sat in the driver's cab of biolab-1, watching the wipers struggle to keep the curving windscreen clear. Their blue-white headlights, and the additional spots on the roof of the cab penetrated no more then ten metres into the maelstrom of snow hurtling along the canyon. The wind was now so fierce it was scouring the snow directly off the frozen river, carving elegant curving forms out of the harder drifts only to pulverize them again in seconds, liberating them into thick cataracts that raced along parallel to the ground. Away with those fast horizontal streamers went any last hope of recovering their food.

Every few seconds the biolab would shudder and growl as a band of denser snow was hammered into it. Vance was waiting for the monster. He almost expected it to walk out of the blizzard to stand in front of the biolab to gloat. Losing half their fuel had been bad, but then to have their food swept away almost as an incidental act of malice was a brutal twist of the knife. For the first time he was considering the prospect of the monster winning, that his command, the people he was responsible for, would not survive. It was a terrible knowledge, corroding his very soul. He knew he mustn't let it show, mustn't be anything less than bullishly confident. The twenty-eight people left alive were his responsibility, they would look to him for that leadership, they'd expect him to find them a way out, some way of delivering them from the cold lingering death so far from home which otherwise awaited them.

He searched round the frenzy of snow again, but saw nothing. Perhaps even the Lord had limits? Certainly Vance could understand if He could no longer find them here. After all, nobody in the convoy knew where *here* was any more. They were lost in so many ways.

Such self-pity offended him. Anger helped him push the sorrow and insecurity to one side. Anger that was mostly directed inward. He was here for a reason. The end was close now, they were drawing towards a final confrontation, the monster was making sure of that. This was the moment Vance Elston was needed the most, the reason his Lord had delivered him to this time and place. The time he would find out if he was truly worthy.

He made his way back into the main cabin, where Smara Jacka was inventorying the meagre collection of silvery packets she and Tamisha and Antrinell had managed to scavenge out of the blizzard. 'Leave that,' he told her. His e-i gave the biolab's net a code, and the door to the little decontam airlock opened.

Antrinell, Tamisha, Roarke, and Camm were inside, sitting together at the bench which ran the length of the lab. Tamisha had spent most of yesterday evening designing the dispersal mechanism which would fit into a hollow-point bullet. The lab's 3D precision printer had churned out the tiny components, which she'd spent hours painstakingly assembling into a small smartpellet that could withstand the pistol's chamber explosion, but would itself detonate a couple of milliseconds after impact. They knew hitting the monster's strangely solid skin would be useless. Instead the mouth slit or eyes would have to provide a route inside its body to the cells. That meant a supremely accurate shot from a distance, or one from point-blank range like Ravi had managed.

Once Tamisha had started producing the bullet dispenser, Vance had authorized access to the snug launch tubes built into the biolab's bulkhead. Antrinell and Camm had removed one of the rockets, and carefully detached the warhead. It had taken hours to extract the phials of zero metavirus from the jetstream release mechanism. There were a lot of very dangerous explosives involved, and it was the middle of the night: nobody wanted to make a mistake.

Now they had one of the phials in a small clean-A chamber, along with the bullet dispensers. Roarke was transferring a tiny droplet of the green-tinted suspension liquid from the phial into each smartpellet.

'I pressure-tested three at random,' Antrinell said as Vance peered over Roarke's shoulder at the small manipulator arms moving about with micrometre precision inside the clean-A chamber. 'They all checked out. There won't be any leakage.'

'Good job,' Vance told Tamisha.

'Thank you, sir. The smartpellet will withstand any ordinary impact, in case you drop the pistol or anything; and they also need an arm code before they'll work.'

'What about cold-exposure?' Vance asked. 'Do we know what temperature renders the metavirus inoperable?'

'Most virus weapons cease to be effective below ten degrees Celsius, and they start dying below fifteen,' Antrinell said. He held up a translucent pistol-shaped rubbery sheath. 'We printed a warmer for your pistol, the battery lasts fifteen hours. It should keep the bullets warm enough outside.'

'Very well,' Vance said. 'How many have you filled?' he asked Roarke.

'Seven, so far, sir.'

'Give me ten. If I can't get a body puncture shot in it by then, I'll be dead anyway.'

Roarke gave him a tight nod. 'Understood.'

'I've decided we're going to stay here,' Vance announced. 'It's basic math. If we don't move, the vehicle fuel cells use up a lot less bioil just supplying electricity and warmth than they will powering the motors. We cannot reach Sarvar on the bioil remaining, so I see no point travelling any further.'

'And the food?' Antrinell asked softly.

'As of now, we're on survival rations. That ought to give us ten to fifteen days with what we have left. Once the blizzard clears properly, we'll launch another comm rocket and let them know we're under attack and low on supplies. The HDA will have to launch a rescue mission. The Berlins are perfectly capable of reaching us from Sarvar, even without a Daedalus tanker refuelling them. It might take a few days, but they just have to establish fuel dumps along the route.'

Antrinell nodded reluctantly. 'So it all depends on the comm rocket punching a signal through to Abellia.'

'Abellia or Sarvar, yes,' Vance said. 'We'll program it to aim at both, of course. They've had Ravi's visual log for a day now. They'll know the guardian is real, and here with us. Rescue is frankly the minimum we should be expecting as soon as the blizzard is over. Vermekia has already arranged for a ski-equipped Daedalus to be put on stand-by to come through the gateway. Ravi's log should give him what he needs to get the General to open a war gateway above us, and drop a whole squadron of ski-equipped Daedaluses into the canyon with enough reinforcements to finish this once and for all.'

'They didn't care about us before,' Tamisha said.

'Because we didn't have the evidence we do now,' Vance replied. 'We'll be out of here soon.'

'If we're going to be staying, we should consider our defensive strategy,' Antrinell said. 'You've got us spread out in two Tropics, the MTJ, both biolabs and the tanker –which only has two people in it. For a static position that leaves us exposed, especially as there are only six Legionnaires left, and only two remote guns working.'

'Okay, what do you suggest?' Vance asked, content with the level of support his decision was being given.

'The biolabs are the most secure vehicles we have,' Antrinell said. 'We know the monster can't get in, it tried before. Once we've finished this procedure, bring people in; we hardly have to maintain the lab's integrity after this. If it's too crowded we can use the MTJ as well, its heater is a lot better than anything the Tropics have. We also need to see if the remote guns can be reactivated. From what Olrg was saying it's probably just ice screwing up the actuators.'

'We'd also get people to bring in what food they gathered,' Camm said. 'That way we'll get a better idea of how much there is left.'

'All right,' Vance said. 'I'll talk with the doctor to see how many we can accommodate in biolab-2 without compromising her patients, then we'll start to dig in for the duration.'

*

The electrical storm raging inside the blizzard began to fire lightning balls down into the canyon around midday. Angela saw the first one streak overhead to strike the canyon wall a couple of hundred metres away. The convoy's minuscule net glitched in response to the EM pulse. A nest of seething lightning braids erupted from the impact point, scrabbling away at the frozen river for several seconds. The serpentine gouge marks they left hissed and steamed before the blizzard quickly obscured them, and the net re-established itself.

'Great, that's all we need,' Angela muttered from the front passenger seat of the Tropic. Ken was up on the roof, trying to fix the remote gun actuators, or at least scrape the ice off them, while Paresh stood guard outside. She didn't like him being out there with his one working arm, everyone knew their firearms had no effect on the monster, but Elston's instructions about withdrawing into the biolabs and MTJ were probably the only good order he'd issued since the convoy began. And she was going to be in the same biolab as Rebka, which was a huge plus point.

Atyeo and Bastian and Garrick had been tasked with filling up the biolab fuel tanks from the tanker's sledge bladders. If she wiped the condensation from the Tropic's windows and squinted, she could sometimes catch a glimpse of their heavy, snow-shrouded figures lumbering round like mythical yetis. Omar and Botin were keeping guard over them.

Rebka, Lulu, and Garrick had just abandoned Tropic-3, their stooped shapes battling the wind as they plodded over to biolab-1. Leora was escorting them. Angela could track their identity icons on her grid, seeing them approaching the safety of the biolab.

She began pulling on her own parka in preparation. They'd be going over there themselves, soon. Their food packets were already in bags ready to carry. Everything else that she couldn't stuff into pockets, all the personal kit, would be abandoned in the Tropic while they waited for some kind of rescue.

The balaclava went on next, then she started jamming her fingers into her gloves. It had taken an age for her to dry them out on the vent, but she couldn't risk them freezing like they had last time when she went chasing food packets. With the inner layer on, she pushed her fingers into the thicker mid-layer, following with the waterproof outer layer. The bag's strap was about the smallest thing she could pick up now, but at least her hands would stay dry and reasonably warm.

Rebka's icon showed her inside biolab-1. Another lightning ball zoomed down from the thick churning sky, erupting like a coronal sunrise on the other side of the parked vehicles. Angela wiped at the condensation and peered out again.

Somebody was walking round the back of the tanker's sledge with its framework of bladders. A dark bulky figure, like everyone in a parka. But her net connection had glitched again, and the identity icons had vanished from the grid. 'Show all last known positions,' she told her e-i.

There was no one near the tanker's sledge. The refuelling crew was over by biolab-2.

'It's back,' Angela yelled.

Sitting in the driver's seat, his parka half on, Forster turned to gape at her. 'What?'

'The monster. It's going after the rest of the bioil.' Angela yanked at the door handle and jumped down onto the hard-packed snow covering the river. 'Paresh!' she screamed. The blizzard buffeted her; high-velocity snow smacked into her face, half-blinding her. She hunched down and began to run as best she could towards the sledge. Another lightning ball zipped across the top of the canyon, bursting against the northern cliff. A plasma rainbow inflated, flaring into lightning tendrils that slithered down the cliff like an incandescent waterfall to ground out among the jagged black rocks at the base.

Angela tugged her outer gloves off and switched her dark weapons to semi-active status. Foreign cells that for the last two months had flourished along her ulna and grown their fronds out along her fingers stirred themselves. The tingling sensation they gave off was exactly as she remembered from twenty years ago. They worked! She hadn't been sure if the old cy-tech would retain its integrity over two decades, but the specialist on New Tokyo had been the very best. All she'd needed was the right activants to resurrect them.

*

Poor old puppy boy Paresh had been ecstatic when they made it back to the hotel that night back in February, just after they'd arrived at Abellia. Angela had been impressed by his stamina. Four clubs, bottle after bottle of beer, several sacs of tox, more beer, dancing hard to get all that alcohol and narcotic pumping fast round his bloodstream – wine followed, then some shots.

In the taxi he'd been pawing at her like the school jock taking the prom queen home. Nothing seemed to have any damping effect on his appallingly fit young body.

They were locked together as they stumbled through the hotel room's door. His tongue was in her mouth and trying to get down into her lungs. Back in the second club, her e-i had used some of Zarleene's dark software to monitor his bodymesh, and reported he'd switched off the medical smartcell routines. So she replicated the passion, and clamped her hands tight on the back of his neck to return the kiss. As she did it, she bumped a sac against his carotid, the sedative she'd extracted from the clinic just after her embarrassing collapse in the mess tent earlier in the week – that day she saw Rebka for the first time.

Paresh was having a grand time with his hand up her blouse. She broke away with a lustful smile. 'Give me one minute,' she told him huskily, and backed towards the en suite. 'And Paresh.'

'Yeah?' he blinked hazily.

'You'd better be naked when I come back in here.'

She closed the door, and started counting. At nine there was the unmistakable thud made by an unconscious Legionnaire corporal hitting the carpet.

When she peeped cautiously back into the bedroom it was difficult not to feel a burst of sympathy. Her lovely puppy boy was sprawled on the floor, his trousers round his ankles.

'Sorry, sweets,' Angela apologized to his snoring form. She took a moment to straighten her own clothes and comb her hair back to something more respectable. Her e-i called a taxi using a trace-avoidance patch from Zarleene's cache. By the time she was striding through the hotel lobby it was pulling up outside.

The taxi's auto management wanted a deposit. Angela accessed one of the small emergency fund accounts Saul had set up in Abellia twenty years ago, pleased she could still remember the code. There was only a couple of hundred Eurofrancs in it, but that was more than enough for the ride to Camilo Beach.

She ordered the taxi to wait at the top of the little village, just off the Rue du Ranelagh, then walked down the sandy road, past the neat whitewashed bungalows that glowed a spectral grey under the bright ringlight, smelling the fresh sea air. The community was typical Saul, a *nice* place, no doubt filled with decent folk bringing up their families as best they could.

Then she arrived at his bungalow, with its tiny rear kitchen patio opening directly onto the beach. Poor old Saul, he'd be so flummoxed by her appearance. The files she'd harvested said he had a wife and children, so she prayed he wouldn't be so stupid as to confess her appearance to them. But knowing Saul there was a good chance he'd do exactly that.

She sat on the low wall surrounding the patio while her e-i called their emergency address code.

'Who is this?' Saul asked thirty seconds later.

At least no light had come on in the house, he wasn't in full freak-out mode. Yet. 'It's me, Saul. It's Angela.'

'But, you're . . . It can't be.'

'They let me out to advise the expedition, darling. I'm officially on probation. Which I've just broken in a spectacular way to come here to see you.'

'Here? Here, where?'

'I'm outside standing on your patio. I didn't want to wake your family up.'

'Ho crap – wait—'

She had to smile fondly, visualizing his panicked face as he tried to slip off the bed without waking Emily. Angela had harvested an image of Mrs Howard number two – she was a real looker. Young, too. That sweet charm of Saul's was still clearly fully charged.

The big glass door slid aside, and he came stumbling out into the night, trying to shove his arms into a baggy old cricket sweater. The sight of him shocked her, causing her smile to diminish. Her husband had *aged* so. Back in Holloway, when she saw Elston again, she'd been quietly smug at his chubby face and frosting of grey on a receding hairline, the heavier build. Now the same illness of entropy had infected her Saul, and there was no triumph in that, only sadness as she finally realized how she was destined to spend her life leaving others behind. *Except Rebka.*

'Oh God, it's really you,' Saul croaked. 'You haven't aged. Not a day. You *are* a one-in-ten aren't you? It's all true.'

Angela summoned up some degree of dignity, and gave him a warm smile as she held out her arms in welcome. 'Hello, babe.'

He stepped into the embrace, but there was so much missing. It was a hug from a long-lost brother, not a lover, not the father of her child. 'I didn't think I'd ever see you again,' he said in a muffled voice.

She could feel him quivering, and knew he'd be crying. 'It's all right,' she said soothingly. 'And before you say anything; I know.'

'You do?' He wiped a hand over his eyes. 'How do you know?'

'Your Abellia Civic Administration files are open, I harvested them as soon as I arrived. Emily looks lovely, well done you. And three children, isn't it?'

His face crumpled in dismay, he was on the verge of tears again. 'No. No . . . That's not – Angela, it's Rebka . . . she didn't make it. My sister called me a year after they caught you. The doctors did their very best, but . . . I'm so sorry.'

'What are you talking about?'

'I couldn't even tell you; there'd been the trial, you were in prison. I followed it all on the transnet news. It was awful. I nearly . . . I didn't know how I survived.'

'Saul, Rebka is very much alive. That's why I broke probation to visit you. She's here on the expedition. I don't know how or why, but she's here. Your daughter is alive and staying at Abellia Airport HDA camp. I've seen her with my own eyes. I damn near had a heart attack. She's beautiful, Saul; she's got my crazy hair, poor thing, but she's got your smile to make up for it.'

'Dearest Angela . . .'

'No!' She swatted away the tentative hand that was reaching out. That sympathy wasn't something she was going to put up with. 'Don't even start down that route. I know what I saw.'

'All right, Angela.'

She gave him a look that was pure contemptuous hatred. He didn't believe her. His life had moved on – no doubt with a great deal of guilt – away from his lost daughter and suspected serial-killer wife. 'Son of a bitch!' She hadn't expected a triumphant 'welcome back' party, but this kind of greeting was pretty shabby. 'Don't worry, I'm going to get out of your life, Saul, for good this time. I just need something first.'

'Of course. I've got some money. It's not much, but you're welcome to it.'

'I don't need money,' she spat. 'I've got to make sure Rebka stays safe. That monster is real, Saul, and it's here on St Libra. Do you even believe that?'

'I know you couldn't have done what they said you did. Not you. I know you better than you think I do.'

'Thank fuck for that. You were smart not going back through the gateway. But then I remember my last message to you. I was being pretty forceful again, wasn't I?'

'Yeah.'

'Always the bitch. But I'm glad you were safe, that you found yourself a life again. You deserve that after everything we went through.'

'Angela,' he said gently. 'If it's not money, what do you want?'

'I came for the activants, Saul.'

'What?' He blurted it out so loud his immediate reaction was to turn and give the bungalow a guilty glance.

'The activants. We had four batches made up in New Tokyo. And I know you. You'll have kept everything from those days. I made you get rid of everything else, everything you were – so you kept whatever relics you had, no matter how small or painful.'

'You can't bump them. Angela, they're twenty years old. They're probably poison now. And the weapons are the same . . .'

'The nuclei threads will still be there in my ulnas. No reason for them not to be. They just need a growth trigger again.'

'Angela, please, don't do this.'

'Saul. You're going to get them for me, and we both know that. So why don't we just cut out the shouting and the threats and move straight to the endgame. Come on, go inside and get them from whatever little secret stash of the past you have. Then I'll be gone.'

'Angela . . .'

'They haven't announced it, of course, but the reason this expedition is being put together is because there was another North murdered by the monster. It's real, Saul, and it took a trip to Earth back in January. The HDA is worried, enough that they busted me out of jail to help them.'

Saul let out a broken sigh. 'Wait here.'

He was gone over ten minutes. Wherever he'd hidden the memorabilia of his earlier life, it was in a deep and difficult to reach place, which was smart of him. But when he returned he was carrying a small plastic box.

'Thank you, Saul,' she said with genuine gratitude. The box had a cradle for four sacs. There were only three left. She picked one out and bumped it against her neck.

Saul winced.

'Still alive,' Angela said brightly.

'Please, Angela—'

'Yeah, I know. When I get back from the jungle I'll go and get me some therapy. That's what you want, isn't it?'

'I'm pleased you're considering it. Angela, they locked you up for *twenty years*.'

'Does it show?' Which was a low blow, especially against him.

'Just be careful out there. Okay?'

'Promise.' She hugged him again. They even kissed – platonically. Then she was walking back up the sand-scattered road to the taxi. She didn't look back. *Just like the last time.*

*

The blizzard punching down the Dolce canyon sent a compact wave of snow slapping against Angela as she tried to hurry towards the tanker's sledge. It almost sent her sprawling on her front. The heavy layers of clothes were conspiring with the wind to make every step an effort. She'd left her goggles behind in the Tropic, forcing her to squint against the whirling ice flecks that filled the air.

Not twenty metres away, the monster swung its arm. Blades hacked into the bladder framework, cutting clean through composite struts and puncturing the rubbery containers themselves. Bioil gushed out, a viscous black liquid splattering down onto the rumpled crust of snow to form a rapidly expanding puddle. Rivulets trickled away across the frozen river.

'Fuck you!' Angela screamed at the monster as it slashed its five-bladed hand through another set of bladders. She kicked her legs as hard as she could, desperate to cover the distance between them. The monster regarded her for a second, pausing with a disdain that was positively human before turning and walking away, leaving the bioil gushing freely onto the ground behind it.

Another ball lightning descended into the canyon, landing on the far side of the circled vehicles. It rebounded, oscillating wildly into a hemisphere before disintegrating into a globular cascade of glaring lightning strands. The entire convoy was illuminated with pure white solar splendour, as if Sirius had returned to its pre-redshift grandeur.

Angela's net link vanished. She saw two figures lying on the snow beside biolab-2, the fuel hose snaking between them. Big patches of crimson blood were growing sluggishly out around each of them. The Legionnaires – Lieutenant Botin and Omar Mihambo were close by – moving as fast as they could in the hurricane wind, their weapons already drawn, thin ruby laser beams tracking round in search of a target. They must have seen the monster at the same time. Their carbines started to level in unison as the monster strode off beyond the sledge, creating its own micro-swirls within the rampaging snow.

'No!' Angela yelled at the top of her lungs. She waved frantically, trying to stop them. But she was too far away, they never saw her.

The carbines opened fire. Thin plumes of ice spiked up out of the ground just short of the sledge, stitching a fast line in pursuit of the monster. Explosive-tipped armour-piercing rounds that shattered the rock-hard snow and ice in small gouts of flame. Three of them struck the spreading pool of bioil as the corona of lightning flares began to fade.

Flames whooshed up from the spilled fuel, blue fire burning bright, sliding inexorably towards the residual torrent still leaking from the bladders. The Legionnaires realized what they'd done and stopped firing. One of them stood perfectly still, watching the flames in horror. The other lunged forwards. Angela watched in dismay as the figure reached the elongated puddle of flame. It skidded to a halt and bent over, dropping the carbine so gauntlets could shove at the snow, trying to create a break in the bioil like a child playing dams and streams on the beach. For a moment it looked like he'd succeed. The flames started to splutter, then suddenly he was lifting his hands, which had become two balls of striking turquoise flame.

A frightened Angela slowed to a halt, and began to run in the other direction. She crashed into Paresh who was heading in to help, sending both of them tumbling onto the unforgiving ground. The lightning died. Leaping blue flames illuminated the scene. They'd burned their way around the Legionnaire, and were racing for the sledge. But the flaming figure rolled over, deliberately crashing down on top of the smooth bright wavefront, extinguishing the blaze. It writhed about, kicking up ridges of saturated snow. The flames began to track wide.

Then the other Legionnaire was racing up to the sledge, snatching a fire extinguisher off the framework. Foam jetted out, smothering the leading edge of the flame. Then he was directing the foam onto the blazing puddles and their splash-pattern rivulets.

Angela's link to the convoy net resurrected. It was instantly full of incoherent shouting. The grid showed her it was Lieutenant Botin in the flames, with his arms still alight, and flaming bioil seeping down his legs. Bioil somehow transferred to his hood, and he was engulfed in a halo of blue flame, the burn accelerated by the howling blizzard.

Paresh was rolling fast, onto his feet to struggle over to Botin. He grabbed a second extinguisher with his functioning arm, and played the foam over the lieutenant while Omar Mihambo battled the slurry of flaming bioil seething over the ground. Flame began to rise up Paresh's own boots, and he fired the extinguisher down.

Angela shamefully shuffled backwards, fearful of the sledge and tanker exploding. The guilt at not helping Paresh was overwhelming, but not enough to push her to her feet. All she could do was squat there in the middle of the inimical blizzard watching the three Legionnaires risk their lives to protect the bioil that everyone else needed to survive another few days.

Eventually it was over, and the flames snuffed out beneath the bubbling foam, itself already starting to freeze. Elston's voice was strong in the net, overridden by Botin's agonized screams. That finally galvanized Angela into action. She put her head down, and pushed through the horizontal snow to reach Paresh. Together with Omar they tugged the lieutenant over to biolab-2.

Coniff and Sakur helped Angela, Paresh, and Omar heave Botin onto the vacant gurney. Ravi was moved aside, while Leora, Winn, Chris, and Juan-Fernando with their serious but non-life-threatening injuries were unceremoniously dispatched into the laboratory section itself to clear some space.

With the snow and ice melting in the cabin's warmth, the damage the flames had done to the lieutenant's hands and arms was becoming apparent. Angela stood as far back as she could, with water dripping off her parka as Sakur cut the crusted, blackened balaclava away from Botin's head. Two sacs of sedative were quickly bumped against the charred skin of his neck, silencing his whimpers.

'We need to strip all his clothes off and apply the flesh membrane seal,' Coniff said. 'Omar, can you help us, please? Take the armour jacket and torso layers, the flames seem to have missed them. Use cutters, don't worry about buttons and zips.'

'Yes ma'am,' Omar said in a hushed, reluctant tone. He pulled his own gloves and parka off, and went to stand at the gurney.

'I'll take the arms and hands,' she said. 'Sakur, legs and feet, please.'

Water and splats of yellow, blood-curdled foam continued to drip off the gurney. Strips of stained cloth followed them, crumpling into a soggy mush on the floor. Angela looked away. There was a smell starting to build up in the biolab's main cabin which the air-con couldn't entirely deal with even though the vent fans were running on high.

The door chamber slid back, and Elston bustled in, unzipping his parka. 'Is he okay?' He craned forward for a look at the lieutenant on the gurney, and blanched when he saw the ruined flesh of both limbs and face.

The doctor was spraying the raw burns with antiseptic oil. She turned to face the colonel, and shook her head, tight-lipped.

It was a wonder Elston didn't slam his fist into the cabin wall. Angela hadn't seen him quite so angry before. Cross, yes, but this was a rage that was consuming him. 'That *thing*,' he choked out.

'Who did it get?' Angela asked quietly. Her grid was showing her identity icons and their status, so she already knew. But there was some kind of primitive belief going on deep in her brain that wanted the deaths confirmed by something other than a machine.

Elston glared at her, then relented. 'Atyeo and Garrick are confirmed dead. You saw them out there. Bastian is missing. It must have carried him off.'

'What does it do with them?' Omar demanded, his ruined face wrinkling up heavily in an expression of frightened dismay. 'Is it eating us? Is that it?'

'It won't be biocompatible at that level,' Coniff said without looking up from her patient. 'Even if it is carnivorous, our protein structures will be all wrong for it.'

'Then what—' Omar began wretchedly.

'I don't fucking know!' Elston shouted back.

Angela realized a mild shock was starting to set in. Her skin was beginning to flush. Somewhere underneath all her layers, her arms were shaking. She wanted to ask Elston what he was going to do about refuelling now. About safeguarding the tanker and the remaining bioil in the sledge. But they were past that now. All they could do was wait in their vehicles for the fury of the blizzard to pass, like peasant primitives, and hope the monster didn't come for them in the meantime. It riled her that she had no other option.

When she looked round the muggy cabin she saw Ravi looking

at her with an unnervingly calm expression. She shuffled her way round to him.

'Thank you again,' the craggy old pilot said.

'Least I could do.' She glanced back at the gurney. 'So what now? You're proper military; what's our best tactical plan?'

'It's going to finish what it just started. I would. Without fuel we're totally screwed. That and the comm rockets. It'll keep going after them until it succeeds, and when it does, we're all dead. Our biggest disadvantage is that none of our weapons work against it. How do you stop something you can't kill or even injure.'

'You're wrong,' Elston said without turning round. 'We do have a weapon that will be utterly lethal to that son of a bitch.' With that he began to pull his outer gauntlets back on in fast angry motions. 'And I'm going to get it, and I will have no hesitation using it on that bastard. If HDA want a living specimen they can come here and collect one for themselves. Because that is now one dead monster walking.' He stomped into the door chamber.

Angela exhaled lightly. She looked down at Ravi, and flexed her fingers, feeling the mild tingle of her dark weapons. 'So if I had a weapon that would kill it, what would I do?'

'There's only one option left,' the pilot said knowingly. 'You have to go on the offensive. Like you did before . . .'

Angela gave him a tight smile. 'Yeah.' The trouble was, she hadn't exactly been on the offensive.

*

After the shock of finding the bodies of the three Norths and Suski in the mansion's lounge, Angela hung on to the door frame for grim life while her nerves steadied fractionally. There was a psycho loose in the mansion, and, like the light, none of the alarms was working. She peered out into the long central corridor. Without ringlight, the only illumination was that provided by the overspill from the lounge lights. She looked up and down the corridor. Five metres away, the door to Bartram's bedroom was opening silently.

The sight of it was all Angela needed to clear her mind and *focus*. All that mattered now was survival. Cost irrelevant. She activated the dark weapons in her hands, and felt eight sharp pricks of pain when the sharp little talons punctured her skin as they rose up from the cy-tech fronds which had twined along her finger bones. Blood began to drip down, adding to the lake of gore around her feet.

There was so much she'd never be able to keep her balance, she realized. She hurried out into the corridor, her feet slapping against the clean marble, gaining traction.

Bartram's door swung right back. A humanoid monster was standing there. Time halted as she stared at the impossibility. It was her own height, though considerably more bulky, with a skin she would always recall as resembling leather turned to stone. Behind it, revealed in the faint wash of light from the lounge, she saw the bodies of Mariangela, Coi, and Bartram. Butchered by the same blades that were now rising up in front of her, the hands of the monster. That motion broke the spell.

She assumed a combat crouch, just as some long-forgotten instructor had taught her and Shasta decades ago, during one of their foolish fads. Studying the monster's movements, waiting for the tell-tale shift that would illustrate its attack.

For some reason it didn't attempt a lunge or swipe with those horrific blades that were poised ready to administer her death. Instead, its head tilted to one side, and it issued the wistful sigh of a thwarted lover, as if it was surprised and gladdened to see her.

Angela jumped, turning sideways as she went, assuming a Soaring Leopard posture. Ducking under the raised arm to unexpectedly jab both sets of fingers into its torso. And trigger—

The cy-tech that had been implanted in New Tokyo, and stimulated by the activants behind Maslen's café, had spent the intervening weeks growing inside her, its quasi-life cells enveloping her ulnas in a sheath of synthetic cells that had been faithfully copied from electric eels. Semi-organic conductor threads had sprouted from them into her hands up to the talon buds in each fingertip.

Five thousand volts slammed into the monster with a blinding violet-white flash. It went flying backwards along the seventh floor's wide central corridor, landing in the long grisly slick of blood and skidding further until it smacked into the wall.

Angela didn't even see the final impact, she was already sprinting for the stairs. The world had gone mad, imploded on her. But that didn't matter, the transfer had gone through. Rebka would get the genetic treatment. Nothing else mattered. A hysterical laugh bubbled out of her rigid throat. *Not even alien killer monsters.*

All she had to do was keep alive, stay ahead of the authorities. Nobody was going to believe her when it came to tonight's events. She couldn't explain them fully unless she told them why she was really here, and that could never happen. Nothing could risk Rebka's treatment. Nothing at all. Her own life was expendable at this point.

She took the stairs three at a time. Couldn't hear anything moving behind her. Not yet. Maybe the charge had killed it? Somehow she knew it hadn't.

There was a bag in her room, one she casually kept packed, one which had items to help any emergency dash to safety. She reached the sixth floor and had a millisecond debate with herself – if she could afford the time to retrieve it. The monster would be after her, she never doubted that for an instant. But she needed the things in that bag if she was to stand any chance of getting away clean.

Angela went for the bag.

*

Inside the biolab's door chamber, Angela ordered her e-i to switch on the identity code in her solid memory cache. She put the little block on a shelf, and deactivated her bodymesh's link to the convoy's net. Not that the net was much use in the bedlam of the lightning storm.

She stepped out into the turmoil of the blizzard. Sirius in its weakened state still hadn't penetrated the cloud, leaving the canyon immersed in a thick gloaming. Gravel-sized snowflakes assailed her parka and quilted trousers, *crackling* against her helmet. As she looked round she could see the white headlight beams pointing ineffectually into the storm, blurring into a haze just a few metres outside the pathetic protective ring the vehicles had once again contracted into.

Atyeo and Garrick still lay on the ground beside biolab-1, with the snow already starting to accumulate along one side of their corpses where the wind blew unceasingly. Most of the hose was already submerged under small ripple-like drifts, while the frozen extinguisher foam looked like another serrated ice ridge, just one more piece of the tormented landscape. None of the remote guns was moving now, leaving the convoy effectively defenceless against the monster. Though in truth, they always had been, she thought.

Angela set off between Tropics-3 and 2. The side windows on both vehicles were covered with pale sheets of ice, fluorescing slightly from the inside lights. Their windscreen wipers were still churning away in pained judders, but all they cleared now was ever-smaller triangles. At this rate the windscreens would be covered in another half-hour.

Nobody saw her, not even when another crazy lightning ball streaked through the turgid clouds far above, throwing down a brighter illumination. She walked unchallenged into the canyon's arctic emptiness where the monster awaited. The solitude was almost refreshing, as was the lack of worry. Her decision had been made, the demon would be faced.

She trudged around the convoy slowly, turning a complete circle every couple of paces so she could see it when it came for her. Ball lightning swooped above her sporadically, revealing the stark ground of broken folds, meandering fissures, and entombed rock. She had to walk, anyone stationary out here would freeze soon enough. The glow of the headlights revealed the vehicles easily enough. An icon in her smartcell grid showed her the net fading in and out as if it was nothing more sophisticated than a shortwave radio signal.

Angela had completed a half-circuit of the vehicles when she saw something moving through the churning snow. A bulky humanoid figure leaning into the wind and abrasive snow. It was heading straight for her. Angela hurriedly pulled off her outer gauntlets.

When it was five metres away, another lightning ball darted above the canyon wall. The figure was coated in a slick black skin, obscuring its features. Snow slithered down it, unable to gain any kind of hold. Several slippery bulges flared out from around the waist, two of them with pistol grips protruding.

'Rebka?'

A secure link quested out from the blank figure. 'Mother, what the hell are you doing out here?'

Angela started stuffing her hands back into the gauntlets. Just a few seconds' exposure had sent the acute cold slithering through the fabric of her inner layers to nip at her fingers. 'Protecting you. It'll come for me. I can deal with it.'

Rebka came right up to her until their faces were centimetres apart; Angela covered by a balaclava wrapped in a scarf, Rebka clad in smooth metamolecule armour.

'I really don't think you can,' Rebka said. 'Come on, come back in.'

'To sit in a biolab until it rips a door off and stabs us while we sleep? Not my style.'

'The biolabs are tough. We can sit out the blizzard in them.'

'It will go for the comm rockets. We need them just as much as the bioil.'

'Mother! Please, I can deal with it.'

'I am not letting you face that thing. I can't. Not after everything we've done to make sure you live.'

'Why won't you trust me? These systems are quite capab— Aye hell.'

'What?' Angela turned to scour the blizzard, fearful what her daughter's sensors had detected.

'You must have two micro-tracers on you. The second one just got triggered.'

'That son of a bitch Elston never did really trust me.'

Rebka slapped her shoulder. 'Can't think why. He'll be out here soon. That's all we need, a Gospel Warrior screwing things up.'

*

As soon as Vance gave the order for everyone to take shelter in the biolabs he found Angela was missing. Her identity icon showed she was in biolab-2 where he'd left her, but Paresh had tried to link to her, to check she'd made it back to the Tropic okay.

Vance didn't know what she was doing, but with his command under deadly assault from the monster, he was long past giving her the benefit of the doubt. He ordered his e-i to trigger the smartmicrobe bug that Antrinell had tagged Angela with.

Even the convoy's decaying, glitching net could still perform a triangulation function. Her location popped up immediately in Vance's iris smartcell grid. Angela was standing twenty-five metres outside the ring of vehicles. At least, he assumed she was standing – there was no medical data to confirm it, just the smartmicrobe's weak ping.

Antrinell and Jay watched him closely as he slipped the pistol into its rubbery heated sheath. His e-i quested a link to the magazine, and gave the bullets their arming code. 'I'm going out there,' he said.

'Keep a link open,' Antrinell said. 'We need to know what's happening.'

'And be careful,' Jay said. 'She's either the murderer or she's helping that thing. There's no other reason for her to be out there.'

'I know,' Vance said. The knowledge came with a heavy heart. Despite their differences, he had come to rely on Angela. And if she was part of whatever conspiracy they were caught up in, why had she brought Ravi back? Was Ravi part of this, too? He hated the fear his paranoia was generating. 'Sweet Jesus, protect me, please,' he whispered.

Ball lightning struck the floor of the canyon several hundred metres away, detonating into a morass of belligerent lightning strands. The vehicles were briefly highlighted in the stark flickering light. He saw Garrick climbing up into biolab-2's door chamber, and his e-i quested a link. 'Did everyone get across okay?' he asked.

'Lulu and Darwin are inside,' Garrick said. 'Madeleine went back for something. I couldn't stop her.'

Vance studied his grid, but Madeleine Hoque's identity icon was missing. 'It's back,' he growled. 'Get inside, now,' he told Garrick.

The lightning rampage died away, leaving Vance alone in the gloom of the savage blizzard. He bent into the wind, and hurried forwards as fast as he could go. Angela's tracer hadn't moved. His e-i activated his iris smartcells' infrared function, shifting his vision to a seething blur-cloud of sapphire and cyan. A slim glimmer of pink fluctuated in and out of existence up in front as the harsh flurries of snow marched across it.

Elston gripped the pistol tightly and slogged forward over the hellish wasteland of the broken ice river. Nothing was going to stop him now, not weather, not monsters. Angela Tramelo was finally going to tell him the truth no matter what. The Good Lord would understand and forgive extreme measures on this day.

As he drew closer, the red glimmer strengthened, widening, resolving out of smeared chaos. Another lightning ball plummeted into the ground behind him. White light flooded out, revealing the canyon. It was two figures up ahead!

Angela was easy enough to identify, she was in a parka with one of those thick scarfs she knitted wrapped round her head. The monster was standing beside her. Its skin was sleeker than the images had shown him, and it wasn't as large as he'd expected.

'I have looked upon you,' Vance snarled into the storm, 'and I have seen the devil.' He raised his pistol and walked forward. He fired. Once. Twice.

The monster bent and ducked. Just as it had been with Ravi, the bullets had no effect. *I have to get closer. Have to get a clean eye shot.* Then Vance realized it didn't have blades for hands. In fact it looked remarkably human, despite being featureless. *There must be different types.*

'Stop stop,' Angela yelled. She was racing forward, waving her arms frantically. 'Elston, for fuck's sake. Stop shooting!'

'You are allied,' he cried in consternation. His pistol swung round, lining up on the traitor woman who had persecuted his dreams for too long. Satan's whore. The arch deceiver.

'She's my daughter,' Angela bellowed.

Vance wouldn't have believed anything could have stopped him from pulling the trigger. Yet his finger now refused to move. 'What?' To know . . . to finally know!

'Madeleine, she's my daughter. That's why I was in the mansion.'

'This is— I don't—' Vance was stricken with doubt. His e-i reported a quest ping emanating from the dark figure. It carried Madeleine Hoque's identity code. 'You can't be—' he blurted.

'I am,' Madeleine said. 'I'm an undercover operative. My real name's Rebka DeVoyal, and Angela is my mother.'

'You're the monster?'

'Crap no. This is metamolecule armour. Constantine North sent me. Jupiter wants to know what's going on.'

'Sweet Jesus,' Vance moaned. But . . . a daughter. 'How?' he pleaded.

'I needed money to save her,' Angela said. 'I was scamming the Norths.'

'You really didn't kill them.' The revelation was almost spiritual. Despite where he was he felt like laughing for the sheer joy of finally understanding.

'Of course I fucking didn't, you cretin,' Angela spat.

Vance grinned. That was Angela. The one and true—

Something moved behind Rebka. 'Look out,' he yelled, and brought the pistol up again.

An arm with five fingerblades slammed into Rebka's side.

*

Rebka guessed it didn't matter any more that her cover was blown. She couldn't see how it compromised her now. And it had certainly stopped that fool of a colonel from shooting at her. He was left begging Angela to explain. While Angela of course was just angry.

Rebka frowned as the two ancient adversaries barked at each other. Her infrared receptors showed her the pistol Elston was carrying was positively hot compared to the rest of him. Then he was yelling directly at her, and his pistol was coming up—

Something smashed against her. Even the armour's amplified muscle functions couldn't keep her upright from such an blow. Rebka toppled over and skidded along the rock-hard ice. Red icons flared in her grid, detailing the damage her net gun had received. It was effectively ruined. That was deliberate. The monster had sliced at it in the holster. *Why that?*

Combat analysis routines slipped up into her optic nerves, analysing every byte of external sensor data, predicting and forecasting options – hers and her opponent's. She spun hard along the ground, using her momentum to give her extra speed, coming round into a crouch. Not quite fast enough.

The monster had followed her. Its hand swung down again, striking against her neck before she was properly balanced again. The metamolecules protected her from the blade edges, but the blow *hurt*. Amber caution icons blinked up. The metamolecules were actually straining to maintain integrity against such impacts.

'Shit,' she grunted. Going with the strike again, falling and rolling. Again, an apparent ungainly struggle to her feet.

The monster loomed large above her, its arm raised to club her down. Standing close.

Rebka's foot lashed out. She saw her foot slide along the program's maximum impact vector, its force amplified by the metamolecules, which even actively corrected her body motion marginally. Her heel connected perfectly against its ankle. The power behind the strike knocked its legs out from under it, sending it crashing down onto the rumpled unforgiving ice. It immediately started to scramble to its feet.

With the metamolecule armour's help Rebka beat it up. Just in time to see Angela sprinting up to help. 'No,' she yelled, flinging out a hand to keep her mother away. That distraction was all the monster needed.

The kick landed full square at the base of her spine. She actually left the ground to half-somersault through the gusting snow.

Ball lightning landed behind the convoy vehicles, detonating into a fountain-spume of lightning fronds that soared twenty metres up into the blizzard. With her enhanced senses, Rebka saw the scene in perfect monochrome light.

The monster turning to follow her. Angela still charging forwards with her hands extended wide. Elston lumbering on behind, trying to keep the warm pistol level on the monster.

'Stay back, Mother,' she cried, as if that would do any good. She watched in disbelief as Angela pulled her gloves off.

Her e-i was throwing up combat options. Weapons were coming on line. She cursed herself for being so slow, for letting emotions interfere with her responses. Without the net gun, capturing the monster wasn't going to be an option any more. Survival was what drove her now. She started to rise.

The lightning withered down, spent against the frozen river. Darkness collapsed in on them again. Elston's muzzle flash was bright in her sensors. Which made the monster turn towards him – and Angela. Those fatal blades swept up. Then Angela was jumping.

Rebka screamed: 'No!'

But Angela reached out, and Rebka's sensors perceived the weirdest pulse of electrical energy surging down her arm.

*

They worked, the old dark cy-tech weapons. Angela felt the tips surge up through the flesh of her fingertips, as she started to jump, to distract the monster from its brutal assault on her daughter. Ten sharp stabs of pain that she ignored. The monster was turning, its blades stretching out as they repeated their ancient dance. And she reached out to stroke its shoulder once again, but this time going low.

The cells discharged. As before, those twenty years ago, there was a blinding flash, and the monster went staggering back through the icy darkness. But this time there was something wrong, some piece of insulation that hadn't quite developed correctly. Fire burned down the inside of her left wrist. Stunning her, stalling the scream of agony that was in her throat. Her senses blanked out for a moment and she hit the ground, sprawling helplessly, heart juddering wildly.

Five blades slid down amid the snowflakes. And she couldn't move.

Elston came hurtling out of the blizzard, shoulder down in the old football tackle. Crunched into the side of the monster, sending them both crashing over together beside Angela. She saw him try to bring his pistol up to the monster's face. Too slow. Five blades jabbed upward, penetrating his parka and the armour vest below, slicing deep into the abdomen.

'NO!' Angela wailed.

Elston's face was inches from her. Shock filled his eyes as he drew down a feeble gasp of air. The blades were withdrawn from his body. He shook uncontrollably as he slumped down onto the ice.

*

Rebka watched in horror as Elston sacrificed himself to deflect the blades from her mother. Then the terrible creature was recovering, pushing the dying colonel to one side, ready to administer the same fatal blow to Angela. Angela who snarled with savage defiance, and brought her weaponized hands up again.

Rebka jumped, effortlessly covering the distance. She landed on both feet directly in front of it, knees bent, fist clenched. Purple and gold kinetic profile projections blossomed in her optic interface as the combat programs ran options. The armour locked into shape as the five-blade hand came slashing round malevolently. The edges hit her upper shoulder and rebounded, slewing the humanoid shape round, trailing projections like neon contrails. Three opportunities opened for a counter-strike. Rebka punched with her right hand, seeing her fist slide along the combat program's trajectory. Impact point was perfect, mid-torso while it was still regaining equilibrium from its deflected attack. It left the ground to fly backwards, thudding down heavily a couple of metres away.

'Enough,' Rebka said coldly. She drew the e-carbine from her waist. Theoretically, it could slice through a two-metre column of metalloceramic armour. But Rebka dialled the power down, and fired. A glaring purple-white beam of electrons stabbed out, hitting the monster's waist. It juddered frantically under the blast. Rebka switched it off. 'Don't like electricity, huh?' She fired again. The monster's fists and heels began to beat against the ice river. Slim serpents of electron currents writhed furiously around it in a splendorous cage of agonizing illumination; its hide was smouldering from the points where it was grounding out, thin wisps of smoke mingling with the steam fizzing up from the ice. 'They want me to keep you alive. I can't do that if you keep up the aggression.' She switched the e-carbine off again. 'What do you say?'

Her e-i reported a link quest from the prone monster, using Bastian North's identification tag. 'I concede your advantage,' he said.

*

Angela knelt beside Elston, and smiled wretchedly at him. 'What did you do that for?' she choked. 'That was so stupid. I had everything under control.'

He smiled weakly and held her hand, turning it round slowly

so he could see her bleeding fingertips with the talons exposed. 'Little girl fought off a monster all by herself. Never did believe it.'

'Good stuff, cy-tech. I'm sure you've got better today.'

'We have.'

'I'll remember that for next time.'

'Angela.'

'I'm not going anywhere.'

He tried to smile again, but a glob of blood spilled out of his mouth. 'You have to see the end of this. I trust you, Angela. The Lord has shown me your true self. You are worthy of His love. Finish this properly. For me.'

'Elston.' Her e-i was questing Coniff, for the others, for help. It reported a file was being sent to her on a secure link from Elston's bodymesh.

'I understand now,' he said. 'She's wonderful. A surprise, just like you. You did the right thing.'

'Hold on,' she urged, and squeezed his hand.

A large spurt of blood gushed out of Elston's mouth. 'My Lord is calling. I will wait for you, Angela. We will meet again in His grace.'

'Vance—'

'Ha, first time . . .'

Angela watched a small smile lift his lips. Then he was staring at something beyond her, an expression of relief and hope filled his pained eyes at the last. In her grid, all his physiological read-outs turned red, then bleached down to white. Her head snapped round to the monster which was standing passively beside Rebka. 'You son of a bitch.' She brought her hands up – and fuck the broken insulation.

'He tried to destroy my world, everything I am,' the monster sent down the link.

'You killed him. You killed everyone.' Confronting her night-mare of twenty years was chilling her far more than any blizzard ever could. She wasn't sure how long she could restrain herself.

'Examine the file he sent you. Examine the genocide weapon

you have in the biolab. Tell me then who is evil, who is the murderer.'

'What? What are you talking about?' Angela regarded the urbane monster in dismay as she hugged her hands to her chest to try and shelter them from the sub-zero wind. She couldn't even feel the pain from the talons any more. Drops of her blood had frozen into lumps around the small tears where they'd punctured her fingertips.

'You were so full of life, Angela. Once. The most delightful human I ever knew; the most human human, despite the deception you were living. Your soul is not something you can disguise. Have you lost that zest? Is it only ever to be the cold-hearted who judge me?'

'What the fuck are you?' she bellowed against the blizzard.

The monster's shape changed – softening.

Angela swayed backwards. Of all the things she'd braced herself for, a North in a parka and quilted trousers wasn't one of them. 'You're not Bastian North,' she said to the thing, forcing herself to believe it. 'So what are you?'

'I speak for this world.'

'Zebediah North.'

'I was. For a long time.' And amid the thick snow and treacherous gloaming illumination the humanoid shape lost cohesion, as if the North had only ever been a spectre. Angela even doubted her brief memory.

'Yet you couldn't be,' she told the monster. 'Because he was never Barclay North to begin with. You murdered Barclay back at the mansion. So what are you? A different kind of clone?'

'I mirror Barclay North. In one respect I still am him, for I retain his essence. You loved me once, Angela, or so I thought. Even in my rage at what your kind had done to me, I cherished that thought.'

'You hesitated,' she said in astonishment. 'That night twenty years ago, when you came out of Bartram's bedroom, you hesitated. That's why I survived.'

'Just like humans, I make mistakes. That and you do pack quite a punch. Who knew?'

'Why did you kill them all? The Norths, those poor helpless girls . . . Why?'

'Why do you kill me? You slash, you burn, you poison; and now you bring a weapon that will destroy all my life on this world.'

'I . . . didn't know that.' She told her e-i to open Elston's file.

*

Angela went in first. Four carbines were aimed at her as she came out of biolab-1's door compartment. Jay, Roarke, Omar and Paresh who were holding them had hyped themselves up on fear and adrenalin. It wasn't a good combination, not if you were facing that many muzzles, all of which were shaking to some degree.

'Come on, guys, it's only me,' Angela said as she carefully unwound the scarf from her face. As soon as she came into contact with the cabin's warm air her frozen blood droplets began to melt, mingling with the ice clinging to her hands. Sensation was creeping back into her extremities, as if she'd been stung by a wasp on each finger.

But they weren't listening to her, they were looking at the other two figures in the door compartment: Rebka in her meta-molecule armour and the hulking Barclay avatar with its five-blade hands.

'Get down,' Paresh pleaded desperately.

'Stop it,' she told him. 'There's nothing to fear, this is Rebka and—'

'Who?'

'Madeleine. You know her as Madeleine.'

Rebka's armour flowed away from her face, and she smiled out stoically. 'Hi.'

Paresh kept looking at Angela along the carbine's barrel. 'Down,' he whispered.

'Listen to me,' Angela said slowly. 'All of you. Put your weapons down. There is to be no more violence. We agreed to that.'

'It killed Elston,' Jay said. 'And you're part of this, you're its partner.'

'A part of what?' Angela studied the fear on Jay's face, and knew she'd never win him over. 'Paresh. Omar. Listen to me, the time for killing and weapons is over. We have to salvage this another way, we have to think and act like rational creatures. Now, please put the weapons down. We all know they're no good against the avatar. The only thing you'll damage with bullets in here is us and the bulkheads.'

Omar glanced at Paresh for a lead, as she knew he would. She kept eye contact with her devoted puppy boy, smiling encouragement. 'It's me, Paresh,' she said. 'I'm telling you this is the only way we're all going to get out of this. And you know I wouldn't lie to you. You know that, don't you? Please. Trust me.' She could see the uncertainty building, his need to believe in her. 'It's me. Okay. Me!'

'What's going to happen if we put the weapons down?' Paresh asked.

'Corporal!' Jay yelled. 'You keep that fucking *thing* covered.'

'Until you have a chance to launch the missiles?' Angela asked sharply. 'That's not going to happen. Not without Elston's codes.'

'How did you know?'

She gave Paresh an expectant glance. 'It'll be all right. Really it will.'

Paresh let out a long sigh, and raised his weapon, engaging the safety. 'Stand down,' he told Omar.

'No,' Jay said.

Paresh put his hand on the barrel of Jay's carbine, and forced it down. 'This is over. You and I don't get to decide this.'

'Thank you,' Angela said. She turned to face the decontam airlock door at the back of the compartment. Her e-i told her it was locked, and not even Elston's code could open it. She quested a link to Antrinell. 'Open it up, please.'

'I always knew you were part of whatever was going on,' Antrinell replied.

'Then you were always wrong. I am not a part of anything. I never have been. Even Elston knew that in the end.'

'Why have you brought that creature here?'

'Because we have to finish this,' she said. 'We have to destroy the zero metavirus.'

'That's the only leverage we have. It's been trying to get in here since the start, so it must fear the weapon. That's all we have left to use against it.'

'No, Antrinell, we have our humanity. We can show St Libra what we really are. That we are mature enough to venture out into the galaxy and take our rightful place in God's creation.'

'What do you know of God, murderess?'

'I have never killed anyone. And I know what you believe, that life – all life – is a precious gift from God. You don't really think, do you, that He wants you to kill all the life on this planet?'

'We picked up some of what you were saying out there,' Antrinell said. 'We heard what it claimed. It's part of the planet, the jungle?'

'Yes,' the Barclay avatar said.

'Then you're some kind of macro-life, just like the Zanth. You're not part of God's creation.'

'I am nothing like the Zanth, I don't even understand where the Zanth came from. I evolved from true biological life, just as you are evolving.'

'So what do you want? Why have you killed so many of us?'

'Because you have destroyed so much of me. This avatar's human nature bestowed me with hatred. I have not hated for a billion years.'

'We did it to ourselves,' Angela said. 'Just like we always screw up. But you've got the chance to make it right, Antrinell. This is why God gave us the greatest gift of all: free will. This is why he brought us to this point, so that you would have to make the decision. We can ally ourselves with St Libra, with life. Without that we will face the Zanth alone and afraid.'

'You can manipulate stars,' Antrinell said. 'You can replicate humans. God alone knows what other abilities you have. And God knows you've shown you have no compunction about slaughtering us. How do we know you won't side with the Zanth?'

'Only a human would ask that question,' the Barclay avatar said.

'Yes, and I'm asking it.'

'We have to show trust to receive trust,' Angela said.

'Then show me some,' Antrinell said.

'I'm supposed to be a bridge,' the Barclay avatar said. 'You tell me why I should be. You who destroy anything you don't comprehend, anything that gets in your way. You who abused this world for your own species and its profit, who replicate that crime across so many worlds. That is why I have no compunction, no remorse. So far all I have seen is vermin, breeding and breeding and desecrating the world, my world, with their own excrement. Yet I have stayed my hand for twenty years trying to reach out to you. I still do. That is my human side, and it grows weary of my failure.'

Angela flinched. She knew damn well that kind of argument wouldn't work on anyone as stubborn as Antrinell. So she played dirty, played to win, just like Angela DeVoyal would do. Her e-i sent Elston's visual log into the ringlink, the one where he lay dying, when he looked up at Angela and said: 'You have to see the end of this. I trust you, Angela. The Lord has shown me your true self. You are worthy of His love. Finish this properly. For me.'

'He gave me his command codes,' she told them all. 'Antrinell cannot launch the missiles without them. I cannot deactivate the warheads without Antrinell's corresponding codes. Vance Elston made that first step, a man who believes as you do, Antrinell, who worshipped with you. A man who revered the sanctity of human life so much he sacrificed himself so I would live. Please, Antrinell, don't betray that sacrament.'

There was a long pause before Antrinell asked: 'What would happen if we destroy the warheads?'

'The arrangement I have with Constantine is that I will provide you with information to help deflect Zanthswarms from the star systems you inhabit,' the Barclay avatar said. 'In return he will assist with the human evacuation of St Libra.'

'Evacuation?' Antrinell said. 'There are millions of people here, most of them political refugees. They won't want to go back. Not even the Norths will be able to make them.'

'If Sirius remains as it is, how many will live? You are running out of food. You can grow no more in this climate. And it will remain like this until I wish it otherwise.'

'Even if we destroy the weapon we've got here, the HDA will send more of it through the gateway as soon as they find out what you are,' Antrinell said.

'Constantine will close the gateway,' the Barclay avatar said. 'Any threat will end with that.'

'This is the first step,' Angela said. 'We both know that the metavirus is ineffective in this climate anyway. You're giving up so little, Antrinell. Doing this is a symbol only, such a small thing, but it will allow a friendship to begin that will endure for aeons. All of us are on the cusp of something extraordinary. Antrinell, you are not betraying yourself or the HDA. You are being true to your real belief, the heart of your religion. All life is sacred. You know this.' She drew a breath, and found herself praying.

The decontam airlock hissed open.

'Thank you,' Angela said. Her legs were so shaky she thought she might fall. Paresh's arm came round her, holding her tight. She glanced up at his tired, worried face with its frost-blackened skin and dirty stubble, and managed a small grateful grin for him. He winked back.

The Barclay avatar walked across the cabin. Just before it reached the airlock it stopped and turned to face Angela. There were human eyes looking out at her from the deep recesses of the stony countenance. 'Did I – did *he*, ever mean anything to you?' it asked.

'I saw him as a means to an end,' she said. It was difficult now even recalling the time she and Barclay had spent together. Before the expedition, she hadn't thought about Barclay for two decades, which in itself was a telling answer. 'At first. But back then I was desperate; I would and did sacrifice anything in order to do what I had to. When you were him, you were not quite the same as your clone brothers. Under different circumstances, in different times, I genuinely don't know what would have happened between us.'

'I thank you for that answer. I have thought about it more than I should for twenty years. That is perhaps why I remain conflicted. There are so many conflicts within a human mind. It is difficult for me to fully comprehend the universe through your eyes.'

Angela glanced at Rebka. 'Yeah, tell me about it.'

Thursday 9th May 2143

The new uniform was stiff; its collar scratched Sid's neck. The cuffs did the same to his wrists. And the trousers weren't cut quite right—

'Stop adjusting yourself,' Jacinta snapped. 'The meshes will pick it up.'

Sid removed his hand from his crotch. At the other end of the big limousine's passenger compartment Chloe Healy was diplomatically looking elsewhere. She'd been the one who delivered the uniform to the house that morning, along with the chauffeured limousine, all courtesy of NorthernMetroServices. He hadn't wanted a new uniform, as there was nothing wrong with the old one. Except when the two of them were hung up side by side, even he had to admit his old one was shabby and worn. The fabric of the one Chloe had brought was a deep black with a lustre that only money could produce in cloth. And actually, when you added all his service ribbons in a discreet band on the breast, it looked very smart indeed. The kind of uniform a competent, dynamic, trustworthy leader would wear.

At least the white shirt was his own.

The limousine crawled along Collingwood Street with its tall grey-brown stone buildings on either side. The stores and businesses all had a picture of Ian in their ground-floor windows, wreathed in black ribbons.

'Did you organize this?' he asked Chloe. It was as if a Catholic saint had died.

'No. It's actually real.'

The second half of Collingwood Street, before the junction with Cathedral Square, had crowd barriers along the edge of the pavement. A lot of people were pressed up behind the waist-high metal meshes, waiting for the hearse.

'My God,' Jacinta muttered.

'He did save the city from a D-bomb,' Chloe said.

Sid and Jacinta looked at each other, then looked away. Their limousine turned right into St Nicholas Street and pulled up outside the cathedral. The majestic old building was isolated by more crowd barriers; uniformed agency constables were lined up along them. Sid couldn't even work out how many people had turned up to pay their respects to the hero who'd sacrificed himself to save the city – but it was certainly in the thousands.

'Now remember, no more than thirty seconds with the Mayor,' Chloe warned as the doors unlocked.

'Aye,' Sid said, with *tone*.

The limousine in front had brought the Mayor to the cathedral. Chloe had negotiated that with the Mayor's office, giving the politician arrival preference, but in return he wasn't to monopolize Sid on the way in to the cathedral. And they weren't going to be sitting together during Ian's memorial service either, that would make it look too much as if Sid was part of the Mayor's ticket. That hadn't been agreed yet.

Sid stepped out onto the pavement. The sun was high in a cloudless azure sky, and the warm air was gusting down New-castle's ancient streets, carrying with it the smell of the city. Leaves on the oak trees along the north side of the cathedral still retained their spring vivacity, producing a bright emerald stipple haze as they were struck by sunlight. It was a lot of rich sensation after the sterility of the limousine, and hundreds of people were staring at him.

The applause began. It took Sid a moment to realize it was directed at him. He managed a discreet smile direct to the crowd, and nodded his appreciation. Faces blurred as he walked past; he was dreading catching sight of one of Ian's girls.

'Detective Hurst.' The Mayor was upon him, hand extended. The large cluster of licensed reporters on either side of the cathedral doors paid very close attention to the greeting.

Sid shook the proffered hand. 'Mayor. Thank you for coming.'

'It's the least I could do. The city owes Detective Lanagin so much. He truly demonstrated why we are right to place so much value on our police force.'

Sid could just picture the mocking grin Ian would have on his face if he could see this, the gesture he'd be making at Sid behind the politician's back. Then he'd be off eyeing the crowd for decent-looking girls to score.

Jacinta smoothly eased forward and offered her hand to the Mayor, who shook it gracefully. 'We should go in,' she said.

'Of course,' the Mayor said, still the epitome of dignity.

They walked away from him. The coffin bearers were waiting just inside the big double door: Eva, Lorelle, Ari, and Royce O'Rouke, who was once again able to show off his old uniform to the transnet news crews. Sid smiled tightly at them, and felt Jacinta's grip squeeze harder. He needed that. It was tougher than he could believe possible simply to walk down the aisle, acknowledging people as he went. That was his job now, being seen and making connections. Ralph Stevens and Sarah Linsell were there, right at the back, as unobtrusive as good spooks should be. Jenson San, the little shit. Hayfa Fullerton, Reannha Hall, Tilly Lewis heading the pew of Market Street personnel. Milligan and his people in the pew behind, making sure they were included. Even Commissioner Passam was there, being ignored by everyone.

So many people he didn't know. Who never knew Ian. Important people to be seen offering their thanks, showing support for the city's finest in these troubled times.

Tallulah was there, several rows from the front. Head down as she sobbed quietly, trying not to make a scene. Grandees on either side, whose polite stiff faces were doing their best to ignore her. Even in distress with tears smearing her make-up she was breathtaking.

Sid stopped, and held out his hand to her. 'Come with me,' he said kindly.

So there was a bit of a commotion as she wormed past people and joined him in the aisle. Sid led her to the front row where Ian's distraught parents were sitting.

'No,' Tallulah began feebly.

'You knew him. You cared about him,' Sid said quietly. 'There's not many of us. We have to stick together.'

She smiled with pathetic gratitude, and sat beside him. He shook hands with the parents, whom he'd met for the first time last night. An awful ninety minutes in their hotel room telling them about all the good parts of their son's life he'd shared.

Jacinta patted his leg. 'That's the man I married,' she whispered.

Sid drew a breath. His e-i told him the coffin had arrived outside. The bearers were gathering to lift it from the hearse.

In front of him, the choir rose. It was the cue for the congregation to stand. Sid slowly got to his feet, the hymn book drooping from his hand. The vast organ began playing the funeral march.

Jacinta's fingers twined through his. 'Forty minutes,' she said. 'And it'll all be over. I'll share it with you.'

'Really? You want all this?'

'For better or worse. I did promise.'

And with that Sid's life was bearable again.

*

The limousine dropped them off outside their Jesmond house at one o'clock. It had proved impossible to get away earlier. Sid couldn't avoid the official reception at Newcastle's Civic Centre. He didn't want to be there, not with all the dignitaries and business leaders and the Bishop of Newcastle. Market Street personnel were having their own wake in a pub down on Quayside beside the Millennium Bridge. There would be genuine laughter, maudlin reminiscences, loud music, too much beer and some tox. Hopefully it would end in a fight, and a whole load of them would wind up being thrown in the cooler cells for the rest of the night. That would be true to Ian. A proper send-off to one of their own.

Instead, he dutifully mingled with the living dead, where it was all small talk, must-be-made introductions by Chloe, and warm white wine served by bored contract waitresses. A midnight shift riding a car round the GSWs would be better than that. Hell, his office on the sixth floor was preferable.

'Cup of tea, pet?' Jacinta asked.

'Yeah, thanks.' Once the front door was closed Sid took the hated uniform jacket off. He rubbed his neck. 'I think I've got an allergy.'

'I'll find you some cream.'

'It's not that bad.'

She rolled her eyes. 'Aye, men! Medicine isn't a weakness you know.'

'I know.' He sat at the breakfast counter on one of the new stools. Jacinta poured boiling water into a china pot – a moving-in present from her parents. 'You know, we haven't had a housewarming party yet.'

'Because we need to decorate everything before I'll let anyone inside,' she replied. 'And once we do that, I'm not having your police friends in here trashing the place. Honestly, pet, they behave worse than a bunch of fresher students once the beer's opened.'

'A fair point, well made.'

She sat down opposite him. 'Do you want to go down to Quayside?'

'Nah, I'd cramp their style. I'm sixth-floor now.'

'You knew him better than all of them.'

'I took him there, into Last Mile. I was the one that wouldn't let the case go.'

'Don't do this to yourself, pet. This case was one big weird disaster right from the start.'

'Aye.' He poured some tea into a cup. 'So the HDA was right. An alien!'

'Have you worked out why it was there, yet?'

'Not a fucking clue.' Sid grinned and drank the tea.

Jacinta reached over the counter and put her hand on top of his. 'Run the cold equation. Are we worse off now than we were before?'

Sid was about to curl his fingers round her hand when his audio smartcells let off a declamatory chime. A bright-red icon flared in the middle of his grid. 'Crap on it!' he exclaimed.

'What?'

'Code red.'

'What's that?'

'An HDA emergency.'

Jacinta's hands flew to her mouth in shock. 'A Zanthswarm?'

'I don't know.'

'Oh God, the children, Sid, we have to get the children.'

'What's happening?' Sid asked his e-i. 'Why is there a code red?'

'HDA's North Europe early warning radar network is detecting spaceships entering Earth's atmosphere.'

'*What?*'

*

Two hundred and eighty-three lightwave ships fell from the zenith of the glorious cerulean sky above Newcastle. They fell silently, discarding their stealth effect as they came swooping down on the unsuspecting city so they blossomed as dark aquamarine shapes in the eyes of the frantic residents staring upwards. Though there were many sizes and profiles, from squat teardrops to giant spheres with stumpy twisted fins protruding from their equator, none of them was small.

A teardrop with fluted contours led the formation, arrowing down towards Last Mile. Similar, people noted, to the mysterious craft that had been glimpsed there exactly a week ago when the D-bomb plot was thwarted by their very own Ian Lanagin. For the final kilometre of its descent, thin trails of vapour sprouted from the tips of the malformed rings extending from its midsection. While its brethren began to slow languidly, this one moved with fast purpose, unwinding five spiralling snow-white contrails as it plummeted down.

The idle workforce of Last Mile's struggling businesses spilled onto the Kingsway to watch the strange armada sink towards them. Images from iris smartcells and the meshes of Last Mile detonated across the transnet, projecting the sight across every trans-space world.

The lead spaceship finally decelerated hard, coming to a halt just above the metal bridge ramp that led into the silver phosphorescence of the gateway itself. With an ease belying its size and mass, it pitched over ninety degrees, presenting its nose to the trans-spacial connection. A moment later it flashed forward, flying through to St Libra.

The rest of the spaceships continued their descent in a more measured, ominous fashion. They came down in a shoal, moving in graceful union, adjusting their position until they engulfed the gateway along with the vast concrete burrow which housed the machinery generating it.

Hundreds of figures sprinted away from the hovering ships, pouring out of the Border Directorate terminal, the cargo-processing halls, the pipeline-control room, the administration offices, and the gateway-engineering centre. They looked back fearfully over their shoulders as they went, seeing fuselage hatches curtain open. Out tumbled an army of cybernetic termites: metre-long machines with spindly flexible legs and a chittering array of mandible tools. They swarmed the gateway, flooding through the open doors along the side and scampering over the concrete roof of the burrow to find vents which they wormed their way into.

Within ten minutes the gateway's remarkable shimmering oval of interdimensional radiance cooled and dimmed, evaporating like a wizard's curtain to reveal a wall of densely packed, high-voltage physics machinery behind. The army of metallic scavengers were already crawling over it, jabbing their tools into the fissures between modules, prising open conduits, tugging out bundles of cabling. Lasers sparkled dazzling red as they sought to cut through the framework girders, sending sparks fountaining down to bounce along the bridge ramp like dying fireworks.

Slowly, and with single machine-purpose intent, they gnawed their way deeper and deeper into the bulk of the generator systems. Liberated sections were lifted out and carried away by the teeming victorious termites, flowing upwards into the waiting spaceships.

With the dismantling process successfully instigated, one teardrop-shaped spaceship rose silently, and streaked away to the north.

*

It had been fifty-five years since Constantine North had seen the truncated pyramid of rainbow prism glass which he and his two siblings had lived in for over forty years while they built their commercial empire. His spaceship came down on the lawn in front of the main doors, and he stepped out to breathe down the air of his birthworld. The smell of mown grass and the last fading cherry blossom summoned up memories and emotional resonances from the older, unreformed sections of his brain. He rather enjoyed the nostalgia, stopping to admire the grounds with their thick fence of trees and two long lakes. The trees had matured nicely over the intervening decades, giving the vista a shaggier, more natural appearance.

Constantine walked up the stone steps to the heavy glass doors of the main entrance, the Aldred-avatar at his side. Augustine was waiting in the cavernous central atrium, where the St Libra vegetation reached almost to the ceiling. Several of his sons were standing beside him, forming an exemplary praetorian guard. Only when his visitors were inside did he start walking, the Rex exoskeleton legs humming quietly. He spared the hulking monster only the briefest of glances, proving to everybody how irrelevant he considered it.

'Brother,' Constantine said. 'You look good. The rejuve treatment is working, yes?'

Augustine stood in front of him not offering any greeting, any acknowledgement of what was happening. 'Aye, but not as well as yours, I see.'

'We refined Bartram's methods, that's all.'

Augustine smiled without humour, and looked at the monster again. 'What the fuck do you think you're doing?' he bellowed, his self-control lost, spittle flying from his mouth. 'You bring this, this . . . *thing* to my house. Our house!'

'Our lives are changing, Augustine. I need you to understand that. What better way . . . ?'

'Your life was nearly over, you stupid shit. I've spent the last ten minutes pleading with General Shaikh not to blow your spaceships to hell.'

'He can't actually do that, but thank you for your intervention. I'll call him myself soon, and offer him the lightwave drive by way of compensation for today. The military do so love shiny new technology, there's always so many ways to abuse it.'

'And the gateway?' Augustine asked dangerously. 'You're destroying it.'

'I'm relocating it. This life is over, Augustine. Northumberland Interstellar, the bioil, the money, let it go. I have a life so much better waiting for both of us.'

'I have spent my life building that company; you spent more than half of yours as well. You can't do this! Give me my gateway back. I'll get the bioil flowing again if I have to nuke Sirius back into life myself.'

'It's *our* gateway, brother, and I need it to save the life of everyone left on St Libra, all the millions of humans cowering in the Independencies as they starve to death. Isn't that a more noble goal to devote yourself to?'

'Save them? How? They can come back the same bloody way they went to their medieval squalor nations if you'd just leave the bloody thing alone.'

Constantine sighed and turned to the Aldred-avatar. 'Show him.'

Behind Augustine, the bullwhip tree growing in the centre of the atrium quivered. One of its lower coiled branches came lashing out, slamming into a marble bench, splitting it in two. Both halves skidded apart over the polished tile flooring, broken pebbles scattering wide. The branch slowly withdrew, coiling itself back up like a serpent returning to slumber.

Two targeting lasers were now shining out of the mansion's pillars, tracking up and down the bullwhip's trunk, trying to find the hidden hostile.

'My son,' Augustine spat at the monster. 'You killed my son. You killed my brother.'

'We're lucky it didn't commit genocide on us,' Constantine said. 'After the crimes we've committed against it.'

Augustine's glare was animated by hatred, never leaving the monster. It was strange, Constantine mused, that so much of human emotion was personalized. To think wide was to dissipate all strength of feeling. But he knew his brother could accomplish the intellectual leap – after all, he had, even though the process had taken fifty years.

'Give us some time,' Constantine said to the hulking Aldred-avatar. 'I have so much to explain to my brother.'

*

By morning the blizzard had subsided. Sirius was shining bright pink across the canyon, darkening its massive walls to a midnight black. Lighter rosy ringlight was washed away behind the most aggressive display of shifting colours the St Libra aurora had ever produced. The vast rivers of ethereal light twirled and looped over the snow-clad roofs of the convoy vehicles, on occasion even reaching down into the canyon itself, a giant's fingers stroking the jumbled white land.

Antrinell led what was left of the convoy personnel out into the clean, calm dawn. Angela followed him out, wishing she

1060

wasn't so tired. Maybe it was just the blues after having achieved so much, but she felt she should be in higher spirits.

There was too much sorrow to overcome, she decided. They'd lost so many people that the accord they'd come to with St Libra didn't settle well, not on the human psyche.

It had taken half of the night to open up the remaining warheads and remove the metavirus containers. One by one their contents had been vaporized under the steady gaze of the hulking Barclay-avatar. All of them knew that something altogether more massive, and possibly quite magical, was looking out at the process through the monster's eyes. Understanding the abstract and acknowledging the fact were quite different things.

Nobody really trusted it. Not the monster who had slain so many of them. So the Barclay-avatar stood to one side while narrow-blade axes were used to chisel the rock-hard bodies of Atyeo and Garrick from the wind-compacted ice that locked them fast against the frozen river. While Angela was taking her turn, on her knees, hammering rhythmically at the ground, she glanced over at the motionless figure standing in front of the overturned Tropic-1. Despite its solidified features, she could tell it was unmoved by the human ritual. Reverence to the dead was clearly not a part of it. But then, would it mourn every leaf that fell from its myriad trees, exhibit sorrow for every spore which didn't germinate? Short individual lives were a forgotten history for it now.

When she'd had enough, she stood up and handed her axe to Ken Schmitt. It was so much easier to move without having to wear the armour, though she noticed not everyone had abandoned it. Paresh was one of them.

'They're on their way,' the Barclay-avatar announced abruptly.

'Who are?' Tamisha asked.

'The Jupiter humans. They have arrived at Newcastle. Constantine has kept his word, and the gateway has been deactivated.'

'Just keeps getting better and better,' Antrinell said bitterly. 'No way home even if we do ever get out of here.'

Rebka put her head close to Angela. 'If a lightwave ship is here, it'll be overhead in less than an hour.'

'What's a lightwave ship?'

'UFO, basically.'

'Cool,' Angela said.

Whatever the avatar's promise, Antrinell insisted they keep working. They refilled the bioil tanks of both biolabs. Atyeo and Garrick were freed from the ice, and wrapped in sleeping bags.

'Take a break for lunch,' Antrinell said when the bodies were put on Tropic-2's sledge, next to Elston and the others. 'When we get back out here we'll launch a comm rocket. This weather's as good as it'll get.'

His voice was swamped by what sounded like a terrific airburst explosion. The canyon walls reverberated, kicking loose several micro-avalanches along the rim. Ice groaned and cracked under Angela's boots. A thin halo of snow puffed off the vehicles.

'What the hell?'

Everyone was cowering, glancing fearfully up at the shimmering curtains of moiré light that danced through the air above. Even the Barclay-avatar had flinched, Angela saw.

'Ya-hey!' Rebka shrieked. She was dancing about like a ten-year-old, waving her arms wide at the sky. 'They're here. Oh wow! Raul's piloting.' She jumped up again, her arms still windmilling excitedly.

Angela stared in astonishment at the dark teardrop shape that was ripping through the aurora's placid streamers along the canyon. Like all castaways devoid of hope, rescue, when it finally came, was hard to believe.

The spaceship slowed and tipped up, presenting its broad base to the ground, then touched down fifty metres away. Tiny emerald sparks skipped along the malformed rings sticking out of its centre, as if it was squeezing the aurora into concentrated droplets. Rebka grabbed Angela's arm, tugging her along. 'Come on, you've got to meet Raul.'

'Who's Raul?'

'My brother. Well . . . he'll probably deny it. To be honest, I was a bit of a pain growing up.' Her face, framed by the wrapped scarf and woolly hat, was so girlishly vibrant that Angela had to smile back, that happiness was like a force of nature.

A hatchway opened and two men stepped out, wearing the same protective oil-slick layer that Rebka's metamolecule cloak could form. They'd left an oval open to show their faces. Rebka squealed and flung her arms round the taller, younger one.

'Mother, this is Raul.'

'Angela DeVoyal,' he said in trepidation. '*The* Angela DeVoyal. Excuse me, but we've all been waiting a very long time to meet you.'

'Of course you have,' Angela told him, and burst out laughing at how ludicrous that statement was.

Nobody had much to take with them. Most didn't even bother delving back into the vehicles to collect their personal kitbags. Angela was one who did. Her bag with the items she'd bought at the Birk-Unwin store were the only possessions she had in the universe, the first she'd owned in twenty years, each one paid for by the money earned in Holloway. Money didn't come harder than that. Which made them important.

After she'd tugged the frost-covered bag out of Tropic-2, she switched the vehicle's power cells off. They'd been on standby since last night. Given the high temperature they operated at, restarting them in sub-zero conditions would probably shatter them. Elston hadn't wanted to risk that. The lights on the dashboard went out. For the first time in eighteen days she didn't have the whiney buzz of machinery in her ears.

Eighteen days?

She found herself trembling. The convoy's journey was too intense, too visceral to be a mere eighteen days. Even the joy of being reunited with Rebka could not compensate for the enormity of everything she'd endured.

Angela backed out of the Tropic, seeing the Barclay-avatar waiting on the frozen river as Ken, Sakur, and Tamisha carried Botin's stretcher to the waiting spaceship. The non-human thing was as impassive as it ever was, standing perfectly still as fat strands of the aurora caressed it as though it communed with the lightstorm. In her mind she saw into the humanoid shell it wore, saw through it, saw how it could be the spirit living in the plants, a fabulously complex life-force swathed round a planet as a corona clung to a star. Immense, immortal, the triumph of an evolution billions of years beyond anything terrestrial biology could aspire to. Rich with abilities that humans couldn't even imagine for their gods. She was standing on it, amid it. Irrelevant, infinitesimal, her time fleeting.

The perspective was draining. Really . . . what was the point to a life as small as hers in a galaxy which held St Libra and the Zanth?

The sound of sobbing broke her miserable reverie. Lulu MacNamara was leaning on the side of Tropic-3, crying her little heart out as she clutched her cheap copy designer bag, not caring the tears froze on her cracked, scabbed cheeks.

Angela walked over. 'What's up, sweets? We're saved. We're out of here.'

'I know,' Lulu whimpered. 'But the gateway's gone, like. I heard the monster say it. I'll never get home now, I'll never see me nan again. She'll be so worried.'

'There's no such thing as never,' Angela told her. 'Look at me, it took twenty years, but I found Rebka again. Your nan, she'll be there waiting for you when you get home.'

'How?' the girl pleaded.

'I've no idea,' Angela said breezily. 'That's the thing about the future: you just take a running jump at it, and see what you can find there. Isn't that kind of wonderful? You want to go home, back to Newcastle: then when we get back to Abellia, stand up and shout out the question as loud as you can: who else wants to come with me? If there's enough of you, then you build that gateway for yourselves.'

'Aye, like I can do that. I'm just a waitress.'

'Lulu, you've come through something that not one of us had any real expectation of surviving. It's been the most remark-able, terrifying, brutal time of my life, and trust me I've been

1064

places and done things you wouldn't believe. That makes you one of the greats, Lulu. Just living is a victory in this universe. Now we're all going to get on the spaceship, and fly back to a city that's going to thaw out nicely. After that, we'll decide where we're going next. Okay? And nobody will decide that for us.'

'Aye, I suppose.'

Angela put an arm round the girl's shoulder and gave a quick squeeze. 'Come on. I've never been in a spaceship before. I want to know what it's like. For one thing, it's going to be warm. Who knows, there might even be a shower.'

The interior didn't seem anything special. The airlock opened into a simple circular compartment with a slightly concave ceiling. Curving couches were arranged in a circle, their grey tough-foam substance blending seamlessly with the floor. The convoy personnel were stripping off their parkas and thick trousers, dripping a small stream of foul slushy ice onto the floor. Advanced spaceship it might be, but the life support was struggling with the smell of so many unwashed people.

'I have a question,' Angela said to the Barclay-avatar.

'Yes?'

'Have you killed the MTJ mutineers?'

'No, Angela. They didn't stand between me and the weapon.'

'Can you feel where they are?'

'Yes. They were hit quite badly by the blizzard. They're still digging themselves out.'

Angela turned to Raul. 'We know the route they took. Let's go get them.'

'They don't deserve it,' Antrinell grunted sourly.

Angela gave him an evil smile. 'I know. But enough people have died on St Libra, so now let's show this planet what being human really means, shall we? Let's go collect them, and give them a hot meal, and take them back to Abellia where they'll be safe and warm, just like us.'

*

As soon as the spaceships appeared, Sid and Jacinta had driven to the school to collect the kids, putting the Toyota Dayon on manual and using Sid's police authority to demand priority in the city's road metamesh. They'd pulled up outside with the siren blaring and strobes flashing, much to Will and Zara's delight. Both children were disappointed when Sid switched them off for the trip back to Jesmond.

'Why?' Will grumped.

'Because I don't think the spaceships are hostile,' Sid explained. He was only half concentrating on the road, which was dangerous when so many people were driving so badly, racing home or to collect loved ones just like him. The streets were rivers of green tail lights, with nobody obeying the metamesh. His attention was mainly on the images playing in his iris smartcell grid. The imposing shoal of spaceships was holding station above and around the gateway, the only objects that were static in the whole area. Their unnerving cybernetic spawn were seething over and inside the massive gateway generator. Sunlight flashed and flickered off the chrome tool mandibles as they writhed incessantly, clawing at the mechanism's seams, prising it apart like mechanical carrion.

'Why, Dad?'

'Because they come from Jupiter. I think.'

'How do you know that, Dad?'

'Because I once met someone who flew in one.'

'Dad!' Zara squawked excitedly. 'When was that?' she asked breathlessly.

'The night Uncle Ian died, okay.'

'Were they part of the D-bomb plot?' Will asked.

'Aye, come on you two, give your father a break,' Jacinta said sternly.

'But Mum—'

'It's all right,' Sid said. 'No, the spaceships didn't have anything to do with the plot. They belong to Constantine North. But I've no idea why they're dismantling the gateway, okay.' *Just like always, we never get to find out what's really going on.*

1066

The sound of jet turbines rolled along the streets. Both kids spent the rest of the journey trying to spot the fighters circling the shoal, vigilantly guarding Newcastle citizens from the invaders blatantly looting their city's greatest asset. Fast, dark delta shapes would flash through the gaps between the rooftops, and they'd point and whoop eagerly.

Back home safely, the Hurst family settled down in the lounge, watching the big wall pane. Media helicopters were venturing ever closer to the floating spaceships, in a quasi-lethal game of dare. Down on Last Mile's streets, a similar charade was being acted out, with reporters attempting to dodge past the nervous agency constables who were trying to close down access roads leading to the gateway. HDA personnel carriers were rumbling along the Kingsway, bringing squads of troopers, with officers not sure what they were supposed to be doing in the absence of definite orders from their command.

Sid's e-i reported a lot of high-priority calls stacking up in his transnet interface. The whole of Market Street's sixth floor were trying to get in touch. He didn't care, he'd run about meekly at the bidding of the rich and powerful for years, playing the game for their benefit, because, as any smart man knew, that was how the world worked.

But on this day he was going to be with his family, because that was what a man should do. Defiance felt good, too.

Northumberland Interstellar made an official statement seventy minutes into the crisis. An amazingly calm Alanzo 2North stood up in front of a media scrum at the company's marketing headquarters in the city centre and announced that the gateway was being dismantled to prevent a humanitarian disaster. That native sentient life had been discovered on St Libra, and an orderly evacuation of the Independencies was being planned.

He wanted to emphasize the spaceships were North-owned, and not a threat to anyone. Yes, they had come from Jupiter. No, he couldn't comment if one of them had been at the Mountain High building the night Ian Lanagin died.

'Is that true, Dad? Have they found aliens?' Will asked.

'Yes. I saw one.'

'Really?'

'Yes. It killed Uncle Ian.'

Jacinta gave him a sharp glance as her elbow nudged him.

'Are they dangerous?'

'Very.'

'Sid!' Jacinta hissed.

He shrugged.

A couple of news-company helicopters had found the spaceship parked outside Augustine North's truncated pyramid mansion beyond Alnwick. Armed security helicopters were buzzing them, but their meshes and lenses were sending back high-resolution images. Several Norths were milling round the base of the craft. Automated trolleys were trundling out of the mansion, laden with crates and pods.

The news switched back to the gateway shoal. Another of the smaller teardrop spaceships was drifting upwards. News copters played chicken with the squadron of HDA's VTOL gunships following it as it began to fly north, a couple of hundred metres above the city.

'It's come over the river,' Will said. 'That's central station, look.'

'What's it doing, Daddy?' Zara asked.

'I've no idea.' Sit watched uneasily as the spaceship slid smoothly over the Civic Centre. That route would bring it very close to—

'Is it following the Metro line?' Jacinta asked.

'Looks like it,' Sid admitted.

Will scrambled to his feet. 'We'll be able to see it!' he yelped.

'No!' Sid said, and lunged, trying to grab his son's arm as the boy charged past with youthful exuberance. 'Come back.'

Sid set off after Will. Jacinta and Zara were on his heels. Will got the front door open, and ran out into the small front garden. Sid was a couple of paces behind him, and finally managed to grab hold of the boy's shoulder. It didn't matter, Will had stopped anyway.

The spaceship with its hornet-swarm of terrestrial aircraft in cautious pursuit was over St George's Terrace, and descending. Sid's neighbours were also outside, staring in quiet awe as the spaceship approached.

'Dad!' Will said in scared delight. 'It's coming *here*.'

Sid's arm went round the amazed boy, his other arm went round his wife and daughter. Twenty metres in front of him, in the middle of a quiet suburban street, a spaceship from Jupiter silently touched down. A circle near the base darkened and dissolved. A North stepped out, wearing a green shirt open at the neck and blue jeans; he grinned at Sid as the news copters and VTOL gunships circled overhead.

Zara pressed into Sid's side, moving slowly behind him as the North walked up to their front gate.

'Hello, Sid,' the North said.

'I've no idea who you are,' Sid told him. 'Not unless you tell me.'

'I understand. I'm Clayton. No subterfuge this time, boss, I owe you that much. That's why I'm here. I know you need answers, and you deserve them.'

'Aye, appreciate that; so what was that thing?'

'An avatar sent by St Libra's dominant life.'

'Did it kill the North?'

'Yes.'

'Who was he; who did we pull out of the Tyne?'

'Aldred. The avatar took on his identity.'

Sid nodded weakly, giddy with the thought that he'd worked right alongside the alien imposter for months, talked to it, sat in cafés with it, accepted its reassurances about his future. And now he knew, he wished it made a difference. Right now he didn't see one. 'Why?'

Clayton pulled a face. 'That's a long answer, and we're leaving as soon as the gateway is dismantled. I can send the file for you. Some of it's quite fascinating, though there's a lot of history involved.'

'Where are you going?' Sid blurted. He couldn't take his eyes from the spaceship. That same sleek machine had been in his dreams for a week, shooting up to the stars, leaving him earthbound and envious. Envious because it wasn't his life.

'The Sirius system,' Clayton said. 'We're going to start a new world, Sid; build a fresh civilization from scratch. Among other things.'

'But you've shut down the gateway. How will you get there?'

'The long way round, I'm afraid.' He gestured at the spaceship with a smile. 'Fortunately they're fast, and it's only eight and a half lightyears away.'

Sid felt his heart leap. Part of him ached with longing at the prospect. He looked at Jacinta, reading the fascination in her expression. 'Take us with you,' he said.

*

The Camilo Village school hall had quickly become their community centre once the snow and ice arrived. It allowed them all to cook big shared meals when the blizzards allowed, there were still classes for the kids, planning sessions for the adults, people coming together to solve problems, organize work parties. If Saul didn't know the farms were buried under metres of snow, that no more food could be grown, he might almost have enjoyed the winter. But as the weeks progressed and they settled into a routine scavenging between storms, snippy rumours started to infiltrate their cosy world, about hoarders, about hidden stashes, about some people not pulling their weight.

Those petty squabbles had instantly become irrelevant when the news came through the remnants of Abellia's net that morning, telling them the Highcastle gateway had shut down. The last images from Newcastle were bewildering. Hundreds of spaceships falling from the sky, then nothing.

Was Earth being invaded?

Camilo villagers didn't care about that. They had all trudged into the school hall without even being summoned. It was a town-council-style meeting, and a lot of fear was being vented in angry exchanges. Everybody in the village agreed they could keep going as they were for another couple of months, though the scavenger parties were now having to venture further each day – and they weren't the only people stripping the unoccupied houses of their food. So far encounters with other groups had been peaceful, even collaborative on occasion. But they admitted that had just ended. They'd have to mark out their territory.

Otto got up and began talking about building greenhouses so they could start growing their own food. People jeered and told him to shut up, told him that Brinkelle was growing food in vats. He yelled back, telling them all to get real; the farms were all under metres of snow and Brinkelle wasn't riding to the rescue; if the Institute could grow food they'd be doing it by now.

Isadora, Jevon, and Clara were quiet and subdued as the shouting grew louder and more acrimonious. Saul was wondering if bringing them to the meeting was a good idea, they deserved the truth, yes, but—

The rancour was inevitable, he supposed, he could still remember the self-preservation frenzy that had possessed everyone on New Florida when the Zanthswarm began. Strange – he hadn't thought of David and Alkhed for decades. Now he found himself wondering if the paramedics had ever made it back to Miami.

Emily leaned over to him. 'You should say something,' she murmured.

'Nobody's listening.'

'They will listen to you.'

Which might have been true, but he didn't know what to say. Maybe when things calmed down he could go round to people individually, try to build a consensus. It was more his style than a public slanging match.

Then his e-i told him he had a call. And nothing mattered any more.

Saul stood up, a look of utter serenity on his face. Otto and Gregor faltered in the middle of an insult storm, giving him puzzled glances, waiting for him to speak.

Instead he smiled at his children. 'Come on,' he said.

'Saul?' Emily asked him nervously.

'It's all right,' he said. 'Someone's here.' He bustled his curious children and concerned wife out, making sure the little ones put their gloves on and pulled their hats down. The rest of the village watched them go in puzzled silence.

'Saul?' Otto queried.

'You might want to see this, too,' he said blithely. Those closest to him caught the glint of moisture in his eyes.

The whole meeting poured out of the school hall, following close behind the Howard family. They were just in time to see a grey-green teardrop-shaped spaceship drop out of the aurora's thrashing streamers to land softly on the ice-swamped beach. Saul walked towards it without hesitation. Isadora, Jevon, and Clara clung to him, awed by the strange wonder from the sky which their daddy knew about. Emily was silent, but sticking with her husband.

As the airlock opened at the base of the spaceship, Saul turned to her. 'I'm so sorry,' he said. 'I never told you about any of this. I thought she was dead. I really did. I thought it was just me and you starting over together.'

Even now he wasn't sure. It was Angela who'd called him, yes, but . . .

Two women walked out of the spacecraft. Angela was one of them, a woolly hat pulled well down against the frigid sea breeze, but still unable to contain her hair. The other had nearly identical hair, just darker and longer. And her face was enchantingly familiar.

Saul burst into tears and opened his arms wide, frightened his legs would give way he was shaking so badly. Then Rebka was pressed up against him, cold nose nuzzling his face, and all emotional herself. 'Hello, Dad.'

*

It was quite a party crammed into the bungalow's lounge. Angela watched Saul putting a couple of new sparpine logs into the stove in the middle of the room. It was make-work; the stove was impressively hot, and this many people in one room wouldn't need any extra heat. The giveaway was how he kept staring at Rebka, the adoration and wonder in his eyes. He didn't know what to say, and clearly wasn't going to be parted from his lost daughter by more than a couple of metres at best. Still, at least he'd stopped crying.

Angela had to admit his other children were quite cute. Isadora, Jevon, and Clara were having their best day since the sunspots emerged. There was an actual spaceship parked outside, they had a brand-new big sister who was exciting and lots of fun, Dad was all funny because he was so happy. A whole bunch of interesting and important strangers were in their house, including an incredibly scary monster. All of which would give them a lot of kudos among their friends in the village afterwards. Angela grinned when little Clara ran up to Rebka and shyly offered up one of her cuddly toys, a green-furred monkey called Bananas One. Rebka was all smiles when she played with the toy, earning even more worship from the girl.

That was the kind of scene that might have belonged to her and Saul if life had been different. Very different, she amended. But then if it had been different Rebka wouldn't have been born.

No regrets.

Coby North and Raul were accepting mugs of tea from Emily. The woman hadn't said much since the spaceship arrived. Angela was aware of some sharp glances being thrown her way. They were clearly going to have to have a long conversation some time soon.

Emily hesitated in front of the Barclay-avatar, clearly wondering if she should offer it a mug. It shook its head fractionally, and Emily hurried on, relieved.

Then there was Otto and Markos who were standing to one side, there to represent the village, but clearly at a loss what to make of their unexpected visitors. The other members of the convoy were being looked after in the school hall where they'd been promised showers in the restrooms. She imagined they'd be subject to a lot of questions right now.

Paresh settled into the settee beside her, wincing as his strapped shoulder touched the armrest.

'You okay?' she asked.

'Sure. It's a lot better now.'

Angela knew he was making a big effort not to look at the Barclay-avatar. It had been quite a step forward for him to leave his carbine and pistol behind in the canyon.

'Good to hear,' she murmured. 'Apparently there are some spare bungalows in Camilo. We'll be moving in to one as soon as we can clear the snow off the roof and get it heated.'

'Oh will we?' he demurred.

Which wasn't her puppy boy at all. 'Rebka and I will,' she teased back. 'I believe there's a spare bedroom.'

'I'll take what I can get.'

'Good.' Her hand closed on his thigh and she lowered her voice. 'And you'd better bring some painkillers for your ribs. Maximum dosage. Do you have any idea how long it's been since you and I have had sex?'

'I am very aware of that number, yes.' He broke off and smiled politely as Emily brought him a mug of tea over. Isadora followed her mother round with a pack of orange chocolate bourbons, eager to please.

Angela took a couple and smiled her thanks at the curious girl.

'If you don't mind,' Coby North said. 'I have to fly over to the mansion and explain what's happening to Brinkelle.'

'What'll happen to us?' Otto asked.

'Ultimately, all humans will be leaving St Libra,' Coby said.

'What?' Otto spluttered.

Coby glanced over at the Barclay-avatar, as if seeking permission. 'We're trespassing here. It's not our world.'

'It might not be yours, but it is mine. My children were born here.'

'So were ours,' Saul said. 'Listen to what's being said, Otto. Listen carefully, because it's not our world to be born into. We don't have that right.'

'Are the sunspots not enough to convince you?' the Barclay-avatar asked.

Otto gave him a frightened look.

'Where are we going to go?' Saul asked. 'The gateway is closed.'

'Sirius XIV,' the Barclay-avatar told him. 'It is further out than St Libra, but well inside this star's life band. The rotation is twenty-three hours nineteen minutes, which I'm sure you can adapt to. And gravity is point-nine Earth standard. It even has iron ores in the crust. It will suit you well.'

'I don't understand,' Emily said. 'That planet has an atmosphere worse than Venus. We can't live there. Nobody can.'

'It is inhospitable now,' the Barclay-avatar said. 'But all things change. I have agreed to modify it for you. All you will need to do is provide the seeds to engender your own biosphere.'

'Which Constantine will fly here,' Coby said. 'We have a gene-bank on the Jupiter habitat for just such an eventuality – well, not quite. But it'll do.'

'The gateway is closed,' Otto growled. 'Nobody can get here.'

'The Jupiter constellation will fly here through interstellar space,' Raul said. 'Most of it is too big to fit through the gateway, anyway. In fact, it's bringing the Newcastle end of the gateway with it.'

'Why?' Paresh asked.

'To reassemble on Sirius XIV,' Coby said. 'That way, everyone on St Libra can walk through. It's a good deal. Without it, Sirius would remain redshifted until the planet is rid of us that way.'

'I have agreed with Constantine to end my disruption of Sirius. The sunspots will decline over the next two months,' the Barclay-avatar said. 'Winter will end. You may spend the intervening years recovering and making ready. I will resume my mission as Zebediah, preparing the people of the Independencies for their departure.'

*

Saul and Emily let Angela have their spare room that night. Rebka was given Clara's room, so the delighted six-year-old got to move in with a less pleased Isadora.

'This stuff really smells,' Paresh complained as he wormed down into their makeshift bed. The spare room only had a single bed, so they'd pulled the mattress on the floor, added cushions from the bungalow's sofas, and zipped a couple of sleeping bags together on top.

Angela had just come back from the bathroom, where every tile seemed to be ingrained with children's toothstik gel. She glanced round the bedroom's walls where Saul had stacked hundreds of sparpine logs so they could dry out, ready for burning in the stove. It was the first time since the sunspot outbreak that she'd experienced any of St Libra's scents. This one was quite acidic. 'Not so bad,' she murmured.

'Have you spoken to Emily yet?' he asked.

'No. I'll do it tomorrow. I think it's best she gets to talk things through with Saul first.'

'Yeah. Boy, has he got some explaining to do.'

'I don't think he has, actually. And what there is, he can blame on me.'

'Hey,' Paresh said. 'I don't think you've done anything wrong.'

Angela grinned down at him. 'Sweets, that list is so long I wouldn't even know where to start.' She shrugged out of her borrowed robe. It would've been nice if she was wearing something thin and lacy for him, but outside the lounge the bungalow wasn't that warm, so she'd settled for some PJ trousers loaned by Emily and Saul's mauve sweatshirt.

'I wasn't kidding about my ribs,' he said glumly as she wiggled down into the sleeping bag beside him. 'They do still hurt. The doc said nothing too strenuous.'

'Hmm, I like a challenge.'

Paresh laughed. 'I still don't understand you.'

'Many have tried.' She turned on her side to look at him. The skin on his face was peeling where it wasn't scabbed. He looked exhausted, a deep-down fatigue that would take a long time to expunge. She realized she could look at that face for a long time without growing tired of it. 'I want you to know this: I am genuinely fond of you. We're not going to get married or anything. Clear? But I'm happy right now. And I can't remember the last time that happened. You're a part of that, so let's keep going with what we've got. I don't want to be unhappy.'

'Sure. I can see why you're happy. Rebka is quite something.'

'She certainly is.'

'So do you trust the avatar?'

'You're looking at and judging the avatar, not the life which animates it. Its shape makes you see human. That's a mistake.'

'That'll be a yes, then.'

She kissed him. 'I think we're going to be okay.'

'Given where we were this time yesterday, you may just be right.'

'Paresh. Thanks for not doubting me, for believing in me back in the canyon. It's meant an awful lot to me these last few months.'

He nodded wisely. 'It's been a strange day, all right. But I'm glad it happened.'

'It's been a strange life,' Angela said. 'So far.'

June 2152

It was Will who got to land the lightwave ship, under supervision from Caspar North – after all he was still only eighteen and therefore officially just a trainee. Zara fumed and sulked the whole way down from the habitat amalgamation in its geostationary orbit around Sirius XIV. At sixteen she was only ranked as a cadet, so all she got to fly was a training-zone virtual.

Sid was very good for the whole eight-minute hop down. He didn't grip the edges of the acceleration couch in terror, or anything.

They touched down on one of the landing field's pads on the outskirts of Burradon, as they'd named the planet's first settlement town. Will joined them in the main passenger cabin, grinning broadly.

'Did you feel a bump?' he asked his family.

'Nothing until you switched the gravity field off,' Jacinta told him. 'I think I can tell the difference from Earth.'

Sid certainly couldn't. After nine years, he was so used to the spin gravity of the big habitat he'd forgotten what straight planetary gravity was like. His inner ear was only mildly perturbed as they walked out of the airlock into the hot air.

Apart from its two oceans, Sirius XIV was a desert from pole to pole. Sid had seen the dazzling ice caps from orbit, but underneath the new glaciers there was only sterile sand. When they arrived a month earlier, taking three days to decelerate the entire Jupiter constellation down from point-nine lightspeed, the planet was completely sterile. Devoid of even a single bacterium.

The ultimate blank canvas, Constantine said. A world where any possibility could be realized.

The powdery sand under Sid's boots was an uninspiring dull ochre, rucked up with footprints, wheel tracks, and rills of rainwater. He had to slip on sunglasses against the sharp glare of the blue-white star which had now regained its former glory. When he stared up into the deep sapphire sky he could just see the spark-point of Sirius B, a thumb's width to the side of its primary. He tracked south. Like a particularly bright star, St Libra twinkled above the horizon. Twenty-three million kilometres away, yet with a distinctive oval profile from its rings. XIV didn't even have a moon.

There were mountains away to the east, a tall range fringed by snowy peaks. Clouds were piling up around them. It rained frequently in Burradon. Fast warm showers several times a day. Perfect for plants and crops and even trees. It also produced a lot of humidity, especially with the sea ten kilometres away.

A buggy pulled up in front of them. Its Hi-Q auto quested a link and told them it was assigned to drive them to their newly constructed house. The landing field octocyber loaded their bags into the boot, and they were off.

Beyond the landing field, the first district was neumanetic, basic cyberblocs producing more of their own. Big cubes with black PV skin splitting off sections like geometric amoeba. Once they were free they absorbed more raw from the thick pipes threading along the side of the dirt track, expanding into set function producers. The initial stages of development had focused on microfacturing houses complete with domestic units, followed by human basics like clothes, furniture, vehicles ... After that, Burradon had concentrated on churning out bioform systems.

Sid watched with delight as they drove past the onion-shaped neumanetics of the bioversity seeders. Aerostats were inflating out of the pinnacles, big oval envelopes with their bulging breeder vats at the bottom, bioreactors that sucked moisture out of the muggy atmosphere to infect with dozens of species of soil bacteria that sprayed out of the bottom like a low-pressure rocket. Bacteria which multiply rapidly, etching nutrients out of the naked minerals, preparing the ground for the next stage.

Algae would come next, establishing a textured biological component in the matrix of sand. Moulds, fungi; all had their slot on the timetable drawn up on the nine-year voyage.

In a couple of years' time the first batches of insects would be released, their eggs gestated in their billions in clone vats to be scattered across the land. Finally, the seeds would come, and flowers would bloom across the desert. Forests and meadows; jungles and savannahs – all would rise to coat the land in a lush emerald terrestrial-growth. Nature's natural order would assume primacy, no longer requiring human assistance, and the bioform would end. Animals would charge out of their pens, enjoying their freedom along with the people who'd been transplanted here.

Just seeing the aerostats floating away to roam across the globe wherever the winds took them, Sid knew he'd made the right decision. Judging by her expression, Jacinta was sharing the thought. They clasped hands, and kissed.

'Urrgh.' Zara wrinkled her nose up and turned away.

'Look,' Will shouted, pointing. 'The gateway.'

Several kilometres beyond the town's expanding boundary, the gateway was slowly being resurrected inside a massive, open-ended building. The components they'd dismantled in Newcastle had been methodically examined, refurbished and upgraded by the constellation's AIs on the voyage. Now a scaffold lattice rippled beneath slick triangular automata that were slowly and carefully locking the individual units back into place.

'There goes the neighbourhood,' Zara said. 'And we only just got here.'

'The migration over will be gradual,' Jacinta said. 'It'll have to be. Even our neumanetics can't cope with everybody all at once.'

'They said Brinkelle will be first across,' Sid said. 'It's supposed to be symbolic. Setting an example.'

'Very symbolic,' Will said. 'The lightwave fleet's been ferrying over key people for a week now.'

'Will the Aldred-avatar be going the other way?' Zara muttered snidely.

'Behave,' Sid told her mildly.

The rolling plain which the bulk of the town was built on began to dip down, and they were on a massive rugged slope which led down to the emerald sea that sparkled enticingly. Streams rippled down gullies, falling down steep sections into small deep pools the water had already eroded. Switchback roads, the envy of any Italian mountain village, criss-crossed the gradient, linking long terraces bulldozed out for a swathe of individual houses.

'It's all freshwater,' Zara exclaimed happily. 'And we don't have to worry about sharks or alligators or jellyfish or adradoth or visimines. Can we go in now, Dad, please? Please-please?'

Sid looked down to the bottom of the slope, where the shore curved into a string of small coves. Ripples lapped against the claggy saturated sand. There were people already down there, splashing about.

'If we can find the swimsuits, sure,' he said.

Zara kissed him happily. 'Thank you, Daddy.'

He smiled back, perfectly content. But part of him was wondering how much longer she'd ask him for permission to do what she wanted.

The house they'd been allocated was a low villa with a lot of glass facing the sea. A long veranda ran along the front, complete with outdoor furniture.

'Wow,' Sid said, as the teenagers ran on ahead, shouting to each other about which room they were going to claim for their own. 'We really did leave Jesmond behind.'

Jacinta's lips pulled back into a rictus smile. 'Looks wrong without any plants,' she said wistfully. 'We need trees – palm trees. Some rose bushes at least.'

'You can always go back.'

'Oh shut up.'

Two women were walking along the terrace towards them. They could have been sisters they were so similar, one looked to be in her early twenties, while the other was probably eighteen. Sid frowned as a memory tickled him; the older one had long blonde hair that blew about a lot in the wind gusting up from the sea.

'Hello there,' she said cheerfully, pushing errant strands away from her face. 'Looks like we're going to be neighbours. Rebka and I just got in from St Libra last night.'

'Hi,' Jacinta said. 'That's great. We've got a couple of kids about your age.'

Sid found himself grinning. 'You're Angela,' he said.

'Yes. How do you know that?'

'I've been reading your file on the voyage from Earth. I'm really pleased to meet you, pet, we have a lot to talk about.'

2377

The ellipsoid lightwave shuttle slipped silently over the rolling landscape that had once been a delightful park. Today, plants and trees from eight different planets, originally selected for their elegant ornamental looks, fought a losing battle against New Monaco's native vegetation that was seeking to reclaim the ground from the exotic foreigners. It looked as if they were sinking under wave after wave of creepers and spindly blue flokgrass.

Angela's ancillary neural plexus directed the shuttle to circle the ruins at the centre of the park. She was surprised and saddened by how much the enormous mansion had decayed. It was over quarter of a millennium now since she'd caught her last glimpse of the scrumptious DeVoyal palace from the rear of Bantri's plane as it flew her to her new life, but even so . . .

Most of the roofing had buckled and fallen in, the shattered panels allowing centuries of rain to gush along the exquisite polished wood flooring, turning the stairs into elaborate curving waterfalls before they rusted and rotted away. That stage of decay gave the plants a better root, allowing bushes and even small trees to grow in the crumbling remains of abandoned furniture and plush fittings.

The stone walls of the central double-H structure had fared a little better, but then they were a metre thick, reinforced by a carbon-meshed concrete core. Wispy flokgrass sprouted from fractured crevices. The creepers which had marched across the parkland now swarmed up the vertical redoubt, their intrusive, persistent stem fronds attacking the stone until it began to flake and fall, carving random organic shapes amid the original gargoyles and fluting. Commanding stately façades that had once known imperial gold light shining from a thousand windows every night were now broken sagging husks of their former selves, the glittering windows empty alcoves devoid of glass.

The shuttle touched down a hundred metres from the end of the west wing. Angela was ready to bounce it back up immediately – she was nervous that any motion would send the whole time-crushed edifice crumbling into its final cataclysm. But nothing moved outside, no tremble shivering along the cracked stonework. The old place was going to survive a few years yet.

'Told you it was real,' she said to the three children clustering round her. 'Come on, let's go take a look.'

They raced out onto what had once been a lawn so flat and smooth you could've used it as a golf green, their shrill happy cries absorbed by the still summer air. Try as she might, Angela couldn't remember if New Monaco had any dangerous animals. Her natural memory was completely shot these days – everything important was stored in her adjuvant neurology, and one day she'd get round to some proper indexing. But the children all had Dn-bands round their wrists, so it didn't matter.

She slipped some sunglasses on, warding off the sun's glare as it blazed down out of the violet-shaded sky.

'Did you really live here, Grandmamma?' little Hollyn asked, her golden hair of coiled ringlets bouncing about as she hopped from foot to foot. Hollyn could never keep still, just like her mother, Scyritha.

Angela searched along the base of the wall, seeing the deep sag in the creeper which must be the archway to the inner courtyard. 'Yes, sweets, I did. In one of the inner sections.'

'So you really are a princess?' Octavio asked with his perpetual cheeky smile.

'I was, darling, a very long time ago.'

'It must have been amazing.'

'The universe was different then, but no, not really. I enjoyed myself, but that was all.'

She allowed them to run on ahead, playing explorers while she made her way over to the grove of eight ancient oaks. This was one place she didn't need to run a request through her adjuvant neurology to find. The last time she'd stood here the oaks were saplings, barely reaching up to her shoulder. Today they were approaching their last decades, with huge gnarled trunks, rotting bark, and dead broken branches stabbing into the quiet violet sky.

Right in the centre of the grove was a simple octagonal black marble pillar. It was on a plinth, she knew, but that had long ago vanished under moss and creepers.

Angela placed a single red rose against the marble's weathered surface. 'Hello Daddy,' she said. 'I'm sorry it took me so long. But oh you should see the life I've had. I think you'd be proud of me. I really do. Our family is so big now, and fabulous. You made it happen, Daddy. You had me, and I'm so grateful for that. Thank you.'

Her hand wiped away a tear which had leaked out from below her sunglasses. Then she turned and went back to the children who had found one of the big fountain ponds. They laughed as they slid down the steep moss-covered slope.

Hollyn grinned as Angela rejoined them. Her little arm waved at the huge palace. 'How many people lived here, Grandmamma? Was our family just as big back then?'

Angela smiled and tucked some of her rebellious hair back behind her ear. 'No, there was just the two of us living here; me and my father.'

The children stared at her goggle-eyed, not sure if she was teasing them.

'Two?' squeaked Shawanna. The little girl looked from her great-ancestor to the looming ruin, then back again. Total disbelief was written all over her.

'And an awful lot of servants – people who looked after us,' Angela explained hurriedly.

'What did you do all day?'

'Good question,' Angela admitted. 'I went to a lot of parties, travelled to all the planets we had in those days. It kept me busy. I even fell in love for the first time.'

'With a prince?' Hollyn asked hopefully.

'Yes, with a prince.'

'Is he our ancestor, too?'

'No darling. I was stupid, I let him get away. But he helped me once, when I really really needed it. That's the reason half of you exist today. He was a true prince, you see.'

'Where is he now?'

'I don't know.' She looked back at the palace, seeing it as it had been in those glory days, its fabulous rooms filled with all those glamorous empty people as they partied the weeks and years away in decadent splendour because they knew nothing else. It was nice to have those memories, but they weren't important, not any more. Just a golden childhood summer day to reminisce about fondly.

'Why aren't you a princess any more?' Octavio asked insistently.

'I grew up, darling. Everybody grew up.'

Which wasn't true, she knew. So many of those faces that danced and laughed for eternity in her mind had gone. She let them brush against her, those dizzy ghosts, Shasta, Matiff, Housden ... such beautiful people ruled by their spent, empty existence. Some redeemed, saved, others lost. And more, those desperately intense souls that shone so bright as they traversed spacetime in their own determined fashion: dear sweet Elston, Ravi, Coniff, Karizma, lovely Paresh, even wonderful old Sid ... everybody she'd slowly lost down the centuries, flittering past unseen yet smiling as she held her arms wide and twirled like a fey dancer. Happy in their own way now. Angela wished them all well wherever they were. This was the one place where it was fitting for her to say goodbye to them, to cast off any lingering sorrows.

'Come along,' she said with a radiant smile, pleased to have shown off the place where it all began to the lovely scamps she was proud to have as descendants. 'We'd better get back, or we'll be in big trouble.'

The Nuii-Zanth conglobate awaited them in geosync orbit, a geode of quantum-three-state matter over a hundred miles across, home to eighty thousand entities who were about to adventure into the galactic core for the first time. Captain Lulu MacNamara had indulged Angela's sentimental diversion for old times' sake, but she was keen for their grand voyage to begin. It didn't do to keep her waiting.

[THE END]